Daughter of Satan

Jean Plaidy

First published in 1952 by Robert Hale Limited

Compass Press Large Print Book Series; an imprint of
ISIS Publishing Ltd, Great Britain, and Bolinda Press, Australia
Published in Large Print 2002 by ISIS Publishing Ltd,
7 Centremead, Osney Mead, Oxford OX2 0ES,
and Bolinda Publishing Pty Ltd,
17 Mohr Street, Tullamarine, Victoria 3043
by arrangement with Robert Hale Limited

British Library Cataloguing in Publication Data
Plaidy, Jean, 1906–
Daughter of Satan. – Large print ed.
1. Witches – Fiction
2. Persecution – Fiction
3. Great Britain – History – 1689–1714 – Fiction
4. Historical fiction
5. Large type books
I. Title
823.9′12 [F]

Australian Cataloguing in Publication Data
Plaidy, Jean
Daughter of Satan / Jean Plaidy.
1. Large type books.
2. Love stories
3. Historical fiction
I. Title
823.912

ISBN 0-7531-6667-4 (hb) ISBN 0-7531-6668-2 (pb)
(ISIS Publishing Ltd)
ISBN 1-74030-765-8 (hb)
(Bolinda Publishing Pty Ltd)

Printed and bound by Antony Rowe, Chippenham

CHAPTER ONE

Tamar was conceived one midsummer's night during the most glorious and triumphant year which England had, up to that time, known.

Her mother was a poor serving-maid, and when she was asked who had fathered the child, she would lower her eyes and do all she could to avoid giving the answer. If she were pressed, she would mutter something to the effect that it had been no fault of hers; the child had been forced on her in the darkness of night and she had not even seen its father's face. But she, the child's own mother, was one of those who believed Tamar's father to be none other than the Devil himself.

*   *   *

It was Whit-Sunday.

The sea sparkled and the sun beat down on the rocks so that it seemed as though they were streaked with amethyst and chrysoprase, rose quartz and jade; the gorse had never seemed so golden as it did that Maytime; even the clumps of sea-pinks — that most modest of flowers — appeared to jut out from the slated rock with a new-born defiance. The haunting fragrance of hawthorn blossom was in the air, mingling with the scents of the sea and land; and the unparalleled charm of English springtime was doubly sweet that year.

On this Sunday morning, Richard Merriman had been unable to remain in his house at Pennicomquick; there was too much excitement in the air; and he, like many others, must go into Plymouth to attend the special church service. He left his horse to be watered and fed at an inn a stone's-throw from the Hoe, and he walked out to face the keen wind and look out across the Sound before making his way back to the town.

One look at him was enough to show him to be a most fastidious man. His breeches were made of velvet and he wore no garters to keep up his stockings, which might have suggested he was rather proud of his calves; the sleeves of his jerkin were open from shoulder to wrist to show the rich cloth of his doublet. He was pale of face, haughty and most elegant; he looked what he was—a mixture of savant and epicurean. His love of learning was not shared by his friend and neighbour, Sir Humphrey Cavill. Sir Humphrey was a man whom all men—and women—understood; a heavy drinker and fast liver, Sir Humphrey had sailed the Spanish Main with John Hawkins and Sir Francis Drake, and it was said that half the children between Stoke and Pennicomquick had the Cavill nose or those deep-set, striking blue eyes of Sir Humphrey's. Richard Merriman was more selective than his friend, who was merely his friend because he was his neighbour.

What a sight it was on that sunny morning! Richard stood on the Hoe, and looked at that array of colourful glory. *Ark*, *Revenge*, *Elizabeth Bonaventure* and *Mary Rose*—there they lay, pulling at their anchors as impatient, it seemed, as Sir Francis certainly was to break away and go out to meet the Spaniard; then *Victory* and *Nonpareil*—all flying the red cross on a white background, the flag of England. And there were many more—a fine fleet, but Richard knew that, on the way to meet them, was what some believed to be an even prouder and more magnificent armada of ships.

At any moment now the first of the Spaniards might appear on the horizon. At dusk that very night the beacons might suddenly begin to blaze along the coasts of Devon and Cornwall.

The bells were pealing as he left the Hoe and walked into the town. He went on to the Barbican and walked thoughtfully along the fishing quay. On such a day as this there was much for a man to think of. On these very cobbles, not so long ago, King Philip of Spain had walked, an honoured guest; for the greatest enemy of the reigning Queen had been the adored husband of Bloody Mary, her predecessor. Times changed and these days were pregnant with great happenings.

He went through the cobbled streets past groups of people who shouted and whispered, laughed and looked grave. From diamond-paned casements girls called to others who leaned towards them across the narrow streets, which were teeming with apprentices and merchants, fishermen and old sailors.

He reached the square, but there was no room inside the Church of St. Andrew on that Sunday morning, and it was necessary for him to take his stand with those outside.

The tension in the crowd was such as he had rarely witnessed. So, he thought, must the burgesses of this old and noble city have felt more than a hundred years before on that sunny Lammas Day when the corsairs of France had tried to subdue them. Excitement was stronger than apprehension, for excitement was what these people craved; here was the cradle of those adventurers who were determined to challenge and subdue the power of Spain.

Among them now, here outside the church, was many a man who had sailed with Drake and hoped to sail again. These men would flock to their ships when the hour for action came. They loathed the Spaniard as only those could who had come into contact with his fanatical cruelty. They knew that when the dignified galleons appeared on the horizon they would bring something besides men and ammunition—thumbscrews, the scourge, the rack and all the instruments of torture of the dreaded Inquisition. They would bring a fanaticism and an intolerance into a land which had had a taste of these things when the wife of the Spanish King had ruled them.

"Never again!" said the men of Devon; and men were saying this all over England. It should not happen again while Sir Francis and his kind lived to prevent it.

The service was at length over and the worshippers were coming out into the sunshine. There was Martin Frobisher, and with him John Hawkins. Cheers went up for these brave men. And now. . . the moment for which they had all been waiting had come, for out of the church came Lord Howard of Effingham and beside him Sir Francis Drake himself.

Here was the idol of Plymouth—the one man among all these great men whom all longed to serve and to follow to the death. His beard touched the fine lace of his ruff; his sweeping moustaches curled jauntily; his full-lidded, twinkling eyes surveyed the crowd, accepting its homage.

"Sir Francis, God bless thee!"

"Sir Francis forever!"

He doffed his cap. Adventurer, charmer, showman, he bowed, and took his companion by the arm as though to introduce him to the crowd; the full lids were lifted as though to say: "You and I, men of Devon, must accept this man. You and I—for the sake of courtesy—will do him honour as the Lord Admiral of the Fleet; but we know, do we not, who will beat the Spaniard. We know whose courage, whose resourcefulness will bring us victory. And you, good men of Devon, while—for courtesy's sake—you will follow him, will truly follow me with all your heart."

A murmur ran through the crowd. Drake commanded and, as ever, Drake would be obeyed.

Drake said: "Homage to my Lord Howard of Effingham," and so the men of Plymouth would do homage to the noble lord. Had Drake said: "To the Devil with Howard. Follow none but your leader!" then there would have been mutiny in the Fleet.

A smile curved Richard's fine, thin lips. How stimulating to contemplate the power that was in this man to set the mood of a mob. The Queen was a woman, and a foolish one at times. Did she not realise how easily she might have lost her throne when she asked Drake to take second place to Howard? She still ran a risk. Noble birth alone could not defeat Spain's Armada. And if Drake was a parson's son of yeoman stock, yet had he the power, as no other had it, to make men follow him. Tradition demanded that the admiral of the fleet should be a noble lord and so here came my Lord Howard of Effingham to take the place which should have belonged to Sir Francis Drake.

Richard shrugged his shoulders and was turning away when he caught sight of two young women in the crowd whom he recognised as serving wenches in his own household. They were giggling and laughing together—two girls on holiday. The big buxom one was eyeing the young men; she had tawny hair cut short like a boy's and eyes to match. But for her short hair, she was a typical Devon maid. The second was a more interesting type. She was dark-eyed and her dark hair was cut short like her companion's. He was amused to see the way in which those dark eyes followed Sir Francis. What adoration! There was scarcely a woman in the town, he supposed, who would not adore Sir Francis, but this girl looked at him as though he were a saint rather than a handsome and charming adventurer. And who but a simple maid would think Sir Francis a saint!

Richard was mildly interested, for the girl had a faint trace of beauty; her face was unmarked by emotion; she was young—not more than fifteen, he supposed. It was a pity that Alton, the housekeeper, cut the girls' hair. Still, it was the woman's business to keep them in order, and he doubted not that she knew her business. She was a stern creature, with a trace of something vicious in her; he guessed that the girls had many a beating to endure, but no doubt they deserved it. Yet, it was a pity she had cut off their hair, for they would have been more pleasant to look at if they had had more of it; and he liked to look at pleasant things. He wondered lightly about them; he was not a sensual man. He had married a wife chosen for him by his grandfather, and he had felt no great emotion when she had died, nor any need to replace her. There was nothing monklike in his attitude to women; he had a friend in Pennie Cross, to see whom he rode there now and then. She was older than he was—charming, serious-minded, interested in matters which interested him. Theirs was hardly a passionate friendship. It was not likely therefore that he would look on the serving girls as Sir Humphrey would have looked. It was merely that the smile on the face of the little dark one amused him, and fleetingly he hoped that if punishment must be inflicted on the girls for coming into the town without Mistress

Alton's permission, the cane would not be allowed to fall too heavily on those slender shoulders.

He forgot the girls as he went for his horse. Looking about him as he rode away from the town, he could see the Tamar winding its way like a silver snake between Devon and Cornwall. The green banks of the lane were rich with bluebells, the red of ragged robin and the white of the stitchwort flowers. It was only a mile or so to his house at Pennicomquick. A pleasant sight was this house of his with its thatched roof, its gables and its latticed windows. It was spacious too, although not so large as Sir Humphrey's over at Stoke, and a comfortable place to live in. He shuddered at the thought of its being ransacked and burned by Spaniards. He rode through the gates, past the yews which Joseph Jubin his gardener had cut into the shapes of birds, past the lavender not yet in flower and the lad's love with its penetrating yet very pleasant odour.

Clem Swann, his groom, came out of the stables to take his horse, and Richard went into the house and up the staircase to his study. This study was a pleasant room with its big diamond-paned windows and oak panelled walls. There was a carpet on the floor and rich hangings on the walls; he could not bear to be surrounded by anything but the most beautiful that could be obtained. There was in this room a big oak chest of which he kept the key; there were shelves of books all exquisitely bound in calf; the stools were tapestry-covered, and there was one elaborately carved chair which, it was understood, no one should sit on but himself.

He realized that he was fatigued. It was the heat and excitement of the morning. He pulled the bell, and when Josiah Hough, his personal servant, appeared, he asked that wine be brought.

"Sir," said Josiah, as he set the wine on the table and poured it out for his master, "you have come from the town. Did you see Sir Francis, sir, might I be so bold as to ask?"

Richard raised his eyebrows. The servants were in awe of him and it was not often that they spoke without being spoken to; but he smiled lightly. This was indeed a very special occasion.

"I saw him, Josiah. The people cheered him mightily."

"The whole country seems in a sort of tremble, sir."

"Not with fear, Josiah. With excitement."

"There's some that say the Spaniards have the best ships in the world, sir."

"That may be, Josiah. But it's men not ships that win a battle. Their ships are like their grandees — very pleasant to look upon, full of dignity. Our English ships may not be so handsome, but sometimes it is better to move with speed than with dignity."

" 'Tis true, master."

Richard folded his long white hands together and smiled at his servant. "They have to face the English in their own waters. Have you any doubt of the issue? They have to face him whom they have named *El*

Draque—the Dragon. They fear him, Josiah, and he is no stranger to them. In their bigotry, in their fanaticism, they believe him to be a magician. Who else, they ask themselves, could score such victories over their Holy Church?"

Josiah drew back astonished; he had never before seen such passion in his master's face. He waited for Richard to go on, but at that moment the sound of sudden shrieks of laughter came floating through the open window.

"Who is that?" asked Richard.

Josiah went to the window. " 'Tis the two maids, sir. I'll put a stick about their shoulders. 'Tis young Betsy Cape and Luce Martin."

To Josiah's surprise. his master rose and came languidly to the window. He looked down on the two girls he had seen in the town.

"A saucy pair of wenches, sir," went on Josiah. "Betsy's a bold thing, and she's showing Luce the way to boldness. I'll have Mistress Alton whip them for shrieking below your window."

"Why do they shriek? It was obviously with pleasure. Do they not realize the import of such a time as this?"

"They realize only the import of a riband or a man's smile, sir."

Betsy's laugh rang out. Richard shuddered as though it grated on his nerves.

"Pray go and tell them to be quiet," he said.

Josiah went, and from the window Richard watched. He was faintly surprised that he should have felt this flicker of interest. He saw each girl receive a slap across her face. Betsy put out a red tongue at Josiah's back and little Luce clapped her hands over her mouth to stop herself laughing.

Even after they had gone into the house Richard continued to think of them. What did the future hold for such as they were? Marriage with one of Clem Swann's boys, life in a cottage close to the house, continuing to work for him mayhap, breeding children—boys who would fight for another hero like Drake against another enemy like the Spaniard; and girls to giggle over a riband and the smile of a sailor.

Then he forgot them. He took a book from the shelf and sat back in his chair. It was difficult to read when at any moment the first of the Spanish ships might be sighted on the horizon.

* * *

Luce Martin was fifteen years old. She had been sent to work at the house of Richard Merriman when she was thirteen. Her father was a fisherman and he lived in a little cottage in Whitsand Bay, on the other side of the Tamar. This made Luce a bit of a foreigner to the people of Devon. Living was hard to get; sometimes the boats went out and returned with little, and if they returned full of fish it seemed that then there was a glut. There were times when the family lived on buttermilk, with nothing to eat but scraps of rye bread. There were many brothers and sisters, so that even their mother had to stop and count them if she were asked their number; they came regularly each year. Luce was one of the middle ones; and when Mistress Alton, who herself came from the Whitsand Bay neighbourhood, offered to take her to the house in Pennicomquick to work under her, Luce's parents agreed with great eagerness.

So she had set out from her home with a small bundle containing her possessions, and for the first time in her life she was ferried over the Tamar; she walked the few remaining miles to her new home.

She had been afraid of Mistress Alton from the moment she had first heard her name, and she had not been reassured by her first meeting with the woman, for Mistress Alton was, in Luce's eyes, terrible to behold. A tall, thin woman with a mouth which scarcely opened even when she talked, and shut up like a trap immediately afterwards, she wore the neatest and most sober clothes Luce had ever seen, and her skin was hideously disfigured by a very bad attack of the pox. But she had a reputation for great piety, though this did not lessen Luce's fears.

As soon as Luce arrived she had been sent into the yard to strip. Her clothes were lousy. She was given garments to wear which had been chosen by Mistress Alton, for such a fastidious gentleman as Mr. Richard Merriman could not demean himself in the affairs of his servants, and he left everything of such a nature to his housekeeper. The clothes were of the same pattern as those worn by Luce's fellow serving maid, Betsy Cape. Then Luce's lovely long hair, which hung curling to her waist, was cut short.

Hair, said Mistress Alton as she cut it, was best cut short, and especially hair that was thick and curly, for that undoubtedly was a gift from Satan.

The Devil's name was more often on Mistress Alton's lips than that of God, who in her eyes seemed to be a superior, vindictive version of the Devil.

So here was Luce, barely thirteen and frightened, never having seen anything as grand as the house in which she now found herself, each day taught her duty to God and her master, but chiefly her duty to Mistress Alton.

Mistress Alton managed the house; she cooked and salted the food and bottled her preserves; she supervised everything that had to be done inside the house and was inordinately proud of her work. She never made a mistake; if mistakes were made, others made them; and faults had to be paid for. It was Mistress Alton's duty to see that they were, and the faults of Luce and Betsy were paid for with beatings administered with the thin cane which hung from the housekeeper's belt together with the keys of her cupboards.

Beatings, which were given for the slightest offence, took place regularly. When Bill Lackwell came to the kitchen to bring fish, and Mistress Alton fancied the girls threw saucy glances at him, they were beaten; once she caught Betsy kissing Charlie Hurly when he came with eggs from his father's farm, and Betsy was treated to a very special beating for that.

It was her duty, said Mistress Alton, to stop that sort of thing. When Betsy was beaten, Luce must be there to look on; and Betsy was always made to witness Luce's punishment.

"It will be a lesson to *you*, my girl!" each would be told.

They were obliged to strip to the waist for the caning, for what was the good of beating through the thickness of cloth? They must hold their bodices over their breasts though, for it was immodest to show them even to members of their own sex. If they dropped the bodice or it slipped out of place, they must be beaten for immodesty.

Mistress Alton kept them working hard. The Devil was forever at their elbows, Mistress Alton explained, waiting to tempt idlers.

So to thirteen-year-old Luce life was all work and beatings. She did not think there was anything strange about that; her father had been wont to beat her merely because he was in the mood. She was lucky, she knew, to get her food and clothing; but now that she was growing older she was a little resentful about the shortness of her hair, and Betsy fostered this discontent.

They slept together in an attic. In some houses all the servants would sleep together in one big room, but Mistress Alton would not have young girls and men sleeping together.

"My dear life!" she said. "What goings-on there would be indeed! I'd not get a wink of sleep for the watch I'd have to keep for wickedness."

Every night the girls were locked into their attic and the windows bolted. "And if," said Mistress Alton, "I should hear of you girls unbolting that window, I'd turn you out of the house, I would. There's some wantonness that can't be beat out, and that sort I would not stand!"

Luce and Betsy would lie on their straw pallets and talk until they fell asleep, which usually they quickly did being tired out after the day's hard work.

On that Whit-Sunday night as they lay together on their pallets waiting for the coming of Mistress Alton, Luce whispered: "Shall us both be beaten to-night?"

"Neither of us will," answered Betsy with such conviction that Luce raised herself to look at her.

"Why not?"

"Because her's too busy to think of caning us."

"How do you know?"

"Charlie Hurly told me." Betsy giggled. "He came up to the house this afternoon. I do think he came to see me. He was out there, trying to get me to go out . . ."

Happy Betsy! A life of hard work and continual punishment could not quell her spirits; she always felt herself to be on the verge of an adventure which involved her seduction, and this evil fate seemed to be what Betsy longed for more than anything.

"You'd taken a bit of the pie," Luce reminded her. "She saw it on your mouth and you'd spilled some on your bodice."

"Well, I got a cut or two for that. Besides, she's too busy, I tell 'ee. 'Sh! Here she comes."

The light in the attic was still good enough for them to see the housekeeper clearly. Betsy was right, thought Luce; something had happened. She looked excited. Luce guessed it was this waiting for the Spaniards to come.

Mistress Alton was wearing her best dress; her ruff was of cambric and her skirt more wired than the one she usually wore; but it was not her dress that Luce noticed so much as her face, for Luce had rarely seen the housekeeper look so pleased. Moreover, nothing was said about their misdeeds of the day, and there were no beatings on that Sunday night.

When she left them, Betsy said, smiling secretly: "I could tell 'ee, Luce Martin, where she be going."

"Where?" demanded Luce.

Betsy continued to smile. "Have you ever thought that there might be witches among us?"

"Witches!" whispered Luce.

"And living close to us. Do you know what witches can do, Luce? They can do anything . . . just anything at all."

Luce did not want to talk about witches; she wanted to continue with the thoughts which had been with her ever since she had seen Sir Francis come out of church. Listening to Betsy's continual talk of men and their ways had aroused Luce's curiosity; and there were things she wished to know and experience. She did not care to make herself understood to Betsy. Better for Betsy to think her cold and prim than that

Betsy should know the real reason why she hated it when she was teased about Ned Swann, who stank of the stables, and Bill Lackwell, who stank of fish. She did not like Ned Swann; still less did she like Bill Lackwell, whose grandmother was a witch. No; Luce's lover must not be as these. She wished for someone great and noble, someone handsome with a lace ruff and a jaunty beard—not Sir Francis, of course, but someone very like him.

Betsy went on with her talk of witches.

"They can rouse a tempest. They can strike down a man or woman with the pox or an ague. They can do devils' work. You're not listening. Why, *you* should listen. Bill Lackwell's got his eyes on you, and if he was to set his heart on 'ee, he'd get you. 'Course he would. Ain't his grandmother one of *them*?"

"I'd have nothing to do with Bill Lackwell."

"That's what you do say now. But what if she was to get to work on 'ee, eh? Witches can do anything. Then there's devils that can creep into your bed at night, and no bolts on doors and windows is going to keep them out. They can come in all shapes. Some come handsome—just the way a woman would look for handsomeness; some comes as toads and hares and cats and dogs. Some comes as the Devil himself."

Betsy's voice had risen to a shriek, and she paused for breath before hurrying on: "I'll tell 'ee something else. I'll tell 'ee why we've been spared the cane. It's because they're going off. . . They're meeting to-night. Charlie. . . he told me. They're going to take old woman Lackwell and look for the Devil's mark . . . teats where she feeds her familiar . . . and then they'll tie her up and duck her. 'Twill be the end of old Granny Lackwell, for if she do float then she be a witch and they'll take her to Witches Gibbet and hang her up by the neck; and if she do sink, well then, she'll be no witch, but she'll be drowned all the same."

Luce began to shiver.

"Don't I wish I were there!" said Betsy. "Why, if we've got one witch among us, then we may have others, and if we have, then we should look for them. It don't do to have witches round us. No wonder Charlie's father lost a whole litter of pigs last month. He says 'twas witches' work, and we ought to find them, if they do be among us."

They were silent.

Darkness fell and the stars came out; there was a thin rind of moon to shed a little light through the diamond panes of the window. They could not sleep, and at last Betsy began to talk of the Spaniards.

"They come to the towns and burn down the houses and ravish the maidens. Well, we couldn't be blamed for that, could we? But some says they ain't human. 'Tain't whores they do want to make of us girls, but Catholics. They give you the scourge and put on the thumbscrews and hang you up by your wrists; and if you was to turn Catholic before they burn you, they strangle you first. If you don't they just roast you alive. Listen. Can you hear those voices? That's them with Granny Lackwell." She leaped up and went to the window. "We couldn't climb out of this window, could we? But if that door was unlocked, I'd be out. I'd be down them stairs. Wouldn't you, Luce? Wouldn't it be worth a bit of trouble to see what they're doing to old Granny Lackwell?"

Luce nodded and Betsy began to giggle. She danced to the door.

"Why," she said, "if that door was unlocked, I'd open it and walk out . . . right down them stairs . . ."

She broke off. She had turned the handle and the door opened, for Mistress Alton had forgotten to lock it.

* * *

Half a mile or so from the big house and the cottages of Pennicomquick some fifteen men and ten women were gathered around an old woman. The light from a flare or two showed the clearing among the trees, and in this clearing was a pond of stagnant water. The faces of these people looked fantastic in the glow; lust of the hunt burned in their eyes, and mingling with it was a gleam of righteousness which made them enjoy their cruelty the more. The Church of England no less than the Church of Rome denounced all witches and sentenced them to ignoble death.

Women were whispering together: "I did see the smoke coming out of her chimney to-day. It did rise in shapes like serpents. 'Twas no ordinary smoke. 'Twas evil she was brewing in her cauldron, I'm sure."

"That cat of hers, 'tis no ordinary cat. 'Tis her familiar and she suckles it. We'll see her float, mark my words."

"And if her floats, what then?"

"What the law won't do for us we must do for ourselves. To the gibbet with her."

They were tying up the old woman now in the traditional manner—her wrists to her ankles; they were attaching a rope about her waist so that they could pull her out of the water and if possible prevent her drowning. They were eager to prove her a witch and hang her on the gibbet.

The poor old creature was moaning softly; a trickle of saliva ran from her lips; she was bemused with fear. She crouched on the grass, stark naked, her withered body seeming inhuman in the light from the flares. They had found a big wart on her back and had declared this to be the Devil's mark, so that there was ample justification for putting to the test one so branded.

The old woman's cat was mewing piteously. They had intended that he should follow his mistress into the water, and a stone was being tied about his neck; he scratched and clawed at his tormentors with what they were certain was more venom than could be displayed by an ordinary cat.

"Send the cat off first," cried a man. "Who knows? It might have powers to help the witch."

This the crowd agreed to do, and the cat was flung into the pond. It went to the bottom immediately.

"Now," cried Mistress Alton, who was well to the fore. "No more delay. Now for the witch. Tom Hurly, you'd better say a word or two before we does it, to show the real reason why we feel we've got to act."

Tom Hurly, a talkative man, was quite prepared to speak.

"We'll ask the blessing of God," he said, "for we know, every one of us, that 'tis His will we should down the Devil and all his friends. Oh Lord, let not this witch escape Thy Vengeance. Let her be shown for what she is by the test of water. Let not the work of Thine enemy Satan come to her aid. If she floats, then Lord, we'll hang her—with Thy help—on the witches gibbet. If she sinks we'll know her for innocent. In Thy Name we seek Thy Help in purging this our land from the Evil One."

Mistress Alton cried: "Come on, friends. In the Name of the Lord."

With a howl of triumph, her persecutors crowded in on the old woman, trying to hustle her to her feet. She could not stand, trussed as she was, and could only crouch on all fours, like an animal in pain.

And then, suddenly, into their midst came Richard Merriman. His presence was so unexpected that the men stopped what they were doing to take off their caps or pull their forelocks, while the women curtsied.

Richard looked with distaste at the naked woman and from her to her persecutors.

"You were making such a devil of a row," he said. "So it's a witch hunt."

"Well, sir," said Tom Hurly the spokesman, "this Granny Lackwell, she be a witch, sir . . ."

"Oh come, Hurly—just a wretched old woman, I am sure."

"No, sir. Not she . . ."

They all began to talk at once.

"My little Jane was took sick with fits, sir, when the old woman looked at her."

"Every pig in a litter lost . . ."

Richard stood there; very elegant he looked in his elaborate breeches slashed and puffed and decorated with gold lace; his doublet was cut in the Italian fashion — dazzling in its richness.

"You disturbed me," he said, "with your howling and shouts. As for the woman, she is no witch. I tell you she is a helpless old woman. Does anyone of you dare to contradict me? Let me tell you that it is not for such as you to take the law into your hands. Untie the ropes, Tom, and one of you take off your gown and wrap it about her. Mistress Alton, I would have thought you might have been looking to your duties rather than mingling with such fools. The two girls should not be allowed to creep out at this hour to witness such things. I am sorry that you do not take better care of them. The rest of you . . . have done with this folly. Take the woman back to her home. If you look for occupation, some of you might keep a watch on the sea. What if the Spaniards should land while you waste your time tormenting an old woman?"

They obeyed him, since it would not have occurred to them to do otherwise. They had always obeyed Mr. Merriman as their forebears had obeyed his.

Richard had no doubt that his orders would be carried out. He walked away.

Poor old woman! he thought. A witch? Well, he had saved her life to-night, but he doubted not that they would murder her one day. She was marked as a witch and it was a sad fate that awaited such a woman. He had been watching them to-night for longer than they realized. They interested him with their superstitions and their cruelty; it seemed to him that the two went often hand in hand.

He smiled, thinking of the two girls. They would be severely punished for this, and so they should be. But he suspected Betsy was the ringleader in this little adventure. Luce had not enjoyed it as her companion had. There was a different quality about Luce.

* * *

The uneasy weeks were passing. June had come, bringing with it the fiercest winds that could be remembered for the time of year. South-westerly gales were keeping the English fleet laid up in harbour, and the stores promised by the Queen and her Council in London had failed to arrive.

Sir Humphrey rode over from Stoke with his son Bartle to call on his friend in Pennicomquick.

Sir Humphrey was the acknowledged father of one boy—Bartle, who was six years old—and was the suspected father of many another child who pulled a forelock and scraped a leg or bobbed a greeting as it stood back from the pounding hoofs of Sir Humphrey's mare. Sir Humphrey was not displeased by the numerous progeny which were put to his account; and if his lady had given him only one son, that was surely a fault to be laid at her door, not his.

He enjoyed life; he was afraid of nothing so long as he understood it—and war, bloodshed and violence he understood perfectly; it was the supernatural which alarmed him. He would face any man with a sword or a blunderbuss; but witches worked in the dark; they attacked a man with a plague or a pox. He was talking of witches to Bartle as they rode over.

Bartle—even at six—was a boy of whom a man such as Sir Humphrey could be proud. He was tall for his years, fair-haired, rosy-cheeked and blue-eyed. He had his mother's looks and his father's spirit. He would be one for the women and the wine of life which was adventure.

Bartle could never hear enough of his father's exploits at sea. He would run his hands over the golden ornaments which his father had brought back from Peru and Hispaniola. He would wrap about him the rich cloth filched from the Spaniards, and he would strut. He was a man in the making.

There was no danger of the boy's turning out to be a scholar; his blue eyes were already turned towards the sea.

They had passed the Lackwell cottage and Sir Humphrey had called out to the boy not to look that way.

"That old woman could put a spell on you, boy. She could turn you from the healthy man you are going to be into a poxy go-by-the-ground . . . or even into a womanish scholar like our friend Merriman."

"I wouldn't mind that, sir, for I should then be able to please my tutor. I'd get through my tasks and not waste so much time on 'em."

"Don't say that, boy. That's tempting the Devil. Stay as you are, and don't give too much thought to your tasks. Just get the way to read and write, and the manners of a gentleman. That's all such as you and me want, boy."

"Look!" cried the boy. "There are ships in the Channel. Over there . . . Bolt Head way . . ."

Sir Humphrey drew up his mare. She stood obedient while he strained his bloodshot eyes, cursing them because they were not so sharp as the boy's.

"There, Father, look! One . . . two . . . three . . . Oh, sir, the Spaniards have come. Let us go to the town. I could do something. I could . . ."

"Be silent, boy. Come on."

They galloped, their hearts beating fast—relief, even joy, showing in their faces.

"The Spaniards have come!" shouted Sir Humphrey. "Out of your houses . . . you oafs . . . you lazy dogs! Now you will have a taste of a fight. By God, my sword will be red before this day is out."

Men, women and children came running from their cottages. Sir Humphrey pointed seawards and rode on.

Richard had come out to meet them. His face was calm and he was smiling in what Sir Humphrey often referred to as that "plaguey superior way of his."

"The Spaniards!" cried Sir Humphrey. "By Christ, man, they're here at last."

Richard continued to smile. "Nonsense, Cavill. It is only the victualling ships from Tilbury."

"By. . . God!" cried Sir Humphrey.

" 'Tis so, sir," shouted Bartle. "I can see the red cross of England."

Richard laid a hand on the boy's shoulder. "So eager, then, for bloodshed? Come into the house for a glass of wine."

They led their horses into the courtyard, where Clem Swann and Ned came to take them; then they went into the house. Richard rang the bell, which Luce answered. He asked for cakes and wine.

Mistress Alton brought the refreshment, with Luce in attendance. Mistress Alton's mouth seemed firmer since the adventure of Whit-Sunday night; there was a faint disapproval in her eyes, and Richard guessed that was for himself because of his leniency towards God's enemies. He smiled at her sardonically. Then his attention went to the girl, and fleetingly he wondered if her back still smarted from the whipping she must have received that night.

Sir Humphrey's attention went immediately to the women, for it was as natural for him to assess women as he assessed his horses. He knew the Alton type; she hated the thought of other people's love-making because she had missed having any of her own. A stick of a woman. No good, no good at all. But the girl? He had not noticed her before; she had always run at his approach, he believed . . . a shy, slip of a girl, hardly ready till now to satisfy his purposes. She was still young, but not too young. Rather like a comely boy with her hair short like that. Sir Humphrey decided to keep an eye on Richard's serving wench. Not that he would go out of his way. . . but if the opportunity came. . . well, he'd be ready for it. And Sir Humphrey was the kind of man whom opportunity invariably favoured.

When the servants went out, Bartle sat entranced, listening to the conversation of his elders.

"By God," Sir Humphrey was saying. "Drake is straining at the leash, man. Of course he is. Does he want to wait in harbour, cowering from the gale like a child behind its nurse's skirts? No, sir. He should out and at 'em! There's restiveness aboard. I know. Drake says, 'We'll go and tackle the Spaniard in his own seas.' But 'No!' says the Queen. And 'No!' says her Council. 'Stay close to the land and protect *us*.' By God, sir, that's not Drake's way. First to the attack; that's our Admiral. And he's right. By God, he's proved it. He's proved it a thousand times."

The boy jumped up and down in his chair.

"It would seem," said Richard, "that it is no good thing to have men of theories impeding men of action. Had he been given his head, I am inclined to think our danger would be past ere this. Sir Francis is manacled by instructions from London. He knows the course he wishes to take. *Fortes fortuna adjuvat.*"

"What's that?" said Sir Humphrey.

"Bartle will tell you," said Richard; "or he should be able to."

But Bartle could not tell his father, and Sir Humphrey was not greatly disturbed on that score.

“Alas! Bartle, it would seem you are a sad pupil. I asked your tutor how you did, and he shook his head in a most melancholy fashion. You dream too much of adventure, of the sea, of bringing home treasure. Is that not so?”

“Then he dreams a man’s dreams,” said Sir Humphrey.

Bartle said: “The coming of these ships will mean that our fleet will sail to the attack.” His face fell. “They will fight away from our coast . . . along the coast of Spain, mayhap in Cadiz Harbour. The Spaniards will see the fight instead of us.”

Sir Humphrey let out a roar of laughter. “They’ll never make a scholar of you, boy. He’d rather see a fight than know the meaning of a Latin tag, wouldn’t you, son?” Sir Humphrey looked into his wine. “There’s something that bothers me, Richard. You know . . . you shouldn’t have stopped ’em the other night. Witches is witches, and the sooner we find out who among us is with the Devil, the better for us all.”

Richard looked at Bartle. “You may find a peach or two in the gardens,” he said.

“Nay!” said Sir Humphrey. “Let the boy stay. I don’t want him made into a mincing dainty who mustn’t hear this and who mustn’t hear that. He knows there are witches, don’t you, boy? And he knows what it’s our bounden duty to do to them.”

Bartle nodded. “I wish I’d been there,” he said. “Why did you stop them, sir? The old woman is a witch.”

"Utterly distasteful!" said Richard. "Good God, we must keep law and order in these parts. It is not for our yokels to take the law into their hands. She is just a foolish old woman who brews herbs and gives charms to lovesick maidens. I heard the shouting and went out. A most disgusting spectacle."

Sir Humphrey looked at his friend. Damn me, thought Sir Humphrey, if I'd be a friend of his but for living so close. Only half a man. Riding over to see that widow woman every so often. A dried-up old widow woman when there's a ripe young virgin under his very roof. Reading his books, scratching away with his quill, can't look on a witch being put to the test without finding it disgusting, distasteful. Give me a man!

Sir Humphrey said: "If there are witches hereabouts, they should be found and finished. We want no trafficking with the Devil."

Richard shrugged his elegant shoulders and gave Sir Humphrey another of his superior smiles. Then he turned the discussion back to the Spaniards, and they were on this when Sir Humphrey rose to go.

When Richard went with his guests to the gate, the girl Luce was in the garden. She had a basket of peaches in her hand, and she coloured and dropped a curtsy as they came out.

"Hey!" said Sir Humphrey. "What you got there, girl?" Richard watched him pretend to peer into the basket while he looked at the opening of her bodice.

"Peaches, sir."

Sir Humphrey took one, and dug his teeth into it. "Why, they're better than ours. Send me over a basket by the girl, will you, Richard?" He gave the peach to Bartle to finish, and slapped Luce's buttocks as she turned away. "Bring them over, girl, and don't give them to anyone but me. You understand?"

Luce looked from Sir Humphrey to her master. Richard nodded and she curtsied again before returning to the house.

When he had waved farewell to Sir Humphrey and his son, Richard came back through the gardens and, as he did so, saw Luce coming out to gather peaches for Sir Humphrey. Richard followed her over to the wall on which the peaches were growing. Luce blushed and fumbled to be so observed.

"Don't give him of our best," he said. "Let us save those for our own table."

She picked the fruit, and when the basket was full he took it from her.

"Go to the stables," he said, "and tell Ned Swann I wish him to take these over to Sir Humphrey."

She curtsied and he watched her as she went into the courtyard.

* * *

In the harbour torches and cressets lighted the sailors loading ships. The Spanish galleons had not come, but the English were going out to meet them, for Drake had won the day. First Howard had agreed to his plan, then the Queen and her Council had followed. Sailors were singing and whistling as they made ready. The suspense of waiting was over.

Mistress Alton had been taken sick. She lay in her bed, muttering prayers which she believed was the only way to counteract a spell. Old woman Lackwell had fixed her sore eyes on Mistress Alton on Whit-Sunday night, and ever since Mistress Alton had been sick. She was certain she had been "overlooked."

Life seemed good to Luce and Betsy without Mistress Alton to watch them, to complain and to cut them across the legs and arms with her cane.

Outside the sun was shining and the gardens were filled with the scent of roses and the lavender which was just breaking into bloom. Betsy sang as she and Luce went from the kitchen to the pastry, and from the pastry to the buttery and back to the kitchen:

"Hyle that the sun with his beames hot
Scorched the fruits in vale and mountain.
Philon the shepherd late forgot,
Sitting beside a crystal fountain."

She taught the words to Luce and they sang them together.

"Sitting beside a crystal fountain
In shadow of a green oak tree,
Upon his pipe this song played he,
Untrue love, untrue love,
Untrue love, adieu, love.
Your mind is light."

They danced round the kitchen, curtsying, dipping, touching hands, bowing.

Charlie Hurly looked through the window and was watching for some minutes before they saw him. Then he clapped his hands, and Luce blushed, while Betsy went to the window and put her hands on her hips, pretending to scold him. But he just laughed and beckoned Betsy out to the shed, for he had something to tell her; she scolded still more and said she would not go, but Luce could not help noticing that she was soon making an excuse to go outside and that she stayed there for a full quarter of an hour.

They had to take it in turns to go up to Mistress Alton's room for instructions. She lay on her pallet, her face greenish yellow, her dry lips muttering prayers to ward off evil.

In the courtyard Charlie Hurly was talking to Ned Swann about what was going on in the harbour; they were nodding their heads, looking grave, looking wise. Charlie would not have dared hang about like that if Mistress Alton had been about. Betsy would not have dared to stay chattering.

And that night, of course, Mistress Alton was unable to lock the two girls in their room.

* * *

The weeks of waiting were not yet done with. The fleet had set out only to be driven back by the gales. Every man and woman of Plymouth shared the impatience of the admirals, and railed against the Queen for her meanness in not sending more of the desperately needed stores. Rations were short on board the ships, and although Drake and Howard were convinced that the winds which were tormenting them were also plaguing the Spaniards, when the opportunity arose to leave the shores of Devon and go into the attack, ill-equipped as they were they were unable to do so. The caution of the Queen, and still more the stinginess of the lady, were preventing a quick victory. It was all very well to make fine speeches at Tilbury, but what folly to let her meanness set her throne and her country in danger!

But in the first week of that July, Howard and Drake could no longer wait; in spite of sickness aboard and shortage of food, they set out for the attack. But before long, back they came dejected and disappointed. The storm-battered Spaniards lay off Corunna, where they would have been at the mercy of the English, but—like a miracle that had worked in the Spaniards' favour—the north wind had suddenly dropped, and the English, in full sight of their enemy, lay becalmed until a south wind arose. They could return or wait—their food and water low, thanks to their Queen—on the pleasure of the winds.

Mistress Alton, now recovered from her mysterious illness, was certain what this meant. It was witchcraft. She knew, if others did not, how the tempest and calm could be controlled by witches. She went about muttering prayers all day; the cane was not used so frequently since she had risen from her sick-bed, but only because she had not the strength in her arms. She had never seen such an addle-pated pair as the two serving wenches had become. There was Betsy going out to get water without a bucket. As for Luce, you could speak to her and she would not seem to hear. These girls had been up to something, Mistress Alton was quick to note, for she was a woman who recognised sin the moment she saw it.

She thought of getting Clem Swann to give them a good beating for her; but she did not trust Clem Swann. He would be gloating over their white shoulders or mayhap trying to get them to expose their bosoms. For modesty's sake, she could not get Clem Swann to punish them; and as for getting him to beat them through their petticoats, that would be just a lark to them. Yet it was a sad thing to let sin go unpunished.

Sir Humphrey was of the same opinion as Mistress Alton regarding the frustrations at sea. This was witches' work. How else could it be explained? He wanted to take old Granny Lackwell and make her talk, make her expose her confederates. He argued the point with Richard; and it was maddening how a scholar could tie up a man with words. He was turning over in his mind whether he would not act in this matter in spite of his friend's disapproval, and one bright Friday afternoon, he decided to ride over to Pennicomquick and tell Richard so.

He did not, however, reach the house, for as he rode the few miles which separated his house from that of Richard, a rider came galloping towards him, and he saw that it was one of his own men whom he had sent that morning into Plymouth on an errand.

"Sir Humphrey," cried the man, "they are coming. Captain Fleming has just come into the harbour. The admirals were at play on the Hoe. The Spaniards are sighted off the Lizard."

Then Sir Humphrey forgot the danger of witches. He lost no time in galloping straight down to the harbour.

* * *

The days that followed saw the defeat of what had been believed to be the greatest armada the world had seen. Much of the battle had been witnessed from the Devon and Cornish coasts before the Spaniards fled up Channel towards the Isle of Wight, pursued by English ships in which men counted their ammunition and were close to starvation, living as they were on half rations. News travelled slowly and it was some time before the people of Plymouth knew the story of the fireships which had finished off the fine work of their seamen.

This was a proud story, but not so proud was the tale of men set ashore to die in the streets of sea-ports from wounds and starvation. Yet England was saved from Spain and the Inquisition in spite of her Queen, who, now that her kingdom was safe, sat shaking her ginger head at the cost of the operations, and grumbling because an ill wind had arisen and carried the battered and beaten ships with their treasure out of her grasp, so that the sea-bed garnered the riches which English seamen had won for their Queen.

Quiet had returned to the town of Plymouth. Nobody talked of the Spaniards now, except the penniless sailors who, their work done, were having to whistle for their pay. Danger of invasion had gone; danger of starvation was less exciting.

It was at the beginning of September when Mistress Alton brought the weeping Luce to her master and bade the girl tell him of her shame.

Richard could see the change in Luce. There were dark shadows under her eyes and her face was set into lines of anxiety.

She was silent, so Mistress Alton spoke for her.

"I have terrible news." The woman's lips could not hide the savage satisfaction she was feeling.

Richard raised his eyebrows. "Indeed? I should have thought it was good news by the look of you."

"Then, sir, my looks belie my feelings. This girl has brought shame on herself and me. On me because she was in my charge; but I lay sick and so she escaped to her wickedness. On herself because the Lord has decided that she shall answer for her sins here below. She thought to escape, but she has learned that sins must be paid for. I have whipped her; she still bleeds from the whipping. And now there is naught to be done but turn her out of doors."

"What great sin is this?" asked Richard, stroking the lace of his ruff with tenderness, as though he were more concerned with its set than with the troubles of a serving girl.

"She is with child, sir. The wicked wanton creature! She's been sneaking out at night to meet her lover, and now it seems he'll have nothing to do with her. So she is left to bring her shame to me."

"Who is your lover?" asked Richard.

Luce hung her head and would not answer. Mistress Alton's clenched fist punched the girl's back.

"Speak, you young hussy, when the master bids you."

Luce lifted her dark eyes to his face. "I . . . I cannot say, master."

"Has he bidden you to silence?"

"I . . . I don't know."

Mistress Alton let out a snort of laughter. "She cannot say his name. It seems he came to her at night. It was no fault of hers, she says. I have heard that tale before. They cast their eyes upon the men; they follow when they're beckoned, and then when they start to grow big, they play the innocent. 'I did not know. . . It was forced upon me . . . 'Twas no fault of mine . . .' "

"Leave the girl with me," said Richard.

The woman hesitated, her mouth working, her eyes gleaming.

"Sir . . ." she began; but he lifted a hand impatiently.

"I pray you leave the girl with me."

When he spoke in that tone—gentle yet very firm with a faintly threatening note in his voice—no one dared disobey him. So Mistress Alton went reluctantly out.

"Now, Luce," he said, when she had gone, "come here. Sit down and tell me exactly what happened."

"I . . . I can't tell you, sir, for I don't rightly know."

"Now, please," he insisted, "that is nonsense. I am afraid you will make me angry if you persist in this silliness. Who is the man? Come along. You must know. Tell me his name at once."

"I . . . I dare not."

"You dare not tell *me*! Now was it Ned Swann?"

She shook her head.

"Luce, listen to me; tell me everything and, who knows, I may decide to help you. Do you think this man would consider marrying you?"

"Oh, no . . . no!"

"He is far above you in station? You must tell him then, and I doubt not that he will find a husband for you. Why, girl, it is not the first time this has happened. Dry your tears, I dare swear a man will be found to marry you."

She looked at him then, shaking her head; and suddenly, tumbling from her lips came the whole story.

It had happened thus:

On the first night of Mistress Alton's sickness, she and Betsy had left their attic and crept out of the house. That day Charlie Hurly had told Betsy that at midnight he was going to witness a very strange sight and he wanted her to accompany him. There were witches in the neighbourhood—many of them—and on certain nights they met to do homage to the Devil, to learn his secrets and to win great powers from him in exchange for their souls.

Betsy had promised to go. She knew that it was possible on this night, and it was too good an opportunity to miss. But when midnight came she was frightened, and she asked Luce to accompany her. Luce did not want to go at first but, after a good deal of persuasion, she did so.

After that the story became still more incoherent. It was obvious to Richard that Charlie had lured Betsy out in order to seduce her; it was small wonder that he was annoyed when she arrived at their tryst with her fellow servant.

Luce then assured him that she had witnessed strange and diabolical things that night, but nothing more strange and more diabolical than the thing which had happened to her.

Charlie had taken them to a clearing in the woods, and they had hidden behind trees and watched. Luce had seen wild figures dancing round a fire; she was sure they were not entirely human beings; some had the heads of animals, and they danced, taking partners and making gestures as though they were . . .

She faltered, but he helped her. "As though they were inviting each other to fornication?" he said.

She hung her head. "Please, sir, I can say no more. Turn me out . . . Let me starve . . . Let me beg . . . But don't ask me to tell you more, for I cannot tell it."

"Nevertheless," he said, "you will tell me, for I insist."

"I should not have left the attic, sir. I knew that was wrong. I knew that was wicked. I shouldn't have watched." She began to sob. "Then it wouldn't have happened to me."

"Go on," he commanded.

And she told him how suddenly she had found that Betsy and Charlie were no longer beside her; she was alone there among the trees, and before her eyes was taking place that weird scene in the clearing. But she was aware suddenly that she was not alone . . . for close to her was a figure, a figure clad in black from head to foot. She could not see his face, or indeed whether he had a face, as men had faces. She knew there were eyes that watched her; there were horns . . . Yes, she saw the horns.

"And, sir," she said, "I was took with trembling, for I did know . . ."

"What did you know, Luce?"

"I knew, sir, that I was in the presence of the Devil himself. He came to me . . . and I tried to run, but I was stuck there . . . like I was chained, sir . . . and he came nearer and nearer . . . and I couldn't cry out . . . nor could I move."

His smile was sardonic. "And then, Luce?"

"He picked me up and threw me over his shoulder."

"So he had a shoulder, then?"

"Yes, sir. I did feel as though I were thrown over his shoulder. I fainted, sir. I fainted right away. I thought, sir, I was being carried straight to eternal damnation as Mistress Alton is always talking of."

"And when you came to?"

"I was lying on the grass, sir. There at the edge of the wood where the bushes is thick . . . and I knew, sir, I knew what had happened to me."

He laid both his hands on her shoulders and looked into her face. "Luce, are you seriously trying to tell me that you believe it was the Devil? Come, girl. You know it was a man dressed up as the Devil. You know it. Admit it. I have an idea that you know who the man is."

"No, sir. I swear I don't."

"Do you swear it? Would you swear it on the Holy Bible?"

"Yes, sir, that I would."

"Luce, you try my patience sorely. It is a trick that has been played on you."

"I do not think so. For there was another time . . ."

"Another time?"

"He came to me in the dark of night when I lay abed."

"What, in this house? Why did you not wake Betsy?"

"Mistress Alton was sick. She was so sick that she wanted one of us to stay with her. So . . . Betsy stayed. I was alone that night. And I woke suddenly. It was dark . . . and I knew he was there."

"Did you faint that time, Luce?"

"No, sir. That time I did not faint. I . . . I was awake all the time . . ."

"And you persist that he was the Devil?"

"Yes, sir. I know he was the Devil."

"Now, listen to me, Luce. I can understand your believing this incredible thing on the night in the wood, but not . . . oh, certainly not . . . when he came to your room. Think of all the men hereabouts who have looked your way and desired you. You must be aware of them."

She shook her head. She was crying silently, the tears spilling over onto her bodice. He looked at her swollen face with distaste and walked away from her to the window.

"I will give you a word of warning," he said. "Tell no one else this incredible tale. If you do, I fear there may be trouble for you . . . greater trouble than this bearing of a child whose father you do not know."

He turned to look at her standing there so miserable, so abject.

"There are some who would say I should send you back to your parents. Would you like that, Luce?"

She began to sob aloud.

He spoke more gently. "Don't make that noise, child. Go now. I shall not send you home if you do not wish to go. Instead, I will do my best to find a man willing to father your child. Come. You have been foolish—for you know you were wrong to leave the house when Mistress Alton forbade you to leave it—and this is the result of your folly. Try to remember that what has happened to you has happened to others before you. Go now. I promise to help you."

He watched her stumble from the room, and he thought how different she was from that graceful girl whom he had seen outside the church on Whit-Sunday morning.

* * *

That was the story of Tamar's conception.

Richard was as good as his word. He chose Ned Swann as a likely husband for Luce, but Ned was reluctant to take her. He had heard whispers as to the paternity of the child that made the marriage necessary.

The Lackwells were not so particular. Bill Lackwell had often cast a lustful eye on the girl, and as Richard offered a small sum of money to go with her, Bill decided it was not a bad match.

So Bill married Luce and almost a year after Luce had watched Sir Francis Drake leave the church with Lord Howard of Effingham, her baby was born.

Tamar was a dark-eyed girl with the marks of beauty on her even in her earliest days. She was a bonny child, and some said that she was actually Bill Lackwell's daughter; but there were many who did not wish to rid themselves of the belief that she was the child of Satan.

CHAPTER TWO

Tamar, being more than ordinarily intelligent, quickly became aware of the difference between herself and other children, for, by the time she was five years old, Luce had three more to litter the one room of the Lackwell cottage. Tamar looked on gravely at the scenes which took place before her young eyes. She had seen the birth of one brother and the death of another. She had sat solemnly in her corner watching, for no one turned her out, and it was then that she first became aware of that awe — which in time grew to fear — with which she was able to inspire those about her.

She made a little corner for herself near the fire — when there was one — the cosiest spot away from the window where the cracked oiled paper, which did the service of glass, let in the draughts. She collected coloured stones and made a boundary with them about her corner.

"Nobody ain't coming inside these stones," she said; and she had said it defiantly, expecting Bill Lackwell to kick the stones from one end of the earthen floor to the other, and to pick her up by her rags and lay about her with his calloused hands before he put her outside the door. But he did no such thing; he merely looked away from her, while her mother watched her with terrified eyes.

Tamar was triumphant. Nobody moved the stones. When the other children came to take them their mother called them away—even their father growled at them; and Tamar kept the cosiest corner in that miserable room to herself.

Tamar was interested in everything that went on in the cottage and outside it. The other children seemed to think of little beyond whether they would eat or whether they would get one of their father's cruel beatings; it was true that Tamar did not have to think of the latter, as Bill Lackwell never touched her, no matter what she did, but food was a matter of great importance to her.

On a stool, from which she rarely moved, sat old Grandmother Lackwell. She could hardly walk now, for when she had been dragged from the cottage to be tested that Whit-Sunday night, her leg had been broken; she could only drag it along as she walked, and that with great pain. She would sit brooding—just sitting, her rheumy old eyes half closed, not seeing the cottage or its inhabitants, as though she were not there in that room but miles away.

Tamar was interested in the old woman; she sensed in her that distinction which had unaccountably been bestowed on herself. The old woman did nothing for her keep, except now and then sell some of the herbs which grew in the patch round the cottage; she would send her customers out with instructions what to pick, and when they had done so, they would bring them into her. Then she would tell them what to do with these plants and what to say while they were doing it. She hardly ever received money, but a few days after these transactions, a gift would be laid at the door — rye bread or an egg or two. Bill Lackwell or Luce took them in and they would all share, no thanks being given to the old woman; but everyone knew that it was due to her that they came.

But, reasoned Tamar, these gifts came too rarely to buy for the old woman her seat in the overcrowded cottage. Yet she was never spoken to harshly, never asked to move. They were afraid of her, as they were beginning to be of Tamar.

One day the child sidled up to the old woman.

"Granny," she said, "tell me about the herbs that grow in our patch."

Then one of the skinny hands touched Tamar's thick black curls.

"Fair and beautiful," mumbled the old woman, so that Tamar had to move close to her to hear what she said. "You will know what you have to do when the time comes."

So Tamar, pondering these words behind her ring of stones, knew that she was a very important person and one day would be more so.

She lived her own secret life. When it was warm she slept out of doors. She liked that, and was sad when the colder nights came to drive her under the Lackwell thatch.

Luce was no longer a slim young girl, but a tired woman, weary with constant child-bearing — her body thickened yet scraggy from the state of semi-starvation which was invariably her lot. The hair, which Mistress Alton had said was a gift from Satan, was now long, but it had lost its lustre and fell untidily to her waist. Out of the horror she had experienced during her first months as Bill Lackwell's wife had grown a dull acceptance of her fate.

She watched her eldest daughter with apprehension. Tamar was named after the river near which her conception had taken place; for such a child, Luce had felt, should not be named with a name that might belong to any child. She had anxiously awaited that moment when the perfectly formed feet might change to cloven hoofs. They remained perfect human feet. She felt the shapely head for those excrescences from which horns might be expected to grow. There was no sign of these. Tamar might have been anybody's child, except that from an early age that brightness of eye, that shapely oval face and the perfectly moulded limbs, as well as a quickness of perception, distinguished her from others. The beauty was an accentuation of that which had been Luce's in the days when she had served under Mistress Alton; but the other qualities did not come from Luce.

Luce wanted to love this daughter, but it was impossible to overcome her apprehension concerning the child, and Tamar could not help but be aware of this.

The little girl had been healthy from the day of her birth; she had remained unswaddled, for in Bill Lackwell's cottage there were no swaddling clothes. This meant that her young limbs were free to kick and feel the fresh air, and certainly to enjoy a modicum of cleanliness which was denied more well-cared-for children.

And so she grew—knowledgeable, longing to use her bright intelligence, missing little that went on around her. She saw the cruel treatment of her half-brothers and sisters by the bully Lackwell; she saw her mother suffering also from his violence, she saw their reconciliations and she knew what frequently happened under the rags on their bed of straw. She saw her mother change gradually from a shrivelled, bony woman to a big one, and she knew what that meant.

She was six years old when the difference between herself and others became fully apparent to her.

Betsy Hurly sometimes came to the cottage. Betsy had done rather well for herself, for she had induced Charlie Hurly to marry her and was now mistress of the Hurly farm. The noisy, full-blooded farmer's wife still hankered after adventures which varied only in a few details from those which had excited her before her marriage.

One day she came to the cottage when only Luce and the old woman—with Tamar sitting in her corner surrounded by her stones—were there.

Betsy brought an air of well-being with her, and in her quick way Tamar was immediately aware of how poor the place was when Betsy sat in it with her coarse worsted garments, which, while not as becoming as those worn by the gentry, looked rich compared with the rags of the other three.

Tamar, polishing her stones, was aware of everything. Outside the cottage, Annis waited. Annis was Betsy's eldest daughter — a few months younger than Tamar. Tamar looked at the child through the open door of the cottage, and Annis put out her tongue. But Tamar was more interested in the grown-ups than in the child.

Betsy was saying: "Come on, Luce. You could if you wanted to. You know how to do it. Where's the good in pretending you don't? I know too much. Don't forget you told me about it. 'Tain't much I'm asking. I'll pay thee well for it."

Luce kept her eyes down. "What is it you want, Betsy?"

Betsy said in a solemn whisper: "Jim Haines. Have you seen him, Luce? Nigh on six feet. What a man! But, my dear life, he don't see none but that young dairy-maid. I do want his affections turned to me."

"But, Betsy, you shouldn't want such things."

"Don't 'ee talk nonsense, Luce Lackwell. Should I be like you . . . let Bill Lackwell beat you sick and then give you child after child as you can't afford to feed?"

" 'Sh!" said Luce.

But Betsy would not be silent. "Well, you did have a bit of glory once, didn't 'ee? I bet *that* were a bit different from Bill Lackwell, weren't it?"

Betsy's eyes slewed round to Tamar, who seemed to be absorbed in her stones.

"Wasn't it, Luce? A bit different, eh?"

"Yes, it was then."

"Must have been. My dear soul! I reckon it must have been just about better than anything."

Luce nodded.

"But it brought you to this. I reckon you'd have had Ned Swann but for *someone's* taking a fancy to 'ee."

Luce said, "Don't say such things. 'Tis like asking for a judgment."

"You'm right. But where's the good pretending you've never had naught to do with such things? Where's the sense? You could give me a charm and bring Jim Haines straight to me arms."

"No, Betsy. 'Twouldn't be right."

"Wouldn't it then? I can tell 'ee Charlie has his larks."

"Come out to the patch," said Luce. "I knows I shouldn't. I know naught of such things. But I heard what the old woman told somebody t'other day."

Betsy glanced towards the old woman, who had sat impassive during this discussion.

"Her don't hear," explained Luce. "Her's very deaf. You have to go right up close and shout to make her hear."

They went out to the patch. Tamar stared after them while Annis looked into the cottage. She again put out her tongue at Tamar, who regarded her with solemn eyes.

"Come here," said Tamar.

"No, I won't."

"Then go away. I don't care."

"I won't."

"You're afraid."

Annis had fair hair and grey eyes; she was quite pretty, but beside Tamar she looked insignificant.

"If you wasn't afraid," said Tamar, "you'd come in."

Annis stepped gingerly into the cottage and cautiously approached the stones.

"What's them?"

"Stones."

"What for?"

"Nobody mustn't come farther than here."

Annis knelt down and looked at the stones; then she looked at Tamar, who smiled suddenly and, picking up one of the stones, gave it to Annis.

When the two women came back into the cottage Betsy looked at her daughter and turned pale. "Annis!" she cried. "What are you doing in here, then? I'll take you home and tan the hide off 'ee."

Annis got up from the floor and ran out of the cottage. Tamar watched her, then started up. "She's got my stone. Give it back. Give it back."

Betsy was out of the door; she had Annis by the shoulder; she shook her until the child's face was red. "Drop it. Drop it quick."

Annis dropped the stone and in triumph Tamar seized it.

"Take that!" said Betsy, and slapped her daughter's face. "And now come home." She pulled at the child's arm. "Good day to you, Luce."

"Goodbye, Betsy."

Tamar looked at her mother, but Luce would not meet her eyes.

I'm different, thought Tamar. Nobody slaps my face. Nobody talks of tanning my hide. I'm different. I'm Tamar. They're afraid of me.

* * *

Down at Sutton Pool people stood about on the cobbles watching the departure of Sir Walter Raleigh and his five ships which were going to explore the Orinoco in the hope of bringing back gold for the Queen.

There was less enthusiasm at such spectacles than there had been a few years ago. Plymouth could not forget the horrible sight of those brave seamen, the heroes of the defeat of the Spanish Armada, now starving in the streets, begging their bread—some cruelly wounded—their services ignored, and what was more important to them, unpaid for by an ungrateful Queen and Council.

These men would have long since died but for men like Drake, Hawkins and Frobisher, who had provided much out of their own pockets, starting a fund for mendicant seamen, building a hospital for mariners; and Sir Francis, when he had left his house in Looe Street to live in Buckland Abbey, had continued with his scheme for bringing water to the town. Now it was conveyed there from the west stream of the River Plym. No wonder they worshipped this man. It was already said—in spite of the digging operations which were to be seen—

that Sir Francis had gone to the river and, bidding it follow him, had galloped into Plymouth. They preferred to think of their benefactor not only as a good brave man, but as a wizard.

And now, with the departure of Sir Walter, there was not the same enthusiasm as when Sir Francis sailed. Adventure was in the blood of these people who lived along the seaboard, but they hated injustice, and they could not forget—being constantly reminded by the sad sights about them, as they were—the callous behaviour of their Queen.

Tamar was there by the Pool. The noble ships rocking so proudly on the water delighted her and she wished that she were sailing with the expedition. It even occurred to her to hide herself in one of the ships. Then she remembered that old Granny Lackwell would be in the cottage alone to-day. Tamar was impulsive, and once an idea had hit her she was eager to put it into practice. She pushed her way through the crowd and ran all the way home.

The old woman was sitting in her accustomed place. Tamar went close to her and shouted in her ear.

"Granny, it's Tamar."

Granny nodded.

"Granny, I've come to ask you things."

She nodded again.

"Why are they afraid of you and me?"

Granny laughed, showing black stumps which fascinated while they horrified the child. "Why are your teeth black?" she asked; but she realised at once that that was a question which could wait, for it had nothing to do with the mystery she was so eager to uncover. "How was I born?" she said quickly.

Old Granny became excited. Her hands were shaking. Tamar looked anxiously about her, for she knew that whatever revelations might take place could only do so if the two of them were alone together.

"Did a man lie with my mother, as Bill Lackwell does under the rags . . . or was it on the grass?"

That made Granny choke with laughter.

"Speak, Granny, speak! I shall be angry if you laugh. I want to know."

Granny sat very still; then she turned her head to look at the child.

"On the grass," she said.

"Why?"

Granny shook her head.

"They like doing that, I think," said Tamar gravely, for she could see that she must continue to prompt the old woman if she were to get her to reveal anything. "It was because they liked it," she went on. "And then my mother grew big and I came out. But . . . why are they afraid of me?"

Granny shook her head, but Tamar lightly slapped the old woman's arm. "Granny, I must know. You are afraid of me. My mother is afraid of me. Even Lackwell is afraid of me. He is big and strong; he has a belt and hard hands, and I am little—see how little I am, Granny!—and he is afraid of me. They are afraid of you too, Granny. It is something you have given me."

Granny shook her head. "I didn't give 'ee nothing. 'Tweren't me."

"Then who was it, Granny? Speak. . . speak. I'll hurt you if you don't tell me."

Granny's eyes grew frightened. "There now. . . there, little beauty. Don't speak so."

"Granny, it was the man on the grass. He gave me something. What is it?"

"He did give you fair looks."

" 'Tain't hair and eyes, Granny. Lackwell wouldn't care about they. Besides, they're afraid of you, Granny, and you'm ugly. You'm terrible ugly."

Granny nodded. She signed, and the black cat at her feet jumped on to her lap. She stroked the cat's back. "Stroke it with me, child," she said; and she took Tamar's little hand and together they stroked the cat.

"You're a witch, Granny," said Tamar.

Granny nodded.

"Granny, have you seen the Devil?"

Granny shook her head.

"Tell me about being a witch. What *is* being a witch?"

"It's having powers as others ain't got. It's powers that be give to the likes of we. We'm Satan's, and he's our master."

"Go on, Granny. Go on. Don't stop."

"We'm devil's children. That be it. We can heal. . . and we can kill. We can turn milk sour before it leaves the cows and goats, and we can do great things. We have Sabbats, child, Sabbats when we do meet, and there we do worship the horned goat who be a messenger from Satan. There's some as say he be one of us . . . dressed up like . . . That may be so, but when he do put on the shape of a goat he be a goat . . . and we do dance about him. Ah! I be too old for dancing now. My days be done. I'm good for naught but to tell others what to brew. 'Twas the night I was took for the test. They'd have done for me then . . . but for a gentleman that stopped 'em. I've been sick and ailing since. But I be a witch, child, and there's none can deny me that."

"Granny . . . am I a witch?"

"Not yet you ain't."

"Shall I be a witch?"

"Like as not you will . . . seeing as you come into the world the way you did."

"How did I come into the world? On the grass, was it? Was my father a witch?"

Granny was solemn. "They do say, child, that he was the greatest of them all . . . under God."

"An angel?"

"Nay. Put thy hand on Toby's back. Come close to me, child . . . closer . . ."

Tamar stood breathless, waiting. "Tell me, Granny. Tell me."

"Your father, child, was none other than the Devil himself."

* * *

The hot sultry July was with them and Tamar was scarcely ever in the cottage, coming in only to snatch a piece of rye bread or salted fish. But if the old woman was alone she would sit with her and they would talk together, for Tamar wished to know all the dark secrets of Granny's devils' world.

Not that Granny was easy to understand; sometimes she mumbled and, even standing so close and suffering the full force of her tainted breath, Tamar could discover very little. But she knew the great secret. People were afraid of her because she was Satan's daughter.

She ran through the grass delighting in its cool caress on her bare feet; she would whisper to the trees: "I am the Devil's daughter. Nothing can hurt me because he looks after me."

She loved the green solitude of the country, and it was her pleasure to collect strange plants and bring them to the old woman to ask what magic properties they contained; but it was the town itself which offered her the greatest delight. She would spend hours lying stretched out on the Hoe, straining her eyes across the sea, trying to picture what lay beyond that line where the sea met the sky. She would stand in the streets, watching the people, listening to their talk; the market delighted her and sometimes there was food to be picked up. There were times when, attracted by her grace and beauty, strangers would throw her a coin. She would watch the men load and unload ships.

There was an ancient seaman who sat on the Hoe with her and told her about his adventures on the Spanish Main. She asked question after question, delighting to listen as he did to talk. They met many times and it seemed to her that he held a new world in his mind to which his voice was the key. But one day when she saw him, he looked away and pretended he did not see her; then she ran to him and tugged his arm. He did not shout at her or curse as he knew so well how to curse; he just turned and would not look at her, gently disengaging himself and hobbling away with his crutch as well as one leg would let him. She knew what had happened; he had discovered who her father was, and he was afraid.

She threw herself down on the grass and sobbed angrily and passionately; but when she saw the old sailor again she stood before him and lifting her flashing eyes to his face, she cursed him. He turned pale and hobbled off. Now she felt triumphant, for she knew he was more afraid of a dark-eyed little girl than the Spanish Inquisition.

One exciting day news came that the Spaniards had landed in Cornwall, that Mousehole was in flames and Penzance under attack.

Tamar watched the ships set out from the Sound to go to the aid of the Cornishmen. They were stimulating days to a child who knew herself to be feared as much as the Spaniards.

August was hot and all through the month Drake and Hawkins were preparing to sail away, and Tamar was there to watch them when they went.

She would never forget the day when the town learned of the death of Drake and Hawkins. Then she saw a city in mourning and longed to be loved as these men had been. It was better to be loved than feared, she felt, for being feared gave you a lonely life.

She listened to people's talk of Drake, for no one talked to her. Her loneliness was becoming more and more marked as she grew older.

Once in the cottage when only her mother and the old woman were there with Tamar, Luce talked of Drake.

"I saw him many times," said Luce, in an unusually talkative mood, no doubt due to the death of the hero. "I remember once . . . it was in the time of our greatest danger. The whole place was waiting . . . waiting for the Spaniards. That was in the days when Spaniards *was* Spaniards."

"Yes?" said Tamar eagerly.

"It was like a sort of fever in the place. The Spaniards had big ships, they said, and ours was little 'uns. That didn't matter, though. We had *him*, you see."

"And he was better than anyone else!" cried Tamar.

"They did go to church . . . him and a great lord. I went to see them . . . with Betsy. I was different then . . ." Her eyes filled with tears as she smoothed her rough hands over her rags. "Yes, I were different. I had me hair cut short like a boy's. Hair like mine was a gift from Satan — so Mistress Alton did say."

"A gift from Satan!" cried Tamar, touching her own abundant curls.

"And she cut it off . . . like a boy's. Betsy's too . . . though Betsy's weren't what mine was."

"Go on!" begged Tamar.

"We went to the church and *he* were there. I saw him. He came out with the noble lord, and women wept to see him and men threw their caps in the air. 'God speed to you, Sir Francis!' they did shout. And now he be dead. The bonny beauty of him rotting on the sea-bed. I never did think that he would die and I be here."

"Tell me more," said Tamar. "Tell me . . . tell me. . . . Tell me about those days and Mistress Alton."

Tears began to run down Luce's cheeks.

"I thought about him too much. 'Tain't right to have the thoughts I had. 'Tis tempting the Devil. That's what it was. I didn't ask much. . . . I only asked a little."

"That's silly," said Tamar. "You must ask for a lot. I shall."

Luce turned to her daughter. "You must not go out at night. You must stay in. I wouldn't like what happened to me to happen to you. Be careful. I wouldn't like you to be caught too young."

Tamar's eyes flashed. "I'd have none of that."

"You don't know what you do say, child. 'Tis something that none of us know about until too late."

"I should know."

"Be careful. It can happen sudden like, and then there's the rest of your life"—she looked down at her garments—"the rest of your life in tatters and rags. You'm caught, and it can happen sudden-like."

"Not to me!" declared Tamar. "There is nobody clever enough to catch me!"

* * *

Once more big ships were in the harbour. Drake was no more; Hawkins had gone; but there were other West Country men waiting to step into the shoes of these men. One of these was Sir Walter Raleigh and people were talking of him now as Drake's Heir. All through the spring, while Plymouth mourned Drake, the fleet was assembling in the Sound. Lord Howard was there and this was yet another great occasion. But the change in the times was obvious to all. Men were no longer flocking to serve in the ships, and Raleigh brought strangers to Plymouth—men who did not speak with the soft Devon burr—sullen strangers who had been pressed into service.

The people murmured. It had not been thus in the days of Drake, who had had to refuse men the honour of sailing with him. What a tragic change this was—when men deserting from their ships were hanged on the Hoe as an example to others of like mind.

It was a day in June. The fleet was ready to sail and Tamar was on the Hoe to watch its departure when close to her she noticed a boy who was so much older than she was that he seemed a man. She knew him for Bartle Cavill, the son of Sir Humphrey. He was thirteen years old, tall, with eyes as blue as the sea, and a shock of yellow hair. She noticed how he gazed at the ships with yearning in his eyes; and understanding that feeling—which was hers also—she moved nearer to him.

She saw that his breeches were puffed and ornamented with mulberry-coloured silk, and she loved its colour and softness. She had to touch the silk to feel if it were as soft as it looked, so she stretched out a hand and felt it. Yes, it was even softer than it looked. There were bars of different colours. Was the green as soft as the mulberry? She had to test it.

But he had become aware of her hands upon him; swift as lightning he caught her by the arm.

"Thief!" he cried. "So I've caught you, thief!"

She lifted her great dark eyes to his face, and said shyly: "I was only feeling the silk."

The blue eyes seemed more brilliant than the sea itself.

"You're hurting me," she said.

"That is my intention!" he retorted. "You'll know what it means to be hurt when they hang you for stealing."

"I stole nothing."

"I'll have you searched. Stand away. Don't dare come close to me, you dirty beggar! What insolence!"

"I'm not a beggar, and I'm not a thief. It is you who should be afraid of me."

"I'll have those rags stripped off you and searched. I'll see you're whipped before they hang you. I'll ask it as a special favour to myself."

She had twisted her arm suddenly and freed herself, but he caught her by her hair.

"See that man hanging there?" he demanded. "He deserted his ship. That's what happens to dirty beggars who steal from their betters."

"I have no betters," she said with dignity while she screwed up her face in pain, for he seemed to be pulling her hair out by the roots.

His eyes blazed with rage. “Insolence! You’ll be sorry for this.”

“You’re the one who’ll be sorry. You don’t know who I am.”

He looked into her face and laughed. “So it’s you . . . the Devil’s own, eh!”

She was shaken, for she saw no fear in his face.

“Now do you know who *I* am?” he asked.

“Yes, I do.”

“Then you know I use no idle words. I’ll have you whipped for your insolence.”

“You wouldn’t dare. No one would dare. I . . . I’d. . . .” She glared at him. “It would be the worse for you if you hurt me.”

He let her go and she ran, and, turning round, saw that he had not moved, but was standing still watching her.

She walked on with slow dignity, but as soon as she felt he could see her no more she broke into a run. She was trembling with fear and hatred, because she was not sure whether or not he had been afraid of her.

* * *

Soon after that she heard that Bartle Cavill had run away to sea, and she was relieved. Afterwards life went on as usual. She was growing up; she was now ten years old.

There seemed less excitement in the town nowadays. King Philip had been dead for a year, and there no longer seemed any great danger of raids on the coast. Just before his death it had been brought home to the King that he would never realise his ambitions. Plymouth had not even seen the ships of his Adelantado, which had come to invade, for a kindly storm had wrecked them in the Bay of Biscay. Such a disaster to ships — as grand and formidable as those of his great Armada — meant the end of his attempt to subdue England. But on the high seas rivalry continued.

Somewhere out there, Tamar sometimes thought, was Bartle Cavill. Perhaps he had left his ship by now and was storming some city; perhaps he was cutting his way through the jungle; perhaps he was being tortured in a dungeon. All of these things might have happened to him. She thought of him with great hatred, not so much for the words he had used to her but for the contempt he had shown her in his brilliant blue eyes.

Her lonely life continued. No children played with her, but she did not wish to play their games. She was learning a good deal from Granny Lackwell, and when people came to the cottage for herbs, Granny would say: "The child will pick them for you. The child knows."

Then Tamar would enjoy afresh that strange power which was hers.

But one day she learned that people hated her because they feared her. The most terrifying experience of her life so far was awaiting her.

It was dusk of an evening in summer and she was walking to a favourite haunt of hers — a shady spot with many trees which overhung a large pond. She often came here; she liked to sit by the pond and watch the birds and insects; she had learned to imitate the calls of the birds so that they answered her; and she liked to watch the ants in the long grass and the spiders in their webs. Sometimes she would dabble her feet in the water. It was a pleasant spot for a hot day such as this had been.

But as she came under the trees she heard a sudden whoop above her, and several small figures—some smaller than herself—dropped from the trees. The children of the neighbourhood were upon her.

She was felled to the ground at once, and although she kicked fiercely and tried to free herself, they were too many for her—and some were quite big boys. While they had her on the ground they blindfolded her by tying a piece of rag about her eyes, and she knew then that they were afraid that she would recognise them. She exulted in that because it showed that they were afraid of her.

"Let me go!" she cried. "I'll curse you. You'll be sorry. I know who you are. I don't have to see you."

They said nothing. One of them kicked her; another punched her back. She felt sick and faint, for although she had often witnessed physical violence she had never before experienced it.

She kicked and screamed, calling: "You'll be sorry. I know you. I know you all."

Still her tormentors did not speak. They forced her to sit on the grass, and when they seized her hands and tied them to her ankles she knew what they planned to do to her.

Many hands touched her, scratching her, tearing her skin. She expected some power to come to her aid, but she had nothing . . . nothing but the strength of a ten-year-old girl to use against them.

A great shout went up from their throats and she felt herself thrown; the waters of the muddy pond splashed about her and she was sitting on its weedy bottom. They had not been able to throw her very far in, and she was only waist-high in the water.

The children on the edge of the pond forgot that she must not hear their voices and they began to shriek:

"She's sinking."

"She's *not*!"

"She'll float all right. She's the Devil's own daughter. He do look after his own."

One of the boys jabbed at her with a long branch of a tree; the skin of her leg was torn as he tried to push her farther out. She was past feeling pain, for she believed she was going to die, since, trussed as she was, she could do nothing to help herself, and the rag about her eyes—now wet and most foul smelling—prevented her from seeing about her.

The shouts went on.

"She's a witch all right."

Someone threw a stone at her. It missed and splashed into the water. More stones came and some of them hit her. She felt herself sinking into the mud. She was half fainting, yet her anger and her belief in herself kept her from doing so. To faint would be to drown, unless the children became frightened and pulled her out. But they would not be frightened, for there was no one to care if she was drowned. Old Granny might care; but the old woman was near death and hardly counted. Her mother? Perhaps she would be a little sorry, but mostly relieved; she would not have to watch her as she did now, waiting for some outward sign of the devil in her daughter. Everyone else would be glad. So there was no one at all who would be really sorry.

And as she gasped and spluttered, she was suddenly aware of silence. The children had stopped shouting.

Then a voice said: "You . . . you . . . and you there, go in and bring the girl out."

She was seized and pulled to the bank. She lay there gasping.

"Take that rag from her eyes and untie her wrists."

Black spots were dancing before her eyes now. The darkening sky seemed to sway above her.

A cultured voice said: "It's the Lackwell girl."

Then Tamar turned over and was violently sick. She groaned and tried to stand up. She saw that the children had scattered but that the man remained. She knew him for Richard Merriman, who lived in the big house.

"You're all right," he said. "Those young devils might have drowned you. Keep out of their way in future."

She heard herself stammer: "They were afraid of me. They had to bind my eyes."

She tottered towards him and he caught her as she almost fell. She was quick enough to see the disgust he felt at her nearness, and she was aware immediately of her verminous rags in contrast with his exquisite garments. With dignity she drew herself away from him.

"Thank you for making them pull me out," she said, and began to totter away.

"Here, child!" he called after her.

But she would not look back.

"What the devil!" he shouted.

The tears were running down her cheeks. She had been deeply insulted, first by the children and then by him; she was not going to let anyone see her tears.

She limped back to the cottage and Granny did her best to comfort her. Granny hobbled from her chair to make some special brew.

"There," muttered the old woman. "You'm doing well. 'Twas your first ducking and you stood up well to it."

When Tamar retired behind her ring of stones, she did not feel the pain of her limbs and the soreness of her wounds. She could only think of the man in the elegant clothes who had been disgusted to have her near him.

* * *

She thought of Richard Merriman a good deal after that. But for him she might have died, for they would have stoned her to death or left her to drown, as they often did stray cats and dogs; she was no more to them than an unwanted animal. Yet they were afraid of her, and that was why they hated her. Perhaps it was not such a good thing to be feared? How much better to be loved!

She must not be angry with Richard Merriman, though, for he had saved her. He could not help it if she disgusted him. She remembered how she had disgusted Bartle Cavill and her eyes blazed with hatred at the thought of him. I hope the Spaniards get him! she thought. I hope they brand him with hot irons and burn him for his faith.

She looked about her, waiting for the earth to open and the Devil to appear, waiting for some animal to come to her and speak with a human voice, and demand her eternal soul in exchange for what she asked. Nothing happened.

"No!" she whispered. "I don't want the Spaniards to get him, for he would never deny his faith and they would burn him alive and I would never seen him again." And she wanted to see him again, so that she could show him in some way how she hated him.

As for the other man, Richard Merriman, she must show her gratitude to him, since he had saved her life. The daughter of Satan must acknowledge her debts.

There was a spot on the cliffs where it was said that it was possible to find seagulls' eggs, although it was rarely anyone went in search of them as the climb was dangerous and the slate and shale cliffs offered scarcely any footing; but the eggs would be all the more appreciated if they were hard to get.

She grew excited at the project. When she took the eggs to him, she would say very haughtily: "You do not like the smell of me, sir, but perhaps you will like the taste of these. They are for you because you saved my life."

The sun was high in the sky when she set out. As she walked to the lonely spot, she kept clear of all trees, for she would never again walk unwarily under trees; she kept turning to make sure she was not being followed. The climb was long and steep, and several times she nearly lost her footing; the birds whirled about her head—gulls and cormorants—shrieking, screaming at her as though indignant at her intrusion. But she was not afraid of the birds.

She pulled her way up, hanging onto the tufts of coarse ling, cutting her feet on jagged rock, scratching her legs on the gorse; once or twice she almost fell, but she went on triumphantly.

Looking down at the rocks below, it occurred to her that if she fell it would be to death; but that was how she would have it, for he had saved her life, and she wished to risk it again in making her thank-offering.

The wind tugged at her thick hair. It was as verminous as her rags, and she hated it to be so; she longed for a gown with puffed sleeves and a skirt cut away to show a splendid undergown. But one thing she had learned from her ducking was that although her clothes smelt of the mud of the pond, many of the lice attached to them had lost their lives in the water. If she dipped her clothes in a clear stream, and her hair too, she might leave some more of the irritating creatures behind; and a clear stream would not leave a smell upon her and her garments as the pond had.

She knew of such a stream; it was in the grounds surrounding none other than the house of Richard Merriman himself. Before she took the eggs to him she would wash her hair and her clothes in the stream.

Such thoughts made her laugh out loud. He would see the change in her. In her imagination the dip in the stream would do more than rid her rags of their pests; it would transform them into silks and velvets.

She went on with vigour, eager to be done with the difficult task and get to the easier and more pleasant one of cleaning herself and her garments in the stream. She clutched at a clump of ling which came away in her hand, but she was able to save herself just in time, though in doing so she scratched her arm badly and it started to bleed.

But she did not care, since she had found her first seagulls' eggs.

Getting down took far longer than the ascent, as now she had the eggs to consider, and she could not have borne the disappointment if she had broken them. She had tied each one separately and skilfully into her rags, for she needed all the help her hands could give her. Gingerly she came, the soft curls at her forehead damp with the sweat of her exertion; and dirty and dishevelled, she eventually reached the grounds about Richard Merriman's house.

The stream at this point was about six feet wide and someone—long ago—had put stepping-stones across it. It was sheltered by trees and shrubs; the grass grew long with weeds and wild flowers between, for Joseph Jubin, at his master's orders, had left this part of the grounds uncultivated.

Delighted to find that only one of the eggs was cracked, very carefully she placed them on the grass while she took off her rags. When she dipped them into the stream the colour of the water changed to a dark brown, and she laughed in quiet pleasure to watch.

She spread them out in the sun, and, cautiously tiptoeing into the stream, she dipped her hair in the water. The cold water took her breath away. She sat down in the stream and rubbed the dirt off her body. Washing seemed a more daring operation than climbing steep cliffs in search of seagulls' eggs.

Stretching herself in the sunshine, waiting for her rags to dry, she thought how pleasant it was to be naked, for thus she would look the same as everyone else. Mistress Alton would look no better, stripped of her good clothes; nor would the wife of Sir Humphrey Cavill, that fine lady who was Bartle's mother!

Her damp hair fell to her waist and she spread it round her to make it dry more easily while she sat hugging her knees, thinking how pleased he would be with the eggs, which must surely be a delicacy even for him. And as she sat there her eyes caught the pale crimson of the betony flower and with a little cry of delight she leaned forward to pick it. He should have that flower, for it would keep evil away from his house.

Neither her rags nor her hair were quite dry, but no matter, she was all impatience now to take him his gift and could wait no longer. She went swiftly towards the house, looking up in admiration at its gabled and diamond-paned windows. It was the most beautiful house she had ever seen; it seemed more beautiful than Sir Humphrey's over at Stoke, because she could never get near enough to Sir Humphrey's to see it as clearly as she could see this. There were big dogs at Cavill House that snarled and snapped and pulled at their chains; and the servants would have no hesitation in turning them loose on anyone like herself who went too close.

She laid the eggs outside the door and put the crimson flower on top of them. Then she lifted the great knocker and let it fall. She heard the sound echoing through the hall and stood there waiting, in spite of her natural boldness, with a quaking heart.

The door opened, but it was not he who opened it; it was a young girl with short hair — cut like a boy's; and she was wearing what seemed to Tamar a very fine gown.

The girl stared at her in dismay. She looked at the eggs on the doorstep and whitened as though Tamar were an emissary from the Devil, which she probably thought the child was.

"What do you want?" asked the girl nervously.

"Your master," answered Tamar boldly.

"You . . . you want to see . . . the master?"

Tamar drew herself up with dignity. "Tell him to come here," she said.

But now Mistress Alton had come to the door. "What's this? What's this?"

The cane and the keys at her waist swung out, and Tamar was aware of them while she kept her eyes on the woman's face.

"I want your master," said Tamar.

"You want . . . what?"

"The master. I got something for him."

Mistress Alton's lips tightened. "I never heard the like! The impertinence. It's that black-eyed daughter of a black-eyed witch! You get out of here and take your filth with you." Her hands reached for her cane.

"I've come to see your master. You'll be sorry if you hurt me."

"You can strike me dead," said Mistress Alton, "but I'll not have you set your evil feet in this house. What's all this mess on my doorstep?"

" 'Tis no mess," said Tamar firmly. " 'Tis what I've brought for your master."

"You've brought . . . *what* for the master?"

"Seagulls' eggs and a flower for luck. I got them myself. Look! I climbed high for them."

"Take those things away."

"I won't. They're for him."

Mistress Alton's face grew red with rage and before Tamar realized what she was about to do, she had stepped forward and stamped on the eggs.

Tamar stared down at the havoc and let out a little cry of anguish; then she rushed at the woman and, catching her skirts in both hands, kicked her.

"Help! Help!" cried Mistress Alton. "I'm set upon. You Moll . . . don't stand there gaping. Get someone quick. My dear life, don't you see the witch is trying to do me some harm?"

At this point Richard Merriman came into the hall, his eyebrows lifted, his eyes puzzled. Tamar released the woman and looked at him through her tangled locks.

"What does this mean?" he asked coldly.

"This . . . witch . . . came here to harm you . . . to harm us all!" cried the housekeeper.

"What a small witch!" he said.

"She was putting eggs on the doorstep. It was a spell, that's what it was. I know their wicked ways."

He had approached to look at the eggs.

Tamar cried out shrilly: "They were seagulls' eggs. I got them for you. It was because you saved me. I went high for them. And the flower was for good luck. It will keep evil away from your house."

"Ah," he said. "You're Luce's girl. What is your name?"

"Tamar."

"A good name," he said; he was smiling. "It was good of you to bring the eggs. I thank you."

"But they are broken. She stamped on them."

"I thank you all the same."

She picked up the flower.

"This is for you too. It will keep evil away."

He took it. "So you pay your debts, then?" he said. And he continued to look at her. Then he seemed to rouse himself from his thoughts; he was haughty and dignified again. "Take her into the house and give her some food," he said. "Give her some clothes too."

"I can't have those rags in the house, sir," declared Mistress Alton. "She should strip outside and put on what I can give her there."

He shrugged his shoulders. "See that she has all she wants to eat."

Tamar lifted her eyes to his face; she was completely fascinated by his clothes, his voice and his manners.

He looked at her again. He said: "Yes, it was good of you to think of bringing me the eggs. Come to the house when you are hungry. Mistress Alton will always give you food when you need it."

He continued to look at her while a faint smile touched his mouth. Then he turned and went away.

"Don't dare set foot in this house," said Mistress Alton. "Don't dare bring your bugs in here. Go round to the back and I'll throw something out to you. You take those rags away with you when you go."

And so, Tamar, as her mother had done when she first came to the house, stripped outside and put on the clothes which were given her. She was a new Tamar now; the clothes were too big for her, but that did not matter, for they were fine good clothes.

Then she was allowed to sit on a stool outside the back door when Moll handed her a bowl of soup.

She had never before had such a glorious adventure, and all the time she ate, occasionally letting her hands stroke the rough worsted of her gown, she thought of Richard Merriman, of his beautiful voice and his rich clothes; and then it seemed to her that he had looked at her in an odd fashion, as though he, like others, realized that there was something strange about her.

* * *

Tamar was just past fourteen when Simon Carter the witch-pricker came to Plymouth.

The old Queen had been dead a year now and a new King had come from Scotland to rule the English and the Scots. Tamar knew this because she never lost an opportunity of listening to the gossip in the streets. She would stand close to men talking outside taverns; she would lie on the Hoe where the seamen gathered, and listen to their talk, keeping her face turned away so that they might not recognise her for the Devil's daughter.

She learned that it was a good thing that they had this James to rule them, for now that the two countries were united under him there would be no more trouble between them. He was a learned man—people were beginning to call him the British Solomon—and, being a fervent believer in the powers of witchcraft, he had determined to do all he could to drive it from his realm.

There were many witches in Scotland, it seemed, as well as in the North of England—far more than there were in the South—and on the continent of Europe there were more than in England and Scotland together. Witches had had an easy time in England compared with their lot in other countries. In their allegiance to the Devil, they denied the Holy Church of Rome and were considered heretics, the greatest criminals of the day. In Catholic countries there was one death only for heretics—the faggots to follow torture.

Tamar heard terrible stories of what happened to witches in other countries and she was glad of that shining strip of Channel which separated her native land from them.

The new King, it appeared, had undeniable evidence of bold witches who had dared work against his own person and that of his Queen. These witches had all but succeeded in drowning Queen Anne when she had set out from Denmark for her marriage to the Scottish King. Twice the Queen had attempted the journey and, just as she was within a few miles of the Scottish coast, a tempest had arisen and blown her squadrons on to the coast of Norway. When the disaster had been repeated, one of her captains admitted having taken on his ship a man who had a witch for a wife; and when a third attempt to reach Scotland was frustrated, there was no doubt in the minds of many that they were the victims of witchcraft.

The witch-wife of the sailor was burned alive with many of her companions, and when the King of Scotland himself set out across the sea to fetch his bride to her new home, his ship was all but wrecked off the coast of Norway.

Convinced that these tempestuous voyages, which had almost resulted in the death by drowning of himself and his Queen, had been the Devil's work, the

King had started an enquiry into the matter as soon as his marriage had been celebrated on Scottish soil. Many well-known witches were seized and under torture confessed to what they had done.

They had baptized a cat, making mock of one of the holy ceremonies of the Church; and then they had stolen parts of the bodies of dead men, and these they had attached to the cat's legs. With the cat they had gone to the end of Leith pier, from where they had thrown the cat into the sea.

The cat had been a strong swimmer and had reached land in spite of its handicaps. The witches declared that this had told them that the new Queen would make port safely. The witches explained that the great Earl of Bothwell had been in communication with them; and it was rumoured that he attended their Sabbats, dressed as the Devil, and that he put on the power of the Evil One with his accoutrements.

The Scottish witches were strangled, and burned till there was nothing left of them but ashes.

This had happened more than ten years ago, and now this King with his wife and family had gone to London.

There were others besides witches to flout the authority of the State. The Puritans, Separatists and Brownists were now continually talked of. Tamar heard terrible stories of the ills these people suffered and had been suffering for years.

Persecution was rife throughout the land; not the hideous bloody persecution which had caused the name of Queen Mary to be spoken with shuddering contempt; but persecution all the same. In Plymouth men had been seized, torn from their families and thrust into prison because they had failed to attend the established church and wished to worship God in their own way. The prisons of London and most other cities were full of such men; they were left to starve in the pits and little eases of those prisons; they were set upon with cudgels and beaten almost to death; some were hanged.

Tamar, at fourteen, was budding into rare beauty, and although she was completely unlettered, her intelligence was fine and quick. She wished, therefore, to know of these matters of religion; and she was saddened because, being suspected of connection with witches, she was hardly ever spoken to.

She knew something of witchcraft, for she had been an eager pupil of Granny Lackwell, who still sat on her stool in the cottage; Granny was getting old now and at times she would sink into a stupor and so remain for hours at a time; she would talk incoherently of flying through the air on a broomstick, of her conversations with Toby, her familiar, and a man in black who, she professed, came to visit her. Tamar had never witnessed any of these visits, and she was inclined to believe that Granny Lackwell was not right in her head.

Bartle was back from his sea voyage — a young man of twenty — tall and strong and very proud of a scar he bore on his cheek. His skin was tanned a light shade of brown which made his blue eyes quite startling. Tamar heard that he was such another as his father and that all the maidens of the town and the surrounding villages were ready to come when he beckoned. It was said that there would be many a child with the Cavill blue eyes roaming the streets and lanes in a year or two.

Once Tamar met him on the Hoe. His lips curled in recognition as she ran past him.

And now. . . Simon Carter the witch-pricker had come to Plymouth. Soberly dressed as became his solemn mission, he carried a Bible in his hand; and with him came a group of men to help in his work.

He stood in the square and told the people of the great work he was doing for God and the King. The country was suffering from witches. He could recognise a witch when he saw one, merely by looking at her; but he believed in justice, so he condemned none before they had been put through the test.

"If any of ye know a witch, do not hold back that knowledge. And if any of ye have suspicions that your neighbour traffics with the Devil, then come forth and name them."

Tamar stood on the edge of the crowd, alert, ready to run if any should look her way.

Simon Carter was a man who knew how to talk to simple people.

God, he explained, was all-powerful, but there was one — turned out from Heaven — who under God was greater than any. Goodness must prevail, because God was the greatest power in the world; but evil unchecked could do great harm. Nor was God one to save from witches those who by their own folly — and he was not sure that he should not say wickedness—abstained from denouncing these creatures. For to give oneself to the Devil was to work against God. They were all God's servants, were they not? Then let them show it by giving the information he sought.

"Good people, have your crops ever failed you and you wondered why? Have your animals died of strange sickness? Have you ever been taken with fits and vomiting and strange sickness? You have! Then, my friends, you may take my word for it, you have been the victims of a witch's spleen. Think, men and women . . . think of those who live around you. Have any of them ever done strange things? Have you seen animals slink into their houses? Have you seen them collecting strange herbs and brewing odd concoctions? Have you ever seen or heard them muttering to themselves? Have you seen them going into the country at dark of moon? Come! As you would serve your King, as you value your health, your good living and that of your little ones . . . come and tell me of those who lead dark lives among you."

Tamar slipped away from the crowd. The streets were deserted. It seemed that everyone was in the square. She knew that she was in danger. The old woman was in danger, and if they tortured her she would say those queer, incoherent things which she had said to Tamar. There was nothing she could do, for how could she take the old woman and hide her? It would be impossible to move her from the cottage.

She did not go back to the cottage, but lay stretched out on the grass, looking at the sea, trying to think clearly, to make some plan to save herself and the old woman.

But the desire to know what was happening in the town was too strong to be resisted, and she went back.

Already Simon Carter had six women gathered together in the Town Hall.

He talked continually.

"Witchcraft, my good friends, is more often found in women than in men. The incubus and the succubus and any devil of Satan's kingdom loves best the women. For women are weak creatures, more given to wickedness than men. They lack the brighter intellect which God has given men; they are more easily persuaded to wickedness. Strip the women of their clothes. My good friends, we will now search for the Devil's mark. He stamps them with it to mark them his forever. He will often put it in the most secret places of the body, so that it is necessary for us to search most diligently."

One woman was protesting; she was young and not uncomely. But one of Simon Carter's men had pinioned her, while another tore her garments from her.

"And what," continued Simon Carter, taking the woman nearest him and forcing her on to her knees while he jerked her face roughly upwards and pulled at her nostrils to peer up them, "and what, my innocent friends, do these creatures do besides the evil tricks they play on you? They wallow in filth, my friends. They entertain strange creatures in their beds. There is the succubus who visits men and draws from them the seed of life; this they pass on to the incubus who visits these women and plants in them the seed contaminated by devils." He pushed the woman to the ground. "Come, woman, don't be shy. Let your evil mind believe that I am the toad you welcome to your bed . . . the devil who comes to pleasure you . . ."

He gave a shout of triumph, for he had found what he called the Devil's Mark. It was behind the woman's knee in the hollow where the leg and thigh join. He chuckled with glee. Each witch he brought to the gallows meant fifteen shillings in his pocket.

"Now, dear people, you shall see how I prick her. She won't bleed, this one, for she has the witches' mark on her. How do I know? Because, men and women, the divine power has been given me. I see a witch; I prick her for the sake of justice. But I know a witch when I see one. Oh, my brothers and sisters of this fair city, you will rejoice in remembering the day that Simon Carter came among you to rid your town of this curse."

He dug a pin into the wart.

"No blood!" he cried. "This is devil's work. If I prick any godly member of this city with a pin, what happens? The blood will spurt. But prick a witch and all the Devil's help cannot save her. She will not bleed, because she is of the devil, and her flesh and blood obey not the rules laid down by God. This witch shall hang on that fair stretch of green which overlooks the sea. Ye shall watch her carcass rot, and then, dear friends, when you have seen how justice can be done, you will bring more and more witches to me."

Tamar could bear no more. She had listened to the horrible obscenities of the lookers-on. She was bewildered, for the name which had been called on more than any other had been that of God.

Nobody noticed Tamar; everybody's eyes were on the naked women; they could only gloat while the searchers handled their victims, crudely exposing them to the eyes of the watchers while they muttered words of righteousness.

Tamar fled and did not stop running until she reached the cottage. Her mother was there with several of her half-brothers and sisters; she ignored them and went to the old woman.

"Granny! Granny!" she cried. "The witch-pricker is in the town. You must make a spell quickly. You must not let him come here . . . or he'll get you . . . he'll get me!"

The old woman was taken with great trembling; her jaw fell and her eyes closed; she sagged on her stool.

The others took no notice.

* * *

A few days later the witch-pricker came to the cottage with two of his men. A crowd from the town followed them.

Tamar heard them coming and made for the door, but she was too late; she could not run away without being seen, and she knew that to attempt to do so would call attention to herself.

Both Luce and Bill Lackwell were in the cottage with three of the children.

Simon Carter threw open the door and stood looking in.

"Ah!" he said, looking straight at Granny. "There sits a witch! 'Twouldn't be necessary to look for the mark on her. Never saw I a witch who was more clearly a witch."

Tamar in her corner, surrounded by her stones which she knew would have no power to protect her now, stared at Granny.

The old woman had recovered a little in the last few days; she had been able to open her eyes, but not to speak. The right side of her face was drawn down and she could not move her right arm or leg. Poor Granny! It was small wonder that Simon Carter was so sure she was a witch.

The two men seized her and pulled her off her stool. She fell forward, a dead weight in their arms.

"She's dead," said one of the men; and it was true.

They let her body slip to the floor.

"It's a trick!" cried Simon. "She's called the aid of her familiar. Take that cat and wring its neck. There's devilry in this place. I can feel it, I can smell it. The Devil is right here . . . close to us, good people. Keep your thoughts holy. Say the Lord's Prayer. That will drive him away quicker than anything. Now we must make sure this woman is dead, for witches play tricks, friends."

They pulled open her rags and felt for poor Granny's heart.

Tamar could not take her eyes from Simon Carter. His mouth was a straight line; his eyes glinted like points of light beneath his bushy brows which almost hid them. He was very angry. A dead witch meant a loss of good money and he had made the journey for nothing.

"Good people," he said, "the Devil has taken this woman. It has pleased him to cheat us of justice." He turned his eyes on Luce, who was cowering against the wall. He continued to stare at her.

Someone in the crowd peering in at the door began to whisper.

"Didn't Luce Lackwell . . . you remember . . . Wasn't it said . . . ?"

Simon Carter, his ears as sharp as his eyes for the hunting of a witch, had swung round.

"What was that, dear friend? The woman there . . ."

A woman was pushed forward. "Well, 'twas said . . . I couldn't swear to the truth of it . . . but 'twas said . . ."

"Come. Speak up, woman dear," begged Simon. "Remember your duty to God and your country."

" 'Twas the woman Luce Lackwell . . ." She pointed at Luce. " 'Twas said she were took by the Devil . . ."

Simon had turned to Luce, his mouth curved in a hopeful leer.

"This woman?" He lifted Luce's hair from her face and peered into her eyes. "You cannot hide it from me. I have seen it in your eyes. There is the guilt. So

’twas you, woman, witch woman, who raised the spell that sent yon older witch to the Devil her master? Come, my men, search for the mark. I’ll warrant you we’ll find it in some secret place, for she is a woman of secrets, this one.”

Luce screamed as they tore off her clothes. In a few seconds they had her naked before them.

Tamar could not bear this. She had to get out of the cottage—not so much because escape was imperative to her safety, but because she could not bear to watch her mother’s shame.

She sidled to the door, and so intent was the crowd on watching Luce and the prickers that they did not notice who she was or what she was doing until she had broken through them.

Someone said then: “That’s the girl . . . the result of her mother’s evil union. Don’t let her go. She should have the test.”

Tamar ran as fast as she could; the thud of footsteps behind her terrified her, but she was fleeter than any of them and no one had any intention of missing the sight to be seen in the cottage.

At length it seemed that Tamar was free of them. The sun beat down on her and she felt sick and faint, gasping as she was to regain her breath. She did not know where to go until she remembered the stream which was in Richard Merriman’s private grounds. She thought of this man now in her extreme need. Not that he had taken very much notice of her when he had seen her; but there had been something in his look which made it different from the looks he bestowed on other children of the place. A faint curving of the lips which might have been a smile. She had often been to his house and received food and clothes, and she guessed that Mistress Alton would not have given those to her if she had not been afraid of offending her master by refraining from so doing. She felt that this gentleman was in some way her friend, so she would hide herself on his land while she thought of something she might do.

She lay down by the stream, cupping the water in her hands and splashing it over her heated face. She listened for the slightest sound, but all was quiet, and when it began to grow dark she hid herself among the bushes and slept.

She awoke at dawn and her longing for food was almost more than she could bear. Wild plans for returning to the cottage came to her, but with them came also the memory of those men who had done shameful things to her mother; she saw the lustful faces of the watchers.

She could not go back to the cottage. Then a wild idea came to her.

There were occasions on summer days when Richard Merriman walked in his garden. This was usually in the late afternoon. Once she had climbed the big oak tree against which she now leaned and she had seen him; after that she had often looked for him and seen him—always at the same hour.

If he came to-day, could she go and ask him to help her? He had saved her life when the children had thrown her into the pond, so perhaps now he would help her to escape from the pricker. Of course it might be that he would hand her to those men, but she did not think so; he hated unpleasantness, and those men, and what they did to women, were unpleasant. She was desperate, for she could not stay here without food much longer, and she could think of no one else whose help she could ask.

How much happier she felt now that she had a plan! First she would wash herself and her garments, for if she were going to ask such a favour of him it would not do to offend him by her smell.

She looked at the sky and guessed that by the time her clothes were dry it would also be the time for him to take his walk. She took off her gown—she wore nothing beneath it—and tried to rub it clean in the stream. It was not very satisfactory, but was the best she could do. She spread it out on the grass and washed herself.

She lay in the sun, her wet hair spread around her, and thought of what she would say to him. Perhaps she would hide behind the bushes in his garden and call to him and, when he was close, whisper: "I am in danger. The witch-pricker is after me. You saved me once. Will you save me again?"

She was sure he could hide her if he wished to, because he was more powerful than anyone she knew; and she believed that he would help her because of the way his lips curled when he glanced at her.

And sitting there, ruminating, she did not hear footsteps approaching until it was too late; then turning she saw, with a horror that numbed her, that between her and her gown spread out on the grass stood Bartle Cavill.

She felt her heart stop and go racing on. There was something in his look which horrified her even as she had been horrified when those men had laid their hands on her mother. Lust had shown in the faces of those men who had looked on her mother's nakedness; the same lust was looking out of those dazzling blue eyes now.

"Well met!" said Bartle with a mocking bow.

She did not move; she tried to cower behind the covering of her hair.

He took a step towards her, the lust deepening in his eyes.

"I have just visited my neighbour—rather a prosy bore. I did not know that such a charming encounter awaited me."

"Keep away!" she said.

"That I declare I won't. It's Tamar, is it not? The witch's girl! By God, you are a beauty without your rags, Tamar."

"Stay where you are . . . or I will put a spell on you."

"If you have such powers, why are you so scared, Tamar?"

He caught her arm and she tried to spring up; but he pulled her down and they rolled over and over on the grass. He was panting and laughing.

"You were waiting for me!" he said. "Yes, you slut, you were. I declare! What immodesty! You trespassed on Merriman's land. Do you know you could be hanged for that?" He tried to kiss her, but she was wriggling madly. "Damn me, if I won't have you hanged for trespass. But no! You waited for me. That was a pretty thing to do. And you took your clothes off. Really, Tamar, it was no use trying to hide yourself with all this beautiful hair . . . You have been a most immodest creature . . ." He yelled suddenly, for she had dug her teeth into his hand. "So you would bite me, eh? It will be the worse for you if you try those tricks . . ."

She spat out his blood.

"I hate you . . . I hate . . ."

"Keep still, you little Devil's imp. Keep still."

With all her strength she kicked him wildly, but the kick went home; she scratched his face and, seizing his nose, she twisted it as though she would wrench it off.

He cursed her, but momentarily she had the advantage, for her violence had had the effect of making him loosen his hold of her. She was up. He caught her ankle, but she swung herself free. Her chance had come. She picked up her gown and sped across the grass in the direction of the cultivated gardens. She had had a good start and she reached them first. Relief filled her heart then, for there, examining his shrubs, was Richard Merriman.

Panting, she threw herself against him.

"Save me!" she cried. "Save me!"

Bartle had pulled up and stood still, breathing heavily and looking like an angry and frustrated bull, while Tamar buried her face in Richard's coat.

"What the devil's this?" began Richard. But there was no need of explanations. One look at Bartle was sufficient to see what he was after, and the child was none other than Luce Lackwell's girl, for whom the witch-pricker was making a search.

"Don't let him . . . get me . . ." panted Tamar. "Don't let him . . . please . . . Hide me."

"Why have you come back, Bartle?" said Richard, trying to gain time, wondering what he was going to do with the child.

"I found her on your ground . . . trespassing, the young devil! She was lying naked on the grass. She saw me come here and she knew I'd go back that way. She was waiting for me."

"I wonder why she took such pains to wait for you and then run away?" said Richard lightly.

"He lies!" cried Tamar.

"Put your gown on, girl," said Richard; and he put her from him.

She blushed and stood behind him while she put on the damp gown.

"Pray, sir," said Bartle with an attempt at a swagger, "there is no need for you to look so shocked. I doubt if I'd have been the first."

"You lie!" flashed Tamar.

"The girl repulsed you—that much is evident," said Richard. "I wish you would not bring your buccaneering manners into my gardens."

"It was just a bit of sport," said Bartle sullenly.

"And after you had had your sport, I suppose you would have handed her over to the witch-pricker."

"Good God, no! I should naturally have hidden her."

"Providing she had been your willing slave! That was your noble plan, I doubt not."

"Oh, she would have been well enough. If she is a virgin, as she protests she is, that state would not have lasted long. And why should not I have been the first?"

Richard looked down at Tamar. "Do not tremble so," he said.

"Give her to me, sir," said Bartle. "I swear I'll hide her. I'll put her somewhere where she can't be found till Simon Carter has gone."

"*No*!" cried Tamar.

"She seems to be as much afraid of you as of Simon Carter. You have been guilty of most discourteous and ungentlemanly behaviour."

"Damme, sir, the girl would have been all right. A little reluctance at first is natural. Many's the time I've found it so, and then it's all hell let loose to turn them off."

"I repeat that you have been unmannerly. Would you like a chance to mend your ways? You know how distasteful to me is the violence of low-born creatures such as this man Carter. Moreover, this one is only a child. I do not think she should be handed over to the pricker."

"I have no wish to hand her over." His mouth curled as he gazed on Tamar's flushed face. "I can think of more pleasant ways for dealing with such a little beauty."

"Don't be afraid," said Richard, looking down at Tamar. "He is a strutting coxcomb who has recently discovered that he is a man and yearns to prove it on every conceivable occasion. Let's forgive him, for now we need his help. Go to the front door, Bartle, engage Alton in conversation and see that you keep her so engaged while I slip up the back staircase with the girl."

"With all my heart, sir."

"And in five minutes come to my study."

Bartle swaggered off, but not before he had thrown a sly glance at Tamar which seemed to say, "You have not seen the last of me!"

"Now," said Richard, looking down at her, "do not speak. Walk behind me, try to make sure you are hidden. Let us hope none from the house has seen this pretty scene from a window."

She followed him to a door at the back. He looked inside, turned and nodded; then swiftly and silently he led the way through a dark passage to the back stairs; they mounted these and were soon in his study.

There was kindness in his eyes as he looked at her.

"You are exhausted, child," he said. "When did you last eat?"

"It was before the pricker came to the cottage."

"Don't be afraid. I will ring for my personal servant. Josiah Hough is a good and obedient man. You need fear nothing from him."

She watched him with wondering eyes as he pulled the bell rope. He seemed god-like to her, all-powerful, kind but in an aloof way, completely incomprehensible.

Josiah appeared; he made no show of surprise at the sight of Tamar in his master's study.

"Bring food and wine at once, Josiah," said Richard. "If any should ask whom it is for, say it is for me. But be quick."

"Yes, sir."

The door shut on him and Richard turned to Tamar. "You are in grave danger, child. I will not attempt to minimize it, because you know full well what it means if this witch-pricker gets you. I am going to hide you."

"You are a good man," she said.

He laughed. "Nay," he said; " that is not so. It is not kindness in me. No matter. You tremble still. It is because you think of that young oaf. Think of him merely as a lusty young man—that is all. He can be trusted not to betray you. I shall not leave you alone with him. I trust his honour in all things but those in which his manly lusts are concerned. If he gives a promise, he will keep it."

Josiah came in with the tray, and when he had gone Richard made her sit at the table. She had never sat at such a table before, and she rubbed her finger wonderingly along its smooth surface. She stared about the room and dropped her eyes to the carpet. She had never imagined a carpet, though she had once heard her mother talk of carpets. Everything was strange, like a daydream, but she was not afraid; as long as he was near her she would not be afraid.

There was a knock on the door and Richard let in Bartle.

Bartle looked at her, but she kept her eyes downcast and began ravenously to eat the food; she found that once she had started she could not care for anything else — not even if the witchprickers were at the door or Bartle in pursuit.

"Pretty manners!" sneered Bartle, indicating Tamar.

"Almost as pretty as your own," retorted Richard. "She knows no better. You should."

"Oh, hang me, sir, draw me and quarter me! A witch's girl! A stay-out-late! A girl who sleeps in hedges! If she's not asking for it, who is? She ought to think herself honoured that I waste my time on her."

"She seems oblivious of the honour," said Richard. "And even when it was almost forced upon her she did not appreciate it. But, Bartle, let us be serious. You know that all this talk of witchcraft wearies me. Of course you are not with me. You are as superstitious as any. Well, let us hope you will grow out of it. In any case, you will help me with this girl for your own reasons. Well, we both have our reasons. Now, promise me you will say nothing to anyone — not even your father — of the girl's being here. Give me your word as a gentleman."

"I give my word. Now have I your leave to retire?"

Richard nodded.

Bartle went on: "Good day to you, sir. Good day, Tamar." He threw her a kiss. "To our next merry meeting. May it be as merry as this one." He held up a hand. “See! It bears the mark of your teeth to remind me of you. Your gown is ugly. I hate your gown. I like you so much better without it.”

The door shut on him and they heard him singing as he went downstairs.

Richard looked at Tamar. What can I do with her? he asked himself. How can I hide her? He shrugged his shoulders. In spite of his outward calm, he was excited. Life had been monotonous since the sudden death of that dear friend of his, the widow who had lived at Pennie Cross.

Tamar was eating noisily. Her eyes met his and she smiled.

Her trust in him was complete; and sensing it, he felt a pleasure which surprised him.

* * *

Tamar remained in Richard’s study for two days before her presence was discovered; and she had herself to blame for that.

She was not yet accustomed to the grandeur of the room, and she would walk about it, touching the furnishings and the table, the bookshelves and the oak chest. She sat on the stools and the chair; she gazed in wonder at the tapestry. There was, moreover, a glass mirror with a most elaborate frame and this gave Tamar the first clear sight of her face; it was so fascinating to see herself as she appeared to others. Indeed, she was so completely occupied with the novelty of being in such a, room that she forgot her fears. Her curiosity was to betray her.

Beyond the study was Richard's bedroom, and she was eager to see this for she was sure it would be wonderful. She had never seen a bedroom used solely for sleeping in; beds to her were pallets of straw on the floors of cottages.

And so, the desire to see a real bedroom became too much for her. She went to the study door and peeped out into the corridor. There was no one about, but from the bottom of the stairs she heard the sound of voices. That came, she guessed, from the servants working in the kitchen.

She tiptoed along the passage until she reached the door next to that from which she had come. She lifted the latch and went in. This WAS his bedroom.

She had only meant to peep, but she could not resist further exploration. There was the bed, its tester and headpiece covered with such intricate carving that she must go near to examine it. The posts were carved with equal beauty. She felt the curtains gleefully and thought how wonderful it would be to sleep in such a bed, to pull the curtains so that she would be shut in a little room of her own. On the floor was a beautiful carpet of Oriental design; not that Tamar knew anything of its origin; she only knew that it was beautiful. There were what she thought of as carpets on the walls, all cleverly worked in *petit point*. There was a mirror of burnished metal in a frame which she thought of as gold. She ran to the chest and knelt to examine the figures carved upon it. She would have enjoyed opening the chest and peeping inside.

And then, suddenly, she felt a chill of horror run down her spine, for she knew, by instinct, that someone was at the door watching her.

She swung round, but she was too late to see who had been there. She only heard the rustle of garments and the sound of quick, light footsteps. Terrified, Tamar dashed to the door, but no one was in sight.

* * *

Tamar heard the shouts in the distance. They came nearer and nearer. Now they were right outside the house.

Richard ran into the study; she had never before seen him in a hurry.

He said: "My child, they have come for you. They are almost here."

In terror she flung herself at him and clung to his doublet. He disengaged her and put her from him, frowning.

"You must stay here," he said. "Don't move. You understand? If they see you, you are lost."

She nodded.

He left her and she leaned against the door, an awful sickness coming over her. She saw herself seized and stripped; she felt the horrible pins jabbing into her. She saw them dragging her to the Hoe, and her body swinging on a gibbet. Tamar . . . dead . . . and the crows pecking at her.

Then she heard Richard's voice; strong, it seemed, and her spirits rose. He was not an ordinary man; he was a god. He was as different from other people as she herself was.

He was leaning over the balustrade of the gallery and looking down on to the hall in which the crowd had assembled.

"What are you doing in my house?" he demanded. "How dare you come breaking in like this? I'll have you whipped, every one of you."

Then Simon Carter spoke in his loud yet gentle voice.

"Be calm, dear friend. We come on a peaceful mission. You know me. I am Simon Carter, and I am here to rid our land of those who do evil in it. We have, two days since, hanged a witch, but before she died she told us of her sins. She had lain with the Devil, and of this unholy union a child was born. This child — Satan's own daughter — must be put to death at once. The town is unsafe while she lives. Nay, the country is unsafe. I have reason to believe she is here, and I must beg of you, good sir, I must entreat you, kind gentleman, to let nothing stand in the way of our taking her."

"Who gave you this news?"

"Those who did would wish that their confidence was not betrayed. I am a respecter of wishes. I respect all those who work in the service of God. It is only those who consort with the Devil that I am here to denounce and punish with death. We know the girl to be in this house. I must, in the name of God and the law, ask you to give her up to me."

"And if I refuse? And if I say she is not here?"

"Dear good sir, we should have no recourse but to search the house. It goes not well with those who obstruct the King's justice."

"So you have come here to take a child and ill-treat her."

"This is no human child, sir. This is the very spawn of the Devil. We are all born in sin, sir, and it is for us to wash ourselves clean of it in our passage through life. But this creature was born in filth, with all the wisdom of hell in her head. Her mother hangs rotting in the sun. I have learned much of her evil ways. We persuaded her to confess her sins. Ah! I have much evidence to take with me when I leave your fair county. The *old* witch worked a spell under our very eyes. She assumed death, but we have strung her up all the same, and she now dangles beside the other. Now, the child, sir . . . I give you a second or two to produce her . . . then we search the house."

There was a short silence. Tamar, cowering behind the door, had heard every word.

They were coming up the stairs. They would take her, for even he could not save her. He was only one; and they were many.

Then he spoke:

"You make a great mistake in coming here for the child. Why should the Devil take a poor silly serving wench and get her with child? Such would be without sense. Is the Devil senseless? If he is like a lustful man and nothing more, you waste your time in seeking out his creatures. Come! Why should the Devil get a girl like Luce Lackwell with child? Why? Why? Do you agree that it is an action without purpose?"

"This man prevaricates," cried Simon Carter. "Let us waste no more time with him. Come, my friends, search the house!"

"Be careful!" commanded Richard. "My friends down there—you who have come to take a child and submit her to indignity before you murder her—take care that I do not have you all thrown into prison for trespass."

"Master!" cried a man in the throng. "We but want the young witch. Give her to us, sir, for that's all we do want."

"You fools!" cried Richard. "Can you understand nothing? Have you not noticed all these years how I have watched over her? Ask the women of my kitchen. She has come here regularly for food. Clothes have been given her. Ask the girls, ask my housekeeper if I did not say that she was never to be turned away. You are stupid people. Is it not clear to you now? You were so anxious to give the girl a devil for a father that you did not see what was under your noses. What has the girl done but be the victim of a filthy story? Her mother lay with the Devil. Is that so?"

There was silence.

"Is that so?" he shouted.

There was still no answer from below, and he went on in a loud and ringing tone: "I demand to know. Is there any other charge against her but that of her mysterious coming into the world? Speak to me there!

You, Hurly. Don't stand gaping at me, man. What charge against the girl?"

"Naught, sir," stammered Hurly, "save that she be the child of the Devil."

Then Richard laughed loudly. "Naught save that! Well, I have the girl here. And here she stays. Have you forgotten that Luce was my serving wench? And a comely one. Think you that I, having lost my wife, have always lived the life of a celibate? Think again, my friends; and this time think with good sense. Luce's daughter is also mine. This girl here in my house is where she has a right to be, since she is my daughter."

"I had the woman's confession!" screamed Simon Carter. "She was at the witches' Sabbat and the Devil pursued her!"

"She dreamed that. I visited her in her room. There was to be a child, so I married her off to Lackwell. Is that such an unusual story, so difficult to believe? Now, Simon Carter, get you out of my house, and if you are not gone in half a minute, I'll have you clapped in gaol. The magistrates of this town are friends of mine. I'll see they show you no mercy. And that is for all of you. Go! Unless there is any among you who dares doubt my story!"

He paused. No one spoke.

"Go then!" he shouted. "But one moment. If any one of you dares harm my daughter, let him know that he will have me to answer to for his offence."

He stood there, watching them turn sheepishly away. He did not move until the last of them had disappeared; then he stood for a moment looking down with disgust at the mess they had made on the tessellated floor of his hall.

He went into his study. He looked at Tamar and she looked at him. Her eyes were wide with faint wonder and disbelief; his held a hint of amusement.

Tamar thought: It is as though I have never really seen him before . . . nor he me.

CHAPTER THREE

When Richard took Tamar down to the kitchen, the two serving girls, Moll Swann and Annis Hurly, were there with Mistress Alton.

Richard said mockingly: "Mistress Alton, I don't doubt that you heard the noise those people were making."

The housekeeper nodded slowly, being too bewildered for speech. Her mind was full of images—the master and Luce Martin! The sly wanton, so mild all the time that she and the master . . . And that black-eyed creature the result! It was more than she could believe. She had known, of course, of the master's visits to the lady of Pennie Cross, who had recently died; but that lady was of the gentry. The master's lapses in that direction were deplorable but understandable. But Luce Martin! That slut! And she had always thought the master so fastidious. What could you know of anybody?

As for the two girls, they could only stare. They had been expecting to see Tamar searched, pricked and hanged; and instead, here she was standing before them.

"If you heard the noise, you doubtless heard what was said," went on Richard. "Then you will know of the relationship between this child and myself. I wish her to help in the house as her mother did, so I shall leave her with you. Teach her to become as thrifty a housekeeper as yourself." He paused at the door. "And, Mistress Alton, I pray you, do not cut off her hair."

Mistress Alton said afterwards to Betsy Hurly, when she came to talk over the affair, that she felt as though the wind had been taken out of her sails by what she'd heard him say to the crowd, so that she felt becalmed. But for that she would have told him she was not going to stay in his house and train his bastards.

As it was, the housekeeper merely nodded and he went out, leaving Tamar in her care.

Tamar advanced towards the table. There was silence in the kitchen. If they were bewildered, she was more so. She had just heard a most astounding revelation, and she knew that if she could have chosen her own father, she would have chosen him. But she did not really believe he had spoken the truth. He had said what he had said because he knew that it was the only thing that could save her. Tamar herself was certain that no human being was her father; and although it would be pleasant to be connected with the gentry, how could she abandon her belief in the secret power which could only come to her through the Devil?

And now, remembering that power in her which set her aside from all others, she was able to face the hostile eyes of the woman whom — ever since she had so callously smashed the seagulls' eggs — Tamar had known to be her enemy.

Mistress Alton's lips were moving; she was saying the Lord's Prayer, so Tamar knew that she herself was not the only one who refused to deny the Devil's part in fathering her.

The two serving girls were waiting for the housekeeper to speak, and Mistress Alton knew that she must exert her authority before those two. She still wore her cane dangling from her waist, and she used it frequently, but not so frequently as she had done on Luce and Annis' mother, Betsy. She was shorter of breath now, and those two were apt to giggle when being belaboured. That was humiliating; still, they were afraid of her tongue, if not of her cane.

"So you've come to work for me in the kitchens, eh?" she said, playing for time.

"Not for you," flashed Tamar. "For him."

"We will see. What are you girls standing about for? Moll, take the key and go to the bolting house. Bring flour and put it into the pastry. I'll be there to do my baking very soon . . . so look sharp. Annis, take the girl and draw some ale. I could do with a drop myself after all I've been through."

Annis came reluctantly towards Tamar.

"Go on! Go on!" cried the housekeeper, sitting down heavily upon a stool and mopping her brow with her apron. "I was all of a tremble," she told Betsy Hurly afterwards. "So I was to have in my kitchen, at best a bastard, at worst a witch!"

Annis took Tamar into the buttery, where Tamar looked eagerly about her, and Annis looked eagerly at Tamar.

"So this is the buttery," said Tamar, dipping her brown finger into a pot of butter and tasting it. She watched Annis draw ale. Then she took that from her and tasted it.

Annis giggled.

"Did she cut your hair like that?" asked Tamar.

Annis nodded.

Tamar tossed her own luxuriant locks. "She cut my mother's. My mother told me."

"The master said not to cut yours."

"If she had tried, it would have been the worse for her."

Annis shivered; then she saw that Tamar's eyes were full of tears. Tamar dashed them angrily away. "I was thinking of my mother . . . in the cottage. They did terrible things to her . . ."

Annis could cry easily. She picked up a corner of her apron and wiped her eyes.

"Why do *you* cry?" asked Tamar curiously.

"She was your mother, even though she was a witch."

Tamar smiled to herself. The world had ceased to be full of hostile people.

"Don't cry," she said. "I won't hurt you. It's only those I hate who need to be afraid."

They had been a long time in the buttery, but Mistress Alton said nothing about that. She was still, as she said, made all of a tremble by this savage creature who had been brought into her kitchen.

* * *

Tamar shared a room with Annis and Moll. Moll was only ten years old — Clem Swann's girl — and she went to sleep as soon as her head touched the straw. But Annis lay awake. So did Tamar.

"Tamar," whispered Annis, "be you really a witch?"

Tamar was silent.

"You know most things, I reckon," said Annis. "Do you know how to make milk turn sour and make cows so that they won't give milk?"

Tamar still said nothing.

"I remember you," went on Annis. "'Twas when my mother came to ask yourn for a charm. 'Twas years ago. I took a stone from 'ee and you thought I'd stole it. You looked like a witch then. My mother said she could see the Devil looking out of your eyes. Natural eyes couldn't look so big and blazing, she said. She got my father to use his belt on me for touching that stone. I ain't forgot."

Tamar contemplated this new friend of hers and felt protective towards her. Apart from Richard Merriman, the girl was the first one who had ever shown friendliness towards her, and she liked friendliness, particularly when it was given with a certain awe and reverence.

"I didn't mean you to get the belt," said Tamar. "But you ought to have give up the stone when I asked for it."

"Was it a magic stone, Tamar?"

Tamar did not answer.

Annis moved nearer to her. "You don't think Moll's awake, do 'ee? I'll whisper . . . in case she is. Could you give me a charm, Tamar, some'at as would make a man turn towards me?"

Tamar shivered, for Annis's words had brought her encounter with Bartle very near. She lay silently thinking of it, seeing him clearly, that smile on his face, the lips half parted, the eyes of blazing blue.

She let herself imagine being caught by him, and she could smell the hot grass, feel his breath on her face . . . just as she had when he had tripped her and fallen on her, pressing her down on the ground.

She said sternly: "Why do you want a man turned towards you?"

"Why? Because I do. 'Tis natural like."

"But . . . you *want* that?"

Annis rolled over and lay staring into the darkness. "Wouldn't matter telling you. I 'spect you do know. 'Tis John Tyler, who do work on the farm with Father. He's terrible handsome. You wait till you see him. Well, John ain't the man a girl can say 'No' to and . . ."

Tamar drew away; she was alarmed by the excited note in Annis's voice. Annis . . . a girl younger than herself . . . and already that which had almost happened to Tamar had happened to her; and it seemed as though she had been far from reluctant.

"You did . . . that?" said Tamar, shaken out of her role of wise woman.

" 'Twas only once. I'd gone over to see my mother and father and to give a hand in the dairy. . . and John, he walked back with me. . . and then well, he being the terrible handsome sort of man a girl couldn't say 'No' to. . . But that Bess Hollicks in the dairy. . . it seems she were after him too, and she'd been down to see old Mother Hartock in Looe Street down in the town, and she got this charm that would take him from me. Old Mother Hartock be caught now. She were one of the first the pricker took; but that don't help me, for the charm do still work; and it be her he takes into the barn. . . not me."

"Did he. . . force you?" asked Tamar, her voice trembling.

Annis laughed softly in the darkness. "Well, I did make a show of being frightened like. . . but I'd always had my eyes on John."

There was a short silence, then Annis said: "Will you give me a charm, Tamar? Will you make a brew for me? For it does seem to me that if you don't I shall never know another man. . . for I do know there be no one in the world for me but John."

"Yes," said Tamar. "I'll make a charm for you. But, Annis, have you thought what happens to girls? Remember my mother. She got a child and then she was married to Bill Lackwell."

"Oh, but she were different. 'Twas the Devil. . . I didn't mean that, Tamar. It sort of slipped out. 'Twas the master. . . not the Devil. But I dunno. Couldn't expect the master to look at the likes of me. If I had John's child, he'd have to marry me."

"Suppose he didn't?"

"He'd have to . . . seeing he works for my father. Besides, John's a good man. He did tell me so. He told me in the barn. He said, ' 'Tis wrong and 'tis wicked, Annis, and I don't want to do it to 'ee, but for the life of me I can't stop myself.' Now, that do show goodness, to my mind. I prayed in church for forgiveness of my sin, I did. 'Dear Lord,' I said, 'I didn't want to sin, but it was so that I couldn't help it . . .' "

Tamar listened to all this, entranced. No one of her own age had ever chatted to her as this girl was chatting. She wanted to stretch out a hand and, taking Annis's, say: "Don't you ever be afraid of me." But caution restrained her; she loved her power too much to throw it lightly away.

"I don't know as I ought to brew for 'ee, Annis," she said.

"Why not?"

"'Tis wrong for 'ee to go in the barn with John Tyler, and I won't help wrong."

"You're a *white* witch, then?"

"I don't want to hurt nobody. . .'cept they hurt me."

" 'Tis a good thing to take John away from Bess Hollicks, for she ain't a good girl. She don't ask the Lord's forgiveness for *her* sin, I reckon."

"Annis, I'll make a brew for 'ee."

"Oh . . . Tamar, will 'ee then?" Annis giggled her pleasure.

"And when you've drunk it, he won't have eyes for anyone else."

There was silence. Annis was thinking what a fine thing it was to have the Devil's daughter working and sleeping beside a girl, so that she could take advantage of the Devil's power without giving up one little bit of her soul for it!

As for Tamar, her thoughts were mixed. She did not know whether she was glad or sorry, happy or unhappy.

*   *   *

The house absorbed her. So many things to learn. So many things she had never seen before.

Friendship with Annis grew. She had gathered the herbs which she would brew to make the charm, though she warned Annis that she must not be impatient, as some of the ingredients were not easy to come by. She needed a hair grown on the nethermost tip of a dog's tail, the brains of a cat or a newt, the bone of a frog whose flesh had been consumed by ants, to say nothing of herbs which did not grow by the wayside. These must be collected before she could begin to brew.

Mistress Alton saw the girls whispering together and made the sign of the Cross, while she went about muttering the Lord's Prayer.

Betsy Hurly came to the kitchen to chat with the housekeeper. Betsy—now a comfortable matron—had aged quickly; she no longer indulged in amorous adventures, and had become a friend of Mistress Alton's. They enjoyed many a gossip together concerning the scandals of the neighbourhood, from which occupation they both derived much pleasure. Mistress Alton was prepared to forget that Betsy had once been what she called "a flighty bit of no-good," because of the news she brought; as for Betsy she had been delighted to find a place for her daughter, and she was ready to forget the cruelty she herself had suffered at the housekeeper's hands.

"Well," said Betsy, sipping her ale, "so you've got that young savage here, I see."

"I was all knocked of a heap," said Mistress Alton. "They came to take her . . . as was right and proper that she should be took . . . and when I heard what *he* had to say . . . well I was as I told you, like a ship without a sail. Bold as brass he said it, leaning over the balustrade. I had the door half open, so I saw. Bold as brass he says, 'She's my daughter,' he says. 'Luce was my serving wench . . . and a comely one . . .' Fancy that Luce! Can you believe it?"

"No, I can't. And what's more I don't. You forget how Luce and me was together. I remember the night . . . I remember her lying there. There was mud on her skirt . . . and bits of leaf clinging to it. She was staring wild like . . . and I got it out of her. She said: 'Big he was . . . and he had horns at the top of his head. His eyes was like a man's eyes . . . shining through the black. I fainted . . . but I knew I'd been took. I knew I'd been ravished by the Devil.' Were that going with the master? Why, 'twould have been a different story then, I reckon. We'd have had her giving herself airs. There was that girl over at Stoke, remember: Sir Humphrey fancied her and for a week or two she couldn't spare a nod for the likes of we. That's how it is when gentry fancies a girl. But the Devil . . . that's another matter."

"'Sh!" said Mistress Alton and recited the Lord's Prayer right through. Betsy followed her, stumbling. Then, feeling herself reinforced against possible evil, the housekeeper gave vent to her feelings: "'Tis terrible. What would happen if I lifted my arm against her? I reckon it would be struck stiff like. My father was struck that way by a witch. Right as rain one day, and the next he fell down . . . never spoke again. We knew he'd been overlooked, for he'd had words with an old woman on the road. We boiled his urine up in a pan over the fire, knowing that, as it boiled, that witch would feel her inside burning. We knew she'd have to come to make us stop, and it would be the first as came to the house after the pan began to boil. It were a steady sort of body that come, and we'd never have thought it of her. We hung her, but even that didn't do no good. She were dead, but 'twere a lifelong spell she'd laid on Father, and he never spoke again."

"Mistress Alton, you do terrify me!"

"And 'tis right that you should be terrified, with witches among us."

"But . . . how could the master . . . ? He be a clever man . . . a gentleman . . . How could he say such things?"

"There's some as gets too clever. It goes to their heads and then they start acting queer. Do you remember the night when we put . . . or was about to put . . . old woman Lackwell to the test? Do you remember how it was him as stopped us?"

"I do indeed," said Betsy.

"It's too much of these books, that's what 'tis . . ."

Tamar knew they talked of her. She watched them maliciously, trying to frighten them with a flash of her black eyes.

Life had changed, but the power was still with her and she was not going to relinquish it without a fight.

One day, when she was set to dust the woodwork of the gallery, she went into the master's study. No one was supposed to go in there except Josiah Hough, but Tamar had once spent two days and nights in there, so she did not think that she need obey the rules which other people must.

What interested her most in this room were the books. She had, when she had been a prisoner here, surreptitiously opened one or two of them, but the letters were quite baffling to her, and no matter how she stared at them or from what angle she studied them, she could make nothing of them. She had felt angry, because power meant so much to her. She believed that if she looked at a book and asked the Devil's aid, he would make her able to understand.

Now, dusting the rail of the gallery, she thought of the books, and the temptation to take another look at them was irresistible.

There was no one in the room, so she sped to the bookcase and opened one at random. She turned it round, staring at the letters.

She was still as ignorant as she had been before. She slapped the page in anger. Earnestly she desired to be able to read the letters, as once she had desired to make herself clean.

Richard came in quietly and found her; he looked very angry.

"What are you doing?" he demanded.

"Looking," she explained.

"Have you not been told that you are not to come here?" he asked coldly.

"No," she answered. "The others have, but I have not been."

"No one from the kitchen is allowed to come in here. Please go."

Her heart was quaking, but she stood boldly before him.

"You are clever," she said. "It is not proper that you should have a daughter who does not know what books mean."

He laughed suddenly, and she saw now that he had ceased to be angry.

"You mean you want to read? Do you think you possibly could?"

"If I wished," she said.

"You must not give yourself airs because I allow you to work in my kitchens."

She repeated stubbornly: "It is not proper for you to have a daughter who does not know what books mean."

"Nonsense!" he retorted. "Very few girls . . . highborn girls at that, not bastards like yourself . . . are taught to read."

"Perhaps they don't want to," she said. "If they did . . . and were clever enough . . . they would learn."

"You are persistent, Tamar," he said.

She smiled dazzlingly, for she could see that he was just a little interested.

"Listen to me; if you were obliged to learn, you would hate it. It is not easy."

"I like to learn. I learned all Granny could tell me."

"This is very different from listening to the chatter of an old woman."

"Old men chatter very like old women."

He looked at her sternly and then suddenly burst into a laugh. "Do you refer to me as an old man?"

"You are not very young."

"And you suggest that *I* should teach *you* how to read?"

"I am your daughter. You have told everybody so. It is not proper that I should not know what these books mean."

He came close to her and looked into her face. "Listen to me," he said. "I will show you that you can never learn to read."

She smiled. "I will show you that I will."

"You will come here for an hour every morning, and I myself will attempt to teach you. I will do this for a week, and at the end of that time you will have discovered that you cannot learn to read and write."

"And write too!" she cried gleefully.

"Do not smile so complacently," he said. "I am a very impatient man and I cannot endure stupidity."

She said: "I am very clever and I will show you how I shall learn."

"We will start to-morrow," he said. "Come here at ten of the clock."

She went out smiling, but in spite of her victory she felt very sad. She could very easily have wept; she did not know why, except that he made her very sad and happy all at once.

* * *

But her learning did not end in a week. Richard was to discover he had no ordinary pupil, and in spite of himself he was aware of a faint excitement when the girl was with him. He was amused by her concentration, delighted to see *her* delight when at length, after what seemed like hours of struggle, she ceased to make her capital J's round the wrong way.

At the end of the week, he said: "Not very amusing, is it?"

She agreed that it was not. "But it will be," she added, "when I know it."

He was secretly pleased that she wished to go on; he enjoyed teaching, and teaching such a strange creature was particularly interesting.

"I'll give you another week," he said grudgingly.

One day he spoke to her very sternly. "I saw you gathering weeds the other day. I suppose it was for some charm or other. That was a very stupid thing to do. Don't you realize what a narrow escape you had?"

"Yes," she said.

"If you got into trouble again, it would not be so easy to get you out of it. Moreover, I might not feel inclined to do so. I did so in the first place because it seemed to me no fault of your own that those fools were after you. But, in the face of what happened, deliberately to go out . . . collecting herbs . . . making charms . . . That I consider the height of folly."

He dismissed her, and she was very sorry that she could not please him in this matter, but she had to keep her promise to Annis, so she went on gathering what she needed for her brew.

The day came when the potion was completed and Annis drank it. She had had to make it at twelve noon, although it should have been midnight; but as they were locked in their room, this could not be.

"I have said a special word about the time," she explained.

"Do you think it'll make any difference?" asked Annis anxiously.

"No. I said that it was because of Mistress Alton, and you can depend upon it those who are helping us will understand."

Annis was delighted. She found it hard to wait until she could see John Tyler again.

Bartle and his father rode over to Pennicomquick, and supper was served to them in the winter parlour, where Moll and Annis waited on them. Richard did not wish Tamar to do so. Tamar went out of the house and into the gardens; she was trembling at the thought of Bartle's being in the house.

It was the silliest thing she could have done, because he saw her from one of the windows, and, making an excuse to the two men, came out to her.

"Hello, Devil's daughter!" he said.

"Don't you dare come near me!" she snapped.

"Have you no kiss for me? 'Twill be a farewell kiss. I am sailing to-morrow."

"I'll never have anything but kicks and scorn for you."

"That's a fool's prophecy . . . doomed to be false."

"I am no fool."

"Tamar, you are the greatest fool in Devon. You might have been my mistress by now. Think of the honour of that to such as you!"

"I see only the shame."

"Think also of the beautiful foreign girls who will be enjoying me. That is what you have to think of, Tamar, until I come back. I have made a vow. When I come back it is the Devil's daughter for me. She may be a little unwilling at first, but afterwards . . . afterwards . . . you will see, Tamar."

"I hate you. I shall always hate you."

"Another false prophecy. And you have changed. Yes, you have. You've got new airs . . . new graces, but damn me, you're as pretty as ever! No! You're more pretty."

She walked past him into the house. She was confident in the knowledge that he dared not touch her now. Life had changed for her. She was learning to be a scholar and a member of the gentry; and at the same time she was not losing any of her magical powers.

Bartle sailed away next day, and for that she was thankful. Now she could enjoy listening to Annis's stories of her love affair with John Tyler.

"Why," said Annis, "I met him there in the hayfield, and I said to him, 'How do 'ee do, John?' and he looked sort of sheepish like, as he has been since he forgot me for Bessie. He said, 'I be well, Annis. And how be you?' And I said, just as I'd said when I drank the brew like as you told me, 'Beautiful and desirable in your eyes, John Tyler.' 'What be that, then?' he asked. I said, ' 'Tis goodbye you've said to your tumbles with Bessie, John; from now on there's no one in this world for you but me.' He said, 'Why's that, then, Annis?' Then I told him. 'For this, John. I've bewitched 'ee. I've taken the draught as Tamar did brew for me. She's charmed you, John.' 'Well, then,' he said, 'there's naught as we can do about it.' So we went to the barn and all is well between us two."

Listening, Tamar was filled with pleasure. She was going to be able to read and write; she was going to be able to talk as easily and cleverly as did the gentry. She was going to be one of those people whom she admired—with this difference: She could work spells, and they could not!

* * *

Tamar was sixteen years old. She had grown taller and plumper in the last two years—the two most important years in her life so far.

There had been no kitchen work for Tamar for a long time. She was accepted as the daughter of the house now. In spite of himself, Richard could not control a growing delight in her. For one thing she was so beautiful—and he had always been susceptible to beauty in any form—so that it was a source of delight merely to look at her. For another she was intelligent; she could amuse and amaze him. She had learned quickly and in a few months after those first lessons she was reading and writing. He had told her then that he did not wish her to waste time in the kitchen; if she cared to study, he would help her.

She did care. She cared deeply.

"You have much to learn besides reading and writing," he said. "You must learn to walk with grace, to act with dignity, to be always poised. And there is your speech. That offends me greatly."

After that she must sit before a mirror mouthing words, taking each vowel and consonant and repeating it until she could say it in a manner which pleased him. She was now speaking in an accent similar to his own, with little trace of soft, cooing Devon in it.

She loved gay colours, and in the blues and scarlets which she favoured her dark hair looked darker, her flashing eyes more bright. When she rode out—for among other things she had learned to ride—people turned to look at her, and swore she had a touch of the Devil in her. She was too beautiful and too clever, they said, to be all human. Look how she had escaped pricking and death, and look what she had made out of it!

Tamar ignored them; she was secretly pleased that they should continue to regard her as the possessor of supernatural powers.

Richard deplored this in her. He would have her sit and talk with him; since the death of his friend in Pennie Cross he needed someone to whom he could talk of the subjects which interested him most and, to his astonishment, Tamar was filling that need. It seemed amazing to him that he could talk thus to the girl who a few years ago had seemed such a little savage.

Sir Humphrey once said: "Merriman, you dote on that girl." He nudged Richard. "Damme! If you hadn't told us she was your daughter, I'd say she was your mistress. Not sure I don't believe it now."

"Nonsense!" he had retorted sharply. "I'm interested. Who could help being interested in a girl like that? Think of her upbringing and look at her now. She's damned unusual."

Sir Humphrey had gone off chuckling.

The fact was that Richard was growing more interested in Tamar than he had thought it possible for him to be in any person. That was why it disturbed him deeply that she could cling so stubbornly to the belief in her supernatural birth. And the reason? Because he feared for her. He feared that if she were in danger again he might not be able to save her, and the thought of losing her, as he said, depressed him; but that, he knew, was a very mild way of expressing what he would feel.

Again and again he remonstrated with her; he was coldly contemptuous; he told her she was being stupid; but nothing he could say could turn her from her beliefs.

One November day he called her to his study.

She noticed that a faint colour burned under his skin, and she knew that something had happened to perturb him.

"Tamar," he said, "sit down, child. I want to talk to you. I've just had news of a diabolical plot in London. It's going to have far-reaching effects on the whole country, you will see."

"What is this plot?" she asked.

"A plot to blow up the King and Parliament, and so rid the country of its rulers at one blow. This is going to mean fresh persecutions."

"Who did this thing?"

"Oh, it was a foolish plot . . . doomed to failure. As I've heard it, a Robert Catesby—a Northamptonshire man and a Catholic—gathered together some fellow Catholics, engaged a man called Guy Fawkes, a soldier of fortune, to secrete himself in the vaults of the Houses of Parliament with a barrel of gunpowder and matches. One of the conspirators warned a friend not to attend Parliament on November the Fifth—the day for which it had been arranged—and so suspicion was aroused, the vaults searched, the plot discovered.

Such folly! This is not the way to get that freedom to live and worship which I long to see in this land."

"Freedom to live and worship," she repeated; and added mischievously: "And to believe in witches . . . if you wish to?"

"How you cling to that stupid belief! There are times, Tamar, when I despair of you."

"It is such a distinction to be the daughter of the Devil. I cannot give it up. And whatever you say, Granny Lackwell's charms did what they were supposed to do. The sick were healed. Some fell sick when she had looked at them . . . or had bad luck."

He looked at her wearily, but even so he could not help smiling at the lovely, animated face. "Sometimes the charms worked," he said; "sometimes they did not. When they did not, it was forgotten; when they did, it was remembered and talked about. That was chance, my dear. We have talked of this many times. But this plot . . . it is going to mean new and severe laws against the Catholics. We shall probably have Catholic-prickers among us as well as witch-prickers."

"At least you need have no anxiety for me when these new prickers come."

He looked at her quizzically. "I fear you are a wild girl, Tamar, and I confess you give me some anxiety. You have learned much, and quickly—no one would guess that you were not born into your present position—and yet you persist stubbornly in clinging to superstitions regarding yourself which can bring at best discomfort, at worst disaster."

"I know," she answered, "that there is a mystery surrounding my birth. You forget that I saw my mother's face when it was referred to. She would not have made up a story about being seized by the Devil in a dark wood."

"There is something I have to say to you, Tamar. I did not mean to . . . yet; but I see I must. I shall have to tell you something of myself. First, I am collecting information of a certain sort. When I have all I need I may have it printed as a book."

"What kind of book?" she asked.

"A book of all times — past and present, of bloodshed and horror."

"Why are you compiling this book?"

"I think it may be because I wish to show what I have found, to others. . . . Perhaps also that I am seeking something myself."

"What do you seek?"

"I am unsure. It may be a religion . . . or it may not be a religion at all. In preparing what I have so far done, it has been necessary for me to have personal experiences and study a good deal. Oh, Tamar, I have often wanted to speak to you of this. There was a time when I would talk of it to a very good friend of mine. Alas! she is now dead, and it is as though you have stepped into her place . . . in one respect. You are eager to know what takes place about you — I do not, of course, mean actual happenings, but in the minds of people, in the trend of the age. You are quick to see a point. Yes, you are a comfort to me."

She was astonished. He had never talked of affection before. A great happiness came to her. She admired him more than anyone she had ever known.

He went on: "There are so few people to whom I could speak of such things. Our friends the Cavills? Well, they are our friends because their lands are not very far distant and it is easy to ride over and be neighbourly. In a way, too, they fit into my picture. They are so much a part of the times in which we now live. Father and son, they are perfect physically; they delight in exercising the body rather than the mind. How like the father the son is! They are buccaneers, both of them. They delight in taking with the strength of their hands what is not theirs, and making it their own."

Tamar felt her cheeks grow hot, as they did whenever Bartle's name was mentioned. She knew she would never forget him and those terrifying moments he had given her; sometimes she dreamed of him. He was far away now; he had been away for two years. Let him stay away.

"Buccaneers, yes!" she said. "Although I confess to a certain liking for Sir Humphrey which I cannot give to his son."

"Sir Humphrey has grown mellow. At Bartle's age he was just such another as Bartle. They have the essence of manhood, and they, Tamar, are the ideals of our times. Such men as they are making our country great, and they will continue to do so. They lead the way to that dominance which our country will attain. Do not despise Bartle too much for what he tried to do to you. Rejoice that he did not succeed. But for Bartle and his kind we should have the Spaniards with us now, and these persecutions of witches and Puritans, Separatists and Catholics — in fact, of all who do not conform to the way laid down by the State and Church — would be a hundred times more rigorous, a thousand times more bloody. You have heard a good deal of the Inquisition in Spain. Let us rejoice that our country has nothing so evil as that. Still, we suffer here, as all the world suffers. I see no way out of suffering until we have learnt tolerance. A man must choose his own religion. Persecution does not — as authority fondly believes — stamp out; it nourishes. King Philip could not drive our men off the seas because of the terrible cruelties he inflicted on those he captured. Men rallied to the ships to fight the Spaniard for revenge as well as gain. My dear child, there are more poor deluded witches in this country since our prickers and suchlike came to seek them out than there ever were before."

"Richard," she said, for as she had explained to him she could never bring herself to call him "Father," and within a month of her coming to his house she had called him by his Christian name. "Richard, how can you know these things?"

"That is at the very root of what I wish to tell you now."

She waited and after a brief hesitation, as though even now he were reluctant to speak of these things, he began to tell her:

"It is a tale of persecution that I wish to tell you—persecution at which I have been a looker-on all my life. A terrible thing happened to me when I was eight years old, and this brought me close to what I have come to see as the scourge of the world, the great impediment to progress. I must tell you of this, Tamar, because it has made me what I am.

"My father was a gentleman of the Court of Queen Mary. . . that Mary of the bloody persecutions. She married, as you know, King Philip of Spain, and when the King came to England, there was a beautiful lady in his retinue with whom my father fell in love. They were married; and when the King returned to Spain, it was necessary that my mother should go back with him, as she was not strong enough to endure the damp of these islands. My father went with her to Madrid and there I was born.

"We were a very happy family until the time when I was seven years old; then my father was arrested and brought before the Inquisition. I had very early become aware of this evil thing; I had seen the furtive horror in people's eyes; but it was only when it touched my own family that I understood what it really meant. My father was taken in the night, and I saw him only once afterwards. That was a year later. I hardly recognised him; his ruddy complexion had become yellow, and he had great difficulty in walking, for he had suffered much torture in the gloomy chambers of the Inquisition.

"A boy of my age should not have been there, of course; but there was fear in our house. My mother lay in her sick bed, and there were leeches ready to say that she was unable to attend; therefore her absence was excusable. But I must not be absent, for if I were, that would be noted, and I should be marked as one who was not being brought up as a good citizen and Catholic.

"Tamar, the memory of that day is always with me. It never fades. Early in the morning I was awakened by the muffled pealing of the bells. I was aroused by the servants, hastily dressed and hurried into the streets.

"The *autos-da-fé* are great holidays in Spain. The population turns out in its best clothes. There is all that pomp and ceremony in which no Church delights as does the Church of Rome.

"I was taken to the gates of the Inquisition so that I might be there to see the tragic procession file out to its doom. Among these miserable men and women was my father. He was dressed hideously in a loose yellow gown; this *sanbenito* was embroidered with busts surrounded with flames, and the flames pointed upwards; figures of horrible devils had also been worked on it, and these were shown as fanning the flames. This particular type of *sanbenito* told the onlookers that my father was one of those condemned to be burned alive. I cannot convey to you the horror of it all, and when I thought of it later, it seemed to me that more horrible than anything, more horrible than even the vile torture to which these people had been submitted, was the religious pomp with which these foul ceremonies were conducted. The working people must be present on pain of having suspicion fall on them; their presence was commanded by their Church. Here was a scene more revolting, I imagined, than those played out in the amphitheatre of Rome under savage Nero and Tiberius. The Romans committed cruelty for what in their view was sport; the Spaniards delighted in it none the less, but they tried to hide their delight in a cloak of piety. In later years I came to believe that the Spaniards were guilty of the greater sin.

"Most of these victims were members of the upper classes; doubtless this was due to the fact that the Inquisition seized all the possessions of those it murdered, and the Inquisition was determined to remain rich and powerful.

"To the *Quemadero*... the place of fire... where the Grand Inquisitor rose and addressed the crowd, enumerating the sins of those about to face most horrible death.

"Then were the fires lighted, and I looked on, Tamar, at those poor bodies, shattered by the rack, burned by fiery pincers, waiting for the final torture which would at last bring a merciful death. Some were strangled before they were burnt—those had turned Catholic at the last moment; the others were roasted alive because they clung to their own faith. My father was of the latter, and I was there... to witness his death..."

Tamar could only look at him, her eyes filled with horror and compassion that blazed into sudden hatred against the tormentors of his father. She could find no words to say to him.

After a pause he continued: "Well, that was many years ago. There have been thousands to suffer torture as my father suffered. Even in this country the scourge of the Holy Roman Church was felt. Fires have blazed at Smithfield and no man has felt safe from his neighbour.

"I was smuggled back to England when my mother died. I had faithful servants—men who had followed my father to Spain and were themselves in fear of the Inquisition, and would, no doubt, have fallen victims to it; the temporary leniency shown to them was due to the fact that there were richer prizes to claim more immediate attention. In England my family owned great estates, and I was brought up by my grandparents in the Protestant religion.

"This seemed a kindlier religion; and one must have religion in this mysterious world into which we come without our own volition, struggle for a few years and then pass on. It is the passing on which makes us long for faith, for we cannot bear that we should die and be no more. Yes, this was a happier reign. Men of England were sickened by the fires of Smithfield, and the men of England are made of different stuff from those of Spain. We do not love solemn ceremonies; we love gay days and holidays; we like our streets to run with wine—not blood. Slow to anger, yet, when aroused, pertinacious in the extreme, we are quick to forget; there is no race in the world as ready to forgive a wrong as the English, providing sufficient time has elapsed for it to be comfortably forgotten. I was happy to be in such a country; but as I grew older I began to hear an echo of those cruelties springing up again in this land. Perhaps they had never really died. The Queen was head of the Church, as her father had made himself, and there were some who would not accept her as such and wished to bring about a greater reformation of the Church.

"I saw the beginning of fresh persecutions. Now it was the Puritans and Separatists who suffered. I saw men thrown into gaol . . . kept in noisome prisons. This was, I assured myself, leniency compared with Spain's horrible methods; still, it was persecution. And one day in Smithfield, I saw two Anabaptists burned to death—the first to suffer since Elizabeth came to the throne; but nevertheless I could feel little satisfaction in a religion which could permit such things . . . even if infrequently.

"I gave myself up then to the study of men and their various faiths since the beginning of time. Among these was the faith of witchcraft."

He paused to pour himself a goblet of wine. Then he looked straight at Tamar.

"Yes," he went on, "I dabbled in witchcraft, for I found it closely connected with the religion of this country. On the Continent horrible torture is inflicted on witches, who are mostly women—sometimes deluded, sometimes completely innocent of the delusion that they possess the powers of evil. And these tortures are inflicted in the name of God.

"Why, I asked myself, do these people confess to witchcraft in some cases before they are put to the torture? Because they believe in it. They die for their faith just as my father died for his. Your attitude, Tamar, has been of great interest to me. You were brought up to believe yourself a child of the Devil, and from this you derived great satisfaction. And even now that you have the benefit of some education, you cling to your beliefs. Small wonder that the ignorant refuse to renounce theirs."

"It is very well for you to disbelieve," she interrupted him. "But I saw Granny Lackwell's charms work. There *is* some power beyond the reach of ordinary men and women, and witches can find it."

"Tamar, I studied witchcraft, and I found it to be linked with the religion of this country before St. Augustine came here with Christianity. Witchcraft as practised to-day has its roots in the days when our forefathers worshipped Woden the All-father, Thor the Thunderer, Tyr the god who gave men wisdom and cunning, Freya the goddess of battle. Witches, it is true, never mention these gods; indeed, they know nothing of them. It is centuries since St. Augustine came here, and then alas! Christianity was *forced* on the inhabitants of this land. That is at the root of all religious conflict. Those in authority will not allow free-will. Through the ages the so-called Christian Church has fiercely, and with bloodshed and torment, denounced witchcraft because witchcraft is a part of a rival faith.

"I have attended witches' Sabbats. I have gone masked in a goat's head. I have seen the dances round a bonfire, and I have recognised these dances as being the same as those performed in this land before Christianity was forced upon its people. In those days our population was very small and there was a desperate need to increase it. These dances, which were in those days performed round the figure of a horned goat, were known as fertility dances. Now they seem lewd in aspect, because their meaning is not understood. They were meant to rouse the participators to an urgency of desire, for it was felt that the greater the desire, the more chance there would be of fertility, and that the children conceived on such nights would be strong—great men to lead their country in war, fine women to breed again such men.

"The witches who dance on their Sabbats do not know all this. They believe that it is the Devil who has called them out to dance. They have been told so, and they are ignorant and credulous. The Church—fearing them—has said: 'You are base. You are possessed by the Devil.' And these people, who would find life drab indeed without their belief in their own supernatural powers, cannot give them up. They are ready to die for them. Imagination can work miracles; it can make the weak-minded see what is not there."

Tamar was looking at him strangely now. He knew that she was picturing him, masked, dancing at a witches' Sabbat, and she was beginning to understand how that which had up till now seemed incredible had come about.

"Yes," he said, with a faint, ironic smile, "now you begin to see. I told no lie when I acknowledged you as my daughter before those people. You *are* my daughter.

"I am not what one would call a sensual man; nor have I lived the life of a monk since the death of my wife. There have been occasional light love affairs, and you have heard of my dear friend now dead. I had seen your mother in the house. She was a dainty creature. She had a quality which was, alas! too slight to grow. I think I probably desired her without realizing that I did, although I did not think very much about her. Others had noticed her also. One was our friend, Sir Humphrey. I guessed that ere long she would fall to him unless some obstacle was put in his way. I had little intention of making that my business, and if Luce had not gone to the Sabbat you would never have been born.

"Those ancient dances were calculated to warm the coldest heart. There are strange chants. There is magic in them—so the witches think. They arouse the dancers to a frenzy. There is fornication on such nights, and each man or woman who participates believes that, through her partner, she has communication with the Devil. In the days when the gods and heroes of Asgard were worshipped, the horned goat represented fertility; in these days the old beliefs are forgotten and only the ritual remains. The Christian interpretation is put on the goat, and that is that he represents the Devil, for men of one faith readily believe all others to be of the Devil. We have seen that even a variation of the same faith suffers the same condemnation. But I must explain to you.

"I wore the black robes which those attending associate with the Devil. There were horns to my cap. I had joined in the dance which to them was witchcraft, but which to me was the fertility dance of my forefathers. It is calculated, as I said, to arouse desire in the coldest man or woman; and this it does. That much is preserved. I was caught up in the primitive urge of my forefathers; and there was Luce in the woods.

"I did not foresee the terrible thing which would happen to her because of this. My conscience at that time worried me little. You know that I found a husband for her. It did not seem to me that what had happened to Luce was worse than what happened to so many more. I meant to take her into my confidence, to talk to her in some way as I have just talked to you, to explain to her that it was I who had seduced her. I even thought of keeping her here as my mistress. She was a dainty creature. I found her stupid, and I had no patience with stupidity. I married her off, and that, I felt, was all that was needed. When I heard that she talked of what had happened that night, I dismissed her as a little fool. I had tried to warn her, but it was impossible to do so without disclosing the identity of her seducer. You are shocked, child. You look at me with horror."

"I saw them come to the cottage. . . I saw them take her."

"I know. I have thought of it often. It was a terrible end for a girl such as Luce had been. I have made excuses for myself, but I see now that what I did to her was far worse than anything Sir Humphrey could have done. I want you to see me as I am. Have no illusions. I sheltered you when they pursued you because of my guilty conscience, not because I had any feeling towards you as a daughter."

"Yet I do not forget that you acknowledged me as your daughter before all those people when I was in my greatest danger."

"That was when I knew they had hanged her; and but for me that would never have happened to her."

"It is all violence and death!" said Tamar. "Perhaps now I understand you more than I did before."

"And to understand me is to despise me?"

"No. I think to love you as well as admire you. You did a great wrong to my mother. . . a very wicked thing. But you were sorry and you took me in and you told all those people that you were my father. How could I despise you?"

He said: "If you had not been beautiful, intelligent and amusing, I should doubtless have left you to work in the kitchens."

She did not speak and he said: "Please say what is in your mind."

"It is that you think me beautiful, intelligent and amusing."

She ran to him and flung her arms about him.

"My beloved daughter!" he said.

And she lifted her face to his. "I never thought to see you weep," she said.

He held her close to him and she felt his lips on her hair.

He put her from him suddenly, as though ashamed of his emotion.

He poured wine into two goblets and handed one to her.

"To Tamar!" he said. "To my daughter. My daughter . . . who now believes that the Devil is exonerated from all responsibility in her birth."

"To you, dear Father," she replied.

He understood the look in her eyes. He said as he put down his glass and took her by the shoulders: "Now you know the truth."

But she continued to smile her secret smile.

"They were afraid of me," she said. "I was protected in my childhood."

"You were protected by the belief of those about you."

"I have seen charms work," she said.

He sighed, and she continued:

"They would say that the Devil was in you that night. And indeed, you will admit that you behaved in a way which was not usual with you."

"I see," he said slowly, "that nothing I can tell you will shift your belief."

She embraced him once more, holding her cheek against his.

"I am glad though that he chose you. I am glad that it was your body he entered."

"Alas!" he answered, "I see your faith is unshakable." He turned her face up to his. "Tamar, can't you give it up?"

Slowly she shook her head.

* * *

Plague came to Plymouth.

In the streets men and women lay dying, calling for help which none dared give. On the doors were large red crosses, warning all to keep away. At night the pest-cart went through the streets. "Bring forth your dead!" was the mournful cry.

The surrounding villages were more fortunate than the town. It was in the cobbled streets with filth running in the gutters that the dread disease flourished. But fear was in every mind; each watched himself or herself for the dreaded signs—the shivering, sickness, headache, and delirium, which must shortly be followed by the fearful sign on the breast which was the grim herald of death.

Into the Sound one hot day came a ship; she rested at anchor while she sent a rowing boat ashore. No citizens were on the quay to greet those three men who came in that boat. The men came ashore, fear in their hearts. It did not take them long to discover why they had received no welcome. They quickly saw the red crosses on the doors, the inert figures of those who had lain down in the streets to die.

They went back to their boat with all possible speed and rowed out to their ship.

* * *

Annis knocked at the door of Tamar's room.

Tamar had her own bedroom now. It contained a four-poster bed, a carved chest, a wardrobe and a press; she had a chair with a tapestry back and there was the great luxury of a carpet on the floor. She delighted in these things to such an extent that Richard had said she must have them. Indeed, she had not yet grown accustomed to them, and would walk round her room examining them, rejoicing in the knowledge that they were hers. There was also a mirror of burnished metal, and in this she enjoyed studying her face; for her beauty delighted her more than her other possessions.

Annis was excited, Tamar saw at once.

"Mistress Tamar, I must tell 'ee what I've found. 'Twere in the barn . . . our barn, you know . . . John's and mine. I did go home and, natural like, I did look for John. He weren't to be seen, so I just put me head in at the barn . . . for memory's sake, you might say . . . and there I did see men! There were three of them . . . all lying down, starving like, they seemed. Queer sort of men. One said: 'Mistress, for the love of the Lord bring us food and drink.' And he said it twice before I could understand . . . he spoke that queer. I didn't know what I should do. I were scared out of my wits."

"Men?" said Tamar. "What sort of men?"

"Strange sort of men . . . and such a way of speaking! I was hard put to it to understand what it was they were saying, and it was guess work that told me. I could see they were starving. I could see they was well-nigh done for."

"Why did you not go to your father or mother?"

"I don't rightly know, 'cept they'd have drove 'em off the farm. Father, he won't have strangers there. He says they steal his roots and corn and suchlike. They'd be stealing the pigs' food—that's what Father would say. I didn't know where to turn, so I come to you."

Tamar smiled, well pleased. She revelled in admiration, and that of Annis was so wholehearted.

"I'll go and see for myself," she said. "I'll ride over. You can follow me. If these men are starving, they'll need help quickly. But we have to be careful, Annis. We don't know who they are."

"I thought mayhap *you* would know," said Annis.

Tamar wrinkled her brows in concentration. "I feel they are good men," she said. "Men we may have to help."

"I'm glad of that," said Annis, "for I might have told me father."

"First of all, I will see them," said Tamar.

The wind pulled at her long black hair as she rode over to the barn. She liked to wear it loose, so that she should be known and recognised at once. She enjoyed Mistress Alton's horrified glances at the offending glory.

Tamar had grown proud in the last few years, for she had risen too quickly in too short a time. In one stride she had left poverty for luxury, physical misery for comfort; she was Richard Merriman's acknowledged daughter, but she was not going to lose one whit of the special prestige among the ignorant which the belief in her satanic parentage had brought her.

She reached the barn, pushed open the door and stood looking at the three wretched men lying in the gloom. Their plight was pitiful, but her eyes had been accustomed to look at such sights.

"Who are you?" she asked.

One of the men who seemed stronger than the others raised himself a little.

"Lady, my name is Humility Brown, and I and my friends have not eaten for . . . we forget how long. For the love of the Lord, bring us food and drink, or we perish."

The man's voice was cultured, which enabled her to understand what he said, but even so it was obvious that he came from another part of the country.

"Tell me first what you do here."

"We rest and shelter against the weather."

"How did you get here?"

"We came off the ship *Adventurer*. We were on our way to Virginia in the New World."

"But where are your shipmates?"

"They would not take us back. We came ashore for stores . . . three of us . . . and when we reached the town we saw its plight. We returned to the ship, but they would not take us back aboard. There was naught we could do . . ."

Tamar slipped outside the door and shut it. These men had been in the polluted town. It might be that already they carried the terrible infection, the token already on their breasts.

She ran to her horse and mounted. She knew that the villages were free of the plague because they had cut off all communication with the stricken town.

She met Annis on the way back.

Annis cried: "Mistress, you saw them? You are going to help?"

"Annis!" cried Tamar. "You must not go near the barn. What shall we do? Those men have been in the town. They left their ship to buy stores and came to the town, so their shipmates would not have them back; but you and I, Annis, have been near them."

Annis began to shiver, but almost immediately she lifted her big grey eyes to Tamar's face and answered cheerfully: "Mistress, *you* can make us clean. We shall be safe because you will see to it."

Tamar's dark eyes were wide, her cheeks flushed. "Why, yes. We shall be safe. I shall see to that. Annis, if I told you to go into the barn and have no fear, would you go?"

"If you would set a charm on me so that I'd come to no harm, I would."

"Then I will. This is what I will do. You can go to the barn now, but do not go inside. Stand outside and let no one enter. I will bring food for the men. I will save their lives, and then no one will doubt my power. But, Annis . . . we shall not tell the master of this until it is done."

Annis nodded.

"Now to the barn. Remember! Stand there and let no one enter. If any come, you must tell them that plague victims are inside. Wait there . . . till I come."

Tamar galloped back to the house, where she went to the kitchen and collected food and wine. She found a piece of charcoal which she took with her when she rode back to the barn, where Annis was standing, placidly obedient to her mistress's command.

"You can go now, Annis. Wait for me at the end of the field."

Annis ran off and Tamar opened the door of the barn.

"Humility Brown," she said, "are you there?"

"Yes, lady."

"Here is food and drink. I will put it by the door. Have you strength to reach it?"

"Yes. And may the good Lord bless you for ever."

"I will bring more food and drink to-morrow. If there is anything else you want, you must ask me for it."

Humility Brown said with much emotion: "My friends, here is an angel from Heaven. Food, friends. This is an answer to prayer."

Tamar shut the door, and she wrote on it in charcoal: "The Lord Have Mercy On Us."

Anyone approaching would know what that meant.

* * *

Tamar was eighteen—wilful and proud. Richard often felt misgivings regarding her. The emotion she aroused in him astonished him. He was beginning to care more for this wild, natural daughter of his than he had ever cared for anyone in the whole of his life.

Her beauty enchanted him; her tortuous nature alarmed him. He had seen her tender and kind, cruel and haughty. She was half cultured, half savage. Her wits were sharp, her mind clear, but nothing he could do or say would rid her of this ridiculous belief in her own supernatural powers. She had, he supposed, found this belief too persistent in her lonely childhood to be able to relinquish it now that she had a comfortable home and an affectionate father to care for her. She was not one to wish to rely on the protection of others.

He had arranged that she should meet all the eligible men of the neighbourhood, but none of them pleased her. There were several who, despite the dark stories which still circulated about her, were so fascinated by all that charm and beauty that willingly would they have married her. But she gave herself the airs of a princess and laughed at the arrangements he would have made for her.

It was not that he wished to lose her; he found her company too entertaining for that; but he had discovered in himself parental feelings which he had not suspected he possessed, and he really wished to do what was best for his daughter. It seemed to him that she would be happier if she were married; he longed to see her with children of her own. If she married and reared a family, she might give up some of her wild ideas; she might accept him as her father, and her own birth as a purely natural event. This he greatly desired, since her persistence in her absurd belief, which proclaimed the savage in her, was at the root of his uneasiness.

Bartle Cavill was home from another voyage, and Bartle was possessed of a pride that equalled Tamar's own. It was clear that he was far from indifferent to Tamar, and Richard would not be displeased by a match between them.

Well, there was nothing he could do but wait and see. To-night he was giving a ball for her. The first ball he had given. Why not? She was eighteen; and he wished all the gentry of the countryside to know that he looked on her as his daughter—illegitimate, it was true, but illegitimacy must be winked at when a man had no legal heirs. Tamar would be rich one day and a fortune would wipe out the stigma of illegitimacy.

From his window now he could see her talking to Humility Brown, who was working in the gardens.

He smiled. Her conduct regarding those three men from *Adventurer* had been brave in the extreme; and yet it may have been her superstitious belief in herself rather than bravery, which had made her act the way she had. He himself had not heard of the affair until it was all over. She had fed those men, who had not been suffering from the plague at all, but from starvation. She had—in that bold, proud way of hers—taken them under her wing. There were only two of them alive, as they had not been discovered in time to save the third—Humility Brown and William Spears. William was working at the Hurly farm and was living in one of the farm cottages with other workers. Humility was working in Richard's own gardens and had been allotted one of the outhouses adjoining the house, for, as Tamar had pointed out, Joseph Jubin really needed assistance.

Tamar's delight in Humility Brown seemed admirable; but was it, Richard wondered. She was a minx, deeply conscious of that rare beauty of hers, and Humility Brown was a Puritan. Her pleasure in saving the man's life shone in her eyes every time she saw him; Richard guessed that Humility did not feel pleasure in Tamar's presence . . . Or was it that he was *afraid* he might feel pleasure? He was a minister from the town of Boston in Lincolnshire, and as fanatical in his beliefs as Tamar was in hers. It was said that there were more Puritans in that part of the country than in any other, and that persecution was more persistent there. Many of Humility's sect had fled to Holland—that centre of Protestantism—and lived there for some time. Richard found conversation with the man interesting, and was often turning over in his mind whether he might not find him some employment more suitable to his learning; but Richard knew himself; he had often decided he would do such-and-such and through sheer inertia had failed to make the necessary arrangements to bring these plans to fruition.

Now he began to wonder what Humility was saying to Tamar.

* * *

Tamar stood watching Humility weeding a flower bed. There were beads of sweat on Humility's brow, and not only his physical exertions had put them there; he always felt uneasy in the presence of his employer's daughter.

"Humility," she persisted, "you are afraid of me."

It was a matter of great secret delight to her that he should want to ignore her and yet find this impossible.

"Nay," said Humility; "I do not fear thee. In my mind's eye I see the Cross, and while I keep that in my mind and heart, I fear nothing."

"Ah, Humility, you are a good man, and I am glad I saved your life. You thought me an angel when I brought you food. Did I look like an angel?"

Humility lifted his eyes to her lovely, laughing face.

"To a starving man, any who brought food would seem like an angel."

"Even if she came from the Devil?"

Humility said a prayer, not aloud; but she knew he said it by the way in which his lips moved.

"What did you think when you heard who I was?" she demanded.

He went on muttering, and she stamped her foot.

"Answer me, Humility! Have you forgotten that I am the mistress here?"

"I would," he said, "that you had allowed me to work on one of the farms . . . or in the town."

"But I saved your life. It is for me to say where you shall work. Humility, if you do not answer when I speak to you I shall have you punished."

"Your father is a just man. I do not think he would agree to punishment which was unmerited."

"If I asked him, he would."

He smiled. "I should not fear punishment," he said.

He continued to weed while she watched him. He both delighted and angered her . . . delighted her because he was a continual reminder of her power, angered her because there was a power in him that rivalled her own.

The minister from Boston was a man yearning to be a martyr. He was the sort who would suffer a thousand tortures and deem himself honoured to die for his faith. He believed the power of God was in him as firmly as Tamar believed she possessed certain powers which were a gift from the Devil.

She knew why he looked at her quickly and looked away. He was a man, and he found her beauty encroaching on his notice; he found her, as most men did, desirable.

It was pleasant to be desired, though she had no wish at present to gratify any man's desires, since she was unsure of her own feelings in this matter; but whereas she could feel fear when the glinting eyes of Bartle Cavill were fixed upon her, she could feel amusement when this man looked quickly and looked away.

He was older than Bartle. He would be about thirty years old, she imagined, which seemed very old to her when she considered the man in the role of a lover. She could guess what sort of life he had led; he was a Puritan child of Puritan parents. Puritans believed that ministers should live frugally, as Jesus Christ had done when He was on Earth. Humility had been brought up to believe that it was sinful to laugh, to enjoy more food than would keep him alive, and as for dancing or making love—these would be mortal sins. She knew that with her flaunting beauty, her quick and ready laughter, her awareness of her own attractions, she must seem like the Devil incarnate to such a man.

She liked to be near him when he was working, just to tease, to taunt. She wished him to know that he was as vulnerable as other men.

She would not have dared to taunt Bartle in such a way.

"Why do you frown at me, good Humility?" she asked. "Why do you stare at my hair as though you hate it?"

"You should cut it short or hide it under a cap."

"Why so? Do you think it is a gift from the Devil?"

He did not answer and she went on imperiously: "Answer when I speak to you. Do you think it is a gift from the Devil?"

Then he said: "That may well be so."

"I thought that God made all beautiful things."

He tried to plead with her, as he had on other occasions: "Do not be deceived. Mend your ways. Renounce the Devil. Embrace the true faith. If you would save yourself from eternal damnation, give up your evil ways."

"Was it evil to save your life?"

"If you called in the aid of the Devil, I had rather you had left me to die."

"It did not seem so when I came to the barn. You called out to me most piteously. I'll warrant you'd have taken food then if imps from Hell had brought it to you."

"You deceive yourself, daughter."

"Don't dare to call me daughter. You know whose daughter I am."

"I know that your birth was the result of sin."

"What if I were to tell your master that?"

"I would tell him so myself."

She gave him a grudging smile of admiration, for she knew that he spoke the truth. He was brave; she must concede that. That was why she felt herself forced to taunt him; his bravery was as great as her own; his belief that he was right as firm as that she held.

"You would, I believe," she said. "Some masters would have you beaten for it. But he is a good man . . . a far better man than you will ever be, Humility Brown."

He was silent.

"Oh," she went on angrily, "he does not go about thanking God that he is saved, that he is so much better than those who risked their lives to save his. He is a good man, I tell you, and if you dare say you are a better, I will whip you with my own hands."

It was at such times that he had the advantage. He was calm, and she could never be calm. He was cold and sure; she was fiery and passionate, though equally sure.

"And you would not care if I did!" Her eyes flashed. "But there are some things I could do which would make you care. Humility Brown, you are a coward. You are afraid to look at me. You take sly glances and look away. Have a care, Humility Brown! I might yet take you to eternal damnation with me. You think me beautiful. Your lips might deny that, but your eyes do not. I might decide to show you that you are but a sinful man, Humility Brown. You have heard talk of who is my real father, have you not? It is true, you know, that I am the Devil's own daughter."

Laughing, she ran into the house and called to Annis to come to her room and help her to dress for the ball.

* * *

She knew that Annis's repeated assertions, that she looked more beautiful than ever to-night, were true.

The dress was of scarlet, blue, and gold—her own choice of colours. The scarlet overgown opened in front to show the deep blue gold-embroidered skirt; her ruff was of finest lace—an upstanding collar that ended on the shoulders, leaving her bosom exposed after the fashion for unmarried ladies. She wore her hair loose, hanging down to the waist. There would be no one else at the ball who would wear her hair as she wore it.

Annis chattered gaily. Annis was now her personal maid, for Tamar, wishing to be known as a lady of fashion, must have such a maid of her own. Richard would have provided her with a trained one had she asked, but loyalty was strong in Tamar, and she wished to remove Annis from the housekeeper's tyranny. Indeed, Annis was more to her than any maid could have been; Annis was her friend.

"You're more beautiful than anyone has ever been," declared Annis. " 'Tis no wonder folks say beauty such as your's ain't of this world."

"You're fond of me, Annis; that's why you think so." It might be true, but Tamar was well pleased with the maid's words all the same.

"Others think it, mistress," explained Annis. "John, he said to me, 'Annis,' he said, 'Mistress Tamar have a beauty which is not of this world.' I spoke to him sharp-like. I said, 'John Tyler, have you been so bold as to cast your eyes that way, then?' And he said, 'Nay, Annis, I dare not. But there ain't another like her, and they do say as there's hardly a gentleman as claps eyes on her that wouldn't give his fortune to marry her, witch though she be.' I said, 'You'd better keep your eyes on me, John Tyler.' To which he answered, 'How could I help doing that, since her give you a charm herself to make me?' "

"Ah!" laughed Tamar. "So that charm still does its work, eh?"

"It does it beautiful, mistress. John's well-nigh beside himself for me some days."

Tamar studied this maid of hers who had experiences such as she herself had not. She thought of Humility Brown, and immediately another figure entered her thoughts—a young man with the most brilliant blue eyes she had ever seen. Then there was another picture in her mind, a picture which had been responsible for many a nightmare.

I hate Bartle Cavill, she told herself.

In the gallery the musicians were already assembling.

"Be quick," said Annis. "You should be there with the master to greet the guests."

Tamar hurried down. Richard was waiting for her at the bottom of the staircase.

She curtsied gaily.

"How do you like me, Richard?"

"You look very beautiful, my dear."

"Then you are not ashamed to own me as your daughter?"

He refused to pander to her demand for compliments. "There is a wildness in your eyes," he said. "What are you plotting this night?"

"I make no plots."

"Perhaps I should make some for you. It would please me very much to see you married."

"I am happy as I am."

"You should marry and have children. It is the duty of a father to choose a husband for his daughter."

She smiled demurely. "You have talked to me so much of the necessity to allow people free-will that I cannot believe you would go against your principles."

"I am very fond of you. It might be that I should consider it my duty. . ."

She took his hand and kissed it. "And I love you dearly," she said. "Nevertheless, I would not allow any to choose for me, or to arrange a marriage I did not want."

"I should not attempt it. But I do confess I should enjoy seeing you and your family riding over to Pennicomquick from Stoke. . ."

"From Stoke?"

He laughed. "I was thinking of Bartle. I am sure he would very gladly marry you."

"Bartle!" She spat out the name. "I would rather die than marry Bartle. He is coarse . . . vulgar . . . lecherous. I wonder that you dare mention his name to me."

"Hush! I crave your pardon. All the same, I think you are hard on the young man. He is brave; he has had many adventures and would be ready to settle down and live the life of a landowner with a family to bring up. Oh, I know he frightened you badly once. He was a clumsy boy, that was all."

"A lustful, lecherous beast!"

"I am sorry. Forget what I said."

"I shall . . . with all speed."

She was trembling, for the guests were arriving, and among the first were Sir Humphrey and Lady Cavill with their son Bartle.

Sir Humphrey's eyes admired Tamar; Lady Cavill kissed her in that half fearful way which Tamar was accustomed to; Bartle bowed over her hand, his eyes brilliant, shining with that blue fire which lit them whenever they fell upon her.

Haughtily she turned from him and talked to Sir Humphrey.

Other guests were arriving—all the gentry within riding distance. Richard had decided that Tamar's first ball should be worthy of his daughter.

When the guests had danced and were eating the rich foods which had been prepared for them—

venison and pies with clouted cream, roast meats of all varieties, to be washed down with wine and ale—morris dancers appeared with gay ribbons in their garments and bells attached to their legs, and they performed before the guests to the playing of musicians in the gallery.

Tamar was gay that night. She told herself it would have been a perfect evening but for the presence of Bartle. When he tried to speak to her she eluded him, and it delighted her to see how this angered him. Deliberately she coquetted with a tall and handsome young man whose large estates lay alongside the Plym. That young man was so fascinated by his beautiful hostess that he asked her to marry him. Then she was immediately sorry, for she had not wished to tease him—only to escape from Bartle.

But close on midnight, when the great fire in the centre of the hall had burned low and some of the guests were half asleep on their stools, indolent with too much rich food and wine, Bartle cornered her. She leaned against the oak panelling of the wall and studied him insolently. He was handsome enough in his swaggering way; his face was red and his eyes had never seemed so blue.

"What Devil's game do you think you're playing with me?" he demanded.

She lifted her hand to brush his aside, but he caught her in a grip which hurt.

"Release me at once or I'll have you thrown out," she retorted.

"It would be wise if you did not goad me too far, as you have been doing this night," he warned.

"I . . . goad you? I can assure you that no one could have been further from my thoughts this night . . . than you!"

"That's a lie and a poor one."

"You have a high conceit of yourself."

"I wonder, does it match yours?"

His eyes explored her face and rested on her bare bosom. She flushed hotly.

"Tamar," he said, "why put off what must certainly come to you?"

"What do you mean?"

"You surely have not forgotten that I made a vow concerning you?"

"Alas for you and your vows! I am not a poor child whom nobody cares for now. You would have to answer to Richard."

"Not if you came to me of your own free-will."

"You would wait a long time for that!"

He brought his face close to hers.

"My dear Tamar, I do not intend to wait. I shall be leaving England in a week. Before that day I shall have what I have long desired."

"You talk without sense."

"We shall see."

"If you dared to try to do to me what you tried once before, I would have no hesitation in killing you."

"But how would you manage that?"

"I should find myself unable to surprise you if I told you that."

"I believe that you have the Devil in you."

"That is the first thing of sense you have said to me to-night."

"But," he went on, "there will be no forcing. It shall be of your own free-will—I promise you that."

"Oh? And have you fixed a day for this voluntary surrender?"

"The day—or night—does not matter, but it shall be before I leave. That I have determined on."

She tried to remain calm, but she was uneasy, and she knew that he was aware of it. She forced herself to laugh, but her laughter was stilled abruptly when he said: "Simon Carter is in Plymouth. The witch-pricker has returned."

"Well?" She knew she had turned pale.

"That frightens you, does it not? Well it might! What if I go to him? What if I tell him that I have seen you making spells? What if I tell him I have seen you changing to a hare?"

"You would be a liar, and that would not help *you*, would it?"

"He would come to you, Tamar. Nothing Richard could do would prevent your being searched. Remember when you were on the point of being searched and pricked before, the only charge against you was your mother's statement that the Devil was your father. Richard declared *he* was, and therefore there was naught against you. But if you had been seen weaving spells . . . consorting with your familiar . . ."

"You . . . beast!"

"I would be kind, if you would but be kind to me. Tamar, why should I want to betray you? It would not be once or twice with me. I know that. To look at you tells me that."

"So," she said, her lips trembling, "you can pick a bedfellow as Simon Carter can pick a witch!"

"Leave your window open. I know which room is yours. I will come to you when the house is quiet. Then you need have no fear. If any attacked you, if any said a word against you, my sword would be ready to defend you . . . for ever, Tamar."

She was staring at him in silent horror, and he went on insolently: "Why, I might even marry you. Richard thinks it is time you married, and he is prepared to be very generous towards the man who marries the witch he is pleased to call his daughter."

"I would rather die than marry you."

"You talk too lightly of death."

"Please let me go. I never want to see your face again."

"You have grown haughty. How will you like the indignity of the search? How will you like to have those foul men exploring your body? How will you like to hang on a gibbet?"

She said coldly, her eyes glittering: "I would prefer torture and death to what you suggest."

He released her then.

His eyes followed her wherever she went for the rest of that evening; when he took his leave they mocked her. She saw his swaggering confidence; he was certain that she would give in to him.

He whispered to her: "Two days in which to come to a decision. No longer, I warn you. Time is precious."

When Annis helped her to undress she made the girl talk of her love affair with John Tyler. She listened with close attention and plagued Annis into giving details which made the girl hang her head and blush.

Then she laughed aloud, dismissed Annis and, throwing herself on the bed, she drew the curtains, shutting herself in.

But she could not shut out the image of Bartle's blazing eyes. And when she slept she dreamed of his pulling aside the curtains and forcing himself upon her. Humility Brown too was in the dream: she forgot what part he had played in it.

* * *

A hundred times Tamar relived that day when she had heard the shouts of the people, with Simon Carter at their head, as they came to the house to take her.

Surely Bartle would not betray her to that man. Once he had helped Richard to hide her. But that was only because he wanted her for himself. He was without pity; he was graceless; he was a boorish lecher; and how she hated him! He wished to treat her as he treated the native girls in those towns which he pillaged and burned. He was a buccaneer, a pirate, for all that he was considered one of King James's brave seamen.

Annis brought her a letter from him. Annis was all secret smiles. "Mistress, I have something for 'ee. 'Tis a note from a gentleman. He bid me give it to you and lose no time. He said 'twere important. Oh, mistress, what a handsome gentleman he be! The sort a woman would be powerless to resist. He gave me a kiss and said he'd warrant I was a pretty bedfellow to some lucky shepherd. I did feel myself shake, mistress, when he did lay his hands upon me."

"Be silent!" cried Tamar shrilly. "You are nothing more than a slut, Annis. If John went with another, you'd be to blame. And it would not surprise me greatly."

"Oh, mistress, you'll not take off the spell!"

"Unless you mend your ways, I swear I will. Now give me the note and leave me. I wish to be alone."

She read it through as soon as Annis had left her.

"I must see you at once," he had written. "It is important. Come to the garden and talk to me. I will wait in sight of the house, so, my chicken-hearted virgin, you need not be afraid. If you ignore this summons, you will be very sorry indeed. I am waiting now and it will not be wise to keep me waiting long. From him who is soon to be your lover."

She went to her window. He was down there, and he looked up and waved impatiently. She saw Humility in the distance.

Hastily she went down.

Elegantly dressed, Bartle was strolling about the gardens. As she approached, he hurried towards her, bowed and kissed her hands.

"Come into the enclosed garden," he said. "That fellow will hear everything if we do not."

She followed him, for she did not wish Humility to know of her predicament. Doubtless he would be pleased if he learned that the witch-pricker was about to be set on her trail.

The garden was secluded, surrounded by a high hedge, and bordering the paths were evergreens cut into fantastic shapes. Soon it would be spring and the first shoots in the flower beds were beginning to show themselves.

Bartle smiled at her mockingly.

"So," he said, "you spoke truth. You would rather die than give yourself to me."

She did not answer, but merely lifted her head and haughtily looked away from him. He took her by the shoulders and forced a rough kiss on her mouth. Her eyes blazed and she kicked him as she had once before. He ignored that, but he released her, though he stood barring her way at the gap in the evergreen hedge which was the only way in or out of the garden.

"We did not come here to fight," he said, "but to talk. Why, my dear Tamar . . ."

"Not *your* Tamar! . . . Never yours!"

"A little too soon perhaps. But this time to-morrow I shall call you my Tamar, and mayhap you will be glad to be so called."

She shrugged her shoulders. "I can see no object in your detaining me here."

"That is because you are so hasty. You never wait to hear: you speak . . . without thinking. You give an opinion on my plans before you have heard them. If I married you, which I have told you I am quite prepared to do and for what reason, I should have to subdue that high temper of yours. I should have to mould you into a meek and loving wife."

"Don't dare to insult me thus. I wonder you are not afraid I shall bewitch you."

"If it had been possible for you to harm me, you would have done so ere this."

"Let me pass, or I shall call to the gardener to come to my rescue."

"What! That meek Puritan! If he dared oppose me I'd slit his throat—and he knows it. Listen sensibly, girl, to what I have to tell you. To-night I shall come to your room. Leave your window open, as I shall come in that way."

She flashed at him: "My window will be barred and bolted to-night . . . and every night until that happy day when you sail away from Plymouth."

"I think, Tamar, that your window will be open to-night."

"Why so?"

"You would rather die than give me what I ask, and you have proved that to me."

"And you have proved your words were idle. You were not going to set Simon Carter upon me. If you were, why have you not done so—as you threatened to do—by this time?"

"Because I have vowed to have you for myself. You yourself are prepared to die rather than concede me what I ask. But are you prepared that others should die?"

"What others?"

"He who calls himself your father."

"I do not understand you."

"Do you not? What if I informed on Richard Merriman?"

"You are completely mad. How could you? And why?"

"The witch Luce said that the Devil was her lover. Richard says *he* was her lover. It is possible that he went to the meeting of witches—because it was at such a meeting that Luce was ravished . . . so she said. You, my beauty, were the result of that unholy union, as you know. I might suggest that Richard is a witch. I might suspect him and, having such suspicions, I should do my duty and go to the pricker and tell him of them. Let him find a mark . . . any mark . . . and I'll warrant that will be the end of Richard Merriman."

"You are vile and I loathe you!"

"Yes. I knew you would. But if you will not love me, then must you be taken loathing me. It will be a change. Too many women have loved me to madness."

"You are a conceited villain."

"I know it well," he mocked.

"Bartle, you would not do this. You cannot mean it. He is your friend!"

"Ah! Now you look at me with soft eyes. Now you plead. Tamar, witch or woman, I have sworn to have you. Never before have I had aught to do with witches, but you have been in my thoughts ever since I found you naked on the grass. I am ready to do anything . . . anything . . . barter my soul for you if necessary."

She felt tears starting to her eyes. "Let me go!" she cried.

He caught her arm as she tried to run past him.

"Leave your window open to-night. I promise you such joy as you have never dreamed of."

She ran past him and into the house.

* * *

She had gone to bed early. She had dismissed Annis, who was quite bewildered. Something ailed her mistress, she knew. Annis wondered what could ail one who had all that Tamar had. And now handsome Bartle Cavill was coming to woo her, and with those two, as Annis said to John Tyler, " 'twould mean a marriage ring and a marriage bed, not a heap of hay in a barn."

Tamar lay shivering. The door was locked and she had drawn the curtains about her bed; they stirred lightly in the breeze from the open window.

The decision had been made for her. He had threatened Richard, and for Richard's sake she must do this thing which was horrible and loathsome to her. It was worse than rape, because it would be done with a semblance of willingness.

"He is a fiend!" she muttered.

She had ill-wished him, but that was of no avail. She had tried to work a spell; but she believed he must have some protection against such things, some secret knowledge which he had picked up from foreign magicians on his travels.

She was dizzy with fear—or excitement.

Any moment now she would hear him, climbing into her bedroom. He would pull aside the curtains and stand there, mocking her in his triumph.

Only for Richard, would she do this. He had saved her life and now she would save his by giving more than her life, for had she not been willing to lose it rather than give in to Bartle for her own sake?

Outside the window she could hear the sounds of the night—the hoot of an owl, the sudden barking of a dog. It sounded as though witches were riding through the air on broomsticks, but it was only the wind in the chimney.

He had not yet come.

She thought—and, to her surprise, the thought angered her: Perhaps he did not mean it. Perhaps he will not come. He was merely teasing. Did he not say once that he would carry tales of me to the pricker?

In the midst of her fearful apprehension she was conscious of a twinge of disappointment.

It is because I wished to make a sacrifice for Richard, she told herself quickly. Even in this most evil thing there is some goodness, for I should have done it for Richard's sake. Had Richard known what wicked bargain Bartle had made with me, he would try to prevent my carrying out my share in it. Richard would let himself be taken by the pricker for my sake. So shall I find satisfaction in giving myself to Bartle . . . for Richard's sake.

And now she could hear a new sound outside her window.

She lay very still. She could hear the thud as he landed on his feet; she could hear his breathing, heavy with the exertion of the climb.

Very slowly, it seemed to her, the curtains were parted. She could not see his face; there was not enough light for that; she was only aware of a broad figure bending over her.

"Tamar!" he said; and his voice was higher than usual, yet thicker, unlike its usual timbre, but she knew it for Bartle's.

She shrank as his hands touched her.

"So," he whispered, "you were waiting for me? I knew you would be."

CHAPTER FOUR

The memory of that night would not leave her.

He had refused to go before dawn was in the sky, and she had no means of making him. There was nothing she could do but lie, quiet and submissive.

She had wept in her anger and he had kissed her tears. But his tenderness quickly changed to mockery.

"You deceive yourself, Tamar! You are as eager for me as I am for you. I certainly shall not go until it pleases me to do so. I meant to stay all through the night. That was our bargain. What a demanding witch you are! Most women ask for a jewel; but you submit for a man's life!"

"You have humiliated me," she answered. "Is that not enough? Go now, I beg of you."

"Come! You know that when you beg me to go, you are really begging me to stay."

"You lie! And stop talking. What if your voice should be heard?"

He put his mouth close to her ear. "They would say 'Tamar has a man in her bed! Well, what do we expect from such as Tamar? Perhaps it is the Devil she has in there? No, not her own father . . . merely some imp from Hell!'"

"If they came and found you here . . . ?"

"Well then, I should tell them how I came to be where I am. I should say, 'I came through the window. Tamar opened it for me.' That is the truth, you know. When I parted the curtains of your bed, you were waiting for me. Can you deny that?"

"You are a devil, I believe."

"Then we are well mated. Of course we are. We know that now. Oh, Tamar, how I love you. This is the beginning. Leave your window open to-morrow and I will come again."

"That was not in the bargain," she said quickly.

"Bargain? Who talks of bargains? You know why I am here."

"Yes! Because you are a traitor . . . a false friend."

"What! To Richard? I'd never have betrayed Richard, sweetheart, and you knew that all the time. I was merely giving you the excuse you wanted for surrender."

"I loathe you. I hate you. You are worse even than I believed you to be. Go at once . . . At once, I say!"

But he had crushed her against him, laughing softly, biting her ear. "You knew I would never have betrayed Richard. He is an old bore, but I'm fond of him. It is not for filthy prickers of the lower orders to use their pins on men of our station. I said what I did to give you an excuse. You knew it. You cannot deceive me. And you were delighted."

She had felt that the humiliation was more than she could tolerate.

When at last he had gone she leaped out of bed and bolted her window. He stood below and bowed mockingly.

Annis was astonished when, pulling back the curtains later that morning, she found Tamar fast asleep, pale-faced and exhausted.

Tamar opened her eyes and looked at her maid.

"Why, mistress, what ails you?" cried Annis. "You look . . . different . . ."

"Don't be a fool. How could I be different?" She rose, her mind full of what had so recently happened to her. "Don't stand there staring at me!" she shouted to Annis. "Help me to dress."

She slapped Annis when the girl fumbled with the fastening of her gown, and, seeing the tears well up in Annis's eyes, she herself began to weep while she embraced her maid.

"Annis, I'm sorry. You're right. I'm not myself."

Annis was all smiles immediately. "I was clumsy. It was just that I couldn't bear you to be cross with me. What ails thee, dear mistress? What has happened to 'ee this night?"

"This night!" cried Tamar. "What do you mean by that?"

"Nothing," said Annis quickly. " 'Twere just that you did seem strange like when I left you for the night, and now you be stranger still."

Tamar kissed Annis's cheek. "Do not speak to me of it," she said. "I am well. I did not sleep well; that is all."

Annis nodded, and it was clear to Tamar that the girl thought she had been up to some Devil's work during the night. And that, Tamar told herself fiercely, would have been a deal more to my liking than what has befallen me.

Bartle dared to ride over to Pennicomquick that morning. "To drink a goblet of wine with the mistress of the house," he told Tamar when Annis brought him into the room.

Tamar regarded him icily. He looked as debonair as ever. There was no novelty for him, she supposed, in such nights.

"How dare you show yourself here!" she demanded.

"I would dare much to see you. I thought you would receive me warmly after last night."

"We were not friends before. We are greater enemies now."

"You cannot be my enemy, and I would never be yours. Oh, Tamar, you are so beautiful and I adore you. I have come to make honourable amends. I have come to ask you to marry me. Custom demands that I go to Richard and tell him what I wish and how I hope he will decide I am a good enough match for his daughter. But that, I know, will not do for Tamar. She must be wooed, then won. Ha! Not so. She must be won, then wooed. So I come to you, Tamar, before I go to your father."

"I would choose my husband and, if I lived until I were fifty and there was no one else in the world, I would never take you."

"Let us have done with quarrels. Let us be reasonable. We are both expected to marry, so why not each other?"

"Because a woman should not marry a man she hates."

"You mean you really hate me?"

"I mean it from the bottom of my heart."

He had become haughty now; he walked to the window and looked out. She remained by the table; and they were thus when Richard came into the room.

Bartle left Plymouth a few days later. Tamar did not know why she felt she must go and see him leave; but she did.

There was the usual bustle such departures always brought with them down there on the causeway. Ships being loaded, sailors shouting to one another, anchors being lifted, sails set.

She had hoped Bartle would not see her, but his sharp eyes found her. He came to her and stood before her, smiling down at her.

"So you have come to see me off on my voyage?"

"To assure myself that you had really gone," she answered caustically. "It gives me great pleasure to know that I shall not see you for a long time."

"I shall soon be back, sweetheart," he said: "and then . . ."

"I beg of you, make no more vows. I assure you there shall be no repetition of that shameful night."

"My lovely Tamar! I shall carry your image in my heart. I expect a dull voyage, for there can be little pleasure for me outside your bed."

He caught her up and kissed her full on the mouth. Then he put her down, bowed low and left her.

She walked up to the Hoe that she might watch the ships until they were specks on the white-flecked sea, while anger, humiliation and something like regret filled her heart.

*   *   *

When she arrived back at the house she saw Humility Brown at work in the garden. She went over to him; by taunting him she thought to regain her self-respect.

"Good day to you, Humility Brown."

"Good day," he answered. But he did not look at her.

She said sharply: "When I speak to you, pray do not go on with your work. Look at me. Smile! Say 'Good day' as though you meant it."

He looked at her gravely, and she felt herself blushing hotly, for she thought he saw the change in her, and visions of Bartle and herself would not be shut out of her mind.

"Do not stare!" she said.

Then he did smile. "I am admonished for not looking, and when I look that does not please you. You are in an ill mood to-day."

"What is that to you?"

"Nothing; but that I am sorry to see you put out."

"*You* . . . sorry for *me*!"

"Ah yes. I am deeply sorry for you."

"And why, pray?"

"Because guilt lies heavy on your soul."

"Who says so? Can you see guilt in my face?"

"You have forsaken true goodness for the evil power which comes to you through the Devil. You have asked for beauty to tempt the senses of men, and it has been given to you."

"It was given without my asking," she retorted. "And does it tempt your senses, Humility Brown?"

His lips moved in silent prayer.

"Stop that!" she cried. "Stop it, I say!"

"My poor erring daughter," he said, "give up your sins. Wash your soul pure in the blood of the Holy Lamb."

She laughed. "Is that what you have done? But you have no sins, I suppose . . . and never have had!"

"We are all sinners."

"It surprises me that you should put yourself into that class. Oh, Humility Brown, sometimes I wish I had left you to starve in the barn."

"Aye! And so do I! Then I should be past my pains . . . safe in the arms of Jesus."

"It might be the fires of Hell for you, Humility Brown."

He bowed his head and once more sought refuge in prayer.

"Oh, I meant not that!" she cried in repentance. "You are a good man and the gates of Heaven will be flung wide for you, I doubt not."

"Daughter," he cried, "repent. Repent while there is yet time."

"Repent of what?"

"Of your sins."

"It might be that I have sinned through no fault of my own."

"It is only the Devil's own who are forced into sin. The Good Shepherd protects His sheep."

"Are you sure of that?"

"As sure as I stand here."

She was silent. It was Humility who spoke first. He leaned on his spade and looked at her earnestly.

"You are a sinner," he said; "that I know. You defy the Holy Gospel. There are many who think you have dealings with witches. You are in peril. Your soul is in danger."

"What can I do about that?"

"Wicked as you are, I know I can trust you with a secret. I will show you how much I am prepared to trust you if you care to let me do so."

She was interested; for the first time since that memorable night, she had forgotten Bartle.

"You would never betray friends," he said, "even though you thought what they did was folly."

"I believe that to be so," she said.

"You are generous and there is kindness in you . . . kindness towards the weak; such kindness was the kindness taught us by our Lord Jesus Christ. Because you possess it, I believe there is hope for you. But you are vain and proud and, I believe, wicked in some strange way. But because of your kindness I wish to save your soul as once you saved my body."

"You must tell me what you mean by that."

"Some of us are meeting together. We meet in secret."

"I see."

He went on: "You know what I mean. William Spears and I, and others here who wish to worship God in the right way, have fixed a meeting-place where we forgather."

"That is a dangerous thing to do, Humility. If you were discovered, it would mean prison—perhaps torture and execution."

He smiled and his smile illumined his face so that it seemed almost beautiful.

"You are a fool!" she said angrily, in sudden fear for him.

"I am the Lord's," he answered.

She was emotional that morning and her eyes filled with tears.

"You are a brave man. I beg of you, take care. I would not care to see you come to harm after I took such pains to save your life."

"We meet in a hut . . . Stoke way. It is on Sir Humphrey Cavill's estate."

"Have a care! Sir Humphrey would have no scruples about denouncing you if he discovered. He is a bigot . . . and so is his son. They are without pity . . . without . . ."

"I know it," he said. "And this we all know: We meet in the name of Truth, in the name of the Lord. We know the risks we run and we are prepared to run them. If the Lord should see fit to make our presence known to those who would persecute us, then we are all ready to accept persecution for His sake."

"Why do you tell me this?"

"That you might join our meeting and perhaps find peace there."

"*I* . . . meet with *Puritans*!" She smoothed the rich stuff of her dress and looked down at it lovingly.

"You would learn that it is folly to lay up for yourself treasures upon earth. You would learn that you should repent of your sins."

She turned from him and hurried into the house. She knew that she would go and see their secret meeting-place. She needed the excitement of new experiences now that Bartle, whose loathsome presence had provided them, had gone away.

* * *

Tamar went once to the meeting-place. Such affairs were not for her. She was like a bird of paradise among sparrows. She sensed the hostility of the Puritans towards her. What, they were asking themselves, was Humility Brown about, to ask a witch to their meetings?

When Humility preached that night he said: "There is none among us who could not reach salvation, an that one wished it."

That she knew was for her.

But she stood apart from them — apart from them as she had been from the people amongst whom she had lived during her childhood. Only Humility wished to befriend her. She listened to his preaching; she watched the earnestness of his expression. He was a bolder man here than in the gardens; there he seemed aptly named; here he was a leader.

She felt a new pride in the fact that she had saved his life. She could look scornfully round her now at the faces of his followers and remind herself that not one of them would have dared to do for him what she had done.

She did not go again to the meeting-place.

Simon Carter had now left Plymouth, and the crow-pecked bodies of several men and women hung rotting from the gibbets.

But for me, thought Tamar, Richard might have been one of them!

Then she must think again of that night which she knew would be the most memorable of her life because it was the most shameful. When she looked out to sea she thought of Bartle. Where was he now? Somewhere on the Spanish Main? Perhaps he had reached land; perhaps he was tricking some other woman to shame as he had tricked her. She might turn angrily away from the sea to the land, but the green grass and the trees reminded her of the day when he had found her naked on the grass and had pursued her. There was no escape from thoughts of Bartle.

Annis came to her room one day; it was easy to see that something was on Annis's mind.

"What is it, Annis?" asked Tamar.

Annis cast down her eyes. "Trouble, mistress. That's what 'tis."

"I know," said Tamar. "You are going to tell me that you are with child."

Annis lifted her wondering eyes to Tamar's face. "You knew afore I did myself, I reckon, mistress."

Tamar could not resist the pleasure of allowing her to think so.

"That this should happen to *me*!" sighed Annis.

"Well, Annis, there was many a meeting in the old barn, I believe."

"You took the spell off, then, did 'ee, mistress?"

"You cannot do what you have been doing so often, with no result. You must tell John and he will have to marry you."

Annis began to cry.

" 'Tis like this, mistress. John, he be sharing a cottage with Will Spears and Dan Layman. John couldn't marry a wife and take her to share with they two."

"But, Annis, John will have to ask for a cottage of his own now."

"There be no empty cottage."

"Your father and mother would let you live at the farm. They surely would when they know how things are."

"My mother said she'd break my neck if aught of this sort ever happened to me. Me father said he'd give me the whipping of me life."

"That's what they said before it happened, Annis. They'll know they will have to look after you now. They'll have to help you and John."

Annis began to cry bitterly. " 'Tis John himself, mistress. You see, I did tell him the charm would look after that there . . . and it looked as though I were right. It certainly looked as though it were. I dursen't tell him. That be the plain truth."

"Annis," said Tamar in exasperation, "you are a little fool!"

"That's what most of us women be, I reckon!" said Annis.

"Please stop crying, Annis. I will think of something to be done."

Annis knelt at Tamar's feet and embraced her knees.

"You'll take it away, mistress. They do say 'tis a thing a witch can do."

"No," said Tamar. "I cannot do that."

All hope faded from Annis's face.

"It would be wrong to do it. But never fear, I will make a plan for you. I will see that you come to no harm. You must trust me."

"Oh, I do, mistress," said Annis fervently, "with the very soul of me!"

* * *

Richard said to Tamar: "Do you know what that fool Humility Brown is doing? He is arranging meetings of the Puritans. Moreover, he is going about the place converting people to his faith. It is a highly dangerous thing to do!"

"He is a very brave but very foolish man, I fear," said Tamar.

"I will speak to him. Ring the bell and ask one of the maids to fetch him."

"I will go myself and bring him to you," she said.

She went into the garden.

"Humility Brown, your master wishes to speak to you. You may well look startled. He has discovered that you are holding meetings and, not content with putting yourself in danger, you go about asking other people to do the same. He is very angry with you."

"If they wish to save their souls, it is of no concern to any but themselves," he said. "The life of the body is transient; that of the soul eternal."

"Well, you must now come and give an account of yourself. I would have you know that I have not betrayed you."

"I did not think for one moment that that was so."

"Thank you," she answered. "Now come this way. Your master does not care to be kept waiting."

She could not help thinking how noble the man looked as he stood before Richard, how cleverly he answered the questions put to him. A brave man . . . this Humility Brown! She compared him with Bartle, and her mouth tightened at the recollection of that which she had tried so hard to forget.

"You are, I know," said Richard, "convinced that you are right. But you are defying the law of this land, and how can that be right?"

"I know of one law only, sir . . . the law of God."

"It would seem," said Richard coldly, "that whether God is on your side or on that of the Church of England is a matter of opinion. But I did not send for you to discuss that. What I wish to say is this: You, my good man, may be made of martyr's stuff, but think you that you do right to involve others?"

“If they wish to save their souls alive, they must worship God in the only true way,” said Humility. “The Carpenter’s Son preached simplicity, but in the Church of England ceremonial rites are practised which are little short of popery. Where does the Church of England differ from the Church of Rome? It would seem in this only: One has a King at its head; one a Pope.”

“You attach too great an importance to the method and ritual of worshipping God. I have little patience with those who would send to their death men and women who have a way of worshipping God which differs from their own. It seems to me the utmost arrogance to say, ‘You are wrong because you do not as I do!’ Arrogance is a sin, is it not? And one Catholics and Puritans are guilty of . . . and all other sects with them. Jesus said, ‘Not everyone that saith unto me, Lord, Lord, shall enter the kingdom of heaven; but he that *doeth* the will of My Father.’ Are you not guilty of the sin of pride when you continually thank God that you are not as other men are? What if I informed against you and your meeting?”

“If you feel that is your duty, then you should do it.”

Tamar said: “Richard, you have always declared that men should be free to worship God in whatever way they wish.”

“I have said that and I believe it.” He turned to Humility. “All I wish to do is to beg you to have a care.”

"I will, sir. And I think you would benefit if you came to our meetings."

"What!" cried Richard. "You dare ask me!"

"You have a soul to save, sir."

"He is a better man than you will ever be, for all your piety!" cried Tamar.

"I did not say that he was not," said Humility.

"But you thought it. I saw it in your eyes."

They made a striking contrast—Tamar and Richard in their gay garments; Humility in his sombre attire.

"It is not sufficient for a man to have a kind heart," said Humility. "It is not sufficient to be courageous and tolerant. It is imperative to worship God in the right way."

"You mean in the Puritan manner," said Richard with a touch of sarcasm.

"That is so, sir."

"You may go now. And remember my warning."

"I thank you, sir."

He bowed gravely to Tamar and to Richard; but as he was about to leave he turned to Tamar.

"Repent," he said. "I beg of you, repent before it is too late. I shall pray for your souls, for you are both in need of salvation."

As he went out Tamar looked at Richard.

"I never knew a man so sure," she said.

"A fanatical fool!" said Richard.

"Yet I have a certain admiration for him."

"That may be because you are also fanatical, also foolish, my dear." He smiled grimly. "He the

Puritan . . . and you the Pagan. And who should be bold enough to say one is right and one is wrong? A cleverer man than I am."

"You are cleverer than any of us and you are the one with doubts." She paused reflectively. "I shall be a little angry if he comes to harm. I did not save his life to have him throw it away."

"If he comes to grief, it is his own fault. My sincere hope is that he does not bring trouble to others in this place."

Tamar went to her own room and had not been there for many minutes when there was a knock on her door.

It was Annis, looking happier than she had for a long time.

"I did see Humility Brown coming from master's study."

"What of that?"

"I was wondering . . . be master saved?"

"Saved from what?"

"Be his soul saved? Has Humility saved it for him?"

"Your master's soul has long been saved. He is the best man in the world, and as such will enter the Kingdom of Heaven before any preaching Puritan!"

Annis would not contradict her; but Tamar saw disbelief in the girl's eyes.

"You, Annis, have been taking a good dose of Mr. Humility Brown, I do believe."

"Oh, mistress, I did mean to tell 'ee. It did happen these several days gone. We'd been to the meetings,

John and me together like . . . and then . . . we found we was saved."

"You and John . . . Puritans!"

"That be the size of it, mistress."

Tamar was angry. She had always felt Humility to be a rival, and Annis belonged to her. She could not help looking upon this as desertion.

"So," she said with a sneer, "'you and John are safe for Heaven, eh?"

"Yes, mistress, we be safe. We only has to worship God as 'tis laid down we should and we be saved."

"As laid down by Master Humility Brown, I suppose."

"That I wouldn't know, mistress. 'Tis as laid down . . . that's all I do know."

"You will not wish to continue to serve me, then."

Annis paled. "Mistress, I would never wish to be parted from you."

"Puritans should have naught to do with those who are in touch with the Devil."

"Oh, mistress, 'tis not so. You be good . . . though not saved yet. I do pray you'll be saved . . . every night I do. Why, I'd rather not be saved than leave 'ee. Nobody ain't ever been so kind to me as you have. I'll give up they meetings if you do forbid me to go."

Tamar laughed in triumph. "No, Annis. You may continue to be a Puritan if you wish it. It makes no difference to me. I am still your friend."

"Well, mistress, 'tis John really. He went to the meeting and got himself saved. He did come to me and say, 'Annis, I be saved, and you'd better be saved too. I shouldn't like to think of your soul in eternal torment, that I shouldn't.' And I said, 'Well, John, 'tis share and share alike with us, and if you be saved then saved I'll be.' So he took me along to the meeting and there I was saved too. Mistress, Master Brown do talk so beautiful . . . he do carry you away, he do. But John says what we've been doing in the barn is sinful like, and now we'm saved we mustn't do it any more."

"You'll have to marry at once, Annis. Puritans must not behave as you've been behaving."

"I know, mistress, but I think the dear Lord will forgive us, for He will know how for the life of us we couldn't say no to it afore we was saved."

"Did you tell John you were with child?"

"In a roundabout way, I did. I said, 'John, if we be saved, we should marry, for we've been sinful and marriage is the only way out of sin like ours.' But John said, ' 'Tis so, Annis. 'Tis fornication that we've been at, and Master Humility Brown did say bitter things about fornication. 'Tis a big sin all right.' ' 'Tis only marriage, John,' I says, 'that'll put us right and save our souls from torment.' John said, 'Aye, 'tis so, but I've been sinful with two others, Annis, so 'tis a terrible problem which the Lord has set before me.' "

"But did you not tell him that there was to be a child?"

"I couldn't find it in my heart to do it, mistress."

"You must do so, Annis, and when John says he'll marry you I'll see what I can do for the pair of you."

"Mistress, you be very good to me. I do hope you'll get saved, for I'm wondering what Heaven will be like without you."

"You need not concern yourself with me," said Tamar. "Depend upon it, when my time comes, I shall know how to take care of myself."

Annis nodded her agreement.

* * *

Annis was weeping bitterly, her head in Tamar's lap. A terrible tragedy had overtaken Annis.

John — the most simple of all the new Puritans — had talked too freely. He had been arrested and taken to the gaol.

When Annis heard the news she was overcome by her grief. In six months' time her baby would be born, and it was unlikely — judging from what had happened in similar cases — that John would be free in time to marry her before the child's birth.

"What'll they do to John?" she wailed. "Mistress Alton has had her eyes on me . . . smiling in a sly, secret sort of way as though to say, 'I knew it would happen to 'ee, Annis Hurly!' "

"Take no notice of that old woman," said Tamar. "You anger me. Why did you not tell John at once so that he might have married you before this happened?"

"I don't know, mistress. I must have been half mazed."

"You must indeed. But your master will be able to help you. I'll have a word with him. I'll warrant John will soon be home and then I swear I'll make him marry you. If you won't tell him, I'll tell him myself."

Annis continued to sob wildly.

"Oh, mistress, you're that good to me!"

"More good to you than Humility Brown with all his fine preaching? But for that man, John would not be in prison to-day. Have you thought of that?"

"He says 'twas God's will, mistress."

"God's will!" snapped Tamar. "Mayhap you should ask God to help you now. . . God or Humility Brown."

"Nobody was ever as good to me as you, mistress," said Annis plaintively.

Tamar went down to Richard.

"You have heard this news?" she asked.

"That fool John Tyler talked too much. He has a head on him like a bundle of hay."

"Richard, what can you do for him?"

Richard shrugged his shoulders. "I think it will be seen that a simpleton such as John Tyler can hardly be dangerous."

"It is necessary that he does not stay away too long. He has to marry Annis."

Richard gave a burst of ironic laughter. "The men and the maidens!" he said.

But she was quick in their defence. "Humility Brown would doubtless say: 'He that is without sin among you, let him first cast a stone.'"

Richard smiled apologetically. "I crave your pardon . . . and theirs. Tell Annis I will do all that can be done."

"I have already told her that."

He raised his eyebrows. “How odd it is that you who persist in your relationship—and shall I say allegiance—to the Devil, should spend so much time bothering yourself with the troubles of others!”

“If Mistress Alton casts her sneering eyes on Annis, I shall take her cane and beat her with it. Why do we not get rid of that woman? I hate her.”

“Sometimes I ask myself that. But she is a good cook and she has learned my tastes. It would not be easy to replace her. I fear I have not the necessary energy to try.”

“Let her be then, but let her remember her place. I’ll not have Annis made more unhappy than she already is. I want you to see what can be done about John’s release. I know you would help me in any case, but I want you to help quickly. I want him to marry Annis. She loves him and will look after him—he needs looking after, it seems. And there is something else. Annis is afraid of her mother and father. She dreads having to live at the farm with them, which is what she and John would have to do if they married. I want to keep Annis with me. She has been with me so long, and I could not fancy replacing her. So I want you to have a cottage built for them. There is a spot not far from the Swanns’. They could live there and John could go on working at the farm and I could keep Annis. Will you do this, Richard?”

He hesitated: then he burst into sudden laughter.

“You take my breath away.”

She kissed him in her impulsive way. He was enchanted, while he still wondered why this should be so.

"You will, then," she said. "I knew you would. Now will you please ride into the town and see what you can do about John's release?"

She went down with him to the stables and watched him ride off.

* * *

Events did not slip into the pleasant pattern which Tamar had planned. For one thing, Richard could not obtain John's release. John had talked seditiously; he had talked against Church and State.

Tamar soothed Annis as best she could. "You must not fret, girl. He'll be out soon."

But he did not come out and the weeks stretched into months. Mistress Alton was now watching her slyly.

"A nice state of affairs!" said Mistress Alton to Moll Swann. "Slip into sin and slip into prosperity, so it would seem. The reward is to the wicked. Have a bastard, and a cottage shall be built for you."

The housekeeper made a face at Tamar when Tamar's back was turned, and only Moll—who was little more than half-witted—and Moll's sister Jane could see her. That was all she dared do. She had been afraid since Tamar had come into the house that the girl would prevail on Richard Merriman to send his housekeeper away. Sometimes Mistress Alton felt that it was only her excellence in running his house and his hatred of being disturbed which were responsible for his keeping her on; she knew she must tread warily, but for the life of her she could not stop herself tattling about Annis. How she wished she had Annis in the kitchens. She would have shown her what she thought of her. As it was, she could not stop talking about her.

"That Annis," she said to Moll and Jane, "got too big for her boots when the *mistress* of the house, the master's *daughter*, took it into her head that she must have a maid to wait on her. Maid indeed! Now we see Annis getting too big for her petticoats, besides her boots!"

Annis was afraid to go home. Her father had threatened, if she did, to tie her to the whipping-post in the yard and give her the biggest whipping of her life; her mother had said she would help him. Mistress Alton, licking her lips, tried to beguile Annis into going home; but Tamar saw that this did not happen.

Tamar was fierce in her defence of Annis. She hated both Mistress Alton and Humility Brown, who were harsh in their condemnation; she wondered at this time how she could ever have thought Humility noble.

She stopped him at his work one day when she was coming from the stables.

"How dare you look as you do at Annis?" she demanded.

He did not answer.

"I hate you when you look like that. Scornful . . . as though . . . as though you would rejoice to see Annis burning slowly in horrible flames that are fanned by devils."

"That will doubtless be her fate."

"I could not accept a God who allowed that."

"You blaspheme," he said.

"Mayhap I do. And you are a tyrant . . . So are all like you. Can you not understand that Annis is a broken-hearted woman?"

"She is a fornicator. She has sinned and cannot hope to escape her punishment."

"She *is* being punished. She loves John Tyler, and they keep him in prison. She is afraid of what they will do to him. She is afraid he will not be released before her baby is born. Is that not enough punishment for anything she has done?" He did not answer, and she went on: "It is you . . . *you* . . . who should be in prison. Not John Tyler. You tricked him into going to your meetings, and he is punished while you go free!"

He said: "If it were the will of God that I should be taken, then it would be I who was in gaol at this moment."

"You madden me! So it is God's will that Annis should suffer thus?"

"How could it be otherwise? Sin brings punishment, and she has been guilty of the greatest sin."

"Have you never committed such a sin?"

He flushed scarlet and looked at her in horror.

"No!" she cried. "*You* have not! You are not man enough. You might take sly glances and think . . . and hope . . . but you escape sin because you are not a man but a . . . a Puritan!"

"You make excuses for your maid, and perhaps . . . yourself."

Her rage was uncontrollable at that moment and, lifting her riding whip, she struck at him. The lash came down on his hand as he stepped back, and, watching the red weal spring up, she was instantly sobered and ashamed.

"You . . . you maddened me!" she said.

"The Devil was at your elbow," he said; and it seemed to Tamar that he regarded his hand with a certain satisfaction.

Her anger returned. "If you dare talk to me in that strain," she said, "I will do it again . . . and again!"

Then she turned and ran into the house.

* * *

Annis's child was a boy, and she called him Christian. "In the hope," said Annis tearfully, "that he will grow up better than his sinful parents."

John was released a month or so after the birth, and he and Annis were married at once, settling into the new cottage near the Swanns'.

The villagers grumbled that the Tylers were the luckiest pair to be met with for many a mile, and it seemed that rewards went to the sinful. That was not what Preacher Brown taught. It was not what the Church taught either! It was easy enough to see what had happened. Tamar had brought this about. Tamar was pleased. Of course she was! Another baby born out of wedlock! Another to be brought up in the service of the Devil!

As for Mistress Alton, she was almost beside herself with annoyance. She chattered to anyone who would listen. It was only when people demanded to know how she could continue to work in a house whose mistress she believed to be a witch that she began to ask herself what she would do if she were turned away. Then she was a little subdued.

Humility Brown was even more dismayed than Mistress Alton. All during the months of Annis's pregnancy he had tried to persuade Tamar not to give the cottage to the Tylers, and she, being contrite because of the mark her whip had made on his hand, was polite to him until the weal had gone. When it had completely disappeared there was many a stormy scene between them.

"What would you do if you were in my place?" she demanded. "Tell me what I should do if I were a good Puritan."

"Pray for the girl."

"Prayers would not build her cottage." She laughed mockingly at him. "My words shock you. You expect the heavens to open and some terrible blight to fall upon me. Annis has sinned, you say; and I will say to you what I have said to others: 'Let him who is without sin cast the first stone.' Would that be you, Humility Brown? I believe it would be. Humility! That should not be your name. Pride should be your name. For the pride of those who are saved, such as you, seems beyond the pride of the damned such as I suppose I am."

"You condone sin," he explained. "There are deserving couples in this place who marry in purity. Could you not have given one such couple a cottage?"

"But I love Annis and Annis is in trouble. But how could you understand that? You never loved anything but good—never hated anything but evil. You would turn Annis out, would you not? Send her home to those wicked parents of hers, whom doubtless you consider good people. It seems to me that your Church has led you a long way from the teachings of Jesus."

"You would glorify evil," he said. "There is no denying that."

With rising temper, she left him.

* * *

One summer's day Bartle came home. Down in the town there was the excitement and bustle which the return of the ships never failed to produce.

The day after his arrival he came riding into the stables at Pennicomquick. Tamar heard the clatter of hoofs and she hurried to her window, for the news of his return had reached her immediately on his arrival and she had been expecting his visit. She saw him leave the stables; she saw him come striding across the lawns in his arrogant way, towards the house. He looked up at her window and she hastily withdrew. She was astonished to see how her hands were trembling as she pulled at her bell-rope.

Annis came, for Annis still worked for Tamar, bringing her baby, who was now a year old, with her from the cottage each day. Christian was at this moment toddling on the lawn, for he was just learning to take a few unsteady steps by himself.

"Annis," said Tamar, "if anyone asks for me, say I am not at home. That is all."

Tamar went back to the window, standing cautiously away, and she saw Bartle approach the child. Little Christian toddled willingly towards him, and Bartle lifted him, and as he held the child high above his head, Tamar heard Christian's shrieks of joy.

Then she stepped back quickly, for Bartle had looked from the child to the window.

He had not been five minutes in the house when Annis came running up.

"Mistress, the master sent me up to find 'ee."

"I told you to say I was not at home."

"Mistress, 'twas a lie. I could not say it."

Tamar laughed angrily. "Here is more of Humility Brown's work! You cannot tell a lie when I bid you!"

"Well, mistress, I did say I would come to your room and, if you were here, tell you that you were wanted below. And, mistress, 'tis a gentleman as the master says you'll be pleased to see."

"I know who is there!" she cried.

Annis kept her eyes downcast. She was a good Puritan now—she and John together—and any manifestation of the peculiar powers of her mistress, while exciting her as they always had done, filled her with apprehension. Humility Brown preached against witchcraft even as the prickers did; and yet one whom Annis loved equally with her husband and child was of that strange and frightening community.

With a suddenness typical of her, Tamar's anger changed to understanding. She laid a hand on Annis's shoulder and said: "I saw him from the window. There was no craft in it; and since you do not wish to lie, you may say that I am here, but that I do not wish to come down."

Annis, smiling gladly with that simplicity which always touched Tamar, went out, but in a little while she was back.

"The master says it is Mr. Cavill returned from the sea, and he thinks that will make you change your mind."

"Go and tell him that that does not make me change my mind."

She stayed in her room for more than an hour and it was only when she had seen Bartle leave that she went downstairs.

Richard was there, sitting thoughtfully in the window-seat of the big room, looking idly out of the window. He raised his eyebrows when he saw her.

"That was most discourteous of you!" he said.

"I had no wish to see him."

"He is our neighbour and there is friendship between our families. He has been away a long time . . . two years, I believe; and when he comes to see us you send down such a message!"

She shrugged her shoulders.

"Tamar," he went on, "why do you continue to hate that young man so vehemently? Can you not forgive him for what he tried to do to you so long ago?"

"No, I cannot."

"But it is so long ago and he was but a wild boy then!"

"He is a wild man now."

"I wish you would marry. You are twenty years old, and that is a marriageable age. You see the happiness of Annis and her John. You are fond of little Christian. Have you no desire to have children of your own?"

"I think when the time comes for me to marry, I shall know. If it does not come"—she shrugged her shoulders again—"well, then I shall not marry." She turned on him fiercely. "Why do you always think about my marrying when Bartle is here?"

"Perhaps because I feel he would make a suitable husband."

"How can you think that? What is your opinion of me, that you think him a match for me? He is nothing but a buccaneer, a pirate! Oh . . . all very legal, because it is only Spanish ships that he robs, Spanish towns that he fires, only Spanish virgins whom he violates! Or are there others who suffer at his hands?"

"I fear you are determined to hate him. It is that pride of yours, which will always be your biggest enemy. You are so sure that you are right when you set yourself to judge such as Bartle, to protect such as Humility Brown; but, do you know, your sense of right and wrong is governed by your emotions? Bartle is a buccaneer; therefore to be despised.

Myself, Annis, John Tyler, have all been guilty of sin, but us you fiercely defend. I wish very much that you would try to be a little more reasonable with Bartle."

"He does not need my kindness!" she said.

The next day she was riding on the moors, thinking of him—as she had not ceased to do for one moment since his return—when she heard the sound of thudding hoofs behind her; and there was Bartle himself.

She drew up and faced him. He had aged a little. He was nearly twenty-seven years old—a man in years. There were more lines about his eyes; his skin was more deeply bronzed; the scar on his cheek seemed less prominent than it had; but his eyes were the same brilliant blue that she remembered. They mocked her now, and she felt the old excited hatred rising within her.

"Well met, Tamar."

"I doubt that it is well."

"What a greeting for your lover!"

"You are no lover of mine!"

"Have you forgotten that night we spent together?"

"I have done my best to wipe the shame of it from my mind."

"At least," he said, "you speak too vehemently for indifference." He smiled. "And that gives me hope."

"Hope? Of what? That you may trick me as you did before?"

"Come, Tamar. Be true to yourself. You saw through the trick. I was merely being generous . . .

giving you a chance to surrender, not for your own sake — for that you were determined not to do in spite of the fact that you found me irresistible — but for the sake of another."

"Your conversation tires me. I am riding back now."

"No," he said. "You will stay awhile and talk with me. Shall we dismount? Let us tie our horses to yonder bush. Then we can make plans more easily."

"I have no plans to make with you."

"That's a pity, for I have plans, and it would be as well for you to know of them."

"I shall not join in them. Nor shall I dismount."

He leaned over and, catching her bridle, laughed up into her face. "You are afraid to dismount. You are afraid that I shall seize you as I almost did that day. . . do you remember when you saw me go to Richard's and were so beside yourself with your desire for me that you stripped and lay in wait to seduce me?"

She looked at him haughtily. "Why do you do everything to increase my hatred for you?"

"Because your hatred is the measure of your love."

"You appear to think you have learned much subtlety from your Spanish conquests. Let me tell you that you are completely ignorant of me and my feelings."

"A Spanish woman and an English one are much the same under the skin, you know. One can divide them into types . . . the clinging types, the meek types.

Then there is your own type, Tamar. The wild ones needing to be tamed."

"Your stupid talk sickens me. I am not a horse to be broken in."

"No indeed. As I told you once before, you are a woman who must be wooed . . . now that she has been won."

"Do you think that, because you once handled me shamefully, it gives you the right to speak to me thus?"

"Ah, Tamar, how I wish that you could see your face. You are excited . . . You are hoping that I will take you now as I did before. Even while you are just a little afraid . . . you hope. Look into your mind, my beauty, and tell me what you see there. Tell the truth. Tell how every detail of our love is cherished in your heart. You have remembered . . . all the time I have been away you have remembered, as I have."

She let her whip cut across her horse's flanks so that it reared and broke away from his hold on the bridle. It galloped off, but Bartle was soon beside her.

He shouted: "I thought the child in the garden was ours."

She looked straight ahead.

"I was disappointed," he continued to shout.

She slowed down her horse to fling at him: "I should have killed myself before I would have borne a child of yours."

"You talk too lightly of death, just as you talk too fervently of hate."

"Go away! Leave me alone."

"I must talk to you."

"You could have nothing to say which could be of the slightest interest to me."

"You are afraid of me."

"I know you so well. You are a brute, a raper of women, a buccaneer, a robber. All that you are I loathe and despise. And I do not trust you. You have more physical strength than I have, and I would not care to be alone with you in lonely places."

She heard his guffaw.

"Oh, Tamar," he cried, "have I ever forced you? Did you not receive me into your bed without a protest?"

She felt hot tears of shame pricking her eyes and she angrily whipped up her horse.

"Come!" she whispered. "Gallop faster. Let us put a great distance between him and us."

But the sweating horses kept level.

Bartle shouted: "Tamar, never fear! It is going to be you and I together . . . for as long as we live."

When they had left the open country behind them and were in the narrow, hilly lanes, it was necessary to walk their horses, and he talked to her with seriousness.

"Tamar, listen to me. I grow old and I must marry. My father is anxious to see my children before he dies. I have thought of this matter while I have been away. I love the sea; but I love you more. You are like the sea, Tamar . . . uncertain . . . beautiful and tender to some, wild and stormy to others. I want you, Tamar."

"You waste your words. And if you would ask my advice I would say this: Yes, you should marry and produce children. There are many girls in this countryside, as well-born as yourself, who would make excellent wives. One of them would doubtless be glad to put up with your crude manners and infidelities, for the sake of one day becoming Lady Cavill."

"I want none but you."

"That may be so, because it would be characteristic of you to want what you cannot have."

"I should not be continually at sea," he said. "We could watch our children grow up. What say you, Tamar?"

"I say you are a fool. In the opinion of your family, I should not be considered worthy of you, and in my opinion you are not worthy of myself. So much unworthiness could not make for happiness, I feel sure."

"My family would forget all those strange stories of your birth once you married me."

"They will never be forgotten."

"Only because you give yourself such airs. You ride about with flying hair so that you may look like a witch, apart from all other witches, with a beauty that fires the blood of men and sickens the hearts of women with envy."

"So you would marry me, knowing me different from other women?"

"I want to marry you," he said firmly.

"Bartle." Her voice softened slightly. "You believe, do you not, that I am no ordinary mortal woman? You believe that I have a power which is not of this Earth. Do you believe that the Devil forced me on my mother that night twenty-one years ago?"

He avoided her eyes. "How should I know what to believe?"

"And yet . . . you would marry me. You would ask me to be the mother of your children!"

"I would," he said solemnly. "There are two loves in my life," he went on slowly, "and I understand myself sufficiently to know that there always will be. One is the sea. You know I ran away to sea when I was fourteen. That was against my father's wishes. I knew that he might disinherit me for this, as he had threatened to do, but I did not care. I had to go to sea. I did not care that for a time I should live the life of a common sailor. I knew my life was in danger; I knew I faced death; but that was what I wanted. And you are my other love, Tamar. Untamed as the sea . . . and as dangerous. I know it, but I must have you. I faced continual dangers on the sea, and I will face them in union with you . . . woman . . . witch . . . devil . . . whatever you be."

She was moved, for she had never before known him speak with such seriousness. Moreover, she could not help feeling proud to see him so humble before her. In some measure that made up for the shame he had inflicted upon her.

She said, and her voice was more gentle than it had ever been when she was addressing him: "If what you say is true, then I am sorry for you. But I will never marry you. You must content yourself with your other love, the sea. You are a fool, Bartle, and I could never love a fool. If you had been kind to me, I might have felt some friendliness towards you; and if you had continued to be kind I might even have married you. Violence . . . shameful violence . . . such as you have dared to show towards me, would never win anything but my contempt."

"So you continue to hate me?"

"I can never love you."

"You forget I have felt you tremble in my arms."

"With hate."

"No," he said, "with passion."

"If that were so, why should I not take advantage of what must seem to you this great and magnanimous offer to make me your wife?"

"Because you do not know yourself. You are determined to hate me, and you cling to hatred as a drowning man clings to a raft, knowing it will soon be swept away from him."

"Know this," she answered. "You have done to me that for which you will never have my forgiveness. You know that I am not like other women. You have said yourself that I have the Devil in me."

He smiled at her—his eyes blazing with that sudden heat of desire which seemed to scorch her, so that for one wild moment she thought it might melt her repulsion and turn it into a fierce capitulation.

Alarmed, she said: "There is nothing more I have to say to you."

And she rode on ahead of him.

* * *

All through that autumn and winter Bartle haunted Pennicomquick. Richard and Tamar were entertained by his family at Stoke. Sir Humphrey had grown very feeble now and watched, with impatience, what he thought to be the courtship of his son and Richard's daughter. He did not like the fact of the girl's illegitimacy, but he was by no means insensible to her charms. She was tall and finely built; he could imagine her producing fine sons; and since Bartle seemed set on having her, Sir Humphrey wished they would not delay in marrying, for if he were to see his grandchildren before he died, there was not much time to be lost.

Tamar, studying the old man, thought: That is what Bartle will be like in thirty years' time. Too much good wine: too much rich food; too many women; a wound or two from a Spaniard's sword, which had seemed to heal, but which left their mark; lecherous eyes for a pretty maid; a wistful eye for the gap between her youth and his age; quick temper; legs swollen with gout. Yes, Bartle would be just like that in thirty years' time. They were of a kind — country gentlemen and buccaneers!

Yet her feelings towards Bartle changed during those months. There were times when he ceased to mock, when he talked of his adventures; often this would be when she sat with him and his family and

Richard in the panelled hall with the Cavill ancestry looking down from the pictures in the gallery above. Then he would make vivid the life at sea which he had so enjoyed, the hundred dangers he had faced, the stories of boarding the Spanish quarry and looting her hold of its treasure. Sir Humphrey would join in with anecdotes from his own adventures, and between them they would turn the hall into a ship for Tamar, and she would feel that she sailed with them upon an ocean. She saw, through their eyes, the Spaniard on the horizon, heard the shout aboard, "A sail! A sail!" She could hear Bartle's voice, his eyes flashing: "Dowse your topsail! Salute him for the sea. Whence is your ship?" And the dreaded yet longed-for answer: "Of Spain. Whence is yours?" She saw the ship shot through and through; the fire that had started in the hold. She saw the surgeon looking to the wounded when the darkness fell. Bartle's voice again: "Keep your berth to windward and see that we lose her not in the night!" She saw the resumption of the fight next day and heard the sound of drums and trumpets, the cry of "St. George for England!"

She was fascinated, in spite of her determination not to be. How his eyes sparkled as he talked; they took on that vivid shade of blue which burned in them when, she knew, he most desired her. He was a man such as Humility Brown could never be.

At Christmas time there was lavish entertainment at Stoke; and the guests of honour were Tamar and her father. There were hunting parties when Tamar and Bartle rode side by side and were always first at the kill. He was more gentle and no longer referred to that night when he had forced himself upon her. He had taken heed of her words; and she was warming towards him.

When he came upon little Christian toddling in the gardens, he would stop and speak to him; he would bring him sweetmeats and fruit, and the child would crow with pleasure at the sight of him. He would take the little boy in his arms and throw him into the air; he would set him upon his mare and hold him there while the mare walked about on the grass. The child adored him.

Annis — now expecting another child — looked on with tears in her eyes.

"He is a good man," she whispered to Tamar; "for only good men are kind to children and the weak."

Then Tamar forced herself to remember an occasion when he had not been so kind to the weak. But was she right in harbouring resentment? Should he not be forgiven if he had repented of his harsh treatment of her?

He was the wooer now. He implied when he entertained her at his father's mansion: This is what I have to offer you. This house and estates will be mine one day.

When they rode to the hunt together he was telling her: We should have a good life together.

When he made much of little Christian he meant: See! How happy we should be if we had children of our own!

But Tamar could not easily forget her distrust of him. There was too much that she could remember vividly.

I do not trust him! she insisted to herself.

And yet, the days when she did not see him were dull days. She was softening towards him and might have softened more, but, naturally, he could not for long keep up this model behaviour.

Several times he had seen her talking to Humility Brown, and on these occasions had spoken slightingly of the man, whereupon Tamar had characteristically sprung to his defence.

One day, at the beginning of the spring, Bartle came to Pennicomquick and found Tamar in the gardens conversing with the Puritan; and when later she and Bartle were riding out together, he said: "You seem very taken with that fellow."

"Taken with him?"

"You cannot hide your feelings from me by repeating what I say. You are *taken* with him! I could see that by the way you looked at him."

"You see too much, Bartle, since you see what is not there."

"You were coquetting with him. By God, you were! Forcing him to look at you, standing there smiling provocatively. You have a fancy for him!" Bartle's face was flushed and distorted with his jealousy. "I believe he is your lover."

She answered coldly: "I had thought your manners improved of late. It seems I am mistaken."

"You cannot deny it. You prevaricate. You cannot hide the truth from me."

"And even if your foul suggestion were truth, why should I wish to hide it from you? What concern would it be of yours?"

"So all this time while I have been playing the mild-mannered suitor, he has been revelling in the pleasures of your bed!"

"If you were nearer, I would strike you for that."

"You need not be so concerned to protect the honour of your sly-eyed Puritan. I always did suspect the meekness of such fellows. They use it to disarm foolish females like yourself. Tell me, does he begin your pleasures by praying first?"

"Stop it!" she screamed at him. "I hate you! What a fool I was to imagine that you were slightly less hateful than I had believed you to be! How dare you utter your coarse thoughts aloud to me! Do you imagine all men are as depraved as yourself!"

He was solemn suddenly. "Tamar, I was wrong. I see it. Forgive me."

"That I will not do. I cannot endure your conversation. Save it, please, for your low-born sailors. I speak to whom I will, and at this moment I do not wish to speak to you."

She was about to whip up her horse when he laid his hand on the bridle.

"Can you not forgive a jealous lover?"

She looked haughtily beyond him. "I can forgive no one who dares say such things."

"Listen, Tamar. I was wrong. I was foolish and jealous. I did not like to see you smile at anyone but me."

"Say no more," she said. "And pray take your hands from my bridle. I wish to go home now."

"First say you forgive me. Say all things are as they were between us."

She met his eyes coolly. "Very well. We were but friendly because our fathers' houses are close, and our fathers wish us to be."

She saw that fierce, angry passion blaze into his eyes.

But he said no more and they rode back to Pennicomquick.

Next day he rode over again. She saw him in the garden with young Christian and noticed how handsome he was, how tall, how strong, and how puny Humility Brown seemed when compared with him.

The child was smiling with pleasure as Bartle lifted him up. He loved children and softened when he was with them—but not too much. He was one of those men who had the power to attract children even when he reprimanded them or scarcely seemed to notice them. He would make a fine father—a father children would be proud of. She pondered: I am twenty, and whom else could I marry if not Bartle? Love, though, should be soft and tender—not fierce, demanding, fostering those tempestuous quarrels which were continually springing up between them. No, she could not love Bartle, but he excited her.

She went down to him and they played with the child together. Humility walked by on his way to the potting sheds, and she smiled at him as he passed; she was thinking of the contrast between him and Bartle, but Bartle saw the smile and misconstrued it. His expression changed, and Tamar felt her anger rising.

Bartle said: "There is to be an expedition at the beginning of the summer. I am asked to captain one of the ships."

"That should be exciting for you," she answered.

"It will. One grows tired of a landsman's life."

They went into the house and she was astonished at her depression which the prospect of losing him had brought with it.

* * *

She thought afterwards how different their lives might have been if they had not, at that point, taken a certain turning.

She was wild, passionate and unaccountable; she had forgotten that Bartle was similar.

If pride was her besetting sin, impatience and violence were his. He was a man of deep and sensuous passions, and he had been celibate too long. It had needed only the smile she had given Humility Brown — that most inoffensive of men — to rekindle the violent passions Bartle had been suppressing all these months.

He sought her out. He must speak to her. Would she walk in the grounds with him?

He took her to that spot by the stream which they both had cause to remember so well; she knew as soon as they reached that spot that she had the old Bartle to deal with. Gone was the tender lover, striving to please; there remained the sensual man determined to have his way. The very manner in which he took her by the shoulders was brutal.

His eyes blazed and she flinched before the passion in them. He kissed her hard on the lips and his kisses were a burning prophecy; he was going to kiss her whether she wanted him to or not.

All her old fear rose within her and, with it, came her passionate hatred.

"Release me at once."

But he kept his hands on her shoulders and looked into her face.

"Did you know," he said, "that that man, Humility Brown . . . *Humility* Brown! . . . dared to hold meetings at a hut on my father's lands?"

She felt a flutter in her stomach.

"Oh yes," he went on; "that sly creature dares to collect his flock together in a hut there. The meek man is a sinner; he is breaking the law. There are some fine new penalties imposed for such law-breakers."

"Why do you tell *me* this?"

"Wait and you will hear. One of my grooms has become a temporary Puritan at my request, and he has told me when the next meeting is to be; so you see I am in the secret."

"I asked you what this has to do with me. What are you threatening to do?"

"As a good servant of my country, what do you expect me to do?"

"You could not do it, Bartle!" she cried. "All those people who have lived among us . . . our friends!"

"Law-breakers! And Humility Brown the biggest one among them. He'll be thrown into gaol. I heard some tales of what they are doing to these people. They leave them to rot in prison. They starve them and beat them. It might even be the rope for such a hardened criminal as Humility Brown! Who knows? Perhaps even the faggots . . ."

"You shall not do this!"

"Why not?"

"I shall stop you. I shall warn him."

"I'll have him taken up in any case. He could not deny what he had been up to."

"Are you really as cruel as you would have me believe?"

He shook her and his eyes blazed forth their passion . . . a passion of hate for Humility Brown, a passion of desire for herself.

"I do not like your feeling for this man," he said.

"You are mad."

"I have seen you together."

"He is a humble gardener. What should I want with him?"

"I am not blind. He is a man of learning. He works in the garden because he lost everything on a ship bound for Virginia. He is biding his time until he can set out again . . . then doubtless he plans to take you with him. Richard invites him to his study. He talks with him. Theirs is not the relationship of master and servant."

"Could not Richard be interested in a servant?"

"Does he invite other servants to talk with him? Nay! Richard and his daughter have an interest in the fellow which I do not like."

"I hate you, Bartle."

"Is that because you love him?"

She brought up her hand to strike him, but he caught it.

"You are hurting me," she said.

"I intend to. You will learn how I can hurt those who insult me by preferring a meek-tongued preacher to a man. When they hang him, I will take you to see the spectacle. I'll warrant there'll be a goodly crowd to cheer him on to hell."

"Bartle," she pleaded, "you don't mean that you will really do this cruel and dastardly thing?"

"You will see what I can do for my country."

He watched her slyly and she should have been warned. When he released her and began to walk away, she ran after him.

"I beg of you not to do this, Bartle."

He turned and smiled slowly, and his smile made her tremble, for she was reminded of another occasion.

He said, "Sweetheart, I can refuse you nothing. If you were to beg of me . . . prettily enough . . . I might reconsider my decision."

He put his arms about her and held her in a grip so tight that she felt as though the blood were being squeezed out of her body.

"For a consideration," he went on, "there is nothing on earth that I would not do for you."

"What . . .?" she began weakly.

"Leave your window open to-night, and I'll swear by God and my fathers that the Puritans shall meet wherever and as often as they like without interference from me."

She looked at him scornfully. "Do you think I would be deceived again and by the same trick?"

"The other *was* a trick, I grant you. I would not have betrayed a friend like Richard. I am fond of Richard. But Humility Brown? Why, I loathe the man; I despise him; and the way in which you smile at him alone would make him my enemy."

"Are you determined to make my hatred burn more fiercely?"

He answered: "If I cannot have you in love, then will I have you in hate; for have you I will, one way or the other."

"Then it is no use my pleading with you?"

"There is only one way."

She tossed her head angrily and walked into the house.

* * *

She lay waiting for him.

There was, she told herself, nothing else she could do. He had tricked her before, but this time he meant what he said. He was brutal; he was callous; he was lecherous. How could she ever have thought of marriage with him?

"I would rather die!" she said into her pillow.

What else could I do but this? How could I let Humility Brown be betrayed? Others would be involved too.

She closed her eyes and tried to see Humility standing in one of the pits of the prisons, knee-deep in water, fighting the rats which tried to attack his starving body. But she could only see Bartle coming towards her, whispering her name.

I hate him! she insisted. This is terrible and shameful. But it is better that this should happen to me than that my friends should lie neglected in prison and then perhaps be taken out to violent death.

He was coming now. It was happening as it had happened before. The curtains parted and she heard his light laugh in the darkness.

His hands were caressing her.

He said: "So, sweetheart, once more you are waiting for me."

* * *

"I hate you! I hate you!" she told him. "I shall hate you for ever for what you have done to me."

He mocked her as he had done before.

"How you longed for me! Do you think you hid your feelings from me? I am too clever for you. Tamar, I know too much of women. Why do you persist in telling me you hate me? You long for me. You burn for me. You knew I cared nothing for Puritans. A plague and a pox on them! I care naught. Let them meet every day. Let them pray till they are hoarse. I'd never betray them. Do I look like a man who would bestir himself to betray miserable Puritans?"

"I believe you would be capable of the utmost cruelty."

He smiled. "Oh, it was a wonderful night, was it not? Better than the first . . . when perhaps you might have been a little reluctant."

"You are coarse and crude and I hate you."

"Constant repetition is not so emphatic as you appear to believe."

"With me it is."

"Marry me, Tamar. I promise to be as faithful as I can."

"Marry you! I would rather die."

"What if there should be a child? Then you would be ready enough, I'll swear."

"If there were a child it would make no difference."

"We will wait and see. When that sly-faced housekeeper starts peeking and prying, I'm ready to wager you'll not be so reluctant."

"You forget that I hate you."

He sighed. "So you have said. When, Tamar, will you be truthful, frank and reasonable? When may I cease thinking up these elaborate schemes so that we can be together?"

"There will never be another time."

"I hope there will be a child," he said. "My God, how I hope for that! There will be time to know before the ships sail. If there is a child, I know you will change your mind. You will be obliged to. It will be a good excuse for you; and how you love excuses! For the child's sake, you will agree to marry me, just as you so charmingly agree to make love with me, first for Richard's sake, then for that of Humility Brown!"

"Marriage with you!" she sneered. "I laugh to contemplate it, though mayhap I should not laugh, for what a bitter tragedy it would be! I should do you some mischief before I had lived a week with you."

"Never fear! I would subdue you. I would have you meek and loving . . . a perfect wife before the week were out."

She felt bruised and wounded, humiliated beyond endurance. He did excite her; she knew the truth now, which was that she half hated, half delighted in his love-making; and that was a shameful conclusion for her to come to.

She was all contrasts during the weeks that followed. She was terrified that there would be a child and yet, at times, she longed that this might be. She pictured herself saying to him: "For the child's sake, then . . ." And she thought of all the attendant excitement which would follow such a decision.

But then her pride arose—that she, whom people had been afraid to cross, even when she was a child, should be so treated, so humiliated, as though she were any low serving girl to be taken at the master's caprice!

No! Fiercely she hated him and what he had done to her; and now again she was terrified that there would be a child.

There was no child.

She mocked him when he came to the house.

"When do you sail?"

"Perhaps," he said, "the next time I sail will be with you up the Thames to London Town."

She laughed exultantly. "I think," she said, "that when the ships sail out you will be with them."

"Oddly enough," he answered, "I would rather marry you. I have had my fill of the sea; you, I have just tasted."

"I hate your coarse words, and I should never have consented to marry you even if there had been a child. But there will be no child."

She laughed loud and long to see his dismay. He understood at last that she had meant what she said when she had told him she hated him.

* * *

He sailed away that summer, and she told herself that she was glad.

But when — only a few weeks after he had been at sea — a ship came limping into the Sound with the news that it was the only one which had escaped after an attack by Algerian or Turkish pirates, she was on the quay with the rest of the town; and her pride suddenly broke when she heard that Bartle was one of those who had not returned.

CHAPTER FIVE

It was Tamar's wedding night.

She was twenty-three years old — old enough to be married — and she thought of the last three years as dull and uneventful.

She had been twenty years old when she had heard that Bartle was lost. The men from that ship which had limped back to Plymouth explained that they had been outnumbered three to one in the Bay of Biscay, and aboard the attacking forces were fierce pirates — Turks or Algerians. Bartle's ship had been fired and all loot taken before it was sunk. It was a fate he had risked many times and now it had overtaken him.

She was numb and listless during those days which had followed. She could not analyse her feelings for Bartle. Her hatred had been fierce because he had so deeply humiliated her. Twice he had tricked her; twice he had cheated her; and he had mocked her mercilessly. He was every bit as cruel as the men who had killed him, and yet . . . how could she understand this feeling which was now hers? Why was it that she hated the bright and shining water which had taken him? Why was it that all the excitement had gone from her life? Was it because there was no one in it who seemed worthy of her hatred?

Whenever a ship came in, she was one of the first to take her stand on Barbican Causeway. She would shade her eyes and watch it as it came towards the land. Surely he must have escaped! He was too young to die. And it was impossible to imagine him dead. She would never be able to do that.

She was restless, yet subdued. There were times when she seemed not to hear, if people spoke to her. Richard was anxious about her, suspecting that she regretted not having married Bartle.

She would not let herself believe that she yearned for that tempestuous existence which marriage with him would have been. How ironical that by marrying him she could have saved him from taking that fatal journey. That first shameful occasion, so she had believed at the time, had saved Richard's life; the second, Humility's; and now, there could be no doubt that, had she given herself to Bartle for ever, she would have saved his.

Often she was at the Tylers' cottage. Annis had another boy now, and at Humility's suggestion they had christened him Restraint. In the old days Tamar would have laughed at that, for the healthy boy, pulling greedily at his mother's breasts, seemed to her most incongruously named. But she had, she realized, little laughter left in her.

Annis in her cottage home, with John a devout Puritan and most faithful husband, was a contented woman. It was irritating to contemplate such contentment, and to envy Annis her home and children just as she envied Richard his calm outlook on life, Humility his faith. This was a strange state for a girl to be in, particularly when a little while ago her life had seemed to be all excitement and pleasure.

Shortly after that day when Bartle had sailed away, Richard put into action a plan which had long been in his mind. He had always taken a keen interest in Humility Brown and had not cared to see him doing rough work under Jubin; he had, therefore, decided that it would be a good plan if Humility — who was a good penman and general scholar — took some of the burden of his estates off his shoulders. Humility was naturally delighted with the change of occupation; and Richard pointed out that he must leave the draughty outhouse for which he had been so grateful when he had first been given work, and one of the attics should be made ready for him. This would not only be more comfortable, but more in keeping with his new status.

It was now that a change seemed to come over Humility. He glowed with something more than his faith. He had some of his meals with Richard and Tamar, and it was one day when they were at supper in the winter parlour that he explained his newly found elation.

"I am a happy man," he declared, his eyes shining with gratitude as they rested on Richard. "I had thought my desires were sinful, but now I know them to be favoured by the Lord. When my friends sailed away to Virginia and left me behind with Will Spears and Spears' boy, I was filled with regret and, in spite of constant prayers, I could not purge my mind of sorrow because I had missed an opportunity of reaching the new land. 'Humility Brown,' I said to myself, 'if it had been God's will that you should have gone to Virginia, do you think He would have sent you into plague-stricken Plymouth?' I knew that it was God's will that I should not go to Virginia then. And I prayed nightly that I might be resigned to my fate. But I hankered. I yearned. I thought of my friends, leading the new life in the new country where they did not find it necessary to creep away and in secret worship God. Oh, to be free and unafraid and to lift up mine eyes to the hills and say 'Holy, Holy, Holy. . .'"

Tamar watched him critically. A born preacher, he was ever carried away by words, and that was a vanity in him surely. He loved the sound of his own voice as dearly as she loved the sight of her face. She would taunt him with that one day when she felt in the mood to do so.

Humility caught the look in her eyes and said: "Forgive me. I grow excited, I fear. I *am* excited. My mind is filled with what I believe to be a message from on High. I have a notion that it may well, after all, be God's will that I go to Virginia. Sir, you have made it possible for me to feed and clothe myself and, by your generous payment, to save money which will enable me to go to the promised land."

"So," said Richard, "that is what you plan. To save, and when you are ready and the opportunity comes, to sail away."

Humility's eyes gleamed. "Ships often come to Plymouth. It is possible to get to Virginia if you have a little money. I rejoice. I see that the Lord did not intend me to miss the promised land."

"Perhaps," said Tamar with a sparkle of her old mischief, "you have been delayed as a punishment, but it may be that, like Moses of old, your sins have been such that it is considered just that you never reach your promised land."

"That may well be," agreed Humility.

"Then you must have sinned greatly—and I wonder how."

That evening she threw off some of her listlessness. She was interested in something once more: Humility's going to Virginia!

She would interrupt him at his work as he sat, quill in hand, and make him talk about Virginia. He was easily tempted to such talk, and it amused her afterwards to see his remorse for the wasted time.

"To steal time," she teased remorselessly, "is as bad as stealing goods. You know that, Humility?"

"You are a temptress!" he said.

And she laughed. Then he whispered a prayer.

"Shall you wear a hair-shirt for this?" she asked; and she was pleased because she could feel amused, teasing Humility Brown.

But when he did not appear at meals next day and she understood he was fasting, she felt sorry for what she had done. Then she discovered that as well as amusement she could feel regret; and it seemed significant that Humility Brown should be the one to make her feel that life was not so dreary after all.

Sometimes they would have serious conversations together. He seemed more human now that he had a goal to work for, and she took an interest in his mounting savings. She would have liked to have given him money, but she knew he would not accept that. He worked assiduously. There never was such a worker, Richard declared, never such a man for denying himself comfort.

"If he were not such a fanatic he would be a great man, I think," said Tamar.

"Great men are often fanatics," Richard reminded her.

Annis and John were saving too. Their simple faith shone in their faces. They were going one day, under the guidance of Humility Brown and accompanied by most of those who joined with them to worship God in secret meeting places, to the new promised land.

"So," Tamar had demanded angrily, "you would leave me, would you, Annis?"

But Annis shook her head. "Mistress, perhaps you will be among those who go with us."

"I? Why. . . the Puritans would not have me."

"They would, mistress, if you were a Puritan."

"You talk like Humility Brown!" snapped Tamar.

"Ah, mistress, if you could but know the peace and joy that has come to me and John! We be saved. Think of it. Happiness has come to us, mistress. I pray on my knees every night that it will come to you."

Tamar left the cottage that day and rode on the moors. The wind caught her long hair as she rode. Here was the spot where Bartle had caught up with her; here he had seized her bridle and laughed up into her face. Now. . . she was alone on the moors and he was alone on the bed of the sea.

She dismounted and tied her horse to a bush. Then she threw herself on to the grass and sobbed brokenheartedly. She thought of Annis and John Tyler, and mostly she thought of Humility Brown. What was it these people had that she had not? Faith! Belief that their souls were saved. Belief in a future life so that what happened here on Earth was of no moment. What an enviable state to be in!

When she was back at the house, she pinned up her hair—not in an elaborate style, but looped over her ears and made into a knot at the nape of her neck. The effect was startling, for she looked almost demure. She was aware of the look of approval which crossed the face of Humility Brown when he saw her.

Annis too was pleased to see her thus. They sat by the chimney-piece in the cottage, and the children—Christian, Restraint and Prudence—played at their feet.

"Annis," said Tamar, "can you truly say that you have never been so happy in your life?"

"I truly can," said Annis.

"But why should a *new* way of worshipping God make you happy?"

"Because 'tis the only true right way," answered Annis.

"Are you right . . . I wonder?"

Annis knelt at Tamar's feet. "Mistress, come to us. Come to our meetings. Listen to the good words and then see if you cannot find the peace which has come to John and me."

"Annis, you must know that when you are in your meeting-place you may be discovered at any time. That may mean prison. John may be taken from you and the children. How can you be happy living in perpetual fear?"

"If John were taken we should know it was the will of the Lord. Good would come of it, for the ways of God are good."

"You might be summoned for failing to appear at church."

Annis nodded and smiled blissfully.

"Annis, sometimes I think you are a fool. Yet you have found happiness and I have not; and since happiness is what we all seek, it must be the wise who find it."

"Mistress, cut yourself off from the Devil. You can do it. I know you are a witch, mistress. You have the powers of witchcraft, but you have never used them for ill; you are a white witch, and prayer could release you from your bondage; it could bring you safe to the arms of Jesus."

Her lips curled. "You talk like Humility Brown."

She could not understand what happened to her during those years—perhaps it was because that which came to her came gradually. She was not wild Tamar one day and Tamar saved the next. Each week saw a little of the old wildness passing, a little of the new quietness gained.

Humility talked with her long and earnestly now that she had ceased to mock him. Who was she to mock? These people had faith, and faith gave them the contentment which she lacked and longed for. She was restless, searching for something which she could never have now that Bartle was dead; and when Bartle was here she had not wanted it.

She was twenty-three and unmarried. Soon she would be qualifying for the title of "ancient maid." She longed for children. Annis had another now—little Felicity. Four children for Annis and not one for Tamar! She was fond of Annis's children and made excuses to visit them at the cottage or have them at the house.

But Tamar was not the sort to live through another woman's experiences.

She wanted this faith; she wanted to escape from restlessness; she longed to be saved so that what happened here on Earth was of no importance since her eyes would be fixed on the happy life to come.

She told Humility this, and he went down on his knees and thanked God.

Tamar's conversion was more enthusiastic than anyone else's, for she could never be half-hearted about anything she took up. Richard watched her with some amusement and a little alarm. He warned her that it was purely dissatisfaction with her present life which was at the root of her acceptance of the faith—

not her belief in it. But she turned from Richard; she turned to Humility.

She listened to him as his followers listened; he was a leader among men. His voice had a power and charm all its own. She saw the goodness in him.

"Oh, Humility," she cried. "I know that what happens to me here matters not. It is the life to come for which we must prepare ourselves."

He embraced her and they knelt in prayer together. The miracle had happened. Tamar was saved.

And then, one day, Humility said an astonishing thing.

"Tamar." He had ceased to call her "daughter." "Tamar, it is the greatest joy the Lord could have given me, to see you turn towards the Truth. You are at peace now. That is natural. But I have had a revelation concerning you. It is this: You are unfulfilled. You are meant to be the mother of children. You are released from the bonds of Satan. God is good; He is all-powerful and through His divine help I have been enabled to free you, for the power of the Devil compared with that of God is like a candle flame to the sun. I could lead you to contentment, to true happiness—which is the suppression of self in the service of God. Would that you would place your hand in mine and I might show you the way."

She held out her hand and he took it.

"Tamar, I did not intend ever to give way to the carnal lusts of the flesh . . . nor will I. But I have seen a new life opening before me. In the new land to which I hope to go, we shall need children . . . good, strong, noble children of the Puritan faith to carry on the work we have started. Each woman should do her share; she must give herself a chance to show her fertility. Each man must do likewise. There need be no lust in a good man and a good woman coming together in matrimony."

She drew away from him. "What do you suggest?"

"That you and I marry and, in the grace of holy wedlock, have children to the glory of God and our faith."

She felt the hot colour in her face. She was shocked by the suggestion; yet this was the answer to her problem. She longed for children, and in having Humility Brown's children she would help to populate the promised land to which one day they would go.

At last there could be a purpose in living. Perhaps for this reason Humility Brown had been sent to Plymouth; perhaps for this reason she had saved his life. At this moment it all seemed so right, so simple and natural.

"I will marry you," she said.

Afterwards she thought of what must be lived through before she reached that happy state of seeing her children round her, contented in a strange land, and she was afraid.

Dreams came to her as she lay in bed. Once she imagined that the curtains round her bed parted. That was a fancy; but she pursued it, and Bartle was standing by her bed. He said: “How can you marry that . . . Puritan! I will not let you!” And in the dream she felt his hands caress her.

Then she jumped out of bed and prayed solemnly and earnestly for the purification of her body and the salvation of her soul.

Queer dreams persisted — fearful dreams of anger and passion.

What have I done? she asked herself. How can I marry Humility Brown?

Richard was against the marriage, and he said so firmly. It was like mating a bird of paradise with a crow.

“You have hurried into this with your usual impetuosity. I know you well — better than you know yourself. You have been depressed — not yourself — and you have been searching for a new interest in life. All this talk of going to Virginia has fired your imagination. I would to God . . .”

“Yes?” she said.

“It was nothing.”

“Tell me. I want to know.”

“Oh, it is foolish of us to make plans for others. I was merely wishing that I had insisted on a father’s right, and married you to Bartle. He would not then have gone away and . . .”

He stopped, for she had buried her face in her hands and was sobbing bitterly.

“Oh, Tamar, my dearest . . .”

“It was just that I could not bear to hear you say it was my fault he is dead.”

"Of course it was not your fault. If you did not want to marry him, you were right not to. What has happened to you, Tamar? You have changed so."

"I don't know what has happened to me," she said.

"I beg of you, my dear, consider this marriage and what it will mean. Consider that seriously. Let us go away for a sea trip. We'll hug the coast and sail up the Thames to London. Or shall we take our horses and ride?"

She shook her head. "My mind is made up. We want children . . . Humility and I. And Richard, when we go to Virginia, *you* must come with us. I could not bear it if you stayed behind." Her eyes shone suddenly. "You are rich. You could finance such an expedition. Richard, could you not tear yourself away from this life—which is not, I believe, very satisfactory to you—and start a new one?"

He answered: "You spring such questions on a man at a minute's notice."

"It would be wonderful!" she cried. "We would all sail out of the Sound together . . . with our stores and all that we should need for our new life. There could not be a more exciting and wonderful adventure than sailing away into the unknown."

Richard let her talk, but he remained uneasy. It seemed to him that a girl should be thinking of her life with her husband rather than a life in new surroundings. Something had happened to change Tamar. Could it be that she had loved Bartle? She was like a person trying to get intoxicated in order to drown a sorrow. Was the hope of children and the new life in Virginia, the wine to make her forget?

As the day fixed for her wedding grew nearer, her mood changed. She rode out to the moors, her hair flying, and it seemed to Richard, watching her, that the old Tamar was not far away. It would not have surprised him if she had decided against the marriage after all. She almost did, when Humility wished them to set up house together in the outhouses, which he suggested could be made into a cottage home for them. Then how her eyes flashed! That was folly, she insisted. They should go on living in the house. If he were to save every penny he could, those pennies should not be spent in the vanity of setting up a home. It would seem that he had forgotten the Virginia project.

"Tamar," said Humility, hurt by the change in her, "it is good that a man and his wife should set up home together . . . however humble that home may be. I do not wish that you should continue to live under your father's roof."

"And there," she answered, "you show your pride. You will have to accept these conditions. You must remember that our plan is to leave this country as soon as it is possible to do so. Did we not plan to marry that we might have children to populate the new country?"

"That was so."

She gave a sudden spurt of laughter. "It is as easy to get children in a comfortable house as in a draughty cottage, I do assure you."

Humility grew pale with alarm. He saw that the Devil was very close to her, and he realized that Tamar was not completely saved. Moreover, he guessed that it would take a lifetime for him to achieve that desired result.

He had to agree. No new arrangements, then. Her room was big enough for both of them. He would share her bed, which was large and comfortable, until they were sure of a child, and when that had happened he could go back to his attic.

He could not understand what was going on in her mind. He did not know that she was most defiant when her fear was greatest. Her frank way of discussing what he felt should not be discussed by unmarried couples worried him. Yet, he assured himself, it was his duty to humour her until he could control her, which, he doubted not, he would be able to do with the Lord's help when they married.

So he must agree to this unnatural arrangement. Well, to some extent she was right. Soon they would be sailing for Virginia.

As the wedding day grew nearer, so did Tamar's fear grow greater. At the back of her mind was a belief that Bartle would reappear; he would explain that some miraculous and incredible thing had happened—the sort of thing which could only happen to Bartle—and he had come back. His blue eyes would flash, and he would have a blackmailing scheme to lay before her which would involve her breaking this incongruous betrothal and marrying him. She would no doubt be forced to do it for the sake of someone other than herself.

But the wedding day came, and she married Humility Brown; and now the house was still and she lay in the bed with the curtains drawn about it, just as she had lain and waited for Bartle.

She could hear the sound of a man's breathing beyond the bed-curtains—but it was not Bartle; it was her husband, Humility Brown.

He had parted the curtains as they had been parted on those other nights and she could see him as only a shape beside the bed—not the big broad shape which she had seen before, but the thin figure of her husband.

How different was this night from those others! Humility did not come eagerly to her; he did not whisper in that passionate voice; he did not caress her with urgent hands. He knelt by the bed and prayed.

"O Heavenly Father, it is because I believe it to be Thy will that I kneel at this bedside to-night. I pray Thee bless this woman, make her fertile, for, O Lord, it is for that reason I am here this night . . . not for carnal lust . . . but for the procreation of children as is laid down in Thy law. Thou knowest how I have grappled with myself . . ."

Tamar could listen to no more. How dare he call her "this woman"! He was not here for love of her, but in the hope of begetting children that they might do their share in populating the new land.

But her anger was lost in the numbness of regret, of a longing for another man, as Humility rose from his knees and came to her.

* * *

A month after her marriage to Humility Brown, Tamar knew that she was pregnant. Now her depression had lifted; she was glad she had married; this new adventure was going to be worth the step she had taken to achieve it.

She lost no time in imparting the news to Humility, and the first thing he did was to go down on his knees and thank God, but when he arose she imagined that he was not so thankful as it had first appeared.

She understood why, for although to Humility, who believed himself to be wise, she was a mysterious creature of odd and unaccountable moods, she was able to read him as easily as a printed sheet.

She was to have a child; the purpose of their nightly embraces was achieved; therefore until after the child was born these must be suspended. How could it be otherwise as, he had so often declared to God in her hearing, they took place for only one reason? That was in the nightly prayer he said at her bedside.

"God has answered our prayer!" he said.

"Now," she told him with a trace of malice, "you may with good conscience go back to your attic."

He was taken aback, but she went on quickly: "That would be wisest. It would be unfortunate if, after all your protestations, you were to give way to carnal lust—which you might well do if you continued to share my bed."

He despaired of her, she knew. She had no modesty, he told her. He pointed out that she said, without thinking, whatever came into her mind. He hoped that one day she would learn from Puritan women to veil her thoughts—even from herself.

She smiled. The last month had brought her soul no nearer to salvation, she feared. It had been very close, she knew, when she had promised to marry him, but alas! it grew farther away.

He went back to his attic and she was relieved; she was mistress of her own domain once more; she had the child safe within her, and that was all she wanted of him.

She would have Annis sent to her room, or go herself to the cottage. They would bend over their sewing and talk incessantly of the baby. Tamar even learned to take a pride in her work, which astonished her, for she had never before been attracted to the needle. She sat and dreamed of the baby, and she believed that she was happier now than she had ever been; she ceased to think of the journey to Virginia, for her only thought was of the child.

How slowly the months passed! Springtime, and it would be December before her baby was born!

Annis said one summer's day as they sat in the garden with their sewing: "It does seem a miracle to me that you and Mr. Brown should be joined together. We did always think 'twould be a *grand* marriage for thee. One of the gentlemen from hereabouts as was mad for 'ee. And then you marry the Puritan! Of course, a finer and more noble gentleman never did live, I do know; and I said to John, I said: 'Happy should a woman be in such a union, but . . ."

"But?" demanded Tamar sharply; and Annis flushed and became intent upon her work. Tamar burst out: "A woman should be happy in such a union, but I am no ordinary woman, am I, Annis? No, I am not! Do not look alarmed. We know — you and I. Oh, Annis, sometimes I think I am bound to the darkness by silken threads which are so light that no one can see them, and only I am aware of them."

"Ain't you saved, then, mistress?"

"No, Annis."

"Oh, 'tis a terrible hard job to save 'ee. The Devil holds fast to his own. But you ain't bad. That's what I say to John: 'There's witchcraft in her, but all witchcraft ain't bad.' If it do help people, how can it be bad?"

"You are a dear creature, Annis."

"I have no wish but to serve you all the days of my life, mistress."

"You are my friend too, Annis."

Annis moved nearer to Tamar. "I did think at one time it would have been Master Bartle Cavill as you would have took. My dear soul! Think of it! If he'd lived and you'd have married him you'd have been Lady Cavill now. You'd have been the Lady of the Manor. I can picture 'ee, sitting there at the head of the table like . . . in your gowns of silk and velvet."

"Yes, Annis."

Annis faltered, remembering that it was sinful to talk of worldly pleasure. "I fear I be a sinful woman," she said. "I'll never learn to be a good Puritan. I be vain and overfond of this world's glories. It'll be a terrible hard struggle for me to climb the golden stairs."

"You'll climb the stairs, I promise you," said Tamar. "As for your sins, no questions will be asked."

Annis opened her eyes very wide. "You couldn't fix that, mistress, for the Devil wouldn't carry no weight up there."

Tamar laughed. "All this talk of Heaven wearies me. I want to be happy here. Oh Annis, I wonder what my baby will be like. A boy or a girl? A girl, I hope, for if it is a boy he might be like Humility. . . and if a girl like me. How wonderful to see yourself in miniature . . . another Tamar . . . but with a Puritan instead of a Devil for her father!"

She laughed so loudly that Annis was frightened, for, as she said to John afterwards: "Women can be awful strange in the waiting months."

The child was born on a snowy December day. Annis was with Tamar, for she had acquired in the last years some competence as a midwife. Richard had engaged the best physician in Plymouth; but it was Annis whom Tamar wanted with her.

The child was a boy, and Tamar, as she lay in what seemed like the best of all worlds, since there was no pain in it and her baby was in her arms, believed that this was the answer to her problem. She had found happiness at last.

He was dark-eyed, that boy; and already there was a good thick down on his head. She laughed with joy to look at him.

Annis said: "Why, mistress, you can't be disappointed in such a bonny boy, for all that you did want a girl."

"I . . . want a girl! Nonsense! I wanted nothing but this one!"

She was absorbed in the child. She had his basket beside her bed, and none but herself must attend to his wants. She would not swaddle him, for she remembered that she herself had not been swaddled, and she did not wish to shut his beautiful limbs away from her sight.

Annis shook her head. That was wrong. He would catch his death.

"He will not catch his death. I will keep him warm. I want him to grow up beautiful like his mother."

"But, mistress . . ." cried Annis, distressed.

"I know what is good for my child." Her eyes flashed and it seemed to Annis, as she told John afterwards, as though the Devil looked out of them. John said: 'Annis, I do know she be the wife of Mr. Brown. I do know she have been good to 'ee. But she can work spells. Didn't she give you one to work on me? And spells ain't Christian, Annis. I would wish to see thee clear of her.' At which Annis's eyes flashed almost as fiercely as those of her mistress, and she answered: 'I'd cut off me right hand rather than leave her, John Tyler.' And John was afraid to say more, for he knew that Annis did not mean she would only give up her right hand for her mistress. And when you have the true faith and you have been saved, you do not want to hear your wife utter blasphemy.

So Tamar brought up her child in her own way, and he thrived; but when the time came for naming him, there was conflict between his parents.

"We will call him Humility," said his father. "Such a name will be to him, as my thoughtful parents knew it would be to me, a constant reminder that he must live up to that quality."

"I will not have him called Humility!" declared Tamar.

"Why not, wife?"

"I have planned to call him Richard, after my father."

"Perhaps I may allow you to call our next boy by that name. Although I would suggest something more appropriate to accompany it."

"What?" she cried. "Restraint? Charity? Virtue? I do not love your Puritan names."

"Do you not then love these qualities in a human being?"

"I do not like them attached as a name is attached. There is something smug about the thing. As though to say, 'I am humble' or 'I am full of restraint.' 'I am charitable and virtuous!' Actions, not words, should proclaim these qualities."

She saw by the flush under his skin that he was trying hard to control himself.

"We will call him Humility," he said. "My dear, the first duty of a wife towards her husband is obedience."

"*I* am no ordinary wife and I would thank you not to speak of me in such terms. This child is mine and I alone will choose his name."

"I regret I must be firm in this," he said. "Had you asked me in humility, I might have allowed him a second name, and, as you wished to name him after your father and that is a pleasant and agreeable thought, I might have given my consent. But in view of your rebellion, your careless words, I can only forbid the use of the name, and I must . . ."

"Pray, do not preach to me!" she cried. "If you attempt to, you will stay in your attic altogether and there will be no more children. That would be a pity, as I wished for more."

"I do not understand you, Tamar."

"No, you do not understand *me*. But understand *this*: The child will be named Richard."

"I cannot countenance such unwifely behaviour," he said; but he stopped short, looking at her.

She was very beautiful with her long black hair upon the pillows, her big luminous eyes flashing, her breast bare in the low-cut bed-gown.

* * *

Little Dick was three years old and Rowan just born when the Indian princess came to Plymouth.

Tamar had left Rowan in the care of Annis and had taken Dick down to Barbican Causeway to see the ships come in.

The little boy, dark-eyed and vivacious, was entirely Tamar's child. She rejoiced to watch him; so must she have been when she was his age. She was determined that none of those hardships which she had had to face should fall to his lot. There seemed hardly anything of Humility in him; indeed, the boy avoided his father whenever possible. He was afraid of the pale, stern-faced man whose every sentence seemed to begin with "Thou shalt not . . ."

He loved the sea, and was never tired of watching it and listening to the tales his mother told him of the Spaniards.

She had taken him down on this occasion, little guessing that such a romantic figure would be on board. There she was — a lovely, dark-eyed girl, a princess from the promised land itself, with straight black hair and strange clothes. Nor was she the only visitor from that distant land, for she, as a princess, had brought her train with her — Indians in brightly coloured clothes that accentuated the darkness of their hair and eyes.

The princess was Pocahontas, now called Rebecca, since she had embraced the Christian faith and had married an Englishman. When the spectators had recovered from their surprise, they welcomed her warmly, for they knew something of her romantic story. Captain John Smith had been in Plymouth a year or so ago, talking to the people. He had, he explained, been travelling through the West Country; his plan was to get people to accompany him to the New World. He scorned those who went in search of gold, for did not many of them return disappointed? There were, he assured them, greater prizes to be taken: trade for England; the development of uncultivated land; an empire. He had been treated badly in Virginia and was anxious to explore new territory. He talked of the place he had christened New England. There was fish in those seas as good—nay, better—than anywhere else in the world. There was one cape which had been called Cape Cod because never before had so many fish been seen as were swimming in the water surrounding it. Corn could be grown there; cattle raised. He explained that he was eager to take out a band of men, and was recruiting for his ships.

Richard had entertained him at Pennicomquick, where Captain Smith had told many a story of the New World; and although Humility had dreamed of going to Virginia, he did not see why New England should not be equally suitable.

Those had been exciting months while Smith made his preparations.

But Richard was against their going. He pointed out again and again that they would be leaving a life of comfort for one of hardship. There might be famine. Had Tamar considered that? Had she imagined her little Dick crying for food? Let those go who found life here intolerable—for they had little to lose. But for those who enjoyed the comfortable life, there should be much consideration before lightly giving it up.

Humility longed to go, for he saw the hand of God in the coming of Captain Smith to Plymouth.

Tamar had then been aware of a growing perversity in herself, which at times made her want to oppose this man whom she had married. She said: "Don't you always see the hand of God when something turns up which you want? It was always Virginia . . . Virginia . . . Virginia . . . I thought that was the place. This New England is virgin soil. Shall we take our child to possible starvation? You may go, but you will go alone."

And then the matter was decided for them. One of the Plymouth ships, which had set out for the New World in search of gold, came back empty and with tales of hardship. Interest in the expedition dropped. Tamar became pregnant again. And when Smith sailed with the two ships which were all he could muster, the family at Pennicomquick was not with him.

But Smith had made known in Plymouth the romantic story of Pocahontas, and when Tamar took the little boy on her horse and rode slowly homewards she told it to him.

"Captain Smith had gone into a strange land, my son," said Tamar, "and with him were many who wished to make the land their own. But there were people—already in the land—people like those you have seen to-day, and they did not wish the white men to take their land from them. And one day Captain Smith was caught by the Indians and they were going to kill him, when the Princess you have seen to-day stepped forward and, just as they were about to kill him, threw herself upon him, so that they had to hold back their blows. Then she begged the King, her father, to save his life; and this he did. So she is remembered in this land as the little girl—for she was only twelve years old—who saved the life of an

Englishman and was a friend to the English. Now, my little Dick, you will be able to tell your grandfather who it was you have seen this day. What is her name? Do you remember?"

"Pocahontas," said Dick; and his eyes were bright. He was filled with excitement by what he had seen. One day *he* would be one of the adventurers of the sea.

There was nothing of his father in him; and she was glad.

* * *

The coming of the Princess excited them.

Humility, his eyes blazing with fervour, declared that this was yet another sign from God. Relations between the Indians and the white settlers were such that an Indian Princess had married a white man and become a Christian and was not afraid to visit the country of the white men. That was a sign. There could be little danger from Indians where such conditions prevailed.

Humility was eager to set out. He declared this was due to his desire to break away from a country whose rulers forbade men to worship God as they wished. But, Tamar asked herself, was that the only reason? Humility did not like their present domestic arrangements, which, she was ready to admit, were unusual and would make a man of Humility's pride uneasy.

No wonder he was eager to get away.

"I would never leave Richard," declared Tamar. "Wait, and he will come with us. He needs a good deal of time to come to such a decision. Moreover, if he came with us, we could go in comfort. He is a rich man and he could use his wealth to give us a well-equipped ship. We cannot go to a strange land and start a settlement there without a good deal of wealth. Believe me, for I know that when the time is ripe Richard will come with us."

Richard went on to talk of comfort *versus* hardship. Was it fair, he demanded, to take women and children to savage lands?

"God would look after them," said Humility.

"The Spaniards, pirates or Indians might arrive on the scene before God," said Tamar, goaded into flippancy by her husband's piety, as she so often was.

Humility prayed silently, and, watching him, Tamar asked herself once more, as she had asked so many times: Why did I marry this man? How could I want to hurt him as I do if I loved him? And yet . . . ever since I saved his life I have been aware of him. I am as happy with him as I could be with any.

"I thought," said Humility, "that you were as eager for this project as I. You talk of risks. Here we risk our lives. We never know when we shall be sent to prison and left to die there. Continually we break the laws of this land. We need only an informer among us, and disaster would be upon us. In the strange land we might find other dangers, but we would hold our heads high and fear none."

Tamar was swayed. "That is so," she agreed. "Richard, there is much to be said for freedom, even if it brings other troubles with it."

But Richard would not be convinced.

"Consider this matter," he said. "You would have me sell my lands, equip a ship, and take with us all our wealth to this new land. Think! First we must make a perilous journey. We must face storm and tempest. Worse still, this ocean we must cross is infested with pirates of all nationalities. Such a ship as ours would be an easy victim. There would be money aboard . . . goods; and pirates would know this. We should have to face death . . . horrible death . . . perhaps worse than horrible death. There may be Spaniards who would hand us over to the Inquisition; Turks who would take us down to the Barbary coast and make slaves of us. As Humility would say, that might be the will of God. But I would not wish such things to happen to myself or Tamar or the children. Dick is three years old; Rowan a baby. Let them grow older. Wait. Let us discover more of this land before we leave the evils we know for those we can only conjecture."

"Just think!" said Tamar. "If you would equip a ship we could begin preparing to-morrow."

"That is why I feel we must give this matter the deepest thought. There is always safety in waiting."

So they waited and the uneventful life continued.

They heard that the little Princess had died at Gravesend just as she was about to return to her native land. She had been unable to endure the damp air of England.

Richard said then that he had been right to oppose the venture.

"Their climate might have the same effect on us," he said.

"Men and women are like plants. They cannot easily be uprooted."

Then Tamar knew that she was to have another child, and temporarily she lost all desire to wander.

* * *

Tamar nearly lost her life when Lorea was born. She lay in bed only half conscious of time and place. For days she remained thus, and in the weeks that followed a listlessness settled upon her.

She heard the voices of those about her without hearing their words: Annis's high-pitched and full of tears; Richard's solemn and full of sorrow; Humility's sad, yet resigned; then Dick aged five and Rowan three, were frightened and bewildered.

She had never been inactive for so long, and inactivity gave her time for thought. She was most unhappily and unsuitably married. How could she ever have been so foolish as to imagine she could have lived a quiet life, that she could have been the meek, submissive Puritan wife of a man like Humility? Often she felt sorry on his account for having married him, and determined to do her best to hide her revulsion.

They had three children now; Humility would not feel he had justified his marrying until they had twelve. Nine more ordeals such as this one she had just passed through! She sighed. Well, it was her duty, and she was committed to it.

Dick and Rowan were *her* children, with rosy cheeks and bright black eyes and dark hair—high-spirited wild young things. She wondered about the new child, little Lorea, born small and puny, not like her brother and sister, who, almost from their birth, had amazed everybody, so that people like Annis and Mistress Alton thought that some devil's power had been used by their mother to make them stronger, more bright and beautiful than others of their age.

When she rose from her bed after the passing of weeks, her mirror showed her how pale and thin she had become. She would sit in her room, deep in thought. Humility was delighted with her. He had returned to her room, as it was time, he said, to get themselves another child.

The memory of the ordeal was still very vividly with her, but she submitted.

Humility went down on his knees and praised God.

"I thank Thee, Lord, for showing this woman Thy ways at last . . ."

Dick and Rowan were bewildered by the change in her; she was too tired to play the games she had once played. They accepted the change, as children will, more readily than the grown-ups. They had lost their bright, gay and exciting mother; and in her place was a quiet stranger.

Little Lorea was a sickly child, over whom all shook their heads. Her poor, pathetic face looked out from the swaddling clothes, and she never smiled; she hardly ever cried.

Humility would sigh, looking at her; he would murmur: "If this be the will of God, then must we bear it."

He turned stern eyes on his two elder children. Violence was something he could never employ, but he saw clearly the need of correction where those two were concerned. Dick, for his sins, was often shut into a dark cupboard, because that, Humility had discovered, was what he feared more than aught else. Rowan, who was always hungry, was sent fasting to bed.

A change had come over the household.

The Devil is in chains! thought Humility.

The summer came, and in the long, hot days Tamar sat out of doors. Then the colour returned to her face and she was aware of a deep delight in the smells of the sun-baked earth and the scent of the flowers. The smell of earth reminded her always of Bartle; she remembered it so well from the day when he had tripped her up and forced her down—and, ever after that, the smell of earth was a smell which excited her; and after those days out of doors, she would feel a little resentful towards Humility. She could not help it if she dreamed of a passionate lover who came to her, most dishonourably it was true, but with what passion, because he desired her, not children!

Then came a day when Dick and Rowan were lost.

They had been caught laughing during prayers that morning and had been called to their father and told to repeat the Lord's Prayer. Humility shared the current belief that inability to say the Lord's Prayer was in itself a confession of wickedness, for there was some magical quality about the words, so that they would not come fluently through impure mouths. When the children faltered, Humility, in deep sorrow, talked to them of the hell which awaited all sinners. Dick, for instance, would be perpetually in the dark, unable to see anything but the eyes of devils who would torment him and pull out his flesh with hot pincers while he burned eternally. Rowan, who was greedy in the extreme, would be sat at a table containing all the food she loved best, and every time she reached out a hand to take some of it, it would be snatched from her. She would starve, but not to death, for she too would suffer the pains of burning for ever.

The thought of burning eternally did not greatly worry the children; they had never been burned. But the thought of being shut in a dark cupboard with devils terrified Dick. Rowan, more sturdily practical than her brother, could imagine no greater torment than going hungry.

In the days before Lorea's birth they might have gone to their mother for comfort, but they sensed, with the quick perception of children, that their mother had changed, and that their father now ruled their lives.

Hell and the supposed horrors devised by their Heavenly Father were in the far distant future; but right before them were the punishments of their earthly one. The dark was not to be faced; and if Rowan was going without her usual food she might as well do it out of doors where there were berries and nuts and plants which were good to eat.

So they ran away.

Tamar was with Annis when the news was brought to her. She had been standing by the basket in which lay her youngest child. Every day Lorea's face took on a more deathly hue. How many weeks of life were left to the child? she wondered.

Annis looked up from some garment she was stitching, and her eyes betrayed the sudden fear which had come to her.

"What ails you, Annis?" asked Tamar.

Annis hesitated, but Tamar insisted that she tell, and at last it came. "I thought, mistress, that you was back with the Devil. I thought you were going to work out one of your spells to save the child."

Tamar's eyes gleamed, but just at that moment Moll Swann came in to say that the children were not to be found. Moll had searched everywhere in the house and grounds. Moll was afraid they were lost.

Then in a moment Tamar threw off the inertia of months as though she were tossing aside a garment.

"Let everyone search," she said. "They must be found at once."

"Where be you going, mistress?" asked Annis.

"To find them," answered Tamar. "Go to the stables and tell them to saddle my horse."

She was in her habit and away in a few minutes, her hair blown loose in the wind as of old. Hundreds of thoughts filled her mind as she rode on. Her children had been frightened because they had missed the mother they had once known; and they had been unable to endure their life at Pennicomquick as the children of Humility Brown. She understood that, and she was to blame.

She rode hard and straight to the spot where the children were — there would be some who would say there was witchcraft in that. Was there? she wondered. Or was it that she herself had taken them there so many times? It was a small grassy plateau on the cliffs, from which it was possible to see, in all its beauty and promise of adventure, that shining expanse of channel. Here she had often told them stories of the sea; and the stories she had told had been those Bartle had told her.

When they saw her coming with her hair flying and the colour in her cheeks, they gave shouts of joy and ran to her.

Dick said: "Rowan, she's come! She's come!"

Tamar held them fiercely against her and she knew that they also meant that she had come back to them. The mother they had once known had returned.

They were delighted to have been found. The dark of the night would have been as frightening as the dark of a cupboard; and starvation in the open air as bad as starvation at home.

She set them on her horse and they went slowly back; but the journey did not seem long to them, for they were all so happy to be reunited.

The children had lost their fears, for their real mother was back and she would protect them from their Puritan father.

The household was in a turmoil when they arrived. Richard saw the trio entering the stable-yard, and knew what had happened. Tamar's health had returned, and with it the true Tamar. The period of submission had been due to her decline in health after the birth of Lorea; just as her conversion had taken place after some deep mental disturbance. He watched the meeting between the returning party and Humility.

Humility had been anxious. He was fond of his children, Richard knew; perhaps he was proud of their fine looks and healthy bodies; but because he was proud of them he considered it necessary to be the sterner with them. Now, though, he had to face their mother, and she stood before him like a tigress with her young.

"Praise be to God!" cried Humility. "The children are safe."

Tamar did not answer. She lifted the children to the ground and called to the gaping Ned Swann to take the horse.

"Dick," said Humility, "Rowan, I can see that you are ashamed of what you have done. That is well. But do not think this can go unpunished."

Tamar said: "They have been sufficiently punished and shall be punished no more."

"Wife," he said, his eyes on her flushed face and wild hair, "you have brought them home. Now you will leave them to me."

"No," she answered, "*you* will leave them to *me*."

She felt the children's hands in hers, clinging hot and tight.

"Annis!" she cried. "Annis, food for the children . . . quickly."

Glances were exchanged among the watching servants. Moll whispered to Jane: "The mistress be back, then." Mistress Alton gave one fearful look at Tamar and began to mutter the Lord's Prayer; and Tamar, watching them, laughed inwardly. They were thinking that the Devil had been in chains, but he had broken free.

Well, at least Dick and Rowan were happy.

"Come, my darlings," she said. "And promise you will never leave your mother again, for she will never leave you."

And they kept their tight grip on her hands as they went past their father, but they could not help throwing triumphant glances at Humility as they did so.

Tamar made them eat in her room instead of in their nursery. As they ate, they told her how frightened they had been, and how they hoped that no one but their mother would find them.

Annis, standing by the baby's basket, shook her head. *She* knew how it was that their mother had been able to go straight to the place where they had been. Annis thought: It is good to have the children home safe, though the Devil is back!

Tamar, reading her thoughts, went over to the basket, and as she stood beside Annis, looking down at the sickly baby, wild thoughts came to her, and with them all the old belief in her powers. She *knew* that she could snatch this child from death.

She picked up Lorea. "Annis," she said quietly, "bring me warm water quickly. Waste no time."

Annis muttered fearfully: "What be you going to do, mistress?"

"Do as I say!"

When Annis returned, Tamar had cut the swaddling clothes from the baby who lay in her lap, her poor, cramped limbs caked and foul with the muck of months.

Annis shrieked; the children stopped eating. "Mistress, you will hasten her to her grave."

"Nay," said Tamar. "I will snatch her from it."

Tenderly and carefully she washed the baby while Annis, standing by, handing her what she asked for, heard the strange words she muttered as she patted and dried the skin which had a look of bad cheese. Then she wrapped the baby in a shawl and held it against her, crooning over it. Annis swore afterwards that from that moment the colour of the baby's face began to change.

Then she fed the baby. It took a little milk and was not sick. All that night Tamar kept her children with her—her baby at her breast, the other two on either side of her.

Humility came in, but she sent him out, and he dared not protest. Annis lay at the end of the bed, and there was no sleep for either her or her mistress that night. Every time the child awakened, Tamar fed her.

Annis was sure she was watching magic. As she said to John later: "It was magic for sure, but *good* magic. Couldn't have been aught else."

"Nay," answered John, " 'was devil's work, for God meant the child to die and she saved her, so how could that be good?"

But Annis believed that the dear Lord would understand and not be too hard on a woman whose sin was to save through witchcraft the baby He had decided to take.

The next day was warm and sunny and Tamar took the baby out into the shade of the garden. And Mistress Alton, watching from the windows with Jane and Moll, was certain that this was witchcraft.

In a week from that day when Dick and Rowan had run away from home, little Lorea was kicking her legs in the sunshine—puny still, but moving slowly away from the grave.

Tamar was triumphant. Her little girl was saved. She herself had worked the miracle and all her old power was back with her.

* * *

Richard saw trouble coming, and spoke of it to Humility.

"Man, you must have a care. From the way things are going I see more and more restrictions coming, more and more persecutions of such as you."

Humility answered as he answered all warnings: "Whatever should come to us would be through the will of God."

Most of the Puritans were attending the service of the Established Church. That was necessary to avoid suspicion. But Humility refused to go. Nothing had happened so far, for nobody had informed against him; but, Richard pointed out, that state of affairs might not last.

"What," he asked, "if you were taken off to prison? You would not escape as easily as John Tyler did. Oh, we are fortunate here, I know. The law is not so strictly enforced in this part of the country. But . . . Humility, if you were taken, I doubt if they would ever set you free." Humility was about to speak, but Richard interrupted impatiently: "I know what you will say. 'It is the will of God!' But what of your family? What of Tamar and the children?"

"They are well looked after here," said Humility. "As you know, I have never supported my family. That I was prepared to do, but Tamar is proud. The life I could offer her was not good enough. She would not renounce her comfort for her duty."

"It may have been the comfort of her children she was thinking of," said Richard coldly. "And it occurs to me that your pride is as great as Tamar's."

Humility was astonished. Richard smiled. It amazed him that Humility—a man of learning and some culture—could be so blind regarding himself, could walk contentedly in the narrow channel he had cut for himself . . . a channel which was bounded on both sides by the strictures of the Puritan faith.

"I . . . proud! Pride is one of the seven deadly sins. If I believed I possessed it . . ."

"I know," said Richard. "You would fast and pray. But sometimes when a man is aware of great goodness in himself he can be blind to that little which is in others. But let us not talk of this. I wish you to take more care, for there are trying times ahead of us."

But what was the use of talking to Humility? He could only fold his hands in prayer and continue in his way of life, so putting himself in perpetual danger of arrest, imprisonment and even death.

Richard was right. The King was not pleased with his Puritans. He had returned from Scotland and had not liked the way the English kept their Sundays. He wished them to attend church, but once divine service was over, there was no need to be glum. In fact, loyal subjects were ordered *not* to be glum.

A proclamation was read throughout the land.

It was His Majesty's pleasure that his people should not be disturbed or discouraged from any lawful recreations, such as dancing, either of men or women, archery, leaping, vaulting or any harmless recreations. Morris dances should be danced and maypoles set up. These sports were within the law.

There was another point in the proclamation. Some people were to be excluded from Sunday sports—those who did not attend service in their parish church, or attended for only part of the service. The name of any man or woman guilty of this should in future be announced from the pulpit.

Richard said to Humility: "Mark my words, this is the beginning of new persecutions."

In East Anglia, where the Separatist movement was at its strongest, persecutions were at their height. In London, where some bold Separatists were preaching their creed in the streets, there were riots and bloodshed. In Devon things were quieter, but to Richard the rumours were like the rumbling of a storm which was coming closer.

And one day two ships sailed into Plymouth Sound, and with the coming of these two ships came raised hopes and new plans to every Puritan who met in secret in that meeting-place which had been founded by Humility Brown.

These ships were the *Mayflower*—a vessel of some one hundred and eighty tons—and her smaller companion, the *Speedwell*.

Here was a great occasion for the town of Plymouth; but for no one more than for Humility Brown and William Spears, because aboard these ships were men they had once known, men from their own county.

Humility had rarely been so excited as he was on that day. Where these men went, would he follow. He was certain now that God had meant him to be left behind so that he might save many souls and take them to the promised land.

Miles Standish, a friend from his past, was delighted to see him. They had long talks together, and Standish gave Humility details of provisions which must be taken on such a trip if there was to be any hope of survival in a new land. Humility listened eagerly, made many notes; and was more than a little sad not to be of their number.

"But," he said to Standish, "I am wrong. I am wicked. It is not for me to rail against the fate which God has ordained for me. I am not ready yet."

"Yea, Humility, my friend," answered Standish. "It is clear that the Lord did not intend you to come with us. The captain of the *Speedwell* is faint of heart and declares his vessel to be unseaworthy. We might have taken you and your family and friends, but as the *Mayflower* goes alone, we have to take on board all those passengers whose hearts do not fail them. Everything must be carried in one ship instead of two, as we planned. Your turn will come, my friend, I doubt not."

It was a moving sight to watch that lonely ship sail off into the unknown. Crowds stood on the Hoe while the *Speedwell* lay in the Sound and the *Mayflower* sailed with those men and women who had said their last farewells to their native land, that they might find a new life, a new country where they could worship God in peace.

* * *

After the Pilgrim Fathers left Plymouth, several years passed uneventfully. There was now a new King on the throne—King Charles the First—but with his reign persecution did not end.

Humility continued to hope that the day was approaching when he would follow in the wake of the Pilgrims; Tamar swayed between him and Richard;

and it was not until a series of disasters occurred that Richard began to change his mind.

The first of these disasters concerned the Puritans. Several of them, it had been noted, were neither attending Sunday service in the church nor Sunday sports; their clothes were too sombre for fashion; they were, in short, living the lives of Puritans and breaking the law of the land.

Josiah Hough discovered that a trap had been laid to catch the Puritans at worship when they met in their barn on Thursday night at eight o'clock. He immediately brought this news to Richard, who lost no time in imparting it to Humility Brown.

"I beg of you, do not go there on Thursday," he said, "and warn all your friends to stay away."

"This," said Humility, "is the protecting arm of God. He does not wish us to rot in prison. He has other plans for us. More and more I am convinced that He wishes us, when the time is ripe, to sail for the New World."

So that Thursday there was no meeting at the barn, and those who had surrounded the place, hoping to make arrests, were so angry that they burned it to the ground.

"You have escaped this time," said Richard. "Let it be a warning to you to take double care in future."

A few months passed during which the Puritans seemed to have been forgotten, for a new witch-hunt was engaging attention.

In Devon this began with Jane Swann. Jane was a pretty girl—golden-haired and blue-eyed, a quiet, good girl. Ned Swann and his wife had been two of the first to turn Puritan, and their girls had been brought up almost from babyhood in the faith. Moll was slow-witted, but Jane was a bright girl and pretty enough in her quiet way to attract the attention of the young men of the neighbourhood.

One afternoon she was gathering wood in a lonely copse which adjoined the Hurlys' farm when she was overtaken by a man. She knew this man to be a merchant of Plymouth, a man of some substance, an ardent church-goer of pious reputation. He stopped and talked to the girl and she, believing him to be all that she had heard, had no fear of him until he made a suggestion which terrified her. She turned to run, but he caught her. She threatened to expose him if he hurt her. He laughed at that.

"Do you think any would believe the word of a girl like you against mine?" he asked.

Poor Jane was bewildered by her fear. She quickly realized that she would be forced to sin; defiled, shamed, damned for ever, she would have to confess at the meeting-place before all the Puritans. To a girl of her upbringing, death seemed preferable, for she would have no wish to live after such shame had overtaken her. She fought with all her might against this man as he tore her clothes from her and flung her to the ground.

He cursed her, but she screamed the louder. He silenced her with a blow that partially stunned her, and proceeded then with his evil work.

He had forgotten that the copse was so close to the farm, and suddenly he heard a rush of footsteps through the undergrowth, and there, standing before him were Peter Hurly and his young brother, George.

The greatly respected citizen was caught in the very act; furiously angry, overcome with shame, he scrambled to his feet and made off—but not before he was recognized—leaving the half-conscious girl lying on the ground.

The boys helped Jane to her feet, and as she could not walk, between them they carried her back to the house at Pennicomquick.

Tamar was horrified at the story they had to tell.

"Bring her to my room," she commanded. "Poor child! I will look after her. And let everyone know what sort of a man this is! He must be punished for this. We will see that he falls from that high pedestal on which he has set himself."

Tenderly she looked after the poor, shocked girl, and all the time she was thinking: This might have happened to me! And the memory of Bartle all those years ago was as vivid as ever.

She herself lost no time in spreading the story of what had happened to Jane; nor did she omit to mention the name of the culprit. "Who could be trusted after this?" everyone was asking.

Mistress Alton blamed the girl, for she persisted in her belief that evil was only suffered by those who deserved so to suffer; but Tamar stood over Jane like an angel with a flaming sword.

It was deeply gratifying to learn that Jane's ravisher was now shunned in the town, that he had ceased to be regarded as a respectable merchant and would not long be a wealthy one, for people did not wish to trade with one who had so deceived them as to his real character.

Poor Jane was recovering under Tamar's care, for Tamar impressed upon her that what had happened to her was due to no fault of hers. "Indeed," said Tamar with flashing eyes, "what happened to you might have happened to any of us!"

Even Humility admitted that what had occurred was Jane's misfortune rather than her fault. He spent long periods praying with her for the purification of her soul, although he thought that only a life of extreme piety could make her pure in the eyes of Jesus.

And one day Jane went out and failed to return.

She was missed early in the afternoon, and when night came and she was not back, Mistress Alton narrowed her eyes and grumbled to Jane's sister Moll: "You can depend upon it, I was right. When that sort of thing happens to a girl there's more in it than meets the eyes. Oh, they are all very innocent when they are caught. It was rape, of course. It is always rape! Mark my words, young Mollie, your sister went out to meet that man and was willing enough until the Hurly boys surprised them. And it wouldn't be such a big surprise to me now if they'd gone off together where they can sin undisturbed."

Tamar went down to the kitchen. "Has Jane returned?"

Mistress Alton smiled her secret smile. "She's well away by now. Like as not they're riding away on the other side of the Tamar. Or mayhap it's across the Plym they've gone. But gone they have . . . and you may be sure they've gone together . . ."

Tamar faced the woman. "I tell you it is not true. I have never seen anyone so distressed as Jane was when the boys brought her home."

"Distressed! Oh . . . aye! They're all distressed when they're caught. And to be caught like that . . ."

"How dare you blame *her*! She was forced. I have talked long with her. *I* could not be mistaken."

"You are too kind to the girl. Forced! Nobody ever tried forcing me."

"That," said Tamar as she swept out of the kitchen, "does not surprise me."

Tamar did not sleep at all that night. She felt convinced that something terrible was happening to Jane; and she believed that she knew this through her secret powers.

Humility, who was sharing her room, hoping for a fourth child, begged her to rest; but she would not rest. She paced up and down the room.

In the early morning, as soon as dawn began to show over Bolt Head, she dressed and went out. That was how it came about that it was Tamar who brought Jane back to the house.

Jane was hardly recognisable as the girl who had left the house yesterday. Her face was red and swollen—blistered and burned. Her bodice had been ripped off her shoulders and there were angry scars on her neck and chest. Across her back were burns which may have been made with a poker or a bar of redhot metal. Tamar could not believe that this was Jane until the girl spoke.

Feeling sick with anger and indignation, Tamar picked up the girl and carried her back to the house, for Jane was in a state of collapse; she had come within a quarter of a mile of the house, but could drag herself no further.

The gentleness of Tamar's hands were a vivid contrast to her angry, flashing eyes. She knew that a cruel and wicked revenge had been taken on an innocent girl.

Jane regained consciousness only to swoon with her pain. Her fair, once lovely, hair had been burned away at one side of her head. She murmured: "They made me say... They made me say..." And then she would slip into unconsciousness.

Tamar took Jane to her room, and, waking Humility, made him get out of the bed, on which she laid the suffering girl.

Humility stared at Jane. "What has happened to her?"

"They have tortured her. Oh, for the love of God, don't start praying now. Get Richard and get Annis. Tell her to bring warm water... and some wine to revive her. Quickly... Quickly. This is no time for prayers, but for action."

Jane was moaning softly in her agony.

"Oh, dear Jane," murmured Tamar while the tears ran down her cheeks. "I will save you. I will ease your pain."

Richard came in and stared at the girl. "Good God!" he cried. "What have they done to her? I will send a groom for a doctor at once."

"I have the ointments to heal these burns," said Tamar. "They are as good as any doctor's. Where is Annis? Oh . . . Annis . . . water . . . warm water . . . and my box of ointments."

"I will see that the doctor is called at once," said Richard; but Tamar laid a hand on his arm.

"We do not yet know the full meaning of this. She muttered something as I carried her in . . . something about a witch. If possible . . . let no one know she is here. I tell you I can do more for her than any doctor."

Annis, her eyes wide with horror, came in with the warm water and the ointments.

"She *must* have a doctor," said Richard. "The girl is near death."

"I saved Lorea, did I not? I tell you I know more than doctors."

Richard could see that there was little a doctor could do for Jane except soothe her burns, and that Tamar's ointments and lotions would do equally well. There had been some treacherous work here, and the fact that Jane had mentioned witches gave a clue to what had been done to her . . . and with what excuse.

Jane moaned softly while the wounds were bathed and Tamar applied the ointments. Wine was forced between Jane's lips; and Annis was bidden to tear up linen so that Tamar might bind the wounds.

Tamar and Annis sat up with Jane, for Tamar refused to have anyone with her but Annis. She wanted Annis's absolute belief in her ability to cure the girl — a belief which the others would not feel; and this lack of belief, Tamar felt, might thwart her success. She felt that, given an atmosphere of confidence and her herbs and ointments, together with magical words, she could carry this thing successfully through.

Soon after Jane had been found, a story was circulating about her. Jane Swann was a witch. She had admitted it. The respected merchant, desolate at losing his good name and his position in the town, had, with the concurrence of some of his friends, captured the girl and questioned her. One or two accepted tests were forced upon her, and after a while she broke down and confessed "the truth."

The merchant — according to this story — had not been in the woods that day. His wife had testified to that. There were others ready to testify. It was said that Jane Swann was in the habit of going into the woods, where she behaved in a very lewd fashion with her familiar — a devil. This devil was at times invisible, but, like all such devils, could change into any shape he chose. One woman swore that on another occasion, as she had walked through the copse, she had seen a girl whom she now believed to have been Jane Swann lying in the grass naked from the waist down, and by her lewd motions it was clear that the girl was having sexual connection with an invisible creature. The woman had watched, and after a while had seen a shape, formed in smoke above the girl, which disappeared into the sky. The girl then got up, rearranged her clothes most demurely and walked away. On this tragic occasion the two boys had seen what the woman had seen; and the girl, knowing that it was too late to hide herself—she had, of course, been unaware that she had been watched before—had pleaded with her familiar for help; whereupon he had changed himself into the shape of the merchant, and, after he was sure that the boys had recognized him as such, had made off. Then the girl told her tale of force and violence. Of course she had seemed stunned! Of course there were bruises! Was she not, on her own confession, a witch? Why, after the confession, she had flown off on a broomstick. There were many who swore they had seen her flying through the sky.

Such was the lying tale which had been put about, and that had restored the merchant's honour.

Richard had already warned Mistress Alton that she would be turned out immediately if she told anyone of Jane's presence in the house. It was thus possible to keep the whole neighbourhood—with the exception of the girl's parents—ignorant of where she was.

After a few weeks of Tamar's nursing, young Jane had recovered from the terrible shock sufficiently to tell the full story of that night of brutality.

Her enemies had watched her leave the house, had stunned her and taken her to a cottage in the town. Here she was made to sit before a fire; her bodice was torn from her back and a red-hot poker applied while she was ordered to confess the story which had been prepared for her.

She was, in spite of the awful agony, able to withstand the torture; it was only when they forced her face downwards on to the fire that she had shrieked for mercy and had given way.

There had been a man present who had taken down her confession in writing, which she had had to repeat at the dictation of her tormentors.

She had become unconscious when they had left her lying on the floor. They intended, she had gathered, to take her in the morning to the Hoe, to proclaim her wickedness to the world and hang her. Believing her to be half-dead already, they had taken no precaution against an escape; but after an hour or so, Jane's young body had somewhat recovered. She prayed for strength, and, feeling that anything was preferable to the ordeal she would have to face on the morrow if she stayed there, had managed to stumble to the door. She was surprised to find that she only had to unlatch this and walk out. And this she did, for the man who had been set to guard her had drunk heavily and was snoring loudly.

It had taken her many hours to crawl towards Pennicomquick, tortured as she was by the cold air making her wounds smart; and it was only her belief in the divine assistance for which she had prayed that enabled her to cling to consciousness as long as she did.

Tamar's one thought was of revenge. She longed to confront that evil man with his sins. But Richard argued with her until he made her see that her interference could only make matters worse for Jane. To let it be known that Jane was safe was to condemn her to the gibbet.

"Oh, Tamar," he said, "the times in which we live are dangerous ones . . . violent and dangerous. Think of the injustice of this! A poor Puritan maiden, wandering in the woods . . . and that to happen to her!" He was silent suddenly, staring before him. "Your mother . . ." he went on quietly, "she . . . wandered in the woods one night; she was seduced by one no better than this merchant . . . and that night her feet were set on a path that led her to the gallows. Who am I to condemn others!"

Tamar went to him and laid a hand on his shoulder. "You were not as this man," she said. "You were thoughtless, careless . . . He is wicked. I will not have you compare yourself with him. Oh, Richard, when I think of what has happened to Jane . . . I want . . . I want to go away. I think of those men and women who sailed from here on that ship. The *Mayflower*, was it not? Think of the dangers they must have faced. Spaniards . . . pirates . . . violence . . . But Richard, if they reached a new country—a country where this which has happened to Jane could not happen . . . then was it worth while."

"Yes," he agreed, "that would be worth while."

"Richard, you too are beginning to think of escape. Yes, I see you are. To a land where meeting-houses are not burned down, where innocent girls are not treated brutally."

They said no more at the time; but that tragic affair was the beginning of Richard's change of mind.

There was continual talk of witches now. Someone saw old Sally Martin at her cottage door talking earnestly to her cat; another saw Maddy Barlow suckling a rabbit. Smoke was seen coming from chimneys, forming itself into shapes of devils. No one dared pick any wild grasses and plants which were well-known remedies for certain ailments. If they were seen picking these things it was very likely that they would be accused of witchcraft. There were furtive glances everywhere. No one was safe from suspicion — neither men, women nor children. Tom Lee, the blacksmith's boy, said, after he had recovered from a fit, that he had been walking in the copse near the Hurly farm when he met an old woman who cursed him before she turned into a dog and ran away. He had clearly been overlooked, said his parents. By whom?

"There is a big witch community among us," it was whispered. "Who knows who these witches are? Children are not safe from their parents, parents from their children; husbands and wives may have the Devil between them."

One day Betsy Hurly, coming to see her daughter, with whom — now that Annis was a wife and mother — she had become reconciled, saw

Jane Swann at the window of Tamar's room. Betsy slyly said nothing of what she had seen, but went out of the house and spread the story all round the place.

The news spread like fire in the wind. Jane Swann was at the house of Richard Merriman. She was in that room which was occupied by Tamar Brown.

Betsy could not stop talking. "My dear, she couldn't hide that she was a witch. Awful she looked. I see her yellow hair showing from under a bandage. Nobody ain't got hair quite Jane Swann's colour. There she was at the window. And what's more . . . I did see *her* . . . Tamar herself . . . gathering herbs . . . her hair wild like as she do love to show it. Muttering she were as she picked the devil's plants."

It was felt that something had to be done and, once more, as had happened years ago when Tamar was fourteen years old, a group of people marched on to the house of Richard Merriman to take a witch. And once more Richard spoke to them; but on this occasion Humility Brown stood beside him.

"Good people," said Richard, "it is true that Jane Swann is here. We have nursed her back to health. You know she was forced in the copse, and you know by whom. She was then taken and most cruelly tortured. We are trying to nurse this poor sick girl back to health. I beg of you to go away and leave us in peace."

They murmured together.

"How do we know he ain't a witch? There be witches among gentry. . ."

"Where be the other one, the black-haired witch? She be the one we ought to be bothering ourselves with."

Then Humility spoke: "Friends, I see among you some who have prayed with me. I have prayed with this poor girl and I believe her story to be true. You know, my friends, that if there were a witch in this house, *I* should know it, and know also my duty, which would be to hand this witch over to you. And do you doubt that, however painful my duty, it would be done?"

There was a short silence. Then a voice said: "You be bewitched, minister. You married a witch."

Humility's eyes flashed wrath. "Purge yourself of your desire to see violence!" he cried, pointing to the man who had spoken. "Ask yourselves this: 'Does the sight of blood please us?' If you look into your hearts and answer that question truthfully, then, friends, you will know that your chances of salvation are slight indeed. I would beg of you to pray with me . . . to ask that your sins may be forgiven. This girl, Jane Swann, was cruelly handled by her ravisher. I saw her with my own eyes when she was brought in by the boys. Peter! George! Stand forth and bear witness. You saw the girl bruised and stunned. Did you not?"

The boys came forward. They said: "Yes, Mr. Brown, we saw her."

"Thank you, George. Thank you, Peter. And these good people think you were deceived, boys. But *I* saw also. That is what they forget. The Devil might deceive *you* into thinking you saw bruises, but would God allow His servant to be so deceived? Nay, the Devil has power, but he is like a man in chains before the strength of Almighty God. If any of you think aught evil goes on in this house, then take me, for I have then deceived you, friends. Take me and crucify me on the nearest tree. Drive the nails into my flesh . . . into my hands, through my feet. Cry, 'Crucify him!' And give me vinegar and gall to drink. Ah, my friends, would that I were worthy of such a death!"

He went on weaving spells through his words, at which the crowd grew quiet, and some wept, while others fell on their knees. And what had begun by being a demand for a girl's life had by his magic oratory been turned into a prayer meeting.

But that was not an end to the matter. On that occasion after prayer with Humility the people had gone quietly away, but they continued to speak together of the witchcraft they feared was in their midst.

It was remembered that Tamar had saved her baby when the child was all but in the grave; it was even said that Lorea had already been dead, and that, by pledging the little girl to the Devil, her mother had brought it to life. They remembered how Simon, the pricker, had wanted to search Tamar and how she had prevailed on Richard Merriman to call her "daughter," and how she had put a spell on him as she did on all men . . . even Humility Brown.

She was more clever than a witch; she was the Devil himself, for the Devil was doubtless like God—three in one, an unholy trinity.

She had turned many people to witchcraft. Look at Annis—getting a cottage, and John Tyler to marry her, even though it was a bit late. Richard Merriman had always been a strange man, and he grew stranger. They had even made Mistress Alton one of them. For did she say anything about that witch, Jane Swann, being in the house? She would have been the first to see justice done before they had made a witch of her.

One night there was an attempt to burn down the house, but the fire was noticed almost at once and put out.

Richard was very thoughtful after that. He made enquiries about chartering ships, and he discussed with Humility what would be needed to fit out an expedition and sail away in the wake of the *Mayflower*.

* * *

John Tyler was arrested for questioning, and all those Puritans who had been attending Humility's meetings were thrown into a panic. They had heard of the way confessions were extracted, and they were afraid that, meek and gentle as John Tyler was, he was hardly the sort to stand up to such questionings. Humility, as the leader, suggested giving himself up; but Richard pointed out the folly of that. If Humility admitted to holding meetings in the place, there would be countless arrests.

Richard himself went to the magistrate in Plymouth, a man whom he had known as a friend.

Richard was frank; he knew that the Government was eager to send men out to the New World to colonize under the English flag. On the Continent, recusants were punished with great severity; but all the English Government wanted to do was to get rid of them. It was ready even to assist those Dissenters who wished to leave the country. So Richard was able to secure John's release by explaining that he was making arrangements to charter a ship in which the Puritan community planned to leave the country for ever.

After that, Richard knew he was committed to proceed with this scheme which he had at first been inclined to treat as a fancy. He went into serious negotiations for a vessel of some one hundred tons, and was arranging with a certain Captain Flame to take her across the ocean.

More people were flocking to the meetings, excited by the rumours of emigration. Life was hard, and wonderful stories were circulated concerning the New World.

And then, as though momentous events could never come singly, a strange ship was one day sighted on the horizon. It was not an English ship—that much was apparent to eyes trained to look on English ships. It was a long, lean galley that cut through the water at astonishing speed and made straight for the Sound.

Bustle and excitement filled the town. Men got out their old guns, and sailors sharpened their cutlasses. But what was there to fear from one ship? Unless, of course, there were others following. The fleet was not in home waters and the sudden violent attack by the corsairs of Brittany was remembered.

Some of the old sailors declared the swiftly moving galley to be a Turk.

Tamar was on the Causeway when the galley came in. A sudden intuition had come to her; and her eyes sought one man among those lean and emaciated figures, but she could not find the one she sought.

But now the men had shipped their oars and were leaping out, embracing those about them. One of them stooped and touched the cobbles with his hands; then knelt and kissed them. In their rags of all shapes and colours, these men were scarcely recognizable as Englishmen; their skins had been burned to a dark brown; their beards were unkempt; and their bare backs showed the marks of the lash and other tortures.

And last to come ashore was the man for whom Tamar had looked. He could not remain unrecognized, this lean, emaciated giant, for his startlingly blue eyes betrayed his identity. He was laughing now; his teeth gleaming white in his lean, brown face, in which the bones seemed ready to pierce the skin. He was looking about him, and Tamar knew he was looking for her.

She ran to him. He caught her and held her; and she felt once more that excitement which she had not known since he went away.

The most bewildering and exhilarating moment of an eventful year was upon her. Bartle had come home.

* * *

He was back in his house at Stoke. Already he had lost that unkempt look. It was said that he and the men who had escaped with him were holding a prolonged feast at his house; he was going to keep them with him, for the ordeals through which they had passed together had made them his friends for ever. His cousin, who had inherited his title and estates when his father had died and he was believed lost, was still at the house, but he was preparing to leave.

Sir Bartle was the hero of the day and the toast of the county. Few men could have lived through what he had lived through; fewer still could have successfully escaped and brought his men home to safety.

It was a stirring story which Bartle and his crew had to tell. A few days out of Plymouth they had found themselves surrounded by Turkish galleys. Some of their crew were drowned, while others were taken prisoner and made to row in the galleys—a hardship such as only the strongest could endure. They were chained to the ship—six at one oar—and given only just enough food and drink to keep them alive. Any faintness or lack of energy was severely punished by the boatswain, who walked the gangway brandishing his lash, bringing it down when the mood took him, lacerating the flesh of his slaves. To this life had proud Bartle been condemned. The galleys only put to sea during the spring and summer, and in winter were laid up, when the galley slaves were confined in a foul prison until they should be needed again.

This life had Bartle and his men somehow miraculously endured for sixteen years; and during the last four Bartle had conceived and prepared the plan of escape, which, with the help of his fellow slaves, he had put into effect.

Discipline in the prison was lax; there were few jailors to be spared—and, seizing an opportunity when a galley lay provisioned for the sea just beyond the walls of their prison, the men had broken out and, experienced as they were in handling this type of craft, were able to make good their escape.

It was a story of adventure, suffering and courage, which was typical of the seamen of the time. They accepted hardship and death as natural; for, as Bartle said, there was not a man of them who did not know before he set sail that he must face them.

Tamar felt that her outlook on life had changed with the coming of the galley. She had been prepared to accept life with Humility; she had been excited by the proposed emigration. But now. . . Bartle had come home.

It was late the very same day of his return that Bartle rode over to Pennicomquick. There had been just that one embrace down on the Causeway; then the crowd had surged round Bartle and she had taken the opportunity to escape, for her one wish at that moment had been to get away, to be alone, to think of the great upheaval which had so suddenly threatened to take place in her life.

She saw him arrive and went down to meet him.

He sat his horse, looking down at her. He had trimmed his beard and was wearing some of the elegant garments which he had worn before he went away. They hung loosely on his thin frame, but they gave him great dignity.

"So," he said, his blue eyes blazing, "you married the Puritan!"

"Yes."

Then Bartle laughed and his laughter was loud and mocking.

"Why should it amuse you so?" she asked.

"Why indeed! The witch . . . and the Puritan!"

"I have three children," she said.

"I congratulate you. How many sons?"

"One son; two daughters."

"A matron now," he said.

She thought: He has not changed at all. I hate him now, just as I always did.

At that moment Ned Swann came from the stables and Bartle dismounted.

" 'Tis good to see you home, Sir Bartle," said Ned.

"Thank you, Swann," said Bartle with one of his charming smiles.

"Come into the house," said Tamar. "Richard is eager to see you and hear of your adventures."

He did not take his eyes from her as they went into the house, where Richard received him warmly.

"Bartle . . . I never thought to have this pleasure . . ."

"Nor I, sir."

"Bartle, my dear boy, come here. Let me look at you. The strength of you! To endure *that* for sixteen years!"

"I'm made of sturdy stuff. I said: 'By God and His Mother, I'll break out of this prison if I kill twenty guards to do it.'"

"And did you?" asked Tamar.

"No," he answered. "Only ten."

Humility came in, and Bartle bowed mockingly. "Why, 'tis the gardener fellow." He looked haughtily down his long nose, while his sensuous lips curled. "I remember you, fellow."

Tamar flushed. Richard said: "Have you not heard? Humility is my son-in-law."

Bartle answered insolently: "Strange things happen at home and abroad, it seems."

Then he sprawled in a chair and drank freely while he talked. He talked of his life as a galley slave, of blood and sweat and the loyalty of his men. He had hardened and coarsened during the years of slavery; his talk was spattered with violent oaths, which made Humility flinch every time they were uttered.

"Mind you," he said, "I did not suffer so acutely as some. I became a Moslem. That gave me a better life. I have scars—I could show you my back—scars that I'll carry to my grave. But I came off lightly. There were some who were beaten to death. Not me. I bowed down to Allah and saved my skin."

Tamar saw that Humility was praying. Bartle saw it too.

"What do you whisper, man?" he demanded.

"Prayers," said Humility.

Bartle was immediately truculent. "I shock you. That is so. My good fellow, you could not endure a day in the galleys, with all your prayers to help you. Why, 'twas a plaguey sight easier to arrange an escape as a good Moslem. A Christian could never have done it. By Christ, I tell you that, had I stuck to my faith and said my prayers, I and my men would be getting ready now for another season in the galleys. It was a far better thing to become a temporary Moslem than that."

"Of course!" said Tamar, looking scornfully at Humility; but as Bartle laughed she gave him a haughty stare; then it seemed to her that she was no longer a woman in her thirties, the mother of three children; she was a young girl again, trembling because a man who had once been her lover had come back.

Richard told Bartle of the proposed expedition to the New World, to which Bartle listened with great interest.

His eyes glittered as they rested on Tamar. "So you are leaving this land. You are going to seek your fortune elsewhere." He lifted his glass and kept his eyes fixed on Tamar's face. "The best of good fortune to you. May you get the good luck you deserve."

Tamar bowed her head because she feared what this man might arouse in her; she said she must leave them, as she had to see to the children. But Bartle said he wished to meet the children, and there was nothing she could do but bring them down.

Dick—who had already heard of his miraculous escape—stood before Bartle, his cheeks rosy with excitement, his dark eyes shining with admiration. Rowan climbed at once on to his knee and, when he asked for a kiss, would not stop kissing him and pulling his beard. Only little Lorea, who was different from the others, hung back shyly; but when he held out a hand and drew her to him even she was overcome by that fascination which he obviously had for all children.

Over their heads Bartle's eyes held Tamar's and they seemed to say: "These should have been ours. The Puritan should have had no hand in making them."

She hurried them away as soon as she could. She was between laughter and tears. She was alive again . . . because Bartle had come home.

* * *

She was afraid to ride out on the moors in case he should follow her there. There were too many vivid memories crowding back. She only dared talk to him when other people were present.

Each day she saw him it was brought home to her how little he had really changed. His eyes mocked her as they had mocked all those years ago. She saw their burning brightness when they rested on her; their contemptuous hatred when they looked towards Humility. One day, she thought, he will come to me with a proposition, as he did before. It will be, "If you do not . . . I will . . ." Yes; he had changed very little.

She tried to shut out from her mind all thought of anything but the expedition. She would sit with Richard and Humility making lists of provisions. It was spring, and they would sail before the summer was over.

Bartle was charming Dick and Rowan; and even Lorea could be induced to ride on his shoulders. Annis's children ran at his heels begging to be allowed to ride on his horse. They all adored him. From the windows, Tamar often watched him, sprawled on the lawn with young Dick beside him, and she knew from the absorbed expression on the boy's face that he was hearing some wild tale of the sea; and she knew that Bartle was thinking: This boy might have been mine.

How glad she was that soon they would sail away from England, away from surroundings which echoed with memories, away from Bartle.

She had lied to Humility, telling him that she was once more pregnant. She could not bear him near her now. She felt that it was better that he should keep away altogether than that, when he knelt by her bedside and prayed for her fertility, she should shout at him something which she would later regret; she might even convey to him that she found him repulsive, or confess her relationship with Bartle before their marriage.

In the quiet of her room, her window barred and bolted, she would say: "I hate the man. I was settling down peaceably before he returned, but now he is back to plague and bewilder me. What a good thing it is that soon I shall sail away and never see him again.

There is no safety from him. He bows formally, but there is nothing formal in the glances he gives me. He is planning all the time how to shame me. I can sense it!"

It was early summer. Their ship—the *Liberty*—lay in the harbour.

In her cottage Annis was packing together her most cherished possessions, telling her children of the new life which would be theirs in the wonderful land across the sea. The Swann family would be going, and forty others. Mistress Alton had begged, with many tears and much humility, to be one of the party. She was suspected of witchcraft after Jane Swann had been tortured and she had said nothing of the girl's presence in the house. What would become of her, she wanted to know, if she were left behind? The answer was obvious. She would be homeless, and to be homeless and suspected of witchcraft was a pitiable plight for any woman to find herself in.

Richard and Tamar had despised this woman; they knew her for a bigot capable of spying and great cruelty. Yet she had become a Puritan and had as much right to make the journey as any other. So even Mistress Alton was preparing to go.

And one day Richard and Humility called Tamar to them.

Richard was very excited. "It seems we have had a very narrow escape. This man, Flame, whose credentials seemed so excellent, is, I hear, nothing but a pirate. He and his men are a band of scoundrels. Their plan undoubtedly was to take us out to sea, murder the lot of us, steal our possessions and go off with the ship on errands of piracy. We have indeed had a lucky escape."

"Glory be to God!" said Humility.

"Does this mean another postponement of our journey?" asked Tamar. "It must, since we shall have to find another captain and crew. And whom can we trust? Captain Flame seemed such a good man."

"There need be no delay," said Richard. "I think we have found a captain and crew whom we can trust."

Tamar looked at him expectantly.

"Bartle," said Richard, "has promised to take the ship to the New World."

CHAPTER SIX

So the *Liberty* was to set sail with Bartle in command. Now she dipped and rose with the tide as she waited on the whim of the winds.

All that morning the last of the stores had gone aboard; legs of mutton minced and stewed and packed in butter and stored in earthen pots; roast beef in vinegar; gammons of bacon; oatmeal and fine wheat flour; wines and ales; butter; ginger; sugar; currants; prunes; cheeses; and the juice of lemons to ward off the scurvy.

The crew, the captain and the master were all on board; the chirurgeon with his physic; the cooper and the carpenter with their tools. The boatswain had tested the tackling and sails; and his mate was waiting to haul up the anchors; the cooper and the carpenter were talking together.

Tamar stood on deck with her children and Richard. Humility was leading a band of Puritans in the singing of psalms; they had just finished praying for a safe journey.

Looking back at the land where she had lived her life so far, Tamar was filled with emotion; and yet, she was not sorry to be going . . . now.

The children were hopping about beside her. Even Lorea could not keep still. Dick was shrilly pointing out the parts of the ship to Rowan. He called her attention to the sails and the rigging. His friend the boatswain had shown him the needles and twine he used for mending sails. "If we had a big storm, the sails would get torn. Then we might have to take to the boats. We may be drowned."

"I wouldn't," said Rowan. "I'd be in the captain's boat."

"So would I," cried Lorea. "I'd be in the captain's boat. So would you, Mamma, wouldn't you?"

Tamar did not answer; she was looking back at the land.

"It's hardly likely we'll get across without one big storm!" said Dick importantly.

And the girls squealed with delight.

Bartle was in deep conversation with the master of the ship.

"He's telling him how to trim his sails!" cried knowledgeable Dick. "He's telling him to what port we're going and to what height!"

Richard said: "You seem to know a good deal about sailing a ship, young Dick."

"Oh yes. Sir Bartle told me. When I grow up, I shall sail with Sir Bartle."

Tamar smiled: "Dear Richard," she said, "how glad I should be to see you as gay and carefree as the children. It has been a wrench, I fear, to sell as much of your land as you have done, and to leave your native country."

Richard shrugged his shoulders; but she knew that he was thinking he would come back home. He had not sold his house, but had handed it over to a distant cousin to hold in trust till his return. If he did not come back, the house would be his cousin's. But Richard was certain he would come back.

The children were dancing round Bartle now.

Tamar saw his hand rest lightly on Dick's shoulder. Dick was asking more of his continual questions.

Richard followed her eyes. "Do you still hate him?" he asked.

She did not answer.

"We have to remember he is our captain now," said Richard. "We have to obey him without question."

"Ah," she answered lightly. "His orders will be for his crew, not for his passengers."

They were silent. The tide was on the turn.

They heard the raucous voices of the sailors and younkers shouting to each other; they heard the singing of a shanty. Then the windlass was heaved round; anchors were being lifted; the yards braced. The sails were now set and the *Liberty* was slipping out of the Sound.

* * *

They had been two days at sea and the wind was freshening. Many of the passengers lay sick in their cabins — so sick that they wished themselves back at home.

Tamar was not sick; she had come on to the upper deck to escape the confined lower quarters and to get a breath of fresh air.

The children were below in the care of Annis; she hoped they were sleeping. Even Dick was a little tired after all the excitement of the last two days.

And as she stood there, Bartle joined her at the bulwarks.

He stood very close to her. "I always planned to make a voyage with you," he said. "But I did not think to bring your husband with us."

She did not answer, but moved away from him. He slipped his hand under her arm and drew her closer to him.

"A stiff gale," he said. "And an overgrowing sea. How like you this, Tamar?"

"It is early yet to say," she answered.

"Early indeed!" He put his lips close to her ear. "Whither are we going, you and I?"

"To the New World, I thought. That is, if you can be trusted to make the voyage."

"But where else do you think? To joy, to pleasure? To continue this miserable frustration?"

"You should know."

"So I thought, but it would seem to be you who calls the tune."

"How is that?"

His voice was hard and angry. "For sixteen years I suffered such misery, such agony, such humiliation as you cannot conceive. That would not have happened . . . but for you. But for you those sixteen years might have been spent at home . . . with you and our children. But your pride and your folly ruined not only my life, but your own. Do you think

I forget that? Do you think that I shall allow you to forget it?"

"You went to sea at your own desire," she said coldly. "You have said that you knew what risks you ran. Was it my fault that the Turks took you? Even had I foreseen it, should I have married you, loathing you?"

"You wanted me. It was only your pride that prevented your admitting it. You are a proud and foolish woman, Tamar, and I will never forgive you for what you have done to us." His voice was tender suddenly. "Why, there are tears on your cheeks."

"Tears!" she cried angrily. "It is the spray. I think I shall go down to the children."

"You will stay here."

"If I wish to go, I shall go. No one shall order me."

"*I* shall order you."

"Ah ! The Captain in command!"

"Exactly. Any who dares disobey him is clapped in irons."

"You would dare to clap me in irons!"

"If it were necessary."

She burst into laughter; he laughed with her.

"You pretend you do not wish to stay," he said, "and yet you cannot tear yourself away."

"What of your duties to your ship? Should they not be engaging your attention?"

"The ship is well looked after."

"What are your plans?"

"To take the ship to the New World."

"I meant. . . concerning yourself. . . and myself?"

She heard his deep, throaty laugh. "My plans concerning you have changed little since I first clapped eyes on you."

"I am waiting. What is it to be? 'If you do not invite me to your cabin, I shall put the whole ship's company in irons. I shall murder them all . . . or hand you over to the Turks!'"

"You put ideas into my head," he warned.

"I have a husband who shares my cabin," she reminded him.

"May God damn the Puritan!" he said. They were silent for a while before he continued: "When I was in captivity, the only way I could endure my life was by imagining another life side by side with my wretched existence. When I was working in the galleys, I pictured myself riding over green turf with you beside me, and that we laughed often together over the follies of our youth. I dreamed that we rode home to Stoke and our children came to meet us. It was a life worth living, and even you—proud as the Devil with your black witch's hair flying in the wind—were contented."

She murmured: "I am sorry for what happened to you, but the fault was not mine. It was yours . . . *yours* . . . It began that day when I was fourteen. Had you but been kind to me when I most needed kindness, ours might have been a very different story. But what use to reproach ourselves? We are as we are and nothing can change us. You are brutal, and you will always be brutal. It is no use crying for a tenderness which only kindness will nourish."

"The fault was yours!" he cried. "Do you think I could not have caught you? A little girl of fourteen! It was because I saw real fear in your eyes that I let you go. As for those nights . . . Why did I force you to do what you did? Because you were longing for me to do so. Because you deceive yourself, it is easy for others to deceive you. Do not think that you will ever escape from me. Do you think I would let your marriage to a Puritan stand in our way? I will tell you something, so that you will understand to what lengths I will go. Captain Flame is a much-maligned man. He is a good captain, a worthy man. But there could only be one captain in charge of the ship which carried Tamar away, and that was myself. So . . . I saw that this was so."

She turned and looked at him in amazement.

"Is there no end to your villainy?" she demanded.

He laughed significantly.

"Only one," he said.

* * *

They had been a month at sea, and Tamar knew with that sure intuition of hers that they were heading for emotional disaster.

Everything that Humility did or said irritated her beyond endurance. Her feeling for him was turning to hatred. She laughed inwardly to contemplate the struggle he was having with himself, confined as they were to the close quarters of their cabin. He believed her to be in a state of pregnancy and he longed for her; she would hear him, praying in the bunk above her own, and she knew she was the subject of his prayers.

It was thoughts of Bartle that disturbed her. She felt that he was in as complete a control of her destiny as he was of this ship. She knew that he was only awaiting his opportunity.

He would humiliate the Puritan whenever he could; and his crew followed his example. When Humility approached a group of sailors, their language would become a shade more obscene. Humility, now as ever conscious of his duty, had ignored their insults and their gibes and had done his best to make Puritans of them.

The conditions of life at sea were having their effects on all those unaccustomed to them. The roughness of the weather, the constant fear of sighting a hostile vessel, the monotony of the diet—all these things, though novelties at first, were beginning to upset the passengers.

The children were the happiest. They suffered less from the rigours of the weather, and as long as they had something to eat they were happy. Annis's five eldest—Christian, Restraint, Prudence, Felicity and Love—made themselves useful looking after the babies; the young ones—Charity, Patience, Joshua, Moses, Matthew, Ruth and little Miriam—played those games in which Dick was generally the leader.

And even watching the children, Tamar knew the tension was increasing. Dick was growing more and more like Bartle; this likeness was not, naturally, one of feature, but of gesture, mannerism and forthright way of speaking. Dick had begun to imitate the Captain in every way he could.

Even now at this moment, Dick was playing Captain, and he had the other children about him, to each of whom he had assigned some role as member of his crew.

Dick, rosy-cheeked, his eyes flashing, was shouting orders, and that manner of standing, legs apart, was Bartle's; that throaty voice was Bartle's.

"A sail, a sail! How stands she, to windward or leeward?"

Annis watched them with her. Annis muttered to herself and cast anxious glances at her mistress.

"And what ails you?" demanded Tamar. "You look sick and sorry, Annis. One would think you had not hoped and planned for this . . . for years . . ."

"I'll be glad enough when we touch land," said Annis, "the new land . . . Aye! I'll be glad enough then. 'Tis this long sea journey, mistress. So full of perils . . . I do shake and shiver in my bunk at night when the ship do roll and I hear the shouts of the men."

"Give chase and fetch her up!" cried Dick. "Come, man! Why do you stand gaping there. By God, I'll clap you in irons. Every man to his charge. Dowse your topsail and salute him for the sea. Whence is your ship?"

Rowan, who had been given the role of Spanish Captain cried: "Of Spain. Whence is yours?"

"Of England!" cried Dick. "Give him a broadside and run ahead. St. George for England!"

"Will you be quiet!" cried Annis. "You and your talk of Spaniards. No wonder we're all wrought up."

Dick said scornfully: "It might happen. You've got to be ready. Sir Bartle says . . ."

But Annis turned away impatiently; her fearful eyes met those of Tamar.

"The boy worships the Captain," she said; and she shivered.

"Annis," said Tamar, "what ails you?"

"You asked me that before, mistress. 'Tis just that there be something about the ship . . ."

"And its Captain?" asked Tamar.

"Aye. Its Captain and its crew. My dear life! I wouldn't care to be the one to cross Sir Bartle."

"Why not, Annis?"

"Because I believe I've seen the Devil look out of those blue eyes of his. He were always wild . . . even before he was took by the Turks, but he has grown wilder."

"It is mostly shouting," said Tamar, with an edge of scorn to her voice. "You can hear his shouting all over the ship."

" 'Tis the way of him. Is he kind to those men of his? No, he is not. He's a hard master; yet they're his men and they'd be for him, no matter what happened or what he did to them. There's magic in him. That's what I do feel . . . and it's the magic of a devil, for look how he do taunt a good man like Mr. Brown. He's put a spell on young Dick . . . and on all the children. You see how their eyes sparkle when he throws a word to them. If they can stand close to him, they're happy, even though he curses them. 'Tis a rare pity he can't be saved. He'd be a conquest for the righteous, he would, and a loss to the Devil."

"The Devil will never loosen his grip on that man!" said Tamar.

"I don't feel safe with all these rough men about," said Annis. "I've a feeling that one day . . . something will break loose. Do you see the way their eyes follow every female of us? Why, I reckon some of them men, in their time, have been to sea and ain't clapped eyes on a woman for months. 'Tis different like . . . with women aboard. And mistress, the Captain . . . he do have his eyes on someone."

"The Captain has his eyes on us all," said Tamar.

"But some more than others. There's Polly Eagel, for one."

"Polly Eagel!"

"That first baby of hers wasn't Tom Eagel's."

"Annis, please stop your tittle-tattle."

"Very well, mistress. I did hear that some of the poultry we've got penned up there on deck is pretty poorly. And there's a winnock in the litter of piglets. My dear life! Ain't there always a winnock in a litter—the little one who hasn't the strength of the others and gets crowded out like and sort of peaky?"

"Are you suggesting that the Captain and Polly Eagel . . . ?"

"Not now, mistress. That was before we sailed. Well, you do know what Polly is with that flaxen hair and baby-blue eyes of hers. Oh . . . not now. There's only one that the Captain has his eyes on now, mistress."

"Well," said Tamar. "Go on."

" 'Tis that that frightens me, mistress. His eyes gleam so in his brown face, and the way he treats Mr. Brown frightens me. 'Tain't right . . . and yet I do know what it means."

"You see too much, Annis."

"That may be so, mistress, but I do beg of 'ee to have a care. You can't play with men like Mr. Brown, because they be too good; and you can't play with men like Sir Bartle, because they be too bad. When you start playing with men like that . . . something bad comes of it. That's what I be feared of, mistress. Something . . . bad!"

"But can you doubt, Annis, that I would be able to deal with whatever might blow up between those two?"

"Nay, mistress. You have your magic, but Sir Bartle too, he have a sort of magic. He has travelled the world and seen sights we have not seen. I did hear that the way those men escaped from prison were a miracle . . . no less. I did think when I watched him shouting to the men: 'Tis the Devil himself who sails this ship! And I asks myself if he bought his freedom from the Turk by setting himself in bondage to the Devil."

"Nay!" cried Tamar, laughing with sudden wildness. "He was the Devil's own before the Turk took him!"

The children came dashing past them.

"Try the pump! We are shot through and through. The ship's on fire!"

Tamar watched them without seeing them, thinking of the Devil who looked out of Bartle's eyes.

"God be thanked!" cried Dick. "The fire is out. Look to the wounded. Swabbers, clean up the deck. Keep your berth to windward. Repair the sails and shrouds. Mend your leaks. St. George for England!"

Something will happen soon, thought Tamar. It comes closer and closer.

* * *

When many of the passengers fell sick, Tamar took it upon herself to help the chirurgeon in curing them. She had her ointments and lotions, and there were many who had greater faith in her skill than in that of the doctor. Most of the sick were suffering from the effects of too much salted food, the fetid atmosphere of some of the quarters, the general insanitary conditions. Humility suffered with the others, but he would not rest. He would go the rounds of the sick and pray with them and talk to them of what work they would be expected to do in the new land.

Bartle sought every opportunity to talk to Tamar, and everything he said convinced her that he intended to ignore her marriage and to have her for himself. There were times when she wondered if he was planning to kill Humility. He had killed many men in his life — so what would one more matter to such as he was?

Her own feelings were difficult to define. She told herself that she was sorry for Humility, that she was filled with admiration for him as he went, pale and wan, about the ship, thinking not of his own suffering, but of that of others. Yet when she was with him she seemed to take a delight in taunting him, in trying to arouse his desire for her, and then remind him of her condition, as he supposed it to be; he irritated her beyond endurance; he maddened her. Bartle, she told herself, she hated; he was a bad man; he was cruel and wicked; yet when she saw him coming towards her, her heart would beat fast with pleasure; and she knew secretly—though she would not admit this—that Bartle's presence on board the *Liberty* made the voyage exhilarating and exciting for her.

"Ah!" said Bartle to her one day, stopping her as she would have walked past him, her box of ointments in her arms. "You should not have come on such a voyage. A woman . . . who is to have a child . . ."

"Who told *you* I was to have a child?"

He smiled insolently. "People talk, you know. John Tyler's wife knows; John Tyler knows also."

"I shall thank John Tyler and his wife to be silent about my affairs. As for you . . . you need not concern yourself with pitying me."

"I do concern myself with you. I shall always concern myself with you as long as we live."

"My child will not be born on this ship!" she said.

"Sometimes journeys such as this take a little longer than we bargain for."

"Nevertheless, my child will not be born on this ship!"

"How can you be so sure?"

"I *am* sure!"

"Mr. Humility Brown praises the Lord for the continued fertility of his wife! So Annis tells us. She also tells us something else. Annis wonders if her mistress may not have made a mistake. She wonders if it may be that there will not be a child after all."

Tamar flushed crimson.

"Ah," he continued, "you must not be angry with these Tylers—such honest, simple folk! Tyler is a talkative devil, and his wife gives him little chance to talk. So when the Captain does him the honour of plying him with questions, it is not easy for him to keep to himself what the Captain wishes to know."

"How dare you discuss me with these people!"

"Have no fear. This is our little secret. Humility Brown is your husband; he is a godly man; he shares your bed for piety, not for passion. Such a good man! No love-making for Humility Brown when the purpose of love-making is achieved."

"I have always loathed your coarseness. If you wish to please me, why not mend your manners?"

"If I wish to please you! Oh, how I please you! So much that you cannot bear to have this man near you when I come home. So you tell him that you are with child, knowing such a tale would keep the pious man away!"

She pushed past him and walked away, holding her head high; but she heard his mocking laughter following her, and she was more uneasy than ever.

* * *

It was on the night of the great storm that Tamar knew how Humility suffered.

The sea had been rough all that day, and towards nightfall all passengers had been ordered below.

Tamar brought the three children into her cabin and kept them close to her. Little Lorea was trembling; even Dick was afraid. It was a different matter to experience a real storm instead of pretending. Besides, he must stay below; Bartle had ordered him there. In the storms of Dick's imagination he had been on deck, shouting orders to his crew.

"How big is this storm?" asked Rowan.

"Not so big as the one Sir Bartle told me about," shouted Dick. "That was in the Bay of Biscay."

"I'm not frightened," said Rowan.

"Who said you were?"

"Well . . . most people are. Annis and John have been praying all the afternoon. What happens when the ship founders?"

"I doubt if Sir Bartle will let it do that."

"He said it was a pox-ridden old bucket—a god-forsaken old bucket. That's what he said it was. I don't think he likes this ship."

Dick laughed. "Captains always talk like that. They love their ships all the same. If it's wrecked, we shall all go in the shallop. Perhaps we'll be picked up by pirates."

Lorea began to cry.

"Be quiet!" said Tamar to the two elder children. "It is all right, my darling. We are not going to be shipwrecked."

"How do you know, Mamma?" asked Dick.

"Because the Captain would not let us be."

She noticed that all the children were ready to accept this.

The rolling of the ship was increasing. The wind howled menacingly, and all about the frail ship *Liberty* the waters seethed and pounded her timbers.

Humility stumbled in.

"This is a terrible night, wife. A terrible night. I have just heard bad news. A man has been washed overboard."

"Man overboard! Man overboard!" shrieked Dick.

"Can't they haul him in?" asked Tamar.

Humility looked at her and did not answer; he did not wish to say before the children that it was impossible to save the man in such a sea.

"One of the sailors," said Humility. "I heard some terrible curses on his lips but yesterday. How do any of us know what is in store for us?"

Tamar thought grimly that if the storm grew worse they would have a shrewd notion of what was in store for them. The *Liberty* was a frail ship; and the strongest ships could not battle indefinitely against storms such as this.

She thought of Bartle and wondered what he was doing now. She was angry suddenly. He would know whether they were in danger or not; he would not be in suspense.

She drew her children closer to her. Lorea began to whimper; the noise and fury and the mad rolling of the ship terrified the little girl.

Humility looked from his wife to his children; he said: "We cannot kneel . . . the ship rolls too much. But God will understand if we say our prayers as we are. He will forgive us this once. Come, children. Pray with me. We will ask God, if it be His wish, to bring us safely through this night."

Tamar said: "If it be His wish, then there is no need to ask Him. And if it is not His wish . . . then it is no use asking Him either. You waste your prayers."

"I like not, wife, to hear such unseemly words on your lips . . . at such a time."

"At such a time! Would you have me snivel, then, when I am in danger? Should I ask God's help then . . . when I have not done so at other times?"

"You wilfully misunderstand."

"No!" she cried. "I understand too well."

Yes, she was thinking, I understand that I hate you, husband. That I am ashamed to have married you and borne your children. It is Bartle I want . . . and I want him as passionately as he wants me. I may not love him. What a fool I was to wait for love! And what a time is this for thinking such thoughts! Who knows . . . in a moment . . . in an hour . . . before morning this ship may be rent in two and my body and Bartle's at the bottom of the sea.

And yet, looking at her husband, gripping the bunk against the heaving of the ship, while his eyes were shut and his lips moving in prayer, great waves of hatred seemed to flow over her—as great and inescapable as the wind that tore at the rigging of the ship and the waves that pounded her sides with malevolent determination to destroy her.

He had opened his eyes and she noticed that he glanced at her and quickly turned away.

He was thinking that she seemed younger than she had for some time—more like the girl she had been before the children were born, the girl who had watched him work in the gardens and had taunted him. Now her cheeks were flushed, her hair in disorder. She refused to cover it or braid it. He knew that she was goading him, luring him to sin. She was tempting him because she knew that the Devil was at his elbow whispering to him as he had once whispered to Jesus. The Devil was showing him his wife as he had shown Jesus the kingdoms of the world. "She is your wife," said the Devil. "Is it then carnal lust for a man to go with his wife?" "For such as I!" was his answer. "For such as I." "She is your wife, your wife . . ." persisted the voice in the darkness. "It was solely because I wished to procreate children for the New World that I took this woman, and I took her not for her beauty, but because she had a wayward soul which must be under constant surveillance, because she has a good, strong body that was obviously meant for the bearing of children. There was no lust . . . no lust . . ."

But when she looked at him with those smouldering lights in her eyes, she was telling him, "Humility, you deceive yourself. Lust there was, and one day you will stand before the throne of Almighty God and you will have to admit it."

He shut his eyes, shut out the sight of her beauty and her wildness and the wanton knowledge in her eyes. He prayed that the ship might weather the storm, that all might be saved to lead good lives in the promised land; and he prayed that he might overcome the temptation which this sensuous, wanton woman was holding out to him; he asked for the salvation of the ship, but his secret prayer was for the salvation of his soul.

* * *

After the storm there were a few days of calm. Now there was hardly a ripple on the water; and the sky was the same colour as the Captain's eyes. The boatswain and his mate sat on deck mending and patching the sails, repairing all the damage which the storm had wrought; the cooper and his mate were busy on their tasks. The cook and the steward were preparing delicacies, on the Captain's orders, for some of the sick among passengers and crew: a little buttered rice flavoured with sugar and cinnamon, a few stewed prunes, or minced mutton and roast beef.

Humility was holding a meeting on the top deck. Tamar could hear them, singing the psalms with feeling. They had come through the storm safely; they were still limp from fear and exhaustion. But this, said Humility, was a sign. The Lord had intended that they should make their homes in the promised land.

Bartle came and stood beside Tamar.

She turned and looked at him. "Rice with sugar and cinnamon!" she said. "And for your most humble sailors. It is a surprise to me to see that you could show such consideration."

"It is no pampering. Merely good sense. Those fellows—wet to the skin, shaking with cold—would fall into a raging fever but for the few comforts I can give them. Such delicacies as buttered rice and mince-meat, green ginger, a little fresh water brewed with sugar, ginger and cinnamon—to say nothing of a little good sack—can save a man's life. Whereas, give him salt fish with oil and mustard or salt and peas . . . and he'll not rally. Such fare is good indeed for ordinary occasions, but after such a storm, if I wish to keep my men with me, I must treat them to their delicacies. This crew of mine is too precious—every man of it—to risk such loss. What if we run into further storms? What if we meet with our enemies? Nay, mere common sense. God! How the preacher rants! Tamar, Tamar, why did you marry him?"

She turned away, but he laid a hand on her arm and, although she tried to shake it off, she could not do so.

"Life at sea," he continued, "is full of dangers. We should have stayed at home . . . both of us . . . Oh, not now. Seventeen years ago."

"How you hark back! I prefer to look forward."

"And so do I now. When, Tamar? *When*?"

"I do not understand you."

"You hold him off. You want me. But what is the use of wanting if we do nothing to ease our desire?"

"As I told you years ago, you have a great conceit of yourself."

"It is justified."

"Are you sure of that?"

"I am. You cannot bear to have him near you, so you lie to him. You tell him you are with child. And you lied for me. Oh, Tamar, I have gone without you too long."

"You might try Polly Eagel for a substitute."

"Who?"

"You feign ignorance, but I know of your adventures. I said Polly Eagel."

"I know her not."

"It is idle to pretend to me that you have not been her lover. I suppose you would have me believe that you have forgotten."

"It matters not whether or no you believe it. It is so. There have been so many, Tamar."

"And you think I should be happy to join such a crowd!"

"Whether you are happy joining it or not, you have already done so."

"There! You see, I can but hate you. You taunt me. You mock me. How could I love such as you?"

"And yet you do."

"Leave me, I beg of you."

"Not till you have heard my plan."

"What plan is this?"

"A plan for us two."

"Such a plan could not interest me."

"You repeat yourself. You have said that to me before."

"Then you invite repetition. You tire me. I pray you, leave me."

"And I pray you, Tamar, for your own sake, not to anger me. When I am truly in a rage, I am incapable of controlling my anger. You *will* listen to me. This is my plan. We shall reach our destination; our passengers will disembark; and you and I, with your children—and Richard if he wishes it—will sail for home. We will leave your husband here with his pilgrims. He shall have them and, as a reward for bringing him safely to port, I shall have you."

"An interesting plan," she said coldly. "But, as I told you, you would be foolish to include me in any plans you might make."

He came closer to her. "I would have you know that I am tired of waiting. We cannot go on like this. One of us . . . will . . . quite soon . . . do something to end this intolerable state of affairs."

She had begun to tremble. She could not meet his eyes, so she stared beyond him, across the translucent water.

*   *   *

It was night and there was tension throughout the ship. Even the sailors were subdued and spoke in whispers.

There were no lights on deck, nor on masts, nor at portholes. The Captain had ordered it so.

"Anyone showing a light," he had bellowed, "be it man, woman or child, will be clapped in irons."

At dusk a ship had been sighted on the horizon, and every seafaring man aboard had known her for a Spaniard.

Below, the passengers muttered together. The old ship was limping along, for she had suffered some damage in the storm. She was not equipped to fight; she carried men and women in search of a home, not a battle and plunder; stores and furniture instead of ordnance. And Catholic Spaniards could strike as deep a note of terror in any heart as could the barbarous Turk.

Annis came to Tamar's cabin, breathless in her agitation. Tamar could hear her panting in the darkness. Poor Annis! She was getting old; she had borne too many children, and of late there had been a bluish tinge about her lips when she was out of breath. Tamar remembered her suddenly as a little yellow-haired girl who had looked in at the Lackwell cottage door and put out her tongue. When death was near, she supposed, you thought back over the past.

Annis said, "Mistress, Mr. Brown is preaching to some on the lower deck. He be a very brave man, for if the Spaniards take him, it'll be burning alive after months of torture that'll be his lot. Sir Bartle—he's on the upper deck. He did ask me to bring you to him there, as he has something to say that is important. He says not to fail . . ."

Tamar put her cloak about her and went on deck. It was a cloudy night with a light fresh breeze which hustled the clouds every now and then bringing a group of stars into view. Bartle had seen her and came swiftly to her side.

"Tamar?"

"Yes, Bartle?"

"Thank God for the dark of night."

"Yes, thank God."

He put an arm about her and she did not resist; she thought of the mighty galleon that might at this moment be sailing towards them.

He said: "With the dawn we shall know. But there is some hope. She may not have seen us. I have changed our course. Tamar, you must not be taken by the Spaniards. Better that you should die by my hand than that."

"Yes," she answered firmly.

"Keep close to me, my love. When the dawn breaks, I wish you to be at my side. We never lived together, and it may be that now we never shall. But we can die together; and that we will do." He had moved his hand up her arm, caressing it. He drew her to him and kissed her with such tenderness as she had never known in him before. "What," he went on, "an unholy mess we have made of our lives! But it is too late for regrets now." He kept his arm about her. "You do not move away from me. I wish I could see your eyes. They are soft and tender, I'll warrant. They do not now flash with pride and anger."

"No," she said. "I do not move away from you now."

"And never will again?"

She did not answer, and he went on: "Tell me that marriage of yours was no true marriage."

"There are children to prove it," she said.

"There may be only a few hours left to us. Let them be truthful hours. What did you feel when you heard that I was lost?"

"Desolation. Yes; I know now that it was desolation. I sought for peace, and I thought that I should find it with Humility Brown."

"As we are given life here on Earth we are surely meant to live it. Why should we be born into this world with its trials and problems if we are to spend our time thinking only of another?"

"Oh," she said, "you are a pagan."

"I should never have thought of that if you had let me live my life. We should have married, done our duty to our line and home. We should have brought our children up to obey the Church and State. You are the pagan, and you have made a pagan of me."

They were silent and she felt his lips on her hair. Then he went on: "Where are we going, you and I? To death when the dawn comes? That will be easy. That will be quick. But if it is not death, what then, Tamar? Where are we going then?"

"We cannot think beyond the morning."

"Why can you be only gentle and truthful with me when we may have to die?"

"Why are *you* different now?"

"Oh, Tamar, let us think of what might have been! Seventeen years ago we had a chance to live. I went to slavery and torture; you to slavery of another kind; but both of our own choosing. We might have been together in our home. We might be there . . . now. Think you that any grass is as green as Devonshire grass, any air as temperate? Nowhere in the world is the sea quite the same colour as that which breaks about our shores. Nowhere else does the mist rise up—so soft and warm—and disappear so suddenly to let the sunshine through, the warm and kindly sun that never burns too fiercely. Yet you threw that life away. You banished me to slavery and yourself to life with a Puritan. I could hate you, Tamar, if I did not love you."

"I could hate you too," she said, "if I did not love you."

They kissed with passion now; and she saw herself regaining all that she had carelessly thrown away; she knew that their kisses were a pledge for the future . . . if they lived through the next day.

She heard Bartle laugh suddenly, and it was a laugh she remembered well.

"Tamar," he said, "we cannot die. We must defy the Spaniard. We have powder and shot, arms and fireworks. We'll give an account of ourselves. You will go to your cabin, take your children with you. You will stay there until I come. For come I will. I promise you I'll fight as I never fought before. I'll not die when I am just about to begin my life with you."

She clung to him. "We must not die. Of course we must not die!"

When dawn broke the whole ship's company was on deck.

Eager eyes scanned the horizon.

The Spaniard had disappeared.

*   *   *

The ship was moving forward.

"How long before we sight land?" Each member of the crew was asked this question every day.

"A week mayhap. Perhaps more . . . perhaps less."

A week! When they had been nearly three months afloat. Excitement ran high. All around them was the heaving water, but any day now land might be sighted.

The map which Captain Smith had made over ten years ago was studied with eagerness. The very names delighted them: Plymouth, Oxford, London; the river Charles and Southampton; and farther along the coast there were Dartmouth, Sandwich, Shooters Hill and Cape Elizabeth. Such names truly had a homely ring.

"See this point, Cape James. That was first called Cape Cod; it was named after the fish that abound there. We shall have fresh cod instead of salted herrings. There will be meat too. No more danger from pirates. No more fear of being captured by the Spaniards or the Turks . . . or the Dutch . . . or the French."

"What of the savages that were first here?"

"Oh . . . a friendly people. Did you not see the little Princess when she came to Plymouth?"

Tamar's uneasiness had grown since that night of fear. Bartle filled her thoughts — not this new country. She had avoided him since that night of mutual understanding, but she could not continue to do so. She could not banish Humility from her thoughts.

What had she done on that night? She had exposed her secrets to Bartle; she could no longer deny her feelings for him.

Yet she had her children. She was married to Humility Brown. How could she return to England with Bartle?

Humility was aware of the change in her. Her temper with him was shorter than ever; she seemed again and again to be endeavouring to make their life more difficult by picking quarrels.

If he were not such a good man, Tamar told herself, I should not feel I wronged him so deeply and I should not hate him so fiercely.

But hate him she did; she wished he were dead. What an easy way out his death would give them. She watched him speculatively. He looked very ill; the journey had tired him, strained him beyond his strength, for he was not a robust man. He fasted a good deal and she believed he did this as a penance; she believed he had been thinking what he would call "evil thoughts," and these thoughts would be concerned with herself.

Perhaps, thought Tamar, he is not such a good man as he thinks himself to be. If I could prove that to him I should not feel I wronged him so deeply in doing what I long to do.

The more she thought of him, the more irresistible was the desire to show him and herself that he was no better than other men. As the ship drew nearer to the New World, she thought continually of this.

One evening, when they were in their cabin, he looked at her intently and said: "Tamar, what has come over you? You have been slowly changing as we have made this journey. You have become more and more like the wild girl you were before your conversion. I feel you have need of guidance. I beg of you to let me give it to you."

"*I* . . . in need of guidance!" she cried. "Look at me! I am well. I never felt better. You look like a death's head. It may be *you* who need guidance from *me*!"

"I was speaking of spiritual guidance. The health of your body is good. But what of the health of your soul?"

Then came the climax to which she afterwards believed the whole of her life with Humility had been leading.

It was a calm night and she was lying in her cabin when Humility came in, as was his custom, to kneel and say a prayer before scrambling into the bunk above hers.

As she watched him, she was sure the Devil was with her, for she decided that now was the time to show him that, for all his fine words and great ideals, he was a man as other men were. She would make him see that he was a man, as Bartle was; the difference being that Bartle strode about the ship not caring who saw him for what he was; whereas Humility hid his inclinations with a cloak of piety. She had vowed she would tear that cloak from him; she would expose him, not only before her eyes, but his own. Then perhaps he would cease to mutter his prayers over her, to offer her guidance, to say in his heart, "Thank God I am not as other men!"

"Humility," she said; and she stretched out a hand to him.

The gentleness of her voice surprised him. The rushlight showed enough of her beauty to excite him. Her long wild hair fell about her shoulders and her breasts were bare.

"Wife," he said hoarsely, "does aught ail you?"

She took his hand. "I know not. Except it may be that I am not a wife. I am treated as a woman to have children, not as one to be loved. You pray before you embrace me. 'Make this woman fertile!' This woman! Fertile! Those are not lovers' words. I am not loved as other women."

"I have loved you," he said. "I do love you . . . as is meet for a man to love his wife."

She leaned forward and, smiling alluringly, put an arm about him.

"You *have* loved me with passion," she said.

He closed his eyes and she laughed inwardly at his cowardice. "I was dedicated to the Lord," he said. "Marriage was not for me. I had eschewed the lusts of the flesh. God blessed our union. Have we not had three children, and is not another on the way?"

She put her lips against his ear and whispered: "I wish to be loved for myself . . . not for the children I may bear."

"You are in great need of prayer, wife."

"Not I!" she said and her voice held a note of excited laughter. "But *you* are, Humility. Pray now. Stay close to me and pray."

"You are a temptress," he said.

"You must not be a coward, Humility. You must look at me. My nights are lonely because I have a husband who thinks of children and not of his wife."

"Why do you tempt me thus?" he asked wonderingly.

"Why indeed! Why do men tempt women or women men? Come nearer, Humility, and I will tell you. I have been left alone too long."

A madness seemed to possess her. Bartle and I are no worse than he is! she thought. None of us is very good . . . no one very bad. I'll not have him thanking God that he is better than others. He shall see here and now that he is not.

She did not love him; she hated him. She did not desire him; he was repulsive to her. But what at this moment she needed beyond love or desire was to show him the truth about himself.

"Come closer, Humility," she murmured.

* * *

She had not known how desperately he had fought against what he considered to be sin. He was no hypocrite, for firmly he believed all that he professed to believe.

She watched him staring blankly before him—his face pale in the wan light.

The desire to mock him was uncontrollable. "So, a man is a man even though he be a Puritan. He knows the same lusts as other men, and when tempted, he can fall just as others."

He covered his face with his hands.

"Would I had died *before* this happened. All the years of purity. . . wiped out . . . by a single act!"

She cried heatedly: "Do not deceive yourself. The temptation never arose before. If it had, you would have fallen into it. When you went to your attic, I was glad that you should go. I made no effort to detain you. If I had wished you to remain . . . if I had wished you to be my lover, have no doubts that you would have been. I beg of you, say no more, 'I am a better man than this one and that one.' For you are not! And it is better for a sinner to say, 'I am a sinner,' than for him to say, 'I am a righteous man!'"

His lips moved in prayer, but she could not stop her tongue.

"You ask the Lord to forgive you. For what? I am your wife. Why should it be righteous to shun me? Stop it! See yourself as you are. A man . . . no more, no less. You are a brave man, but others are brave. You are a Puritan, but others are Puritans. You are lustful, and so are other men. There is as much joy for you in your plain garments as there is for me in my colours and silks and velvets. You are not different from others. Know this: If at any time I had tempted you as I did to-night, you would have fallen. Do not judge others lest you be judged yourself."

He did not seem to be aware of her. He murmured: "I am unworthy. I have shown myself to be unworthy. I have fallen from God's grace and there is no health in me."

He went out and she lay thinking of him. Now he would know himself. When she told him of her future plans he would not be able to talk of her sin, for if he did she would remind him of his. Some would say he had not sinned, but he believed he had; and surely sin was in the motive rather than the deed.

But later she softened towards him. He was a good man; he was even a noble man. Perhaps when she saw him again she would try to persuade him that there could be no sin in normal acts. She would say to him: "If God did not wish us to act so, why should He have given us desires?" She feared she would not be able to comfort him, but the next time she saw him she would try.

She never saw Humility again.

John Tyler was the last to see him alive.

"It were early morning," said John. "I couldn't sleep, so I came on deck to see what I could see. I thought mayhap I should be the first to sight land. And there he was . . . Mr. Brown . . . leaning over the side, looking at the water. I said: 'Good morning to 'ee, Mr. Brown. A fine good morning.' But he answered me not, and it did seem to me that he were in deep communion with the Lord. I wouldn't be the one to interrupt him at that, so I passed on. I took a look at the pigs and the poultry penned up there. I looked round. He were still there . . . but a minute later when I did glance over my shoulder, he'd gone. I stared like. There was no sign of him. He couldn't have gone below in the time. Then I was struck all of a tremble . . . for something did tell me that he had gone overboard.

"Well, you do know the rest. I raised the alarm, but 'twas too late. No sign of him . . . and the ship travelling fast before a strong wind."

Humility Brown . . . lost! The news spread through the ship. A terrible and most shocking accident. There was sincere mourning among the Puritans for one whom many considered their leader. But there was none who mourned him so deeply as did his wife.

Her guilt lay heavily upon her.

She blamed herself. I sent him to his death as surely as if I pushed him over the side. There will never be happiness for me, since, when I stretch out to take it, he will be there to remind me of my sin. I cannot escape my guilt, because I wanted him out of the way. I believe I knew that he would do this thing if I offered him a temptation which he would be unable to resist.

But even the tragic loss of Humility Brown was forgotten when land was sighted. At last, before these sea-weary people lay the promised land. But Humility, like Moses, was denied the sight of the land for which he had longed.

For ever this sense of guilt will lie on my conscience! thought Tamar.

CHAPTER SEVEN

To look on a strange land which might become home should he a wonderful experience. Tamar stood on deck with Richard and Bartle beside her, and gazed at the coastline which, as they grew nearer, became more and more distinct.

The *Liberty* was anchored now, and galleys and shallops were coming out to meet and greet her. The sailors were lowering the ship's own boats. A group of people was assembling on the shore, eager and excited, for the coming of friends from home was a great occasion indeed.

It was impossible not to experience a feeling of pride to be one of this band of adventurers; but it seemed to Tamar, as she stood there, that a shadowy figure was beside her—a thin man in wet garments and with a look of bewildered horror in his eyes.

She turned at once to look at Bartle. His eyes gleamed. He was the true adventurer, eager for new sights. From Bartle her eyes went to Richard, and she saw in his face the hope that he might play a useful part in this founding of a new community.

How wonderful it was to set foot on *terra firma* after all those months at sea, to be free from the stale smell from below decks which seemed for ever in the nostrils in spite of the fresh sea air! How pleasant to smell the air which had blown across meadow and forest!

Eagerly they were taken to the settlement, where the Elders of the Church and the Governor himself came to welcome them. The settlement consisted of one street which stretched for just over a thousand feet up the slope of a hill from the sandy beach. The houses were roughly made of hewn planks, but each had its garden reminding all the newcomers suddenly and poignantly of home. And even as they looked along that street—the result of much loving toil, hopes and hardship—they noticed the square enclosure in which cannons were mounted, so placed that they could, at a moment's notice, defend the street against attack from any direction. They had not done with danger; they knew that. There would be perils ashore to vie with those of the sea.

But now was the time for rejoicing. Friends from home were in the settlement, and although most of the newcomers were strangers to those who had already made their home in this spot, this was like a family reunion. Tamar herself remembered some of these men, for she had met them before the sailing of the *Mayflower*. Prominent among these were Captain Standish, Edward Winslow and Governor Bradford.

They asked after Humility, and she found she was too overcome by emotion to speak of him to them. Richard spoke for her.

"It was a terrible accident. A great shock to us all. And such a tragedy that it should have happened the night before land was sighted. For years he had thought and worked for this."

"Doubtless," said Governor Bradford, "it was the will of God."

And then, before food was prepared to welcome the newcomers, thanks must be given to God for their safe arrival.

It was an impressive scene—the ship's company and the settlers gathered there together on the beach at the bottom of Leyden Street, while the Elders gave thanks and all the population joined in the hymns of praise and glory to God.

After the service of thanksgiving, there was bustle and activity throughout the little township. The newcomers should see what Puritan hospitality meant. There was great delight when it was learned what the ship carried. Poultry! Pigs! Gold could not have pleased them more.

This was indeed a special occasion. Each housewife was busy in a little house, preparing her contribution to the feast of welcome. The newcomers were divided up among the households, and each woman vied with the others in providing a feast of feasts. No mere hasty pudding for the guests! No maize cakes or codfish! Nothing would suit the occasion but the great festivity dish of beans baked with pork and succotash.

There were so many wonderful things to be seen while the feast was in preparation. The children were running wild about the place, lifting handfuls of sand

and letting it trickle through their fingers, gazing with longing eyes towards the forest, aching to explore after months of confinement at sea. The settlers' children watched gravely, and some joined in; those who remembered home asked many questions.

The grown-ups talked; they could not stop talking; they talked of the first terrible winter, when more than half their number had died; they talked of the fire which had almost been a final disaster. Mr. Carver and Mr. Bradford, who had been sick in bed at the time, had all but lost their lives as well as their homes. Ah! That had been a terrible time—and all because of a spark that lighted the thatch of a cottage. But the Lord had looked after them; terrible tribulations had been theirs, but they had come through with His help and His grace.

Talk went on and on; and it was talk that raised laughter and tears—laughter for the tragedies which had brought sorrow at the time, but, in retrospect, could amuse; sorrow for the loss of so many who now lay buried in the New England soil. They told of the making of the plantation; of how they trapped fish in the shallow, rapid river which could be seen from where they stood, emptying itself into the sea; they told how they had discovered that the maize, which they needed so badly, would not grow in the sandy, stony soil until they had planted fish from the sea in the land; then did the maize grow in abundance.

Fish! The newcomers would soon realize that there never was such fish as that which abounded in the neighbourhood of Cape James. There was the

Cape itself, clearly to be seen on such a bright day as this. It was shaped like an arm crooked about a corner of the sea. They would see that the cod found in these parts were twice as large as those found elsewhere. What labour that saved in hooking and splitting! Oh, the Lord was looking after them. In the summer, besides the cod, came mullet and sturgeon. And what caviare and puttargo could be made from the roes! The savages said that the fish in these waters could be compared in numbers with the hairs on men's heads.

Fruit there was in plenty—mulberries, gooseberries, plums, strawberries, pumpkins and gourds; walnut and chestnut trees abounded in the forests; flax grew freely, and from it they were able to make the strongest of ropes and nets. Then there were beavers and otters, foxes and martens—and in the Old Country good money was paid for the skins of such animals.

It was indeed a "land flowing with milk and honey."

Oh, but those first months! Not then had the fruits of this land been discovered. Meat and meal had been sadly missed; there were too few clothes and bedding; no yarn for lamps; no oiled paper for the windows of the houses which must be built. The cruel cold had overtaken them, had found them unready; but their determination had been stronger than the harsh winds and bitter snows. They would never, they vowed, return to England or Holland; they had vowed to make this country their own, to build a new freedom in a new land; and this, with the help of God, they were doing.

The first settlers had discovered during their second winter that the first winter had been a mild one; then, in spite of the winds and snow they had had to endure, they knew that God was with them, for if they had been obliged to face a normal winter during their first months in the new land, not merely half of the new colony would have perished, but the whole of it.

There was much to tell, so much to listen to. They must tell of the great day of Thanksgiving when Governor Bradford had decided there should be a feast. It should be a sober feast—a solemn rejoicing, a means of showing gratitude to the Almighty for having brought them through great trials.

So Governor Bradford sent men into the forest to kill wild fowl, and there was rejoicing for three whole days.

The Puritans smiled in delighted reminiscence.

"My friends, what think you? Massasoit came to the feast. Massasoit was an Indian chief who had become our friend through the Grace of God and the diplomacy of our Governor and Captain Standish—and mayhap by the sight of our cannon. There was dancing and singing, and we were much put out, as you can guess, for this was a solemn feast, a tribute to Almighty God; and here in our midst were savages worshipping their own heathen gods . . . barbarians and pagans, showing us their dancing, their faces painted, their bodies all but naked. But we trust the Lord understood that they were our guests and that we must humour them. And their dancing and their nakedness was apart from the thankfulness which was in our hearts."

Now to the feast. The pork and beans and fowls cooked together tasted delicious. There was ale and gin to drink; and when they had eaten and drunk they got into little groups and talk broke out once more; and now most of this talk was of home—not the new home, but the home across the sea to which most of them had said farewell for ever.

Yes, it was a wonderful country to which they had come, but they thought of home continually. Here there was fish in abundance—lobsters, clams and oysters besides cod and mullet—but how often did they think of the rich red beef of England and good English ale! Nostalgia was like a disease; it attacked some more than others. Some had died, it was believed, of melancholy, because they missed the richly green fields of England.

Tamar, watching it all, was fired with enthusiasm. She wanted to live here among these brave men and women; she visualized a town which was not merely a street with its plantation and its little houses; she visualized a town—a great town where there was friendship for all, and no cruelty, no brutality. . . but freedom. Yes, freedom was the most important thing—freedom to live one's own life, to think one's own thoughts.

They went back to the *Liberty* to sleep, as there was not sufficient accommodation in the settlement.

Bartle talked to her when they were back on the ship.

"A noble venture that!" he said. "But not for us."

"Why not?"

"Pagans cannot make their homes with Puritans."

"Anyone can hope for freedom," she said. "Why should we not become Puritans?"

"You know that we never could be."

"They are a wonderful people. When I think of their arriving and seeing it, not as we see it now, but just a waste land, a sandy bank about which the water breaks . . . a gentle hill on which to build a town, and the forests in the distance in which the savages abound! What had they but their courage and a sea full of fish! I wish I had been one of them in the beginning."

"What has come over you?" he asked. "You change from one day to another. Have you forgotten that night when we thought the Spaniard was upon us? Then you promised that we should be together. You would leave your husband and come back with me. Now that he is gone, that surely makes everything easier for us. We need not consider him now."

"We have to consider him," she said dully.

"You talk in riddles."

"No. He is dead and I killed him."

"*You* . . . killed him!"

She blurted out an account of what had happened in the cabin on the night before Humility's death.

He was scornful. She was fanciful, he said.

"He killed himself. What nonsense is this! He killed himself because he lacked the courage to live."

"I killed him," she said stonily. "Almost in sight of the land he had longed for."

"You deceive yourself. As usual, your emotions cloud your vision. You think with the heart . . . not with the mind. How could you know that he would kill himself? Why did he kill himself? Because he lacked the courage to live. He brooded so continually on sin, that he saw it where it was not. Think no more of him. He was a weak man. If God decided he should not come to this land, then it was because he was unworthy. This is a land for brave men and women."

"I feel that there is a great weight about my neck. I killed him, and I must pay for my sin. I can find no happiness until I do. I knew that to-day, when I listened to what these people had to tell. If I stay here, if I try to do Humility's work, then I shall in some measure atone for my sin."

He turned on her angrily. "I do not know you. What of us? What of our life together . . . the life you promised me if we should escape the Spaniard to enjoy it? Why is it that when the road is clear for us you must build up these obstacles?"

"I am not young and foolish any more . . . not the woman to be excited by a lover."

He took her into his arms. "I will soon alter that!" he said grimly.

But she was determined. "Leave me alone for a while. I wish to think of this. I do not understand my feelings. Just now I can see nothing but his poor white face, his eyes so sorrowful, looking into mine. I can hear only my own voice saying cruel, brutal things to him; they cut into his heart like a knife; and they were the instruments that killed him."

Bartle turned from her in a passion. He was speechless with anger. He strode away from her.

She went back to her cabin and looked about her with fearful eyes, and it seemed to her that the spirit of Humility Brown was in that cabin. She lay sleepless, turning from one side to another in a vain effort to reach sleep.

It was dawn before she dozed; and then she dreamed that Humility was in the cabin, the water dripping from his sombre garments, while his hair hung dank about his death-pale face.

"Only by a life of piety," said the spirit of Humility, "can you atone for your sin."

* * *

Early next morning Richard came to her cabin.

"Do I disturb you, Tamar?"

"No."

"But you look tired. You have scarcely slept. I have slept little myself. Yesterday was a day I shall remember all my life."

"And I," she said.

"Tamar, you are going to be happy here."

She shook her head, but he did not notice; he seemed to be looking beyond her into a future which pleased him.

"When I saw the town they had made," he went on, as though speaking to himself, "I was filled with emotion. Their simple houses . . . small, bare and only just adequate. But think! They must first have cut the trees before they could begin to build. Winslow was telling me that in those days they worked from sunrise to sunset, felling, sawing and carrying timber. He told me that, before the building could begin, many of the men fell sick, and some died. Those who were well enough worked when the weather would allow them. They worked with a will. I would I had been one of them. These men will be remembered as long as men are remembered. And what impresses me most is that on that first Sabbath day, although the need to get those houses built was great, greater still was their faith and their belief that the Sabbath day should be kept holy. There was no work on the first Sunday. I picture them; they had no meeting house—no house at all. I can see them giving thanks in the open air. Tamar, there is a greatness in these men which I have never seen before. Often I have thought I could worship the Carpenter's Son. It was not His own simple doctrines which I could not accept; it was the various complicated versions laid down by different Churches which I rejected one by one. But surely this simple life—this life of goodness and restraint—is the true life. The religion these men brought with them is the true religion."

"I feel you may be right," said Tamar.

"These first settlers were bolder than the Puritans we have known. The large majority of them spent years of exile in Holland. They did not wish merely to simplify the ritual of the existing Church, but to form a new one. That was why it was first of all necessary to fly the country; then to form a new community of their own."

"You wish to become one of them, Richard. I think that is what I wish. To work with them, to watch a great town grow here, a town where there is kindness instead of brutality, freedom to take the place of persecution. I wish to live here simply, as these people do. I *must* do that, because Humility did not live to do it."

Now Richard was watching her closely.

"I have been thinking of you . . . and Bartle," he said.

"What of us?"

"That you would now doubtless marry. He loves you and I believe you love him."

"I do not know," she said.

"You must be happy here, Tamar. It is necessary that you should be. You must make Bartle happy here. You need him, for I do not believe you can be happy without him. I think too that, although it is difficult for us to imagine him in this place, living the life of a Puritan, he may attempt it . . . for your sake. He could go back to England; he could resume the life which would naturally be his, the country squire, the lord of the manor. But, Tamar, you dare not go back. They would have taken you some time or other had you stayed. I always knew it. I was never at peace thinking of it. It might not have been for years . . . but do it they would. One day they would have hanged you. They would never have forgotten that you had the reputation of being a witch. That was why I agreed to come here. I knew you would never be safe at home."

"Yes," she said. "I felt that too. They looked at me slyly. They were awaiting their opportunity, waiting to find me defenceless. I often pictured them, coming to take me, as they came to the house that day, Simon Carter leading the way. And not myself only. There is poor Jane Swann. They would have had her. Perhaps even Mistress Alton and you, Richard. None of us was safe. And John Tyler and Annis, and Annis's children . . . they might have been taken for their religion."

"It is all religious persecution," said Richard vehemently. "You persist in believing yourself of the witch community because of an old religion whose rites and remedies have become known to you. It is all persecution. Religious persecution . . . from which we are escaping."

"Richard, I know I must stay. I must drive the Devil out of my soul."

Richard sighed. "So even now that you are a woman and a mother of children, you believe in black magic?"

"I know I am of the Devil," she said. "That is why I have murder on my soul." She went on before he could interrupt. "There is much that you do not know of me. I am full of wickedness. So is Bartle. That is why we cannot resist each other. He is brutal and cruel, barbarous and murderous. I am the same. Yes, I am. Let me explain; then you will understand. Bartle was my lover . . . years and years ago. I did not want him to be, but he forced that on me. Not as it almost was on that occasion when you saved me . . . but more subtly. And I—I know now—was secretly delighted that this should be so. I deceived myself into thinking that I hated him, but that was not so. Then I married Humility. I had no right to marry Humility. It was the Devil who persuaded me to do it. I see that now. If I had married Bartle, I should have had no influence over Humility. Bartle belonged to the Devil already and it was Humility's soul the Devil wanted."

"What are you saying, Tamar? You are hysterical."

"You think you are wise, Richard. So you are . . . wise in book-learning. But you know nothing of women like me. I saved Humility's life and I was proud of that; and it seemed to me that because I had saved it, that life belonged to me. I know now that that was the Devil whispering in my ear. I deceived myself into thinking that my soul was saved, so that my marriage should not seem incongruous. I see it all so clearly now—my cruelty, my barbarity. You know what happened. Then Bartle came home. Of course I wanted Bartle. We were of a kind. We quarrelled; we hated; and we loved each other madly. It was always like that. And coming over on the ship I knew that I wanted Bartle and I wanted my children . . . but I did not want Humility—so I killed him!"

"You are not talking sense, Tamar. John Tyler saw the end of Humility."

"John Tyler was there when he fell overboard. But why did he fall overboard? There was no reason for it. It was a calm morning. Why should he have fallen overboard? He deliberately went over; he killed himself because I had seen to it that his life was impossible to live."

"I can see that you are working yourself into a passion of grief. It was no fault of yours that he went overboard. He loved you; you had given him children; you were accompanying him to the land he had always longed for. His dearest dreams were all about to be realized."

"I killed him, I tell you! I taunted him to his death! His prayers angered me, hurt my pride in myself. It was not for love of me that he had married me. He told me that continually. . . not for the love of my body but for the sake of the children we must have to populate the colony. I could not bear it, so I proved to him that he was as lustful as any man, that he deceived himself but he did not deceive me. Then I taunted him. He was, I told him, not only a sinner, but a hypocrite. The truth was too much for him. He believed he was going to eternal damnation. He was guilty of one of those seven deadly sins about which he was always preaching—Lust. All the years he had been practising lust—not as Bartle practised it, boasting, swaggering, showing himself to the world for what he was. No! He practised it under a cloak of piety. . . under cover of darkness. Those were the words I used to him. And so he went out and killed himself."

Richard took her by the shoulders and shook her gently. "Tamar, what are you saying? I am going to get you a glass of spirits. Then I am going to make you lie down. I am going to make you rest and, when you have recovered, I shall talk to you. You have let yourself become overwrought by this terrible tragedy. You have been over-excited by the last few days. When I have talked to you, you will see this more clearly. Humility's death was an accident. He would never have killed himself because of what you call a lustful act. You were his wife."

"He thought I was with child. I had lied to him . . . because I did not want him. He thought I was with child, I say . . . and still he . . ."

"You must be calm, Tamar, or you will be ill."

She took his hand; hers was quite cold.

"I am calm," she said, "and in my calmness I see myself a murderess. I sent him to his death, and all the work that was to have been done will be left undone. I can only be at peace if I take on that work. Richard . . . Father . . . try to understand me. Try to help me."

He put his lips against her forehead.

"I understand, my dearest child," he said. "I understand. I will help you. Together we will do his work."

* * *

The days passed rapidly. Stores were unloaded, pens set up for the pigs and poultry. There was timber to be felled, as many more houses would be needed. Then there was the perpetual hunt for food. If they had been content to eat the fish which abounded off their shores, they might have saved much time, for it was only necessary for a few small boats to go out for a day's fishing to bring back enough to feed the community. But they felt the need of flesh. Lobsters, oysters, clams and cod could not completely satisfy them; they must hunt the deer of the forest.

The children were made to work, fetching and carrying. Tamar watched Dick and Rowan running hither and thither with the younger members of Annis's large family and others. Even Lorea was given small tasks to perform.

"There is no idleness here," was the rule. "There is no privilege. Those who would live in houses must build them; those who would eat must work."

But the children were delighted with their new life. Everything was so strange and exciting; the changing colours of the sea, which was somehow different from that sea of Devon; the sandy bank on which the water broke violently; the ship lying there between the bank and the land, the ship which had meant adventure and exploration; the Cape which could easily be seen on clear days; the swiftly flowing river emptying itself into the sea; the Cheuyot Mountains in the distance; the town itself spreading on the hillside; the wild birds—geese, cranes, herons; and beyond, the forest. Dick's eyes were turned again and again towards the forest—the enchanted forest in which lurked red-skinned men. Dick was awake early every morning, was tired out every night. Dick was enchanted with the new life.

Richard had plans which had met with the approval of the Governor and those in charge of the settlement. Richard had brought carefully chosen books with him and proposed teaching the children. It was absolutely necessary that they should learn to read and write. They could not be allowed to grow up ignorant, or they would not be able to read the Bible and teach their children to do the same.

That, it was confessed, had been a matter of great anxiety to the leaders of the Pilgrims. There had been little time to think of education; they had been too busy trying to keep alive. Richard, finding that he could be useful in the new community, was in high delight. Tamar announced her desire to help him; and, Richard said, as there was now quite a large juvenile section of the population, he would need a helper, and who better than his own daughter, whom he himself had taught?

This suggestion was received with slightly less enthusiasm than the first. A certain James Milroy, a middle-aged widower, whose wife had died the previous winter, volunteered the suggestion that it might not be meet in the eyes of the Lord that a woman should teach male members of the community.

Richard challenged this view, declaring that he would need help and that it was for him to choose his helper; he chose his daughter. The matter was allowed to rest there, but, looking round at those stern faces, Tamar felt sudden anger rising within her. She must keep her lips tightly pressed together to stop the flow of words which afterwards she would wish she had not uttered, for even as she opened her mouth, she had seemed to see Humility standing among those men.

So instead of making angry retorts, she determined to show by her ability that a woman could do the work as well as any man, and that, providing she was a good and enthusiastic teacher, her sex could be of no moment.

Richard's house was to be the first of the new houses, as it was also to be the schoolhouse. While it was being built, a few Indians came to watch. They stood about, their faces painted vermilion to show they came in peace; they smiled and chattered together. They offered wampum and deerskins in exchange for saws and oiled paper. "*Mawchick chammay*!" they insisted. "Best of friends!" They laughed as they watched, for it seemed to them that the ways of the white men were strange and wonderful.

Annis and her family were split up between other families so that they might have a roof over their heads while they were waiting for a house of their own. Annis went about in a state of bliss.

"Why, mistress," she said to Tamar, "this is indeed a great land. I know now how feared I was, every time John went out, that they would have taken him for questioning. If you did but know how wonderful it is to have lost that fear. And they do think a lot of John here. He be so good with the land. The Governor, he did say to me: 'Your man is the kind we want here!' Yes, he did. And Christian and Restraint are fine workers too. And he said: 'And you, daughter, with your fine family. You are the sort of woman we want, a woman who knows her duty to God, a pure woman who has given us children.' Oh, mistress, I be so happy. This be the promised land."

Mistress Alton was living with another family until the time when Richard's house should be built; then she would become his housekeeper. In the house where Mistress Alton dwelt, James Milroy also lived; and Tamar had heard that James Milroy was looking for a wife.

"Who knows?" said Tamar to Richard. "Mistress Alton may find a husband in her new country!"

Bartle was giving Tamar cause for anxiety. He was even more apart from this community than she was. He was accepted as the Captain of the ship bringing stores and colonists. He never attended prayer meetings, and was not expected to. He had said that when the spring came he would take the *Liberty* back to England, report on the colony to London, and arrange either to bring or send the stores and cattle which New Plymouth needed.

But Bartle, of course, had no wish to become a part of this community, whereas Tamar was growing more and more certain that within it lay her salvation.

Bartle was angry. This, he declared, was yet another phase of her perversity — the perversity which had dogged them since their first meeting and ruined their lives. Would she never learn her lesson? It was always wait . . . wait . . . wait. Did she not know that her prevaricating had been responsible for all the misery they had endured?

"*Now* is the time!" cried Bartle. "Not to-morrow. . . or next year! Now! *Now*!"

"You must try to be understanding," she said. "You must help me."

"Humility Brown was in our way when I came home. He is no longer in our way. We are free . . . free to marry, and still you say, 'Wait!' We grow old, waiting. We are both past the first flush of our youth, and still you say, 'Wait!'"

"We are *not* free, Bartle. Humility is between us."

"He is dead!"

"He lives on to haunt me because I killed him."

"What nonsense! He killed himself. Or it was an accident. Yes! It was an accident."

"You cannot say it was an accident just because it makes a prettier story."

"I can and I will. He is dead; his life is done with; and ours are short. You try my patience as you ever did. You know what I am like when I get impatient. I refuse to wait. I refuse to waste my life."

Her eyes filled with tears. "Oh, Bartle, I beg of you . . ."

"It is no use begging of me! I ask you to marry me, to sail back with me to England in the spring. Come! That is the life for us. We will stay there."

"Richard says I shall never be safe in England. They know me for a witch. They will remember always."

"Do you think that any would dare hurt my wife?"

"I should never be safe in Devon where they know me."

"That is not why you will not go back. You would not be afraid of them!"

"I will not go back because I want to live here. I want to be of these people. I must live a life of sacrifice and restraint. I know it. It has been revealed to me. They have revealed it to me by their goodness."

"You will change your mind."

"I do not think so."

He caught her hand in a grip that hurt. "You are a fool, Tamar. You set yourself ideals which you cannot live up to. You think with your emotions. *You* can never live among Puritans. There is nothing of the Puritan in you. You belong to me as I do to you. I marvel at my patience. One of these days I will make you see how wrong you have been to waste our time. Indeed, I will not allow much more time to be wasted. Do not stand there looking sad and holy, or by God, I will take it upon myself to show you that there is nothing holy about you . . . and no need for sadness!" He turned away, but before he had gone a few paces he turned once more to face her. "Think not that I shall endure this state of affairs. You will see."

She was trembling. She remembered that smile so well, that flash of the intensely blue eyes. Her heart was beating fast, and she knew that she wanted him to come back, to repeat that he would wait no longer. But Humility seemed close then, Humility, with his white face and wet clinging garments—a sad, repentant ghost. "Pray," said the ghost of Humility, "pray for help to fight your lust."

She prayed as she turned and ran back to watch the builders at work on that house in which she would work with Richard for the good of the colony.

However, it seemed that even Bartle had a place in this community. He went off into the forest with the hunters. He was an expert shot, and there was meat in plenty whenever he was of the party.

"You are a mighty hunter, friend," he was told. Shrewd eyes smiled kindly on him. "Stay with us!" said those eyes. "There is work for you here; and in time God may see fit to save your soul from eternal damnation. He has given you the eyes of a hawk, the fleetness of an Indian, the strength of three men. There is work for you here."

But Bartle saw no permanent place for himself with them. It was merely that he could not resist the thrill of the hunt, and it gave him great pleasure to come back after a good day in the forest and see the eyes of the people glisten in anticipation as they gazed on the spoils.

One day Dick was missing, and Tamar was frantic with anxiety.

It was a bright winter's day with a keen frost in the air. She imagined her son lost in the forest, injured perhaps, unable to move, spending the night there . . . the cold night. It would kill him. The winters of this land were more rigorous than the winters of Devon. It was realized by many that the winters they had known at home had scarcely been winters at all. In Devonshire a whole winter could pass without a sight of snow; it was one of the most temperate spots in a temperate island. Now they were learning what a real winter could be, and it was harder to bear for those who came from Devonshire than for the men from colder East Anglia and Holland.

She must find her child, but she dared not let it be known that he was missing, for fear he had transgressed the rules; and if he had gone into the forest, he certainly had. They were right, of course, these men with their sternness. Children, they said, were born in sin and must be led away from it. This often meant harsh correction; and there were a good many beatings administered on the instructions of the Elders of the Church. But even if they were right, it must not happen to Dick, for he was a proud child, deeply conscious of his dignity. He was herself all over again, and he had learned to be like Bartle too. He would be resentful of public humiliation, since he thought himself a man already, worthy of a man's privileges.

If she found Bartle, he would help her to search for the boy and bring him back so that his misdemeanour might not be known.

She made her way down to the shore, determined to row out to the *Liberty*, find Bartle and ask his help. Her heart-beats quickened. She could imagine Bartle, cruel as ever, making conditions. "I will find the boy, and in payment for returning him to you and keeping his sins from the Puritans, I demand . . ."

Someone was calling her name and, turning, she saw coming towards her, James Milroy, that middle-aged widower who had objected to a woman's teaching boys.

"You are anxious on account of your son," he said. "I can tell you where he is."

His eyes studied her with disapproval and she put up her hand to tuck a straying curl under her cap.

"You know?" she cried. "He . . . is safe?"

"It would seem so. Sir Bartle has taken a party on a day's hunting in the forest and the boy is with them."

She was filled with relief, but James Milroy shook his head sternly.

"If you would care to take the advice of a friend who wishes you well, this is it. The boy should not be allowed to spend so much time with the Captain. That man is a sinner and he will lead the boy into temptation. His language offends the ears of all men of God. He has an evil reputation."

"I thank you, sir," she said, and her eyes flashed, "but the boy is mine and I think I know what is good for him."

"There I disagree, and so would the Elders. The boy should not have absented himself without permission. I insist that on his return the necessary correction shall be administered."

"You mean . . ."

"'He that spareth his rod hateth his son.' That boy is already spoiled. He needs a father."

"I assure you that I am the best judge of how a child of mine shall be brought up."

She turned and walked away, her head held high. Had she stayed another moment, she would have been unable to control her furious anger.

The hunting party returned at the end of that day with enough meat to provide the whole settlement with a good meal. Tamar saw them coming, saw Dick striding along beside Bartle; and she felt a pride rise up in her. Dick was almost a man.

James Milroy was there to watch the return of the party, and the very way in which his thin lips were pressed together told Tamar that he was going to demand the punishment of her son.

She saw the man approach the boy and lay his hand on his shoulder. She saw the boy's eyes flash as he moved closer to Bartle.

Then she heard Dick's voice, high-pitched and indignant. " 'Twas hunting! 'Twas finding food! That is a good thing to do."

Tamar's heart leaped, for Bartle now faced James Milroy, and Bartle, drawing himself up to his full height, was laughing in the face of the man, with that bold insolence which Tamar knew well.

There was a hush about them. Pleasure in the return of the hunters with good meat was lost, for here was a troublous note introduced into the harmony of the occasion.

"I took the boy with me," said Bartle. "If any has to answer for his going, then that is myself. What do you wish, sir—to challenge me? Come then, I am ready. Shall we fight with the sword or the fist? It matters not to me. Nor will it to you in less than a minute for, by God, I swear . . ."

But one of the Elders had approached them, had laid a hand on Bartle's arm.

"Sir Bartle, I beg of you, restrain yourself."

Bartle growled: "Let him leave the boy alone, then. Anyone who dares lay a hand on him answers to me."

"It is forbidden," said James Milroy, "that children should go into the forest without the consent of parents or the authorities."

"He came with his parent's consent," said Bartle.

"I know that to be an untruth."

"You dare insult me?"

But James Milroy, although he knew himself to be no match for the great blustering Captain, was not a coward. He would not have been of this community if he had not been a brave man. He fervently believed in the righteousness of what he was doing.

"It is you who insult the truth, Sir Bartle. His mother was anxious. She was looking for him. I met her and told her where he was."

Bartle's eyes narrowed. He would have laid his hands on the man, but the Elder said: "His mother is here; she will tell us of this matter. You were anxious, were you not, Mistress Brown? You had not given the child permission and it was for you to give it, as the child, alas, has no father to guide him."

Tamar glared angrily at the Puritan, James Milroy.

"The boy had my permission to go. He is allowed to hunt with Sir Bartle whenever he wishes."

James Milroy looked at her in startled horror. He would not have been surprised if the heavens had opened and Tamar had been struck dumb or even dead.

What is the use of my trying to be one of them? Tamar asked herself.

She was a pagan; she and Bartle were of a kind. What cared she if she must tell a lie to save her son pain and humiliation! And what cared Bartle?

* * *

Afterwards she was remorseful. She had been wrong. Better for Dick to have taken his beating than for her to have perjured her soul.

Moreover, she had given way to Bartle; she had sided with him and the old ways against the Puritans and the new.

"The idea," said Bartle, "of wanting to punish a boy because he goes off for a day's hunting! Leave him to me and I will make a man of him."

"He must learn to obey rules . . . the rules of the community in which he lives."

"He will learn what it is good for him to learn, with me as his teacher."

"I would have him grow up good and noble."

"As his father?" said Bartle. "A poor frail thing of a man who jumps into the sea because he is tempted to make love to his wife!"

"How dare you!"

"Now that is more like yourself. By God, I'd a thousand times rather see you stormy than pious."

She was about to blaze at him when she seemed to see the ghost of Humility standing beside him; and it was as though she saw Bartle through Humility's eyes—the Devil incarnate, there to tempt her.

She turned away, but she heard Bartle's laughter following her; and she guessed that plans were forming in his mind.

After that Dick hardly ever left Bartle's side. Dick worshipped Bartle. Once the boy looked at his mother critically and said "*You* used to be more like Sir Bartle, Mamma. Now you are becoming like these people."

"Dick," she asked earnestly, "don't you like living here with these people?"

"I like living here," he said significantly, "because I like hunting with Sir Bartle. One day. . . I shall go sailing with him. When he goes back to England, he's promised that I. . ."

The boy stopped. But she understood. Bartle was winning the boy from her.

She was tormented by the thought. She prayed constantly. She could not talk to Richard of this matter, for Richard wished her to marry Bartle. Richard had not believed in her first conversion; he did not believe in this one.

A few weeks after the arrival of the *Liberty* another ship called at New Plymouth, and aboard her were Dutch settlers from farther along the coast. Great hospitality was shown to the guests, for, as the Governor said, he and the entire colony were happy when people came as friends instead of enemies.

These Dutchmen expressed great admiration for the New Plymouth way of life; they were astonished that the Pilgrims had experienced so little trouble with the red-skinned men; the French and Dutch in other parts of this great continent had not found the natives so amenable.

Tamar knew then that this was due to the example of goodness and honour set by the men of New Plymouth. So pronounced and unswerving was this code that it was one which savages could see was desirable. These Englishmen were born colonizers, as was no other nation on Earth; they possessed a natural dignity and a way of straight-dealing which was apparent to all men, whatever their colour, whatever their creed. Brave they were; but so were other settlers who had left their homes for a new life in a strange land. But Tamar saw this quality, which they possessed in a larger degree than men of other nations, as a calm dignity, an ability to suppress feelings, whether of anger or joy, so that those who gave vent to such feelings must inevitably find themselves at a disadvantage when opposing such men; there was a slowness to anger in these men, but once righteous indignation was aroused, there was in them a determination of purpose, stubborn insistence on finishing what they had begun; and these qualities made of them men to respect and to fear. Among such men—and such men only—could she follow magnificent examples and work out her salvation.

Christmas was near and Tamar planned a celebration for the children. There should be, she promised them, dancing, games and feasting. The children went dancing down Leyden Street, all chattering about the Christmas feast.

Word came to Tamar that one of the Elders wished to speak to her, and she went along to his house.

"Sit down, dear sister," he said. "I must have speech with thee. I have heard of the feast you would give on Christ's birthday."

Tamar waited and, after a pause, he went on: "Our Lord Jesus, sister, was a Man of Sorrows, and it is not meet that the day of His birth should be celebrated with feasting and games. That day should be given to prayer."

"But . . ." she began.

He lifted his hand. "Hear me out, I pray you. I thought I would tell you first, before it is explained to the children that there cannot be this . . . this bacchanalia. You have, I fear—in your ignorance, I know, and not from wanton guilt—imbued them with the wrong ideas. Fear not, sister, we do not blame you. We merely wish to show you the folly of your ways."

"But it is simple fun for the children. It is no . . . bacchanalia. It is just a little pleasure . . . a little fun."

"Dear sister, you have brought old ideas with you from England. All that wickedness we left behind us. There is not room for it in the New World. Do not fret. We have seen you striving to become one of us and are pleased with your progress. We wish to help you, and that is why, in addition to explaining to you your mistake about Christ's birthday, I have asked you to come here."

She lifted her eyes to his face; she knew they were beginning to blaze. She wanted to run out of this room, which seemed suddenly oppressive. She noted the shelf which contained a few books, chief of which was a translation of the Bible done in Holland; she looked down at the rushes on the floor, and from the floor to the windows with their oiled paper; and she suddenly remembered with an almost intolerable nostalgia her bedroom in the house at Pennicomquick with the carpet on the floor and real glass in the window, and the bed with its rich curtains. She wanted to escape from this restricted, primitive life; she wanted to be free. Free? But it was to this land she had come in search of freedom.

She suppressed the thought. Humility seemed to be there, pointing an accusing finger at her. She waited as patiently as she could.

"You are a young woman still. You are a strong woman. You have bred children and could breed more. It is your duty to God and to your new country to have children to worship Him and cultivate your adopted land. You are too young to remain unmarried. Pray do not look startled. I have good news for you. There is one among us who is prepared to marry you, to guide you, and to be a father to those children you already have, while he will endeavour to give you more."

She felt her lips curl in uncontrollable scorn. "And who is this man?"

"James Milroy. A good man, a noble man, a man who has long dedicated his life to the service of God. He has watched you protectively since you have been here. He has felt you and your children to be in need of correction and guidance; and he feels that God has selected him for the task. He is willing — nay, anxious — to obey the will of the Lord."

"If he looks for a wife," she said, "there are others more worthy than I."

But the Elder did not notice the edge on her voice. "That may be. But our dear brother Milroy was never a man to shirk his duty when he sees it plain before him. He is therefore willing to take you to him as his wife."

"That is generous of him indeed. You may tell him this: When I marry, and if I marry, I shall choose my own husband."

"You make many mistakes, sister. Your life is full of mistakes. You have brought evil ideas with you from the Old World, and you cling to them. You have set yourself up to teach our boys. We like that not. A woman's duty is not to instruct men, and these boys will one day be men. Nay! We would see you as other women — at your spinning wheel, helping in the fields at harvest, and, above all, a wife to give us children. Yes, dear sister, we have accepted you. One of us offers to take care of your life, to guide you into the paths which will lead to your salvation and the glorification of God."

She was too dazed to speak. She could only think: James Milroy! That man!

And when she pictured him, the quiet, solemn-eyed man changed in her mind's eye to Humility Brown.

The voice went on: "You are of the weaker sex, dear sister; and it is easy to see that in the Old Country you have been spoiled. Your father continues to spoil you. We are pleased with him and the work he is doing for us, and we know that one day he will be completely with us. We shall rejoice on that day. But there is much he too has to learn. You have been unfortunate in your upbringing and we are sorry for you. You have been given beauty; and beauty, dear sister, is not always a gift from God. Or it may be that it is given by the Almighty as a special burden to be carried through a life. Women are frail creatures. We must never forget that they are not the equals of men. They must never forget that they are the weaker vessels. They must remain subservient to the good men who marry them. Never forget that it was Eve who listened to the temptation of the serpent. It was due to Eve that Adam, our forefather, was turned out of Eden. Adam was weak; but Eve was wicked; and all women are descendants of Eve as all men are of Adam. Women are more easily tempted to sin, being of weaker intellect than men, and therefore must obey their husbands in all things. Children are born in sin and must be sternly led to righteousness. It is a great task which falls upon us men."

"A great task doubtless!" she said.

"And you will allow me to send Master Milroy along to your father's house?"

She lowered her lids that he might not see the blaze of her eyes, and when she spoke her voice was scarcely audible, such an effort did she have to make to control it. “I am too sinful for such a man,” she said. “It will be well for such an Adam to find a more worthy Eve, someone who has not had to carry this heavy burden of beauty through her life.”

“Your modesty is not unbecoming . . .” began the Elder.

But she said hastily as she turned to the door: “I will bid you good day.”

She hurried to the beach and dragged the nearest boat to the water. Furiously she rowed out to the *Liberty*.

Scrambling aboard, she cried to one of the sailors: “Tell Sir Bartle I am here. I wish to see him . . . at once!”

She leaned over the bulwarks waiting, but she did not have to wait for long. He gave a mighty roar of laughter when he saw her. Unlike the Elder, he knew her rages when he saw them.

He took her hands. “This is a joy, to have you visit me.” Then he pulled her towards him and kissed her firmly on the mouth.

She held him off. “I . . . I have just come from the Elder . . .” she said breathlessly.

“I do not think that Elder has pleased you greatly.”

“Pleased me! I am infuriated!”

“That delights me. It is so long since I have seen you in a rage . . . much too long.”

“I am sinful! I am a descendant of Eve, who is responsible for all the sin in the world. I have been handicapped by the burden of my beauty. And now . . . *now* . . . it pleases Brother Milroy . . . *dear*

Brother Milroy. . . to guide me into the paths of righteousness! He will look after my children and give me more. In short, he is prepared to marry me . . . for the sake of my soul, I am told, and so that I can supply more children for the colony!"

"Ha! Yet another Humility Brown! And what said you to this dazzling proposal?"

"I said I would choose my own husband."

"That was well spoken. And you told them, I believe, that you had chosen already."

"I did not."

"That," he said, "was remiss of you." He drew her to him once more and this time kissed her tenderly. "No matter, we will tell them together."

"I do not mean . . ." she began.

"But I do. The time has come, and you can no longer delay. They are right when they say such as you should not remain unmarried. Plague on them! They would marry you off to their Elders! And in your mood of these last weeks you'd have had another Humility Brown if I had not been here to stop you. Listen, sweetheart. You don't belong here. We don't belong here. We'll marry and sail away. Would we could go to-night! But that's impossible. We'll not tempt death when life looks good. But as soon as these gales cease . . . as soon as the sun begins to smile again . . ."

"Brother Milroy !" she cried. "That man! You can imagine how he would look after my children. Poor Dick! Poor Rowan! Poor little Lorea!"

"Think how delighted *they* will be when they know about us! It is their dearest wish that I should be their father."

"You have put a spell upon them."

"As I have on you . . . and as you have on me, Tamar."

"Was it magic you learned in foreign places?"

"I know not. I only know that I love them and they love me; and that I love their mother . . . as she loves me."

"If I married you . . . would you . . . could you give up all thought of returning to England? I mean, would you stay here? Of course you will sail back to get stores . . . and mayhap to adventure up the coast. That you should do, and I would go with you. What I mean is: Could you make this place your *home*?"

"Is that what you want?"

"I feel this place has something to show me. I think of Humility. Oh, do not be impatient. You say I did not kill him, but I know I sent him to his death. That hangs heavily on my conscience, and I should never be happy if I did not do what I feel I must do. And now I know that I want to stay here and try to lead a better life than I have so far lived."

He took her face in his hands and his blue eyes gleamed with great tenderness.

"Once I said I would go to hell for you. Well, if I would do that, surely I could endure a Puritan settlement."

"I will marry you, Bartle."

He held her tightly against him and his laugh was one of great joy and triumph.

"We'll get married," he said, "and we'll build a little house. We'll start it to-morrow. We'll live in a little Puritan house among Puritans . . . for as long as you want to . . . but I know that won't be for the rest of our lives. And one day you'll say, 'Let us sail away. There are other places in the world.' I would not take you back to England to live, though, for Richard is right. But mayhap we might sail into the Sound one day . . . just to see Devon again . . . that greenest of green grass, the coombs and hills, that rich red soil . . . But we should not stay, for I should be afraid of their witch-prickers and what they would do to you, since, if aught happened to you, what would be my life? What has it been without you ever since I met you?"

She tried to stem the great excitement which was creeping over her.

"So you want me, Bartle, not because it is good for a woman, a descendant of Eve, to have a husband to guide her; not so that you can give children to the colony. You want *me* . . . because I am myself . . . because you cannot be happy without me? That seems a good reason."

When he rowed her back to the shore they talked about the cottage they would build.

"It will be like a cottage on your estate at home," she reminded him.

"It'll be as no other place on Earth!" he answered.

Richard was delighted with the news. As for the two elder children, they were so enchanted that they must dance about the room; and Lorea could not keep still, so excited was she at the prospect of owning such a father.

It was unfortunate that the Elder, misunderstanding Tamar's meaning, should have sent James Milroy along to make an offer for her hand, and that he should have arrived just as Bartle and Tamar were making their announcement.

Tamar smiled pertly at the man, disliking him through no great fault of his own but because he reminded her of Humility.

Bartle's eyes, as they fell on the man, were full of malice.

"Here comes Master Milroy to have a word with you, Richard," he said.

"Pray, sit down," said Richard. "You must drink with us."

"I wish to speak to you in private," said James.

"Can it be," said Tamar, "that you have come to ask my father for my hand in marriage?"

The Puritan flushed.

"Ah ! I see that is so. I have been told of your desire to guide me, to save my soul, and to make my body fruitful. You are too late with your offer, sir. I have decided to marry Sir Bartle Cavill."

There was silence in the little room. Richard looked with dismay from the newly affianced couple to the Puritan. The latter, poor man, was very shocked, and the colour stayed in his face. Bartle and

Tamar looked completely mischievous. Ah! thought Richard. This then is the end of another phase in Tamar's life. She is no longer going to be a Puritan; she is now going to be herself.

Dick was so excited by the great news that he forgot the presence of the Puritan. "Sir Bartle, I shall call you Father from now on. I shan't wait."

"I shall call you Father too!" declared Rowan.

"Lorea too!" said Lorea.

And the children seized Bartle's hands, and danced round him as though he were a pole and they Maytime revellers.

James Milroy looked on the scene with horror.

He rose and said calmly: "I beg your pardon. I have made a mistake."

And as the door shut behind him, Bartle swept Tamar into his arms and kissed her hungrily, while the children applauded. But Richard looked on uneasily.

* * *

Their house was made ready for them. They had declared their desire to be married before the magistrate, and the simple Puritan ceremony was over.

Tamar no longer thought of being a Puritan; she only thought of being happy. This, she realized, was what she had been wanting all through the years. It did not matter now that it had come late; it was never too late. She had almost forgotten that a man named Humility Brown had ever existed.

They lay in their small room in their tiny cottage, and both of them thought of another room, with a curtained bed and a wide open window. But never had they known such happiness as this.

In the bitterly cold first weeks of their marriage they were snug in their little house. There was no need to think beyond the winter. They were happy now. In the spring the *Liberty* would return to England and Bartle would take Tamar with him, for they had agreed that never again would they be parted for long.

There were times when Bartle went off on a hunting expedition into the forest. Once he was away two days and a night. Those were the longest hours she had known since her marriage. But home he came safely, with meat for the settlement.

It was pleasant for Tamar to slip into Annis's cottage and sit by her fireside and see her contentment, enjoying contentment herself.

"Ah!" said Annis. "You be happy now. At last you be happy. . . happy as you never were before. Sir Bartle, he be the man for you; and 'tis right and proper that you should be Lady Cavill. I always knew he were the man for you, wild though he be, for you be wild too, mistress my lady."

"No," she said. "I *was* wild, Annis. I have changed. I want quiet happiness and peace now and for evermore."

Annis did not speak, but she knew that peace was not what Tamar would find with Sir Bartle. He wasn't the one for peace. Humility Brown was the one for that.

"Don't mention *his* name to me!" cried Tamar.

Annis trembled. She was always frightened by Tamar's way of reading her thoughts.

"He were a good man," said Annis, "and happy he'll be at this moment, I'll be ready to swear, to look out through the golden gates and see you happy."

"I said don't speak of him!" cried Tamar; and she got up and went home.

Then for a while it seemed that Humility Brown was in the cottage. She was happy, yes. But she had bought this happiness with the death of Humility Brown. He would always be there, she believed, to mock her at odd moments, ready to spoil her pleasure in the new life.

It was not a good life, she feared. It was gay and full of laughter; full of passion and quarrels too. Bartle was quickly jealous. He even accused her of smiling in too friendly a fashion at James Milroy, which infuriated her while it sent her into mocking laughter, so that he in his turn was infuriated. But such scenes ended in passionate embraces. She herself was jealous at times, accusing him of infidelities, remembering the reputation he had had in England and reminding him of it.

So after those first weeks of blissful contentment there came those sudden gusts of anger and passion; they were two violent natures let loose and enjoying their anger when they both knew that it would end in passionate reunion.

Not a tranquil life — a wild and exciting life, even here in a Puritan settlement, just as she had always known it would be with Bartle. Yet how had she ever lived without it?

Only when there was trouble with the Indians and Bartle went off with some ten men under Captain Standish with muskets and cutlasses — only then did she know the depth of her love for him, only then did she realize that she would rather die than lose him again as she had once before.

John Tyler was one of the men who went with Captain Standish, and that brought Annis even closer. During those eight days they were together constantly, exchanging confidences, telling each other of their love and the life they led with these men, while the children played noisily outside and only little Lorea sat on a stool listening to them.

Back came the men, victorious — only one of them, who had caught an arrow in his back, the worse for the expedition.

She clung to Bartle, and there were many days and nights when they were gentle with one another, all violence forgotten.

Then she fancied that Bartle was becoming resigned to this life of hunting and protecting the settlement from the native redskins. Why should he not? It was a man's life.

She was happy at the thought of their living in the little cottage until they went to their graves — she with her children about her, tending her garden, cooking maize cakes, perhaps learning to spin with the expert touch most women acquired.

She should have known such a life could not be for her, nor for Bartle. They were not of these people, and they were tolerated only because they were known to be birds of passage. Bartle had never pretended to be one of them. He was Captain of the ship which had brought them; he had built a house, it was true, but when he had gone it would still be a house, and houses were desperately needed in New Plymouth.

And then occurred an incident which shocked Tamar as she had not been shocked since the day she had found poor Jane Swann escaping from her tormentors.

It concerned Polly Eagel. Polly's husband was a quiet man, and Polly would never have thought of becoming a Puritan if she had not married him. Polly was flighty, fond of admiration; and James Milroy for one was deeply aware of sin such as Polly brought into the settlement. It was not the original Pilgrims, serious-minded, righteous, ready to die for their faith whom he felt needed supervision; they were as stalwart as ever. But newcomers had emigrated for a variety of reasons—for the love of adventure, to make a change because life was hard at home. The Captain and the crew of his ship were evil men. As for Tamar—and he thanked God nightly that he had been saved from the calamity of marrying her—she was a wanton creature. She had lured him on, he knew now, not because she wanted a good man to instruct and guide her, but that she might tempt him to lust. Much wickedness had come into Plymouth with the *Liberty*. It must be stamped out, and James

Milroy was going to do his duty and see that this was done.

He had been suspicious of Polly Eagel for some time. She was a pretty, fluffy-haired little woman, forever fingering her hair and letting it peep out from under her cap as if by accident. He had set a watch upon Polly Eagel and—glory be to God!—he had himself been led by divine guidance to discover her immorality with one of the sailors from the ship.

Now the sailors did not come under Puritan law. Their souls were their own, which meant that they were the Devil's. Eternal damnation was to be their lot in any case. But Polly Eagel was a member of the Puritan Church, and as such must suffer the necessary correction.

Annis came bursting into Tamar's cottage to tell her the news.

Annis was excited. This was like something that might have happened at home.

"Mistress, have 'ee heard? Have 'ee heard what Polly Eagel have been up to? Caught she were . . . by Master Milroy. Caught right in the act, so I did hear. Oh my lady, he has told the Elders, and Polly have been taken off. It seems that one thing she'll have to do is to confess her sin before us at the meeting house. Then she'll take her punishment. My dear life! The shame of it would wellnigh kill a woman! Not that Polly Eagel's the sort to die for such. She's a brazen piece and no mistake. It's poor Bill Eagel I'm sorry for."

On the day of Polly's confession, the meeting house was full of an expectant congregation. Tamar was there with Richard. Bartle never attended at the meeting house.

Tamar was struck by the gloating anticipation showing in the faces about her; she felt sickened by the scene. Perhaps that was because she was a sinner herself, and felt she was no better than Polly Eagel. Polly had committed adultery; Tamar was guilty of causing her husband's death; perhaps that was why she could feel no pleasure in watching a sinner brought to justice, as these righteous people could.

The Elder talked for a long time. In the front row of seats sat Polly Eagel; her face was white, her head downcast. She did not look the same gay girl who had come out from England, and whom Tamar had noticed during the voyage when she had heard that Bartle had once been interested in her. Now was Polly brought low. In the front row, near her, sat her accuser, James Milroy, his arms folded, his eyes lifted to the rafters of the hall as though he knew God to be up there, smiling down His approval on the acts of James Milroy.

The Elder preached of sin . . . sin that had crept like a fog into their midst, sin that must be crushed and defeated. Of all the great sins of the world, there were few to be compared with Adultery; and there was one among them who stood guilty of this sin. She had confessed and repented, and that was a matter for rejoicing; but God was a just God, and such sins could not in His name be allowed to go unpunished. It might be that through a life of devotion to duty this miserable sinner would come to salvation. This was for God and herself to decide. Her partner in sin was not here to stand beside her. His was a lost soul. But let no one imagine he would escape the wages of his sin. He would burn eternally in Hell, though he thought here on Earth to continue his evil life. Polly Eagel would now stand forth.

Polly stood up and turned to face the congregation.

She was scarlet and pale in turn, and she spoke so low that those at the back of the hall had to crane forward to hear her words.

She was a miserable sinner; she had defiled her marriage bed. She gave details of the place and occasion when her sin had taken place, as she had been told to do. Eyes glistened. Puritan hearts beat fast. Tamar watching, thought: it would be better if they might dance now and then, or see a play acted. Then they would not be so eager to take their entertainment from another's misery.

And suddenly, in an overwhelming pity for Polly Eagel, she hated them all, hated the Elder with his hands piously folded, hated James Milroy with his eyes turned piously upwards, hated all those who stood in judgment, with their sly eyes and their tight mouths. But almost at once she realized that she hated them because she should be standing there beside Polly Eagel, for she was a greater sinner than Polly.

Polly's confession was over, but that was preliminary to her punishment. A solemn procession went from the meeting place, led by the Elders and dignitaries of the settlement, Polly among them; other important members of the community followed, and after them came the congregation.

They went to that raised platform whose significance Tamar had not realized before. The post there was, of course, a whipping post. As for the gallows, she had accepted such an erection as a necessary part of any community; it was just that in such a one as this, it had seemed to have been put there merely as a warning. Gallows and whipping posts were a part of the Old Country; she had thought they had no place in the New.

Polly's hands were tied behind her back and she was forced on to a stool. Tamar saw the brazier, the hot irons; she heard Polly Eagel give one wild, protesting shriek before she fainted and fell back into the arms of one of the Elders.

It was some time before Polly appeared in public, for she had had to serve a month in the house of correction. Tamar had looked once into that poor mutilated face, and she could never bring herself to look again. Clearly she had seen branded on Polly's forehead the letter A; and the sight of the scorched and tortured flesh had enraged her.

She was weary and disillusioned. She was like a traveller who thought he had travelled far along a road that was beset with hardship, only to find that he had been walking round in a circle and had moved only a very short distance from the starting point.

* * *

The snows had disappeared and the harsh winds had softened. Spring was coming to New England.

Polly mingled with the people, the A standing out clearly on her forehead, her head downcast and all the natural joy drained out of her. Whenever Tamar saw her she averted her eyes. She felt as she did when she was with Jane Swann — poor Jane, who had become vague, hiding in quiet corners, not hearing when spoken to. She sat in her father's house, spinning. When other women sat at their spinning wheels the sound of their singing would mingle with the hum of the wheel. Jane was never heard singing.

It was perhaps easier to live a Puritan life in the cold of winter. But when the bluebirds and the robins were building in the forest and their songs filled the air, when the fruit trees were in blossom, the young men and maidens would look towards each other and think that life could not be all work and prayer, as their serious Elders seemed to believe it should be.

Two young people were whipped publicly for the sin of fornication. They had, they declared, every intention of marrying, but spring had taken them unaware. That was no excuse; so they were punished before they went through the simple marriage ceremony. They were told that their sin merited death, but since they were members of a new colony which needed children, they would be given a chance to regain salvation through a life of piety and devotion to God.

The Elders were deeply concerned at this time by what seemed to them a hideous menace. It was not fear of famine or hostile Indians that gave them their greatest anxiety; it was a certain Thomas Morton.

To the Puritans this man was the Devil in person. He was a swaggering fellow very proud of his scholarship, describing himself as "Of Clifford's Inne, Gent." He had come to New England a few years before with a Captain Wollaston and a company of men, their idea being to start a plantation. This they had set about doing not very far from Plymouth, at a spot which they had named Mount Wollaston. But Wollaston had grown tired of the hardship such a project had entailed and had sailed off to Virginia in the hope of finding an easier fortune. The same Morton—as the Puritans said—had, by some evil means, ousted those left in charge by Wollaston, and taken over command of the place himself. And the first thing he had done—and this in the eyes of New Plymouth was an indication of his character—was to rename the place "Merry Mount."

The state of affairs between New Plymouth and Merry Mount was far from cordial. Morton accused the Puritans of disregarding the laws of England by denying the marriage ceremony to the colonists and supplying some simple form of their own. The Puritans retaliated by accusing Morton of selling firearms and strong drink to the Indians and so endangering the lives of all the settlers in New England. The real cause of the trouble was that the people of New Plymouth were Separatist and those of Merry Mount, Episcopalian.

As the days grew warmer, Bartle made preparations for the journey back to England. All day the small boats were busy, transferring stores from land to the *Liberty.* Many turned away from the sight of the ship, for it made them think of home. Polly Eagel would shudder when she saw it, and touch the letter on her forehead. Annis took her youngest down to the beach to show her what was going on; but Annis was sad, seeing the ship's preparations, because her beloved mistress was sailing away on that ship. Tamar had said she would come back, but who could know what might happen to prevent her?

Yes, indeed, spring was a time of disquiet, for spring was to be enjoyed by youth and lovers. There were many marriages, and it was said that there should have been many a whipping to precede those marriages, if the watchful Puritans could but have found sufficient evidence.

Mistress Alton and Brother Milroy were friends together; they were of one mind, devoted to the Puritan cause, so eager to bring straying footsteps back to the path of righteousness.

It was Thomas Morton, the Episcopalian of Merry Mount, who now also took a part in the shaping of many lives.

The Elders were storming against him at the meeting place, but the young and the lively could not help it if their eyes turned towards Merry Mount; and they whispered together of the goings-on at the "Mount of Sin" as an Elder had called it.

For Thomas Morton was setting up a maypole on Merry Mount. At home they had danced round the maypole for many years, since it was an old English custom to make merry in the early days of May as a welcome to the spring, a thanksgiving for the burgeon of the year. The master of Merry Mount was a merry man, and there was drinking and carousing in his settlement.

He had set up an idol, thundered the Elders; yea, a calf of Horeb. He would realize he had made a woeful place indeed of his Merry Mount when he felt the vengeance of the Lord.

But Thomas Morton cared nothing for the Elders. He had come to the New World to make a fortune, trapping animals for their skins and trading with the old country; and doubtless he had found the Indians' desire for what they called "the firewater," and their keen delight in European firearms, very profitable. And now he had committed as great a sin in the eyes of the Elders of New Plymouth as any, so far, in setting up a maypole.

Excitement was high in New Plymouth. All the men from the ship had decided to pay their homage to the "Calf of Horeb." It would be like a bit of home, they said, to dance round a maypole.

All through the days before the first of May there were sounds of revelry on Merry Mount. There were shots from cannon to herald the frivolity, and the sound of drums came over the clear air. The maypole was a pine tree to which had been nailed a pair of buckshorns. It could be seen for miles.

In the morning Bartle took Tamar out to the *Liberty* to show her how far preparations for the return journey had gone.

"In a few weeks we shall sail for England!" he said, and excitement gleamed in his eyes.

But when she thought of England she must think also of terrible things; of her mother in the cottage, of the women she had seen at the town hall being searched by the prickers, of the seamen begging in the streets. She looked back at the land and thought how fair it was in the morning sunshine, with the faint mist rising from the meadows and the sparkling river losing itself in the sea, and the nearby forest and the distant mountains. The settlement itself was not exactly beautiful, but there was about it something which moved her more deeply than the beauties of nature. Those little houses represented bravery, courage, sacrifice. She wished her gaze would not stray to that spot where the platform would be with its whipping post and its gallows. She wished she could shut out of her mind the memory of Polly Eagel's scream as the hot iron touched her forehead. She wished she need not think of Polly, walking through the village street, her head downcast, all the saucy gaiety gone from her, branded for life.

But Polly had sinned, she reminded herself.

So have we all! came back the answer.

And then: But this is not cruelty such as I have seen at home. Nevertheless, it is cruelty.

She told Bartle of her thoughts, and he laughed and caught her to him.

"You want a land of your own," he said. "There will be no winter in such a land. It shall always be springtime, and there we shall be eternally young. Food grows on the trees and you and I stretch ourselves out on the grass and love and love and love . . ."

Then she laughed with him that she, the most imperfect of beings, should demand a perfect world.

Bartle said: "We will call at Merry Mount and dance round the maypole. It will bring memories of home; and when you see the merrymaking you will be as eager to slip away from these shores as I am."

She could not help being excited at the prospect of hearing merry laughter, of dancing at Bartle's side. She had missed these things; she had missed them too long.

She wanted to ask Annis to go with them, for Annis loved gaiety; she was on the point of suggesting it, but she refrained. It would not be good to tempt Annis; Annis was so happy in the new life; she was saved, and she would not have the same inclination towards frivolity that she had once had. Had she forgotten, wondered Tamar, those occasions when she had met John in the barn on her father's land? She made no reference to them when she had heard that the young people were to make public confession and suffer a whipping for doing what she and John had once done.

Bartle and Tamar took one of the boats and went along the coast to Merry Mount. It was late afternoon and all the settlers on Merry Mount had turned out to help in the preparations for the fun. Indians, naked but for their belts of wampum, stood about watching: some with solemn faces, some smiling at the antics of the white men.

Thomas Morton welcomed Bartle and Tamar.

"Come, my friends, laugh and be merry with us. Life was meant to be enjoyed."

He knew Bartle as the Captain of the ship which was shortly to sail away, and he knew Tamar was his wife. So this was not such a victory as it would have been had he, with his maypole, been able to lure some of the Puritan young people over to his Mount. Still, all were welcome.

A pageant had been planned by Morton; there was a special song compiled for the occasion in which every man took part: there were old dances which had been danced in England as long as any could remember.

Dusk came, and with it the festivity was at its height. Flares were lighted. Indians crept in with their women and danced their native dances. In the light from the flares, the painted faces of the Indians glowed, their bodies gleamed—some naked, some adorned with deerskins; their heads and faces oiled; their straight black hair cut in the style of their tribe; the paint on their faces, red and vermilion, to show all who looked their way that they came in peace and not in war. About their necks were beads of *wampompeag* to match the belts about their loins.

It was a strange, fantastic sight, with the lights from the flares shining alike on the faces of white men and red men.

Morton had provided a good deal of drink, and the Indians cried out in joy at the prospect of indulging in some of the white man's "fire-water." To them this magic water, which burned the throat and intoxicated the mind so that those who took it seemed filled with great joy, was the most wonderful thing the white men had brought with them.

The Indians sprawled on the ground near the maypole, clapping their hands in time with the songs, ecstatic smiles on their faces, delighted to be present at this feast of the white men. The maypole they imagined to be a god of the white men as were Kitan the good god and Hobbamocco the evil god of their own. They were ready to pay homage to this strange god while never swerving in their devotion to their own, for gods were gods and must be treated with respect, to whatever men they belonged.

The song of the day was sung again and again:

"Nectar is the thing assigned,
By the Deity's own mind,
To cure the heart opprest with grief,
And of good liquors is the chief."

Voices were raised in the chorus:

"Then drink and be merry, merry,
merry, boys. . . ."

Both Bartle and Tamar were caught up in the excitement all about them. They danced with the rest, round and round the maypole. In the light from the flares Tamar saw some of the young people from New Plymouth, furtive yet determined. They had risked a terrible punishment in order to dance round a maypole.

And then, among the milling crowd of sweating men and women and painted Indians, Tamar caught sight of James Milroy. His eyes glared at her as he watched her and Bartle, dancing with their arms about each other.

She laughed with a wonderful sense of freedom. It had occurred to her that James Milroy desired her even as had Humility Brown; and the knowledge had come to her that she would be able to forget the death of her first husband for long periods at a time during the years to come. These men who had seemed so saintly were hardly different from their fellow men whom they despised. Such thoughts brought relief with them and she asked herself slyly: Does Brother Milroy come to watch the merrymaking or to spy? And in any case, whatever he comes for, he comes for his own pleasure, as do the rest. Where is the difference then between one and another of us?

She was sick of the hot smell of bodies, and the fumes of gammedes and Jupiter were in her head. That liquor had been potent.

"Come," she said to Bartle. "Let us seek the cool of the forest. I am hot and tired, and weary of the noise and singing. I have had enough and would rest."

He was nothing loth, and they went together into the forest, where he laid his cloak on the grass that they might lie down together.

It was peaceful in the forest, lying there among the trees; there was no sound but the call of a bird, the murmur of insects, a rustle in the undergrowth that might have been made by musk-rat or beaver. Now and then they heard the sound of human voices whispering, and they knew that they were not the only lovers to steal away from the merrymaking for the sake of the peace of the forest.

Through the darkness came the sound of fresh outbursts of revelry.

> "Give to the melancholy man
> A cup or two of it now and then;
> This physic will soon revive his blood
> And make him of a merrier mood.
> Then drink and be merry, merry, merry,
> boys . . ."

Tamar thought that the Elders had spoken aptly when they had compared the revellers of Merry Mount with the Children of Israel dancing round the golden calf. But people must sometimes laugh and be merry. Life should not be all drabness surely; and if the Lord of Merry Mount worshipped drink and riches as the Puritans said he did, had not the Puritans set up their own golden calf of pride, bigotry and intolerance?

Where had these thoughts come from so suddenly? She did not know; and Bartle was close to her, and they were alone — or almost alone — in the forest.

* * *

May Day brought a climax. Life became furtive and sly after that. There were more punishments in the weeks following that May Day than there had been since the *Liberty* had arrived. Confessions were made in the meeting place and it was clear to Tamar — who felt that everything about her was becoming gradually clearer — that these stern-faced Puritans and their hardmouthed wives were going to the meeting place with more alacrity than they had before. Some of those who had sinned gave details of their sins; they received their whippings and were married.

Tamar had been seen at the revelries, but she had been there with her husband, and Sir Bartle was not of the community, although Tamar was considered to be. Her marriage was deplored, and she was looked upon with suspicion, but she was in the charge of her husband and no punishment was suggested for her to endure.

It was discovered that two people among them were Quakers, and these two were tied to a cart's tail and whipped out of New Plymouth. They were warned that if they came back they would be hanged.

There were great crowds to witness the whipping of the Quakers.

And then Mistress Alton began to recall the iniquities of Annis's past life, and she spoke of these — as she felt it her duty to do — to Brother

Milroy, with the result that John and Annis Tyler were summoned before the Elders.

Tamar was in the meeting place, and Richard was with her when Annis and John made their confession.

Richard had tried to persuade Tamar not to go, for he saw in her eyes something which alarmed him. He knew that since the death of Humility she had been trying to become a good Puritan, and he knew also that this was because of some twisted notion that by doing so she could expiate her sin. She had, by long and arduous practice, suppressed something which was essentially herself; but that which had taken months to cover up, could leap out without a moment's warning.

Richard kept close to her. He knew that she was very concerned, because her affection for Annis went deep.

Annis had changed since the accusation had been made against her. She had become like an old woman; the flaming colour in her cheeks was tinged with purple and her eyes showed her bewilderment. She had tried so hard to win respect; she had been so ready to love the new land and the new way of life; and now to hear that her old sin was remembered against her, brought her such shame that she could not hold up her head. She had neither slept nor eaten since the terrible accusation had been made.

Young Dick was with Tamar and Richard as they made their way to the meeting house; but as they were about to enter, Richard said to Tamar: "Go on,

Tamar. I'll be with you in a moment. And Dick . . . here a moment, please."

Tamar, who could think of nothing but Annis at this time, hardly noticed what was said and went on into the meeting house.

When she had gone, Richard said to Dick: "Your father is on the *Liberty.* Go out to him and tell him that he must come at once. It's very important, I feel, that he should be here. Tell him I have sent you to fetch him and that he must come at once. If we should be in the meeting house he should go to the whipping post and wait for us there. Tell him he must be here for your mother's sake. He must be at hand when Annis is punished, in case he is needed. Tell him I am afraid . . . afraid for Tamar."

Dick ran off, thrilled by what seemed an important mission.

Richard went into the meeting house.

"Where is Dick?" asked Tamar.

"I sent him away. It is not good for him to witness such spectacles."

She nodded. She had caught sight of the bowed back of Annis, and tears had started to her eyes.

She listened to the droning voice of the Elder. Sin, sin, sin . . . ! she thought. They think of nothing but sin! They are obsessed with sin, so that they see it all around them.

"This is a long-ago sin, but sin does not grow less with the years. It lies across the soul like an ugly mark on a clean garment. It is necessary to dip that garment in the blood of the Lamb if it should be whiter than the snow. Repentance is not enough. Repentance there must be, but expiation also . . . Brothers and sisters, among us of late, sin has been rampant. Since our wicked neighbour of the Mount of Woe set up a golden calf and worshipped it, there has been evil even here among us!"

Tamar was clenching and unclenching her hands. Richard took the hand nearest his and pressed it.

"Calm," he whispered. "Be calm, my darling."

"Richard . . . not Annis. I *love* Annis. She is like a sister to me. She is my friend . . ."

"We live in an imperfect world," he said.

Angry glances were directed towards them. Whispering in the meeting house was a sin as deserving of punishment as any other sin. But now they were forgotten, for Annis and John Tyler had stood up and were about to confess their sin.

Tamar heard Annis's voice as though it were coming to her over the years.

"We was young . . . and we was sinful . . . and we did meet in the barn . . . and because we did know no better, there was great sin between us . . ."

Tamar seemed to be reliving the past, seeing herself in Pennicomquick, mixing a potion, muttering a charm, listening to Annis's confidences as they lay on their straw pallets together.

Not Annis! This could not happen to Annis. She wanted to shout: "Do not be ashamed, Annis. It is they who should be ashamed. You are a good woman, however you sinned in your youth. You and John were happy. You loved this land. You asked for nothing but to work here and be happy and good . . ." But her lips were dry, her mouth parched and her voice lost to her.

Annis was going on: " 'Twas no fault of John's. He had no say in it. The sin was mine, so I hope you'll not punish him. It was a charm I got from a witch. So John had no say in it. There was a child . . . my first, my Christian. I named him Christian so's he could be better than his mother were, and so he is. 'Twere no fault of John's that our boy were born out of wedlock. He were took off to prison for going to the meeting house, and so we couldn't be married . . . and our child were born . . ."

The Elder spoke. It was true, as in so many cases, that the woman was at fault. He did not doubt that. She had, on her own admission, consorted with witches in the hope of leading a man to damnation. For that she should have her strokes increased. But the man could not go without punishment. The godly are free from any spells that might be made from witchcraft, since the Devil sows his seed in fertile ground.

As they left the meeting house for the platform, Tamar tried to call out to Annis, but no words would come. She saw Annis walking into the bright, hard light of day and she felt that her heart was breaking, for she had not known until now how she had loved this friend of her childhood, girlhood and maturity. Words crowded into her mind: "Take me! Whip me! I gave her the charm." And then: "Whip me if you dare! Judge me . . . judge us both . . . if you dare!"

Annis's back was bare for the lash. A garment had been discreetly laid across her breast with a string to tie it about her neck and keep it secure. She was tied to the whipping post, and she did not look like Annis. Her plump face sagged and there was a hideous purple colour in her cheeks and on her lips—a dark and ugly colour.

Tamar would have run forward, but Richard was holding her firmly by the hand.

"Let us go," he said. "You do not want to see this."

He was looking anxiously about him to see if Bartle had come.

"I will stay!" she said. "I *will* stay. I must be near her. I cannot run away because I dare not look."

She turned to him with blazing hatred in her eyes.

"Do you know what I would do if I had the strength of ten men?" she demanded. She did not wait for him to answer: "I would leap up there. I would tie the Elders and Brother Milroy to that post. I would use the whip on *them*!" Her voice broke and tears ran down her cheeks. "Annis!" she whispered. "But what has *Annis* done? What did she ever do . . . but want to live and be happy?"

The whip whistled in the air. It seemed to be poised above Annis's bare back for a long time before it fell.

A weal leaped up on the tender flesh. There was a heartrending cry as Annis slumped at the post.

The whip came down again, but this time there was no cry.

Tamar wrenched herself free.

"I must go to her! I *must* go to her. What am I doing standing by. . . while they do that to her?"

She had pushed her way through the crowds before Richard could stop her; she was mounting the platform. The man with the whip was standing back a little, staring at Annis's body, for he had noticed something strange about her inert figure, her purple face, her lips which hung open and her staring eyes. Annis was curiously still.

Tamar knelt beside her.

"Annis," she murmured. "Dearest Annis, speak to me. It is your own Tamar. What have these murderous brutes done to you? Annis. . . look at me. . . speak. . . speak. I command you, Annis! Don't dare disobey me. It is I. . . Tamar." She was sobbing because she knew what those about her had yet to learn. She did not need to put her hand on Annis's heart to know that it had stopped. They had killed Annis; they had piled such shame and ignominy upon her that they had broken her heart.

Out of her grief grew a mad and uncontrollable rage. She snatched the whip from the hand of the man who had used it; she lifted it and would have struck him had not someone seized her and taken it from her.

She cried out: "You have murdered Annis. You have killed my friend. I hate you. I wish I had never seen your smug faces. You are cruel. . . evil and wicked. I hate you. I hate you. I hope you will all rot in hell as you deserve to do. . . you. . . and you. . . and you. . ."

One of the Elders knelt down by Annis and untied the ropes which bound her to the post. There was a deep silence everywhere as he laid Annis gently down, and looked into her face.

"I fear she is dead," he said slowly.

"Dead! Dead!" cried Tamar. "And you killed her."

Richard was standing beside her on the platform. "Come away, Tamar. Come away."

But she would not move. She stared at the dead body of Annis while memories, bitter, poignant and sweet, crowded in on her.

What right had these people to stand in judgment on dear sweet Annis?

Words fell from her lips. Her eyes flashed and her hair fell about her face. Many watching began to pray, for they were sure that the woman who stood before them was a witch.

She shouted: "You murdered her . . . all of you. Do you think I am deceived by you? Do you think I have not seen Brother Milroy's sly eyes upon me? You men have desires as other men have! Oh, but you are so pure, are you not? We must have children for the colony. . . not a woman's body to caress and give you pleasure. I hate you. I loathe you. You sin equally with the men of Merry Mount; but they sin merrily, and I could be happier with merry sinners than with brutal murdering ones. Freedom! What freedom is there here? Look at Polly Eagel! Have none of you ever sinned . . . in thought perhaps, since you would lack the courage to sin in deed? Freedom! You speak of freedom to worship God. Yes! Freedom to worship Him as you would have us worship Him! We are offered that at home in England. What of the Quakers you whipped out of Plymouth? What had they done but worshipped God in a way different from your own?"

Brother Milroy had caught her by the arm; another helped him to hold her.

Mistress Alton, her voice high-pitched with excitement, shouted from the crowd: "She is a witch. The Devil forced her on her mother. We knew her for a witch in the old country."

"So it is you!" shouted Tamar. "You . . . you wicked old woman. You . . . who killed Annis with your cruelty. You wanted James Milroy for yourself, did you not? But his lustful eyes were turned on me. The Devil gave me my beauty, they say; and they would enjoy it . . . ah, only for the sake of the *colony*! You sent the pricker after me when we were in Pennicomquick. Do you think that I did not know that? I despised you. Till now I did not know that you were worth hating."

"Witchcraft!" screamed Mistress Alton. "Witchcraft! She is a witch. She it was who gave Annis Tyler the charm which led John Tyler to sin with her. She is a witch on her own confession. Hang her quickly . . . before she casts her spells upon us. Look for the mark. Strip her, find it . . . and then . . . prick it! You will find that she is a witch. To the gallows! To the gallows! Lose no time, for she is evil. She is the Devil's own."

"Witch! Witch!" It grew in volume as thunder rolls. Tamar saw the gleaming eyes, the cruel mouths, and she thought: They have not had such excitement since they landed here. What is the beating of Annis, the branding of Polly, compared with the hanging of a witch?

Richard was trying to speak; he was holding up his hand and his eyes were full of agony. Dear Richard! To avoid this he had left his native land, and now it had caught up with them, as it seemed it must.

"Listen to me!" Richard was shouting. But his voice was lost in the cry of angry voices chanting: "A witch! A witch! To the gallows with the witch. The Devil's own. The Devil's own daughter. To the gallows! To the gallows!"

Tamar felt the breath of those who would seize her; her gown was torn. The more brutal among the crowd were surging on to the platform, and she felt she had seen these faces before. Puritans were no different from others.

But now someone was forcing his way to her. An arm was about her. One of the men who had pulled at her bodice was sent hurtling off the platform.

She was aware of the glitter of blue eyes and the flash of a sword; she felt weak with sudden emotion.

In the last few seconds she had forgotten Bartle.

CHAPTER EIGHT

The *Liberty* had rounded Cape James and was sailing down towards Chesapeake Bay.

With her sailed all those who wished to leave the settlement; the Swanns and their family; John Tyler and his, for they could not bear to stay with people who had killed Annis; there was Tom Eagel with his wife Polly; and there were some of the young couples who had danced at Merry Mount and been brought to shame through the prying eyes of Brother Milroy. There was Richard, with Tamar and her children.

The sun was sinking in a sky of blood-red which was staining the waters; soon the *Liberty* would be shut in by darkness.

Tamar came on deck and stood beside Bartle. He put an arm about her and held her tightly against him. He laughed then; for he was not displeased to feel his ship beneath him.

And she laughed with him, sharing in his mood of exultation. For the second time in her life she had narrowly missed the gallows. She would never forget that moment when Bartle had stood beside her on the platform, his sword flashing in the sunlight with a promise of death to any who dared lay a hand upon her. And those people had fallen back, afraid, until the Elders, who did not love violence, had commanded order. Richard had spoken then and told them that he and his daughter were going to leave New Plymouth, and that they would never return. The *Liberty* was theirs; they had brought provisions with them, and they would take away as much as they had brought. Then they would go in peace.

"We came here to escape violence and intolerance," Richard had said. "We thought we had made that escape, but we find we were wrong. The small Church is as intolerant as its bigger sister. We have but escaped from one to another of the same kind. We shall sail forth in the *Liberty.* We shall try to find a place for ourselves somewhere in this great country. The way may be long; our path may be set with dangers; but liberty will be the reward, and liberty must be fought for and won by bitter fighting, great hardship; it may be constant hardship; that we cannot say, for having fought and won we may have to continue fighting to retain this precious gift. Only those who are ready to fight the fight should come with us."

There were some, it seemed, who were ready.

Bartle gripped Tamar's hand as they watched the sun begin to dip into the sea; they watched until the pink stain on the waters turned to a dark green.

"Whither are we going?" asked Bartle. "Whither will this pox-ridden bucket carry us?"

"She will carry us whither we should go," answered Tamar. "Somewhere in this vast land we will find freedom, for in our thoughts we have already made it the land of freedom."

The water was changing colour once more; away to the east it was now an inky black.

Bartle mused: "She's a frail thing, this *Liberty*, to face wind and rain, pirates and savages."

"We are in danger," said Tamar. "We all know that. From hour to hour, minute to minute, we are in danger. But what we seek is worth facing all the dangers the world can offer us."

They were both silent while the darkness came down upon them and wrapped itself about them so that they could no longer see the heaving water.

But the *Liberty* went steadily on.

THE END

The publishers hope that this large print book has brought you pleasurable reading. Each title is designed to make the text as easy to read as possible.

For further information on backlist or forthcoming titles please write or telephone:

In the British Isles and its territories, customers should contact:

ISIS Publishing Ltd
7 Centremead
Osney Mead
Oxford OX2 0ES
England
Telephone: (01865) 250 333 Fax: (01865) 790 358

In Australia and New Zealand, customers should contact:

Bolinda Publishing Pty Ltd
17 Mohr Street
Tullamarine Victoria 3043
Australia
Telephone: (03) 9338 0666 Fax: (03) 9335 1903
Toll Free Telephone: 1800 335 364
Toll Free Fax: 1800 671 4111

In New Zealand:

Toll Free Telephone: 0800 44 5788
Toll Free Fax: 0800 44 5789

DATABASE SYSTEM CONCEPTS

McGraw-Hill Series in Computer Science

Senior Consulting Editor

C.L. Liu, *University of Illinois at Urbana-Champaign*

Consulting Editor

Allen B. Tucker, *Bowdoin College*

Fundamentals of Computing and Programing
Computer Organization and Architecture
Computers in Society/Ethics
Systems and Languages
Theoretical Foundations
Software Engineering and Database
Artificial Intelligence
Networks, Parallel and Distributed Computing
Graphics and Visualization
The MIT Electrical and Computer Science Series

Software Engineering and Database

Cohen: *Ada as a Second Language*
Fairley: *Software Engineering Concepts*
Silberschatz, Korth, and Sudarshan: *Database System Concepts*
Musa, Iannino, and Okumoto: *Software Reliability*
Pressman: *Software Engineering: A Beginner's Guide*
Pressman: *Software Engineering: A Practitioner's Approach*
Wiederhold: *Database Design*

DATABASE SYSTEM CONCEPTS

Third Edition

Abraham Silberschatz

Bell Laboratories

Henry F. Korth

Bell Laboratories

S. Sudarshan

Indian Institute of Technology, Bombay

The McGraw-Hill Companies, Inc.

New York St. Louis San Francisco Auckland Bogotá Caracas
Lisbon London Madrid Mexico City Milan Montreal New Delhi
San Juan Singapore Sydney Tokyo Toronto

McGraw-Hill
A Division of The ***McGraw-Hill*** *Companies*

DATABASE SYSTEM CONCEPTS
International Editions 1997

9 0 KKP PMP 20 9

This book was set in Times Roman by ETP Harrison.
The editor was Eric M. Munson;
the production supervisor was Leroy A. Young.
The cover was designed by Christopher Brady.
Project supervision was done by ETP Harrison (Portland, Oregon).

Library of Congress Cataloging-in-Publication Data

Silberschatz, Abraham.
Database system concepts / Abraham Silberschatz, Henry F. Korth, S. Sudarshan. – 3rd ed.
p. cm. – (McGraw-Hill series in computer science)
Korth's name appears first on earlier editions.
Includes bibliographical references and index.
ISBN 0-07-044756-X
1. Database management. I. Korth, Henry F. II. Sudarshan S. III. Title. IV. Series: McGraw-Hill computer science series.
QA76.9.D3S5737 1996
005.74–dc21 96-44015

When ordering this title, use ISBN 0-07-114810-8

Printed in Singapore

In memory of my father Joseph Silberschatz,
and my grandparents Stepha and Aaron Rosenblum

Avi Silberschatz

In memory of my grandparents:
Giuseppa and Anthony Affatigato and Gertrude and Frank Korth

Hank Korth

In memory of my grandfather, S. Mahalingam

S. Sudarshan

CONTENTS

Preface xv

1 Introduction 1
- 1.1 Purpose of Database Systems 1
- 1.2 View of Data 4
- 1.3 Data Models 7
- 1.4 Database Languages 12
- 1.5 Transaction Management 13
- 1.6 Storage Management 14
- 1.7 Database Administrator 15
- 1.8 Database Users 15
- 1.9 Overall System Structure 16
- 1.10 Summary 19
- Exercises 20
- Bibliographic Notes 20

2 Entity–Relationship Model 23
- 2.1 Basic Concepts 23
- 2.2 Design Issues 28
- 2.3 Mapping Constraints 30
- 2.4 Keys 34
- 2.5 Entity–Relationship Diagram 36
- 2.6 Weak Entity Sets 37
- 2.7 Extended E-R Features 41
- 2.8 Design of an E-R Database Schema 47
- 2.9 Reduction of an E-R Schema to Tables 52

2.10	Summary	58
	Exercises	59
	Bibliographic Notes	62

3 Relational Model 63

3.1	Structure of Relational Databases	63
3.2	The Relational Algebra	71
3.3	The Tuple Relational Calculus	86
3.4	The Domain Relational Calculus	90
3.5	Extended Relational-Algebra Operations	94
3.6	Modification of the Database	100
3.7	Views	102
3.8	Summary	106
	Exercises	107
	Bibliographic Notes	110

4 SQL 111

4.1	Background	111
4.2	Basic Structure	113
4.3	Set Operations	120
4.4	Aggregate Functions	122
4.5	Null Values	124
4.6	Nested Subqueries	125
4.7	Derived Relations	129
4.8	Views	130
4.9	Modification of the Database	131
4.10	Joined Relations	136
4.11	Data-Definition Language	140
4.12	Embedded SQL	145
4.13	Other SQL Features	148
4.14	Summary	148
	Exercises	149
	Bibliographic Notes	152

5 Other Relational Languages 153

5.1	Query-by-Example	153
5.2	Quel	165
5.3	Datalog	174
5.4	Summary	188
	Exercises	188
	Bibliographic Notes	190

6 Integrity Constraints 193

6.1	Domain Constraints	193
6.2	Referential Integrity	195
6.3	Assertions	200
6.4	Triggers	201
6.5	Functional Dependencies	202
6.6	Summary	210
	Exercises	211
	Bibliographic Notes	213

7 Relational Database Design 215

7.1 Pitfalls in Relational-Database Design 215
7.2 Decomposition 217
7.3 Normalization Using Functional Dependencies 221
7.4 Normalization Using Multivalued Dependencies 231
7.5 Normalization Using Join Dependencies 239
7.6 Domain-Key Normal Form 242
7.7 Alternative Approaches to Database Design 244
7.8 Summary 246
Exercises 247
Bibliographic Notes 250

8 Object-Oriented Databases 251

8.1 New Database Applications 251
8.2 The Object-Oriented Data Model 253
8.3 Object-Oriented Languages 262
8.4 Persistent Programming Languages 263
8.5 Persistent C++ Systems 267
8.6 Summary 271
Exercises 272
Bibliographic Notes 272

9 Object-Relational Databases 275

9.1 Nested Relations 275
9.2 Complex Types and Object Orientation 278
9.3 Querying with Complex Types 283
9.4 Creation of Complex Values and Objects 287
9.5 Comparison of Object-Oriented and Object-Relational Databases 288
9.6 Summary 289
Exercises 289
Bibliographic Notes 290

10 Storage and File Structure 293

10.1 Overview of Physical Storage Media 293
10.2 Magnetic Disks 296
10.3 RAID 301
10.4 Tertiary Storage 307
10.5 Storage Access 309
10.6 File Organization 312
10.7 Organization of Records in Files 318
10.8 Data-Dictionary Storage 322
10.9 Storage Structures for Object-Oriented Databases 324
10.10 Summary 332
Exercises 333
Bibliographic Notes 336

11 Indexing and Hashing 339

11.1 Basic Concepts 339
11.2 Ordered Indices 340

11.3 B+-Tree Index Files 346
11.4 B-Tree Index Files 356
11.5 Static Hashing 358
11.6 Dynamic Hashing 362
11.7 Comparison of Ordered Indexing and Hashing 369
11.8 Index Definition in SQL 371
11.9 Multiple-Key Access 372
11.10 Summary 377
Exercises 378
Bibliographic Notes 379

12 Query Processing 381
12.1 Overview 381
12.2 Catalog Information for Cost Estimation 384
12.3 Measures of Query Cost 386
12.4 Selection Operation 386
12.5 Sorting 394
12.6 Join Operation 397
12.7 Other Operations 410
12.8 Evaluation of Expressions 413
12.9 Transformation of Relational Expressions 418
12.10 Choice of Evaluation Plans 426
12.11 Summary 432
Exercises 434
Bibliographic Notes 437

13 Transactions 439
13.1 Transaction Concept 439
13.2 Transaction State 443
13.3 Implementation of Atomicity and Durability 445
13.4 Concurrent Executions 447
13.5 Serializability 451
13.6 Recoverability 456
13.7 Implementation of Isolation 457
13.8 Transaction Definition in SQL 458
13.9 Testing for Serializability 459
13.10 Summary 465
Exercises 467
Bibliographic Notes 468

14 Concurrency Control 471
14.1 Lock-Based Protocols 471
14.2 Timestamp-Based Protocols 482
14.3 Validation-Based Protocols 485
14.4 Multiple Granularity 487
14.5 Multiversion Schemes 490
14.6 Deadlock Handling 492
14.7 Insert and Delete Operations 497
14.8 Concurrency in Index Structures 500

14.9 Summary 503
Exercises 504
Bibliographic Notes 508

15 Recovery System 511
15.1 Failure Classification 511
15.2 Storage Structure 512
15.3 Recovery and Atomicity 516
15.4 Log-Based Recovery 517
15.5 Shadow Paging 525
15.6 Recovery with Concurrent Transactions 528
15.7 Buffer Management 531
15.8 Failure with Loss of Nonvolatile Storage 534
15.9 Advanced Recovery Techniques 535
15.10 Summary 539
Exercises 540
Bibliographic Notes 541

16 Database System Architectures 543
16.1 Centralized Systems 544
16.2 Client–Server Systems 545
16.3 Parallel Systems 549
16.4 Distributed Systems 555
16.5 Network Types 558
16.6 Summary 560
Exercises 561
Bibliographic Notes 562

17 Parallel Databases 565
17.1 Introduction 565
17.2 I/O Parallelism 566
17.3 Interquery Parallelism 569
17.4 Intraquery Parallelism 570
17.5 Intraoperation Parallelism 571
17.6 Interoperation Parallelism 579
17.7 Design of Parallel Systems 582
17.8 Summary 583
Exercises 583
Bibliographic Notes 585

18 Distributed Databases 587
18.1 Distributed Data Storage 588
18.2 Network Transparency 593
18.3 Distributed Query Processing 596
18.4 Distributed Transaction Model 599
18.5 Commit Protocols 604
18.6 Coordinator Selection 612
18.7 Concurrency Control 613
18.8 Deadlock Handling 617
18.9 Multidatabase Systems 622
18.10 Summary 626

	Exercises	628
	Bibliographic Notes	631
19	**Special Topics**	633
19.1	Security and Integrity	633
19.2	Standardization	644
19.3	Performance Benchmarks	647
19.4	Performance Tuning	650
19.5	Time in Databases	655
19.6	User Interfaces	657
19.7	Active Databases	660
19.8	Summary	663
	Exercises	664
	Bibliographic Notes	666
20	**Advanced Transaction Processing**	669
20.1	Remote Backup Systems	669
20.2	Transaction-Processing Monitors	672
20.3	High-Performance Transaction Systems	676
20.4	Long-Duration Transactions	679
20.5	Real-Time Transaction Systems	685
20.6	Weak Levels of Consistency	686
20.7	Transactional Workflows	687
20.8	Summary	693
	Exercises	694
	Bibliographic Notes	695
21	**New Applications**	697
21.1	Decision-Support Systems	698
21.2	Data Analysis	700
21.3	Data Mining	702
21.4	Data Warehousing	708
21.5	Spatial and Geographic Databases	710
21.6	Multimedia Databases	719
21.7	Mobility and Personal Databases	722
21.8	Information-Retrieval Systems	726
21.9	Distributed Information Systems	731
21.10	The World Wide Web	733
21.11	Summary	740
	Exercises	741
	Bibliographic Notes	743
A	**Network Model**	747
A.1	Basic Concepts	747
A.2	Data-Structure Diagrams	748
A.3	The DBTG CODASYL Model	750
A.4	Implementation Techniques	752
A.5	Discussion	752
B	**Hierarchical Model**	755
B.1	Basic Concepts	755

B.2 Tree-Structure Diagrams 756
B.3 Implementation Techniques 759
B.4 The IMS Database System 760
B.5 Discussion 761

Bibliography 763

Index 809

PREFACE

Database management has evolved from a specialized computer application to a central component of a modern computing environment. As such, knowledge about database systems has become an essential part of an education in computer science. Our purpose in this text is to present the fundamental concepts of database management. These concepts include aspects of database design, database languages, and database-system implementation.

This text is intended for a first course in databases at the junior or senior undergraduate, or first-year graduate, level. In addition to basic material for a first course, the text also contains advanced material that can be used for course supplements, or as introductory material for an advanced course.

We assume only a familiarity with basic data structures, computer organization, and a high-level (Pascal-like) programming language. Concepts are presented using intuitive descriptions, many of which are based on our running example of a bank enterprise. Important theoretical results are covered, but formal proofs are omitted. The bibliographic notes contain pointers to research papers in which results were first presented and proved, as well as references to material for further reading. In place of proofs, figures and examples are used to suggest why we should expect the result in question to be true.

The fundamental concepts and algorithms covered in the book are often based on those used in existing commercial or experimental database systems. Our aim is to present these concepts and algorithms in a general setting that is not tied to one particular database system.

In this third edition of *Database System Concepts*, we have retained the overall style of the first and second editions, while addressing the evolution of database management. Every chapter has been edited, and most have been modified extensively. We shall describe the changes in detail shortly.

Organization

The text is organized in eight major parts, plus two appendices:

- **Overview** (Chapters 1 and 2). Chapter 1 provides a general overview of the nature and purpose of database systems. We explain how the concept of a database system has developed, what the common features of database systems are, what a database system does for the user, and how a database system interfaces with operating systems. We also introduce an example database application: a banking enterprise consisting of multiple bank branches. This example is used as a running example throughout the book. This chapter is motivational, historical, and explanatory in nature. Chapter 2 presents the entity–relationship model. This model provides a high-level view of the issues in database design, and of the problems that we encounter in capturing the semantics of realistic applications within the constraints of a data model.
- **Relational model** (Chapters 3 through 5). Chapter 3 focuses on the relational data model, covering the relevant relational algebra and relational calculus. Chapter 4 focuses on the most influential of the user-oriented relational languages: SQL. Chapter 5 covers other relational languages. These three chapters describe data manipulation: queries, updates, insertions, and deletions. Algorithms and design issues are deferred to later chapters. Thus, these chapters are suitable for those individuals or lower-level classes who want to learn what a database system is, without getting into the details of what the internal algorithms and structure are.
- **Database constraints** (Chapters 6 and 7). Chapter 6 presents constraints from the standpoint of database integrity; Chapter 7 shows how constraints can be used in the design of a relational database. Functional dependencies and referential integrity are presented in Chapter 6, as are mechanisms for integrity maintenance, such as triggers and assertions. The theme of this chapter is the protection of the database from accidental damage. Chapter 7 introduces the theory of relational database design. Such topics as normalization and data dependencies are covered, with emphasis on the motivation for each normal form and on the intuitive meaning of each type of data dependency.
- **Object-based systems** (Chapters 8 and 9). Chapter 8 covers object-oriented databases. It introduces the concepts of object-oriented programming, and shows how these concepts form the basis for a data model. No prior knowledge of object-oriented languages is assumed. Chapter 9 covers object-relational databases, and shows how we can extend the relational data model to include object-oriented features, such as inheritance and complex types.
- **Data storage and retrieval** (Chapters 10 through 12). Chapter 10 deals with disk, file, and file-system structure, and with the mapping of relational and object data to a file system. A variety of data-access techniques are presented in Chapter 11, including hashing, B^+-tree indices, and grid file indices. Chapter 12 addresses query-evaluation algorithms, and query optimization based on equivalence-preserving query transformations. These chapters are targeted

at people who want to gain an understanding of the internals of the storage and retrieval components of a database.

- **Transaction management** (Chapters 13 through 15). Chapter 13 focuses on the fundamentals of a transaction-processing system, including transaction atomicity, consistency, isolation, and durability, as well as the notion of serializability. It is suitable for those individuals or classes that need an introduction to the issues of transaction management, yet do not require the details of concurrency-control and recovery protocols. In Chapter 14, we focus on concurrency control, and present several techniques for ensuring serializability, including locking, timestamping, and optimistic (validation) techniques. Deadlock issues are also covered in that chapter. Chapter 15 covers the primary techniques for ensuring correct transaction execution despite system crashes and disk failures. These techniques include logs, shadow pages, checkpoints, and database dumps.
- **Parallel and distributed systems** (Chapters 16 through 18). Chapter 16 covers computer-system architecture, and describes the influence of the underlying computer system on the database system. We discuss centralized systems, client–server systems, parallel and distributed architectures, and network types. In Chapter 17, on parallel databases, we explore a variety of parallelizing techniques, including I/O parallelism, interquery and intraquery parallelism, and interoperation and intraoperation parallelism. We also discuss cost estimation, query optimization, and parallel-system design. Chapter 18 revisits issues of database design, transaction management, and query evaluation and optimization, in the context of a distributed database system.
- **Advanced topics** (Chapters 19 through 21). Chapter 19 covers numerous special topics, including security and integrity, standardization, performance benchmarks and performance tuning, time in databases, user interfaces, and active databases. Chapter 20 deals with advanced transaction processing. We discuss transaction-processing monitors, high-performance transaction systems, real-time transaction systems, and transactional workflows. In Chapter 21, we introduce numerous new applications for database systems. First, we discuss decision-support systems, including data-analysis, data-mining, and data-warehousing applications. We then examine spatial and geographic databases, multimedia databases, and mobile and personal databases. Finally, we investigate information-retrieval systems for textual data, and distributed information systems, including the World Wide Web.
- **Appendices**. Although most new database applications use either the relational model or the object-oriented model, the network and hierarchical data models are still in use. As we did in the second edition, we have covered systems based on the network and hierarchical models in Appendices A and B, respectively. However, due to a decline in interest in teaching these older models, the full text of these appendices has been moved to the internet, with only a summary appearing in the printed text. The full version of the appendices is available on the web (http://www.bell-labs.com/topic/books/db-book) or via anonymous FTP from ftp.research.bell-labs.com in directory dist/db-book.

The Third Edition

Many comments and suggestions were forwarded to us concerning the first and second editions. These inputs — coupled with our own observations while teaching at the University of Texas, IIT Bombay, and IBM, and with our analysis of the directions in which database technology is evolving — have prodded us to produce this third edition, and have guided us in its production. Our basic procedure was to rewrite the material in each chapter, bringing the older material up to date, adding discussions on recent developments in database technology, improving the exercises, and adding new references. We have also restructured the organization of parts of the book. For the benefit of those readers familiar with the second edition, we explain the main changes here.

- **Entity–Relationship model**. We have improved our coverage of the entity–relationship (E-R) model. Chapter 2 in the third edition is similar to the previous Chapter 2; however, we have expanded coverage of issues in E-R database design. Design issues are discussed throughout the chapter, and are addressed in particular in two new sections, 2.2 and 2.8. Extended E-R features are discussed in more detail than in the second edition, as is reduction of an E-R schema to tables (Sections 2.7 and 2.9, respectively).

- **Relational databases**. In the second edition, we expanded our coverage of the relational model. In the third edition, we again devote Chapter 3 to the relational model and to the formal relational languages: the relational algebra and the relational calculus. In Section 3.5, we have added discussions of the generalized projection, outer-join operations, and aggregation. Chapter 4 now covers SQL exclusively. Our coverage of SQL has been significantly expanded to include features of the SQL-92 standard, in addition to the existing coverage based on the SQL-89. Some SQL implementations may support only SQL-89 and not SQL-92; we explicitly identify those features of SQL-92 that are not supported in SQL-89. We now cover QBE, and Quel, in Chapter 5. The research language Datalog, which had been presented in the second edition in Chapter 14, is included now in Chapter 5, and receives a more detailed discussion. Chapter 6 covers integrity constraints; Chapter 7 covers database-design issues and normal forms. These chapters were Chapters 5 and 6, respectively, in the second edition.

- **Object-based databases**. Expansions to our coverage of the object-oriented data model appear in Chapters 8, 9, and 10. In Chapter 8, we augment the material from Chapter 13 in the second edition with a discussion of object-oriented programming languages. Chapter 9 is a new chapter in which we present object-relational data models. These models extend the relational data model by providing a richer type system, including object orientation, and add constructs to relational query languages, such as SQL, to deal with the added data types. Chapter 10 now includes a section on the storage structures for object-oriented databases (Section 10.9).

- **Query processing**. Our treatment of query processing has been greatly expanded from the second edition. In Chapter 12, we now present detailed explanations of what different ways we have for implementing various relational operations, and of how to estimate their execution costs. We have also expanded our coverage of query transformations that preserve equivalence of the query results, and have incorporated new material on query optimization. Chapter 17 now has expanded coverage of parallel query processing.
- **Transaction processing**. As we did for the second edition, we have reorganized and slightly expanded our coverage of transaction processing (Chapters 13 through 15). Some of the advanced material on transaction processing from Chapter 12 in the second edition is now organized in a new chapter on advanced transaction processing: Chapter 20 (see the note on advanced topics that follows). Chapter 13 introduces issues in all aspects of transaction management, with details deferred to later chapters. This organization allows instructors to choose between just introducing transaction-processing concepts (by covering only Chapter 13), or offering detailed coverage (based on Chapters 13 through 15).
- **Computer architectures and parallel systems**. Chapter 16 is a new chapter that covers computer-system architecture and the influence of the underlying computer system on the database system. We discuss centralized systems, client–server systems, and network types. We also present parallel and distributed architectures; we cover these systems in detail in Chapters 17 and 18, respectively. Chapter 17 is also a new chapter; it covers parallel databases. We explore a variety of parallelizing techniques, including I/O parallelism, interquery and intraquery parallelism, and interoperation and intraoperation parallelism. We also discuss cost evaluation, query optimization, and parallel-system design. New material on disk organization based on the RAID architectures is included in Chapter 10.
- **Advanced topics**. Although we have modified and updated the entire text, we concentrate our presentation of material pertaining to ongoing database research and new database applications in three new chapters.

  We present numerous special topics in Chapter 19. Chapter 16 in the second edition on security and integrity, now appears as Section 19.1. The remaining sections are new material pertaining to standardization projects, performance benchmarks, performance tuning, time in databases, user interfaces, and active databases.

  Some of the material on transaction processing in Chapter 20 appeared previously in Chapter 12 in the second edition; Section 20.1 on transaction processing monitors, Section 20.2 on high-performance transaction systems, Section 20.4 on real-time transaction systems, and Section 20.6 on transactional workflows are all new.

  In Chapter 21, we introduce several new applications for database systems; the material in this chapter is all new. First, we discuss decision-support systems, including data-analysis, data-mining, and data-warehousing applications. We then discuss spatial and geographic databases, multimedia databases, and mobile and personal databases. Finally, we discuss information-retrieval systems for textual data, and distributed information systems, including the World Wide Web.

Instructor's Note

The book contains both basic and advanced material, which might not be covered in a single semester. It is possible to design courses using various subsets of the chapters. We outline possibilities here:

- Chapter 5 can be omitted if students will not be using QBE, Quel, or Datalog as part of the course.
- Chapter 7 contains a series of normal forms, in decreasing order of practical importance. Later sections (Section 7.4 on) may be omitted, if desired.
- If object-orientation is to be covered in a separate advanced course, Chapters 8 and 9, and Section 10.9, can be omitted. Alternatively, they could constitute the foundation of an advanced course in object databases.
- Chapters 11 and 12 contain some material that may be more suitable for an advanced course. You might choose to omit some or all of Sections 11.6, 11.9, 12.7, 12.8, and 12.10.
- Both our coverage of transaction processing (Chapters 13 through 15) and our coverage of database-system architecture (Chapters 16 through 18) consist of an overview chapter (Chapters 13 and 16, respectively), followed by chapters with details. You might choose to use Chapters 13 and 16, while omitting Chapters 14, 15, 17, and 18, if you defer these latter chapters to an advanced course.
- The sections of the final three chapters (Chapters 19 through 21) are largely independent. Based on instructor or student interest, a custom-tailored set of subsections may be chosen as end-of-semester enrichment material. Those chapters as a whole are suitable for an advanced topics course.

Model course syllabi, based on the text, can be found on the World Wide Web home page of the book (see following section).

Supplements and Mailing List

For information about the teaching supplements that complement this book, send electronic mail to CompSci_college@mcgraw-hill.com.

We also now provide an environment in which users can communicate among themselves and with us. We have created a mailing list consisting of users of our book with the electronic mail address db-book@research.bell-labs.com. If you wish to be on the list, please send a message to db-book@research.bell-labs.com, include your name, affiliation, title, and electronic mail address.

Home Page

A World Wide Web home page for the book is available with the URL:

http://www.bell-labs.com/topic/books/db-book

The home page contains information about the book, such as up-to-date errata, model course syllabi, and information about teaching supplements.

Errata

We have endeavored to eliminate typos, bugs, and the like from the text. But, as in new releases of software, bugs probably remain. We would appreciate it if you would notify us of any errors or omissions in the book. An updated errata page will be accessible from the book's WWW home page. Also, if you would like to suggest improvements or to contribute exercises, we would be glad to hear from you. Any correspondence should be sent to Avi Silberschatz, Bell Laboratories, Lucent Technologies Inc., 700 Mountain Avenue, Murray Hill, NJ 07974, USA. Internet electronic mail should be addressed to db-book@research.bell-labs.com.

Acknowledgments

This edition is based on the two previous editions, so we thank once again the many people who helped us with the first and second editions, including Don Batory, Haran Boral, Robert Brazile, Sara Strandtman, Won Kim, Anil Nigam, Bruce Porter, Carol Kroll, Jim Peterson, Fletcher Mattox, Ron Hitchens, Alberto Mendelzon, Alan Fekete, Hyoung-Joo Kim, Keith Marzullo, Mark Roth, Greg Speegle, and Henry Korth (father of Henry F.)

Greg Speegle and Dawn Bezviner helped us to prepare the instructor's manual for the first edition. Their work served as the basis for the new instructor's manual for the third edition, which was prepared with the help of K. V. Raghavan.

This edition has benefited from the many useful comments provided to us by the numerous students who have used the second edition in our classes at the University of Texas and at IBM, or have used drafts of the third edition at IIT Bombay. In addition, numerous people have written or spoken to us about the book, and have offered suggestions and comments. Although we cannot mention all these people here, we especially thank R. B. Abhyankar, Paul Bourgeois, Michael Carey, J. Edwards, Christos Faloutsos, Homma Farian, Shashi Gadia, Jim Gray, Le Gruenwald, Yannis Ioannidis, Gary Lindstrom, Dave Maier, Hector Garcia-Molina, Ami Motro, Cyril Orji, K. V. Raghavan, Marek Rusinkiewicz, S. Seshadri, Shashi Shekhar, Amit Sheth, Nandit Soparkar, and Marianne Winslett.

Lyn Dupré copyedited the book. Sara Strandtman edited our text into the LaTeXformat, and helped us prepare the revised text for this edition. Sara also edited the instructor's manual and transparencies.

The new cover—an evolution of the covers of the first two editions—was drawn by Chris Brady of McGraw-Hill. Marilyn Turnamian created an early draft of the cover design. The idea of using ships as part of the cover concept was originally suggested to us by Bruce Stephan. We would also like to thank our editor, Eric Munson, for his wisdom and patience.

Finally, Sudarshan would like to acknowledge his brother, Mohan, and mother, Indira, for their support. Hank would like to acknowledge his wife, Joan, and his children, Abby and Joe, for their love and understanding. Avi would like to acknowledge his mother for her love and support.

A. S.
H. F. K.
S. S.

CHAPTER 1

INTRODUCTION

A *database-management system* (DBMS) consists of a collection of interrelated data and a set of programs to access those data. The collection of data, usually referred to as the *database*, contains information about one particular enterprise. The primary goal of a DBMS is to provide an environment that is both *convenient* and *efficient* to use in retrieving and storing database information.

Database systems are designed to manage large bodies of information. The management of data involves both the definition of structures for the storage of information and the provision of mechanisms for the manipulation of information. In addition, the database system must provide for the safety of the information stored, despite system crashes or attempts at unauthorized access. If data are to be shared among several users, the system must avoid possible anomalous results.

The importance of information in most organizations—which determines the value of the database—has led to the development of a large body of concepts and techniques for the efficient management of data. In this chapter, we present a brief introduction to the principles of database systems.

1.1 Purpose of Database Systems

Consider part of a savings-bank enterprise that keeps information about all customers and savings accounts. One way to keep the information on a computer is to store it in permanent system files. To allow users to manipulate the information, the system has a number of application programs that manipulate the files, including

- A program to debit or credit an account
- A program to add a new account

- A program to find the balance of an account
- A program to generate monthly statements

These application programs have been written by system programmers in response to the needs of the bank organization.

New application programs are added to the system as the need arises. For example, suppose that new government regulations allow the savings bank to offer checking accounts. As a result, new permanent files are created that contain information about all the checking accounts maintained in the bank, and new application programs may need to be written to deal with situations that do not arise in savings accounts, such as handling overdrafts. Thus, as time goes by, more files and more application programs are added to the system.

The typical *file-processing system* just described is supported by a conventional operating system. Permanent records are stored in various files, and different application programs are written to extract records from, and to add records to, the appropriate files. Before the advent of DBMSs, organizations typically stored information using such systems.

Keeping organizational information in a file-processing system has a number of major disadvantages

- **Data redundancy and inconsistency**. Since the files and application programs are created by different programmers over a long period, the various files are likely to have different formats and the programs may be written in several programming languages. Moreover, the same information may be duplicated in several places (files). For example, the address and telephone number of a particular customer may appear in a file that consists of savings-account records and in a file that consists of checking-account records. This redundancy leads to higher storage and access cost. In addition, it may lead to *data inconsistency*; that is, the various copies of the same data may no longer agree. For example, a changed customer address may be reflected in savings-account records but not elsewhere in the system.
- **Difficulty in accessing data**. Suppose that one of the bank officers needs to find out the names of all customers who live within the city's 78733 zip code. The officer asks the data-processing department to generate such a list. Because this request was not anticipated when the original system was designed, there is no application program on hand to meet it. There is, however, an application program to generate the list of *all* customers. The bank officer has now two choices: Either obtain the list of all customers and have the needed information extracted manually, or ask the data-processing department to have a system programmer write the necessary application program. Both alternatives are obviously unsatisfactory. Suppose that such a program is written, and that, several days later, the same officer needs to trim that list to include only those customers who have an account balance of $10,000 or more. As expected, a program to generate such a list does not exist. Again, the officer has the preceding two options, neither of which is satisfactory.

The point here is that conventional file-processing environments do not allow needed data to be retrieved in a convenient and efficient manner. More responsive data-retrieval systems must be developed for general use.

- **Data isolation**. Because data are scattered in various files, and files may be in different formats, it is difficult to write new application programs to retrieve the appropriate data.
- **Integrity problems**. The data values stored in the database must satisfy certain types of *consistency constraints*. For example, the balance of a bank account may never fall below a prescribed amount (say, \$25). Developers enforce these constraints in the system by adding appropriate code in the various application programs. However, when new constraints are added, it is difficult to change the programs to enforce them. The problem is compounded when constraints involve several data items from different files.
- **Atomicity problems**. A computer system, like any other mechanical or electrical device, is subject to failure. In many applications, it is crucial to ensure that, once a failure has occurred and has been detected, the data are restored to the consistent state that existed prior to the failure. Consider a program to transfer \$50 from account *A* to *B*. If a system failure occurs during the execution of the program, it is possible that the \$50 was removed from account *A* but was not credited to account *B*, resulting in an inconsistent database state. Clearly, it is essential to database consistency that either both the credit and debit occur, or that neither occur. That is, the funds transfer must be *atomic*—it must happen in its entirety or not at all. It is difficult to ensure this property in a conventional file-processing system.
- **Concurrent-access anomalies**. So that the overall performance of the system is improved and a faster response time is possible, many systems allow multiple users to update the data simultaneously. In such an environment, interaction of concurrent updates may result in inconsistent data. Consider bank account *A*, containing \$500. If two customers withdraw funds (say \$50 and \$100 respectively) from account *A* at about the same time, the result of the concurrent executions may leave the account in an incorrect (or inconsistent) state. Suppose that the programs executing on behalf of each withdrawal read the old balance, reduce that value by the amount being withdrawn, and write the result back. If the two programs run concurrently, they may both read the value \$500, and write back \$450 and \$400, respectively. Depending on which one writes the value last, the account may contain either \$450 or \$400, rather than the correct value of \$350. To guard against this possibility, the system must maintain some form of supervision. Because data may be accessed by many different application programs that have not been coordinated previously, however, supervision is difficult to provide.
- **Security problems**. Not every user of the database system should be able to access all the data. For example, in a banking system, payroll personnel need to see only that part of the database that has information about the various bank employees. They do not need access to information about customer

accounts. Since application programs are added to the system in an ad hoc manner, it is difficult to enforce such security constraints.

These difficulties, among others, have prompted the development of DBMSs. In what follows, we shall see the concepts and algorithms that have been developed for database systems to solve the problems mentioned. In most of this book, we use a bank enterprise as a running example of a typical data-processing application found in a corporation. A typical data-processing application stores a large number of records, each of which is fairly simple and small.

In Chapters 8 and 9, we consider different classes of database applications, such as interactive design applications. Applications in these categories typically deal with more complex and larger records, such as a complete building design, but there are fewer records. There is a substantial amount of research and development work underway to provide database systems that are both sufficiently powerful and sufficiently flexible to manage these applications.

1.2 View of Data

A DBMS is a collection of interrelated files and a set of programs that allow users to access and modify these files. A major purpose of a database system is to provide users with an *abstract* view of the data. That is, the system hides certain details of how the data are stored and maintained.

1.2.1 Data Abstraction

For the system to be usable, it must retrieve data efficiently. This concern has led to the design of complex data structures for the representation of data in the database. Since many database-systems users are not computer trained, developers hide the complexity from users through several levels of abstraction, to simplify users' interactions with the system:

- **Physical level.** The lowest level of abstraction describes *how* the data are actually stored. At the physical level, complex low-level data structures are described in detail.
- **Logical level.** The next-higher level of abstraction describes *what* data are stored in the database, and what relationships exist among those data. The entire database is thus described in terms of a small number of relatively simple structures. Although implementation of the simple structures at the logical level may involve complex physical-level structures, the user of the logical level does not need to be aware of this complexity. The logical level of abstraction is used by database administrators, who must decide what information is to be kept in the database.
- **View level.** The highest level of abstraction describes only part of the entire database. Despite the use of simpler structures at the logical level, some complexity remains, because of the large size of the database. Many users of the database system will not be concerned with all this information. Instead,

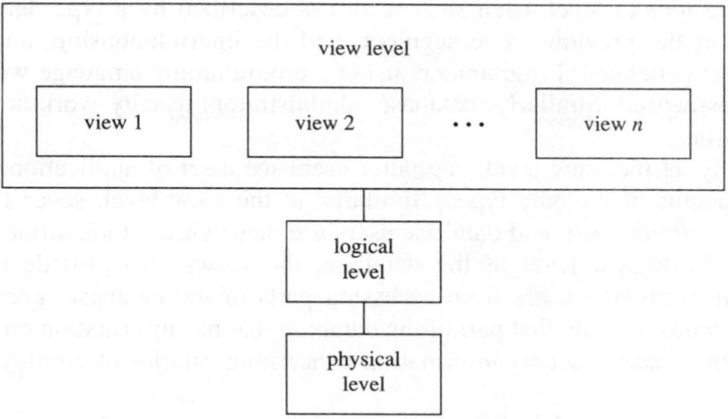

Figure 1.1 The three levels of data abstraction.

such users need to access only a part of the database. So that their interaction with the system is simplified, the view level of abstraction is defined. The system may provide many views for the same database.

The interrelationship among these three levels of abstraction is illustrated in Figure 1.1.

An analogy to the concept of data types in programming languages may clarify the distinction among levels of abstraction. Most high-level programming languages support the notion of a record type. For example, in a Pascal-like language, we may declare a record as follows:

```
type customer = record
        customer-name : string;
        sociai-security : string;
        customer-street : string;
        customer-city : string;
    end;
```

This code defines a new record called *customer* with three fields. Each field has a name and a type associated with it. A banking enterprise may have several such record types, including

- *account*, with fields *account-number* and *balance*
- *employee*, with fields *employee-name* and *salary*

At the physical level, a *customer*, *account*, or *employee* record can be described as a block of consecutive storage locations (for example, words or bytes). The language compiler hides this level of detail from programmers. Similarly, the database system hides many of the lowest-level storage details from database programmers. Database administrators may be aware of certain details of the physical organization of the data.

At the logical level, each such record is described by a type definition, as illustrated in the previous code segment, and the interrelationship among these record types is defined. Programmers using a programming language work at this level of abstraction. Similarly, database administrators usually work at this level of abstraction.

Finally, at the view level, computer users see a set of application programs that hide details of the data types. Similarly, at the view level, several views of the database are defined, and database users see these views. In addition to hiding details of the logical level of the database, the views also provide a security mechanism to prevent users from accessing parts of the database. For example, tellers in a bank see only that part of the database that has information on customer accounts; they cannot access information concerning salaries of employees.

1.2.2 Instances and Schemas

Databases change over time as information is inserted and deleted. The collection of information stored in the database at a particular moment is called an *instance* of the database. The overall design of the database is called the database *schema*. Schemas are changed infrequently, if at all.

Analogies to the concepts of data types, variables, and values in programming languages is useful here. Returning to the *customer*-record type definition, note that, in declaring the type *customer*, we have *not* declared any variables. To declare such variables in a Pascal-like language, we write

var *customer*1 : *customer*;

Variable *customer*1 now corresponds to an area of storage containing a *customer* type record.

A database schema corresponds to the programming-language type definition. A variable of a given type has a particular value at a given instant. Thus, the value of a variable in programming languages corresponds to an *instance* of a database schema.

Database systems have several schemas, partitioned according to the levels of abstraction that we discussed. At the lowest level is the *physical schema*; at the intermediate level is the *logical schema*; and at the highest level is a *subschema*. In general, database systems support one physical schema, one logical schema, and several subschemas.

1.2.3 Data Independence

The ability to modify a schema definition in one level without affecting a schema definition in the next higher level is called *data independence*. There are two levels of data independence:

1. **Physical data independence** is the ability to modify the physical schema without causing application programs to be rewritten. Modifications at the physical level are occasionally necessary to improve performance.

2. **Logical data independence** is the ability to modify the logical schema without causing application programs to be rewritten. Modifications at the logical level are necessary whenever the logical structure of the database is altered (for example, when money-market accounts are added to a banking system).

Logical data independence is more difficult to achieve than is physical data independence, since application programs are heavily dependent on the logical structure of the data that they access.

The concept of data independence is similar in many respects to the concept of *abstract data types* in modern programming languages. Both hide implementation details from the users, to allow users to concentrate on the general structure, rather than on low-level implementation details.

1.3 Data Models

Underlying the structure of a database is the *data model*: a collection of conceptual tools for describing data, data relationships, data semantics, and consistency constraints. The various data models that have been proposed fall into three different groups: object-based logical models, record-based logical models, and physical models.

1.3.1 Object-Based Logical Models

Object-based logical models are used in describing data at the logical and view levels. They are characterized by the fact that they provide fairly flexible structuring capabilities and allow data constraints to be specified explicitly. There are many different models, and more are likely to come. Several of the more widely known ones are

- The entity–relationship model
- The object-oriented model
- The semantic data model
- The functional data model

In this book, we examine the *entity–relationship model* and the *object-oriented model* as representatives of the class of the object-based logical models. The entity–relationship model, explored in Chapter 2, has gained acceptance in database design and is widely used in practice. The object-oriented model, examined in Chapter 8, includes many of the concepts of the entity–relationship model, but represents executable code as well as data. It is rapidly gaining acceptance in practice. We shall give brief descriptions of both models next.

1.3.1.1 The Entity–Relationship Model

The entity–relationship (E-R) data model is based on a perception of a real world that consists of a collection of basic objects, called *entities*, and of *relationships*

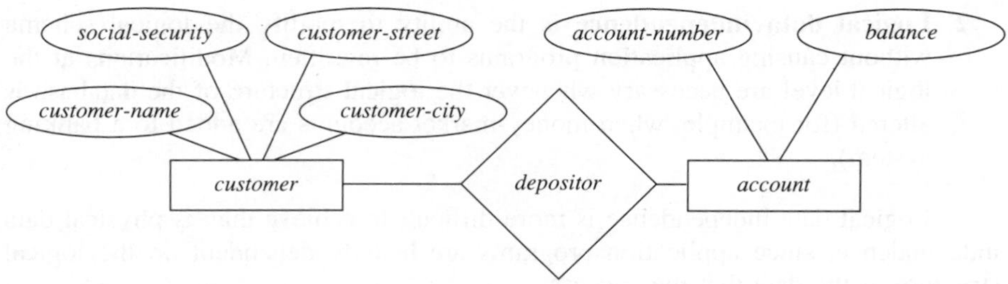

Figure 1.2 A sample E-R diagram.

among these objects. An entity is a "thing" or "object" in the real world that is distinguishable from other objects. For example, each person is an entity, and bank accounts can be considered to be entities. Entities are described in a database by a set of *attributes*. For example, the attributes *account-number* and *balance* describe one particular account in a bank. A *relationship* is an association among several entities. For example, a *Depositor* relationship associates a customer with each account that she has. The set of all entities of the same type, and the set of all relationships of the same type, are termed an *entity set* and *relationship set*, respectively.

In addition to entities and relationships, the E-R model represents certain constraints to which the contents of a database must conform. One important constraint is *mapping cardinalities*, which express the number of entities to which another entity can be associated via a relationship set.

The overall logical structure of a database can be expressed graphically by an E-R *diagram*, which is built up from the following components:

- **Rectangles**, which represent entity sets
- **Ellipses**, which represent attributes
- **Diamonds**, which represent relationships among entity sets
- **Lines**, which link attributes to entity sets and entity sets to relationships

Each component is labeled with the entity or relationship that it represents.

An an illustration, consider part of a database banking system consisting of customers and of the accounts that these customers have. The corresponding E-R diagram is shown in Figure 1.2. This example is extended in Chapter 2.

1.3.1.2 The Object-Oriented Model

Like the E-R model, the object-oriented model is based on a collection of objects. An object contains values stored in *instance variables* within the object. An object also contains bodies of code that operate on the object. These bodies of code are called *methods*.

Objects that contain the same types of values and the same methods are grouped together into *classes*. A class may be viewed as a type definition for objects. This combination of data and methods comprising a type definition is similar to a programming-language abstract data type.

The only way in which one object can access the data of another object is by invoking a method of that other object. This action is called *sending a message* to the object. Thus, the call interface of the methods of an object defines that object's externally visible part. The internal part of the object—the instance variables and method code—are not visible externally. The result is two levels of data abstraction.

To illustrate the concept, let us consider an object representing a bank account. Such an object contains instance variables *account-number* and *balance*. It contains a method *pay-interest*, which adds interest to the balance. Assume that the bank had been paying 6-percent interest on all accounts, but now is changing its policy to pay 5 percent if the balance is less than $1000 or 6 percent if the balance is $1000 or greater. Under most data models, making this adjustment would involve changing code in one or more application programs. Under the object-oriented model, the only change is made within the *pay-interest* method. The external interface to the objects remains unchanged.

Unlike entities in the E-R model, each object has its own unique identity, independent of the values that it contains. Thus, two objects containing the same values are nevertheless distinct. The distinction among individual objects is maintained in the physical level through the assignment of distinct object identifiers.

1.3.2 Record-Based Logical Models

Record-based logical models are used in describing data at the logical and view levels. In contrast to object-based data models, they are used both to specify the overall logical structure of the database and to provide a higher-level description of the implementation.

Record-based models are so named because the database is structured in fixed-format records of several types. Each record type defines a fixed number of fields, or attributes, and each field is usually of a fixed length. As we shall see in Chapter 10, the use of fixed-length records simplifies the physical-level implementation of the database. This simplicity is in contrast to many of the object-based models, whose richer structure often leads to variable-length records at the physical level.

The three most widely accepted record-based data models are the relational, network, and hierarchical models. The relational model, which has gained favor over the other two in recent years, is examined in detail in Chapters 3 through 7. The network and hierarchical models, still used in a large number of older databases, are described in the appendices. Here, we present a brief overview of each model.

1.3.2.1 Relational Model

The relational model uses a collection of tables to represent both data and the relationships among those data. Each table has multiple columns, and each column has a unique name. Figure 1.3 presents a sample relational database comprising of two tables: one shows bank customers, and the other shows the accounts that belong to those customers. It shows, for example, that customer Johnson, with

customer-name	*social-security*	*customer-street*	*customer-city*	*account-number*
Johnson	192-83-7465	Alma	Palo Alto	A-101
Smith	019-28-3746	North	Rye	A-215
Hayes	677-89-9011	Main	Harrison	A-102
Turner	182-73-6091	Putnam	Stamford	A-305
Johnson	192-83-7465	Alma	Palo Alto	A-201
Jones	321-12-3123	Main	Harrison	A-217
Lindsay	336-66-9999	Park	Pittsfield	A-222
Smith	019-28-3746	North	Rye	A-201

account-number	*balance*
A-101	500
A-215	700
A-102	400
A-305	350
A-201	900
A-217	750
A-222	700

Figure 1.3 A sample relational database.

social-security number 321-12-3123, lives on Main in Harrison, and has two accounts: A-101, with a balance of $500, and A-201, with a balance of $900. Note that customers Johnson and Smith share account number A-201 (they may share a business venture).

1.3.2.2 Network Model

Data in the network model are represented by collections of *records* (in the Pascal sense), and relationships among data are represented by *links*, which can be viewed as pointers. The records in the database are organized as collections of arbitrary graphs. Figure 1.4 presents a sample network database using the same information as in Figure 1.3.

1.3.2.3 Hierarchical Model

The hierarchical model is similar to the network model in the sense that data and relationships among data are represented by records and links, respectively. It differs from the network model in that the records are organized as collections of trees rather than arbitrary graphs. Figure 1.5 presents a sample hierarchical database with the same information as in Figure 1.4.

1.3.2.4 Differences Among the Models

The relational model differs from the network and hierarchical models in that it does not use pointers or links. Instead, the relational model relates records by the

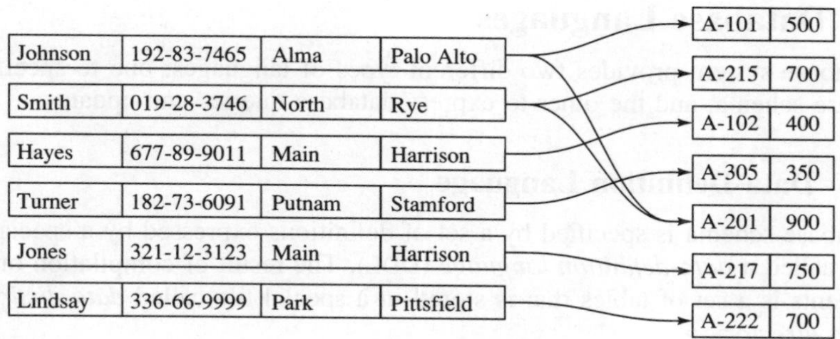

Figure 1.4 A sample network database.

values that they contain. This freedom from the use of pointers allows a formal mathematical foundation to be defined.

1.3.3 Physical Data Models

Physical data models are used to describe data at the lowest level. In contrast to logical data models, there are few physical data models in use. Two of the widely known ones are the *unifying model* and the *frame-memory model*.

Physical data models capture aspects of database-system implementation that are not covered in this book.

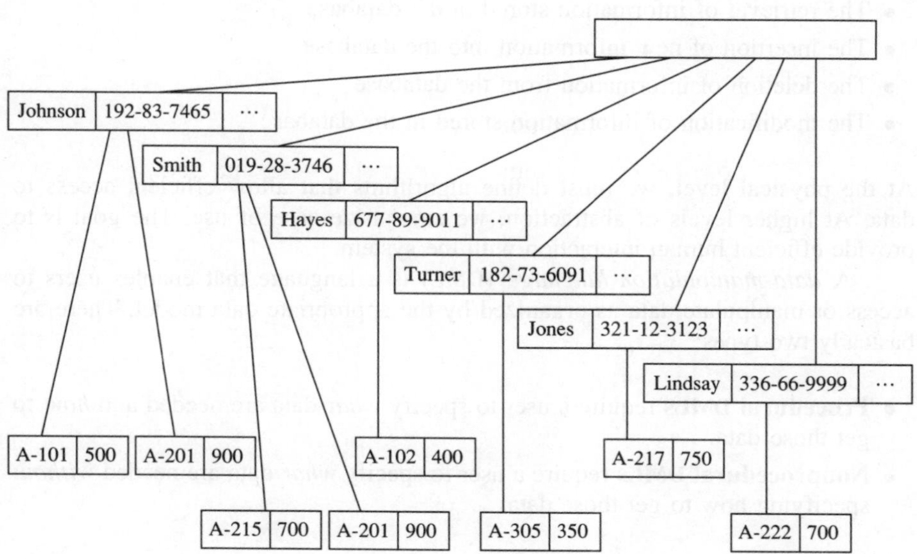

Figure 1.5 A sample hierarchical database.

1.4 Database Languages

A database system provides two different types of languages: one to specify the database schema, and the other to express database queries and updates.

1.4.1 Data-Definition Language

A database schema is specified by a set of definitions expressed by a special language called a *data-definition language* (DDL). The result of compilation of DDL statements is a set of tables that is stored in a special file called *data dictionary*, or *data directory*.

A data dictionary is a file that contains *metadata*—that is, data about data. This file is consulted before actual data are read or modified in the database system.

The storage structure and access methods used by the database system are specified by a set of definitions in a special type of DDL called a *data storage and definition* language. The result of compilation of these definitions is a set of instructions to specify the implementation details of the database schemas—details are usually hidden from the users.

1.4.2 Data-Manipulation Language

The levels of abstraction that we discussed in Section 1.2 apply not only to the definition or structuring of data, but also to the manipulation of data. By *data manipulation*, we mean

- The retrieval of information stored in the database
- The insertion of new information into the database
- The deletion of information from the database
- The modification of information stored in the database

At the physical level, we must define algorithms that allow efficient access to data. At higher levels of abstraction, we emphasize ease of use. The goal is to provide efficient human interaction with the system.

A *data-manipulation language* (DML) is a language that enables users to access or manipulate data as organized by the appropriate data model. There are basically two types:

- **Procedural DMLs** require a user to specify *what* data are needed and *how* to get those data.
- **Nonprocedural DMLs** require a user to specify *what* data are needed *without* specifying how to get those data.

Nonprocedural DMLs are usually easier to learn and use than are procedural DMLs. However, since a user does not have to specify how to get the data, these languages may generate code that is not as efficient as that produced by procedural languages. We can remedy this difficulty through various optimization techniques, several of which we discuss in Chapter 12.

A *query* is a statement requesting the retrieval of information. The portion of a DML that involves information retrieval is called a *query language*. Although technically incorrect, it is common practice to use the terms *query language* and *data-manipulation language* synonymously.

1.5 Transaction Management

Often, several operations on the database form a single logical unit of work. An example that we saw earlier is a funds transfer, in which one account (say A) is debited and another account (say B) is credited. Clearly, it is essential that either both the credit and debit occur, or that neither occur. That is, the funds transfer must happen in its entirety or not at all. This all-or-none requirement is called *atomicity*. In addition, it is essential that the execution of the fund transfer preserve the consistency of the database. That is, the value of the sum $A + B$ must be preserved. This correctness requirement is called *consistency*. Finally, after the successful execution of a funds transfer, the new values of accounts A and B must persist, despite the possibility of system failure. This persistency requirement is called *durability*.

A *transaction* is a collection of operations that performs a single logical function in a database application. Each transaction is a unit of both atomicity and consistency. Thus, we require that transactions do not violate any database-consistency constraints. That is, if the database was consistent when a transaction started, the database must be consistent when the transaction successfully terminates. However, during the execution of a transaction, it may be necessary temporarily to allow inconsistency. This temporary inconsistency, although necessary, may lead to difficulty if a failure occurs.

It is the responsibility of the programmer to define properly the various transactions, such that each preserves the consistency of the database. For example, the transaction to transfer funds from account A to account B could be defined to be composed of two separate programs: one that debits account A, and another that credits account B. The execution of these two programs one after the other will indeed preserve consistency. However, each program by itself does not transform the database from a consistent state to a new consistent state. Thus, those programs are not transactions.

Ensuring the atomicity and durability properties is the responsibility of the database system itself—specifically, of the *transaction-management component*. In the absence of failures, all transactions complete successfully, and atomicity is achieved easily. However, due to various types of failure, a transaction may not always complete its execution successfully. If we are to ensure the atomicity property, a failed transaction must have no effect on the state of the database. Thus, the database must be restored to the state in which it was before the transaction in question started executing. It is the responsibility of the database system to detect system failures and to restore the database to a state that existed prior to the occurrence of the failure.

Finally, when several transactions update the database concurrently, the consistency of data may no longer be preserved, even though each individual transaction is correct. It is the responsibility of the *concurrency-control manager* to control the interaction among the concurrent transactions, to ensure the consistency of the database.

Database systems designed for use on small personal computers may not have all the features noted. For example, many small systems impose the restriction of only one user being allowed to access the database at a time. Others leave the tasks of backup and recovery to the user. This setup allows for a smaller data manager, with fewer requirements for physical resources—especially main memory. Although such a low-cost, low-feature approach is sufficient for small personal databases, it is inadequate to meet the needs of a medium- to large-scale enterprise.

1.6 Storage Management

Databases typically require a large amount of storage space. Corporate databases are usually measured in terms of *gigabytes* or, for the largest databases, *terabytes* of data. A gigabyte is 1000 megabytes (1 billion bytes), and a terabyte is 1 million megabytes (1 trillion bytes). Since the main memory of computers cannot store this much information, the information is stored on disks. Data are moved between disk storage and main memory as needed. Since the movement of data to and from disk is slow relative to the speed of the central processing unit, it is imperative that the database system structure the data so as to minimize the need to move data between disk and main memory.

The goal of a database system is to simplify and facilitate access to data. High-level views help to achieve this goal. Users of the system should not be burdened unnecessarily with the physical details of the implementation of the system. Nevertheless, a major factor in a user's satisfaction or lack thereof with a database system is that system's performance. If the response time for a request is too long, the value of the system is diminished. The performance of a system depends on what the efficiency is of the data structures used to represent the data in the database, and on how efficiently the system is able to operate on these data structures. As is the case elsewhere in computer systems, a tradeoff must be made not only between space and time, but also between the efficiency of one kind of operation and that of another.

A *storage manager* is a program module that provides the interface between the low-level data stored in the database and the application programs and queries submitted to the system. The storage manager is responsible for the interaction with the file manager. The raw data are stored on the disk using the file system, which is usually provided by a conventional operating system. The storage manager translates the various DML statements into low-level file-system commands. Thus, the storage manager is responsible for storing, retrieving, and updating of data in the database.

1.7 Database Administrator

One of the main reasons for using DBMSs is to have central control of both the data and the programs that access those data. The person who has such central control over the system is called the *database administrator* (DBA). The functions of the DBA include the following:

- **Schema definition**. The DBA creates the original database schema by writing a set of definitions that is translated by the DDL compiler to a set of tables that is stored permanently in the *data dictionary*.
- **Storage structure and access-method definition**. The DBA creates appropriate storage structures and access methods by writing a set of definitions, which is translated by the data-storage and data-definition–language compiler.
- **Schema and physical-organization modification**. Programmers accomplish the relatively rare modifications either to the database schema or to the description of the physical storage organization by writing a set of definitions that is used by either the DDL compiler or the data-storage and data-definition–language compiler to generate modifications to the appropriate internal system tables (for example, the data dictionary).
- **Granting of authorization for data access**. The granting of different types of authorization allows the database administrator to regulate which parts of the database various users can access. The authorization information is kept in a special system structure that is consulted by the database system whenever access to the data is attempted in the system.
- **Integrity-constraint specification**. The data values stored in the database must satisfy certain consistency constraints. For example, perhaps the number of hours an employee may work in 1 week may not exceed a specified limit (say, 80 hours). Such a constraint must be specified explicitly by the database administrator. The integrity constraints are kept in a special system structure that is consulted by the database system whenever an update takes place in the system.

1.8 Database Users

A primary goal of a database system is to provide an environment for retrieving information from and storing new information into the database. There are four different types of database-system users, differentiated by the way that they expect to interact with the system.

- **Application programmers** are computer professionals who interact with the system through DML calls, which are embedded in a program written in a *host* language (for example, Cobol, PL/I, Pascal, C). These programs are commonly referred to as *application programs*. Examples in a banking system include programs that generate payroll checks, that debit accounts, that credit accounts, or that transfer funds between accounts.

Since the DML syntax is usually markedly different from the host language syntax, DML calls are usually prefaced by a special character so that the appropriate code can be generated. A special preprocessor, called the *DML precompiler*, converts the DML statements to normal procedure calls in the host language. The resulting program is then run through the host-language compiler, which generates appropriate object code.

There are special types of programming languages that combine control structures of Pascal-like languages with control structures for the manipulation of a database object (for example, relations). These languages, sometimes called *fourth-generation languages*, often include special features to facilitate the generation of forms and the display of data on the screen. Most major commercial database systems include a fourth-generation language.

- **Sophisticated users** interact with the system without writing programs. Instead, they form their requests in a database query language. Each such query is submitted to a *query processor* whose function is to break down DML statement into instructions that the storage manager understands. Analysts who submit queries to explore data in the database fall in this category.

- **Specialized users** are sophisticated users who write specialized database applications that do not fit into the traditional data-processing framework. Among these applications are computer-aided design systems, knowledge-base and expert systems, systems that store data with complex data types (for example, graphics data and audio data), and environment-modeling systems. Several of these applications are covered in Chapters 8 and 9.

- **Naive users** are unsophisticated users who interact with the system by invoking one of the permanent application programs that have been written previously. For example, a bank teller who needs to transfer $50 from account *A* to account *B* invokes a program called *transfer*. This program asks the teller for the amount of money to be transferred, the account from which the money is to be transferred, and the account to which the money is to be transferred.

1.9 Overall System Structure

A database system is partitioned into modules that deal with each of the responsibilities of the overall system. Some of the functions of the database system may be provided by the computer's operating system. In most cases, the computer's operating system provides only the most basic services, and the database system must build on that base. Thus, the design of a database system must include consideration of the interface between the database system and the operating system.

The functional components of a database system can be broadly divided into query processor components and storage manager components. The query processor components include

- **DML compiler**, which translates DML statements in a query language into low-level instructions that the query evaluation engine understands. In addition, the DML compiler attempts to transform a user's request into an equivalent but more efficient form, thus finding a good strategy for executing the query.
- **Embedded DML precompiler**, which converts DML statements embedded in an application program to normal procedure calls in the host language. The precompiler must interact with the DML compiler to generate the appropriate code.
- **DDL interpreter**, which interprets DDL statements and records them in a set of tables containing *metadata*.
- **Query evaluation engine**, which executes low-level instructions generated by the DML compiler.

The storage manager components provides the interface between the low-level data stored in the database and the application programs and queries submitted to the system. The storage manager components include

- **Authorization and integrity manager**, which tests for the satisfaction of integrity constraints and checks the authority of users to access data.
- **Transaction manager**, which ensures that the database remains in a consistent (correct) state despite system failures, and that concurrent transaction executions proceed without conflicting.
- **File manager**, which manages the allocation of space on disk storage and the data structures used to represent information stored on disk.
- **Buffer manager**, which is responsible for fetching data from disk storage into main memory, and deciding what data to cache in memory.

In addition, several data structures are required as part of the physical system implementation:

- **Data files**, which store the database itself.
- **Data dictionary**, which stores metadata about the structure of the database. The data dictionary is used heavily. Therefore, great emphasis should be placed on developing a good design and efficient implementation of the dictionary.
- **Indices**, which provide fast access to data items that hold particular values.
- **Statistical data**, which store statistical information about the data in the database. This information is used by the query processor to select efficient ways to execute a query.

Figure 1.6 shows these components and the connections among them.

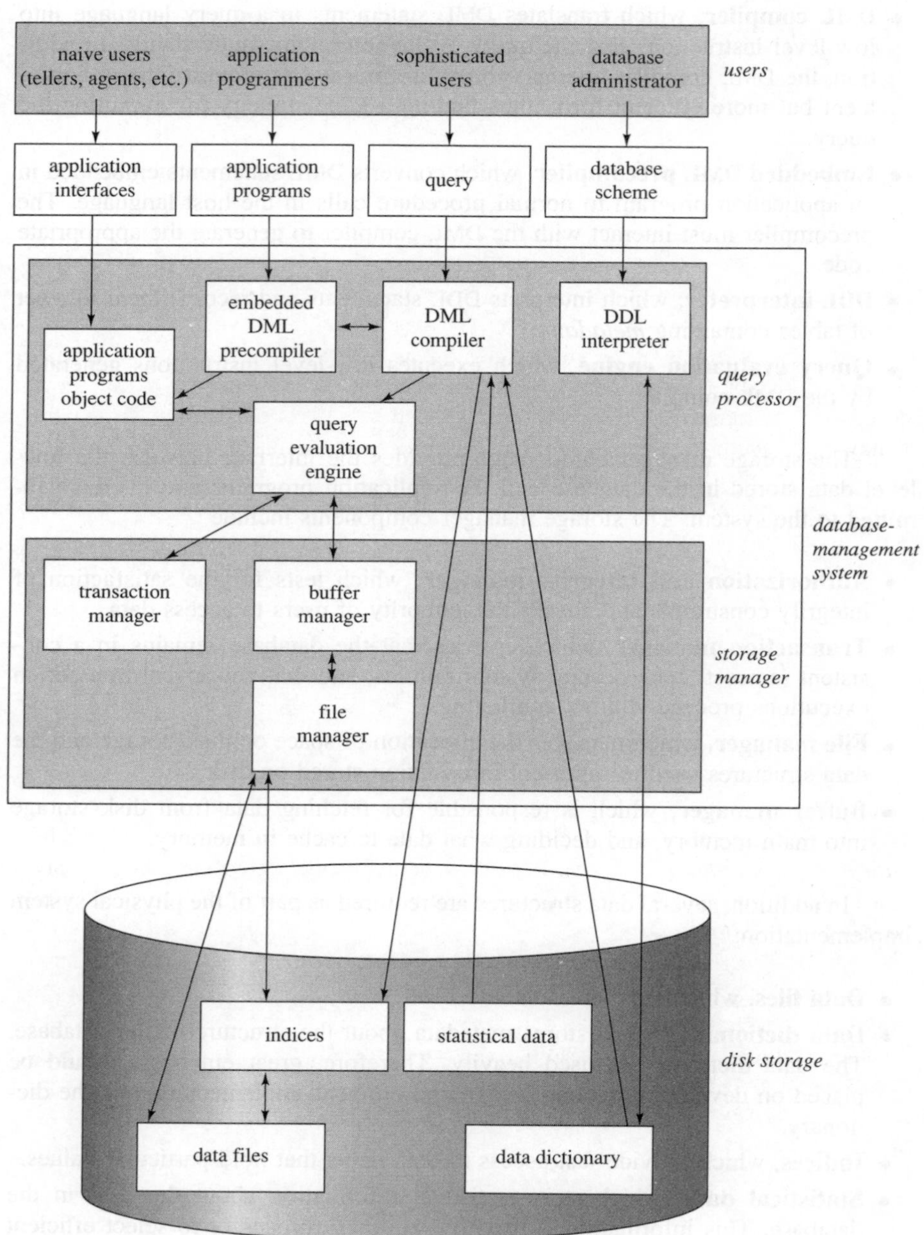

Figure 1.6 System structure.

1.10 Summary

A *database-management system* (DBMS) consists of a collection of interrelated data and a collection of programs to access that data. The data describe one particular enterprise. The primary goal of a DBMS is to provide an environment that is both *convenient* and *efficient* for people to use in retrieving and storing information.

Database systems are designed to store large bodies of information. The management of data involves both the definition of structures for the storage of information and the provision of mechanisms for the manipulation of information. In addition, the database system must provide for the safety of the information stored, in the face of system crashes or attempts at unauthorized access. If data are to be shared among several users, the system must avoid possible anomalous results.

A major purpose of a database system is to provide users with an abstract view of the data. That is, the system hides certain details of how the data are stored and maintained. It does so by defining three levels of abstraction at which it may be viewed: the *physical level*, the *logical level*, and the *view level*.

Underlying the structure of a database is the *data model*: a collection of conceptual tools for describing data, data relationships, data semantics, and data constraints. The various data models that have been proposed fall into three different groups: *object-based logical models*, *record-based logical models*, and *physical data models*.

Databases change over time as information is inserted and deleted. The collection of information stored in the database at a particular moment is called an *instance* of the database. The overall design of the database is called the database *schema*. The ability to modify a schema definition in one level without affecting a schema definition in the next-higher level is called *data independence*. There are two levels of data independence: *physical* data independence and *logical* data independence.

A database schema is specified by a set of definitions that are expressed by a *data-definition language* (DDL). DDL statements are compiled into a set of tables that is stored in a special file called the *data dictionary*; the data dictionary thus contains *metadata*.

A *data-manipulation language* (DML) is a language that enables users to access or manipulate data. There are basically two types: procedural DMLs, which require a user to specify what data are needed and how to get those data, and nonprocedural DMLs, which require a user to specify what data are needed without specifying how to get those data.

The *transaction manager* is responsible for ensuring that the database remains in a consistent (correct) state despite system failures. The transaction manager also ensures that concurrent transaction executions proceed without conflicting.

A *storage manager* is a program module that provides the interface between the low-level data stored in the database and the application programs and queries submitted to the system. The storage manager is responsible for interaction with the data stored on disk.

Exercises

1.1. What are four main differences between a file-processing system and a DBMS?

1.2. This chapter has described several major advantages of a database system. What are two disadvantages?

1.3. Explain the difference between physical and logical data independence.

1.4. List five responsibilities of the database manager. For each responsibility, explain the problems that would arise if the responsibility were not discharged.

1.5. What are five main functions of a database administrator?

1.6. List seven programming languages that are procedural, and two that are nonprocedural. Which group is easier to learn and use? Explain your answer.

1.7. List six major steps that you would take in setting up a database for a particular enterprise.

1.8. Consider a two-dimensional integer array of size $n \times m$ that is to be used in your favorite programming language. Using the array as an example, illustrate the difference (a) between the three levels of data abstraction, and (b) between a schema and instances.

Bibliographic Notes

Discussions concerning the evolution of DBMSs and the development of database technology are offered by Fry and Sibley [1976] and by Sibley [1976].

The three levels of data abstraction were introduced in the CODASYL DBTG report [CODASYL 1971]. A similar proposal was put forward in the ANSI/SPARC report, in which these levels were termed *internal*, *conceptual*, and *external* [ANSI 1975].

The entity–relationship, object-oriented, relational, network, and hierarchical models are covered in other chapters of this book. More extensive bibliographic references are provided in later chapters of this book.

Semantic data models are based on data models that were initially developed in connection with research in artificial intelligence. Discussion concerning the various models can be found in Roussopoulos and Mylopoulos [1975], Wong and Mylopoulos [1977], and Hammer and McLeod [1981]. Surveys of semantic data models are provided by Hull and King [1987] and by Peckham and Maryanski [1988].

The functional data model was proposed by Sibley and Kerschberg [1977], and has been extended by Shipman [1981]. Several functional query languages have been proposed, including FQL [Buneman and Frankel 1979] and DAPLEX [Shipman 1981].

The unifying model was introduced by Batory and Gotlieb [1982]. The frame memory structure was introduced by March et al. [1981].

Database-administration issues are covered in Weldon [1981]. Other textbooks covering database systems include Abiteboul et al. [1995], Date [1995], Elmasri and Navathe [1994], O'Neil [1994], and Ullman [1988].

Several books contain collections of research papers on database management. Among these are Bancilhon and Buneman [1990], Date [1986, 1990], Kim et al. [1985], Kim [1995], and Stonebraker [1994]. A review of accomplishments in database management and an assessment of future research challenges appears in Silberschatz et al. [1990, 1996].

CHAPTER 2

ENTITY–RELATIONSHIP MODEL

The entity–relationship (E-R) data model is based on a perception of a real world that consists of a set of basic objects called *entities*, and of *relationships* among these objects. It was developed to facilitate database design by allowing the specification of an *enterprise schema*, which represents the overall logical structure of a database. The E-R data model is one of several semantic data models; the semantic aspect of the model lies in the attempt to represent the meaning of the data. The E-R model is extremely useful in mapping the meanings and interactions of real-world enterprises onto a conceptual schema. Because of this utility, many database-design tools draw on concepts from the E-R model.

2.1 Basic Concepts

There are three basic notions that the E-R data model employs: entity sets, relationship sets, and attributes.

2.1.1 Entity Sets

An *entity* is a "thing" or "object" in the real world that is distinguishable from all other objects. For example, each person in an enterprise is an entity. An entity has a set of properties, and the values for some set of properties may uniquely identify an entity. For example, the social-security number 677-89-9011 uniquely identifies one particular person in the enterprise.† Similarly, loans can be thought

†In the United States, the government assigns to each person in the country a unique number, called a social-security number, to identify them uniquely. Each person is supposed to have only one social-security number, and no two people are supposed to have the same social-security number.

Jones	321-12-3123	Main	Harrison
Smith	019-28-3746	North	Rye
Hayes	677-89-9011	Main	Harrison
Jackson	555-55-5555	Dupont	Woodside
Curry	244-66-8800	North	Rye
Williams	963-96-3963	Nassau	Princeton
Adams	335-57-7991	Spring	Pittsfield

customer

L-17	1000
L-23	2000
L-15	1500
L-14	1500
L-93	500
L-11	900
L-16	1300

loan

Figure 2.1 Entity sets *customer* and *loan*.

of as entities, and loan number L-15 at the Perryridge branch uniquely identifies a loan entity. An entity may be concrete, such as a person or a book, or it may be abstract, such as a loan, or a holiday or a concept. In this text, we assume for simplicity that the enterprises with which we are dealing are located in the United States, and that all the person entities with which we deal have social-security numbers. We address the problem of choosing unique identifiers in Section 2.4.1.

An *entity set* is a set of entities of the same type that share the same properties, or attributes. The set of all persons who are customers at a given bank, for example, can be defined as the entity set *customer*. Similarly, the entity set *loan* might represent the set of all loans awarded by a particular bank. The individual entities that constitute a set are said to be the *extension* of the entity set. Thus, all the individual bank customers are the extension of the entity set *customer*.

Entity sets do not need to be disjoint. For example, it is possible to define the entity set of all employees of a bank (*employee*) and the entity set of all customers of the bank (*customer*). A *person* entity may be an *employee* entity, a *customer* entity, both, or neither.

An entity is represented by a set of *attributes*. Attributes are descriptive properties possessed by each member of an entity set. The designation of an attribute for an entity set expresses that the database stores similar information concerning each entity in the entity set; however, each entity may have its own value for each attribute. Possible attributes of the *customer* entity set are *customer-name*, *social-security*, *customer-street*, and *customer-city*. Possible attributes of the *loan* entity set are *loan-number* and *amount*. For each attribute, there is a set of permitted values, called the *domain*, or *value set*, of that attribute. The domain of attribute *customer-name* might be the set of all text strings of a certain length. Similarly, the domain of attribute *loan-number* might be the set of all positive integers.

A database thus includes a collection of entity sets each of which contains any number of entities of the same type. Figure 2.1 shows part of a bank database which consists of two entity sets: *customer* and *loan*.

Formally, an attribute of an entity set is a function that maps from the entity set into a domain. Since an entity set may have several attributes, each entity can be described by a set of (attribute, data value) pairs, one pair for each attribute of the entity set. For example, a particular *customer* entity may be described by the set {(*name*, Hayes), (*social-security*, 677-89-9011), (*customer-street*, Main), (*customer-city*, Harrison)}, meaning that the entity describes a person named Hayes who holds social-security number 677-89-9011, and resides at Main Street in Harrison. We can see, at this point, an integration of the abstract schema with the actual enterprise being modeled. The attribute values describing an entity will constitute a significant portion of the data stored in the database.

An attribute, as used in the E-R model, can be characterized by the following attribute types.

- **Simple** and **composite** attributes. In our examples thus far, the attributes have been simple; that is, they are not divided into subparts. Composite attributes, on the other hand, can be divided into subparts (that is, other attributes). For example, *customer-name* could be structured as a composite attribute consisting of *first-name*, *middle-initial*, and *last-name*. Using composite attributes in a design schema is a good choice if a user will wish to refer to an entire attribute on some occasions, and to only a component of the attribute on other occasions. Suppose we were to substitute for the *customer* entity-set attributes *customer-street* and *customer-city*, the composite attribute *customer-address* with the attributes *street*, *city*, *state*, and *zip-code*.† Composite attributes help us to group together related attributes, making the modeling cleaner.

  Note also that a composite attribute may appear as a hierarchy. Returning to our example composite attribute of *customer-address*, its component attribute *street* can be further divided into *street-number*, *street-name*, and *apt-number*. These examples of composite attributes, for the *customer* entity set, are depicted in Figure 2.2.

- **Single-valued** and **multivalued** attributes. The attributes that we have specified in our examples all have a single value for a particular entity. For instance, the *loan-number* attribute for a specific loan entity refers to only one loan number. Such attributes are said to be *single valued.* There may be instances where an attribute has a set of values for a specific entity. Consider an *employee* entity set with the attribute *dependent-name*. Any particular employee may have zero, one, or more dependents; therefore, different employee entities within the entity set will have different numbers of values for the *dependent-name* attribute. This type of attribute is said to be *multivalued.* Where appropriate, upper and lower bounds may be placed on the number of values in a multivalued attribute. For example, a bank may limit the number of addresses recorded for a single customer to two. Placing bounds in this

†We assume the *customer-street* and address format used in the United States, which includes a numeric postal code called a "zip code."

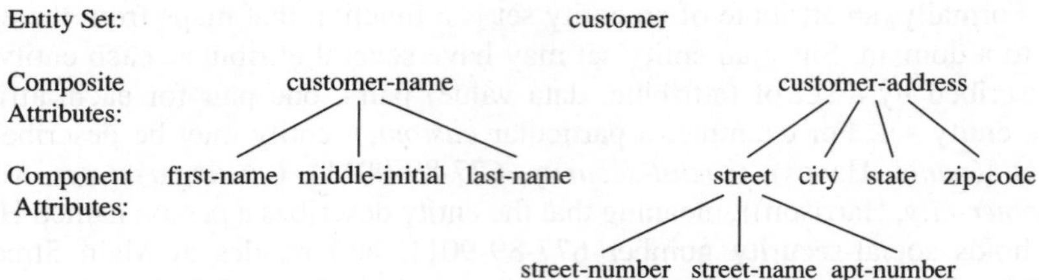

Figure 2.2 Composite attributes *customer-name* and *customer-address*.

case expresses that the *customer-address* attribute of the *customer* entity set may have between zero and two values.

- **Null** attributes. A *null* value is used when an entity does not have a value for an attribute. As an illustration, if a particular employee has no dependents, the *dependent-name* value for that employee will be *null*, and will have the meaning of "not applicable." *Null* can also designate that an attribute value is unknown. An unknown value may be either *missing* (the value does exist, but we do not have that information) or *not known* (we do not know whether or not the value actually exists). For instance, if the *social-security* value for a particular customer is *null*, we assume that the value is missing, since it is required for tax reporting. A null value for the *apt-number* attribute could mean that the address does not include an apartment number, that an apartment number exists but we do not know what it is, or that we do not know whether or not an apartment number is part of the customer's address.
- **Derived** attribute. The value for this type of attribute can be derived from the values of other related attributes or entities. For instance, let us say that the *customer* entity set has an attribute *loans-held*, which represents how many loans a customer has from the bank. we can derive the value for this attribute by counting the number of *loan* entities associated with that customer. As another example, consider that the *employee* entity set has the related attributes *start-date* and *employment-length*, which represent the first day an employee began working for the bank and the total length of time an employee has worked for the bank, respectively. The value for *employment-length* can be derived from the value for *start-date* and the current date. In this case, *start-date* may be referred to as a *base* attribute, or a *stored* attribute.

A database for a banking enterprise may include a number of different entity sets. For example, in addition to keeping track of customers and loans, the bank also provides accounts, which are represented by the entity set *account* with attributes *account-number* and *balance*. Also, if the bank has a number of different branches, then we may keep information about all the branches of the bank. Each *branch* entity set may be described by the attributes *branch-name*, *branch-city*, and *assets*.

In this chapter, we shall be dealing with various different entity sets. To avoid confusion, unique attribute names are used. We shall define the new entity sets as the occasion arises.

2.1.2 Relationship Sets

A *relationship* is an association among several entities. For example, we can define a relationship that associates customer Hayes with loan L-15. This relationship specifies that Hayes is a customer with loan number L-15.

A *relationship set* is a set of relationships of the same type. Formally, it is a mathematical relation on $n \geq 2$ (possibly nondistinct) entity sets. If $E_1, E_2, \ldots, E_n$ are entity sets, then a relationship set R is a subset of

$$\{(e_1, e_2, \ldots, e_n) \mid e_1 \in E_1, e_2 \in E_2, \ldots, e_n \in E_n\}$$

where $(e_1, e_2, \ldots, e_n)$ is a relationship.

Consider the two entity sets *customer* and *loan* in Figure 2.1. We define the relationship set *borrower* to denote the association between customers and the bank loans that the customers have. This association is depicted in Figure 2.3.

As another example, consider the two entity sets *loan* and *branch*. We can define the relationship set *loan-branch* to denote the association between a bank loan and the branch in which that loan is maintained.

The association between entity sets is referred to as *participation*; that is, the entity sets $E_1, E_2, \ldots, E_n$ *participate* in relationship set R. A relationship instance in an E-R schema represents that an association exists between the named entities in the real-world enterprise that is being modeled. As an illustration, the individual *customer* entity Hayes, who has social-security number 677-89-9011, and the *loan* entity L-15 participate in a relationship instance of *borrower*. This relationship instance represents that, in the real-world enterprise, the person called Hayes who holds social-security number 677-89-9011 has taken the loan that is numbered L-15.

The function that an entity plays in a relationship is called that entity's *role*. Since entity sets participating in a relationship set are generally distinct, roles are implicit and are not usually specified. However, they are useful when the meaning of a relationship needs clarification. Such is the case when the entity

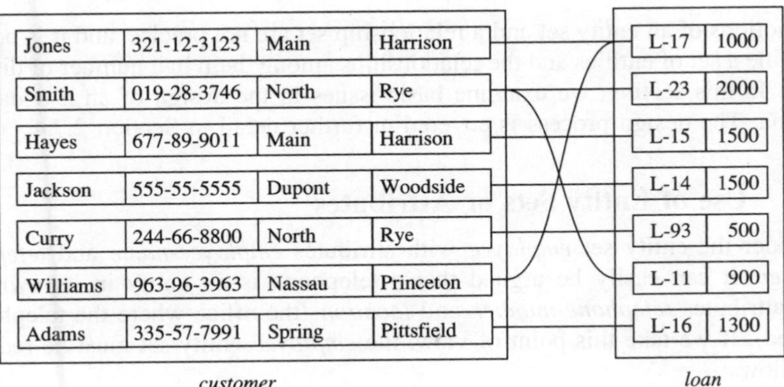

Figure 2.3 Relationship set *borrower*.

sets of a relationship set are not distinct; that is, the same entity set participates in a relationship set more than once, in different roles. In this type of relationship set, which is sometimes called a *recursive* relationship set, explicit role names are necessary to specify how an entity participates in a relationship instance. For example, consider an entity set *employee* that records information about all the employees of the bank. We may have a relationship set *works-for* that is modeled by ordered pairs of *employee* entities. The first employee of a pair takes the role of manager, whereas the second takes the role of worker. In this way, all relationships of *works-for* are characterized by (manager, worker) pairs; (worker, manager) pairs are excluded.

A relationship may also have *descriptive attributes*. Consider a relationship set *depositor* with entity sets *customer* and *account*. We could associate the attribute *access-date* to that relation to specify the most recent date on which a customer accessed an account. The *depositor* relationship among the entities corresponding to customer Jones and account A-217 is described by {(*access-date*, 23 May 1996)}, which means that the most recent time that Jones accessed account A-217 was on 23 May 1996.

The relationship sets *borrower* and *loan-branch* provide an example of a *binary* relationship set—that is, one that involves two entity sets. Most of the relationship sets in a database system are binary. Occasionally, however, relationship sets involve more than two entity sets. As an example, we could combine the *borrower* and *loan-branch* relationship sets to form a ternary relationship set *CLB* involving the entity sets *customer*, *loan*, and *branch*. Thus, the ternary relationship among the entities corresponding to customer Hayes, loan L-15, and the Perryridge branch specifies that customer Hayes has loan L-15 at the Perryridge branch.

The number of entity sets that participate in a relationship set is also the *degree* of the relationship set. A binary relationship set is of degree 2; a ternary relationship set is of degree 3.

2.2 Design Issues

The notions of an entity set and a relationship set are not precise, and it is possible to define a set of entities and the relationships among them in a number of different ways. In this section, we examine basic issues in the design of an E-R database schema. The design process is covered in further detail in Section 2.7.4.

2.2.1 Use of Entity Sets or Attributes

Consider the entity set *employee* with attributes *employee-name* and *telephone-number*. It can easily be argued that a telephone is an entity in its own right with attributes *telephone-number* and *location* (the office where the telephone is located). If we take this point of view, the *employee* entity set must be redefined as follows:

- The *employee* entity set with attribute *employee-name*

- The *telephone* entity set with attributes *telephone-number* and *location*
- The relationship set *emp-telephone*, which denotes the association between employees and the telephones that they have

What, then, is the main difference between these two definitions of an employee? In the first case, the definition implies that every employee has precisely one telephone number associated with him. In the second case, however, the definition states that employees may have several telephone numbers (including zero) associated with them. Thus, the second definition is more general than the first one, and may more accurately reflect the real-world situation.

Even if we are given that each employee has precisely one telephone number associated with him, the second definition may still be more appropriate if the telephone is shared among several employees.

It would not be appropriate, however, to apply the same technique to the attribute *employee-name*; it is difficult to argue that *employee-name* is an entity in its own right (in contrast to the telephone). Thus, it is appropriate to have *employee-name* as an attribute of the *employee* entity set.

Two natural questions thus arise: What constitutes an attribute, and what constitutes an entity set? Unfortunately, there are no simple answers. The distinctions mainly depend on the structure of the real-world enterprise being modeled, and on the semantics associated with the attribute in question.

2.2.2 Use of Entity Sets or Relationship Sets

It is not always clear whether an object is best expressed by an entity set or a relationship set. In Section 2.1.1, we assumed that a bank loan is modeled as an entity. An alternative is to model a loan not as an entity, but rather as a relationship between customers and branches, with *loan-number* and *amount* as descriptive attributes. Each loan is represented by a relationship between a customer and a branch.

If every loan is held by exactly one customer and is associated with exactly one branch, we may find satisfactory the design where a loan is represented as a relationship. However, with this design, we cannot represent conveniently a situation in which several customers hold a loan jointly. We must define a separate relationship for each holder of the joint loan. Then, we must replicate the values for the descriptive attributes *loan-number* and *amount* in each such relationship. Each such relationship must, of course, have the same value for the descriptive attributes *loan-number* and *amount*. Two problems arise as a result of the replication: (1) the data are stored multiple times, wasting storage space; and (2) updates potentially leave the data in an inconsistent state, where the values differ in two relationships for attributes that are supposed to have the same value. The issue of how to avoid such replication is treated formally by *normalization theory*, discussed in Chapter 7. The problem of replication of the attributes *loan-number* and *amount* is absent in the original design of Section 2.1.1, because there *loan* is an entity set.

One possible guideline in determining whether to use an entity set or a relationship set is to designate a relationship set to describe an action that occurs between entities. This approach can also be useful in deciding whether certain attributes may be more appropriately expressed as relationships.

2.2.3 Binary Versus *n*-ary Relationship Sets

It is always possible to replace a nonbinary (n-ary, for $n > 2$) relationship set by a number of distinct binary relationship sets. For simplicity, consider the abstract ternary ($n = 3$) relationship set R, relating entity sets A, B, and C. We replace the relationship set R by an entity set E, and create three relationship sets:

- R_A, relating E and A
- R_B, relating E and B
- R_C, relating E and C

If the relationship set R had any attributes, these are assigned to entity set E; otherwise, a special identifying attribute is created for E (since every entity set must have at least one attribute to distinguish members of the set). For each relationship (a_i, b_i, c_i) in the relationship set R, we create a new entity e_i in the entity set E. Then, in each of the three new relationship sets, we insert a relationship as follows:

- (e_i, a_i) in R_A
- (e_i, b_i) in R_B
- (e_i, c_i) in R_C

We can generalize this process in a straightforward manner to n-ary relationship sets. Thus, conceptually, we can restrict the E-R model to include only binary relationship sets. However, this restriction is not always desirable.

- An identifying attribute may have to be created for the entity set created to represent the relationship set. This attribute, along with the extra relationship sets required, increase the complexity of the design and (as we shall see in Section 2.9) overall storage requirements.
- A n-ary relationship set shows more clearly that several entities participate in a single relationship. In the corresponding design using binary relationships, it is more difficult to enforce this participation constraint.

2.3 Mapping Constraints

An E-R enterprise schema may define certain constraints to which the contents of a database must conform. In this section, we examine mapping cardinalities and existence dependencies—two of the most important types of constraints.

2.3.1 Mapping Cardinalities

Mapping cardinalities, or cardinality ratios, express the number of entities to which another entity can be associated via a relationship set.

Mapping cardinalities are most useful in describing binary relationship sets, although occasionally they contribute to the description of relationship sets that involve more than two entity sets. In this section, we shall concentrate on only binary relationship sets.

For a binary relationship set R between entity sets A and B, the mapping cardinality must be one of the following:

- **One to one**. An entity in A is associated with at most one entity in B, and an entity in B is associated with at most one entity in A. (See Figure 2.4a.)
- **One to many**. An entity in A is associated with any number of entities in B. An entity in B, however, can be associated with at most one entity in A. (See Figure 2.4b.)
- **Many to one**. An entity in A is associated with at most one entity in B. An entity in B, however, can be associated with any number of entities in A. (See Figure 2.5a.)
- **Many to many**. An entity in A is associated with any number of entities in B, and an entity in B is associated with any number of entities in A. (See Figure 2.5b.)

The appropriate mapping cardinality for a particular relationship set is obviously dependent on the real-world situation that is being modeled by the relationship set.

As an illustration, consider the *borrower* relationship set. If, in a particular bank, a loan can belong to only one customer, and a customer can have several loans, then the relationship set from *customer* to *loan* is one to many. This type of relationship is depicted in Figure 2.3. If a loan can belong to several customers (as can loans taken jointly by several business partners), the relationship set is many to many.

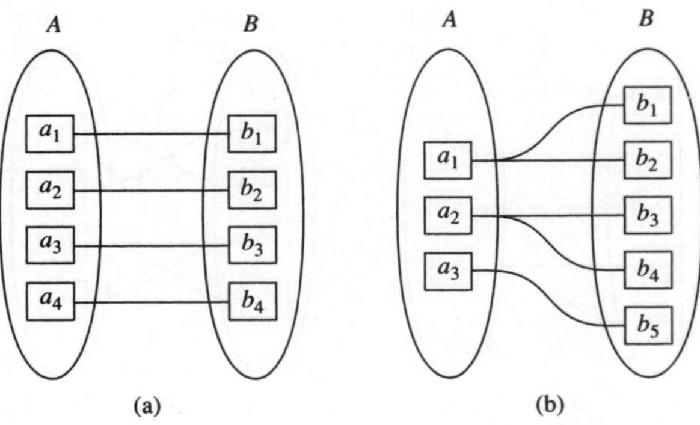

Figure 2.4 Mapping cardinalities. (a) One to one. (b) One to many.

The cardinality ratio of a relationship can affect the placement of relationship attributes. Attributes of one-to-one or one-to-many relationship sets can be associated with one of the participating entity sets, rather than with the relationship set. For instance, let us specify that *depositor* is a one-to-many relationship set such that one customer may have several accounts, but each account is held by only one customer. In this case, the attribute *access-date* could be associated with the *account* entity set, as depicted in Figure 2.6; to keep the figure simple, only some of the attributes of the two entity sets are shown. Since each *account* entity participates in a relationship with at most one instance of *customer*, making this attribute designation would have the same meaning as would placing *access-date* with the *depositor* relationship set. Attributes of a one-to-many relationship set can be repositioned to only the entity set on the "many" side of the relationship. For one-to-one relationship sets, the relationship attribute can be associated with either one of the participating entities.

The design decision of where to place descriptive attributes in such cases—as a relationship or entity attribute—should reflect the characteristics of the enterprise being modeled. The designer may choose to retain *access-date* as an attribute of *depositor* to express explicitly that an access occurs at the point of interaction between the *customer* and *account* entity sets.

The choice of attribute placement is more clearcut for many-to-many relationship sets. Returning to our example, let us specify the perhaps more realistic case that *depositor* is a many-to-many relationship set expressing that a customer may have one or more accounts, and that an account can be held by one or more customers. If we are to express the date on which a specific customer last accessed a specific account, *access-date* must be an attribute of the *depositor* relationship set, rather than either one of the participating entities. If *access-date* were an attribute of *account*, for instance, we could not determine which customer made the most recent access to a joint account. When an attribute is determined by the combination of participating entity sets, rather than by either entity separately, that attribute must be associated with the many-to-many relationship set. The placement of *access-date* as a relationship attribute is depicted in Figure 2.7;

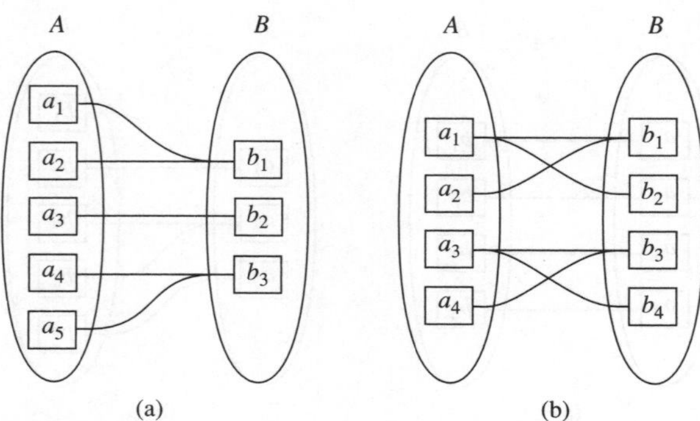

Figure 2.5 Mapping cardinalities. (a) Many to one. (b) Many to many.

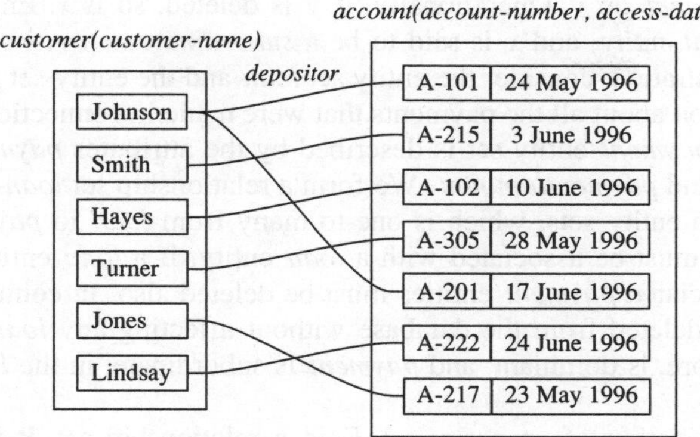

Figure 2.6 *Access-date* as attribute of the *account* entity set.

again, to keep the figure simple, only some of the attributes of the two entity sets are shown.

2.3.2 Existence Dependencies

Another important class of constraints is *existence dependencies*. Specifically, if the existence of entity x depends on the existence of entity y, then x is said to be

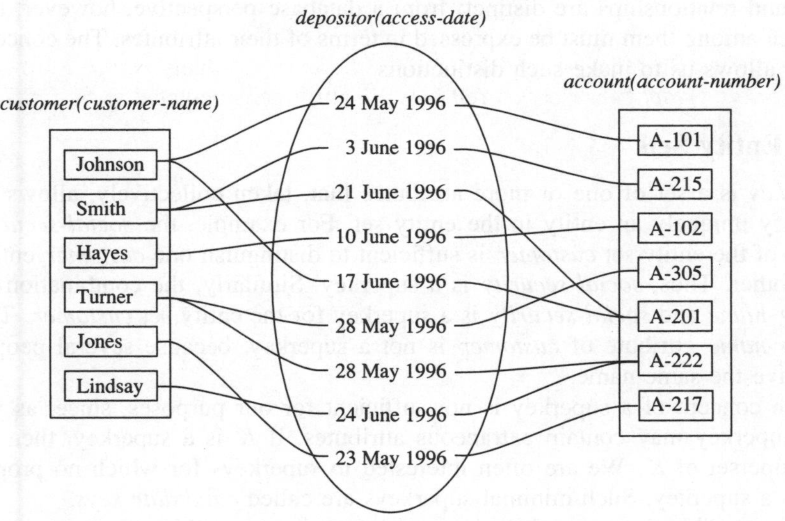

Figure 2.7 *Access-date* as attribute of the *depositor* relationship set.

existence dependent on *y*. Operationally, if *y* is deleted, so is *x*. Entity *y* is said to be a *dominant entity*, and *x* is said to be a *subordinate entity*.

As an illustration, consider the entity set *loan* and the entity set *payment* that keeps information about all the payments that were made in connection to a particular loan. The *payment* entity set is described by the attributes *payment-number*, *payment-date*, and *payment-amount*. We form a relationship set *loan-payment* between these two entity sets, which is one-to-many from *loan* to *payment*. Every *payment* entity must be associated with a *loan* entity. If a *loan* entity is deleted, then all its associated *payment* entities must be deleted also. In contrast, *payment* entities can be deleted from the database without affecting any *loan*. The entity set *loan*, therefore, is dominant, and *payment* is subordinate, in the *loan-payment* relationship set.

The participation of an entity set *E* in a relationship set *R* is said to be *total* if every entity in *E* participates in at least one relationship in *R*. If only some entities in *E* participate in relationships in *R*, the participation of entity set *E* in relationship *R* is said to be *partial*. Total participation is closely related to existence dependency. For example, since every payment entity must be related to some loan entity by the *loan-payment* relationship, the participation of *payment* in the relationship set *loan-payment* is total. In contrast, an individual can be a bank customer whether or not she has a loan with the bank. Hence, it is possible that only a partial set of the *customer* entities relate to the *loan* entity set, and the participation of *customer* in the *borrower* relationship set is therefore partial.

2.4 Keys

It is important to be able to specify how entities within a given entity set and relationships within a given relationship set are distinguished. Conceptually, individual entities and relationships are distinct; from a database perspective, however, the difference among them must be expressed in terms of their attributes. The concept of a *key* allows us to make such distinctions.

2.4.1 Entity Sets

A *superkey* is a set of one or more attributes that, taken collectively, allows us to identify uniquely an entity in the entity set. For example, the *social-security* attribute of the entity set *customer* is sufficient to distinguish one *customer* entity from another. Thus, *social-security* is a superkey. Similarly, the combination of *customer-name* and *social-security* is a superkey for the entity set *customer*. The *customer-name* attribute of *customer* is not a superkey, because several people might have the same name.

The concept of a superkey is not sufficient for our purposes, since, as we saw, a superkey may contain extraneous attributes. If *K* is a superkey, then so is any superset of *K*. We are often interested in superkeys for which no proper subset is a superkey. Such minimal superkeys are called *candidate keys*.

It is possible that several distinct sets of attributes could serve as a candidate key. Suppose that a combination of *customer-name* and *customer-street* is sufficient to distinguish among members of the *customer* entity set. Then, both {*social-security*} and {*customer-name*, *customer-street*} are candidate keys. Although the attributes *social-security* and *customer-name* together can distinguish *customer* entities, their combination does not form a candidate key, since the attribute *social-security* alone is a candidate key.

Candidate keys must be designated with care. As we noted, the name of a person is obviously not sufficient, because there may be many people with the same name. In the U. S., the social-security number may be a candidate key. Since non-U.S. residents usually do not have social-security numbers, enterprises may generate their own unique identifiers, such as customer numbers or student-id numbers, or may use some unique combination of other attributes as a key. One that is often used is the combination of name, date of birth, and address, since it is extremely unlikely that two people will have the same values for all these attributes.

We shall use the term *primary key* to denote a candidate key that is chosen by the database designer as the principal means of identifying entities within an entity set. A key (primary, candidate, and super) is a property of the entity set, rather than of the individual entities. Any two individual entities in the set are prohibited from having the same value on the key attributes at the same time. The designation of a key represents a constraint in the real-world enterprise being modeled.

2.4.2 Relationship Sets

The primary key of an entity set allows us to distinguish among the various entities of the set. We need a similar mechanism to distinguish among the various relationships of a relationship set.

Let R be a relationship set involving entity sets $E_1, E_2, \ldots, E_n$. Let $primary\text{-}key(E_i)$ denote the set of attributes that forms the primary key for entity set E_i. Assume that the attribute names of all primary keys are unique (if they are not, use an appropriate renaming scheme). The composition of the primary key for a relationship set depends on the structure of the attributes associated with the relationship set R.

If the relationship set R has no attributes associated with it, then the set of attributes

$$primary\text{-}key(E_1) \cup primary\text{-}key(E_2) \cup \ldots \cup primary\text{-}key(E_n)$$

describes an individual relationship in set R.

If the relationship set R has attributes $a_1, a_2, \ldots, a_m$ associated with it, then the set of attributes

$$primary\text{-}key(E_1) \cup primary\text{-}key(E_2) \cup \ldots \cup primary\text{-}key(E_n) \cup \{a_1, a_2, \ldots, a_m\}$$

describes an individual relationship in set R.

In both of the above cases, the set of attributes

$$primary\text{-}key(E_1) \cup primary\text{-}key(E_2) \cup \ldots \cup primary\text{-}key(E_n)$$

form a superkey for the relationship set.

The structure of the primary key for the relationship set depends on the mapping cardinality of the relationship set. As an illustration, consider the entity sets *customer* and *employee*, and a relationship set *cust-banker* that represents an association between a customer and her banker (an employee entity). Suppose that the relationship set is many to many, and also suppose that the relationship set has the attribute *type* associated with it, representing the nature of the relationship (such as loan officer or personal banker). Then the primary key of *cust-banker* consists of the union of the primary keys of *customer* and *employee*. However, if a customer can have only one banker—that is, if the *cust-banker* relationship is many to one—then the primary key of *cust-banker* is simply the primary key of *customer*. For one-to-one relationships either primary key can be used.

The designation of primary keys is more complicated for non-binary relationships. We consider the issue in more detail in Chapter 7.

2.5 Entity–Relationship Diagram

As we saw briefly in Section 1.3, the overall logical structure of a database can be expressed graphically by an E-R *diagram*. The relative simplicity and pictorial clarity of this diagramming technique may well account in large part for the widespread use of the E-R model. Such a diagram consists of the following major components:

- **Rectangles**, which represent entity sets
- **Ellipses**, which represent attributes
- **Diamonds**, which represent relationship sets
- **Lines**, which link attributes to entity sets and entity sets to relationship sets
- **Double ellipses**, which represent multivalued attributes
- **Dashed ellipses**, which denote derived attributes
- **Double Lines**, which indicate total participation of an entity in a relationship set

As depicted in Figure 2.8, attributes of an entity set that are members of the primary key are underlined.

Consider the entity-relationship diagram in Figure 2.8, which consists of two entity sets, *customer* and *loan*, related through a binary relationship set *borrower*. The attributes associated with *customer* are *customer-name*, *social-security*, *customer-street*, and *customer-city*. The attributes associated with *loan* are *loan-number* and *amount*.

The relationship set *borrower* may be many-to-many, one-to-many, many-to-one, or one-to-one. To distinguish among these types, we draw either a directed line (→) or an undirected line (—) between the relationship set and the entity set in question.

- A directed line from the relationship set *borrower* to the entity set *loan* specifies that *borrower* is either a one-to-one, or many-to-one relationship

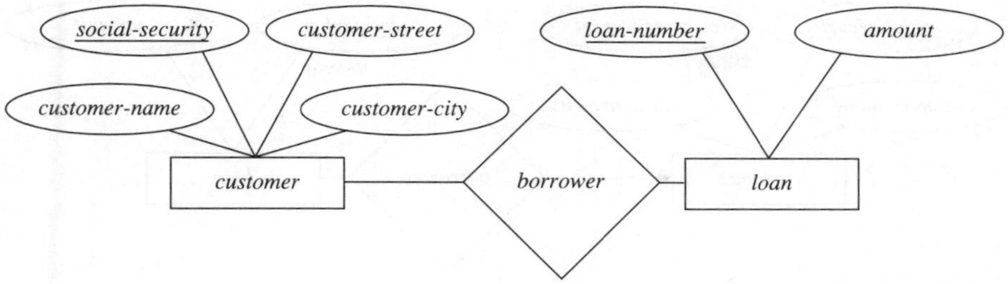

Figure 2.8 E-R diagram corresponding to customers and loans.

set, from *customer* to *loan*; *borrower* cannot be a many-to-many or a one-to-many relationship set, from *customer* to *loan*.

- An undirected line from the relationship set *borrower* to the entity set *loan* specifies that *borrower* is either a many-to-many, or one-to-many relationship set, from *customer* to *loan*.

Returning to the E-R diagram of Figure 2.8, we see that the relationship set *borrower* is many to many. If the relationship set *borrower* were one to many, from *customer* to *loan*, then the line from *borrower* to *customer* would be directed, with an arrow pointing to the *customer* entity set (Figure 2.9a). Similarly, if the relationship set *borrower* were many to one from *customer* to *loan*, then the line from *borrower* to *loan* would have an arrow pointing to the *loan* entity set (Figure 2.9b). Finally, if the relationship set *borrower* were one to one, then both lines from *borrower* would have arrows: one pointing to the *loan* entity set, and one pointing to the *customer* entity set (Figure 2.10).

If a relationship set has also some attributes associated with it, then we link these attributes to that relationship set. For example, in Figure 2.11, we have the *access-date* descriptive attribute attached to the relationship set *depositor* to specify the most recent date on which a customer accessed that account.

We indicate roles in E-R diagrams by labeling the lines that connect diamonds to rectangles. Figure 2.12 shows the role indicators *manager* and *worker* between the *employee* entity set and the *works-for* relationship set.

Nonbinary relationship sets can be specified easily in an E-R diagram. Figure 2.13 consists of the three entity sets *customer*, *loan*, and *branch*, related through the relationship set *CLB*. This diagram specifies that a customer may have several loans, and that loan may belong to several different customers. Further, the arrow pointing to *branch* indicates that each customer–loan pair is associated with a specific bank branch. If the diagram had an arrow pointing to *customer*, in addition to the arrow pointing to *branch*, the diagram would specify that each loan is associated with a specific customer and a specific bank branch.

2.6 Weak Entity Sets

An entity set may not have sufficient attributes to form a primary key. Such an entity set is termed a *weak entity set*. An entity set that has a primary key is termed

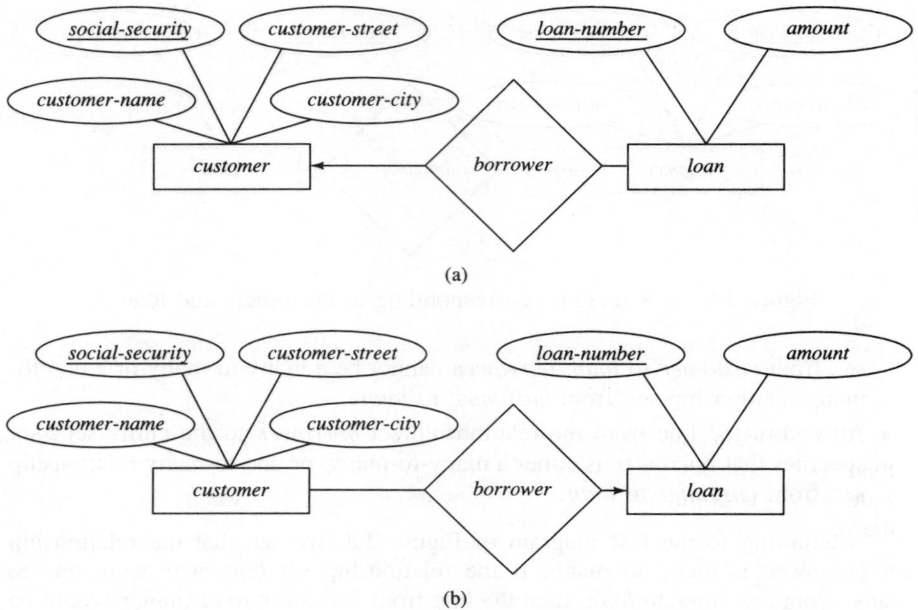

Figure 2.9 Relationships. (a) One to many. (b) Many to one.

a *strong entity set*. As an illustration, consider the entity set *payment*, which has the three attributes: *payment-number*, *payment-date*, and *payment-amount*. Although each *payment* entity is distinct, payments for different loans may share the same payment number. Thus, this entity set does not have a primary key; it is a weak entity set. For a weak entity set to be meaningful, it must be part of a one-to-many relationship set. This relationship set should have no descriptive attributes, since any required attributes can be associated with the weak entity set (see the discussion of moving relationship-set attributes to participating entity sets in Section 2.3.1).

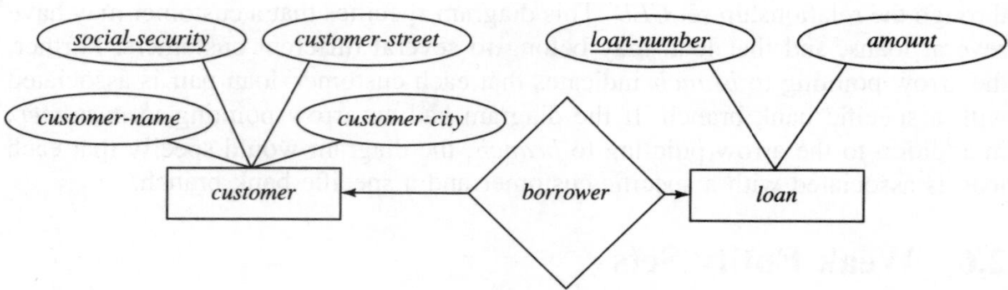

Figure 2.10 One-to-one relationship.

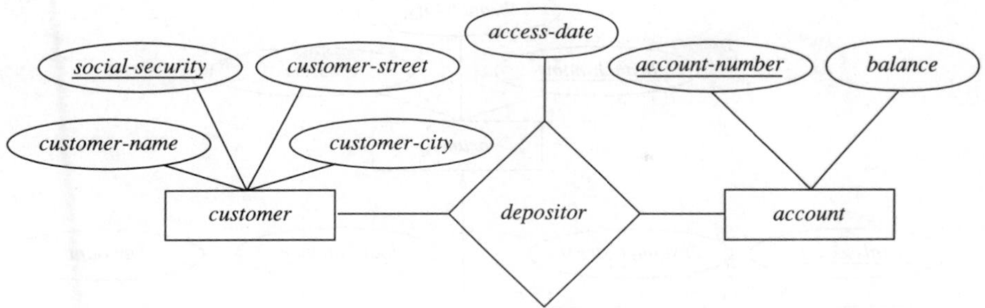

Figure 2.11 E-R diagram with an attribute attached to a relationship set.

The concepts of strong and weak entity sets are related to the existence dependencies introduced in Section 2.3.2. A member of a strong entity set is by definition a dominant entity, whereas a member of a weak entity set is a subordinate entity.

Although a weak entity set does not have a primary key, we nevertheless need a means of distinguishing among all those entities in the entity set that depend on one particular strong entity. The *discriminator* of a weak entity set is a set of attributes that allows this distinction to be made. For example, the discriminator of the weak entity set *payment* is the attribute *payment-number*, since, for each loan, a payment number uniquely identifies one single payment for that loan. The discriminator of a weak entity set is also called the *partial key* of the entity set.

The primary key of a weak entity set is formed by the primary key of the strong entity set on which the weak entity set is existence dependent, plus the weak entity set's discriminator. In the case of the entity set *payment*, its primary key is {*loan-number*, *payment-number*}, where *loan-number* identifies the dominant entity of a *payment*, and *payment-number* distinguishes *payment* entities within the same loan.

The identifying dominant entity set is said to *own* the weak entity set that it identifies. The relationship that associates the weak entity set with an owner

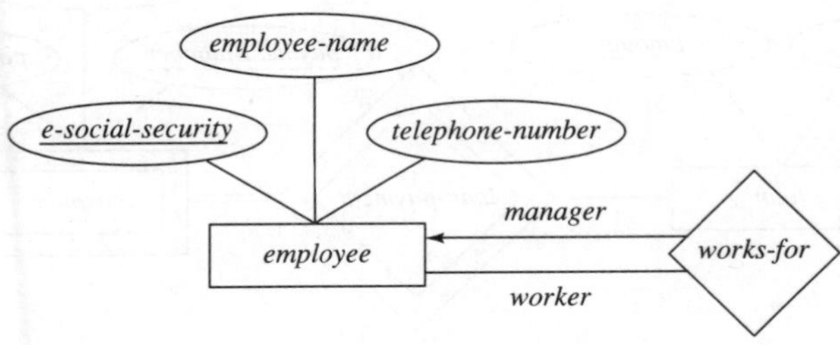

Figure 2.12 E-R diagram with role indicators.

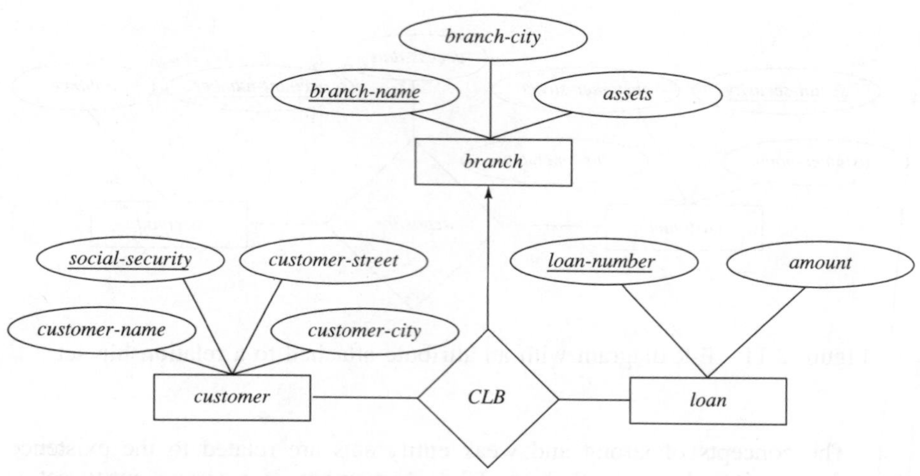

Figure 2.13 E-R diagram with a ternary relationship.

is the *identifying relationship*. In our example, *loan-payment* is the identifying relationship for *payment*.

A weak entity set is indicated in E-R diagrams by a doubly outlined box, and the corresponding identifying relationship by a doubly outlined diamond. In Figure 2.14, the weak entity set *payment* is dependent on the strong entity set *loan* via the relationship set *loan-payment*. The figure also illustrates the use of double lines to indicate *total participation*—the participation of the (weak) entity set *payment* in the relationship *loan-payment* is total, meaning that every payment must be related via *loan-payment* to some account. Finally, the arrow from *loan-payment* to *loan* indicates that each payment is for a single loan. The discriminator of a weak entity set also is underlined, but with a dashed, rather than a solid, line.

A weak entity set may participate as owner in an identifying relationship with another weak entity set. Even though a weak entity set is always existence de-

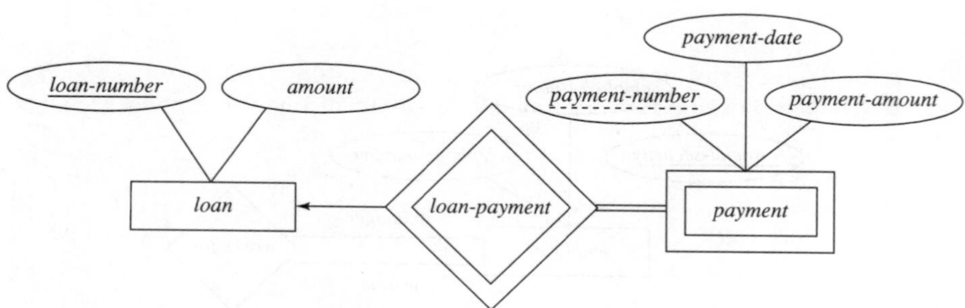

Figure 2.14 E-R diagram with a weak entity set.

pendent on a dominant entity, an existence dependency does not necessarily result in a weak entity set; that is, the subordinate entity set may have a primary key.

In some cases, the database designer may choose to express a weak entity set as a multivalued, composite attribute of the owner entity set. In our example, this alternative would require that the entity set *loan* have a multivalued, composite attribute *payment*, consisting of *payment-number*, *payment-date*, and *payment-amount*. A weak entity set may be more appropriately modeled as an attribute if it participates in only the identifying relationship, and if it has few attributes. Conversely, a weak-entity-set representation will more aptly model a situation where the set participates in relationships other than the identifying relationship, and where the weak entity set has several attributes.

2.7 Extended E-R Features

Although the basic E-R concepts can model most database features, some aspects of a database may be more aptly expressed by certain extensions to the basic E-R model. In this section, we discuss the extended E-R features of specialization, generalization, higher- and lower-level entity sets, attribute inheritance, and aggregation.

2.7.1 Specialization

An entity set may include subgroupings of entities that are distinct in some way from other entities in the set. For instance, a subset of entities within an entity set may have attributes that are not shared by all the entities in the entity set. The E-R model provides a means for representing these distinctive entity groupings.

Consider the entity set *account* with attributes *account-number* and *balance*. An account is further classified as being one of the following:

- *savings-account*
- *checking-account*

Each of these account types is described by a set of attributes that includes all the attributes of entity set *account* plus additional attributes. For example, *savings-account* entities are described further by the attribute *interest-rate*, whereas *checking-account* entities are described further by the attribute *overdraft-amount*. The process of designating subgroupings within an entity set is *specialization*. The specialization of *account* allows us to distinguish among accounts based on the type of account.

An entity set may be specialized by more than one distinguishing feature. In our example, the distinguishing feature among account entities is the type of account. Another, coexistent, specialization could be based on the type of account ownership, and would result in the entity sets *commercial-account* and *personal-account*. When more than one specialization is formed on an entity set, a particular entity may belong to both of the specializations. For instance, a given account may be both a personal account and a checking account.

We can apply specialization repeatedly to refine the design scheme. For instance, the bank may offer the following three types of checking accounts.

1. A *standard* checking account with a \$3.00 monthly service charge and 25 free checks each month. For these accounts, the bank keeps track of the number of checks written from an account each month.
2. A *gold* checking account that requires a \$1000.00 minimum balance, pays 2-percent interest, and offers unlimited free check writing. In this case, the bank monitors the minimum balance and the interest paid for each month.
3. A *senior* checking account for customers aged 65 years or older that has no monthly service charge, and that allows unlimited free check writing each month. A record of the customer's date of birth is associated with this type of account.

The specialization of *checking-account* by account type yields the following entity sets.

1. *standard*, with attribute *num-checks*
2. *gold*, with attributes *min-balance* and *interest-payment*
3. *senior*, with attribute *date-of-birth*

In terms of an E-R diagram, specialization is depicted by a *triangle* component labeled ISA, as shown in Figure 2.15. The label ISA stands for "is a" and represents, for example, that a savings account "is an" account. The ISA relationship may also be referred to as a superclass–subclass relationship. Higher- and lower-level entity sets are depicted as regular entity sets—that is, as rectangles containing the name of the entity set.

2.7.2 Generalization

The refinement from an initial entity set into successive levels of entity subgroupings represents a *top-down* design process in which distinctions are made explicit. The design process may also proceed in a *bottom-up* manner, in which multiple entity sets are synthesized into a higher-level entity set based on common features. The database designer may have first identified a *checking-account* entity set with the attributes *account-number*, *balance*, and *overdraft-amount*, and a *savings-account* entity set with the attributes *account-number*, *balance*, and *interest-rate*.

There are similarities between the *checking-account* entity set and the *savings-account* entity set in the sense that they have several attributes in common. This commonality can be expressed by *generalization*, which is a containment relationship that exists between a *higher-level* entity set and one or more *lower-level* entity sets. In our example, *account* is the higher-level entity set and *savings-account* and *checking-account* are lower-level entity sets. Higher- and lower-level entity sets also may be designated by the terms *superclass* and *sub-*

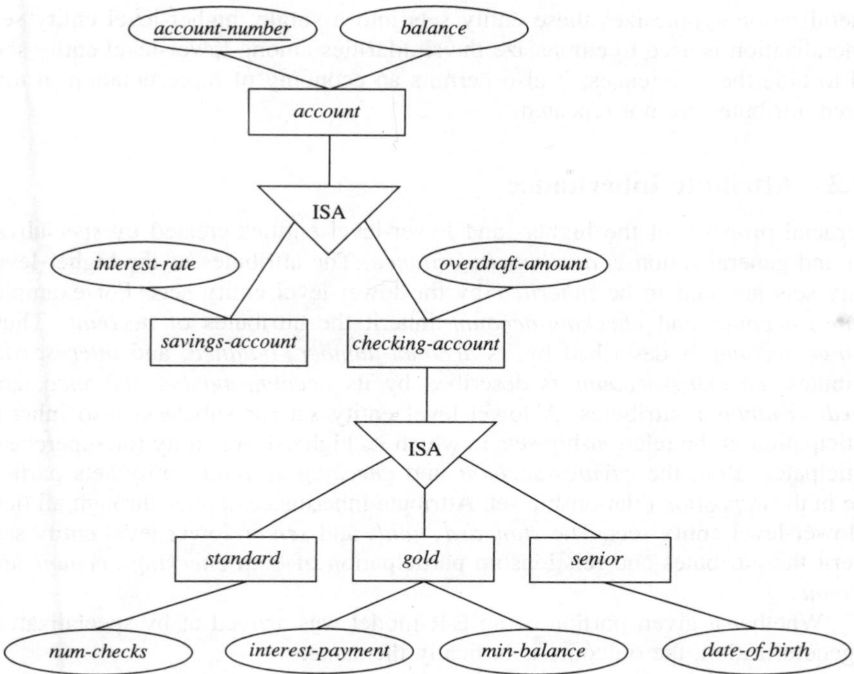

Figure 2.15 Specialization and generalization.

class, respectively. The *account* entity set is the superclass of the *savings-account* and *checking-account* subclasses.

For all practical purposes, generalization is a simple inversion of specialization. We will apply both processes, in combination, in the course of designing the E-R schema for an enterprise. In terms of the E-R diagram itself, we do not distinguish between specialization and generalization. New levels of entity representation will be distinguished (specialization) or synthesized (generalization) as the design schema comes to express fully the database application and the user requirements of the database. Differences in the two approaches may be characterized by their starting point and overall goal.

Specialization stems from a single entity set; it emphasizes differences among entities within the set by creating distinct lower-level entity sets. These lower-level entity sets may have attributes, or may participate in relationships, that do not apply to all the entities in the higher-level entity set. Indeed, the reason a designer applies specialization is to represent such distinctive features. If *savings-account* and *checking-account* did not each have unique attributes, there would be no need to specialize the *account* entity set.

Generalization proceeds from the recognition that a number of entity sets share some common features (namely, they are described by the same attributes and participate in the same relationship sets). Based on their commonalities, generalization synthesizes these entity sets into a single, higher-level entity set. Generalization is used to emphasize the similarities among lower-level entity sets and to hide the differences; it also permits an economy of representation in that shared attributes are not repeated.

2.7.3 Attribute Inheritance

A crucial property of the higher- and lower-level entities created by specialization and generalization is *attribute inheritance*. The attributes of the higher-level entity sets are said to be *inherited* by the lower-level entity sets. For example, *savings-account* and *checking-account* inherit the attributes of *account*. Thus, *savings-account* is described by its *account-number*, *balance*, and *interest-rate* attributes; *checking-account* is described by its *account-number*, *balance*, and *overdraft-amount* attributes. A lower-level entity set (or subclass) also inherits participation in the relationship sets in which its higher-level entity (or superclass) participates. Both the *savings-account* and *checking-account* entity sets participate in the *depositor* relationship set. Attribute inheritance applies through all tiers of lower-level entity sets. The *standard*, *gold*, and *senior* lower-level entity sets inherit the attributes and relationship participation of both *checking-account* and *account*.

Whether a given portion of an E-R model was arrived at by specialization or generalization, the outcome is basically the same:

- A higher-level entity set with attributes and relationships that apply to all of its lower-level entity sets
- Lower-level entity sets with distinctive features that apply only within a particular lower-level entity set

In what follows, although we often refer to only generalization, the properties that we discuss belong fully to both processes.

Figure 2.15 depicts a *hierarchy* of entity sets. In the figure, *checking-account* is a lower-level entity set of *account* and a higher-level entity set of the *standard, gold*, and *senior* entity sets. In a hierarchy, a given entity set may be involved as a lower-level entity set in only one ISA relationship. If an entity set is a lower-level entity set in more than one ISA relationship, the resulting structure is said to be a *lattice*.

2.7.4 Design Constraints

To model an enterprise more accurately, the database designer may choose to place certain constraints on a particular generalization. One type of constraint involves determining which entities can be members of a given lower-level entity set. Such membership may be one of the following:

- **Condition-defined**. In condition-defined lower-level entity sets, membership is evaluated on the basis of whether or not an entity satisfies an explicit condition or predicate. For example, assume that the higher-level entity set *account* has the attribute *account-type*. All *account* entities are evaluated on the defining *account-type* attribute. Only those entities that satisfy the condition *account-type* = "savingsaccount" are allowed to belong to the lower-level entity set *savings-account*. All entities that satisfy the condition *account-type* = "checkingaccount" are included in *checking account*. Since all the lower-level entities are evaluated on the basis of the same attribute (in this case, on *account-type*), this type of generalization is said to be *attribute-defined*.

- **User-defined**. User-defined lower-level entity sets are not constrained by a membership condition; rather, entities are assigned to a given entity set by the database user. For instance, let us assume that, after 3 months of employment, bank employees are assigned to one of four work teams. The teams are represented as four lower-level entity sets of the higher-level *employee* entity set. The specific team entity set to which a given employee is assigned is not evaluated automatically based on an explicit defining condition. Instead, team assignment is made on an individual basis by the user in charge of this decision, and is implemented by an operation that adds an entity to an entity set.

A second type of constraint relates to whether or not entities may belong to more than one lower-level entity set within a single generalization. The lower-level entity sets may be one of the following:

- **Disjoint**. A disjointness constraint requires that an entity belong to no more than one lower-level entity set. In our example, an *account* entity can satisfy only one condition for the *account-type* attribute; an entity can be either a savings account or a checking account, but cannot be both.
- **Overlapping**. In overlapping generalizations, the same entity may belong to more than one lower-level entity set within a single generalization. For an illustration, let us return to the employee workteam example, and assume that certain managers participate in more than one workteam. A given employee may therefore appear in more than one of the team entity sets.

Lower-level entity overlap is the default case; a disjointness constraint must be placed explicitly on a generalization (or specialization).

A final constraint, the *completeness constraint* on a generalization, specifies whether or not an entity in the higher-level entity set must belong to at least one of the lower-level entity sets within a generalization. This constraint may be one of the following:

- **Total**. Each higher-level entity must belong to a lower-level entity set.
- **Partial**. Some higher-level entities may not belong to any lower-level entity set.

The *account* generalization is total: All account entities must be either a savings account or a checking account. Because the higher-level entity set arrived at through generalization is generally composed of only those entities in the lower-level entity sets, the completeness constraint for a generalized higher-level entity set is usually total. When the constraint is partial, a higher-level entity is not constrained to appear in a lower-level entity set. The workteam entity sets illustrate a partial specialization. Since employees are assigned to a team only after 3 months on the job, some *employee* entities may not be members of any of the lower-level team entity sets.

We may characterize the team entity sets more fully as a partial, overlapping specialization of *employee*. The generalization of *checking-account* and *savings-account* into *account* is a total, disjoint generalization. The completeness and disjointness constraints, however, are not dependent on each other. Constraint patterns may also be partial–disjoint and total–overlapping.

We can see that certain insertion and deletion requirements follow from the constraints that apply to a given generalization or specialization. For instance, when a total completeness constraint is in place, an entity inserted in a higher-level entity set must also be inserted in at least one of the lower-level entity sets. With a condition-defined constraint, all higher-level entities that satisfy the condition must be inserted in that lower-level entity set. Finally, an entity that is deleted from a higher-level entity set also is deleted from all the associated lower-level entity sets to which it belongs.

2.7.5 Aggregation

One limitation of the E-R model is that it is not possible to express relationships among relationships. To illustrate the need for such a construct, we consider again a database describing information about customers and their loans. Suppose that each customer–loan pair may have a bank employee who is the loan officer for that particular pair. Using our basic E-R modeling constructs, we obtain the E-R diagram of Figure 2.16. It appears that the relationship sets *borrower* and *loan-officer* can be combined into one single relationship set. Nevertheless, we should not combine them, because doing so would obscure the logical structure of this schema. For example, if we combine the *borrower* and *loan-officer* relationship sets, then this combination specifies that a loan officer must be assigned to every customer–loan pair, which is not true. The separation into two different relationship sets solves this problem.

There is redundant information in the resultant figure, however, since every customer-loan pair in *loan-officer* is also in *borrower*. If the loan officer were a value rather than an *employee* entity, we could instead make *loan-officer* a multivalued attribute of the relationship *borrower*. But doing so makes it more difficult (logically as well as in execution cost) to find, for example, customer–loan pairs for which an employee is responsible. Since the loan officer is an *employee* entity, this alternative is ruled out in any case.

The best way to model a situation such as the one just described is to use aggregation. *Aggregation* is an abstraction through which relationships are

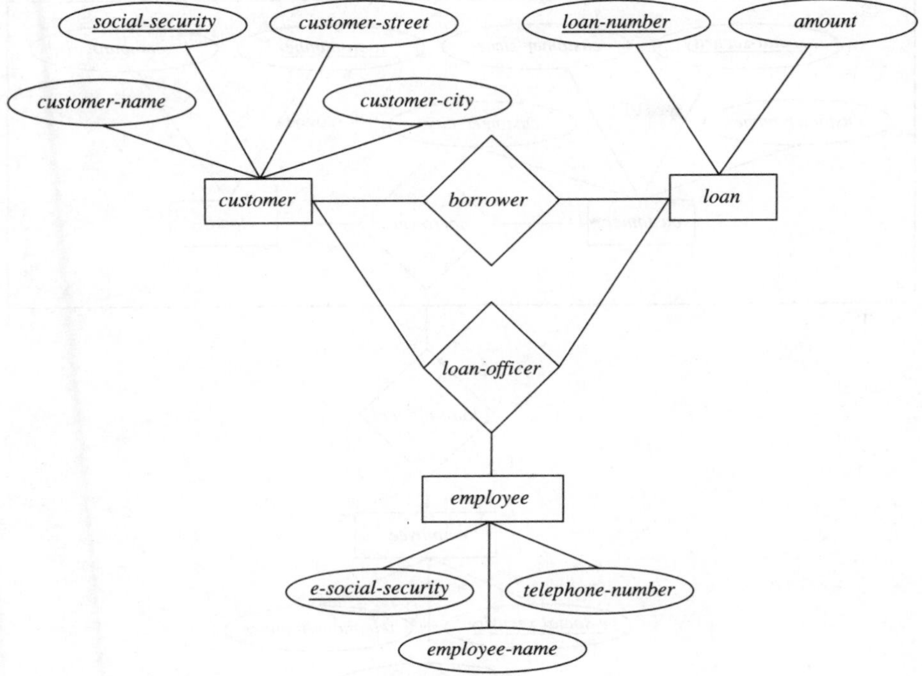

Figure 2.16 E-R diagram with redundant relationships.

treated as higher-level entities. Thus, for our example, we regard the relationship set *borrower* and the entity sets *customer* and *loan* as a higher-level entity set called *borrower*. Such an entity set is treated in the same manner as is any other entity set. A common notation for aggregation is shown in Figure 2.17.

2.8 Design of an E-R Database Schema

The E-R data model gives us substantial flexibility in designing a database schema to model a given enterprise. In this section, we consider how a database designer may select from the wide range of alternatives. Among the decisions to be made are the following:

- Whether to use an attribute or an entity set to represent an object (discussed earlier in Section 2.2.1)
- Whether a real-world concept is expressed most accurately by an entity set or by a relationship set (Section 2.2.2)
- Whether to use a ternary relationship or a pair of binary relationships (Section 2.2.3)

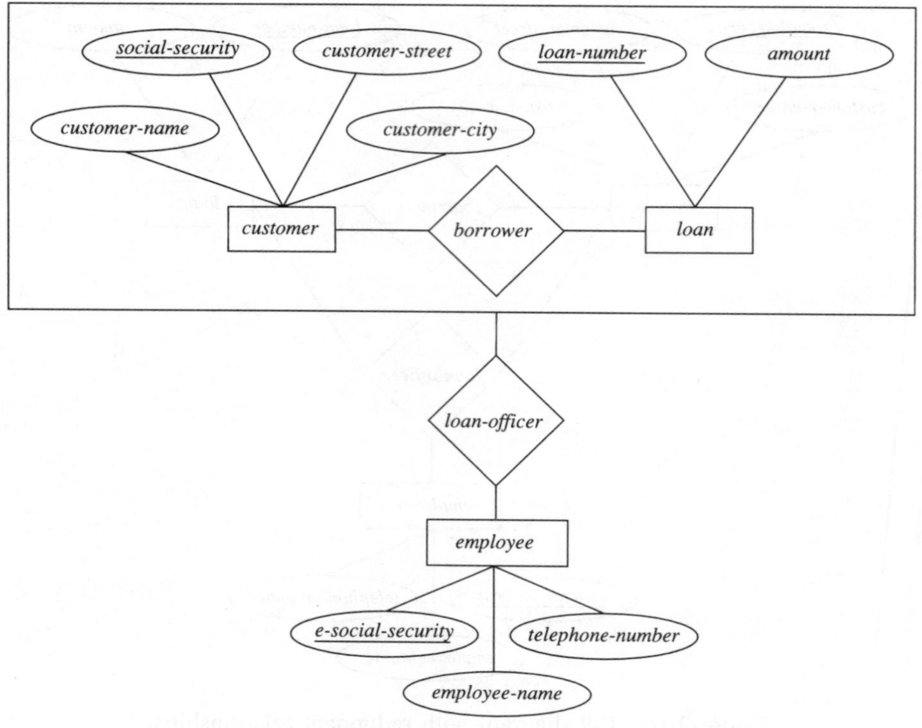

Figure 2.17 E-R diagram with aggregation.

- Whether to use a strong or a weak entity set (Section 2.6); a strong entity set and its dependent weak entity sets may be regarded as a single "object" in the database, since weak entities are existence dependent on a strong entity
- Whether using generalization (Section 2.7.2) is appropriate; generalization, or a hierarchy of ISA relationships, contributes to modularity by allowing common attributes of similar entity sets to be represented in one place in an E-R diagram
- Whether using aggregation (Section 2.7.5) is appropriate; aggregation groups a part of an E-R diagram into a single entity set, allowing us to treat the aggregate entity set as a single unit without concern for the details of its internal structure.

We shall see that the database designer needs a good understanding of the enterprise being modeled to make these decisions.

2.8.1 Design Phases

A high-level data model serves the database designer by providing a conceptual framework in which to specify, in a systematic fashion, what the data requirements of the database users are, and how the database will be structured to fulfill these requirements. The initial phase of database design, then, is to characterize fully the data needs of the prospective database users. The outcome of this phase is a *specification of user requirements*.

Next, the designer chooses a data model, and by applying the concepts of the chosen data model, translates these requirements into a conceptual schema of the database. The schema developed at this *conceptual-design* phase provides a detailed overview of the enterprise. Since we have studied only the E-R model so far, we shall use it to develop the conceptual schema. Stated in terms of the E-R model, the schema specifies all entity sets, relationship sets, attributes, and mapping constraints. The designer reviews the schema to confirm that all data requirements are indeed satisfied and are not in conflict with one another. She can also examine the design to remove any redundant features. Her focus at this point is describing the data and their relationships, rather than on specifying physical storage details.

A fully developed conceptual schema will also indicate the functional requirements of the enterprise. In a *specification of functional requirements*, users describe the kinds of operations (or transactions) that will be performed on the data. Example operations include modifying or updating data, searching for and retrieving specific data, and deleting data. A review of the schema for meeting functional requirements can be made at this stage of conceptual design.

The process of moving from an abstract data model to the implementation of the database proceeds in two final design phases. In the *logical-design* phase, the high-level conceptual schema is mapped onto the implementation data model of the DBMS that will be used. The resulting DBMS-specific database schema is used in the subsequent *physical-design* phase, in which the physical features of the database are specified. These features include the form of file organization and the internal storage structures; they are discussed in Chapter 10.

In this chapter, we cover only the concepts of the E-R model as used in the conceptual-schema-design phase. We have presented a brief overview of the database-design process to provide a context for the discussion of the E-R data model. Database design receives a full treatment in Chapter 7.

In Sections 2.8.2 and 2.8.3, we apply the two initial database-design phases to our banking-enterprise example. We employ the E-R data model to translate user requirements into a conceptual design schema that is depicted as an E-R diagram.

2.8.2 Data Requirements for Banking Enterprise

The initial specification of user requirements may be based on interviews with the database users, and on the designer's own analysis of the enterprise. The description that arises from this design phase serves as the basis for specifying the conceptual structure of the database. The following list itemizes the major requirements for the banking enterprise.

- The bank is organized into branches. Each branch is located in a particular city and is identified by a unique name. The bank monitors the assets of each branch.
- Bank customers are identified by their social-security numbers. The bank stores each customer's name, and the street and city where the customer lives. Customers may have accounts, and can take out loans. A customer may be associated with a particular banker, who may act as a loan officer or personal banker for that customer.
- Bank employees are also identified by their social-security numbers. The bank administration stores the name and telephone number of each employee, the names of the employee's dependents, and the social-security number of the employee's manager. The bank also keeps track of the employee's start date and, thus, length of employment.
- The bank offers two types of accounts—savings and checking accounts. Accounts can be held by more than one customer, and a customer can have more than one account. Each account is assigned a unique account number. The bank maintains a record of each account's balance, and the most recent date on which the account was accessed by each customer holding the account. In addition, each savings account has an interest rate, and overdrafts are recorded for each checking account.
- A loan originates at a particular branch and can be held by one or more customers. A loan is identified by a unique loan number. For each loan, the bank keeps track of the loan amount and the loan payments. Although a loan-payment number does not uniquely identify a particular payment among those for all the bank's loans, a payment number does identify a particular payment for a specific loan. The date and amount are recorded for each payment.

In a real banking enterprise, the bank would keep track of deposits and withdrawals from savings and checking accounts, just as it keeps track of payments to loan accounts. Since the modeling requirements for that tracking are similar, and we would like to keep our example application small, we do not keep track of such deposits and withdrawals in our model.

2.8.3 Entity-Sets Designation of Banking Enterprise

Our specification of data requirements serves as the starting point for constructing a conceptual schema for the database. From the specifications listed in Section 2.8.2, we begin to identify entity sets and their attributes.

- The *branch* entity set, with attributes *branch-name*, *branch-city*, and *assets*
- The *customer* entity set, with attributes:

  customer-name, *social-security*, *customer-street*; and *customer-city*

  A possible additional attribute is *banker-name*
- The *employee* entity set, with attributes:

  e-social-security, *employee-name*, *telephone-number*, *salary*, and *manager*

Additional descriptive features are the multivalued attribute *dependent-name*, the base attribute *start-date*, and the derived attribute *employment-length*

- Two account entity sets—*savings-account* and *checking-account*—with the common attributes of *account-number* and *balance*; in addition, *savings-account* has the attribute *interest-rate*, and *checking-account* has the attribute *overdraft-amount*
- The *loan* entity set, with the attributes:

  loan-number, *amount*, and *originating-branch*

  A possible additional attribute is the multivalued composite attribute *loan-payment*, with component attributes:

  payment-number, *payment-date*, and *payment-amount*

2.8.4 Relationship Sets Designation of Banking Enterprise

We now return to the rudimentary design scheme of Section 2.8.3 and specify the following relationship sets and mapping cardinalities.

- *borrower*, a many-to-many relationship set between *customer* and *loan*
- *loan-branch*, a many-to-one relationship set that indicates in which branch a loan originated
- *loan-payment*, a one-to-many relationship from *loan* to *payment*, which documents that a payment is made on a loan
- *depositor*, with relationship attribute *access-date*, a many-to-many relationship set between *customer* and *account*, indicating that a customer owns an account
- *cust-banker*, with relationship attribute *type*, a many-to-one relationship set expressing that a customer can be advised by a bank employee, and that a bank employee can advise one or more customers
- *works-for*, a relationship set between *employee* entities with role indicators *manager* and *worker*; the mapping cardinalities express that an employee works for only one manager, and that a manager supervises one or more employees

Note that we have replaced the *banker-name* attribute of the *customer* entity set by the *cust-banker* relationship set, and the *manager* attribute of the *employee* entity set by the *works-for* relationship set. We have chosen to retain *loan* as an entity set. The relationship sets *loan-branch* and *loan-payment* have replaced, respectively, the *originating-branch* and *loan-payment* attributes of the *loan* entity set.

2.8.5 E-R Diagram for Banking Enterprise

Drawing on the discussions presented in Section 2.8.4, we now present the completed E-R diagram for our example banking enterprise. Figure 2.18 depicts the full representation of a conceptual model of a bank, expressed in terms of E-R concepts. The diagram includes the entity sets, attributes, relationship sets, and

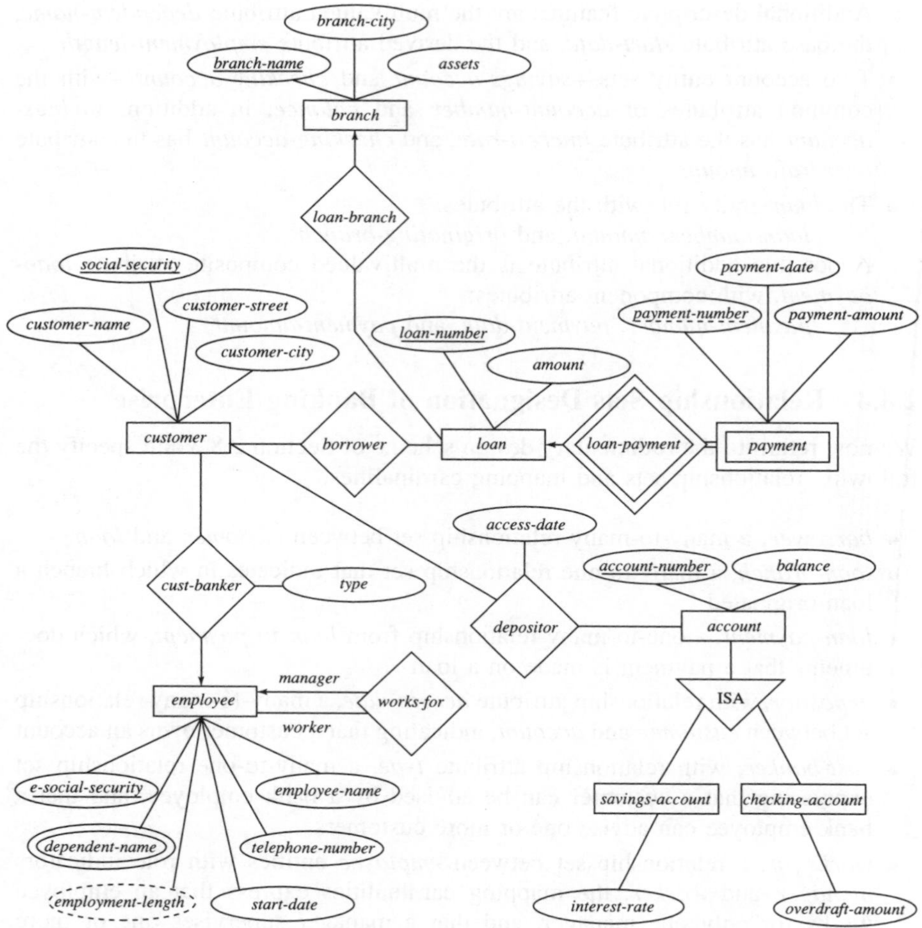

Figure 2.18 E-R diagram for banking enterprise.

mapping cardinalities arrived at through the design processes of Sections 2.8.2 and 2.8.3, and refined in Section 2.8.4.

2.9 Reduction of an E-R Schema to Tables

A database that conforms to an E-R database schema can be represented by a collection of tables. For each entity set and for each relationship set in the database, there is a unique table that is assigned the name of the corresponding entity set or relationship set. Each table has multiple columns, each of which has a unique name.

Both the E-R model and the relational-database model are abstract, logical representations of real-world enterprises. Because the two models employ similar design principles, we can convert an E-R design into a relational design. Converting a database representation from an E-R diagram to a table format is the basis for deriving a relational-database design from an E-R diagram. Although important differences exist between a relation and a table, informally, a relation can be considered to be a table of values. In this section, we describe how an E-R schema can be represented by tables; and in Chapter 3, we show how to generate a relational-database schema from an E-R schema.

2.9.1 Tabular Representation of Strong Entity Sets

Let E be a strong entity set with descriptive attributes $a_1, a_2, \ldots, a_n$. We represent this entity by a table called E with n distinct columns, each of which corresponds to one of the attributes of E. Each row in this table corresponds to one entity of the entity set E.

As an illustration, consider the entity set *loan* of the E-R diagram shown in Figure 2.8. This entity set has two attributes: *loan-number* and *amount*. We represent this entity set by a table called *loan*, with two columns, as shown in Figure 2.19. The row

(L-17, 1000)

in the *loan* table means that loan number L-17 has a loan amount of $1000. We can add a new entity to the database by inserting a row into a table. We can also delete or modify rows.

Let D_1 denote the set of all loan numbers, and let D_2 denote the set of all balances. Any row of the *loan* table must consist of a 2-tuple (v_1, v_2), where v_1 is a loan (that is, v_1 is in set D_1) and v_2 is an amount (that is, v_2 is in set D_2). In general, the *loan* table will contain only a subset of the set of all possible rows. We refer to the set of all possible rows of *loan* as the *Cartesian product* of D_1 and D_2, denoted by

$$D_1 \times D_2$$

In general, if we have a table of n columns, we denote the Cartesian product of $D_1, D_2, \ldots, D_n$ by

$$D_1 \times D_2 \times \ldots \times D_{n-1} \times D_n$$

loan-number	*amount*
L-17	1000
L-23	2000
L-15	1500
L-14	1500
L-93	500
L-11	900
L-16	1300

Figure 2.19 The *loan* table.

customer-name	*social-security*	*customer-street*	*customer-city*
Jones	321-12-3123	Main	Harrison
Smith	019-28-3746	North	Rye
Hayes	677-89-9011	Main	Harrison
Curry	244-66-8800	North	Rye
Lindsay	336-66-9999	Park	Pittsfield
Turner	182-73-6091	Putnam	Stamford
Williams	963-96-3963	Nassau	Princeton
Adams	335-57-7991	Spring	Pittsfield
Johnson	192-83-7465	Alma	Palo Alto

Figure 2.20 The *customer* table.

As another example, consider the entity set *customer* of the E-R diagram shown in Figure 2.8. This entity set has the attributes *customer-name*, *social-security*, *customer-street*, and *customer-city*. The table corresponding to *customer* has four columns, as shown in Figure 2.20.

2.9.2 Tabular Representation of Weak Entity Sets

Let A be a weak entity set with attributes $a_1, a_2, \ldots, a_m$. Let B be the strong entity set on which A is dependent. Let the primary key of B consist of attributes b_1, $b_2, \ldots, b_n$. We represent the entity set A by a table called A with one column for each attribute of the set:

$$\{a_1, a_2, \ldots, a_m\} \cup \{b_1, b_2, \ldots, b_n\}$$

As an illustration, consider the entity set *payment* shown in the E-R diagram of Figure 2.14. This entity set has three attributes: *payment-number*, *payment-date*, and *payment-amount*. The primary key of the *loan* entity set, on which *payment* is dependent, is *loan-number*. Thus, *payment* is represented by a table with four columns labeled *loan-number*, *payment-number*, *payment-date*, and *payment-amount*, as depicted in Figure 2.21.

2.9.3 Tabular Representation of Relationship Sets

Let R be a relationship set, let $a_1, a_2, \ldots, a_m$ be the set of attributes formed by the union of the primary keys of each of the entity sets participating in R, and let the descriptive attributes (if any) of R be $b_1, b_2, \ldots, b_n$. We represent this relationship set by a table called R with one column for each attribute of the set:

$$\{a_1, a_2, \ldots, a_m\} \cup \{b_1, b_2, \ldots, b_n\}$$

loan-number	*payment-number*	*payment-date*	*payment-amount*
L-17	5	10 May 1996	50
L-23	11	17 May 1996	75
L-15	22	23 May 1996	300
L-14	69	28 May 1996	500
L-93	103	3 June 1996	900
L-17	6	7 June 1996	50
L-11	53	7 June 1996	125
L-93	104	13 June 1996	200
L-17	7	17 June 1996	100
L-16	58	18 June 1996	135

Figure 2.21 The *payment* table.

As an illustration, consider the relationship set *borrower* in the E-R diagram of Figure 2.8. This relationship set involves the following two entity sets:

- *customer*, with the primary key *social-security*
- *loan*, with the primary key *loan-number*

Since the relationship set has no attributes, the *borrower* table has two columns labeled *social-security* and *loan-number*, as shown in Figure 2.22.

2.9.3.1 Redundancy of Tables

The case of a relationship set linking a weak entity set to the corresponding strong entity set is special. As we noted earlier, these relationships are many to one and have no descriptive attributes. Furthermore, the primary key of a weak entity set includes the primary key of the strong entity set. In the E-R diagram of Figure 2.14, the weak entity set *payment* is dependent on the strong entity set *loan* via the relationship set *loan-payment*. The primary key of *payment* is {*loan-number*, *payment-number*}, and the primary key of *loan* is {*loan-number*}. Since *loan-payment* has no descriptive attributes, the table for *loan-payment* would

social-security	*loan-number*
321-12-3123	L-17
019-28-3746	L-23
677-89-9011	L-15
555-55-5555	L-14
244-66-8800	L-93
019-28-3746	L-11
963-96-3963	L-17
335-57-7991	L-16

Figure 2.22 The *borrower* table.

have two columns, *loan-number* and *payment-number*. The table for the entity set *payment* has four columns, *loan-number*, *payment-number*, *payment-date*, and *payment-amount*. Thus, the *loan-payment* table is redundant. In general, the table for the relationship set linking a weak entity set to its corresponding strong entity set is redundant and does not need to be present in a tabular representation of an E-R diagram.

2.9.3.2 Combination of Tables

Consider a many-to-one relationship set *AB* from entity set *A* to entity set *B*. Using our table-construction scheme outlined previously, we get three tables: *A*, *B*, and *AB*. However, if there is an existence dependency of *A* on *B* (that is, for each entity *a* in *A*, the existence of *a* depends on the existence of some entity *b* in *B*), then we can combine the tables *A* and *AB* to form a single table consisting of the union of columns of both tables.

As an illustration, consider the E-R diagram of Figure 2.23. The relationship set *account-branch* is many to one from *account* to *branch*. Further, the double line in the E-R diagram indicates that the participation of *account* in the *account-branch* is total. Hence, an account cannot exist without being associated with a particular branch. Therefore, we require only the following two tables:

- *account*, with attributes *account-number*, *balance*, and *branch-name*
- *branch*, with attributes *branch-name*, *branch-city*, and *assets*

2.9.4 Multivalued Attributes

We have seen that attributes in an E-R diagram generally map directly into columns for the appropriate tables. Multivalued attributes, however, are an exception; new tables are created for these attributes.

For a multivalued attribute *M*, we create a table *T* with a column *C* that corresponds to *M* and columns corresponding to the primary key of the entity set or relationship set of which *M* is an attribute. As an illustration, consider the E-R diagram depicted in Figure 2.18. The diagram includes the multivalued attribute *dependent-name*. For this multivalued attribute, we create a table *dependent-name*,

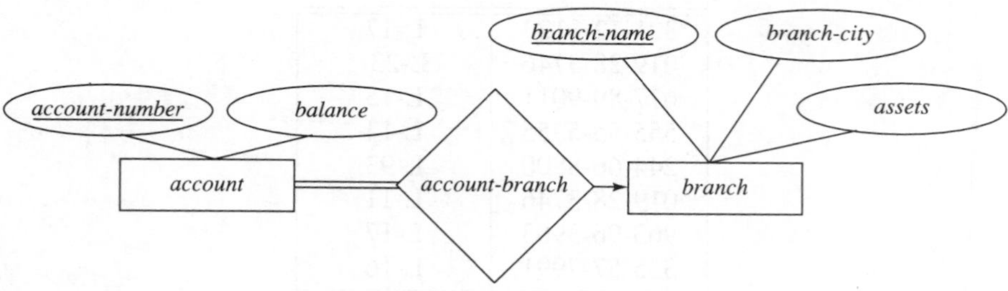

Figure 2.23 E-R diagram.

with columns *dname*, referring to the *dependent-name* attribute of *employee*, and *e-social-security*, representing the primary key of the entity set *employee*. Each dependent of an employee is represented as a unique row in the table.

2.9.5 Tabular Representation of Generalization

There are two different methods for transforming to a tabular form an E-R diagram that includes generalization. Although we refer to the generalization depicted in Figure 2.15, we have chosen to simplify this discussion by including only the first tier of lower-level entity sets—that is, *savings-account* and *checking-account*.

1. Create a table for the higher-level entity set. For each lower-level entity set, create a table that includes a column for each of the attributes of that entity set plus a column for each attribute of the primary key of the higher-level entity set. Thus, for the E-R diagram of Figure 2.15, we have three tables:
   - *account*, with attributes *account-number* and *balance*
   - *savings-account*, with attributes *account-number* and *interest-rate*
   - *checking-account*, with attributes *account-number* and *overdraft-amount*
2. If the generalization is disjoint and complete—that is, if no entity is a member of two lower-level entity sets directly below a higher-level entity set, and if every entity in the higher level entity set is also a member of one of the lower-level entity sets—then an alternative representation is possible. Here, create no table for the higher-level entity set. Instead, for each lower-level entity set, create a table that includes a column for each of the attributes of that entity set plus a column for *each* attribute of the higher-level entity set. Then, for the E-R diagram of Figure 2.15, we have two tables.
   - *savings-account*, with attributes *account-number*, *balance*, and *interest-rate*
   - *checking-account*, with attributes *account-number*, *balance*, and *overdraft-amount*

   The *savings-account* and *checking-account* relations corresponding to these tables both have *balance* as the primary key.

If the second method were used for an overlapping generalization, some values such as *balance* would be stored twice unnecessarily. Similarly, if the generalization were not complete—that is, if some accounts were neither savings nor checking accounts—then such accounts could not be represented with the second method.

2.9.6 Tabular Representation of Aggregation

Transforming to a tabular form an E-R diagram which includes aggregation is straightforward. Consider the diagram of Figure 2.17. The table for the relationship set *loan-officer* includes a column for each attribute in the primary key of the entity set *employee* and the relationship set *borrower*. It would also include a column for any descriptive attributes, if they existed, of the relationship set *loan-officer*. Using the same procedure as before for the rest of the diagram, we create the following tables:

- *customer*, with attributes *customer-name*, *social-security*, *customer-street*, and *customer-city*
- *loan*, with attributes *loan-number* and *amount*
- *borrower*, with attributes *social-security* and *loan-number*
- *employee*, with attributes *e-social-security*, *employee-name*, and *telephone-number*
- *loan-officer*, with attributes *social-security*, *loan-number*, and *e-social-security*.

2.10 Summary

The entity–relationship (E-R) data model is based on a perception of a real world that consists of a set of basic objects called *entities*, and of *relationships* among these objects. The model is intended primarily for the database-design process. It was developed to facilitate database design by allowing the specification of an *enterprise schema*. Such a schema represents the overall logical structure of the database. This overall structure can be expressed graphically by an E-R *diagram*.

An *entity* is an object that exists and is distinguishable from other objects. We accomplish the distinction by associating with each entity a set of attributes that describes the object. A *relationship* is an association among several entities. The collection of all entities of the same type is an *entity set*, and the collection of all relationships of the same type is a *relationship set*.

Mapping cardinalities express the number of entities to which another entity can be associated via a relationship set. Another form of constraint is *existence dependency*, which specifies that the existence of entity x depends on the existence of entity y.

An important task in database modeling is to specify how entities and relationships are distinguished. Conceptually, individual entities and relationships are distinct; from a database perspective, however, their difference must be expressed in terms of their attributes. To make such distinctions, we assign a *primary key* to each entity set. The primary key is a set of one or more attributes that, taken collectively, allows us to identify uniquely an entity in the entity set and a relationship in a relationship set. An entity set that does not have sufficient attributes to form a primary key is termed a *weak entity set*. An entity set that has a primary key is termed a *strong entity set*.

Specialization and *generalization* define a containment relationship between a higher-level entity set and one or more lower-level entity sets. Specialization is the result of taking a subset of a higher-level entity set to form a lower-level entity set. Generalization is the result of taking the union of two or more disjoint (lower-level) entity sets to produce a higher-level entity set. The attributes of higher-level entity sets are inherited by lower-level entity sets.

One limitation of the E-R model is that it cannot express relationships among relationships. The solution is to use *aggregation*; an abstraction in which relationship sets are treated as higher-level entity sets. Thus, a relationship set and its associated entity sets can be viewed as a higher-level entity that is treated in the same manner as any other entity.

The various features of the E-R model offer the database designer numerous choices in how best to represent the enterprise being modeled. Concepts and objects may, in certain cases, be represented by entities, relationships, or attributes. Aspects of the overall structure of the enterprise may be best described using weak entity sets, generalization, specialization, or aggregation. Often, the designer must weigh the merits of a simple, compact model versus those of a more precise, but more complex, one.

A database that conforms to an E-R diagram can be represented by a collection of tables. For each entity set and for each relationship set in the database, there is a unique table that is assigned the name of the corresponding entity set or relationship set. Each table has a number of columns, each of which, has a unique name. Converting of database representation from an E-R diagram to a table format is the basis for deriving a relational-database design from an E-R diagram.

Exercises

2.1. Explain the distinctions among the terms primary key, candidate key, and superkey.

2.2. Construct an E-R diagram for a university registrar's officeof Exercise 2.2. The office maintains data about each class, including the instructor, the enrollment, and the time and place of the class meetings. For each student–class pair, a grade is recorded. Document all assumptions that you make about the mapping constraints.

2.3. Construct an E-R diagram for a car-insurance company that has a set of customers, each of whom owns one or more cars. Each car has associated with it zero to any number of recorded accidents.

2.4. Construct an E-R diagram for a hospital with a set of patients and a set of medical doctors. Associate with each patient a log of the various tests and examinations conducted.

2.5. Construct appropriate tables for each of the E-R diagrams in Exercises 2 to 4.

2.6. Explain the difference between a weak and a strong entity set.

2.7. We can convert any weak entity set to a strong entity set by simply adding appropriate attributes. Why, then, do we have weak entity sets?

2.8. Define the concept of aggregation. Give two examples of where this concept is useful.

2.9. Consider an E-R diagram in which the same entity set appears several times. Why is allowing this redundancy a bad practice that one should avoid whenever possible?

2.10. Consider a university database for the scheduling of classrooms for final exams. This database could be modeled as the single entity set *exam*, with attributes *course-name*, *section-number*, *room-number*, and *time*. Alternatively, one or more additional entity sets could be defined, along with relationship sets to replace some of the attributes of the *exam* entity set, as

- *course* with attributes *name*, *department*, and *c-number*
- *section* with attributes *s-number* and *enrollment*, and dependent as a weak entity set on *course*
- *room* with attributes *r-number*, *capacity*, and *building*

(*a*) Show an E-R diagram illustrating the use of all three additional entity sets listed.

(*b*) Explain what application characteristics would influence a decision to include or not to include each of the additional entity sets.

2.11. When designing an E-R diagram for a particular enterprise, you have several alternatives from which to choose.

(*a*) What criteria should you consider in making the appropriate choice?

(*b*) Design three alternative E-R diagrams to represent the university registrar's office of Exercise 2.2. List the merits of each. Argue in favor of one of the alternatives.

2.12. An E-R diagram can be viewed as a graph. What do the following mean in terms of the structure of an enterprise schema?

(*a*) The graph is disconnected.

(*b*) The graph is acyclic.

2.13. In Section 2.2.3, we represented a ternary relationship (Figure 2.24a) using binary relationships, as shown in Figure 2.24b. Consider the alternative

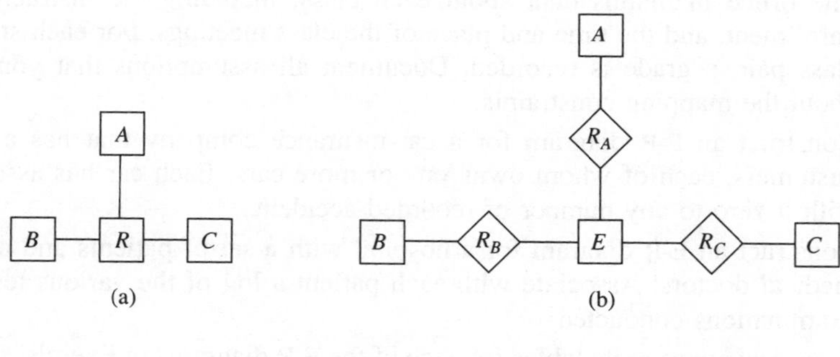

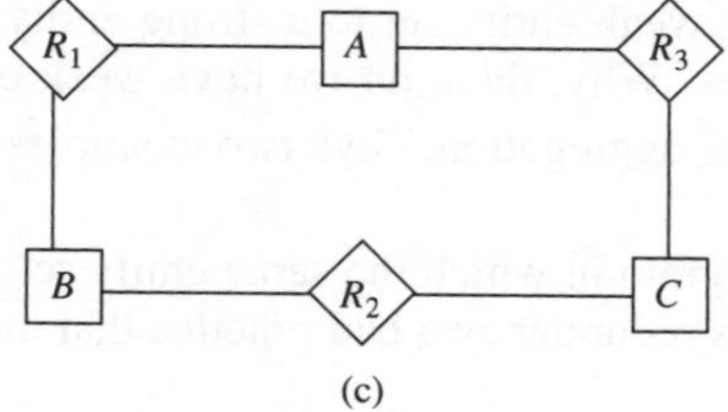

Figure 2.24 E-R diagram for Exercise 2.13. (attributes not shown)

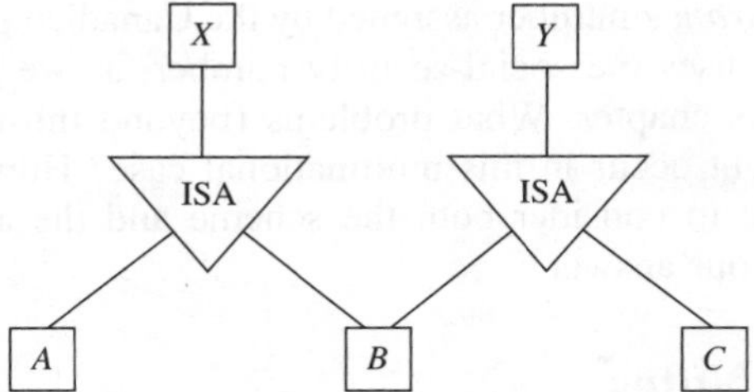

Figure 2.25 E-R diagram for Exercise 2.18 (attributes not shown).

shown in Figure 2.24c. Discuss the relative merits of these two alternative representations of a ternary relationship by binary relationships.

2.14. Design a generalization–specialization hierarchy for a motor-vehicle sales company. The company sells motorcycles, passenger cars, vans, and buses. Justify your placement of attributes at each level of the hierarchy. Explain why they should not be placed at a higher or lower level.

2.15. Explain the distinction between condition-defined and user-defined design constraints. Which of these constraints can the system check automatically? Explain your answer.

2.16. Explain the distinction between disjoint and overlapping design constraints. Explain your answer.

2.17. Explain the distinction between total and partial design constraints. Explain your answer.

2.18. Figure 2.25 shows a lattice structure of generalization and specialization. For entity sets A, B, and C, explain how attributes are inherited from the higher-level entity sets X and Y. Discuss how to handle a case where an attribute of X has the same name as some attribute of Y.

2.19. Consider two separate banks that decide to merge. Assume that both banks use exactly the same E-R database schema—the one in Figure 2.18. (This assumption is, of course, highly unrealistic; we consider the more realistic case in Section 18.9.) If the merged bank is to have a single database, there are several potential problems:

- The possibility that the two original banks have branches with the same name
- The possibility that some customers are customers of both original banks
- The possibility that some loan or account numbers were used at both original banks (for different loans or accounts, of course)

For each of these potential problems, describe why there is indeed a potential for difficulties. Propose a solution to the problem. For your solution, explain any changes that would have to be made, and describe what their affect would be on the schema and the data.

2.20. Reconsider the situation described for Exercise 2.19 under the assumption that one bank is in the U.S., and the other is in Canada. As before, the banks use the schema of Figure 2.18, except that the Canadian bank uses the *social-insurance* number assigned by the Canadian government, whereas the U.S. bank uses the social-security number, as we have been assuming throughout this chapter. What problems (beyond those identified in Exercise 2.19) might occur in this multinational case? How would you resolve them? Be sure to consider both the scheme and the actual data values in constructing your answer.

Bibliographic Notes

The E-R data model was introduced by Chen [1976]. A logical design methodology for relational databases using the extended E-R model is presented by Teorey et al. [1986]. Mapping from extended E-R models to the relational model is discussed by Lyngbaek and Vianu [1987], and by Markowitz and Shoshani [1992].

Various data-manipulation languages for the E-R model have been proposed: GERM [Benneworth et al. 1981], GORDAS [ElMasri and Wiederhold 1981], and ERROL [Markowitz and Raz 1983]. A graphical query language for the E-R database was proposed by Zhang and Mendelzon [1983], and by ElMasri and Larson [1985]. An algebra for a general E-R model is presented by Parent and Spaccapietra [1985]. Campbell et al. [1985] present a language for the E-R model that is equivalent in expressive power to the relation algebra and calculus (see Chapter 3). An E-R language with formal mathematical semantics is given in Gogolla and Hohenstein [1991].

The concepts of generalization, specialization, and aggregation were introduced by Smith and Smith [1977], and were expanded in Hammer and McLeod [1981]. Lenzerini and Santucci [1983] have used these concepts in defining cardinality constraints in the E-R model. Logic-based semantics for a variant of the E-R model is given by Di Battista and Lenzerini [1989].

Basic textbook discussions are offered by Batini et al. [1992], and ElMasri and Navathe [1994].

CHAPTER 3

RELATIONAL MODEL

The relational model has established itself as the primary data model for commercial data-processing applications. The first database systems were based on either the network model (see Appendix A) or the hierarchical model (see Appendix B). Those two older models are tied more closely to the underlying implementation of the database than is the relational model.

A substantial theory exists for relational databases. This theory assists in the design of relational databases and in the efficient processing of user requests for information from the database. We shall examine this theory in Chapters 6 and 7.

The relational model is now being used in numerous applications outside the domain of traditional data processing. We shall consider extensions to the relational model required to handle these newer applications in Chapter 9.

3.1 Structure of Relational Databases

A relational database consists of a collection of *tables*, each of which is assigned a unique name. Each table has a structure similar to that presented in Chapter 2, where we represented E-R databases by tables. A row in a table represents a *relationship* among a set of values. Since a table is a collection of such relationships, there is a close correspondence between the concept of *table* and the mathematical concept of *relation*, from which the relational data model takes its name. In what follows, we introduce the concept of relation.

In this chapter, we shall be using a number of different relations to illustrate the various concepts underlying the relational data model. These relations represent part of a banking enterprise. They differ slightly from the tables that were used in Chapter 2, so that we can simplify our presentation. We shall discuss criteria for the appropriateness of relational structures in great detail in Chapter 7.

3.1.1 Basic Structure

Consider the *account* table of Figure 3.1. It has three column headers: *branch-name*, *account-number*, and *balance*. Following the terminology of the relational model, we refer to these headers as attributes (as we did for the E-R model in Chapter 2). For each attribute, there is a set of permitted values, called the *domain* of that attribute. For the attribute *branch-name*, for example, the domain is the set of all branch names. Let D_1 denote this set, D_2 denote the set of all account numbers, and D_3 the set of all balances. As we saw in Chapter 2, any row of *account* must consist of a 3-tuple (v_1, v_2, v_3), where v_1 is a branch name (that is, v_1 is in domain D_1), v_2 is an account number (that is, v_2 is in domain D_2), and v_3 is a balance (that is, v_3 is in domain D_3). In general, *account* will contain only a subset of the set of all possible rows. Therefore, *account* is a subset of

$$D_1 \times D_2 \times D_3$$

In general, a table of n attributes must be a subset of

$$D_1 \times D_2 \times \ldots \times D_{n-1} \times D_n$$

Mathematicians define a relation to be a subset of a Cartesian product of a list of domains. This definition corresponds almost exactly with our definition of *table*. The only difference is that we have assigned names to attributes, whereas mathematicians rely on numeric "names," using the integer 1 to denote the attribute whose domain appears first in the list of domains, 2 for the attribute whose domain appears second, and so on. Because tables are essentially relations, we shall use the mathematical terms *relation* and *tuple* in place of the terms *table* and *row*.

In the *account* relation of Figure 3.1, there are seven tuples. Let the *tuple variable t* refer to the first tuple of the relation. We use the notation t[*branch-name*] to denote the value of t on the *branch-name* attribute. Thus, t[*branch-name*]

branch-name	*account-number*	*balance*
Downtown	A-101	500
Mianus	A-215	700
Perryridge	A-102	400
Round Hill	A-305	350
Brighton	A-201	900
Redwood	A-222	700
Brighton	A-217	750

Figure 3.1 The *account* relation.

= "Downtown," and $t[balance] = 500$. Alternatively, we may write $t[1]$ to denote the value of tuple t on the first attribute (*branch-name*), $t[2]$ to denote *account-number*, and so on. Since a relation is a set of tuples, we use the mathematical notation of $t \in r$ to denote that tuple t is in relation r.

We shall require that, for all relations r, the domains of all attributes of r be atomic. A domain is *atomic* if elements of the domain are considered to be indivisible units. For example, the set of integers is an atomic domain, but the set of all sets of integers is a nonatomic domain. The distinction is that we do not normally consider integers to have subparts, but we consider sets of integers to have subparts—namely, the integers comprising the set. The important issue is not what the domain itself is, but rather how we use domain elements in our database. The domain of all integers would be nonatomic if we considered each integer to be an ordered list of digits. In all our examples, we shall assume atomic domains. In Chapter 9, we shall discuss the *nested relational* data model, which allows nonatomic domains.

It is possible for several attributes to have the same domain. For example, suppose that we have a relation *customer* that has the three attributes·*customer-name*, *customer-street*, and *customer-city*, and a relation *employee* that includes the attribute *employee-name*. It is possible that the attributes *customer-name* and *employee-name* will have the same domain: the set of all person names. The domains of *balance* and *branch-name*, on the other hand, certainly ought to be distinct. It is perhaps less clear whether *customer-name* and *branch-name* should have the same domain. At the physical level, both customer names and branch names are character strings. However, at the logical level, we may want *customer-name* and *branch-name* to have distinct domains.

One domain value that is a member of any possible domain is the *null* value, which signifies that the value is unknown or does not exist. For example, suppose that we include the attribute *telephone-number* in the *customer* relation. It may be that a customer does not have a telephone number, or that the telephone number is unlisted. We would then have to resort to null values to signify that the value is unknown or does not exist. We shall see later that null values cause a number of difficulties when we access or update the database, and thus should be eliminated if at all possible.

3.1.2 Database Schema

When we talk about a database, we must differentiate between the *database schema*, or the logical design of the database, and a *database instance*, which is a snapshot of the data in the database at a given instant in time.

The concept of a relation corresponds to the programming-language notion of a variable. The concept of a *relation schema* corresponds to the programming-language notion of type definition.

It is convenient to give a name to a relation schema, just as we give names to type definitions in programming languages. We adopt the convention of using lowercase names for relations, and names beginning with an uppercase letter for

branch-name	*branch-city*	*assets*
Downtown	Brooklyn	9000000
Redwood	Palo Alto	2100000
Perryridge	Horseneck	1700000
Mianus	Horseneck	400000
Round Hill	Horseneck	8000000
Pownal	Bennington	300000
North Town	Rye	3700000
Brighton	Brooklyn	7100000

Figure 3.2 The *branch* relation.

relation schemas. Following this notation, we use *Account-schema* to denote the relation schema for relation *account*. Thus,

Account-schema = (*branch-name*, *account-number*, *balance*)

We denote the fact that *account* is a relation on *Account-schema* by

account(*Account-schema*)

In general, a relation schema comprises a list of attributes and their corresponding domains. We shall not be concerned about the precise definition of the domain of each attribute until we discuss the SQL language in Chapter 4.

The concept of a *relation instance* corresponds to the programming language notion of a value of a variable. The value of a given variable may change with time; similarly the contents of a relation instance may change with time as the relation is updated. However, we often simply say "relation" when we actually mean "relation instance."

As an example of a relation instance, consider the *branch* relation of Figure 3.2. The schema for that relation is

Branch-schema = (*branch-name*, *branch-city*, *assets*)

Note that the attribute *branch-name* appears in both *Branch-schema* and *Account-schema*. This duplication is not a coincidence. Rather, using common attributes in relation schemas is one way of relating tuples of distinct relations. For example, suppose we wish to find the information about all of the accounts maintained in branches located in Brooklyn. We look first at the *branch* relation to find the names of all the branches located in Brooklyn. Then, for each such branch, we would look in the *account* relation to find the information about the accounts maintained at that branch. Using the terminology of the E-R model, we say that the attribute *branch-name* represents the same entity set in both relations.

Let's continue our banking example. We need a relation to describe information about customers. The relation schema is

Customer-schema = (*customer-name*, *customer-street*, *customer-city*)

A sample relation *customer* (*Customer-schema*) is shown in Figure 3.3.

customer-name	*customer-street*	*customer-city*
Jones	Main	Harrison
Smith	North	Rye
Hayes	Main	Harrison
Curry	North	Rye
Lindsay	Park	Pittsfield
Turner	Putnam	Stamford
Williams	Nassau	Princeton
Adams	Spring	Pittsfield
Johnson	Alma	Palo Alto
Glenn	Sand Hill	Woodside
Brooks	Senator	Brooklyn
Green	Walnut	Stamford

Figure 3.3 The *customer* relation.

We also need a relation to describe the association between customers and accounts. The relation schema to describe this association is

Depositor-schema = (*customer-name*, *account-number*)

A sample relation *depositor* (*Depositor-schema*) is shown in Figure 3.4.

It would appear that, for our banking example, we could have just one relation schema, rather than several. That is, it may be easier for a user to think in terms of one relation schema, rather than in terms of several. Suppose that we used only one relation for our example, with schema

(*branch-name*, *branch-city*, *assets*, *customer-name*, *customer-street* *customer-city*, *account-number*, *balance*)

Observe that, if a customer has several accounts, we must list her address once for each account. That is, we must repeat certain information several times. This repetition is wasteful and is avoided by the use of several relations, as in our example.

In addition, if a branch has no accounts (a newly created branch, say, that has no customers yet), we cannot construct a complete tuple on the preceding single

customer-name	*account-number*
Johnson	A-101
Smith	A-215
Hayes	A-102
Turner	A-305
Johnson	A-201
Jones	A-217
Lindsay	A-222

Figure 3.4 The *depositor* relation.

branch-name	*loan-number*	*amount*
Downtown	L-17	1000
Redwood	L-23	2000
Perryridge	L-15	1500
Downtown	L-14	1500
Mianus	L-93	500
Round Hill	L-11	900
Perryridge	L-16	1300

Figure 3.5 The *loan* relation.

relation, because no data concerning *customer* and *account* are available yet. To represent incomplete tuples, we must use *null* values that signify that the value is unknown or does not exist. Thus, in our example, the values for *customer-name*, *customer-street*, and so on must be null. By using several relations, we can represent the branch Information for a bank with no customers without using null values. We simply use a tuple on *Branch-schema* to represent the information about the branch, and create tuples on the other schemas only when the appropriate information becomes available.

In Chapter 7, we shall study criteria to help us decide when one set of relation schemas is more appropriate than another, in terms of information repetition and the existence of null values. For now, we shall assume that the relation schemas are given.

We include two additional relations to describe data about loans maintained in the various branches in the bank:

Loan-schema = (*branch-name*, *loan-number*, *amount*)
Borrower-schema = (*customer-name*, *loan-number*)

The sample relations *loan* (*Loan-schema*) and *borrower* (*Borrower-schema*) are shown in Figures 3.5 and 3.6, respectively.

The banking enterprise that we have described is derived from the E-R diagram shown in Figure 3.7. The relation schemas correspond to the set of tables

customer-name	*loan-number*
Jones	L-17
Smith	L-23
Hayes	L-15
Jackson	L-14
Curry	L-93
Smith	L-11
Williams	L-17
Adams	L-16

Figure 3.6 The *borrower* relation.

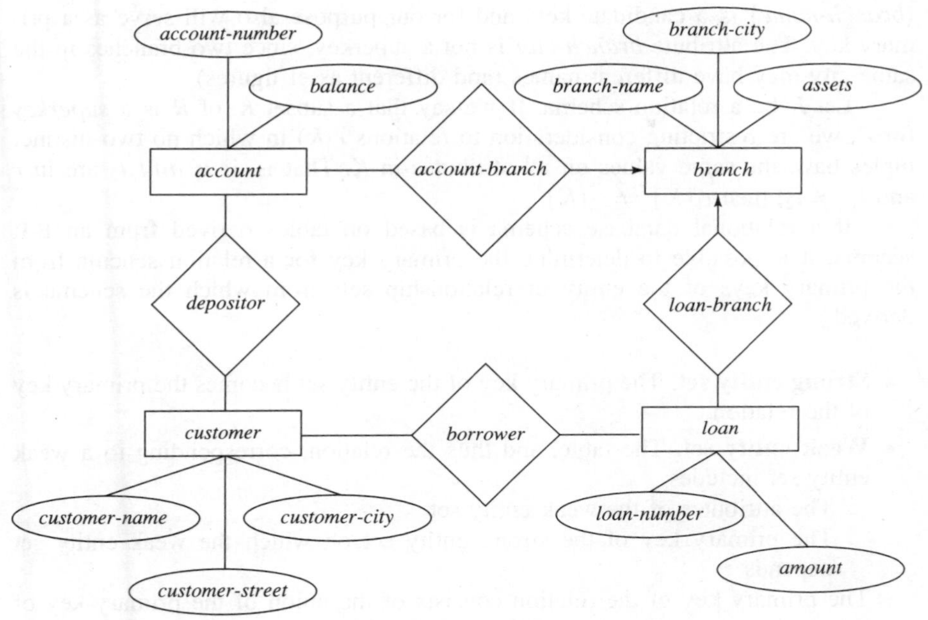

Figure 3.7 E-R diagram for the banking enterprise.

that we might generate using the method outlined in Section 2.9. We assume that the primary key for the *branch* entity set is *branch-name*. The primary key for *Customer-schema* is *customer-name*. We are not using the *social-security* attribute, as we did in Chapter 2, because now we want to have smaller relation schemas in our running example of a bank database. We expect that, in a real-world database, the *social-security* attribute would serve as a primary key. The primary key for the *account* entity set and the *loan* entity set are *account-number* and *loan-number*, respectively.

Finally, we note that the *customer* relation may contain information about customers who have neither an account nor a loan at the bank.

The banking enterprise described here will serve as our primary example in this chapter and in subsequent ones. On occasion, we shall need to introduce additional relation schemas to illustrate particular points.

3.1.3 Keys

The notions of *superkey*, *candidate key*, and *primary key*, as discussed in Chapter 2, are also applicable to the relational model. For example, in *Branch-schema*, {*branch-name*} and {*branch-name, branch-city*} are both superkeys. {*branch-name*, *branch-city*} is not a candidate key, because {*branch-name*} is a subset of {*branch-name, branch-city*} and {*branch-name*} itself is a superkey. However, {*branch-name*} *is* a candidate key, and for our purpose also will serve as a primary key. The attribute *branch-city* is not a superkey, since two branches in the same city may have different names (and different asset figures).

Let R be a relation schema. If we say that a subset K of R is a *superkey* for R, we are restricting consideration to relations $r(R)$ in which no two distinct tuples have the same values on all attributes in K. That is, if t_1 *and* t_2 are in r and $t_1 \neq t_2$, then $t_1[K] \neq t_2[K]$.

If a relational database schema is based on tables derived from an E-R schema, it is possible to determine the primary key for a relation schema from the primary keys of the entity or relationship sets from which the schema is derived:

- **Strong entity set.** The primary key of the entity set becomes the primary key of the relation.
- **Weak entity set.** The table, and thus the relation, corresponding to a weak entity set includes
  - The attributes of the weak entity set
  - The primary key of the strong entity set on which the weak entity set depends

  The primary key of the relation consists of the union of the primary key of the strong entity set and the discriminator of the weak entity set.
- **Relationship set.** The union of the primary keys of the related entity sets becomes a superkey of the relation. If the relationship is many-to-many, this superkey is also the primary key. Section 2.4.2 describes how to determine the primary keys in other cases. Recall from Section 2.9.3 that no table is generated for relationship sets linking a weak entity set to the corresponding strong entity set.
- **Combined tables.** Recall from Section 2.9.3 that a binary many-to-one relationship set from A to B can be represented by a table consisting of the attributes of A and attributes (if any exist) of the relationship set. The primary key of the "many" entity set becomes the primary key of the relation (that is, if the relationship set is many to one from A to B, the primary key of A is the primary key of the relation). For one-to-one relationship sets, the relation is constructed like that for a many-to-one relationship set. However, either entity set's primary key can be chosen as the primary key of the relation, since both are candidate keys.
- **Multivalued attributes.** Recall from Section 2.9.4 that a multivalued attribute M is represented by a table consisting of the primary key of the entity set or relationship set of which M is an attribute plus a column C holding an individual value of M. The primary key of the entity or relationship set together with the attribute C becomes the primary key for the relation.

From the preceding list, we see that a relation schema may include among its attributes the primary key of another schema. This key is is called a *foreign key*. For example, the attribute *branch-name* in *Account-schema* is a foreign key, since *branch-name* is the primary key of *Branch-schema*.

3.1.4 Query Languages

A *query language* is a language in which a user requests information from the database. These languages are typically of a level higher than that of a standard programming language. Query languages can be categorized as being either procedural or nonprocedural. In a *procedural language*, the user instructs the system to perform a sequence of operations on the database to compute the desired result. In a *nonprocedural language*, the user describes the information desired without giving a specific procedure for obtaining that information.

Most commercial relational-database systems offer a query language that includes elements of both the procedural and the nonprocedural approaches. We shall study several commercial languages in Chapters 4 and 5. In this chapter, we examine "pure" languages: The relational algebra is procedural, whereas the tuple relational calculus and the domain relational calculus are nonprocedural. These query languages are terse and formal, lacking the "syntactic sugar" of commercial languages, but they illustrate the fundamental techniques for extracting data from the database.

Initially, we shall be concerned with only queries. A complete data-manipulation language includes not only a query language, but also a language for database modification. Such languages include commands to insert and delete tuples, as well as commands to modify parts of existing tuples. We shall examine database modification after we complete our discussion of "pure" query languages.

3.2 The Relational Algebra

The relational algebra is a *procedural* query language. It consists of a set of operations that take one or two relations as input and produce a new relation as their result. The fundamental operations in the relational algebra are *select, project*, *union*, *set difference*, *Cartesian product,* and *rename*. In addition to the fundamental operations, there are several other operations—namely, set intersection, natural join, division, and assignment. These operations will be defined in terms of the fundamental operations.

3.2.1 Fundamental Operations

The select, project, and rename operations are called *unary* operations, because they operate on one relation. The other three operations operate on pairs of relations and are, therefore, called *binary* operations.

3.2.1.1 The Select Operation

The *select* operation selects tuples that satisfy a given predicate. We use the lowercase Greek letter sigma (σ) to denote selection. The predicate appears as

branch-name	*loan-number*	*amount*
Perryridge	L-15	1500
Perryridge	L-16	1300

Figure 3.8 Result of $\sigma_{branch\text{-}name = \text{"Perryridge"}}\ (loan)$.

a subscript to σ. The argument relation is given in parentheses following the σ. Thus, to select those tuples of the *loan* relation where the branch is "Perryridge," we write

$$\sigma_{branch\text{-}name = \text{"Perryridge"}}\ (loan)$$

If the *loan* relation is as shown in Figure 3.5, then the relation that results from the preceding query is as shown in Figure 3.8.

We can find all tuples in which the amount lent is more than $1200 by writing

$$\sigma_{amount > 1200}\ (loan)$$

In general, we allow comparisons using $=$, $\neq$, $<$, $\leq$, $>$, $\geq$ in the selection predicate. Furthermore, we can combine several predicates into a larger predicate using the connectives *and* ($\wedge$) and *or* ($\vee$). Thus, to find those tuples pertaining to loans of more than $1200 made by the Perryridge branch, we write

$$\sigma_{branch\text{-}name = \text{"Perryridge"} \wedge amount > 1200}\ (loan)$$

The selection predicate may include comparisons between two attributes. To illustrate, consider the relation *loan-officer* that consists of three attributes: *customer-name*, *banker-name*, and *loan-number*, which specifies that a particular banker is the loan officer for a loan that belong to some customer. To find all customers who have the same name as their loan officer, we can write

$$\sigma_{customer\text{-}name = banker\text{-}name}(loan\text{-}officer)$$

Since the special value *null* indicates "value unknown or non-existent," any comparisons involving a null value evaluate to **false**.

3.2.1.2 The Project Operation

Suppose we want to list all loan numbers and the amount of the loans, but do not care about the branch name. The *project* operation allows us to produce this relation. The project operation is a unary operation that returns its argument relation, with certain attributes left out. Since a relation is a set, any duplicate rows are eliminated. Projection is denoted by the Greek letter pi (π). We list those attributes that we wish to appear in the result as a subscript to π. The argument relation follows in parentheses. Thus, the query to list all loan numbers and the amount of the loan can be written as

$$\pi_{loan\text{-}number,\ amount}\ (loan)$$

The relation that results from this query is shown in Figure 3.9.

loan-number	*amount*
L-17	1000
L-23	2000
L-15	1500
L-14	1500
L-93	500
L-11	900
L-16	1300

Figure 3.9 Loan number and the amount of the loan.

3.2.1.3 Composition of Relational Operations

The fact that the result of a relational operation is itself a relation is important. Let us consider the more complicated query "Find those customers who live in "Harrison." We write:

$$\Pi_{customer\text{-}name}\ (\sigma_{customer\text{-}city\,=\,\text{"Harrison"}}\ (customer))$$

Notice that, instead of giving the name of a relation as the argument of the projection operation, we give an expression that evaluates to a relation.

In general, since the result of a relational-algebra operation is of the same type (relation) as its inputs, relational-algebra operations can be composed together into a *relational-algebra expression*. Composing relational-algebra operations into relational-algebra expressions is just like composing arithmetic operations (such as $+$, $-$, $*$ and $\div$) into arithmetic expressions. We study the formal definition of relational-algebra expressions in Section 3.2.2.

3.2.1.4 The Union Operation

Consider a query to find the names of all bank customers who have either an account or a loan or both. Note that the *customer* relation does not contain the information, since a customer does not need to have either an account or a loan at the bank. To answer this query, we need the information in the *depositor* relation (Figure 3.4) and in the *borrower* relation (Figure 3.6). We know how to find the names of all customers with a loan in the bank:

$$\Pi_{customer\text{-}name}\ (borrower)$$

We also know how to find the names of all customers with an account in the bank:

$$\Pi_{customer\text{-}name}\ (depositor)$$

To answer the query, we need the *union* of these two sets; that is, we need all customer names that appear in either or both of the two relations. We find these data by the binary operation union, denoted, as in set theory, by $\cup$. So the

customer-name
Johnson
Smith
Hayes
Turner
Jones
Lindsay
Jackson
Curry
Williams
Adams

Figure 3.10 Names of all customers who have either a loan or an account.

expression needed is

$$\Pi_{customer\text{-}name}\ (borrower) \cup \Pi_{customer\text{-}name}\ (depositor)$$

The result relation for this query appears in Figure 3.10. Notice that there are 10 tuples in the result, even though there are seven distinct borrowers and six depositors. This apparent discrepancy occurs because Smith, Jones, and Hayes are borrowers as well as depositors. Since relations are sets, duplicate values are eliminated.

Observe that, in our example, we took the union of two sets, both of which consisted of *customer-name* values. In general, we must ensure that unions are taken between *compatible* relations. For example, it would not make sense to take the union of the *loan* relation and the *borrower* relation. The former is a relation of three attributes; the latter is a relation of two. Furthermore, consider a union of a set of customer names and a set of cities. Such a union would not make sense in most situations. Therefore, for a union operation $r \cup s$ to be valid, we require that two conditions hold:

1. The relations r and s must be of the same arity. That is, they must have the same number of attributes.
2. The domains of the ith attribute of r and the ith attribute of s must be the same, for all i.

Note that r and s can be, in general, temporary relations that are the result of relational-algebra expressions.

3.2.1.5 The Set Difference Operation

The *set-difference* operation, denoted by $-$, allows us to find tuples that are in one relation but are not in another. The expression $r - s$ results in a relation containing those tuples in r but not in s.

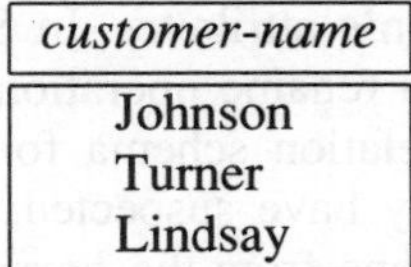

customer-name
Johnson
Turner
Lindsay

Figure 3.11 Customers with an account but no loan.

We can find all customers of the bank who have an account but not a loan by writing

$$\Pi_{customer\text{-}name}\ (depositor) - \Pi_{customer\text{-}name}\ (borrower)$$

The result relation for this query appears in Figure 3.11.

As was the case with the union operation, we must ensure that set differences are taken between *compatible* relations. Therefore, for a set difference operation $r - s$ to be valid, we require that the relations r and s be of the same arity, and that the domains of the ith attribute of r and the ith attribute of s be the same.

3.2.1.6 The Cartesian-Product Operation

The *Cartesian-product* operation, denoted by a cross ($\times$), allows us to combine information from any two relations. We write the Cartesian product of relations r_1 and r_2 as $r_1 \times r_2$.

Recall that a relation is defined to be a subset of a Cartesian product of a set of domains. From that definition, we should already have an intuition about the definition of the Cartesian-product operation. However, since the same attribute name may appear in both r_1 and r_2, we need to devise a naming schema to distinguish between these attributes. We do so here by attaching to an attribute the name of the relation from which the attribute originally came. For example, the relation schema for $r = borrower \times loan$ is

(*borrower.customer-name*, *borrower.loan-number*, *loan.branch-name*, *loan.loan-number*, *loan.amount*)

With this schema, we can distinguish *borrower.loan-number* from *loan.loan-number*. For those attributes that appear in only one of the two schemas, we shall usually drop the relation-name prefix. This simplification does not lead to any ambiguity. We can then write the relation schema for r as

(*customer-name*, *borrower.loan-number*, *branch-name*, *loan.loan-number*, *amount*)

This above naming convention *requires* that the relations that are the arguments of the Cartesian-product operation have distinct names. This requirement causes problems in some cases, such as if the Cartesian product of a relation with itself is desired. A similar problem arises if we use the result of a relational-algebra expression in a Cartesian product, since we will need a name for the relation so that we can refer to ther relation's attributes. In Section 3.2.1.7, we see how to avoid these problems by using a rename operation.

Now that we know the relation schema for r = *borrower* × *loan*, what tuples appear in r? As you may have suspected, we construct a tuple of r out of each possible pair of tuples: one from the *borrower* relation and one from the *loan* relation. Thus, r is a large relation, as you can see from Figure 3.12, where we included only a portion of the tuples that comprise r.

Assume that we have n_1 tuples in *borrower* and n_2 tuples in *loan*. Then, there are $n_1 * n_2$ ways of choosing a pair of tuples—one tuple from each relation; so there are $n_1 * n_2$ tuples in r. In particular, note that for some tuples t in r, it may be that $t[borrower.loan\text{-}number] \neq t[loan.loan\text{-}number]$.

In general, if we have relations $r_1(R_1)$ and $r_2(R_2)$, then $r_1 \times r_2$ is a relation whose schema is the concatenation of R_1 and R_2. Relation R contains all tuples t for which there is a tuple t_1 in r_1, and t_2 in r_2 for which $t[R_1] = t_1[R_1]$ and $t[R_2] = t_2[R_2]$.

Suppose that we want to find the names of all customers who have a loan at the Perryridge branch. We need the information in both the *loan* relation and the *borrower* relation to do so. If we write

$$\sigma_{branch\text{-}name = \text{"Perryridge"}}(borrower \times loan)$$

then the result is the relation shown in Figure 3.13. We have a relation that pertains to only the Perryridge branch. However, the *customer-name* column may contain customers who do not have a loan at the Perryridge branch. (If you do not see why that is true, recall that the Cartesian product takes all possible pairings of one tuple from *borrower* with one tuple of *loan*.)

Since the Cartesian-product operation associates *every* tuple of *loan* with every tuple of *borrower*, we know that, if a customer has a loan in the Perryridge branch, then there is some tuple in *borrower* × *loan* that contains his name, and *borrower.loan-number* = *loan.loan-number*. So, if we write

$$\sigma_{borrower.loan\text{-}number = loan.loan\text{-}number}\\ (\sigma_{branch\text{-}name = \text{"Perryridge"}}(borrower \times loan))$$

we get only those tuples of *borrower* × *loan* that pertain to customers that have a loan at the Perryridge branch.

Finally, since we want only *customer-name*, we do a projection:

$$\Pi_{customer\text{-}name}\ (\sigma_{borrower.loan\text{-}number = loan.loan\text{-}number}\\ (\sigma_{branch\text{-}name = \text{"Perryridge"}}\ (borrower \times loan)))$$

The result of this expression is shown in Figure 3.14 and is the correct answer to our query.

3.2.1.7 The Rename Operation

Unlike relations in the database, the results of relational-algebra expressions do not have a name that we can use to refer to them. It is useful to be able to give

customer-name	*borrower. loan-number*	*branch-name*	*loan. loan-number*	*amount*
Jones	L-17	Downtown	L-17	1000
Jones	L-17	Redwood	L-23	2000
Jones	L-17	Perryridge	L-15	1500
Jones	L-17	Downtown	L-14	1500
Jones	L-17	Mianus	L-93	500
Jones	L-17	Round Hill	L-11	900
Jones	L-17	Perryridge	L-16	1300
Smith	L-23	Downtown	L-17	1000
Smith	L-23	Redwood	L-23	2000
Smith	L-23	Perryridge	L-15	1500
Smith	L-23	Downtown	L-14	1500
Smith	L-23	Mianus	L-93	500
Smith	L-23	Round Hill	L-11	900
Smith	L-23	Perryridge	L-16	1300
Hayes	L-15	Downtown	L-17	1000
Hayes	L-15	Redwood	L-23	2000
Hayes	L-15	Perryridge	L-15	1500
Hayes	L-15	Downtown	L-14	1500
Hayes	L-15	Mianus	L-93	500
Hayes	L-15	Round Hill	L-11	900
Hayes	L-15	Perryridge	L-16	1300
...	...	...	...	...
...	...	...	...	...
...	...	...	...	...
Williams	L-17	Downtown	L-17	1000
Williams	L-17	Redwood	L-23	2000
Williams	L-17	Perryridge	L-15	1500
Williams	L-17	Downtown	L-14	1500
Williams	L-17	Mianus	L-93	500
Williams	L-17	Round Hill	L-11	900
Williams	L-17	Perryridge	L-16	1300
Adams	L-16	Downtown	L-17	1000
Adams	L-16	Redwood	L-23	2000
Adams	L-16	Perryridge	L-15	1500
Adams	L-16	Downtown	L-14	1500
Adams	L-16	Mianus	L-93	500
Adams	L-16	Round Hill	L-11	900
Adams	L-16	Perryridge	L-16	1300

Figure 3.12 Result of *borrower* × *loan*.

customer-name	*loan-number*	*branch-name*	*loan-number*	*amount*
Jones	L-17	Perryridge	L-15	1500
Jones	L-17	Perryridge	L-16	1300
Smith	L-23	Perryridge	L-15	1500
Smith	L-23	Perryridge	L-16	1300
Hayes	L-15	Perryridge	L-15	1500
Hayes	L-15	Perryridge	L-16	1300
Jackson	L-14	Perryridge	L-15	1500
Jackson	L-14	Perryridge	L-16	1300
Curry	L-93	Perryridge	L-15	1500
Curry	L-93	Perryridge	L-16	1300
Smith	L-11	Perryridge	L-15	1500
Smith	L-11	Perryridge	L-16	1300
Williams	L-17	Perryridge	L-15	1500
Williams	L-17	Perryridge	L-16	1300
Adams	L-16	Perryridge	L-15	1500
Adams	L-16	Perryridge	L-16	1300

Figure 3.13 Result of $\sigma_{branch\text{-}name = \text{"Perryridge"}} (borrower \times loan)$.

them names; the *rename* operator, denoted by the lower-case Greek letter rho (ρ), lets us perform this task. Given a relational-algebra expression E, the expression

$$\rho_x (E)$$

returns the result of expression E under the name x.

A relation r by itself is considered to be a (trivial) relational-algebra expression. Thus, we can also apply the rename operation to a relation r to get the same relation under a new name.

A second form of the rename operation is as follows. Assume that a relational-algebra expression E has arity n. Then, the expression

$$\rho_{x(A_1, A_2, \ldots, A_n)} (E)$$

returns the result of expression E under the name x, and with the attributes renamed to $A_1, A_2, \ldots, A_n$.

To illustrate the use of renaming a relation, we consider the query "Find the largest account balance in the bank." Our strategy is to compute first a temporary

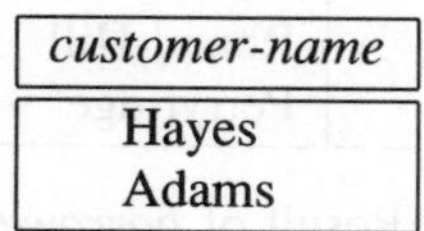

customer-name
Hayes
Adams

Figure 3.14 Result of

$$\Pi_{customer\text{-}name} (\sigma_{borrower.loan\text{-}number = loan.loan\text{-}number} (\sigma_{branch\text{-}name = \text{"Perryridge"}} (borrower \times loan))).$$

relation consisting of those balances that are *not* the largest, and then to take the set difference between the relation $\Pi_{balance}$ (*account*) and the temporary relation just computed, to obtain the result. To compute the temporary relation, we need to compare the values of all account balances. We can do this comparison by computing the Cartesian product *account* $\times$ *account* and forming a selection to compare the value of any two balances appearing in one tuple. First, we need to devise a mechanism to distinguish between the two *balance* attributes. We shall use the rename operation to rename one reference to the account relation; thus we can reference the relation twice without ambiguity.

The temporary relation that consists of the balances that are not the largest can now be written as

$$\Pi_{account.balance}\ (\sigma_{account.balance\ <\ d.balance}\ (account\ \times\ \rho_d\ (account)))$$

This expression gives those balances in the *account* relation for which a larger balance appears somewhere in the *account* relation (renamed as d). The result contains all balances *except* the largest one. This relation is shown in Figure 3.15. The query to find the largest account balance in the bank can be written as follows:

$$\begin{array}{l} \Pi_{balance}\ (account)\ - \\ \quad \Pi_{account.balance}\ (\sigma_{account.balance\ <\ d.balance}\ (account\ \times\ \rho_d\ (account))) \end{array}$$

Figure 3.16 shows the result of this query.

Let us present one more example to illustrate the rename operation. Consider the query "Find the names of all customers who live on the same street and in the same city as Smith." We can obtain the street and city of Smith by writing

$$\Pi_{customer\text{-}street,\ customer\text{-}city}\ (\sigma_{customer\text{-}name\ =\ \text{"Smith"}}\ (customer))$$

However, to find other customers with this street and city, we must reference the *customer* relation a second time. In the following query, we use the rename operation on the preceding expression to give its result the name *smith-addr*, and to rename its attributes to *street* and *city*, instead of *customer-street* and

balance
500
700
400
350
750

Figure 3.15 Result of subexpression
$\Pi_{account.balance}\ (\sigma_{account.balance\ <\ d.balance}\ (account\ \times\ \rho_d\ (account)))$.

balance
900

Figure 3.16 Largest account balance in the bank.

customer-city:

$$\Pi_{customer.customer\text{-}name} \\ (\sigma_{customer.customer\text{-}street=smith\text{-}addr.street \wedge customer.customer\text{-}city=smith\text{-}addr.city} \\ (customer \times \rho_{smith\text{-}addr(street, city)} \\ (\Pi_{customer\text{-}street,\ customer\text{-}city}\ (\sigma_{customer\text{-}name\ =\ \text{"Smith"}}(customer)))))$$

The result of this query, when we apply it to the *customer* relation of Figure 3.3, is shown in Figure 3.17.

The rename operation is not strictly required, since it is possible to use a positional notation for attributes. We can name attributes of a relation implicitly using a positional notation, where \$1, \$2, ... refer to the first attribute, the second attribute, and so on. The positional notation also applies to results of relational-algebra operations. The following relational-algebra expression illustrates the use of positional notation with the unary operator σ:

$$\sigma_{\$2=\$3}(R \times R)$$

If a binary operation needs to distinguish between its two operand relations, a similar positional notation can be used for relation names as well. For example, $\$R1$ could refer to the first operand, and $\$R2$ could refer to the second operand. However, the positional notation is inconvenient for humans, since the position of the attribute is a number, rather than an easy-to-remember attribute name. Hence, we do not use the positional notation in this textbook.

3.2.2 Formal Definition of the Relational Algebra

The operations that we saw in Section 3.2.1 allow us to give a complete definition of an expression in the relational algebra. A basic expression in the relational algebra consists of either one of the following:

- A relation in the database
- A constant relation

A general expression in the relational algebra is constructed out of smaller subexpressions. Let E_1 and E_2 be relational-algebra expressions. Then, the following

customer-name
Smith
Curry

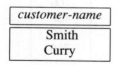

Figure 3.17 Customers who live on the same street and in the same city as Smith.

are all relational-algebra expressions:

- $E_1 \cup E_2$
- $E_1 - E_2$
- $E_1 \times E_2$
- $\sigma_P(E_1)$, where P is a predicate on attributes in E_1
- $\Pi_S(E_1)$, where S is a list consisting of some of the attributes in E_1
- $\rho_x\ (E_1)$, where x is the new name for the result of E_1

3.2.3 Additional Operations

The fundamental operations of the relational algebra are sufficient to express any relational-algebra query.[†] However, if we restrict ourselves to just the fundamental operations, certain common queries are lengthy to express. Therefore, we define additional operations that do not add any power to the algebra, but that simplify common queries. For each new operation, we give an equivalent expression using only the fundamental operations.

3.2.3.1 The Set-Intersection Operation

The first additional-relational algebra operation that we shall define is *set intersection* ($\cap$). Suppose that we wish to find all customers who have both a loan and an account. Using set intersection, we can write

$$\Pi_{customer\text{-}name}\ (borrower) \cap \Pi_{customer\text{-}name}\ (depositor)$$

The result relation for this query appears in Figure 3.18.

Note that we can rewrite any relational algebra expression using set intersection by replacing the intersection operation with a pair of set-difference operations as follows:

$$r \cap s = r - (r - s)$$

Thus, set intersection is not a fundamental operation and does not add any power to the relational algebra. It is simply more convenient to write $r \cap s$ than to write $r - (r - s)$.

customer-name
Hayes
Jones
Smith

Figure 3.18 Customers with both an account and a loan at the bank.

[†]In Section 3.5, we introduce operations that extend the power of the relational algebra to handle null and aggregate values.

3.2.3.2 The Natural-Join Operation

It is often desirable to simplify certain queries that require a Cartesian product. Typically, a query that involves a Cartesian product includes a selection operation on the result of the Cartesian product. Consider the query "Find the names of all customers who have a loan at the bank, and find the amount of the loan." We first form the Cartesian product of the *borrower* and *loan* relations. Then, we select those tuples that pertain to only the same *loan-number*, followed by the projection of the resulting *customer-name*, *loan-number*, and *amount*:

$$\Pi_{customer\text{-}name,\ loan.loan\text{-}number,\ amount} \\ (\sigma_{borrower.loan\text{-}number\ =\ loan.loan\text{-}number}\ (borrower\ \times\ loan))$$

The *natural join* is a binary operation that allows us to combine certain selections and a Cartesian product into one operation. It is denoted by the "join" symbol $\bowtie$. The natural-join operation forms a Cartesian product of its two arguments, performs a selection forcing equality on those attributes that appear in both relation schemas, and finally removes duplicate attributes.

Although the definition of natural join is complicated, the operation is easy to apply. As an illustration, let us consider again the example "Find the names of all customers who have a loan at the bank, and find the amount of the loan." This query can be expressed using the natural join as follows:

$$\Pi_{customer\text{-}name,\ loan\text{-}number,\ amount}\ (borrower \bowtie loan)$$

Since the schemas for *borrower* and *loan* (that is, *Borrower-schema* and *Loan-schema*) have the attribute *loan-number* in common, the natural-join operation considers only pairs of tuples that have the same value on *loan-number*. It combines each such pair of tuples into a single tuple on the union of the two schemas (that is, *customer-name, branch-name, loan-number, amount*). After performing the projection, we obtain the relation shown in Figure 3.19.

Consider two relation schemas R and S—which are, of course, lists of attribute names. If we consider the schemas to be *sets*, rather than lists, we can denote those attribute names that appear in both R and S by $R \cap S$, and denote those attribute names that appear in R, in S, or in both by $R \cup S$. Similarly, those

customer-name	*loan-number*	*amount*
Jones	L-17	1000
Smith	L-23	2000
Hayes	L-15	1500
Jackson	L-14	1500
Curry	L-93	500
Smith	L-11	900
Williams	L-17	1000
Adams	L-16	1300

Figure 3.19 Result of $\Pi_{customer\text{-}name,\ loan\text{-}number,\ amount}\ (borrower \bowtie loan)$.

branch-name
Brighton
Perryridge

Figure 3.20 Result of
$\Pi_{branch\text{-}name}(\sigma_{customer\text{-}city\,=\,\text{“Harrison”}}\ (customer \bowtie account \bowtie depositor))$.

attribute names that appear in R but not S are denoted by $R - S$, whereas $S - R$ denotes those attribute names that appear in S but not in R. Note that the union, intersection, and difference operations here are on sets of attributes, rather than on relations.

We are now ready for a formal definition of the natural join. Consider two relations $r(R)$ and $s(S)$. The *natural join* of r and s, denoted by $r \bowtie s$ is a relation on schema $R \cup S$ formally defined as follows:

$$r \bowtie s = \Pi_{R \cup S}\ (\sigma_{r.A_1 = s.A_1 \wedge r.A_2 = s.A_2 \wedge \ldots \wedge r.A_n = s.A_n}\ r \times s)$$

where $R \cap S = \{A_1,\ A_2, \ldots, A_n\}$.

Because the natural join is central to much of relational-database theory and practice, we give several examples of its use.

- Find the names of all branches with customers who have an account in the bank and who live in Harrison.

  $$\Pi_{branch\text{-}name}\ (\sigma_{customer\text{-}city\,=\,\text{“Harrison”}}\ (customer \bowtie account \bowtie depositor))$$

  The result relation for this query appears in Figure 3.20.

  Notice that we wrote *customer* ⋈ *account* ⋈ *depositor* without inserting parentheses to specify the order in which the natural-join operations on the three relations be executed. In the preceding case, there are two possibilities:
  - (*customer* ⋈ *account*) ⋈ *depositor*
  - *customer* ⋈ (*account* ⋈ *depositor*)

  We did not specify which expression we intended, because the two are equivalent. That is, the natural join is *associative*.

- Find all customers who have *both* a loan and an account at the bank.

  $$\Pi_{customer\text{-}name}\ (borrower \bowtie depositor)$$

  Note that in Section 3.2.3.1, we wrote an expression for this query using set intersection. We repeat this expression here.

  $$\Pi_{customer\text{-}name}\ (borrower) \cap \Pi_{customer\text{-}name}\ (depositor)$$

  The result relation for this query was shown earlier in Figure 3.18. This example illustrates a general fact about the relational algebra: It is possible to write several equivalent relational-algebra expressions that are quite different from one another.

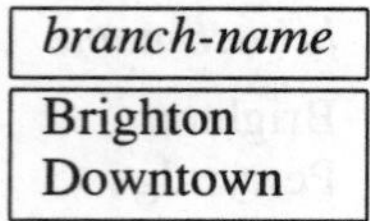

branch-name
Brighton
Downtown

Figure 3.21 Result of $\Pi_{branch\text{-}name}$ ($\sigma_{branch\text{-}city = \text{"Brooklyn"}}$ (*branch*)).

- Let $r(R)$ and $s(S)$ be relations without any attributes in common; that is, $R \cap S = \emptyset$. ($\emptyset$ denotes the empty set.) Then, $r \bowtie s = r \times s$.

The theta join operation is an extension to the natural-join operation that allows us to combine a selection and a Cartesian product into a single operation. Consider relations $r(R)$ and $s(S)$, and let θ be a predicate on attributes in the schema $R \cup S$, The *theta join* operation $r \bowtie_\theta s$, is defined as follows:

$$r \bowtie_\theta s = \sigma_\theta(r \times s)$$

3.2.3.3 The Division Operation

The *division* operation, denoted by $\div$, is suited to queries that include the phrase "for all." Suppose that we wish to find all customers who have an account at *all* the branches located in Brooklyn. We can obtain all branches in Brooklyn by the expression

$$r_1 = \Pi_{branch\text{-}name} \ (\sigma_{branch\text{-}city = \text{"Brooklyn"}} \ (branch))$$

The result relation for this expression appears in Figure 3.21.

We can find all (*customer-name, branch-name*) pairs for which the customer has an account at a branch by writing

$$r_2 = \Pi_{customer\text{-}name,\ branch\text{-}name} \ (depositor \bowtie account)$$

Figure 3.22 shows the result relation for this expression.

Now, we need to find customers who appear in r_2 with *every* branch name in r_1. The operation that provides exactly those customers is the divide operation.

customer-name	*branch-name*
Johnson	Downtown
Smith	Mianus
Hayes	Perryridge
Turner	Round Hill
Williams	Perryridge
Lindsay	Redwood
Johnson	Brighton
Jones	Brighton

Figure 3.22 Result of $\Pi_{customer\text{-}name,\ branch\text{-}name}$ (*depositor* $\bowtie$ *account*).

We formulate the query by writing

$$\Pi_{customer\text{-}name,\ branch\text{-}name}\ (depositor \bowtie account)$$
$$\div\ \Pi_{branch\text{-}name}\ (\sigma_{branch\text{-}city\ =\ \text{“Brooklyn”}}\ (branch))$$

The result of this expression is a relation that has the schema (*customer-name*) and that contains the tuple (Johnson).

Formally, let $r(R)$ and $s(S)$ be relations, and let $S \subseteq R$; that is every attribute of schema S is also in schema R. The relation $r \div s$ is a relation on schema $R - S$—that is, on the schema containing all attributes of schema R that are not in schema S. A tuple t is in $r \div s$ if and only if both of two conditions hold:

1. t is in $\Pi_{R-S}(r)$
2. For every tuple t_s in s, there is a tuple t_r in r satisfying both of the following:
   a. $t_r[S] = t_s[S]$
   b. $t_r[R - S] = t$

It may surprise you to discover that, given a division operation and the schemas of the relations, we can, in fact, define the division operation in terms of the fundamental operations. Let $r(R)$ and $s(S)$ be given, with $S \subseteq R$:

$$r \div s = \Pi_{R-S}\ (r)\ -\ \Pi_{R-S}\ (\ (\Pi_{R-S}\ (r)\ \times\ s)\ -\ \Pi_{R-S,S}(r))$$

To see that this expression is true, we observe that $\Pi_{R-S}\ (r)$ gives us all tuples t that satisfy the first condition of the definition of division. The expression on the right side of the set difference operator,

$$\Pi_{R-S}\ (\ (\Pi_{R-S}\ (r)\ \times\ s)\ -\ \Pi_{R-S,S}(r)),$$

serves to eliminate those tuples that fail to satisfy the second condition of the definition of division. Let us see how it does so. Consider $\Pi_{R-S}\ (r)\ \times\ s$. This relation is on schema R, and pairs every tuple in $\Pi_{R-S}\ (r)$ with every tuple in s. The expression $\Pi_{R-S,S}(r)$ merely reorders the attributes of r.

Thus, $(\Pi_{R-S}\ (r)\ \times\ s)\ -\ \Pi_{R-S,S}(r)$ gives us those pairs of tuples from $\Pi_{R-S}\ (r)$ and s that do not appear in r. If a tuple t_j is in

$$\Pi_{R-S}\ (\ (\Pi_{R-S}\ (r)\ \times\ s)\ -\ \Pi_{R-S,S}(r)),$$

then there is some tuple t_s in s that does not combine with tuple t_j to form a tuple in r. Thus, t_j holds a value for attributes $R - S$ that does not appear in $r \div s$. It is these values that we eliminate from $\Pi_{R-S}\ (r)$.

3.2.3.4 The Assignment Operation

It is convenient at times to write a relational-algebra expression in parts using assignment to a temporary relation variable. The *assignment* operation denoted by $\leftarrow$, works in a manner similar to assignment in a programming language. To illustrate this operation, we consider the definition of division given in Section 3.2.3.3.

We could write $r \div s$ as

$$\begin{aligned} temp1 &\leftarrow \Pi_{R-S}(r) \\ temp2 &\leftarrow \Pi_{R-S}((temp1 \times s) - r) \\ result &= temp1 - temp2 \end{aligned}$$

The evaluation of an assignment does not result in any relation being displayed to the user. Rather, the result of the expression to the right of the $\leftarrow$ is assigned to the relation variable on the left of the $\leftarrow$. This relation variable may be used in subsequent expressions.

With the assignment operation, a query can be written as a sequential program consisting of a series of assignments followed by an expression whose value is displayed as the result of the query. For relational-algebra queries, assignment must always be made to a temporary relation variable. Assignments to permanent relations constitute a database modification. We discuss this issue in Section 3.6. Note that the assignment operation does not provide any additional power to the algebra. It is, however, a convenient way to express complex queries.

3.3 The Tuple Relational Calculus

When we write a relational-algebra expression, we provide a sequence of procedures that generates the answer to our query. The tuple relational calculus, by contrast, is a *nonprocedural* query language. It describes the desired information without giving a specific procedure for obtaining that information.

A query in the tuple relational calculus is expressed as

$$\{t \mid P(t)\}$$

that is, it is the set of all tuples t such that predicate P is true for t. Following our earlier notation, we use $t[A]$ to denote the value of tuple t on attribute A, and we use $t \in r$ to denote that tuple t is in relation r.

Before we give a formal definition of the tuple relational calculus, we return to some of the queries for which we wrote relational-algebra expressions in Section 3.2.

3.3.1 Example Queries

Say that we want to find the *branch-name*, *loan-number*, and *amount* for loans of over \$1200:

$$\{t \mid t \in loan \wedge t[amount] > 1200\}$$

Suppose that we want only the *loan-number* attribute, rather than all attributes of the *loan* relation. To write this query in the tuple relational calculus, we need to write an expression for a relation on the schema (*loan-number*). We need those tuples on (*loan-number*) such that there is a tuple in *loan* with the *amount* attribute > 1200. To express this request, we need the construct "there exists" from mathematical logic. The notation

$$\exists\, t \in r\ (Q(t))$$

means "there exists a tuple t in relation r such that predicate $Q(t)$ is true."

Using this notation, we can write the query "Find the loan number for each loan of an amount greater than \$1200" as

$$\{t \mid \exists\, s \in \mathit{loan}\ (t[\mathit{loan\text{-}number}] = s[\mathit{loan\text{-}number}] \\ \wedge\ s[\mathit{amount}] > 1200)\}$$

In English, we read the preceding expression as "the set of all tuples t such that there exists a tuple s in relation *loan* for which the values of t and s for the *loan-number* attribute are equal, and the value of s for the *amount* attribute is greater than \$1200."

Tuple variable t is defined on only the *loan-number* attribute, since that is the only attribute for which a condition is specified for t. Thus, the result is a relation on (*loan-number*).

Consider the query "Find the names of all customers who have a loan from the Perryridge branch." This query is slightly more complex than the previous queries, since it involves two relations: *borrower* and *loan*. As we shall see, however, all it requires is that we have two "there exists" clauses in our tuple-relational-calculus expression, connected by *and* ($\wedge$). We write the query as follows:

$$\{t \mid \exists\, s \in \mathit{borrower}\ (t[\mathit{customer\text{-}name}] = s[\mathit{customer\text{-}name}] \\ \wedge\ \exists\, u \in \mathit{loan}\ (u[\mathit{loan\text{-}number}] = s[\mathit{loan\text{-}number}] \\ \wedge\ u[\mathit{branch\text{-}name}] = \text{"Perryridge"}))\}$$

In English, this expression is "the set of all (*customer-name*) tuples for which the customer has a loan that is at the Perryridge branch." Tuple variable u ensures that the customer is a borrower at the Perryridge branch. Tuple variable s is restricted to pertain to the same loan number as s. The result of this query is shown in Figure 3.23.

To find all customers who have a loan, an account, or both at the bank, we used the union operation in the relational algebra. In the tuple relational calculus, we shall need two "there exists" clauses, connected by *or* ($\vee$):

$$\{t \mid \exists\, s \in \mathit{borrower}\ (t[\mathit{customer\text{-}name}] = s[\mathit{customer\text{-}name}]) \\ \vee\ \exists\, u \in \mathit{depositor}\ (t[\mathit{customer\text{-}name}] = u[\mathit{customer\text{-}name}])\}$$

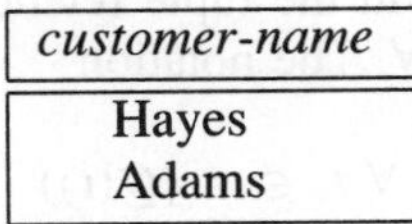

customer-name
Hayes
Adams

Figure 3.23 Names of all customers who have a loan at the Perryridge branch.

This expression gives us the set of all *customer-name* tuples such that at least one of the following holds:

- The *customer-name* appears in some tuple of the *borrower* relation as a borrower from the bank.
- The *customer-name* appears in some tuple of the *depositor* relation as a depositor of the bank.

If some customer has both a loan and an account at the bank, that customer appears only once in the result, because the mathematical definition of a set does not allow duplicate members. The result of this query was shown earlier in Figure 3.10.

If we now want *only* those customers that have *both* an account and a loan at the bank, all we need to do is to change the *or* ($\vee$) to *and* ($\wedge$) in the preceding expression.

$$\{t \mid \exists\, s \in borrower\ (t[customer\text{-}name] = s[customer\text{-}name]) \\ \wedge \exists\, u \in depositor\ (t[customer\text{-}name] = u[customer\text{-}name])\}$$

The result of this query was shown in Figure 3.18.

Now consider the query "Find all customers who have an account at the bank but do not have a loan from the bank." The tuple-relational-calculus expression for this query is similar to the expressions that we have just seen, except for the use of the *not* ($\neg$) symbol:

$$\{t \mid \exists\, u \in depositor\ (t[customer\text{-}name] = u[customer\text{-}name]) \\ \wedge \neg \exists\, s \in borrower\ (t[customer\text{-}name] = s[customer\text{-}name])\}$$

The preceding tuple-relational-calculus expression uses the $\exists\, u \in depositor\ (\ldots)$ clause to require that the customer have an account at the bank, and it uses the $\neg \exists\, s \in borrower\ (\ldots)$ clause to eliminate those customers who appear in some tuple of the *borrower* relation as having a loan from the bank. The result of this query appeared in Figure 3.11.

The query that we shall consider next uses implication, denoted by $\Rightarrow$. The formula $P \Rightarrow Q$ means "P implies Q;" that is, "if P is true, then Q must be true." Note that $P \Rightarrow Q$ is logically equivalent to $\neg P \vee Q$. The use of implication rather than *not* and *or* often suggests a more intuitive interpretation of a query in English.

Consider the query that we used in Section 3.2.3 to illustrate the division operation: "Find all customers who have an account at all branches located in Brooklyn." To write this query in the tuple relational calculus, we introduce the "for all" construct, denoted by $\forall$. The notation

$$\forall\, t \in r\ (Q(t))$$

means "Q is true for all tuples t in relation r."

We write the expression for our query as follows:

$$\{t \mid \forall\, u \in \mathit{branch}\ (u[\mathit{branch\text{-}city}] = \text{“Brooklyn”} \Rightarrow$$
$$\exists\, s \in \mathit{depositor}\ (t[\mathit{customer\text{-}name}] = s[\mathit{customer\text{-}name}]$$
$$\wedge\ \exists\, w \in \mathit{account}\ (w[\mathit{account\text{-}number}] = s[\mathit{account\text{-}number}]$$
$$\wedge\ w[\mathit{branch\text{-}name}] = u[\mathit{branch\text{-}name}]))))\}$$

In English, we interpret this expression as "the set of all customers, (that is, (*customer-name*) tuples t) such that, for *all* tuples u in the *branch* relation, if the value of u on attribute *branch-city* is Brooklyn, then the customer has an account at the branch whose name appears in the *branch-name* attribute of u."

3.3.2 Formal Definition

We are now ready for a formal definition. A tuple-relational-calculus expression is of the form

$$\{t \mid P(t)\}$$

where P is a *formula*. Several tuple variables may appear in a formula. A tuple variable is said to be a *free variable* unless it is quantified by a $\exists$ or $\forall$. Thus, in

$$t \in \mathit{loan} \wedge \exists\, s \in \mathit{customer}(t[\mathit{branch\text{-}name}] = s[\mathit{branch\text{-}name}])$$

t is a free variable. Tuple variable s is said to be a *bound* variable.

A tuple-relational-calculus formula is built up out of *atoms*. An atom has one of the following forms:

- $s \in r$, where s is a tuple variable and r is a relation (we do not allow use of the $\notin$ operator)
- $s[x]\ \Theta\ u[y]$, where s and u are tuple variables, x is an attribute on which s is defined, y is an attribute on which u is defined, and Θ is a comparison operator ($<, \leq, =, \neq, >, \geq$); we require that attributes x and y have domains whose members can be compared by Θ
- $s[x]\ \Theta\ c$, where s is a tuple variable, x is an attribute on which s is defined, Θ is a comparison operator, and c is a constant in the domain of attribute x

We build up formulae from atoms using the following rules:

- An atom is a formula.
- If P_1 is a formula, then so are $\neg P_1$ and (P_1).
- If P_1 and P_2 are formulae, then so are $P_1 \vee P_2$, $P_1 \wedge P_2$, and $P_1 \Rightarrow P_2$.
- If $P_1(s)$ is a formula containing a free tuple variable s, and r is a relation, then

$$\exists\, s \in r\ (P_1(s))\ \textit{and}\ \forall\, s \in r\ (P_1(s))$$

are also formulae.

As we could for the relational algebra, we can write equivalent expressions that are not identical in appearance. In the tuple relational calculus, these equivalences include the following three rules:

1. $P_1 \wedge P_2$ is equivalent to $\neg (\neg P_1 \vee \neg P_2)$.
2. $\forall t \in r\ (P_1(t))$ is equivalent to $\neg \exists t \in r\ (\neg P_1(t))$.
3. $P_1 \Rightarrow P_2$ is equivalent to $\neg P_1 \vee P_2$.

3.3.3 Safety of Expressions

There is one final issue to be addressed. A tuple-relational-calculus expression may generate an infinite relation. Suppose that we wrote the expression

$$\{t \mid \neg (t \in loan)\}$$

There are infinitely many tuples that are not in *loan*. Most of these tuples contain values that do not even appear in the database! Clearly, we do not wish to allow such expressions.

To assist us in defining a restriction of the tuple relational calculus, we introduce the concept of the *domain* of a tuple relational formula, P. Intuitively, the domain of P, denoted $dom(P)$, is the set of all values referenced by P. These include values mentioned in P itself, as well as values that appear in a tuple of a relation mentioned in P. Thus, the domain of P is the set of all values that appear explicitly in P or that appear in one or more relations whose names appear in P. For example, $dom(t \in loan \wedge t[amount] > 1200)$ is the set containing 1200 as well as the set of all values appearing in *loan*. Also, $dom(\neg\ (t \in loan))$ is the set of all values appearing in *loan*, since the relation *loan* is mentioned in the expression.

We say that an expression $\{t \mid P(t)\}$ is *safe* if all values that appear in the result are values from $dom(P)$. The expression $\{t \mid \neg\ (t \in loan)\}$ is not safe. Note that $dom(\neg\ (t \in loan))$ is the set of all values appearing in *loan*. However, it is possible to have a tuple t not in *loan* that contains values that do not appear in *loan*. The other examples of tuple-relational-calculus expressions that we have written in this section are safe.

3.3.4 Expressive Power of Languages

The tuple relational calculus restricted to safe expressions is equivalent in expressive power to the relational algebra. Thus, for every relational-algebra expression, there is an equivalent expression in the tuple relational calculus, and for every tuple-relational-calculus expression, there is an equivalent relational-algebra expression. We will not prove this assertion here; the bibliographic notes contain references to the proof. Some parts of the proof are included in the exercises.

3.4 The Domain Relational Calculus

There is a second form of relational calculus called *domain relational calculus*. This form uses *domain* variables that take on values from an attribute's domain, rather than values for an entire tuple. The domain relational calculus, however, is closely related to the tuple relational calculus.

3.4.1 Formal Definition

An expression in the domain relational calculus is of the form

$$\{< x_1, x_2, \ldots, x_n > \mid P(x_1, x_2, \ldots, x_n)\}$$

where $x_1, x_2, \ldots, x_n$ represent domain variables. P represents a formula composed of atoms, as was the case in the tuple relational calculus. An atom in the domain relational calculus has one of the following forms:

- $< x_1, x_2, \ldots, x_n > \in r$, where r is a relation on n attributes and $x_1, x_2, \ldots, x_n$ are domain variables or domain constants.
- $x \ \Theta \ y$, where x and y are domain variables and Θ is a comparison operator ($<, \leq, =, \neq, >, \geq$). We require that attributes x and y have domains that can be compared by Θ.
- $x \ \Theta \ c$, where x is a domain variable, Θ is a comparison operator, and c is a constant in the domain of the attribute for which x is a domain variable.

We build up formulae from atoms using the following rules:

- An atom is a formula.
- If P_1 is a formula, then so are $\neg P_1$ and (P_1).
- If P_1 and P_2 are formulae, then so are $P_1 \vee P_2$, $P_1 \wedge P_2$, and $P_1 \Rightarrow P_2$.
- If $P_1(x)$ is a formula in x, where x is a domain variable, then

  $$\exists \ x \ (P_1(x)) \text{ and } \forall \ x \ (P_1(x))$$

  are also formulae.

As a notational shorthand, we write

$$\exists \ a, b, c \ (P(a, b, c))$$

for

$$\exists \ a \ (\exists \ b \ (\exists \ c \ (P(a, b, c))))$$

3.4.2 Example Queries

We now give domain-relational-calculus queries for the examples that we considered earlier. Note the similarity of these expressions and the corresponding tuple-relational-calculus expressions

- Find the branch name, loan number, and amount for loans of over \$1200:

  $$\{< b, l, a > \mid < b, l, a > \in loan \wedge a > 1200\}$$

- Find all loan numbers for loans with an amount greater than \$1200:

$$\{< l > \mid \exists\, b, a\ (< b, l, a > \in\ loan\ \wedge\ a\ >\ 1200)\}$$

Although the second query appears similar to the one that we wrote for the tuple relational calculus, there is an important difference. In the tuple calculus, when we write $\exists\ s$ for some tuple variable s, we bind it immediately to a relation by writing $\exists\ s\ \in\ r$. However, when we write $\exists\ b$ in the domain calculus, b refers not to a tuple, but rather to a domain value. Thus, the domain of variable b is unconstrained until the subformula $b, l, a\ \in\ loan$ constrains b to branch names that appear in the *loan* relation.

- Find the names of all customers who have a loan from the Perryridge branch and find the loan amount:

$$\{< c, a > \mid \exists\ l\ (< c, l > \in\ borrower \\ \wedge\ \exists\ b\ (< b, l, a > \in\ loan\ \wedge\ b\ =\ \text{"Perryridge"}))\}$$

- Find the names of all customers who have a loan, an account, or both at the Perryridge branch:

$$\{< c > \mid \exists l\ (< c, l > \in\ borrower \\ \wedge \exists b, a\ (< b, l, a > \in\ loan\ \wedge\ b\ =\ \text{"Perryridge"})) \\ \vee \exists a\ (< c, a > \in\ depositor \\ \wedge \exists b, n\ (< b, a, n > \in\ account\ \wedge\ b = \text{"Perryridge"}))\}$$

- Find the names of all customers who have an account at all the branches located in Brooklyn:

$$\{< c > \mid \forall\ x, y, z\ (< x, y, z > \in\ branch)\ \wedge\ y\ =\ \text{"Brooklyn"}\ \Rightarrow \\ \exists\ a, b\ (< x, a, b > \in\ account\ \wedge\ < c, a > \in\ depositor)\}$$

In English, we interpret the preceding expression as "the set of all (*customer-name*) tuples c such that, for all (*branch-name*, *branch-city, assets*) tuples, x, y, z, if the branch city is Brooklyn, then the following is true":

- There exists a tuple in the relation *account* with account number a and branch name x
- There exists a tuple in the relation *depositor* with customer c and account number a

3.4.3 Safety of Expressions

We noted that, in the tuple relational calculus, it is possible to write expressions that may generate an infinite relation. That led us to define *safety* for tuple-relational-calculus expressions. A similar situation arises for the domain relational calculus. An expression such as

$$\{< b, l, a > \mid \neg(< b, l, a > \in \ loan)\}$$

is unsafe, because it allows values in the result that are not in the domain of the expression.

For the domain relational calculus, we must be concerned also about the form of formulae within "there exists" and "for all" clauses. Consider the expression

$$\{< x > \mid \exists\, y\ (x, y \in\ r)\ \wedge\ \exists\, z\ (\neg(< x,\ z > \in\ r)\ \wedge\ P(x, z))\}$$

where P is some formula involving x and z. We can test the first part of the formula, $\exists\, y\ (< x,\ y > \in\ r)$, by considering only the values in r. However, to test the second part of the formula, $\exists\, z\ (\neg\ (< x,\ z > \in\ r)\ \wedge\ P(x, z))$, we must consider values for z that do not appear in r. Since all relations are finite, an infinite number of values do not appear in r. Thus, it is not possible, in general, to test the second part of the formula, without considering an infinite number of potential values for z. Instead, we add restrictions to prohibit expressions such as the preceding one.

In the tuple relational calculus, we restricted any existentially quantified variable to range over a specific relation. Since we did not do so in the domain calculus, we add rules to the definition of safety to deal with cases like our example. We say that an expression

$$\{< x_1,\ x_2, \ldots, x_n > \ \mid P\ (x_1,\ x_2, \ldots, x_n)\}$$

is safe if all of the following hold:

1. All values that appear in tuples of the expression are values from $dom(P)$.
2. For every "there exists" subformula of the form $\exists\, x\ (P_1(x))$, the subformula is true if and only if there is a value x in $dom(P_1)$ such that $P_1(x)$ is true.
3. For every "for all" subformula of the form $\forall x\ (P_1(x))$, the subformula is true if and only if $P_1(x)$ is true for all values x from $dom(P_1)$.

The purpose of the additional rules is to ensure that we can test "for all" and "there exists" subformulae without having to test infinitely many possibilities. Consider the second rule in the definition of safety. For $\exists\, x\ (P_1(x))$ to be true, we need to find only one x for which $P_1(x)$ is true. In general, there would be infinitely many values to test. However, if the expression is safe, we know that we can restrict our attention to values from $dom(P_1)$. This restriction reduces to a finite number the tuples we must consider.

The situation for subformulae of the form $\forall x\ (P_1(x))$ is similar. To assert that $\forall x\ (P_1(x))$ is true, we must, in general, test all possible values, so we must examine infinitely many values. As before, if we know that the expression is safe, it is sufficient for us to test $P_1(x)$ for those values taken from $dom(P_1)$.

All the domain-relational-calculus expressions that we have written in the example queries of this section are safe.

3.4.4 Expressive Power of Languages

When the domain relational calculus is restricted to safe expressions, it is equivalent in expressive power to the tuple relational calculus restricted to safe expressions. Since we noted earlier that the restricted tuple relational calculus is equivalent to the relational algebra, all three of the following are equivalent:

- The relational algebra
- The tuple relational calculus restricted to safe expressions
- The domain relational calculus restricted to safe expressions

3.5 Extended Relational-Algebra Operations

The basic relational algebra operations have been extended in several ways. A simple extension is to allow arithmetic operations as part of projection. An important extension is to allow *aggregate operations*, such as computing the sum of the elements of a set, or their average. Another important extension is the *outer-join* operation, which allows relational-algebra expressions to deal with null values, which model missing information.

3.5.1 Generalized Projection

The *generalized-projection* operation extends the projection operation by allowing arithmetic functions to be used in the projection list. The generalized projection operation has the form

$$\Pi_{F_1, F_2, \ldots, F_n}(E)$$

where E is any relational-algebra expression, and each of $F_1, F_2, \ldots, F_n$ are arithmetic expressions involving constants and attributes in the schema of E. As a special case, the arithmetic expression may be simply an attribute or a constant.

The following example demonstrates the basis for the use of the generalized projection operation. Suppose we have a relation *credit-info*, as depicted in Figure 3.24, which lists the credit limit and expenses so far (the *credit-balance* on the account). If we want to find how much more each person can spend, we can write the following expression:

$$\Pi_{customer\text{-}name,\ limit\ -\ credit\text{-}balance}\ (credit\text{-}info)$$

customer-name	*limit*	*credit-balance*
Jones	6000	700
Smith	2000	400
Hayes	1500	1500
Curry	2000	1750

Figure 3.24 The *credit-info* relation.

customer-name	*limit* − *credit-balance*
Jones	5300
Smith	1600
Hayes	0
Curry	250

Figure 3.25 The result of $\Pi_{customer\text{-}name,\ limit\ -\ credit\text{-}balance}$ (*credit-info*).

Figure 3.25 shows the result of applying this expression to the relation in Figure 3.24.

3.5.2 Outer Join

The *outer-join* operation is an extension of the join operation to deal with missing information. Suppose that we have the relations with the following schemas, which contain data on full-time employees:

employee (*employee-name, street, city*)
ft-works (*employee-name, branch-name, salary*)

Let us consider the *employee* and *ft-works* relations shown in Figure 3.26. Suppose that we want to generate a single relation with all the information (street, city, branch name, and salary) about full-time employees. A possible approach would be to use the natural-join operation as follows:

$$employee \bowtie ft\text{-}works$$

The result of this expression is shown in Figure 3.27. Notice that we have lost the street and city information about Smith, since the tuple describing Smith is absent from the *ft-works* relation; similarly, we have lost the branch name and salary information about Gates, since the tuple describing Gates is absent from the *employee* relation.

employee-name	*street*	*city*
Coyote	Toon	Hollywood
Rabbit	Tunnel	Carrotville
Smith	Revolver	Death Valley
Williams	Seaview	Seattle

employee-name	*branch-name*	*salary*
Coyote	Mesa	1500
Rabbit	Mesa	1300
Gates	Redmond	5300
Williams	Redmond	1500

Figure 3.26 The *employee* and *ft-works* relations.

employee-name	*street*	*city*	*branch-name*	*salary*
Coyote	Toon	Hollywood	Mesa	1500
Rabbit	Tunnel	Carrotville	Mesa	1300
Williams	Seaview	Seattle	Redmond	1500

Figure 3.27 The result of *employee* ⋈ *ft-works*.

We can use the *outer-join* operation to avoid this loss of information. There are actually three forms of the operation: *left outer join*, denoted ⟕; *right outer join*, denoted ⟖; and *full outer join*, denoted ⟗. All three forms of outer join compute the join, and add extra tuples to the result of the join. The results of the expressions *employee* ⟕ *ft-works*, *employee* ⟖ *ft-works* and *employee* ⟗ *ft-works* are shown in Figures 3.28, 3.29, and 3.30, respectively.

The left outer join takes all tuples in the left relation that did not match with any tuple in the right relation, pads the tuples with null values for all other attributes from the right relation, and adds them to the result of the natural join. In Figure 3.28, tuple (Smith, Revolver, Death Valley, *null*, *null*) is such a tuple. All information from the left relation is present in the result of the left outer join.

The right outer join is symmetric with the left outer join: Tuples from the right relation that did not match any from the left relation are padded with nulls and added to the result of the natural join. In Figure 3.29, tuple (Gates, *null*, *null*, Redmond, 5300) is such a tuple. Thus, all information from the right relation is present in the result of the right outer join.

The full outer join does both of those operations, padding tuples from left relation that did not match any from the right relation, as well as tuples from the right relation that did not match any from the left relation, and adding them to the result of the join. Figure 3.30 shows the result of a full outer join.

3.5.3 Aggregate Functions

Aggregate functions are functions that take a collection of values and return a single value as a result. For example, the aggregate function **sum** takes a collection of values and returns the sum of the values. Thus, the function **sum** applied on the collection

$$< 1, 1, 3, 4, 4, 11 >$$

employee-name	*street*	*city*	*branch-name*	*salary*
Coyote	Toon	Hollywood	Mesa	1500
Rabbit	Tunnel	Carrotville	Mesa	1300
Williams	Seaview	Seattle	Redmond	1500
Smith	Revolver	Death Valley	*null*	*null*

Figure 3.28 Result of *employee* ⟕ *ft-works*.

employee-name	*street*	*city*	*branch-name*	*salary*
Coyote	Toon	Hollywood	Mesa	1500
Rabbit	Tunnel	Carrotville	Mesa	1300
Williams	Seaview	Seattle	Redmond	1500
Gates	*null*	*null*	Redmond	5300

Figure 3.29 Result of *employee* ⟕ *ft-works*.

returns the value 24. The aggregate function **avg** returns the average of the values. When applied to the preceding collection, it returns the value 4. The aggregate function **count** returns the number of the elements in the collection, and would return 6 on the preceding collection. Other common aggregate functions include **min** and **max**, which return the minimum and maximum values in a collection; they return 1 and 11, respectively on the preceding collection.

The collections on which aggregate functions are used can have multiple occurrences of a value; the order in which the values appear is not relevant. Such collections are called *multisets*. Sets are a special case of multisets, where there is only one copy of each element.

To illustrate the concept of aggregation, we shall use the *pt-works* relation depicted in Figure 3.31, showing part-time employees. Suppose that we wanted to find out the total sum of salaries of all the part-time employees in the bank. The relational-algebra expression for this query is:

$$\mathbf{sum}_{\,salary}(pt\text{-}works)$$

The result of this query is a relation with a single attribute, containing a single row with a numerical value corresponding to the sum of all the salaries of all employees working part-time in the bank.

There are cases where we must eliminate multiple occurrences of a value prior to computing an aggregate function. If we do want to eliminate duplicates, we use the same function names as before, with the addition of the hyphenated string "**distinct**" appended to the end of the function name (for example, **count-distinct**). An example arises in the query "Find the number of branches appearing

employee-name	*street*	*city*	*branch-name*	*salary*
Coyote	Toon	Hollywood	Mesa	1500
Rabbit	Tunnel	Carrotville	Mesa	1300
Williams	Seaview	Seattle	Redmond	1500
Smith	Revolver	Death Valley	*null*	*null*
Gates	*null*	*null*	Redmond	5300

Figure 3.30 Result of *employee* ⟗ *ft-works*

employee-name	*branch-name*	*salary*
Johnson	Downtown	1500
Loreena	Downtown	1300
Peterson	Downtown	2500
Sato	Austin	1600
Rao	Austin	1500
Gopal	Perryridge	5300
Adams	Perryridge	1500
Brown	Perryridge	1300

Figure 3.31 The *pt-works* relation.

in the *pt-works* relation." In this case, a branch name counts only once, regardless of the number of employees working that branch. We write this query as follows:

$$\textbf{count-distinct}_{\,branch\text{-}name}(pt\text{-}works)$$

For the relation shown in Figure 3.31, the result of this query is the value 3.

There are circumstances where we would like to apply the aggregate function not only to a single set of tuples, but also to several groups, where each group is a set of tuples; we do so by using an operation called *grouping*. For example, we may want to find the total salary sum of all part-time employees at each branch of the bank individually, rather than in the entire bank. To do so, we need to partition the relation *pt-works* into *groups* based on the branch, and to apply the aggregate function on each group.

The following expression using the aggregation operator $\mathcal{G}$ achieves the desired result:

$$_{branch\text{-}name}\mathcal{G}\textbf{sum}_{\,salary}(pt\text{-}works)$$

The meaning of the expression is as follows. The attribute *branch-name* to the

employee-name	*branch-name*	*salary*
Johnson	Downtown	1500
Loreena	Downtown	1300
Peterson	Downtown	2500
Sato	Austin	1600
Rao	Austin	1500
Gopal	Perryridge	5300
Adams	Perryridge	1500
Brown	Perryridge	1300

Figure 3.32 The *pt-works* relation after grouping.

branch-name	*sum of salary*
Downtown	5300
Austin	3100
Perryridge	8100

Figure 3.33 Result of ${}_{branch\text{-}name}\mathcal{G}_{\mathbf{sum}\ salary}\,(pt\text{-}works)$.

left of the $\mathcal{G}$ indicates that the input relation *pt-works* must be divided into groups based on the value of *branch-name*. The resulting groups are shown in Figure 3.32. The expression $\mathbf{sum}_{salary}\,(pt\text{-}works)$ to the right of the $\mathcal{G}$ indicates that, for each group of tuples (that is, each branch), the aggregation function **sum** must be applied on the collection of values of the *salary* attribute. The output relation consists of tuples with the branch name, and the sum of the salaries for the branch; it is shown in Figure 3.33.

The general form of the *aggregation operation* $\mathcal{G}$ is as follows:

$$_{G_1, G_2, \ldots, G_n}\mathcal{G}_{F_1\ A_1,\ F_2\ A_2, \ldots,\ F_m\ A_m}(E)$$

where E is any relational-algebra expression, $G_1, G_2, \ldots, G_n$ constitute a list of attributes on which to group, each F_i is an aggregate function, and each A_i is an attribute name. The meaning of the operation is defined as follows. The tuples in result of expression E are partitioned into groups such that

1. All tuples in a group have the same values for $G_1, G_2, \ldots, G_n$.
2. Tuples in different groups have different values for $G_1, G_2, \ldots, G_n$.

Thus, the groups can be identified by the values of attributes $G_1, G_2, \ldots, G_n$. For each group $(g_1, g_2, \ldots, g_n)$, the result has a tuple $(g_1, g_2, \ldots, g_n, a_1, a_2, \ldots, a_m)$ where, for each i, a_i is the result of applying the aggregate function F_i on the multiset of values for attribute A_i in the group.

Going back to our earlier example, if we wanted to find the maximum salary for part-time employees at each branch, in addition to the sum of the salaries, we would write the expression

$$_{branch\text{-}name}\mathcal{G}_{\mathbf{sum}\ salary,\ \mathbf{max}\ salary}\,(pt\text{-}works)$$

The result of the expression is shown in Figure 3.34.

branch-name	*sum of salary*	*max of salary*
Downtown	5500	2500
Austin	3100	1600
Perryridge	7900	5300

Figure 3.34 Result of ${}_{branch\text{-}name}\mathcal{G}_{\mathbf{sum}\ salary,\ \mathbf{max}\ salary}\,(pt\text{-}works)$.

3.6 Modification of the Database

We have limited our attention until now to the extraction of information from the database. In this section, we address how to add, remove, or change information in the database.

We express database modifications using the assignment operation. We make assignments to actual database relations using the same notation as that described in Section 3.2.3 for assignment.

3.6.1 Deletion

A delete request is expressed in much the same way as a query. However, instead of displaying tuples to the user, we remove the selected tuples from the database. We can delete only whole tuples; we cannot delete values on only particular attributes. In relational algebra, a deletion is expressed by

$$r \leftarrow r - E$$

where r is a relation and E is a relational-algebra query.

Here are several examples of relational-algebra delete requests:

- Delete all of Smith's accounts.

$$account \leftarrow account - \sigma_{customer\text{-}name = \text{"Smith"}}(account)$$

- Delete all loans with amount in the range 0 to 50.

$$loan \leftarrow loan - \sigma_{amount \geq 0 \text{ and } amount \leq 50}(loan)$$

- Delete all accounts at branches located in Needham.

$$\begin{aligned} r_1 &\leftarrow \sigma_{branch\text{-}city = \text{"Needham"}}(account \bowtie branch) \\ r_2 &\leftarrow \Pi_{branch\text{-}name,\, account\text{-}number,\, balance}(r_1) \\ account &\leftarrow account - r_2 \end{aligned}$$

Note that, in the final example, we simplified our expression by using assignment to temporary relations (r_1 and r_2).

3.6.2 Insertion

To insert data into a relation, we either specify a tuple to be inserted or write a query whose result is a set of tuples to be inserted. Obviously, the attribute values for inserted tuples must be members of the attribute's domain. Similarly, tuples inserted must be of the correct arity. In relational algebra, an insertion is expressed by

$$r \leftarrow r \cup E$$

where r is a relation and E is a relational-algebra expression. We express the insertion of a single tuple by letting E be a constant relation containing one tuple.

Suppose that we wish to insert the fact that Smith has $1200 in account A-973 at the Perryridge branch. We write

$$account \leftarrow account \cup \{(\text{“Perryridge”}, \text{A-973}, 1200)\}$$
$$depositor \leftarrow depositor \cup \{(\text{“Smith”}, \text{A-973})\}$$

More generally, we might want to insert tuples based on the result of a query. Suppose that we want to provide as a gift for all loan customers of the Perryridge branch, a new \$200 savings account. Let the loan number serve as the account number for this savings account. We write

$$r_1 \leftarrow (\sigma_{branch\text{-}name = \text{“Perryridge”}} (borrower \bowtie loan))$$
$$r_2 \leftarrow \Pi_{branch\text{-}name,\ loan\text{-}number} (r_1)$$
$$account \leftarrow account \cup (r_2 \times \{(200)\})$$
$$depositor \leftarrow depositor \cup \Pi_{customer\text{-}name,\ loan\text{-}number} (r_1)$$

Instead of specifying a tuple as we did earlier, we specify a set of tuples that is inserted into both the *account* and *depositor* relation. Each tuple in the *account* relation has the *branch-name* (Perryridge), a *account-number* (which is the same as the loan number), and the initial balance of the new account (\$200). Each tuple in the *depositor* relation has as *customer-name* the name of the loan customer who is being given the new account and the same account number as the corresponding *account* tuple.

3.6.3 Updating

In certain situations, we may wish to change a value in a tuple without changing *all* values in the tuple. We can use the generalized projection operator to do this task:

$$r \leftarrow \Pi_{F_1, F_2, \ldots, F_n}(r)$$

where each F_i is either the ith attribute of r, if the ith attribute is not updated, or, if the attribute is to be updated, F_i is an expression, involving only constants and the attributes of r, which gives the new value for the attribute.

If we want to select some tuples from r and to update only them, we can use the following expression; here, P denotes the selection condition that chooses which tuples to update:

$$r \leftarrow \Pi_{F_1, F_2, \ldots, F_n}(\sigma_P(r)) \cup (r - \sigma_P(r))$$

To illustrate the use of the update operation, we suppose that interest payments are being made, and that all balances are to be increased by 5 percent. We write

$$account \leftarrow \Pi_{branch\text{-}name,\ account\text{-}number,\ balance\ \leftarrow\ balance\ *1.05} (account)$$

Let us now suppose that accounts with balances over \$10,000 receive 6-percent interest, whereas all others receive 5 percent. We write

$$account \leftarrow \Pi_{BN, AN, balance\ \leftarrow\ balance\ *1.06} (\sigma_{balance > 10000} (account))$$
$$\cup\ \Pi_{BN,\ AN,\ balance\ \leftarrow\ balance\ *1.05} (\sigma_{balance \leq 10000} (account))$$

where the abbreviations BN and AN stand for *branch-name* and *account-number*, respectively.

3.7 Views

In our examples up to this point, we have operated at the logical-model level. That is, we have assumed that the collection of relations we are given are the actual relations stored in the database.

It is not desirable for all users to see the entire logical model. Security considerations may require that certain data be hidden from users. Consider a person who needs to know a customer's loan number but has no need to see the loan amount. This person should see a relation described, in the relational algebra, by

$$\Pi_{customer\text{-}name,\ loan\text{-}number}\ (borrower \bowtie loan)$$

Aside from security concerns, we may wish to create a personalized collection of relations that is better matched to a certain user's intuition than is the logical model. An employee in the advertising department, for example, might like to see a relation consisting of the customers who have either an account or a loan at the bank, and the branches with which they do business. The relation that we would create for that employee is

$$\Pi_{branch\text{-}name,\ customer\text{-}name}\ (depositor \bowtie account)$$
$$\cup\ \Pi_{branch\text{-}name,\ customer\text{-}name}\ (borrower \bowtie loan)$$

Any relation that is not part of the logical model but is made visible to a user as a virtual relation, is called a *view*. It is possible to support a large number of views on top of any given set of actual relations.

3.7.1 View Definition

We define a view using the **create view** statement. To define a view, we must give the view a name, and must state the query that computes the view. The form of the **create view** statement is

create view *v* **as** <query expression>

where <query expression> is any legal relational-algebra query expression. The view name is represented by *v*.

As an example, consider the view consisting of branches and their customers. Assume that we wish this view to be called *all-customer*. We define this view as follows:

create view *all-customer* **as**

$$\Pi_{branch\text{-}name,\ customer\text{-}name}\ (depositor \bowtie account)$$
$$\cup\ \Pi_{branch\text{-}name,\ customer\text{-}name}\ (borrower \bowtie loan)$$

Once we have defined a view, we can use the view name to refer to the virtual relation that the view generates. Using the view *all-customer*, we can find all customers of the Perryridge branch by writing

$$\Pi_{customer\text{-}name}\ (\sigma_{branch\text{-}name = \text{"Perryridge"}}\ (all\text{-}customer))$$

Recall that we wrote the same query in Section 3.2.1 without using views.

View names may appear in any place that a relation name may appear, so long as no update operations are executed on the views. We study the issue of update operations on views in Section 3.7.2.

View definition differs from the relational-algebra assignment operation. Suppose that we define relation $r1$ as follows:

$$r1 \leftarrow \Pi_{branch\text{-}name,\ customer\text{-}name}\ (depositor \bowtie\ account)$$
$$\cup\ \Pi_{branch\text{-}name,\ customer\text{-}name}(borrower \bowtie\ loan)$$

The assignment operation is evaluated once, and $r1$ does not change when the relations *depositor*, *account*, *loan* or *borrower* are updated. In contrast, if there is any modification to these relations, the set of tuples in the view *all-customer* changes as well. Intuitively, at any given time, the set of tuples in the view relation is defined as the result of evaluation of the query expression that defines the view at that time.

Thus, if a view relation is computed and stored, it may become out of date if the relations used to define it are modified. Instead, views are typically implemented as follows. When a view is defined, the database system stores the definition of the view itself, rather than the result of evaluation of the relational-algebra expression that defines the view. Wherever a view relation is used in a query, it is replaced by the stored query expression. Thus, whenever the query is evaluated, the view relation is recomputed.

Certain database systems allow view relations to be stored, but they make sure that, if the actual relations used in the view definition change, the view is kept up to date. Such views are called *materialized views*. Applications in which a view is used frequently benefit from the use of materialized views, as do applications in which response time to certain view-based queries is of utmost importance. The benefits to queries from the materialization of a view must be weighed against the storage costs and the added overhead for updates.

3.7.2 Updates Through Views and Null Values

Although views are a useful tool for queries, they present significant problems if updates, insertions, or deletions are expressed with them. The difficulty is that a modification to the database expressed in terms of a view must be translated to a modification to the actual relations in the logical model of the database.

To illustrate the problem, we consider a clerk who needs to see all loan data in the *loan* relation, except *loan-amount*. Let *branch-loan* be the view given to the clerk. We define this view as

create view *branch-loan* **as**
$\Pi_{branch\text{-}name,\ loan\text{-}number}\ (loan)$

Since we allow a view name to appear wherever a relation name is allowed, the clerk can write:

$$branch\text{-}loan\ \leftarrow\ branch\text{-}loan \cup \{(\text{“Perryridge”, L-37})\}$$

This insertion must be represented by an insertion into the relation *loan*, since *loan* is the actual relation from which the view *branch-loan* is constructed. However, to insert a tuple into *loan*, we must have some value for *amount*. There are two reasonable approaches to dealing with this insertion:

- Reject the insertion, and return an error message to the user.
- Insert a tuple ("Perryridge", L-37, *null*) into the *loan* relation.

Let us illustrate another problem resulting from modification of the database through views:

create view *loan-info* **as**
$$\Pi_{customer\text{-}name,\ amount}(borrower \bowtie loan)$$

This view lists the loan amount for each loan that any customer of the bank has. Consider the following insertion through this view:

$$loan\text{-}info \leftarrow loan\text{-}info \cup \{(\text{"Johnson"}, 1900)\}$$

The only possible method of inserting tuples into the *borrower* and *loan* relations is to insert ("Johnson", *null*) into *borrower* and (*null*, *null*, 1900) into *loan*. Then, we obtain the relations shown in Figure 3.35. However, this update does not have the desired effect, since the view relation *loan-info* still does *not* include the tuple ("Johnson", 1900). (Recall that all comparisons involving *null* are defined to be **false**, so the natural join of *borrower* and *loan* does not contain the required tuple.) Thus, there is no way to update the relations *borrower* and *loan* using nulls to get the desired update on *loan-info*. borrower

branch-name	*loan-number*	*amount*
Downtown	L-17	1000
Redwood	L-23	2000
Perryridge	L-15	1500
Downtown	L-14	1500
Mianus	L-93	500
Round Hill	L-11	900
Perryridge	L-16	1300
null	*null*	1900

customer-name	*loan-number*
Jones	L-17
Smith	L-23
Hayes	L-15
Jackson	L-14
Curry	L-93
Smith	L-11
Williams	L-17
Adams	L-16
Johnson	*null*

Figure 3.35 Tuples inserted into *loan* and *borrower*.

Due to problems such as these, modifications are generally not permitted on view relations, except in limited cases. The general problem of database modification through views has been the subject of substantial research. The bibliographic notes mention recent works on this subject.

3.7.3 Views Defined Using Other Views

In Section 3.7.1, we mentioned that view relations may appear in any place that a relation name may appear, except for restrictions on the use of views in update expressions. Thus, one view may be used in the expression defining another view. For example, we can define the view *perryridge-customer* as follows:

create view *perryridge-customer* **as**

$$\Pi_{customer\text{-}name}\ (\sigma_{branch\text{-}name\,=\,\text{"Perryridge"}}\ (all\text{-}customer))$$

where *all-customer* is itself a view relation.

A view relation v_1 is said to *depend directly on* a view relation v_2 if v_2 is used in the expression defining v_1. An example of view dependency is shown pictorially in Figure 3.36. The figure indicates that the view *all-customer* depends directly on the relations *borrower* and *loan*, since the expression defining *all-customer* uses the other two views. Similarly the view *perryridge-customer* depends on the view *all-customer*. A graph such as the one shown in the figure is called a *dependency graph*; it has a node for each view, and a directed edge from view v_2 to view v_1 if v_1 depends directly on v_2.

A view relation v_1 is said to *depend on* view relation v_2 if and only if there is a path in the dependency graph from v_2 to v_1. In other words, view v_1 depends on view v_2 if either v_1 depends directly on v_2, or there is a sequence of view relations $r_1, r_2, \ldots, r_{n-1}, r_n$ such that v_1 depends directly on r_1, r_1 depends directly on r_2, and so on, until r_{n-1} depends directly on r_n, and r_n depends directly on v_2.

A view relation v is said to be *recursive* if it depends on itself. Pictorially, the dependency graph would have a cycle involving v if and only if v is recursive. In Chapter 5, we consider the meaning of recursive views; for now, we simply require that view definitions not be recursive.

View expansion is one way to define the meaning of views defined in terms of other views. Let view v_1 be defined by an expression e_1 that may itself contain uses of view relations. A view relation stands for the expression defining the view, and therefore a view relation can be replaced by the expression that defines it. If we modify an expression by replacing a view relation by the latter's definition, the

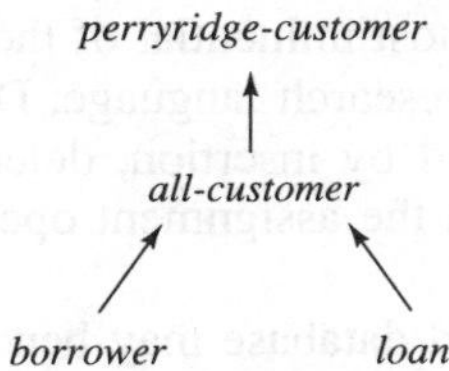

Figure 3.36 Dependency of views.

resultant expression may still contain other view relations. Hence, view expansion of an expression repeats the replacement step as follows:

repeat
 Find any view relation v_i in e_1
 Replace the view relation v_i by the expression defining v_i
until no more view relations are present in e_1

As long as the view definitions are not recursive, this loop will terminate. Thus, an expression e containing view relations can be understood as the expression resulting from view expansion of e, which does not contain any view relations.

We illustrate view expansion using the following expression:

$$\sigma_{customer\text{-}name=\text{"John"}}(perryridge\text{-}customer)$$

The view-expansion procedure initially generates

$$\sigma_{customer\text{-}name=\text{"John"}}(\Pi_{customer\text{-}name}\ (\sigma_{branch\text{-}name\ =\text{"Perryridge"}}\ (all\text{-}customer)))$$

it then generates

$$\sigma_{customer\text{-}name=\text{"John"}}\ (\Pi_{customer\text{-}name}\ (\sigma_{branch\text{-}name\ =\text{"Perryridge"}}\ (\Pi_{branch\text{-}name,\ customer\text{-}name}\ (depositor \bowtie account) \cup \Pi_{branch\text{-}name,\ customer\text{-}name}\ (borrower \bowtie loan))))$$

There are no more uses of view relations, and view expansion terminates.

3.8 Summary

The relational data model is based on a collection of tables. The user of the database system may query these tables, insert new tuples, delete tuples, and update (modify) tuples. There are several languages for expressing these operations. The tuple relational calculus and the domain relational calculus are nonprocedural languages that represent the basic power required in a relational query language. The relational algebra is a procedural language that is equivalent in power to both forms of the relational calculus when they are restricted to safe expressions. The algebra defines the basic operations used within relational query languages.

The relational algebra and the relational calculi are terse, formal languages that are inappropriate for casual users of a database system. Commercial database systems, therefore, use languages with more "syntactic sugar." In Chapters 4 and 5, we shall consider the three most influential of the commercial languages: SQL, QBE, and Quel, as well as the research language, Datalog.

Databases can be modified by insertion, deletion, or update of tuples. We used the relational algebra with the assignment operator to express these modifications.

Different users of a shared database may benefit from individualized views of the database. Views are "virtual relations" defined by a query expression. We used relational algebra as an example to show how such views can be defined and used. We evaluate queries involving views by replacing the view with the expression that defines the view. Views are useful mechanisms for simplifying database queries, but modification of the database through views may have potentially disadvantageous consequences. Therefore, database systems severely restrict updates through views. For reasons of query-processing efficiency, a view may be materialized—that is, stored physically. Updates that affect materialized views incur additional overhead.

Exercises

3.1. Design a relational database for a university registrar's office. The office maintains data about each class, including the instructor, the number of students enrolled, and the time and place of the class meetings. For each student–class pair, a grade is recorded.

3.2. Describe the differences in meaning between the terms *relation* and *relation schema*. Illustrate your answer by referring to your solution to Exercise 3.1

3.3. Design a relational database corresponding to the E-R diagram of Figure 3.37.

3.4. In Chapter 2, we showed how to represent many-to-many, many-to-one, one-to-many, and one-to-one relationship sets. Explain how primary keys help us to represent such relationship sets in the relational model.

3.5. Consider the relational database of Figure 3.38. For each of the following queries, give an expression in the relational algebra, the tuple relational calculus, and the domain relational calculus:

(*a*) Find the names of all employees who work for First Bank Corporation.

(*b*) Find the names and cities of residence of all employees who work for First Bank Corporation.

(*c*) Find the names, street address, and cities of residence of all employees who work for First Bank Corporation and earn more than $10,000 per annum.

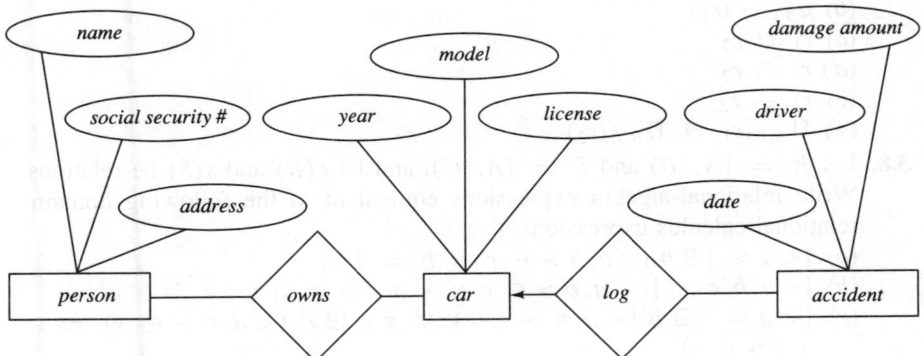

Figure 3.37 E-R diagram.

employee (*employee-name*, *street*, *city*)
works (*employee-name*, *company-name*, *salary*)
company (*company-name*, *city*)
manages (*employee-name*, *manager-name*)

Figure 3.38 Relational database for Exercises 3.5 and 3.12.

(*d*) Find the names of all employees in this database who live in the same city as the company for which they work.
(*e*) Find the names of all employees who live in the same city and on the same street as do their managers.
(*f*) Find the names of all employees in this database who do not work for First Bank Corporation.
(*g*) Find the names of all employees who earn more than every employee of Small Bank Corporation.
(*h*) Assume the companies may be located in several cities. Find all companies located in every city in which Small Bank Corporation is located.

3.6. Let the following relation schemas be given:

$$R = (A, B, C)$$

$$S = (D, E, F)$$

Let relations $r(R)$ and $s(S)$ be given. Give an expression in the tuple relational calculus that is equivalent to each of the following:
(*a*) $\Pi_A(r)$
(*b*) $\sigma_{B=17}\ (r)$
(*c*) $r \times s$
(*d*) $\Pi_{A,F}\ (\sigma_{C=D}(r \times s))$

3.7. Let $R = (A, B, C)$, and let r_1 and r_2 both be relations on schema R. Give an expression in the domain relational calculus that is equivalent to each of the following:
(*a*) $\Pi_A(r_1)$
(*b*) $\sigma_{B=17}\ (r_1)$
(*c*) $r_1 \cup r_2$
(*d*) $r_1 \cap r_2$
(*e*) $r_1 - r_2$
(*f*) $\Pi_{A,B}(r_1) \bowtie \Pi_{B,C}(r_2)$

3.8. Let $R = (A, B)$ and $S = (A, C)$, and let $r(R)$ and $s(S)$ be relations. Write relational-algebra expressions equivalent to the following domain-relational-calculus expressions:
(*a*) $\{< a > \mid \exists\, b\ (< a, b > \in r \wedge b = 17)\}$
(*b*) $\{< a, b, c > \mid < a, b > \in r \wedge < a, c > \in s\}$
(*c*) $\{< a > \mid \exists\, b\ (< a, b > \in r) \vee \forall\, c\ (\exists\, d\ (< d, c > \in s) \Rightarrow < a, c > \in s)\}$
(*d*) $\{< a > \mid \exists\, c\ (< a, c > \in s \wedge \exists\, b_1, b_2\ (< a, b_1 > \in r \wedge < c, b_2 > \in r \wedge b_1 > b_2))\}$

3.9. Let $R = (A, B)$ and $S = (A, C)$, and let $r(R)$ and $s(S)$ be relations. Using the special constant *null*, write tuple-relational-calculus expressions equivalent to each of the following:
(*a*) r ⟕ s
(*b*) r ⟗ s
(*c*) r ⟖ s

3.10. Consider the relation of Figure 3.19, which shows the result of the query "Find the names of all customers who have a loan at the bank." Rewrite the query to include not only the name, but also the city of residence for each customer. Observe that now customer Jackson no longer appears in the result, even though Jackson does in fact have a loan from the bank.
(*a*) Explain why Jackson does not appear in the result.
(*b*) Suppose that you want Jackson to appear in the result. How would you modify the database to achieve this effect?
(*c*) Again, suppose that you want Jackson to appear in the result. Write a query using an outer join that accomplishes this desire without your having to modify the database.

3.11. The outer-join operations extend the natural-join operation so that tuples from the participating relations are not lost in the result of the join. Describe how the theta join operation can be extended so that tuples from the left, right, or both relations are not lost from the result of a theta join.

3.12. Consider the relational database of Figure 3.38. Give an expression in the relational algebra for each request:
(*a*) Modify the database such that Jones now lives in Newtown.
(*b*) Give all employees of First Bank Corporation a 10-percent salary raise.
(*c*) Give all managers in this database a 10-percent salary raise.
(*d*) Give all managers in this database a 10-percent salary raise, unless the salary would be greater than \$100,000. In such cases, give only a 3-percent raise.
(*e*) Delete all tuples in the *works* relation for employees of Small Bank Corporation.

3.13. List two reasons why null values might be introduced into the database.

3.14. Certain systems allow *marked* nulls. A marked null $\perp_i$ is equal to itself, but if $i \neq j$, then $\perp_i \neq \perp_j$. One application of marked nulls is to allow certain updates through views. Consider the view *loan-info* (Section 3.7). Show how you can use marked nulls to allow the insertion of the tuple ("Johnson", 1900) through *loan-info*.

3.15. Using the bank example, write relational-algebra queries to find out how many accounts are held by more than two customers in the following ways:
(*a*) using an aggregate function.
(*b*) without using any aggregate functions.

3.16. Consider the relational database of Figure 3.38. Give a relational-algebra expression for each of the following queries:
(*a*) Find the company with the most employees.
(*b*) Find the company with the smallest payroll.

(*c*) Find those companies whose employees earn a higher salary, on average, than the average salary at First Bank Corporation.

3.17. List two reasons why we may choose to define a view.

3.18. List two major problems with processing update operations expressed in terms of views.

Bibliographic Notes

The relational model was proposed by E. F. Codd of the IBM San Jose Research Laboratory in the late 1960s [Codd 1970]. This work led to Codd's receipt of the prestigious ACM Turing Award in 1981 (Codd [1982]). Following Codd's original paper, several research projects were formed with the goal of constructing practical relational database systems, including System R at the IBM San Jose Research Laboratory, Ingres at the University of California at Berkeley, Query-by-Example at the IBM T. J. Watson Research Center, and the Peterlee Relational Test Vehicle (PRTV) at the IBM Scientific Center in Peterlee, United Kingdom. System R is discussed in Astrahan et al. [1976, 1979], and Chamberlin et al. [1981]. Ingres is discussed in Stonebraker [1980, 1986b] and Stonebraker et al. [1976]. Query-by-example is described in Zloof [1977]. PRTV is described in Todd [1976].

Numerous relational-database products are now commercially available. These include IBM's DB2, Ingres, Oracle, Sybase, Informix, Microsoft SQL Server. Database products for personal computers include Microsoft Access, dBase, and FoxPro. Information about the products can be found in their respective manuals. Textbooks devoted to specific commercial systems include Malamud [1989] and Date [1987], covering Ingres; Martin et al. [1989] and Date and White [1993], covering IBM's DB2 product; Date and White [1989] covering SQL/DS; and Corrigan and Gurry [1993] and Koch and Loney [1995], covering Oracle.

General discussion of the relational data model appears in most database texts. Gardarin and Valduriez [1989], Valduriez and Gardarin [1989], Atzeni and De Antonellis [1993], and Maier [1983] are texts devoted exclusively to the relational data model.

The original definition of relational algebra is given in Codd [1970]; that of tuple relational calculus is given in Codd [1972b]. A formal proof of the equivalence of tuple relational calculus and relational algebra was given in Codd [1972b]. Several extensions to the relational calculus have been proposed. Klug [1982] and Escobar-Molano et al. [1993] describe extensions to scalar aggregate functions. Extensions to the relational model and discussions concerning incorporation of null values in the relational algebra (the RM/T model), as well as outer joins, are presented in Codd [1979]. Codd [1990] is a compendium of E. F. Codd's papers on the relational model. Outer joins are also discussed in Date [1983b].

The problem of updating relational databases through views is addressed by Barsalou et al. [1991], Bancilhon and Spyratos [1981], Cosmadakis and Papadimitriou [1984], Dayal and Bernstein [1978, 1982], Keller [1985], and Langerak [1990].

Blakeley et al. [1986, 1989] and Griffin and Libkin [1995] describe techniques for maintenance of materialized views. Gupta and Mumick [1995] provide a recent survey of materialized view maintenance.

CHAPTER 4

SQL

The formal languages described in Chapter 3 provide a concise notation for representing queries. However, commercial database systems require a query language that is more user-friendly. In this chapter, we study the most influential commercially marketed product language, SQL. SQL uses a combination of relational-algebra and relational-calculus constructs.

Although we refer to the SQL language as a "query language," it contains many other capabilities besides querying a database. It includes features for defining the structure of the data, for modifying data in the database, and for specifying security constraints.

It is not our intention to provide a complete users' guide for SQL. Rather, we present SQL's fundamental constructs and concepts. Individual implementations of SQL may differ in details, or may support only a subset of the full language.

In Chapter 5, we present two other influential commercial languages, QBE and Quel, and a language used in research systems, Datalog. These languages represent a variety of styles. QBE is based on the domain relational calculus, Quel is based on the tuple relational calculus, and Datalog is based on the logic-programming language Prolog. All three languages have been influential in research database systems; the first two have also been influential in commercially marketed systems.

4.1 Background

SQL has clearly established itself as *the* standard relational-database language. There are numerous versions of SQL. The original version was developed at IBM's San Jose Research Laboratory (now the Almaden Research Center). This language, originally called Sequel, was implemented as part of the System R project in the early 1970s. The Sequel language has evolved since then, and its name has changed to SQL (Structured Query Language). Numerous products now support the SQL language.

In 1986, the American National Standards Institute (ANSI) and the International Standards Organization (ISO) published an SQL standard, called SQL-86. IBM published its own corporate SQL standard, the Systems Application Architecture Database Interface (SAA-SQL) in 1987. An extended standard for SQL, SQL-89, was published in 1989, and database systems today typically support at least the features of SQL-89. The current version of the ANSI/ISO SQL standard is the SQL-92 standard. The bibliographic notes provide references to these standards, as well as to ongoing standardization work on the SQL-3 standard.

In this section, we present a survey of SQL, based on the SQL-89 and SQL-92 standards. You should be aware that some SQL implementations may support only SQL-89, and thus will not support SQL-92. Features of SQL-92 that are not supported in SQL-89 are identified explicitly as SQL-92 features, for the benefit of those people who use database systems that do not fully support SQL-92.

The SQL language has several parts:

- **Data-definition language** (DDL). The SQL DDL provides commands for defining relation schemas, deleting relations, creating indices, and modifying relation schemas.

- **Interactive data-manipulation language** (DML). The SQL DML includes a query language based on both the relational algebra and the tuple relational calculus. It includes also commands to insert tuples into, delete tuples from, and to modify tuples in the database.

- **Embedded DML**. The embedded form of SQL is designed for use within general-purpose programming languages, such as PL/I, Cobol, Pascal, Fortran, and C.

- **View definition**. The SQL DDL includes commands for defining views.

- **Authorization**. The SQL DDL includes commands for specifying access rights to relations and views.

- **Integrity**. The SQL DDL includes commands for specifying integrity constraints that the data stored in the database must satisfy. Updates that violate integrity constraints are disallowed.

- **Transaction control**. SQL includes commands for specifying the beginning and ending of transactions. Several implementations also allow explicit locking of data for concurrency control.

In this chapter, we cover the interactive DML and the basic DDL feature of SQL.

The enterprise that we use in the examples in this chapter, as well as in Chapter 5, is the banking enterprise, with the following relation schemas:

Branch-schema = (*branch-name, branch-city, assets*)
Customer-schema = (*customer-name, customer-street, customer-city*)
Loan-schema = (*branch-name, loan-number, amount*)
Borrower-schema = (*customer-name, loan-number*)
Account-schema = (*branch-name, account-number, balance*)
Depositor-schema = (*customer-name, account-number*)

In Chapter 6, we discuss SQL's features regarding integrity. Transactions are covered in Chapters 13 and 14. Security and authorization are discussed in Chapter 19. In this chapter, as elsewhere in the text, we use hyphenated names for schema, relations, and attributes for ease of reading. In actual SQL systems, however, the underscore ("_") must be used instead.

4.2 Basic Structure

A relational database consists of a collection of relations, each of which is assigned a unique name. Each relation has a structure similar to that presented in Chapter 3. SQL allows the use of null values to indicate that the value either is unknown or does not exist. Provisions are made to allow a user to specify which attributes cannot be assigned null values, as we shall discuss in Section 4.11.

The basic structure of an SQL expression consists of three clauses: **select**, **from**, and **where**.

- The **select** clause corresponds to the projection operation of the relational algebra. It is used to list the attributes desired in the result of a query.
- The **from** clause corresponds to the Cartesian-product operation of the relational algebra. It lists the relations to be scanned in the evaluation of the expression.
- The **where** clause corresponds to the selection predicate of the relational algebra. It consists of a predicate involving attributes of the relations that appear in the **from** clause.

That the term *select* has different meaning in SQL and in the relational algebra is an unfortunate historical fact. We emphasize the different interpretations here to minimize potential confusion.

A typical SQL query has the form

select $A_1, A_2, \ldots, A_n$
from $r_1, r_2, \ldots, r_m$
where P

Each A_i represents an attribute, and each r_i a relation. P is a predicate. The query is equivalent to the relational-algebra expression

$$\Pi_{A_1,\ A_2,\ldots,A_n}(\sigma_P\,(r_1 \times r_2 \times \ldots \times r_m))$$

If the **where** clause is omitted, the predicate *P* is **true**. However, unlike that of a relational-algebra expression, the result of the SQL query may contain multiple copies of some tuples; we return to this issue in Section 4.2.8.

SQL forms the Cartesian product of the relations named in the **from** clause, performs a relational-algebra selection using the **where** clause predicate, and then projects the result onto the attributes of the **select** clause. In practice, SQL may convert the expression into an equivalent form that can be processed more efficiently. However, we shall defer concerns about efficiency to Chapter 12.

4.2.1 The select Clause

The result of an SQL query is, of course, a relation. Let us consider a simple query using our banking example, "Find the names of all branches in the *loan* relation":

select *branch-name*
from *loan*

The result is a relation consisting of a single attribute with the heading *branch-name*.

Formal query languages are based on the mathematical notion of a relation being a set. Thus, duplicate tuples never appear in relations. In practice, duplicate elimination is relatively time consuming. Therefore, SQL (like most other commercial query languages) allows duplicates in relations as well as in the results of SQL expressions. Thus, the preceding query will list each *branch-name* once for every tuple in which it appears in the *loan* relation.

In those cases where we want to force the elimination of duplicates, we insert the keyword **distinct** after **select**. We can rewrite the preceding query as

select distinct *branch-name*
from *loan*

if we want duplicates removed.

Note that SQL allows us to use the keyword **all** to specify explicitly that duplicates are not removed:

select all *branch-name*
from *loan*

Since duplicate retention is the default, we will not use **all** in our examples. To ensure the elimination of duplicates in the results of our example queries, we will use **distinct** whenever it is necessary. In most queries where **distinct** is not used, the exact number of duplicate copies of each tuple present in the query result is not important. However, the number is important in certain applications; we return to this issue in Section 4.2.8.

The asterisk symbol "*" can be used to denote "all attributes." Thus, the use of *loan*.* in the preceding **select** clause would indicate that all attributes of *loan* should be selected. A select clause of the form **select** * indicates that all attributes of all relations appearing in the **from** clause must be selected.

The **select** clause can also contain arithmetic expressions involving the operators, +, −, ∗, and /, and operating on constants or attributes of tuples. For example, the query

```
select branch-name, loan-number, amount * 100
from loan
```

will return a relation that is the same as the *loan* relation, except that the attribute *amount* is multiplied by 100.

SQL-92 also provides special data types, such as various forms of the *date* type, and allows several arithmetic functions to operate on these types.

4.2.2 The where Clause

Let us illustrate the use of the **where** clause in SQL. Consider the query "Find all loan numbers for loans made at the Perryridge branch with loan amounts greater that $1200." This query can be written in SQL as:

```
select loan-number
from loan
where branch-name = "Perryridge" and amount > 1200
```

SQL uses the logical connectives **and**, **or**, and **not**—rather than the mathematical symbols ∧, ∨, and ¬—in the **where** clause. The operands of the logical connectives can be expressions involving the comparison operators <, <=, >, >=, =, and <>. SQL allows us to use the comparison operators to compare strings and arithmetic expressions, as well as special types, such as date types.

SQL includes a **between** comparison operator to simplify **where** clauses that specify that a value be less than or equal to some value and greater than or equal to some other value. If we wish to find the loan number of those loans with loan amounts between $90,000 and $100,000, we can use the **between** comparison to write

```
select loan-number
from loan
where amount between 90000 and 100000
```

instead of

```
select loan-number
from loan
where amount <= 100000 and amount >= 90000
```

Similarly, we can use the **not between** comparison operator.

4.2.3 The from Clause

Finally, let us discuss the use of the **from** clause. The **from** clause by itself defines a Cartesian product of the relations in the clause. Since the natural join is defined in terms of a Cartesian product, a selection, and a projection, it is a relatively simple matter to write an SQL expression for the natural join.

We write the relational-algebra expression

$$\Pi_{customer\text{-}name,\, loan\text{-}number}\ (borrower\ \bowtie\ loan)$$

for the query "For all customers who have a loan from the bank, find their names and loan numbers." In SQL, this query can be written as

select distinct *customer-name, borrower.loan-number*
from *borrower, loan*
where *borrower.loan-number* = *loan.loan-number*

Notice that SQL uses the notation *relation-name.attribute-name*, as does the relational algebra, to avoid ambiguity in cases where an attribute appears in the schema of more than one relation. We could have written *borrower.customer-name* instead of *customer-name* in the **select** clause. However, since the attribute *customer-name* appears in only one of the relations named in the **from** clause, there is no ambiguity when we write *customer-name*.

Let us extend the preceding query, and consider a more complicated case in which we require also that customers have a loan from the Perryridge branch: "Find the names and loan numbers of all customers who have a loan at the Perryridge branch." To write this query, we shall need to state two constraints in the **where** clause, connected by the logical connective **and**:

select distinct *customer-name, borrower.loan-number*
from *borrower, loan*
where *borrower.loan-number* = *loan.loan-number* **and**
branch-name = "Perryridge"

SQL-92 includes extensions to perform natural joins, and outer joins in the **from** clause. We discuss these extensions in Section 4.10.

4.2.4 The Rename Operation

SQL provides a mechanism for renaming both relations and attributes. It uses the **as** clause, taking the form:

old-name **as** *new-name*

The **as** clause can appear in both the **select** and **from** clauses.

Consider again the query that we used earlier:

select distinct *customer-name, borrower.loan-number*
from *borrower, loan*
where *borrower.loan-number* = *loan.loan-number* **and**
branch-name = "Perryridge"

The result of this query is a relation with the following two attributes:

customer-name, loan-number.

The names of the attributes in the result are derived from the names of the attributes in the relations in the **from** clause.

We cannot, however, always derive names in this way. First, two relations in the **from** clause may have attributes with the same name, in which case a attribute name is duplicated in the result. Second, if we used an arithmetic expression in the **select** clause, the resultant attribute does not have a name. Third, even if a attribute name can be derived from the base relations as in the preceding example, we may want to change the attribute name in the result. Hence, SQL provides a way of renaming the attributes of a result relation.

For example, if we want the attribute name *loan-number* to be replaced with the name *loan-id*, we can rewrite the preceding query as

select distinct *customer-name, borrower.loan-number* **as** *loan-id*
from *borrower, loan*
where *borrower.loan-number* = *loan.loan-number* **and**
branch-name = "Perryridge"

4.2.5 Tuple Variables

The **as** clause is particularly useful in defining the notion of tuple variables, as is done in the tuple relational calculus. A tuple variable in SQL must be associated with a particular relation. Tuple variables are defined in the **from** clause via the use of the **as** clause. To illustrate, we rewrite the query "For all customers who have a loan from the bank, find their names and loan numbers" as

select distinct *customer-name, T.loan-number*
from *borrower* **as** *T, loan* **as** *S*
where *T.loan-number* = *S.loan-number*

Note that we define a tuple variable in the **from** clause by placing it after the name of the relation with which it is associated, with the keyword **as** in between (the keyword **as** is optional). When we write expressions of the form *relation-name.attribute-name*, the relation name is, in effect, an implicitly defined tuple variable.

Tuple variables are most useful for comparing two tuples in the same relation. Recall that, in such cases, we could use the rename operation in the relational algebra. Suppose that we want the query "Find the names of all branches that have assets greater than at least one branch located in Brooklyn." We can write the SQL expression

select distinct *T.branch-name*
from *branch* **as** *T, branch* **as** *S*
where *T.assets* > *S.assets* **and** *S.branch-city* = "Brooklyn"

Observe that we could not use the notation *branch.asset*, since it would not be clear which reference to *branch* is intended.

SQL-92 permits us to use the notation $(v_1, v_2, \ldots, v_n)$ to denote a tuple of arity n containing values $v_1, v_2, \ldots, v_n$. The comparison operators can be used on tuples, and the ordering is defined lexicographically. For example, $(a_1, a_2) <= (b_1, b_2)$ is true if $a_1 < b_1$, or $(a_1 = b_1) \wedge (a_2 <= b_2)$; similarly, the two tuples are equal if all their attributes are equal.

4.2.6 String Operations

The most commonly used operation on strings is pattern matching using the operator **like**. We describe patterns using two special characters:

- Percent (%): The % character matches any substring.
- Underscore (_): The _ character matches any character.

Patterns are case sensitive; that is, uppercase characters do not match lowercase characters, or vice versa. To illustrate pattern matching, we consider the following examples:

- "Perry%" matches any string beginning with "Perry".
- "%idge%" matches any string containing "idge" as a substring, for example, "Perryridge", "Rock Ridge", "Mianus Bridge", and "Ridgeway".
- "_ _ _" matches any string of exactly three characters.
- "_ _ _%" matches any string of at least three characters.

Patterns are expressed in SQL using the **like** comparison operator. Consider the query "Find the names of all customers whose street address includes the substring 'Main'." This query can be written as

select *customer-name*
from *customer*
where *customer-street* **like** "%Main%"

For patterns to include the special pattern characters (that is, %, and _), SQL allows the specification of an escape character. The escape character is used immediately before a special pattern character to indicate that the special pattern character is to be treated like a normal character. We define the escape character for a **like** comparison using the **escape** keyword. To illustrate, consider the following patterns, which use a backslash (\) as the escape character:

- **like** "ab\%cd%" **escape** "\" matches all strings beginning with "ab%cd".
- **like** "ab\\cd%" **escape** "\" matches all strings beginning with "ab\cd".

SQL allows us to search for mismatches instead of matches by using the **not like** comparison operator.

SQL also permits a variety of functions on character strings, such as concatenating (using "||"), extracting substrings, finding the length of strings, converting between uppercase and lowercase, and so on.

4.2.7 Ordering the Display of Tuples

SQL offers the user some control over the order in which tuples in a relation are displayed. The **order by** clause causes the tuples in the result of a query to appear in sorted order. To list in alphabetic order all customers who have a loan at the Perryridge branch, we write

```
select distinct customer-name
from borrower, loan
where borrower.loan-number = loan.loan-number and
        branch-name = "Perryridge"
order by customer-name
```

By default, the **order by** clause lists items in ascending order. To specify the sort order, we may specify **desc** for descending order or **asc** for ascending order. Furthermore, ordering can be performed on multiple attributes. Suppose that we wish to list the entire *loan* relation in descending order of *amount*. If several loans have the same amount, we order them in ascending order by loan number. We express this query in SQL as follows:

```
select *
from loan
order by amount desc, loan-number asc
```

To fulfill an **order by** request, SQL must perform a sort. Since sorting a large number of tuples may be costly, it is desirable to sort only when necessary.

4.2.8 Duplicates

The use of relations with duplicates has proved useful in several situations. SQL formally defines not only what tuples are in the result of a query, but also how many copies of each of those tuples appears in the result. We can define the duplicate semantics of an SQL query using *multiset* versions of the relational operators. We define the multiset versions of several of the relational-algebra operators here. Given multiset relations r_1 and r_2,

1. If there are c_1 copies of tuple t_1 in r_1, and t_1 satisfies selection σ_θ, then there are c_1 copies of t_1 in $\sigma_\theta(r_1)$.
2. For each copy of tuple t_1 in r_1, there is a copy of tuple $\Pi_A(t_1)$ in $\Pi_A(r_1)$, where $\Pi_A(t_1)$ denotes the projection of the single tuple t_1.
3. If there are c_1 copies of tuple t_1 in r_1 and c_2 copies of tuple t_2 in r_2, there are $c_1 * c_2$ copies of the tuple $t_1.t_2$ in $r_1 \times r_2$.

For example, suppose that relations r_1 with schema (A, B) and r_2 with schema (C) are the following multisets:

$$r_1 = \{(1, a), (2, a)\} \qquad r_2 = \{(2), (3), (3)\}$$

Then, $\Pi_B(r_1)$ would be $\{(a), (a)\}$, whereas $\Pi_B(r_1) \times r_2$ would be

$$\{(a, 2), (a, 2), (a, 3), (a, 3), (a, 3), (a, 3)\}$$

We can now define the how many copies of each tuple occur in the result of an SQL query. An SQL query of the form

select $A_1,\ A_2, \ldots, A_n$
from $r_1,\ r_2, \ldots, r_m$
where P

is equivalent to the relational-algebra expression

$$\Pi_{A_1,\ A_2,\ldots,A_n}(\sigma_P\ (r_1\ \times\ r_2\ \times\ \ldots\ \times\ r_m))$$

using the multiset versions of the relational operators σ, Π, and $\times$.

4.3 Set Operations

The SQL-92 operations **union**, **intersect**, and **except** operate on relations and correspond to the relational-algebra operations $\cup$, $\cap$, and $-$. Like union, intersection, and set difference in relational algebra, the relations participating in the operations must be *compatible*; that is, they must have the same set of attributes. SQL-89 has several restrictions on the use of the **union**, **intersect**, and **except** operations, and certain products do not support these operations.

Let us demonstrate how several of the example queries that we considered in Chapter 3 can be written in SQL. We will construct queries involving the **union**, **intersect**, and **except** operations of two sets: the set of all customers who have an account at the bank, which can be derived by

select *customer-name*
from *depositor*

and the set of customers who have a loan at the bank, which can be derived by

select *customer-name*
from *borrower*

We shall refer to the relations obtained as the result of the preceding queries as *d* and *b*, respectively.

4.3.1 The Union Operation

To find all customers having a loan, an account, or both at the bank, we write

(**select** *customer-name*
from *depositor*)
union
(**select** *customer-name*
from *borrower*)

The **union** operation automatically eliminates duplicates, unlike the **select** clause. Thus, in the preceding query, if a customer—say, Jones—has several accounts or loans (or both) at the bank, then Jones will appear only once in the result.

If we want to retain all duplicates, we must write **union all** in place of **union**:

```
(select customer-name
 from depositor)
union all
(select customer-name
 from borrower)
```

The number of duplicate tuples in the result is equal to the total number of duplicates that appear in both *d* and *b*. Thus, if Jones has three accounts and two loans at the bank, then there will be five tuples with the name Jones in the result.

4.3.2 The Intersect Operation

To find all customers who have both a loan and an account at the bank, we write

```
(select distinct customer-name
 from depositor)
intersect
(select distinct customer-name
 from borrower)
```

The **intersect** operation automatically eliminates duplicates. Thus, in the preceding query, if a customer—say, Jones—has several accounts and loans at the bank, then Jones will appear only once in the result.

If we want to retain all duplicates, we must write **intersect all** in place of **intersect**:

```
(select customer-name
 from depositor)
intersect all
(select customer-name
 from borrower)
```

The number of duplicate tuples that appear in the result is equal to the minimum number of duplicates in both *d* and *b*. Thus, if Jones has three accounts and two loans at the bank, then there will be two tuples with the name Jones in the result.

4.3.3 The Except Operation

To find all customers who have an account but no loan at the bank, we write

```
(select distinct customer-name
 from depositor)
except
(select customer-name
 from borrower)
```

The **except** operation automatically eliminates duplicates. Thus, in the preceding query, a tuple with customer name Jones will appear (exactly once) in the result only if Jones has an account at the bank, but has no loan at the bank.

If we want to retain all duplicates, we must write **except all** in place of **except**:

> (**select** *customer-name*
> **from** *depositor*)
> **except all**
> (**select** *customer-name*
> **from** *borrower*)

The number of duplicate copies of a tuple in the result is equal to the number of duplicate copies of the tuple in *d* minus the number of duplicate copies of the tuple in *b*, provided that the difference is positive. Thus, if Jones has three accounts and one loan at the bank, then there will be two tuples with the name Jones in the result. If, instead, this customer has two accounts and three loans at the bank, there will be no tuple with the name Jones in the result.

4.4 Aggregate Functions

Aggregate functions are functions that take a collection (a set or multiset) of values as input and return a single value. SQL offers five built-in aggregate functions:

- Average: **avg**
- Minimum: **min**
- Maximum: **max**
- Total: **sum**
- Count: **count**

The input to **sum** and **avg** must be a collection of numbers, but the other operators can operate on collections of nonnumeric data types, such as strings, as well.

As an illustration, consider the query "Find the average account balance at the Perryridge branch." We write this query as follows:

> **select avg** (*balance*)
> **from** *account*
> **where** *branch-name* = "Perryridge"

The result of this query is a relation with a single attribute, containing a single row with a numerical value corresponding to the average balance at the Perryridge branch. We can optionally give a name to the attribute of the result relation using the **as** clause.

There are circumstances where we would like to apply the aggregate function not only to a single set of tuples, but also to a group of sets of tuples; we specify this wish in SQL using the **group by** clause. The attribute or attributes given in the **group by** clause are used to form groups. Tuples with the same value on all attributes in the **group by** clause are placed in one group.

As an illustration, consider the query "Find the average account balance at each branch." We write this query as follows:

select *branch-name*, **avg** (*balance*)
from *account*
group by *branch-name*

Retaining of duplicates is important in computing an average. Suppose that the account balances at the (small) Brighton branch are \$1000, \$3000, \$2000, and \$1000. The average balance is \$7000/4 = \$1750.00. If duplicates were eliminated, we would obtain the wrong answer (\$6000/3 = \$2000).

There are cases where we must eliminate duplicates prior to computing an aggregate function. If we do want to eliminate duplicates, we use the keyword **distinct** in the aggregate expression. An example arises in the query "Find the number of depositors for each branch." In this case, a depositor counts only once, regardless of the number of accounts that depositor may have. We write this query as follows:

select *branch-name*, **count** (**distinct** *customer-name*)
from *depositor*, *account*
where *depositor.account-number* = *account.account-number*
group by *branch-name*

At times, it is useful to state a condition that applies to groups rather than to tuples. For example, we might be interested in only those branches where the average account balance is more than \$1200. This condition does not apply to a single tuple; rather, it applies to each group constructed by the **group by** clause. To express such a query, we use the **having** clause of SQL. Predicates in the **having** clause are applied after the formation of groups, so aggregate functions may be used. We express this query in SQL as follows:

select *branch-name*, **avg** (*balance*)
from *account*
group by *branch-name*
having avg (*balance*) > 1200

At times, we wish to treat the entire relation as a single group. In such cases, we do not use a **group by** clause. Consider the query "Find the average balance for all accounts." We write this query as follows:

select avg (*balance*)
from *account*

We use the aggregate function **count** frequently to count the number of tuples in a relation. The notation for this function in SQL is **count** (*). Thus, to find the number of tuples in the *customer* relation, we write

select count (*)
from *customer*

SQL does not allow the use of **distinct** with **count**(*). It is legal to use **distinct** with **max** and **min**, even though the result does not change. We can use the keyword **all** in place of **distinct** to specify duplicate retention, but, since **all** is the default, there is no need to do so.

If a **where** clause and a **having** clause appear in the same query, the predicate in the **where** clause is applied first. Tuples satisfying the **where** predicate are then placed into groups by the **group by** clause. The **having** clause, if it is present, is then applied to each group; the groups that do not satisfy the **having** clause predicate are removed. The remaining groups are used by the **select** clause to generate tuples of the result of the query.

To illustrate the use of both a **having** clause and a **where** clause in the same query, we consider the query "Find the average balance for each customer who lives in Harrison and has at least three accounts."

> **select** *depositor.customer-name*, **avg** (*balance*)
> **from** *depositor, account, customer*
> **where** *depositor.account-number* = *account.account-number* **and**
> *depositor.customer-name* = *customer.customer-name* **and**
> *customer-city* = "Harrison"
> **group by** *depositor.customer-name*
> **having count** (**distinct** *depositor.account-number*) >= 3

4.5 Null Values

As we indicated earlier, SQL allows the use of *null* values to indicate absence of information about the value of an attribute.

We can use the special keyword **null** in a predicate to test for a null value. Thus, to find all loan numbers that appear in the *loan* relation with null values for *amount*, we write

> **select** *loan-number*
> **from** *loan*
> **where** *amount* **is null**

The predicate **is not null** tests for the absence of a null value.

The use of a *null* value in arithmetic and comparison operations causes several complications. The result of an arithmetic expressions (involving, for example +, −, ∗ or /) is null if any of the input values is null. The result of any comparison involving a *null* value can be thought of as being **false**. More precisely, SQL-92 treats the result of such comparisons as **unknown**, which is neither **true** nor **false**. SQL-92 also allows us to test whether the result of a comparison is unknown, rather than being true or false. In almost all other cases, however, **unknown** is treated just like **false**. Details are provided in references cited in the bibliographic notes.

The existence of null values also complicates the processing of aggregate operators. Assume that some tuples in the *loan* relation have a null value for *amount*. Consider the following query to total all loan amounts:

select sum (*amount*)
from *loan*

The values to be summed in the preceding query include null values, since some tuples have a null value for *amount*. Rather than say that the overall sum is itself *null*, the SQL standard says that the **sum** operator should ignore *null* values in its input.

In general, aggregate functions treat nulls using the following rule: All aggregate functions except **count(*)** ignore null values in their input collection. As a result of null values being ignored, the collection of values may be empty. The **count** of an empty collection is defined to be 0, and all other aggregate operations return a value of null when applied on an empty collection. The effect of null values on some of the more complicated SQL constructs can be subtle.

4.6 Nested Subqueries

SQL provides a mechanism for the nesting of subqueries. A subquery is a **select-from-where** expression that is nested within another query. A common use of subqueries is to perform tests for set membership, set comparisons, and set cardinality. We study these uses in subsequent sections.

4.6.1 Set Membership

SQL draws on the relational calculus for operations that allow testing tuples for membership in a relation. The **in** connective tests for set membership, where the set is a collection of values produced by a **select** clause. The **not in** connective tests for the absence of set membership. As an illustration, reconsider the query "Find all customers who have both a loan and an account at the bank." Earlier, we wrote such a query by intersecting two sets: the set of depositors at the bank, and the set of borrowers from the bank. We can take the alternative approach of finding all account holders at the bank who are members of the set of borrowers from the bank. Clearly, this formulation generates the same results as did the previous one, but it leads us to write our query using the **in** connective of SQL. We begin by finding all account holders, and we write the subquery

(**select** *customer-name*
from *depositor*)

We then need to find those customers who are borrowers from the bank and who appear in the list of account holders obtained in the subquery. We do so by nesting the subquery in an outer **select**. The resulting query is

select distinct *customer-name*
from *borrower*
where *customer-name* **in** (**select** *customer-name*
from *depositor*)

This example shows that it is possible to write the same query several ways in SQL. This flexibility is beneficial, since it allows a user to think about the query in the way that appears most natural. We shall see that there is a substantial amount of redundancy in SQL.

In the preceding example, we tested membership in a one-attribute relation. It is also possible to test for membership in an arbitrary relation in SQL-92. We can thus write the query "Find all customers who have both an account and a loan at the Perryridge branch," which we saw earlier, in yet another way:

```
select distinct customer-name
from borrower, loan
where borrower.loan-number = loan.loan-number and
      branch-name = "Perryridge" and
      (branch-name, customer-name) in
            (select branch-name, customer-name
             from depositor, account
             where depositor.account-number = account.account-number)
```

We now illustrate the use of the **not in** construct. To find all customers who do have a loan at the bank, but do not have an account at the bank, we can write

```
select distinct customer-name
from borrower
where customer-name not in (select customer-name
                            from depositor)
```

The **in** and **not in** operators can also be used on enumerated sets. The following query selects the names of customers who have a loan at the bank, and whose names are neither "Smith" nor "Jones".

```
select distinct customer-name
from borrower
where customer-name not in ("Smith", "Jones")
```

4.6.2 Set Comparison

Consider the query "Find the names of all branches that have assets greater than those of at least one branch located in Brooklyn." In Section 4.2.5, we wrote this query as follows:

```
select distinct T.branch-name
from branch as T, branch as S
where T.assets > S.assets and S.branch-city = "Brooklyn"
```

SQL does, however, offer an alternative style for writing the preceding query. The phrase "greater than at least one" is represented in SQL by > **some**. This construct allows us to rewrite the query in a form that resembles closely our formulation of the query in English.

```
select branch-name
from branch
where assets > some (select assets
                     from branch
                     where branch-city = "Brooklyn")
```

The subquery

```
(select assets
 from branch
 where branch-city = "Brooklyn")
```

generates the set of all asset values for all branches in Brooklyn. The > **some** comparison in the **where** clause of the outer **select** is true if the *assets* value of the tuple is greater than at least one member of the set of all asset values for branches in Brooklyn.

SQL also allows < **some**, <= **some**, >= **some**, = **some**, and <> **some** comparisons. As an exercise, verify that = **some** is identical to **in**, whereas <> **some** is *not* the same as **not in**. The keyword **any** is synonymous to **some** in SQL. Early versions of SQL allowed only **any**. Later versions added the alternative **some** to avoid the linguistic ambiguity of the word *any* in English.

Now let us modify our query slightly. Let us find the names of all branches that have assets greater than that of each branch in Brooklyn. The construct > **all** corresponds to the phrase "greater than all." Using this construct, we write the query as follows:

```
select branch-name
from branch
where assets > all (select assets
                    from branch
                    where branch-city = "Brooklyn")
```

As it does for **some**, SQL also allows < **all**, <= **all**, >= **all**, = **all**, and <> **all** comparisons. As an exercise, verify that <> **all** is identical to **not in**.

As another example of set comparisons, consider the query "Find the branch that has the highest average balance." Aggregate functions cannot be composed in SQL. Thus, use of **max** (**avg** (. . .)) is not allowed. Instead, our strategy is as follows. We begin by writing a query to find all average balances, and then nest it as a subquery of a larger query that finds those branches for which the average balance is greater than or equal to all average balances:

```
select branch-name
from account
group by branch-name
having avg (balance) >= all (select avg (balance)
                             from account
                             group by branch-name)
```

4.6.3 Test for Empty Relations

SQL includes a feature for testing whether a subquery has any tuples in its result. The **exists** construct returns the value **true** if the argument subquery is nonempty. Using the **exists** construct, we can write the query "Find all customers who have both an account and a loan at the bank" in still another way:

```
select customer-name
from borrower
where exists (select *
              from depositor
              where depositor.customer-name = borrower.customer-name)
```

We can test the nonexistence of tuples in a subquery by using the **not exists** construct. We can use the **not exists** construct to simulate the set containment (that is, superset) operation: We can write "relation *A* contains relation *B*" as "**not exists** (B **except** A)". Although it is not part of the SQL-92 standard, the **contains** operator was present in some early relational systems. To illustrate the **not exists** operator, let us consider again the query "Find all customers who have an account at all the branches located in Brooklyn." For each customer, we need to see whether the set of all branches at which that customer has an account contains the set of all branches in Brooklyn. Using the **except** construct, we can write the query as follows:

```
select distinct S.customer-name
from depositor as S
where not exists ((select branch-name
                   from branch
                   where branch-city = "Brooklyn")
                  except
                  (select R.branch-name
                   from depositor as T, account as R
                   where T.account-number = R.account-number and
                         S.customer-name = T.customer-name))
```

Here, the subquery

```
(select branch-name
 from branch
 where branch-city = "Brooklyn")
```

finds all the branches in Brooklyn. The subquery

```
(select R.branch-name
 from depositor as T, account as R
 where T.account-number = R.account-number and
       S.customer-name = T.customer-name)
```

finds all the branches at which customer *S.customer-name* has an account. Thus, the outer **select** takes each customer and tests whether the set of all branches at which that customer has an account contains the set of all branches located in Brooklyn.

In queries that contain subqueries, a scoping rule applies for tuple variables. In a subquery, it is legal to use only tuple variables defined in the subquery itself or in any query that contains the subquery. If a tuple variable is defined both locally in a subquery and globally in a containing query, the local definition applies. This rule is analogous to the usual scoping rules used for variables in programming languages.

4.6.4 Test for the Absence of Duplicate Tuples

SQL includes a feature for testing whether a subquery has any duplicate tuples in its result. The **unique** construct returns the value **true** if the argument subquery contains no duplicate tuples. Using the **unique** construct, we can write the query "Find all customers who have only one account at the Perryridge branch," as follows:

```
select T.customer-name
from depositor as T
where unique (select R.customer-name
              from account, depositor as R
              where T.customer-name = R.customer-name and
                    R.account-number = account.account-number and
                    account.branch-name = "Perryridge")
```

We can test for the existence of duplicate tuples in a subquery by using the **not unique** construct. To illustrate this construct, consider the query "Find all customers who have at least two accounts at the Perryridge branch," which we write as

```
select distinct T.customer-name
from depositor T
where not unique (select R.customer-name
                  from account, depositor as R
                  where T.customer-name = R.customer-name and
                        R.account-number = account.account-number and
                        account.branch-name = "Perryridge")
```

Formally, the **unique** test on a relation is defined to fail if and only if the relation contains two tuples t_1 and t_2 such that $t_1 = t_2$. Since the test $t_1 = t_2$ fails if any of the fields of t_1 or t_2 are null, it is possible for **unique** to be true even if there are multiple copies of a tuple, as long as at least one of the attributes of the tuple is null.

4.7 Derived Relations

SQL-92 allows a subquery expression to be used in the **from** clause. If such an expression is used, then the result relation must be given a name, and the attributes can be renamed. We accomplish this renaming by using the **as** clause. For example, consider the subquery

```
(select branch-name, avg (balance)
 from depositor
 group by branch-name)
 as result (branch-name, avg-balance)
```

This subquery generates a relation consisting of the names of all branches and their corresponding average account balances. This temporary relation is named *result*, with the attributes *branch-name* and *avg-balance*.

Let us illustrate the use of a subquery expression in the **from** clause by considering the query "Find the average account balance of those branches where the average account balance is greater than $1200." We wrote this query in Section 4.4 using the **having** clause. We can now rewrite this query, without using the **having** clause, as follows:

```
select branch-name, avg-balance
from (select branch-name, avg (balance)
      from depositor
      group by branch-name)
      as result (branch-name, avg-balance)
where avg-balance > 1200
```

Note that we do not need to use the **having** clause, since we compute in the **from** clause the temporary relation *result*, and the attributes of *result* can be used directly in the **where** clause.

4.8 Views

We define a view in SQL using the **create view** command. To define a view, we must give the view a name, and must state the query that computes the view. The form of the **create view** command is

```
create view v as <query expression>
```

where <query expression> is any legal query expression. The view name is represented by *v*. Observe that the notation that we used for view definition in the relational algebra (see Chapter 3) is based on that of SQL.

As an example, consider the view consisting of branch names and the names of customers who have either an account or a loan at that branch. Assume that we want this view to be called *all-customer*. We define this view as follows:

```
create view all-customer as
    (select branch-name, customer-name
     from depositor, account
     where depositor.account-number = account.account-number)
   union
    (select branch-name, customer-name
     from borrower, loan
     where borrower.loan-number = loan.loan-number)
```

The attribute names of a view can be specified explicitly as follows:

```
create view branch-total-loan(branch-name, total-loan) as
select branch-name, sum(amount)
from loan
groupby branch-name
```

The preceding view gives for each branch the sum of the amounts of all the loans at the branch. Since the expression **sum**(*amount*) does not have a name, the attribute name is specified explicitly in the view definition.

View names may appear in any place that a relation name may appear. Using the view *all-customer*, we can find all customers of the Perryridge branch by writing

```
select customer-name
from all-customer
where branch-name = "Perryridge"
```

Complex queries are much easier to write and to understand if we structure them by breaking them into smaller views that we then combine, just as we structure programs by breaking their task into procedures. However, unlike a procedure definition, a **create view** clause creates a view definition in the database, and the view definition stays in the database until a command **drop view** *view-name* is executed. The SQL-3 standard, which is currently being developed, includes a proposal to support temporary views, which are not stored in the database.

4.9 Modification of the Database

We have restricted our attention until now to the extraction of information from the database. We show now how to add, remove, or change information using SQL.

4.9.1 Deletion

A delete request is expressed in much the same way as a query. We can delete only whole tuples; we cannot delete values on only particular attributes. In SQL, a deletion is expressed by

```
delete from r
where P
```

where P represents a predicate and r represents a relation. The **delete** statement first finds all tuples t in r for which $P(t)$ is true, and then deletes them from r. The **where** clause can be omitted, in which case all tuples in P are deleted.

We note that a **delete** command operates on only one relation. If we want to delete tuples from several relations, we must use one **delete** command for each relation. The predicate in the **where** clause may be as complex as a **select** command's **where** clause. At the other extreme, we can have an empty **where** clause. The request

```
delete from loan
```

deletes all tuples from the *loan* relation. (Well-designed systems will seek confirmation from the user before executing such a devastating request.)

Here are examples of SQL delete requests.

- Delete all of Smith's account records.

```
delete from depositor
where customer-name = "Smith"
```

- Delete all loans with loan amounts between \$1300 and \$1500.

```
delete from loan
where amount between 1300 and 1500
```

- Delete all accounts at every branch located in Perryridge.

```
delete from account
where branch-name in (select branch-name
                      from branch
                      where branch-city = "Perryridge")
```

The preceding **delete** request first finds all branches in Perryridge, and then deletes all *account* tuples pertaining to those branches.

Note that, although we may delete tuples from only one relation at a time, we may reference any number of relations in a **select-from-where** nested in the **where** clause of a **delete**. The **delete** request can contain a nested **select** that references the relation from which tuples are to be deleted. For example, suppose that we want to delete the records of all accounts with balances below the average at the bank. We could write

```
delete from account
where balance < (select avg (balance)
                 from account)
```

The **delete** statement first tests each tuple in the relation *accounts* to check whether the account has a balance less than the average at the bank. Then, all tuples that fail the test are deleted. Performing all the tests before performing any deletion is important—if some tuples were deleted before other tuples were tested, the average balance could have changed, and the final result of the **delete** would depend on the order in which the tuples were processed!

4.9.2 Insertion

To insert data into a relation, we either specify a tuple to be inserted or write a query whose result is a set of tuples to be inserted. Obviously, the attribute values for inserted tuples must be members of the attribute's domain. Similarly, tuples inserted must be of the correct arity.

The simplest **insert** statement is a request to insert one tuple. Suppose that we wish to insert the fact that there is an account A-9732 at the Perryridge branch and that is has a balance of $1200. We write

> **insert into** *account*
> **values** ("Perryridge", "A-9732", 1200)

In the preceding example, the values are specified in the order in which the corresponding attributes are listed in the relation schema. For the benefit of users who may not remember the order of the attributes, SQL allows the attributes to be specified as part of the **insert** statement. The following are SQL **insert** statements identical in function to the preceding one

> **insert into** *account* (*branch-name, account-number, balance*)
> **values** ("Perryridge", "A-9732", 1200)

> **insert into** *account* (*account-number, branch-name, balance*)
> **values** ("A-9732", "Perryridge", 1200)

More generally, we might want to insert tuples based on the result of a query. Suppose that we want to provide as a gift for all loan customers of the Perryridge branch, a new $200 savings account for each loan account they have. Let the loan number serve as the account number for the savings account. We write

> **insert into** *account*
> **select** *branch-name, loan-number*, 200
> **from** *loan*
> **where** *branch-name* = "Perryridge"

Instead of specifying a tuple as we did earlier in this section, we use a **select** to specify a set of tuples. The **select** statement is evaluated first, giving a set of tuples that is then inserted into the *account* relation. Each tuple has the *branch-name* (Perryridge), a *loan-number* (which serves as the account number for the new account), and an initial balance of the new account ($200).

We also need to add tuples to the *depositor* relation; we do so by writing

```
insert into depositor
    select customer-name, loan-number
    from borrower, loan
    where borrower.loan-number = loan.loan-number and
          branch-name = "Perryridge"
```

The preceding query inserts a tuple (*customer-name, loan-number*) into the *depositor* relation for each *customer-name* who has a loan in the Perryridge branch with loan number *loan-number*.

It is important that we evaluate the **select** statement fully before we carry out any insertions. If some insertions were carried out even as the **select** statement were being evaluated, a request such as

```
insert into account
    select *
    from account
```

might insert an infinite number of tuples! The first tuple in *account* would be inserted again into *account*, creating a second copy of the tuple. Since this second copy is part of *account* now, the **select** statement may find it, and a third copy will be inserted into *account*. This third copy may then be found by the **select** statement, and a fourth copy inserted, and so on, forever. Evaluating the **select** statement completely before performing insertions avoids such problems.

Our discussion of the **insert** statement considered only examples in which a value is given for every attribute in inserted tuples. It is possible, as we saw in Chapter 3, for inserted tuples to be given values on only some attributes of the schema. The remaining attributes are assigned a null value denoted by *null*. Consider the request

```
insert into account
    values (null, "A-401", 1200)
```

We know that account A-401 has $1200, but the branch name is not known. Consider the query

```
select account-number
from account
where branch-name = "Perryridge"
```

Since the branch at which account A-401 is maintained is not known, we cannot determine whether it is equal to "Perryridge".

We can prohibit the insertion of null values using the SQL DDL, which we discuss in Section 4.11.

4.9.3 Updates

In certain situations, we may wish to change a value in a tuple without changing *all* values in the tuple. For this purpose, the **update** statement can be used. As we could for **insert** and **delete**, we can choose the tuples to be updated using a query.

Suppose that annual interest payments are being made, and all balances are to be increased by 5 percent. We write

```
update account
set balance = balance * 1.05
```

The preceding statement is applied once to each tuple in *account*.

Let us now suppose that accounts with balances over $10,000 receive 6 percent interest, whereas all others receive 5 percent. We write two **update** statements:

```
update account
set balance = balance * 1.06
where balance > 10000

update account
set balance = balance * 1.05
where balance <= 10000
```

Note that, as we saw in Chapter 3, the order in which the two **update** statements are written is important. If we changed the order of the two statements, an account with a balance just under $10,000 would receive 11.3 percent interest. SQL-92 offers a **case** construct, which we can use to perform both the preceding updates in a single **update** statement; see Exercise 4.11.

In general, the **where** clause of the **update** statement may contain any construct legal in the **where** clause of the **select** statement (including nested **select**s). As with **insert** and **delete**, a nested **select** within an **update** statement may reference the relation that is being updated. As before, all tuples in the relation are first tested to see whether they should be updated, and the updates are carried out afterward. For example, the request "Pay 5 percent interest on accounts whose balance is greater than average" can be written as follows:

```
update account
set balance = balance * 1.05
where balance > select avg (balance)
                from account
```

4.9.4 Update of a View

The view-update anomaly that we discussed in Chapter 3 exists also in SQL. As an illustration, consider the following view definition:

```
create view branch-loan as
        select branch-name, loan-number
        from loan
```

Since SQL allows a view name to appear wherever a relation name is allowed, we can write

insert into *branch-loan*
values ("Perryridge", "L-307")

This insertion is represented by an insertion into the relation *loan*, since *loan* is the actual relation from which the view *branch-loan* is constructed. We must, therefore, have some value for *amount*. This value is a null value. Thus, the preceding **insert** results in the insertion of the tuple

("Perryridge", "L-307", *null*)

into the *loan* relation.

As we saw in Chapter 3, the view-update anomaly becomes more difficult to handle when a view is defined in terms of several relations. As a result, many SQL-based database systems impose the following constraint on modifications allowed through views:

- A modification is permitted through a view only if the view in question is defined in terms of one relation of the actual relational database—that is, of the logical-level database.

Under this constraint, the **update**, **insert**, and **delete** operations would be forbidden on the example view *all-customer* that we defined previously.

4.10 Joined Relations

In addition to providing the basic Cartesian-product mechanism for joining tuples of relations provided by earlier versions of SQL, SQL-92 also provides various other mechanisms for joining relations, including condition joins, and natural joins, as well as various forms of outer joins. These additional operations are typically used as subquery expressions in the **from** clause.

4.10.1 Examples

We illustrate the various join operations using the relations *loan* and *borrower* in Figure 4.1. We start with a simple example of inner joins. Figure 4.2 shows the

branch-name	*loan-number*	*amount*
Downtown	L-170	3000
Redwood	L-230	4000
Perryridge	L-260	1700

loan

customer-name	*loan-number*
Jones	L-170
Smith	L-230
Hayes	L-155

borrower

Figure 4.1 The *loan* and *borrower* relations.

branch-name	*loan-number*	*amount*	*customer-name*	*loan-number*
Downtown	L-170	3000	Jones	L-170
Redwood	L-230	4000	Smith	L-230

Figure 4.2 Result of *loan* **inner join** *borrower* **on** *loan.loan-number* = *borrower.loan-number*.

result of the expression

loan **inner join** *borrower* **on** *loan.loan-number* = *borrower.loan-number*

The expression computes the theta join of the *loan* and the *borrower* relations, with the join condition being *loan.loan-number* = *borrower.loan-number*. The attributes of the result consist of the attributes of the left-hand-side relation followed by the attributes of the right-hand-side relation. Note that the attribute *loan-number* appears twice in the figure—the first occurrence is from *loan*, and the second is from *borrower*.

We rename the result relation of a join and the attributes of the result relation using an **as** clause, as illustrated here:

loan **inner join** *borrower* **on** *loan.loan-number* = *borrower.loan-number*
as *lb(branch, loan-number, amount, cust, cust-loan-num)*

The second occurrence of *loan-number* has been renamed to *cust-loan-num*. The ordering of the attributes in the result of the join is important for the renaming.

Next, we consider an example of the use of the **left outer join** operation:

loan **left outer join** *borrower* **on** *loan.loan-number* = *borrower.loan-number*

The left outer join is computed as follows. First, the result of the inner join is computed as before. Then, for every tuple *t* in the left-hand-side relation *loan* that did not match any tuple in the right-hand-side relation *borrower* in the inner join, a tuple *r* is added to the result of the join as follows. The attributes of tuple *r* that are derived from the left-hand-side relation are filled in with the values from tuple *t*, and the remaining attributes of *r* are filled with null values. The resultant relation is shown in Figure 4.3. The tuples (Downtown, L-170, 3000) and (Redwood, L-230, 4000) are joined with tuples from *borrower* and appear in the result of the inner join, and hence in the result of the left outer join. On the other hand, the tuple (Perryridge, L-260, 1700) did not match any tuple from

branch-name	*loan-number*	*amount*	*customer-name*	*loan-number*
Downtown	L-170	3000	Jones	L-170
Redwood	L-230	4000	Smith	L-230
Perryridge	L-260	1700	*null*	*null*

Figure 4.3 Result of *loan* **left outer join** *borrower* **on** *loan.loan-number* = *borrower.loan-number*.

branch-name	*loan-number*	*amount*	*customer-name*
Downtown	L-170	3000	Jones
Redwood	L-230	4000	Smith

Figure 4.4 Result of *loan* **natural inner join** *borrower*.

borrower in the inner join, and hence a tuple (Perryridge, L-260, 1700, null, null) is present in the result of the left outer join.

Finally, we consider an example of the use of the **natural join** operation.

loan **natural inner join** *borrower*

This expression computes the natural join of the two relations. The only attribute name common to *loan* and *borrower* is *loan-number*. The result of the expression is shown in Figure 4.4. The result is similar to the result of the inner join with the **on** condition shown in Figure 4.2, since they have, in effect, the same join condition. However, the attribute *loan-number* appears only once in the result of the natural join, whereas it appears twice in the result of the join with the **on** condition.

4.10.2 Join Types and Conditions

In Section 4.10.1, we saw examples of the join operations permitted in SQL-92. Join operations take two relations and return as a result another relation. Although outer-join expressions are typically used in the **from** clause, they can be used anywhere that a relation can be used.

Each of the variants of the join operations in SQL-92 consists of a *join type* and a *join condition*. The join condition defines which tuples in the two relations match, and what attributes are present in the result of the join. The join type defines how tuples in each relation that do not match any tuple in the other relation (based on the join condition) are treated. Figure 4.5 shows some of the allowed join types and join conditions. The first join type is the inner join, and the other three are the three types of outer joins. The three join conditions are the **natural** join and the **on** condition, which we have seen before, and the **using** condition, which we discuss later.

The use of a join condition is mandatory for outer joins, but is optional for inner joins (if it is omitted, a Cartesian product results). Syntactically, the

Join types
inner join
left outer join
right outer join
full outer join

Join Conditions
natural
on <predicate>
using $(A_1, A_2, \ldots, A_n)$

Figure 4.5 Join types and join conditions.

keyword **natural** appears before the join type, as illustrated earlier, whereas the **on** and **using** conditions appear at the end of the join expression. The keywords **inner** and **outer** are optional, since the rest of the join type enables us to deduce whether the join is an inner join or an outer join.

The meaning of the join condition **natural**, in terms of which tuples from the two relations match, is straightforward. The ordering of the attributes in the result of a natural join is as follows. The join attributes (that is, the attributes common to both relations) appear first, in the order in which they appear in the left-hand-side relation. Next come all nonjoin attributes of the left-hand-side relation, and finally all nonjoin attributes of the right-hand-side relation.

The **right outer join** join type is symmetric to the **left outer join**. Tuples from the right-hand-side relation that do not match any tuple in the left-hand-side relation are padded with nulls and are added to the result of the right outer join.

The following expression is an example of combining the natural join condition with the right outer join type.

loan **natural right outer join** *borrower*

The result of the expression is shown in Figure 4.6. The attributes of the result are defined by the join type, which is a natural join; hence, *loan-number* appears only once. The first two tuples in the result are from the inner natural join of *loan* and *borrower*. The tuple (Hayes, L-155) from the right-hand-side relation does not match any tuple from the left-hand-side relation *loan* in the natural inner join. Hence, the tuple (null, L-155, Hayes) appears in the join result.

The join condition **using**($A_1, A_2, \ldots, A_n$) is similar to the natural join condition, except that the join attributes are the attributes $A_1, A_2, \ldots, A_n$, rather than all attributes that are common to both relations. The attributes $A_1, A_2, \ldots, A_n$ must consist of only attributes that are common to both relations, and they appear only once in the result of the join.

The **full outer join** join type is a combination of the left and right outer-join types. After the result of the inner join is computed, tuples from the left-hand-side relation that did not match with any from the right-hand-side are extended with nulls and are added to the result. Similarly, tuples from the right-hand-side relation that did not match with any tuples from the left-hand-side relation are also extended with nulls, and are added to the result.

For example, the result of the expression

loan **full outer join** *borrower* **using** (loan-number)

is shown in Figure 4.7.

branch-name	*loan-number*	*amount*	*customer-name*
Downtown	L-170	3000	Jones
Redwood	L-230	4000	Smith
null	L-155	null	Hayes

Figure 4.6 Result of *loan* **natural right outer join** *borrower*

branch-name	*loan-number*	*amount*	*customer-name*
Downtown	L-170	3000	Jones
Redwood	L-230	4000	Smith
Perryridge	L-260	1700	*null*
null	L-155	null	Hayes

Figure 4.7 Result of *loan* **full outer join** *borrower* **using**(*loan-number*)

As another example of the use of the outer-join operation, the query "Find all customers who have an account but no loan at the bank," can be written as

> **select** *d*-CN
> **from** (*depositor* **left outer join** *borrower*
> **on** *depositor.customer-name* = *borrower.customer-name*)
> **as** *db*1 (*d*-CN, *account-number*, *b*-CN, *loan-number*)
> **where** *b*-CN **is** *null*

Similarly, the query "Find all customers who have either an account or a loan (but not both) at the bank," can be written using natural full outer joins as:

> **select** *customer-name*
> **from** (*depositor* **natural full outer join** *borrower*)
> **where** *account-number* **is** *null* **or** *loan-number* **is** *null*

SQL-92 also provides two other join types, called **cross join** and **union join**. The first is equivalent to an inner join without a join condition; the second is equivalent to a full outer join on the "false" condition—that is, where the inner join is empty.

4.11 Data-Definition Language

In most of our discussions concerning SQL and relational databases, we have accepted a set of relations as given. Of course, the set of relations in a database must be specified to the system by means of a data definition language (DDL).

The SQL DDL allows the specification of not only a set of relations, but also information about each relation, including

- The schema for each relation
- The domain of values associated with each attribute
- The integrity constraints
- The set of indices to be maintained for each relation
- The security and authorization information for each relation
- The physical storage structure of each relation on disk

We shall discuss here schema definition and domain values; we defer discussion of the other SQL DDL features to Chapter 6.

4.11.1 Domain Types in SQL

The SQL-92 standard supports a variety of built-in domain types, including the following:

- **char**(n) is a fixed-length character string, with user-specified length n. The full form, **character**, can be used instead.
- **varchar**(n) is a variable-length character string, with user-specified maximum length n. The full form, **character varying**, is equivalent.
- **int** is an integer (a finite subset of the integers that is machine-dependent). The full form, **integer**, is equivalent.
- **smallint** is a small integer (a machine-dependent subset of the integer domain type).
- **numeric**(p, d) is a fixed-point number, with user-specified precision. The number consists of p digits (plus a sign), and d of the p digits are to the right of the decimal point. Thus, **numeric**(3,1) allows 44.5 to be stored exactly, but neither 444.5 or 0.32 can be stored exactly in a field of this type.
- **real, double precision** are floating-point and double-precision floating-point numbers, with machine-dependent precision.
- **float**(n) is a floating-point number, with user-specified precision of at least n digits.
- **date** is a calendar date, containing a (four digit) year, month, and day of the month.
- **time** is the time of day, in hours, minutes, and seconds.

Varying-length character strings, date, and time were not part of the SQL-89 standard.

SQL allows arithmetic and comparison operations on the various numeric domains, and comparison operations on all the domains listed here. SQL also provides a data type called **interval**, and allows computations based on dates and times, and on intervals. For example, if x and y are of type **date**, then $x - y$ is an interval whose value is the number of days from date x to date y. Similarly, adding or subtracting an interval to a date or time gives back a date or time, respectively.

It is often useful to be able to compare values from *compatible* domains. For example, since every small integer is an integer, a comparison $x < y$, where x is a small integer and y is an integer (or vice versa), makes sense. We make such a comparison by casting small integer x as an integer. A transformation of this sort is called a *type coercion*. Type coercion is used routinely in common programming languages, as well as in database systems.

As an illustration, suppose that the domain of *customer-name* is a character string of length 20, and the domain of *branch-name* is a character string of length 15. We see that, although the string lengths might differ, standard SQL will consider the two domains compatible.

As we discussed in Chapter 3, the *null* value is a member of all domains. For certain attributes, however, null values may be inappropriate. Consider a tuple in the *customer* relation where *customer-name* is null. Such a tuple gives a street and city for an anonymous customer; thus, it does not contain useful information. In cases such as this, we wish to forbid null values, by restricting the domain of *customer-name* to exclude null values.

SQL allows the domain declaration of an attribute to include the specification **not null**, and thus prohibits the insertion of a null value for this attribute. Any database modification that would cause a null to be inserted in a **not null** domain generates an error diagnostic. There are many situations where the prohibition of null values is desirable. A particular case where it is essential to prohibit null values is in the primary key of a relation schema. Thus, in our bank example, in the *customer* relation, we must prohibit a null value for the attribute *customer-name*, which is the primary key for *customer*.

The SQL-92 allows us to define domains using a **create domain** clause, as shown in the following example:

create domain *person-name* **char**(20)

We can then use the domain name *person-name* to define the type of an attribute, just like a built-in domain.

4.11.2 Schema Definition in SQL

We define an SQL relation using the **create table** command:

create table $r\,(A_1 D_1, A_2 D_2, \ldots, A_n D_n,$
$\langle$integrity-constraint$_1\rangle$,
$\ldots$,
$\langle$integrity-constraint$_k\rangle)$

where r is the name of the relation, each A_i is the name of an attribute in the schema of relation r, and D_i is the domain type of values in the domain of attribute A_i. The allowed integrity constraints include

primary key $(A_{j_1}, A_{j_2}, \ldots, A_{j_m})$

and

check(P)

The **primary key** specification says that attributes $A_{j_1}, A_{j_2}, \ldots, A_{j_m}$ form the primary key for the relation. Although the primary key specification is optional, it is generally a good idea to specify a primary key for each relation. The **check** clause specifies a predicate P that must be satisfied by every tuple in the relation; it

```
create table customer
    (customer-name   char(20) not null,
     customer-street char(30),
     customer-city   char(30),
     primary key (customer-name))

create table branch
    (branch-name     char(15) not null,
     branch-city     char(30),
     assets          integer,
     primary key (branch-name),
     check (assets >= 0))

create table account
    (account-number  char(10) not null,
     branch-name     char(15),
     balance         integer,
     primary key (account-number),
     check (balance >= 0))

create table depositor
    (customer-name   char(20) not null,
     account-number  char(10) not null,
     primary key (customer-name, account-number))
```

Figure 4.8 SQL data definition for part of the bank database.

was introduced in SQL-92. The **create table** command also includes other integrity constraints, which we shall discuss in Chapter 6.

Figure 4.8 presents a partial SQL DDL definition of our bank database. Recall that **null** is a legal value for every type in SQL, unless the type is specifically stated to be **not null**, as shown in the figure.

The attributes of a relation that are declared to be a primary key are required to be *nonnull* and *unique*; that is, no two tuples in the relation can be equal on all the primary-key attributes. If a newly inserted or modified tuple in a relation has null values for any primary-key attribute, or if the tuple has the same value on the primary-key attributes as does another tuple in the relation, an error is flagged, and the update is prevented. Similarly, an error is flagged, and the update prevented, if the **check** condition on the tuple fails. Note that the **not null** declarations that are shown in Figure 4.8 are redundant in SQL-92, since they are specified on attributes that are also part of the primary keys. However, in SQL-89, primary-key attributes were required to be declared **not null** explicitly in the manner shown in the figure.

A common use of the **check** clause is to ensure that attribute values satisfy specified conditions, in effect creating a powerful type system. For instance, the **check** clause in the **create table** command for relation *branch* checks that the value of **assets** is nonnegative. As another example, consider the following:

> **create table** *student*
> (*name* **char**(15) **not null**,
> *student-id* **char**(10) **not null**,
> *degree-level* **char**(15) **not null**,
> **primary key** (*student-id*),
> **check** (*degree-level* **in** ("Bachelors", "Masters", "Doctorate")))

Here, we use the **check** clause to simulate an enumerated type, by specifying that *degree-level* must be one of "Bachelors", "Masters", or "Doctorate".

The preceding **check** conditions can be tested quite easily, when a tuple is inserted or modified. However, in general, the **check** conditions can be more complex (and harder to check), since subqueries that refer to other relations are permitted in the **check** condition. For example, the following **check** condition could be specified on the relation *deposit*:

> **check** (*branch-name* **in** (**select** *branch-name* **from** *branch*))

The preceding **check** condition verifies that the *branch-name* in each tuple in the *deposit* relation is actually the name of a branch in the *branch* relation. Thus, the preceding **check** has to be checked not only when a tuple is inserted or modified in *deposit*, but also when the relation *branch* changes (in this case, when a tuple is deleted or modified in relation *branch*). The preceding condition is an example of a class of conditions called *foreign-key* constraints, which we discuss in Chapter 6. Complex **check** conditions, such as the preceding one, can be useful when we want to ensure integrity of data, but we should use them with care, since they may be costly to test.

A newly created relation is empty initially. We can use the **insert** command to load data into the relation. Many relational-database products have special bulk loader utilities to load an initial set of tuples into a relation.

To remove a relation from an SQL database, we use the **drop table** command. The **drop table** command deletes all information about the dropped relation from the database. The command

> **drop table** *r*

is a more drastic action than

> **delete from** *r*

The latter retains relation *r*, but deletes all tuples in *r*. The former deletes not only all tuples of *r*, but also the schema for *r*. After *r* is dropped, no tuples can be inserted into *r* unless it is recreated with the **create table** command.

We use the **alter table** command in SQL-92 to add attributes to an existing relation. All tuples in the relation are assigned *null* as the value for the new attribute. The form of the **alter table** command is

> **alter table** *r* **add** *A D*

where *r* is the name of an existing relation, *A* is the name of the attribute to be added, and D is the domain of the added attribute. We can drop attributes from a relation using a command

alter table r **drop** A

where r is the name of an existing relation, and A is the name of an attribute of the relation.

4.12 Embedded SQL

SQL provides a powerful declarative query language. Writing queries in SQL is typically much easier than is coding the same queries in a general-purpose programming language. However, access to a database from a general-purpose programming language is required for at least two reasons:

1. Not all queries can be expressed in SQL, since SQL does not provide the full expressive power of a general-purpose language. That is, there exist queries that can be expressed in a language such as Pascal, C, Cobol, or Fortran that cannot be expressed in SQL. To write such queries, we can embed SQL within a more powerful language.

   SQL is designed such that queries written in it can be optimized automatically and executed efficiently—and providing the full power of a programming language makes automatic optimization exceedingly difficult.

2. Nondeclarative actions—such as printing a report, interacting with a user, or sending the results of a query to a graphical user interface—cannot be done from within SQL. Applications typically have several components, and querying or updating data is only one component; other components are written in general-purpose programming languages. For an integrated application, the programs written in the programming language must be able to access the database.

The SQL standard defines embeddings of SQL in a variety of programming languages, such as Pascal, PL/I, Fortran, C, and Cobol. A language in which SQL queries are embedded is referred to as a *host* language, and the SQL structures permitted in the host language constitute *embedded* SQL.

Programs written in the host language can use the embedded SQL syntax to access and update data stored in a database. This embedded form of SQL extends the programmer's ability to manipulate the database even further. In embedded SQL, all query processing is performed by the database system. The result of the query is then made available to the program one tuple (record) at a time.

An embedded SQL program must be processed by a special preprocessor prior to compilation. Embedded SQL requests are replaced with host-language declarations and procedure calls that allow run-time execution of the database accesses. Then, the resulting program is compiled by the host-language compiler. To identify embedded SQL requests to the preprocessor, we use the EXEC SQL statement; it has the form:

EXEC SQL <embedded SQL statement > END-EXEC

The exact syntax for embedded SQL requests depends on the language in which SQL is embedded. For instance, a semi-colon is used instead of END-EXEC when SQL is embedded in C or Pascal.

We place the statement SQL INCLUDE in the program to identify the place where the preprocessor should insert the special variables used for communication between the program and the database system. Variables of the host language can be used within embedded SQL statements, but they must be preceded by a colon (:) to distinguish them from SQL variables.

Embedded SQL statements are of a form similar to the SQL statements that we described in this chapter. There are, however, several important differences, as we note here.

To write a relational query, we use the **declare cursor** statement. The result of the query is not yet computed. Rather, the program must use the **open** and **fetch** commands (discussed later in this section) to obtain the result tuples.

Consider the banking schema that we have used in this chapter. Assume that we have a host-language variable *amount*, and that we wish to find the names and cities of residence of customers who have more than *amount* dollars in any account. We can write this query as follows:

```
EXEC SQL
    declare c cursor for
    select customer-name, customer-city
    from deposit, customer
    where deposit.customer-name = customer.customer-name and
              deposit.balance > :amount
END-EXEC
```

The variable *c* in the preceding expression is called a *cursor* for the query. We use this variable to identify the query in the **open** statement, which causes the query to be evaluated, and in the **fetch** statement, which causes the values of one tuple to be placed in host-language variables.

The **open** statement for our sample query is as follows:

EXEC SQL **open** *c* END-EXEC

This statement causes the database system to execute the query and to save the results within a temporary relation. If the SQL query results in an error, the database system stores an error diagnostic in the SQL communication-area (SQLCA) variables, whose declarations are inserted by the SQL INCLUDE statement.

A series of **fetch** statements is executed to make tuples of the result available to the program. The **fetch** statement requires one host-language variable for each attribute of the result relation. For our example query, we need one variable to hold the *customer-name* value, and another to hold the *customer-city* value. Suppose that those variables are *cn* and *cc*, respectively. A tuple of the result relation is obtained by the statement:

EXEC SQL **fetch** *c* **into** *:cn*, *:cc* END-EXEC

The program can then manipulate the variables *cn* and *cc* using the features of the host programming language.

A single **fetch** request returns only one tuple. If we are to obtain all tuples of the result, the program must contain a loop to iterate over all tuples. Embedded SQL assists the programmer in managing this iteration. Although a relation is conceptually a set, the tuples of the result of a query are in some fixed physical order. When an **open** statement is executed, the cursor is set to point to the first tuple of the result. When a **fetch** statement is executed, the cursor is updated to point to the next tuple of the result. A variable in the SQLCA is set to indicate that no further tuples remain to be processed. Thus, we can use a **while** loop (or the equivalent, depending on the host language) to process each tuple of the result.

The **close** statement must be used to tell the database system to delete the temporary relation that held the result of the query. For our example, this statement takes the form

EXEC SQL **close** *c* END-EXEC

Embedded SQL expressions for database modification (**update**, **insert**, and **delete**) do not return a result. Thus, they are somewhat simpler to express. A database-modification request takes the form

EXEC SQL < any valid **update, insert,** or **delete**> END-EXEC

Host-language variables, preceded by a colon, may appear in the SQL database-modification expression. If an error condition arises in the execution of the statement, a diagnostic is set in the SQLCA.

The *dynamic* SQL component of SQL-92 allows programs to construct and submit SQL queries at run time. In contrast, embedded SQL statements must be completely present at compile time, and are compiled by the embedded SQL preprocessor. Using dynamic SQL, programs can create SQL queries as strings at run time (perhaps based on input from the user), and can either have them executed immediately, or have them *prepared* for subsequent use. Preparing a dynamic SQL statement compiles it, and subsequent uses of the prepared statement use the compiled version. The following is an example of the use of dynamic SQL from within a C program:

```
char * sqlprog = "update account set balance = balance *1.05
        where account-number = ?"
EXEC SQL prepare dynprog from :sqlprog;
char account[10] = "A-101";
EXEC SQL execute dynprog using :account;
```

The dynamic SQL program contains a ?, which is a place holder for a value that is provided when the SQL program is executed.

SQL-92 also contains a *module* language, which allows procedures to be defined in SQL. A module typically contains multiple SQL procedures. Each procedure has a name, optional arguments, and a single SQL statement. The procedures can be called directly from an external language without any special syntax.

4.13 Other SQL Features

Embedded SQL allows a host-language program to access the database, but it provides no assistance in presenting results to the user or in generating reports. Most commercial database products include a special language to assist application programmers in creating templates on the screen for a user interface, and in formatting data for report generation. These special languages are called *fourth-generation languages*.

Some fourth-generation languages also include high-level constructs to allow iteration over relations to be expressed directly, without forcing programmers to deal with the details of cursor management. However, unlike for SQL and embedded SQL, no single accepted standard currently exists for fourth-generation languages. Rather, each product provides its own proprietary language.

The SQL-92 standard defines the concepts of SQL sessions and SQL environments. SQL sessions provide the abstraction of a client and a server (which could possibly be remote). The client *connects* to an SQL server, establishing a session, executes a series of statements, and finally *disconnects* the session. In addition to the normal SQL commands, a session can also contain commands to *commit* the work carried out in the session, or to *rollback* the work carried out in the session.

An SQL environment contains several components, including a user identifier, and a *schema*. The presence of multiple schemas allows different applications and different users to work independently. All the usual SQL statements, including the DDL and DML statements, operate in the context of a schema. Schemas can be created and dropped by means of **create schema** and **drop schema** statements. If a schema is not set explicitly, a default schema associated with the user identifier is used, so different users see their own schemas. Another use of schemas is to allow multiple versions of an application—one a production version, and others versions being tested—to run on the same database system.

4.14 Summary

Commercial database systems do not use the terse, formal query languages of Chapter 3. Instead, they use languages based on the formal languages, but including much "syntactic sugar." Commercial database languages include constructs for update, insertion, and deletion of information, as well as for queries to the database. We have discussed the language SQL which has gained wide acceptance in commercial products.

We saw how to express queries and to modify the database in SQL. Modifications to the database may lead to the generation of null values in tuples. We discussed how nulls can be introduced, and how the SQL query language handles queries on relations containing null values. We showed how to define relations and create views. Further details on the SQL DDL appear in Chapters 6 and 19.

person (<u>*ss#*</u>, *name*, *address*)
car (<u>*license*</u>, *year*, *model*)
accident (<u>*date*</u>, <u>*driver*</u>, *damage-amount*)
owns (<u>*ss#*</u>, <u>*license*</u>)
log (<u>*license*</u>, <u>*date*</u>, <u>*driver*</u>)

Figure 4.9 Insurance database.

Exercises

4.1. Consider the insurance database of Figure 4.9, where the primary keys are underlined. Construct the following SQL queries for this relational database.
(*a*) Find the total number of people whose cars were involved in accidents in 1989.
(*b*) Find the number of accidents in which the cars belonging to "John Smith" were involved.
(*c*) Add a new customer to the database.
(*d*) Delete the Mazda belonging to "John Smith."
(*e*) Add a new accident record for the Toyota belonging to "Jones."

4.2. Consider the employee database of Figure 4.10. Give an expression in SQL for each of the following queries.
(*a*) Find the names of all employees who work for First Bank Corporation.
(*b*) Find the names and cities of residence of all employees who work for First Bank Corporation.
(*c*) Find the names, street address, and cities of residence of all employees who work for First Bank Corporation and earn more than $10,000.
(*d*) Find all employees in the database who live in the same cities as the companies for which they work.
(*e*) Find all employees in the database who live in the same cities and on the same streets as do their managers.
(*f*) Find all employees in the database who do not work for First Bank Corporation.
(*g*) Find all employees in the database who earn more than every employee of Small Bank Corporation.
(*h*) Assume that the companies may be located in several cities. Find all companies located in every city in which Small Bank Corporation is located.

employee (*employee-name*, *street*, *city*)
works (*employee-name*, *company-name*, *salary*)
company (*company-name*, *city*)
manages (*employee-name*, *manager-name*)

Figure 4.10 Employee database.

(*i*) Find all employees who earn more than the average salary of all employees of their company.
(*j*) Find the company that has the most employees.
(*k*) Find the company that has the smallest payroll.
(*l*) Find those companies whose employees earn a higher salary, on average, than the average salary at First Bank Corporation.

4.3. Consider the relational database of Figure 4.10. Give an expression in SQL for each of the following queries.
(*a*) Modify the database so that Jones now lives in Newtown.
(*b*) Give all employees of First Bank Corporation a 10-percent raise.
(*c*) Give all managers of First Bank Corporation a 10-percent raise.
(*d*) Give all managers of First Bank Corporation a 10-percent raise unless the salary becomes greater than $100,000; in such cases, give only a 3-percent raise.
(*e*) Delete all tuples in the *works* relation for employees of Small Bank Corporation.

4.4. Let the following relation schemas be given:

$$R = (A, B, C)$$
$$S = (D, E, F)$$

Let relations $r(R)$ and $s(S)$ be given. Give an expression in SQL that is equivalent to each of the following queries.
(*a*) $\Pi_A(r)$
(*b*) $\sigma_{B=17}\ (r)$
(*c*) $r\ \times\ s$
(*d*) $\Pi_{A,F}\ (\sigma_{C=D}(r\ \times\ s))$

4.5. Let $R = (A, B, C)$, and let r_1 and r_2 both be relations on schema R. Give an expression in SQL that is equivalent to each of the following queries.
(*a*) $r_1 \cup r_2$
(*b*) $r_1 \cap r_2$
(*c*) $r_1 - r_2$
(*d*) $\Pi_{AB}(r_1) \bowtie \Pi_{BC}(r_2)$

4.6. Let $R = (A, B)$ and $S = (A, C)$, and let $r(R)$ and $s(S)$ be relations. Write an expression in SQL for each of the queries below:
(*a*) $\{< a > \mid \exists\, b\ (< a, b > \in r \wedge b = 17)\}$
(*b*) $\{< a, b, c > \mid\ < a, b > \in r \wedge\ < a, c > \in s\}$
(*c*) $\{< a > \mid \exists\, c\ (< a, c > \in s \wedge \exists\, b_1, b_2\ (< a, b_1 > \in r \wedge\ < c, b_2 > \in r \wedge b_1 > b_2))\}$

4.7. Show that, in SQL, <> **all** is identical to **not in**.

4.8. Consider the relational database of Figure 4.10. Using SQL, define a view consisting of *manager-name* and the average salary of all employees who work for that manager. Explain why the database system should not allow updates to be expressed in terms of this view.

4.9. Consider the SQL query

> **select** $p.a1$
> **from** p, $r1$, $r2$
> **where** $p.a1 = r1.a1$ **or** $p.a1 = r2.a1$

Under what conditions does the preceding query select values of $p.a1$ that are either in $r1$ or in $r2$? Examine carefully the cases where one of $r1$ or $r2$ may be empty.

4.10. SQL-92 provides an operation called **case**, which is defined as follows:

> **case**
>   **when** $pred_1$ **then** $result_1$
>   **when** $pred_2$ **then** $result_2$
>   ...
>   **when** $pred_n$ **then** $result_n$
>   **else** $result_0$
> **end**

The operation returns $result_i$, where i is the first of $pred_1, pred_2, \ldots, pred_b$ that is satisfied; if none of the predicates is satisfied, the operation returns $result_0$.

Suppose that we have a relation *marks*(*student-id*, *score*) and we wish to assign grades to students based on the score as follows: grade F if $score < 40$, grade C if $40 \leq score < 60$, grade B if $60 \leq score < 80$, and grade A if $80 \leq score$. Write queries to do the following:

(*a*) Display the grade for each student, based on the *marks* relation.

(*b*) Find the number of students with each grade.

4.11. Use the **case** operation described in Exercise 4.10 to perform, in a single update statement, the following update to each tuple in the *account* relation: "Add 6-percent to *balance* if $balance > 10000$; add 5-percent if $balance \leq 10000$.

4.12. SQL-92 provides an n-ary operation called **coalesce**, which is defined as follows: **coalesce**($A_1, A_2, \ldots, A_n$) returns the first nonnull A_i in the list $A_1, A_2, \ldots, A_n$, and returns null if all of $A_1, A_2, \ldots, A_n$ are null. Show how to express the **coalesce** operation using the **case** operation.

4.13. Let a and b be relations with the schemas A(*name*, *address*, *title*) and B(*name*, *address*, *salary*), respectively. Show how to express a **natural full outer join** b using the **full outer join** operation with an **on** condition and the **coalesce** operation. Make sure that the result relation does not contain two copies of the attributes *name* and *address*, and that the solution is correct even if some tuples in a and b have null values for attributes *name* or *address*.

4.14. Give an SQL schema definition for the employee database of Figure 4.10. Choose an appropriate domain for each attribute and an appropriate primary key for each relation schema.

4.15. Write **check** conditions for the schema you defined in Exercise 4.14 to ensure that:

(*a*) Every employee works for a company located in the same city as the city in which the employee lives.

(*b*) No employee earns a salary higher than that of his manager.

4.16. Describe the circumstances in which you would choose to use embedded SQL rather than using SQL alone or using only a general-purpose programming language.

Bibliographic Notes

The original version of SQL, called Sequel 2, is described by Chamberlin et al. [1976]. Sequel 2 was derived from the languages Square [Boyce et al. 1975] and Sequel [Chamberlin and Boyce 1974]. The American National Standard SQL-86 is described in ANSI [1986]. The IBM Systems Application Architecture definition of SQL is defined by IBM [1987]. The official standards for SQL-89 and SQL-92 are available as ANSI [1989] and ANSI [1992], respectively. SQL92 is also described in U. S. Dept. of Commerce [1992], and in X/Open [1992, 1993]. The next version of the SQL standard, tentatively called SQL-3, is currently under development.

Cannan and Otten [1993] is a text devoted to SQL. Textbook descriptions of the SQL-92 language include Date and Darwen [1993] and Melton and Simon [1993]. Date and Darwen [1993] and Date [1993] include a critique of SQL-92. SQL-3 is discussed in Melton [1993] and Melton [1996].

Many database products support SQL features beyond those specified in the standards. More information on these features may be found in the SQL user manuals of the respective products. Date and White [1993] and Martin et al. [1989] cover SQL as implemented in DB2. Several relational database systems are surveyed in Valduriez and Gardarin [1989].

The processing of SQL queries, including algorithms and performance issues, is discussed in Chapter 12. Bibliographic references on these matters appear in that chapter as well.

CHAPTER 5

OTHER RELATIONAL LANGUAGES

In Chapter 4, we have described SQL—the most influential commercially marketed relational-database language. In this chapter, we study three additional languages: QBE, Quel and Datalog. We have chosen these languages because they represent a variety of styles. QBE is based on the domain relational calculus; Quel is based on the tuple relationa l calculus. These two languages have been influential not only in research database systems, but also in commercially marketed systems. Datalog has a syntax modeled after the Prolog language. Although not used commercially at present, Datalog has been used in several research database systems.

Like SQL, QBE and Quel contain many other capabilities besides querying a database. They include features for defining the structure of the data, for modifying data in the database, and for specifying security constraints.

It is not our intention to provide a complete users' guide for these languages. Rather, we present fundamental constructs and concepts. Individual implementations of a language may differ in details, or may support only a subset of the full language.

5.1 Query-by-Example

Query-by-Example (*QBE*) is the name of both a data-manipulation language and the database system that included this language. The QBE database system was developed at IBM's T. J. Watson Research Center in the early 1970s. The QBE data-manipulation language was later used in IBM's Query Management Facility

(QMF). Today, some database systems for personal computers support variants of QBE language. In this section, we consider only the data-manipulation language. It has two distinctive features:

1. Unlike most query languages and programming languages, QBE has a *two-dimensional* syntax: Queries *look* like tables. A query in a one-dimensional language (for example, SQL) *can* be written in one (possibly long) line. A two-dimensional language *requires* two dimensions for its expression. (There is a one-dimensional version of QBE, but we shall not consider it in our discussion).
2. QBE queries are expressed "by example." Instead of giving a procedure for obtaining the desired answer, the user gives an example of what is desired. The system generalizes this example to compute the answer to the query.

Despite these unusual features, there is a close correspondence between QBE and the domain relational calculus.

We express queries in QBE using *skeleton tables*. These tables show the relation schema, as presented in Figure 5.1. Rather than clutter the display with all skeletons, the user selects those skeletons needed for a given query and fills in the skeletons with *example rows*. An example row consists of constants and *example elements*, which are domain variables. To avoid confusion, in QBE domain variables are preceded by an underscore character (_), as in _*x*, and constants appear without any qualification. This convention is in contrast to those in most other languages, in which constants are quoted and variables appear without any qualification.

5.1.1 Queries on One Relation

Returning to our ongoing bank example, to find all loan numbers at the Perryridge branch, we bring up the skeleton for the *loan* relation, and fill it in as follows:

loan	*branch-name*	*loan-number*	*amount*
	Perryridge	P._*x*	

The preceding query causes the system to look for tuples in *loan* that have "Perryridge" as the value for the *branch-name* attribute. For each such tuple, the value of the *loan-number* attribute is assigned to the variable *x*. The value of the variable *x* is "printed" (actually, displayed), because the command P. appears in the *loan-number* column next to the variable *x*. Observe that this result is similar to what would be done to answer the domain-relational calculus query

$$\{\langle x\rangle \mid \exists\, b, a(\langle b, x, a\rangle \in loan \land b = \text{"Perryridge"})\}$$

QBE assumes that a blank position in a row contains a unique variable. As a result, if a variable does not appear more than once in a query, it may be omitted.

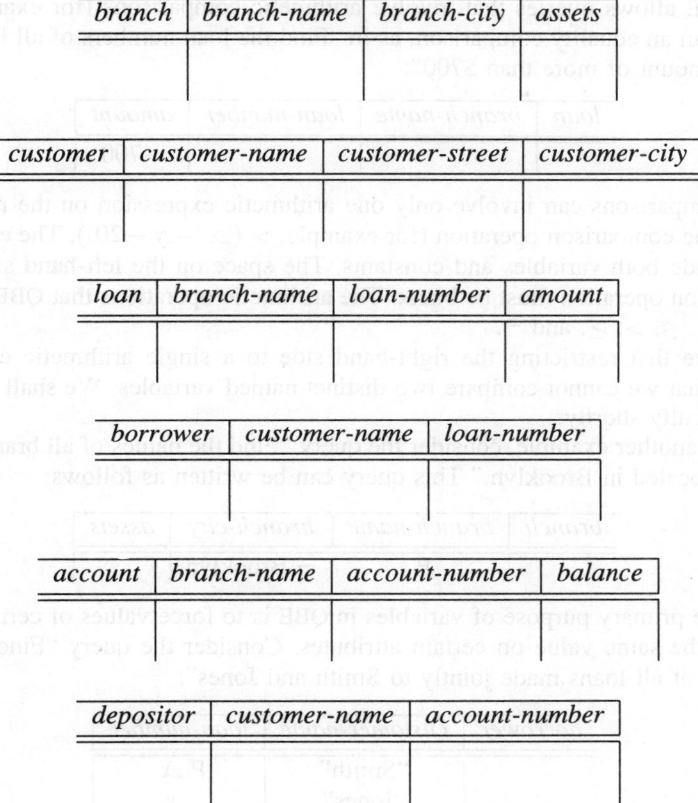

Figure 5.1 QBE skeleton tables for the bank example.

Our previous query could thus be rewritten as

loan	branch-name	loan-number	amount
	Perryridge	P.	

QBE (unlike SQL) performs duplicate elimination automatically. To suppress duplicate elimination, we insert the command ALL. after the P. command:

loan	branch-name	loan-number	amount
	Perryridge	P.ALL.	

To display the entire *loan* relation, we can create a single row consisting of P. in every field. Alternatively, we can use a shorthand notation by placing a single P. in the column headed by the relation name:

loan	branch-name	loan-number	amount
P.			

QBE allows queries that involve arithmetic comparisons (for example, >), rather than an equality comparison, as in "Find the loan numbers of all loans with a loan amount of more than $700":

loan	*branch-name*	*loan-number*	*amount*
		P.	>700

Comparisons can involve only one arithmetic expression on the right-hand side of the comparison operation (for example, $> (\_x + \_y - 20)$). The expression can include both variables and constants. The space on the left-hand side of the comparison operation must be blank. The arithmetic operations that QBE supports are $=, <, \leq, >, \geq$, and $\neg$.

Note that restricting the right-hand side to a single arithmetic expression implies that we cannot compare two distinct named variables. We shall deal with this difficulty shortly.

As another example, consider the query "Find the names of all branches that are not located in Brooklyn." This query can be written as follows:

branch	*branch-name*	*branch-city*	*assets*
	P.	¬ Brooklyn	

The primary purpose of variables in QBE is to force values of certain tuples to have the same value on certain attributes. Consider the query "Find the loan numbers of all loans made jointly to Smith and Jones":

borrower	*customer-name*	*loan-number*
	"Smith"	P._*x*
	"Jones"	_*x*

To execute the preceding query, the system finds all pairs of tuples in *borrower* that agree on the *loan-number* attribute, where the value for the *customer-name* attribute is "Smith" for one tuple and "Jones" for the other. The value of the *loan-number* attribute is then displayed.

Contrast the preceding query with "Find the loan numbers of all loans made to Smith, to Jones, or to both jointly," which can be written as

borrower	*customer-name*	*loan-number*
	"Smith"	P._*x*
	"Jones"	P._*y*

The critical distinction between these two queries lies in the use of the same domain variable (x) for both rows in the former query, but of distinct domain variables (x and y) in the latter query. Note that, in the domain relational calculus, the former query would be written as

$$\{\langle l\rangle \mid \exists\, x\ (\langle x, l\rangle \in borrower \wedge x = \text{"Smith"})$$

$$\wedge\ \exists\, x\ (\langle x, l\rangle \in borrower \wedge x = \text{"Jones"})\}$$

whereas the latter query would be written as

$$\{\langle l \rangle \mid \exists\, x\ (\langle x, l \rangle \in \textit{borrower} \wedge x = \text{“Smith”})$$

$$\vee\ \exists\, x\ (\langle x, l \rangle \in \textit{borrower} \wedge x = \text{“Jones”})\}$$

As another example, consider the query “Find all customers who live in the same city as Jones”:

customer	*customer-name*	*customer-street*	*customer-city*
	P._x		_y
	Jones		_y

5.1.2 Queries on Several Relations

QBE allows queries that span several different relations (analogous to Cartesian product or natural join in the relational algebra). The connections among the various relations are achieved through variables that force certain tuples to have the same value on certain attributes. As an illustration, suppose that we want to find the names of all customers who have a loan from the Perryridge branch. This query can be written as

loan	*branch-name*	*loan-number*	*amount*
	Perryridge	_x	

borrower	*customer-name*	*loan-number*
	P._y	_x

To evaluate the preceding query, the system finds tuples in *loan* with “Perryridge” as the value for the *branch-name* attribute. For each such tuple, the system finds tuples in *borrower* with the same value for the *loan-number* attribute as the *loan* tuple. The values for the *customer-name* attribute are displayed.

We can use a technique similar to the preceding one to write the query “Find the names of all customers who have both an account and a loan at the bank”:

depositor	*customer-name*	*account-number*
	P._x	

borrower	*customer-name*	*loan-number*
	_x	

Let us now consider the query “Find the names of all customers who have an account at the bank, but who do not have a loan from the bank.” We express queries that involve negation in QBE by placing a **not** sign (¬) under the relation name and next to an example row:

depositor	*customer-name*	*account-number*
	P._x	

borrower	*customer-name*	*loan-number*
¬	_x	

Compare the preceding query with our earlier query "Find the names of all customers who have both an account and a loan at the bank." The only difference is the ¬ appearing next to the example row in the *borrower* skeleton. This difference, however, has a major effect on the processing of the query. QBE finds all x values for which

1. There is a tuple in the *depositor* relation whose *customer-name* is the domain variable x.
2. There is no tuple in the *borrower* relation whose *customer-name* is the same as in the domain variable x.

The ¬ can be read as "there does not exist."

The fact that we placed the ¬ under the relation name, rather than under an attribute name, is important. A ¬ under an attribute name is a shorthand for $\neq$. Thus, to find all customers who have at least two accounts, we write

depositor	*customer-name*	*account-number*
	P._x	_y
	_x	¬ _y

In English, the preceding query reads "Display all *customer-name* values that appear in at least two tuples, with the second tuple having an *account-number* different from the first."

5.1.3 The Condition Box

At times, it is either inconvenient or impossible to express all the constraints on the domain variables within the skeleton tables. To overcome this difficulty, QBE includes a *condition box* feature that allows the expression of general constraints over any of the domain variables. Suppose that we modify the final query in Section 5.1.2 to be "Find all customers who are not named 'Jones' and who have at least two accounts." We want to include an "$x \neq$ Jones" constraint in this query. We do that by bringing up the condition box and entering the constraint "x ¬ = Jones":

conditions
x ¬ = Jones

Turning to another example, to find all account numbers with a balance between $1300 and $1500, we write

account	*branch-name*	*account-number*	*balance*
		P.	_x

conditions
_x ≥ 1300
_x ≤ 1500

As another example, consider the query "Find all branches that have assets greater than those of at least one branch located in Brooklyn." This query can be written as

branch	*branch-name*	*branch-city*	*assets*
	P._x		_y
		Brooklyn	_z

conditions
_y > _z

QBE allows complex arithmetic expressions to appear in a condition box. We can write the query "Find all branches that have assets that are at least twice as large as the assets of one of the branches located in Brooklyn" much as we did in the preceding query, by modifying the condition box to

conditions
_y ≥ 2 * _z

QBE also allows logical expressions to appear in a condition box. The logical operators are the words **and** and **or**, or the symbols "&" and "|". To find all account numbers of account with a balance between $1300 and $2000, but not exactly $1500, we write

account	*branch-name*	*account-number*	*balance*
		P.	_x

conditions
_x = (≥ 1300 **and** ≤ 2000 **and** ¬1500)

QBE includes an unconventional use of the **or** construct to allow comparison with a set of constant values. To find all branches that are located in either Brooklyn or Queens, we write

branch	*branch-name*	*branch-city*	*assets*
	P.	_x	

conditions
_x = (Brooklyn **or** Queens)

5.1.4 The Result Relation

The queries that we have written thus far have one characteristic in common: The results to be displayed appear in a single relation schema. If the result of a query includes attributes from several relation schemas, we need a mechanism to display the desired result in a single table. For this purpose, we can declare a temporary *result* relation that includes all the attributes of the result of the query. We print the desired result by including the command P. in only the *result* skeleton table.

As an illustration, consider the query "Find the *customer-name*, *account-number*, and *balance* for all accounts at the Perryridge branch." In relational algebra, we would accomplish this query as follows:

1. Join *depositor* and *account*.
2. Project *customer-name*, *account-number*, and *balance*.

To accomplish this query in QBE, we proceed as follows:

1. Create a skeleton table, called *result*, with attributes *customer-name*, *account-number*, and *balance*. The name of the newly created skeleton table (that is, *result*) must be different from any of the previously existing database relation names.
2. Write the query.

The resulting query is

account	*branch-name*	*account-number*	*balance*
	Perryridge	_y	_z

depositor	*customer-name*	*account-number*
	_x	_y

result	*customer-name*	*account-number*	*balance*
P.	_x	_y	_z

5.1.5 Ordering of the Display of Tuples

QBE offers the user some control over the order in which tuples in a relation are displayed. We gain this control by inserting either the command AO. (ascending order) or the command DO. (descending order) in the appropriate column. Thus, to list in ascending alphabetic order all customers who have an account at the bank, we write

depositor	*customer-name*	*account-number*
	P.AO.	

QBE provides a mechanism for sorting and displaying data in multiple columns. We specify the order in which the sorting should be carried out by including, with each sort operator (AO or DO), an integer surrounded by parentheses. Thus, to list all account numbers at the Perryridge branch in ascending alphabetic order with their respective account balances in descending order, we write

account	*branch-name*	*account-number*	*balance*
	Perryridge	P.AO(1).	P.DO(2).

The command P.AO(1). specifies that the account number should be sorted first; the command P.DO(2). specifies that the balances for each account should then be sorted.

5.1.6 Aggregate Operations

QBE includes the aggregate operators AVG, MAX, MIN, SUM, and CNT. We must postfix these operators with ALL. to create a multiset on which the aggregate operation is evaluated. The ALL. operator ensures that duplicates are not eliminated. Thus, to find the total balance of all the accounts maintained at the Perryridge branch, we write

account	*branch-name*	*account-number*	*balance*
	Perryridge		P.SUM.ALL.

Suppose that we wish to eliminate duplicates when an aggregate operator is used. Since all aggregate operators must be postfixed with ALL, we must add a new operator, UNQ, to specify that we want duplicates eliminated. Thus, to find the total number of customers who have an account at the bank, we write

depositor	*customer-name*	*account-number*
	P.CNT.UNQ.ALL.	

QBE also offers the ability to compute functions on groups of tuples using the G. operator, which is analogous to SQL's **group by** construct. Thus, to find the average balance at each branch, we can write

account	*branch-name*	*account-number*	*balance*
	P.G.		P.AVG.ALL._*x*

The average balance is computed on a branch-by-branch basis. The ALL. in the P.AVG.ALL. entry in the *balance* column ensures that all the balances are considered. If we wish to display the branch names in ascending order, we replace P.G. by P.AO.G.

To find the average account balance at only those branches where the average account balance is more than $1200, we add the following condition box:

conditions
AVG.ALL._*x* > 1200

To find the name, street and city of all customers who have more than one account at the bank, we write

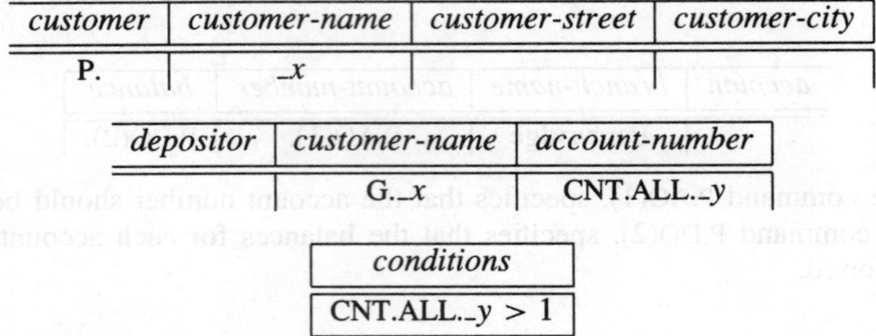

customer	*customer-name*	*customer-street*	*customer-city*
P.	_x		

depositor	*customer-name*	*account-number*
	G._x	CNT.ALL._y

conditions
CNT.ALL._y > 1

The approach is to count the number of *depositor* tuples pertaining to each customer of the bank. The condition box selects the names of the desired customers and the join with *customer* gives the required information.

As a final example, consider the query "Find all customers who have accounts at each of the branches located in Brooklyn":

depositor	*customer-name*	*account-number*
	P.G._x	_y

account	*branch-name*	*account-number*	*balance*
	CNT.UNQ.ALL._z	_y	

branch	*branch-name*	*branch-city*	*assets*
	_z	Brooklyn	
	_w	Brooklyn	

conditions
CNT.UNQ.ALL._z = CNT.UNQ.ALL._w

The domain variable *w* can hold the value of names of branches located in Brooklyn. Thus, CNT.UNQ.ALL._*w* is the number of distinct branches in Brooklyn. The domain variable *z* can hold the value of branches such that both of the following hold:

- The branch is located in Brooklyn.
- The customer whose name is *x* has an account at the branch.

Thus, CNT.UNQ.ALL._*z* is the number of distinct branches in Brooklyn at which customer *x* has an account. If CNT.UNQ.ALL._*z* = CNT.UNQ.ALL._*w*, then customer *x* must have an account at all of the branches located in Brooklyn. In such a case, *x* is included in the displayed result (because of the P.).

5.1.7 Modification of the Database

In this section, we show how to add, remove, or change information using QBE.

5.1.7.1 Deletion

Deletion of tuples from a relation is expressed in much the same way as a query. The major difference is the use of D. in place of P. In QBE (unlike in SQL), we can delete whole tuples, as well as values in selected columns. When we delete information in only some of the columns, null values, specified by –, are inserted.

We note that a D. command operates on only one relation. If we want to delete tuples from several relations, we must use one D. operator for each relation.

Here are some examples of QBE delete requests:

- Delete customer Smith.

customer	*customer-name*	*customer-street*	*customer-city*
D.	Smith		

- Delete the *branch-city* value of the branch whose name is "Perryridge."

branch	*branch-name*	*branch-city*	*assets*
	Perryridge	D.	

Thus, if before the delete operation the *branch* relation contains the tuple (Perryridge, Brooklyn, 50000), the delete results in the replacement of the preceding tuple with the tuple (Perryridge, –, 50000).

- Delete all loans with a loan amount between \$1300 and \$1500.

loan	*branch-name*	*loan-number*	*amount*
D.		_y	_x

borrower	*customer-name*	*loan-number*
D.		_y

conditions
$\_x = (\geq 1300$ **and** $\leq 1500)$

Note that, to delete loans we must delete tuples from both the *loan* and *borrower* relations.

- Delete all accounts at all branches located in Brooklyn.

account	*branch-name*	*account-number*	*balance*
D.	_x	_y	

depositor	*customer-name*	*account-number*
D.		_y

branch	*branch-name*	*branch-city*	*assets*
	_x	Brooklyn	

Note that, in expressing a deletion, we can reference relations other than those from which we are deleting information.

5.1.7.2 Insertion

To insert data into a relation, we either specify a tuple to be inserted or write a query the result of which is a set of tuples to be inserted. We do the insertion by placing the I. operator in the query expression. Obviously, the attribute values for inserted tuples must be members of the attribute's domain.

The simplest insert is a request to insert one tuple. Suppose that we wish to insert that account A-9732 at the Perryridge branch has a balance of $700. We write

account	*branch-name*	*account-number*	*balance*
I.	Perryridge	A-9732	700

We can also insert a tuple that contains only partial information. To insert into the *branch* relation information about a new branch with name "Capital" and city "Queens," but with a null asset value, we write

branch	*branch-name*	*branch-city*	*assets*
I.	Capital	Queens	

More generally, we might want to insert tuples based on the result of a query. Let us consider again the situation where we want to provide as a gift for all loan customers of the Perryridge branch, a new $200 savings account for every loan account that they have, with the loan number serving as the account number for the savings account. We write

account	*branch-name*	*account-number*	*balance*
I.	Perryridge	_x	200

depositor	*customer-name*	*account-number*
I.	_y	_x

loan	branch-name	loan-number	amount
	Perryridge	_x	

borrower	customer-name	loan-number
	_y	_x

To execute the preceding insertion request, the system must get the appropriate information from the *borrower* relation, then must use that information to insert the appropriate new tuple in the *depositor* and *account* relations.

5.1.7.3 Updates

There are situations in which we wish to change one value in a tuple without changing *all* values in the tuple. For this purpose, we use the U. operator. As we could for insert and delete, we can choose the tuples to be updated using a query. QBE, however, does not allow users to update the primary key fields.

Suppose that we want to update the asset value of the of the Perryridge branch to $10,000,000. This update is expressed as

branch	branch-name	branch-city	assets
	Perryridge		U.10000000

The blank field of attribute *branch-city* implies that no updating of that value is required.

The preceding query updates the assets of the Perryridge branch to $10,000,000, regardless of the old value. There are circumstances, however, where we need to update a value using the previous value. We must express such a request using two rows: one specifying the old tuples that need to be updated, and the other indicating the new updated tuples to be inserted in the database.

Suppose that interest payments are being made, and all balances are to be increased by 5 percent. We write

account	branch-name	account-number	balance
U.			_x * 1.05
			_x

This query specifies that we retrieve one tuple at a time from the *account* relation, determine the balance *x*, and update that balance to *x* * 1.05.

5.2 Quel

Quel was introduced as the query language for the Ingres database system, developed at the University of California, Berkeley. The basic structure of Quel closely parallels that of the tuple relational calculus. We express most Quel queries using three types of clauses: **range of**, **retrieve**, and **where**.

- Each tuple variable is declared in a **range of** clause. We write

  range of t **is** r

  to declare t to be a tuple variable restricted to take on values of tuples in relation r.
- The **retrieve** clause is similar in function to the **select** clause of SQL.
- The **where** clause contains the selection predicate.

A typical Quel query is of the form

range of t_1 **is** r_1
range of t_2 **is** r_2
.
.
.
range of t_m **is** r_m
retrieve $(t_{i_1}.A_{j_1},\ t_{i_2}.A_{j_2},\ \ldots,\ t_{i_n}.A_{j_n})$
where P

Each t_i is a tuple variable, each is a r_i relation, and each A_{j_k} is an attribute. Quel, like SQL, uses the notation

$$t.A$$

to denote the value of tuple variable t on attribute A. This expressions has the same meaning as $t[A]$ in the tuple relational calculus.

Quel does not include relational algebra operations such as **intersect, union**, and **minus**. Furthermore, Quel (unlike SQL), does not allow nested subqueries. That is, we *cannot* have a nested **retrieve-where** clause inside a **where** clause. These limitations do not reduce the expressive power of Quel, although they may sometimes make writing a query more complicated.

5.2.1 Simple Queries

Let us return to our bank example, and write several of our earlier queries using Quel. First, we find the names of all customers who have a loan at the bank:

range of t **is** *borrower*
retrieve (*t.customer-name*)

The preceding query does not eliminate duplicates. Thus, the name of a customer who has several loans from the bank will appear several times. To remove duplicates, we must add the keyword **unique** to the **retrieve** clause:

range of t **is** *borrower*
retrieve unique (*t.customer-name*)

Although duplicate elimination imposes additional overhead in query processing, we shall specify duplicate elimination when necessary in our examples.

Let us consider a more complicated example to find all loan numbers for loans made at the Perryridge branch that have loan amounts greater than $700. This query can be written in Quel as

> **range of** *t* **is** *loan*
> **retrieve** (*t.loan-number*)
> **where** *t.branch-name* = "Perryridge" **and** *t.amount* > 700

To show a Quel query involving more than one relation, let us consider the query "Find the names of all customers who have a loan at the Perryridge branch."

> **range of** *t* **is** *borrower*
> **range of** *s* **is** *loan*
> **retrieve unique** (*t.customer-name*)
> **where** *s.branch-name* = "Perryridge" **and**
> *t.loan-number* = *s.loan-number*

Note that Quel, like SQL, uses the logical connectives **and**, **or**, and **not**, rather than the mathematical symbols $\wedge$, $\vee$, and $\neg$, as are used in the tuple relational calculus. We need to express the join predicate explicitly. Quel does not have a special notation for natural join. Like SQL, it includes pattern-matching comparisons, but we shall not cover them here.

As another example involving two relations, consider the query "Find the names of all customers who have both a loan and an account at the bank":

> **range of** *s* **is** *borrower*
> **range of** *t* **is** *depositor*
> **retrieve unique** (*s.customer-name*)
> **where** *t.customer-name* = *s.customer-name*

In SQL, we had the option of writing such a query by using the relational-algebra operation **intersect**. As we noted, Quel does not include this operation.

5.2.2 Tuple Variables

For certain queries, we need to have two distinct tuple variables ranging over the same relation. Consider the query "Find the names of all customers who live in the same city as Jones does." We write this query as follows:

> **range of** *s* **is** *customer*
> **range of** *t* **is** *customer*
> **retrieve unique** (*s.customer-name*)
> **where** *t.customer-name* = "Jones" **and**
> *s.customer-city* = *t.customer-city*

Since the preceding query requires us to compare tuples pertaining to Jones with every *customer* tuple, we need two distinct tuple variables ranging over *customer*. However, a query often requires only one tuple variable ranging over a relation. In such cases, we may omit the **range of** statement for that relation, and use the relation name itself as an implicitly declared tuple variable. Following this convention, we rewrite the query "Find the names of all customers who have both a loan and an account at the bank" as follows:

> **retrieve unique** (*borrower.customer-name*)
> **where** *depositor.customer-name* = *borrower.customer-name*

The original academic Quel does not allow the use of implicitly declared tuple variables.

5.2.3 Aggregate Functions

Aggregate functions in Quel compute functions on groups of tuples. However, they take a form different from that of SQL. In SQL, a **group by** clause is part of the query itself, resulting in a single grouping of tuples for all aggregate functions in the query. In Quel, grouping is specified as part of each aggregate expression.

Quel aggregate expressions can take the following forms:

> *aggregate function* (*t.A*)
> *aggregate function* (*t.A* **where** *P*)
> *aggregate function* (*t.A* **by** $s.B_1$, $s.B_2, \ldots, s.B_n$ **where** *P*)

where

- *aggregate function* is one of **count**, **sum**, **avg**, **max**, **min**, **countu**, **sumu**, **avgu**, or **any**.
- *t* and *s* are tuple variables.
- $A, B_1, B_2, \ldots, B_n$ are attributes.
- *P* is a predicate similar to the **where** clause in a **retrieve**.

An aggregate expression can appear anywhere a constant can appear. The intuitive meaning of **count**, **sum**, **avg**, **max**, and **min** should be clear. We shall explain **any** later in this section. The functions **countu**, **sumu**, and **avgu** are identical to **count**, **sum**, and **avg**, respectively, except that they remove duplicates from their operands.

To find the average account balance for all accounts at the Perryridge branch, we write

> **range of** *t* **is** *account*
> **retrieve avg** (*t.balance*
> **where** *t.branch-name* = "Perryridge")

Aggregates can appear in the **where** clause. Suppose that we wish to find all accounts that have a balance higher than the average of all balances at the bank. We write

> **range of** *u* **is** *account*
> **range of** *t* **is** *account*
> **retrieve** (*t.account-number*)
> **where** *t.balance* > **avg** (*u.balance*)

The preceding **avg** (...) expression computes the average balance of all accounts at the bank.

Let us now consider a modification to the preceding query. Instead of using the average balance at the bank, we consider only the Perryridge branch. Thus, we are finding all accounts whose balance is higher than the average balance of Perryridge-branch accounts. We write this query as follows:

> **range of** *u* **is** *account*
> **range of** *t* **is** *account*
> **retrieve** (*t.account-number*)
> **where** *t.balance* > **avg** (*u.balance*
> **where** *u.branch-name* = "Perryridge")

Let us modify our query further. We now wish to find all accounts whose balance is higher than the average balance at the branch where the account is held. In this case, we need to compute, for each tuple *t* in *account*, the average balance at branch *t.branch-name*. To form these groups of tuples, we need to use the **by** construct in our aggregate expression:

> **range of** *u* **is** *account*
> **range of** *t* **is** *account*
> **retrieve** (*t.account-number*)
> **where** *t.balance* > **avg** (*u.balance* **by** *t.branch-name*
> **where** *u.branch-name* = *t.branch-name*)

The effect of the **by** construct in Quel differs from that of the **group by** clause in SQL. The primary source of this distinction is the role of tuple variables. The tuple variable *t* used in **by** is the same one that is used in the rest of the query. However, all other tuple variables are local to the aggregate expression even if a variable with the same name appears elsewhere in the query. Thus, in the preceding Quel query, if we removed "**by** *t.branch-name*" from the expression, we would turn tuple variable *t* into a local variable of the aggregate expression that is not bound to the tuple variable *t* of the outer query.

Let us consider the query "Find the names of all customers who have an account at the bank, but who do not have a loan from the bank." In the relational algebra, we wrote this query using the set difference operation. We can write this query in Quel using the **count** aggregate operation if we think of the query as "Find the names of all customers who have an account at the bank, and for whom the count of the number of loans from the bank is zero."

> **range of** *t* **is** *depositor*
> **range of** *u* **is** *borrower*
> **retrieve unique** (*t.customer-name*)
> **where count** (*u.loan-number* **by** *t.customer-name*
> **where** *u.customer-name* = *t.customer-name*) = 0

Quel offers another aggregate function that is applicable to this example, called **any**. If we replace **count** in the preceding query with **any**, we obtain 1 if the count is greater than 0; otherwise, we obtain 0. The **any** function allows faster execution of the query, in that processing can stop as soon as one tuple is found. The use of a comparison with **any** is analogous to the "there exists" quantifier of the relational calculus. Thus, we can rewrite our query as

> **range of** *t* **is** *depositor*
> **range of** *u* **is** *borrower*
> **retrieve unique** (*t.customer-name*)
> **where any** (*u.loan-number* **by** *t.customer-name*
>   **where** *u.customer-name* = *t.customer-name*) = 0

As a more complicated example, consider the query "Find the names of all customers who have accounts at each of the branches located in Brooklyn." Our strategy for expressing this query in Quel is as follows: First find out how many branches there are in Brooklyn. Then, compare this number with the number of distinct branches in Brooklyn at which each customer has an account. The **count** aggregate function that we used earlier counts duplicates. Therefore, we use the **countu** function, which counts unique values.

> **range of** *t* **is** *depositor*
> **range of** *u* **is** *account*
> **range of** *s* **is** *branch*
> **range of** *w* **is** *branch*
> **retrieve unique** (*t.customer-name*)
> **where countu** (*s.branch-name* **by** *t.customer-name*
>   **where** *u.account-number* = *t.account-number*
>   **and** *u.branch-name* = *s.branch-name*
>   **and** *s.branch-city* = "Brooklyn") =
>   **countu** (*w.branch-name* **where** *w.branch-city* = "Brooklyn")

We use **by** in the first **countu** expression, since we must restrict consideration to a single customer at a time. However, we do not use **by** in the latter **countu** expression, since we are interested in counting all branches in Brooklyn independent of the bindings of tuple variables external to this **countu** expression.

5.2.4 Modification of the Database

Database modification in Quel is similar to modification in SQL, although the syntax differs slightly.

5.2.4.1 Deletion

The form of a Quel deletion is

> **range of** *t* **is** *r*
> **delete** *t*
> **where** *P*

The tuple variable *t* can be defined implicitly. The predicate *P* can be any valid Quel predicate. If the **where** clause is omitted, all tuples in the relation are deleted.

Here are examples of Quel delete requests.

- Delete all tuples in the *loan* relation:

```
range of t is loan
delete t
```

- Delete all Smith's account records:

```
range of t is depositor
delete t
where t.customer-name = "Smith"
```

- Delete all accounts at branches located in Needham:

```
range of t is account
range of u is branch
delete t
where t.branch-name = u.branch-name
      and u.branch-city = "Needham"
```

5.2.4.2 Insertion

Insertion in Quel takes two general forms: insertion of a single tuple, and insertion of a set of tuples. Quel uses the keyword **append** for insertion. Here are examples of Quel insert requests:

- Insert that account A-9732 at the Perryridge branch has a balance of $700:

```
append to account (branch-name = "Perryridge",
                   account-number = A-9732,
                   balance = 700)
```

- Provide as a gift for all loan customers of the Perryridge branch, a new $200 savings account for every loan account that they have. Let the loan numbers serve as the account numbers for the new savings accounts.

```
range of t is loan
range of s is borrower
append to account (branch-name = t.branch-name,
                   account-number = t.loan-number,
                   balance = 200)
where t.branch-name = "Perryridge"
append to depositor (customer-name = s.customer-name,
                     account-number = s.loan-number)
where t.branch-name = "Perryridge" and t.loan-number = s.loan-number
```

Note that we need two **append** to statements to record information on the new account in both the *account* and *depositor* relations.

5.2.4.3 Updates

We express updates in Quel using the **replace** command. Examples of Quel update requests follow:

- Pay 5-percent interest (increase all account balances by 5 percent):

  range of *t* **is** *account*
  replace *t* (*balance* = 1.05 ∗ *t.balance*)

- Pay 6-percent interest on accounts that have balances over $10,000, and 5 percent on all other accounts:

  range of *t* **is** *account*
  replace *t* (*balance* = 1.06 ∗ *balance*)
  where *t.balance* > 10000
  replace *t* (*balance* = 1.05 ∗ *balance*)
  where *t.balance* ≤ 10000

Recall that the order of these two interest payments matters for amounts with a balance just under $10,000.

5.2.5 Set Operations

Let us consider a query for which we used the **union** operation in SQL: "Find the names of all customers who have an account, a loan, or both at the bank." Since we do not have a **union** operation in Quel, and we know that Quel is based on the tuple relational calculus, we might be guided by our tuple-relational-calcuius expression for this query:

$$\{t \mid \exists\, s \in borrower\ (t[customer\text{-}name] = s[customer\text{-}name]) \\ \lor \exists\, u \in depositor\ (t[customer\text{-}name] = u[customer\text{-}name])\}$$

Unfortunately, the preceding expression does not lead us to a Quel query. The problem is that, in the tuple-relational-calculus query, we obtain customers from *both* tuple variable *s* (whose range is *borrower*) and tuple variable *u* (whose range is *depositor*). In Quel, our **retrieve** clause must be one of the following:

- **retrieve** *s.customer-name*
- **retrieve** *u.customer-name*

If we choose the former, we exclude those depositors who are not borrowers. If we choose the latter, we exclude those borrowers who are not depositors.

To write this query in Quel, we must create a new relation, and must insert tuples into this new relation. Let us call this new relation *temp*. We obtain all depositors of the bank by writing

> **range of** *u* **is** *depositor*
> **retrieve into** *temp* **unique** (*u.customer-name*)

The **into** *temp* clause causes a new relation, *temp*, to be created to hold the result of this query. Now, we can find all borrowers of the bank, and can insert them in the newly created relation *temp*. We do so using the **append** command:

> **range of** *s* **is** *borrower*
> **append to** *temp* **unique** (*s.customer-name*)

We now have a relation *temp* that contains all customers who have an account, a loan, or both at the bank. Our use of the keyword **unique** in both the **retrieve** and **append** requests ensures that any duplicates have been removed.

The relation *temp* contains the desired list of customers. We thus can now write

> **range of** *t* **is** *temp*
> **retrieve unique** (*t.customer-name*)

to complete our query.

The strategy of using **append** allows us to perform unions in Quel. To perform a set difference $r - s$ (**minus** in SQL), we create a temporary relation representing *r*, and delete tuples of this temporary relation that are also in *s*. To illustrate this strategy, let us consider the query, "Find the names of all customers who have an account at the bank, but who do not have a loan from the bank." We begin by writing the following to create the temporary relation:

> **range of** *u* **is** *depositor*
> **retrieve into** *temp* (*u.customer-name*)

At this point, *temp* contains all customers who have an account at the bank, including those who possibly have a loan from the bank. We now delete those customers who do have a loan.

> **range of** *s* **is** *borrower*
> **range of** *t* **is** *temp*
> **delete** *t*
> **where** *t.customer-name* = *s.customer-name*

The relation *temp* now contains the desired list of customers. We thus can now write

> **range of** *t* **is** *temp*
> **retrieve unique** (*t.customer-name*)

to complete our query.

5.2.6 Quel and the Tuple Relational Calculus

To see more clearly the relationship between Quel and the tuple relational calculus, we consider the following Quel query

range of t_1 **is** r_1
range of t_2 **is** r_2
.
.
.
range of t_m **is** r_m
retrieve unique $(t_{i_1}.A_{j_1},\ t_{i_2}.A_{j_2}, \ldots, t_{i_n}.A_{j_n})$
where P

The preceding Quel query would be expressed in the tuple relational calculus as

$$\{t \mid \exists\, t_1 \in r_1,\ t_2 \in r_2, \ldots, t_m \in r_m\ ($$
$$t[r_{i_1}.A_{j_1}] = t_{i_1}[A_{j_1}] \wedge t[r_{i_2}.A_{j_2}] = t_{i_2}[A_{j_2}] \wedge \ldots \wedge$$
$$t[r_{i_n}.A_{j_n}] = t_{i_n}[A_{j_n}] \wedge P(t_1,\ t_2, \ldots, t_m))\}$$

We can understand this expression by looking at the formula within the "there exists" formula in three parts:

- $t_1 \in r_1 \wedge t_2 \in r_2 \wedge \ldots \wedge t_m \in r_m$. This part constrains each tuple in $t_1, t_2, \ldots, t_m$ to take on values of tuples in the relation over which it ranges.
- $t[r_{i_1}.A_{j_1}] = t_{i_1}[A_{j_1}] \wedge t_{i_2}[A_{j_2}] = t[r_{i_2}.A_{j_2}] \wedge \ldots \wedge t[r_{i_n}.A_{j_n}] = t_{i_n}[A_{j_n}]$. This part corresponds to the **retrieve** clause of the Quel query. We need to ensure that the kth attribute in tuple t corresponds to the kth entry in the **retrieve** clause. Consider the first entry: $t_{i_1}.A_{j_1}$. This entry is the value of some tuple of r_{i_1} (since the range of t_{i_1} is r_{i_1}) on attribute A_{j_1}. Thus, we need $t[A_{j_1}] = t_{i_1}[A_{j_1}]$. We used the more cumbersome notation $t[r_{i_1}.A_{j_1}] = t_{i_1}[A_{j_1}]$ to deal with the possibility that the same attribute name appears in more than one relation.
- $P(t_1,\ t_2, \ldots, t_m)$. This part expresses the constraint on acceptable values for $t_1,\ t_2, \ldots, t_m$ imposed by the **where** clause in the Quel query.

There are no representations of "for all" and of "there does not exist" in the relational-calculus formulation for the preceding Quel query. Quel achieves the power of the relational algebra by means of the **any** aggregate function and by the use of insertion and deletion on temporary relations.

5.3 Datalog

Datalog is a nonprocedural query language that is based on the logic-programming language Prolog. As she does in the relational calculus, a user describes the information desired without giving a specific procedure for obtaining that information. The syntax of Datalog resembles that of Prolog. However, the meaning of Datalog programs is defined in a purely declarative manner, unlike the more procedural semantics of Prolog, so Datalog simplifies writing simple queries and makes query optimization easier.

5.3.1 Basic Structure

A Datalog program consists of a set of *rules*. Before presenting a formal definition of Datalog rules and their formal meaning, we consider examples. The following is an example of a Datalog rule to define a view relation *v1* containing account numbers and balances for accounts at the Perryridge branch with a balance of over $700:

$$v1(A, B) \;:-\; account(\text{“Perryridge”}, A, B),\; B > 700$$

Datalog rules define views; the preceding rule *uses* the relation *account*, and *defines* the view relation *v1*. The symbol :– is read as "if," and the comma separating the "*account*("Perryridge", *A*, *B*)" from "*B* > 700" is read as "and." Intuitively, the rule is understood as follows:

for all *A*, *B*
if ("Perryridge", *A*, *B*) ∈ *account* **and** *B* > 700
then (*A*, *B*) ∈ *v1*

Suppose that the relation *account* is as shown in Figure 5.2. Then, the view relation *v1* contains the tuples shown in Figure 5.3.

To retrieve the balance of account number A-217 in the view relation *v1*, we can write the following query:

$$?\; v1(\text{“A-217”}, B)$$

The answer to the query is

(A-217, 750)

To get the account number and balance of all accounts in relation *v1*, where the balance is greater than 800, we can write

$$?\; v1(A, B),\; B > 800$$

branch-name	*account-number*	*balance*
Downtown	A-101	500
Mianus	A-215	700
Perryridge	A-102	400
Round Hill	A-305	350
Perryridge	A-201	900
Redwood	A-222	700
Perryridge	A-217	750

Figure 5.2 The *account* relation.

account-number	*balance*
A-201	900
A-217	750

Figure 5.3 The *v1* relation.

The answer to this query is

(A-201, 900)

In general, we may need more than one rule to define a view relation. Each rule defines a set of tuples that the view relation must contain. The set of tuples in the view relation is then defined as the union of all these sets of tuples. The following Datalog program specifies the interest rates for accounts. The program has two rules defining a view relation *interest-rate*, whose attributes are the account number and the interest rate. The rules say that, if the balance is less that $2000, then the interest rate is 0; if the balance is greater than or equal to $2000, the interest rate is 5 percent.

interest-rate(*A*, 0) :– *account*(*N*, *A*, *B*), *B* < 2000
interest-rate(*A*, 5) :– *account*(*N*, *A*, *B*), *B* >= 2000

Datalog rules can also use negation. The following rules define a view relation *c* that contains the names of all customers who have a deposit, but have no loan, at the bank:

c(*N*) :– *depositor*(*N*,*A*), **not** *is-borrower*(*N*)
is-borrower(*N*) :– *borrower*(*N*, *L*),

In Prolog and in most Datalog implementations, attributes of a relation are recognized by position, and attribute names are omitted. Thus, Datalog rules are compact, compared to SQL queries. However, when relations have a large number of attributes, or the order or number of attributes of relations may change, the positional notation can be cumbersome and error prone. It is not hard to create a variant of Datalog syntax using named attributes, rather than positional attributes. In such a system, the Datalog rule defining *v1* can be written as

v1(*account-number A*, *balance B*) :–
  account(*branch-name* "Perryridge", *account-number A*, *balance B*),
  B > 700

Translation between the two forms can be done without significant effort, given the relation schema.

5.3.2 Syntax of Datalog Rules

Now that we have informally explained rules and queries, let us formally define their syntax; we discuss their meaning in Section 5.3.3. We use the same conventions as in the relational algebra for denoting relation names, attribute names, constants (such as numbers or quoted strings), and variable names. Examples of constants are 4, which is a number, and "John," which is a string; X and *Name* are variables. A *positive literal* has the form

$$p(t_1, t_2, \ldots, t_n)$$

where p is the name of a relation with n attributes, and $t_1, t_2, \ldots, t_n$ are either constants or variables. A *negative literal* has the form

$$\textbf{not}\ p(t_1, t_2, \ldots, t_n)$$

where relation p has n attributes. The following is an example of a literal:

account("Perryridge", A, B)

Literals involving arithmetic operations are treated specially. For example, the literal $B > 700$, although not in the syntax just described, can be conceptually understood to stand for $>(B, 700)$, which *is* in the required syntax, and where $>$ is a relation.

But what does this notation mean for arithmetic operations such as "$>$"? The relation $>$ (conceptually) contains tuples of the form (x, y) for every possible pair of values x, y such that $x > y$. Thus, (2, 1) and (5, −33) are both tuples in $>$. Clearly, the (conceptual) relation $>$ is infinite. Other arithmetic operations (such as $>$, $=$, $+$ or $-$) are also treated conceptually as relations. For example, $A = B + C$ stands conceptually for $+(B, C, A)$, where the relation $+$ contains every tuple (x, y, z) such that $z = x + y$.

A *fact* is written in the form

$$p(v_1, v_2, \ldots, v_n).$$

and denotes that the tuple $(v_1, v_2, \ldots, v_n)$ is in relation p. A set of facts for a relation can also be written in the usual tabular notation. A *set of facts* for the relations in a database schema is equivalent to an instance of the database schema. *Rules* are built out of literals and have the form

$$p(t_1, t_2, \ldots, t_n) :\!-\ L_1, L_2, \ldots, L_n$$

where each L_i is a (positive or negative) literal. The literal $p(t_1, t_2, \ldots, t_n)$ is referred to as the *head* of the rule, and the rest of the literals in the rule constitute the *body* of the rule.

A Datalog *program* consists of a set of rules; the order in which the rules are written has no significance. As mentioned earlier, there may be several rules defining a relation.

Figure 5.4 shows an example of a relatively complex Datalog program, which defines the interest on each account in the Perryridge branch. The first rule of the program defines a view relation *interest*, whose attributes are the account number and the interest earned on the account. The view relations *interest-rate* and *perryridge-account* are used in the rule. The second rule defines the view

$$
\begin{aligned}
&\textit{interest}(A, I) \text{ :- } \textit{perryridge-account}(A, B),\\
&\qquad\qquad\qquad \textit{interest-rate}(A, R), I = B * R/100.\\
&\textit{perryridge-account}(A, B) \text{ :- } \textit{account}(\text{“Perryridge”}, A, B).\\
&\textit{interest-rate}(A, 0) \text{ :- } \textit{account}(N, A, B), B < 2000.\\
&\textit{interest-rate}(A, 5) \text{ :- } \textit{account}(N, A, B), B >= 2000.
\end{aligned}
$$

Figure 5.4 Datalog program that defines interest on Perryridge accounts.

relation *perryridge-account*, using the database relation *account*. The final two rules of the program are rules that we saw earlier.

In Section 3.7.3, we defined when a view *depends on* another view, and when a view is *recursive*. Although the syntax for view definitions in Datalog differs from the syntax used for view definition in Section 3.7.3, the definitions depends-on and recursive views are applicable to Datalog views. For example, in the program in Figure 5.4, relation *interest* depends (directly) on relations *interest-rate* and *perryridge-account*. Relation *interest-rate* in turn depends directly on *account*, as does *perryridge-account*. Since we have a chain of dependencies from *interest* to *interest-rate* to *account*, relation *interest* depends (indirectly) on *account*.

The program in Figure 5.4 is nonrecursive. However, the program in Figure 5.5 is recursive, since *empl* depends on itself (due to the second rule).

5.3.3 Semantics of Nonrecursive Datalog

We consider the formal semantics of Datalog programs. For now, we consider only programs that are nonrecursive. The semantics of recursive programs is somewhat more complicated; it is discussed in Section 5.3.6. We define the semantics of a program by starting with the semantics of a single rule.

5.3.3.1 Semantics of a Rule

A *ground instantiation of a rule* is the result of replacing each variable in the rule by some constant. If a variable occurs multiple times in a rule, all occurrences of the variable must be replaced by the same constant. Ground instantiations are often simply called *instantiations*.

Our example rule defining *v1*, and an instantiation of the rule, are shown here:

$$
\begin{aligned}
&\textit{v1}(A, B) \text{ :- } \textit{account}(\text{“Perryridge”}, A, B), B > 700\\
&\textit{v1}(\text{“A-217”}, 750) \text{ :- } \textit{account}(\text{“Perryridge”}, \text{“A-217”}, 750), 750 > 700
\end{aligned}
$$

Here, variable A was replaced by "A-217," and variable B by 750.

$$
\begin{aligned}
&\textit{empl}(X, Y) \text{ :- } \textit{manager}(X, Y).\\
&\textit{empl}(X, Y) \text{ :- } \textit{manager}(X, Z), \textit{empl}(Z, Y).
\end{aligned}
$$

Figure 5.5 Recursive Datalog program.

A rule typically has many possible instantiations. These instantiations correspond to the various ways of assigning values to each variable in the rule.

Suppose that we are given a rule R,

$$p(t_1, t_2, \ldots, t_n) \text{ :– } L_1, L_2, \ldots, L_n$$

and a set of facts I for the relations used in the rule (I can also be thought of as a database instance). Consider any instantiation R' of rule R:

$$p(v_1, v_2, \ldots, v_n) \text{ :– } l_1, l_2, \ldots, l_n$$

where each literal l_i is either of the form $q_i(v_{i,1}, v_{1,2}, \ldots, v_{i,n_i})$ or of the form **not** $q_i(v_{i,1}, v_{1,2}, \ldots, v_{i,n_i})$, and where each v_i and each $v_{i,j}$ is a constant.

We say that the body of rule instantiation R' is *satisfied* in I if

1. For each positive literal $q_i(v_{i,1}, \ldots, v_{i,n_i})$ in the body of R', the set of facts I contains the fact $q(v_{i,1}, \ldots, v_{i,n_i})$.
2. For each negative literal **not** $q_j(v_{j,1}, \ldots, v_{j,n_j})$ in the body of R', the set of facts I does not contain the fact $q_j(v_{j,1}, \ldots, v_{j,n_j})$.

We define the set of facts that can be *inferred* from a given set of facts I using rule R as

$$\begin{aligned} \textit{infer}(R, I) = \{p(t_1, \ldots, t_{n_i}) \mid & \text{ there is an instantiation } R' \text{ of } R, \\ & \text{where } p(t_1, \ldots, t_{n_i}) \text{ is the head of } R', \text{ and} \\ & \text{the body of } R' \text{ is satisfied in } I\}. \end{aligned}$$

Given a set of rules $\mathcal{R} = \{R_1, R_2, \ldots, R_n\}$, we define

$$\textit{infer}(\mathcal{R}, I) = \textit{infer}(R_1, I) \cup \textit{infer}(R_2, I) \cup \ldots \cup \textit{infer}(R_n, I)$$

Suppose that we are given a set of facts I containing the tuples for relation *account* shown in Figure 5.2. One possible instantiation of our running-example rule R is

v1("A-217", 750) :– *account*("Perryridge", "A-217", 750), 750 > 700.

The fact *account*("Perryridge", "A-217", 750) is in the set of facts I. Further, 750 is greater than 700, and hence conceptually (750,700) is in the relation ">". Hence, the body of the rule instantiation is satisfied in I. There are other possible instantiations of R, and using them we find that $\textit{infer}(R, I)$ has exactly the set of facts for *v1* that is shown in Figure 5.6.

account-number	*balance*
A-201	900
A-217	750

Figure 5.6 Result of $\textit{infer}(R, I)$.

5.3.3.2 Semantics of a Program

When a view relation is defined in terms of another view relation, the set of facts in the first view depends on the set of facts in the second one. We have assumed, in this section, that the definition is nonrecursive; that is, no view relation depends (directly or indirectly) on itself. Hence, we can layer the view relations as follows, and can use the layering to define the semantics of the program:

- A relation is in layer 1 if all relations used in the bodies of rules defining it are stored in the database.
- A relation is in layer 2 if all relations used in the bodies of rules defining it either are stored in the database, or are in layer 1.
- In general, a relation p is in layer $i+1$ if (1) it is not in layers $1, 2, \ldots, i$, and (2) all relations used in the bodies of rules defining p either are stored in the database, or are in layers $1, 2, \ldots, i$.

Consider the program in Figure 5.4. The layering of view relations in the program is shown in Figure 5.7. The relation *account* is in the database. Relation *interest-rate* is in level 1, since all the relations used in the two rules defining it are in the database. Relation *perryridge-account* is similarly in layer 1. Finally, relation *interest* is in layer 2, since it is not in layer 1 and all the relations used in the rule defining it are in the database or in layers less than 2.

We can now define the semantics of a datalog program in terms of the layering of view relations. Let the layers in a given program be $1, 2, \ldots, n$. Let $\mathcal{R}_i$ denote the set of all rules defining view relations in layer i.

- We define I_0 to be the set of facts stored in the database, and define I_1 as

$$I_1 = I_0 \cup \mathit{infer}(\mathcal{R}_1, I_0)$$

- We proceed in a similar fashion, defining I_2 in terms of I_1 and $\mathcal{R}_2$, and so on, using the following definition:

$$I_{i+1} = I_i \cup \mathit{infer}(\mathcal{R}_{i+1}, I_i)$$

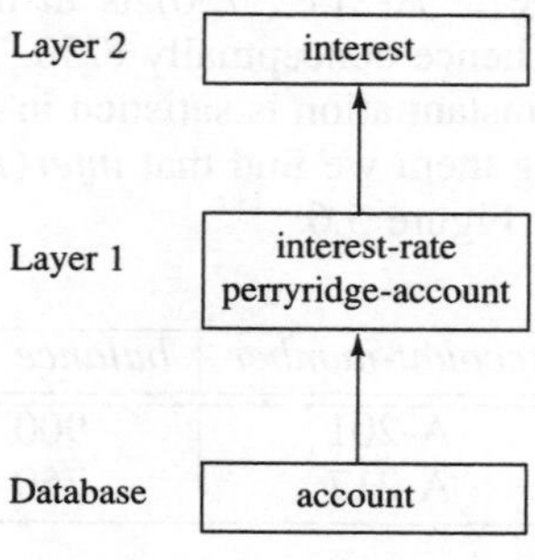

Figure 5.7 Layering of view relations.

- Finally, the set of facts in the view relations defined by the program (also called the *semantics of the program*) is given by the set of facts I_n corresponding to the highest layer n.

For the program in Figure 5.4, I_0 is the set of facts in the database, and I_1 is the set of facts in the database along with all facts that we can infer from I_0 using the rules for relations *interest-rate* and *perryridge-account*. Finally, I_2 contains the facts in I_1 along with the facts for relation *interest* that we can infer from the facts in I_1 using the rule defining *interest*. The semantics of the program—that is, the set of those facts that are in each of the view relations—is defined as the set of facts I_2.

Recall that, in Section 3.7.3, we saw how to define the meaning of nonrecursive relational-algebra views using a technique known as view expansion. View expansion, can be used with nonrecursive Datalog views as well; conversely, the layering technique described here can also be used with relational-algebra views. However, the layering technique can be used with certain extensions of Datalog, where view expansion cannot be used.

5.3.4 Safety

It is possible to write rules that generate an infinite number of answers. Consider the rule

$$gt(X, Y) \ :\!-\ X > Y$$

Since the relation defining > is infinite, this rule would generate an infinite number of facts for the relation *gt*, which calculation would, correspondingly, take an infinite amount of time and space.

The use of negation can also cause similar problems. Consider the following rule:

$$not\text{-}in\text{-}loan(B, L) \ :\!-\ \mathbf{not}\ loan(B, L)$$

The idea is that a tuple *(branch, loan-number)* is in view relation *not-in-loan* if the tuple is not present in the *loan* relation. However, if the set of possible branch names or account numbers is infinite, the relation *not-in-loan* may be infinite as well.

Finally, if we have a variable in the head that does not appear in the body, we may get an infinite number of facts where the variable is instantiated to different values.

So that these possibilities are avoided, Datalog rules are required to satisfy the following *safety* conditions:

1. Every variable that appears in the head of the rule also appears in a nonarithmetic positive literal in the body of the rule.
2. Every variable appearing in a negative literal in the body of the rule also appears in some positive literal in the body of the rule.

If all the rules in a nonrecursive Datalog program satisfy the preceding safety conditions, then all the view relations defined in the program can be shown to be finite, as long as all the database relations are finite. The conditions can be weakened somewhat to allow variables in the head to appear only in an arithmetic literal in the body in some cases. For example, in the rule

$$p(A) \ :\!-\ q(B),\ A = B + 1$$

we can see that if relation q is finite, then so is p, based on the properties of addition, even though variable A appears in only an arithmetic literal.

5.3.5 Relational Operations in Datalog

Nonrecursive Datalog expressions without arithmetic operations are equivalent in expressive power to expressions using the basic operations in relational algebra (excluding the modification operations). We shall not formally prove this assertion here. Rather, we shall show through examples how the various relational-algebra operations can be expressed in Datalog. In all cases, we define a view relation called *query* to illustrate the operations.

We have already seen how to do selection using Datalog rules. We perform projections simply by using only the required attributes in the head of the rule. To project out attribute *account-name* from account, we use

$$query(A) \ :\!-\ account(N,\ A,\ B)$$

We can obtain the Cartesian product of two relations r_1 and r_2 in Datalog as follows:

$$query(X_1, X_2, \ldots, X_n, Y_1, Y_2, \ldots, Y_m) :\!- r_1(X_1, X_2, \ldots, X_n), r_2(Y_1, Y_2, \ldots, Y_m)$$

where r_1 is of arity n, and r_2 is of arity m, and the $X_1, X_2, \ldots, X_n, Y_1, Y_2, \ldots, Y_m$ are all distinct variable names.

The union of two relations r_1 and r_2 (both of arity n) is formed as follows:

$$query(X_1, X_2, \ldots, X_n) :\!- r_1(X_1, X_2, \ldots, X_n)$$
$$query(X_1, X_2, \ldots, X_n) :\!- r_2(X_1, X_2, \ldots, X_n)$$

Finally, the set difference of two relations r_1 and r_2 is formed as follows:

$$query(X_1, X_2, \ldots, X_n) :\!- r_1(X_1, X_2, \ldots, X_n),\ \textbf{not}\ r_2(X_1, X_2, \ldots, X_n)$$

It is possible to show that we can express any nonrecursive Datalog query without arithmetic using the relational-algebra operations. We leave this demonstration as an exercise for you to carry out. You can thus establish the equivalence of the basic operations of relational algebra and nonrecursive Datalog without arithmetic operations.

The extended relational update operations of insertion, deletion, and update are supported in certain extensions to Datalog. The syntax for such operations varies from implementation to implementation. Some systems allow the use of +

or – in rule heads to denote relational insertion and deletion. For example,

$$+\ account(\text{“Johnstown”}, A, B)\ \text{:--}\ account(\text{“Perryridge”}, A, B)$$

inserts all Perryridge accounts into the set of Johnstown accounts. The aggregation operation of extended relational algebra is supported in some implementations of Datalog. Again, there is no standard syntax for this operation.

5.3.6 Recursion in Datalog

Several database applications deal with structures that are similar to tree data structures. For example, consider employees in an organization. Some of the employees are managers. Each manager manages a set of people who report to him or her. But each of these people may in turn be managers, and they in turn may have other people who report to them. Thus employees may be organized in a structure similar to a tree.

Suppose that we have a relation schema

$$\textit{Manager-schema} = (\textit{employee-name}, \textit{manager-name})$$

Let *manager* be a relation on the preceding schema.

Suppose now, that we want to find out which employees are supervised, directly or indirectly by a given manager—say, Jones. Thus, if the manager of Alon is Barinsky, and the manager of Barinsky is Estovar, and the manager of Estovar is Jones, then Alon, Barinsky, and Estovar are the employees controlled by Jones. People often write programs to manipulate tree data structures using recursion. Using the idea of recursion, we can define the set of people controlled by Jones as follows. The people supervised by Jones are (1) people whose manager is Jones, and (2) people whose manager is supervised by Jones. Note that case (2) is recursive.

We can encode the preceding recursive definition as a recursive Datalog view, called *empl-jones*, as follows.

$$\textit{empl-jones}(X)\ \text{:--}\ \textit{manager}(X, \text{“Jones”})$$
$$\textit{empl-jones}(X)\ \text{:--}\ \textit{manager}(X, Y), \textit{empl-jones}(Y)$$

The first rule corresponds to case (1); the second rule corresponds to case (2). The view *empl-jones* depends on itself due to the second rule; hence, the preceding Datalog program is recursive.

We *assume* that recursive Datalog programs contain no rules with negative literals. The reason will become clear later. The bibliographic notes refer to papers that describe where negation can be used in recursive Datalog programs.

The view relations of a recursive program that contains a set of rules $\mathcal{R}$ are defined to contain exactly the set of facts I computed by the iterative procedure Datalog-Fixpoint shown in Figure 5.8. The recursion in the Datalog program has been turned into an iteration in the procedure. At the end of the procedure, $\textit{infer}(\mathcal{R}, I) = I$, and I is called a *fixed point* of the program.

Consider the program defining *empl-jones*, with the relation *manager*, as shown in Figure 5.9. The set of facts computed for the view relation *empl-jones*

procedure Datalog-Fixpoint
I = set of facts in the database
repeat
$Old\_I = I$
$I = I \cup infer(\mathcal{R}, I)$
until $I = Old\_I$

Figure 5.8 Datalog-Fixpoint procedure.

in each iteration is shown in Figure 5.10. In each iteration, one more level of employees under Jones is computed, and is added to the set *empl-jones*. The procedure is terminated when there is no change to the set *empl-jones*, which the system detects by finding $I = Old\_I$. Such a termination point must be reached, since the set of managers and employees is finite. On the given *manager* relation, the procedure Datalog-Fixpoint terminates after iteration 4, when it detects that no new facts have been inferred.

You should verify that, at the end of the iteration, the view relation *empl-jones* contains exactly those employees who work under Jones. To print out the names of the employees supervised by Jones defined by the view, you can use the following query:

? *empl-jones*(N)

To understand procedure Datalog-Fixpoint, we recall that a rule infers new facts from a given set of facts. Iteration starts with a set of facts I_0 set to the facts in the database. These facts are all known to be true, but there may be other facts that are true as well.† Next, the set of rules $\mathcal{R}$ in the given Datalog program is used to infer what facts are true, given that facts in I_0 are true. We can show that, as long as no rule in the program contains a negative literal, any facts in $infer(\mathcal{R}, I_0)$ also will be present in $infer(\mathcal{R}, J)$ for any set of facts J that contain

employee-name	*manager-name*
Alon	Barinsky
Barinsky	Estovar
Corbin	Duarte
Duarte	Jones
Estovar	Jones
Jones	Klinger
Rensal	Klinger

Figure 5.9 The *manager* relation.

†The word "fact" is used in a technical sense to note membership of a tuple in a relation. Thus, in the Datalog sense of "fact," a fact may be true (the tuple is indeed in the relation) or false (the tuple is not in the relation).

Iteration number	Tuples in *empl-jones*
0	
1	(Duarte), (Estovar)
2	(Duarte), (Estovar), (Barinsky), (Corbin)
3	(Duarte), (Estovar), (Barinsky), (Corbin), (Alon)
4	(Duarte), (Estovar), (Barinsky), (Corbin), (Alon)

Figure 5.10 Employees of Jones in iterations of procedure Datalog-Fixpoint.

I_0. From this assertion, it follows that every fact in $infer(\mathcal{R}, I_0)$ is true, regardless of what other facts also are inferred to be true later.

Let $I_1 = I_0 \cup infer(\mathcal{R}, I_0)$; based on the preceding argument, all facts in I_1 are known to be true. Now, I_1 corresponds to the value of I in the fixed-point procedure at the end of the first iteration; hence, all the facts inferred by the end of first iteration of the fixed-point procedure are true.

Since facts in I_1 are all true, we can deduce that all the facts in $I_2 = I_1 \cup infer(\mathcal{R}, I_1)$ also are true. In general, let

$$I_{i+1} = I_i \cup infer(\mathcal{R}, I_i)$$

The set of facts I_i corresponds to the value of I in the fixed-point procedure, at the end of the ith iteration. At each iteration i, we can infer that, all facts in I_i are true. Further, it is clear that $I_{i+1} \supseteq I_i$, that is, the set of facts known to be true increases in successive iterations.

For safe Datalog programs, we can show that there will be some point where no more new facts can be derived; that is, for some k, $I_{k+1} = I_k$. At this point, then, we have the final set of true facts. Further, given a Datalog program and a database, the fixed-point procedure infers all the facts that can be inferred to be true.

Since procedure Datalog-Fixpoint computes only true facts, so long as no rule in the program has a negative literal, it is said to be *sound* for such programs. Further, it can be shown that the procedure computes all true facts that can be inferred from the given database and Datalog program; hence, procedure Datalog-Fixpoint is also said to be *complete*.

Instead of creating a view for the employees supervised by a specific manager Jones, we can create a more general view relation *empl* that contains every tuple (X, Y) such that X is directly or indirectly managed by Y, using the following program (also shown in Figure 5.5):

$$empl(X,Y) \text{ :- } manager(X,Y)$$
$$empl(X,Y) \text{ :- } manager(X,Z),\ empl(Z,Y)$$

To find the direct and indirect subordinates of Jones, we simply use the query

? $empl(X, \text{"Jones"})$

which gives the same set of values for X as the view *empl-jones*. Most Datalog implementations have sophisticated query optimizers and evaluation engines that can run the preceding query at about the same speed as they could evaluate the view *empl-jones*.

The view *empl* defined previously is called the *transitive closure* of the relation *manager*. If the relation *manager* were replaced by any other binary relation *R*, the preceding program would define the transitive closure of *R*.

5.3.7 The Power of Recursion

Datalog with recursion has more expressive power than Datalog without recursion. In other words, there are queries on the database that we can answer using recursion, but cannot answer without using it. For example, we cannot express transitive closure in Datalog without using recursion (or for that matter, SQL, QBE or Quel without recursion). Consider the transitive closure of the relation *manager*. Intuitively, a fixed number of joins can find only those employees that are some (other) fixed number of levels down from any manager (we will not attempt to prove this result here). Since any given nonrecursive query has a fixed number of joins, there is a limit on how many levels of employees the query can find. If the number of level of employees in the *manager* relation is more than the limit of the query, the query will miss some levels of employees. Thus, a nonrecursive Datalog program cannot express transitive closure.

An alternative to recursion is to use an external mechanism, such as embedded SQL, to iterate on a nonrecursive query. The iteration in effect implements the fixed-point loop of Figure 5.8. In fact, that is how such queries are implemented on database systems that do not support recursion. However, writing such queries using iteration is more complicated than using recursion, and evaluation using recursion can be optimized to run faster than evaluation using iteration.

The expressive power provided by recursion must be used with care. It is relatively easy to write recursive programs that will generate an infinite number of facts, as the following program illustrates:

$$number(0)$$
$$number(A) \text{ :- } number(B),\ A = B + 1$$

The program generates *number*(n) for all positive n, which is clearly infinite, and will not terminate. The second rule of the program does not satisfy the safety condition described in Section 5.3.4. Programs that satisfy the safety condition will terminate, even if they are recursive, provided that all database relations are finite. For such programs, tuples in view relations can contain only constants from the database, and hence the view relations must be finite. The converse is not true; that is, there are programs that do not satisfy the safety conditions, but that do terminate.

The procedure Datalog-Fixpoint iteratively uses the function *infer*$(\mathcal{R}, I)$ to compute what facts are true. Although we considered only the case of Datalog programs without negative literals, the procedure can also be used on views defined using other languages, such as relational algebra, provided that the views satisfy the conditions described next. Regardless of the language used to define a view V, the view can be thought of as being defined by an expression E_V that given a set of facts I returns a set of facts $E_V(I)$ for the view relation V. Given a set of view definitions $\mathcal{R}$ (in any language), we can define a function *infer*$(\mathcal{R}, I)$ that returns $I \cup \bigcup_{V \in \mathcal{R}} E_V(I)$. The preceding function is of the same form as the *infer* function for Datalog.

A view V is said to be *monotonic* if, given any two sets of facts I_1 and I_2 such that $I_1 \subseteq I_2$, then $E_V(I_1) \subseteq E_V(I_2)$, where E_V is the expression used to define V. Similarly, the function *infer* is said to be monotonic if

$$I_1 \subseteq I_2 \Rightarrow \mathit{infer}(\mathcal{R}, I_1) \subseteq \mathit{infer}(\mathcal{R}, I_2)$$

Thus, if *infer* is monotonic, given a set of facts I_0 that is a subset of the true facts, we can be sure that all facts in *infer*$(\mathcal{R}, I_0)$ are also true. Using the same reasoning as in Section 5.3.6, we can then show that procedure Datalog-Fixpoint is sound (that is, it computes only true facts) provided that the function *infer* is monotonic.

Relational-algebra expressions that use only the operators Π, σ, $\times$, $\bowtie$, $\cup$, $\cap$, or ρ are monotonic. Recursive views can be defined using such expressions.

However, relational expressions that use the operator $-$ are not monotonic. For example, let $\mathit{manager}_1$ and $\mathit{manager}_2$ be relations with the same schema as the *manager* relation. Let

$$\begin{aligned} I_1 = \{ & \mathit{manager}_1(\text{“Alon”}, \text{“Barinsky”}), \mathit{manager}_1(\text{“Barinsky”}, \text{“Estovar”}), \\ & \mathit{manager}_2(\text{“Alon”}, \text{“Barinsky”}) \} \end{aligned}$$

and let

$$\begin{aligned} I_2 = \{ & \mathit{manager}_1(\text{“Alon”}, \text{“Barinsky”}), \mathit{manager}_1(\text{“Barinsky”}, \text{“Estovar”}), \\ & \mathit{manager}_2(\text{“Alon”}, \text{“Barinsky”}), \mathit{manager}_2(\text{“Barinsky”}, \text{“Estovar”}) \} \end{aligned}$$

Consider the expression $\mathit{manager}_1 - \mathit{manager}_2$. Now the result of the preceding expression on I_1 is (“Barinsky”, “Estovar”), whereas the result of the expression on I_2 is the empty relation. But $I_1 \subseteq I_2$; hence, the expression is not monotonic. Expressions using the grouping operation of extended relational algebra are also nonmonotonic.

The fixed-point technique does not work on recursive views defined with nonmonotonic expressions. However, there are instances where such views are useful, particularly for defining aggregates on part–subpart relationships. Such relationships define of what subparts each part is composed. Subparts themselves may have further subparts, and so on; hence, the relationships, like the manager relationship, have a natural recursive structure. The bibliographic notes provide references to research on defining such views.

It is possible to define some kinds of recursive queries without using views. For example, extended relational operations have been proposed to define transitive closure, and extensions to the SQL syntax to specify (generalized) transitive closure have been proposed. However, recursive view definitions provide more expressive power than do the other forms of recursive queries.

5.4 Summary

We have considered three query languages: QBE, Quel, and Datalog. QBE is based on a visual paradigm: The queries look much like tables. QBE and its variants have become popular with nonexpert database users due to the intuitive simplicity of the visual paradigm. Quel is based on the tuple relational calculus, and is similar in many respects to SQL, but avoids much of the latter's complexity. Datalog is derived from Prolog, but unlike Prolog, it has a declarative semantics, making simple queries easier to write and query evaluation easier to optimize. Defining views is particularly easy in Datalog, and the recursive views that Datalog supports makes it possible to write queries, such as transitive-closure queries, that cannot be written without recursion or iteration. However, no accepted standards exist for important features, such as grouping and aggregation, in Datalog. Datalog remains mainly a research language.

Exercises

5.1. Consider the insurance database of Figure 5.11, where the primary keys are specified with leading capital letters. Construct the following QBE queries for this relational-database system.

(*a*) Find the total number of people whose car was involved in an accident in 1989.

(*b*) Find the number of accidents in which at least one car belonging to "John Smith" were involved.

(*c*) Add a new policy holder to the database.

(*d*) Delete the car "Mazda" that belongs to "John Smith."

(*e*) Add a new accident record for the Toyota that belongs to "Williams."

5.2. Consider the employee database of Figure 5.12. Give expressions in QBE, Quel, and Datalog for each of the following queries:

(*a*) Find the names of all employees who work for First Bank Corporation.

(*b*) Find the names and cities of residence of all employees who work for First Bank Corporation.

(*c*) Find the names, street addresses, and cities of residence of all employees who work for First Bank Corporation and earn more than $10,000 per annum.

(*d*) Find all employees who live in the city where the company for which they work is located.

person (SS#, name, address)
car (License, year, model)
accident (Date, Driver, damage-amount)
owns (SS#, License)
log (License, Date, Driver)

Figure 5.11 Insurance database.

employee (*person-name*, *street*, *city*)
works (*person-name*, *company-name*, *salary*)
company (*company-name*, *city*)
manages (*person-name*, *manager-name*)

Figure 5.12 Employee database.

(*e*) Find all employees who live in the same city and on the same street as their managers.
(*f*) Find all employees in the database who do not work for First Bank Corporation.
(*g*) Find all employees who earn more than every employee of Small Bank Corporation.
(*h*) Assume that the companies may be located in several cities. Find all companies located in every city in which Small Bank Corporation is located.

5.3. Consider the relational database of Figure 5.12. Give expressions in QBE and Quel for each of the following queries:
(*a*) Find all employees who earn more than the average salary of all employees of their company.
(*b*) Find the company that has the most employees.
(*c*) Find the company that has the smallest payroll.
(*d*) Find those companies whose employees earn a higher salary, on average, than the average salary at First Bank Corporation.

5.4. Consider the relational database of Figure 5.12. Give expressions in QBE and Quel for each of the following queries:
(*a*) Modify the database so that Jones now lives in Newtown.
(*b*) Give all employees of First Bank Corporation a 10-percent raise.
(*c*) Give all managers in the database a 10-percent raise.
(*d*) Give all managers in the database a 10-percent raise, unless the salary would be greater than $100,000. In such cases, give only a 3-percent raise.
(*e*) Delete all tuples in the *works* relation for employees of Small Bank Corporation.

5.5. Let the following relation schemas be given:

$$R = (A, B, C)$$
$$S = (D, E, F)$$

Let relations *r*(*R*) and *s*(*S*) be given. Give expressions in QBE, Quel, and Datalog equivalent to each of the following queries:
(*a*) $\Pi_A(r)$
(*b*) $\sigma_{B=17}\ (r)$
(*c*) $r \times s$
(*d*) $\Pi_{A,F}\ (\sigma_{C=D}(r \times s))$

5.6. Let $R = (A, B, C)$, and let r_1 and r_2 both be relations on schema R. Give expressions in QBE, Quel, and Datalog equivalent to each of the following queries:
(*a*) $r_1 \cup r_2$
(*b*) $r_1 \cap r_2$
(*c*) $r_1 - r_2$
(*d*) $\Pi_{AB}(r_1) \bowtie \Pi_{BC}(r_2)$

5.7. Let $R = (A, B)$ and $S = (A, C)$, and let $r(R)$ and $s(S)$ be relations. Write expressions in QBE, Quel, and Datalog for each of the following queries:
(*a*) $\{< a > \mid \exists\, b\, (< a, b > \in r \wedge b = 17)\}$
(*b*) $\{< a, b, c > \mid < a, b > \in r \wedge < a, c > \in s\}$
(*c*) $\{< a > \mid \exists\, c\, (< a, c > \in s \wedge \exists\, b_1, b_2\, (< a, b_1 > \in r \wedge < c, b_2 > \in r \wedge b_1 > b_2))\}$

5.8. In Section 5.2.3, on page 169, we wrote a Quel expression to find all accounts whose balance is higher than the average balance at the branch where the account is held. That query included a use of **by**. Explain what would be retrieved if "**by** *t.branch-name*" were not included in the statement of the query.

5.9. Consider the relational database of Figure 5.12. Write a Datalog program for each of the following queries:
(*a*) Find all employees who work (directly or indirectly) under the manager "Jones".
(*b*) Find all cities of residence of all employees who work (directly or indirectly) under the manager "Jones".
(*c*) Find all pairs of employees who have a (direct or indirect) manager in common.
(*d*) Find all pairs of employees who have a (direct or indirect) manager in common, and are at the same number of levels of supervision below the common manager.

5.10. Write an extended relational-algebra view equivalent to the Datalog rule

$$p(A, C, D) \text{ :- } q1\,(A, B),\ q2\,(B, C),\ q3\,(4, B),\ D = B + 1\ .$$

5.11. Describe how an arbitrary Datalog rule can be expressed as an extended relational-algebra view.

Bibliographic Notes

The experimental version of Query-by-Example is described in Zloof [1977]; the commercial version is described in IBM [1978b]. Numerous database systems—in particular, database systems that run on personal computers—implement QBE or variants. Quel is defined by Stonebraker et al. [1976]. Stonebraker [1986b] provides a collection of research and survey papers related to the Ingres system. Ingres is now owned by Computer Associates.

Implementations of Datalog include LDL system (described in Tsur and Zaniolo [1986] and Naqvi and Tsur [1988]), Nail! (described in Derr et al. [1993]), and Coral (described in Ramakrishnan et al. [1992a, 1993]). Early discussions concerning logic databases were presented in Gallaire and Minker [1978] and in Gallaire et al. [1984]. A collection of selected papers on this subject is given in Minker [1988]. Ullman [1988, 1989] provides extensive textbook discussions of logic query languages and implementation techniques; these are the sources of the Datalog syntax we have used. Ramakrishnan and Ullman [1995] provide a more recent survey on deductive databases. Further coverage of query-processing techniques for Datalog is given by Bancilhon and Ramakrishnan [1986], Beeri and Ramakrishnan [1991], Ramakrishnan et al. [1992b], Srivastava et al. [1995], and Mumick et al. [1996]. Datalog programs that have both recursion and negation can be assigned a simple semantics if the negation is "stratified"—that is, if there is no recursion through negation. Stratified negation is discussed by Chandra and Harel [1982], and by Apt and Pugin [1987]. An important extension, called the *modular-stratification semantics*, which handles a class of recursive programs with negative literals, is discussed in Ross [1990]; an evaluation technique for such programs is described by Ramakrishnan et al. [1992c].

CHAPTER 6

INTEGRITY CONSTRAINTS

Integrity constraints provide a means of ensuring that changes made to the database by authorized users do not result in a loss of data consistency. Thus, integrity constraints guard against accidental damage to the database.

We have already seen a form of integrity constraint for the E-R model in Chapter 2. These constraints were in the following forms:

- **Key declarations**—the stipulation that certain attributes form a candidate key for a given entity set. The set of legal insertions and updates is constrained to those that do not create two entities with the same value on a candidate key.
- **Form of a relationship**—many to many, one to many, one to one. A one-to-one or one-to-many relationship restricts the set of legal relationships among entities of a collection of entity sets.

In general, an integrity constraint can be an arbitrary predicate pertaining to the database. However, arbitrary predicates may be costly to test. Thus, we usually limit ourselves to integrity constraints that can be tested with minimal overhead.

6.1 Domain Constraints

We have seen that a domain of possible values must be associated with every attribute. In Chapter 4, we saw how such constraints are specified in the SQL DDL. Domain constraints are the most elementary form of integrity constraint. They are tested easily by the system whenever a new data item is entered into the database.

It is possible for several attributes to have the same domain. For example, the attributes *customer-name* and *employee-name* might have the same domain: the set of all person names. However, the domains of *balance* and *branch-name* certainly ought to be distinct. It is perhaps less clear whether *customer-name* and *branch-name* should have the same domain. At the implementation level, both customer names and branch names are character strings. However, we would normally not consider the query "Find all customers who have the same name as a branch" to be a meaningful query. Thus, if we view the database at the conceptual, rather than the physical, level, *customer-name* and *branch-name* should have distinct domains.

From the previous discussion, we can see that a proper definition of domain constraints not only allows us to test values inserted in the database, but also permits us to test queries to ensure that the comparisons made make sense.

The principle behind attribute domains is similar to that behind typing of variables in programming languages. Strongly typed programming languages allow the compiler to check the program in greater detail. However, strongly typed languages inhibit "clever hacks" that are often required for systems programming. Since database systems are designed to support users who are not computer experts, the benefits of strong typing often outweigh the disadvantages. Nevertheless, many existing systems allow only a small number of types of domains. Newer systems, particularly object-oriented database systems, offer a rich set of domain types that can be extended easily. Object-oriented databases are discussed in Chapters 8 and 9.

The **check** clause in SQL-92 permits domains to be restricted in powerful ways that most programming language type systems do not permit. Specifically, the **check** clause permits the schema designer to specify a predicate that must be satisfied by any value assigned to a variable whose type is the domain. For instance, a **check** clause can ensure that an hourly wage domain allows only values greater than a specified value (such as the minimum wage), as illustrated here:

create domain *hourly-wage* **numeric**(5,2)
  constraint *wage-value-test* **check(value** >= 4.00)

The domain *hourly-wage* is declared to be a decimal number with a total of five digits, two of which are placed after the decimal point, and the domain has a constraint that ensures that the hourly wage is greater than 4.00. The clause **constraint** *wage-value-test* is optional, and is used to give the name *wage-value-test* to the constraint. The name is used to indicate which constraint an update violated.

The **check** clause can also be used to restrict a domain to not contain any null values, as illustrated here:

create domain *account-number* **char**(10)
  constraint *account-number-null-test* **check(value not null**)

As another example, the domain can be restricted to contain only a specified set of values by using the **in** clause:

create domain *account-type* **char**(10)
  constraint *account-type-test*
    check(value in ("Checking", "Saving"))

6.2 Referential Integrity

Often, we wish to ensure that a value that appears in one relation for a given set of attributes also appears for a certain set of attributes in another relation. This condition is called *referential integrity*.

6.2.1 Basic Concepts

Consider a pair of relations $r(R)$ and $s(S)$, and the natural join $r \bowtie s$. There may be a tuple t_r in r that does not join with any tuple in s. That is, there is no t_s in s such that $t_r[R \cap S] = t_s[R \cap S]$. Such tuples are called *dangling* tuples. Depending on the entity set or relationship set being modeled, dangling tuples may or may not be acceptable. In Section 3.5.2, we considered a modified form of join—the outer join—to operate on relations containing dangling tuples. Here, our concern is not with queries, but rather with the matter of when we are willing to permit dangling tuples to exist in the database.

Suppose there is a tuple t_1 in the *account* relation with $t_1[branch\text{-}name]$ = "Lunartown," but there is no tuple in the *branch* relation for the Lunartown branch. This situation would be undesirable. We expect the *branch* relation to list all bank branches. Therefore, tuple t_1 would refer to an account at a branch that does not exist. Clearly, we would like to have an integrity constraint that prohibits dangling tuples of this sort.

Not all instances of dangling tuples are undesirable, however. Assume that there is a tuple t_2 in the *branch* relation with $t_2[branch\text{-}name]$ = "Mokan," but there is no tuple in the *account* relation for the Mokan branch. In this case, a branch exists that has no accounts. Although this situation is not common, it may arise when a branch is opened or is about to close. Thus, we do not want to prohibit this situation.

The distinction between these two examples arises from two facts:

- The attribute *branch-name* in *Account-schema* is a foreign key referencing the primary key of *Branch-schema*.
- The attribute *branch-name* in *Branch-schema* is not a foreign key.

(Recall from Section 3.1.3 that a foreign key is a set of attributes in a relation schema that forms a primary key for another schema.)

In the Lunartown example, tuple t_1 in *account* has a value on the foreign key *branch-name* that does not appear in *branch*. In the Mokan-branch example, tuple t_2 in *branch* has a value on *branch-name* that does not appear in *account*, but *branch-name* is not a foreign key. Thus, the distinction between our two examples of dangling tuples is the presence of a foreign key.

Let $r_1(R_1)$ and $r_2(R_2)$ be relations with primary keys K_1 and K_2, respectively. We say that a subset α of R_2 is a *foreign key* referencing K_1 in relation r_1 if it is required that, for every t_2 in r_2, there must be a tuple t_1 in r_1 such that $t_1[K_1] = t_2[\alpha]$. Requirements of this form are called *referential integrity constraints*, or *subset dependencies*. The latter term arises because the preceding referential-integrity constraint can be written as $\Pi_\alpha\ (r_2) \subseteq \Pi_{K_1}\ (r_1)$. Note that, for a referential-integrity constraint to make sense, either α must be equal to K_1, or α and K_1 must be compatible sets of attributes.

6.2.2 Referential Integrity in the E-R Model

Referential-integrity constraints arise frequently. If we derive our relational-database schema by constructing tables from E-R diagrams, as we saw in Chapter 2, then every relation arising from a relationship set has referential-integrity constraints. Figure 6.1 shows an N-ary relationship set R, relating entity sets $E_1, E_2, \ldots, E_n$. Let K_i denote the primary key of E_i. The attributes of the relation schema for relationship set R include $K_1 \cup K_2 \cup \ldots \cup K_n$. Each K_i in the schema for R is a foreign key that leads to a referential-integrity constraint.

Another source of referential-integrity constraints is weak entity sets. Recall from Chapter 2 that the relation schema for a weak entity set must include the primary key of the entity set on which the weak entity set depends. Thus, the relation schema for each weak entity set includes a foreign key that leads to a referential-integrity constraint.

6.2.3 Database Modification

Database modifications can cause violations of referential integrity. We list here the test that we must make for each type of database modification to preserve the following referential-integrity constraint:

$$\Pi_\alpha\ (r_2) \subseteq \Pi_K\ (r_1)$$

- Insert. If a tuple t_2 is inserted into r_2, the system must ensure that there is a tuple t_1 in r_1 such that $t_1[K] = t_2[\alpha]$. That is,

$$t_2[\alpha] \in \Pi_K\ (r_1)$$

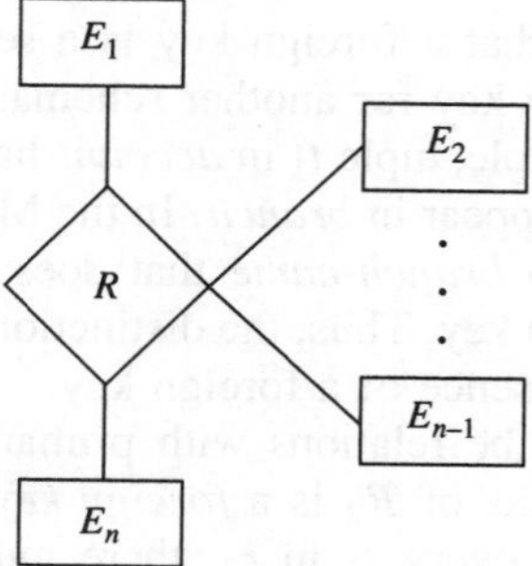

Figure 6.1 An N-ary relationship set.

- Delete. If a tuple t_1 is deleted from r_1, the system must compute the set of tuples in r_2 that reference t_1:

$$\sigma_{\alpha\ =\ t_1[K]}\ (r_2)$$

If this set is not empty, either the delete command is rejected as an error, or the tuples that reference t_1 must themselves be deleted. The latter solution may lead to cascading deletions, since tuples may reference tuples that reference t_1, and so on.

- Update. We must consider two cases for update: updates to the referencing relation (r_2), and updates to the referenced relation (r_1).
  - If a tuple t_2 is updated in relation r_2, and the update modifies values for the foreign key α, then a test similar to the insert case is made. Let t_2' denote the new value of tuple t_2. The system must ensure that

$$t_2'[\alpha] \in \Pi_K\ (r_1)$$

  - If a tuple t_1 is updated in r_1, and the update modifies values for the primary key (K), then a test similar to the delete case is made. The system must compute

$$\sigma_{\alpha\ =\ t_1[K]}\ (r_2)$$

using the old value of t_1 (the value before the update is applied). If this set is not empty, the update is rejected as an error, or the update is cascaded in a manner similar to delete.

6.2.4 Referential Integrity in SQL

Primary and candidate keys and foreign keys can be specified as part of the SQL **create table** statement:

- The **primary key** clause of the **create table** statement includes a list of the attributes that constitute the primary key.
- The **unique** clause of the **create table** statement includes a list of the attributes that constitute a candidate key.
- The **foreign key** clause of the **create table** statement includes both a list of the attributes that constitute the foreign key and the name of the relation referenced by the foreign key.

We illustrate primary- and foreign-key declarations using the partial SQL DDL definition of our bank database shown in Figure 6.2. Note that, as in earlier chapters, we do not attempt to model precisely the real world in the bank-database example. In the real world, multiple people may have the same name, so *customer-name* would not be a primary key for *customer*. In the real world, some other attribute, such as the social-security number, or a combination of attributes such as name and address, would be used as a primary key. We use *customer-name* as a primary key to keep our database schema simple and short.

```
create table customer
    (customer-name   char(20) not null,
     customer-street char(30),
     customer-city   char(30),
     primary key (customer-name))

create table branch
    (branch-name  char(15) not null,
     branch-city  char(30),
     assets       integer,
     primary key (branch-name),
     check (assets >= 0))

create table account
    (account-number char(10) not null,
     branch-name    char(15),
     balance        integer,
     primary key (account-number),
     foreign key (branch-name) references branch,
     check (balance >= 0))

create table depositor
    (customer-name  char(20) not null,
     account-number char(10) not null,
     primary key (customer-name, account-number),
     foreign key (customer-name) references customer,
     foreign key (account-number) references account)
```

Figure 6.2 SQL data definition for part of the bank database.

We can use the following short form to declare that a single column is a foreign key:

```
branch-name     char(15) references branch
```

SQL also supports a version of the foreign-key clause where a list of attributes of the referenced relation can be specified explicitly, and these attributes are used instead of the primary key; the specified list of attributes must be declared as a candidate key of the referenced relation.

When a referential-integrity constraint is violated, the normal procedure is to reject the action that caused the violation. However, a **foreign key** clause in SQL-92 can specify that, if a delete or update action on the referenced relation violates the constraint, then, instead of rejecting the action, steps are to be taken to change the tuple in the referencing relation to restore the constraint. Consider the following definition of an integrity constraint on the relation *account*:

```
create table account
   ...
   foreign key (branch-name) references branch
                             on delete cascade
                             on update cascade,
   ... )
```

Due to the clause **on delete cascade** associated with the foreign-key declaration, if a delete of a tuple in *branch* results in the preceding referential-integrity constraint being violated, the delete is not rejected. Instead, the delete "cascades" to the *account* relation, deleting the tuple that refers to the branch that was deleted. Similarly, an update to a field referenced by the constraint is not rejected if it violates the constraint; instead, the field *branch-name* in the referencing tuples in *account* are updated to the new value as well. SQL-92 also allows the **foreign key** clause to specify actions other than cascade, such as setting the referencing field (here, *branch-name*) to null, or to a default value, if the constraint is violated.

If there is a chain of foreign-key dependencies across multiple relations, a deletion or update at one end of the chain can propagate across the entire chain. An interesting case where the **foreign key** constraint on a relation references the same relation is considered in Exercise 6.4. If a cascading update or delete causes a constraint violation that cannot be handled by a further cascading operation, the system aborts the transaction. As a result, all the changes caused by the transaction and its cascading actions are undone.

The semantics of the keys in SQL is complicated by the fact that SQL allows null values. The following rules, some of which are arbitrary, are used to deal with null values:

- All attributes of the primary key are implicitly declared to be **not null**.
- Attributes of a **unique** declaration (that is, attributes of a candidate key) are allowed to be null, provided that they have not otherwise been declared to be nonnull. The uniqueness constraint on a relation is violated only if two tuples in the relation have the same values for all the attributes in a **unique** constraint, and all the values are nonnull. Thus, any number of tuples can be equal on all columns declared to be unique without violating the constraint, provided that at least one of the columns has a null value. The treatment of nulls here is the same as that of the **unique** construct defined in Section 4.6.4.
- Attributes of foreign keys are allowed to be null, provided that they have not otherwise been declared to be nonnull. If all the columns of a foreign key are nonnull in a given tuple, the usual definition of foreign-key constraints is used for that tuple. If any of the foreign-key columns is null, the tuple is defined automatically to satisfy the constraint. This definition is arbitrary and may not always be the right choice, so SQL also provides constructs that allow you to change the behavior with null values; we do not discuss the constructs here.

Given the complexity and arbitrary nature of the way constraints in SQL behave with null values, it is best to ensure that all columns of **unique** and **foreign key** specifications are declared to be nonnull.

6.3 Assertions

An *assertion* is a predicate expressing a condition that we wish the database always to satisfy. Domain constraints and referential-integrity constraints are special forms of assertions. We have paid substantial attention to these forms of assertion because they are easily tested and apply to a wide range of database applications. However, there are many constraints that we cannot express using only these special forms. Examples of such constraints include

- The sum of all loan amounts for each branch must be less than the sum of all account balances at the branch.
- Every loan has at least one customer who maintains an account with a minimum balance of $1000.00.

An assertion in SQL-92 takes the form

create assertion <assertion-name> **check** <predicate>

The two constraints mentioned can be written as shown next. Since SQL does not provide a "for all X, $P(X)$" construct (where P is a predicate), we are forced to implement the construct using then equivalent "not exists X such that not $P(X)$" construct, which can be written in SQL.

```
create assertion sum-constraint check
    (not exists (select * from branch
        where (select sum(amount) from loan
                where loan.branch-name = branch.branch-name)
            >= (select sum(amount) from account
                where loan.branch-name = branch.branch-name)))

create assertion balance-constraint check
    (not exists (select * from loan
        where not exists ( select *
            from borrower, depositor, account
            where loan.loan-number = borrower.loan-number
                and borrower.customer-name = depositor.customer-name
                and depositor.account-number = account.account-number
                and account.balance >= 1000)))
```

When an assertion is created, the system tests it for validity. If the assertion is valid, then any future modification to the database is allowed only if it does not cause that assertion to be violated. This testing may introduce a significant amount of overhead if complex assertions have been made. Hence, assertions should be used with great care. The high overhead of testing and maintaining assertions has led some system developers to omit support for general assertions, or to provide specialized forms of assertions that are easier to test.

6.4 Triggers

A *trigger* is a statement that is executed automatically by the system as a side effect of a modification to the database. To design a trigger mechanism, we must meet two requirements:

1. Specify the conditions under which the trigger is to be executed.
2. Specify the actions to be taken when the trigger executes.

Triggers are useful mechanisms for alerting humans, or for performing certain tasks automatically when certain conditions are met. As an illustration, suppose that, instead of allowing negative account balances, the bank deals with overdrafts by setting the account balance to zero, and creating a loan in the amount of the overdraft. This loan is given a loan number identical to the account number of the overdrawn account. For this example, the condition for executing the trigger is an update to the *account* relation that results in a negative *balance* value. Suppose that Jones withdrew some money from an account that resulted in the account balance being negative. Let t denote the account tuple with a negative *balance* value. The actions to be taken are as follows:

- Insert a new tuple s in the *loan* relation with

$$s[branch\text{-}name] = t[branch\text{-}name]$$
$$s[loan\text{-}number] = t[account\text{-}number]$$
$$s[amount] = -t[balance]$$

  (Note that, since $t[balance]$ is negative, we negate $t[balance]$ to get the loan amount—a positive number.)

- Insert a new tuple u in the *borrower* relation with

$$u[customer - name] = \text{“Jones”}$$
$$u[loan\text{-}number] = t[account\text{-}number]$$

- Set $t[balance]$ to 0.

The SQL-92 standard does not include triggers, although the original System R SQL proposal included a limited trigger feature. Several existing systems have their own nonstandard trigger features. Here, we illustrate how the account-overdraft trigger would be written in the original version of SQL:

define trigger *overdraft* **on update of** *account T*
  (if new *T.balance* < 0
  then (insert into *loan* **values**
      (*T.branch-name, T.account-number*, − **new** *T.balance*)
    insert into *borrower*
      (select *customer-name, account-number*
      from *depositor*
      where *T.account-number* = *depositor.account-number*)
    update *account S*
    set *S.balance* = 0
    where *S.account-number* = *T.account-number*))

The keyword **new** used before *T.balance* indicates that the value of *T.balance* after the update should be used; if it is omitted, the value before the update is used.

Triggers are sometimes called *rules*, or *active rules*, but should not be confused with Datalog rules (see Section 5.3), which are really view definitions.

6.5 Functional Dependencies

This section focuses on a particular kind of constraint called a *functional dependency*. The notion of functional dependency is a generalization of the notion of *key*, as discussed in Chapters 2 and 3. Functional dependencies play an important role in database design, which we study in Chapter 7.

6.5.1 Basic Concepts

Functional dependencies are constraints on the set of legal relations. They allow us to express facts about the enterprise that we are modeling with our database.

In Chapter 2, we defined the notion of a *superkey* as follows. Let R be a relation schema. A subset K of R is a *superkey* of R if, in any legal relation $r(R)$, for all pairs t_1 and t_2 of tuples in r such that $t_1 \neq t_2$, then $t_1[K] \neq t_2[K]$. That is, no two tuples in any legal relation $r(R)$ may have the same value on attribute set K.

The notion of functional dependency generalizes the notion of superkey. Let $\alpha \subseteq R$ and $\beta \subseteq R$. The *functional dependency*

$$\alpha \rightarrow \beta$$

holds on R if, in any legal relation $r(R)$, for all pairs of tuples t_1 and t_2 in r such that $t_1[\alpha] = t_2[\alpha]$, it is also the case that $t_1[\beta] = t_2[\beta]$.

Using the functional-dependency notation, we say that K is a superkey of R if $K \rightarrow R$. That is, K is a superkey if, whenever $t_1[K] = t_2[K]$, it is also the case that $t_1[R] = t_2[R]$ (that is, $t_1 = t_2$).

Functional dependencies allow us to express constraints that we cannot express using superkeys. Consider the schema

Loan-info-schema = (*branch-name, loan-number, customer-name, amount*).

The set of functional dependencies that we expect to hold on this relation schema is

loan-number → *amount*
loan-number → *branch-name*

We would not, however, expect the functional dependency

loan-number → *customer-name*

to hold, since, in general, a given loan can be made to more than one customer (for example, to both members of a husband–wife pair).

We shall use functional dependencies in two ways:

1. We use them to specify constraints on the set of legal relations. We shall thus concern ourselves with *only* those relations that satisfy a given set of functional dependencies. If we wish to constrain ourselves to relations on schema R that satisfy a set F of functional dependencies, we say that F *holds* on R.

2. We use them to test relations to see whether the latter are legal under a given set of functional dependencies. If a relation r is legal under a set F of functional dependencies, we say that r *satisfies* F.

Let us consider the relation r of Figure 6.3, to see which functional dependencies are satisfied. Observe that $A \rightarrow C$ is satisfied. There are two tuples that have an A value of a_1. These tuples have the same C value—namely, c_1. Similarly, the two tuples with an A value of a_2 have the same C value, c_2. There are no other pairs of distinct tuples that have the same A value. The functional dependency $C \rightarrow A$ is not satisfied, however. To see that is is not, consider the tuples $t_1 = (a_2, b_3, c_2, d_3)$ and $t_2 = (a_3, b_3, c_2, d_4)$. These two tuples have the same C values, c_2, but they have different A values, a_2 and a_3, respectively. Thus, we have found a pair of tuples t_1 and t_2 such that $t_1[C] = t_2[C]$, but $t_1[A] \neq t_2[A]$.

Many other functional dependencies are satisfied by r, including, for example, the functional dependency $AB \rightarrow D$. Note that we use AB as a shorthand for $\{A,B\}$, to conform with standard practice. Observe that there is no pair of distinct tuples t_1 and t_2 such that $t_1[AB] = t_2[AB]$. Therefore, if $t_1[AB] = t_2[AB]$, it must be that $t_1 = t_2$ and, thus, $t_1[D] = t_2[D]$. So, r satisfies $AB \rightarrow D$.

A	B	C	D
a_1	b_1	c_1	d_1
a_1	b_2	c_1	d_2
a_2	b_2	c_2	d_2
a_2	b_3	c_2	d_3
a_3	b_3	c_2	d_4

Figure 6.3 Sample relation r.

customer-name	*customer-street*	*customer-city*
Jones	Main	Harrison
Smith	North	Rye
Hayes	Main	Harrison
Curry	North	Rye
Lindsay	Park	Pittsfield
Turner	Putnam	Stamford
Williams	Nassau	Princeton
Adams	Spring	Pittsfield
Johnson	Alma	Palo Alto
Glenn	Sand Hill	Woodside
Brooks	Senator	Brooklyn
Green	Walnut	Stamford

Figure 6.4 The *customer* relation.

Some functional dependencies are said to be *trivial* because they are satisfied by all relations. For example, $A \rightarrow A$ is satisfied by all relations involving attribute A. Reading the definition of functional-dependency literally, we see that, for all tuples t_1 and t_2 such that $t_1[A] = t_2[A]$, it is the case that $t_1[A] = t_2[A]$. Similarly, $AB \rightarrow A$ is satisfied by all relations involving attribute A. In general, a functional dependency of the form $\alpha \rightarrow \beta$ is trivial if $\beta \subseteq \alpha$.

To distinguish between the concepts of a relation satisfying a dependency and a dependency holding on a schema, we return to the banking example. If we consider the *customer* relation (on *Customer-schema*) as shown in Figure 6.4, we see that *customer-street* → *customer-city* is satisfied. However, we believe that, in the real world, two cities can have streets with the same name. Thus, it is possible, at some time, to have an instance of the *customer* relation in which *customer-street* → *customer-city* is not satisfied. So, we would not include *customer-street* → *customer-city* in the set of functional dependencies that hold on *Customer-schema*.

In the *loan* relation (on *Loan-schema*) of Figure 6.5, we see that *loan-number* → *amount* is satisfied. Unlike the case of *customer-city* and *customer-street* in *Customer-schema*, we do believe that the real-world enterprise that we are modeling requires each loan to have only one amount. Therefore, we want to require that *loan-number* → *amount* be satisfied by the *loan* relation at all times. In other words, we require that the constraint that *loan-number* → *amount* hold on *Loan-schema*.

In the *branch* relation of Figure 6.6, we see that *branch-name* → *assets* is satisfied, as is *assets* → *branch-name*. We want to require that *branch-name* → *assets* hold on *Branch-schema*. However, we do not wish to require that *assets* → *branch-name* hold, since it is possible to have several branches that have the same asset value.

Although SQL does not provide a simple way of specifying functional dependencies, we can write queries to test for functional dependencies, as well as to create assertions that enforce functional dependencies, as discussed in Exercise 6.19.

branch-name	*loan-number*	*amount*
Downtown	L-17	1000
Redwood	L-23	2000
Perryridge	L-15	1500
Downtown	L-14	1500
Mianus	L-93	500
Round Hill	L-11	900
Pownal	L-29	1200
North Town	L-16	1300
Downtown	L-18	2000
Perryridge	L-25	2500
Brighton	L-10	2200

Figure 6.5 The *loan* relation.

In what follows, we assume that, when we design a relational database, we first list those functional dependencies that must always hold. In the banking example, our list of dependencies includes the following:

- On *Branch-schema*:

$$\begin{array}{l} \textit{branch-name} \rightarrow \textit{branch-city} \\ \textit{branch-name} \rightarrow \textit{assets} \end{array}$$

- On *Customer-schema*:

$$\begin{array}{l} \textit{customer-name} \rightarrow \textit{customer-city} \\ \textit{customer-name} \rightarrow \textit{customer-street} \end{array}$$

- On *Loan-schema*:

$$\begin{array}{l} \textit{loan-number} \rightarrow \textit{amount} \\ \textit{loan-number} \rightarrow \textit{branch-name} \end{array}$$

branch-name	*branch-city*	*assets*
Downtown	Brooklyn	9000000
Redwood	Palo Alto	2100000
Perryridge	Horseneck	1700000
Mianus	Horseneck	400000
Round Hill	Horseneck	8000000
Pownal	Bennington	300000
North Town	Rye	3700000
Brighton	Brooklyn	7100000

Figure 6.6 The *branch* relation.

- On *Borrower-schema*:

  no functional dependencies

- On *Account-schema*:

  account-number → *branch-name*
  account-number → *balance*

- On *Depositor-schema*:

  no functional dependencies

6.5.2 Closure of a Set of Functional Dependencies

It is not sufficient to consider the given set of functional dependencies. Rather, we need to consider *all* functional dependencies that hold. We shall see that, given a set F of functional dependencies, we can prove that certain other functional dependencies hold. We say that such functional dependencies are *logically implied* by F.

Suppose we are given a relation schema $R = (A, B, C, G, H, I)$ and the set of functional dependencies

$$\begin{array}{l} A \rightarrow B \\ A \rightarrow C \\ CG \rightarrow H \\ CG \rightarrow I \\ B \rightarrow H \end{array}$$

The functional dependency

$$A \rightarrow H$$

is logically implied. That is, we can show that, whenever our given set of functional dependencies holds, $A \rightarrow H$ must hold also. Suppose that t_1 and t_2 are tuples such that

$$t_1[A] = t_2[A]$$

Since we are given that $A \rightarrow B$, it follows from the definition of functional dependency that

$$t_1[B] = t_2[B]$$

Then, since we are given that $B \rightarrow H$, it follows from the definition of functional dependency that

$$t_1[H] = t_2[H]$$

Therefore, we have shown that, whenever t_1 and t_2 are tuples such that $t_1[A] = t_2[A]$, it must be that $t_1[H] = t_2[H]$. But that is exactly the definition of $A \rightarrow H$.

Let F be a set of functional dependencies. The closure of F is the set of all functional dependencies logically implied by F. We denote the *closure* of F by F^+. Given F, we can compute F^+ directly from the formal definition of functional dependency. If F were large, this process would be lengthy and difficult. Such a computation of F^+ requires arguments of the type given previously to show that $A \rightarrow H$ is in the closure of our example set of dependencies. There are simpler techniques for reasoning about functional dependencies.

The first technique is based on three *axioms* or rules of inference for functional dependencies. By applying these rules repeatedly, we can find all of F^+ given F. In the rules that follow, we adopt the convention of using Greek letters (α, β, γ, ...) for sets of attributes, and uppercase Roman letters from the beginning of the alphabet for individual attributes. We use $\alpha\beta$ to denote $\alpha \cup \beta$.

- **Reflexivity rule**. If α is a set of attributes and $\beta \subseteq \alpha$, then $\alpha \rightarrow \beta$ holds.
- **Augmentation rule**. If $\alpha \rightarrow \beta$ holds and γ is a set of attributes, then $\gamma\alpha \rightarrow \gamma\beta$ holds.
- **Transitivity rule**. If $\alpha \rightarrow \beta$ holds and $\beta \rightarrow \gamma$ holds, then $\alpha \rightarrow \gamma$ holds.

These rules are *sound*, because they do not generate any incorrect functional dependencies. The rules are *complete*, because, for a given set F of functional dependencies, they allow us to generate all F^+. This collection of rules is called *Armstrong's axioms* in honor of the person who first proposed it.

Although Armstrong's axioms are complete, it is tiresome to use them directly for the computation of F^+. To simplify matters further, we list additional rules. It is possible to use Armstrong's axioms to prove that these rules are correct (see Exercises 6.12, 6.13, and 6.14).

- **Union rule**. If $\alpha \rightarrow \beta$ holds and $\alpha \rightarrow \gamma$ holds, then $\alpha \rightarrow \beta\gamma$ holds.
- **Decomposition rule**. If $\alpha \rightarrow \beta\gamma$ holds, then $\alpha \rightarrow \beta$ holds and $\alpha \rightarrow \gamma$ holds.
- **Pseudotransitivity rule**. If $\alpha \rightarrow \beta$ holds and $\gamma\beta \rightarrow \delta$ holds, then $\alpha\gamma \rightarrow \delta$ holds.

Let us apply our rules to the example that we presented earlier of schema $R = (A, B, C, G, H, I)$ and the set F of functional dependencies $\{A \rightarrow B, A \rightarrow C, CG \rightarrow H, CG \rightarrow I, B \rightarrow H\}$. We list several members of F^+ here:

- $A \rightarrow H$. Since $A \rightarrow B$ and $B \rightarrow H$ holds, we apply the transitivity rule. Observe that it was much easier to use Armstrong's axioms to show that $A \rightarrow H$ holds than it was to argue directly from the definitions, as we did earlier.
- $CG \rightarrow HI$. Since $CG \rightarrow H$ and $CG \rightarrow I$, the union rule implies that $CG \rightarrow HI$.
- $AG \rightarrow I$. Since $A \rightarrow C$ and $CG \rightarrow I$, the pseudotransitivity rule implies that $AG \rightarrow I$ holds.

6.5.3 Closure of Attribute Sets

To test whether a set α is a superkey, we must devise an algorithm for computing the set of attributes functionally determined by α. We shall see that such an algorithm is useful also as part of the computation of the closure of a set F of functional dependencies.

Let α be a set of attributes. We call the set of all attributes functionally determined by α under a set F of functional dependencies the *closure* of α under F; we denote it by α^+. Figure 6.7 shows an algorithm, written in pseudo-Pascal, to compute α^+. The input is a set F of functional dependencies and the set α of attributes. The output is stored in the variable *result*.

To illustrate how the algorithm of Figure 6.7 works, we shall use the algorithm to compute $(AG)^+$ with the functional dependencies defined previously. We start with *result* $= AG$. The first time that we execute the **while** loop to test each functional dependency, we find that

- $A \rightarrow B$ causes us to include B in *result*. To see this fact, we observe that $A \rightarrow B$ is in F, $A \subseteq$ *result* (which is AG), so *result* := *result* $\cup B$.
- $A \rightarrow C$ causes *result* to become $ABCG$.
- $CG \rightarrow H$ causes *result* to become $ABCGH$.
- $CG \rightarrow I$ causes *result* to become $ABCGHI$.

The second time that we execute the **while** loop, no new attributes are added to *result*, and the algorithm terminates.

Let us see why the algorithm of Figure 6.7 is correct. The first step is correct, since $\alpha \rightarrow \alpha$ always holds (by the reflexivity rule). We claim that, for any subset β of *result*, $\alpha \rightarrow \beta$. Since we start the **while** loop with $\alpha \rightarrow$ *result* being true, we can add γ to *result* only if $\beta \subseteq$ *result* and $\beta \rightarrow \gamma$. But then *result* $\rightarrow \beta$ by the reflexivity rule, so $\alpha \rightarrow \beta$ by transitivity. Another application of transitivity shows that $\alpha \rightarrow \gamma$ (using $\alpha \rightarrow \beta$ and $\beta \rightarrow \gamma$). The union rule implies that $\alpha \rightarrow$ *result* $\cup\ \gamma$, so α functionally determines any new result generated in the **while** loop. Thus, any attribute returned by the algorithm is in α^+.

It is easy to see that the algorithm finds all α^+. If there is an attribute in α^+ that is not yet in *result*, then there must be a functional dependency $\beta \rightarrow \gamma$ for which $\beta \subseteq$ *result*, and at least one attribute in γ is not in *result*.

It turns out that, in the worst case, this algorithm may take time quadratic in the size of F. There is a faster (although slightly more complex) algorithm that runs in time linear in the size of F; that algorithm is presented as part of Exercise 6.18.

```
result := α;
while (changes to result) do
    for each functional dependency β → γ in F do
      begin
        if β ⊆ result then result := result ∪ γ;
      end
```

Figure 6.7 An algorithm to compute α^+, the closure of α under F.

6.5.4 Canonical Cover

Suppose that we have a set of functional dependencies F on a relation schema. Whenever an update is performed on the relation, the database system must ensure that all the functional dependencies in F are satisfied in the new database state, and must rollback the update if they are not. We can reduce the effort required to perform the test by simplifying the given set of functional dependencies without changing that set's closure. Any database that satisfies the simplified set of functional dependencies will also satisfy the original set, and vice versa, since the two sets have the same closure. However, the simplified set is easier to test. The simplified set can be constructed as we shall describe in a moment. First, we need some definitions.

An attribute of a functional dependency is *extraneous* if we can remove it without changing the closure of the set of functional dependencies. Formally, extraneous attributes are defined as follows. Consider a set F of functional dependencies and the functional dependency $\alpha \rightarrow \beta$ in F.

- Attribute A is extraneous in α if $A \in \alpha$, and F logically implies $(F - \{\alpha \rightarrow \beta\}) \cup \{(\alpha - A) \rightarrow \beta\}$.
- Attribute A is extraneous in β if $A \in \beta$, and the set of functional dependencies $(F - \{\alpha \rightarrow \beta\}) \cup \{\alpha \rightarrow (\beta - A)\}$ logically implies F.

A *canonical cover* F_c for F is a set of dependencies such that F logically implies all dependencies in F_c, and F_c logically implies all dependencies in F. Furthermore, F_c must have the following properties:

- No functional dependency in F_c contains an extraneous attribute.
- Each left side of a functional dependency in F_c is unique. That is, there are no two dependencies $\alpha_1 \rightarrow \beta_1$ and $\alpha_2 \rightarrow \beta_2$ in F_c such that $\alpha_1 = \alpha_2$.

A canonical cover for a set of functional dependencies F can be computed as follows:

repeat
  Use the union rule to replace any dependencies in F of the form
    $\alpha_1 \rightarrow \beta_1$ and $\alpha_1 \rightarrow \beta_2$ with $\alpha_1 \rightarrow \beta_1 \beta_2$.
  Find a functional dependency $\alpha \rightarrow \beta$ with an extraneous
    attribute either in α or in β.
  If an extraneous attribute is found, delete it from $\alpha \rightarrow \beta$.
until F does not change.

The canonical cover of F, F_c, can be shown to have the same closure as F; hence, testing whether F_c is satisfied is equivalent to testing whether F is satisfied. However, F_c is minimal in a certain sense—it does not contain extraneous attributes, and functional dependencies with the same left side have been combined. It is cheaper to test F_c than it is to test F itself.

Consider the following set F of functional dependencies on schema (A, B, C):

$$A \rightarrow BC$$
$$B \rightarrow C$$
$$A \rightarrow B$$
$$AB \rightarrow C$$

Let us compute the canonical cover for F.

- There are two functional dependencies with the same set of attributes on the left side of the arrow:

  $$A \rightarrow BC$$
  $$A \rightarrow B$$

  We combine these functional dependencies into $A \rightarrow BC$.
- A is extraneous in $AB \rightarrow C$ because F logically implies $(F - \{AB \rightarrow C\}) \cup \{B \rightarrow C\}$. This assertion is true because $B \rightarrow C$ is already in our set of functional dependencies.
- C is extraneous in $A \rightarrow BC$, since $A \rightarrow BC$ is logically implied by $A \rightarrow B$ and $B \rightarrow C$.

Thus, our canonical cover is

$$A \rightarrow B$$
$$B \rightarrow C$$

Given a set F of functional dependencies, it may be that an entire functional dependency in the set is extraneous, in the sense that dropping it does not change the closure of F. We can show that a canonical cover F_c of F contains no such extraneous functional dependency. Suppose that, to the contrary, there was such an extraneous functional dependency in F_c. The right side attributes of the dependency would then be extraneous, which is not possible by the definition of canonical covers.

6.6 Summary

Integrity constraints ensure that changes made to the database by authorized users do not result in a loss of data consistency. In earlier chapters, we considered several forms of constraints, including key declarations and the declaration of the form of a relationship (many to many, many to one, one to one). In this chapter, we considered several additional forms of constraints, and discussed mechanisms for ensuring the maintenance of these constraints.

Domain constraints specify the set of possible values that may be associated with an attribute. Such constraints may also prohibit the use of null values for particular attributes.

Referential-integrity constraints ensure that a value that appears in one relation for a given set of attributes also appears for a certain set of attributes in another relation.

Functional dependencies are a generalization of key dependencies. They require that the value for a certain set of attributes determines uniquely the value for another set of attributes. Using the formal definition of functional dependencies, we saw how to determine the set of all functional dependencies logically implied by a given set F of functional dependencies. This set is called the closure of F. We also saw a way to reduce the size of a set F of functional dependencies without changing the closure. This set is called a canonical cover F_c for F.

Domain constraints, referential-integrity constraints, and functional dependencies are relatively easy to test. Use of more complex constraints may lead to substantial overhead. We saw two ways to express more general constraints. Assertions are declarative expressions that state predicates that we require always to be true. Triggers are procedures to be executed when certain events occur.

Exercises

6.1. Complete the SQL DDL definition of the bank database of Figure 6.2 to include the relations *loan* and *borrower*.

6.2. Consider the following relational database:

employee (*person-name*, *street*, *city*)
works (*person-name*, *company-name*, *salary*)
company (*company-name*, *city*)
manages (*person-name*, *manager-name*)

Give an SQL DDL definition of this database. Identify referential-integrity constraints that should hold, and include them in the DDL definition.

6.3. Referential-integrity constraints as defined in this chapter involve exactly two relations. Consider a database that includes the following relations:

salaried-worker (*name, office, phone, salary*)
hourly-worker (*name, hourly-wage*)
address (*name, street, city*)

Suppose that we wish to require that every name that appears in *address* appear in either *salaried-worker* or *hourly-worker*, but not necessarily in both.

(*a*) Propose a syntax for expressing such constraints.
(*b*) Discuss the actions that the system must take to enforce a constraint of this form.

6.4. The SQL-92 standard allows a foreign-key dependency to refer to the same relation, as in the following example:

```
create table manager
    (employee-name  char(20) not null
    manager-name    char(20) not null,
    primary key employee-name,
    foreign key (manager-name) references manager
                               on delete cascade )
```

Here, *employee-name* is a key to the table *manager*, meaning that each employee has at most one manager. The foreign-key clause requires that every manager also be an employee. Explain exactly what happens when a tuple in the relation *manager* is deleted.

6.5. Suppose there are two relations r and s, such that the foreign key B of r references the primary key A of s. Describe how the trigger mechanism can be used to implement the **on delete cascade** option, when a tuple is deleted from s.

6.6. Write an assertion for the bank database to ensure that the assets value for the Perryridge branch is equal to the sum of all the amounts lent by the Perryridge branch.

6.7. Why are certain functional dependencies called *trivial* functional dependencies?

6.8. List all functional dependencies satisfied by the relation of Figure 6.8.

6.9. Use the definition of functional dependency to argue that each of Armstrong's axioms (reflexivity, augmentation, and transitivity) is sound.

6.10. Explain how functional dependencies can be used to indicate the following:

- A one-to-one relationship set exists between entity sets *student* and *advisor*.
- A many-to-one relationship set exists between entity sets *student* and *advisor*.

6.11. Consider the following proposed rule for functional dependencies: If $\alpha \rightarrow \beta$ and $\gamma \rightarrow \beta$, then $\alpha \rightarrow \gamma$. Prove that this rule is *not* sound by showing a relation r that satisfies $\alpha \rightarrow \beta$ and $\gamma \rightarrow \beta$, but does not satisfy $\alpha \rightarrow \gamma$.

6.12. Use Armstrong's axioms to prove the soundness of the union rule. (Hint: Use the augmentation rule to show that, if $\alpha \rightarrow \beta$, then $\alpha \rightarrow \alpha\beta$. Apply the augmentation rule again, using $\alpha \rightarrow \gamma$, and then apply the transitivity rule.)

6.13. Use Armstrong's axioms to prove the soundness of the decomposition rule.

6.14. Use Armstrong's axioms to prove the soundness of the pseudotransitivity rule.

A	B	C
a_1	b_1	c_1
a_1	b_1	c_2
a_2	b_1	c_1
a_2	b_1	c_3

Figure 6.8 Relation of Exercise 6.8.

6.15. Compute the closure of the following set F of functional dependencies for relation schema $R = (A, B, C, D, E)$.

$$A \rightarrow BC$$
$$CD \rightarrow E$$
$$B \rightarrow D$$
$$E \rightarrow A$$

List the candidate keys for R.

6.16. Using the functional dependencies of Exercise 6.15, compute B^+.

6.17. Using the functional dependencies of Exercise 6.15, compute the canonical cover F_c.

6.18. Consider the algorithm shown in Figure 6.9 to compute α^+. Show that this algorithm is more efficient than is the one presented in Figure 6.7 (Section 6.5.3) and that it computes α^+ correctly.

6.19. Given the database schema $R(a, b, c)$, and a relation r on the schema R, write an SQL query to test whether the functional dependency $b \rightarrow c$ holds on relation r. Also write an SQL assertion that enforces the functional dependency. Assume that no null values are present.

Bibliographic Notes

Discussions concerning integrity constraints in the relational model are offered by Hammer and McLeod [1975], Stonebraker [1975], Eswaran and Chamberlin [1975], Schmid and Swenson [1975], and Codd [1979].

Functional dependencies were originally defined by Codd [1970]. Armstrong's axioms were introduced by Armstrong [1974]. The theory of functional dependencies is discussed in Maier [1983]. Formal aspects of the concept of a legal relation are discussed by Graham et al. [1986]. Application of functional dependencies to semantic data models is discussed in Weddell [1992].

The original SQL proposals for assertions and triggers are discussed in Astrahan et al. [1976], Chamberlin et al. [1976], and Chamberlin et al. [1981]. See the bibliographic notes of Chapter 4 for references to SQL standards.

Discussions concerning efficient maintenance and checking of semantic-integrity assertions is offered by Hammer and Sarin [1978], Badal and Popek [1979], Bernstein et al. [1980b], Hsu and Imielinski [1985], McCune and Henschen [1989], and Chomicki [1992a, 1992b]. Active databases are discussed in McCarthy and Dayal [1989], Gehani and Jagadish [1991], and Gehani et al. [1992].

An alternative to using run-time integrity checking is certifying the correctness of programs that access the database. This approach is discussed by Sheard and Stemple [1989].

```
result := Ø;
/* fdcount is an array whose ith element contains the number
   of attributes on the left side of the ith FD that are
   not yet known to be in α+ */
for i := 1 to |F| do
   begin
      let β → γ denote the ith FD;
      fdcount [i] := |β|;
   end
/* appears is an array with one entry for each attribute. The
   entry for attribute A is a list of integers. Each integer
   i on the list indicates that A appears on the left side
   of the ith FD */
for each attribute A do
   begin
      appears [A] := NIL;
      for i := 1 to |F| do
         begin
            let β → γ denote the ith FD;
            if A ∈ β then add i to appears [A];
         end
   end
addin (α);
return (result);

procedure addin (α);
for each attribute A in α do
begin
   if A ∉ result then
      begin
         result := result ∪ {A};
         for each element i of appears[A] do
            begin
               fdcount [i] := fdcount [i] − 1;
               if fdcount [i] := 0 then
                  begin
                     let β → γ denote the ith FD;
                     addin (γ);
                  end
            end
      end
end
```

Figure 6.9 An algorithm to compute α^+.

CHAPTER 7

RELATIONAL DATABASE DESIGN

This chapter continues our discussion of design issues in relational databases. In general, the goal of a relational-database design is to generate a set of relation schemas that allows us to store information without unnecessary redundancy, yet also allows us to retrieve information easily. One approach is to design schemas that are in an appropriate *normal form*. To determine whether a relation schema is in one of the normal forms, we need additional information about the real-world enterprise that we are modeling with the database. We have already seen how we can use functional dependencies to express facts about the data. In this chapter, we define normal forms using functional dependencies and using other types of data dependencies.

7.1 Pitfalls in Relational-Database Design

Before we begin our discussion of normal forms and data dependencies, let us look at what can go wrong in a bad database design. Among the undesirable properties that a bad design may have are

- Repetition of information
- Inability to represent certain information

We shall discuss these problems using a modified database design for our banking example; in contrast to the relation schema used in Chapters 3 to 6, the information concerning loans is now kept in one single relation, *lending*, which is defined over

branch-name	*branch-city*	*assets*	*customer-name*	*loan-number*	*amount*
Downtown	Brooklyn	9000000	Jones	L-17	1000
Redwood	Palo Alto	2100000	Smith	L-23	2000
Perryridge	Horseneck	1700000	Hayes	L-15	1500
Downtown	Brooklyn	9000000	Jackson	L-14	1500
Mianus	Horseneck	400000	Jones	L-93	500
Round Hill	Horseneck	8000000	Turner	L-11	900
Pownal	Bennington	300000	Williams	L-29	1200
North Town	Rye	3700000	Hayes	L-16	1300
Downtown	Brooklyn	9000000	Johnson	L-23	2000
Perryridge	Horseneck	1700000	Glenn	L-25	2500
Brighton	Brooklyn	7100000	Brooks	L-10	2200

Figure 7.1 Sample *lending* relation.

the relation schema

Lending-schema = (*branch-name, branch-city, assets, customer-name, loan-number, amount*)

Figure 7.1 shows an instance of the relation *lending* (*Lending-schema*). A tuple *t* in the *lending* relation has the following intuitive meaning:

- *t*[*assets*] is the asset figure for the branch named *t*[*branch-name*].
- *t*[*branch-city*] is the city in which the branch named *t*[*branch-name*] is located.
- *t*[*loan-number*] is the number assigned to a loan made by the branch named *t*[*branch-name*] to the customer named *t*[*customer-name*].
- *t*[*amount*] is the amount of the loan whose number is *t*[*loan-number*].

Suppose that we wish to add a new loan to our database. Say that the loan is made by the Perryridge branch to Adams in the amount of $1500. Let the *loan-number* be L-31. In our design, we need a tuple with values on all the attributes of *Lending-schema*. Thus, we must repeat the asset and city data for the Perryridge branch, and must add the tuple

(Perryridge, Horseneck, 1700000, Adams, L-31, 1500)

to the *lending* relation. In general, the asset and city data for a branch must appear once for each loan made by that branch.

The repetition of information required by the use of our alternative design is undesirable. Repeating information wastes space. Furthermore, it complicates updating the database. Suppose, for example, that the Perryridge branch moves from Horseneck to Newtown. Under our original design, one tuple of the *branch* relation needs to be changed. Under our alternative design, many tuples of the *lending* relation need to be changed. Thus, updates are more costly under the alternative design than under the original design. When we perform the update in the alternative database, we must ensure that *every* tuple pertaining to the Perryridge branch is updated, or else our database will show two cities for the Perryridge branch.

That observation is central to understanding why the alternative design is bad. We know that a bank branch is located in exactly one city. On the other hand, we know that a branch may make many loans. In other words, the functional dependency

$$branch\text{-}name \rightarrow branch\text{-}city$$

holds on *Lending-schema*, but we do not expect the functional dependency *branch-name* → *loan-number* to hold. The fact that a branch is located in a city and the fact that a branch makes a loan are independent, and, as we have seen, these facts are best represented in separate relations. We shall see that we can use functional dependencies to specify formally when a database design is good.

Another problem with the *Lending-schema* design is that we cannot represent directly the information concerning a branch (*branch-name*, *branch-city*, *assets*) unless there exists at least one loan at the branch. The problem is that tuples in the *lending* relation require values for *loan-number*, *amount*, and *customer-name*.

One solution to this problem is to introduce *null values* to handle updates through views. Recall, however, that null values are difficult to handle. If we are not willing to deal with null values, then we can create the branch information only when the first loan application at that branch is made. Worse, we would have to delete this information when all the loans have been paid. Clearly, this situation is undesirable, since, under our original database design, the branch information would be available regardless of whether or not loans are currently maintained in the branch, and without resorting to the use of null values.

7.2 Decomposition

The example of Section 7.1 of a bad design suggests that we should *decompose* a relation schema that has many attributes into several schemas with fewer attributes. Careless decomposition, however, may lead to another form of bad design.

Consider an alternative design in which *Lending-schema* is decomposed into the following two schemas:

Branch-customer-schema = (*branch-name, branch-city, assets, customer-name*)
Customer-loan-schema = (*customer-name, loan-number, amount*)

Using the *lending* relation of Figure 7.1, we construct our new relations *branch-customer* (*Branch-customer*) and *customer-loan* (*Customer-loan-schema*) as follows:

$$branch\text{-}customer = \Pi_{branch\text{-}name,\ branch\text{-}city,\ assets,\ customer\text{-}name}\ (lending)$$
$$customer\text{-}loan = \Pi_{customer\text{-}name,\ loan\text{-}number,\ amount}\ (lending)$$

We show the resulting *branch-customer* and *customer-name* relations in Figures 7.2 and 7.3, respectively.

branch-name	*branch-city*	*assets*	*customer-name*
Downtown	Brooklyn	9000000	Jones
Redwood	Palo Alto	2100000	Smith
Perryridge	Horseneck	1700000	Hayes
Downtown	Brooklyn	9000000	Jackson
Mianus	Horseneck	400000	Jones
Round Hill	Horseneck	8000000	Turner
Pownal	Bennington	300000	Williams
North Town	Rye	3700000	Hayes
Downtown	Brooklyn	9000000	Johnson
Perryridge	Horseneck	1700000	Glenn
Brighton	Brooklyn	7100000	Brooks

Figure 7.2 The relation *branch-customer*.

Of course, there are cases in which we need to reconstruct the *loan* relation. For example, suppose that we wish to find all branches that have loans with amounts less than $1000. No relation in our alternative database contains these data. We need to reconstruct the *lending* relation. It appears that we can do so by writing

$$branch\text{-}customer \bowtie customer\text{-}loan$$

Figure 7.4 shows the result of computing *branch-customer* ⋈ *customer-loan*. When we compare this relation and the *lending* relation with which we started (Figure 7.1), we notice some differences. Although every tuple that appears in *lending* appears in *branch-customer* ⋈ *customer-loan*, there are tuples in *branch-customer* ⋈ *customer-loan* that are not in *lending*. In our example,

customer-name	*loan-number*	*amount*
Jones	L-17	1000
Smith	L-23	2000
Hayes	L-15	1500
Jackson	L-14	1500
Jones	L-93	500
Turner	L-11	900
Williams	L-29	1200
Hayes	L-16	1300
Johnson	L-23	2000
Glenn	L-25	2500
Brooks	L-10	2200

Figure 7.3 The relation *customer-loan*.

branch-name	*branch-city*	*assets*	*customer-name*	*loan-number*	*amount*
Downtown	Brooklyn	9000000	Jones	L-17	1000
Downtown	Brooklyn	9000000	Jones	L-93	500
Redwood	Palo Alto	2100000	Smith	L-23	2000
Perryridge	Horseneck	1700000	Hayes	L-15	1500
Perryridge	Horseneck	1700000	Hayes	L-16	1300
Downtown	Brooklyn	9000000	Jackson	L-14	1500
Mianus	Horseneck	400000	Jones	L-17	1000
Mianus	Horseneck	400000	Jones	L-93	500
Round Hill	Horseneck	8000000	Turner	L-11	900
Pownal	Bennington	300000	Williams	L-29	1200
North Town	Rye	3700000	Hayes	L-15	1500
North Town	Rye	3700000	Hayes	L-16	1300
Downtown	Brooklyn	9000000	Johnson	L-23	2000
Perryridge	Horseneck	1700000	Glenn	L-25	2500
Brighton	Brooklyn	7100000	Brooks	L-10	2200

Figure 7.4 The relation *branch-customer* ⋈ *customer-loan*.

branch-customer ⋈ *customer-loan* has the following additional tuples:

(Downtown, Brooklyn, 9000000, Jones, L-93, 500)
(Perryridge, Horseneck, 1700000, Hayes, L-16, 1300)
(Mianus, Horseneck, 400000, Jones, L-17, 1000)
(North Town, Rye, 3700000, Hayes, L-15, 1500)

Consider the query, "Find all branches that have made a loan in an amount less than \$1000." If we look back at Figure 7.1, we see that the only branches with loan amounts less than \$1000 are Mianus and Round Hill. However, when we apply the expression

$$\Pi_{branch\text{-}name}\ (\sigma_{amount\ <\ 1000}\ (branch\text{-}customer \bowtie customer\text{-}loan))$$

we obtain *three* branch names: Mianus, Round Hill, and Downtown.

Let us examine this example more closely. If a customer happens to have several loans from different branches, we cannot tell which loan belongs to which branch. Thus, when we join *branch-customer* and *customer-loan*, we obtain not only the tuples we had originally in *lending*, but also several additional tuples. Although we have *more* tuples in *branch-customer* ⋈ *customer-loan*, we actually have *less* information. We are no longer able, in general, to represent in the database information about which customers are borrowers from which branch. Because of this loss of information, we call the decomposition of *Lending-schema* into *Branch-customer-schema* and *customer-loan-schema* a *lossy decomposition*, or a *lossy-join decomposition*. A decomposition that is not a lossy-join decomposition is a *lossless-join decomposition*. It should be clear from our example that a lossy-join decomposition is, in general, a bad database design.

Let us examine the decomposition more closely to see why it is lossy. There is one attribute in common between *Branch-customer-schema* and *Customer-loan-schema*:

$$\textit{Branch-customer-schema} \cap \textit{Customer-loan-schema} = \{\textit{customer-name}\}$$

The only way that we can represent a relationship between, for example, *loan-number* and *branch-name* is through *customer-name*. This representation is not adequate because a customer may have several loans, yet these loans are not necessarily obtained from the same branch.

Let us consider another alternative design, in which *Lending-schema* is decomposed into the following two schemas:

Branch-schema = (*branch-name, branch-city, assets*)
Loan-info-schema = (*branch-name, customer-name, loan-number, amount*)

There is one attribute in common between these two schemas:

$$\textit{Branch-loan-schema} \cap \textit{Customer-loan-schema} = \{\textit{branch-name}\}$$

Thus, the only way that we can represent a relationship between, for example, *customer-name* and *assets* is through *branch-name*. The difference between this example and the preceding one is that the assets of a branch are the same, regardless of the customer to which we are referring, whereas the lending branch associated with a certain loan amount *does* depend on the customer to which we are referring. For a given *branch-name*, there is exactly one *assets* value and exactly one *branch-city*; whereas a similar statement cannot be made for *customer-name*. That is, the functional dependency

$$\textit{branch-name} \rightarrow \textit{assets branch-city}$$

holds, but *customer-name* does not functionally determine *loan-number*.

The notion of lossless joins is central to much of relational-database design. Therefore, we restate the preceding examples more concisely and more formally. Let R be a relation schema. A set of relation schemas $\{R_1, R_2, \ldots, R_n\}$ is a *decomposition* of R if

$$R = R_1 \cup R_2 \cup \ldots \cup R_n$$

That is, $\{R_1, R_2, \ldots, R_n\}$ is a decomposition of R if, for $i = 1, 2, \ldots, n$, each R_i is a subset of R, and every attribute in R appears in at least one R_i.

Let r be a relation on schema R, and let $r_i = \Pi_{R_i}(r)$ for $i = 1, 2, \ldots, n$. That is, $\{r_1, r_2, \ldots, r_n\}$ is the database that results from decomposing R into $\{R_1, R_2, \ldots, R_n\}$. It is always the case that

$$r \subseteq r_1 \bowtie r_2 \bowtie \ldots \bowtie r_n$$

To see that this assertion is true, consider a tuple t in relation r. When we compute the relations $r_1, r_2, \ldots, r_n$, the tuple t gives rise to one tuple t_i in each r_i, $i = 1, 2, \ldots, n$. These n tuples combine to regenerate t when we compute $r_1 \bowtie r_2 \bowtie$

$\ldots \bowtie r_n$. The details are left for you to complete as an exercise. Therefore, every tuple in r appears in $r_1 \bowtie r_2 \bowtie \ldots \bowtie r_n$.

In general, $r \neq r_1 \bowtie r_2 \bowtie \ldots \bowtie r_n$. As an illustration, consider our earlier example, in which

- $n = 2$.
- R = *Lending-schema*.
- R_1 = *Branch-customer-schema*.
- R_2 = *Customer-loan-schema*.
- r = the relation shown in Figure 7.1.
- r_1 = the relation shown in Figure 7.2.
- r_2 = the relation shown in Figure 7.3.
- $r_1 \bowtie r_2$ = the relation shown in Figure 7.4.

Note that the relations in Figures 7.1 and 7.4 are not the same.

To have a lossless-join decomposition, we need to impose constraints on the set of possible relations. We found that the decomposition of *Lending-schema* into *Branch-schema* and *Loan-info-schema* is lossless because the functional dependency

branch-name → *branch-city assets*

holds on *Branch-schema*.

Later in this chapter, we shall introduce constraints other than functional dependencies. We say that a relation is *legal* if it satisfies all rules, or constraints, that we impose on our database.

Let C represent a set of constraints on the database. A decomposition $\{R_1, R_2, \ldots, R_n\}$ of a relation schema R is a *lossless-join decomposition* for R if, for all relations r on schema R that are legal under C,

$$r = \Pi_{R_1}(r) \bowtie \Pi_{R_2}(r) \bowtie \ldots \bowtie \Pi_{R_n}(r)$$

We shall show how to test whether a decomposition is a lossless-join decomposition in the next few sections. A major part of this chapter is concerned with the questions of how to specify constraints on the database, and how to obtain lossless-join decompositions that avoid the pitfalls represented by the examples of bad database designs that we have seen in this section.

7.3 Normalization Using Functional Dependencies

We can use a given set of functional dependencies in designing a relational database in which most of the undesirable properties discussed in Section 7.1 do not occur. When we design such systems, it may become necessary to decompose a relation into several smaller relations. Using functional dependencies, we can define several *normal forms* that represent "good" database designs. There are many normal forms. The ones that we shall cover here are BCNF (Section 7.3.2) and 3NF (Section 7.3.3).

7.3.1 Desirable Properties of Decomposition

In this subsection, we shall illustrate our concepts by considering the *Lending-schema* schema of Section 7.1:

Lending-schema = (*branch-name, branch-city, assets, customer-name, loan-number, amount*)

The set F of functional dependencies that we require to hold on *Lending-schema* are

branch-name → *assets branch-city*
loan-number → *amount branch-name*

As we discussed in Section 7.1, the *Lending-schema* is an example of a bad database design. Assume that we decompose it to the following three relations:

Branch-schema = (*branch-name, assets, branch-city*)
Loan-schema = (*branch-name, loan-number, amount*)
Borrower-schema = (*customer-name, loan-number*)

We claim that this decomposition has several desirable properties, which we discuss next. Note that these three relation schemas are precisely the ones that we used previously, in Chapters 3 through 5.

7.3.1.1 Lossless-Join Decomposition

In Section 7.1, we argued that, when decomposing a relation into a number of smaller relations, it is crucial that the decomposition be lossless. We claim that the decomposition in Section 7.3.1 is indeed lossless. To demonstrate our claim, we must first present a criterion for determining whether a decomposition is lossy.

Let R be a relation schema, and let F be a set of functional dependencies on R. Let R_1 and R_2 form a decomposition of R. This decomposition is a lossless-join decomposition of R if at least one of the following functional dependencies are in F^+:

- $R_1 \cap R_2 \rightarrow R_1$
- $R_1 \cap R_2 \rightarrow R_2$

We now show that our decomposition of *Lending-schema* is a lossless-join decomposition by showing a sequence of steps that generate the decomposition. We begin by decomposing *Lending-schema* into two schemas:

Branch-schema = (*branch-name, branch-city, assets*)
Loan-info-schema = (*branch-name, customer-name, loan-number, amount*)

Since *branch-name* → *branch-city assets*, the augmentation rule for functional dependencies (Section 6.5.2) implies that

branch-name → *branch-name branch-city assets*

Since *Branch-schema* ∩ *Loan-info-schema* = {*branch-name*}, it follows that our initial decomposition is a lossless-join decomposition.

Next, we decompose *Loan-info-schema* into

Loan-schema = (*branch-name*, *loan-number*, *amount*)
Borrower-schema = (*customer-name*, *loan-number*)

This step results in a lossless-join decomposition, since *loan-number* is a common attribute and *loan-number* → *amount branch-name*.

7.3.1.2 Dependency Preservation

There is another goal in relational-database design: *dependency preservation*. When an update is made to the database, the system should be able to check that the update will not create an illegal relation—that is, one that does not satisfy all the given functional dependencies. If we are to check updates efficiently, we should design relational-database schemas that allow update validation without the computation of joins.

To decide whether joins must be computed, we need to determine what functional dependencies may be tested by checking each relation individually. Let F be a set of functional dependencies on a schema R, and let $R_1, R_2, \ldots, R_n$ be a decomposition of R. The *restriction* of F to R_i is the set F_i of all functional dependencies in F^+ that include *only* attributes of R_i. Since all functional dependencies in a restriction involve attributes of only one relation schema, it is possible to test satisfaction of such a dependency by checking only one relation.

The set of restrictions $F_1, F_2, \ldots, F_n$ is the set of dependencies that can be checked efficiently. We now must ask whether testing only the restrictions is sufficient. Let $F' = F_1 \cup F_2 \cup \ldots \cup F_n$. F' is a set of functional dependencies on schema R, but, in general, $F' \neq F$. However, even if $F' \neq F$, it may be that $F'^+ = F^+$. If the latter is true, then every dependency in F is logically implied by F', and, if we verify that F' is satisfied, we have verified that F is satisfied. We say that a decomposition having the property $F'^+ = F^+$ is a *dependency-preserving* decomposition. Figure 7.5 shows an algorithm for testing dependency preservation. The input is a set $D = \{R_1, R_2, \ldots, R_n\}$ of decomposed relation schemas, and a set F of functional dependencies.

We can now show that our decomposition of *Lending-schema* is dependency preserving. We consider each member of the set F of functional dependencies that we require to hold on *Lending-schema*, and show that each one can be tested in at least one relation in the decomposition.

- We can test the functional dependency: *branch-name* → *branch-city assets* using *Branch-schema* = (*branch-name*, *branch-city*, *assets*).
- We can test the functional dependency: *loan-number* → *amount branch-name* using *Loan-schema* = (*branch-name*, *loan-number*, *amount*).

As the preceding example shows, it is often easier not to apply the algorithm of

```
compute F+;
for each schema Ri in D do
    begin
        Fi : = the restriction of F+ to Ri;
    end
F' := ∅
for each restriction Fi do
    begin
        F' = F' ∪ Fi
    end
compute F'+;
if (F'+ = F+) then return (true)
              else return (false);
```

Figure 7.5 Testing for dependency preservation.

Figure 7.5 to test dependency preservation, since the first step—computation of F^+—takes exponential time.

7.3.1.3 Repetition of Information

The decomposition of *Lending-schema* does not suffer from the problem of repetition of information that we discussed in Section 7.1. In *Lending-schema*, it was necessary to repeat the city and assets of a branch for each loan. The decomposition separates branch and loan data into distinct relations, thereby eliminating this redundancy. Similarly, observe that, if a single loan is made to several customers, we must repeat the amount of the loan once for each customer (as well as the city and assets of the branch). In the decomposition, the relation on schema *Borrower-schema* contains the *loan-number*, *customer-name* relationship, and no other schema does. Therefore, we have one tuple for each customer for a loan in only the relation on *Borrower-schema*. In the other relations involving *loan-number* (those on schemas *Loan-schema* and *Borrower-schema*), only one tuple per loan needs to appear.

Clearly, the lack of redundancy exhibited by our decomposition is desirable. The degree to which we can achieve this lack of redundancy is represented by several *normal forms*, which we shall discuss in the remainder of this chapter.

7.3.2 Boyce–Codd Normal Form

One of the more desirable normal forms that we can obtain is *Boyce–Codd normal form* (*BCNF*). A relation schema R is in BCNF with respect to a set F of functional dependencies if for all functional dependencies in F^+ of the form $\alpha \rightarrow \beta$, where $\alpha \subseteq R$ and $\beta \subseteq R$, at least one of the following holds:

- $\alpha \rightarrow \beta$ is a trivial functional dependency (that is, $\beta \subseteq \alpha$).
- α is a superkey for schema R.

A database design is in BCNF if each member of the set of relation schemas that constitutes the design is in BCNF.

As an illustration, let us consider the following relation schemas, and their respective functional dependencies:

- *Customer-schema* = (*customer-name*, *customer-street*, *customer-city*)
  customer-name → *customer-street customer-city*
- *Branch-schema* = (*branch-name*, *assets*, *branch-city*)
  branch-name → *assets branch-city*
- *Loan-info-schema* = (*branch-name*, *customer-name*, *loan-number*, *amount*)
  loan-number → *amount branch-name*

We claim that *Customer-schema* is in BCNF. We note that a candidate key for the schema is *customer-name*. The only nontrivial functional dependencies that hold on *Customer-schema* have *customer-name* on the left side of the arrow. Since *customer-name* is a candidate key, functional dependencies with *customer-name* on the left side do not violate the definition of BCNF. Similarly, it can be shown easily that the relation schema *Branch-schema* is in BCNF.

The schema, *Loan-info-schema*, however, is *not* in BCNF. First, note that *loan-number* is not a superkey for *Loan-info-schema*, since we *could* have a pair of tuples representing a single loan made to two people—for example,

(Downtown, Mr. Bell, L-44, 1000)
(Downtown, Ms. Bell, L-44, 1000)

Because we did not list functional dependencies that rule out the preceding case, *loan-number* is not a candidate key. However, the functional dependency *loan-number* → *amount* is nontrivial. Therefore, *Loan-info-schema* does not satisfy the definition of BCNF.

We claim that *Loan-info-schema* is not in a desirable form, since it suffers from the problem of *repetition of information* that we described in Section 7.1. We observe that, if there are several customer names associated with a loan, in a relation on *Loan-info-schema*, then we are forced to repeat the branch name and the amount once for each customer. We can eliminate this redundancy by redesigning our database such that all schemas are in BCNF. One approach to this problem is to take the existing non-BCNF design as a starting point, and to decompose those schemas that are not in BCNF. Consider the decomposition of *Loan-info-schema* into two schemas:

Loan-schema = (*branch-name*, *loan-number*, *amount*)
Borrower-schema = (*customer-name*, *loan-number*)

This decomposition is a lossless-join decomposition.

```
result := {R};
done := false;
compute F+;
while (not done) do
   if (there is a schema Ri in result that is not in BCNF)
     then begin
            let α → β be a nontrivial functional dependency that holds
            on Ri such that α → Ri is not in F+, and α ∩ β = Ø;
            result := (result − Ri) ∪(Ri − β) ∪(α, β);
          end
     else done := true;
```

Figure 7.6 BCNF decomposition algorithm.

To determine whether these schemas are in BCNF, we need to determine what functional dependencies apply to them. In this example, it is easy to see that

loan-number → *amount branch-name*

applies to *Loan-schema,* and that only trivial functional dependencies apply to *Borrower-schema*. Although *loan-number* is not a superkey for *Loan-info-schema*, it is a candidate key for *Loan-schema*. Thus, both schemas of our decomposition are in BCNF.

It is now possible to avoid redundancy in the case where there are several customers associated with a loan. There is exactly one tuple for each loan in the relation on *Loan-schema,* and one tuple for each customer of each loan in the relation on *Borrower-schema*. Thus, we do not have to repeat the branch name and the amount once for each customer associated with a loan.

We are now able to state a general method to generate a collection of BCNF schemas. If R is not in BCNF, we can decompose R into a collection of BCNF schemas $R_1, R_2, \ldots, R_n$ using the algorithm of Figure 7.6, which generates not only a BCNF decomposition, but also a lossless-join decomposition. To see why our algorithm generates only lossless-join decompositions, we note that, when we replace a schema R_i with $(R_i - \beta)$ and (α, β), the dependency $\alpha \rightarrow \beta$ holds, and $(R_i - \beta) \cap (\alpha, \beta) = \alpha$.

Let us apply the BCNF decomposition algorithm to the *Lending-schema* schema that we used in Section 7.1 as an example of a poor database design:

Lending-schema = (*branch-name, branch-city, assets, customer-name, loan-number, amount*)

The set of functional dependencies that we require to hold on *Lending-schema* are

branch-name → *assets branch-city*
loan-number → *amount branch-name*

A candidate key for this schema is {*loan-number, customer-name*}.

We can apply the algorithm of Figure 7.6 to the *Lending-schema* example as follows:

- The functional dependency

  branch-name → *assets branch-city*

  holds on *Lending-schema*, but *branch-name* is not a superkey. Thus, *Lending-schema* is not in BCNF. We replace *Lending-schema* by

  Branch-schema = (*branch-name*, *branch-city*, *assets*)
  Loan-info-schema = (*branch-name*, *customer-name*, *loan-number*, *amount*)

- The only nontrivial functional dependencies that hold on *Branch-schema* include *branch-name* on the left side of the arrow. Since *branch-name* is a key for *Branch-schema*, the relation *Branch-schema* is in BCNF.

- The functional dependency

  loan-number → *amount branch-name*

  holds on *Loan-info-schema*, but *loan-number* is not a key for *Loan-info-schema*. We replace *Loan-info-schema* by

  Loan-schema = (*branch-name*, *loan-number*, *amount*)
  Borrower-schema = (*customer-name*, *loan-number*)

- *Loan-schema* and *Borrower-schema* are in BCNF.

Thus, the decomposition of *Lending-schema* results in the three relation schemas *Branch-schema*, *Loan-schema*, and *Borrower-schema*, each of which is in BCNF. These relation schemas are the same as those used in Section 7.3.1. We demonstrated in that section that the resulting decomposition is both a lossless-join decomposition and a dependency-preserving decomposition.

Not every BCNF decomposition is dependency preserving. As an illustration, consider the relation schema

Banker-schema = (*branch-name*, *customer-name*, *banker-name*)

which indicates that a customer has a "personal banker" in a particular branch. The set F of functional dependencies that we require to hold on the *Banker-schema* is

banker-name → *branch-name*
branch-name customer-name → *banker-name*

Clearly, *Banker-schema* is not in BCNF since *banker-name* is not a superkey.

If we apply the algorithm of Figure 7.6, we obtain the following BCNF decomposition:

Banker-branch-schema = (*banker-name*, *branch-name*)
Customer-banker-schema = (*customer-name*, *banker-name*)

The decomposed schemas preserve only *banker-name* $\rightarrow$ *branch-name* (and trivial dependencies), but the closure of {*banker-name* $\rightarrow$ *branch-name*} does not include *customer-name branch-name* $\rightarrow$ *banker-name*. The violation of this dependency cannot be detected unless a join is computed.

To see why the decomposition of *Banker-schema* into the schemas *Banker-branch-schema* and *Customer-banker-schema* is not dependency preserving, we apply the algorithm of Figure 7.5. We find that the restrictions F_1 and F_2 of F to each schema are as follows (for brevity, we show only a canonical cover):

F_1 = {*banker-name* $\rightarrow$ *branch-name*}
$F_2 = \emptyset$ (only trivial dependencies hold on *Customer-banker-schema*)

Thus, a canonical cover for the set F' is F_1.

It is easy to see that the dependency *customer-name branch-name* $\rightarrow$ *banker-name* is not in F'^{+} even though it *is* in F^{+}. Therefore, $F'^{+} \neq F^{+}$, and the decomposition is not dependency preserving.

The preceding example demonstrates that not every BCNF decomposition is dependency preserving. Moreover, it demonstrates that we cannot always satisfy all three design goals:

1. BCNF
2. Lossless join
3. Dependency preservation

We cannot do so here because every BCNF decomposition of *Banker-schema* must fail to preserve *customer-name branch-name* $\rightarrow$ *banker-name*.

7.3.3 Third Normal Form

In those cases where we cannot meet all three design criteria, we abandon BCNF and accept a weaker normal form called *third normal form* (*3NF*). We shall see that it is always possible to find a lossless-join, dependency-preserving decomposition that is in 3NF.

BCNF requires that all nontrivial dependencies be of the form $\alpha \rightarrow \beta$, where α is a superkey. 3NF relaxes this constraint slightly by allowing nontrivial functional dependencies whose left side is not a superkey.

A relation schema R is in 3NF with respect to a set F of functional dependencies if, for all functional dependencies in F^{+} of the form $\alpha \rightarrow \beta$, where $\alpha \subseteq R$ and $\beta \subseteq R$, at least one of the following holds:

- $\alpha \rightarrow \beta$ is a trivial functional dependency.

- α is a superkey for R.
- Each attribute A in $\beta - \alpha$ is contained in a candidate key for R.

The definition of 3NF allows certain functional dependencies that are not allowed in BCNF. A dependency $\alpha \rightarrow \beta$ that satisfies only the third condition of the 3NF definition is not allowed in BCNF, but is allowed in 3NF. These dependencies are examples of *transitive dependencies* (see Exercise 7.13).

Observe that, if a relation schema is in BCNF, then all functional dependencies are of the form "superkey determines a set of attributes," or the dependency is trivial. Thus, a BCNF schema cannot have *any* transitive dependencies. As a result, every BCNF schema is also in 3NF, and BCNF is therefore a more restrictive constraint than is 3NF.

Let us return to our *Banker-schema* example (Section 7.3.2). We have shown that this relation schema does not have a dependency-preserving, lossless-join decomposition into BCNF. This schema, however, turns out to be in 3NF. To see that is is, we note that {*customer-name, branch-name*} is a candidate key for *Banker-schema*, so the only attribute not contained in a candidate key for *Banker-schema* is *banker-name*. The only nontrivial functional dependencies of the form

$$\alpha \rightarrow \textit{banker-name}$$

include {*customer-name, branch-name*} as part of α. Since {*customer-name, branch-name*} is a candidate key, these dependencies do not violate the definition of 3NF.

Figure 7.7 shows an algorithm for finding a dependency-preserving, lossless-join decomposition into 3NF. The fact that each relation schema R_i is in 3NF follows directly from our requirement that the set F of functional dependencies be in canonical form (Section 6.5.4). The algorithm ensures preservation of dependencies by building explicitly a schema for each given dependency. It ensures that the decomposition is a lossless-join decomposition by guaranteeing that at least one schema contains a candidate key for the schema being decomposed. Exercise 7.6 provides some insight into the proof that this suffices to guarantee a lossless join.

To illustrate the algorithm of Figure 7.7, we consider the following extension to the *Banker-schema* introduced in Section 7.3.2:

Banker-info-schema = (*branch-name*, *customer-name*, *banker-name*, *office-number*)

The main difference here is that we include the banker's office number as part of the information. The functional dependencies for this relation schema are

banker-name → *branch-name office-number*
customer-name branch-name → *banker-name*

The **for** loop in the algorithm causes us to include the following schemas in our decomposition:

Banker-office-schema = (*banker-name*, *branch-name*, *office-number*)
Banker-schema = (*customer-name*, *branch-name*, *banker-name*)

let F_c be a canonical cover for F;
$i := 0$;
for each functional dependency $\alpha \rightarrow \beta$ in F_c **do**
  if none of the schemas $R_j, j = 1, 2, \ldots, i$ contains $\alpha\,\beta$
    then begin
      $i := i + 1$;
      $R_i := \alpha\,\beta$;
    end
if none of the schemas $R_j, j = 1, 2, \ldots, i$ contains a candidate key for R
  then begin
    $i := i + 1$;
    $R_i :=$ any candidate key for R;
  end
return $(R_1, R_2, \ldots, R_i)$

Figure 7.7 Dependency-preserving, lossless-join decomposition into 3NF.

Since *Banker-schema* contains a candidate key for *Banker-info-schema*, we are finished with the decomposition process.

7.3.4 Comparison of BCNF and 3NF

We have seen two normal forms for relational-database schemas: 3NF and BCNF. There is an advantage to 3NF in that we know that it is always possible to obtain a 3NF design without sacrificing a lossless join or dependency preservation. Nevertheless, there is a disadvantage to 3NF. If we do not eliminate all transitive dependencies, we may have to use null values to represent some of the possible meaningful relationships among data items, and there is the problem of repetition of information.

As an illustration, consider again the *Banker-schema* and its associated functional dependencies. Since *banker-name* → *branch-name*, we may want to represent relationships between values for *banker-name* and values for *branch-name* in our database. If we are to do so, however, either there must be a corresponding value for *customer-name*, or we must use a null value for the attribute *customer-name*.

The other difficulty with the *Banker-schema* is repetition of information. As an illustration, consider an instance of *Banker-schema* shown in Figure 7.8. Notice that the information indicating that Johnson is working at the Perryridge branch is repeated.

If we are forced to choose between BCNF and dependency preservation with 3NF, it is generally preferable to opt for 3NF. If we cannot test for dependency preservation efficiently, we either pay a high penalty in system performance or risk the integrity of the data in our database. Neither of these alternatives is attractive. With such alternatives, the limited amount of redundancy imposed by transitive

customer-name	*banker-name*	*branch-name*
Jones	Johnson	Perryridge
Smith	Johnson	Perryridge
Hayes	Johnson	Perryridge
Jackson	Johnson	Perryridge
Curry	Johnson	Perryridge
Turner	Johnson	Perryridge

Figure 7.8 An instance of *Banker-schema*.

dependencies allowed under 3NF is the lesser evil. Thus, we normally choose to retain dependency preservation and to sacrifice BCNF.

In summary, we repeat that our three design goals for a relational-database design are

1. BCNF
2. Lossless join
3. Dependency preservation

If we cannot achieve all three, we accept

1. 3NF
2. Lossless join
3. Dependency preservation

7.4 Normalization Using Multivalued Dependencies

There are relation schemas that are in BCNF that do not seem to be sufficiently normalized, in the sense that they still suffer from the problem of repetition of information. Consider again our banking example. Let us assume that, in an alternative design for the bank database schema, we have the schema

BC-schema = (*loan-number, customer-name, customer-street, customer-city*)

The astute reader will recognize this schema as a non-BCNF schema because of the functional dependency

$$customer\text{-}name \rightarrow customer\text{-}street\ customer\text{-}city$$

that we asserted earlier, and because *customer-name* is not a key for *BC-schema*. However, let us assume that our bank is attracting wealthy customers who have several addresses (say, a winter home and a summer home). Then, we no longer wish to enforce the functional dependency *customer-name* → *customer-street customer-city*. If we remove this functional dependency, we find *BC-schema* to be in BCNF with respect to our modified set of functional dependencies. Yet, even though *BC-schema* is now in BCNF, we still have the problem of repetition of information that we had earlier.

To deal with this problem, we must define a new form of constraint, called a *multivalued dependency*. As we did for functional dependencies, we shall use multivalued dependencies to define a normal form for relation schemas. This normal form, called *fourth normal form* (*4NF*), is more restrictive than BCNF. We shall see that every 4NF schema is also in BCNF, but there are BCNF schemas that are not in 4NF.

7.4.1 Multivalued Dependencies

Functional dependencies rule out certain tuples from being in a relation. If $A \rightarrow B$, then we cannot have two tuples with the same A value but different B values. Multivalued dependencies do not rule out the existence of certain tuples. Instead, they *require* that other tuples of a certain form be present in the relation. For this reason, functional dependencies sometimes are referred to as equality-generating dependencies, and multivalued dependencies are referred to as tuple-generating dependencies.

Let R be a relation schema and let $\alpha \subseteq R$ and $\beta \subseteq R$. The *multivalued dependency*

$$\alpha \twoheadrightarrow \beta$$

holds on R if, in any legal relation $r(R)$, for all pairs of tuples t_1 and t_2 in r such that $t_1[\alpha] = t_2[\alpha]$, there exist tuples t_3 and t_4 in r such that

$$\begin{aligned}
&t_1[\alpha] = t_2[\alpha] = t_3[\alpha] = t_4[\alpha] \\
&t_3[\beta] = t_1[\beta] \\
&t_3[R - \beta] = t_2[R - \beta] \\
&t_4[\beta] = t_2[\beta] \\
&t_4[R - \beta] = t_1[R - \beta]
\end{aligned}$$

This definition is less complicated than it appears to be. In Figure 7.9, we give a tabular picture of t_1, t_2, t_3, and t_4. Intuitively, the multivalued dependency $\alpha \twoheadrightarrow \beta$ says that the relationship between α and β is independent of the relationship between α and $R - \beta$. If the multivalued dependency $\alpha \twoheadrightarrow \beta$ is satisfied by all relations on schema R, then $\alpha \twoheadrightarrow \beta$ is a *trivial* multivalued dependency on schema R. Thus, $\alpha \twoheadrightarrow \beta$ is trivial if $\beta \subseteq \alpha$ or $\beta \cup \alpha = R$.

	α	β	$R - \alpha - \beta$
t_1	$a_1 \ldots a_i$	$a_{i+1} \ldots a_j$	$a_{j+1} \ldots a_n$
t_2	$a_1 \ldots a_i$	$b_{i+1} \ldots b_j$	$b_{j+1} \ldots b_n$
t_3	$a_1 \ldots a_i$	$a_{i+1} \ldots a_j$	$b_{j+1} \ldots b_n$
t_4	$a_1 \ldots a_i$	$b_{i+1} \ldots b_j$	$a_{j+1} \ldots a_n$

Figure 7.9 Tabular representation of $\alpha \twoheadrightarrow \beta$.

loan-number	*customer-name*	*customer-street*	*customer-city*
L-23	Smith	North	Rye
L-23	Smith	Main	Manchester
L-93	Curry	Lake	Horseneck

Figure 7.10 Relation *bc*: An example of redundancy in a BCNF relation.

To illustrate the difference between functional and multivalued dependencies, we consider again the *BC-schema*, and the relation *bc* (*BC-schema*) of Figure 7.10. We must repeat the loan number once for each address a customer has, and we must repeat the address for each loan a customer has. This repetition is unnecessary, since the relationship between a customer and his address is independent of the relationship between that customer and a loan. If a customer (say, Smith) has a loan (say, loan number L-23), we want that loan to be associated with all Smith's addresses. Thus, the relation of Figure 7.11 is illegal. To make this relation legal, we need to add the tuples (L-23, Smith, Main, Manchester) and (L-27, Smith, North, Rye) to the *bc* relation of Figure 7.11.

Comparing the preceding example with our definition of multivalued dependency, we see that we want the multivalued dependency

$$\textit{customer-name} \rightarrow\!\!\!\rightarrow \textit{customer-street customer-city}$$

to hold. (The multivalued dependency *customer-name* $\rightarrow\!\!\!\rightarrow$ *loan-number* will do as well. We shall soon see that they are equivalent.)

As was the case for functional dependencies, we shall use multivalued dependencies in two ways:

1. To test relations to determine whether they are legal under a given set of functional and multivalued dependencies

2. To specify constraints on the set of legal relations; we shall thus concern ourselves with *only* those relations that satisfy a given set of functional and multivalued dependencies

Note that, if a relation r fails to satisfy a given multivalued dependency, we can construct a relation r' that *does* satisfy the multivalued dependency by adding tuples to r.

loan-number	*customer-name*	*customer-street*	*customer-city*
L-23	Smith	North	Rye
L-27	Smith	Main	Manchester

Figure 7.11 An illegal *bc* relation.

7.4.2 Theory of Multivalued Dependencies

As we did for functional dependencies and 3NF and BCNF, we shall need to determine all the multivalued dependencies that are logically implied by a given set of multivalued dependencies.

We take the same approach here that we did earlier for functional dependencies. Let D denote a set of functional and multivalued dependencies. The closure D^+ of D is the set of all functional and multivalued dependencies logically implied by D. As we did for functional dependencies, we can compute D^+ from D, using the formal definitions of functional dependencies and multivalued dependencies. However, it is usually easier to reason about sets of dependencies using a system of inference rules.

The following list of inference rules for functional and multivalued dependencies is *sound* and *complete*. Recall that *sound* rules do not generate any dependencies that are not logically implied by D, and *complete* rules allow us to generate all dependencies in D^+. The first three rules are Armstrong's axioms, which we saw earlier in Chapter 6.

1. **Reflexivity rule**. If α is a set of attributes, and $\beta \subseteq \alpha$, then $\alpha \rightarrow \beta$ holds.
2. **Augmentation rule**. If $\alpha \rightarrow \beta$ holds, and γ is a set of attributes, then $\gamma\alpha \rightarrow \gamma\beta$ holds.
3. **Transitivity rule**. If $\alpha \rightarrow \beta$ holds, and $\beta \rightarrow \gamma$ holds, then $\alpha \rightarrow \gamma$ holds.
4. **Complementation rule**. If $\alpha \twoheadrightarrow \beta$ holds, then $\alpha \twoheadrightarrow R - \beta - \alpha$ holds.
5. **Multivalued augmentation rule**. If $\alpha \twoheadrightarrow \beta$ holds, and $\gamma \subseteq R$ and $\delta \subseteq \gamma$, then $\gamma\alpha \twoheadrightarrow \delta\beta$ holds.
6. **Multivalued transitivity rule**. If $\alpha \twoheadrightarrow \beta$ holds, and $\beta \twoheadrightarrow \gamma$ holds, then $\alpha \twoheadrightarrow \gamma - \beta$ holds.
7. **Replication rule**. If $\alpha \rightarrow \beta$ holds, then $\alpha \twoheadrightarrow \beta$.
8. **Coalescence rule**. If $\alpha \twoheadrightarrow \beta$ holds, and $\gamma \subseteq \beta$, and there is a δ such that $\delta \subseteq R$, and $\delta \cap \beta = \emptyset$, and $\delta \rightarrow \gamma$, then $\alpha \rightarrow \gamma$ holds.

The bibliographic notes provide references to proofs that the preceding rules are sound and complete. The following examples provide insight into how the formal proofs proceed.

Let $R = (A, B, C, G, H, I)$ be a relation schema. Suppose that $A \twoheadrightarrow BC$ holds. The definition of multivalued dependencies implies that, if $t_1[A] = t_2[A]$, then there exist tuples t_3 and t_4 such that

$$\begin{aligned}
&t_1[A] = t_2[A] = t_3[A] = t_4[A] \\
&t_3[BC] = t_1[BC] \\
&t_3[GHI] = t_2[GHI] \\
&t_4[GHI] = t_1[GHI] \\
&t_4[BC] = t_2[BC]
\end{aligned}$$

The complementation rule states that, if $A \twoheadrightarrow BC$, then $A \twoheadrightarrow GHI$. Observe that t_3 and t_4 satisfy the definition of $A \twoheadrightarrow GHI$ if we simply change the subscripts.

We can provide similar justification for rules 5 and 6 (see Exercise 7.17) using the definition of multivalued dependencies.

Rule 7, the replication rule, involves functional and multivalued dependencies. Suppose that $A \rightarrow BC$ holds on R. If $t_1[A] = t_2[A]$ and $t_1[BC] = t_2[BC]$, then t_1 and t_2 themselves serve as the tuples t_3 and t_4 required by the definition of the multivalued dependency $A \rightarrow\rightarrow BC$.

Rule 8, the coalescence rule, is the most difficult of the eight rules to verify (see Exercise 7.19).

We can simplify the computation of the closure of D by using the following rules, which we can prove using rules 1 to 8 (see Exercise 7.20):

- **Multivalued union rule**. If $\alpha \rightarrow\rightarrow \beta$ holds, and $\alpha \rightarrow\rightarrow \gamma$ holds, then $\alpha \rightarrow\rightarrow \beta\gamma$ holds.
- **Intersection rule**. If $\alpha \rightarrow\rightarrow \beta$ holds, and $\alpha \rightarrow\rightarrow \gamma$ holds, then $\alpha \rightarrow\rightarrow \beta \cap \gamma$ holds.
- **Difference rule**. If $\alpha \rightarrow\rightarrow \beta$ holds, and $\alpha \rightarrow\rightarrow \gamma$ holds, then $\alpha \rightarrow\rightarrow \beta - \gamma$ holds and $\alpha \rightarrow\rightarrow \gamma - \beta$ holds.

Let us apply our rules to the following example. Let $R = (A, B, C, G, H, I)$ with the following set of dependencies D given:

$$A \rightarrow\rightarrow B$$
$$B \rightarrow\rightarrow HI$$
$$CG \rightarrow H$$

We list several members of D^+ here:

- $A \rightarrow\rightarrow CGHI$: Since $A \rightarrow\rightarrow B$, the complementation rule (rule 4) implies that $A \rightarrow\rightarrow R - B - A$. $R - B - A = CGHI$, so $A \rightarrow\rightarrow CGHI$.
- $A \rightarrow\rightarrow HI$: Since $A \rightarrow\rightarrow B$ and $B \rightarrow\rightarrow HI$, the multivalued transitivity rule (rule 6) implies that $A \rightarrow\rightarrow HI - B$. Since $HI - B = HI$, $A \rightarrow\rightarrow HI$.
- $B \rightarrow H$: To show this fact, we need to apply the coalescence rule (rule 8). $B \rightarrow\rightarrow HI$ holds. Since $H \subseteq HI$ and $CG \rightarrow H$ and $CG \cap HI = \emptyset$, we satisfy the statement of the coalescence rule, with α being B, β being HI, δ being CG, and γ being H. We conclude that $B \rightarrow H$.
- $A \rightarrow\rightarrow CG$: We already know that $A \rightarrow\rightarrow CGHI$ and $A \rightarrow\rightarrow HI$. By the difference rule, $A \rightarrow\rightarrow CGHI - HI$. Since $CGHI - HI = CG$, $A \rightarrow\rightarrow CG$.

7.4.3 Fourth Normal Form

Let us return to our *BC-schema* example in which the multivalued dependency *customer-name* $\rightarrow\rightarrow$ *customer-street customer-city* holds, but no nontrivial functional dependencies hold. We saw earlier that, although *BC-schema* is in BCNF, the design is not ideal, since we must repeat a customer's address information for each loan. We shall see that we can use the given multivalued dependency to improve the database design, by decomposing *BC-schema* into a *fourth normal form* (4NF) decomposition.

A relation schema R is in 4NF with respect to a set D of functional and multivalued dependencies if, for all multivalued dependencies in D^+ of the form $\alpha \twoheadrightarrow \beta$, where $\alpha \subseteq R$ and $\beta \subseteq R$, at least one of the following holds

- $\alpha \twoheadrightarrow \beta$ is a trivial multivalued dependency.
- α is a superkey for schema R.

A database design is in 4NF if each member of the set of relation schemas that constitutes the design is in 4NF.

Note that the definition of 4NF differs from the definition of BCNF in only the use of multivalued dependencies instead of functional dependencies. Every 4NF schema is in BCNF. To see this fact, we note that, if a schema R is not in BCNF, then there is a nontrivial functional dependency $\alpha \rightarrow \beta$ holding on R, where α is not a superkey. Since $\alpha \rightarrow \beta$ implies $\alpha \twoheadrightarrow \beta$ (by the replication rule), R cannot be in 4NF.

The analogy between 4NF and BCNF applies to the algorithm for decomposing a schema into 4NF. Figure 7.12 shows the 4NF decomposition algorithm. It is identical to the BCNF decomposition algorithm of Figure 7.6, except for the use of multivalued, instead of functional, dependencies.

If we apply the algorithm of Figure 7.12 to *BC-schema*, we find that *customer-name* $\twoheadrightarrow$ *loan-number* is a nontrivial multivalued dependency, and *customer-name* is not a superkey for *BC-schema*. Following the algorithm, we replace *BC-schema* by two schemas:

Borrower-schema = (*customer-name*, *loan-number*)
Customer-schema = (*customer-name*, *customer-street*, *customer-city*).

This pair of schemas, which is in 4NF, eliminates the problem we encountered earlier with the redundancy of *BC-schema*.

As was the case when we were dealing solely with functional dependencies, we are interested in decompositions that are lossless-join decompositions and that

```
result := {R};
done := false;
compute D+;
while (not done) do
  if (there is a schema Ri in result that is not in 4NF)
    then begin
           let α →→ β be a nontrivial multivalued dependency that holds
           on Ri such that α → Ri is not in D+, and α ∩ β = ∅;
           result := (result − Ri) ∪ (Ri − β) ∪ (α, β);
         end
    else done := true;
```

Figure 7.12 4NF decomposition algorithm.

preserve dependencies. The following fact about multivalued dependencies and lossless joins shows that the algorithm of Figure 7.12 generates only lossless-join decompositions:

- Let R be a relation schema, and let D be a set of functional and multivalued dependencies on R. Let R_1 and R_2 form a decomposition of R. This decomposition is a lossless-join decomposition of R if and only if at least one of the following multivalued dependencies is in D^+:

$$R_1 \cap R_2 \rightarrow\!\!\!\rightarrow R_1$$
$$R_1 \cap R_2 \rightarrow\!\!\!\rightarrow R_2$$

Recall that we stated earlier that, if $R_1 \cap R_2 \rightarrow R_1$ or $R_1 \cap R_2 \rightarrow R_2$, then R_1 and R_2 are a lossless-join decomposition of R. The preceding fact regarding multivalued dependencies is a more general statement about lossless joins. It says that, for *every* lossless-join decomposition of R into two schemas R_1 and R_2, one of the two dependencies $R_1 \cap R_2 \rightarrow\!\!\!\rightarrow R_1$ or $R_1 \cap R_2 \rightarrow\!\!\!\rightarrow R_2$ must hold.

The question of dependency preservation when we have multivalued dependencies is not as simple as it is when we have only functional dependencies. Let R be a relation schema, and let $R_1, R_2, \ldots, R_n$ be a decomposition of R. Recall that, for a set F of functional dependencies, the restriction F_i of F to R_i is all functional dependencies in F^+ that include *only* attributes of R_i. Now consider a set D of both functional and multivalued dependencies. The *restriction* of D to R_i is the set D_i, consisting of

- All functional dependencies in D^+ that include only attributes of R_i
- All multivalued dependencies of the form

$$\alpha \rightarrow\!\!\!\rightarrow \beta \cap R_i$$

  where $\alpha \subseteq R_i$ and $\alpha \rightarrow\!\!\!\rightarrow \beta$ is in D^+

A decomposition of schema R into schemas $R_1, R_2, \ldots, R_n$ is a *dependency-preserving decomposition* with respect to a set D of functional and multivalued dependencies if, for every set of relations $r_1(R_1), r_2(R_2), \ldots, r_n(R_n)$ such that for all i, r_i satisfies D_i, there exists a relation $r(R)$ that satisfies D and for which $r_i = \Pi_{R_i}(r)$ for all i.

Let us apply the 4NF decomposition algorithm of Figure 7.12 to our example of $R = (A, B, C, G, H, I)$ with $D = \{A \rightarrow\!\!\!\rightarrow B, B \rightarrow\!\!\!\rightarrow HI, CG \rightarrow H\}$. We shall then test the resulting decomposition for dependency preservation.

R is not in 4NF. Observe that $A \rightarrow\!\!\!\rightarrow B$ is not trivial, yet A is not a superkey. Using $A \rightarrow\!\!\!\rightarrow B$ in the first iteration of the **while** loop, we replace R with two schemas, (A, B) and (A, C, G, H, I). It is easy to see that (A, B) is in 4NF since all multivalued dependencies that hold on (A, B) are trivial. However, the schema (A, C, G, H, I) is not in 4NF. Applying the multivalued dependency $CG \rightarrow\!\!\!\rightarrow H$ (which follows from the given functional dependency $CG \rightarrow H$ by the

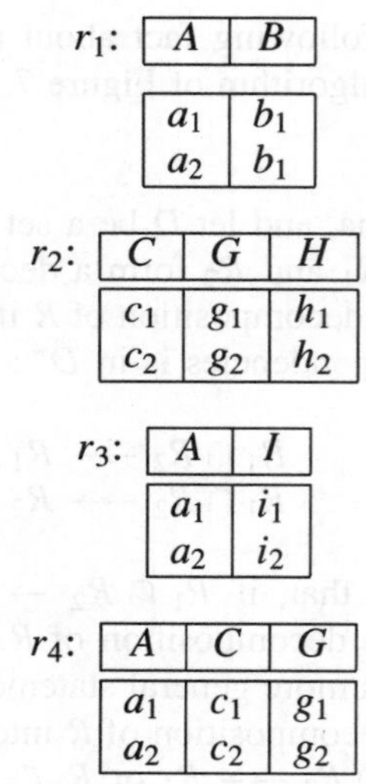

r_1:

A	B
a_1	b_1
a_2	b_1

r_2:

C	G	H
c_1	g_1	h_1
c_2	g_2	h_2

r_3:

A	I
a_1	i_1
a_2	i_2

r_4:

A	C	G
a_1	c_1	g_1
a_2	c_2	g_2

Figure 7.13 Projection of relation r onto a 4NF decomposition of R.

replication rule), we replace (A, C, G, H, I) by the two schemas (C, G, H) and (A, C, G, I). Schema (C, G, H) is in 4NF, but schema (A, C, G, I) is not. To see that (A, C, G, I) is not in 4NF, we recall that we showed earlier that $A \twoheadrightarrow HI$ is in D^+. Therefore, $A \twoheadrightarrow I$ is in the restriction of D to (A, C, G, I). Thus, in a third iteration of the **while** loop, we replace (A, C, G, I) by two schemas (A, I) and (A, C, G). The algorithm then terminates and the resulting 4NF decomposition is $\{(A, B), (C, G, H), (A, I), (A, C, G)\}$.

This 4NF decomposition is not dependency preserving, since it fails to preserve the multivalued dependency $B \twoheadrightarrow HI$. Consider Figure 7.13, which shows the four relations that may result from the projection of a relation on (A, B, C, G, H, I) onto the four schemas of our decomposition. The restriction of D to (A, B) is $A \twoheadrightarrow B$ and some trivial dependencies. It is easy to see that r_1 satisfies $A \twoheadrightarrow B$, because there is no pair of tuples with the same A value. Observe that r_2 satisfies *all* functional and multivalued dependencies, since no two tuples in r_2 have the same value on any attribute. A similar statement can be made for r_3 and r_4. Therefore, the decomposed version of our database satisfies all the dependencies in the restriction of D. However, there is no relation r on (A, B, C, G, H, I) that satisfies D and decomposes into r_1, r_2, r_3, and r_4. Figure 7.14 shows the relation $r = r_1 \bowtie r_2 \bowtie r_3 \bowtie r_4$. Relation r does not satisfy $B \twoheadrightarrow HI$. Any relation s containing r and satisfying $B \twoheadrightarrow HI$ must include the tuple $(a_2, b_1, c_2, g_2, h_1, i_1)$. However, $\Pi_{CGH}(s)$ includes a tuple (c_2, g_2, h_1) that is not in r_2. Thus, our decomposition fails to detect a violation of $B \twoheadrightarrow HI$.

We have seen that, if we are given a set of multivalued and functional dependencies, it is advantageous to find a database design that meets the three criteria of

A	B	C	G	H	I
a_1	b_1	c_1	g_1	h_1	i_1
a_2	b_1	c_2	g_2	h_2	i_2

Figure 7.14 A relation $r(R)$ that does not satisfy $B \twoheadrightarrow HI$.

1. 4NF
2. Dependency preservation
3. Lossless join

If all we have are functional dependencies, then the first criterion is just BCNF.

We have seen also that it is not always possible to meet all three of these criteria. We succeeded in finding such a decomposition for the bank example, but failed for the example of schema $R = (A, B, C, G, H, I)$.

When we cannot achieve our three goals, we compromise on 4NF, and accept BCNF or even 3NF, if necessary, to ensure dependency preservation.

7.5 Normalization Using Join Dependencies

We have seen that the lossless-join property is one of several properties of a good database design. Indeed, this property is essential: Without it, information is lost. When we restrict the set of legal relations to those satisfying a set of functional and multivalued dependencies, we are able to use these dependencies to show that certain decompositions are lossless-join decompositions.

Because of the importance of the concept of lossless join, it is useful to be able to constrain the set of legal relations over a schema R to those relations for which a given decomposition is a lossless-join decomposition. In this section, we define such a constraint, called a *join dependency*. Just as types of dependency led to other normal forms, join dependencies will lead to a normal form called *project-join normal form* (*PJNF*).

7.5.1 Join Dependencies

Let R be a relation schema and $R_1, R_2, \ldots, R_n$ be a decomposition of R. The join dependency $*(R_1, R_2, \ldots, R_n)$ is used to restrict the set of legal relations to those for which $R_1, R_2, \ldots, R_n$ is a lossless-join decomposition of R. Formally, if $R = R_1 \cup R_2 \cup \ldots \cup R_n$, we say that a relation $r(R)$ satisfies the *join dependency* $*(R_1, R_2, \ldots, R_n)$ if

$$r = \Pi_{R_1}(r) \bowtie \Pi_{R_2}(r) \bowtie \ldots \bowtie \Pi_{R_n}(r)$$

A join dependency is *trivial* if one of the R_i is R itself.

Consider the join dependency $*(R_1, R_2)$ on schema R. This dependency requires that, for all legal $r(R)$,

$$r = \Pi_{R_1}(r) \bowtie \Pi_{R_2}(r)$$

	$R_1 - R_2$	$R_1 \cap R_2$
$\Pi_{R_1}(t_1)$	$a_1 \; \ldots \; a_i$	$a_{i+1} \; \cdots \; a_j$
$\Pi_{R_1}(t_2)$	$b_1 \; \ldots \; b_i$	$a_{i+1} \; \cdots \; a_j$

	$R_1 \cap R_2$	$R_2 - R_1$
$\Pi_{R_2}(t_1)$	$a_{i+1} \; \ldots \; a_j$	$a_{j+1} \; \ldots \; a_n$
$\Pi_{R_2}(t_2)$	$a_{i+1} \; \ldots \; a_j$	$b_{j+1} \; \ldots \; b_n$

Figure 7.15 $\Pi_{R_1}(r)$ *and* $\Pi_{R_2}(r)$.

Let r contain the two tuples t_1 and t_2, defined as follows:

$$t_1[R_1 - R_2] = (a_1, a_2, \ldots, a_i) \qquad t_2[R_1 - R_2] = (b_1, b_2, \ldots, b_i)$$
$$t_1[R_1 \cap R_2] = (a_{i+1}, \ldots, a_j) \qquad t_2[R_1 \cap R_2] = (a_{i+1}, \ldots, a_j)$$
$$t_1[R_2 - R_1] = (a_{j+1}, \ldots, a_n) \qquad t_2[R_2 - R_1] = (b_{j+1}, \ldots, b_n)$$

Thus, $t_1[R_1 \cap R_2] = t_2[R_1 \cap R_2]$, but t_1 and t_2 have different values on all other attributes. Let us compute $\Pi_{R_1}(r) \bowtie \Pi_{R_2}(r)$. Figure 7.15 shows $\Pi_{R_1}(r)$ and $\Pi_{R_2}(r)$. When we compute the join, we get two tuples in addition to t_1 and t_2, shown by t_3 and t_4 in Figure 7.16.

If $*(R_1, R_2)$ holds, then, whenever we have tuples t_1 and t_2, we must also have t_3 and t_4. Thus, Figure 7.16 shows a tabular representation of the join dependency $*(R_1, R_2)$. Compare Figure 7.16 with Figure 7.9, in which we gave a tabular representation of $\alpha \rightarrow\!\!\!\rightarrow \beta$. If we let $\alpha = R_1 \cap R_2$ and $\beta = R_1$, then we can see that the two tabular representations in these figures are the same. Indeed, $*(R_1, R_2)$ is just another way of stating $R_1 \cap R_2 \rightarrow\!\!\!\rightarrow R_1$. Using the complementation and augmentation rules for multivalued dependencies, we can show that $R_1 \cap R_2 \rightarrow\!\!\!\rightarrow R_1$ implies $R_1 \cap R_2 \rightarrow\!\!\!\rightarrow R_2$. Thus, $*(R_1, R_2)$ is equivalent to $R_1 \cap R_2 \rightarrow\!\!\!\rightarrow R_2$. This observation is not surprising in light of the fact we noted earlier that R_1 and R_2 form a lossless-join decomposition of R if and only if $R_1 \cap R_2 \rightarrow\!\!\!\rightarrow R_2$ or $R_1 \cap R_2 \rightarrow\!\!\!\rightarrow R_1$.

Every join dependency of the form $*(R_1, R_2)$ is therefore equivalent to a multivalued dependency. However, there are join dependencies that are not equivalent to any multivalued dependency. The simplest example of such a dependency is on schema $R = (A, B, C)$. The join dependency

$$*((A, B), (B, C), (A, C))$$

	$R_1 - R_2$	$R_1 \cap R_2$	$R_2 - R_1$
t_1	$a_1 \; \ldots \; a_i$	$a_{i+1} \; \ldots \; a_j$	$a_{j+1} \; \ldots \; a_n$
t_2	$b_1 \; \ldots \; b_i$	$a_{i+1} \; \ldots \; a_j$	$b_{j+1} \; \ldots \; b_n$
t_3	$a_1 \; \ldots \; a_i$	$a_{i+1} \; \ldots \; a_j$	$b_{j+1} \; \ldots \; b_n$
t_4	$b_1 \; \ldots \; b_i$	$a_{i+1} \; \ldots \; a_j$	$a_{j+1} \; \ldots \; a_n$

Figure 7.16 Tabular representation of $*(R_1, R_2)$.

A	B	C
a_1	b_1	c_2
a_2	b_1	c_1
a_1	b_2	c_1
a_1	b_1	c_1

Figure 7.17 Tabular representation of $*((A,\ B),\ (B,\ C),\ (A,\ C))$.

is not equivalent to any collection of multivalued dependencies. Figure 7.17 shows a tabular representation of this join dependency. To see that no set of multivalued dependencies logically implies $*((A,\ B),\ (B,\ C),\ (A,\ C))$, we consider Figure 7.17 as a relation $r\ (A,\ B,\ C)$ as shown in Figure 7.18. Relation r satisfies the join dependency $*((A,\ B),\ (B,\ C),\ (A,\ C))$, as we can verify by computing

$$\Pi_{AB}\ (r) \bowtie \Pi_{BC}\ (r) \bowtie \Pi_{AC}\ (r)$$

and by showing that the result is exactly r. However, r does not satisfy any nontrivial multivalued dependency. To see that it does not, we verify that r fails to satisfy any of $A \twoheadrightarrow B$, $A \twoheadrightarrow C$, $B \twoheadrightarrow A$, $B \twoheadrightarrow C$, $C \twoheadrightarrow A$, or $C \twoheadrightarrow B$.

Just as a multivalued dependency is a way of stating the independence of a pair of relationships, a join dependency is a way of stating that the members of a *set* of relationships are all independent. This notion of independence of relationships is a natural consequence of the way that we generally define a relation. Consider

Loan-info-schema = (*branch-name, customer-name, loan-number, amount*)

from our banking example. We can define a relation *loan-info* (*Loan-info-schema*) as the set of all tuples on *Loan-info-schema* such that

- The loan represented by *loan-number* is made by the branch named *branch-name*.
- The loan represented by *loan-number* is made to the customer named *customer-name*.
- The loan represented by *loan-number* is in the amount given by *amount*.

The preceding definition of the *loan-info* relation is a conjunction of three predicates: one on *loan-number* and *branch-name*, one on *loan-number* and *customer-name*, and one on *loan-number* and *amount*. Surprisingly, it can be shown that

A	B	C
a_1	b_1	c_2
a_2	b_1	c_1
a_1	b_2	c_1
a_1	b_1	c_1

Figure 7.18 Relation $r\ (A,\ B,\ C)$.

the preceding intuitive definition of *loan-info* logically implies the join dependency *((*loan-number, branch-name*), (*loan-number, customer-name*), (*loan-number, amount*)).

Thus, join dependencies have an intuitive appeal and correspond to one of our three criteria for a good database design.

For functional and multivalued dependencies, we were able to give a system of inference rules that are sound and complete. Unfortunately, no such set of rules is known for join dependencies. It appears that we must consider more general classes of dependencies than join dependencies to construct a sound and complete set of inference rules. The bibliographic notes contain references to research in this area.

7.5.2 Project-Join Normal Form

Project-join normal form (*PJNF*) is defined in a manner similar to BCNF and 4NF, except that join dependencies are used. A relation schema R is in PJNF with respect to a set D of functional, multivalued, and join dependencies if, for all join dependencies in D^+ of the form $*(R_1, R_2, \ldots, R_n)$, where each $R_i \subseteq R$ and $R = R_1 \cup R_2 \cup \ldots \cup R_n$, at least one of the following holds:

- $*(R_1, R_2, \ldots, R_n)$ is a trivial join dependency.
- Every R_i is a superkey for R.

A database design is in PJNF if each member of the set of relation schemas that constitutes the design is in PJNF. PJNF is called *fifth normal form* (*5NF*) in some of the literature on database normalization.

Let us return to our banking example. Given the join dependency *((*loan-number, branch-name*), (*loan-number, customer-name*), (*loan-number, amount*)), *Loan-info-schema* is not in PJNF. To put *Loan-info-schema* into PJNF, we must decompose it into the three schemas specified by the join dependency: (*loan-number, branch-name*), (*loan-number, customer-name*), and (*loan-number, amount*).

Because every multivalued dependency is also a join dependency, it is easy to see that every PJNF schema is also in 4NF. Thus, in general, we may not be able to find a dependency-preserving decomposition into PJNF for a given schema.

7.6 Domain-Key Normal Form

The approach we have taken to normalization is to define a form of constraint (functional, multivalued, or join dependency), and then to use that form of constraint to define a normal form. *Domain-key normal form* (*DKNF*) is based on three notions.

1. **Domain declaration**. Let A be an attribute, and let **dom** be a set of values. The domain declaration $A \subseteq$ **dom** requires that the A value of all tuples be values in **dom**.

2. **Key declaration**. Let R be a relation schema with $K \subseteq R$. The key declaration **key** (K) requires that K be a superkey for schema R—that is, $K \rightarrow R$. Note that all key declarations are functional dependencies but not all functional dependencies are key declarations.
3. **General constraint**. A *general constraint* is a predicate on the set of all relations on a given schema. The dependencies that we have studied in this chapter are examples of general constraints. In general, a general constraint is a predicate expressed in some agreed-on form, such as first-order logic.

We now give an example of a general constraint that is not a functional, multivalued, or join dependency. Suppose that all accounts whose *account-number* begins with the digit 9 are special high-interest accounts with a minimum balance of $2500. Then, we include as a general constraint, "If the first digit of t[*account-number*] is 9, then t[*balance*] $\geq$ 2500."

Domain declarations and key declarations are easy to test in a practical database system. General constraints, however, may be extremely costly (in time and space) to test. The purpose of a DKNF database design is to allow us to test the general constraints using only domain and key constraints.

Formally, let **D** be a set of domain constraints and let **K** be a set of key constraints for a relation schema R. Let **G** denote the general constraints for R. Schema R is in DKNF if $\mathbf{D} \cup \mathbf{K}$ logically imply **G**.

Let us return to the general constraint that we gave on accounts. The constraint implies that our database design is not in DKNF. To create a DKNF design, we need two schemas in place of *Account-schema*:

Regular-acct-schema = (*branch-name*, *account-number*, *balance*)
Special-acct-schema = (*branch-name*, *account-number*, *balance*)

We retain all the dependencies that we had on *Account-schema* as general constraints. The domain constraints for *Special-acct-schema* require that, for each account,

- The account number begins with 9.
- The balance is greater than 2500.

The domain constraints for *Regular-acct-schema* require that the account number does not begin with 9. The resulting design is in DKNF, although the proof of this fact is beyond the scope of this text.

Let us compare DKNF to the other normal forms that we have studied. Under the other normal forms, we did not take into consideration domain constraints. We assumed (implicitly) that the domain of each attribute was some infinite domain, such as the set of all integers or the set of all character strings. We allowed key constraints (indeed, we allowed functional dependencies). For each normal form, we allowed a restricted form of general constraint (a set of functional, multivalued, or join dependencies). Thus, we can rewrite the definitions of PJNF, 4NF, BCNF, and 3NF in a manner that shows them to be special cases of DKNF.

branch-name	*loan-number*
Round Hill	L-58

loan-number	*amount*

loan-number	*customer-name*
L-58	Johnson

Figure 7.19 Decomposition in PJNF.

The following is a DKNF-inspired rephrasing of our definition of PJNF. Let $R = (A_1, A_2, \ldots, A_n)$ be a relation schema. Let $\text{dom}(A_i)$ denote the domain of attribute A_i, and let all these domains be infinite. Then all domain constraints **D** are of the form $A_i \subseteq \text{dom}(A_i)$. Let the general constraints be a set **G** of functional, multivalued, or join dependencies. If F is the set of functional dependencies in **G**, let the set **K** of key constraints be those nontrivial functional dependencies in F^+ of the form $\alpha \rightarrow R$. Schema R is in PJNF if and only if it is in DKNF with respect to **D**, **K**, and **G**.

A consequence of DKNF is that all insertion and deletion anomalies are eliminated.

DKNF represents an "ultimate" normal form because it allows arbitrary constraints, rather than dependencies, yet it allows efficient testing of these constraints. Of course, if a schema is not in DKNF, we may be able to achieve DKNF via decomposition, but such decompositions, as we have seen, are not always dependency-preserving decompositions. Thus, although DKNF is a goal of a database designer, it may have to be sacrificed in a practical design.

7.7 Alternative Approaches to Database Design

In this section, we reexamine normalization of relation schemas with an emphasis on the effects of normalization on the design of practical database systems.

We have taken the approach of starting with a single relation schema and decomposing it. One of our goals in choosing a decomposition was that the decomposition be a lossless-join decomposition. To consider losslessness, we assumed that it is valid to talk about the join of all the relations of the decomposed database.

Consider the database of Figure 7.19, showing a *loan-info* relation decomposed in PJNF. In Figure 7.19, we represent a situation in which we have not yet determined the amount of loan L-58, but wish to record the remainder of the data on the loan. If we compute the natural join of these relations, we discover that all tuples referring to loan L-58 disappear. In other words, there is no *loan-info* relation corresponding to the relations of Figure 7.19. Tuples that disappear when we compute the join are *dangling tuples* (see Section 6.2.1). Formally, let $r_1(R_1),\ r_2(R_2), \ldots, r_n(R_n)$ be a set of relations. A tuple t of relation r_i is a dangling tuple if t is not in the relation

$$\Pi_{R_i} \ (r_1 \bowtie r_2 \bowtie \ldots \bowtie r_n)$$

Dangling tuples may occur in practical database applications. They represent incomplete information, as they do in our example, where we wish to store data about a loan that is still in the process of being negotiated. The relation $r_1 \bowtie r_2 \bowtie \ldots \bowtie r_n$ is called a *universal relation*, since it involves all the attributes in the universe defined by $R_1 \cup R_2 \cup \ldots \cup R_n$.

The only way that we can write a universal relation for the example of Figure 7.19 is to include *null values* in the universal relation. We saw in Chapter 3 that null values present serious difficulties. Research regarding null values and universal relations is discussed in the bibliographic notes. Because of the difficulty of managing null values, it may be desirable to view the relations of the decomposed design as representing the database, rather than the universal relation whose schema we decomposed during the normalization process.

Note that we cannot enter all incomplete information into the database of Figure 7.19 without resorting to the use of null values. For example, we cannot enter a loan number unless we know at least one of the following:

- The customer name
- The branch name
- The amount of the loan

Thus, a particular decomposition defines a restricted form of incomplete information that is acceptable in our database.

The normal forms that we have defined generate good database designs from the point of view of representation of incomplete information. Returning again to the example of Figure 7.19, we would not want to allow storage of the following fact: "There is a loan (whose number is unknown) to Jones in the amount of $100." Since

$$\textit{loan-number} \rightarrow \textit{customer-name amount},$$

the only way that we can relate *customer-name* and *amount* is through *loan-number*. If we do not know the loan number, we cannot distinguish this loan from other loans with unknown numbers.

In other words, we do not want to store data for which the key attributes are unknown. Observe that the normal forms that we have defined do not allow us to store that type of information unless we use null values. Thus, our normal forms allow representation of acceptable incomplete information via dangling tuples, while prohibiting the storage of undesirable incomplete information.

If we allow dangling tuples in our database, we may prefer to take an alternative view of the database-design process. Instead of decomposing a universal relation, we may *synthesize* a collection of normal-form schemas from a given set of attributes. We are interested in the same normal forms, regardless of whether we use decomposition or synthesis. The decomposition approach is better understood and is more widely used. The bibliographic notes provide references to research into the synthesis approach.

Another consequence of our approach to database design is that attribute names must be unique in the universal relation. We cannot use *name* to refer to both *customer-name* and to *branch-name*. It is generally preferable to use unique names, as we have done. Nevertheless, if we defined our relation schemas directly, rather than in terms of a universal relation, we could obtain relations on schemas such as the following for our banking example:

branch-loan (*name, number*)
loan-customer (*number, name*)
amt (*number, amount*)

Observe that, with the preceding relations, expressions such as *branch-loan* ⋈ *loan-customer* are meaningless. Indeed, the expression *branch-loan* ⋈ *loan-customer* finds loans made by branches to customers who have the same name as the name of the branch.

In a language such as SQL, however, there is no natural-join operation, so, in a query involving *branch-loan* and *loan-customer*, we must disambiguate references to *name* by prefixing the relation name. In such environments, the multiple roles for *name* (as branch name and as customer name) are less troublesome and may be simpler to use.

We believe that using the *unique-role assumption*—that each attribute name has a unique meaning in the database—is generally preferable to reusing of the same name in multiple roles. When the unique-role assumption is not made, the database designer must be especially careful when constructing a normalized relational-database design.

7.8 Summary

In this chapter, we have presented three criteria for a good database design:

1. PJNF, BCNF, 4NF, or 3NF
2. Lossless join
3. Dependency preservation

We have shown how to achieve these goals, and how to find a good compromise when we cannot achieve all of them.

To represent these criteria, we defined several types of data dependencies:

- Functional dependencies (defined in Chapter 5)
- Multivalued dependencies
- Join dependencies

We studied the properties of these dependencies, with emphasis on what dependencies are logically implied by a set of dependencies.

DKNF is an idealized normal form that may be difficult to achieve in practice. Yet DKNF has desirable properties that should be included to the extent possible in a good database design.

Conspicuous by their absence from our discussion of 3NF, 4NF, and so on, are first and second normal forms. The reason for not discussing *second normal form (2NF)* is that this form is of historical interest only. We simply define it, and let you experiment with it in Exercise 7.14. Although we have not mentioned first normal form, we have assumed it since we introduced the relational model in Chapter 3. We say that a relation schema R is in *first normal form (1NF)* if the domains of all attributes of R are atomic. A domain is *atomic* if elements of the domain are considered to be indivisible units. We discuss non-atomic domains further in Chapter 8.

In reviewing the issues that we have discussed in this chapter, note that the reason we could define rigorous approaches to relational-database design is that the relational data model rests on a firm mathematical foundation. That is one of the primary advantages of the relational model, as compared with the other data models that we have studied.

Exercises

7.1. Explain what is meant by *repetition of information* and *inability to represent information*. Explain why each of these properties may indicate a bad relational-database design.

7.2. Suppose that we decompose the schema $R = (A, B, C, D, E)$ into

$$(A, B, C)$$
$$(A, D, E).$$

Show that this decomposition is a lossless-join decomposition if the following set F of functional dependencies holds:

$$A \rightarrow BC$$
$$CD \rightarrow E$$
$$B \rightarrow D$$
$$E \rightarrow A$$

7.3. Show that the following decomposition of the schema R of Exercise 7.2 is not a lossless-join decomposition:

$$(A, B, C)$$
$$(C, D, E).$$

Hint: Give an example of a relation r on schema R such that

$$\Pi_{A,B,C}\ (r)\ \bowtie\ \Pi_{C,D,E}\ (r)\ \neq\ r$$

7.4. Let $R_1, R_2, \ldots, R_n$ be a decomposition of schema U. Let $u(U)$ be a relation, and let $r_i = \Pi_{R_i}(u)$. Show that

$$u \subseteq r_1 \bowtie r_2 \bowtie \ldots \bowtie r_n$$

7.5. Show that the decomposition in Exercise 7.2 is not a dependency-preserving decomposition.

7.6. Show that it is possible to ensure that a decomposition into 3NF is a lossless-join decomposition by guaranteeing that at least one schema contains a candidate key for the schema being decomposed. (*Hint*: Show that the join of all the projections onto the schemas of the decomposition cannot have more tuples than the original relation.)

7.7. List the three design goals for relational databases, and explain why each is desirable.

7.8. Give a lossless-join decomposition into BCNF of the schema R of Exercise 7.2.

7.9. Give an example of a relation schema R' and set F' of functional dependencies such that there are at least two distinct lossless-join decompositions of R' into BCNF.

7.10. In designing a relational database, why might we choose a non-BCNF design?

7.11. Give a lossless-join, dependency-preserving decomposition into 3NF of the schema R of Exercise 7.2.

7.12. Show that, if a relation schema is in BCNF, then it is also in 3NF.

7.13. Let a *prime* attribute be one that appears in at least one candidate key. Let α and β be sets of attributes such that $\alpha \rightarrow \beta$ holds, but $\beta \rightarrow \alpha$ does not hold. Let A be an attribute that is not in α, is not in β, and for which $\beta \rightarrow A$ holds. We say that A is *transitively dependent* on α. We can restate our definition of 3NF as follows: A relation schema R is in 3NF with respect to a set F of functional dependencies if there are no nonprime attributes A in R for which A is transitively dependent on a key for R.

Show that this new definition is equivalent to the original one.

7.14. A functional dependency $\alpha \rightarrow \beta$ is called a *partial* dependency if there is a proper subset γ of α such that $\gamma \rightarrow \beta$. We say that β is *partially dependent* on α. A relation schema R is in second normal form (*2NF*) if each attribute A in R meets one of the following criteria:

- It appears in a candidate key.
- It is not partially dependent on a candidate key.

Show that every 3NF schema is in 2NF. (*Hint*: Show that every partial dependency is a transitive dependency.)

7.15. Given the three goals of relational-database design, is there any reason to design a database schema that is in 2NF, but is in no higher-order normal form? (See Exercise 7.14 for the definition of 2NF.)

7.16. List all the nontrivial multivalued dependencies satisfied by the relation of Figure 7.20.

A	B	C
a_1	b_1	c_1
a_1	b_1	c_2
a_2	b_1	c_1
a_2	b_1	c_3

Figure 7.20 Relation of Exercise 7.16.

7.17. Use the definition of multivalued dependency (Section 7.4) to argue that each of the following axioms is sound:
(*a*) The complementation rule
(*b*) The multivalued augmentation rule
(*c*) The multivalued transitivity rule

7.18. Use the definitions of functional and multivalued dependencies (Sections 6.5 and 7.4) to show the soundness of the replication rule.

7.19. Show that the coalescence rule is sound. (*Hint*: Apply the definition of $\alpha \twoheadrightarrow \beta$ to a pair of tuples t_1 and t_2 such that $t_1[\alpha] = t_2[\alpha]$. Observe that since $\delta \cap \beta = \emptyset$, if two tuples have the same value on $R - \beta$, then they have the same value on δ.)

7.20. Use the axioms for functional and multivalued dependencies to show that each of the following rules is sound:
(*a*) The multivalued union rule
(*b*) The intersection rule
(*c*) The difference rule

7.21. Let $R = (A, B, C, D, E)$, and let M be the following set of multivalued dependencies

$$A \twoheadrightarrow BC$$
$$B \twoheadrightarrow CD$$
$$E \twoheadrightarrow AD$$

List the nontrivial dependencies in M^+.

7.22. Give a lossless-join decomposition of schema R in Exercise 7.21 into 4NF.

7.23. Give an example of a relation schema R and a set of dependencies such that R is in BCNF, but is not in 4NF.

7.24. Explain why 4NF is a normal form more desirable than is BCNF.

7.25. Give an example of relation schema R and a set of dependencies such that R is in 4NF, but is not in PJNF.

7.26. Explain why PJNF is a normal form more desirable than is 4NF.

7.27. Rewrite the definitions of 4NF and BCNF using the notions of domain constraints and general constraints.

7.28. Explain why DKNF is a highly desirable normal form, yet is one that is difficult to achieve in practice.

7.29. Explain how dangling tuples may arise. Explain problems that they may cause.

Bibliographic Notes

The first discussion of relational-database design theory appeared in an early paper by Codd [1970]. In that paper, Codd also introduced first, second, and third normal forms.

BCNF was introduced in Codd [1972a]. The desirability of BCNF is discussed in Bernstein and Goodman [1980b]. A polynomial-time algorithm for BCNF decomposition appears in Tsou and Fischer [1982]. Biskup et al. [1979] give the algorithm we used to find a lossless-join dependency-preserving decomposition into 3NF. Fundamental results on the lossless-join property appear in Aho et al. [1979b].

Multivalued dependencies are discussed by Zaniolo [1976]. Beeri et al. [1977] give a set of axioms for multivalued dependencies, and prove that their axioms are sound and complete. Our axiomatization is based on theirs.

The notions of 4NF, PJNF, and DKNF are from Fagin [1977], Fagin [1979], and Fagin [1981], respectively. The synthesis approach to database design is discussed in Bernstein [1976].

Join dependencies were introduced by Rissanen [1979]. Sciore [1982] gives a set of axioms for a class of dependencies that properly includes the join dependencies. In addition to their use in PJNF, join dependencies are central to the definition of universal relation databases. Fagin et al. [1982] introduces the relationship between join dependencies and the definition of a relation as a conjunction of predicates (see Section 7.5.1). This use of join dependencies has led to a large amount of research into *acyclic* database schemas. Intuitively, a schema is acyclic if every pair of attributes is related in a unique way. Formal treatment of acyclic schemas appears in Fagin [1983], and in Beeri et al. [1983].

Additional dependencies are discussed in detail in Maier [1983]. Inclusion dependencies are discussed by Casanova et al. [1984] and Cosmadakis et al. [1990]. Template dependencies are covered by Sadri and Ullman [1982]. Mutual dependencies are examined by Furtado [1978], and by Mendelzon and Maier [1979].

Maier [1983] presents the design theory of relational databases in detail. Ullman [1988], and Abiteboul et al. [1995] present a more theoretic coverage of many of the dependencies and normal forms presented here.

CHAPTER 8

OBJECT-ORIENTED DATABASES

In recent years, several new application areas for database systems have emerged that are limited by restrictions imposed by the relational data model. As a result, several new data models have been proposed to deal with these new application domains. In this chapter, as well as in Chapter 9, we present the basic underlying concepts of these new data models. This chapter concentrates on the *object-oriented model*, which is based on the object-oriented–programming paradigm. This approach to programming was first introduced by the language Simula 67, which was designed for programming of simulations. More recently, the languages C++ and Smalltalk have become the most widely known object-oriented programming languages. In this chapter, we introduce the concepts of object-oriented programming and then consider the use of these concepts in database systems.

8.1 New Database Applications

The purpose of database systems is the management of large bodies of information. Early databases developed from file-management systems. These systems evolved first into either network (see Appendix A) or hierarchical (see Appendix B) databases, and later, into relational databases. Among the common features of these "old" applications are the following:

- **Uniformity**. There are large numbers of similarly structured data items, all of which have the same size (in bytes).
- **Record orientation**. The basic data items consist of fixed-length records.

- **Small data items**. Each record is short—records are rarely more than a few hundred bytes long.
- **Atomic fields**. Fields within a record are short and of fixed length. There is no structure within fields. In other words, first normal form holds (see Chapter 7).

In recent years, however, database technology has been applied to applications outside the realm of data processing that, in general, fail to have at least one of the preceding features. These new applications include the following:

- **Computer-aided design (CAD)**. A CAD database stores data pertaining to an engineering design, including the components of the item being designed, the interrelationship of components, and old versions of designs.
- **Computer-aided software engineering (CASE)**. A CASE database stores data required to assist software developers. These data include source code, dependencies among software modules, definitions and uses of variables, and the development history of the software system.
- **Multimedia databases**. A multimedia database contains image, spatial data, audio data, video data, and the like. Databases of this sort arise from the need to store photographs, and geographical data, and from voice-mail systems, graphics applications, and video-on-demand systems.
- **Office information systems (OIS)**. Office automation includes workstation-based tools for document creation and document retrieval, tools for maintaining appointment calendars, and so on. An OIS database must allow queries pertaining to schedules, documents, and contents of documents.
- **Hypertext databases**. Hypertext is text that is enriched with links that point to other documents. The world-wide web is an example of hypertext (or, more accurately, hypermedia, since web documents may be multimedia documents). Hypertext documents may also be structured in specific ways that help index them. Hypertext database must support the ability to retrieve documents based on links, and to query documents based on their structure.

These new applications of databases were not considered in the 1970s, when most current commercial database systems were initially designed. They are now practical owing to the increase in available main memory and disk size, the speedup of central processing units, the lower cost of hardware, and the improved understanding of database management that has developed in recent years.

The relational model and entity-relationship models are not sufficient to model the data requirements of these new applications. Moreover, the modeling requirements of even traditional business applications has grown more complex over time, and it is hard to express some of their requirements in the relational model. For instance, today's business applications often have to deal with image data and hypertext databases.

In this chapter, as well as in Chapter 9, we consider several data-modeling concepts that have been developed to meet the needs of these applications. We shall not discuss the features of all the preceding applications in detail. Rather, we shall use a few of them as examples of those concepts not well illustrated by our bank example. Here, we consider these concepts as they relate to the object-oriented paradigm. In Chapter 9, we consider these concepts as they relate to the object-relational paradigm.

8.2 The Object-Oriented Data Model

The object-oriented data model has several aspects, which we study in the following sections.

8.2.1 Object Structure

Loosely speaking, an *object* corresponds to an entity in the E-R model. The object-oriented paradigm is based on *encapsulating* data and code related to an object into a single unit. Conceptually, all interactions between an object and the rest of the system are via messages. Thus, the interface between an object and the rest of the system is defined by a set of allowed *messages*.

In general, an object has associated with it

- A set of *variables* that contain the data for the object; variables correspond to attributes in the E-R model
- A set of *messages* to which the object responds; each message may have zero, one, or more *parameters*
- A set of *methods*, each of which is a body of code to implement a message; a method returns a value as the *response* to the message

The term *message* in an object-oriented context does not imply the use of a physical message in a computer network. Rather, it refers to the passing of requests among objects without regard to specific implementation details. The term *invoke a method* is sometimes used to denote the act of sending a message to an object and the execution of the corresponding method.

We can illustrate the motivation for using this approach by considering *employee* entities in a bank database. Suppose the annual salary of an employee is calculated in different ways for different employees. For instance, managers may get a bonus depending on the bank's performance, while tellers may get a bonus depending on how many hours they have worked. We can (conceptually) encapsulate the code for computing the salary with each employee as a method that is executed in response to an *annual-salary* message.

All *employee* objects respond to the *annual-salary* message, but they do so in different ways. By encapsulating within the *employee* object itself the information about how to compute the annual salary, all employee objects present the same interface. Since the only external interface presented by an object is the set of messages to which that object responds, it is possible to modify the definitions of methods and variables without affecting the rest of the system. The ability to modify the definition of an object without affecting the rest of the system is considered to be one of the major advantages of the object-oriented–programming paradigm.

Methods of an object may be classified as either *read-only* or *update*. A read-only method does not affect the values of the variables in an object, whereas an update method may change the values of the variables. The messages to which an object responds can be similarly classified as read-only or update, based on the method that implements the message.

Derived attributes of an entity in the E-R model can be expressed in the object-oriented model as read-only messages. For example, the derived attribute *employment-length* of an *employee* entity can be expressed as an *employment-length* message of an *employee* object. The method implementing the message may determine the employment length by subtracting the *start-date* of the employee from the current date.

Strictly speaking, every attribute of an entity must be expressed as a variable and a pair of messages of the corresponding object in the object-oriented model. The variable is used to store the value of the attribute, one message is used to read the value of the attribute, and the other method is used to update the value. For instance, the attribute *address* of the *employee* entity can be represented by:

- A variable *address*
- A message *get-address* the response to which is the address
- A message *set-address*, which takes a parameter *new-address*, to update the address

However, for simplicity, many object-oriented data models allow variables to be read or updated directly, without having to define messages to read and update them.

8.2.2 Object Classes

Usually, there are many similar objects in a database. By *similar*, we mean that they respond to the same messages, use the same methods, and have variables of the same name and type. It would be wasteful to define each such object separately. Therefore, we group similar objects to form a *class*. Each such object is called an *instance* of its class. All objects in a class share a common definition, although they differ in the values assigned to the variables.

The notion of a class in the object-oriented data model corresponds to the notion of an entity-set in the E-R model. Examples of classes in our bank database are employees, customers, accounts, and loans.

We show below the definition of the class *employee*, written in pseudocode. The definition shows the variables and the messages to which the objects of the class respond; the methods for handling the messages are not shown here.

```
class employee {
    /* Variables */
        string name;
        string address;
        date   start-date;
        int    salary;
    /* Messages */
        int    annual-salary();
        string get-name();
        string get-address();
        int    set-address(string new-address);
        int    employment-length();
};
```

In the above definition, each object of the class *employee* contains the variables *name* and *address*, both of which are strings, *start-date*, which is a date, and *salary*, which is an integer. Each object responds to the five messages shown, namely *annual-salary*, *get-name*, *get-address*, *set-address* and *employment-length*. The type name before each message name indicates the type of the response to the message. Also observe that the message *set-address* takes a parameter *new-address*, which specifies the new value of the address.

The concept of classes is similar to the concept of abstract data types. However, there are several additional aspects to the class concept, beyond those of abstract data types. To represent these additional properties, we treat each class as itself being an object. A class object includes

- A set-valued variable whose value is the set of all objects that are instances of the class
- Implementation of a method for the message *new*, which creates a new instance of the class

We return to these features in Section 8.5.2.

8.2.3 Inheritance

An object-oriented database schema typically requires a large number of classes. Often, however, several classes are similar. For example, assume that we have an object-oriented database for our bank application. We would expect the class of bank customers to be similar to the class of bank employees, in that both define variables for *name*, *address*, and so on. However, there are variables specific to employees (*salary*, for example) and variables specific to customers (*credit-rating*, for example). It would be desirable to define a representation for the common variables in one place. We can define one only if we combine employees and customers into one class.

To allow the direct representation of similarities among classes, we need to place classes in a specialization hierarchy (the "ISA" relationship) like that defined

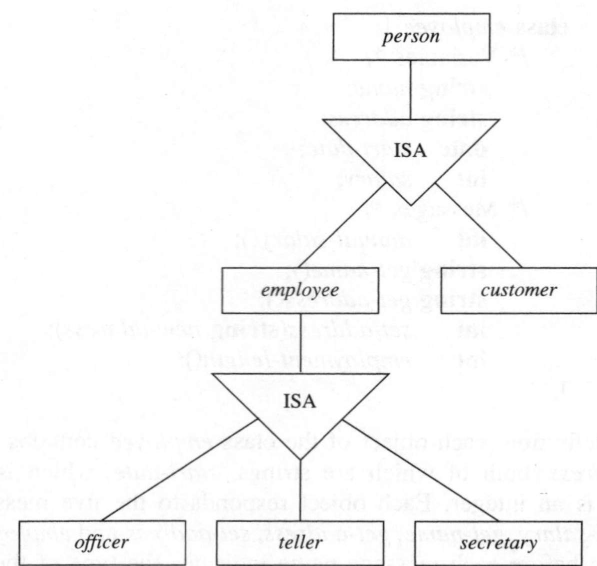

Figure 8.1 Specialization hierarchy for the bank example.

in Chapter 2 for the entity–relationship model. For instance, we say that *employee* is a specialization of *person*, because the set of all employees is a subset of the set of all persons. That is, every employee is a person. Similarly, *customer* is a specialization of *person*.

The concept of a class hierarchy is similar to the concept of specialization in the entity–relationship model. Employees and customers can be represented by classes that are specializations of a *person* class. Variables and methods specific to employees are associated with the *employee* class. Variables and methods specific to customers are associated with the *customer* class. Variables and methods that apply both to employees and to customers are associated with the *person* class.

Figure 8.1 shows an E-R diagram with a specialization hierarchy to represent people involved in the operation of our bank example. Figure 8.2 shows the corresponding class hierarchy. The classes shown in the hierarchy can be defined in pseudocode as shown in Figure 8.3. For brevity, we do not present the methods associated with these classes, although they would be included in a full definition of the bank database.

The keyword **isa** is used to indicate that a class is a specialization of another class. The specializations of a class are called *subclasses*. Thus, for example, *employee* is a subclass of *person*, and *teller* is a subclass of *employee*. Conversely, *employee* is a *superclass* of *teller*, and *person* is a superclass of *employee*.

An object representing an officer contains all the variables of class *officer*; in addition the object representing an officer also contains all the variables of classes *employee* and *person*. This is because every officer is defined to be an

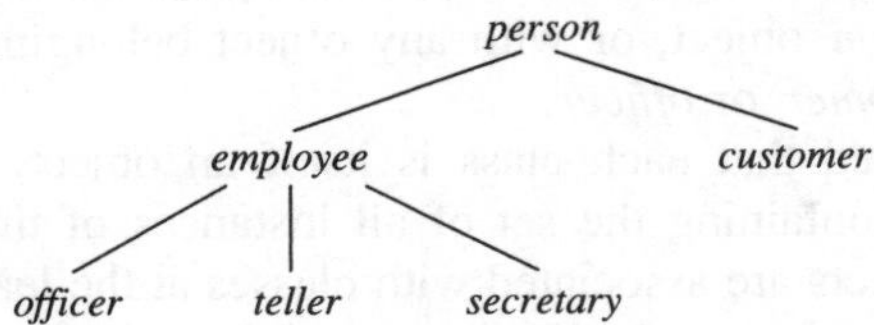

Figure 8.2 Class hierarchy corresponding to Figure 8.1.

employee, and since in turn every employee is defined to be a person, we can infer that every officer is also a person. This property that objects of a class contain variables defined in its superclasses is referred to as the *inheritance* of variables.

Methods are inherited in a manner identical to inheritance of variables. An important benefit of inheritance in object-oriented systems is the notion of *substitutability*: Any method of a class—say, *A* (or a function that takes an object of a class *A* as an argument)—can equally well be invoked with any object belonging to any subclass *B* of *A*. This characteristic leads to code reuse, since the methods and functions do not have to be written again for objects of class *B*.

```
class person {
    string name;
    string address;
};
class customer isa person {
    int    credit-rating;
};
class employee isa person {
    date   start-date;
    int    salary;
};
class officer isa employee {
    int    office-number;
    int    expense-account-number;
};
class teller isa employee {
    int    hours-per-week;
    int    station-number;
};
class secretary isa employee {
    int    hours-per-week;
    string manager;
};
```

Figure 8.3 Definition of class hierarchy in pseudocode.

For instance, if the method *get-name*() is defined for the class *person*, it can be invoked with a *person* object, or with any object belonging to any subclass of *person*, such as *customer* or *officer*.

Earlier, we noted that each class is itself an object, and that that object includes a variable containing the set of all instances of the class. It is easy to determine which objects are associated with classes at the leaves of the hierarchy. For example, we associate with the *customer* class the set of all customers of the bank. For nonleaf classes, however, the issue is more complex. In the hierarchy of Figure 8.2, there are two plausible ways of associating objects with classes:

1. We could associate with the *employee* class all employee objects including those that are instances of *officer*, *teller*, and *secretary*.
2. We could associate with the *employee* class only those employee objects that are instances of neither *officer* nor *teller* nor *secretary*.

Typically, the latter choice is made in object-oriented systems. It is possible to determine the set of all employee objects in this case by taking the union of those objects associated with all subclasses of *employee*. Most object-oriented systems allow the specialization to be partial; that is, they allow objects that belong to a class such as *employee* but that do not belong to any of that class's subclasses.

8.2.4 Multiple Inheritance

In most cases, a tree-structured organization of classes is adequate to describe applications. In such cases, all superclasses of a class are ancestors or descendants of one another in the hierarchy. However, there are situations that cannot be represented well in a such tree-structured class hierarchy.

Suppose that we wish to distinguish between full-time and part-time tellers and secretaries in our example of Figure 8.2. Further assume that we require different variables and methods to represent full-time and part-time employees. Thus, each of these employees is classified in two different ways. We could create subclasses: *part-time-teller*, *full-time-teller*, *part-time-secretary* and *full-time-secretary*. The resulting hierarchy shown in Figure 8.4 has a few drawbacks:

- As we noted, there are certain variables and methods specific to full-time employment, and others specific to part-time employment. In Figure 8.4, the variables and methods for full-time employees must be defined twice: once for *full-time-secretary*, and once for *full-time-teller*. A similar redundancy exists for part-time employees. Redundancy of this form is undesirable, since any change to the properties of full- or part-time employees must be made in two places, leading to potential inconsistency. Furthermore, the hierarchy fails to exploit potential code reuse.

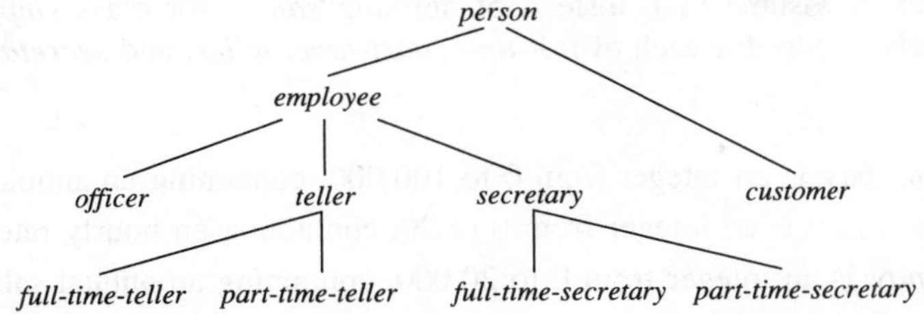

Figure 8.4 Class hierarchy for full- and part-time employees.

- The hierarchy has no means of representing employees who are not officers, tellers or secretaries, unless we expand the hierarchy further to include the classes *full-time-employee* and *part-time-employee*.

If we had several job classifications, instead of the two in our simple example, the limitations of the model would become even more apparent.

The difficulties that we have just observed are dealt with in the object-oriented model by the concept of *multiple inheritance*, which is the ability of a class to inherit variables and methods from multiple superclasses. The class–subclass relationship is represented by a *directed acyclic graph* (*DAG*), in which a class may have more than one superclass. Let us return to our bank example. Using a DAG, we can define properties of full- and part-time employment in one place. As shown in Figure 8.5, we define a class *part-time*, which defines those variables and methods specific to part-time employment, and a class *full-time*, which defines those variables and methods specific to full-time employment. The class *part-time-teller* is a subclass of both *teller* and *part-time*. It inherits from *teller* those variables and methods pertaining to tellers, and from *part-time* those variables and methods pertaining to part-time employment. The redundancy of the hierarchy of Figure 8.4 is eliminated.

Using the DAG of Figure 8.5, we can represent full- and part-time employees who are neither tellers nor secretaries as instances of classes *full-time* and *part-time*, respectively.

When multiple inheritance is used, there is potential ambiguity if the same variable or method can be inherited from more than one superclass. In our bank

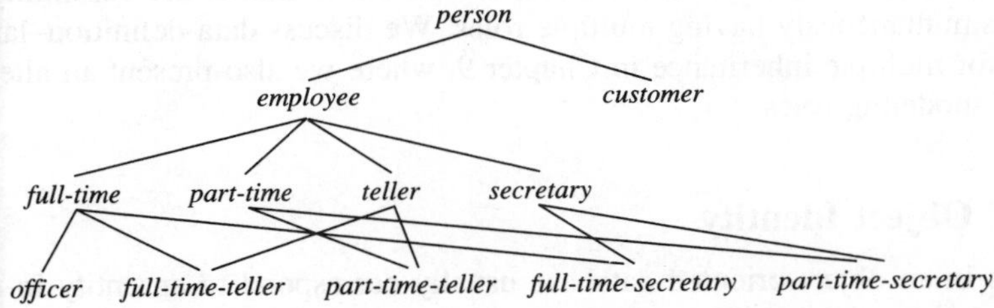

Figure 8.5 Class DAG for the bank example.

example, let us assume that, instead of defining *salary* for class *employee*, we define a variable *pay* for each of *full-time*, *part-time*, *teller*, and *secretary*, as follows:

- *full-time*: *pay* is an integer from 0 to 100,000, containing an annual salary.
- *part-time*: *pay* is an integer from 0 to 20, containing an hourly rate of pay.
- *teller*: *pay* is an integer from 0 to 20,000, containing an annual salary.
- *secretary*: *pay* is an integer from 0 to 25,000, containing an annual salary.

Consider the class *part-time-secretary*. It could inherit the definition of *pay* from either *part-time* or *secretary*. The result is different, depending on the choice made. Among the options chosen by various implementations of the object-oriented model are the following:

- Include both variables, renaming them to *part-time.pay* and *secretary.pay*.
- Choose one or the other, based on the order in which the classes *part-time* and *secretary* were created.
- Force the user to make a choice explicitly in the definition of the class *part-time-secretary*.
- Treat the situation as an error.

No single solution has been accepted as best, and different systems make different choices.

Not all cases of multiple inheritance lead to ambiguity. If, instead of defining *pay*, we retain the definition of variable *salary* in class *employee*, and define it nowhere else, then classes *part-time*, *full-time*, *secretary*, and *teller* all inherit *salary* from *employee*. Since all four of these classes share the same definition of *salary*, no ambiguity results from the inheritance of *salary* by *part-time-secretary*, *full-time-secretary*, and so on.

We can use multiple inheritance to model the concept of "roles." To understand the concept, we consider a university database. The database may have several subclasses of *person*, such as *student*, *teacher*, and *footballPlayer*. An object can belong to several of these categories at once, and each of these categories is called a *role*. We can use multiple inheritance to create subclasses such as *student-teacher*, *student-footballPlayer*, and so on, to model the possibility of an object simultaneously having multiple roles. We discuss data-definition–language issues for multiple inheritance in Chapter 9, where we also present an alternative way of modeling roles.

8.2.5 Object Identity

Objects in an object-oriented database usually correspond to an entity in the enterprise being modeled by the database. An entity retains its identity even if some of its properties change over time. Likewise, an object retains its identity even if some or all of the values of variables or definitions of methods change over time. This concept of identity does not apply to tuples of a relational database. In relational systems, the tuples of a relation are distinguished only by the values that they contain.

Object identity is a stronger notion of identity than that typically found in programming languages or in data models not based on object orientation. We illustrate several forms of identity next.

- **Value**. A data value is used for identity. This form of identity is used in relational systems. For instance, the primary key value of a tuple identifies the tuple.
- **Name**. A user-supplied name is used for identity. This form of identity typically is used for files in file systems. Each file is given a name that uniquely identifies the file, regardless of the contents of the file.
- **Built-in**. A notion of identity is built into the data model or programming language, and no user-supplied identifier is required. This form of identity is used in object-oriented systems. Each object is automatically given an identifier by the system when that object is created.

The identity of objects is a conceptual notion; actual systems require a physical mechanism to *identify* objects uniquely. For humans, names along with other information, such as date and place of birth, are often used as identifiers. Object-oriented systems provide a notion of an *object identifier* to identify objects. Object identifiers are *unique*; that is, each object has a single identifier, and no two objects have the same identifier. Object identifiers are not necessarily in a form with which humans are comfortable—they could be long numbers, for example. The ability to store the identifier of an object as a field of another object is more important than is having a name that is easy to remember.

As an example of the use of object identifiers, one of the attributes of a *person* object may be a *spouse* attribute, which is actually an identifier of the *person* object corresponding to the first person's spouse. Thus, the *person* object can store a *reference* to the object representing the person's spouse.

Usually, the identifier is generated automatically by the system. In contrast, in a relational database, the *spouse* field of a *person* relation would typically be a unique identifier (perhaps a social-security number) of the person's spouse, generated external to the database system. There are many situations where having the system generate identifiers automatically is a benefit, since it frees humans from performing that task. However, this ability should be used with care. System-generated identifiers are usually specific to the system, and have to be translated if data are moved to a different database system. System-generated identifiers may be redundant if the entities being modeled already have unique identifiers external to the system. For example, social-security numbers are often used as unique identifiers for people in the United States.

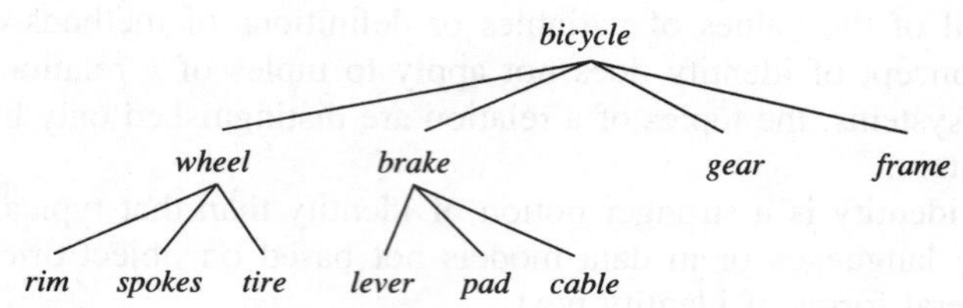

Figure 8.6 Containment hierarchy for bicycle-design database.

8.2.6 Object Containment

References between objects can be used to model different real world concepts. One such concept is that of *object containment*. To illustrate containment, we consider the simplified bicycle-design database of Figure 8.6. Each bicycle design contains wheels, a frame, brakes, and gears. Wheels, in turn, contain a rim, a set of spokes, and a tire. Each of the components of the design can be modeled as an object, and the containment of components can be modeled as containment of objects.

Objects that contain other objects are called *complex* or *composite* objects. There can be multiple levels of containment, as shown in Figure 8.6. This situation creates a *containment hierarchy* among objects.

The hierarchy of Figure 8.6 shows the containment relationship among objects in a schematic way by listing class names, rather than individual objects. The links between classes must be interpreted as **is-part-of**, rather than the **is-a** interpretation of links in an inheritance hierarchy.

The variables of the various classes are not shown in the figure. Consider the class *bicycle*. It may include variables such as *brand-name* containing descriptive data about an instance of the class *bicycle*. In addition, class *bicycle* includes variables that contain a reference, or a set of references, to objects from the classes *wheel*, *brake*, *gear*, and *frame*.

Containment is an important concept in object-oriented systems because it allows data to be viewed at different granularities by different users. A wheel designer can focus on instances of class *wheel* without much, if any, concern about the objects of class *gear* or *brake*. A marketing-staff person, attempting to price an entire bicycle, can reference all data pertaining to the bicycle by referencing the appropriate instance of class *bicycle*. The containment hierarchy is used to find all objects contained in a *bicycle* object.

In certain applications, an object may be contained in several objects. In such cases, the containment relationship is represented by a DAG, rather than by a hierarchy.

8.3 Object-Oriented Languages

Until now, we have covered the basic concepts of object orientation at an abstract level. To be used in practice in a database system, the concepts have to be expressed in some language. This expression can be done in one of two ways.

1. The concepts of object-orientation are used purely as a design tool, and are encoded into, for example, a relational database. This approach is followed when entity–relationship diagrams are used to model data, and are then manually converted into a set of relations.

2. The concepts of object orientation are incorporated into a language that is used to manipulate the database.

   With this approach, there are several possible languages into which the concepts can be integrated.

   - One choice is to extend a data-manipulation language such as SQL by adding complex types and object-orientation. Systems that provide object-oriented extensions to relational systems are called *object-relational* systems. We describe object-relational systems, and in particular object-oriented extensions to SQL, in Chapter 9.
   - Another choice is to take an existing object-oriented programming language and to extend it to deal with databases. Such languages are called persistent programming languages.

   We study the latter approach in succeeding sections of this chapter. There are different situations in which each approach is better. We discuss their relationship in Chapter 9, after describing object-relational systems.

8.4 Persistent Programming Languages

Databases languages differ from traditional programming languages in that they directly manipulate data that are persistent—that is, data that continue to exist even after the program that created it has terminated. A relation in a database and tuples in a relation are examples of persistent data. In contrast, the only persistent data that traditional programming languages directly manipulate are files.

Access to a database is only one component of any real-world application. While a data manipulation language like SQL is quite effective for accessing data, a programming language is required for implementing other components of the application such as user interfaces or communication with other computers. The traditional way of interfacing database to programming languages is by embedding SQL within the programming language.

A *persistent programming language* is a programming language extended with constructs to handle persistent data. Persistent programming languages can be distinguished from languages with embedded SQL in at least two ways:

1. With an embedded language, the type system of the host language usually differs from the type system of the data manipulation language. The programmer is responsible for any type conversions between the host language and the data manipulation language. Requiring the programmer to carry out this task has several drawbacks:

   - The code to convert between objects and tuples operates outside the object-oriented type system, and hence has a higher chance of having undetected errors.

- Conversion between the object-oriented format and the relational format of tuples in the database takes a substantial amount of code. The format translation code, along with the code for loading and unloading data from a database, can form a significant percentage of the total code required for an application.

  In contrast, in a persistent programming language, the query language is fully integrated with the host language, and both share the same type system. Objects can be created and stored in the database without any explicit type or format changes; any format changes required are carried out transparently.

2. The programmer using an embedded query language is responsible for writing explicit code to fetch data from the database into memory. If any updates are performed, the programmer must write code explicitly to store the updated data back in the database.

   In contrast, in a persistent programming language, the programmer can manipulate persistent data without having to write code explicitly to fetch it into memory or store it back to disk.

Persistent versions of programming languages such as Pascal have been proposed in the past. In recent years, persistent versions of object-oriented languages such as C++ or Smalltalk have received much attention. They allow programmers to manipulate data directly from the programming language, without having to go through a data-manipulation language such as SQL. Thereby, they provide tighter integration of the programming languages with the database than, for example, embedded SQL.

There are certain drawbacks to persistent programming languages, however, that we must keep in mind when deciding whether to use them. Since the programming language is typically powerful, it is relatively easy to make programming errors that damage the database. The complexity of the language makes automatic high-level optimization, such as to reduce disk I/O, harder. Support for declarative querying is important for many applications, but persistent programming languages currently do not support declarative querying well.

8.4.1 Persistence Of Objects

Object-oriented programming languages already have a concept of objects, a type system to define object types, and constructs to create objects. However, these objects are *transient*—they vanish when the program terminates, just as variables in a Pascal or C program vanish when the program terminates. If we wish to turn such a language into a database programming language, the first step is to provide a way to make objects persistent. Several approaches have been proposed.

- **Persistence by class**. The simplest, but least convenient, approach is to declare that a class is persistent. All objects of the class are then persistent objects by default. Objects of nonpersistent classes are all transient.

This approach is not flexible, since it is often useful to have both transient and persistent objects in a single class. In many object-oriented database systems, declaring a class to be persistent is interpreted as saying that objects in the class potentially can be made persistent, rather than that all objects in the class are persistent. Such classes might more appropriately have been called "persistable" classes.

- **Persistence by creation**. In this approach, new syntax is introduced to create persistent objects, by extending the syntax for creating transient objects. Thus, an object is either persistent or transient, depending on how it was created. This approach is followed in several object-oriented database systems.
- **Persistence by marking**. A variant of the preceding approach is to mark objects as persistent after they are created. All objects are created as transient objects, but, if an object is to persist beyond the execution of the program, it must be marked explicitly as persistent before the program terminates. Unlike the previous approach, the decision on persistence or transience is postponed until after the object is created.
- **Persistence by reference**. One or more objects are explicitly declared as (root) persistent objects. All other objects are persistent if (and only if) they are referred to directly, or indirectly, from a root persistent object.

  Thus, all objects referenced from the root persistent objects are persistent. But also, all objects referenced from these objects are persistent, and objects to which they refer are in turn persistent, and so on.

  This scheme has the benefit that it is easy to make entire data structures persistent by merely declaring the root of such structures as persistent. However, the database system has the burden of following chains of references to detect which objects are persistent, and that can be expensive.

8.4.2 Object Identity and Pointers

When a persistent object is created, it is assigned a persistent object identifier. In an object-oriented programming language that has not been extended to handle persistence, when an object is created, a transient object identifier is returned. The only difference between the two identifiers is that the transient object identifier is valid only when the program that created it is executing; after that program terminates, the object is deleted, and the identifier is meaningless.

The notion of object identity has an interesting relationship to pointers in programming languages. A simple way to achieve built-in identity is through pointers to physical locations in storage. In particular, in many object-oriented languages such as C++, an object identifier is actually an in-memory pointer.

However, the association of an object with a physical location in storage may change over time. There are several degrees of permanence of identity:

- **Intraprocedure**. Identity persists only during the execution of a single procedure. Examples of intraprogram identity are local variables within procedures.
- **Intraprogram**. Identity persists only during the execution of a single program or query. Examples of intraprogram identity are global variables in

programming languages. Main-memory or virtual-memory pointers offer only intraprogram identity.

- **Interprogram**. Identity persists from one program execution to another. Pointers to file-system data on disk offer interprogram identity, but they may change if the way data is stored in the file system is changed.
- **Persistent**. Identity persists not only among program executions, but also among structural reorganizations of the data. It is the persistent form of identity that is required for object-oriented systems.

In persistent extensions of languages such as C++, object identifiers for persistent objects are implemented as "persistent pointers." A *persistent pointer* is a type of pointer that, unlike in-memory pointers, remains valid even after the end of a program execution, and across some forms of data reorganization. A programmer may use a persistent pointer in the same ways that she may use an in-memory pointer in a programming language. Conceptually, we may think of a persistent pointer as a pointer to an object in the database.

8.4.3 Storage and Access of Persistent Objects

What does it mean to store an object in a database? Clearly, the data part of an object has to be stored individually for each object. Logically, the code that implements methods of a class should be stored in the database as part of the database schema, along with the type definitions of the classes. However, many implementations simply store the code in files outside the database, to avoid having to integrate system software such as compilers with the database system.

There are several ways to find objects in the database. One approach is to give names to objects, just as we give names to files. This approach works for a relatively small number of objects, but does not scale to millions of objects. A second approach is to expose object identifiers or persistent pointers to the objects, which can be stored externally. Unlike names, these pointers do not have to be mnemonic, and can even be physical pointers pointers into a database.

A third approach is to store collections of objects, and to allow programs to iterate over the collections to find required objects. Collections of objects can themselves be modeled as objects of a *collection type*. Collection types include sets, multisets (that is, sets with possibly many occurrences of a value), lists, and so on. A special case of a collection is a *class extent*, which is the collection of all objects belonging to the class. If a class extent is present for a class, then, whenever an object of the class is created that object is inserted in the class extent automatically, and, whenever an object is deleted, that object is removed from the class extent. Class extents allow classes to be treated like relations in that it is possible to examine all objects in the class, just as we can examine all tuples in a relation.

Most object-oriented database systems support all three ways of accessing persistent objects. All objects have object identifiers. Names are typically given only to class extents and other collection objects, and perhaps to other selected objects, but most objects are not given names. Class extents are usually maintained for all classes that can have persistent objects, but, in many of the implementations, they contain only persistent objects of the class.

8.5 Persistent C++ Systems

Several object-oriented databases based on persistent extensions to C++ have appeared in the past few years (see the bibliographic notes). There are differences between them in terms of the system architecture, yet they have many common features in terms of the programming language.

Several of the object-oriented features of the C++ language help in providing a good deal of support for persistence without changing the language itself. For example, we can declare a class called `Persistent_Object` with attributes and methods to support persistence; any other class that should be persistent can be made a subclass of this class, and thereby inherit the support for persistence. The C++ language (like other modern programming languages) also provides the ability to redefine standard function names and operators—such as +, −, the pointer dereference operator `->`, and so on—based on the type of the operands on which they are applied. This ability is called *overloading*, and is used to redefine operators to behave in the required manner when they are operating on persistent objects. Examples of the use of such features are presented in the next section.

Providing persistence support via class libraries has the benefit of making minimal changes to C++, and is relatively easy to implement. However, it has the drawback that the programmer has to spend much more time to write a program that handles persistent objects, and it is not easy to specify integrity constraints on the schema, or to provide support for declarative querying. Most of the persistent C++ implementations therefore extend the C++ syntax, at least to some extent.

8.5.1 The ODMG C++ Object-Definition Language

The Object Database Management Group (ODMG) has been working on standardizing language extensions to C++ and Smalltalk to support persistence, and on defining class libraries to support persistence. The ODMG standard attempts to extend C++ as little as possible, providing most functionality via class libraries. We describe the ODMG standard using examples. You must have prior knowledge of the C++ programming language to understand the examples fully. (See the bibliographic notes for references to C++ texts.)

There are two parts to the ODMG C++ extension: (1) the *C++ Object Definition Language* (*C++ ODL*), and (2) the *C++ Object Manipulation Language* (*C++ OML*). The C++ ODL extends the C++ type definition syntax.

Figure 8.7 shows a sample of code written in the ODMG C++ ODL. The schema of four classes are defined in the code. Each class is defined as a subclass of `Persistent_Object`, and objects in the class can therefore be made persistent. The classes `Person`, `Branch`, and `Account` are direct subclasses of

```
class Person : public Persistent_Object {
public:
   String name;
   String address;
};

class Customer : public Person {
public:
   Date member_from;
   int customer_id;
   Ref<Branch> home_branch;
   Set<Ref<Account>> accounts inverse Account::owners;
};

class Branch : public Persistent_Object {
public:
   String name;
   String address;
   int assets;
};

class Account : public Persistent_Object {
private:
   int balance;
public:
   int number;
   Set<Ref<Customer>> owners inverse Customer::accounts;
   int find_balance();
   int update_balance(int delta);
};
```

Figure 8.7 Example of ODMG C++ Object Definition Language.

Persistent_Object. The class Customer is a subclass of Person and is therefore indirectly also a subclass of Persistent_Object.

C++ does not support the concept of messages directly. Instead, methods may be directly invoked, and behave like procedure calls. The keyword private indicates that the following attributes or methods are visible to only methods of the class; public indicates that the attributes or methods are visible to other code as well. The use of the keyword public just before the name of a superclass indicates that public attributes or methods inherited from the superclass remain public in the subclass. These features are part of standard C++.

The attribute definitions of type int, String, and Date are in standard C++ syntax; the types String and Date are among the standard types defined by ODMG. Type Ref<Branch> is a *reference*, or persistent pointer, to an object of type Branch. Type Set<Ref<Account>> is a set of persistent pointers to objects of type Account. We use the notation **inverse** to specify referential integrity constraints. Consider any Customer object. Specifying **inverse** Account::owners for the attribute accounts says that, for each account object referenced in the accounts set of the Customer object, the field owners of the account object must contain a reference back to the Customer object.

The classes Ref<T> and Set<T> are *template* classes defined in the ODMG standard; they are defined in a type-independent way, and are instantiated to the required types (such as Ref<Account>) as desired. The template class Set<T> provides functions such as insert_element and delete_element.

The declaration of class Account also illustrates the "encapsulation" features of C++. The attribute balance of Account is declared to be private, meaning that no function other than methods of the class can read or write it. The class also has two methods: find_balance() and update_balance(int delta). These methods can read and write the balance attribute; we shall use them to read and update the balance of the account (we have not presented their code).

The only extension to the C++ syntax in the preceding example is the syntax for declaring inverse relationships to ensure referential integrity. All other functionality added by ODMG is provided by means of class libraries.

Planned extensions to the standard include replacement of Ref<T> by the usual C++ notation T *, to improve readability. Certain systems, such as ObjectStore, provide this enhancement already. To the programmer, pointers to persistent objects appear to be the same as pointers to regular in-memory objects, and that makes programming much easier. This functionality is implemented by means of a translation mechanism called *swizzling*, which converts between persistent pointers and in-memory pointers; swizzling is described in Chapter 10.

8.5.2 The ODMG C++ Object Manipulation Language

Figure 8.8 shows an example of code written in the ODMG C++ OML. First, a database is opened, and a transaction is started.

The notion of transactions is covered in detail in Chapter 13. Briefly, a *transaction* is a sequence of steps, demarcated by a call to begin a transaction and a call to commit or abort the transaction. The steps of the transaction are treated as an atomic unit; the database system guarantees that either all the steps are executed successfully, or, if any step cannot be executed for any reason, the effect of already-executed steps is undone in the database. The transaction is said to have *committed* in the first case, and to have *aborted* in the second case.

As the next step, an account and an owner object are created and are initialized as part of the transaction. Finally, the transaction is committed. The class Persistent_Object implements several methods, including the persistent version of the C++ memory-allocation operator new that is used in the example code. This version of the new operator allocates the object in the specified database, rather than in memory. We use the method insert_element of the template class Set<> to insert customer and account references in the appropriate sets after creating the customer and account objects. If only one of the two inserts was executed, a referential-integrity violation will be detected when the transaction commit occurs, and the transaction will be aborted.

The example code in Figure 8.8 is incomplete in that, after the end of the transaction, there is no way to get back to the customer and account objects that we just created. We can fix this problem by inserting the references to the customer and account objects in persistent sets that contain all customer and account objects. We can then give these sets names, and look them up by name, or we can associate them with the classes `Customer` and `Account` by adding an attribute declaration of the form

```
static Ref<Set<Ref<Customer>>> all_customers;
```

to the `Customer` class, and a similar one to the `Account` class. The collection is initially allocated in the database and set to be empty. We can insert a customer object in the preceding set by using a statement of the form

```
Customer::all_customers.insert_element(cust);
```

A *constructor* for a class is a special method that is used to initialize objects when they are created, and is called automatically when the `new` operator is executed. Similarly, a *destructor* for a class is a special method that is called when objects in the class are deleted. By adding the preceding statement to the constructors of a class, and adding a corresponding `delete_element` statement to the destructor of the class, a programmer can ensure that the collection `Customer::all_customers` is maintained correctly. In certain persistent C++ extensions, class extents (that is, collections containing all persistent objects in a class) are created and maintained automatically for every class that can have persistent objects. The programmer then does not have to write code to insert or delete objects from the class extents.

We can iterate over a collection of references using an *iterator*, as shown in Figure 8.9. We create an iterator using the method `create_iterator()`

```
int create_account_owner(String name, String address) {
   Database * bank_db;
   bank_db = Database::open("Bank-DB");
   Transaction Trans;
   Trans.begin();

   Ref<Account> account = new(bank_db) Account;
   Ref<Customer> cust = new(bank_db) Customer;
   cust->name = name;
   cust->address = address;
   cust->accounts.insert_element(account);
   account->owners.insert_element(cust);
   ... Code to initialize customer_id, account number etc.
   Trans.commit();
}
```

Figure 8.8 Example of ODMG C++ Object Manipulation Language.

```
int print_customers() {
    Database * bank_db;
    bank_db = Database::open("Bank-DB");
    Transaction Trans;
    Trans.begin();

    Iterator<Ref<Customer>> iter =
        Customer::all_customers.create_iterator();
    Ref<Customer> p;
    while(iter.next(p)) {
        print_cust(p);
    }
    Trans.commit();
}
```

Figure 8.9 Example of use of ODMG C++ iterators.

provided by the class `Collection` and by that class's subclasses, such as `Set`. We use the method `next()`, provided by the iterator, to step through consecutive elements of the collection of customers. For each customer, the method `print_cust` (which we assume has been defined elsewhere) is called to print out the customer.

8.6 Summary

Database applications in such areas as computer-aided design, software engineering, and office information systems do not fit the set of assumptions made for older, data-processing–style applications. The object-oriented data model has been proposed to deal with several of these new type of applications.

The object-oriented data model is an adaptation to database systems of the object-oriented–programming paradigm. It is based on the concept of encapsulating in an object the data, and the code that operates on those data. Similarly structured objects are grouped into classes. The set of classes is structured into sub- and superclasses based on an extension of the ISA concept of the entity–relationship model. Since the value of a data item in an object is also an object, it is possible to represent object containment, resulting in a composite object.

There are two approaches to creating an object-oriented database: We can add the concepts of object orientation to existing database languages, or we can extend existing object-oriented languages to deal with databases by adding concepts such as persistence and collections. Extended relational databases take the former approach. Persistent programming languages follow the latter approach. Persistent extensions to C++ have made significant progress in recent years. Integrating persistence seamlessly and orthogonally with existing language constructs is important for ease of use.

Exercises

8.1. For each of the following application areas, explain why a relational database system would be inadequate. List all specific system components that would need to be modified.
(*a*) Computer-aided design
(*b*) Computer-aided software engineering
(*c*) Multimedia databases
(*d*) Office information systems

8.2. How does the concept of an object in the object-oriented model differ from the concept of an entity in the entity–relationship model?

8.3. A car-rental company maintains a vehicle database for all vehicles in its current fleet. For all vehicles, it includes the vehicle identification number, license number, manufacturer, model, date of purchase, and color. Special data are included for certain types of vehicles:
- Trucks: cargo capacity
- Sports cars: horsepower, renter age requirement
- Vans: number of passengers
- Off-road vehicles: ground clearance, drivetrain (four- or two-wheel drive)

Construct an object-oriented database schema definition for this database. Use inheritance where appropriate.

8.4. Explain why ambiguity potentially exists with multiple inheritance. Illustrate your explanation with an example.

8.5. Explain how the concept of object identity in the object-oriented model differs from the concept of tuple equality in the relational model.

8.6. Explain the distinction in meaning between edges in a DAG representing inheritance and a DAG representing object containment.

8.7. Consider a system that provides persistent objects. Is such a system necessarily a database system? Explain your answer.

8.8. Let O_1 and O_2 be composite objects that contain the same set of objects. Must O_1 be identical to O_2? Explain your answer.

8.9. Why do persistent programming languages allow transient objects? Might it be simpler to use only persistent objects, with unneeded objects deleted at the end of an execution? Explain your answer.

8.10. Explain how a persistent pointer is implemented. Contrast this implementation with that of pointers as they exist in general-purpose languages, such as C or Pascal.

8.11. If an object is created without any references to it, how can that object be deleted?

Bibliographic Notes

Applications of database concepts to CAD are discussed in Haskin and Lorie [1982], Kim et al. [1984], Lorie et al. [1985], Ranft et al. [1990], and Bancilhon et al. [1985a, 1985b].

Object-oriented programming is discussed in Goldberg and Robson [1983], Cox [1986], Stefik and Bobrow [1986], and Stroustrup [1988]. Stroustrup [1992] describes the C++ programming language. There are numerous implemented object-oriented database systems, including (in alphabetical order) Cactis (Hudson and King [1989]), E/Exodus, developed at the University of Wisconsin (Carey et al. [1990]), Gemstone (Maier et al. [1986]), Iris, developed at Hewlett-Packard (Fishman et al. [1990]), Jasmine, developed at Fujitsu Labs (Ishikawa et al. [1993]), O_2 (Lecluse et al. [1988]), ObjectStore (Lamb et al. [1991]), Ode, developed at Bell Laboratories (Agrawal and Gehani [1989]), Ontos, Open-OODB, Orion (Banerjee et al. [1987a], Kim et al. [1988] and Kim [1990a]), Versant, and others.

Overviews of object-oriented database research include Kim and Lochovsky [1989], Kim [1990b], Zdonik and Maier [1990], and Dittrich [1988]. Object identity is characterized in detail by Khoshafian and Copeland [1990]. Further discussion of object identity appears in Abiteboul and Kanellakis [1989]. The object database standard ODMG-93 is described in detail in Cattell [1994]. Recent advances in object-oriented database systems are discussed in Dogac et al. [1994].

Schema modification in object-oriented databases is more complicated than schema modification in relational databases, since object-oriented databases have complex type systems with inheritance. Schema modification is discussed in Banerjee et al. [1987b] as it pertains to Orion, and in Penney and Stein [1987] as it pertains to Gemstone. Other discussions of schema modification and semantics appear in Skarra and Zdonik [1986].

Goodman [1995] describes the benefits and drawbacks of using an object-oriented databases in a genome database application.

CHAPTER 9

OBJECT-RELATIONAL DATABASES

Persistent programming languages add persistence and other database features to existing programming languages with an existing object-oriented type system. In contrast, *object-relational data models* extend the relational data model by providing a richer type system including object orientation, and add constructs to relational query languages, such as SQL to deal with the added data types. The extended type systems allow attributes of tuples to have complex types. Such extensions attempt to preserve the relational foundations—in particular, the declarative access to data—while extending the modeling power. Object-relational database systems (that is, database systems based on the object-relation model) provide a convenient migration path for users of relational databases who wish to use object-oriented features.

We first present the motivation for the nested relational model, which allows relations that are not in first normal form, and allows direct representation of hierarchical structures. We then show how we can extend the SQL DDL by adding a rich type system and object orientation. Next, we show how we can extend the SQL query language to deal with complex types, including nested relations, and objects. Finally, we discuss differences between persistent programming languages and object-relational systems, and mention criteria for choosing between them.

9.1 Nested Relations

In Chapter 7, we defined *first normal form* (1NF), which requires that all attributes have *atomic domains*. A domain is *atomic* if elements of the domain are considered to be indivisible units.

For example, the set of integers is an atomic domain, but the set of all sets of integers is a nonatomic domain. The distinction is that we do not normally consider integers to have subparts, but we consider set of integers to have subparts—namely, the integers constituting the set. If we were to consider each integer to be an ordered list of digits, then the domain of all integers would be considered nonatomic. Thus, the important issue in 1NF is not the domain itself, but rather the way we use domain elements in the database.

We have not drawn attention to the 1NF assumption until now because the assumption of 1NF is a natural one in the bank examples we have considered. However, not all applications are compatible with the 1NF assumption. Rather than viewing the database as a set of records, users of certain applications view the database as a set of objects. These objects may require several records for their representation. We shall see that a simple, easy-to-use interface requires a one-to-one correspondence between the user's intuitive notion of an object and the database system's notion of a data item.

The nested relational model is an extension of the relational model in which domains may be either atomic or relation valued. Thus, the value of a tuple on an attribute may be a relation, and relations may be stored within relations. A complex object thus can be represented by a single tuple of a nested relation. If we view a tuple of a nested relation as a data item, we have a one-to-one correspondence between data items and objects in the user's view of the database.

We illustrate nested relations by an example drawn from office information systems. Consider a document-retrieval system in which we store, for each document, the following information:

- Document title
- Author list
- Date acquired
- Keyword list

We can see that, if we define a relation for the preceding information, several domains will be nonatomic.

- **Authors**. A document may have a set of authors. Nevertheless, we may want to find all documents of which Jones was one of the authors. Thus, we are interested in a subpart of the domain element "set of authors."
- **Keywords**. If we store a set of keywords for a document, we expect to be able to retrieve all documents whose keywords include one or more keywords. Thus, we view the domain of *keyword-list* as nonatomic.
- **Date**. Unlike *keywords* and *authors*, *date* does not have a set-valued domain. However, we may view *date* as consisting of the subfields *day*, *month*, and *year*. This view makes the domain of *date* nonatomic.

Figure 9.1 shows an example document relation, *doc*. The *doc* relation can be represented in 1NF, as shown in Figure 9.2. Since we must have atomic domains

title	*author-list*	*date*	*keyword-list*
		(*day, month, year*)	
salesplan	{Smith, Jones}	(1, April, 89)	{profit, strategy}
status report	{Jones, Frick}	(17, June, 94)	{profit, personnel}

Figure 9.1 Non-1NF document relation, *doc*.

in 1NF, yet want access to individual authors and to individual keywords, we need one tuple for each (keyword, author) pair. The *date* attribute is replaced in the 1NF version by three attributes: one for each subfield of *date*.

Much of the awkwardness of the *flat-doc* relation in Figure 9.2 is removed if we assume that the following multivalued dependencies hold:

- *title* $\rightarrow\!\!\rightarrow$ *author*
- *title* $\rightarrow\!\!\rightarrow$ *keyword*
- *title* $\rightarrow$ *day month year*

Then, we can decompose the relation into 4NF using the schemas:

- (*title, author*)
- (*title, keyword*)
- (*title, day, month, year*)

Figure 9.3 shows the projection of the relation *flat-doc* of Figure 9.2 onto the preceding decomposition.

Although 1NF can represent our example document database adequately, the non-1NF representation may be an easier-to-understand model, since the typical user of a document-retrieval system thinks of the database in terms of our non-1NF design. The 4NF design would require users to include joins in their queries, thereby complicating interaction with the system. We could define a nonnested relational view that eliminates the need for users to write joins in their query. In

title	*author*	*day*	*month*	*year*	*keyword*
salesplan	Smith	1	April	89	profit
salesplan	Jones	1	April	89	profit
salesplan	Smith	1	April	89	strategy
salesplan	Jones	1	April	89	strategy
status report	Jones	17	June	94	profit
status report	Frick	17	June	94	profit
status report	Jones	17	June	94	personnel
status report	Frick	17	June	94	personnel

Figure 9.2 *flat-doc*, a 1NF version of non-1NF relation *doc*.

title	*author*
salesplan	Smith
salesplan	Jones
status report	Jones
status report	Frick

title	*keyword*
salesplan	profit
salesplan	strategy
status report	profit
status report	personnel

title	*day*	*month*	*year*
salesplan	1	April	89
status report	17	June	94

Figure 9.3 4NF version of the relation *flat-doc* of Figure 9.2.

such a view, however, we lose the one-to-one correspondence between tuples and documents.

9.2 Complex Types and Object Orientation

Nested relations are just one example of extensions to the basic relational model. Other nonatomic data types, such as nested records, have also proved useful. The object-oriented data model has caused a need for features such as inheritance and references to objects. Complex type systems and object orientation enable E-R model concepts, such as identity of entities, multivalued attributes, and generalization and specialization to be represented directly without a complex translation to the relational model.

In this section, we describe extensions to SQL to allow complex types, including nested relations, and object-oriented features. Several such extensions have been proposed, and a standardization effort is under way. Our presentation is based loosely on a preliminary draft of the SQL-3 standard, which is likely to be finalized in a few years. We stress that our presentation does not strictly follow the current draft, and moreover the draft is evolving and changes are likely. Our presentation also incorporates features of other proposed extensions, such as XSQL, and the query language of the Illustra database system. XSQL is a research language that extends SQL with powerful object-oriented features. Illustra is the commercial version of the Postgres database system, developed at the University of California at Berkeley, which was one of the early systems to extend the relational model with object-oriented features. See the bibliographic notes for references to these languages.

9.2.1 Structured and Collection Types

Consider the following statements, which define a relation *doc* with the complex attributes described in the previous section.

```
create type MyString char varying.
create type MyDate
    ( day integer,
      month char(10),
      year integer)
create type Document
    (name MyString,
     author-list setof(MyString),
     date MyDate,
     keyword-list setof(MyString))
create table doc of type Document
```

The first statement defines a type *MyString*, which is a variable-length character string. The next statement defines a type called *MyDate*, which has three components: day, month, and year. The third statement defines a type *Document*, which contains a *name*, an *author-list*, which is a set of authors, a date of type *MyDate*, and a set of keywords. Finally, the table *doc* containing tuples of type *Document* is created. The preceding table definition differs from table definitions in ordinary relational databases, since it allows attributes that are sets, and attributes such as *MyDate* that are structured. These features allow composite attributes and multivalued attributes of E-R diagrams to be represented directly.

An important point to note is that the types created using the preceding statements are recorded in the schema stored in the database. Thus, other statements that access the database can make use of the type definitions. Type definitions in programming languages (including persistent programming languages) typically are not stored in a database, and can be seen only by programs that include a textual file containing the definitions.

We can also create tables directly, without creating an intermediate type for the table. For example, the table *doc* could also be defined as follows:

```
create table doc
    (name MyString,
     author-list setof(MyString),
     date MyDate,
     keyword-list setof(MyString))
```

Complex type systems usually support other collection types, such as arrays and multisets (that is, unordered collections, where an element may occur multiple times). The following attribute definitions illustrate the use of such collection types:

```
author-array MyString[10]
print-runs multiset(integer)
```

Here, *author-array* is an array of author names. As we cannot do from a set of author names, from an array we can determine who is the first author, who is the second author, and so on. The second attribute, *print-runs*, is a multiset of integers, which could represent the number of copies of a document printed in each printing run of the document. Since two printing runs may have the same number of copies, a multiset should be used, rather than a set.

9.2.2 Inheritance

Inheritance can be at the level of types, or at the level of tables. Let us first consider inheritance of types. Suppose that we have the following type definition for people:

create type *Person*
(*name MyString*,
social-security **integer**)

We may want to store extra information in the database about people who are students, and about people who are teachers. Since students and teachers are also people, we can use inheritance to define the student and teacher types as follows:

create type *Student*
(*degree MyString*,
department MyString)
under *Person*
create type *Teacher*
(*salary* **integer**,
department MyString)
under *Person*

Both *Student* and *Teacher* inherit the attributes of *Person*—namely, *name* and *social-security*. *Student* and *Teacher* are said to be subtypes of *Person*, and *Person* is a supertype of *Student*, as well as of *Teacher*.

Now suppose that we want to store information about teaching assistants, who are simultaneously students and teachers, perhaps even in different departments. Recall the idea of multiple inheritance, which we studied in Chapter 8. If our type system supports multiple inheritance, we can try to define a type for teaching assistant as follows:

create type *TeachingAssistant*
under *Student*, *Teacher*

TeachingAssistant ought to inherit all the attributes of *Student* and *Teacher*. There is a problem, however, since the attributes *social-security*, *name*, and *department* are present in *Student*, as well as in *Teacher*.

The attributes *social-security* and *name* are actually inherited from a common source, *Person*. So there is no conflict caused by inheriting them from *Student* as well as *Teacher*. However, the attribute *department* is defined separately in *Student* and *Teacher*. In fact, a teaching assistant may be a student of one department and a teacher in another department. To avoid a conflict between the two occurrences of *department*, we can rename them using an **as** clause, as shown in the following definition of the type *TeachingAssistant*:

> **create type** *TeachingAssistant*
> **under** *Student* **with** (*department* **as** *student-dept*),
> *Teacher* **with** (*department* **as** *teacher-dept*)

Inheritance of types should be used with care. A university database may have many subtypes of *Person*, such as *Student*, *Teacher*, *FootballPlayer*, *ForeignCitizen*, and so on. *Student* may itself have subtypes such as *UndergraduateStudent*, *GraduateStudent*, and *PartTimeStudent*. Clearly, a person can belong to several of these categories at once. As mentioned in Chapter 8, each of these categories is sometimes called a *role*.

In most programming languages, an entity must have exactly one *most specific type*; that is, if an entity has more than one type, there must be a single type to which the entity belongs, and that single type must be a subtype of all the types to which the entity belongs. For example, suppose that an entity has the type *Person*, as well as the type *Student*. Then, the most specific type of the entity is *Student*, since *Student* is a subtype of *Person*. However, an entity cannot have the type *Student*, as well as the type *Teacher*, unless it has a type, such as *TeachingAssistant*, that is a subtype of *Teacher*, as well as of *Student*.

For each entity to have exactly one most specific type, we would have to create a subtype for every possible combination of the supertypes. In the preceding example, we would have subtypes such as *ForeignUndergraduateStudent*, *ForeignGraduateStudentFootballPlayer*, and so on. Unfortunately, we would end up with an enormous number of subtypes of *Person*.

A better approach in the context of database systems is to allow an object to have multiple types, without having a most specific type. Object-relational systems can model such a feature by using inheritance at the level of tables, rather than of types, and allowing an entity to exist in more than one table at once. We can rephrase the preceding example of students and teachers as follows. First, we define the *people* table as follows:

> **create table** *people*
> (*name MyString*,
> *social-security* **integer**)

Then, we define the *students* and *teachers* tables as follows:

> **create table** *students*
> (*degree MyString*,
> *department MyString*)
> **under** *people*
> **create table** *teachers*
> (*salary* **integer**,
> *department MyString*)
> **under** *people*

The subtables *students* and *teachers* inherit all the attributes of the table *people*. There is no need to create further subtables, such as *teaching-assistants*, that inherit from both *students* and *teachers*, unless there are attributes specific to entities that are *students* as well as *teachers*.

There are consistency requirements on subtables and supertables. We illustrate them using the same example.

- Each tuple of the supertable *people* can correspond to (that is, have the same values for all inherited attributes as) at most one tuple in each of the tables *students* and *teachers*.
- Each tuple in *students* and *teachers* must have exactly one corresponding tuple (that is, with the same values for all inherited attributes) in *people*.

Without the first condition, we could have two tuples in *students* (or *teachers*) that correspond to the same person. Without the second condition, we could have a tuple in *students* or in *teachers* that does not correspond to any tuple in *people*, or that corresponds to several tuples in *people*. These states cannot correspond to the real world, and are hence erroneous.

Subtables can be stored in an efficient manner without replication of all inherited fields. Inherited attributes other than the primary key of the supertable do not need to be stored, and can be derived by means of a join with the supertable, based on the primary key.

Multiple inheritance is possible with tables, just as it is possible with types. A teaching-assistant entity can simply belong to the table *students*, as well as to the table *teachers*. However, if we want, we can create a table for teaching-assistant entities as follows:

> **create table** *teaching-assistants*
> **under** *students* **with** (*department* **as** *student-dept*),
> *teachers* **with** (*department* **as** *teacher-dept*)

The consistency requirements for subtables ensure that, if an entity is present in the *teaching-assistants* table, it is also present in the *teachers* and in the *students* table.

Inheritance makes schema definition more natural. Without inheritance of tables, the schema designer has to link tables corresponding to subtables explicitly with tables corresponding to supertables via primary keys, and to define constraints between the tables to ensure referential and cardinality constraints. The use of inheritance enables the use of functions defined for supertypes on objects belonging to subtypes, allowing the orderly extension of a database system to incorporate new types.

9.2.3 Reference Types

Object-oriented languages provide the ability to refer to objects. An attribute of a type can be a reference to an object of a specified type. For example, references to people are of the type **ref**(*Person*). The author-list field of the type *Document* can be redefined as

author-list **setof**(**ref**(*Person*))

which is a set of references to *Person* objects.

Tuples of a table can also have references to them. References to tuples of the table *people* have the type **ref**(*people*). We can implement references to tuples of a table by using the primary key of the table. Alternatively, each tuple of a table may have a tuple identifier as an implicit attribute, and a reference to a tuple is simply the tuple identifier. Subtables implicitly inherit the tuple identifier attribute, just as they inherit other attributes from supertables.

The **ref** notation is used in the Illustra database system. In the preliminary draft of SQL-3 "**ref**(*Person*)" is written as "*Person* **identity**." The identifiers of tuples and objects can be accessed through special attributes **identity** and **oid** (that is, object identifier), respectively. The SQL-3 standard may require that, if we are to allow references to objects of a data type, the data type must be declared to be "**with oid**." Similarly, if we are to allow references to tuples of a table, the table may be required to be declared "**with identity**."

9.3 Querying with Complex Types

In this section, we present an extension of the SQL query language to deal with complex types. Let us start with a simple example: Find the name and year of publication of each document. The following query carries out the task:

select *name*, *date.year*
from *doc*

Notice that the field *year* of the composite attribute *date* is referred to using a dot notation. (A double dot (..) notation has been proposed for SQL-3 , instead of the dot notation.)

9.3.1 Relation-Valued Attributes

Our extended SQL allows an expression evaluating to a relation to appear anywhere that a relation name may appear, such as in a **from** clause. The ability to use subexpressions freely makes it possible to take advantage of the structure of nested relations, as the following example shows.

Suppose that we are given a relation *pdoc* with a schema created as follows:

create table *pdoc*
(*name MyString*,
author-list **setof**(**ref**(*people*)),
date MyDate,
keyword-list **setof**(*MyString*))

If we want to find all documents that have the word "database" as one of their keywords, we can use the following query:

```
select name
from pdoc
where "database" in keyword-list
```

Note that we have used the relation-valued attribute *keyword-list* in a position where SQL without nested relations would have required a **select-from-where** subexpression.

Now, suppose that we want a relation containing pairs of the form "document-name, author-name" for each document and each author of the document. We can use the following query:

```
select B.name, Y.name
from pdoc as B, B.author-list as Y
```

Since the *author-list* attribute of *pdoc* is a set-valued field, it can be used in a **from** clause where a relation is expected.

Aggregate functions (for example, **min**, **max**, and **count**) take a collection of values as an argument and return a single value as their result. They can be applied to any relation-valued expression. The query, "Find the name, and the number of authors for each document" can be written as

```
select name, count(author-list)
from pdoc
```

Since *author-list* is a set-valued attribute containing one tuple for each author, a count of the set provides the number of authors.

9.3.2 Path Expressions

The dot notation for referring to composite attributes can be used with references. Suppose that we have the table *people* as defined earlier, and a table *phd-student* defined as here:

```
create table phd-students
        (advisor ref(people))
        under people
```

Then, we can use the following query to find the names of the advisors of all doctoral students:

```
select phd-students.advisor.name
from phd-students
```

Since *phd-students.advisor* is a reference to tuple in the *people* table, the attribute *name* in the preceding query is the *name* attribute of the tuple from the *people* table. References can be used to hide join operations; in the preceding example, without the use of references, the *advisor* field of *phd-students* would be a foreign key of the table *people*. To find the name of the advisor of a doctoral student, we would require an explicit join of *phd-students* with the *people* relation based on the foreign key. The use of references simplifies the query considerably.

An expression of the form "*students.advisor.name*" is called a *path expression*. In the preceding example, each attribute in the path expression has a single value (a reference in the case of advisor). In general, attributes used in a path expression can be a collection, such as a set or a multiset. If we want to get the names of all authors of documents in the *pdoc* relation, we can write the following query:

```
select Y.name
from pdoc.author-list as Y
```

The variable *Y* ranges over each author of each document in the *pdoc* relation.

9.3.3 Nesting and Unnesting

The transformation of a nested relation into 1NF is called *unnesting*. The *doc* relation has two attributes *author-list* and *keyword-list*, which are nested relations, and two attributes, *name* and *date*, which are not. Suppose that we want to convert the relation into a single flat relation, with no nested relations or structured types as attributes. We can use the following query to carry out the task:

```
select name, A as author, date.day, date.month, date.year,
       K as keyword
from doc as B, B.author-list as A, B.keyword-list as K
```

The variable *B* in the from clause is declared to range over *doc*. The variable *A* is declared to range over the authors in *author-list* for that document, and *K* is declared to range over the keywords in the *keyword-list* of the document. Figure 9.1 (in Section 9.1) shows an instance *doc* relation, and Figure 9.2 shows the 1NF relation that is the result of the preceding query.

The reverse process of transforming a 1NF relation into a nested relation is called *nesting*. Nesting can be carried out by an extension of grouping in SQL. In the normal use of grouping in SQL, a temporary multiset relation is (logically) created for each group, and an aggregate function is applied on the temporary relation. By returning the multiset instead of applying the aggregate function, we can create a nested relation. Suppose that we are given a 1NF relation *flat-doc*, as shown in Figure 9.2. The following query nests the relation on the attribute *keyword*:

```
select title, author, (day, month, year) as date,
       set(keyword) as keyword-list
from flat-doc
groupby title, author, date
```

The result of the query on the *doc* relation from Figure 9.2 is shown in Figure 9.4. If we want to nest the author attribute as well, and thereby to convert the 1NF table *flat-doc* in Figure 9.2 back to the nested table *doc* shown in Figure 9.1, we

title	*author*	*date* (*day, month, year*)	*keyword-list*
salesplan	Smith	(1, April, 89)	{profit, strategy}
salesplan	Jones	(1, April, 89)	{profit, strategy}
status report	Jones	(17, June, 94)	{profit, personnel}
status report	Frick	(17, June, 94)	{profit, personnel}

Figure 9.4 A partially nested version of the *flat-doc* relation.

can use the following query:

> **select** *title*, **set**(*author*) **as** *author-list*, (*day, month, year*) **as** *date*,
> **set**(*keyword*) **as** *keyword-list*
> **from** *flat-doc*
> **groupby** *title, date*

9.3.4 Functions

Object-relational systems allow functions to be defined by users. These functions can be defined either in a programming language such as C or C++, or in a data-manipulation language such as SQL. We look at function definitions in our extended SQL first.

Suppose that we want a function that, given a document, returns the count of the number of authors. We can define the function as follows:

> **create function** *author-count*(*one-doc Document*)
> **returns integer as**
> **select count**(*author-list*)
> **from** *one-doc*

Recall that *Document* is a type name. The function is invoked with a single document object, and the **select** statement is executed with a relation *one-doc* containing only a single tuple—namely, the argument of the function. The result of the **select** statement is a single value; strictly speaking, it is a tuple with a single attribute, whose type is converted into a value.

The preceding function can be used in a query that returns the names of all documents that have more than one author:

> **select** *name*
> **from** *doc*
> **where** *author-count*(*doc*) > 1

Note that, in the preceding SQL expression, although *doc* refers to a relation in the **from** clause, it is treated implicitly as a tuple variable in the **where** clause, and can therefore be used as an argument to the *author-count* function.

In general, a select statement can return a collection of values. If the return type of the function is a collection type, the result of the function is the entire collection. If the return type is not a collection type, as is the case in the preceding example, the collection generated by the **select** statement should contain only one tuple, which is returned as the answer. If there is more than one tuple in the result of the **select** statement, the system has two choices: either it can treat this situation as an error, or it can select an arbitrary tuple from the collection and return that tuple as the answer.

Some database systems allow us to define functions using a programming language such as C or C++. Functions defined in this fashion can be more efficient than functions defined using SQL, and computations that cannot be carried out in SQL can be executed by these functions. An example of the use of such functions would be to perform a complex arithmetic computation on the data in a tuple.

Functions defined using a programming language and compiled external to the database system need to be loaded and executed with the database system code. This process carries the risk that a bug in the program can corrupt the database internal structures, and can bypass the access-control functionality of the database system. Certain systems, such as Illustra, that are designed to be extensible typically allow such functions, whereas database systems that emphasize security of data do not.

It may appear that using functions defined in a programming language is not unlike using embedded SQL, in which database queries are included within a general-purpose program. There is, however, an important distinction here. In embedded SQL, the query is passed by the user program to the database system to be run. The results are returned (one tuple at a time) to the program. Therefore, user-written code never needs access to the database itself. The operating system thus can protect the database from access by any user process.

When user-coded functions are employed within queries, either that code must be run by the database system itself, or the data on which the function operates must be copied into a separate data space. The latter imposes an extraordinarily high overhead, whereas the former incurs potential vulnerability in terms of integrity (through bugs in the user code) and in terms of security (through maliciously implanted actions as part of the user code).

9.4 Creation of Complex Values and Objects

So far, we have seen how to create complex type definitions and query relations defined using complex types. We now see how to create and update tuples in relations that have complex types.

We can create a tuple of the type defined by the *doc* relation as follows:

("salesplan", **set**("Smith", "Jones"), (1, "April", 89), **set**("profit", "strategy"))

The preceding tuple illustrates several aspects of the creation of complex types. We create the value for the composite attribute *date* by listing the latter's attributes—day, month, and year—within parentheses. We create the set-valued attributes *author-list* and *keyword-list* by enumerating their elements within parentheses following the keyword **set**.

We can use complex values constructed as shown here in a number of ways. If we want to insert the preceding tuple into the relation *doc*, we could execute the statement

insert into doc
values
("salesplan", **set**("Smith", "Jones"), (1, "April", 89), **set**("profit", "strategy"))

We can also use complex values in queries. For example, anywhere in a query where a set is expected, we can enumerate a set, as illustrated in the following query:

select *name*, *date*
from *doc*
where *name* **in set**("salesplan", "opportunities", "risks")

The preceding query finds the names and dates of all documents whose name is one of "salesplan", "opportunities", or "risks".

We can create multiset values just like set values, by replacing **set** by **multiset**. A list or array of values can be created just like a tuple values.

To create new objects, we can use *constructor* functions. The constructor function for an object of type T is $T()$; when it is invoked it creates a new uninitialized object of type T, fills in its **oid** field, and returns the object. The fields of the object must then be initialized.

We can carry updates of complex relations using the usual SQL **update** clause; such updates are very similar to updates of 1NF relations.

9.5 Comparison of Object-Oriented and Object-Relational Databases

We have now studied object-oriented databases built around persistent programming languages, as well as object-relational databases, which are object-oriented databases built on top of the relation model. Database systems of both types are on the market, and a database designer needs to choose the kind of system that is appropriate to the needs of the application.

Persistent extensions to programming languages and object-relational systems have targeted different markets. The declarative nature and limited power (compared to a programming language) of the SQL language provides good protection of data from programming errors, and makes high-level optimizations, such as reducing I/O, relatively easy. (We cover optimization of relational expressions in Chapter 12.) Object-relational systems aim at making data modeling and querying easier by using complex data types. Typical applications include storage and querying of complex data, including multimedia data.

A declarative language such as SQL, however, imposes a significant performance penalty for certain kinds of applications that run primarily in main memory, and that perform a large number of accesses to the database. Persistent programming languages target applications of that form that have high performance requirements. They provide low-overhead access to persistent data, and eliminate the need for data translation if the data are to be manipulated using a programming language. However, they are more susceptible to data corruption due to programming errors, and usually do not have a powerful querying capability. Typical applications include CAD databases.

The strengths of the various kinds of database systems can be summarized as follows:

- **Relational systems**: simple data types, powerful query languages, high protection
- **Persistent programming language based OODBs**: complex data types, integration with programming language, high performance
- **Object-relational systems**: complex data types, powerful query languages, high protection

These descriptions hold in general, but keep in mind that some database systems blur these boundaries. For example, some object-oriented database systems built around a persistent programming language are implemented on top of a relational database system. Such systems may provide lower performance than object-oriented database systems built directly on a storage system, but provide some of the stronger protection guarantees of relational systems.

9.6 Summary

Complex types such as nested relations, are useful for modeling complex data in many applications. The relational model is extended beyond 1NF, to allow nonatomic types. Object-relational systems combine complex data based on an extended relational model with object-oriented concepts such as object identity and inheritance. The SQL data-definition and query languages have been extended to deal with complex types and object orientation. We saw a variety of features of the extended data-definition language, as well as the query language, and in particular support for set-valued attributes, inheritance, and object and tuple references.

Exercises

9.1. Consider the database schema

Emp = (ename, **setof***(Children),* **setof***(Skills))*
Children = (name, Birthday)
Birthday = (day, month, year)
Skills = (type, **setof***(Exams))*
Exams = (year, city)

Write the following queries in the extended SQL for the relation *emp (Emp)*.

(*a*) Find the names of all employees who have a child who has a birthday in March.

(*b*) Find those employees who took an examination for the skill type "typing" in the city "Dayton."

(*c*) List all skill types in the relation *emp*.

9.2. Redesign the database of Exercise 9.1 into first normal form and fourth normal form. List any functional or multivalued dependencies that you assume. Also list all referential-integrity constraints that should be present in the first- and fourth-normal-form schemas.

9.3. Consider the schemas for the table *person*, and the tables *student* and *teacher*, which were created under *person*, in Section 9.2.2. Give a relational schema in third normal form that represents the same information. Recall the constraints on subtables, and give all constraints that must be imposed on the relational schema so that every database instance of the relational schema can also be represented by an instance of the schema with inheritance.

9.4. A car-rental company maintains a vehicle database for all vehicles in its current fleet. For all vehicles, it includes the vehicle identification number, license number, manufacturer, model, date of purchase, and color. Special data are included for certain types of vehicles:

- Trucks: cargo capacity
- Sports cars: horsepower, renter age requirement
- Vans: number of passengers
- Off-road vehicles: ground clearance, drivetrain (four- or two-wheel drive)

Construct an extended SQL schema definition for this database. Use inheritance where appropriate.

9.5. Explain the distinction between a type x and a reference type **ref**(x). Under what circumstances would you choose to use a reference type?

9.6. Compare the use of embedded SQL with the use in SQL of functions defined using a general-purpose programming language. Under what circumstances would you use each of these features?

9.7. Suppose that you have been hired as a consultant to choose a database system for your client's application. For each of the following applications, state what type of database system (relational, persistent-programming-language–based OODB, object relational; do not specify a commercial product) you would recommend. Justify your recommendation.

(*a*) A computer-aided design system for a manufacturer of airplanes

(*b*) A system to track contributions made to candidates for public office

(*c*) A system to aid managers of highway-construction projects

(*d*) An information system to support the making of movies

Bibliographic Notes

The nested relational model was introduced in Makinouchi [1977] and Jaeschke and Schek [1982]. Various algebraic query languages are presented in Fischer and Thomas [1983], Zaniolo [1983], Ozsoyoglu et al. [1987], Van Gucht [1987], and Roth et al. [1988]. The management of null values in nested relations is discussed in Roth et al. [1989]. Design and normalization issues are discussed in Ozsoyoglu and Yuan [1987], Roth and Korth [1987], and Mok et al. [1996]. A collection of papers on nested relations appears in Abiteboul et al. [1989]. Sacks-Davis et al. [1995] present an application of the nested relational model to databases containing documents.

Several object-oriented extensions to SQL have been proposed. POSTGRES (Stonebraker and Rowe [1986], Stonebraker [1986a, 1987], and Stonebraker et al. [1987a, 1987b]) was an early implementation of an object-relational system. Illustra is the commercial object-relational system that is the successor of POSTGRES. The Iris database system from Hewlett-Packard (Fishman et al. [1990], and Wilkinson et al. [1990]) provides object-oriented extensions on top of a relational database system. Iris supports a language called Object SQL (OSQL), which is an object-oriented extension of SQL. The O_2 query language described in Bancilhon et al. [1989], and in Deux et al. [1991], is an object-oriented extension of SQL implemented in the O_2 object-oriented database system. UniSQL is described in [UniSQL 1991]. Triggers in object-oriented database systems are discussed in Gehani and Jagadish [1991], Gehani et al. [1992], and Jagadish and Qian [1992].

XSQL is an object-oriented extension of SQL proposed by Kifer et al. [1992]. Kim [1995] contains a collection of papers on modern database systems, including descriptions of OSQL and ZQL[C++], which integrates declarative querying with C++. Standardization projects for object-oriented extensions to SQL are underway as part of the SQL-3 standard, which is currently being developed.

CHAPTER 10

STORAGE AND FILE STRUCTURE

In preceding chapters, we have emphasized the higher-level models of a database. At the *conceptual* or *logical* level, we viewed the database, in the relational model, as a collection of tables. The logical model of the database is the correct level for database *users* to focus on. The goal of a database system is to simplify and facilitate access to data. Users of the system should not be burdened unnecessarily with the physical details of the implementation of the system.

In this chapter, as well as in Chapters 11 and 12, we describe various methods for implementing the data models and languages presented in preceding chapters. We start with characteristics of the underlying storage media, such as disk and tape systems. We then define various data structures that will allow fast access to data. We consider several alternative structures, each best suited to a different kind of access to data. The final choice of data structure needs to be made on the basis of the expected use of the system and of the physical characteristics of the specific machine.

10.1 Overview of Physical Storage Media

Several types of data storage exist in most computer systems. These storage media are classified by the speed with which data can be accessed, by the cost per unit of data to buy the medium, and by the medium's reliability. Among the media typically available are these:

- **Cache**. The cache is the fastest and most costly form of storage. Cache memory is small; its use is managed by the operating system. We shall not be concerned about managing cache storage in the database system.
- **Main memory**. The storage medium used for data that are available to be operated on is main memory. The general-purpose machine instructions operate on main memory. Although main memory may contain many megabytes of data, it is generally too small (or too expensive) to store the entire database. The contents of main memory are usually lost if a power failure or system crash occurs.
- **Flash memory**. Also known as *electrically erasable programmable read-only memory* (*EEPROM*), flash memory differs from main-memory in that data survive power failure. Reading data from flash memory takes less than 100 nanoseconds (a nanosecond is 0.001 microsecond), which is roughly as fast as is reading data from main memory. However, writing data to flash memory is more complicated—data can be written once, which takes about 4 to 10 microseconds, but cannot be over written directly. To overwrite memory that has been written already, we have to erase an entire bank of memory at once; it is then ready to be written again. A drawback of flash memory is that it can support a only limited number of erase cycles, ranging from 10,000 to 1 million. Flash memory has found popularity as a replacement for magnetic disks for storing small volumes of data (5 to 10 megabytes) in low-cost computer systems, such as computer systems that are embedded in other devices.
- **Magnetic-disk storage**. The primary medium for the long-term on-line storage of data is the magnetic disk. Typically, the entire database is stored on magnetic disk. Data must be moved from disk to main memory to be accessed. After operations are performed, the data that have been modified must be written to disk. Disk storage is referred to as *direct-access* storage, because it is possible to read data on disk in any order (unlike sequential-access storage). Disk storage survives power failures and system crashes. Disk-storage devices themselves may sometimes fail and thus destroy data, but such failures usually occur much less frequently than do system crashes.
- **Optical storage**. The most popular form of optical storage is the *compact-disk read-only memory* (*CD-ROM*). Data are stored optically on a disk, and are read by a laser. The optical disks used in CD-ROM storage cannot be written, but are supplied with data prerecorded, and can be loaded into or removed from a drive. Another version of optical storage is the *write-once, read-many* (*WORM*) disk, which allows data to be written once, but does not allow them to be erased and rewritten; this medium is used for archival storage of data. There are also combined magnetic–optical storage devices that use optical means to read magnetically encoded data, and that allow overwriting of old data.

  Most types of optical storage allow the disks to be removed from the drive and replaced by other disks. *Jukebox* systems contain a few drives and numerous disks that can be loaded into one of the drives automatically (by a robot arm) on demand.

- **Tape storage**. Tape storage is used primarily for backup and archival data. Although magnetic tape is much cheaper than disks, access to data is much slower, because the tape must be accessed sequentially from the beginning. For this reason, tape storage is referred to as *sequential-access* storage. Tapes have a high capacity (5-gigabyte tapes are commonly available), and can be removed from the tape drive, facilitating cheap archival storage. Tape jukeboxes are used to hold exceptionally large collections of data, such as remote-sensing data from satellites, which could include as much as 12 terabytes (10^{12} bytes) in the near future.

The various storage media can be organized in a hierarchy (Figure 10.1) according to their speed and their cost. The higher levels are expensive, but are fast. As we move down the hierarchy, the cost per bit decreases, whereas the access time increases. This tradeoff is reasonable; if a given storage system were both faster and less expensive than another—other properties being the same—then there would be no reason to use the slower, more expensive memory. In fact, many early storage devices, including paper tape and core memories, are relegated to museums now that magnetic tape and semiconductor memory have become faster and cheaper. Magnetic tapes themselves were used to store active data back when disks were expensive and had low storage capacity. Today, almost

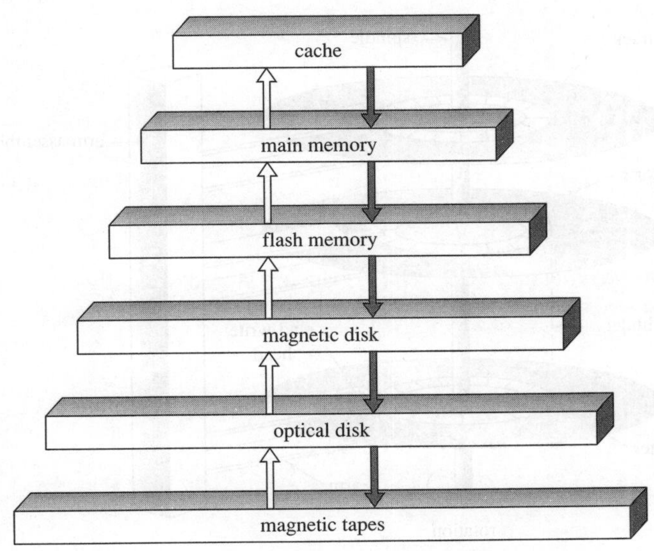

Figure 10.1 Storage-device hierarchy.

all active data are stored on disks, except in rare cases where they are stored on tape or in optical jukeboxes.

The fastest storage media—for example, cache and main memory—are referred to as *primary storage*. The media in the next level in the hierarchy—for example, magnetic disks—are referred to as *secondary storage*, or *on-line storage*. The media in the lowest level in the hierarchy—for example, magnetic tape and optical-disk jukeboxes—are referred to as *tertiary storage*, or *off-line storage*.

In addition to the speed and cost of the various storage systems, there is also the issue of storage volatility. *Volatile storage* loses its contents when the power to the device is removed. In the absence of expensive battery and generator backup systems, data must be written to nonvolatile storage for safekeeping. In the hierarchy shown in Figure 10.1, the storage systems from main memory up are volatile, whereas the storage systems below main memory are nonvolatile. We shall return to this subject in Chapter 15.

10.2 Magnetic Disks

Magnetic disks provide the bulk of secondary storage for modern computer systems. The storage capacity of a single disk ranges from 10 megabytes to 10 gigabytes. A typical large commercial database may require hundreds of disks.

10.2.1 Physical Characteristics of Disks

Physically, disks are relatively simple (Figure 10.2). Each disk *platter* has a flat circular shape. Its two surfaces are covered with a magnetic material, and infor-

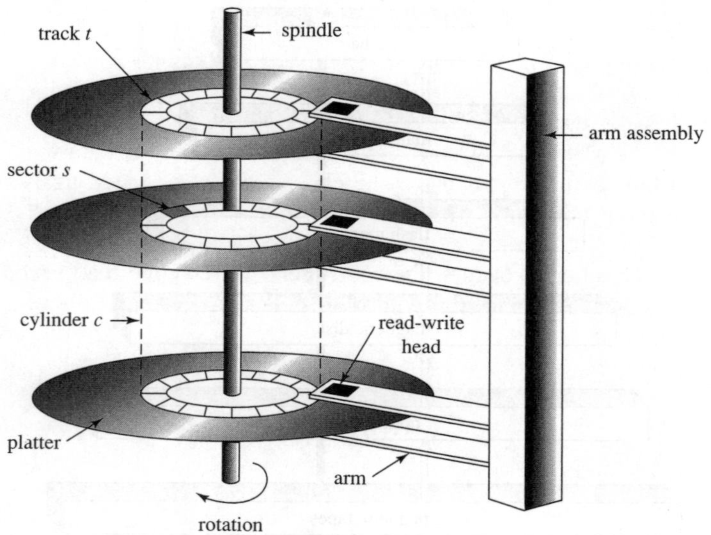

Figure 10.2 Moving-head disk mechanism.

mation is recorded on the surfaces. Platters are made from rigid metal or glass and are covered (usually on both sides) with magnetic recording material. We call such magnetic disks *hard disks*, to distinguish them from *floppy disks*, which are made from flexible material.

When the disk is in use, a drive motor spins it at a constant high speed (usually 60, 90, or 120 revolutions per second). There is a read–write head positioned just above the surface of the platter. The disk surface is logically divided into *tracks*, which are subdivided into *sectors*. A *sector* is the smallest unit of information that can be read from or written to the disk. Depending on the disk type, sectors vary from 32 bytes to 4096 bytes; usually, they are 512 bytes. There are 4 to 32 sectors per track, and from 20 to 1500 tracks per disk surface. The *read–write head* stores information on a sector magnetically as reversals of the direction of magnetization of the magnetic material. There may be hundreds of concentric tracks on a disk surface, containing thousands of sectors.

Each side of a platter of a disk has a read–write head, which is moved across the platter to access different tracks. A disk typically contains many platters, and the read–write heads of all the tracks are mounted on a single assembly called a *disk arm*, and move together. The disk platters, mounted on a spindle and surrounded by heads driven by a motor, are known as *head–disk assemblies* and come in a complete package. Since the heads on all the platters move together, when the head on one platter is on the ith track, the heads on all other platters are also on the ith track of their respective platters. Hence, the ith tracks of all the platters together are called the ith *cylinder*.

Disk platters range from 1.8 inches to 14 inches in diameter. Today, 5 1/4- and 3 1/2-inch disks dominate, since they have a lower cost and faster seek times (due to smaller seek distances) than do larger disks, yet they provide high storage capacity.

A *disk controller* interfaces between the computer system and the actual hardware of the disk drive. It accepts high-level commands to read or write a sector, and initiates actions, such as moving the disk arm to the right track and actually reading or writing the data. Disk controllers also attach *checksums* to each sector that is written; the checksum is computed from the data written to the sector. When the sector is read back, the checksum is computed again from the retrieved data and is compared with the stored checksum; if the data are corrupted, with a high probability the newly computed checksum will not match the stored checksum. If such an error occurs, the controller will retry the read several times; if the error continues to occur, the controller will signal a read failure.

Another interesting task performed by disk controllers is *remapping of bad sectors*. If the controller detects that a sector is damaged when the disk is initially formatted, or when an attempt is made to write the sector, it can logically map the sector to a different physical location (allocated from a pool of extra sectors set aside for this purpose). The remapping is noted on disk or in nonvolatile memory, and the write is carried out on the new location.

Figure 10.3 shows how disks are connected to a computer system. Like other storage units, disks are connected to a computer system or to a controller through a high-speed interconnection. The *small computer-system interconnect*

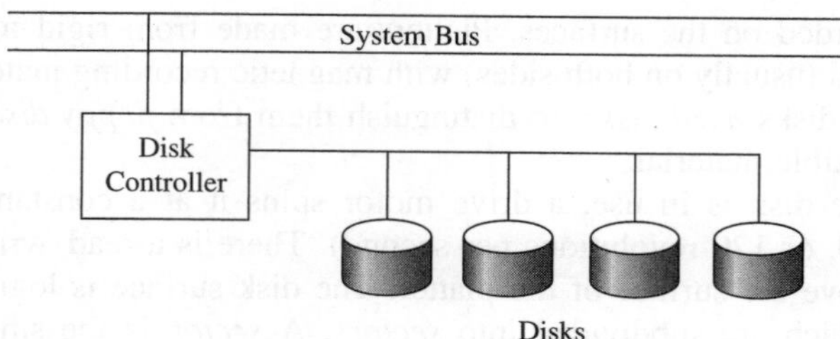

Figure 10.3 Disk subsystem.

(*SCSI*; pronounced "scuzzy") is commonly used to connect disks to personal computers and workstations. Mainframe and server systems usually have a faster and more expensive bus to connect to the disks.

The read–write heads are kept as close as possible to the disk surface to increase the recording density. Often, the head floats or flies only microns from the disk surface, supported by a cushion of air. Because the head floats so close to the surface, platters must be machined carefully to be flat. Head crashes can be a problem. If the head contacts the disk surface (due to a power failure, for example), the head will scrape the recording medium off the disk, destroying the data that had been there. Usually, the head touching the surface causes the removed medium to become airborne and to come between the other heads and their platters, causing more crashes. Under normal circumstances, a head crash results in the entire disk failing and needing to be replaced.

A *fixed-head disk* has a separate head for each track. This arrangement allows the computer to switch from track to track quickly, without having to move the head assembly, but it requires a large number of heads, making the device extremely expensive. Some disk systems have multiple disk arms, allowing more than one track on the same platter to be accessed at a time. Fixed-head disks and multiple arm disks were used in high-performance mainframe systems, but are relatively rare today.

10.2.2 Performance Measures of Disks

The main measures of the qualities of a disk are capacity, access time, data-transfer rate, and reliability.

Access time is the time from when a read or write request is issued to when data transfer begins. To access (that is, to read or write) data on a given sector of a disk, the arm first must move so that it is positioned over the correct track, and then must wait for the sector to appear under it as the disk rotates. The time for repositioning the arm is called the *seek time*, and it increases with the distance that the arm must move. Typical seek times range from 2 to 30 milliseconds, depending on how far the track is from the initial arm position. Smaller disks tend to have lower seek times since the head has to travel a smaller distance.

The *average seek time* is the average of the seek times, measured over a sequence of (uniformly distributed) random requests, and is about one-third of the worst-case seek time. If the head were positioned at one end (inner or outer) before an access, the average seek time would be one-half of the worst-case seek time; if it were positioned exactly in between the innermost and outermost tracks, the average seek time would be one-fourth of the worst-case seek time. Averaging over all positions of the head, the average seek time is one-third of the worst case.

Once the seek has occurred, the time spent waiting for the sector to be accessed to appear under the head is called the *rotational latency time*. Typical rotational speeds of disks today range from 60 to 120 rotations per second, or, equivalently, 8.35 to 16.7 milliseconds per rotation. On an average, one-half of a rotation of the disk is required for the beginning of the desired sector to appear under the head. Thus, the *average latency time* of the disk is one-half of the time for a full rotation of the disk.

The access time is then the sum of the seek time and the latency, and ranges from 10 to 40 milliseconds. Once the first sector of the data to be accessed has come under the head, data transfer begins. The *data-transfer rate* is the rate at which data can be retrieved from or stored to the disk. Current disk systems support transfer rates from 1 to 5 megabytes per second.

The final commonly used measure of a disk is the *mean time to failure*, which is a measure of the reliability of the disk. The mean time to failure of a disk (or of any other system) is the amount of time that, on average, we can expect the system to run continuously without any failure. The typical mean time to failure of disks today ranges from 30, 000 to 800, 000 hours— about 3.4 to 91 years.

10.2.3 Optimization of Disk-Block Access

Requests for disk I/O are generated both by the file system and by the virtual memory manager found in most operating systems. Each request specifies the address on the disk to be referenced; that address is in the form of a *block number*. A *block* is a contiguous sequence of sectors from a single track of one platter. Block sizes range from 512 bytes to several kilobytes. Data are transferred between disk and main memory in units of blocks. The lower levels of the file-system manager convert block addresses into the hardware-level cylinder, surface, and sector number.

Since access to data on disk is several orders of magnitude slower than is access to data in main memory, much attention has been paid to improving the speed of access to blocks on disk. Buffering of blocks in memory to satisfy future requests is discussed in Section 10.5. Here, we discuss several other techniques.

- **Scheduling**. If several blocks from a cylinder need to be transferred from disk to main memory, we may be able to save access time by requesting the blocks in the order in which they will pass under the heads. If the desired blocks are on different cylinders, it is advantageous to request the blocks in an order that minimizes disk-arm movement. *Disk-arm–scheduling* algorithms attempt to order accesses to tracks in a fashion that increases the number of accesses that can be processed. A commonly used algorithm is the *elevator algorithm*, which works in a manner similar to many elevators. Suppose that, initially, the arm is moving from the innermost track toward the outside of the disk. For each track for which there is an access request, it stops at that track, services requests for the track, and then continues moving outward until there are no waiting requests for tracks farther out. At this point, the arm changes direction, and moves toward the inside, again stopping at each track for which there is a request, until it reaches a track where there is no request for tracks farther toward the center. Now, it reverses direction and starts a new cycle. Disk controllers usually perform the task of reordering read requests to improve performance, since they are intimately aware of the organization of blocks on disk, of the rotational position of the disk platters, and of the position of the disk arm.

- **File organization**. To reduce block-access time, we can organize blocks on disk in a way that corresponds closely to the manner in which we expect data to be accessed. For example, if we expect a file to be accessed sequentially, then we should ideally keep all the blocks of the file sequentially on adjacent cylinders. Older operating systems, such as the IBM mainframe operating systems, provided programmers fine control on placement of files, allowing a programmer to reserve a set of cylinders for storing a file. However, this control places a burden on the programmer or system administrator to decide, for example, how many cylinders to allocate for a file, and may require costly reorganization if data are inserted to or deleted from the file.

  Subsequent operating systems, such as Unix and personal-computer operating systems, hide the disk organization from users, and manage the allocation internally. However, over time, a sequential file may become *fragmented*; that is, its blocks become scattered all over the disk. To reduce fragmentation, the system can make a back-up copy of the data on disk and restore the entire disk. The restore operation writes back the blocks of each file contiguously (or nearly so). Some systems (such as MS-DOS) have utilities that scan the disk and then move blocks to decrease the fragmentation. The performance increases realized from these techniques can be large, but the system is generally unusable while these utilities operate.

- **Nonvolatile write buffers**. Since the contents of main memory are lost in a power failure, information about database updates has to be recorded on disk to survive possible system crashes. Hence, the performance of update-intensive database applications, such as transaction-processing systems, is heavily dependent on the speed of disk writes.

  We can use *nonvolatile random-access memory* (*nonvolatile RAM*) to speed up disk writes drastically. The contents of nonvolatile RAM are not lost in power failure. A common way to implement nonvolatile RAM is to use battery-backed-up RAM. The idea is that, when the database system (or the operating system) requests that a block be written to disk, the disk controller writes the block to a nonvolatile RAM buffer, and immediately notifies the operating system that the write completed successfully. The controller writes the data to their destination on disk whenever the disk does not have any other requests, or when the nonvolatile RAM buffer becomes full. When the database system requests a block write, it notices a delay only if the nonvolatile RAM buffer is full. On recovery from a system crash, any pending buffered writes In the nonvolatile RAM are written back to the disk.

The degree to which nonvolatile RAM improves performance is illustrated by the following example. Assume that write requests are received in a random (uniformly distributed) fashion, with the disk being busy on average 90 percent of the time. If we have a nonvolatile RAM buffer of 50 blocks, then, on average, only once per minute will a write find the buffer to be full (and therefore have to wait for a disk write to finish). Thus, in most cases, disk writes can be executed without the database system waiting for a seek or rotational latency. If the disk and the disk controller do not have a nonvolatile RAM write buffer, some operating systems (such as Solaris) can perform write buffering using nonvolatile RAM in the computer system itself.

- **Log disk**. Another approach to reducing write latencies is to use a *log disk*—that is, a disk devoted to writing a sequential log—in much the same way as a nonvolatile RAM buffer. All access to the log disk is sequential, essentially eliminating seek time, and several consecutive blocks can be written at once, making writes to the log disk several times faster than random writes. As before, the data have to be written to their actual location on disk as well, but this write can be done without the database system having to wait for it to complete. After a system crash, the system reads the log disk to find those writes that had not been completed, and carries them out then.

  The *log-based file system* is an extreme version of the log-disk approach. Data are not written back to their original destination on disk; instead, the file system keeps track of where in the log disk the blocks were written most recently, and retrieves them from that location. The log disk itself is compacted periodically, so that old writes that have subsequently been overwritten can be removed. This approach improves write performance, but generates a high degree of fragmentation for files that are updated often. As we noted earlier, such fragmentation increases seek time for sequential reading of files.

10.3 RAID

Disk drives have continued to get smaller and cheaper in recent years, so it is now economically feasible to attach a large number of disks to a computer system. Small disks are now mass produced and are relatively inexpensive. Using a large number of cheap small disks to store data may be more cost effective than is using a smaller number of expensive large disks.

Having a large number of disks in a system presents opportunities for improving the rate at which data can be read or written, if the disks are operated in parallel. Furthermore, this setup offers the potential for improving the reliability of data storage, because redundant information can be stored on multiple disks. Thus, failure of one disk does not lead to loss of data. A variety of disk-organization techniques, collectively called *redundant arrays of inexpensive disks* (RAIDs), have been proposed to address the performance and reliability issues.

In the past, RAIDs composed of small cheap disks were viewed as a cost-effective alternative to large, expensive disks; today, large disks are used rarely, and RAIDs are used for their higher reliability and higher data transfer rate, rather than for economic reasons. Hence, the I in RAID now stands for *independent*, instead of *inexpensive*.

10.3.1 Improvement of Reliability via Redundancy

Let us first consider reliability. The chance that some disk out of a set of N disks will fail is much higher than the chance that a specific single disk will fail. Suppose that the mean time to failure of a single disk is 100,000 hours, or approximately 11.4 years. Further assume that the probability that the disk will fail in a given unit of time does not change with time. (This assumption is not valid in practice, since the probability of failure of a disk is highest late in its life as well as when it is first used, but relatively low in between. We make the assumption for simplicity.) Then, the mean time to failure of some disk in an array of 100 disks will be $100,000/100 = 1000$ hours, or 41.66 days, which is not long at all! If we store only one copy of the data, then each disk failure will result in loss of a significant amount of data (as discussed earlier in Section 10.2.1) and, such a high rate of data loss is unacceptable.

The solution to the problem of reliability is to introduce *redundancy*; that is, we store extra information that is not needed normally, but that can be used in the event of failure of a disk to rebuild the lost information. Thus, even if a disk fails, data are not lost, so the effective mean time to failure is increased, provided that we count only failures that lead to loss of data or to nonavailability of data.

The simplest (but most expensive) approach to introducing redundancy is to duplicate every disk. This technique is called *mirroring* or *shadowing*. A logical disk then consists of two physical disks, and every write is carried out on both disks. If one of the disks fails, the data can be read from the other. Data will be lost only if the second disk fails before the first failed disk is repaired.

The mean time to failure (where failure is the loss of data) of a mirrored disk depends on the mean time to failure of the individual disks, as well as on the *mean time to repair*, which is the time it takes (on an average) to replace a failed disk and to restore the data on it. Suppose that the failures of the two disks are *independent*; that is, there is no connection between the failure of one disk and the failure of the other. Then, if the mean time to failure of a single disk is 100,000 hours, and the mean time to repair is 10 hours, then the *mean time to data loss* of a mirrored disk system is $100000^2/2 * 10 = 500 * 10^6$ hours, or 57,000 years! (We do not go into the derivations here; references in the bibliographic notes provide the details.)

You should be aware that the assumption of independence of disk failures is not valid. Power failures, and natural disasters such as earthquakes, fires, and floods, may result in damage to both disks at the same time. As disks age, the probability of failure increases, increasing the chance that a second disk will fail while the first is being repaired. In spite of all these considerations, however, mirrored-disk systems offer much higher reliability than do single-disk systems. Mirrored-disk systems with mean time to data loss of about 500,000 to 1000,000 hours, or 55 to 110 years, are available today.

Power failures are a particular source of concern, since they occur far more frequently than do natural disasters. Power failures are not a concern if there is no data transfer to disk in progress when they occur. However, even with mirroring of disks, if writes are in progress to the same block in both disks, and power fails before both blocks are fully written, the two blocks can be in an inconsistent state. The solution to this problem is to write one copy first, then the next, so that one of the two copies is always consistent. Some extra actions are required when we restart after a power failure, to recover from incomplete writes. This matter is examined in Exercise 10.4.

10.3.2 Improvement in Performance via Parallelism

Now let us consider the benefit of parallel access to multiple disks. With disk mirroring, the rate at which read requests can be handled is doubled, since read requests can be sent to either disk (as long as both disks in a pair are functional, as is almost always the case). The transfer rate of each read is the same as in a single-disk system, but the number of reads per unit time has doubled.

With multiple disks, we can improve the transfer rate as well (or instead) by striping data across multiple disks. In its simplest form, *data striping* consists of splitting the bits of each byte across multiple disks; such striping is called *bit-level striping*. For example, if we have an array of eight disks, we write bit i of each byte to disk i. The array of eight disks can be treated as a single disk with sectors that are eight times the normal size, and, more important, that have eight times the access rate. In such an organization, every disk participates in every access (read or write), so the number of accesses that can be processed per second is about the same as on a single disk, but each access can read eight times as many data in the same time as on a single disk.

Bit-level striping can be generalized to a number of disks that either is a multiple of 8 or divides 8. For example, if we use an array of four disks, bits i and $4+i$ of each byte go to disk i. Further, striping does not need to be at the level of bits of a byte: For example, in *block-level striping*, blocks of a file are striped across multiple disks; with n disks, block i of a file goes to disk $(i \bmod n) + 1$. Other levels of striping, such as bytes of a sector or sectors of a block also are possible.

In summary, there are two main goals of parallelism in a disk system:

1. Load balance multiple small accesses (that is, page accesses), so that the throughput of such accesses increases.
2. Parallelize large accesses so that the response time of large accesses is reduced.

10.3.3 RAID Levels

Mirroring provides high reliability, but it is expensive. Striping provides high data-transfer rates, but does not improve reliability. Numerous schemes to provide redundancy at lower cost by using the idea of disk striping combined with "parity" bits (which we describe next) have been proposed. These schemes have different cost–performance tradeoffs, and are classified into levels called *RAID Levels*. We describe the various levels here; Figure 10.4 shows these levels pictorially (in the figure, P indicates error-correcting bits, and C indicates a second copy of the data). In all cases depicted in the figure, four disks worth of data is stored, and the extra disks are used to store redundant information for failure recovery.

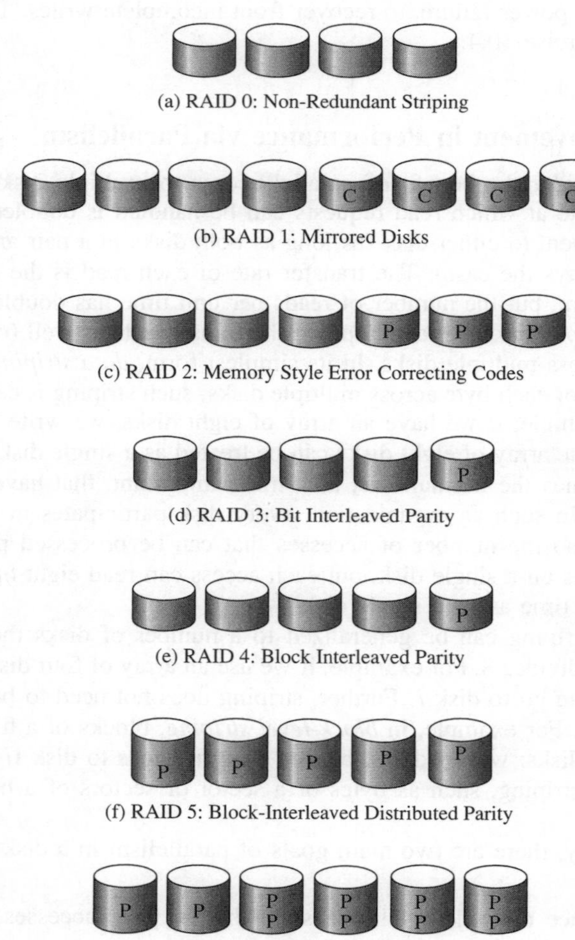

Figure 10.4 RAID levels.

- **RAID level 0** refers to disk arrays with striping at the level of blocks, but without any redundancy (such as mirroring or parity bits). Figure 10.4a shows an array of size 4.
- **RAID level 1** refers to disk mirroring, which we discussed earlier. Figure 10.4b shows a mirrored organization that holds four disks worth of data.
- **RAID level 2** is also known as memory-style error-correcting-code (ECC) organization. Memory systems have long implemented error detection using parity bits. Each byte in a memory system may have a parity bit associated with it that records whether the numbers of bits in the byte that are set to 1 is even (parity=0) or odd (parity=1). If one of the bits in the byte gets damaged (either a 1 becomes a 0, or a 0 becomes a 1), the parity of the byte changes and thus will not match the stored parity. Similarly, if the stored parity bit gets damaged, it will not match the computed parity. Thus, all 1-bit errors are detected by the memory system. Error-correcting schemes store 2 or more extra bits, and can reconstruct the data if a single bit gets damaged. The idea of error-correcting codes can be used directly in disk arrays via striping of bytes across disks. For example, the first bit of each byte could be stored in disk 1, the second bit in disk 2, and so on until the eighth bit is stored in disk 8, and the error-correction bits are stored in further disks. This scheme is shown pictorially in Figure 10.4, where the disks labeled *P* store the error-correction bits. If one of the disks fails, the remaining bits of the byte and the associated error-correction bits can be read from other disks, and can be used to reconstruct the damaged data. Figure 10.4c shows an array of size 4; note RAID level 2 requires only three disks' overhead for four disks of data, unlike RAID level 1, which required four disks' overhead.
- **RAID level 3**, or bit-interleaved parity organization, improves on level 2 by noting that, unlike memory systems, disk controllers can detect whether a sector has been read correctly, so a single parity bit can be used for error correction, as well as for detection. The idea is as follows. If one of the sectors gets damaged, we know exactly which sector it is, and, for each bit in the sector, we can figure out whether it is a 1 or a 0 by computing the parity of the corresponding bits from sectors in the other disks. If the parity of the remaining bits is equal to the stored parity, the missing bit is 0; otherwise, it is 1. RAID level 3 is as good as level 2, but is less expensive in the number of extra disks (it has only a one disk overhead), so level 2 is not used in practice. This scheme is shown pictorially in Figure 10.4d.

  RAID level 3 has two benefits over level 1. Only one parity disk is needed for several regular disks, unlike one mirror disk for every disk in level 1, thus reducing the storage overhead. Since reads and writes of a byte are spread out over multiple disks, with N-way striping of data, the transfer rate is N times as fast as with a single disk. On the other hand, RAID level 3 supports a lower number of I/Os per second, since every disk has to participate in every I/O request.
- **RAID Level 4**, or block-interleaved parity organization, stores blocks just like in regular disks, without striping them across disks, but keeps a parity block

on a separate disk for corresponding blocks from N other disks. This scheme is shown pictorially in Figure 10.4e. If one of the disks fails, the parity block can be used with the corresponding blocks from the other disks to restore the blocks of the failed disk.

A block read accesses only one disk, allowing other requests to be processed by the other disks. Thus, the data-transfer rate for each access is slower, but multiple read accesses can proceed in parallel, leading to a higher overall I/O rate. The transfer rates for large reads is high, since all the disks can be read in parallel; large writes also have high transfer rates, since the data and parity can be written in parallel.

Small independent writes, on the other hand, cannot be performed in parallel. A write of a block has to access the disk on which the block is stored, as well as the parity disk, since the parity block has to be updated. Moreover, both the old value of the parity block and the old value of the block being written have to be read for the new parity to be computed. Thus, a single write requires four disk accesses: two to read the two old blocks, and two to write the two blocks.

- **RAID level 5**, or block-interleaved distributed parity, improves on level 4 by partitioning data and parity among all $N + 1$ disks, rather than storing data in N disks and parity in one disk. In level 5, all disks can participate in satisfying read requests, unlike in RAID level 4, where the parity disk cannot participate, so level 5 increases the total number of requests that can be met in a given amount of time. For each block, one of the disks stores the parity, and the others store data. For example, with an array of five disks, the parity for the nth block is stored in disk $(n \bmod 5) + 1$; the nth blocks of the other four disks store actual data for that block. This setup is denoted pictorially in Figure 10.4f, where the Ps are distributed across all the disks. Note that a parity block cannot store parity for blocks in the same disk, since then a disk failure would result in loss of data as well as of parity, and hence would not be recoverable. Level 5 subsumes level 4, since it offers better read–write performance at the same cost, so level 4 is not used in practice.
- **RAID Level 6**, also called the P+Q redundancy scheme, is much like RAID level 5, but stores extra redundant information to guard against multiple disk failures. Instead of using parity, error-correcting codes such as the Reed–Solomon codes (see the bibliographic notes) are used. In the scheme shown in Figure 10.4g, 2 bits of redundant data are stored for every 4 bits of data—unlike 1 parity bit in level 5—and the system can tolerate two disk failures.

Finally, we note that numerous improvements have been proposed to the basic RAID schemes described here. As a result, sometimes there is confusion about the exact definitions of the different RAID levels.

10.3.4 Choice of the Correct RAID Level

If a disk fails, the time to rebuild its data can be significant, and will vary with the RAID level that is used. Rebuilding is easiest for RAID level 1, since data can be copied from another disk; for the other levels, we need to access all the other disks in the array to rebuild data in a failed disk. The rebuild performance of a RAID system may be an important factor if continuous supply of data is required, as it is in high-performance or interactive database systems. Furthermore, rebuild performance influences the mean time to failure.

Since RAID levels 2 and 4 are subsumed by RAID levels 3 and 5, the choice of RAID levels is restricted to the remaining levels. RAID level 0 is used in high-performance applications where data loss is not critical. RAID level 1 is popular for applications such as storage of log files in a database system, since it offers the best write performance. Due to level 1's high overhead, levels 3 and 5 are often preferred for storing large volumes of data. The difference between levels 3 and 5 is the data-transfer rate versus the overall I/O rate. Level 3 is preferred if a high data-transfer is required; level 5 is preferred if random reads are important, as they are in most database systems. Level 6 is not supported currently by many RAID implementations, but it offers better reliability than level 5.

RAID system designers have to make several other decisions as well. For example, how many disks should there be in an array? How many bits should be protected by each parity bit? If there are more disks in an array, data-transfer rates are higher but, overall, fewer I/O operations can be performed per second. If there are more bits protected by a parity bit, the space overhead due to parity bits is lower, but there is an increased chance that a second disk will fail before the first failed disk is repaired, and that will result in data loss.

10.3.5 Extensions

The concepts of RAID have been generalized to other storage devices, including arrays of tapes, and even to the broadcast of data over wireless systems. When applied to arrays of tapes, the RAID structures are able to recover data even if one of the tapes in an array of tapes is damaged. When applied to broadcast of data, a block of data is split into short units and is broadcast along with a parity unit; if one of the units is not received for any reason, it can be reconstructed from the other units.

10.4 Tertiary Storage

In a large database system, some of the data may have to reside on tertiary storage. The two most common tertiary storage media are optical disks and magnetic tapes.

10.4.1 Optical Disks

CD-ROM has become a popular medium for distributing software, multimedia data such as audio and images, and other electronically published information. CD-ROM has the benefit that the disks can be loaded into or removed from a drive, and the disks have a high storage capacity (about 500 megabytes on a single disk, several hundred times the capacity of a floppy disk). Further, disks are cheap to mass produce, and the drives themselves are cheaper than are magnetic-disk drives.

CD-ROM drives have much longer seek times (250 milliseconds is common) than do magnetic-disk drives; lower rotational speeds (about 400 rpm), leading to a high latency; and lower data-transfer rates (about 150 kilobytes per second). Rotational speeds initially corresponded to the audio CD standards, but drives that spin disks at eight times the standard speed are available today, and thereby provide increased data-transfer rates. More recently, a new optical format, *digital video disk* (*DVD*) has become a standard. These disks hold between 4.7 and 17 gigabytes of data.

Write-once, read-many (*WORM*) disks can be written by the same drive from which they are read, but differ from magnetic disks in that they can be written only once, and their data cannot be erased; they can be read as many times as desired, however. WORM disks are popular for archival storage of data, since they have a high capacity (about 500 megabytes per disk), have a longer lifetime than magnetic disks, and, like tapes, can be removed from the drive. Moreover, since they cannot be overwritten, they provide an audit trail with which it is hard to tamper. *WORM jukeboxes* are devices that can store a large number of WORM disks, and can load the disks automatically on demand to one of a few WORM drives.

10.4.2 Magnetic Tapes

Magnetic tape has long history of use as a secondary-storage medium. Although it is relatively permanent, and can hold large volumes of data, magnetic tape is slow in comparison to magnetic and optical disks. Even more important, magnetic tape is limited to sequential access. Thus, it is unsuitable for providing the random access to meet for most secondary-storage requirements. Tapes are used mainly for backup, for storage of infrequently used information, and as an off-line medium for transferring information from one system to another.

A tape is kept in a spool, and is wound or rewound past a read–write head. Moving to the correct spot on a tape can take minutes rather than milliseconds; once positioned, however, tape drives can write data at densities and speeds approaching those of disk drives. Capacities vary depending on the length and width of the tape, and on the density at which the head can read and write. A tape drive is usually named by its width. Thus, there are 8-millimeter, 1/4-inch, and 1/2-inch (also known as nine-track) tape drives. The 8-millimeter tape drives have the highest density, due to the technology that they use; they currently store 5 gigabytes of data on a 350-foot tape. Tape devices are reliable, but tapes have limits on the number of times that they can be read or written reliably.

Tapes are also used for storage of large volumes of data, such as video or image data that either do not need to be accessible quickly or are so voluminous that magnetic-disk storage would be too expensive. *Tape jukeboxes* hold large numbers of tapes, with a few drives onto which the tapes can be mounted; they are used for storing large volumes of data, ranging up to many terabytes (10^{12} bytes), with access times on the order of seconds to a few minutes. Applications that need such enormous data storage include imaging systems that gather data by remote-sensing satellites.

10.5 Storage Access

A database is mapped into a number of different files, which are maintained by the underlying operating system. These files resides permanently on disks, with backups on tapes. Each file is partitioned into fixed-length storage units called *blocks*, which are the units of both storage allocation and data transfer. We shall discuss in Section 10.6 various ways to organize the data logically in files.

A block may contain several data items. The exact set of data items that a block contains is determined by the form of physical data organization being used (see Section 10.6). We shall assume that no data item spans two or more blocks. This assumption is realistic for most data-processing applications, such as our banking example.

A major goal of the database system is to minimize the number of block transfers between the disk and memory. One way to reduce the number of disk accesses is to keep as many blocks as possible in main memory. The goal is to maximize the chance that, when a block is accessed, it is already in main memory, and, thus, no disk access is required.

Since it is not possible to keep all blocks in main memory, we need to manage the allocation of the space available in main memory for the storage of blocks. The *buffer* is that part of main memory available for storage of copies of disk blocks. There is always a copy kept on disk of every block, but the copy on disk may be a version of the block older than the version in the buffer. The subsystem responsible for the allocation of buffer space is called the *buffer manager*.

10.5.1 Buffer Manager

Programs in a database system make requests (that is, calls) on the buffer manager when they need a block from disk. If the block is already in the buffer, the requester is passed the address of the block in main memory. If the block is not in the buffer, the buffer manager first allocates space in the buffer for the block, throwing out some other block, if required, to make space for the new block. The block that is thrown out is written back to disk only if it was modified since the most recent time that it was written to the disk. Then, the buffer manager reads in the block from the disk to the buffer, and passes the address of the block in main memory to the requester. The internal actions of the buffer manager are transparent to the programs that issue disk-block requests.

If you are familiar with operating-system concepts, you will note that the buffer manager appears to be nothing more than a virtual-memory manager, like those found in most operating systems. One difference is that the size of the database may be much more than the hardware address space of a machine, so memory addresses are not sufficient to address all disk blocks. Further, to serve the database system well, the buffer manager must use techniques more sophisticated than typical virtual-memory management schemes:

- **Replacement strategy**. When there is no room left in the buffer, a block must be removed from the buffer before a new one can be read in. Typically, operating systems use a least recently used (LRU) scheme, in which the block that was referenced least recently is written back to disk and is removed from the buffer. This simple approach can be improved on for database applications.

- **Pinned blocks**. For the database system to be able to recover from crashes (Chapter 15), it is necessary to restrict those times when a block may be written back to disk. A block that is not allowed to be written back to disk is said to be *pinned*. Although many operating systems do not provide support for pinned blocks, such a feature is essential for the implementation of a database system that is resilient to crashes.
- **Forced output of blocks**. There are situations in which it is necessary to write back the block to disk, even though the buffer space that it occupies is not needed. This write is called the *forced output* of a block. We shall see the reason for requiring forced output in Chapter 15; briefly, main-memory contents and thus buffer contents are lost in a crash, whereas data on disk usually survive a crash.

We discuss buffer-replacement issues next.

10.5.2 Buffer-Replacement Policies

The goal of a replacement strategy for blocks in the buffer is the minimization of accesses to the disk. For general-purpose programs, it is not possible to predict accurately which blocks will be referenced. Therefore, operating systems use the past pattern of block references as a predictor of future references. The assumption that is generally made is that blocks that have been referenced recently are likely to be referenced again. Therefore, if a block must be replaced, the least recently referenced block is replaced. This approach is called the *LRU block-replacement scheme*.

LRU is an acceptable replacement scheme in operating systems. However, a database system is able to predict the pattern of future references more accurately than is an operating system. A user request to the database system involves several steps. The database system is often able to determine in advance which blocks will be needed by looking at each of the steps required to perform the user-requested operation. Thus, unlike operating systems, which must rely on the past to predict the future, database systems may have information regarding at least the short-term future.

To illustrate how information about future block access allows us to improve the LRU strategy, we consider the processing of the relational-algebra expression

$$borrower \bowtie customer$$

Assume that the strategy chosen to process this request is given by the pseudocode program shown in Figure 10.5. (We shall study other strategies in Chapter 12.)

Assume that the two relations of this example are stored in separate files. In this example, we can see that, once a tuple of *borrower* has been processed, that tuple is not needed again. Therefore, once processing of an entire block of

```
for each tuple b of borrower do
    for each tuple c of customer do
        if b[customer-name] = c[customer-name]
        then begin
                let x be a tuple defined as follows:
                x[customer-name] := b[customer-name]
                x[loan-number] := b[loan-number]
                x[customer-street] := c[customer-street]
                x[customer-city] := c[customer-city]
                include tuple x as part of result of borrower ⋈ customer
            end
    end
end
```

Figure 10.5 Procedure for computing join.

borrower tuples is completed, that block is no longer needed in main memory, even though it has been used recently. The buffer manager should be instructed to free the space occupied by a *borrower* block as soon as the final tuple has been processed. This buffer-management strategy is called the *toss-immediate* strategy.

Now consider blocks containing *customer* tuples. We need to examine every block of *customer* tuples once for each tuple of the *borrower* relation. When processing of a *customer* block is completed, we know that that block will not be accessed again until all other *customer* blocks have been processed. Thus, the most recently used *customer* block will be the final block to be re-referenced, and the least recently used *customer* block is the block that will be referenced next. This assumption set is the exact opposite of the one that forms the basis for the LRU strategy. Indeed, the optimal strategy for block replacement is the *most recently used* (*MRU*) *strategy*. If a *customer* block must be removed from the buffer, the MRU strategy chooses the most recently used block.

For the MRU strategy to work correctly for our example, the system must pin the *customer* block currently being processed. After the final *customer* tuple has been processed, the block is unpinned, and it becomes the most recently used block.

In addition to using knowledge that the system may have about the request being processed, the buffer manager can use statistical information regarding the probability that a request will reference a particular relation. The data dictionary is one of the most frequently accessed parts of the database. Thus, the buffer manager should try not to remove data-dictionary blocks from main memory, unless other factors dictate that it do so. In Chapter 11, we discuss indices for files. Since an index for a file may be accessed more frequently than the file itself, the buffer manager should, in general, not remove index blocks from main memory if alternatives are available.

The ideal database block-replacement strategy needs knowledge of the database operations being performed. No single strategy is known that handles all the possible scenarios well. Indeed, a surprisingly large number of database systems use LRU, despite that strategy's faults. The exercises explore alternative strategies.

The strategy used by the buffer manager for block replacement is influenced by factors other than the time at which the block will be referenced again. If the system is processing requests by several users concurrently, the concurrency-control subsystem (Chapter 14) may need to delay certain requests, to ensure preservation of database consistency. If the buffer manager is given information from the concurrency-control subsystem indicating which requests are being delayed, it can use this information to alter its block-replacement strategy. Specifically, blocks needed by active (nondelayed) requests can be retained in the buffer at the expense of blocks needed by the delayed requests.

The crash-recovery subsystem (Chapter 15) imposes stringent constraints on block replacement. If a block has been modified, the buffer manager is not allowed to write back the new version of the block in the buffer to disk, since that would destroy the old version. Instead, the block manager must seek permission from the crash-recovery subsystem before writing out a block. The crash-recovery subsystem may demand that certain other blocks be force output before it grants permission to the buffer manager to output the block requested. In Chapter 15, we define precisely the interaction between the buffer manager and the crash-recovery subsystem.

10.6 File Organization

A *file* is organized logically as a sequence of records. These records are mapped onto disk blocks. Files are provided as a basic construct in operating systems, so we shall assume the existence of an underlying *file system*. We need to consider ways of representing logical data models in terms of files.

Although blocks are of a fixed size determined by the physical properties of the disk and by the operating system, record sizes vary. In a relational database, tuples of distinct relations are generally of different sizes.

One approach to mapping the database to files is to use several files, and to store records of only one fixed length in any given file. An alternative is to structure our files such that we can accommodate multiple lengths for records. Files of fixed-length records are easier to implement than are files of variable-length records. Many of the techniques used for the former can be applied to the variable-length case. Thus, we begin by considering a file of fixed-length records.

10.6.1 Fixed-Length Records

As an example, let us consider a file of *account* records for our bank database. Each record of this file is defined as follows:

type *deposit* = **record**
branch-name : char (22);
account-number : char(10);
balance : real;
end

record 0	Perryridge	A-102	400
record 1	Round Hill	A-305	350
record 2	Mianus	A-215	700
record 3	Downtown	A-101	500
record 4	Redwood	A-222	700
record 5	Perryridge	A-201	900
record 6	Brighton	A-217	750
record 7	Downtown	A-110	600
record 8	Perryridge	A-218	700

Figure 10.6 File containing *account* records.

If we assume that each character occupies 1 byte and that a real occupies 8 bytes, our *account* record is 40 bytes long. A simple approach is to use the first 40 bytes for the first record, the next 40 bytes for the second record, and so on (Figure 10.6). However, there are two problems with this simple approach:

1. It is difficult to delete a record from this structure. The space occupied by the record to be deleted must be filled with some other record of the file, or we must have a way of marking deleted records so that they can be ignored.
2. Unless the block size happens to be a multiple of 40 (which is unlikely), some records will cross block boundaries. That is, part of the record will be stored in one block and part in another. It would thus require two block accesses to read or write such a record.

When a record is deleted, we could move the record that came after it into the space formerly occupied by the deleted record, and so on, until every record following the deleted record has been moved ahead (Figure 10.7). Such an approach requires moving a large number of records. It might be easier simply to move the final record of the file into the space occupied by the deleted record, as shown in Figure 10.8.

It is undesirable to move records to occupy the space freed by a deleted record, since doing so requires additional block accesses. Since insertions tend to be more frequent than deletions, it is acceptable to leave open the space occupied

record 0	Perryridge	A-102	400
record 1	Round Hill	A-305	350
record 3	Downtown	A-101	500
record 4	Redwood	A-222	700
record 5	Perryridge	A-201	900
record 6	Brighton	A-217	750
record 7	Downtown	A-110	600
record 8	Perryridge	A-218	700

Figure 10.7 File of Figure 10.6, with record 2 deleted and all records moved.

record 0	Perryridge	A-102	400
record 1	Round Hill	A-305	350
record 8	Perryridge	A-218	700
record 3	Downtown	A-101	500
record 4	Redwood	A-222	700
record 5	Perryridge	A-201	900
record 6	Brighton	A-217	750
record 7	Downtown	A-110	600

Figure 10.8 File of Figure 10.6, with record 2 deleted and final record moved.

by the deleted record, and to wait for a subsequent insertion before reusing the space. A simple marker on a deleted record is not sufficient, since it is hard to find this available space when an insertion is being done. Thus, we need to introduce an additional structure.

At the beginning of the file, we allocate a certain number of bytes as a *file header*. The header will contain a variety of information about the file. For now, all we need to store there is the address of the first record whose contents are deleted. We use this first record to store the address of the second available record, and so on. Intuitively, we can think of these stored addresses as *pointers*, since they point to the location of a record. The deleted records thus form a linked list, which is often referred to as a *free list*. Figure 10.9 shows the file of Figure 10.6 after records 1, 4, and 6 have been deleted.

On insertion of a new record, we use the record pointed to by the header. We change the header pointer to point to the next available record. If no space is available, we add the new record to the end of the file.

The use of pointers requires careful programming. If we move or delete a record, a pointer to which another record contains, that pointer becomes incorrect in the sense that it no longer points to the desired record. Such pointers are called *dangling pointers*; in effect, they point to garbage. To avoid the dangling-pointer problem, we must avoid moving or deleting records that are pointed to by other records. We say that such records are *pinned*.

header				
record 0	Perryridge	A-102	400	
record 1				
record 2	Mianus	A-215	700	
record 3	Downtown	A-101	500	
record 4				
record 5	Perryridge	A-201	900	
record 6				
record 7	Downtown	A-110	600	
record 8	Perryridge	A-218	700	

Figure 10.9 File of Figure 10.6, after deletion of records 1, 4, and 6.

Insertion and deletion for files of fixed-length records are simple to implement, because the space made available by a deleted record is exactly the space needed to insert a record. If we allow records of variable length in a file, this match no longer holds. An inserted record may not fit in the space left free by a deleted record, or it may fill only part of that space.

10.6.2 Variable-Length Records

Variable-length records arise in database systems in several ways:

- Storage of multiple record types in a file
- Record types that allow variable lengths for one or more fields
- Record types that allow repeating fields

Different techniques for implementing variable-length records exist. For purposes of illustration, we shall use one example to demonstrate the various implementation techniques. We shall consider a different representation of the *deposit* information stored in the file of Figure 10.6, in which we use one variable-length record for each branch name and for all the account information for that branch. The format of the record is

```
type account-list = record
                        branch-name : char (22);
                        account-info : array [1 .. ∞] of
                                           record;
                                               account-number : char(10);
                                               balance : real;
                                           end
                    end
```

We define *account-info* as an array with an arbitrary number of elements, so that there is no limit on how large a record can be (up to, of course, the size of the disk!).

10.6.2.1 Byte-String Representation

A simple method for implementing variable-length records is to attach a special *end-of-record* (⊥) symbol to the end of each record. We can then store each record as a string of consecutive bytes. Figure 10.10 shows such an organization to represent the file of fixed-length records of Figure 10.6 using variable-length records. An alternative version of the byte-string representation stores the record length at the beginning of each record, instead of using end-of-record symbols.

The byte-string representation as we have discussed it has disadvantages:

- It is not easy to reuse space occupied formerly by a deleted record. Although techniques exist to manage insertion and deletion, they lead to a large number of small fragments of disk storage that are wasted.

0	Perryridge	A-102	400	A-201	900	A-218	700	⊥
1	Round Hill	A-305	350	⊥				
2	Mianus	A-215	700	⊥				
3	Downtown	A-101	500	A-110	600	⊥		
4	Redwood	A-222	700	⊥				
5	Brighton	A-217	750	⊥				

Figure 10.10 Byte-string representation of variable-length records.

- There is no space, in general, for records to grow longer. If a variable-length record becomes longer, it must be moved, and movement is costly if the record is pinned.

Thus, the basic byte-string representation as we described it is not usually used for implementing variable-length records. However, a modified form of the byte-string representation, called the slotted-page structure, is commonly used for organizing records *within* a single block.

The *slotted-page structure* is shown in Figure 10.11. There is a header at the beginning of each block, containing the following information:

1. The number of record entries in the header
2. The end of free space in the block
3. An array whose entries contain the location and size of each record

The actual records are allocated *contiguously* in the block, starting from the end of the block. The free space in the block is contiguous, between the final entry in the header array, and the first record. If a record is inserted, space is allocated for it at the end of free space, and an entry containing its size and location is added to the header.

If a record is deleted, the space that it occupies is freed, and its entry is set to deleted (its size is set to −1, for example). Further, the records in the block before the deleted record are moved, so that the free space created by the deletion gets occupied, and all free space is again between the final entry in the header array and the first record. The end-of-free-space pointer in the

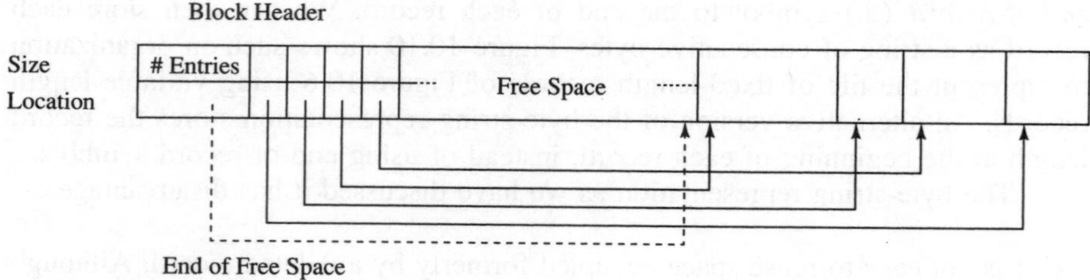

Figure 10.11 Slotted-page structure.

header is appropriately updated as well. Records can be grown or shrunk using similar techniques, as long as there is space in the block. The cost of moving the records is not too high, since the size of a block is limited: A typical value is 4 kilobytes.

The slotted-page structure requires that there be no pointers that point directly to records. Instead, pointers must point to the entry in the header that contains the actual location of the record. This level of indirection allows records to be moved to prevent fragmentation of space inside a block, while supporting indirect pointers to the record.

10.6.2.2 Fixed-Length Representation

Another way to implement variable-length records efficiently in a file system is to use one or more fixed-length records to represent one variable-length record.

There are two techniques for implementing files of variable-length records using fixed-length records:

1. **Reserved space**. If there is a maximum record length that is never exceeded, we can use fixed-length records of that length. Unused space (for records shorter than the maximum space) is filled with a special null, or end-of-record, symbol.
2. **Pointers**. The variable-length record is represented by a list of fixed-length records, chained together via pointers.

If we choose to apply the reserved-space method to our account example, we need to select a maximum record length. Figure 10.12 shows how the file of Figure 10.6 would be represented if we allowed a maximum of three accounts per branch. A record in this file is of the *account-list* type, but with the array containing exactly three elements. Those branches with fewer than three accounts (for example, Round Hill) have records with null fields. We use the symbol ⊥ to represent this situation in Figure 10.12. In practice, a particular value that can never represent real data is used (for example, a negative "account number" or a "name" beginning with an "*").

The reserved-space method is useful when most records are of length close to the maximum. Otherwise, a significant amount of space may be wasted. In our bank example, some branches may have many more accounts than others. This situation leads us to consider use of the pointer method. To represent the file using

0	Perryridge	A-102	400	A-201	900	A-218	700
1	Round Hill	A-305	350	⊥	⊥	⊥	⊥
2	Mianus	A-215	700	⊥	⊥	⊥	⊥
3	Downtown	A-101	500	A-110	600	⊥	⊥
4	Redwood	A-222	700	⊥	⊥	⊥	⊥
5	Brighton	A-217	750	⊥	⊥	⊥	⊥

Figure 10.12 File of Figure 10.6, using the reserved-space method.

0	Perryridge	A-102	400	
1	Round Hill	A-305	350	
2	Mianus	A-215	700	
3	Downtown	A-101	500	
4	Redwood	A-222	700	
5		A-201	900	
6	Brighton	A-217	750	
7		A-110	600	
8		A-218	700	

Figure 10.13 File of Figure 10.6, using the pointer method.

the pointer method, we add a pointer field as we did in Figure 10.9. The resulting structure is shown in Figure 10.13.

In effect, the file structures of Figures 10.9 and 10.13 are the same, except that, in Figure 10.9, we used pointers only to chain together deleted records, whereas in Figure 10.13, we chain together all records pertaining to the same branch.

A disadvantage to the structure of Figure 10.13 is that we waste space in all records except the first in a chain. The first record needs to have the *branch-name* value, but subsequent records do not. Nevertheless, we need to include a field for *branch-name* in all records, lest the records not be of fixed length. This wasted space is significant, since we expect, in practice, that each branch has a large number of accounts. To deal with this problem, we allow two kinds of blocks in our file:

1. **Anchor block**, which contains the first record of a chain
2. **Overflow block**, which contains records other than those that are the first record of a chain

Thus, all records *within a block* have the same length, even though not all records in the file have the same length. Figure 10.14 shows this file structure.

10.7 Organization of Records in Files

So far, we have studied how records are represented in a file structure. An instance of a relation is a set of records. Given a set of records, the next question is how to organize them in a file. Several of the ways of organizing records in files follow:

- **Heap file organization**. In this organization, any record can be placed anywhere in the file where there is space for the record. There is no ordering of records. Typically, there is a single file for each relation
- **Sequential file organization**. In this organization, records are stored in sequential order, based on the value of the search key of each record. The implementation of this organization is described in Section 10.7.1.

anchor block

Perryridge	A-102	400
Round Hill	A-305	350
Mianus	A-215	700
Downtown	A-101	500
Redwood	A-222	700
Brighton	A-217	750

overflow block

A-201	900
A-218	700
A-110	600

Figure 10.14 Anchor-block and overflow-block structures.

- **Hashing file organization**. In this organization, a hash function is computed on some attribute of each record. The result of the hash function specifies in which block of the file the record should be placed. This organization is described in Chapter 11; it is closely related to the indexing structures described in that chapter.
- **Clustering file organization**. In this organization, records of several different relations can be stored in the same file. Related records of the different relations are stored on the same block, so that one I/O operation fetches related records from all the relations. This organization is described in Section 10.7.2.

10.7.1 Sequential File Organization

A *sequential file* is designed for efficient processing of records in sorted order based on some *search key*. To permit fast retrieval of records in search-key order, we chain together records by pointers. The pointer in each record points to the next record in search-key order. Furthermore, to minimize the number of block accesses in sequential file processing, we store records physically in search-key order, or as close to search-key order as possible.

Figure 10.15 shows a sequential file of *account* records taken from our banking example. In that example, the records are stored in search-key order, using *branch-name* as the search key.

The sequential file organization allows records to be read in sorted order; that can be useful for display purposes, as well as for certain query-processing algorithms that we shall study in Chapter 12.

It is difficult, however, to maintain physical sequential order as records are inserted and deleted, since it is costly to move many records as a result of a single insertion or deletion. We can manage deletion using pointer chains, as we saw previously. For insertion, we apply the following rules:

1. Locate the record in the file that comes before the record to be inserted in search-key order.

Brighton	A-217	750	
Downtown	A-101	500	
Downtown	A-110	600	
Mianus	A-215	700	
Perryridge	A-102	400	
Perryridge	A-201	900	
Perryridge	A-218	700	
Redwood	A-222	700	
Round Hill	A-305	350	

Figure 10.15 Sequential file for *account* records.

2. If there is a free record (that is, space left after a deletion) within the same block as this record, insert the new record there. Otherwise, insert the new record in an *overflow block*. In either case, adjust the pointers so as to chain together the records in search-key order.

Figure 10.16 shows the file of Figure 10.15 after the insertion of the record (North Town, A-888, 800). The structure in Figure 10.16 allows fast insertion of new records, but forces sequential file-processing applications to process records in an order that does not match the physical order of the records.

If relatively few records need to be stored in overflow blocks, this approach works well. Eventually, however, the correspondence between search-key order and physical order may be totally lost, in which case sequential processing will become significantly less efficient. At this point, the file should be *reorganized* such that it is once again physically in sequential order. Such reorganizations are costly, and must be done during times when the system load is low. The frequency with which reorganizations are needed depends on the frequency of insertion of new records. In the extreme case in which insertions rarely occur, it is possible

Brighton	A-217	750	
Downtown	A-101	500	
Downtown	A-110	600	
Mianus	A-215	700	
Perryridge	A-102	400	
Perryridge	A-201	900	
Perryridge	A-218	700	
Redwood	A-222	700	
Round Hill	A-305	350	

North Town	A-888	800	

Figure 10.16 Sequential file after an insertion.

always to keep the file in physically sorted order. In such a case, the pointer field shown in Figure 10.15 is not needed.

10.7.2 Clustering File Organization

Many relational-database systems store each relation in a separate file, so that they can take full advantage of the file system provided as part of the operating system. Usually, tuples of a relation can be represented as fixed-length records. Thus, relations can be mapped to a simple file structure. This simple implementation of a relational database system is well suited to database systems designed for personal computers. In such systems, the size of the database is small, so little is gained from a sophisticated file structure. Furthermore, in some personal computers, small overall size of the object code for the database system is essential. A simple file structure reduces the amount of code needed to implement the system.

This simple approach to relational-database implementation becomes less satisfactory as the size of the database increases. We have seen that there are performance advantages to be gained from careful assignment of records to blocks, and from careful organization of the blocks themselves. Thus, it is apparent that a more complicated file structure may be beneficial, even if we retain the strategy of storing each relation in a separate file.

However, many large-scale database systems do not rely directly on the underlying operating system for file management. Instead, one large operating-system file is allocated to the database system. All relations are stored in this one file, and the management of this file is left to the database system. To see the advantage of storing many relations in one file, we consider the following SQL query for the bank database:

> **select** *account-number, customer-name, customer-street, customer-city*
> **from** *depositor, customer*
> **where** *depositor.customer-name* = *customer.customer-name*

This query computes a join of the *depositor* and *customer* relations. Thus, for each tuple of *depositor*, the system must locate the *customer* tuples with the same value for *customer-name*. Ideally, these records will be located with the help of *indices*, which we shall discuss in Chapter 11. Regardless of how these records are located, however, they need to be transferred from disk into main memory. In the worst case, each record will reside on a different block, forcing us to do one block read for each record required by the query.

As a concrete example, consider the *depositor* and *customer* relations of Figures 10.17 and 10.18, respectively. In Figure 10.19, we show a file structure designed for efficient execution of queries involving *depositor* ⋈ *customer*. The *depositor* tuples for each *customer-name* are stored near the *customer* tuple for the corresponding *customer-name*. This structure mixes together tuples of two relations, but allows for efficient processing of the join. When a tuple of the *customer* relation is read, the entire block containing that tuple is copied from disk into main memory. Since the corresponding *depositor* tuples are stored on

customer-name	*account-number*
Hayes	A-102
Hayes	A-220
Hayes	A-503
Turner	A-305

Figure 10.17 The *depositor* relation.

the disk near the *customer* tuple, the block containing the *customer* tuple contains tuples of the *depositor* relation needed to process the query. If a customer has so many accounts that the *depositor* records do not fit in one block, the remaining records appear on nearby blocks. This file structure, called *clustering*, allows us to read many of the required records using one block read. Thus, we are able to process this particular query more efficiently.

Our use of clustering has enhanced processing of a particular join (*depositor* ⋈ *customer*), but it results in slowing processing of other types of query. For example,

select *
from *customer*

requires more block accesses than it did in the scheme under which we stored each relation in a separate file. Instead of several *customer* records appearing in one block, each record is located in a distinct block. Indeed, simply finding all the *customer* records is not possible without some additional structure. To locate all tuples of the *customer* relation in the structure of Figure 10.19, we need to chain together all the records of that relation using pointers, as shown in Figure 10.20.

The determination of when clustering is to be used depends on the types of query that the database designer believes to be most frequent. Careful use of clustering can produce significant performance gains in query processing.

10.8 Data-Dictionary Storage

So far, we have considered only the representation of the relations themselves. A relational-database system needs to maintain data *about* the relations, such as the schema of the relations. This information is called the *data dictionary*, or *system catalog*. Among the types of information that the system must store are

customer-name	*customer-street*	*customer-city*
Hayes	Main	Brooklyn
Turner	Putnam	Stamford

Figure 10.18 The *customer* relation.

Hayes	Main	Brooklyn
Hayes	A-102	
Hayes	A-220	
Hayes	A-503	
Turner	Putnam	Stamford
Turner	A-305	

Figure 10.19 Clustering file structure.

these:

- Names of the relations
- Names of the attributes of each relation
- Domains and lengths of attributes
- Names of views defined on the database, and definitions of those views
- Integrity constraints (for example, key constraints)

In addition, many systems keep the following data on users of the system:

- Names of authorized users
- Accounting information about users

Further, statistical and descriptive data about relations may be kept on these matters:

- Number of tuples in each relation
- Method of storage used for each relation (for example, clustered or nonclustered)

In Chapter 11, in which we study indices, we shall see a need to store information about each index on each of the relations:

- Name of the index
- Name of the relation being indexed
- Attributes on which the index is defined
- Type of index formed

Hayes	Main	Brooklyn	
Hayes	A-102		
Hayes	A-220		
Hayes	A-503		
Turner	Putnam	Stamford	
Turner	A-305		

Figure 10.20 Clustering file structure with pointer chains.

All this information comprises, in effect, a miniature database. Some database systems store this information using special-purpose data structures and code. It is generally preferable to store the data about the database in the database itself. By using the database to store system data, we simplify the overall structure of the system and allow the full power of the database to be used to permit fast access to system data.

The exact choice of how to represent system data using relations must be made by the system designer. One possible representation follows:

System-catalog-schema = (*relation-name, number-of-attributes*)
Attribute-schema = (*attribute-name, relation-name, domain-type, position, length*)
User-schema = (*user-name, encrypted-password, group*)
Index-schema = (*index-name, relation-name, index-type, index-attributes*)
View-schema = (*view-name, definition*)

10.9 Storage Structures for Object-Oriented Databases

The file-organization techniques described earlier—such as the heap, sequential, hashing and clustering organizations—can also be used for storing objects in an object-oriented databases. However, extra features are needed to support object-oriented database features, such as set-valued fields and persistent pointers.

10.9.1 Mapping of Objects to Files

The mapping of objects to files has many similarities to the mapping of tuples to files in a relational system. At the lowest level of data representation, both tuples and the data parts of objects are simply sequences of bytes. We can therefore store object data using the file structures described in earlier sections, with some modifications that we note next.

Objects in object-oriented databases may lack the uniformity of tuples in relational databases. For example, fields of records may be sets, unlike in relational databases, where data are typically required to be (at least) in first normal form. Furthermore, objects may be extremely large. Such objects have to be managed differently from records in a relational system.

We can implement set fields that have a small number of elements using data structures such as linked lists. Set fields that have a larger number of elements can be implemented as B-trees, or as separate relations in the database. Set fields can also be eliminated at the storage level by normalization. The storage system gives the upper levels of the database system the view of a set field, even though the set field has actually been normalized to create a new relation.

Some applications include extremely large objects that are not easily decomposed into smaller components. Such large objects may each be stored in a separate file. We discuss this idea further in Section 10.9.5.

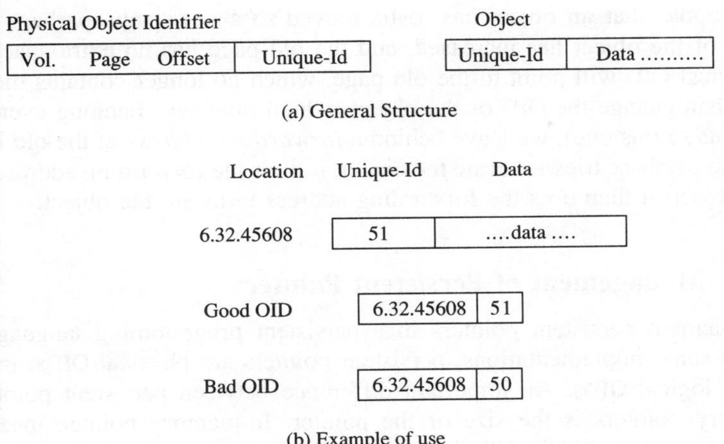

Figure 10.21 Unique identifiers in an OID.

10.9.2 Implementation of Object Identifiers

Since objects are identified by object identifiers (OID), an object-storage system needs a mechanism to locate an object given an OID. If the OIDs are *logical*—that is, they do not specify the location of the object—then the storage system must maintain an index that maps OIDs to the actual location of the object. If the OIDs are *physical*—that is, they encode the location of the object—then the object can be found directly. Physical OIDs typically have the following three parts:

1. A volume or file identifier.
2. A page identifier within the volume or file
3. An offset within the page

In addition, physical OIDs may contain a *unique identifier*, which is an integer that distinguishes the OID from the identifiers of other objects that happened to be stored at the same location earlier, and were deleted or moved elsewhere. The unique identifier is also stored with the object, and the identifiers in an OID and the corresponding object should match. If the unique identifier in a physical OID does not match the unique identifier in the object to which that OID points, the system detects that the pointer is a dangling pointer, and signals an error. Figure 10.21 illustrates this scheme.

Such pointer errors occur when physical OIDs corresponding to old objects that have been deleted are used accidentally. If the space occupied by the object had been reallocated, there may be a new object in the location, and it may get incorrectly addressed by the identifier of the old object. If not detected, the use of dangling pointers could result in corruption of a new object stored at the same location. The unique identifier helps to detect such errors, since the unique identifiers of the old physical OID and the new object will not match.

Suppose that an object has to be moved to a new page, perhaps because the size of the object has increased, and the old page has no extra space. Then, the physical OID will point to the old page, which no longer contains the object. Rather than change the OID of the object (which involves changing every object that points to this one), we leave behind a *forwarding address* at the old location. When the database tries to locate the object, it finds the forwarding address instead of the object; it then uses the forwarding address to locate the object.

10.9.3 Management of Persistent Pointers

We implement persistent pointers in a persistent programming language using OIDs. In some implementations, persistent pointers are physical OIDs; in others, they are logical OIDs. An important difference between persistent pointers and in-memory pointers is the size of the pointer. In-memory pointers need to be only big enough to address all virtual memory. On current computers, in-memory pointers are 4 bytes long, which is sufficient to address 4 gigabytes of memory. Persistent pointers need to address all the data in a database. Since database systems are often bigger than 4 gigabytes, persistent pointers are typically at least 8 bytes long. Many object-oriented databases also provide unique identifiers in persistent pointers, to catch dangling references. This feature further increases the size of persistent pointers. Thus, persistent pointers are substantially longer than are in-memory pointers.

10.9.3.1 Pointer Swizzling

The action of looking up an object given its identifier is called *dereferencing*. Given an in-memory pointer (as in C++), looking up the object is merely a memory reference. Given a persistent pointer, dereferencing an object has an extra step—we have to find the actual location of the object in memory by looking up the persistent pointer in a table. If the object is not already in memory, it has to be loaded from disk. We can implement the table lookup fairly efficiently using hashing, but the lookup is still slow compared to a pointer dereference, even if the object is already in memory.

Pointer swizzling is a way to cut down the cost of locating persistent objects that are already present in memory. The idea is that, when a persistent pointer is first dereferenced, the object is located and is brought into memory if it is not already there. Now an extra step is carried out—an in-memory pointer to the object is stored in place of the persistent pointer. The next time that the *same* persistent pointer is dereferenced, the in-memory location can be read out directly, so the costs of locating the object are avoided. (In the case where persistent objects may be moved from memory back to disk to make space for other persistent objects, an extra step to ensure that the object is still in memory also must be carried out.) Correspondingly, when an object is written out, any persistent pointers that it contained and that were swizzled have to be *unswizzled* and thus converted back to their persistent representation. Pointer swizzling on pointer dereference, as described here, is called *software swizzling*.

Buffer management is more complicated if pointer swizzling is used, since the physical location of an object must not change once that object is brought into the buffer. One way to ensure that it will not change is to pin pages containing swizzled objects in the buffer pool, so that they are never replaced until the program that performed the swizzling was finished. See the bibliographic notes for more complex buffer-management schemes, involving virtual-memory mapping techniques, that remove the requirement of pinning the buffer pages.

10.9.3.2 Hardware Swizzling

Having two types of pointers, persistent and transient (in-memory), is rather inconvenient. Programmers have to remember the type of the pointers, and may have to write code twice—once for the persistent pointers and once for the in-memory pointers. It would be more convenient if both persistent and in-memory pointers were of the same type.

A simple way to merge persistent and in-memory pointer types is simply to extend the length of in-memory pointers to the same size as persistent pointers, and to use 1 bit of the identifier to distinguish between persistent and in-memory pointers. However, the storage cost of longer persistent pointers will have to be borne by in-memory pointers as well; hence, this scheme is unpopular.

We shall describe a technique called *hardware swizzling*, which uses the memory-management hardware present in most current computer systems to address this problem.

Hardware swizzling has two major advantages over software swizzling. First, it is able to store persistent pointers in objects in the same amount of space as in-memory pointers require (along with extra storage external to the object). Second, it transparently converts between persistent pointers and in-memory pointers in a clever and efficient way. Software written to deal with in-memory pointers can thereby deal with persistent pointers as well, without any changes.

Hardware swizzling uses the following representation of persistent pointers contained in objects that are on disk. A persistent pointer is conceptually split into two parts: a page identifier in the database, and an offset within the page. The page identifier is actually a small indirect pointer: Each page (or other unit of storage) has a translation table that provides a mapping from the short page identifiers to full database page identifiers. The system has to look up the small page identifier in a persistent pointer in the translation table to find the full page identifier.

The translation table, in the worst case, will be only as big as the maximum number of pointers that can be contained in objects in a page; with a page size of 4096, and a pointer size of 4 bytes, the maximum number of pointers is 1024. In practice, the translation table is likely to contain many fewer than the maximum number of elements (1024 in our example), and will not consume excessive space. The small page identifier needs to have only enough bits to identify a row in the table; with a maximum table size of 1024, only 10 bits are required. Hence, a small number of bits is enough to store the small page identifier. Thus, the translation table permits an entire persistent pointer to fit into the same space as an in-memory pointer. Even though only a few bits are needed for the short page identifier, all

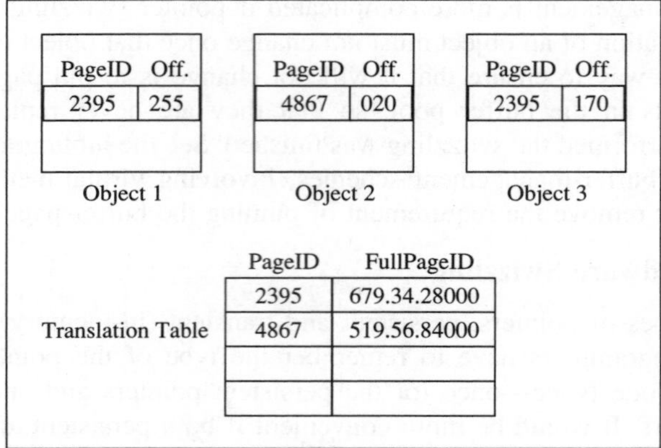

Figure 10.22 Page image before swizzling.

the bits of an in-memory pointer, other than the page-offset bits, are used as the short page identifier. This architecture facilitates swizzling, as we shall see.

The persistent-pointer representation scheme is shown in Figure 10.22, where there are three objects in the page, each containing a persistent pointer. The translation table gives the mapping between short page identifiers and the full database page identifiers for each of the short page identifiers in these persistent pointers. The database page identifiers are shown in the format *volume.file.offset*.

Extra information is maintained with each page so that all persistent pointers in the page can be found. The information is updated when an object is created or deleted in the page. The need to locate all persistent pointers in a page will become clear later.

When an in-memory pointer is dereferenced, if the operating system detects that the page in virtual address space that is pointed to does not have storage allocated for it, or has been access protected, then a *segmentation violation* is said to occur. (Many descriptions of hardware swizzling use the term *page fault* instead of *segmentation violation*.) Many operating systems provide a mechanism to specify a function to be called when a segmentation violation occurs, and a mechanism to allocate storage for a page in virtual address space, and to set that pages's access permissions. In most Unix systems, the `mmap` system call provides this latter functionality, and is used to implement hardware swizzling.

Consider the first time that an in-memory pointer to a page v is dereferenced, when storage has not yet been allocated for the page. As we described, a segmentation violation will occur, and will result in a function call on the database system. The database system first determines what database page was allocated to virtual-memory page v; let the full page identifier of the database page be P. If there was no database page allocated to v, an error is flagged. Otherwise, the database system allocates storage space for page v, and loads the database page P into page v.

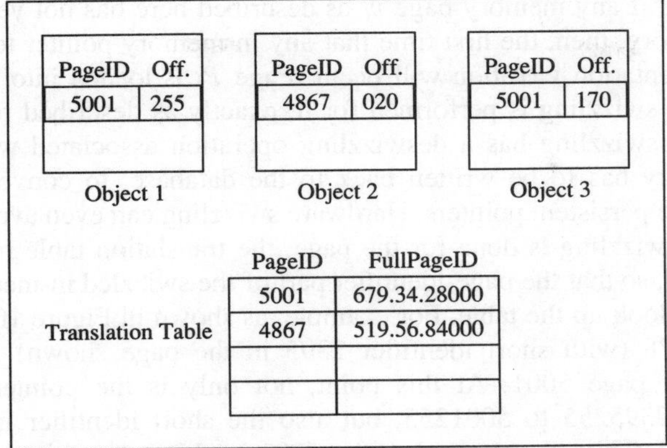

Figure 10.23 Page image after swizzling.

Pointer swizzling is now done for page P, as follows. The system locates all persistent pointers contained in objects in page P, using the extra information stored in the page. Consider each such pointer; call it $\langle p_i, o_i \rangle$, where p_i is the short page identifier and o_i is the offset within the page. Let P_i be the full page identifier of p_i, found in the translation table in page P.

If page P_i does not already have a virtual-memory page allocated to it, a free page in virtual address space is now allocated to it. The page P_i will reside at this virtual address location if and when it is brought in. At this point, the page in virtual address space does not have any storage allocated for it, either in memory or on disk; it is merely a range of addresses reserved for the database page.

Let the virtual-memory page allocated (either earlier or in the previous step) for P_i be v_i. We update the pointer $\langle p_i, o_i \rangle$ being considered by replacing p_i with v_i. Finally, after swizzling all persistent pointers in P, the pointer dereference that resulted in the segmentation violation is allowed to continue, and will find the object for which it was looking loaded in memory.

Figure 10.23 shows the state of the page from Figure 10.22 after that page has been brought into memory and the pointers in it have been swizzled. Here, we assume that the page whose database page identifier is 679.342.78 has been mapped to page 5001 in memory, whereas the page whose identifier is 519.568.50 has been mapped to page 4867 (which is the same as the short page identifier). All the pointers in objects have been updated to reflect the new mapping, and can now be used as in-memory pointers.

At the end of the translation phase for a page, the objects in the page satisfy an important property: All persistent pointers contained in objects in the page have been converted to in-memory pointers. Thus, objects in in-memory pages contain only in-memory pointers. Routines that use these objects do not even need to know about the existence of persistent pointers! For example, existing libraries written for in-memory objects can be used unchanged for persistent objects. That is indeed an important advantage!

Note that, if any memory page v_i as described here has not yet been loaded in virtual memory, then, the first time that any in-memory pointer to it is dereferenced, a segmentation violation will occur. Page P_i is loaded into memory page v_i, and pointer swizzling is performed for it, exactly as described for page P.

Software swizzling has a deswizzling operation associated with it when a page in memory has to be written back to the database, to convert in-memory pointers back to persistent pointers. Hardware swizzling can even avoid this step—when pointer swizzling is done for the page, the translation table for the page is simply updated, so that the page-identifier part of the swizzled in-memory pointers can be used to look up the table. For example, as shown in Figure 10.23, database page 679.342.78 (with short identifier 2395 in the page shown) is mapped to virtual-memory page 5001. At this point, not only is the pointer in object 1 updated from 2395255 to 5001255, but also the short identifier in the table is updated to 5001. Thus, the short identifier 5001 in object 1 and in the table match each other again. Therefore, the page can be written back to disk without any deswizzling.

Several optimizations can be carried out on the basic scheme described here. When swizzling is done for page P, for each page P' referred to by any persistent pointer in P, the system attempts to allocate P' to the virtual address location indicated by the short page identifier of P' on page P. If the page can be allocated as attempted, pointers to it do not need to be updated. In our swizzling example, page 519.568.50 with short page identifier 4867 was mapped to virtual-memory page 4867, which is the same as its short page identifier. We can see that the pointer in object 2 to this page did not need to be changed during swizzling. If every page can be allocated to its appropriate location in virtual address space, none of the pointers need to be translated, and the cost of swizzling is reduced significantly.

Hardware swizzling works even if the database is bigger than virtual memory, but only as long as all the pages that a particular process accesses fit into the virtual memory of the process. If they do not, a page that has been brought into virtual memory will have to be replaced, and that replacement is hard, since there may be in-memory pointers to objects in that page. Hardware swizzling can also be used conceptually at the level of sets of pages (often called segments), instead of for a single page, as long as the short page identifier, with the page offset, does not exceed the length of an in-memory pointer.

10.9.4 Disk Versus Memory Structure of Objects

The format in which objects are stored in memory may be different from the format in which they are stored on disk in the database. One reason may be the use of software swizzling, where the structures of persistent and in-memory pointers are different. Another reason may be that we want to have the database accessible from different machines, possibly based on different architectures, and from different languages, and from programs compiled under different compilers, all of which result in differences in the in-memory representation.

Consider for example a data-structure definition in a programming language, such as C++. The physical structure (such as sizes and representation of integers) in the object are dependent on the machine on which the program is run.† Further, the physical structure may also depend on which compiler is used—in a language as complex as C++, different choices for translation from the high-level description to the physical structure are possible, and each compiler can make its own choice.

The solution to this problem is to make the physical representation of objects in the database independent of the machine and of the compiler. The object can be converted from the disk representation to the form that is required on the specific machine, language, and compiler, when that object is brought into memory. This conversion can be done transparently at the same time that pointers in the object are swizzled, so the programmer does not need to worry about the conversion.

The first step in implementing such a scheme is to define a common language for describing the structure of objects—that is, a data-definition language. Several proposals have been made, one of which is the Object Definition Language (ODL) developed by the Object Database Management Group (ODMG). ODL has mappings defined to C++ and to Smalltalk, so potentially we may manipulate objects in an ODMG-compliant database using either C++ or Smalltalk.

The definition of the structure of each class in the database is stored (logically) in the databases. The code to translate an object in the database to the representation that is manipulated with the programming language (and vice versa) is dependent on the machine as well as on the compiler for the language. We can generate this code automatically, using the stored definition of the class of the object.

An unexpected source of differences between the disk and in-memory representations of data are the hidden-pointers in objects. *Hidden pointers* are transient pointers that are generated by compilers and are stored in objects. These pointers point (indirectly) to tables used to implement certain methods of the object. The tables are typically compiled into executable object code, and the exact location of the tables depends on the executable object code, and hence may be different for different processes. Hence, when an object is accessed by a process, the hidden pointers must be fixed to point to the correct location. The hidden pointers can be initialized at the same time that data-representation conversions are carried out.

10.9.5 Large Objects

Objects may also be extremely large; for instance, multimedia objects may occupy several megabytes of space. Exceptionally large data items, such as video sequences, may run into gigabytes, although they are usually split into into multiple objects, each on the order of a few megabytes or fewer. Large objects are called *binary large objects* (*blobs*) because they typically contain binary data.

†For instance, the Motorola 680x0 architectures, the IBM 360 architecture, and the Intel 80386/80486/Pentium architectures all have 4-byte integers. However, they differ in how the bits of an integer are laid out within a word. In earlier-generation personal computers, integers were 2 bytes long; in newer workstation architectures, such as the DEC Alpha, integers can be 8 bytes long.

In relational systems, record fields that are extremely large are also called *long fields*.

Most relational databases restrict the size of a record to be no larger than the size of a page, to simplify buffer management and free-space management. Large objects and long fields are often stored in a special file (or collection of files) reserved for long-field storage.

A problem with managing large objects is presented by the allocation of buffer pages. Large objects must be stored in a contiguous sequence of bytes when they are brought into memory; if an object is bigger than a page, contiguous pages of the buffer pool must be allocated to store it, which makes buffer management more difficult.

We often modify large objects by updating part of the object, or by inserting or deleting parts of the object, rather than by writing the entire object. If inserts and deletes need to be supported, we can implement large objects using B-tree structures (which we study in Chapter 11). B-tree structures permit us to read the entire object, as well as to insert and delete parts of the object.

For practical reasons, we may manipulate large objects using application programs, rather than doing so within the database:

- **Text data**. Text is usually treated as a byte string manipulated by editors and formatters.
- **Graphical data**. Graphical data may be represented as a bitmap or as a set of lines, boxes, and other geometric objects. Although some graphical data often are managed within the database system itself, special application software is used for many cases. An example of the latter is a VLSI design.
- **Audio and video data**. Audio and video data are typically a digitized, compressed representation created and displayed by separate application software. Modification of data is usually performed with special-purpose editing software, outside the database system.

The most widely used method for updating such data is the *checkout/checkin* method. A user or an application *checks out* a copy of a long-field object, operates on this copy using special-purpose application programs, and then *checks in* the modified copy. The notions of a *checkout* and a *checkin* correspond roughly to those of a read and a write. In some systems, a checkin may create a new version of the object without deleting the old version.

10.10 Summary

Several types of data storage exist in most computer systems. These storage media are classified by the speed with which data be accessed, by the cost per unit of data to buy the memory, and by their reliability. Among the media typically available are cache, main memory, flash memory, magnetic disks, optical disks, and magnetic tapes.

Reliability of storage media is determined by two factors: whether a power failure or system crash causes data to be lost, and what the likelihood is of physical failure of the storage devise. We can reduce the likelihood of physical failure by retaining multiple copies of data. For disks, mirroring can be used. A more sophisticated set of approaches is based on redundant arrays of inexpensive disks (RAIDs). By striping data across disks, they offer high throughput rates on large accesses; by introducing redundancy across disks, they improve reliability greatly. Several different RAID organizations have been proposed, with differing cost, performance and reliability characteristics. RAID level 1 (mirroring) and RAID level 5 are the most commonly used.

A *file* is organized logically as a sequence of records mapped onto disk blocks. One approach to mapping the database to files is to use several files, and to store records of only one fixed length in any given file. An alternative is to structure files such that they can accommodate multiple lengths for records. There are different techniques for implementing variable-length records, including the slotted-page method, the pointer method, and the reserved-space method.

Since data are transferred between disk storage and main memory in units of a block, it is worthwhile to assign file records to blocks such that a single block contains related records. If we can access several of the records desired using only one block access, we save disk accesses. Since disk accesses are usually the bottleneck in the performance of a database system, careful assignment of records to blocks can pay significant performance dividends.

One way to reduce the number of disk accesses is to keep as many blocks as possible in main memory. Since it is not possible to keep all blocks in main memory, we need to manage the allocation of the space available in main memory for the storage of blocks. The *buffer* is that part of main memory available for storage of copies of disk blocks. The subsystem responsible for the allocation of buffer space is called the *buffer manager*.

Storage systems for object-oriented databases are somewhat different from storage systems for relational databases: They must deal with large objects, for example, and must support persistent pointers. There are schemes to detect dangling persistent pointers, and software- and hardware-based swizzling schemes for efficient dereferencing of persistent pointers. The hardware-based schemes use the virtual-memory-management support implemented in hardware, and made accessible to user programs by many current-generation operating systems.

Exercises

10.1. List the physical storage media available on the computers you use routinely. Give the speed with which data can be accessed on each medium.

10.2. How does the remapping of bad sectors by disk controllers affect data-retrieval rates?

10.3. Consider the following data and parity-block arrangement on four disks:

Disk 1	Disk 2	Disk 3	Disk 4
B_1	B_2	B_3	B_4
P_1	B_5	B_6	B_7
B_8	P_2	B_9	B_{10}
⋮	⋮	⋮	⋮

The B_is represent data blocks; the P_is represent parity blocks. Parity block P_i is the parity block for data blocks B_{4i-3} to B_{4i}. What, if any, problem might this arrangement present?

10.4. A power failure that occurs while a disk block is being written could result in the block being only partially written. Assume that partially written blocks can be detected. An atomic block write is one where either the disk block is fully written or nothing is written (i.e., there are no partial writes). Suggest schemes for getting the effect of atomic block writes with the following RAID schemes. Your schemes should involve work on recovery from failure.
(*a*) RAID level 1 (mirroring)
(*b*) RAID level 5 (block interleaved, distributed parity)

10.5. RAID systems typically allow you to replace failed disks without stopping access to the system. Thus, the data in the failed disk must be rebuilt and written to the replacement disk while the system is in operation. With which of the RAID levels is the amount of interference between the rebuild and on-going disk accesses least? Explain your answer.

10.6. Give an example of a relational-algebra expression and a query-processing strategy in each of the following situations:
(*a*) MRU is preferable to LRU.
(*b*) LRU is preferable to MRU.

10.7. Define the term *pinned record*.

10.8. Consider the deletion of record 5 from the file of Figure 10.8. Compare the relative merits of the following techniques for implementing the deletion:
(*a*) Move record 6 to the space occupied by record 5, and move record 7 to the space occupied by record 6.
(*b*) Move record 7 to the space occupied by record 5.
(*c*) Mark record 5 as deleted, and move no records.

10.9. Show the structure of the file of Figure 10.9 after each of the following steps:
(*a*) Insert (Brighton, A-323, 1600).
(*b*) Delete record 2.
(*c*) Insert (Brighton, A-626, 2000).

10.10. Give an example of a database application in which the reserved-space method of representing variable-length records is preferable to the pointer method. Explain your answer.

10.11. Give an example of a database application in which the pointer method of representing variable-length records is preferable to the reserved-space method. Explain your answer.

10.12. Show the structure of the file of Figure 10.12 after each of the following steps:
(*a*) Insert (Mianus, A-101, 2800).
(*b*) Insert (Brighton, A-323, 1600).
(*c*) Delete (Perryridge, A-102, 400).

10.13. What happens if you attempt to insert the record

(Perryridge, A-929, 3000)

into the file of Figure 10.12?

10.14. Show the structure of the file of Figure 10.13 after each of the following steps:
(*a*) Insert (Mianus, A-101, 2800).
(*b*) Insert (Brighton, A-323, 1600).
(*c*) Delete (Perryridge, A-102, 400).

10.15. Explain why the allocation of records to blocks affects database-system performance significantly.

10.16. If a block becomes empty as a result of deletions, for what purposes should the block be reused? Explain your answer. If possible, determine the buffer-management strategy used by the operating system running on your local computer system. Discuss how useful this strategy would be for the implementation of database systems.

10.17. In the sequential file organization, why is an overflow *block* used even if there is, at the moment, only one overflow record?

10.18. List two advantages and two disadvantages of each of the following strategies for storing a relational database:
(*a*) Store each relation in one file.
(*b*) Store multiple relations (perhaps even the entire database) in one file.

10.19. Consider a relational database with two relations:

course (*course-name, room, instructor*)
enrollment (*course-name, student-name, grade*)

Define instances of these relations for three courses, each of which enrolls five students. Give a file structure of these relations that uses clustering.

10.20. Explain why a physical OID must contain more information than a pointer to a physical storage location.

10.21. If physical OIDs are used, is it possible to relocate an object? If so, explain what actions must be taken by the system to relocate an object correctly. If not, explain why relocation is not possible.

10.22. Define the term *dangling pointer*. Describe how the unique-id scheme helps in detecting dangling pointers in an object-oriented database.

10.23. Consider the example on page 330, which shows that there is no need for deswizzling if hardware swizzling is used. Explain why, in that example, it is safe to change the short identifier of page 679.342.78 from 2395 to 5001. Can some other page already have short identifier 5001? If one could, how can you handle that situation?

Bibliographic Notes

Cache memories, including associative memory, are described and analyzed by Smith [1982]. This paper also includes an extensive bibliography on the subject. Patterson and Hennessy [1995] discuss the hardware aspects of translation lookaside buffers, caches, and memory-management units.

Discussions concerning magnetic-disk technology are presented by Freedman [1983], and by Harker et al. [1981]. Optical disks are covered by Kenville [1982], Fujitani [1984], O'Leary and Kitts [1985], Gait [1988], and Olsen and Kenley [1989]. Ruemmler and Wilkes [1994] present an excellent survey of magnetic-disk technology. ¡Wiederhold [1983], Bohl [1981], Trivedi et al. [1980] and ElMasri and Navathe [1994] discuss the physical properties of disks. Discussions of floppy disks are offered by Pechura and Schoeffler [1983] and Sarisky [1983]. Flash memory is discussed by Dippert and Levy [1993].

Ammon et al. [1985] discuss a high-speed, large-capacity, jukebox optical-disk system. An example of an application of optical storage is given in Christodoulakis and Faloutsos [1986]. General discussions concerning mass-storage technology are offered by Chi [1982], and by Hoagland [1985].

Alternative disk organizations that provide a high degree of fault tolerance include those developed by Gray et al. [1990], and by Bitton and Gray [1988]. Disk striping was described by Salem and Garcia-Molina [1986]. Discussions of redundant arrays of inexpensive disks (RAID) were presented by Patterson et al. [1988] and by Chen and Patterson [1990]. Chen et al. [1994] presents an excellent survey of RAID principles and implementation. Reed-Solomon codes are covered in Pless [1989].

Disk-system architectures for high-performance computing are discussed by Katz et al. [1989]. Nelson and Cheng [1992] compare the performance of IPI and SCSI disks and controllers in a real system. The Loge project [English and Stepanov 1992] experimented with adding intelligence to the disk controller. The log-based file system, which makes disk access sequential, is described in Rosenblum and Ousterhout [1991].

In systems that support mobile computing, data may be broadcast repeatedly. The broadcast medium can be viewed as a level of the storage hierarchy — as a broadcast disk with high latency. These issues are discussed in Acharya et al. [1995]. Caching and buffer management for mobile computing is discussed in Barbará and Imielinski [1994]. Further discussion of storage issues in mobile computing appears in Douglis et al. [1994].

Basic data structures are discussed in Knuth [1973], Aho et al. [1983], and Horowitz and Sahni [1976]. Textbook discussions of file organization and access methods for database systems include those of Teorey and Fry [1982], Smith and Barnes [1987], and Ullman [1988].

There are several papers describing the storage structure of specific database systems. Astrahan et al. [1976] discuss System R. Chamberlin et al. [1981] review System R in retrospect. Stonebraker et al. [1976] describe the implementation of Ingres. The *Oracle 7 Concepts Manual* (Oracle [1992]) describes the storage organization of the Oracle 7 database system. The structure of the Wisconsin Storage System (WiSS) is described in Chou et al. [1985]. A software tool for the physical design of relational database is described by Finkelstein et al. [1988].

Buffer management is discussed in most operating system texts, including in Silberschatz and Galvin [1994]. Stonebraker [1981] discusses the relationship between database-system buffer managers and operating-system buffer managers. Chou and DeWitt [1985] present algorithms for buffer management in database systems, and describe a performance evaluation.

Descriptions and performance comparisons of different swizzling techniques are given in Wilson [1990], Moss [1990], and White and DeWitt [1992]. White and DeWitt [1994] describe the virtual-memory-mapped buffer-management scheme used in the ObjectStore OODB system and in the QuickStore storage manager. Using this scheme, we can map disk pages to a fixed virtual-memory address, even if they are not pinned in the buffer. The Exodus object storage manager is described in Carey et al. [1986]. Biliris and Orenstein [1993] provide a survey of storage systems for object-oriented databases. Jagadish et al. [1994] describe a storage manager for main-memory databases.

CHAPTER

11

INDEXING AND HASHING

Many queries reference only a small proportion of the records in a file. For example, the query "Find all accounts at the Perryridge branch" references only a fraction of the account records. It is inefficient for the system to have to read every record and to check the *branch-name* field for the name "Perryridge." Ideally, the system should be able to locate these records directly. To allow these forms of access, we design additional structures that we associate with files.

11.1 Basic Concepts

An index for a file in the system works in much the same way as a catalog for a book in a library. If we are looking for a book by a particular author, we look in the author catalog, and a card in the catalog tells us where to find the book. To assist us in searching the catalog, the library keeps cards in alphabetic order, so we do not have to check every card to find the one we want.

In real-world databases, indices of the type just described may be too large to be handled efficiently. Instead, more sophisticated indexing techniques may be used. We shall discuss several of these techniques subsequently. There are two basic kinds of indices:

- **Ordered indices**. Such indices are based on a sorted ordering of the values.
- **Hash indices**. Such indices are based on the values being distributed uniformly across a range of buckets. The bucket to which a value is assigned is determined by a function, called a *hash function*.

We shall consider several techniques for both ordered indexing and hashing. No one technique is the best. Rather, each technique is best suited to particular database applications. Each technique must be evaluated on the basis of these factors:

- **Access types**: The types of access that are supported efficiently. These types could include finding records with a specified attribute value, or finding records whose attribute values fall in a specified range.
- **Access time**: The time it takes to find a particular data item, or set of items, using the technique in question.
- **Insertion time**: The time it takes to insert a new data item. This value includes the time it takes to find the correct place to insert the new data item, as well as the time it takes to update the index structure.
- **Deletion time**: The time it takes to delete a data item. This value includes the time it takes to find the item to be deleted, as well as the time it takes to update the index structure.
- **Space overhead**: The additional space occupied by an index structure. Provided that the amount of additional space is moderate, it is usually worthwhile to sacrifice the space to achieve improved performance.

We often want to have more than one index for a file. Returning to the library example, we note that most libraries maintain several card catalogs: for author, for subject, and for title. The attribute or set of attributes used to look up records in a file is called a *search key*. Note that this definition of *key* differs from that used in *primary key*, *candidate key*, and *superkey*. This duplicate meaning for *key* is (unfortunately) well established in practice. Using our notion of a search key, we see that, if there are several indices on a file, there are several search keys.

11.2 Ordered Indices

To gain fast random access to records in a file, we can use an index structure. Each index structure is associated with a particular search key. Just like a library catalog, an index stores the values of the search keys in sorted order, and associates with each search key the records that contain that search key.

The records in the indexed file may themselves be stored in some sorted order, just like books in a library are stored sorted by some attribute such as the Dewey decimal number. A file may have several indices, on different search keys. If the file containing the records is sequentially ordered, the index whose search key specifies the sequential order of the file is the *primary index*. (The term *primary index* is sometimes used to mean an index on a primary key. However, such usage is nonstandard and should be avoided). Primary indices are also called *clustering indices*. The search key of a primary index is usually the primary key, although that is not necessarily so. Indices whose search key specifies an order different from the sequential order of the file are called *secondary indices*, or *nonclustering* indices.

Brighton	A-217	750
Downtown	A-101	500
Downtown	A-110	600
Mianus	A-215	700
Perryridge	A-102	400
Perryridge	A-201	900
Perryridge	A-218	700
Redwood	A-222	700
Round Hill	A-305	350

Figure 11.1 Sequential file for *account* records.

11.2.1 Primary Index

In this section, we assume that all files are ordered sequentially on some search key. Such files, with a primary index on the search key, are called *index-sequential files*. They represent one of the oldest index schemes used in database systems. They are designed for applications that require both sequential processing of the entire file and random access to individual records.

Figure 11.1 shows a sequential file of *account* records taken from our banking example. In the example of Figure 11.1, the records are stored in search-key order, with *branch-name* used as the search key.

11.2.1.1 Dense and Sparse Indices

There are two types of ordered indices that we can use:

- **Dense index**. An *index record* (or *index entry*) appears for every search-key value in the file. The index record contains the search-key value and a pointer to the first data record with that search-key value. (Some authors use the term *dense index* to mean an index where an index record appears for every *record* in the file.)
- **Sparse index**. An index record is created for only some of the values. As is true in dense indices, each index record contains a search-key value and a pointer to the first data record with that search-key value. To locate a record, we find the index entry with the largest search-key value that is less than or equal to the search-key value for which we are looking. We start at the record pointed to by that index entry, and follow the pointers in the file until we find the desired record.

Figures 11.2 and 11.3 show dense and sparse indices, respectively, for the *account* file. Suppose that we are looking up records for the Perryridge branch. Using the dense index of Figure 11.2, we follow the pointer directly to the first Perryridge record. We process this record, and follow the pointer in that record to locate the next record in search-key (*branch-name*) order. We continue processing records until we encounter a record for a branch other than Perryridge.

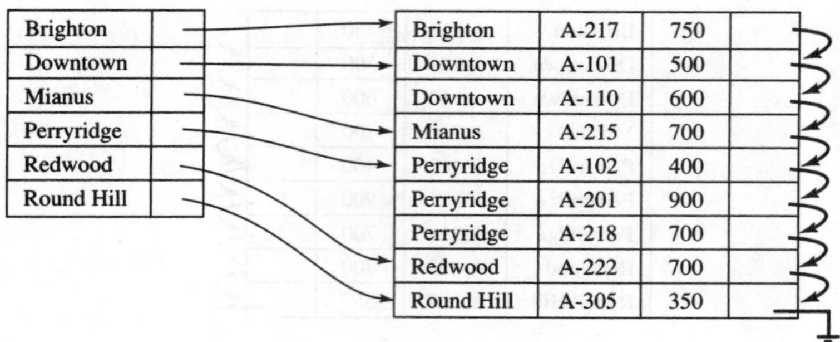

Figure 11.2 Dense index.

If we are using the sparse index (Figure 11.3), we do not find an index entry for "Perryridge." Since the last entry (in alphabetic order) before "Perryridge" is "Mianus," we follow that pointer. We then read the *account* file in sequential order until we find the first Perryridge record, and begin processing at that point.

As we have seen, it is generally faster to locate a record if we have a dense index rather than a sparse index. However, sparse indices have advantages over dense indices in that they require less space and they impose less maintenance overhead for insertions and deletions.

There is a tradeoff that the system designer must make between access time and space overhead. Although the decision regarding this tradeoff is dependent on the specific application, a good compromise is to have a sparse index with one index entry per block. The reason this design is a good tradeoff is that the dominant cost in processing a database request is the time that it takes to bring a block from disk into main memory. Once we have brought in the block, the time to scan the entire block is negligible. Using this sparse index, we locate the block containing the record that we are seeking. Thus, unless the record is on an overflow block (see Section 10.7.1), we minimize block accesses while keeping the size of the index (and thus, our space overhead) as small as possible.

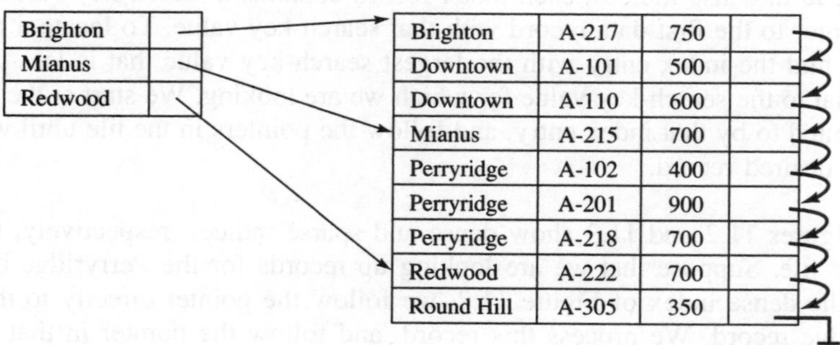

Figure 11.3 Sparse index.

For the preceding technique to be fully general, we must consider the case where records for one search-key value occupy several blocks. It is easy to modify our scheme to handle this situation.

11.2.1.2 Multilevel Indices

Even if we use a sparse index, the index itself may become too large for efficient processing. It is not unreasonable, in practice, to have a file with 100,000 records, with 10 records stored in each block. If we have one index record per block, the index has 10,000 records. Index records are smaller than data records, so let us assume that 100 index records fit on a block. Thus, our index occupies 100 blocks. Such large indices are stored as sequential files on disk.

If an index is sufficiently small to be kept in main memory, search time to find an entry is low. However, if the index is so large that it must be kept on disk, a search for an entry requires several disk block reads. Binary search can be used on the index file to locate an entry, but the search still has a large cost. If the index occupies b blocks, binary search requires as many as $\lceil \log_2(b) \rceil$ blocks to be read. ($\lceil x \rceil$ denotes the least integer that is greater than or equal to x; that is, we round upward.) For our 100-block index, binary search requires seven block reads. On a disk system where a block read takes 30 milliseconds, the search will take 210 milliseconds, which is long. Note that, if overflow blocks have been used, binary search will not be possible. In that case, a sequential search is typically used, and that requires b block reads, which will take even longer. Thus, the process of searching a large index may be costly.

To deal with this problem, we treat the index just as we would treat any other sequential file, and we construct a sparse index on the primary index, as shown in Figure 11.4. To locate a record, we first use binary search on the outer index to find the record for the largest search-key value less than or equal to the one that we desire. The pointer points to a block of the inner index. We scan this block until we find the record that has the largest search-key value less than or equal to the one that we desire. The pointer in this record points to the block of the file that contains the record for which we are looking.

Using the two levels of indexing, we have read only one index block, rather than the seven we read with binary search, if we assume that the outer index is already in main memory. If our file is extremely large, even the outer index may grow too large to fit in main memory. In such a case, we can create yet another level of index. Indeed, we can repeat this process as many times as necessary. Indices with two or more levels are called *multilevel* indices. Searching for records using a multilevel index requires significantly fewer I/O operations than does searching for records using binary search. Each level of index could correspond to a unit of physical storage. Thus, we may have indices at the track, cylinder, and disk levels.

Multilevel indices are closely related to tree structures, such as the binary trees used for in-memory indexing. We shall examine the relationship later, in Section 11.3.

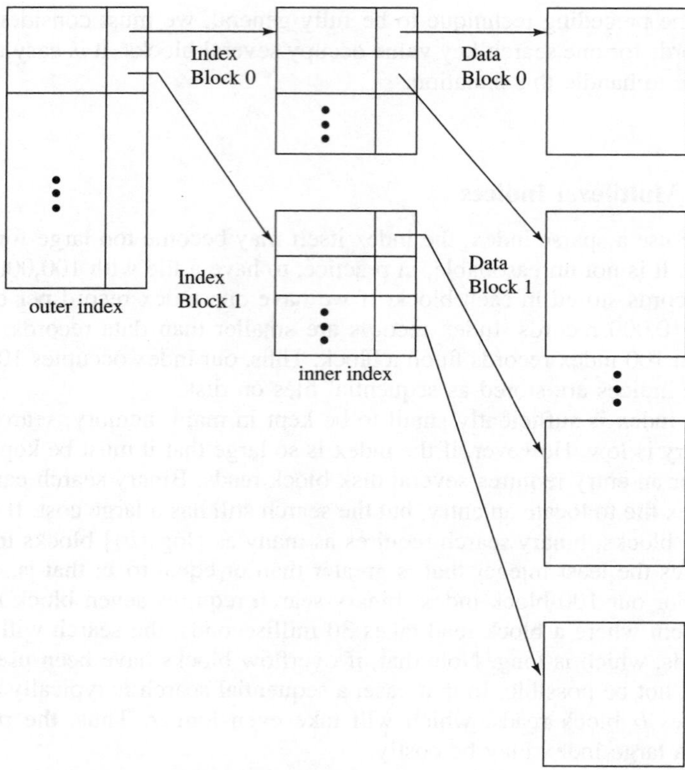

Figure 11.4 Two-level sparse index.

11.2.1.3 Index Update

Regardless of what form of index is used, every index must be updated whenever a record is either inserted into or deleted from the file. We describe algorithms for updating single-level indices next.

- **Deletion**. To delete a record, we first look up the record to be deleted. If the deleted record was the only record with its particular search-key value, then the search-key value is deleted from the index. For dense indices, deletion of a search-key value is similar to deletion of a record from a file. For sparse indices, we delete a key value by replacing its entry (if one exists) in the index with the next search-key value (in search-key order). If the next search-key value already has an index entry, the entry is deleted instead of being replaced.
- **Insertion**. First, we perform a lookup using the search-key value that appears in the record to be inserted. If the index is dense, and the search-key value does not appear in the index, the latter is inserted in the index. If the index is sparse and stores an entry for each block, no change needs to be made

to the index unless a new block is created. In this case, the first search-key value (in search-key order) appearing in the new block is inserted into the index.

Insertion and deletion algorithms for multilevel indices are a simple extension of the scheme just described. On deletion or insertion, the lowest-level index is updated as described. As far as the second level is concerned, the lowest-level index is merely a file containing records—thus, if there is any change in the lowest-level index, the second-level index is updated as described. The same technique applies to further levels of the index, if there are any.

11.2.2 Secondary Indices

A secondary index on a candidate key looks just like a dense primary index, except that the records pointed to by successive values in the index are not stored sequentially. In general, however, secondary indices may be structured differently from primary indices. If the search key of a primary index is not a candidate key, it suffices if the index points to the first record with a particular value for the search key, since the other records can be fetched by a sequential scan of the file.

However, if the search key of a secondary index is not a candidate key, it is not enough to point to just the first record with each search-key value. The remaining records with the same search-key value could be anywhere in the file, since the records are ordered by the search key of the primary index, rather than by the search key of the secondary index. Therefore, a secondary index must contain pointers to all the records. We can use an extra level of indirection to implement secondary indices on search keys that are not candidate keys. The pointers in such a secondary index do not point directly to the file. Instead, each points to a bucket that contains pointers to the file. Figure 11.5 shows the structure of a secondary

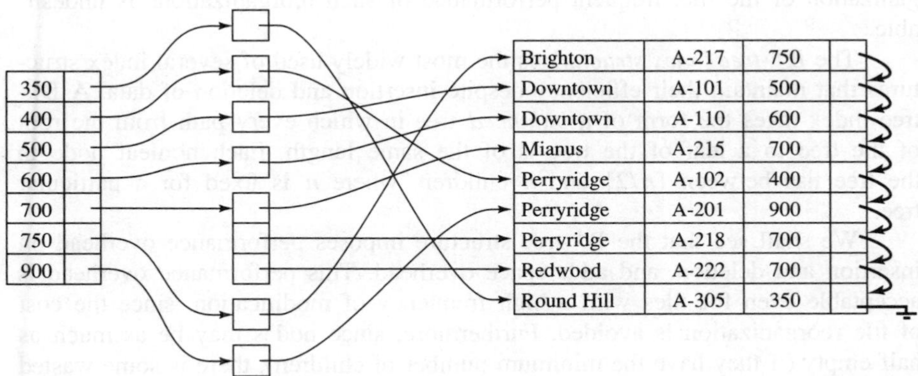

Figure 11.5 Secondary index on *account* file, on non-candidate key *balance*.

index that uses an extra level of indirection on the *account* file, on the search key *balance*.

A *sequential scan* in primary index order is efficient because records in the file are stored physically in the same order as the index order. However, we cannot (except in rare special cases) store a file physically ordered both by the search key of the primary index, and the search key of a secondary index. Because secondary-key order and physical-key order differ, if we attempt to scan the file sequentially in secondary-key order, the reading of each record is likely to require the reading of a new block from disk.

A sparse primary index may store only some of the search-key values, since it is always possible to find records with intermediate search-key values by a sequential access to a part of the file, as described earlier. If a secondary index stores only some of the search-key values, records with intermediate search-key values may be anywhere in the file and, in general, we cannot find them without searching the entire file. Secondary indices must therefore be dense, with an index entry for every search-key value, and a pointer to every record in the file.

The procedure described earlier for deletion and insertion can be applied to a file with multiple indices. Whenever the file is modified, *every* index must be updated.

Secondary indices improve the performance of queries that use keys other than the search key of the primary index. However, they impose a significant overhead on modification of the database. The designer of a database decides which secondary indices are desirable on the basis of an estimate of the relative frequency of queries and modifications.

11.3 B$^+$-Tree Index Files

The main disadvantage of the index-sequential file organization is that performance degrades as the file grows, both for index lookups and for sequential scans through the data. Although this degradation can be remedied by reorganization of the file, frequent performance of such reorganizations is undesirable.

The *B$^+$-tree index structure* is the most widely used of several index structures that maintain their efficiency despite insertion and deletion of data. A B$^+$-tree index takes the form of a *balanced* tree in which every path from the root of the tree to a leaf of the tree is of the same length. Each nonleaf node in the tree has between $\lceil n/2 \rceil$ and n children, where n is fixed for a particular tree.

We shall see that the B$^+$-tree structure imposes performance overhead on insertion and deletion, and adds space overhead. This performance overhead is acceptable even for files with a high frequency of modification, since the cost of file reorganization is avoided. Furthermore, since nodes may be as much as half empty (if they have the minimum number of children), there is some wasted space. This space overhead, too, is acceptable given the performance benefits of the B$^+$-tree structure.

P_1	K_1	P_2	...	P_{n-1}	K_{n-1}	P_n

Figure 11.6 Typical node of a B$^+$-tree.

11.3.1 Structure of a B$^+$-Tree

A B$^+$-tree index is a multilevel index, but it has a structure that differs from that of the multilevel index-sequential file. A typical node of a B$^+$-tree is shown in Figure 11.6. It contains up to $n - 1$ search-key values K_1, K_2, ..., K_{n-1}, and n pointers P_1, P_2, ..., P_n. The search-key values within a node are kept in sorted order; thus, if $i < j$, then $K_i < K_j$.

We consider first the structure of the leaf nodes. For $i = 1, 2, \ldots, n-1$, pointer P_i points to either a file record with search-key value K_i or to a bucket of pointers, each of which points to a file record with search-key value K_i. The bucket structure is used only if the search key does not form a primary key, and if the file is not sorted in the search-key value order. Pointer P_n has a special purpose that we shall discuss shortly.

Figure 11.7 shows one leaf node of a B$^+$-tree for the *account* file, in which we have chosen n to be 3, and the search key is *branch-name*. Note that, since the account file is ordered by *branch-name*, the pointers in the leaf node point directly to the file.

Now that we have seen the structure of a leaf node, let us consider how search-key values are assigned to particular nodes. Each leaf can hold up to $n - 1$ values. We allow leaf nodes to contain as few as $\lceil (n-1)/2 \rceil$ values. The ranges of values in each leaf do not overlap. Thus, if L_i and L_j are leaf nodes and $i < j$, then every search-key value in L_i is less than every search-key value in L_j. If the B$^+$-tree index is to be a dense index, every search-key value must appear in some leaf node.

Now we can explain the use of the pointer P_n. Since there is a linear order on the leaves based on the search-key values that they contain, we use P_n to chain together the leaf nodes in search-key order. This ordering allows for efficient sequential processing of the file.

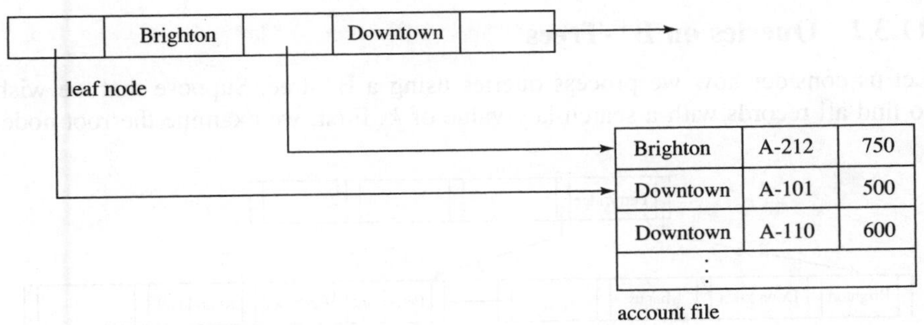

Figure 11.7 A leaf node for *account* B$^+$-tree index ($n = 3$).

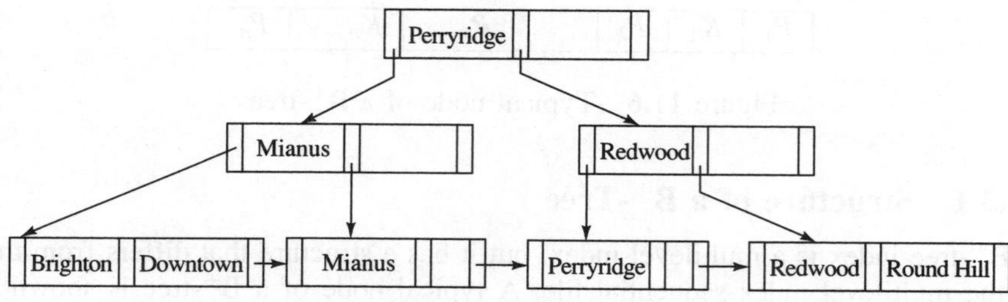

Figure 11.8 B^+-tree for *account* file ($n = 3$).

The nonleaf nodes of the B^+-tree form a multilevel (sparse) index on the leaf nodes. The structure of nonleaf nodes is the same as that for leaf nodes, except that all pointers are pointers to tree nodes. A nonleaf node may hold up to n pointers, and *must* hold at least $\lceil n/2 \rceil$ pointers. The number of pointers in a node is called the *fanout* of the node.

Let us consider a node containing m pointers. For $i = 2, 3, \ldots, m - 1$, pointer P_i points to the subtree that contains search-key values less than K_i and greater than or equal to K_{i-1}. Pointer P_m points to the part of the subtree that contains those key values greater than or equal to K_{m-1}, and pointer P_1 points to the part of the subtree that contains those search-key values less than K_1.

The requirement that each nonleaf node hold at least $\lceil n/2 \rceil$ pointers is imposed at all levels of the tree except for the root. Figure 11.8 shows a complete B^+-tree for the *account* file ($n = 3$). For simplicity, we have omitted both the pointers to the file itself and the null pointers. As an example of a B^+-tree for which the root must have less than $\lceil n/2 \rceil$ values, in Figure 11.9 we show a B^+-tree for the *account* file with $n = 5$. It is always possible to construct a B^+-tree, for any n, in which all nonroot nodes contain at least $\lceil n/2 \rceil$ pointers.

The examples that we have given of B^+-trees have all been balanced. That is, the length of every path from the root to a leaf node is the same. This property is a requirement for a B^+-tree. Indeed, the "B" in B^+-tree stands for "balanced." It is the balance property of B^+-trees that ensures good performance for lookup, insertion, and deletion.

11.3.2 Queries on B^+-Trees

Let us consider how we process queries using a B^+-tree. Suppose that we wish to find all records with a search-key value of k. First, we examine the root node,

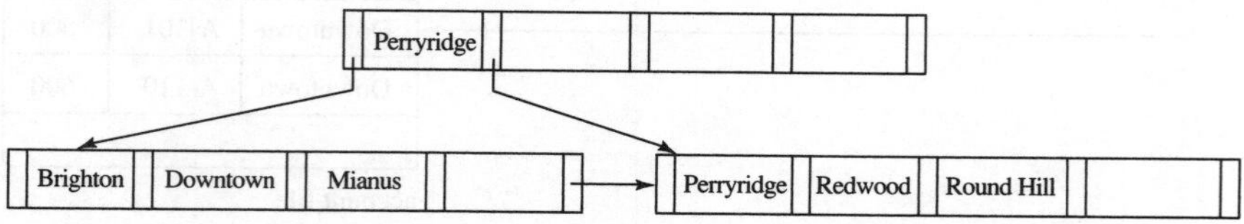

Figure 11.9 B^+-tree for *account* file with $n = 5$.

looking for the smallest search-key value greater than k. Assume that this search-key value is K_i. We follow pointer P_i to another node. If $K < K_1$, then we follow P_1 to another node. If we have m pointers in the node, and $K \geq K_{m-1}$, then we follow P_m to another node. Once again, we look for the smallest search-key value greater than k, and follow the corresponding pointer. Eventually, we reach a leaf node, at which point the pointer directs us to the desired record or bucket.

Thus, in the processing of a query, a path is traversed in the tree from the root to some leaf node. If there are K search-key values in the file, the path is no longer than $\lceil \log_{\lceil n/2 \rceil}(K) \rceil$.

In practice, only a few nodes need to be accessed, Typically, a node is made to be the same size as a disk block, which is typically 4 kilobytes. With a search-key size of 12 bytes, and a disk-pointer size of 8 bytes, n is around 200. Even with a more conservative estimate of 32 bytes for the search-key size, n is around 100. With $n = 100$, if we have 1 million search-key values in the file, a lookup requires only $\lceil \log_{50}(1{,}000{,}000) \rceil = 4$ nodes to be accessed. Thus, at most four blocks need to be read from disk for the lookup. The root node of the tree is usually heavily accessed and is likely to be in the buffer, so typically only three or fewer blocks need to be read from disk.

An important difference between B$^+$-tree structures and in-memory tree structures, such as binary trees, is the size of a node, and as a result, the height of the tree. In a binary tree, each node is small, and has at most two pointers. In a B$^+$-tree, each node is large—typically a disk block—and a node can have a large number of pointers. Thus, B$^+$-trees tend to be fat and short unlike thin and tall binary trees. In a balanced binary tree, the path for a lookup can be of length $\lceil \log_2(K) \rceil$, where K is the number of search-key values. With $K = 1{,}000{,}000$ as in the previous example, a balanced binary tree requires around 20 node accesses. If each node were on a different disk block, 20 block reads would be required to process a lookup, in contrast to the four block reads for the B$^+$-tree.

11.3.3 Updates on B$^+$-Trees

Insertion and deletion are more complicated than lookup, since it may be necessary to *split* a node that becomes too large as the result of an insertion, or to *combine* nodes if a node becomes too small (fewer than $\lceil n/2 \rceil$ pointers). Furthermore, when a node is split or a pair of nodes is combined, we must ensure that balance is preserved. To introduce the idea behind insertion and deletion in a B$^+$-tree, we shall assume temporarily that nodes never become too large or too small. Under this assumption, insertion and deletion are performed as defined next.

- **Insertion**. Using the same technique as for lookup, we find the leaf node in which the search-key value would appear. If the search-key value already appears in the leaf node, we add the new record to the file and, if necessary, a pointer to the bucket. If the search-key value does not appear, we insert the value in the leaf node, and position it such that the search keys are still in order. We then insert the new record in the file and, if necessary, create a new bucket with the appropriate pointer.

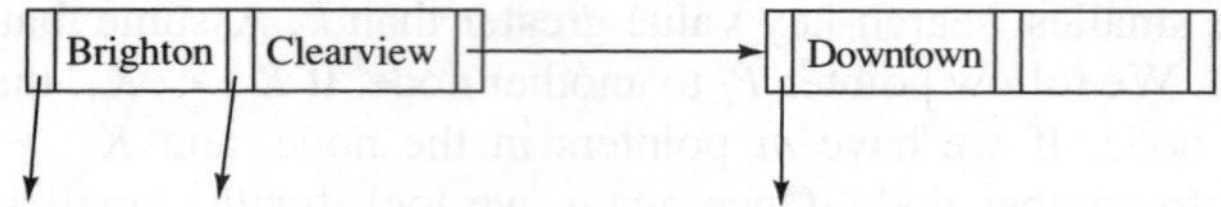

Figure 11.10 Split of leaf node on insertion of "Clearview."

- **Deletion**. Using the same technique as for lookup, we find the record to be deleted, and remove it from the file. The search-key value is removed from the leaf node if there is no bucket associated with that search-key value or if the bucket becomes empty as a result of the deletion.

We now consider an example in which a node must be split. Assume that we wish to insert a record with a *branch-name* value of "Clearview" into the B^+-tree of Figure 11.8. Using the algorithm for lookup, we find that "Clearview" should appear in the node containing "Brighton" and "Downtown." There is no room to insert the search-key value "Clearview." Therefore, the node is *split* into two nodes. Figure 11.10 shows the two leaf nodes that result from inserting "Clearview" and splitting the node containing "Brighton" and "Downtown." In general, we take the n search-key values (the $n - 1$ values in the leaf node plus the value being inserted), and put the first $\lceil n/2 \rceil$ in the existing node and the remaining values in a new node.

Having split a leaf node, we must insert the new leaf node into the B^+-tree structure. In our example, the new node has "Downtown" as its smallest search-key value. We need to insert this search-key value into the parent of the leaf node that was split. The B^+-tree of Figure 11.11 shows the result of the insertion. The search-key value "Downtown" was inserted into the parent. It was possible to perform this insertion because there was room for an added search-key value. If there were no room, the parent would have had to be split. In the worst case, all nodes along the path to the root must be split. If the root itself is split, the entire tree becomes deeper.

The general technique for insertion into a B^+-tree is to determine the leaf node l into which insertion must occur. If a split results, insert the new node

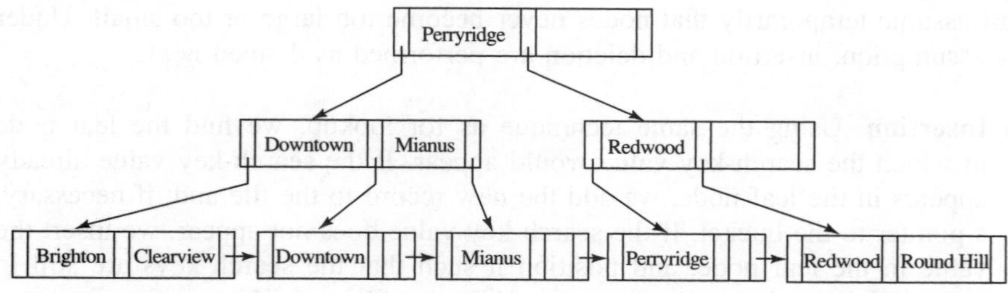

Figure 11.11 Insertion of "Clearview" into the B^+-tree of Figure 11.8.

into the parent of node l. If this insertion causes a split, proceed recursively until either an insertion does not cause a split or a new root is created.

Figure 11.12 outlines the insertion algorithm in pseudocode. In the pseudocode $L.K_i$ and $L.P_i$ denote the ith value and the ith pointer in node L, respectively. The pseudocode also makes use of the function *parent*(L) to find the parent of a node L. We can compute a list of nodes in the path from the root to the leaf while initially finding the leaf node, and can use it later to find the parent of any node in the path efficiently. The pseudocode refers to inserting an entry (V, P) into a node. In the case of leaf nodes, the pointer to an entry actually precedes the key value, so the leaf node actually stores P preceding V. For internal nodes, P is stored just after V.

We now consider deletions that cause tree nodes to contain too few pointers. First, let us delete "Downtown" from the B$^+$-tree of Figure 11.11. We locate the entry for "Downtown" using our lookup algorithm. When we delete the entry for "Downtown" from its leaf node, the leaf becomes empty. Since, in our example, $n = 3$ and $0 < \lceil (n-1)/2 \rceil$, this node must be eliminated from the B$^+$-tree. To delete a leaf node, we must delete the pointer to it from its parent. In our example, this deletion leaves the parent node, which formerly contained three pointers, with only two pointers. Since $2 \geq \lceil n/2 \rceil$, the node is still sufficiently large, and the deletion operation is complete. The resulting B$^+$-tree is shown in Figure 11.13.

When a deletion is made to a parent of a leaf node, the parent node itself may become too small. That is exactly what happens if we delete "Perryridge" from the B$^+$-tree of Figure 11.13. Deletion of the Perryridge entry causes a leaf node to become empty. When we delete the pointer to this node in the latter's parent, the parent is left with only one pointer. Since $n = 3$, $\lceil n/2 \rceil = 2$, and thus only one pointer is too few. However, since the parent node contains useful information, we cannot simply delete it. Instead, we look at the sibling node (the nonleaf node containing the one search key, Mianus). This sibling node has room to accommodate the information contained in our now-too-small node, so we coalesce these nodes, such that the sibling node now contains the keys "Mianus" and "Redwood." The other node (the node containing only the search key "Redwood") now contains redundant information and can be deleted from its parent (which happens to be the root in our example). Figure 11.14 shows the result. Notice that the root has only one child pointer after the deletion, so it is deleted and its sole child becomes the root. So the depth of the B$^+$-tree has been decreased by 1.

It is not always possible to coalesce nodes. As an illustration, let us delete "Perryridge" from the B$^+$-tree of Figure 11.11. In this example, the "Downtown" entry is still part of the tree. Once again, the leaf node containing "Perryridge" becomes empty. The parent of the leaf node becomes too small (only one pointer). However, in this example, the sibling node already contains the maximum number of pointers: three. Thus, it cannot accommodate an additional pointer. The solution in this case is to *redistribute* the pointers such that each sibling has two pointers. The result is shown in Figure 11.15. Note that the redistribution of values necessitates a change of a search-key value in the parent of the two siblings.

```
procedure insert(value V, pointer P)
    find the leaf node L that should contain value V
    insert_entry(L, V, P)
end procedure

procedure insert_entry(node L, value V, pointer P)
    if (L has space for (V, P))
        then insert (V, P) in L
        else begin /* Split L */
            Create node L'
            if (L is a leaf) then begin
                Let V' be the value such that ⌈n/2⌉ of the values
                    L.K_1, ..., L.K_{n-1}, V are less than V'
                Let m be the lowest value such L.K_m ≥ V'
                move L.P_m, L.K_m, ..., L.P_{n-1}, L.K_{n-1} to L'
                if (V < V') then insert (P, V) in L
                else insert (P, V) in L'
            end
            else begin
                Let V' be the value such that ⌈n/2⌉ of the values
                    L.K_1, ..., L.K_{n-1}, V are greater than or equal to V'
                Let m be the lowest value such L.K_m ≥ V'
                add Nil, L.K_m, ..., L.P_{n-1}, L.K_{n-1}, L.P_n to L'
                delete L.K_m, ..., L.P_{n-1}, L.K_{n-1}, L.P_n from L
                if (V < V') then insert (V, P) in L
                else insert (V, P) in L'
                delete (Nil, V') from L'
            end
            if (L is not the root of the tree)
                then insert_entry(parent(L), V', L');
                else begin
                    create a new node R with child nodes L and L' and
                        the single value V'
                    make R the root of the tree
                end
                if (L) is a leaf node then begin /* Fix next child pointers */
                    set L'.P_n = L.P_n;
                    set L.P_n = L'
                end
        end
end procedure
```

Figure 11.12 Insertion of entry in a B^+-tree.

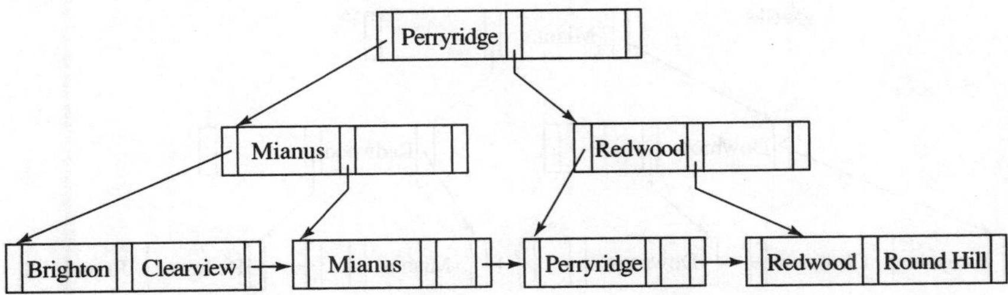

Figure 11.13 Deletion of "Downtown" from the B$^+$-tree of Figure 11.11.

In general, to delete a value in a B$^+$-tree, we perform a lookup on the value and delete it. If the node is too small, we delete it from its parent. This deletion results in recursive application of the deletion algorithm until the root is reached, a parent remains adequately full after deletion, or redistribution is applied.

Figure 11.16 outlines pseudocode for deletion from a B$^+$-tree. The procedure swap_variables(L, L') merely swaps the values of the (pointer) variables L and L'; this swap has no effect on the tree itself. The pseudocode uses the condition "too few pointers/values." For nonleaf nodes, this criterion means less than $\lceil n/2 \rceil$ pointers; for leaf nodes, it means less than $\lceil (n-1)/2 \rceil$ values. The pseudocode performs redistribution by borrowing a single entry from an adjacent node. We can also do redistribution by repartitioning entries equally between the two nodes. The pseudocode refers to deleting an entry (V, P) from a node. In the case of leaf nodes, the pointer to an entry actually precedes the key value, so the pointer P precedes the key value V. For internal nodes, P follows the key value V.

Although insertion and deletion operations on B$^+$-trees are complicated, they require relatively few operations. It can be shown that the number of operations needed for a worst-case insertion or deletion is proportional to $\log_{\lceil n/2 \rceil}(K)$, where n is the maximum number of pointers in a node, and K is the number of search key values. In other words, the cost of insertion and deletion operations is proportional to the height of the B$^+$-tree, and is therefore low. It is the speed of operation on B$^+$-trees that makes them a frequently used index structure in database implementations.

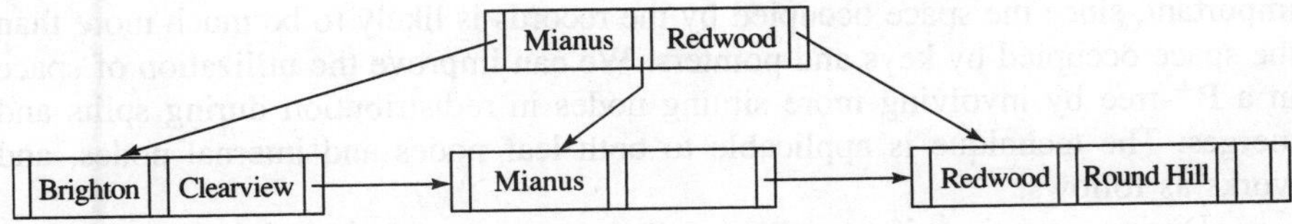

Figure 11.14 Deletion of "Perryridge" from the B$^+$-tree of Figure 11.13.

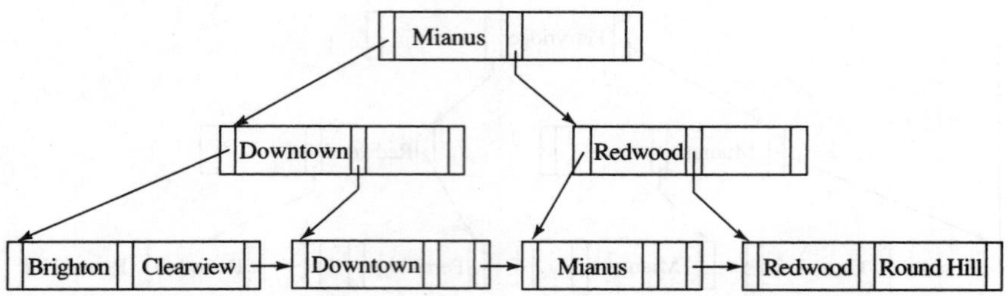

Figure 11.15 Deletion of "Perryridge" from the B$^+$-tree of Figure 11.11.

11.3.4 B$^+$-Tree File Organization

As mentioned earlier, the drawback of index-sequential file organization is the degradation of performance as the file grows. We solve the degradation of index lookups by using B$^+$-tree indices on the file. We solve the degradation problem for storing the actual records by using the leaf level of the B$^+$-tree to organize the blocks containing the actual records. In such structures, the B$^+$-tree structure is used not only as an index, but also as an organizer for records into a file.

In a *B$^+$-tree file organization*, the leaf nodes of the tree store records, instead of storing pointers to records. Figure 11.17 shows an example of a B$^+$-tree file organization. Since records are usually larger than pointers, the maximum number of records that can be stored in a leaf node is less than the number of pointers in a nonleaf node. However, the leaf nodes are still required to be at least half full.

Insertion and deletion from a B$^+$-tree file organization are handled in the same way as insertion and deletion of entries in a B$^+$-tree index. When a record with a given key value v is inserted, we locate the block that should contain the record by searching the B$^+$-tree for the largest key in the tree that is $\leq v$. If the block located has enough free space for the record, the record is stored in the block. Otherwise, as in B$^+$-tree insertion, the block is split in two, and the records in it are redistributed (in the B$^+$-tree–key order) to create space for the new record. The split propagates up the B$^+$-tree in the normal fashion. When a record is deleted, it is first removed from the block containing it. If a block B becomes less than half full as a result, the records in B are redistributed with the records in an adjacent block B'. Assuming fixed-sized records, each block will hold at least one-half as many records as the maximum that it can hold. The nonleaf nodes of the B$^+$-tree are then updated in the usual fashion.

When a B$^+$-tree is used for file organization, space utilization is particularly important, since the space occupied by the records is likely to be much more than the space occupied by keys and pointers. We can improve the utilization of space in a B$^+$-tree by involving more sibling nodes in redistribution during splits and merges. The technique is applicable to both leaf nodes and internal nodes, and works as follows.

During insertion, if a node is full we attempt to redistribute some of its entries to one of the adjacent nodes, to make space for a new entry. If this

```
procedure delete(value V, pointer P)
    find the leaf node L that contains (V, P)
    delete_entry(L, V, P)
end procedure
procedure delete_entry(node L, value V, pointer P)
    delete (V, P) from L
    if (L is the root and L has only one remaining child)
    then make the child of L the new root of the tree and delete L
    else if (L has too few values/pointers) then begin
        Let L' be the previous or next child of parent(L)
        Let V' be the value between pointers L and L' in parent(L)
        if (entries in L and L' can fit in a single node)
            then begin /* Coalesce nodes */
                if (L is a predecessor of L') then swap_variables(L, L')
                if (L is not a leaf)
                    then append V' and all pointers and values in L to L'
                    else append all (K_i, P_i) pairs in L to L'; set L'.P_n = L.P_n
                delete_entry(parent(L), V', L); delete node L
            end
        else begin /* Redistribution: borrow an entry from L' */
            if (L' is a predecessor of L) then begin
                if (L is a non-leaf node) then begin
                    let m be such that L'.P_m is the last pointer in L'
                    remove (L'.K_m-1, L'.P_m) from L'
                    insert (L'.P_m, V') as the first pointer and value in L,
                        by shifting other pointers and values right
                    replace V' in parent(L) by L'.K_m-1
                end
                else begin
                    let m be such that (L'.P_m, L'.K_m) is the last pointer/value
                        pair in L'
                    remove (L'.P_m, L'.K_m) from L'
                    insert (L'.P_m, L'.K_m) as the first pointer and value in L,
                        by shifting other pointers and values right
                    replace V' in parent(L) by L'.K_m
                end
            end
            else ... symmetric to the then case ...
        end
    end
end procedure
```

Figure 11.16 Deletion of entry from a B^+-tree.

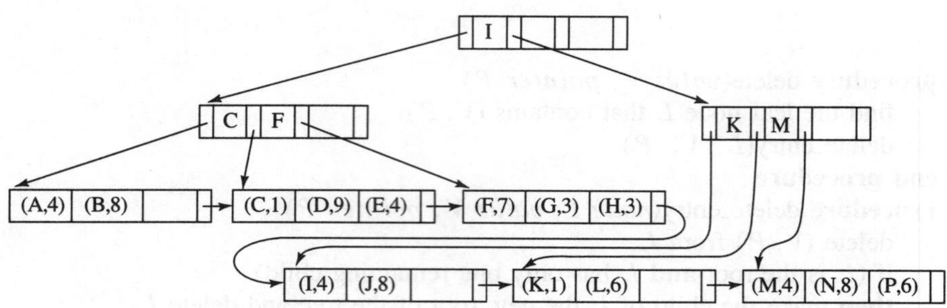

Figure 11.17 B$^+$-tree file organization.

attempt fails because the adjacent nodes are themselves full, we split the node, and split the entries evenly among one of the adjacent nodes and the two nodes that we obtained by splitting the original node. Since the three nodes together contain one more record than can fit in two nodes, each node will be about two thirds full. More precisely, each node will have at least $\lfloor 2n/3 \rfloor$ entries, where n is the maximum number of entries that the node can hold.

During deletion of a record, if the occupancy of a node falls below $\lfloor 2n/3 \rfloor$, we attempt to borrow an entry from one of the sibling nodes. If both sibling nodes have $\lfloor 2n/3 \rfloor$ records, instead of borrowing an entry, we redistribute the entries in the node and in the two siblings evenly between two of the nodes, and we delete the third node. We can use this approach because the total number of entries is $3\lfloor 2n/3 \rfloor - 1$, which is less than $2n$. With three adjacent nodes used for redistribution, each node can be guaranteed to have $\lfloor 3n/4 \rfloor$ entries. In general, if m nodes ($m - 1$ siblings) are involved in redistribution, each node can be guaranteed to contain at least $\lfloor (m-1)n/m \rfloor$ entries. However, the cost of update becomes higher as more sibling nodes are involved in the redistribution.

11.4 B-Tree Index Files

B-tree indices are similar to B$^+$-tree indices. The primary distinction between the two approaches is that a B-tree eliminates the redundant storage of search-key values. In the B$^+$-tree of Figure 11.11, the search keys "Downtown," "Mianus," "Redwood," and "Perryridge" appear twice. Every search-key value appears in some leaf node; several are repeated in nonleaf nodes.

A B-tree allows search-key values to appear only once. Figure 11.18 shows a B-tree that represents the same search keys as does the B$^+$-tree of Figure 11.11. Since search keys are not repeated in the B-tree, we may be able to store the index using fewer tree nodes than in the corresponding B$^+$-tree index. However, since search keys that appear in nonleaf nodes appear nowhere else in the B-tree, we are forced to include an additional pointer field for each search key in a nonleaf node. These additional pointers point to either file records or buckets for the associated search key.

A generalized B-tree leaf node appears in Figure 11.19a; a nonleaf node appears in Figure 11.19b. The pointers P_i are the tree pointers that we used

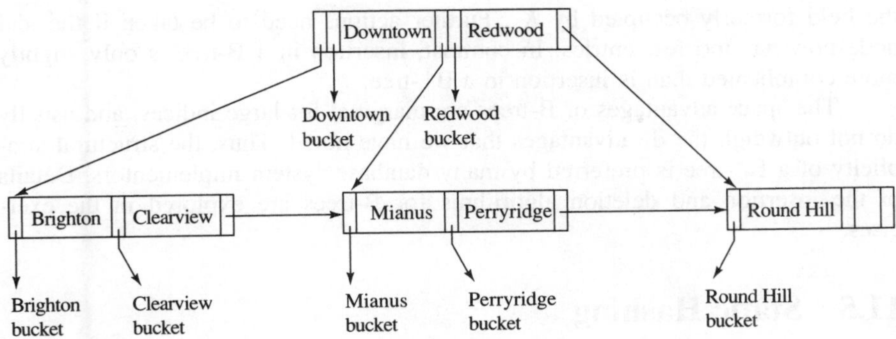

Figure 11.18 B-tree equivalent of B^+-tree in Figure 11.11.

also for B^+-trees. The pointers B_i in the nonleaf nodes are the bucket or file-record pointers. In the generalized B-tree in the figure, there are $n - 1$ keys in the leaf node, but there are $m - 1$ keys in the nonleaf node. This discrepancy occurs because nonleaf nodes must include pointers B_i, thus reducing the number of search keys that can be held in these nodes. Clearly, $m < n$, but the exact relationship between m and n depends on the relative size of search keys and pointers.

The number of nodes accessed in a lookup in a B-tree depends on where the search key is located. A lookup on a B^+-tree requires traversal of a path from the root of the tree to some leaf node. In contrast, it is sometimes possible to find the desired value in a B-tree before reaching a leaf node. However, roughly n times as many keys are stored in the leaf level of a B-tree as in the nonleaf levels, and, since n is typically large, the benefit of finding certain values early is relatively small. Moreover, the fact that fewer search keys appear in a nonleaf B-tree node, as compared to in B^+-trees, implies that a B-tree has a smaller fanout and therefore may have depth greater than that of the corresponding B^+-tree. Thus, lookup in a B-tree is faster for some search keys but slower for others, although, in general, lookup time is still proportional to the logarithm of the number of search keys.

Deletion in a B-tree is more complicated. In a B^+-tree, the deleted entry always appears in a leaf. In a B-tree, the deleted entry may appear in a nonleaf node. The proper value must be selected as a replacement from the subtree of the node containing the deleted entry. Specifically, if search key K_i is deleted, the smallest search key appearing in the subtree of pointer P_{i+1} must be moved to

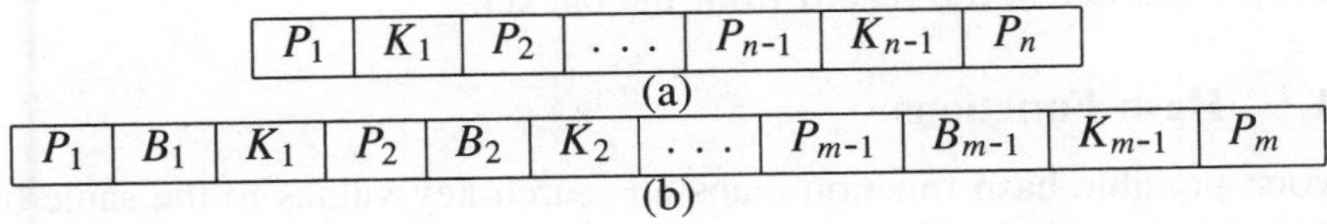

Figure 11.19 Typical nodes of a B-tree. (a) Leaf node. (b) Nonleaf node.

the field formerly occupied by K_i. Further actions need to be taken if the leaf node now has too few entries. In contrast, insertion in a B-tree is only slightly more complicated than is insertion in a B^+-tree.

The space advantages of B-trees are marginal for large indices, and usually do not outweigh the disadvantages that we have noted. Thus, the structural simplicity of a B^+-tree is preferred by many database system implementors. Details of the insertion and deletion algorithms for B-trees are explored in the exercises.

11.5 Static Hashing

One disadvantage of sequential file organization is that we must access an index structure to locate data, or must use binary search, and that results in more I/O operations. File organizations based on the technique of *hashing* allow us to avoid accessing an index structure. Hashing also provides a way of constructing indices. We study file organizations and indices based on hashing in the following sections.

11.5.1 Hash File Organization

In a hash file organization, we obtain the address of the disk block containing a desired record directly by computing a function on the search-key value of the record. In our description of hashing, we shall use the term *bucket* to denote a unit of storage that can store one or more records. A bucket is typically a disk block, but could be chosen to be smaller or larger than a disk block.

Formally, let K denote the set of all search-key values, and let B denote the set of all bucket addresses. A *hash function* h is a function from K to B. Let h denote a hash function.

To insert a record with search key K_i, we compute $h(K_i)$, which gives the address of the bucket for that record. Assume for now that there is space in the bucket to store the record. Then, the record is stored in that bucket.

To perform a lookup on a search-key value K_i, we simply compute $h(K_i)$, then search the bucket with that address. Suppose that two search keys, K_5 and K_7, have the same hash value; that is, $h(K_5) = h(K_7)$. If we perform a loyokup on K_5, the bucket $h(K_5)$ contains records with search-key values K_5 and records with search-key values K_7. Thus, we have to check the search-key value of every record in the bucket to verify that the record is one that we want.

Deletion is equally straightforward. If the search-key value of the record to be deleted is K_i, we compute $h(K_i)$, then search the corresponding bucket for that record, and delete the record from the bucket.

11.5.1.1 Hash Functions

The worst possible hash function maps all search-key values to the same bucket. This function is undesirable because all the records have to be kept in the same bucket. A lookup has to examine every such record to find the one desired. An ideal hash function distributes the stored keys uniformly across all the buckets, so that every bucket has the same number of records.

Since we do not know at design time precisely which search-key values will be stored in the file, we want to choose a hash function that assigns search-key values to buckets such that the following hold:

- The distribution is uniform. That is, each bucket is assigned the same number of search-key values from the set of *all* possible search-key values.
- The distribution is random. That is, in the average case, each bucket will have nearly the same number of values assigned to it, regardless of the actual distribution of search-key values. More precisely, the hash value will not be correlated to any externally visible ordering on the search-key values, such as alphabetic ordering or ordering by the length of the search keys; the hash function will appear to be random.

As an illustration of these principles, let us choose a hash function for the *account* file using the search key *branch-name*. The hash function that we choose must have the desirable properties not only on the example *account* file that we have been using, but also on an *account* file of realistic size for a large bank with many branches.

Assume that we decide to have 26 buckets, and we define a hash function that maps names beginning with the ith letter of the alphabet to the ith bucket. This hash function has the virtue of simplicity, but it fails to provide a uniform distribution, since we expect more branch names to begin with such letters as "B" and "R" than "Q" and "X," for example.

Now suppose that we want a hash function on the search key *balance*. Suppose that the minimum balance is 1 and the maximum balance is 100,000, and we use a hash function that divides the values into 10 ranges, 1–10,000, 10,001–20,000 and so on. The distribution of search-key values is uniform (since each bucket has the same number of different *balance* values), but is not random. But records with balances between 1 and 10,000 are far more common than are records with balances between 90,001 and 100,000. As a result, the distribution of records is not uniform—some buckets receive more records than others do. If the function has a random distribution, even if there are such correlations in the search keys, the randomness of the distribution will make it likely that all buckets will have roughly the same number of records.

Typical hash functions perform computation on the internal binary machine representation of characters in the search key. A simple hash function of this type first computes the sum of the binary representations of the characters of a key, then returns the sum modulo the number of buckets. Figure 11.20 shows the application of such a scheme, using 10 buckets, to the *account* file, under the assumption that the ith letter in the alphabet is represented by the integer i.

Hash functions require careful design. A bad hash function may result in lookup taking time proportional to the number of search keys in the file. A well-designed function gives an average-case lookup time that is a (small) constant, independent of the number of search keys in the file.

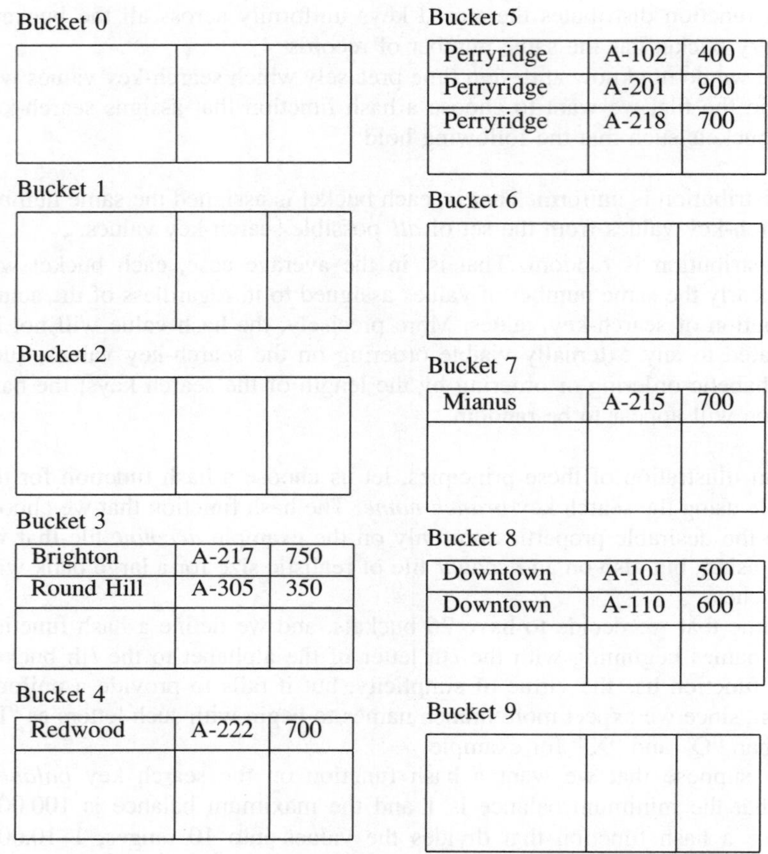

Bucket 0
Bucket 1
Bucket 2
Bucket 3
Brighton A-217 750
Round Hill A-305 350
Bucket 4
Redwood A-222 700
Bucket 5
Perryridge A-102 400
Perryridge A-201 900
Perryridge A-218 700
Bucket 6
Bucket 7
Mianus A-215 700
Bucket 8
Downtown A-101 500
Downtown A-110 600
Bucket 9

Figure 11.20 Hash organization of *account* file, using *branch-name* as the key.

11.5.1.2 Handling of Bucket Overflows

So far, we have assumed that, when a record is inserted, the bucket to which it is mapped has space to store the record. If the bucket does not have enough space, a *bucket overflow* is said to occur. Bucket overflow can occur for several reasons:

- **Insufficient buckets**. The number of buckets, which we denote n_B, must be chosen such that $n_B > n_r/f_r$, where n_r denotes the total number of records that will be stored, and f_r denotes the number of records that will fit in a bucket. This designation, of course, is under the assumption that the total number of records is known when the hash function is chosen.
- **Skew**. Some buckets are assigned more records than are others, so a bucket may overflow even when other buckets still have space. This situation is called bucket *skew*. Skew can occur for two reasons:
  1. Multiple records may have the same search key.

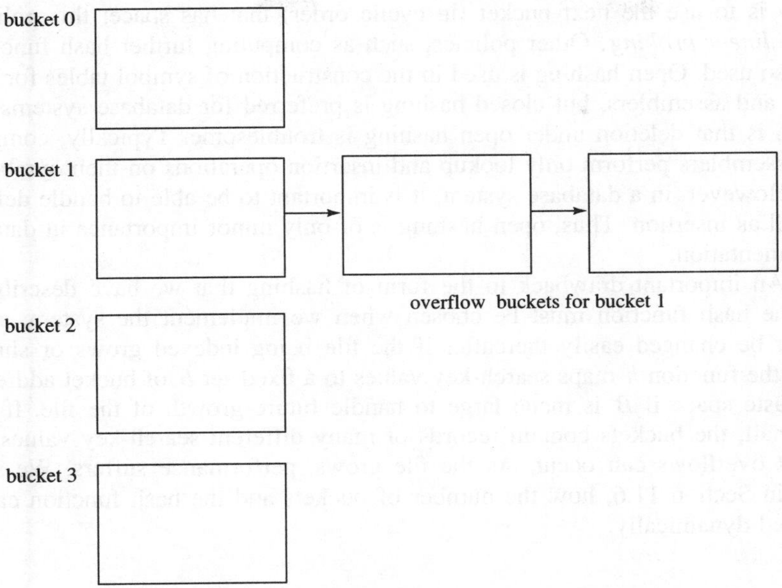

Figure 11.21 Overflow chaining in a hash structure.

2. The chosen hash function may result in nonuniform distribution of search keys.

So that the probability of bucket overflow is reduced, the number of buckets is chosen to be $(n_r/f_r) * (1 + d)$, where d is a fudge factor, typically around 0.2. Some space is wasted: About 20 percent of the space in the buckets will be empty. But the benefit is that the probability of overflow is reduced.

Despite allocation of a few more buckets than required, bucket overflow can still occur. We handle bucket overflow using *overflow buckets*. If a record must be inserted into a bucket b, and b is already full, an overflow bucket is provided for b, and the record is inserted into the overflow bucket. If the overflow bucket is also full, another overflow bucket is provided, and so on. All the overflow buckets of a given bucket are chained together in a linked list, as shown in Figure 11.21. Overflow handling using such a linked list is called *overflow chaining*.

We must change the lookup algorithm slightly to handle overflow chaining. As before, the hash function is used on the search key to identify a bucket b. We must examine all the records in bucket b to see whether they match the search key, as before. In addition, if bucket b has overflow buckets, the records in all the overflow buckets of b must also be examined.

The form of hash structure that we have just described is sometimes referred to as *closed hashing*. Under an alternative approach, called *open hashing*, the set of buckets is fixed, and there are no overflow chains. Instead, if a bucket is full, records are inserted in some other bucket in the initial set of buckets B. One policy is to use the next bucket (in cyclic order) that has space; this policy is called *linear probing*. Other policies, such as computing further hash functions, are also used. Open hashing is used in the construction of symbol tables for compilers and assemblers, but closed hashing is preferred for database systems. The reason is that deletion under open hashing is troublesome. Typically, compilers and assemblers perform only lookup and insertion operations on their symbol tables. However, in a database system, it is important to be able to handle deletion as well as insertion. Thus, open hashing is of only minor importance in database implementation.

An important drawback to the form of hashing that we have described is that the hash function must be chosen when we implement the system, and it cannot be changed easily thereafter if the file being indexed grows or shrinks. Since the function h maps search-key values to a fixed set B of bucket addresses, we waste space if B is made large to handle future growth of the file. If B is too small, the buckets contain records of many different search-key values, and bucket overflows can occur. As the file grows, performance suffers. We study later, in Section 11.6, how the number of buckets and the hash function can be changed dynamically.

11.5.2 Hash Indices

Hashing can be used not only for file organization, but also for index-structure creation. A *hash index* organizes the search keys, with their associated pointers, into a hash file structure. We construct a hash index as follows. We apply a hash function on a search key to identify a bucket, and store the key and its associated pointers in the bucket (or in overflow buckets). Figure 11.22 shows a secondary hash index on the *account* file, for the search key *account-number*. The hash function used computes the sum of the digits of the account number modulo 7. The hash index has seven buckets, each of size 2 (realistic indices would, of course, have much larger bucket sizes). One of the buckets has three keys mapped to it, so it has an overflow bucket. In this example, *account-number* is a primary key for *account*, so each search-key has only one associated pointer. In general, multiple pointers can be associated with each key.

We use the term *hash index* to denote hash file structures as well as secondary hash indices. Strictly speaking, hash indices are only secondary index structures. A hash index is never needed as a primary index structure, since, if a file itself is organized using hashing, there is no need for a separate hash index structure on it. However, since hash file organization provides the same direct access to records that is provided by indexing, we pretend that a file organized by hashing also has a virtual primary hash index on it.

11.6 Dynamic Hashing

As we have seen, the need to fix the set B of bucket addresses presents a serious problem with the static hashing technique of the previous section. Most databases grow larger over time. If we are to use static hashing for such a database, we

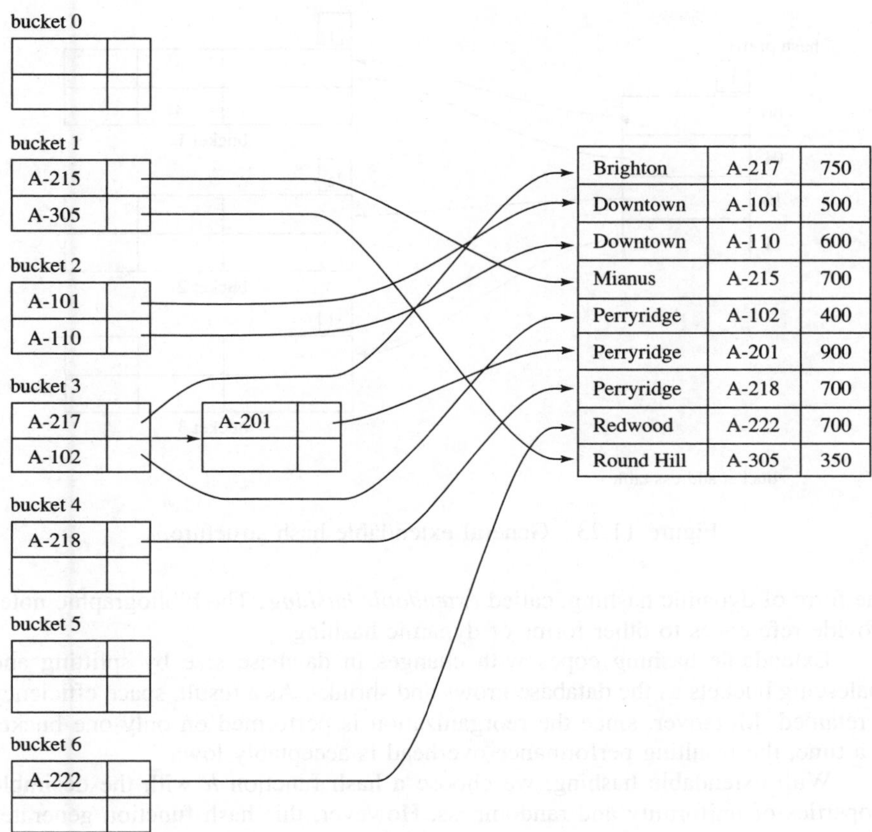

Figure 11.22 Hash index on search key *account-number* of *account* file.

have three classes of options:

1. Choose a hash function based on the current file size. This option will result in performance degradation as the database grows.
2. Choose a hash function based on the anticipated size of the file at some point in the future. Although performance degradation is avoided, a significant amount of space may be wasted initially.
3. Periodically reorganize the hash structure in response to file growth. Such a reorganization involves choosing a new hash function, recomputing the hash function on every record in the file, and generating new bucket assignments. This reorganization is a massive, time-consuming operation. Furthermore, it is necessary to forbid access to the file during reorganization.

Several *dynamic hashing techniques* allow the hash function to be modified dynamically to accommodate the growth or shrinkage of the database. We describe

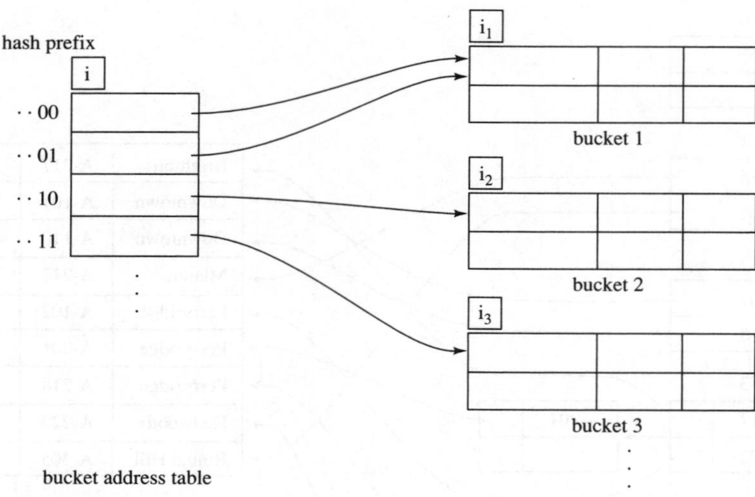

Figure 11.23 General extendable hash structure.

one form of dynamic hashing, called *extendable hashing*. The bibliographic notes provide references to other forms of dynamic hashing.

Extendable hashing copes with changes in database size by splitting and coalescing buckets as the database grows and shrinks. As a result, space efficiency is retained. Moreover, since the reorganization is performed on only one bucket at a time, the resulting performance overhead is acceptably low.

With extendable hashing, we choose a hash function h with the desirable properties of uniformity and randomness. However, this hash function generates values over a relatively large range—namely, b-bit binary integers. A typical value for b is 32.

We do not create a bucket for each hash value. Indeed, 2^{32} is over 4 billion, and that many buckets is unreasonable for all but the largest databases. Instead, we create buckets on demand, as records are inserted into the file. We do not use the entire b bits of the hash value initially. At any point, we use i bits, where $0 \leq i \leq b$. These i bits are used as an offset into an additional table of bucket addresses. The value of i grows and shrinks with the size of the database.

Figure 11.23 shows a general extendable hash structure. The i appearing above the bucket address table in the figure indicates that i bits of the hash value $h(K)$ are required to determine the correct bucket for K. This number will, of course, change as the file grows. Although i bits are required to find the correct entry in the bucket address table, several consecutive table entries may point to the same bucket. All such entries will have a common hash prefix, but the length of this prefix may be less than i. Therefore, we associate with each bucket an integer giving the length of the common hash prefix. In Figure 11.23 the integer associated with bucket j is shown as i_j. The number of bucket-address-table entries that point to bucket j is

$$2^{(i - i_j)}$$

To locate the bucket containing search-key value K_l, we take the first i high-order bits of $h(K_l)$, look at the corresponding table entry for this bit string, and follow the bucket pointer in the table entry.

To insert a record with search-key value K_l, we follow the same procedure for lookup as before, ending up in some bucket—say, j. If there is room in the bucket, we insert the record in the bucket. If, on the other hand, the bucket is full, we must split the bucket and redistribute the current records, plus the new one. To split the bucket, we must first determine from the hash value whether we need to increase the number of bits that we use.

- If $i = i_j$, only one entry in the bucket address table points to bucket j. Therefore, we need to increase the size of the bucket address table so that we can include pointers to the two buckets that result from splitting bucket j. We do so by considering an additional bit of the hash value. We increment the value of i by 1, thus doubling the size of the bucket address table. Each entry is replaced by two entries, both of which contain the same pointer as the original entry. Now two entries in the bucket address table point to bucket j. We allocate a new bucket (bucket z), and set the second entry to point to the new bucket. We set i_j and i_z to i. Next, each record in bucket j is rehashed and, depending on the first i bits (remember we have added 1 to i), is either kept in bucket j or allocated to the newly created bucket.

  We now reattempt the insertion of the new record. Usually, the attempt will succeed. However, if all the records in bucket j, as well as the new record, have the same hash-value prefix, it will be necessary to split a bucket again, since all the records in bucket j and the new record are assigned to the same bucket. If the hash function has been chosen carefully, it is unlikely that a single insertion will require that a bucket be split more than once, unless there are a large number of records with the same search key. If all the records in bucket j have the same search-key value, no amount of splitting will help. In such cases, overflow buckets are used to store the records, as in static hashing.

- If $i > i_j$, then more than one entry in the bucket address table points to bucket j. Thus, we can split bucket j without increasing the size of the bucket address table. Observe that all the entries that point to bucket j correspond to hash prefixes that have the same value on the leftmost i_j bits. We allocate a new bucket (bucket z), and set i_j and i_z to the value that results from adding 1 to the original i_j value. Next, we need to adjust the entries in the bucket address table that previously pointed to bucket j. (Note that with the new value for i_j, not all the entries correspond to hash prefixes that have the same value on the leftmost i_j bits.) We leave the first half of the entries as they were (pointing to bucket j), and set all the remaining entries to point to the newly created bucket (bucket z). Next, as in the case we saw previously, each record in bucket j is rehashed, and is allocated either to bucket j or to the newly created bucket z.

  The insert is then reattempted. In the unlikely case that it again fails, we apply one of the two cases, $i = i_j$ or $i > i_j$, as appropriate.

Brighton	A-217	750
Downtown	A-101	500
Downtown	A-110	600
Mianus	A-215	700
Perryridge	A-102	400
Perryridge	A-201	900
Perryridge	A-218	700
Redwood	A-222	700
Round Hill	A-305	350

Figure 11.24 Sample *account* file.

Note that, in both cases, we need to recompute the hash function on only the records in bucket j.

To delete a record with search-key value K_l, we follow the same procedure for lookup as before, ending up in some bucket—say, j. We remove both the search key from the bucket and the record from the file. The bucket too is removed if it becomes empty. Note that, at this point, several buckets can be coalesced, and the size of the bucket address table can be cut in half. The procedure for deciding on when and how to coalesce buckets is left to your to do as an exercise.

We illustrate the operation of insertion using our example *account* file (Figure 11.24). The 32-bit hash values on *branch-name* are shown in Figure 11.25. We assume that, initially, the file is empty, as shown in Figure 11.26. We insert the records one by one. To illustrate all the features of extendable hashing using a small structure, we shall make the unrealistic assumption that a bucket can hold only two records.

Let us insert the record (Brighton, A-217, 750). The bucket address table contains a pointer to the one bucket, and the record is inserted. Next, let us insert the record (Downtown, A-101, 500). This record also is placed in the one bucket of our structure.

When we attempt to insert the next record (Downtown, A-110, 600), we find that the bucket is full. Since $i = i_0$, we need to increase the number of bits

branch-name	h(*branch-name*)
Brighton	0010 1101 1111 1011 0010 1100 0011 0000
Downtown	1010 0011 1010 0000 1100 0110 1001 1111
Mianus	1100 0111 1110 1101 1011 1111 0011 1010
Perryridge	1111 0001 0010 0100 1001 0011 0110 1101
Redwood	0011 0101 1010 0110 1100 1001 1110 1011
Round Hill	1101 1000 0011 1111 1001 1100 0000 0001

Figure 11.25 Hash function for *branch-name*.

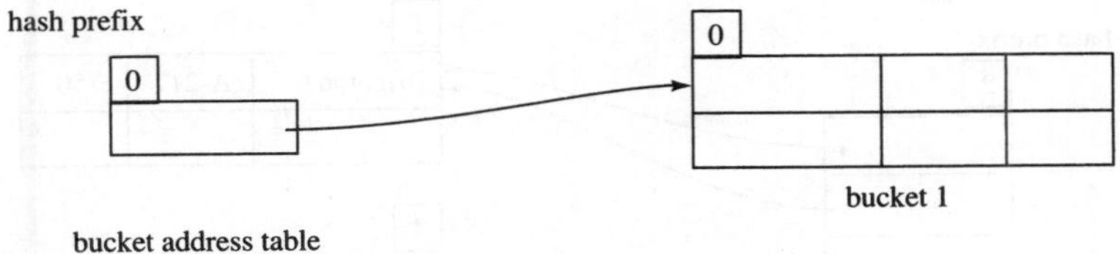

Figure 11.26 Initial extendable hash structure.

that we use from the hash value. We now use 1 bit, allowing us $2^1 = 2$ buckets. This increase in the number of bits necessitates doubling the size of the bucket address table to two entries. We split the bucket, placing in the new bucket those records whose search key has a hash value beginning with 1, and leaving in the original bucket the other records. Figure 11.27 shows the state of our structure after the split.

Next, we insert (Mianus, A-215, 700). Since the first bit of h(Mianus) is 1, we must insert this record into the bucket pointed to by the "1" entry in the bucket address table. Once again, we find the bucket full and $i = i_1$. We increase the number of bits that we use from the hash to 2. This increase in the number of bits necessitates doubling the size of the bucket address table to four entries, as shown in Figure 11.28. Since the bucket of Figure 11.27 for hash prefix 0 was not split, the two entries of the bucket address table of 00 and 01 both point to this bucket.

For each record in the bucket of Figure 11.27 for hash prefix 1 (the bucket being split), we examine the first 2 bits of the hash value to determine which bucket of the new structure should hold it.

Next, we insert (Perryridge, A-102, 400), which goes in the same bucket as Mianus. The following insertion, of (Perryridge, A-201, 900), results in a bucket overflow, leading to an increase in the number of bits, and a doubling of the size of the bucket address table. The insertion of the third Perryridge record, (Perryridge, A-218, 700), leads to another overflow. However, this overflow cannot be handled

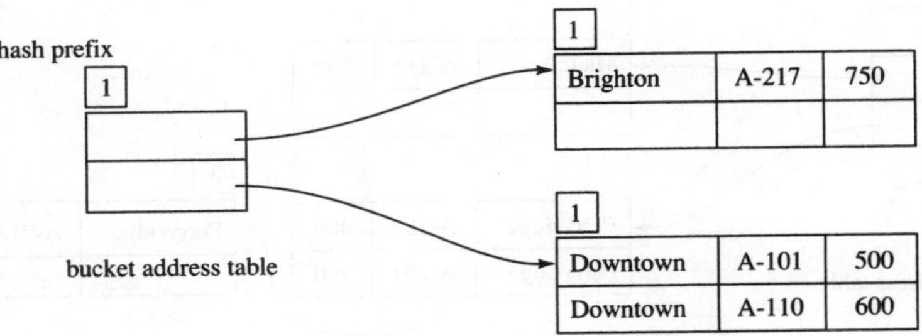

Figure 11.27 Hash structure after three insertions.

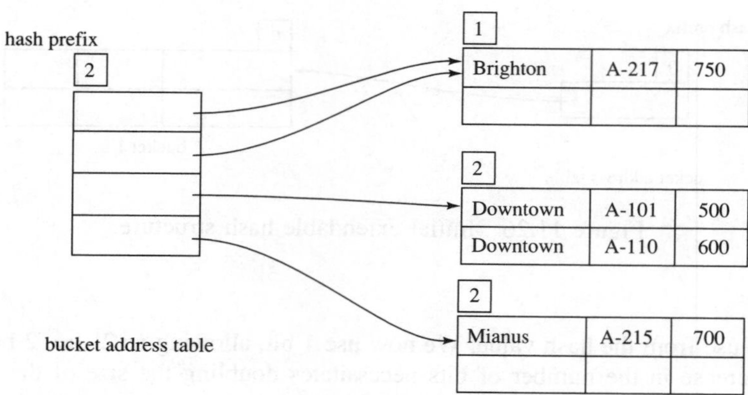

Figure 11.28 Hash structure after four insertions.

by increasing the number of bits, since there are three records with exactly the same hash value. Hence an overflow bucket is used, as shown in Figure 11.29.

We continue in this manner until we have inserted all the *account* records of Figure 11.24. The resulting structure is shown in Figure 11.30.

Let us now examine the advantages and disadvantages of extendable hashing, as compared with the other schemes that we have discussed. The main advantage of extendable hashing is that performance does not degrade as the file grows. Furthermore, there is minimal space overhead. Although the bucket address table incurs additional overhead, it contains one pointer for each hash value for the

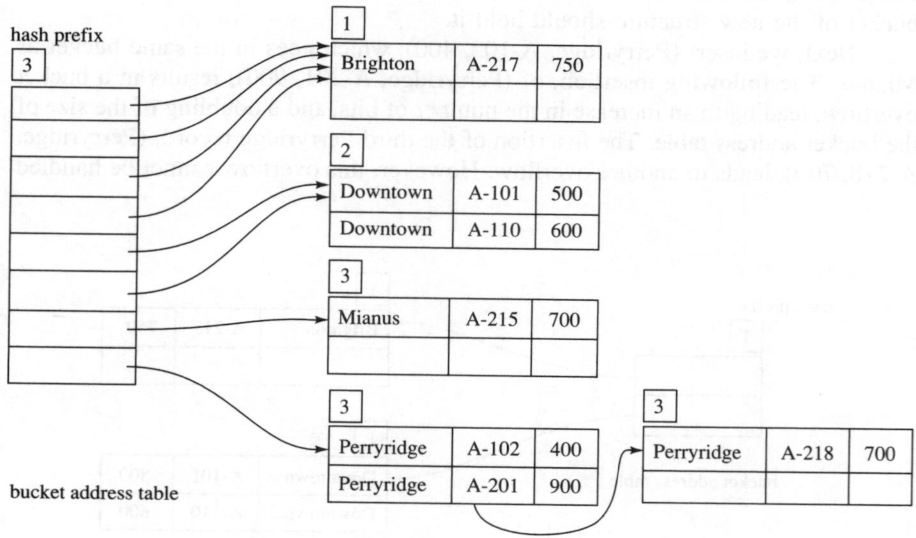

Figure 11.29 Hash structure after seven insertions.

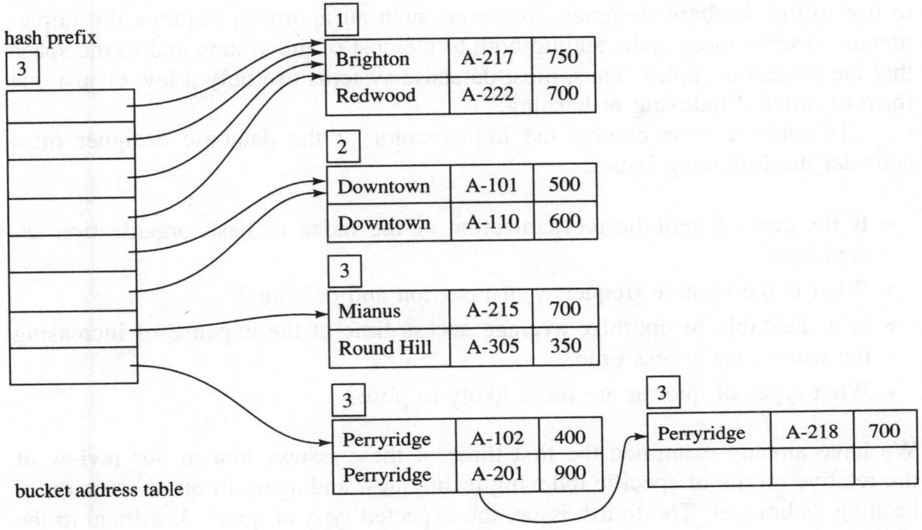

Figure 11.30 Extendable hash structure for the *account* file.

current prefix length. This table is thus small. The main space saving of extendable hashing over other forms of hashing is that no buckets need to be reserved for future growth; rather, buckets can be allocated dynamically.

A disadvantage of extendable hashing is that lookup involves an additional level of indirection, since we must access the bucket address table before accessing the bucket itself. This extra reference has only a minor effect on performance. Although the hash structures that we discussed earlier do not have this extra level of indirection, they lose their minor performance advantage as they become full.

Thus, extendable hashing appears to be a highly attractive technique, provided that we are willing to accept the added complexity involved in its implementation. More detailed descriptions of the implementation of extendable hashing are referenced in the bibliographic notes. The bibliographic notes also provide references to another form of dynamic hashing called *linear hashing*, which avoids the extra level of indirection associated with extendable hashing, at the possible cost of more overflow buckets.

11.7 Comparison of Ordered Indexing and Hashing

We have seen several ordered-indexing schemes and several hashing schemes. We can organize files of records as ordered files, using index-sequential organization, or using B^+-tree organizations. Alternatively, we can organize the files using hashing. Finally, we can organize them as heap files, where the records are not ordered in any particular way.

Each scheme has advantages in certain situations. A database-system implementor could provide many schemes, leaving the final decision of which schemes to use to the database designer. However, such an approach requires the implementor to write more code, adding both to the cost of the system and to the space that the system occupies. Thus, most database systems use only a few or just one form of ordered indexing or hashing.

To make a wise choice, the implementor or the database designer must consider the following issues:

- Is the cost of periodic reorganization of the index or hash organization acceptable?
- What is the relative frequency of insertion and deletion?
- Is it desirable to optimize average access time at the expense of increasing the worst-case access time?
- What types of queries are users likely to pose?

We have already examined the first three of these issues, first in our review of the relative merits of specific indexing techniques, and again in our discussion of hashing techniques. The fourth issue, the expected type of query, is critical to the choice of ordered indexing or hashing.

If most queries are of the form

select $A_1, A_2, ..., A_n$
from r
where $A_i = c$

then, to process this query, the system will perform a lookup on an ordered index or a hash structure for attribute A_i, for value c. For queries of this form, a hashing scheme is preferable. An ordered-index lookup requires time proportional to the log of the number of values in r for A_i. In a hash structure, however, the average lookup time is a constant independent of the size of the database. The only advantage to an index over a hash structure for this form of query is that the worst-case lookup time is proportional to the log of the number of values in r for A_i. By contrast, if hashing is used, the worst-case lookup time is proportional to the number of values in r for A_i. However, the worst-case lookup time is unlikely to occur with hashing, and hashing is preferable in this case.

Ordered-index techniques are preferable to hashing in cases where a range of values is specified in the query. Such a query takes the following form:

select $A_1, A_2, ..., A_n$
from r
where $A_i \leq c_2$ **and** $A_i \geq c_1$

In other words, the preceding query finds all records with A_i values between c_1 and c_2.

Let us consider how we process this query using an ordered index. First, we perform a lookup on value c_1. Once we have found the bucket for value c_1, we follow the pointer chain in the index to read the next bucket in order, and we continue in this manner until we reach c_2.

If, instead of an ordered index, we have a hash structure, we can perform a lookup on c_1 and can locate the corresponding bucket—but it is not easy, in general, to determine the next bucket that must be examined. The difficulty arises because a good hash function assigns values randomly to buckets. Thus, there is no simple notion of "next bucket in sorted order." The reason we cannot chain buckets together in sorted order on A_i is that each bucket is assigned many search-key values. Since values are scattered randomly by the hash function, the values in the specified range are likely to be scattered across many or all of the buckets. Therefore, we have to read all the buckets to find the required search keys.

Typically, ordered indexing is used unless it is known in advance that range queries will be infrequent, in which case hashing is used. Hash organizations are particularly useful for temporary files created during query processing, if lookups based on a key value are required, but no range queries will be performed.

11.8 Index Definition in SQL

The SQL standard does not provide any way for the database user or administrator to control what indices are created and maintained in the database system. Indices are not required for correctness, since they are redundant data structures. However, indices are important for efficient processing of transactions, including both update transactions and queries. Indices are also important for efficient enforcement of integrity constraints. For example, typical implementations enforce a key declaration (Chapter 6) by creating an index with the declared key as the search key of the index.

In principle, a database system can decide automatically what indices to create. However, due to the space cost of indices, as well as to the effect of indices on update processing, it is not easy to make the right choices automatically on what indices to maintain. Therefore, most SQL implementations provide the programmer control over creation and removal of indices via data-definition-language commands. We illustrate the syntax of these commands next. Although the syntax that we show is not part of the SQL-92 standard, it is widely used and supported by many database systems.

An index is created by the **create index** command, which takes the form

create index <index-name> **on** <relation-name> (<attribute-list>)

The *attribute-list* is the list of attributes of the relations that form the search key for the index.

To define an index name *b-index* on the *branch* relation with *branch-name* as the search key, we write

create index *b-index* **on** *branch* (*branch-name*)

If we wish to declare that the search key is a candidate key, we add the attribute **unique** to the index definition. Thus, the command

create unique index *b-index* **on** *branch* (*branch-name*) declares *branch-name* to be a candidate key for *branch*. If, at the time the **create unique index** command is entered, *branch-name* is not a candidate key, an error message will be displayed, and the attempt to create the index will fail. If the index-creation attempt succeeds, any subsequent attempt to insert a tuple that violates the key declaration will fail. Note that the **unique** feature is redundant if the **unique** declaration of the SQL standard is supported by the database system.

The index name specified for an index is required so that it is possible to drop indices. The **drop index** command takes the form:

drop index <index-name>

11.9 Multiple-Key Access

Until now, we have assumed implicitly that only one index (or hash table) is used to process a query on a relation. However, for certain types of queries, it is advantageous to use multiple indices if they exist.

Assume that the *account* file has two indices: one for *branch-name* and one for *balance*. Consider the following query: "Find all account numbers at the Perryridge branch with balances equal to $1000." We write

select *loan-number*
from *account*
where *branch-name* = "Perryridge" **and** *balance* = 1000

There are three strategies possible for processing this query:

1. Use the index on *branch-name* to find all records pertaining to the Perryridge branch. Examine each such record to see whether *balance* = 1000.
2. Use the index on *balance* to find all records pertaining to accounts with balances of $1000. Examine each such record to see whether *branch-name* = "Perryridge."
3. Use the index on *branch-name* to find *pointers* to all records pertaining to the Perryridge branch. Also, use the index on *balance* to find pointers to all records pertaining to accounts with a balance of $1000. Take the intersection of these two sets of pointers. Those pointers that are in the intersection point to records pertaining to both Perryridge and accounts with a balance of $1000.

The third strategy is the only one of the three that takes advantage of the existence of multiple indices. However, even this strategy may be a poor choice if all of the following hold:

- There are many records pertaining to the Perryridge branch.
- There are many records pertaining to accounts with a balance of $1000.
- There are only a few records pertaining to *both* the Perryridge branch and accounts with a balance of $1000.

If these conditions hold, we must scan a large number of pointers to produce a small result.

A more efficient strategy for this case is to create and use an index on a search key (*branch-name*, *balance*)—that is, the search key consisting of the branch name concatenated with the account balance. The structure of the index is the same as that of any other index, the only difference being that the search key is not a single attribute, but rather is a list of attributes. The search key can be represented as a tuple of values, of the form $(a_1, \ldots, a_n)$, where the indexed attributes are $A_1, \ldots, A_n$. The ordering of search-key values is the *lexicographic ordering*. For example, for the case of two attribute search keys, $(a_1, a_2) < (b_1, b_2)$ if either $a_1 < b_1$, or $a_1 = b_1$ and $a_2 < b_2$. Lexicographic ordering is basically the same as alphabetic ordering of words.

The use of an ordered-index structure on multiple attributes has a few shortcomings. As an illustration, consider the query

> **select** *loan-number*
> **from** *account*
> **where** *branch-name* < "Perryridge" **and** *balance* = 1000

We can answer this query using an ordered index on the search key (*branch-name*, *balance*) as follows: For each value of *branch-name* that is less than "Perryridge" in alphabetic order, records with a *balance* value of 1000 are located. However, each record is likely to be in a different disk block, due to the ordering of records in the file, leading to many I/O operations.

The difference between this query and the previous one is that the condition on *branch-name* is a comparison condition, rather than an equality condition.

To speed the processing of general multiple search-key queries (which can involve one or more comparison operations), we can use several special structures. We shall consider two such structures: the *grid file* and *partitioned hashing*. There is another structure, called the *R-tree*, which can be used for this purpose. Since it is a comparatively complex structure, we postpone its description to Chapter 21.

11.9.1 Grid Files

Figure 11.31 shows part of a grid file for the search keys *branch-name* and *balance* on the *account* file. The two-dimensional array in the figure is called the *grid array*, and the one-dimensional arrays are called *linear scales*. The grid file has a single grid array, and one linear scale for each search-key attribute.

Search keys are mapped to cells in a manner described next. Each cell in the grid array has a pointer to a bucket that contains the search-key values and pointers to records. Only some of the buckets and pointers from the cells are shown in the figure. So that space is conserved, multiple elements of the array can point to the same bucket. The dotted boxes in the figure indicate which cells point to the same bucket.

Suppose that we want to insert in the grid-file index a record whose search-key value is ("Brighton", 500000). To find the cell to which the key is mapped, we independently locate the row and column to which the cell belongs.

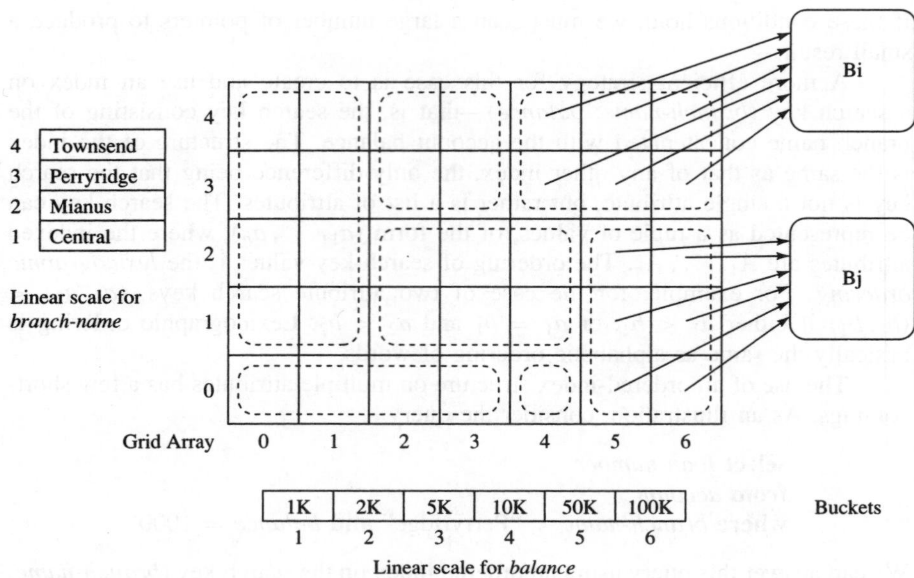

Figure 11.31 Grid file on keys *branch-name* and *balance* of the *account* file.

We first use the linear scales on *branch-name* to locate the row of the cell to which the search key maps. To do so, we search the array to find the least element that is greater than "Brighton". In this case, it is the first element, so the search key maps to the row marked 0. If it were the ith element, the search key would map to row $i-1$. If the search key is greater than or equal to all elements in the linear scale, it maps to the final row. Next, we use the linear scale on *balance* to find out similarly to which column the search key maps. In this case, the balance 500,000 maps to column 6.

Thus, the search-key value ("Brighton", 500000) maps to the cell in row 0, column 6. Similarly, ("Downtown", 60000) would map to the cell in row 1 column 5. Both cells point to the same bucket (as indicated by the dotted box), so, in both cases, the search-key values and the pointer to the record are stored in the bucket labeled B_j in the figure.

To perform a lookup to answer our example query, with the search condition of

$$branch\text{-}name < \text{"Perryridge"} \textbf{ and } balance = 1000$$

we find all rows that can contain branch names less than "Perryridge", using the linear scale on *branch-name*. In this case, these rows are 0, 1, and 2. Rows 3 and beyond contain branch names greater than or equal to "Perryridge". Similarly, we find that only column 1 can contain a *balance* value of 1000. In this case, only column 1 satisfies this condition. Thus, only the cells in column 1, rows 0, 1, and 2 can contain entries that satisfy the search condition.

We therefore look up all entries in the buckets pointed to from these three cells. In this case, there are only two buckets, since two of the cells point to the same bucket, as indicated by the dotted boxes in the figure. The buckets may contain some search keys that do not satisfy the required condition, so each search key in the buckets must be tested again to see whether it satisfies the search condition. We have to examine only a small number of buckets, however, to answer this query.

The linear scales must be chosen such that the records are uniformly distributed across the cells. If the bucket—call it A—becomes full and an entry has to be inserted in it, an extra bucket B is allocated. If more than one cell points to A, the cell pointers are changed such that some point to A and others to B. The entries in the bucket A and the new entry are then redistributed between A and B based on to which cells they map. If only one cell points to bucket A, B becomes an overflow bucket for A. To improve performance in such a situation, we must reorganize the grid file, with an expanded grid array and expanded linear scales. The process is much like the expansion of the bucket address table in extensible hashing, and is left for you to do as an exercise.

It is conceptually simple to extend the grid-file approach to any number of search keys. If we want our structure to be used for queries on n keys, we construct an n-dimensional grid array with n linear scales.

The grid structure is suitable also for queries involving one search key. Consider this query:

select *
from *account*
where *branch-name* = "Perryridge"

The linear scale on *branch-name* tells us that only cells in row 3 can satisfy this condition. Since there is no condition on *balance*, we examine all buckets pointed to by cells in row 3 to find entries pertaining to Perryridge. Thus, we can use a grid-file index on two search keys to answer queries on either search key by itself, as well as to answer queries on both search keys. Thus, a single grid-file index can serve the role of three separate indices. If each index were maintained separately, the three together would occupy more space, and the cost of updating them would be high.

Grid files provide a significant decrease in processing time for multiple-key queries. However, they impose a space overhead (the grid directory can become large), as well as a performance overhead on record insertion and deletion. Further, it is hard to choose partitioning ranges for the keys such that the distribution of records is uniform. If insertions to the file are frequent, reorganization will have to be carried out periodically, and that can have a high cost.

11.9.2 Partitioned Hashing

Partitioned hashing is an extension of hashing that allows indexing on multiple attributes. A partitioned hash structure allows queries on individual attributes, as well as queries that involve multiple attributes, although it does not support range

search-key value	*hash value*
(Main, Harrison)	101 111
(North, Rye)	110 101
(Main, Brooklyn)	101 001
(North, Princeton)	110 000
(Park, Palo Alto)	010 010
(Putnam, Stamford)	011 001
(Nassau, Princeton)	011 000
(Spring, Brooklyn)	001 001
(Alma, Palo Alto)	110 010

Figure 11.32 Partitioned hash function for key (*customer-street*, *customer-city*).

queries. Suppose that we wish to construct a structure suitable for queries on the *customer* file involving *customer-name*, *customer-street*, and *customer-city*. We construct a hash structure for the key (*customer-street, customer-city*). The only difference between the structure that we shall create and those we saw earlier is that we impose an additional constraint on the hash function h. Hash values are split into two parts. The first part depends on only the *customer-street* value; the second part depends on only the *customer-city* value. The hash function is called *partitioned* because the hash values are split into segments that depend on each element of the key.

Figure 11.32 shows a sample hash function in which the first 3 bits depend on *customer-street*, and the final 3 bits depend on *customer-city*. Thus, the hash values for (Main, Harrison) and (Main, Brooklyn) agree on the first 3 bits, and the hash values for (Park, Palo Alto) and (Alma, Palo Alto) agree on the last 3 bits.

We can use the partitioned hash function of Figure 11.32 to answer the query, "Find the names of all customers who live on Main Street in Brooklyn." We simply compute h(Main, Brooklyn), and access the hash structure. The same hash structure is suitable for a query involving only one of the two search keys. To find all records pertaining to the customers who live in Brooklyn, we compute *part* of the partitioned hash. Since we have only the *customer-city* value, we are able to compute only the last 3 bits of the hash. For the value "Brooklyn," these 3 bits are 001. We access the hash structure, then scan those buckets for which the last 3 bits of the hash value are 001. In the example of Figure 11.32, we access the buckets for hash values 101 001, 011 001, and 001 001.

Partitioned hashing extends to an arbitrary number of attributes. There are several improvements that we can make in partitioned hashing if we know how frequently a user will specify each attribute in a query. The bibliographic notes reference these techniques. Using partitioned hashing is similar to using grid files, with two differences. First, hash partitioning is used on the key values, instead of range partitioning. Second, there is no directory; instead, the hash value directly gives a bucket address.

Several other hybrid techniques for processing multiple-key queries exist. Such techniques may be useful in applications where the system implementor knows that most queries will be of a restricted form. Again, references to some of the more interesting techniques appear in the bibliographic notes.

11.10 Summary

Many queries reference only a small proportion of the records in a file. To reduce the overhead in searching for these records, we can construct *indices* for the files that store the database.

Index-sequential files are one of the oldest index schemes used in database systems. They are designed for applications that require both sequential processing of the entire file and random access to individual records. To permit fast retrieval of records in search-key order, we chain together records by pointers. To allow fast random access, we use an index structure. There are two types of indices that we can use: dense indices and sparse indices.

In a standard index-sequential file, only one index is maintained. If several indices on different search keys are used, the index whose search key specifies the sequential order of the file is the *primary index*. The other indices are called *secondary indices*. Secondary indices improve the performance of queries that use search keys other than the primary one. However, they impose an overhead on modification of the database.

The primary disadvantage of the index-sequential file organization is that performance degrades as the file grows. To overcome this deficiency, we can use a B^+*-tree index*. A B^+-tree index takes the form of a *balanced* tree, in which every path from the root of the tree to a leaf of the tree is of the same length. Lookup in this scheme is straightforward and efficient. Insertion and deletion, however, are more complicated. Nevertheless, the number of operations required for insertion and deletion on B^+-trees is proportional to the logarithm to the base N of the size of the database, where each nonleaf node stores N pointers. Thus, B^+-trees are shorter than other balanced binary-tree structures such as AVL trees, and therefore require fewer disk accesses to locate records. We can use B^+-trees for indexing a file containing records, as well as to organize records into a file.

B-tree indices are similar to B^+-tree indices. The primary advantage of a B-tree is that the B-tree eliminates the redundant storage of search-key values. The major disadvantages are overall complexity and reduced fanout for a given node size. B^+-tree indices are almost universally preferred over B-tree indices in practice.

Sequential file organizations require an index structure to locate data. File organizations based on hashing, by contrast, allow us to find the address of a data item directly by computing a function on the search-key value of the desired record. Since we do not know at design time precisely which search-key values will be stored in the file, a good hash function to choose is one that assigns search-key values to buckets such that the distribution is both uniform and random.

Static hashing uses hash functions in which the set of bucket addresses is fixed. Such hash functions cannot easily accommodate databases that grow significantly larger over time. There are several *dynamic hashing techniques* that allow the hash function to be modified. One example is *extendable hashing*, which copes with changes in database size by splitting and coalescing buckets as the database grows and shrinks.

We can also use hashing to create secondary indices; such indices are called *hash indices*. For notational convenience, hash file organizations are assumed to have an implicit hash index on the search key used for hashing.

Ordered indices such as B^+-trees and hash indices can be used for indexing based on equality conditions involving multiple attributes. Indexing techniques such as the grid file and partitioned hashing handle the general case of indexing with multiple attributes.

Exercises

11.1. When is it preferable to use a dense index rather than a sparse index? Explain your answer.

11.2. Since indices speed query processing, why might they not be kept on several search keys? List as many reasons as possible.

11.3. What is the difference between a primary index and a secondary index?

11.4. Is it possible in general to have two primary indices on the same relation for different search keys? Explain your answer.

11.5. Construct a B^+-tree for the following set of key values:

$$(2, 3, 5, 7, 11, 17, 19, 23, 29, 31)$$

Assume that the tree is initially empty and values are added in ascending order. Construct B^+-trees for the cases where the number of pointers that will fit in one node is as follows:

(*a*) four
(*b*) six
(*c*) eight

11.6. For each B^+-tree of Exercise 11.5, show the steps involved in the following queries:

(*a*) Find records with a search-key value of 11.
(*b*) Find records with a search-key value between 7 and 17, inclusive.

11.7. For each B^+-tree of Exercise 11.5, show the form of the tree after each of the following series of operations:

(*a*) Insert 9.
(*b*) Insert 11.
(*c*) Insert 11.
(*d*) Delete 23.
(*e*) Delete 19.

11.8. Consider the modified redistribution scheme for B^+-trees described in page 354. What is the expected height of the tree as a function of n?

11.9. Repeat Exercise 11.5 for a B-tree.

11.10. Explain the distinction between closed and open hashing. Discuss the relative merits of each technique in database applications.

11.11. What are the causes of bucket overflow in a hash file organization? What can be done to reduce the occurrence of bucket overflows?

11.12. Suppose that we are using extendable hashing on a file that contains records with the following search-key values:

2, 3, 5, 7, 11, 17, 19, 23, 29, 31.

Show the extendable hash structure for this file if the hash function is $h(x) = x \bmod 8$ and buckets can hold three records.

11.13. Show how the extendable hash structure of Exercise 11.12 changes as the result of each of the following steps:
(*a*) Delete 11.
(*b*) Delete 31.
(*c*) Insert 1.
(*d*) Insert 15.

11.14. Why is a hash structure not the best choice for a search key on which range queries are likely?

11.15. Consider a grid file in which we wish to avoid overflow buckets for performance reasons. In cases where an overflow bucket would be needed, we instead reorganize the grid file. Present an algorithm for such a reorganization.

Bibliographic Notes

Discussions concerning the basic data structures used in indexing and hashing can be found in Cormen et al. [1990]. B-tree indices were first introduced in Bayer [1972] and Bayer and McCreight [1972], B^+-trees are discussed in Comer [1979], Bayer and Unterauer [1977], and Knuth [1973]. Bayer and Schkolnick [1977] and Shasha and Goodman [1988] analyze the problem of managing a B-tree index for a file updated concurrently by several processes. Other discussions of concurrency control within B-trees and similar data structures include those of Lehman and Yao [1981], Kung and Lehman [1980], and Ford and Calhoun [1984]. Gray and Reuter [1993] provide a good description of issues in the implementation of B^+-trees.

Several alternative tree and treelike search structures have been proposed. Tries are trees whose structure is based on the "digits" of keys (for example, a dictionary thumb index, which has one entry for each letter). Such trees may not be balanced in the sense that B^+-trees are. Tries are discussed by Ramesh et al. [1989], Orestein [1982], Litwin [1981], and Fredkin [1960]. Related work includes the digital B-trees of Lomet [1981].

Knuth [1973] analyzes a large number of different hashing techniques. Several dynamic hashing schemes exist. Extendable hashing was introduced by Fagin et al. [1979]. Linear hashing was introduced by Litwin [1978, 1980]; a performance analysis of that scheme was presented by Larson [1982]. Concurrency with linear hashing is examined by Ellis [1987]. A variant of linear hashing is presented by Larson [1988]. Another scheme, called dynamic hashing, was proposed by Larson [1978]. An alternative given by Ramakrishna and Larson [1989] allows retrieval in a single disk access at the price of a high overhead for a small fraction of database modifications.

The grid file structure appears in Nievergelt et al. [1984], and in Hinrichs [1985]. Partitioned hash functions have been applied to several index structures. Partial-match retrieval uses a partitioned hash function to limit the number of buckets to be searched when a multiple-key query is processed; see Rivest [1976], Burkhard [1976, 1979], and Ullman [1988]. King et al. [1983] use a combination of extendable hashing and partitioned hash functions in an index structure designed for multiple-key queries that include subset queries (as in keyword-based retrieval). Optimal choice of partitioning for a partitioned hash function is discussed in Bolour [1979], and in Aho and Ullman [1979].

CHAPTER
12

QUERY PROCESSING

Query processing refers to the range of activities involved in extracting data from a database. These activities include translation of queries expressed in high-level database languages into expressions that can be implemented at the physical level of the file system, a variety of query-optimizing transformations, and actual evaluation of queries.

The cost of processing a query is usually dominated by disk access, which is slow compared to memory access. There are usually many possible strategies for processing a given query, especially if the query is complex. The difference between a good strategy and a bad strategy, in terms of the number of disk accesses required, is often substantial, and may be several orders of magnitude. Hence, it is worthwhile for the system to spend a substantial amount of time on the selection of a good strategy for processing a query, even if the query is executed only once.

12.1 Overview

The steps involved in processing a query are illustrated in Figure 12.1. The basic steps are

1. Parsing and translation
2. Optimization
3. Evaluation

Before query processing can begin, the system must translate the query into a usable form. A language such as SQL is suitable for human use, but is ill-suited

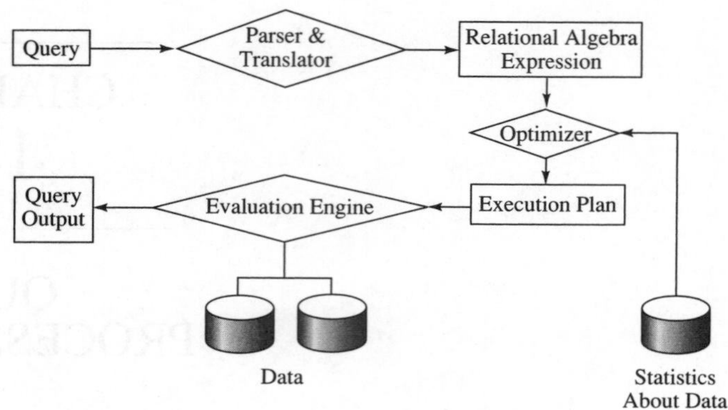

Figure 12.1 Steps in query processing.

to be the system's internal representation of a query. A more useful internal representation is one based on the extended relational algebra.

Thus, the first action the system must take in query processing is to translate a given query into its internal form. This translation process is similar to the work performed by the parser of a compiler. In generating the internal form of the query, the parser checks the syntax of the user's query, verifies that the relation names appearing in the query are names of relations in the database, and so on. A parse-tree representation of the query is constructed, which is then translated into a relational-algebra expression. If the query was expressed in terms of a view, the translation phase also replaces all uses of the view by the relational-algebra expression that defines the view.† Parsing is covered in most compiler texts (see the bibliographic notes), and is outside the scope of this book.

In the network and hierarchical models (discussed in Appendices A and B), query optimization is left, for the most part, to the application programmer. That choice is made because the data-manipulation–language statements of these two models are usually embedded in a host programming language, and it is not easy to transform a network or hierarchical query into an equivalent one without knowledge of the entire application program. In contrast, relational-query languages are either declarative or algebraic. Declarative languages permit users to specify what a query should generate without saying how the system should do the generating. Algebraic languages allow for algebraic transformation of users' queries. Based on the query specification, it is relatively easy for an optimizer to generate a variety of equivalent plans for a query, and to choose the least expensive one.

† For materialized views, the expression defining the view has already been evaluated and stored. Therefore, the stored relation can be used, instead of uses of the view being replaced by the expression defining the view. Recursive views are handled differently, via a fixpoint procedure, as discussed in Section 5.3.6.

In this chapter, we assume the relational model. We shall see that the algebraic basis provided by this model is of considerable help in query optimization. Given a query, there is generally a variety of methods for computing the answer. For example, we have seen that, in SQL, a query could be expressed in several different ways. Each SQL query can itself be translated into a relational-algebra expression in one of several ways. Furthermore, the relational-algebra representation of a query specifies only partially how to evaluate a query; there are usually several ways to evaluate relational-algebra expressions. As an illustration, consider the query

```
select balance
from account
where balance < 2500
```

This query can be translated into either of the following relational-algebra expressions:

- $\sigma_{balance<2500}(\pi_{balance}(account))$
- $\pi_{balance}(\sigma_{balance<2500}(account))$

Further, we can execute each relational-algebra operation using one of several different algorithms. For example, to implement the preceding selection, we can search every tuple in *account* to find tuples with balance less than 2500. If a B+-tree index is available on the attribute *balance*, we can use the index instead to locate the tuples.

To specify fully how to evaluate a query, we need not only to provide the relational-algebra expression, but also to annotate it with instructions specifying how to evaluate each operation. Annotations may state the algorithm to be used for a specific operation, or the particular index or indices to use. A relational-algebra operation annotated with instructions on how to evaluate it is called an *evaluation primitive*. Several primitives may be grouped together into a *pipeline*, in which several operations are performed in parallel. A sequence of primitive operations that can be used to evaluate a query is a *query-execution plan* or *query-evaluation plan*. Figure 12.2 illustrates an evaluation plan for our example query, in which a particular index (denoted in the figure as "index 1") is specified for the selection operation. The *query-execution engine* takes a query-evaluation plan, executes that plan, and returns the answers to the query.

The different evaluation plans for a given query can have different costs. We do not expect users to write their queries in a way that suggests the most

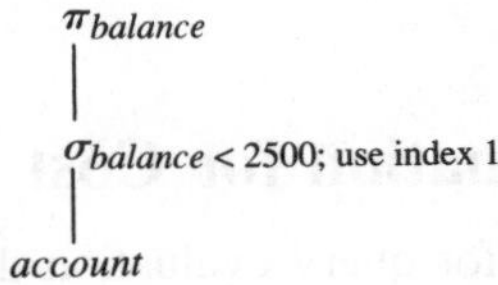

Figure 12.2 A query-evaluation plan.

efficient evaluation plan. Rather, it is the responsibility of the system to construct a query-evaluation plan that minimizes the cost of query evaluation. As we explained, the most relevant performance measure is usually the number of disk accesses.

Query optimization is the process of selecting the most efficient query-evaluation plan for a query. One aspect of optimization occurs at the relational-algebra level. An attempt is made to find an expression that is equivalent to the given expression, but that is more efficient to execute. We shall discuss equivalent expressions in greater detail in Section 12.9. The other aspect involves the selection of a detailed strategy for processing the query, such as choosing the algorithm to use for executing an operation, choosing the specific indices to use, and so on.

To choose among different query-evaluation plans, the optimizer has to *estimate* the cost of each evaluation plan. Computing the precise cost of evaluation of a plan is usually not possible without actually evaluating the plan. Instead, optimizers make use of statistical information about the relations, such as relation sizes and index depths, to make a good estimate of the cost of a plan.

Consider the preceding example of a selection applied to the *account* relation. The optimizer estimates the cost of the different evaluation plans. If an index is available on attribute *balance* of *account*, then the evaluation plan shown in Figure 12.2, in which the selection is done using the index, is likely to have the lowest cost, and, thus, to be chosen.

Once the query plan is chosen, the query is evaluated with that plan, and the result of the query is output.

The sequence of steps already described for processing a query is representative; not all databases exactly follow those steps. For instance, instead of using the relational-algebra representation, several databases use an annotated parse-tree representation based on the structure of the given SQL query. However, the concepts that we describe here form the basis of query processing in databases.

In Section 12.2, we construct a cost model that allows us to estimate the cost of various operations. Using this cost measure, we address the optimal evaluation of individual operations in Sections 12.3 through 12.7. In Section 12.8, we examine the efficiencies that we can achieve by combining multiple operations into one pipelined operation. These tools allow us to determine the approximate cost of evaluating a given relational-algebra expression optimally. Finally, in Sections 12.9 and 12.10, we show equivalences among relational-algebra expressions. We can use these equivalences to replace a relational-algebra expression constructed from a user's query with an equivalent expression whose estimated cost of evaluation is lower.

12.2 Catalog Information for Cost Estimation

The strategy that we choose for query evaluation depends on the estimated cost of the strategy. Query optimizers make use of of statistical information stored in the DBMS catalog to estimate the cost of a plan. The relevant catalog information about relations includes

- n_r is the number of tuples in the relation r.
- b_r is the number of blocks containing tuples of relation r.
- s_r is the size of a tuple of relation r in bytes.
- f_r is the blocking factor of relation r—that is, the number of tuples of relation r that fit into one block.
- $V(A, r)$ is the number of distinct values that appear in the relation r for attribute A. This value is the same as the size of $\Pi_A(r)$. If A is a key for relation r, $V(A, r)$ is n_r.
- $SC(A, r)$ is the selection cardinality of attribute A of relation r. Given a relation r and an attribute A of the relation, $SC(A, r)$ is the average number of records that satisfy an equality condition on attribute A, given that at least one record satisfies the equality condition. For example, $SC(A, r) = 1$ if A is a key attribute of r; for a nonkey attribute, we estimate that the $V(A, r)$ distinct values are distributed evenly among the tuples, yielding $SC(A, r) = (n_r / V(A, r))$.

The last two statistics, $V(A, r)$ and $SC(A, r)$, can also be maintained for sets of attributes if desired, instead of just for individual attributes. Thus, given a set of attributes $\mathcal{A}$, $V(\mathcal{A}, r)$ is the size of $\Pi_{\mathcal{A}}(r)$.

If we assume that the tuples of relation r are stored together physically in a file, the following equation holds:

$$b_r = \left\lceil \frac{n_r}{f_r} \right\rceil$$

In addition to catalog information about relations, the following catalog information about indices is also used:

- f_i is the average fan-out of internal nodes of index i, for tree-structured indices such as B+-trees.
- HT_i is the number of levels in index i—that is, the height of index i. For a balanced tree index (such as a B+-tree) on attribute A of relation r, $HT_i = \lceil \log_{f_i}(V(A, r)) \rceil$. For a hash index, HT_i is 1.
- LB_i is the number of lowest-level index blocks in index i—that is, the number of blocks at the leaf level of the index.

We use the statistical variables to estimate the size of the result and the cost for various operations and algorithms, as we shall see in the following sections. We refer to the cost estimate of algorithm A as E_A.

If we wish to maintain accurate statistics, then, every time a relation is modified, we must also update the statistics. This update incurs a substantial amount of overhead. Therefore, most systems do not update the statistics on every modification. Instead, the updates are done during periods of light system load.

As a result, the statistics used for choosing a query-processing strategy may not be completely accurate. However, if not too many updates occur in the intervals between the updates of the statistics, the statistics will be sufficiently accurate to provide a good estimation of the relative costs of the different plans.

The statistical information noted here is simplified. Real-world optimizers often maintain further statistical information to improve the accuracy of their cost estimates of evaluation plans.

12.3 Measures of Query Cost

The cost of query evaluation can be measured in terms of a number of different resources, including disk accesses, CPU time to execute a query, and, in a distributed or parallel database system, the cost of communication (which we discuss later, in Chapters 17 and 18). The response time for a query-evaluation plan (that is, the clock time required to execute the plan), assuming no other activity is going on on the computer, would account for all these costs, and could be used as a good measure of the cost of the plan.

In large database systems, however, disk accesses (which we measure as the number of transfers of blocks from disk) are usually the most important cost, since disk accesses are slow compared to in-memory operations. Moreover, CPU speeds have been improving much faster than have disk speeds. Thus, it is likely that the time spent in disk activity will continue to dominate the total time to execute a query. Finally, estimating the CPU time is relatively hard, compared to estimating the disk-access cost. Therefore, the disk-access cost is considered a reasonable measure of the cost of a query-evaluation plan.

To simplify our computation of disk-access cost, we assume that all transfers of blocks have the same cost. This assumption ignores the variance arising from rotational latency (waiting for the desired data to spin under the read–write head) and seek time (the time that it takes to move the head over the desired track or cylinder). Although these factors are significant, they are difficult to estimate in a shared system. Therefore, we simply use the *number of block transfers* from disk as a measure of the actual cost.

We also ignore the cost of writing the final result of an operation back to disk. Whatever the query-evaluation plan used, this cost does not change; hence, ignoring it does not affect the choice of a plan.

The costs of all the algorithms that we consider depend significantly on the size of the buffer in main memory. In the best case, all data can be read into the buffers, and the disk does not need to be accessed again. In the worst case, we assume that the buffer can hold only a few blocks of data—approximately one block per relation. When presenting cost estimates, we generally assume the worst case.

12.4 Selection Operation

In query processing, the *file scan* is the lowest-level operator to access data. File scans are search algorithms that locate and retrieve records that fulfill a selection condition. In relational systems, file scan allows an entire relation to be read in those cases where the relation is stored in a single, dedicated file.

12.4.1 Basic Algorithms

Consider a selection operation on a relation whose tuples are stored together in one file. Two scan algorithms to implement the selection operation are as follows:

- **A1** (*linear search*). In a linear search, each file block is scanned, and all records[†] are tested to see whether they satisfy the selection condition. Since all blocks have to be read, $E_{A1} = b_r$. (Recall that E_{A1} denotes the estimated cost of algorithm $A1$.) For a selection on a key attribute, we assume that one-half of the blocks will be searched before the record is found, at which point the scan can terminate. The estimate in this case is $E_{A1} = (b_r/2)$.

  Although it may be inefficient in many cases, the linear search algorithm can be applied to any file, regardless of the ordering of the file or of the availability of indices.
- **A2** (*binary search*). If the file is ordered on an attribute, and the selection condition is an equality comparison on the attribute, we can use a binary search to locate records that satisfy the selection. The binary search is performed on the blocks of the file, giving the following estimate for the file blocks to be scanned:

  $$E_{A2} = \lceil \log_2(b_r) \rceil + \left\lceil \frac{SC(A,r)}{f_r} \right\rceil - 1$$

  The first term, $\lceil \log_2(b_r) \rceil$, accounts for the cost of locating the first tuple by a binary search on the blocks. The total number of records that will satisfy the selection is $SC(A,r)$, and these records will occupy $\lceil SC(A,r)/f_r \rceil$ blocks,[‡] of which one has already been retrieved, giving the preceding estimate.

  If the equality condition is on a key attribute, then $SC(A,r) = 1$, and the estimate reduces to $E_{A2} = \lceil \log_2(b_r) \rceil$.

The cost estimates for binary search are based on the assumption that the blocks of a relation are stored contiguously on disk. Otherwise, the cost of looking up the file-access structures (which may be on disk) to locate the physical address of a block in a file must be added to the estimates. The cost estimates also depend on the size of the result of the selection.

If we assume uniform distribution of values (that is, each value appears with equal probability), then the query $\sigma_{A=a}(r)$ is estimated to have

$$SC(A,r) = \frac{n_r}{V(A,r)}$$

[†] We are assuming that the file contains a relation, so each record corresponds to exactly one tuple.

[‡] This formula is based on the (often-valid) assumption that the set of records for a given value start at a block boundary. If this assumption does not hold, one additional block access is required in the worst case.

tuples, assuming that the value a appears in attribute A of some record of r. The assumption that the value a in the selection appears in some record is generally true, and cost estimates often make it implicitly. However, it is often not realistic to assume that each value appears with equal probability. The *branch-name* attribute in the *account* relation is an example where the assumption is not valid. There is one tuple in the *account* relation for each account. It is reasonable to expect that the large branches have more accounts than smaller branches. Therefore, certain *branch-name* values appear with greater probability than do others. Despite the fact that the uniform-distribution assumption is often not correct, it is a reasonable approximation of reality in many cases, and it helps us to keep our presentation relatively simple.

As an illustration of this use of the cost estimates, suppose that we have the following statistical information about the *account* relation:

- $f_{account} = 20$ (that is, 20 tuples of *account* fit in one block).
- $V(branch\text{-}name, account) = 50$ (that is, there are 50 different branches).
- $V(balance, account) = 500$ (that is, there are 500 different *balance* values).
- $n_{account} = 10000$ (that is, the *account* relation has 10,000 tuples).

Consider the query

$$\sigma_{branch\text{-}name=\text{"Perryridge"}}(account)$$

Since the relation has 10,000 tuples, and each block holds 20 tuples, the number of blocks is $b_{account} = 500$. A simple file scan on *account* therefore takes 500 block accesses.

Suppose that *account* is sorted on *branch-name*. Since V(branch-name, *account*) is 50, we expect that $10000/50 = 200$ tuples of the *account* relation pertain to the Perryridge branch. These tuples would fit in $200/20 = 10$ blocks. A binary search to find the first record would take $\lceil log_2(500) \rceil = 9$ block accesses. Thus, the total cost would be $9 + 10 - 1 = 18$ block accesses.

12.4.2 Selections Using Indices

Index structures are referred to as *access paths*, since they provide a path through which data can be located and accessed. In Chapter 11, we pointed out that it is efficient to read the records of a file in an order corresponding closely to physical order. Recall that a *primary index* is an index that allows the records of a file to be read in an order that corresponds to the physical order in the file. An index that is not a primary index is called a *secondary index*.

Search algorithms that use an index are referred to as *index scans*. Ordered indices, such as B+-trees, also permit access to tuples in a sorted order, which is useful for implementing range queries. Although indices can provide fast, direct, and ordered access, their use imposes the overhead of access to those blocks containing the index. We need to take into account these block accesses when we estimate the cost of a strategy that involves the use of indices. We use the selection predicate to guide us in the choice of the index to use in processing the query.

- **A3** (*primary index, equality on key*). For an equality comparison on a key attribute with a primary index, we can use the index to retrieve a single record that satisfies the corresponding equality condition. To retrieve a single record, we need to retrieve one block more than the number of index levels (HT_i); the cost is $E_{A3} = HT_i + 1$.
- **A4** (*primary index, equality on nonkey*). We can retrieve multiple records by using a primary index when the selection condition specifies an equality comparison on a nonkey attribute, A. $SC(A, r)$ records will satisfy an equality condition, and $\lceil SC(A, r)/f_r \rceil$ file blocks will be accessed; hence,

$$E_{A4} = HT_i + \left\lceil \frac{SC(A, r)}{f_r} \right\rceil$$

- **A5** (*secondary index, equality*). Selections specifying an equality condition can use a secondary index. This strategy can retrieve a single record if the indexing field is a key; multiple records can be retrieved if the indexing field is not a key. For an equality condition on attribute A, $SC(A, r)$ records satisfy the condition. Given that the index is a secondary index, we assume the worst-case scenario that each matching record resides on a different block, yielding $E_{A5} = HT_i + SC(A, r)$, or, for a key indexing attribute, $E_{A5} = HT_i + 1$.

We assume the same statistical information about *account* as used in the earlier example. We also suppose that the following indices exist on *account*:

- A primary, B$^+$-tree index for attribute *branch-name*
- A secondary, B$^+$-tree index for attribute *balance*†

As mentioned earlier, we make the simplifying assumption that values are distributed uniformly.

Consider the query

$$\sigma_{branch\text{-}name=\text{“Perryridge”}}(account)$$

Since $V(branch\text{-}name, account) = 50$, we expect that $10000/50 = 200$ tuples of the *account* relation pertain to the Perryridge branch. Suppose that we use the index on *branch-name*. Since the index is a clustering index, $200/20 = 10$ block reads are required to read the *account* tuples. In addition, several index blocks must be read. Assume that the B$^+$-tree index stores 20 pointers per node. Since

†In practice, it is unlikely that an index would be maintained on *balance*, since balances change frequently. However, the example is useful here to illustrate the relative costs of various access plans.

there are 50 different branch names, the B$^+$-tree index must have between three and five leaf nodes. With this number of leaf nodes, the entire tree has a depth of 2, so two index blocks must be read. Thus, the preceding strategy requires 12 total block reads.

12.4.3 Selections Involving Comparisons

Consider a selection of the form $\sigma_{A \leq v}(r)$. In the absence of any further information about the comparison, we assume that approximately one-half of the records will satisfy the comparison condition; hence, the result has $n_r/2$ tuples.

If the actual value used in the comparison (v) is available at the time of cost estimation, a more accurate estimate can be made. The lowest and highest values ($min(A, r)$ and $max(A, r)$) for the attribute can be stored in the catalog. Assuming that values are uniformly distributed, we can estimate the number of records that will satisfy the condition $A \leq v$ as 0 if $v < min(A, r)$, as n_r if $v \geq max(A, r)$, and $n_r \cdot \frac{v - min(A,r)}{max(A,r) - min(A,r)}$ otherwise.

We can implement selections involving comparisons either using a linear or binary search, or using indices in one of the following ways:

- **A6** (*primary index, comparison*). A primary ordered index (for example, a primary B$^+$-tree index) can be used when the selection condition is a comparison. For comparison conditions of the form $A > v$ or $A \geq v$, the primary index can be used to direct the retrieval of tuples, as follows. For $A \geq v$, we look up the value v in the index to find the first tuple in the file that has a value of $A = v$. A file scan starting from that tuple up to the end of the file returns all tuples that satisfy the condition. For $A > v$, the file scan starts with the first tuple such that $A > v$.

  For comparisons of the form $A < v$ or $A \leq v$, an index lookup is not required. For $A < v$, we use a simple file scan starting from the beginning of the file, and continuing up to (but not including) the first tuple with attribute $A = v$. The case of $A \leq v$ is similar, except that the scan continues up to (but not including) the first tuple with attribute $A > v$. In either case, the index is not useful.

  We assume that approximately one-half of the records will satisfy one of the conditions. Under this assumption, retrieval using the index has the following cost:

$$E_{A6} = HT_i + \frac{b_r}{2}$$

  If the actual value used in the comparison is available at the time of cost estimation, a more accurate estimate can be made. Let the estimated number of values that satisfy the condition (as described earlier) be c. Then,

$$E_{A6} = HT_i + \left\lceil \frac{c}{f_r} \right\rceil$$

- **A7** (*secondary index, comparison*). We can use a secondary ordered index to guide retrieval for comparison conditions involving $<, \leq, \geq$, or $>$. The lowest-level index blocks are scanned, either from the smallest value up to v (for $<$ and $\leq$), or from v up to the maximum value (for $>$ and $\geq$). For these comparisons, if we assume that at least one-half of the records satisfy the condition, then one-half of the lowest-level index blocks are accessed and, via the index, one-half of the file records are accessed. Furthermore, a path must be traversed in the index from the root block to the first leaf block to be used. Thus, the cost estimate is the following:

$$E_{A7} = HT_i + \frac{LB_i}{2} + \frac{n_r}{2}$$

As we can with nonequality comparisons on clustering indices, we can get a more accurate estimate if we know the actual value used in the comparison at the time of cost estimation.

In Tandem's Non-Stop SQL System, B^+-trees are used both for primary data storage and as secondary access paths. The primary indices are clustering indices, whereas the secondary ones are not. Rather than pointers to records' physical location, the secondary indices contains keys to search the primary B^+-tree. The cost formulae described previously for secondary indices will have to be modified slightly if such indices are used.

Although the preceding algorithms show that indices are helpful in processing selections with comparisons, they are not always so useful. As an illustration, consider the query

$$\sigma_{balance<1200}(account)$$

Suppose that the statistical information about the relations is the same as that used earlier. If we have no information about the minimum and maximum balances in the *account* relation, we assume that one-half of the tuples satisfy the selection.

If we use the index for *balance*, we estimate the number of block accesses as follows. Let us assume that 20 pointers fit into one node of the B^+-tree index for *balance*. Since there are 500 different balance values, and each leaf node of the tree must be at least half-full, the tree has between 25 and 50 leaf nodes. So, as was the case for the index on *branch-name*, the index for *balance* has a depth of 2, and two block accesses are required to read the first index block. In the worst case, there are 50 leaf nodes, one-half of which must be accessed. This accessing leads to 25 more block reads. Finally, for each tuple that we locate in the index, we have to retrieve that tuple from the relation. We estimate that 5000 tuples (one-half of the 10,000 tuples) satisfy the condition. Since the index is nonclustering, in the worst case each of these tuple accesses will require a separate block access. Thus, we get a total of 5027 block accesses.

In contrast, a simple file scan will take only $10000/20 = 500$ block accesses. In this case, it is clearly not wise to use the index, and we should use the file scan instead.

12.4.4 Implementation of Complex Selections

So far, we have considered only simple selection conditions of the form A *op* B, where *op* is an equality or comparison operation. We now consider more complex selection predicates.

- **Conjunction:** A *conjunctive selection* is a selection of the form

$$\sigma_{\theta_1 \wedge \theta_2 \wedge \ldots \wedge \theta_n}(r)$$

We can estimate the result size of such a selection as follows. For each θ_i, we estimate the size of the selection $\sigma_{\theta_i}(r)$, denoted by s_i, as described previously. Thus, the probability that a tuple in the relation satisfies selection condition θ_i is s_i/n_r.

The preceding probability is called the *selectivity* of the selection $\sigma_{\theta_i}(r)$. Assuming that the conditions are *independent* of each other, the probability that a tuple satisfies all the conditions is simply the product of all these probabilities. Thus, we estimate the size of the full selection as

$$n_r * \frac{s_1 * s_2 * \ldots * s_n}{n_r^n}$$

- **Disjunction:** A *disjunctive selection* is a selection of the form

$$\sigma_{\theta_1 \vee \theta_2 \vee \ldots \vee \theta_n}(r)$$

A disjunctive condition is satisfied by the union of all records satisfying the individual, simple conditions θ_i.

As before, let s_i/n_r denote the probability that a tuple satisfies condition θ_i. The probability that the tuple will satisfy the disjunction is then 1 minus the probability that it will satisfy *none* of the conditions, or

$$1 - (1 - \frac{s_1}{n_r}) * (1 - \frac{s_2}{n_r}) * \ldots * (1 - \frac{s_n}{n_r})$$

Multiplying this value by n_r gives us the number of tuples that satisfy the selection.

- **Negation:** The result of a selection $\sigma_{\neg\theta}(r)$ is simply the tuples of r that are not in $\sigma_\theta(r)$. We already know how to estimate the size of $\sigma_\theta(r)$. The size of $\sigma_{\neg\theta}(r)$ is therefore estimated to be

$$size(r) - size(\sigma_\theta(r))$$

We can implement a selection operation involving either a conjunction or a disjunction of simple conditions using one of the following algorithms:

- **A8** (*conjunctive selection using one index*). We first determine whether an access path is available for an attribute in one of the simple conditions. If one is, one of the selection algorithms A2 through A7 can retrieve records satisfying that condition. We complete the operation by testing, in the memory buffer, whether or not each retrieved record satisfies the remaining simple conditions.

Selectivity is central to determining in what order the the simple conditions in a conjunctive selection should tested. The most selective condition (that is, the one with the smallest selectivity) will retrieve the smallest number of records; hence, that condition should constitute the first scan.

- **A9** (*conjunctive selection using composite index*). An appropriate *composite index* may be available for some conjunctive selections. If the selection specifies an equality condition on two or more attributes, and a composite index exists on these combined attribute fields, then the index can be searched directly. The type of index determines which of algorithms *A*3, *A*4, or *A*5 will be used.
- **A10** (*conjunctive selection by intersection of identifiers*). Another alternative for implementing conjunctive selection operations involves the use of record pointers or record identifiers. This algorithm requires indices with record pointers, on the fields involved in the individual conditions. Each index is scanned for pointers to tuples that satisfy an individual condition. The intersection of all the retrieved pointers is the set of pointers to tuples that satisfy the conjunctive condition. We then use the pointers to retrieve the actual records. If indices are not available on all the individual conditions, then the retrieved records are tested against the remaining conditions.
- **A11** (*disjunctive selection by union of identifiers*). If access paths are available on all the conditions of a disjunctive selection, each index is scanned for pointers to tuples that satisfy the individual condition. The union of all the retrieved pointers yields the set of pointers to all tuples that satisfy the disjunctive condition. We then use the pointers to retrieve the actual records.

  However, if even one of the conditions does not have an access path, we will have to perform a linear scan of the relation to find tuples that satisfy the condition. Therefore, if there is even one such condition in the disjunct, the most efficient access method is a linear scan, with the disjunctive condition tested on each tuple during the scan.

The implementation of selections with negation conditions is left to you as an exercise (Exercise 12.15). Also left to you as an exercise are conditions that combine conjunctions and disjunctions (Exercise 12.16).

To illustrate the preceding algorithms, we suppose that we have the query

> **select** *account-number*
> **from** *account*
> **where** *branch-name* = "Perryridge" **and** *balance* = 1200

We assume that the statistical information about the *account* relation is the same as that in the earlier example.

If we use the index on *branch-name*, we will have a total of 12 block reads, as discussed in the previous section. If we use the index for *balance*, we estimate the number of block accesses as follows. Since $V(balance, account) = 500$, we expect that $10000/500 = 20$ tuples of the *account* relation will have a balance of \$1200. However, since the index for *balance* is nonclustering, we anticipate that one block read will be required for each tuple. Thus, 20 block reads are required just to read the *account* tuples.

Let us assume that 20 pointers fit into one node of the B^+-tree index for *balance*. Since there are 500 different balance values, the tree has between 25 and 50 leaf nodes. So, as was the case for the B^+-tree index on *branch-name*, the index for *balance* has a depth of 2, and two block accesses are required to read the necessary index blocks. Therefore, this strategy requires a total of 22 block reads.

Thus, we conclude that it is preferable to use the index for *branch-name*. Observe that, if both indices were nonclustering, we would prefer to use the index on *balance*, since we would expect only 10 tuples to have $balance = 1200$, versus 200 tuples with *branch-name* = "Perryridge". Without the clustering property, our first strategy could require as many as 200 block accesses to read the data, since, in the worst case, each tuple is on a different block. We add these 200 accesses to the 2 index block accesses, for a total of 202 block reads. However, because of the clustering property of the *branch-name* index, it is actually less expensive in this example to use the *branch-name* index.

Another way in which we could use the indices to process our example query is by using intersection of identifiers. We use the index for *balance* to retrieve pointers to records with $balance = 1200$, rather than retrieving the records themselves. Let S_1 denote this set of pointers. Similarly, we use the index for *branch-name* to retrieve pointers to records with *branch-name* = "Perryridge". Let S_2 denote this set of pointers. Then, $S_1 \cap S_2$ is a set of pointers to records with *branch-name* = "Perryridge" and $balance = 1200$.

This technique requires both indices to be accessed. Both indices have a height of 2, and, for each index, the number of pointers retrieved, estimated earlier as 20 and 200, will fit into a single leaf page. Thus, we read a total of four index blocks to retrieve the two sets of pointers. The intersection of the two sets of pointers can be computed with no further disk I/O. We estimate the number of blocks that must be read from the *account* file by estimating the number of pointers in $S_1 \cap S_2$.

Since $V(branch\text{-}name, account) = 50$ and $V(balance, account) = 1000$, we estimate that one tuple in $50 * 1000$ or one in $50,000$ has both *branch-name* = "Perryridge" and $balance = 1200$. This estimate is based on an assumption of uniform distribution (which we made earlier), and on an added assumption that the distribution of branch names and balances are independent. Based on these assumptions, $S_1 \cap S_2$ is estimated to have only one pointer. Thus, only one block of *account* needs to be read. The total estimated cost of this strategy is five block reads.

12.5 Sorting

Sorting of data plays an important role in database systems for two reasons. First, SQL queries can specify that the output be sorted. Second, and equally important for query processing, several of the relational operations, such as joins, can be implemented efficiently if the input relations are first sorted. Thus, we discuss sorting prior to discussing the join operation in Section 12.6.

We can accomplish sorting by building an index on the sort key, and then using that index to read the relation in sorted order. However, such a process orders the relation only *logically*, through an index, rather than *physically*. Hence, the reading of tuples in the sorted order may lead to a disk access for each tuple. For this reason, it may be desirable to order the tuples physically.

The problem of sorting has been studied extensively, both for the case where the relation fits entirely in main memory, and for the case where the relation is bigger than memory. In the first case, standard sorting techniques such as quick-sort can be used. Here, we discuss how to handle the second case.

Sorting of relations that do not fit in memory is called *external sorting*. The most commonly used technique for external sorting is the *external sort–merge* algorithm. We describe the external sort–merge algorithm next. Let M denote the number of page frames in the main-memory buffer (the number of disk blocks whose contents can be buffered in main memory).

1. In the first stage, a number of sorted *runs* are created.

```
i = 0;
repeat
    read M blocks of the relation, or the rest of the relation,
        whichever is smaller;
    sort the in-memory part of the relation;
    write the sorted data to run file R_i;
    i = i + 1;
until the end of the relation
```

2. In the second stage, the runs are *merged*. Suppose, for now, that the total number of runs, N, is less than M, so that we can allocate one page frame to each run and have space left to hold one page of output. The merge stage operates as follows:

```
read one block of each of the N files R_i into a buffer page in memory;
repeat
    choose the first tuple (in sort order) among all buffer pages;
    write the tuple to the output, and delete it from the buffer page;
    if the buffer page of any run R_i is empty and not end-of-file(R_i)
        then read the next block of R_i into the buffer page;
until all buffer pages are empty
```

The output of the merge stage is the sorted relation. The output file is buffered to reduce the number of disk write operations. The preceding merge operation is a generalization of the two-way merge used by the standard in-memory sort–merge algorithm; it merges N runs, so it is called an *n-way merge*.

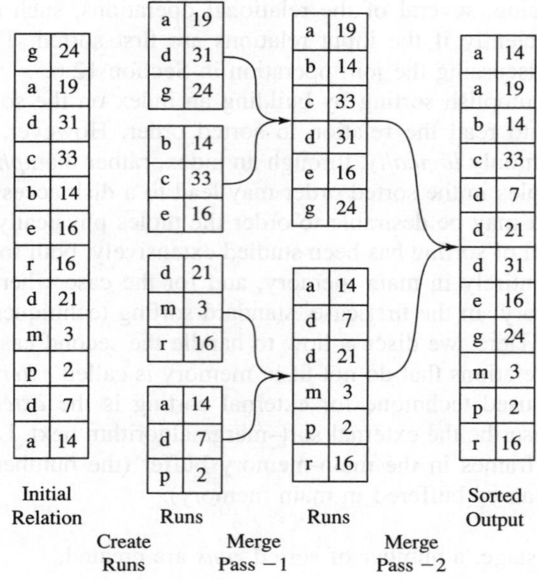

Figure 12.3 External sorting using sort–merge.

In general, if the relation is much larger than memory, there may be M or more runs generated in the first stage, and it is not possible to allocate a page frame for each run during the merge stage. In this case, the merge operation is done in multiple passes. Since there is enough memory for $M - 1$ input buffer pages, each merge can take $M - 1$ runs as input.

The initial *pass* functions as follows. The first $M - 1$ runs are merged (as described previously) to get a single run for the next pass. Then, the next $M - 1$ runs are similarly merged, and so on, until all the initial runs have been processed. At this point, the number of runs has been reduced by a factor of $M - 1$. If this reduced number of runs is still greater than or equal to M, another pass is made, with the runs created by the first pass as input. Each pass reduces the number of runs by a factor of $M - 1$. These passes are repeated as many times as required, until the number of runs is less than M; a final pass then generates the sorted output.

Figure 12.3 illustrates the steps of the external sort–merge of an example relation. For illustration purposes, we assume that only one tuple fits in a block ($f_r = 1$), and we assume that memory holds at most three page frames. During the merge stage, two page frames are used for input and one for output.

Let us compute how many block transfers are required for the external sort merge. In the first stage, every block of the relation is read and is written out again, giving a total of $2b_r$ disk accesses. The initial number of runs is $\lceil b_r/M \rceil$. Since the number of runs is decreased by a factor of $M - 1$ in each merge pass, the total number of merge passes required is given by $\lceil \log_{M-1}(b_r/M) \rceil$. Each of these passes reads every block of the relation once and writes it out once, with two exceptions. First, the final pass can produce the sorted output without writing its result to disk. Second, there may be runs that are not read in or written out during a pass—for example, if there are M runs to be merged in a pass, $M - 1$ are read in and merged, and one run is not accessed during the pass. Ignoring the (relatively small) savings due to the latter effect, the total number of disk accesses for external sorting of the relation is

$$b_r(2\lceil \log_{M-1}(b_r/M)\rceil + 1)$$

Applying this equation to the example in Figure 12.3, we get a total of $12 * (4+1) = 60$ block transfers, as you can verify from the figure. Note that this value does not include the cost of writing out the final result.

12.6 Join Operation

In this section, we first show how to estimate the size of the result of a join. We then study several algorithms for computing the join of relations, and analyze their respective costs. We use the word *equi-join* to refer to a join of the form $r \bowtie_{r.A=s.B} s$, where A and B are attributes or sets of attributes of relations r and s respectively.

We use as a running example the expression

$$depositor \bowtie customer$$

We assume the following catalog information about the two relations:

- $n_{customer} = 10,000$.
- $f_{customer} = 25$, which implies that $b_{customer} = 10000/25 = 400$.
- $n_{depositor} = 5000$.
- $f_{depositor} = 50$, which implies that $b_{depositor} = 5000/50 = 100$.
- V(customer-name, depositor) $= 2500$, which implies that, on average, each customer has two accounts.

We also assume that *customer-name* in *depositor* is a foreign key on *customer*.

12.6.1 Estimation of the Size of Joins

The Cartesian product $r \times s$ contains $n_r * n_s$ tuples. Each tuple of $r \times s$ occupies $s_r + s_s$ bytes, from which we can calculate the size of the Cartesian product.

Estimation of the size of a natural join is somewhat more complicated than is estimation of the size of a selection or of a Cartesian product. Let $r(R)$ and $s(S)$ be relations.

- If $R \cap S = \emptyset$—that is, the relations have no attribute in common—then $r \bowtie s$ is the same as $r \times s$, and we can use our estimation technique for Cartesian products.

- If $R \cap S$ is a key for R, then we know that a tuple of s will join with at most one tuple from r. Therefore, the number of tuples in $r \bowtie s$ is no greater than the number of tuples in s. If $R \cap S$ is a foreign key for R, then the number of tuples in $r \bowtie s$ is exactly the same as the number of tuples in s. The case where $R \cap S$ is a key for S is symmetric to the case just described.

  In our example of *depositor* $\bowtie$ *customer*, *customer-name* in *depositor* is a foreign key of *customer*; hence, the size of the result is exactly $n_{depositor}$, which is 5000.

- The most difficult case to consider is when $R \cap S$ is a key for neither R nor S. In this case, we assume, as we did for selections, that each value appears with equal probability. Consider a tuple t of r, and assume $R \cap S = \{A\}$. We estimate that tuple t produces

$$\frac{n_s}{V(A, s)}$$

  tuples in $r \bowtie s$, since this number is the average number of tuples in s with a given value for the attributes A. Considering all the tuples in r, we estimate that there are

$$\frac{n_r * n_s}{V(A, s)}$$

  tuples in $r \bowtie s$. Observe that, if we reverse the roles of r and s in the preceding estimate, we obtain an estimate of

$$\frac{n_r * n_s}{V(A, r)}$$

  tuples in $r \bowtie s$. These two estimates differ if $V(A, r) \neq V(A, s)$. If this situation occurs, there are likely to be dangling tuples that do not participate in the join. Thus, the lower of the two estimates is probably the more accurate one.

  The preceding estimate of join size may be too high if the $V(A, r)$ values for attribute A in r have few values in common with the $V(A, s)$ values for attribute A in s. However, this situation is unlikely to happen in the real world, since dangling tuples either do not exist, or constitute only a small fraction of the tuples, in most real-world relations. More important, the preceding estimate depends on the assumption that each value appears with equal probability. More sophisticated techniques for size estimation have to be used if this assumption does not hold.

Let us now compute the size estimates for *depositor* $\bowtie$ *customer* without using information about foreign keys. Since V(*customer-name, depositor*) = 2500, and V(*customer-name, customer*) = 10000, the two estimates we get are $5000 * 10000/2500 = 20,000$ and $5000 * 10000/10000 = 5000$, and we choose the lower one. In this case, the lower of these estimates is the same as that which we computed earlier using information about foreign keys.

12.6.2 Nested-Loop Join

The procedure in Figure 12.4 shows a simple algorithm to compute the theta join, $r \bowtie_\theta s$, of two relations r and s. This algorithm is called the *nested-loop join* algorithm, since it basically consists of a pair of nested **for** loops. As shown in the procedure, r is called the *outer* relation and s the *inner* relation of the join, since the loop for r encloses the loop for s. The algorithm uses the notation $t_r \cdot t_s$, where t_r and t_s are tuples; $t_r \cdot t_s$ denotes the tuple constructed by concatenating the attribute values of tuples t_r and t_s.

Like the linear file-scan algorithm for selection, the nested-loop join algorithm requires no indices, and it can be used regardless of what the join condition is. Extending the algorithm to compute the natural join is straightforward, since the natural join can be expressed as a theta join followed by elimination of repeated attributes by a projection. The only change required is an extra step of deleting repeated attributes from the tuple $t_r \cdot t_s$, before adding it to the result.

The nested-loop join algorithm is expensive, since it examines every pair of tuples in the two relations. Consider the cost of the nested-loop join algorithm. The number of pairs of tuples to be considered is $n_r * n_s$. For each record in r, we have to perform a complete scan on s. In the worst case, the buffer can hold only one block of each relation, and a total of $n_r * b_s + b_r$ block accesses will be required. In the best case, there is enough space for both relations to fit in memory, so each block will have to be read only once; hence, only $b_r + b_s$ block accesses will be required.

If the smaller relation fits entirely in main memory, it is beneficial to use that relation as the inner relation. This format speeds query processing significantly, since it is necessary to read the inner-loop relation only once. Therefore, if s is small enough to fit in main memory, our strategy requires only a total $b_r + b_s$ accesses—the same cost as that for the case where both relations fit in memory.

Now consider the natural join of *depositor* and *customer*. Let us assume, for now, that we have no indices whatsoever on either relation, and that we are not willing to create any index. We can use the nested loops to compute the join; let us assume that *depositor* is the outer relation, and *customer* is the inner relation, in the join. We will have to examine $5000 * 10000 = 50 * 10^6$ pairs of tuples. In the worst case, the number of block accesses is $5000 * 400 + 100 = 2{,}000{,}100$. In the best-case scenario, however, we can read both relations only once, and perform the computation. This computation requires at most $100 + 400 = 500$ block accesses—a significant improvement over the worst-case scenario. If we had used *customer*

for each tuple t_r **in** r **do begin**
    for each tuple t_s **in** s **do begin**
        test pair (t_r, t_s) to see if they satisfy the join condition θ
        if they do, add $t_r \cdot t_s$ to the result.
    end
end

Figure 12.4 Nested-loop join.

```
for each block Br of r do begin
    for each block Bs of s do begin
        for each tuple tr in Br do begin
            for each tuple ts in Bs do begin
                test pair (tr, ts) to see if they satisfy the join condition
                if they do, add tr · ts to the result.
            end
        end
    end
end
```

Figure 12.5 Block nested-loop join.

as the relation for the outer loop and *depositor* for the inner loop, the worst-case cost of our final strategy would have been lower: $10000*100+400 = 1,000,400$.

12.6.3 Block Nested-Loop Join

If the buffer is too small to hold both relations entirely in memory, we can still obtain a major saving in block accesses if we process the relations on a per-block basis, rather than on a per-tuple basis. The procedure of Figure 12.5 shows a variant of the nested-loop join, where every block of the inner relation is paired with every block of the outer relation. Within each pair of blocks, every tuple in one block is paired with every tuple in the other block, to generate all pairs of tuples. As before, all pairs of tuples that satisfy the join condition are added to the result.

The primary difference in cost between the block nested-loop join and the basic nested-loop join is that, in the worst case, each block in the inner relation s is read only once for each *block* in the outer relation, instead of once for each *tuple* in the outer relation. Thus, in the worst case, there will be a total of $b_r * b_s + b_r$ block accesses. Clearly, it is most efficient to use the smaller relation as the outer relation. In the best case, there will be $b_r + b_s$ block accesses.

Let us return to our example of computing *depositor* $\bowtie$ *customer*, using the block nested-loop join algorithm. In the worst case we have to read each block of *customer* once for each block of *depositor*. Thus, in the worst case, a total of $100 * 400 + 100 = 40,100$ block accesses are required. This cost is a significant improvement over the $5000 * 400 + 100 = 2,000,100$ block accesses needed in the worst case for the basic nested-loop join. The number of block accesses in the best case remains the same—namely, $100 + 400 = 500$.

The performance of the nested-loop and block nested-loop procedures can be further improved:

- If the join attributes in a natural join or an equi-join form a key on the inner relation, then the inner loop can terminate as soon as the first match is found.
- In the block nested-loop algorithm, instead of using disk blocks as the blocking unit for the outer relation, we can use the biggest size that can fit in memory,

while leaving enough space for the buffers of the inner relation and the output. This change reduces the number of times that the inner relation is scanned.

- We can scan the inner loop alternately forward and backward. This scanning method orders the requests for disk blocks such that the data remaining in the buffer from the previous scan can be reused, thus reducing the number of disk accesses needed.
- If an index is available on the inner loop's join attribute, more efficient index lookups can replace file scans. This optimization is described in Section 12.6.4.

12.6.4 Indexed Nested-Loop Join

In a nested-loop join (Figure 12.4), if an index (either permanent or temporary) is available on the inner loop's join attribute, index lookups can replace file scans. For each tuple t_r in the outer relation r, the index is used to look up tuples in s that will satisfy the join condition with tuple t_r.

The preceding join method is called an *indexed nested-loop join*; it can be used with existing indices, as well as with temporary indices created for the sole purpose of evaluating the join.

Looking up tuples in s that will satisfy the join conditions with a given tuple t_r is essentially a selection on s. For example, consider *depositor* ⋈ *customer*. Suppose that we have a *depositor* tuple with *customer-name* "John". Then, the relevant tuples in s are those that satisfy the selection "*customer-name* = John".

The cost of index nested-loops join can be computed as follows. For each tuple in the outer relation r, a lookup is performed on the index for s, and the relevant tuples are retrieved. In the worst case, there is space in the buffer for only one page of r and one page of the index. Then, b_r disk accesses are needed to read relation r, and, for each tuple in r, we perform an index lookup on s. Then, the cost of the join can be computed as $b_r + n_r * c$, where c is the cost of a single selection on s using the join condition. We have already seen how to compute the cost of a single selection on a relation using indices of various types, which computation gives us the value of c. The cost formula indicates that, if indices are available on both relations r and s, it is generally most efficient to use the one with fewer tuples as the outer relation.

For example, consider an index nested-loop join of *depositor* ⋈ *customer*, with *depositor* as the outer relation. Suppose also that *customer* has a primary B+-tree index on the join attribute *customer-name*, which contains 20 entries in each index node. Since *customer* has 10,000 tuples, the height of the tree is 4, and one more access is needed to find the actual data. Since $n_{depositor}$ is 5000, the total cost is $100 + 5000 * 5 = 25,100$ disk accesses. This cost is lower than the 40,100 accesses needed for a block nested-loop join.

12.6.5 Merge–Join

The *merge–join* algorithm (also called the *sort–merge-join* algorithm) can be used to compute natural joins and equi-joins. Let $r(R)$ and $s(S)$ be the relations whose natural join is to be computed, and let $R \cap S$ denote their common attributes.

```
pr := address of first tuple of r;
ps := address of first tuple of s;
while (ps ≠ null and pr ≠ null) do
    begin
        t_s := tuple to which ps points;
        S_s := {t_s};
        set ps to point to next tuple of s;
        done := false;
        while (not done and ps ≠ null) do
            begin
                t_s' := tuple to which ps points;
                if (t_s'[JoinAttrs] = t_s[JoinAttrs])
                then begin
                        S_s := S_s ∪ {t_s'};
                        set ps to point to next tuple of s;
                    end
                else done := true;
            end
        t_r := tuple to which pr points;
        while (pr ≠ null and t_r[JoinAttrs] < t_s[JoinAttrs]) do
            begin
                set pr to point to next tuple of r;
                t_r := tuple to which pr points;
            end
        while (pr ≠ null and t_r[JoinAttrs] = t_s[JoinAttrs]) do
            begin
                for each t_s in S_s do
                    begin
                        add t_s ⋈ t_r to result ;
                    end
                set pr to point to next tuple of r;
                t_r := tuple to which pr points;
            end
    end.
```

Figure 12.6 Merge-join.

Suppose that both relations are sorted on the attributes $R \cap S$. Then, their join can be computed by a process much like the merge stage in the merge–sort algorithm.

The merge–join algorithm is shown in Figure 12.6. In the algorithm, *JoinAttrs* refers to the attributes in $R \cap S$, and $t_r \bowtie t_s$, where t_r and t_s are tuples that have the same values for *JoinAttrs*, denotes the concatenation of the attributes of the tuples, followed by projecting out repeated attributes. The merge–join algorithm associates one pointer with each relation. These pointers point initially to the first tuple of the respective relations. As the algorithm proceeds, the pointers move through the relation. A group of tuples of one relation with the same value on

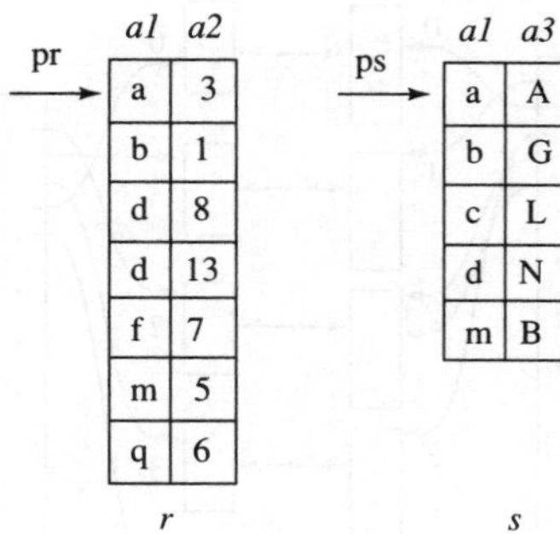

Figure 12.7 Sorted relations for merge–join.

the join attributes is read into S_s. The algorithm shown in Figure 12.6 *requires* that every set of tuples S_s fit in main memory; we shall look at extensions of the algorithm to avoid this assumption later in this section. Then, the corresponding tuples (if any) of the other relation are read in, and are processed as they are read.

Figure 12.7 shows two relations that are sorted on their join attribute $a1$. It is instructive to go through the steps of the merge–join algorithm on the relations shown in the figure.

Since the relations are in sorted order, tuples with the same value on the join attributes are in consecutive order. Thereby, each tuple in the sorted order needs to be read only once, and, as a result, each block is also read only once. Since only a single pass is made through both files, the merge–join method is efficient; the number of block accesses is equal to the sum of the number of blocks in both files, $b_r + b_s$.

If either of the input relations r and s is not sorted on the join attributes, they can be sorted first, and then the merge–join algorithm can be used. The merge–join algorithm can also be easily extended from natural joins to the more general case of equi-joins.

Suppose the merge–join scheme is applied to our example of *depositor* ⋈ *customer*. The join attribute here is *customer-name*. Suppose that the relations are already sorted on the join attribute *customer-name*. In this case, the merge–join takes a total of $400 + 100 = 500$ block accesses. Suppose the relations are not sorted, and the memory size is the worst case of three blocks. Sorting *customer* takes $400 * (2\lceil log_2(400/3)\rceil + 1)$, or 6800, block transfers, with 400 more transfers to write out the result. Similarly, sorting *depositor* takes $100 * (2\lceil log_2(100/3)\rceil + 1)$, or 1300, transfers, with 100 more transfers to write it out. Thus, the total cost is 9100 block transfers if the relations are not sorted.

As mentioned earlier, the merge–join algorithm of Figure 12.6 requires that the set S_s of all tuples with the same value for the join attributes must fit in main memory. This requirement can usually be met, even if the relation s is large. If it cannot be met, a block nested-loop join must be performed between S_s and the tuples in r with the same values for the join attributes. The overall cost of the merge–join increases as a result.

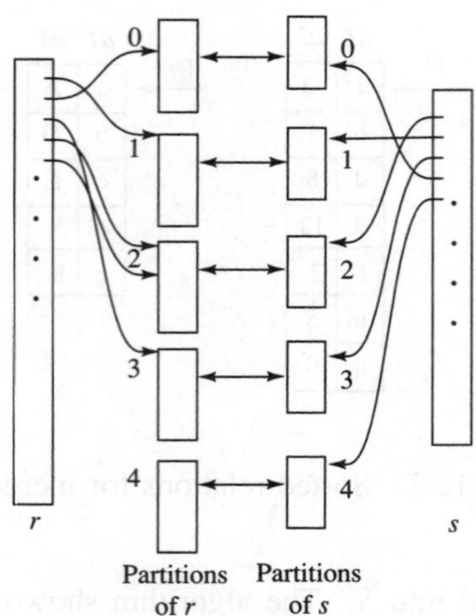

Figure 12.8 Hash partitioning of relations.

It is also possible to perform a variation of the merge–join operation on unsorted tuples, if secondary indices exist on both join attributes. The records are scanned through the indices, resulting in their being retrieved in sorted order. This variation presents a significant drawback, however, since records may be scattered throughout the file blocks. Hence, each tuple access could involve accessing a disk block, and that is costly.

To avoid this cost, we can use a hybrid merge–join technique, which combines indices with merge–join. Suppose that one of the relations is sorted; the other is unsorted, but has a secondary B^+-tree index on the join attributes. The *hybrid merge–join algorithm* merges the sorted relation with the leaf entries of the secondary B^+-tree index. The result file contains tuples from the sorted relation and addresses for tuples of the unsorted relation. The result file is then sorted on the addresses of tuples of the unsorted relation, allowing efficient retrieval of the corresponding tuples, in physical storage order, to complete the join. Extensions of the technique to handle two unsorted relations are left as an exercise for you.

12.6.6 Hash–Join

Like the merge–join algorithm, the hash–join algorithm can be used to implement natural joins and equi-joins. In the hash–join algorithm, a hash function h is used to partition tuples of both relations. The basic idea is to partition the tuples of each of the relations into sets that have the same hash value on the join attributes.

We assume that

- h is a hash function mapping *JoinAttrs* values to $\{0, 1, \ldots, max\}$, where *JoinAttrs* denotes the common attributes of r and s used in the natural join.
- $H_{r_0}, H_{r_1}, \ldots, H_{r_{max}}$ denote partitions of r tuples, each initially empty. Each tuple $t_r \in r$ is put in partition H_{r_i}, where $i = h(t_r[JoinAttrs])$.

```
/* Partition s */
for each tuple t_s in s do begin
    i := h(t_s[JoinAttrs]);
    H_si := H_si ∪ {t_s};
end
/* Partition r */
for each tuple t_r in r do begin
    i := h(t_r[JoinAttrs]);
    H_ri := H_ri ∪ {t_r};
end
/* Perform join on each partition */
for i := 0 to max do begin
    read H_si and build an in-memory hash index on it
    for each tuple t_r in H_ri do begin
        probe the hash index on H_si to locate all tuples t_s
            such that t_s[JoinAttrs] = t_r[JoinAttrs]
        for each matching tuple t_s in H_si do begin
            add t_r ⋈ t_s to the result
        end
    end
end
```

Figure 12.9 Hash–join.

- $H_{s_0}, H_{s_1}, \ldots, H_{s_{max}}$ denote partitions of s tuples, each initially empty. Each tuple $t_s \in s$ is put in partition H_{s_i}, where $i = h(t_s[JoinAttrs])$.

The hash function h should have the "goodness" properties of randomness and uniformity that we discussed in Chapter 11. The partitioning of the relations is shown pictorially in Figure 12.8.

The idea behind the hash-join algorithm is as follows. Suppose that an r tuple and an s tuple satisfy the join condition; then, they will have the same value for the join attributes. If that value is hashed to some value i, the r tuple has to be in H_{r_i} and the s tuple in H_{s_i}. Therefore, r tuples in H_{r_i} need only to be compared with s tuples in H_{s_i}; they do not need to be compared with s tuples in any other partition.

For example, if d is a tuple in *depositor*, c a tuple in *customer*, and h a hash function on the *customer-name* attributes of the tuples, then d and c must be tested only if $h(c) = h(d)$. If $h(c) \neq h(d)$, then c and d must have different values for *customer-name*. However, if $h(c) = h(d)$, we must test c and d to see whether the values in their join attributes are the same, since it is possible that c and d have different *customer-name*s that have the same hash value.

Figure 12.9 shows the details of the hash–join algorithm to compute the natural join of relations r and s. As in the merge-join algorithm, $t_r \bowtie t_s$ denotes the concatenation of the attributes of tuples t_r and t_s, followed by projecting out repeated attributes. After the partitioning of the relations, the rest of the hash–join code performs a separate indexed nested-loop join on each of the partition pairs i, for $i = 0 \ldots max$. To do so, it first *builds* a hash index on each H_{s_i}, and then *probes* (that is, looks up H_{s_i}) with tuples from H_{r_i}. The relation s is the *build input*, and r is the *probe input*.

The hash index on H_{s_i} is built in memory, so there is no need to access the disk to retrieve the tuples. The hash function used to build this hash index is different from the hash function h used earlier, but is still applied to only the join attributes. In the course of the indexed nested-loop join, the system uses this hash index to retrieve records that will match records in the probe input.

The build and probe phases require only a single pass through both the build and probe inputs. It is straightforward to extend the hash–join algorithm to compute general equi-joins.

The value *max* must be chosen to be large enough such that, for each i, the tuples in the partition H_{s_i} of the build relation, along with the hash index on the partition, will fit in memory. It is not necessary for the partitions of the probe relation to fit in memory. Clearly, it is best to use the smaller input relation as the build relation. If the size of the build relation is b_s blocks, then, for each of the *max* partitions to be of size less than or equal to M, *max* must be at least $\lceil b_s/M \rceil$. More precisely stated, we have to account for the extra space occupied by the hash index on the partition as well, so *max* should be correspondingly larger. For simplicity, we sometimes ignore the space requirement of the hash index in our analysis.

12.6.6.1 Recursive Partitioning

If the value of *max* is greater than or equal to the number of page frames of memory, partitioning of the relations cannot be done in one pass, since there will not be enough buffer pages. Instead, partitioning has to be done by repeated passes. In one pass, the input can be split into at most as many partitions as there are page frames available for use as output buffers. Each bucket generated by one pass is separately read in and partitioned again in the next pass, to create smaller partitions. The hash function used in a pass is, of course, different from the one used in the previous pass. This splitting of the input is repeated until each partition of the build input fits in memory. Such partitioning is called *recursive partitioning*.

A relation does not need recursive partitioning if $M > max + 1$, or equivalently $M > (b_s/M) + 1$, which simplifies (approximately) to $M > \sqrt{b_s}$. For example, consider a memory size of 12 megabytes, divided into 4-kilobyte blocks; it would contain a total of 3000 blocks. We can use a memory of this size to partition relations of size 9 million blocks, which is 36 gigabytes. Similarly, a relation of size 1 gigabyte requires $\sqrt{250,000}$ blocks, or about 2 megabytes.

12.6.6.2 Handling of Overflows

Hash-table overflow occurs in partition i of the build relation s if the hash index on H_{s_i} is larger than main memory. Hash-table overflow can occur if there are many tuples in the build relation with the same values for the join attributes, or if the hash function does not have the property of randomness and uniformity. In either case, some of the partitions will have more tuples than the average, whereas others will have fewer; partitioning is then said to be *skewed*.

We can handle a small amount of skew by increasing the number of partitions such that the expected size of each partition (including the hash index on the partition) is somewhat less than the size of memory. The number of partitions is therefore increased by a small value called the *fudge factor*, which is usually about 20 percent of the number of hash partitions computed as described earlier.

Even if we are conservative on the sizes of the partitions, by using a fudge factor, overflows can still occur. Hash-table overflows can be handled by either *resolution* or *avoidance*. Overflow resolution is performed during the build phase, if a hash-index overflow is detected. Overflow resolution is done as follows. If H_{s_i}, for any i, is found to be too large, we further partition it into smaller partitions using a different hash function. Similarly, we also partition H_{r_i} using the new hash function, and only tuples in the matching partitions need to be joined.

In contrast, overflow avoidance performs the partitioning carefully, such that overflows never occur during the build phase. We implement overflow avoidance by partitioning the build relation s initially into many small partitions, and then combining some partitions such that each combined partition fits in memory. The probe relation r must be partitioned in the same way as the combined partitions on s, but the sizes of H_{r_i} do not matter.

If a large number of tuples in s have the same value for the join attributes, the resolution and avoidance techniques may fail on some partitions. In that case, instead of creating an in-memory hash index and using a nested-loop join to join the partitions, we can use other join techniques, such as block nested-loop join, on those partitions.

12.6.6.3 Cost of Hash–Join

We now consider the cost of a hash–join. Our analysis assumes that there is no hash-table overflow. First, consider the case where recursive partitioning is not required. The partitioning of the two relations r and s calls for a complete reading of both relations, and a subsequent writing back of them. This operation requires $2(b_r + b_s)$ block accesses. The build and probe phases read each of the partitions once, calling for a further $b_r + b_s$ accesses. The number of blocks occupied by partitions could be slightly more than $b_r + b_s$, due to partially filled blocks. Accessing such partially filled blocks can add an overhead of at most $2 * max$, since each of the *max* partitions could have a partially filled block that has to be written and read back. Thus, the cost estimate for a hash–join is

$$3(b_r + b_s) + 2 * max$$

Now consider the case where recursive partitioning is required. Each pass reduces the size of each of the partitions by an expected factor of $M - 1$; this size reduction is repeated until each partition is of size at most M blocks. The expected number of passes required for partitioning s is therefore $\lceil log_{M-1}(b_s) - 1 \rceil$. Since, in each pass, every block of s is read in and written out, the total block transfers for partitioning of s is $2b_s \lceil log_{M-1}(b_s) - 1 \rceil$. The number of passes for partitioning of r is the same as the number of passes for partitioning of s, giving the following cost estimate for the join:

$$2(b_r + b_s)\lceil log_{M-1}(b_s) - 1\rceil + b_r + b_s$$

Consider, for example, the join *customer* ⋈ *depositor*. With a memory size of 20 blocks, *depositor* can be partitioned into five partitions, each of size 20 blocks, which size will fit into memory. Only one pass is required for the partitioning. The relation *customer* is similarly partitioned into five partitions, each of size 80. Ignoring the cost of writing partially filled blocks, the cost is 3(100+400) = 1500 block transfers.

The hash–join can be improved if the main memory size is large. When the entire build input can be kept in main memory, *max* can be set to 0; then, the hash–join algorithm executes quickly, without partitioning the relations into temporary files, regardless of the probe input's size. The cost estimate goes down to $b_r + b_s$.

12.6.6.4 Hybrid Hash–Join

The *hybrid hash–join* algorithm performs another optimization; it is useful when memory sizes are relatively large, but not all the build relation fits in memory. The partitioning phase of the hash–join algorithm needs one block of memory as a buffer for each partition that is created, and one block of memory as an input buffer. Hence, a total of *max*+1 blocks of memory are needed for the partitioning the two relations. If memory is larger than *max*+1, we can use the rest of memory ($M - max - 1$ blocks) to buffer the first partition of the build input (that is, H_{s_0}), so that it will not need to be written out and read back in. Further, the hash function is designed such that the hash index on H_{s_0} fits in $M - max - 1$ blocks, so that, at the end of partitioning of s, H_{s_0} is completely in memory and a hash index can be built on H_{s_0}.

When r is partitioned, tuples in H_{r_0} are again not written to disk; instead, as they are generated, the system uses them to probe the memory-resident hash index on H_{s_0}, and to generate output tuples of the join. After being used for probing, the tuples can be discarded, so the partition H_{r_0} does not occupy any memory space. Thus, a write and a read access have been saved for each block of both H_{r_0} and H_{s_0}. Tuples in the other partitions are written out as usual, and are joined later. The savings of hybrid hash–join can be significant if the build input is only slightly bigger than memory.

If the size of the build relation is b_s, *max* is approximately equal to b_s/M. Thus, hybrid hash–join is most useful if $M >> b_s/M$, or $M >> \sqrt{b_s}$, where the notation $>>$ denotes *much larger than.* For example, suppose the block size is 4 kilobytes, and the build relation is of size 1 gigabyte. Then, the hybrid hash–join algorithm is useful if the size of memory is significantly more than 2 megabytes; memory sizes of 50 to 100 megabytes or more are common on computers today.

Consider the join *customer* ⋈ *depositor* again. With a memory size of 25 blocks, *depositor* can be partitioned into five partitions, each of size 20 blocks, and the first of the partitions of the build relation can be kept in memory. It occupies 20 blocks of memory; one block is used for input, and one block each is used for buffering the other four partitions. The relation *customer* is similarly partitioned into five partitions each of size 80, the first of which is used right away for probing, instead of being written out and read back in. Ignoring the cost of writing partially filled blocks, the cost is $3(80+320)+20+80 = 1300$ block transfers, instead of 1500 block transfers without the hybrid hashing optimization.

12.6.7 Complex Joins

Nested-loop and block nested-loop joins can be used regardless of the join conditions. The other join techniques are more efficient than are the nested-loop join and its variants, but can handle only simple join conditions, such as natural joins or equi-joins. We can implement joins with complex join conditions, such as conjunctions and disjunctions, using the efficient join techniques, by applying the techniques developed in Section 12.4.4 for handling complex selections.

Consider the following join with a conjunctive condition:

$$r \bowtie_{\theta_1 \wedge \theta_2 \wedge \ldots \wedge \theta_n} s$$

One or more of the join techniques described earlier may be applicable for joins on the individual conditions $r \bowtie_{\theta_1} s$, $r \bowtie_{\theta_2} s$, $r \bowtie_{\theta_3} s$, and so on. We can compute the overall join by first computing the result of one of these simpler joins $r \bowtie_{\theta_i} s$; each pair of tuples in the intermediate result is composed of one tuple from r and one from s. The result of the complete join consists of those tuples in the intermediate result that satisfy the remaining conditions

$$\theta_1 \wedge \ldots \wedge \theta_{i-1} \wedge \theta_{i+1} \wedge \ldots \wedge \theta_n$$

These conditions can be tested as tuples in $r \bowtie_{\theta_i} s$ are being generated.

A join whose condition is disjunctive can be computed as follows. Consider

$$r \bowtie_{\theta_1 \vee \theta_2 \vee \ldots \vee \theta_n} s$$

The join can be computed as the union of the records in individual joins $r \bowtie_{\theta_i} s$:

$$(r \bowtie_{\theta_1} s) \cup (r \bowtie_{\theta_2} s) \cup \ldots \cup (r \bowtie_{\theta_n} s)$$

Algorithms for computing the union of relations are described in Section 12.7.

Let us now consider a join involving three relations:

$$loan \bowtie depositor \bowtie customer$$

Not only do we have a choice of strategy for join processing; we also have a choice of which join to compute first. There are many possible strategies to consider. We describe a few here and leave another as an exercise for you (Exercise 12.4).

- **Strategy 1**. Compute the join *depositor* ⋈ *customer* using one of the techniques that we presented. Using this intermediate result, compute

$$loan \bowtie (depositor \bowtie customer)$$

- **Strategy 2**. Proceed as in strategy 1, but compute *loan* ⋈ *depositor* first, and then join the result with *customer*. The joins can be computed in other orders as well.
- **Strategy 3**. Instead of performing two joins, perform the pair of joins at once. The technique involves first building two indices:
  - On *loan* for *loan-number*
  - On *customer* for *customer-name*

  Next, consider each tuple *t* in *depositor*. For each *t*, look up the corresponding tuples in *customer* and the corresponding tuples in *branch*. Thus, each tuple of *depositor* is examined exactly once.

Strategy 3 represents a form that we have not considered before. It does not correspond directly to a relational-algebra operation. Instead, it combines two operations into one special-purpose operation. With this strategy, it is often possible to perform a join of three relations more efficiently than we can by using two joins of two relations. The relative costs depend on the way in which the relations are stored, the distribution of values within columns, and the presence of indices. Exercise 12.5 provides an opportunity to compute these costs.

12.7 Other Operations

Other relational operations and extended relational operations—such as duplicate elimination, projection, set operations, outer join, and aggregation—can be implemented as outlined in Sections 12.7.1 through 12.7.5.

12.7.1 Duplicate Elimination

We can implement duplicate elimination easily using sorting. Identical tuples will appear adjacent to each other during sorting, and all but one copy can be removed. With external sort–merge, duplicates found while a run is being created can be removed before the run is written to disk, thereby reducing the number of block transfers. The remaining duplicates can be eliminated during merging, and the final sorted run will have no duplicates. The worst-case cost estimate for duplicate elimination is the same as the worst-case cost estimate for sorting of the relation.

We can also implement duplicate elimination using hashing, in a manner similar to the hash–join algorithm. First, the relation is partitioned based on a hash function on the whole tuple. Then, each partition is read in, and an in-memory hash index is constructed. While the hash index is being constructed, a tuple is inserted only if it is not already present. Otherwise, it is discarded. After all tuples in the partition have been processed, the tuples in the hash index are written to the result. The cost estimate is the same as the cost of processing (partitioning and reading each partition) of the build relation in a hash–join.

Because of the relatively high cost of duplicate elimination, commercial query languages require an explicit request by the user to remove duplicates; otherwise, the duplicates are retained.

12.7.2 Projection

We can implement projection easily by performing projection on each tuple, which gives a relation that could have duplicate records, and then removing duplicate records. Duplicate elimination can be done as described in Section 12.7.1. If the attributes in the projection list include a key of the relation, no duplicates will exist; hence, duplicate elimination is not required. Generalized projection (which was discussed in Section 3.5.1) can be implemented in the same way as projection. The size of a projection of the form $\Pi_A(r)$ is estimated as $V(A, r)$, since projection eliminates duplicates.

12.7.3 Set Operations

We can implement the *union*, *intersection*, and *set-difference operations* by first sorting both relations, and then scanning once through each of the sorted relations to produce the result. In $r \cup s$, when a concurrent scan of both relations reveals the same tuple in both files, only one of the tuples is retained. The result of $r \cap s$ will contain only those tuples that appear in both relations. We implement *set difference*, $r - s$, similarly, by retaining tuples in r only if they are absent in s.

For all these operations, only one scan of the two input relations is required, so the cost is $b_r + b_s$. If the relations are not sorted initially, the cost of sorting has to be included. Any sort order can be used in evaluation of set operations, provided that both inputs have that same sort order.

Hashing provides another way to implement these set operations. The first step in each case is to partition the two relations using the same hash function, and thereby to create the partitions $H_{r_0}, \ldots, H_{r_{max}}$ and $H_{s_0}, \ldots, H_{s_{max}}$. The following is then done on each partition $i = 0 \ldots max$.

- $r \cup s$
  1. Build an in-memory hash index on H_{r_i}.
  2. Add the tuples in H_{s_i} to the hash index only if they are not already present.
  3. Add the tuples in the hash index to the result.
- $r \cap s$
  1. Build an in-memory hash index on H_{r_i}.
  2. For each tuple in H_{s_i}, probe the hash index, and output the tuple to the result only if it is already present in the hash index.
- $r - s$
  1. Build an in-memory hash index on H_{r_i}.
  2. For each tuple in H_{s_i}, probe the hash index, and, if the tuple is present in the hash index, delete it from the hash index.
  3. Add the tuples remaining in the hash index to the result.

12.7.4 Outer Join

Recall the *outer-join operations*, which were described in Section 3.5.2. For example, the natural left outer join *customer* ⟕ *depositor* contains the join of *customer* and *depositor*, and, in addition, for each *customer* tuple t that has no matching tuple in *depositor* (that is, where *customer-name* is not in *depositor*), the following tuple t_1 is added to the result. For all attributes in the schema of *customer*, tuple t_1 has the same values as tuple t. The remaining attributes (from the schema of *depositor*) of tuple t_1 contain the value null.

We can implement the outer-join operations using one of two strategies. The first strategy is to compute the corresponding join, and then to add further tuples to the join result to get the outer-join result. Consider the left outer-join operation and two relations: $r(R)$ and $s(S)$. To evaluate $r ⟕_\theta s$, we first compute $r \bowtie_\theta s$, and save that result as temporary relation q_1. Next, we compute $r - \Pi_R(q_1)$, which gives tuples in r that did not participate in the join. We can use any of the algorithms for computing the joins, projection, and set difference described earlier to compute the outer joins. We pad each of these tuples with null values for attributes from s, and add it to q_1 to get the result of the outer join.

The right outer-join operation $r ⟖_\theta s$ is equivalent to $s ⟕_\theta r$, and can therefore be implemented in a symmetric fashion to the left outer join. We can implement the full outer-join operation $r ⟗_\theta s$ by computing the join $r \bowtie s$, and then adding the extra tuples of both the left and right outer-join operations, as before.

The second strategy for implementing outer joins is to modify the join algorithms. It is easy to extend the nested-loop join algorithms to compute the left outer join: Tuples in the outer relation that do not match any tuple in the inner relation are written to the output after being padded with null values. However, it is hard to extend the nested-loop join to compute the full outer join.

Natural outer joins and outer joins with an equi-join condition can be computed by extensions of the merge–join and hash–join algorithms. Merge–join can be extended to compute the full outer join as follows. When the merge of the two relations is being done, tuples in either relation that did not match any tuple in the other relation can be padded with nulls and written to the output. Similarly, we can extend merge–join to compute the left and right outer joins by writing out nonmatching tuples (padded with nulls) from only one of the relations. Since the relations are sorted, it is easy to detect whether or not a tuple matches any tuples from the other relation. For example, when a merge–join of *customer* and *depositor* is done, the tuples are read in sorted order of *customer-name*, and it is easy to check, for each tuple, whether there is a matching tuple in the other.

The cost estimates for implementing outer joins using the merge–join algorithm are the same as are those for the corresponding join. The only difference lies in size of the result, and therefore in the block transfers for writing it out, which we did not count in our earlier cost estimates.

The extension of the hash–join algorithm to compute outer joins is left for you to do as an exercise (Exercise 12.17).

12.7.5 Aggregation

Recall the aggregation operator $\mathcal{G}$, discussed in Section 3.5.3. For example, the operation

$$_{branch\text{-}name}\mathcal{G}_{\mathbf{sum}(balance)}(account)$$

groups *account* tuples by branch, and computes the total balance of all the accounts at each branch.

The aggregation operation can be implemented in a manner similar to duplicate elimination. We use either sorting or hashing, just as we did for duplicate elimination, but based on the grouping attributes (*branch-name* in the preceding example). However, instead of eliminating tuples with the same value for the grouping attribute, we gather them into groups, and apply the aggregation operations on each group to get the result.

The size of $_A\mathcal{G}_F(r)$ is simply $V(A, r)$, since there is one tuple in $_A\mathcal{G}_F(r)$ for each distinct value of A. The cost estimate for implementing the aggregation operation is the same as the cost of duplicate elimination, for aggregate functions such as **min**, **max**, **sum**, **count**, and **avg**.

Instead of gathering all the tuples in a group and then applying the aggregation operations, we can implement the aggregation operations **sum**, **min**, **max**, **count**, and **avg** on the fly as the groups are being constructed. For the case of **sum**, **min**, and **max**, when two tuples in the same group are found, they are replaced by a single tuple containing the **sum**, **min**, or **max**, respectively, of the columns being aggregated. For the **count** operation, a running count is maintained for each group for which a tuple has been found. Finally, we implement the **avg** operation by computing the sum and the count values on the fly, and finally dividing the sum by the count to get the average.

If $V(A, r)$ tuples of the result will fit in memory, both the sort-based and the hashing-based implementations do not need to write any tuples to disk. As the tuples are read in, they can be inserted in a sorted tree structure or in a hash index. When we use on the fly aggregation techniques, only one tuple needs to be stored for each of the $V(A, r)$ groups. Hence, the sorted tree-structure or hash index will fit in memory, and the aggregation can be processed with just b_r block transfers, instead of with the $3b_r$ transfers that would be required otherwise.

12.8 Evaluation of Expressions

So far, we have studied how individual relational operations are carried out. Now we consider how to evaluate an expression containing multiple operations. The obvious way to evaluate an expression is simply to evaluate one operation at a time, in an appropriate order. The result of each evaluation is *materialized* in a temporary relation for subsequent use. A disadvantage to this approach is the need to construct the temporary relations, which (unless they are small) must be written to disk. An alternative approach is to evaluate several operations simultaneously in a *pipeline*, with the results of one operation passed on to the next, without the need to store a temporary relation.

In Sections 12.8.1 and 12.8.2, we consider both the *materialization* approach and the *pipelining* approach. We shall see that the costs of these approaches can differ substantially, but also that there are cases where only the materialization approach is feasible.

12.8.1 Materialization

It is easiest to understand intuitively how to evaluate an expression by looking at a pictorial representation of the expression in an *operator tree*. Consider the expression

$$\Pi_{customer\text{-}name}\ (\sigma_{balance<2500}\ (account) \bowtie\ customer)$$

shown in Figure 12.10.

If we apply the materialization approach, we start from the lowest-level operations in the expression (at the bottom of the tree). In our example, there is only one such operation; the selection operation on *account*. The inputs to the lowest-level operations are relations in the database. We execute these operations using the algorithms that we studied earlier, and we store the results in temporary relations. We can use these temporary relations to execute the operations at the next level up in the tree, where the inputs now are either temporary relations or relations stored in the database. In our example, the inputs to the join are the *customer* relation and the temporary relation created by the selection on *account*. The join can now be evaluated, creating another temporary relation.

By repeating the process, we will eventually evaluate the operation at the root of the tree, giving the final result of the expression. In our example, we get the final result by executing the the projection operation at the root of the tree, using as input the temporary relation created by the join.

Evaluation as just described is called *materialized evaluation*, since the results of each intermediate operation are created (materialized) and then are used for evaluation of the next-level operations.

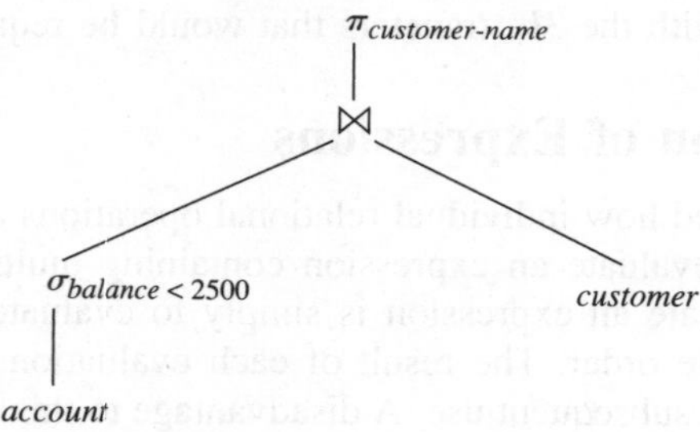

Figure 12.10 Pictorial representation of an expression.

The cost of a materialized evaluation is not simply the sum of the costs of the operations involved. When we computed the cost estimates of algorithms, we ignored the cost of writing the result of the operation to disk. To compute the cost of evaluating an expression as done here, we have to add the costs of all the operations, as well as the cost of writing the intermediate results to disk. We assume that the records of the result accumulate in a buffer, and, when the buffer is full, they are written to disk. The cost of writing out the result can be estimated as n_r/f_r, where n_r is the estimated number of tuples in the result relation, and f_r is the blocking factor of the result relation. Double buffering (using two buffers, with one continuing execution of the algorithm while the other is being written out) allows the algorithm to execute more quickly by performing CPU activity in parallel with I/O activity.

12.8.2 Pipelining

We can improve query-evaluation efficiency by reducing the number of temporary files that are produced. We achieve this reduction by combining several relational operations into a *pipeline* of operations, in which the results of one operation are passed along to the next operation in the pipeline. Combining operations into a pipeline eliminates the cost of reading and writing temporary relations.

For example, consider a join on a pair of relations followed by a projection ($\Pi_{a1,a2}(r \bowtie s)$). If materialization were applied, evaluation would involve creating a temporary relation to hold the result of the join, and then reading back in the result to perform the projection. These operations can be combined as follows. When the join operation generates a tuple of its result, that tuple is passed immediately to the project operation for processing. By combining the join and the projection, we avoid creating the intermediate result, and instead create the final result directly.

12.8.2.1 Implementation of Pipelining

We can implement a pipeline by constructing a single, complex operation that combines the operations that constitute the pipeline. Although this approach may be feasible for various frequently occurring situations, it is desirable in general to reuse the code for individual operations in the construction of a pipeline. Therefore, each operation in the pipeline is modeled as a separate process or thread within the system, which takes a stream of tuples from its pipelined inputs, and generates a stream of tuples for its output. For each pair of adjacent operations in the pipeline, a buffer is created to hold tuples being passed from one operation to the next.

In the example of Figure 12.10, all three operations can be placed in a pipeline, in which the results of the selection are passed to the join as they are generated. In turn, the results of the join are passed to the projection as they are generated. The memory requirements are low, since results of an operation are not stored for long. However, as a result of pipelining, the inputs to the operations are not available all at once for processing.

Pipelines can be executed in one of two ways:

1. Demand driven
2. Producer driven

In a *demand-driven* pipeline, the system makes repeated requests for tuples from the operation at the top of the pipeline. Each time that an operation receives a request for tuples, it computes the next tuple (or tuples) to be returned, and then returns that tuple. If the inputs of the operation are not pipelined, the next tuple(s) to be returned can be computed from the input relations, while we keep track of what has been returned so far. If some of its inputs are pipelined, the operation also makes requests for tuples from its pipelined inputs. Using the tuples received from its pipelined inputs, the operation computes tuples for its output, and passes them up to its parent.

In a *producer-driven* pipeline, operations do not wait for requests to produce tuples, but instead generate the tuples *eagerly*. Each operation at the bottom of a pipeline continually generates output tuples, and puts them in its output buffer, until the buffer is full. An operation at any other level of a pipeline generates output tuples when it gets input tuples from lower down in the pipeline, until its output buffer is full. Once the operation uses a tuple from a pipelined input, it removes the tuple from its input buffer. In either case, once the output buffer is full, the operation waits until tuples are removed from the buffer by its parent operation, so the buffer has space for more tuples. At this point, the operation generates more tuples, until the buffer is full again. This process is repeated by an operation until all the output tuples have been generated.

It is necessary for the system to switch between operations only when an output buffer is full, or an input buffer is empty and more input tuples are needed to generate any more output tuples. In a parallel-processing system, operations in a pipeline may be run concurrently on distinct processors (see Chapter 17).

Using producer-driven pipelining can be thought of as *pushing* data up an operation tree from below, whereas using demand-driven pipelining can be thought of as *pulling* data up an operation tree from the top. Each operation in a demand-driven pipeline can be implemented as an *iterator*, which provides the following functions: *open, next*, and *close*. After a call to *open*, each call to *next* returns the next output tuple of the operation. The implementation of the operation in turn calls *next* on its inputs, to get its input tuples when required. The function *close* tells an iterator that no more tuples are required. The iterator maintains the *state* of its execution in between calls, so that successive *next* requests receive successive result tuples. Details of the implementation of an iterator are left for you to complete in Exercise 12.18. Demand-driven pipelining is used more commonly than producer-driven pipelining, because it is easier to implement.

12.8.2.2 Evaluation Algorithms for Pipelining

Consider a join operation whose left-hand–side input is pipelined. Since it is pipelined, the input is not available all at once for processing by the join operation. This unavailability limits the choice of join algorithm to be used. Merge–join, for example, cannot be used if the inputs are not sorted, since it is not possible to sort a relation until all the tuples are available – thus, in effect, turning pipelining into materialization. However, indexed nested-loop join can be used: As tuples are received for the left-hand side of the join, they can be used to index the right-hand–side relation, and to generate tuples in the join result. This example illustrates that choices regarding the algorithm used for an operation and choices regarding pipelining are not independent.

The restrictions on the evaluation algorithms that can be used is a limiting factor for pipelining. As a result, despite the apparent advantages of pipelining, there are cases where materialization achieves lower overall cost. Suppose that the join of r and s is required, and input r is pipelined. If indexed nested-loop join is used to support pipelining, one access to disk may be needed for every tuple in the pipelined input relation. The cost of this technique is $n_r * HT_i$, where HT_i is the height of the index on s. With materialization, the cost of writing out r would be b_r. With a join technique such as hash–join, it may be possible to perform the join with a cost of about $3(b_r + b_s)$. If n_r is substantially more than $4b_r + 3b_s$, materialization would be cheaper.

The effective use of pipelining requires the use of evaluation algorithms that can generate output tuples even as tuples are received for the inputs to the operation. We can distinguish between two cases:

1. Only one of the inputs to a join is pipelined.
2. Both inputs to the join are pipelined.

If only one of the inputs to a join is pipelined, indexed nested-loop join is a natural choice. If the pipelined input tuples are sorted on the join attributes, and the join condition is an equi-join, merge–join can also be used. Hybrid hash–join can be used, with the pipelined input as the probe relation. However, tuples that are not in the first partition will be output only after the entire pipelined input relation is received. Hybrid hash–join is useful if the nonpipelined input fits entirely in memory, or if at least most of that input fits in memory.

If both inputs are pipelined, the choice of join algorithms is more restricted. If both inputs are sorted on the join attribute, and the join condition is an equi-join, merge–join can be used. Another alternative is the *pipelined-join* technique, shown in Figure 12.11. The algorithm assumes that the input tuples for both input relations, r and s, are pipelined. Tuples made available for both relations are queued for processing in a single queue. Special queue entries, called End_r and End_s, which serve as end-of-file markers, are inserted in the queue after all tuples from r and s (respectively) have been generated. For efficient evaluation, appropriate indices should be built on the relations r and s. As tuples are added to r and s, the indices must be kept up to date.

```
done_r := false;
done_s := false;
r := ∅;
s := ∅;
result := ∅;
while not done_r or not done_s do
    begin
        if queue is empty, then wait until queue is not empty;
        t := top entry in queue;
        if t = End_r then done_r := true
            else if t = End_s then done_s := true
                else if t is from input r then
                    begin
                        r := r ∪ {t};
                        result := result ∪ ({t} ⋈ s);
                    end
                else /* t is from input s */
                    begin
                        s := s ∪ {t};
                        result := result ∪ (r ⋈ {t});
                    end
    end
```

Figure 12.11 Pipelined join algorithm.

12.9 Transformation of Relational Expressions

So far, we have studied algorithms to evaluate extended relational-algebra operations, and have estimated their costs. As we mentioned earlier, a query can be expressed in several different ways, with different costs of evaluation. In this section, rather than taking the relational expression as given, we consider alternative, equivalent expressions.

12.9.1 Equivalence of Expressions

Consider the relational-algebra expression for the query "Find the names of all customers who have an account at any branch located in Brooklyn."

$$\Pi_{customer\text{-}name}\ (\sigma_{branch-city = \text{"Brooklyn"}}\ (branch \bowtie\ (account \bowtie\ depositor)))$$

This expression constructs a large intermediate relation, *branch* ⋈ *account* ⋈ *depositor*. However, we are interested in only a few tuples of this relation (those pertaining to branches located in Brooklyn), and in only one of the six attributes of this relation. Since we are concerned with only those tuples in the *branch* relation that pertain to branches located in Brooklyn, we do not need to consider

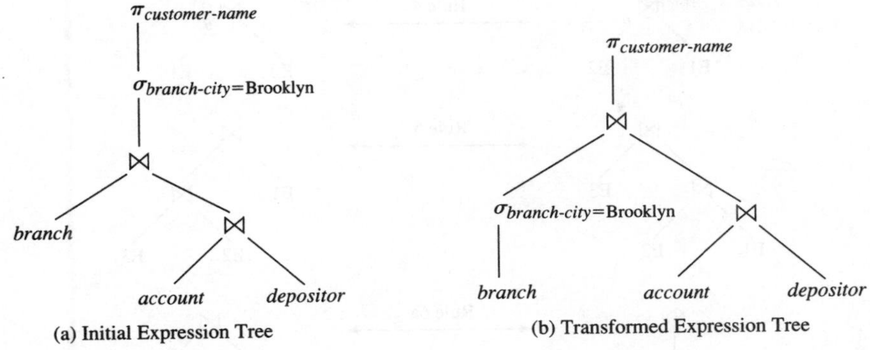

Figure 12.12 Equivalent expressions.

those tuples that do not have *branch-city* = "Brooklyn." By reducing the number of tuples of the *branch* relation that we need to access, we reduce the size of the intermediate result. Our query is now represented by the relational-algebra expression

$$\Pi_{customer\text{-}name}\ (\ (\sigma_{branch\text{-}city\ =\text{"Brooklyn"}}\ (branch))\ \bowtie\ (account \bowtie depositor))$$

which is equivalent to our original algebra expression, but which generates smaller intermediate relations. The initial and transformed expressions are shown pictorially in Figure 12.12.

Given a relational-algebra expression, it is the job of the query optimizer to come up with a query-evaluation plan that computes the same result as the given expression, and is the least costly way of generating the result (or, at least, is not much costlier than the least costly way).

To find the least costly query-evaluation plan, the optimizer needs to generate alternative plans that produce the same result as the given expression, and to choose the least costly one. Generation of query-evaluation plans involves two steps: (1) generating expressions that are logically equivalent to the given expression, and (2) annotating the resultant expressions in alternative ways to generate alternative query plans. The two steps are interleaved in the query optimizer—some expressions are generated and annotated, then further expressions are generated and annotated, and so on.

To implement the first step, the query optimizer must generate expressions equivalent to a given expression. It does so by means of *equivalence rules* that specify how to transform an expression into a logically equivalent one. We describe these rules next. In Section 12.10, we describe how to choose a query-evaluation plan. We can choose one based on the *estimated* cost of the plans. Since the cost is an estimate, the selected plan is not necessarily the least costly plan; however, as long as the estimates are good, the plan is likely to be the least costly one, or not much more costly than that one. Such optimization is called *cost-based optimization*, and is described in Section 12.10.2.

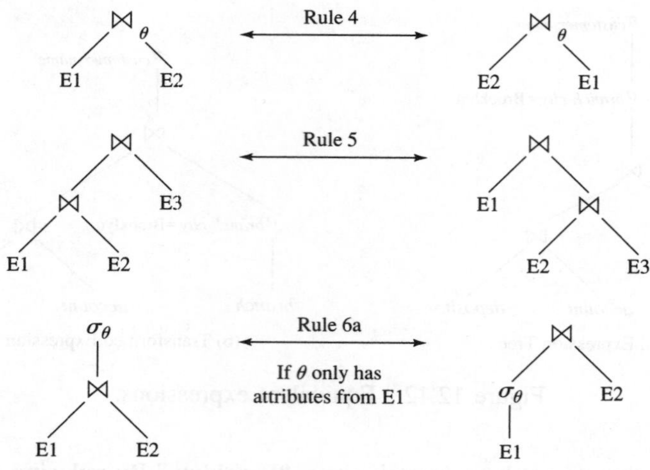

Figure 12.13 Pictorial representation of equivalences.

12.9.2 Equivalence Rules

An *equivalence rule* says that expressions of two forms are equivalent: We can transform either to the other while preserving equivalence. By *preserve equivalence* we mean that relations generated by the two expressions have the same set of attributes and contain the same set of tuples, although their attributes may be ordered differently. Equivalence rules are used by the optimizer to transform expressions into other logically equivalent expressions.

We now list a number of general equivalence rules on relational-algebra expressions. Some of the equivalences listed are also illustrated in Figure 12.13. We use $\theta, \theta_1, \theta_2$, and so on to denote predicates, L_1, L_2, L_3, and so on to denote lists of attributes, and E, E_1, E_2, and so on to denote relational-algebra expressions. A relation name r is simply a special case of a relational-algebra expression, and can be used wherever E appears.

1. Conjunctive selection operations can be deconstructed into a sequence of individual selections. This transformation is referred to as a cascade of σ.

$$\sigma_{\theta_1 \wedge \theta_2}(E) = \sigma_{\theta_1}(\sigma_{\theta_2}(E))$$

2. Selection operations are commutative.

$$\sigma_{\theta_1}(\sigma_{\theta_2}(E)) = \sigma_{\theta_2}(\sigma_{\theta_1}(E))$$

3. Only the final operations in a sequence of projection operations is needed, the others can be omitted. This transformation can also be referred to as a cascade of Π.

$$\Pi_{L_1}(\Pi_{L_2}(\ldots(\Pi_{L_n}(E))\ldots)) = \Pi_{L_1}(E)$$

4. Selections can be combined with Cartesian products and theta joins.

a. $\sigma_\theta(E_1 \times E_2) = E_1 \bowtie_\theta E_2$

This expression is just the definition of the theta join.

b. $\sigma_{\theta_1}(E_1 \bowtie_{\theta_2} E_2) \;=\; E_1 \bowtie_{\theta_1 \wedge \theta_2} E_2$

5. Theta-join operations are commutative.

$$E_1 \bowtie_\theta E_2 \;=\; E_2 \bowtie_\theta E_1$$

Recall that the natural-join operator is simply a special case of the theta-join operator; hence, natural joins are also commutative.

6. a. Natural-join operations are associative.

$$(E_1 \bowtie E_2) \bowtie E_3 \;=\; E_1 \bowtie (E_2 \bowtie E_3)$$

b. Theta joins are associative in the following manner:

$$(E_1 \bowtie_{\theta_1} E_2) \bowtie_{\theta_2 \wedge \theta_3} E_3 \;=\; E_1 \bowtie_{\theta_1 \wedge \theta_3} (E_2 \bowtie_{\theta_2} E_3)$$

where θ_2 involves attributes from only E_2 and E_3. Any of these conditions may be empty; hence, it follows that the Cartesian product ($\times$) operation is also associative. The commutativity and associativity of join operations are important for join reordering in query optimization.

7. The selection operation distributes over the theta join operation under the following two conditions:

a. It distributes when all the attributes in selection condition θ_0 involve only the attributes of one of the expressions (E_1) being joined.

$$\sigma_{\theta_0}(E_1 \bowtie_\theta E_2) = \;(\sigma_{\theta_0}(E_1)) \bowtie_\theta E_2$$

b. It distributes when selection condition θ_1 involves only the attributes of E_1 and θ_2 involves only the attributes of E_2.

$$\sigma_{\theta_1 \wedge \theta_2}(E_1 \bowtie_\theta E_2) = \;(\sigma_{\theta_1}(E_1)) \bowtie_\theta (\sigma_{\theta_2}(E_2))$$

8. The projection operation distributes over the theta join operation.

a. Let L_1 and L_2 be attributes of E_1 and E_2, respectively. Suppose that the join condition θ involves only attributes in $L_1 \cup L_2$. Then,

$$\Pi_{L_1 \cup L_2}(E_1 \bowtie_\theta E_2) = (\Pi_{L_1}(E_1)) \bowtie_\theta (\Pi_{L_2}(E_2))$$

b. Consider a join $E_1 \bowtie_\theta E_2$. Let L_1 and L_2 be sets of attributes from E_1 and E_2, respectively. Let L_3 be attributes of E_1 that are involved in join condition θ, but are not in $L_1 \cup L_2$, and let L_4 be attributes of E_2 that are involved in join condition θ, but are not in $L_1 \cup L_2$. Then,

$$\Pi_{L_1 \cup L_2}(E_1 \bowtie_\theta E_2) = \Pi_{L_1 \cup L_2}((\Pi_{L_1 \cup L_3}(E_1)) \bowtie_\theta (\Pi_{L_2 \cup L_4}(E_2)))$$

9. The set operations union and intersection are commutative.

$$E_1 \cup E_2 = E_2 \cup E_1$$

$$E_1 \cap E_2 = E_2 \cap E_1$$

Set difference is not commutative.

10. Set union and intersection are associative.

$$(E_1 \cup E_2) \cup E_3 = E_1 \cup (E_2 \cup E_3)$$

$$(E_1 \cap E_2) \cap E_3 = E_1 \cap (E_2 \cap E_3)$$

11. The selection operation distributes over the union, intersection, and set-difference operations.

$$\sigma_P(E_1 - E_2) = \sigma_P(E_1) - E_2 = \sigma_P(E_1) - \sigma_P(E_2)$$

Similarly, for union and intersection, the preceding equivalence, with set difference ($-$) replaced with either one of $\cup$ or $\cap$, also holds.

12. The projection operation distributes over the union operation.

$$\Pi_L(E_1 \cup E_2) = (\Pi_L(E_1)) \cup (\Pi_L(E_2))$$

The preceding list is only a partial list of equivalences. More equivalences involving extended relational operators, such as the outer join and aggregation, are discussed in the exercises.

12.9.3 Examples of Transformations

We now illustrate the use of the equivalence rules. We use our bank example with the relation schemas:

Branch-schema = (*branch-name, branch-city, assets*)
Account-schema = (*branch-name, account-number, balance*)
Depositor-schema = (*customer-name, account-number*)

The relations *branch*, *account*, and *depositor* are instances of these schemas.

In our earlier example, the expression

$$\Pi_{customer\text{-}name}(\sigma_{branch\text{-}city = \text{"Brooklyn"}}(branch \bowtie (account \bowtie depositor)))$$

was transformed into the following expression,

$$\Pi_{customer\text{-}name}((\sigma_{branch\text{-}city = \text{"Brooklyn"}}(branch)) \bowtie (account \bowtie depositor))$$

which is equivalent to our original algebra expression, but generates smaller intermediate relations. We can carry out this transformation using rule 7a. Remember that the rule merely says that the two expressions are equivalent; it does not say that one is better than the other.

Multiple equivalence rules can be used, one after the other, on a query or on parts of the query. As an illustration, suppose that we modify our original query to restrict attention to customers who have a balance over $1000. The new relational-algebra query is

$$\Pi_{customer\text{-}name}\ (\sigma_{branch\text{-}city\,=\,\text{"Brooklyn"}\ \wedge\ balance\ >1000}\ (branch \bowtie (account \bowtie depositor)))$$

We cannot apply the selection predicate directly to the *branch* relation, since the predicate involves attributes of both the *branch* and *account* relation. However, we can first apply rule 6a (associativity of natural join) to transform the join *branch* ⋈ (*account* ⋈ *depositor*) into (*branch* ⋈ *account*) ⋈ *depositor*:

$$\Pi_{customer\text{-}name}\ (\sigma_{branch\text{-}city\,=\,\text{"Brooklyn"}\ \wedge\ balance\ >1000}\ ((branch \bowtie account) \bowtie depositor))$$

Then, using rule 7a, we can rewrite our query as

$$\Pi_{customer\text{-}name}\ ((\sigma_{branch\text{-}city\,=\,\text{"Brooklyn"}\wedge\ balance>1000}\ (branch \bowtie account)) \bowtie depositor)$$

Let us examine the selection subexpression within this expression. Using rule 1, we can break the selection into two selections, to get the following subexpression:

$$\sigma_{branch\text{-}city\,=\,\text{"Brooklyn"}}\ (\sigma_{balance\ >\ 1000}\ (branch \bowtie account))$$

Both of the preceding expressions select tuples with *branch-city* = "Brooklyn" and *balance* > 1000. However, the latter form of the expression provides a new opportunity to apply the "perform selections early" rule, resulting in the subexpression

$$\sigma_{branch\text{-}city\,=\,\text{"Brooklyn"}}\ (branch) \bowtie \sigma_{balance>1000}\ (account)$$

The initial expression and the final expression after all the preceding transformations are shown pictorially in Figure 12.14. We could equally well have used rule 7b to get the final expression directly, without using rule 1 to break the selection into two selections. In fact, rule 7b can itself be derived from rules 1 and 7a

A set of equivalence rules is said to be *minimal* if no rule can be derived from any combination of the others. The preceding example illustrates that the set of equivalence rules in Section 12.9.2 is not minimal.

Now consider the following form of our example query:

$$\Pi_{customer\text{-}name}\ ((\sigma_{branch\text{-}city\,=\,\text{"Brooklyn"}}\ (branch) \bowtie account) \bowtie depositor)$$

When we compute the subexpression

$$(\sigma_{branch\text{-}city\,=\,\text{"Brooklyn"}}\ (branch) \bowtie account)$$

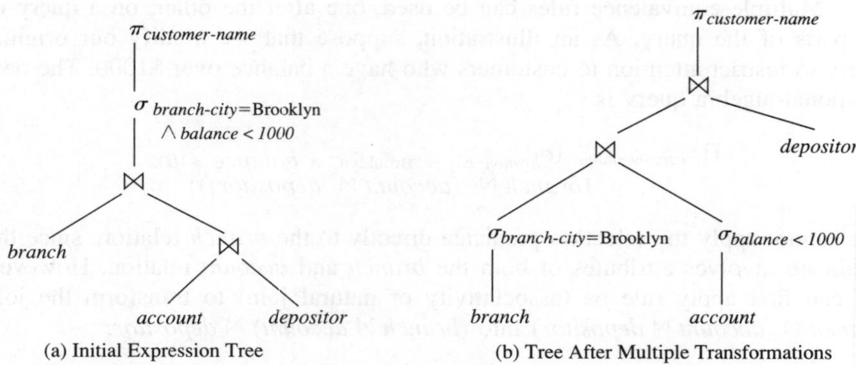

Figure 12.14 Multiple transformations.

we obtain a relation whose schema is

$$(\textit{branch-name, branch-city, assets, account-number, balance})$$

We can eliminate several attributes from the schema, by pushing projections using equivalence rules 8a and 8b. The only attributes that we must retain are those that either appear in the result of the query or are needed to process subsequent operations. By eliminating unneeded attributes, we reduce the number of columns of the intermediate result. Thus, the size of the intermediate result is reduced. In our example, the only attribute we need from the join of *branch* and *account* is *account-number*. Therefore, we can modify the expression to

$$\Pi_{customer\text{-}name} \; (\\ (\; \Pi_{account\text{-}number} \;((\sigma_{branch\text{-}city\,=\,\text{"Brooklyn"}}\;(branch)) \bowtie \; account)) \\ \bowtie \; depositor)$$

The projection $\Pi_{account\text{-}number}$ reduces the size of the intermediate join results.

12.9.4 Join Ordering

A good ordering of join operations is important for reducing the size of temporary results; hence, most query optimizers pay a lot of attention to the join order. As mentioned in Chapter 3 and in equivalence rule 6a, the natural-join operation is associative. Thus, for all relations r_1, r_2, and r_3,

$$(r_1 \bowtie r_2) \bowtie r_3 \;=\; r_1 \bowtie (r_2 \bowtie r_3)$$

Although these expressions are equivalent, the costs of computing them may differ. Consider again the expression

$$\Pi_{customer\text{-}name}\;((\sigma_{branch\text{-}city\,=\,\text{"Brooklyn"}}\;(branch)) \bowtie \; account \bowtie \; depositor)$$

We could choose to compute *account* ⋈ *depositor* first, and then to join the result with

$$\sigma_{branch\text{-}city\,=\,\text{"Brooklyn"}}\;(branch)$$

However, *ilmaccount* ⋈ *depositor* is likely to be a large relation, since it contains one tuple for every account. In contrast,

$$\sigma_{branch\text{-}city = \text{"Brooklyn"}} \ (branch) \bowtie \ account$$

is probably a small relation. To see that it is, we note that, since the bank has a large number of widely distributed branches, it is likely that only a small fraction of the bank's customers have accounts in branches located in Brooklyn. Thus, the preceding expression results in one tuple for each account held by a resident of Brooklyn. Therefore, the temporary relation that we must store is smaller than it would have been had we computed *account* ⋈ *depositor* first.

There are other options to consider for evaluating our query. We do not care about the order in which attributes appear in a join, since it is easy to change the order before displaying the result. Thus, for all relations r_1 and r_2,

$$r_1 \bowtie \ r_2 \ = \ r_2 \bowtie \ r_1$$

That is, natural join is commutative (equivalence rule 5).

Using the associativity and commutativity of the natural join (Rules 5 and 6), we can consider rewriting our relational-algebra expression as

$$\Pi_{customer\text{-}name} \ (((\sigma_{branch\text{-}city = \text{"Brooklyn"}} \ (branch)) \bowtie \ depositor) \bowtie \ account)$$

That is, we could compute

$$(\sigma_{branch\text{-}city = \text{"Brooklyn"}} \ (branch)) \bowtie \ depositor$$

first, and, after that, join the result with *account*. Note, however, that there are no attributes in common between *Branch-schema* and *Depositor-schema*, so the join is just a Cartesian product. If there are b branches in Brooklyn and d tuples in the *depositor* relation, this Cartesian product generates $b * d$ tuples, one for every possible pair of depositor tuple and branches (without regard for whether the account in *depositor* is maintained at the branch). Thus, it appears that this Cartesian product will produce a large temporary relation. As a result, we would reject this strategy. However, if the user had entered the preceding expression, we could use the associativity and commutativity of the natural join to transform this expression to the more efficient expression that we used earlier.

12.9.5 Enumeration of Equivalent Expressions

Query optimizers use equivalence rules to generate systematically expressions equivalent to the given query expression. Conceptually, the process is carried out as follows. Given an expression, if any subexpression matches one side of an equivalence rule, a new expression is generated, where the subexpression is transformed to match the other side of the rule. This process continues until no more new expressions can be generated.

The preceding process is costly both in space and in time. The space requirement is reduced as follows. If we generate an expression E_1 from an expression

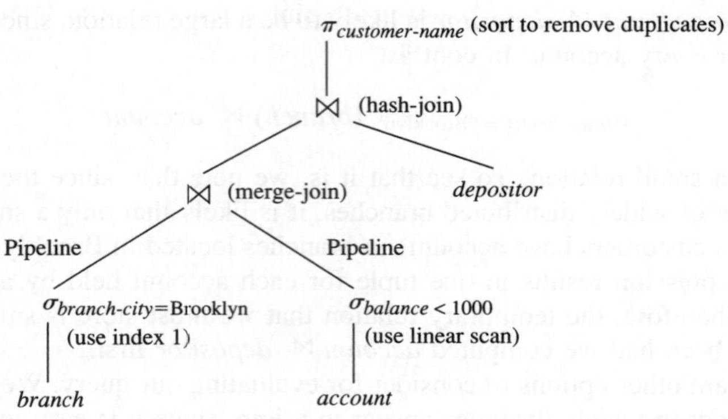

Figure 12.15 An evaluation plan.

E_2 using an equivalence rule, then E_1 and E_2 are similar in structure, and have subexpressions that are identical. Expression-representation techniques that allow both expressions to point to shared subexpressions can reduce the space requirement significantly, and are used in many query optimizers.

Moreover, it is not always necessary to generate every expression that can be generated using the equivalence rules. If cost estimates of evaluation are taken into account, an optimizer may be able to avoid examining some of the expressions, as we shall see in Section 12.10. We can reduce the time required for optimization using techniques such as the ones just described.

12.10 Choice of Evaluation Plans

Generation of expressions is only part of the query-optimization process. Each operation in the expression can be implemented with different algorithms. An evaluation plan defines exactly what algorithm is used for each operation, and how the execution of the operations is coordinated. Figure 12.15 illustrates one possible evaluation plan for the expression from Figure 12.14. As we have seen, several different algorithms can be used for each relational operation, giving rise to alternative evaluation plans. Further, decisions about pipelining have to be made. In the figure, the edges from the selection operations to the merge–join operation are marked as pipelined; pipelining is feasible if the selection operations generate their output sorted on the join attributes. They would do so if the indices on *branch* and *account* store records with equal values for the index attributes sorted by *branch-name*.

12.10.1 Interaction of Evaluation Techniques

One way to choose an evaluation plan for a query expression is simply to choose for each operation the cheapest algorithm for evaluating it. We can choose any ordering of the operations consistent with operations lower in the tree being executed before operations higher in the tree.

However, choosing the cheapest algorithm for each operation independently is not necessarily a good idea. Although a merge–join at a given level may be costlier than a hash–join, it may provide a sorted output that makes evaluating a later operation (such as duplicate elimination, intersection, or another merge–join) cheaper. Similarly, a nested-loop join with indexing may provide opportunities for pipelining the results to the next operation, and thus may be useful even if it is not the cheapest way of performing the join. To choose the best overall algorithm, we must consider even nonoptimal algorithms for individual operations.

Thus, in addition to considering alternative expressions for a query, we must also consider alternative algorithms for each operation in an expression. We can use rules much like the equivalence rules to define what are the possible algorithms for each operation, including whether or not to pipeline that operation with another expression. We can use these rules to evaluate systematically all the query-evaluation plans for a given expression.

Given an evaluation plan, we can use the techniques discussed earlier in the chapter to estimate its cost. That still leaves the problem of choosing the best evaluation plan for a query. There are two broad approaches: the first searches all the plans, and chooses the best plan in a cost-based fashion. The second uses heuristics to choose a plan. We discuss these approaches next. Practical query optimizers incorporate elements of both approaches.

12.10.2 Cost-Based Optimization

A cost-based optimizer generates a range of query-evaluation plans from the given query by using the equivalence rules, and chooses the one with the least cost. For a complex query, the number of different query plans that are equivalent to a given plan can be large. As an illustration, consider the expression

$$r_1 \bowtie r_2 \bowtie \cdots \bowtie r_n$$

where the joins are expressed without any ordering. With $n = 3$, there are 12 different join orderings:

$r_1 \bowtie (r_2 \bowtie r_3)$	$r_1 \bowtie (r_3 \bowtie r_2)$	$(r_2 \bowtie r_3) \bowtie r_1$	$(r_3 \bowtie r_2) \bowtie r_1$
$r_2 \bowtie (r_1 \bowtie r_3)$	$r_2 \bowtie (r_3 \bowtie r_1)$	$(r_1 \bowtie r_3) \bowtie r_2$	$(r_3 \bowtie r_1) \bowtie r_2$
$r_3 \bowtie (r_1 \bowtie r_2)$	$r_3 \bowtie (r_2 \bowtie r_1)$	$(r_1 \bowtie r_2) \bowtie r_3$	$(r_2 \bowtie r_1) \bowtie r_3$

In general, with n relations, there are $(2(n-1))!/(n-1)!$ different join orders. (We leave the computation of this expression for you to do in Exercise 12.23.) For joins involving small numbers of relations, this number is acceptable; for example, with $n = 5$, the number is 1680. However, as n increases, this number rises quickly. With $n = 7$, the number is 665280; with $n = 10$, the number is greater than 176 billion!

Luckily, it is not necessary to generate all the expressions equivalent to a given expression. For example, suppose that we want to find the best join order for the form:

$$(r_1 \bowtie r_2 \bowtie r_3) \bowtie r_4 \bowtie r_5$$

which represents all join orders where r_1, r_2, and r_3 are joined first (in some order), and the result is joined (in some order) with r_4 and r_5. There are 12 different join orders for computing $r_1 \bowtie r_2 \bowtie r_3$, and 12 orders for computing the join of this result with r_4 and r_5. Thus, there appear to be 144 join orders to examine. However, once we have found the best join order for the subset of relations $\{r_1, r_2, r_3\}$, we can use that order for further joins with r_4 and r_5, and can ignore all costlier join orders of $r_1 \bowtie r_2 \bowtie r_3$. Thus, instead of 144 choices to examine, we need to examine only $12 + 12$ choices. Using this idea, we can develop a dynamic-programming algorithm for finding optimal join orders, which approach greatly reduces the number of expressions examined. The algorithm computes the best join order for each subset of the given set of n relations. (See Exercise 12.24.)

Actually, the order in which tuples are generated by the join of $r_1 \bowtie r_2 \bowtie r_3$ is also important for finding the best overall join order, since it can affect the cost of further joins (for instance, if merge–join is used). A particular sort order of the tuples is said to be an *interesting sort order* if it could be useful for a later operation. For instance, given the result of $r_1 \bowtie r_2 \bowtie r_3$, sorting on the common attributes with r_4 or r_5 may be useful, but sorting on the attributes common to only r_1 and r_2 is not useful. Using merge–join when computing $r_1 \bowtie r_2 \bowtie r_3$ may be costlier than using some other join technique, but may provide an output sorted in an interesting order.

Hence, it is not sufficient to find the best join order for each subset of the set of n given relations. Instead, we have to find the best join order for each subset, for each interesting sort order of the join result for that subset. The number of subsets of n relations is 2^n. The number of interesting sort orders is generally not large. Thus, about 2^n join expressions need to be stored. The dynamic-programming algorithm for finding the best join order can be easily extended to handle sort orders, and has a time cost of around 3^n. (See Exercise 12.25.)

With $n = 10$, this number is around 59000, which is much better than the 176 billion different join orders. More important, the storage required is much less than before, since we need to store only one join order for each interesting order of each of 1024 subsets of $r_1, \ldots, r_{10}$. Although both numbers still increase rapidly with n, commonly occurring joins usually have less than 10 relations, and can be handled easily.

We can use several techniques to reduce further the cost of searching through a large number of plans. For instance, when examining the plans for an expression, we can terminate after we examine only a part of the expression, if we determine that the cheapest plan for that part is already costlier than the cheapest evaluation plan for a full expression examined earlier. Similarly, suppose that we determine that the cheapest way of evaluating a subexpression is costlier than the cheapest evaluation plan for a full expression examined earlier. Then, no full expression involving that subexpression needs to be examined. We can further reduce the number of evaluation plans that need to be considered fully by first making a heuristic guess of a good plan, and estimating that plan's cost. Then, only a few competing plans will require a full analysis of cost. These optimizations can reduce the overhead of query optimization significantly.

12.10.3 Heuristic Optimization

A drawback of cost-based optimization is the cost of optimization itself. Although the cost of query processing can be reduced by clever optimizations, cost-based optimization is still expensive. Hence, many systems use *heuristics* to reduce the number of choices that must be made in a cost-based fashion. Some systems even choose to use only heuristics, and do not used cost-based optimization at all.

An example of a heuristic rule is the following rule for transforming relational-algebra queries:

- Perform selection operations as early as possible.

A heuristic optimizer would use this rule without finding out whether the cost is reduced by this transformation. In the first transformation example in Section 12.9, the selection operation was pushed into a join.

We say that the preceding rule is a heuristic because it usually, but not always, helps to reduce the cost. For an example of where it can result in an increase in cost, consider an expression $\sigma_\theta(r \bowtie s)$, where the condition θ refers to only attributes in s. The selection can certainly be performed before the join. However, if r is extremely small compared to s, and if there is an index on the join attributes of s, but no index on the attributes used by θ, then it is probably a bad idea to perform the selection early. Performing the selection early—that is, directly on s—would require doing a scan of all tuples in s. It is probably cheaper, in this case, to compute the join using the index, and then to reject tuples that fail the selection.

The projection operation, like the selection operation, reduces the size of relations. Thus, whenever we need to generate a temporary relation, it is advantageous to apply immediately any projections that are possible. This advantage suggests a companion to the "perform selections early" heuristic that we stated earlier:

- Perform projections early.

It is usually better to perform selections earlier than projections, since selections have the potential to reduce the sizes of relations greatly, and selections enable the use of indices to access tuples. An example similar to the one used for the selection heuristic should convince you that this heuristic does not always reduce the cost.

Drawing on the equivalences discussed in Section 12.9.2, a heuristic optimization algorithm will reorder the components of an initial query tree to achieve improved query execution. We now present an overview of the steps in a typical heuristic optimization algorithm. You can understand the heuristics by visualizing a query expression as a tree, as illustrated earlier.

1. Deconstruct conjunctive selections into a sequence of single selection operations. Based on equivalence rule 1, this step facilitates moving selection operations down the query tree.
2. Move selection operations down the query tree for the earliest possible execution. This step uses the commutativity and distributivity properties of the selection operation noted in equivalence rules 2, 7a, 7b, and 11.

For instance, $\sigma_\theta(r \bowtie s)$ is transformed into either $\sigma_\theta(r) \bowtie s$ or $r \bowtie \sigma_\theta(s)$ whenever possible. Performing value-based selections as early as possible reduces the cost of sorting and merging intermediate results. The degree of reordering permitted for a particular selection is determined by the attributes involved in that selection condition.

3. Determine which selection operations and join operations will produce the smallest relations—that is, will produce the relations with the least number of tuples. Using associativity of the $\bowtie$ operation, rearrange the tree such that the leaf-node relations with these restrictive selections are executed first.

   This step considers the selectivity of a selection or join condition. Recall that the most restrictive selection—that is, the condition with the smallest selectivity—retrieves the fewest records. This step relies on the associativity of binary operations given in equivalence rules 6 and 10

4. Replace with join operations Cartesian product operations that are followed by a selection condition (rule 4a). As demonstrated in Section 12.9.4, the Cartesian product operation is often expensive to implement. In $r_1 \times r_2$, not only does the result include a record for each combination of records from r_1 and r_2, but also the result attributes include all the attributes of r_1 and r_2. Therefore, it is advisable to avoid using the Cartesian product operation.

5. Deconstruct and move as far down the tree as possible lists of projection attributes, creating new projections where needed. This step draws on the properties of the projection operation given in equivalence rules 3, 8a, 8b, and 12.

6. Identify those subtrees whose operations can be pipelined, and execute them using pipelining.

In summary, the heuristics listed here reorder an initial query-tree representation such that the operations that reduce the size of intermediate results are applied first; early selection reduces the number of tuples, and early projection reduces the number of attributes. The heuristic transformations also restructure the tree such that the most restrictive selection and join operations are performed before other similar operations.

Heuristic optimization further maps the heuristically transformed query expression into alternative sequences of operations to produce a set of candidate evaluation plans. An evaluation plan includes not only the relational operations to be performed, but also the indices to be used, the order in which tuples are to be accessed, and the order in which the operations are to be performed. The *access-plan–selection* phase of a heuristic optimizer chooses the most efficient strategy for each operation.

12.10.4 Structure of Query Optimizers

So far, we have described the two basic approaches to choosing an evaluation plan. Most practical query optimizers combine elements of both approaches. Certain query optimizers, such as the System R optimizer, do not consider all join orders,

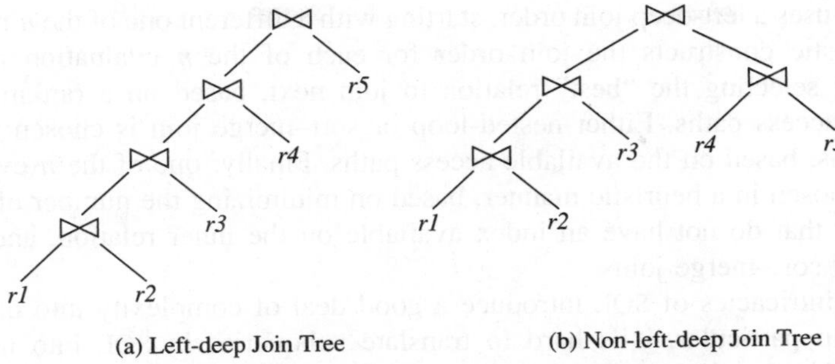

(a) Left-deep Join Tree (b) Non-left-deep Join Tree

Figure 12.16 Left-deep join trees.

but rather restrict the search to particular kinds of join orders. The System R optimizer considers only those join orders where the right operand of each join is one of the initial relations $r_1, \ldots, r_n$. Such join orders are called *left-deep join orders*. Left-deep join orders are particularly convenient for pipelined evaluation, since the right operand is a stored relation, and thus only one input to each join is pipelined.

Figure 12.16 illustrates the difference between left-deep join trees and non–left-deep join trees. The time it takes to consider all left-deep join orders is $O(n!)$, which is much less than the time to consider all join orders. With the use of some optimizations, the System R optimizer can find the best join order in time approximately $O(2^n)$. Contrast this cost with the 3^n time required to find the best overall join order. The System R optimizer uses heuristics to push selections and projections down the query tree.

The cost estimate that we presented for scans using secondary indices assumed that every tuple access results in an I/O operation. The estimate is likely to be accurate with small buffers; with large buffers, however, the page containing the tuple may already be in the buffer. The Sybase optimizer incorporates a better cost-estimation technique for such scans: It takes into account the probability that the page containing the tuple is in the buffer.

Query optimization approaches that integrate heuristic selection and the generation of alternative access plans have been adopted in several systems. The approach used in System R and in its successor, the Starburst project, consists of a hierarchical procedure based on the nested-block concept of SQL. The cost-based optimization techniques described here are used for each block of the query separately. Ingres uses heuristic decomposition to reduce a query to a set of subqueries containing no more than two relations. Detailed access plans are then generated for each of these subqueries.

The Oracle7 optimizer has two components: one is based on heuristic rules, and the other is cost based.† The heuristic approach works roughly as we shall describe. For an n-way join, it considers n evaluation plans constructed as follows.

†The details that we describe apply to the Oracle7 release of December 1992. Later versions may follow other optimization techniques.

Each plan uses a left-deep join order, starting with a different one of the n relations. The heuristic constructs the join order for each of the n evaluation plans by repeatedly selecting the "best" relation to join next, based on a ranking of the available access paths. Either nested-loop or sort–merge join is chosen for each of the joins, based on the available access paths. Finally, one of the n evaluation plans is chosen in a heuristic manner, based on minimizing the number of nested-loop joins that do not have an index available on the inner relation, and on the number of sort–merge joins.

The intricacies of SQL introduce a good deal of complexity into query optimizers. In particular, it is hard to translate subqueries in SQL into relational algebra. Many optimizers, such as System R and Starburst, attempt to rewrite SQL queries to transform subqueries into joins where possible. Where the transformation is not possible, the subqueries are kept as separate expressions, and are optimized separately. The chosen evaluation plans are then combined via special evaluation algorithms. Similarly, for compound SQL queries (using the $\cup$, $\cap$, or $-$ operation), each component is optimized separately, and the evaluation plans are combined to form the overall evaluation plan.

Even with the use of heuristics, cost-based query optimization imposes a substantial overhead on query processing. However, the added cost of cost-based query optimization is usually more than offset by the saving at query-execution time, which is dominated by slow disk accesses. The difference in execution time between a good plan and a bad one may be huge, making query optimization essential. The achieved saving is magnified in those applications that run on a regular basis, where the query can be optimized once, and the selected query plan can be used on each run. Therefore, most commercial systems include relatively sophisticated optimizers. The bibliographic notes give references to descriptions of the query optimizers of actual database systems.

12.11 Summary

The first action that the system must perform on a query is to translate the query into its internal form, which (for relational database systems) is usually based on the relational algebra. In the process of generating the internal form of the query, the parser checks the syntax of the user's query, verifies that the relation names appearing in the query are names of relations in the database, and so on. If the query was expressed in terms of a view, the parser replaces all references to the view name with the relational-algebra expression to compute the view.

Given a query, there is generally a variety of methods for computing the answer. It is the responsibility of the system to transform the query as entered by the user into an equivalent query that can be computed more efficiently. This *optimizing* or, more accurately, improving of the strategy for processing a query is called *query optimization*.

The evaluation of complex queries involves many accesses to disk. Since the transfer of data from disk is slow relative to the speed of main memory and the CPU of the computer system, it is worthwhile to allocate a considerable amount of processing to choose a method that minimizes disk accesses.

The strategy that we choose for evaluating an operation depends on the size of each relation and on the distribution of values within columns. So that they can choose a strategy based on reliable information, database systems may store statistics for each relation *r*. These statistics include

- The number of tuples in the relation *r*
- The size of a record (tuple) of relation *r* in bytes
- The number of distinct values that appear in the relation *r* for a particular attribute

These statistics allow us to estimate the sizes of the results of various operations, as well as the cost of executing the operations. Statistical information about relations is particularly useful when several indices are available to assist in the processing of a query. The presence of these structures has a significant influence on the choice of a query-processing strategy.

We can process queries involving simple selections by performing a linear scan, by doing a binary search, or by making use of indices. We can handle complex selections by computing unions and intersections of the results of simple selections. We can sort relations larger than memory using the external merge–sort algorithm. Queries involving a natural join may be processed in several ways, depending on the availability of indices and the form of physical storage used for the relations. If the join result is almost as large as the Cartesian product of the two relations, a *block nested-loop* join strategy may be advantageous. If indices are available, the *indexed nested-loop* join can be used. If the relations are sorted, a *merge–join* may be desirable. It may be advantageous to sort a relation prior to join computation (so as to allow use of the merge–join strategy). It may also be advantageous to compute a temporary index for the sole purpose of allowing a more efficient join strategy to be used. The *hash–join* algorithm partitions the relations into several pieces, such that each piece of one of the relations fits in memory. The partitioning is carried out with a hash function on the join attributes, so that corresponding pairs of partitions can be joined independently. Hashing and sorting are dual, in the sense that many operations such as duplicate elimination, aggregation, joins, and outer joins can be implemented via either hashing or sorting.

Each relational-algebra expression represents a particular sequence of operations. The first step in selecting a query-processing strategy is to find a relational-algebra expression that is equivalent to the given expression and is estimated to cost less to execute. There are a number of equivalence rules that we can use to transform an expression into an equivalent one. We use these rules to generate systematically all expressions equivalent to the given query, and we choose the cheapest expression. Alternative evaluation plans for each expression can be generated by similar rules, and the cheapest plan across all expressions can be chosen. Several optimization techniques are available to reduce the number of alternative expressions and plans that need to be generated.

We use heuristics to reduce the number of plans considered, and thereby to reduce the cost of optimization. Heuristic rules for transforming relational-algebra queries include "perform selection operations as early as possible," "perform projections early," and "avoid Cartesian products."

Exercises

12.1. At what point during query processing does optimization occur?

12.2. Why is it not desirable to force users to make an explicit choice of a query-processing strategy? Are there cases in which it *is* desirable for users to be aware of the costs of competing query-processing strategies? Explain your answer.

12.3. Consider the following SQL query for our bank database:

> **select** *T.branch-name*
> **from** *branch T*, *branch S*
> **where** *T.assets* > *S.assets* **and** *S.branch-city* = "Brooklyn"

Write an efficient relational-algebra expression that is equivalent to this query. Justify your choice.

12.4. Consider the relations $r_1(A, B, C)$, $r_2(C, D, E)$, and $r_3(E, F)$, with primary keys A, C, and E, respectively. Assume that r_1 has 1000 tuples, r_2 has 1500 tuples, and r_3 has 750 tuples. Estimate the size of $r_1 \bowtie r_2 \bowtie r_3$, and give an efficient strategy for computing the join.

12.5. Consider the relations $r_1(A, B, C)$, $r_2(C, D, E)$, and $r_3(E, F)$ of Exercise 12.4. Assume that there are no primary keys, except the entire schema. Let $V(C, r_1)$ be 900, $V(C, r_2)$ be 1100, $V(E, r_2)$ be 50, and $V(E, r_3)$ be 100. Assume that r_1 has 1000 tuples, r_2 has 1500 tuples, and r_3 has 750 tuples. Estimate the size of $r_1 \bowtie r_2 \bowtie r_3$, and give an efficient strategy for computing the join.

12.6. Clustering indices may allow faster access to data than is afforded by a nonclustering index. When must we create a nonclustering index, despite the advantages of a clustering index? Explain your answer.

12.7. What are the advantages and disadvantages of hash indices relative to B^+-tree indices? How might the type of index available influence the choice of a query-processing strategy?

12.8. Assume (for simplicity in this exercise) that only one tuple fits in a block and memory holds at most 3 page frames. Show the runs created on each pass of the sort-merge algorithm, when applied to sort the following tuples on the first attribute: (kangaroo, 17), (wallaby, 21), (emu, 1), (wombat,13), (platypus, 3), (lion, 8), (warthog, 4), (zebra, 11), (meerkat, 6), (hyena, 9), (hornbill, 2), (baboon, 12).

12.9. Let relations $r_1(A, B, C)$ and $r_2(C, D, E)$ have the following properties: r_1 has 20,000 tuples, r_2 has 45,000 tuples, 25 tuples of r_1 fit on one block, and 30 tuples of r_2 fit on one block. Estimate the number of block accesses

required, using each of the following join strategies for $r_1 \bowtie r_2$:
(*a*) Nested-loop join
(*b*) Block nested-loop join
(*c*) Merge–join
(*d*) Hash–join

12.10. Design a variant of the hybrid merge–join algorithm for the case where both relations are not physically sorted, but both have a sorted secondary index on the join attributes.

12.11. The indexed nested-loop join algorithm described in Section 12.6.4 can be inefficient if the index is a secondary index, and there are multiple tuples with the same value for the join attributes. Why is it inefficient? Describe a way, using sorting, to reduce the cost of retrieving tuples of the inner relation. Under what conditions would this algorithm be more efficient than hybrid merge–join?

12.12. Estimate the number of block accesses required by your solution to Exercise 12.10 for $r_1 \bowtie r_2$, where r_1 and r_2 are as defined in Exercise 12.9.

12.13. Consider relations r_1 and r_2 of Exercise 12.9, with a relation $r_3(E, F)$. Assume that r_3 has 30,000 tuples, and that 40 tuples of r_3 fit on one block. Estimate the costs of the three strategies of Section 12.6.7 for computing $r_1 \bowtie r_2 \bowtie r_3$.

12.14. Let r and s be relations with no indices, and assume that the relations are not sorted. Assuming infinite memory, what is the lowest cost way (in terms of I/O operations) to compute $r \bowtie s$? What is the amount of memory required for this algorithm?

12.15. Suppose that a B^+-tree index on *branch-name* is available on relation *branch*, and that no other index is available. What would be the best way to handle the following selections that involve negation?
(*a*) $\sigma_{\neg(branch\text{-}city < \text{"Brooklyn"})}(branch)$
(*b*) $\sigma_{\neg(branch\text{-}city = \text{"Brooklyn"})}(branch)$
(*c*) $\sigma_{\neg(branch\text{-}city < \text{"Brooklyn"} \vee assets < 5000)}(branch)$

12.16. Suppose that a B^+-tree index on *branch-name* is available on relation *branch*, and that no other index is available. What would be the best way to handle the following selection?

$$\sigma_{(branch\text{-}city < \text{"Brooklyn"}) \vee assets < 5000) \wedge (branch\text{-}name1 \neq \text{"Downtown"}}(branch)$$

12.17. The hash–join algorithm as described in Section 12.6.6 computes the natural join of two relations. Describe how to extend the hash–join algorithm to compute the natural left outer join, the natural right outer join and the natural full outer join. (Hint: Keep extra information with each tuple in the hash index, to detect whether any tuple in the probe relation matches the tuple in the hash index.) Try out your algorithm on the *customer* and *depositor* relations.

12.18. Write pseudocode for an iterator that implements indexed nested-loop join, where the outer relation is pipelined. Use the standard iterator functions in your pseudocode. Show what state information the iterator must maintain between calls.

12.19. Show that the following equivalences hold. Explain how you can apply then to improve the efficiency of certain queries:
(*a*) $E_1 \bowtie_\theta (E_2 - E_3) = (E_1 \bowtie_\theta E_2 - E_1 \bowtie_\theta E_3)$.
(*b*) $\sigma_\theta({}_A\mathcal{G}_F(E)) = {}_A\mathcal{G}_F(\sigma_\theta(E))$, where θ uses only attributes from A.
(c) $\sigma_\theta(E_1 ⟕ E_2) = \sigma_\theta(E_1) ⟕ E_2$ where θ uses only attributes from E_2.

12.20. Show how to derive the following equivalences by a sequence of transformations using the equivalence rules in Section 12.9.2.
(*a*) $\sigma_{\theta_1 \wedge \theta_2 \wedge \theta_3}(E) = \sigma_{\theta_1}(\sigma_{\theta_2}(\sigma_{\theta_3}(E)))$
(*b*) $\sigma_{\theta_1 \wedge \theta_2}(E_1 \bowtie_{\theta_3} E_2) = \sigma_{\theta_1}(E_1 \bowtie_{\theta_3}(\sigma_{\theta_2}(E_2)))$, where θ_2 involves only attributes from E_2

12.21. For each of the following pairs of expressions, give instances of relations that show the expressions are not equivalent.
(*a*) $\Pi_A(R - S)$ and $\Pi_A(R) - \Pi_A(S)$
(*b*) $\sigma_{B<4}({}_A\mathcal{G}_{max(B)}(R))$ and ${}_A\mathcal{G}_{max(B)}(\sigma_{B<4}(R))$
(*c*) $\sigma_{B<4}({}_A\mathcal{G}_{min(B)}(R))$ and ${}_A\mathcal{G}_{min(B)}(\sigma_{B<4}(R))$
(*d*) $(R ⟕ S) ⟕ T$ and $R ⟕ (S ⟕ T)$
In other words, the natural left outer join is not associative. (Hint: Assume that the schemas of the three relations are $R(a, b1)$, $S(a, b2)$, and $T(a, b3)$, respectively.)
(*e*) $\sigma_\theta(E_1 ⟕ E_2)$ and $E_1 ⟕ \sigma_\theta(E_2)$, where θ uses only attributes from E_2

12.22. The SQL language allows relations with duplicates (Chapter 4).
(*a*) Define versions of the basic relational-algebra operations σ, Π, $\times$, $\bowtie$, $-$, $\cup$, and $\cap$ that work on relations with duplicates, in a way consistent with SQL.
(*b*) Check which of the equivalence rules 1 through 7b hold for the multiset version of the relational-algebra defined in part a.

12.23. Show that, with n relations, there are $(2(n-1))!/(n-1)!$ different join orders.

12.24. Describe a dynamic-programming algorithm for finding the most efficient join order for the join of n relations. Assume that there is only one interesting sort order. (Hint: Show how to derive the lowest cost join order (and its cost) for a set of n relations, given the lowest cost join order (and its cost) for each subset of the n relations.)

12.25. Show that the lowest cost join order can be computed in time $O(3^n)$. Assume that you can store and look up information about a set of relations (such as the optimal join order for the set, and the cost of that join order) in constant time. (If you find this exercise difficult, at least show the looser time bound of $O(2^{2n})$.)

12.26. Show that, if only left-deep join trees are considered, as in the System R optimizer, the time taken to find the most efficient join order is around 2^n. Assume that there is only one interesting sort order.

12.27. A set of equivalence rules is said to be *complete* if, whenever two expressions are equivalent, one can be derivedfrom the other by a sequence of uses of the equivalence rules. Is the set of equivalence rules that we considered in Section 12.9.2 complete? Hint: Consider the equivalence $\sigma_{3=5}(r) = \{\ \}$.

Bibliographic Notes

A query processor must parse statements in the query language, and must translate them into an internal form. Parsing of query languages differs little from parsing of traditional programming languages. Most compiler texts, including Aho et al. [1986] and Tremblay and Sorenson [1985], cover the main parsing techniques. These two texts also present optimization from a programming-languages point of view.

Knuth [1973] presents an excellent description of external sorting algorithms, including an optimization that can create initial runs that are (on the average) twice the size of memory. Based on performance studies conducted in the mid-1970s, database systems used only nested-loop join and merge–join. These studies, which were related to the development of System R, determined that either the nested-loop join or merge–join nearly always provided the optimal join method [Blasgen and Eswaran 1976]; hence, these two were the only join algorithms implemented in System R.

The System R study, however, did not include an analysis of hash–join algorithms. Today, hash–joins are considered to be highly efficient. Hash–join algorithms were initially developed for parallel database systems. Experimental systems using hash–join methods were developed in the mid-1980s; notable among these systems are the Grace database machine (Kitsuregawa et al. [1983], Fushimi et al. [1986]) and the Gamma database machine (DeWitt et al. [1986, 1990]). Hash–join techniques are described in Kitsuregawa et al. [1983], and extensions including hybrid hash–join are described in Shapiro [1986]. More recent results by Zeller and Gray [1990] and Davison and Graefe [1994] describe hash–join techniques that can adapt to the available memory, which is important in systems where multiple queries may be running at a time.

Query processing in main memory database is covered by DeWitt et al. [1984], and Whang and Krishnamurthy [1990]. Kim [1982, 1984] describes join strategies and the optimal use of available main memory. Processing of queries using outer joins is described in Rosenthal and Reiner [1984], Galindo-Legaria and Rosenthal [1992] and Galindo-Legaria [1994]. Klug [1982] discusses optimization of relational-algebra expressions with aggregate functions. Theoretical results on the complexity of the computation of relational-algebra operations appear in Gotlieb [1975], Pecherer [1975], and Blasgen and Eswaran [1976]. A comparison of various query-evaluation algorithms is given by Yao [1979b]. Additional discussions are presented in Kim et al. [1985].

Graefe [1993] presents an excellent survey of query-evaluation techniques. An earlier survey of query-processing techniques appears in Jarke and Koch [1984].

The seminal work of Selinger et al. [1979] describes access-path selection in the System R optimizer, which was one of the earliest relational-query optimizers. Wong and Youssefi [1976] describe a technique called *decomposition*, which is used in the Ingres query optimizer. Query processing in Starburst is described in Haas et al. [1989]. Query optimization in Oracle is briefly outlined in Oracle [1992].

Graefe and McKenna [1993] describe the extensibility and search-efficiency features of Volcano, a rule-based query optimizer. Exhaustive searching of all query plans is impractical for optimization of joins involving many relations, and techniques based on randomized searching, which do not examine all alternatives, have been proposed. Ioannidis and Wong [1987], Swami and Gupta [1988], and Ioannidis and Kang [1990] present results in this area. Parametric query-optimization techniques have been proposed by Ioannidis et al. [1992], to handle query processing when relation sizes change frequently. A set of plans—one for each of several different sizes of relations—is computed, and is stored by the optimizer, at compile time. One of these plans is chosen at run time, based on the actual relation sizes, avoiding the cost of full optimization at run time. Nonuniform distributions of values causes problems for estimation of query size and cost. Cost-estimation techniques that use histograms of value distributions have been proposed to tackle the problem. Ioannidis and Christodoulakis [1993], Ioannidis and Poosala [1995], and Poosala et al. [1996] present results in this area.

The SQL language poses several challenges for query optimization, including the presence of duplicates and nulls, and the semantics of nested subqueries. Extension of relational algebra to duplicates is described in Dayal et al. [1982]; optimization of nested subqueries is discussed in Kim [1982], Ganski and Wong [1987], and Dayal [1987]. Chaudhuri and Shim [1994] describe techniques for optimization of queries that use aggregation.

Sellis [1988] describes multiquery optimization, which is the problem of optimizing the execution of several queries as a group. If an entire group of queries is consider ed, it is possible to discover *common subexpressions* that can be evaluated once for the entire group. Finkelstein [1982] and Hall [1976] consider optimization of a group of queries and the use of common subexpressions.

Query optimization can make use of semantic information, such as functional dependencies and other integrity constraints. Semantic-query optimization in relational databases is covered by King [1981]. Malley and Zdonick [1986] present a knowledge-based approach to query optimization. Chakravarthy et al. [1990] use integrity constraints to assist in query optimization.

Query processing for object-oriented databases is discussed in Maier and Stein [1986], Beech [1988], Bertino and Kim [1989], Cluet et al. [1989], Kim [1989], and Kim et al. [1989].

When queries are generated through views, more relations often are joined than is necessary for computation of the query. A collection of techniques for join minimization has been grouped under the name *tableau optimization*. The notion of a tableau was introduced by Aho et al. [1979a, 1979c], and was further extended by Sagiv and Yannakakis [1981]. Ullman [1988] and Maier [1983] provide a textbook coverage of tableaux.

CHAPTER 13

TRANSACTIONS

Often, a collection of several operations on the database is considered to be a single unit from the point of view of the database user. For example, a transfer of funds from a checking account to a savings account is a single operation when viewed from the customer's standpoint; within the database system, however, it comprises several operations. Clearly, it is essential that all these operations occur, or that, in case of a failure, none occur. It would be unacceptable if the checking account were debited, but the savings account were not credited.

Collections of operations that form a single logical unit of work are called *transactions*. A database system must ensure proper execution of transactions despite failures—either the entire transaction executes, or none of it does. Furthermore, it must manage concurrent execution of transactions in a way that avoids the introduction of inconsistency. Returning to our funds-transfer example, a transaction computing the customer's total money might see the checking-account balance before it is debited by the funds-transfer transaction, but see the savings balance after it is credited. As a result, it would obtain an incorrect result.

This chapter provides an introduction to the basic concepts of transaction processing. Details on concurrent transaction processing and recovery from failures are covered in Chapters 14 and 15, respectively. Further topics in transaction processing are discussed in Chapter 20.

13.1 Transaction Concept

A *transaction* is a *unit* of program execution that accesses and possibly updates various data items. A transaction usually results from the execution of a user program written in a high-level data-manipulation language or programming language (for example, SQL, COBOL, C, or Pascal), and is delimited by statements (or function calls) of the form **begin transaction** and **end transaction**. The transaction consists of all operations executed between the begin and end of the transaction.

To ensure integrity of the data, we require that the database system maintains the following properties of the transactions:

- **Atomicity.** Either all operations of the transaction are reflected properly in the database, or none are.
- **Consistency.** Execution of a transaction in isolation (that is, with no other transaction executing concurrently) preserves the consistency of the database.
- **Isolation.** Even though multiple transactions may execute concurrently, the system guarantees that, for every pair of transactions T_i and T_j, it appears to T_i that either T_j finished execution before T_i started, or T_j started execution after T_i finished. Thus, each transaction is unaware of other transactions executing concurrently in the system.
- **Durability.** After a transaction completes successfully, the changes it has made to the database persist, even if there are system failures.

These properties are often called the ACID properties; the acronym is derived from the first letter of each of the four properties.

To gain a better understanding of ACID properties and the need for these properties, let us consider a simplified banking system consisting of several accounts and a set of transactions that access and update those accounts. For the time being, we assume that the database permanently resides on disk, but that some portion of it is temporarily residing in main memory.

Access to the database is accomplished by the following two operations:

- **read**(X), which transfers the data item X from the database to a local buffer belonging to the transaction that executed the **read** operation.
- **write**(X), which transfers the data item X from the the local buffer of the transaction that executed the **write** back to the database.

In a real database system, the **write** operation does not necessarily result in the immediate update of the data on the disk; the **write** operation may be temporarily stored in memory and executed on the disk later. For now, however, we shall assume that the **write** operation updates the database immediately. We shall return to this subject in Chapter 15.

Let T_i be a transaction that transfers \$50 from account A to account B. This transaction can be defined as

T_i: **read**(A);
$A := A - 50$;
write(A);
read(B);
$B := B + 50$;
write(B).

Let us now consider each of the ACID requirements. (For ease of presentation, we consider them in an order different from the order A-C-I-D).

- **Consistency**: The consistency requirement here is that the sum of A and B be unchanged by the execution of the transaction. Without the consistency requirement, money could be created or destroyed by the transaction! It can be verified easily that, if the database is consistent before an execution of the transaction, the database remains consistent after the execution of the transaction.

  Ensuring consistency for an individual transaction is the responsibility of the application programmer who codes the transaction. This task may be facilitated by automatic testing of integrity constraints, as we discussed in Chapter 6.

- **Atomicity**: Suppose that, just prior to the execution of transaction T_i the values of accounts A and B are \$1000 and \$2000, respectively. Now suppose that, during the execution of transaction T_i, a failure has occurred that prevented T_i from completing its execution successfully. Examples of such failures include power failures, hardware failures, and software errors. Further, suppose that the failure happened after the **write**(A) operation was executed, but before the **write**(B) operation was executed. In this case, the value of accounts A and B reflected in the database are \$950 and \$2000. We have destroyed \$50 as a result of this failure. In particular, we note that the sum $A + B$ is no longer preserved.

  Thus, as the result of the failure, the state of the system no longer reflects a real state of the world that the database is supposed to capture. We term such a state an *inconsistent* state. We must ensure that such inconsistencies are not visible in a database system. Note, however, that the system must at some point be in an inconsistent state. Even if transaction T_i is executed to completion, there exists a point at which the value of account A is \$950 and the value of account B is \$2000, which is clearly an inconsistent state. This state, however, is eventually replaced by the consistent state where the value of account A is \$950, and the value of account B is \$2050. Thus, if the transaction never started or was guaranteed to complete, such an inconsistent state would not be visible except during the execution of the transaction. That is the reason for the atomicity requirement: If the atomicity property is provided, all actions of the transaction are reflected in the database, or none are.

  The basic idea behind ensuring atomicity is as follows. The database system keeps track (on disk) of the old values of any data on which a transaction performs a write, and, if the transaction does not complete its execution, the old values are restored to make it appear as though the transaction never executed. We discuss these ideas further in Section 13.2. Ensuring atomicity is the responsibility of the database system itself; specifically, it is handled by a component called the *transaction-management component*, which we describe in detail in Chapter 15.

- **Durability:** Once the execution of the transaction completes successfully, and the user who initiated the transaction has been notified that the transfer of funds has taken place, it must be the case that no system failure will result in a loss of data corresponding to this transfer of funds.

  The durability property guarantees that, once a transaction completes successfully, all the updates that it carried out on the database persist, even if there is a system failure after the transaction completes execution.

  We assume for now that a failure of the computer system may result in loss of data in main memory, but data written to disk are never lost. We can guarantee durability by ensuring that either

  1. The updates carried out by the transaction have been written to disk before the transaction completes.
  2. Information about the updates carried out by the transaction and written to disk is sufficient to enable the database to reconstruct the updates when the database system is restarted after the failure.

  Ensuring durability is the responsibility of a component of the database system called the *recovery-management component*. The transaction-management component and the recovery-management component are closely related, and we describe their implementation in Chapter 15.

- **Isolation:** Even if the consistency and atomicity properties are ensured for each transaction, if several transactions are executed concurrently, their operations may interleave in some undesirable way, resulting in an inconsistent state.

  For example, as we saw earlier, the database is temporarily inconsistent while the transaction to transfer funds from A to B is executing, with the deducted total written to A and the increased total yet to be written to B. If a second concurrently running transaction reads A and B at this intermediate point and computes $A + B$, it will observe an inconsistent value. Furthermore, if this second transaction then performs updates on A and B based on the inconsistent values that it read, the database may be left in an inconsistent state even after both transactions have completed.

  A solution to the problem of concurrently executing transactions is to execute transactions serially—that is, one after the other. However, concurrent execution of transactions provides significant performance benefits, as we shall see in Section 13.4. Other solutions have therefore been developed; they allow multiple transactions to execute concurrently.

  We discuss the problems caused by concurrently executing transactions in Section 13.4. The isolation property of a transaction ensures that the concurrent execution of transactions results in a system state that is equivalent to a state that could have been obtained had these transactions executed one at a time in some order. We shall discuss the principles of isolation further in Section 13.5. Ensuring the isolation property is the responsibility of a component of the database system called the *concurrency-control component*, which we discuss later, in Chapter 14.

13.2 Transaction State

In the absence of failures, all transactions complete successfully. However, as we noted earlier, a transaction may not always complete its execution successfully. Such a transaction is termed *aborted*. If we are to ensure the atomicity property, an aborted transaction must have no effect on the state of the database. Thus, any changes that the aborted transaction made to the database must be undone. Once the changes caused by an aborted transaction have been undone, we say that the transaction has been *rolled back*. It is part of the responsibility of the recovery scheme to manage transaction aborts.

A transaction that completes its execution successfully is said to be *committed*. A committed transaction that has performed updates transforms the database into a new consistent state, which must persist even if there is a system failure.

Once a transaction has committed, we cannot undo its effects by aborting it. The only way to undo the effects of a committed transaction is to execute a *compensating transaction*; however, it is not always possible to create such a compensating transaction. Therefore, the responsibility of writing and executing a compensating transaction is left to the user, and is not handled by the database system. Chapter 20 includes a discussion of compensating transactions.

We need to be more precise about what we mean by *successful completion* of a transaction. We therefore establish a simple abstract transaction model. A transaction must be in one of the following states:

- **Active**, the initial state; the transaction stays in this state while it is executing
- **Partially committed**, after the final statement has been executed
- **Failed**, after the discovery that normal execution can no longer proceed
- **Aborted**, after the transaction has been rolled back and the database has been restored to its state prior to the start of the transaction
- **Committed**, after successful completion

The state diagram corresponding to a transaction is shown in Figure 13.1. We say that a transaction has committed only if it has entered the committed state. Similarly, we say that a transaction has aborted only if it has entered the aborted state. A transaction is said to have *terminated* if has either committed or aborted.

A transaction starts in the active state. When it finishes its final statement, it enters the partially committed state. At this point, the transaction has completed its execution, but it is still possible that it may have to be aborted, since the actual output may still be temporarily residing in main memory, and thus a hardware failure may preclude its successful completion.

The database system then writes out enough information to disk that, even in the event of a failure, the updates performed by the transaction can be recreated when the system restarts after the failure. When the last of this information is written out, the transaction enters the committed state.

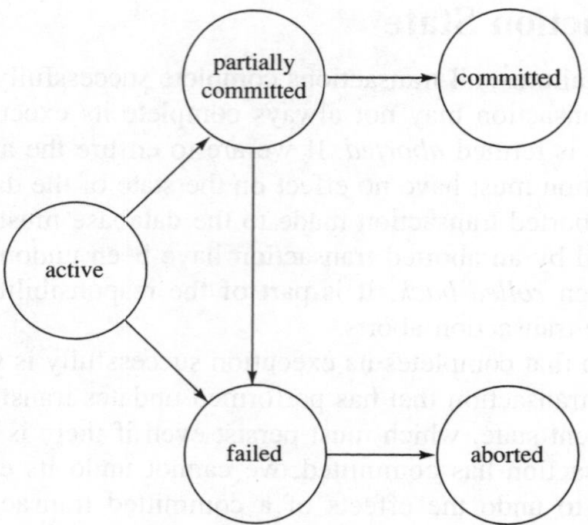

Figure 13.1 State diagram of a transaction.

As mentioned earlier, we assume for now that failures do not result in loss of data on disk. Techniques to deal with loss of data on disk are discussed in Chapter 15.

A transaction enters the failed state after the system determines that the transaction can no longer proceed with its normal execution (for example, because of hardware or logical errors). Such a transaction must be rolled back. Then, it enters the aborted state. At this point, the system has two options:

- It can **restart the transaction**, but only if the transaction was aborted as a result of some hardware or software error that was not created through the internal logic of the transaction. A restarted transaction is considered to be a new transaction.
- It can **kill the transaction**. It usually does so because of some internal logical error that can be corrected only by rewriting of the application program, or because the input was bad, or because the desired data were not found in the database.

We must be cautious when dealing with *observable external writes*, such as writes to a terminal or printer. Once such a write has occurred, it cannot be erased, since it may have been seen external to the database system. Most systems allow such writes to take place only after the transaction has entered the committed state. One way to implement such a scheme is for the database system to store any value associated with such external writes temporarily in nonvolatile storage, and to perform the actual writes only after the transaction enters the committed state. If the system should fail after the transaction has entered the committed state, but before it could complete the external writes, the database system will carry out the external writes (using the data in nonvolatile storage) when the system is restarted.

For certain applications, it may be desirable to allow active transactions to display data to users, particularly for long-duration transactions that run for minutes or hours. Unfortunately, we cannot allow such output of observable data unless we are willing to compromise transaction atomicity. Most current transaction systems ensure atomicity and, therefore, forbid this form of interaction with users. In Chapter 20, we discuss alternative transaction models that support long-duration, interactive transactions.

13.3 Implementation of Atomicity and Durability

The recovery-management component of a database system implements the support for atomicity and durability. We first consider a simple, but extremely inefficient, scheme. This scheme assumes that only one transaction is active at a time, and is based on making copies of the database, called *shadow* copies. The scheme assumes that the database is simply a file on disk. A pointer called db_pointer is maintained on disk; it points to the current copy of the database.

In the shadow-database scheme, a transaction that wants to update the database first creates a complete copy of the database. All updates are done on the new database copy, leaving the original copy, called the *shadow copy*, untouched. If at any point the transaction has to be aborted, the new copy is merely deleted. The old copy of the database has not been affected.

If the transaction completes, it is committed as follows. First, the operating system is asked to make sure that all pages of the new copy of the database have been written out to disk. On Unix systems, the flush command is used for this purpose. After the flush has completed, the pointer db_pointer is updated to point to the new copy of the database; the new copy then becomes the current copy of the database. The old copy of the database is then deleted. The scheme is depicted pictorially in Figure 13.2, where the database state before and after the update are shown.

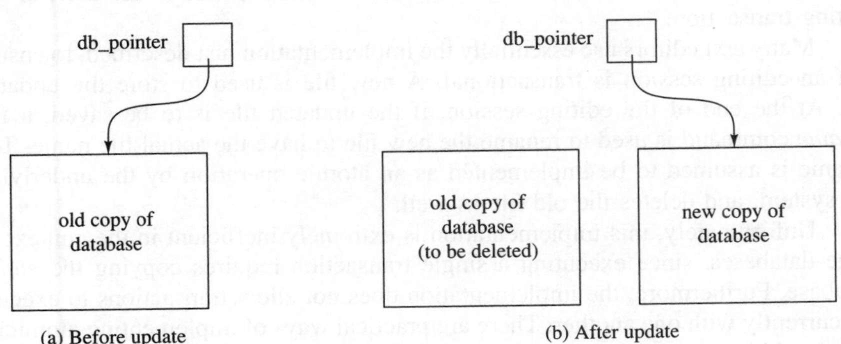

Figure 13.2 Shadow-copy technique for atomicity and durability.

The transaction is said to have been *committed* at the point where the updated db_pointer is written to disk. We now consider how transaction and system failures are handled by this technique. First, consider transaction failure. If the transaction fails at any time before db_pointer is updated, the old contents of the database are not affected. We can abort the transaction by deleting simply the new copy of the database. Once the transaction has been committed, all the updates that it performed are in the database pointed to by db_pointer. Thus, either all updates of the transaction are reflected, or none of the effects are reflected, regardless of transaction failure.

Now consider the issue of system failure. Suppose that the system fails at any time before the updated db_pointer is written to disk. Then, when the system restarts, it will read db_pointer, and will thus see the original contents of the database, and none of the effects of the transaction will be visible on the database. Next, suppose that the system fails after db_pointer has been updated on disk. Before the pointer is updated, all updated pages of the new copy of the database were written to disk. As mentioned earlier, we assume that, once a file is written to disk, its contents will not be damaged even if there is a system failure. Therefore, when the system restarts, it will read db_pointer, and will thus see the contents of the database *after* all the updates performed by the transaction.

The implementation actually depends on the write to db_pointer being atomic; that is, either all its bytes are written or none of its bytes are written. If some of the bytes of the pointer were updated by the write, but others were not, the pointer is meaningless, and neither old nor new versions of the database may be found when the system restarts. Luckily, disk systems provide atomic updates to entire blocks, or at least to a disk sector. In other words, the disk system guarantees that it will update db_pointer atomically.

Thus, the atomicity and durability properties of transactions are ensured by the shadow-copy implementation of the recovery-management component.

As a simple example of a transaction outside the database domain, consider a text-editing session. An entire editing session can be modeled as a transaction. The actions executed by the transaction are reading and updating the file. Saving the file at the end of editing corresponds to a commit of the editing transaction; quitting the editor session without saving the file corresponds to an abort of the editing transaction.

Many text editors use essentially the implementation just described, to ensure that an editing session is transactional. A new file is used to store the updated file. At the end of the editing session, if the updated file is to be saved, a file *rename* command is used to rename the new file to have the actual file name. The rename is assumed to be implemented as an atomic operation by the underlying file system, and deletes the old file as well.

Unfortunately, this implementation is extremely inefficient in the context of large databases, since executing a single transaction requires copying the *entire* database. Furthermore, the implementation does not allow transactions to execute concurrently with one another. There are practical ways of implementing atomicity and durability that are much less expensive and more powerful. We study these recovery techniques in Chapter 15.

13.4 Concurrent Executions

Transaction-processing systems usually allow multiple transactions to run concurrently. Allowing multiple transactions to update data concurrently causes several complications with consistency of the data, as we saw earlier. Ensuring consistency in spite of concurrent execution of transactions requires extra work; it is far easier to insist that transactions run *serially*—that is, one at a time, each starting only after the previous one has completed. However, there are two good reasons for allowing concurrency.

- A transaction consists of multiple steps. Some involve I/O activity; others involve CPU activity. The CPU and the disks in a computer system can operate in parallel. Therefore, I/O activity can be done in parallel with processing at the CPU. The parallelism of the CPU and the I/O system can therefore be exploited to run multiple transactions in parallel. While a read or write on behalf of one transaction is in progress on one disk, another transaction can be running in the CPU, while another disk may be executing a read or write on behalf of a third transaction. Thereby, there is an increase in the *throughput* of the system—that is, in the number of transactions that can be executed in a given amount of time. Correspondingly, the processor and disk *utilization* also increase; in other words, the processor and disk spend less time idle, or not performing any useful work.
- There may be a mix of transactions running on a system, some short and some long. If transactions are run serially, a short transaction may have to wait for a preceding long transaction to complete, which can lead to unpredictable delays in running a transaction. If the transactions are operating on different parts of the database, it is better to let them run concurrently, sharing the CPU cycles and disk accesses among them. Concurrent execution reduces the unpredictable delays in running transactions. Moreover, it also reduces the *average response time*: the average time for a transaction to be completed after it has been submitted.

The motivation for using concurrent execution in a database is essentially the same as the motivation for using *multiprogramming* in an operating system.

When several transactions run concurrently, database consistency can be destroyed despite the correctness of each individual transaction. In this section, we present the concept of schedules to help identify those executions that are guaranteed to ensure consistency.

The database system must control the interaction among the concurrent transactions to prevent them from destroying the consistency of the database. It does so through a variety of mechanisms called *concurrency-control* schemes. We study concurrency-control schemes in Chapter 14; for now, we focus on the concept of correct concurrent execution.

Consider again the simplified banking system of Section 13.1, which has several accounts, and a set of transactions that access and update those accounts. Let T_1 and T_2 be two transactions that transfer funds from one account to another. Transaction T_1 transfers \$50 from account A to account B and is defined as

T_1: **read**(A);
$A := A - 50$;
write(A);
read(B);
$B := B + 50$;
write(B).

Transaction T_2 transfers 10 percent of the balance from account A to account B, and is defined as

T_2: **read**(A);
$temp := A * 0.1$;
$A := A - temp$;
write(A);
read(B);
$B := B + temp$;
write(B).

Let the current values of accounts A and B be \$1000 and \$2000, respectively. Suppose that the two transactions are executed one at a time in the order T_1 followed by T_2. This execution sequence is represented in Figure 13.3. In the figure, the sequence of instruction steps is in chronological order from top to bottom, with instructions of T_1 appearing in the left column, and instructions of T_2 appearing in the right column. The final values of accounts A and B, after the execution in Figure 13.3 takes place, are \$855 and \$2145, respectively. Thus, the total amount of money in accounts A and B—that is, the sum $A + B$—is preserved after the execution of both transactions.

T_1	T_2
read(A)	
$A := A - 50$	
write(A)	
read(B)	
$B := B + 50$	
write(B)	
	read(A)
	$temp := A * 0.1$;
	$A := A - temp$
	write(A)
	read(B)
	$B := B + temp$
	write(B)

Figure 13.3 Schedule 1 — a serial schedule in which T_1 is followed by T_2.

T_1	T_2
	read(A) $temp$:= A * 0.1; A := A − $temp$ **write**(A) **read**(B) B := B + $temp$ **write**(B)
read(A) A := A − 50 **write**(A) **read**(B) B := B + 50 **write**(B)	

Figure 13.4 Schedule 2—a serial schedule in which T_2 is followed by T_1.

Similarly, if the transactions are executed one at a time in the order T_2 followed by T_1, then the corresponding execution sequence is that of Figure 13.4. Again, as expected, the sum $A + B$ is preserved, and the final values of accounts A and B are \$850 and \$2150, respectively.

The execution sequences just described are called *schedules*. They represent the chronological order in which instructions are executed in the system. Clearly, a schedule for a set of transactions must consist of all instructions of those transactions, and must preserve the order in which the instructions appear in each individual transaction. For example, in transaction T_1, the instruction **write**(A) must appear before the instruction **read**(B), in any valid schedule. In the following discussion, we shall refer to the first execution sequence (T_1 followed by T_2) as schedule 1, and to the second execution sequence (T_2 followed by T_1) as schedule 2.

These schedules are *serial*. Each serial schedule consists of a sequence of instructions from various transactions, where the instructions belonging to one single transaction appear together in that schedule. Thus, for a set of n transactions, there exist $n!$ different valid serial schedules.

When several transactions are executed concurrently, the corresponding schedule no longer needs to be serial. If two transactions are running concurrently, the operating system may execute one transaction for a little while, then perform a context switch, execute the second transaction for some time, and then switch back to the first transaction for some time, and so on. With multiple transactions, the CPU time is shared among all the transactions.

Several execution sequences are possible, since the various instructions from both transactions may now be interleaved. In general, it is not possible to predict exactly how many instructions of a transaction will be executed before the CPU switches to another transaction. Thus, the number of possible schedules for a set of n transactions is much larger than $n!$.

T_1	T_2
read(A)	
$A := A - 50$	
write(A)	
	read(A)
	$temp := A * 0.1;$
	$A := A - temp$
	write(A)
read(B)	
$B := B + 50$	
write(B)	
	read(B)
	$B := B + temp$
	write(B)

Figure 13.5 Schedule 3—a concurrent schedule equivalent to schedule 1.

Returning to our previous example, suppose that the two transactions are executed concurrently. One possible schedule is shown in Figure 13.5. After this execution takes place, we arrive at the same state as the one in which the transactions are executed serially in the order T_1 followed by T_2. The sum $A + B$ is indeed preserved.

Not all concurrent executions result in a correct state. To illustrate, consider the schedule of Figure 13.6. After the execution of this schedule, we arrive at a state where the final values of accounts A and B are \$950 and \$2100, respectively. This final state is an *inconsistent state*, since we have gained \$50 in the process of

T_1	T_2
read(A)	
$A := A - 50$	
	read(A)
	$temp := A * 0.1;$
	$A := A - temp$
	write(A)
	read(B)
write(A)	
read(B)	
$B := B + 50$	
write(B)	
	$B := B + temp$
	write(B)

Figure 13.6 Schedule 4—a concurrent schedule.

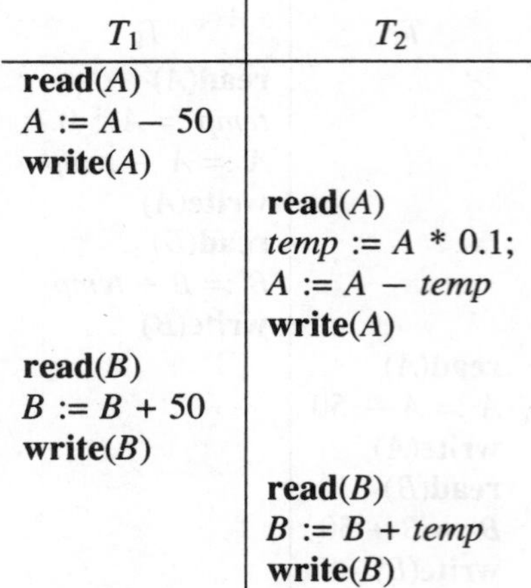

the concurrent execution. Indeed, the sum $A + B$ is not preserved by the execution of the two transactions.

If control of concurrent execution is left entirely to the operating system, many possible schedules, including ones that leave the database in an inconsistent state, such as the one just described, are possible. It is the job of the database system to ensure that any schedule that gets executed will leave the database in a consistent state. The component of the database system that carries out this task is called the *concurrency-control* component.

We can ensure consistency of the database under concurrent execution by making sure that any schedule that executed has the same effect as a schedule that could have occurred without any concurrent execution. That is, the schedule should, in some sense, be equivalent to a serial schedule. We examine this idea in Section 13.5.

13.5 Serializability

The database system must control concurrent execution of transactions, to ensure that the database state remains consistent. Before we examine how the database system can carry out this task, we must first understand which schedules will ensure consistency, and which schedules will not.

Since transactions are programs, it is computationally difficult to determine what are the exact operations that a transaction performs, and how operations of various transactions interact. For this reason, we shall not interpret the type of operations that a transaction can perform on a data item. Instead, we consider only two operations: **read** and **write**. We thus assume that, between a **read**(Q) instruction and a **write**(Q) instruction on a data item Q, a transaction may perform an arbitrary sequence of operations on the copy of Q that is residing in the local buffer of the transaction. Thus, the only significant operations of a transaction, from a scheduling point of view, are its **read** and **write** instructions. We shall therefore usually show only **read** and **write** instructions in schedules, as we do in the representation of schedule 3 that is shown in Figure 13.7.

In this section, we discuss different forms of schedule equivalence; they lead to the notions of *conflict serializability* and *view serializability*.

T_1	T_2
read(A)	
write(A)	
	read(A)
	write(A)
read(B)	
write(B)	
	read(B)
	write(B)

Figure 13.7 Schedule 3—showing only the **read** and **write** instructions.

13.5.1 Conflict Serializability

Let us consider a schedule S in which there are two consecutive instructions I_i and I_j, of transactions T_i and T_j, respectively ($i \neq j$). If I_i and I_j refer to different data items, then we can swap I_i and I_j without affecting the results of any instruction in the schedule. However, if I_i and I_j refer to the same data item Q, then the order of the two steps may matter. Since we are dealing with only **read** and **write** instructions, there are four cases that we need to consider:

1. I_i = **read**(Q), I_j = **read**(Q). The order of I_i and I_j does not matter, since the same value of Q is read by T_i and T_j, regardless of the order.
2. I_i = **read**(Q), I_j = **write**(Q). If I_i comes before I_j, then T_i does not read the value of Q that is written by T_j in instruction I_j. If I_j comes before I_i, then T_i reads the value of Q that is written by T_j. Thus, the order of I_i and I_j matters.
3. I_i = **write**(Q), I_j = **read**(Q). The order of I_i and I_j matters for reasons similar to those of the previous case.
4. I_i = **write**(Q), I_j = **write**(Q). Since both instructions are **write** operations, the order of these instructions does not affect either T_i or T_j. However, the value obtained by the next **read**(Q) instruction of S is affected, since the result of only the latter of the two **write** instructions is preserved in the database. If there is no other **write**(Q) instruction after I_i and I_j in S, then the order of I_i and I_j directly affects the final value of Q in the database state that results from schedule S.

Thus, only in the case where both I_i and I_j are **read** instructions does the relative order of their execution not matter.

We say that I_i and I_j *conflict* if they are operations by different transactions on the same data item, and at least one of these instructions is a **write** operation.

To illustrate the concept of conflicting instructions, we consider schedule 3, as shown in Figure 13.7. The **write**(A) instruction of T_1 conflicts with the **read**(A) instruction of T_2. However, the **write**(A) instruction of T_2 does not conflict with the **read**(B) instruction of T_1, because the two instructions access different data items.

Let I_i and I_j be consecutive instructions of a schedule S. If I_i and I_j are instructions of different transactions and I_i and I_j do not conflict, then we can swap the order of I_i and I_j to produce a new schedule S'. We expect S to be equivalent to S', since all instructions appear in the same order in both schedules except for I_i and I_j, whose order does not matter.

Since the **write**(A) instruction of T_2 in schedule 3 of Figure 13.7 does not conflict with the **read**(B) instruction of T_1, we can swap these instructions to generate an equivalent schedule, schedule 5, as shown in Figure 13.8. Regardless of the initial system state, schedules 3 and 5 both produce the same final system state.

T_1	T_2
read(A)	
write(A)	
	read(A)
read(B)	
	write(A)
write(B)	
	read(B)
	write(B)

Figure 13.8 Schedule 5—schedule 3 after swapping of a pair of instructions.

Let us continue to swap nonconflicting instructions as follows:

- Swap the **read**(B) instruction of T_1 with the **read**(A) instruction of T_2.
- Swap the **write**(B) instruction of T_1 with the **write**(A) instruction of T_2.
- Swap the **write**(B) instruction of T_1 with the **read**(A) instruction of T_2.

The final result of these swaps, as shown in schedule 6 of Figure 13.9, is a serial schedule. Thus, we have shown that schedule 3 is equivalent to a serial schedule. This equivalence implies that, regardless of the initial system state, schedule 3 will produce the same final state as will some serial schedule.

If a schedule S can be transformed into a schedule S' by a series of swaps of nonconflicting instructions, we say that S and S' are *conflict equivalent*.

Returning to our previous examples, we note that schedule 1 is not conflict equivalent to schedule 2. However, schedule 1 is conflict equivalent to schedule 3, because the **read**(B) and **write**(B) instruction of T_1 can be swapped with the **read**(A) and **write**(A) instruction of T_2.

The concept of conflict equivalence leads to the concept of conflict serializability. We say that a schedule S is *conflict serializable* if it is conflict equivalent to a serial schedule. Thus, schedule 3 is conflict serializable, since it is conflict equivalent to the serial schedule 1.

T_1	T_2
read(A)	
write(A)	
read(B)	
write(B)	
	read(A)
	write(A)
	read(B)
	write(B)

Figure 13.9 Schedule 6—a serial schedule that is equivalent to schedule 3.

T_3	T_4
read(Q)	
	write(Q)
write(Q)	

Figure 13.10 Schedule 7.

Finally, consider schedule 7 of Figure 13.10; it consists of only the significant operations (that is, the **read** and **write**) of transactions T_3 and T_4. This schedule is not conflict serializable, since it is not equivalent to either the serial schedule $<T_3,T_4>$ or the serial schedule $<T_4,T_3>$.

It is possible to have two schedules that produce the same outcome, but that are not conflict equivalent. For example, consider transaction T_5, which transfers \$10 from account B to account A. Let schedule 8 be as defined in Figure 13.11. We claim that schedule 8 is not conflict equivalent to the serial schedule $<T_1,T_5>$, since, in schedule 8, the **write**(B) instruction of T_5 conflicts with the **read**(B) instruction of T_1. Thus, we cannot move all the instructions of T_1 before those of T_5 by swapping consecutive nonconflicting instructions. However, the final values of accounts A and B after the execution of either schedule 8 or the serial schedule $<T_1,T_5>$ are the same—namely, \$960 and \$2040, respectively.

We can see from this example that there are less stringent definitions of schedule equivalence than there are of conflict equivalence. For the system to determine that schedule 8 produces the same outcome as the serial schedule $<T_1,T_5>$, it must analyze the computation performed by T_1 and T_5, rather than just the **read** and **write** operations. In general, such analysis is hard to implement and is computationally expensive. However, there are other definitions of schedule equivalence

T_1	T_5
read(A)	
$A := A - 50$	
write(A)	
	read(B)
	$B := B - 10$
	write(B)
read(B)	
$B := B + 50$	
write(B)	
	read(A)
	$A := A + 10$
	write(A)

Figure 13.11 Schedule 8.

based purely on the **read** and **write** operations. We will consider one such definition in the next section.

13.5.2 View Serializability

In this section, we consider a form of equivalence that is less stringent than conflict equivalence, but that, like conflict equivalence, is based on only the **read** and **write** operations of transactions.

Consider two schedules S and S', where the same set of transactions participates in both schedules. The schedules S and S' are said to be *view equivalent* if the following three conditions are met:

1. For each data item Q, if transaction T_i reads the initial value of Q in schedule S, then transaction T_i must, in schedule S', also read the initial value of Q.
2. For each data item Q, if transaction T_i executes **read**(Q) in schedule S, and that value was produced by transaction T_j (if any), then transaction T_i must, in schedule S', also read the value of Q that was produced by transaction T_j.
3. For each data item Q, the transaction (if any) that performs the final **write**(Q) operation in schedule S must perform the final **write**(Q) operation in schedule S'.

Conditions 1 and 2 ensure that each transaction reads the same values in both schedules and, therefore, performs the same computation. Condition 3, coupled with conditions 1 and 2, ensures that both schedules result in the same final system state.

Returning to our previous examples, we note that schedule 1 is not view equivalent to schedule 2, since, in schedule 1, the value of account A read by transaction T_2 was produced by T_1, whereas this case does not hold in schedule 2. However, schedule 1 is view equivalent to schedule 3, because the values of account A and B read by transaction T_2 were produced by T_1 in both schedules.

The concept of view equivalence leads to the concept of view serializability. We say that a schedule S is *view serializable* if it is view equivalent to a serial schedule.

As an illustration, suppose that we augment schedule 7 with transaction T_6, and obtain schedule 9, as depicted in Figure 13.12. schedule 9 is view serializable. Indeed, it is view equivalent to the serial schedule $<T_3, T_4, T_6>$, since the one **read**(Q) instruction reads the initial value of Q in both schedules, and T_6 performs the final write of Q in both schedules.

Every conflict-serializable schedule is view serializable, but there are view-serializable schedules that are not conflict serializable. Indeed, schedule 9 is not conflict serializable, since every pair of consecutive instructions conflicts, and, thus, no swapping of instructions is possible.

Observe that, in schedule 9, transactions T_4 and T_6 perform **write**(Q) operations without having performed a **read**(Q) operation. Writes of this sort are called *blind writes*. Blind writes appear in any view-serializable schedule that is not conflict serializable.

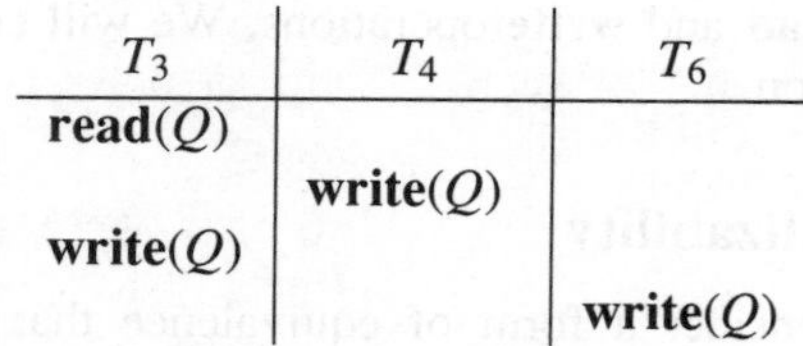

T_3	T_4	T_6
read(Q)		
	write(Q)	
write(Q)		
		write(Q)

Figure 13.12 Schedule 9—a view-serializable schedule.

13.6 Recoverability

So far, we have studied what schedules are acceptable from the viewpoint of consistency of the database, assuming implicitly that there are no transaction failures. We now address the effect of transaction failures during concurrent execution.

If a transaction T_i fails, for whatever reason, we need to undo the effect of this transaction to ensure the atomicity property of the transaction. In a system that allows concurrent execution, it is necessary also to ensure that any transaction T_j that is dependent on T_i (that is, T_j has read data written by T_i) is also aborted. To achieve this surety, we need to place restrictions on the type of schedules permitted in the system.

In the following two subsections, we address the issue of what schedules are acceptable from the viewpoint described. As mentioned earlier, we describe in Chapter 14 how to ensure that only such acceptable schedules are generated.

13.6.1 Recoverable Schedules

Consider schedule 11, shown in Figure 13.13, in which T_9 is a transaction that performs only one instruction: **read**(A). Suppose that the system allows T_9 to commit immediately after executing the **read**(A) instruction. Thus, T_9 commits before T_8 does. Now suppose that T_8 fails before it commits. Since T_9 has read the value of data item A written by T_8, we must abort T_9 to ensure transaction atomicity. However, T_9 has already committed and cannot be aborted. Thus, we have a situation where it is impossible to recover correctly from the failure of T_8.

Schedule 11, with the commit happening immediately after the **read**(A) instruction, is an example of a *nonrecoverable* schedule, which should be not allowed. Most database system require that all schedules be *recoverable*. A re-

T_8	T_9
read(A)	
write(A)	
	read(A)
read(B)	

Figure 13.13 Schedule 11.

T_{10}	T_{11}	T_{12}
read(A)		
read(B)		
write(A)		
	read(A)	
	write(A)	
		read(A)

Figure 13.14 Schedule 12.

coverable schedule is one where, for each pair of transactions T_i and T_j such that T_j reads a data items previously written by T_i, the commit operation of T_i appears before the commit operation of T_j.

13.6.2 Cascadeless Schedules

Even if a schedule is recoverable, to recover correctly from the failure of a transaction T_i, we may have to roll back several transactions. Such situations occur if transactions have read data written by T_i. As an illustration, consider the partial schedule of Figure 13.14. Transaction T_{10}, writes a value of A that is read by transaction T_{11}. Transaction T_{11} writes a value of A that is read by transaction T_{12}. Suppose that, at this point, T_{10} fails. T_{10} must be rolled back. Since T_{11} is dependent on T_{10}, T_{11} must be rolled back. Since T_{12} is dependent on T_{11}, T_{12} must be rolled back. This phenomenon, in which a single transaction failure leads to a series of transaction rollbacks, is called *cascading rollback*.

Cascading rollback is undesirable, since it leads to the undoing of a significant amount of work. It is desirable to restrict the schedules to those where cascading rollbacks cannot occur. Such schedules are called *cascadeless* schedules. A cascadeless schedule is one where, for each pair of transactions T_i and T_j such that T_j reads a data item previously written by T_i, the commit operation of T_i appears before the read operation of T_j. It is easy to verify that every cascadeless schedule is also recoverable.

13.7 Implementation of Isolation

So far, we have seen what properties a schedule must have if it is to leave the database in a consistent state, and to allow transaction failures to be handled in a safe manner. Specifically, schedules that are conflict or view serializable and cascadeless satisfy these requirements.

There are various *concurrency-control* schemes that we can use to ensure that, even when multiple transactions are executed concurrently, only acceptable schedules are generated, regardless of how the operating-system time-shares resources (such as CPU time) among the transactions.

As a trivial example of a concurrency-control scheme, consider this scheme: A transaction acquires a *lock* on the entire database before it starts, and releases the lock after it has committed. While a transaction holds a lock, no other transaction is allowed to acquire the lock, and all must therefore wait for the lock to be released. As a result of the locking policy, only one transaction can execute at a time. Therefore, only serial schedules are generated. These are trivially serializable, and it is easy to verify that they are cascadeless as well.

A concurrency-control scheme such as this one leads to poor performance, since it forces transactions to wait for preceding transactions to finish before they can start. In other words, it provides a poor degree of concurrency. As explained in Section 13.4, concurrent execution has several performance benefits.

The goal of concurrency-control schemes is to provide a high degree of concurrency, while ensuring that all schedules that can be generated are conflict or view serializable, and are cascadeless.

We study a number of concurrency-control schemes in Chapter 14. The schemes have different tradeoff in terms of the amount of concurrency they allow and the amount of overhead that they incur. Some of them allow only conflict-serializable schedules to be generated; others allow view-serializable schedules that are not conflict-serializable to be generated.

13.8 Transaction Definition in SQL

A data-manipulation language must include a construct for specifying the set of actions that constitute a transaction.

The SQL standard specifies that a transaction begins implicitly. Transactions are ended by one of the following SQL statements:

- **Commit work** commits the current transaction and begins a new one.
- **Rollback work** causes the current transaction to abort.

The keyword **work** is optional in both the statements. If a program terminates without either of these commands, the updates are either committed or rolled back—which of the two happens is not specified by the standard, and is implementation dependent.

The standard also specifies that the system must ensure both serializability and freedom from cascading rollback. The definition of *serializability* used by the standard is that a schedule must have the *same effect* as would a serial schedule. Thus, conflict and view serializability are both acceptable.

The SQL-92 standard also allows a transaction to specify that it may be executed in a manner that causes it to become nonserializable with respect to other transactions. For instance, a transaction may operate at the level of **read uncommitted**, which permits the transaction to read records even if they have not been committed. Such features are provided for long transactions whose results do not need to be precise. For instance, approximate information is usually sufficient for statistics used for query optimization. If these transactions were to execute in a serializable fashion, they could interfere with other transactions, causing the others execution to be delayed.

The levels of consistency specified by SQL-92 are as follows:

- **Serializable** is the default.
- **Repeatable read** allows only committed records to be read, and further requires that, between two reads of a record by a transaction, no other transaction is allowed to update the record. However, the transaction may not be serializable with respect to other transactions. For instance, when it is searching for records satisfying some conditions, a transaction may find some of the records inserted by a committed transaction, but may not find others.
- **Read committed** allows only committed records to be read, but does not require even repeatable reads. For instance, between two reads of a record by the transaction, the records may have been updated by other committed transactions.
- **Read uncommitted** allows even uncommitted records to be read. It is the lowest level of consistency allowed by SQL-92.

13.9 Testing for Serializability

When designing concurrency control schemes, we must show that schedules generated by the scheme are serializable. To do that, we must first understand how to determine, given a particular schedule S, whether the schedule is serializable. In this section, we shall present methods for determining conflict and view serializability. We will show that there exists a simple and efficient algorithm to determine conflict serializability. However, there is no efficient algorithm for determining view serializability.

13.9.1 Test for Conflict Serializability

Let S be a schedule. We construct a directed graph, called a *precedence graph*, from S. This graph consists of a pair $G = (V,E)$, where V is a set of vertices, and E is a set of edges. The set of vertices consists of all the transactions participating in the schedule. The set of edges consists of all edges $T_i \rightarrow T_j$ for which one of the following three conditions hold

1. T_i executes **write**(Q) before T_j executes **read**(Q).
2. T_i executes **read**(Q) before T_j executes **write**(Q).
3. T_i executes **write**(Q) before T_j executes **write**(Q).

If an edge $T_i \rightarrow T_j$ exists in the precedence graph, then, in any serial schedule S' equivalent to S, T_i must appear before T_j.

For example, the precedence graph for schedule 1 is shown in Figure 13.15a. It contains the single edge $T_1 \rightarrow T_2$, since all the instructions of T_1 are executed before the first instruction of T_2 is executed. Similarly, Figure 13.15b shows the precedence graph for schedule 2 with the single edge $T_2 \rightarrow T_1$, since all the instructions of T_2 are executed before the first instruction of T_1 is executed.

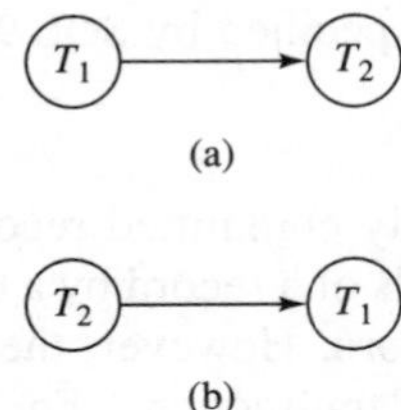

Figure 13.15 Precedence graph for (a) schedule 1 and (b) schedule 2.

The precedence graph for schedule 4 is depicted in Figure 13.16. It contains the edge $T_1 \rightarrow T_2$, because T_1 executes **read**(A) before T_2 executes **write**(A). It also contains the edge $T_2 \rightarrow T_1$, because T_2 executes **read**(B) before T_1 executes **write**(B).

If the precedence graph for S has a cycle, then schedule S is not conflict serializable. If the graph contains no cycles, then the schedule S is conflict serializable. The serializability order can be obtained through *topological sorting*, which determines a linear order consistent with the partial order of the precedence graph. There are, in general, several possible linear orders that can be obtained through a topological sorting. For example, the graph of Figure 13.17a has two acceptable linear orderings, as illustrated in Figures 13.17b and 13.17c.

Thus, to test for conflict serializability, we need to construct the precedence graph and to invoke a cycle-detection algorithm. Cycle-detection algorithms can be found in standard textbooks on algorithms. Cycle-detection algorithms, such as those based on depth-first search, require on the order of n^2 operations, where n is the number of vertices in the graph (that is, the number of transactions). Thus, we have a practical scheme for determining conflict serializability.

Returning to our previous examples, note that the precedence graphs for schedules 1 and 2 (Figure 13.15) indeed do not contain cycles. The precedence graph for schedule 4 (Figure 13.16), on the other hand, contains a cycle, indicating that this schedule is not conflict serializable.

13.9.2 Test for View Serializability

We can modify the precedence-graph test for conflict serializability to test for view serializability, as we show next. However, the resultant test is expensive in CPU time. In fact, testing for view serializability is computationally an expensive problem, as we shall see later.

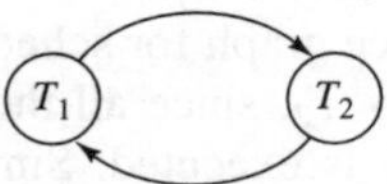

Figure 13.16 Precedence graph for schedule 4.

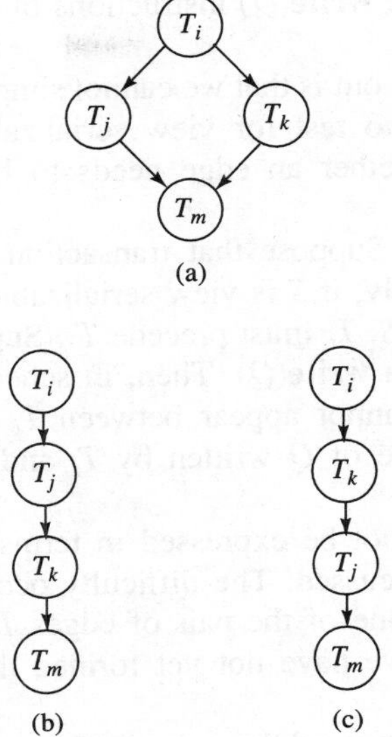

Figure 13.17 Illustration of topological sorting.

In the case of testing for conflict serializability, we know that, if two transactions, T_i and T_j, access a data item Q, and at least one of these transactions writes Q, then either the edge, $T_i \rightarrow T_j$ or the edge $T_j \rightarrow T_i$ is inserted in the precedence graph. This situation, however, is no longer the case when we are testing for view serializability. As we shall see shortly, this difference is the cause of our inability to come up with an efficient algorithm for such a test.

Consider schedule 9, which we saw earlier in Figure 13.12. If we follow the rule in the conflict-serializability test for forming the precedence graph, we get the graph of Figure 13.18. This graph contains a cycle, indicating that schedule 9 is not conflict serializable. However, as we saw earlier, schedule 9 is view serializable, since it is view equivalent to the serial schedule $<T_3,T_4,T_6>$. The edge $T_4 \rightarrow T_3$ should *not* have been inserted in the graph, since the values of item Q produced by T_3 and T_4 were never used by any other transaction, and T_6 produced

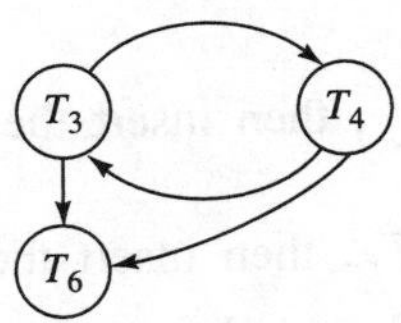

Figure 13.18 Precedence graph for schedule 9.

a new final value of Q. The **write**(Q) instructions of T_3 and T_4 are called *useless writes*.

What we have pointed out is that we cannot simply use the precedence-graph scheme of Section 13.9.1 to test for view serializability. We need to develop a scheme for deciding whether an edge needs to be inserted in a precedence graph.

Let S be a schedule. Suppose that transaction T_j reads the value of data item Q written by T_i. Clearly, if S is view serializable, then, in any serial schedule S' that is equivalent to S, T_i must precede T_j. Suppose now that, in schedule S, transaction T_k executed a **write**(Q). Then, in schedule S', T_k must either precede T_i or follow T_j. It cannot appear between T_i and T_j, because otherwise T_j would not read the value of Q written by T_i and thus S would not be view equivalent to S'.

These constraints cannot be expressed in terms of the simple precedence-graph model previously discussed. The difficulty occurs because we know that, in the preceding example, one of the pair of edges $T_k \rightarrow T_i$, $T_j \rightarrow T_k$ must be inserted in the graph, but we have not yet formed the rule for determining the appropriate choice.

To form it, we need to extend the precedence graph to include labeled edges. We term such a graph a *labeled precedence graph*. As before, the nodes of the graph are the transactions participating in the schedule. The rules for inserting labeled edges are described next.

Let S be a schedule consisting of transactions $\{T_1, T_2, \ldots, T_n\}$. Let T_b and T_f be two dummy transactions such that T_b issues **write**(Q) for each Q accessed in S, and T_f issues **read**(Q) for each Q accessed in S. We construct a new schedule S' from S by inserting T_b at the beginning of S, and appending T_f to the end of S. We construct the labeled precedence graph for schedule S' as follows:

1. Add an edge $T_i \xrightarrow{0} T_j$, if transaction T_j reads the value of data item Q written by transaction T_i.

2. Remove all the edges incident on useless transactions. A transaction T_i is *useless* if there exists no path, in the precedence graph, from T_i to transaction T_f.

3. For each data item Q such that T_j reads the value of Q written by T_i, and T_k executes **write**(Q) and $T_k \neq T_b$, do the following:

   a. If $T_i = T_b$ and $T_j \neq T_f$, then insert the edge $T_j \xrightarrow{0} T_k$ in the labeled precedence graph.

   b. If $T_i \neq T_b$ and $T_j = T_f$, then insert the edge $T_k \xrightarrow{0} T_i$ in the labeled precedence graph.

   c. If $T_i \neq T_b$ and $T_j \neq T_f$, then insert the pair of edges $T_k \xrightarrow{p} T_i$, and $T_j \xrightarrow{p} T_k$ in the labeled precedence graph where p is a unique integer larger than 0 that has not been used earlier for labeling edges.

Rule 3c reflects that, if T_i writes a data item that T_j reads, then a transaction T_k that writes the same data item must come before T_i or after T_j. Rules 3a and 3b are special cases that result from the fact that T_b and T_f are necessarily the first and final transactions, respectively. When we apply rule 3c, we are *not* requiring T_k to be *both* before T_i *and* after T_j. Rather, we have a choice of where T_k may appear in an equivalent serial ordering.

As an illustration, consider again schedule 7 (Figure 13.10). The graph constructed in steps 1 and 2 is depicted in Figure 13.19a. It contains the edge $T_b \xrightarrow{0} T_3$, since T_3 reads the value of Q written by T_b. It contains the edge $T_3 \xrightarrow{0} T_f$, since T_3 was the final transaction that wrote Q and, thus, T_f read that value. The final graph corresponding to schedule 7 is depicted in Figure 13.19b. It contains the edge $T_3 \xrightarrow{0} T_4$ as a result of step 3a. It contains the edge $T_4 \xrightarrow{0} T_3$ as a result of step 3b.

Consider now schedule 9 (Figure 13.12). The graph constructed in steps 1 and 2 is depicted in Figure 13.20a. The final graph is shown in Figure 13.20b. It contains the edges $T_3 \xrightarrow{0} T_4$ and $T_3 \xrightarrow{0} T_6$ as a result of step 3a. It contains the edges $T_3 \xrightarrow{0} T_6$ (already in the graph) and $T_4 \xrightarrow{0} T_6$ as a result of step 3b.

Finally, consider schedule 10 of Figure 13.21. Schedule 10 is view serializable, since it is view equivalent to the serial schedule $<T_3,T_4,T_7>$. The corresponding labeled precedence graph, constructed in steps 1 and 2, is depicted in Figure 13.22a. The final graph is depicted in Figure 13.22b. The edges $T_3 \xrightarrow{0} T_4$ and $T_3 \xrightarrow{0} T_7$ were inserted as a result of rule 3a. The pair of edges $T_3 \xrightarrow{1} T_4$ and $T_7 \xrightarrow{1} T_3$ was inserted as the result of a *single* application of rule 3c.

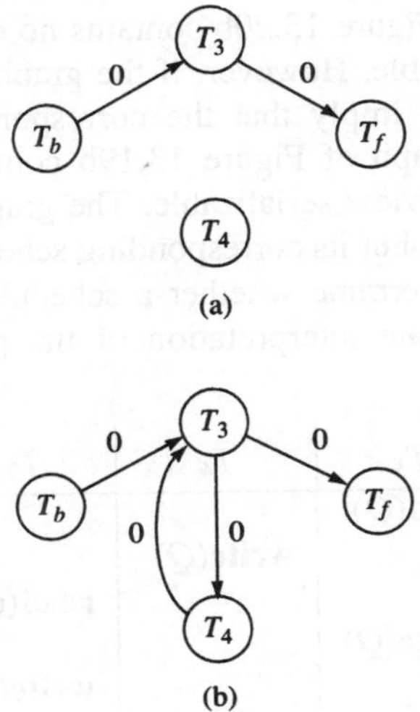

Figure 13.19 Labeled precedence graph of schedule 7.

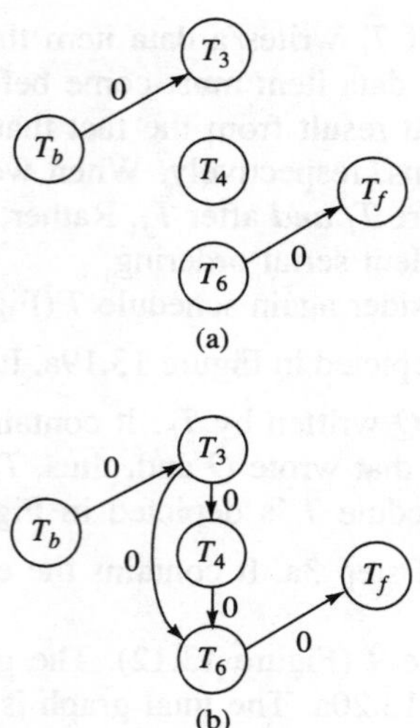

Figure 13.20 Labeled precedence graph of schedule 9.

The graphs depicted in Figures 13.19b and 13.22b contain the following minimal cycles, respectively:

- $T_3 \xrightarrow{0} T_4 \xrightarrow{0} T_3$
- $T_3 \xrightarrow{0} T_7 \xrightarrow{1} T_3$

The graph in Figure 13.20b, on the other hand, contains no cycles.

If the graph contains no cycle, the corresponding schedule is view serializable. Indeed, the graph of Figure 13.20b contains no cycle, and its corresponding schedule 9 is view serializable. However, if the graph contains a cycle, that condition does *not* necessarily imply that the corresponding schedule is not view serializable. Indeed, the graph of Figure 13.19b contains a cycle, yet its corresponding schedule 7 is not view serializable. The graph of Figure 13.22b, on the other hand, contains a cycle, but its corresponding schedule 10 is view serializable.

How, then, do we determine whether a schedule is view serializable? The answer lies in an appropriate interpretation of the precedence graph. Suppose

T_3	T_4	T_7
read(Q)		
	write(Q)	
		read(Q)
write(Q)		
		write(Q)

Figure 13.21 Schedule 10.

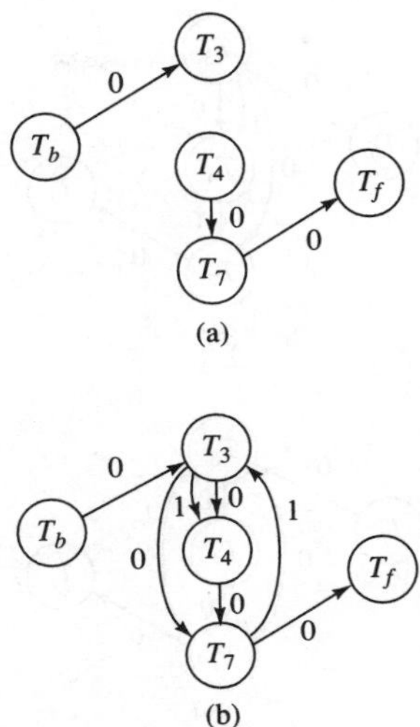

Figure 13.22 Labeled precedence graph of schedule 10.

that there are n distinct edge pairs. That is, we applied rule 3c n times in the construction of the precedence graph. Then, there exist 2^n different graphs, where each graph contains only one edge from each pair. If any one of these graphs is acyclic, then the corresponding schedule is view serializable. The serializability order is determined by the removal of the dummy transactions T_b and T_f, and by the topological sorting of the remaining acyclic graph.

Return to the graph of Figure 13.22b. Since there is exactly one distinct pair, there are two different graphs that need to be considered. The two graphs are depicted in Figure 13.23. Since the graph of Figure 13.23a is acyclic, we know that the corresponding schedule 10 is view serializable.

The algorithm just described requires exhaustive testing of all possible distinct graphs. It has been shown that the problem of testing for an acyclic graph in this set falls in the class of *NP*-complete problems (see the bibliographic notes for references to discussion of the theory of *NP*-complete problems). Any algorithm for an *NP*-complete problem will almost certainly take time that is exponential in the size of the problem.

In fact, it has been shown that the problem of testing for view serializability is itself *NP*-complete. Thus, almost certainly there exists no efficient algorithm to test for view serializability. However, concurrency-control schemes can still use *sufficient conditions* for view serializability. That is, if the sufficient conditions are satisfied, the schedule is view serializable, but there may be view-serializable schedules that do not satisfy the sufficient conditions.

13.10 Summary

A *transaction* is a *unit* of program execution that accesses and possibly updates various data items. Understanding the concept of a transaction is critical for un-

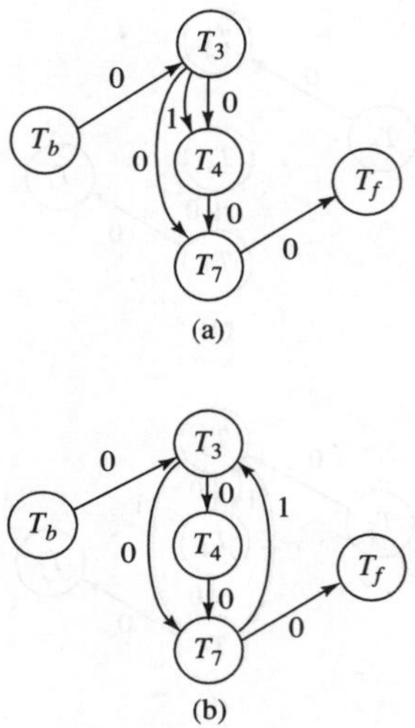

Figure 13.23 Two distinct precedence graphs.

derstanding and implementing updates of data in a database, such that concurrent executions and failures of various forms do not result inthe database becoming inconsistent. Transactions are required to have the ACID properties: atomicity, consistency, isolation and durability.

Atomicity ensures that either all the effects of a transaction are reflected in the database, or none are; a failure cannot leave the database in a state where a transaction is partially executed. Consistency ensures that, if the database is initially consistent, the execution of the transaction (by itself) leaves the database in a consistent state. Isolation ensures that concurrently executing transactions are isolated from one another, such that each has the impression that no other transaction is executing concurrently with it. Durability ensures that, once a transaction has been committed, that transaction's updates do not get lost, even if there is a system failure.

When several transactions execute concurrently in the database, the consistency of data may no longer be preserved. It is therefore necessary for the system to control the interaction among the concurrent transactions. Since a transaction is a unit that preserves consistency, a serial execution of transactions guarantees that consistency is preserved. We therefore require that any schedule produced by concurrent processing of a set of transactions will have an effect equivalent to a schedule produced when these transactions are run serially in some order. A system that guarantees this property is said to ensure *serializability*. There are several different notions of equivalence leading to the concepts of *conflict serializability* and *view serializability*.

Serializability of schedules generated by concurrently executing transactions can be ensured through one of a variety of mechanisms called *concurrency-control* schemes. The concurrency-control–management component of the database is responsible for handling the concurrency-control schemes. The recovery-management component of a database is responsible for ensuring the atomicity and durability properties of transactions.

We can test a given schedule for conflict serializability by constructing a *precedence graph* for the schedule, and by searching for absence of cycles in the graph. The time taken for the test is of the order of n^2, where n is the number of transactions. We can test for view serializability in order 2^n time by constructing a *labeled precedence graph* and searching over all possible distinct labeled graphs for a graph without a cycle.

Exercises

13.1. List the ACID properties. Explain the usefulness of each.

13.2. Suppose that there is a database system that never fails. Is a recovery manager required for this system?

13.3. Consider a file system such as the one on your favorite operating system. Are the issues of atomicity and durability relevant to the following? Explain your answer.
(*a*) A user of the file system
(*b*) An implementor of the file system

13.4. Database-system implementors have paid much more attention to the ACID properties than have file-system implementors. Why does that make sense?

13.5. During its execution, a transaction passes through several states, until it finally commits or aborts. List all possible sequences of states through which a transaction may pass. Explain why each state transition may occur.

13.6. Explain the distinction between the terms *serial schedule* and *serializable schedule*.

13.7. Consider the following two transactions:

T_1: **read**(A);
read(B);
if $A = 0$ **then** $B := B + 1$;
write(B).

T_2: **read** (B);
read (A);
if $B = 0$ **then** $A := A + 1$;
write(A).

Let the consistency requirement be $A = 0 \vee B = 0$, with $A = B = 0$ the initial values.

(*a*) Show that every serial execution involving these two transactions preserves the consistency of the database.

(*b*) Show a concurrent execution of T_1 and T_2 that produces a nonserializable schedule.

(*c*) Is there a concurrent execution of T_1 and T_2 that produces a serializable schedule?

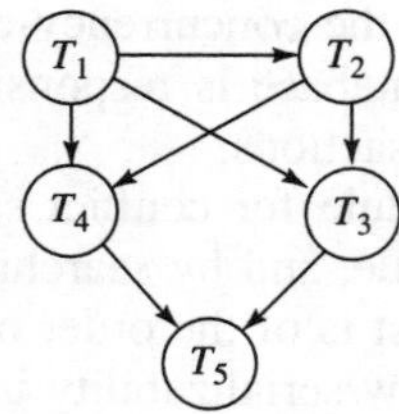

Figure 13.24 Precedence graph.

13.8. Since every conflict-serializable schedule is view serializable, why do we emphasize conflict serializability rather than view serializability?

13.9. Consider the precedence graph of Figure 13.24. Is the corresponding schedule conflict serializable? Explain your answer.

13.10. Consider the labeled precedence graph of Figure 13.25. Is the corresponding schedule view serializable? Explain your answer.

13.11. What is a recoverable schedule? Why is recoverability of schedules desirable? Are there any circumstances under which it would be desirable to allow nonrecoverable schedules? Explain your answer.

13.12. What is a cascadeless schedule? Why is cascadelessness of schedules desirable? Are there any circumstances under which it would be desirable to allow noncascadeless schedules? Explain your answer.

Bibliographic Notes

Textbook discussions of concurrency control and recovery are given by Bernstein et al. [1987] and Papadimitriou [1986]. A comprehensive survey paper on implementation issues in concurrency control and recovery is presented by Gray [1978]. Gray and Reuter [1993] provide extensive textbook coverage of transaction-processing concepts and techniques, including recovery and concurrency-control issues. Lynch et al. [1994] provide extensive textbook coverage of atomic transactions.

The concept of serializability was formulated by Eswaran et al. [1976] in connection to their work on concurrency control for System R. The results con-

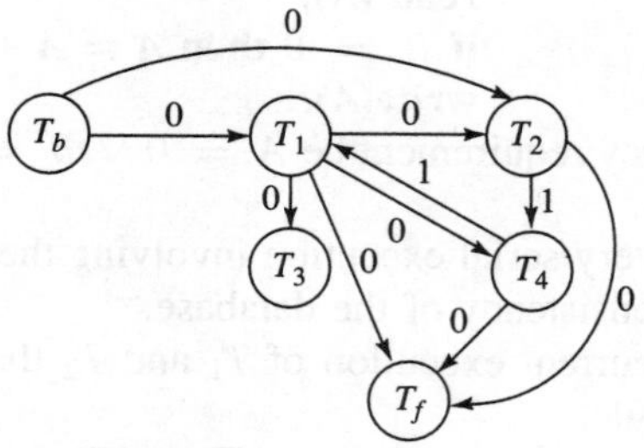

Figure 13.25 Labeled precedence graph.

cerning serializability testing are from Papadimitriou et al. [1977], and Papadimitriou [1979]. Cycle-detection algorithms can be found in standard algorithm textbooks, such as Cormen et al. [1990], and Aho et al. [1983].

Papadimitriou [1979] shows that testing for view serializability is NP-complete. (The theory of NP-completeness is presented in Aho et al. [1974], and in Garey and Johnson [1979].)

References covering specific aspects of transaction processing are cited in Chapters 14, 15, and 20.

CHAPTER 14

CONCURRENCY CONTROL

We saw in Chapter 13 that one of the fundamental properties of a transaction is isolation. When several transactions execute concurrently in the database, the isolation property may no longer be preserved. It is necessary for the system to control the interaction among the concurrent transactions; this control is achieved through one of a variety of mechanisms called *concurrency-control* schemes.

The concurrency-control schemes that we discuss in this chapter are all based on the serializability property. That is, all the schemes presented here ensure that the schedules are serializable. In Chapter 20, we discuss concurrency control schemes that admit nonserializable schedules. In this chapter, we consider the management of concurrently executing transactions, and we ignore failures. In Chapter 15, we shall see how the system can recover from failures.

14.1 Lock-Based Protocols

One way to ensure serializability is to require that access to data items be done in a mutually exclusive manner; that is, while one transaction is accessing a data item, no other transaction can modify that data item. The most common method used to implement this requirement is to allow a transaction to access a data item only if it is currently holding a lock on that item.

14.1.1 Locks

There are various modes in which a data item may be locked. In this section, we restrict our attention to two modes:

1. **Shared**. If a transaction T_i has obtained a shared-mode lock (denoted by S) on item Q, then T_i can read, but cannot write, Q.
2. **Exclusive**. If a transaction T_i has obtained an exclusive-mode lock (denoted by X) on item Q, then T_i can both read and write Q.

We require that every transaction *request* a lock in an appropriate mode on data item Q, depending on the types of operations that it will perform on Q. The request is made to the concurrency-control manager. The transaction can proceed with the operation only after the concurrency-control manager *grants* the lock to the transaction.

Given a set of lock modes, we can define a *compatibility function* on them as follows. Let A and B represent arbitrary lock modes. Suppose that a transaction T_i requests a lock of mode A on item Q on which transaction T_j ($T_i \neq T_j$) currently holds a lock of mode B. If transaction T_i can be granted a lock on Q immediately, in spite of the presence of the mode B lock, then we say mode A is *compatible* with mode B. Such a function can be represented conveniently by a matrix. The compatibility relation between the two modes of locking used in this section is given by the matrix **comp** of Figure 14.1. An element **comp**(A,B) of the matrix has the value *true* if and only if mode A is compatible with mode B.

Note that shared mode is compatible with shared mode, but not with exclusive mode. At any time, several shared-mode locks can be held simultaneously (by different transactions) on a particular data item. A subsequent exclusive-mode lock request has to wait until the currently held shared-mode locks are released.

A transaction requests a shared lock on data item Q by executing the **lock-S**(Q) instruction. Similarly, an exclusive lock is requested through the **lock-X**(Q) instruction. A data item Q can be unlocked via the **unlock**(Q) instruction.

To access a data item, transaction T_i must first lock that item. If the data item is already locked by another transaction in an incompatible mode, the concurrency-control manager will not grant the lock until all incompatible locks held by other transactions have been released. Thus, T_i is made to *wait* until all incompatible locks held by other transactions have been released.

Transaction T_i may unlock a data item that it had locked at some earlier point. Note that a transaction must hold a lock on a data item as long as it accesses that item. Moreover, for a transaction to unlock a data item immediately after its final access of that data item is not always desirable, since serializability may not be ensured.

	S	X
S	true	false
X	false	false

Figure 14.1 Lock-compatibility matrix **comp**.

As an illustration, consider again the simplified banking system that we introduced in Chapter 13. Let A and B be two accounts that are accessed by transactions T_1 and T_2. Transaction T_1 transfers \$50 from account B to account A, and is defined as

T_1: **lock-X**(B);
read(B);
$B := B - 50$;
write(B);
unlock(B);
lock-X(A);
read(A);
$A := A + 50$;
write(A);
unlock(A).

Transaction T_2 displays the total amount of money in accounts A and B—that is, the sum $A + B$—and is defined as

T_2: **lock-S**(A);
read(A);
unlock(A);
lock-S(B);
read(B);
unlock(B);
display($A + B$).

Suppose that the values of accounts A and B are \$100 and \$200, respectively. If these two transactions are executed serially, either in the order T_1, T_2 or the order T_2, T_1, then transaction T_2 will display the value \$300. If, however, these transactions are executed concurrently, then schedule 1, as shown in Figure 14.2, is possible. In this case, transaction T_2 displays \$250, which is incorrect. The reason for this mistake is that the transaction T_1 unlocked data item B too early, as a result of which T_2 saw an inconsistent state.

The schedule shows the actions executed by the transactions, as well as the points when the locks are granted by the concurrency-control manager. The transaction making a lock request cannot execute its next action until the lock is granted by the concurrency-control manager; hence, the lock must be granted in the interval of time between the lock-request operation and the following action of the transaction. Exactly when within this interval the lock is granted is not important; the lock can be safely assumed to be granted just before the following action of the transaction. Hence, we shall drop the column depicting the actions of the concurrency-control manager from all schedules depicted in the rest of the chapter. We let you infer when locks are granted.

Suppose now that unlocking is delayed to the end of the transaction. Transaction T_3 corresponds to T_1 with unlocking delayed, and is defined as

T_3: **lock-X**(B);
read(B);
$B := B - 50$;
write(B);
lock-X(A);
read(A);
$A := A + 50$;
write(A);
unlock(B);
unlock(A).

Transaction T_4 corresponds to T_2 with unlocking delayed, and is defined as

T_4: **lock-S**(A);
read(A);
lock-S(B);
read(B);
display($A + B$);
unlock(A);
unlock(B).

T_1	T_2	concurrency-control manager
lock-X(B)		
		grant-X(B,T_1)
read(B)		
$B := B - 50$		
write(B)		
unlock(B)		
	lock-S(A)	
		grant-S(A,T_2)
	read(A)	
	unlock(A)	
	lock-S(B)	
		grant-S(B,T_2)
	read(B)	
	unlock(B)	
	display($A + B$)	
lock-X(A)		
		grant-X(A,T_2)
read(A)		
$A := A + 50$		
write(A)		
unlock(A)		

Figure 14.2 Schedule 1.

T_3	T_4
lock-X(B)	
read(B)	
$B := B - 50$	
write(B)	
	lock-S(A)
	read(A)
	lock-S(B)
lock-X(A)	

Figure 14.3 Schedule 2.

You should verify that the sequence of reads and writes in schedule 1, which lead to an incorrect total of $250 being displayed, is no longer possible with T_3 and T_4. Other schedules are possible. T_4 will not print out an inconsistent result in any of them; we shall see why later.

Unfortunately, the use of locking can lead to an undesirable situation. Consider the partial schedule of Figure 14.3 for T_3 and T_4. Since T_3 is holding an exclusive-mode lock on B and T_4 is requesting a shared-mode lock on B, T_4 is waiting for T_3 to unlock B. Similarly, since T_4 is holding a shared-mode lock on A and T_3 is requesting an exclusive-mode lock on A, T_3 is waiting for T_4 to unlock A. Thus, we have arrived at a state where neither of these transactions can ever proceed with its normal execution. This situation is called *deadlock*. When deadlock occurs, the system must roll back one of the two transactions. Once a transaction has been rolled back, the data items that were locked by that transaction are unlocked. These data items are then available to the other transaction, which can continue with its execution. We shall return to the issue of deadlock handling in Section 14.6.

If we do not use locking, or unlock data items as soon as possible after reading or writing them, we may get inconsistent states. On the other hand, if we do not unlock a data item before requesting a lock on another data item, deadlocks may occur. There are ways to avoid deadlock in some situations, as we shall see in Section 14.1.4. However, in general, deadlocks are a necessary evil associated with locking, if we want to avoid inconsistent states. Deadlocks are definitely preferable to inconsistent states, since they can be handled by rolling back of transactions, whereas inconsistent states may lead to real-world problems that cannot be handled by the database system.

We shall require that each transaction in the system follow a set of rules, called a *locking protocol*, indicating when a transaction may lock and unlock each of the data items. Locking protocols restrict the number of possible schedules. The set of all such schedules is a proper subset of all possible serializable schedules. We shall present several locking protocols that allow only conflict-serializable schedules. Before doing so, we need a few definitions.

Let $\{T_0, T_1, ..., T_n\}$ be a set of transactions participating in a schedule S. We say that T_i *precedes* T_j in S, written $T_i \rightarrow T_j$, if there exists a data item Q such that T_i has held lock mode A on Q, and T_j has held lock mode B on Q later, and **comp**(A,B) = false. If $T_i \rightarrow T_j$, then that precedence implies that in any equivalent serial schedule, T_i must appear before T_j. Observe that this graph is similar to the precedence graph that we used in Section 13.9.1 to test for conflict serializability. Conflicts between instructions correspond to noncompatibility of lock modes.

We say that a schedule S is *legal* under a given locking protocol if S is a possible schedule for a set of transactions following the rules of the locking protocol. We say that a locking protocol *ensures conflict serializability* if and only if, for all legal schedules, the associated $\rightarrow$ relation is acyclic.

14.1.2 Granting of Locks

When a transaction requests a lock on a data item in a particular mode, and no other transaction has a lock on the same data item in a conflicting mode, the lock can be granted. However, care must be taken to avoid the following scenario. Suppose a transaction T_2 has a shared-mode lock on a data item, and another transaction T_1 requests an exclusive-mode lock on the data item. Clearly, T_1 has to wait for T_2 to release the shared-mode lock. Meanwhile, a transaction T_3 may request a shared-mode lock on the same data item. The lock request is compatible with the lock granted to T_2, so T_3 may be granted the shared-mode lock. At this point T_2 may release the lock, but still T_1 has to wait for T_3 to finish. But again, there may be a new transaction T_4 that requests a shared-mode lock on the same data item, and is granted the lock before T_3 releases it. In fact, it is possible that there is a sequence of transactions that each requests a shared-mode lock on the data item, and each transaction releases the lock a short while after it is granted, but T_1 never gets the exclusive-mode lock on the data item. The transaction T_1 may never make progress, and is said to be *starved.*

We can avoid starvation of transactions by granting locks as follows. When a transaction T_i requests a lock on a data item Q in a particular mode M, the lock is granted provided that

1. There is no other other transaction holding a lock on Q in a mode that conflicts with M.
2. There is no other transaction that is waiting for a lock on Q, and that made its lock request before T_i.

14.1.3 The Two-Phase Locking Protocol

One protocol that ensures serializability is the *two-phase locking protocol.* This protocol requires that each transaction issue lock and unlock requests in two phases:

1. **Growing phase**. A transaction may obtain locks, but may not release any lock.

2. **Shrinking phase**. A transaction may release locks, but may not obtain any new locks.

Initially, a transaction is in the growing phase. The transaction acquires locks as needed. Once the transaction releases a lock, it enters the shrinking phase, and it can issue no more lock requests.

For example, transactions T_3 and T_4 (see page 474) are two phase. On the other hand, transactions T_1 and T_2 (see page 473) are not two phase. Note that the unlock instructions do not need to appear at the end of the transaction. For example, in the case of transaction T_3, we could move the **unlock**(B) instruction to just after the **lock-X**(A) instruction, and still retain the two-phase locking property.

We can show that the two-phase locking protocol ensures conflict serializability. Consider any transaction. The point in the schedule where the transaction has obtained its final lock (the end of its growing phase) is called the *lock point* of the transaction. Now, transactions can be ordered according to their lock points—this ordering is, in fact, a serializability ordering for the transactions. We leave the proof as an exercise for you to do (see Exercise 14.1).

Two-phase locking does *not* ensure freedom from deadlock. Observe that transactions T_3 and T_4 are two-phase, but, in schedule 2 (Figure 14.3), they are deadlocked.

Recall from Section 13.6.2 that, in addition to their being serializable, it is desirable that schedules be cascadeless. Cascading rollback may occur under two-phase locking. As an illustration, consider the partial schedule of Figure 14.4. Each transaction observes the two-phase locking protocol, but the failure of T_5 after the **read**(A) step of T_7 leads to cascading rollback of T_6 and T_7.

Cascading rollbacks can be avoided by a modification of two-phase locking called the *strict two-phase locking* protocol. The strict two-phase locking protocol, requires, that in addition to locking being two-phase, all exclusive-mode locks taken by a transaction must be held until that transaction commits. This

T_5	T_6	T_7
lock-X(A)		
read(A)		
lock-S(B)		
read(B)		
write(A)		
unlock(A)		
	lock-X(A)	
	read(A)	
	write(A)	
	unlock(A)	
		lock-S(A)
		read(A)

Figure 14.4 Partial schedule under two-phase locking.

requirement ensures that any data written by an uncommitted transaction are locked in exclusive mode until the transaction commits, preventing any other transaction from reading the data.

Another variant of two-phase locking is the *rigorous two-phase* locking protocol, which requires all locks to be held until the transaction commits. It can be easily verified that, with rigorous two-phase locking, transactions can be serialized in the order in which they commit. Most database systems implement either strict or rigorous two-phase locking.

Consider the following two transactions for which we have shown only some of the significant **read** and **write** operations. Transaction T_8 is defined as

T_8: **read**(a_1);
read(a_2);
. . .
read(a_n);
write(a_1).

Transaction T_9 is defined as

T_9: **read**(a_1);
read(a_2);
display($a_1 + a_2$).

If we employ the two-phase locking protocol, then T_8 must lock a_1 in exclusive mode. Therefore, any concurrent execution of both transactions amounts to a serial execution. Notice, however, that T_8 needs an exclusive lock on a_1 only at the end of its execution, when it writes a_1. Thus, if T_8 could initially lock a_1 in shared mode, and then could later change the lock to exclusive mode, we could get more concurrency, since T_8 and T_9 could access a_1 and a_2 simultaneously.

This observation leads us to a refinement of the basic two-phase locking protocol, in which lock *conversions* are allowed. We shall provide a mechanism for upgrading a shared lock to an exclusive lock, and downgrading an exclusive lock to a shared lock. We denote conversion from shared to exclusive modes by **upgrade**, and from exclusive to shared by **downgrade**. Lock conversion cannot be allowed to occur arbitrarily. Rather, upgrading can take place in only the growing phase, whereas downgrading can take place in only the shrinking phase.

Returning to our example, transactions T_8 and T_9 can run concurrently under the refined two-phase locking protocol, as shown in the incomplete schedule of Figure 14.5, where only some of the locking instructions are shown.

Note that a transaction attempting to upgrade a lock on an item Q may be forced to wait. This enforced wait occurs if Q is currently locked by *another* transaction in shared mode.

Just like the basic two-phase locking protocol, two-phase locking with lock conversion generates only conflict-serializable schedules, and transactions can be serialized by their lock points. Further, if exclusive locks are held until the end of the transaction, the schedules are cascadeless.

T_8	T_9
lock-S(a_1)	
	lock-S(a_1)
lock-S(a_2)	
	lock-S(a_2)
lock-S(a_3)	
lock-S(a_4)	
	unlock(a_1)
	unlock(a_2)
lock-S(a_n)	
upgrade(a_1)	

Figure 14.5 Incomplete schedule with a lock conversion.

We now describe a simple but widely used scheme that automatically generates the appropriate lock and unlock instructions for a transaction. When a transaction T_i issues a **read**(Q) operation, the system issues a **lock-S**(Q) instruction followed by the **read**(Q) instruction. When T_i issues a **write**(Q) operation, the system checks to see whether T_i already holds a shared lock on Q. If it does, then the system issues an **upgrade**(Q) instruction, followed by the **write**(Q) instruction. Otherwise, the system issues a **lock-X**(Q) instruction, followed by the **write**(Q) instruction. All locks obtained by a transaction are unlocked after that transaction commits or aborts.

For a set of transactions, there may be conflict-serializable schedules that cannot be obtained through the two-phase locking protocol. However, to obtain conflict-serializable schedules through non-two-phase locking protocols, we need either to have additional information about the transactions or to impose some structure or ordering on the set of data items in the database. In the absence of such information, two-phase locking is necessary for conflict serializability—if T_i is a non–two-phase transaction, it is always possible to find another transaction T_j that is two-phase such that there is a schedule possible for T_i and T_j that is not conflict serializable.

Strict two-phase locking and rigorous two-phase locking (with lock conversions) are used extensively in commercial database systems.

14.1.4 Graph-Based Protocols

As we pointed out, in the absence of information concerning the manner in which data items are accessed, the two-phase locking protocol is both necessary and sufficient for ensuring serializability. Thus, if we wish to develop protocols that are not two-phase, we need additional information on how each transaction will access the database. There are various models that differ in the amount of such information provided. The simplest model requires that we have prior knowledge about the order in which the database items will be accessed. Given such information, it is possible to construct locking protocols that are not two-phase, but that, nevertheless, ensure conflict serializability.

To acquire such prior knowledge, we impose a partial ordering $\rightarrow$ on the set $\mathbf{D} = \{d_1, d_2, ..., d_h\}$ of all data items. If $d_i \rightarrow d_j$, then any transaction accessing both d_i and d_j must access d_i before accessing d_j. This partial ordering may be the result of either the logical or the physical organization of the data, or it may be imposed solely for the purpose of concurrency control.

The partial ordering implies that the set **D** may now be viewed as a directed acyclic graph, called a *database graph*. In this section, for the sake of simplicity, we will restrict our attention to only those graphs that are rooted trees. We will present a simple protocol, called the *tree protocol*, which is restricted to employ only *exclusive* locks. References to other, more complex, graph-based locking protocols are provided in the bibliographic notes.

In the tree protocol, the only lock instruction allowed is **lock-X**. Each transaction T_i can lock a data item at most once, and must observe the following rules:

1. The first lock by T_i may be on any data item.
2. Subsequently, a data item Q can be locked by T_i only if the parent of Q is currently locked by T_i.
3. Data items may be unlocked at any time.
4. A data item that has been locked and unlocked by T_i cannot subsequently be relocked by T_i.

As we stated earlier, all schedules that are legal under the tree protocol are conflict serializable.

To illustrate this protocol, consider the database graph of Figure 14.6. The following four transactions follow the tree protocol on this graph. We have shown

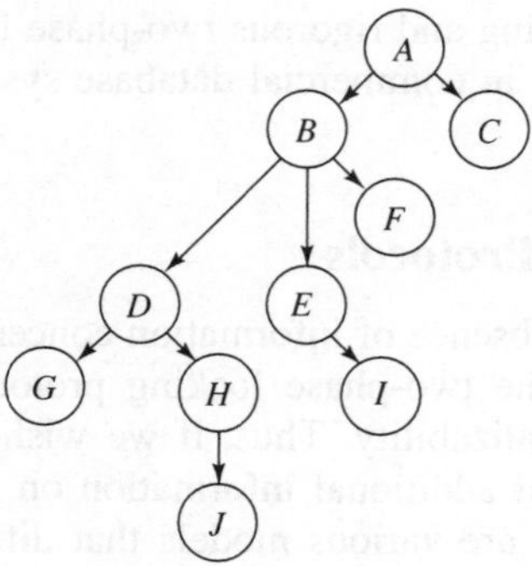

Figure 14.6 Tree structured database graph.

only the lock and unlock instructions:

T_{10}: **lock-X(*B*); lock-X(*E*); lock-X(*D*); unlock(*B*); unlock(*E*); lock-X(*G*); unlock(*D*); unlock(*G*).**

T_{11}: **lock-X(*D*); lock-X(*H*); unlock(*D*); unlock(*H*).**

T_{12}: **lock-X(*B*); lock-X(*E*); unlock(*E*); unlock(*B*).**

T_{13}: **lock-X(*D*); lock-X(*H*); unlock(*D*); unlock(*H*).**

One possible schedule in which these four transactions participated is depicted in Figure 14.7. Note that, during its execution, transaction T_{10} holds locks on two *disjoint* subtrees.

Observe that the schedule of Figure 14.7 is conflict serializable. It can be shown not only that the tree protocol ensures conflict serializability, but also that this protocol ensures freedom from deadlock.

The tree-locking protocol has an advantage over the two-phase locking protocol in that unlocking may occur earlier. Earlier unlocking may lead to shorter waiting times, and to an increase in concurrency. In addition, since the protocol is deadlock-free, no rollbacks are required. However, the protocol has the disadvantage that, in some cases, a transaction may have to lock data items that it does not access. For example, a transaction that needs to access data items *A* and *J* in the database graph of Figure 14.6 must lock not only *A* and *J*, but also data items *B*, *D*, and *H*. This additional locking results in increased locking

T_{10}	T_{11}	T_{12}	T_{13}
lock-X(*B*)			
	lock-X(*D*)		
	lock-X(*H*)		
	unlock(*D*)		
lock-X(*E*)			
lock-X(*D*)			
unlock(*B*)			
unlock(*E*)			
		lock-X(*B*)	
		lock-X(*E*)	
	unlock(*H*)		
lock-X(*G*)			
unlock(*D*)			
			lock-X(*D*)
			lock-X(*H*)
			unlock(*D*)
			unlock(*H*)
		unlock(*E*)	
		unlock(*B*)	
unlock(*G*)			

Figure 14.7 Serializable schedule under the tree protocol.

overhead, the possibility of additional waiting time, and a potential decrease in concurrency. Further, without prior knowledge of what data items will need to be locked, transactions will have to lock the root of the tree, and that can reduce concurrency greatly.

For a set of transactions, there may be conflict-serializable schedules that cannot be obtained through the tree protocol. Indeed, there are schedules possible under the two-phase locking protocol that are not possible under the tree protocol, and vice versa. Examples of such schedules are explored in the exercises.

14.2 Timestamp-Based Protocols

In the locking protocols that we have described thus far, the order between every pair of conflicting transactions is determined at execution time by the first lock that they both request that involves incompatible modes. Another method for determining the serializability order is to select an ordering among transactions in advance. The most common method for doing so is to use a *timestamp-ordering* scheme.

14.2.1 Timestamps

With each transaction T_i in the system, we associate a unique fixed timestamp, denoted by $\text{TS}(T_i)$. This timestamp is assigned by the database system before the transaction T_i starts execution. If a transaction T_i has been assigned timestamp $\text{TS}(T_i)$, and a new transaction T_j enters the system, then $\text{TS}(T_i) < \text{TS}(T_j)$. There are two simple methods for implementing this scheme:

1. Use the value of the *system clock* as the timestamp; that is, a transaction's timestamp is equal to the value of the clock when the transaction enters the system.
2. Use a *logical counter* that is incremented after a new timestamp has been assigned; that is, a transaction's timestamp is equal to the value of the counter when the transaction enters the system.

The timestamps of the transactions determine the serializability order. Thus, if $\text{TS}(T_i) < \text{TS}(T_j)$, then the system must ensure that the produced schedule is equivalent to a serial schedule in which transaction T_i appears before transaction T_j.

To implement this scheme, we associate with each data item Q two timestamp values:

- **W-timestamp**(Q) denotes the largest timestamp of any transaction that executed **write**(Q) successfully.
- **R-timestamp**(Q) denotes the largest timestamp of any transaction that executed **read**(Q) successfully.

These timestamps are updated whenever a new **read**(Q) or **write**(Q) instruction is executed.

14.2.2 The Timestamp-Ordering Protocol

The *timestamp-ordering protocol* ensures that any conflicting **read** and **write** operations are executed in timestamp order. This protocol operates as follows:

1. Suppose that transaction T_i issues **read**(Q).
   a. If TS(T_i) $<$ W-timestamp(Q), then T_i needs to read a value of Q that was already overwritten. Hence, the **read** operation is rejected, and T_i is rolled back.
   b. If TS(T_i) $\geq$ W-timestamp(Q), then the **read** operation is executed, and R-timestamp(Q) is set to the maximum of R-timestamp(Q) and TS(T_i).
2. Suppose that transaction T_i issues **write**(Q).
   a. If TS(T_i) $<$ R-timestamp(Q), then the value of Q that T_i is producing was needed previously, and the system assumed that that value would never be produced. Hence, the **write** operation is rejected, and T_i is rolled back.
   b. If TS(T_i) $<$ W-timestamp(Q), then T_i is attempting to write an obsolete value of Q. Hence, this **write** operation is rejected, and T_i is rolled back.
   c. Otherwise, the **write** operation is executed, and W-timestamp(Q) is set to TS(T_i).

A transaction T_i, that is rolled back by the concurrency-control scheme as result of either a **read** or **write** operation being issued, is assigned a new timestamp and is restarted.

To illustrate this protocol, we consider transactions T_{14} and T_{15}. Transaction T_{14} displays the contents of accounts A and B, and is defined as

T_{14}: **read**(B);
read(A);
display($A + B$).

Transaction T_{15} transfers \$50 from account A to account B, and then displays the contents of both:

T_{15}: **read**(B);
$B := B - 50$;
write(B);
read(A);
$A := A + 50$;
write(A);
display($A + B$).

In presenting schedules under the timestamp protocol, we shall assume that a transaction is assigned a timestamp immediately before its first instruction. Thus, in schedule 3 of Figure 14.8, TS(T_{14}) $<$ TS(T_{15}), and the schedule is possible under the timestamp protocol.

We note that the preceding execution can also be produced by the two-phase locking protocol. There are, however, schedules that are possible under the two-

T_{14}	T_{15}
read(B)	
	read(B)
	$B := B - 50$
	write(B)
read(A)	
	read(A)
display($A + B$)	
	$A := A + 50$
	write(A)
	display($A + B$)

Figure 14.8 Schedule 3.

phase locking protocol, but are not possible under the timestamp protocol, and vice versa (see Exercise 14.20).

The timestamp-ordering protocol ensures conflict serializability. This assertion follows from the fact that conflicting operations are processed in timestamp order. The protocol ensures freedom from deadlock, since no transaction ever waits. The protocol can generate schedules that are not recoverable; however it can be extended to make the schedules cascadeless (see Exercise 14.23).

14.2.3 Thomas' Write Rule

We now present a modification to the timestamp-ordering protocol that allows greater potential concurrency than does the protocol of Section 14.2.2. Let us consider schedule 4 of Figure 14.9, and apply the timestamp-ordering protocol. Since T_{16} starts before T_{17}, we shall assume that TS(T_{16}) < TS(T_{17}). The **read**(Q) operation of T_{16} succeeds, as does the **write**(Q) operation of T_{17}. When T_{16} attempts its **write**(Q) operation, we find that TS(T_{16}) < W-timestamp(Q), since W-timestamp(Q) = TS(T_{17}). Thus, the **write**(Q) by T_{16} is rejected and transaction T_{16} must be rolled back.

Although the rollback of T_{16} is required by the timestamp-ordering protocol, it is unnecessary. Since T_{17} has already written Q, the value that T_{16} is attempting to write is one that will never need to be read. Any transaction T_i with TS(T_i) < TS(T_{17}) that attempts a **read**(Q) will be rolled back, since TS(T_i) < W-timestamp(Q). Any transaction T_j with TS(T_j) > TS(T_{17}) must read the value of Q written by T_{17}, rather than the value written by T_{16}.

T_{16}	T_{17}
read(Q)	
	write(Q)
write(Q)	

Figure 14.9 Schedule 4.

This observation leads to a modified version of the timestamp-ordering protocol in which obsolete **write** operations can be ignored under certain circumstances. The protocol rules for **read** operations remain unchanged. The protocol rules for **write** operations, however, are slightly different from the timestamp-ordering protocol of Section 14.2.2.

Suppose that transaction T_i issues **write**(Q).

1. If TS(T_i) < R-timestamp(Q), then the value of Q that T_i is producing was previously needed, and it was assumed that the value would never be produced. Hence, the **write** operation is rejected, and T_i is rolled back.
2. If TS(T_i) < W-timestamp(Q), then T_i is attempting to write an obsolete value of Q. Hence, this **write** operation can be ignored.
3. Otherwise, the **write** operation is executed, and W-timestamp(Q) is set to TS(T_i).

The difference between the preceding rules and those of Section 14.2.2 lies in the second rule. The timestamp-ordering protocol requires that T_i be rolled back if T_i issues **write**(Q) and TS(T_i) < W-timestamp(Q). However, here, in those cases where TS(T_i) ≥ R-timestamp(Q), we ignore the obsolete **write**. This modification to the timestamp-ordering protocol is called *Thomas' write rule*.

Thomas' write rule makes use of view serializability by, in effect, deleting obsolete **write** operations from the transactions that issue them. This modification of transactions makes it possible to generate serializable schedules that would not be possible under the other protocols presented in this chapter. For example, schedule 4 of Figure 14.9 is not conflict serializable and, thus, is not possible under any of two-phase locking, the tree protocol, or the timestamp-ordering protocol. Under Thomas' write rule, the **write**(Q) operation of T_{16} would be ignored. The result is a schedule that is view equivalent to the serial schedule <T_{16},T_{17}>.

14.3 Validation-Based Protocols

In cases where the majority of transactions are read-only transactions, the rate of conflicts among transactions may be low. Thus, many of these transactions, if executed without the supervision of a concurrency-control scheme, would nevertheless leave the system in a consistent state. A concurrency control scheme imposes overhead of code execution and possible delay of transactions. It may be desirable to use an alternative scheme that imposes less overhead. A difficulty in reducing the overhead is that we do not know in advance which transactions will be involved in a conflict. To gain that knowledge, we need a scheme for *monitoring* the system.

We assume that each transaction T_i executes in two or three different phases in its lifetime, depending on whether it is a read-only or an update transaction. The phases are, in order, as follows:

1. **Read phase**. During this phase, the execution of transaction T_i takes place. The values of the various data items are read, and are stored in variables

local to T_i. All **write** operations are performed on temporary local variables, without updates of the actual database.

2. **Validation phase**. Transaction T_i performs a validation test to determine whether it can copy to the database the temporary local variables that hold the results of **write** operations without causing a violation of serializability.
3. **Write phase**. If transaction T_i succeeds in validation (step 2), then the actual updates are applied to the database. Otherwise, T_i is rolled back.

Each transaction must go through the three phases in the order shown. However, all three phases of concurrently executing transactions can be interleaved.

The read and write phases are self-explanatory. The only phase that needs further discussion is the validation phase. To perform the validation test, we need to know when the various phases of transactions T_i took place. We shall, therefore, associate three different timestamps with transaction T_i:

1. **Start**(T_i), the time when T_i started its execution
2. **Validation**(T_i), the time when T_i finished its read phase and started its validation phase
3. **Finish**(T_i), the time when T_i finished its write phase

We determine the serializability order by the timestamp-ordering technique using the value of the timestamp Validation(T_i). Thus, the value TS(T_i) = Validation(T_i) and, if TS(T_j) < TS(T_k), then any produced schedule must be equivalent to a serial schedule in which transaction T_j appears before transaction T_k. The reason we have chosen Validation(T_i), rather than Start(T_i), as the timestamp of transaction T_i is that we can expect faster response time provided that conflict rates among transactions are indeed low.

The validation test for transaction T_j requires that, for all transactions T_i with TS(T_i) < TS(T_j), one of the following two conditions must hold:

1. Finish(T_i) < Start(T_j). Since T_i completes its execution before T_j started, the serializability order is indeed maintained.
2. The set of data items written by T_i does not intersect with the set of data items read by T_j, and T_i completes its write phase before T_j starts its validation phase (Start(T_j) < Finish(T_i) < Validation(T_j)). This condition ensures that the writes of T_i and T_j do not overlap. Since the writes of T_i do not affect the read of T_j, and since T_j cannot affect the read of T_i, the serializability order is indeed maintained.

As an illustration, consider again transactions T_{14} and T_{15}. Suppose that TS(T_{14}) < TS(T_{15}). Then, the validation phase succeeds in producing schedule 5, which is depicted in Figure 14.10. Note that the writes to the actual variables are performed only after the validation phase of T_{15}. Thus, T_{14} reads the old values of B and A, and this schedule is serializable.

T_{14}	T_{15}
read(B)	
	read(B)
	$B := B - 50$
	read(A)
	$A := A + 50$
read(A)	
⟨ *validate* ⟩	
display($A + B$)	
	⟨ *validate* ⟩
	write(B)
	write(A)

Figure 14.10 Schedule 5, a schedule produced using validation.

The validation scheme automatically guards against cascading rollbacks, since the actual writes take place only after the transaction issuing the write has committed.

14.4 Multiple Granularity

In the concurrency control schemes described thus far, we have used each individual data item as the unit on which synchronization is performed.

There are circumstances, however, where it would be advantageous to group several data items, and to treat them as one individual synchronization unit. For example, if a transaction T_i needs to access the entire database, and a locking protocol is used, then T_i must lock each item in the database. Clearly, executing these locks is time consuming. It would be better if T_i could issue a *single* lock request to lock the entire database. On the other hand, if transaction T_j needs to access only a few data items, it should not be required to lock the entire database, since otherwise concurrency is lost.

What is needed is a mechanism to allow the system to define multiple levels of *granularity*. We can make one by allowing data items to be of various sizes and defining a hierarchy of data granularities, where the small granularities are nested within larger ones. Such a hierarchy can be represented graphically as a tree. Note that the tree that we describe here is significantly different from that used by the tree protocol (Section 14.1.4). A nonleaf node of the multiple-granularity tree represents the data associated with its descendants. In the tree protocol, each node is an independent data item.

As an illustration, consider the tree of Figure 14.11, which consists of four levels of nodes. The highest level represents the entire database. Below it are nodes of type *area*; the database consists of exactly these areas. Each area in turn has nodes of type *file* as its children. Each area contains exactly those files that are its child nodes. No file is in more than one area. Finally, each file has nodes of type *record*. As before, the file consists of exactly those

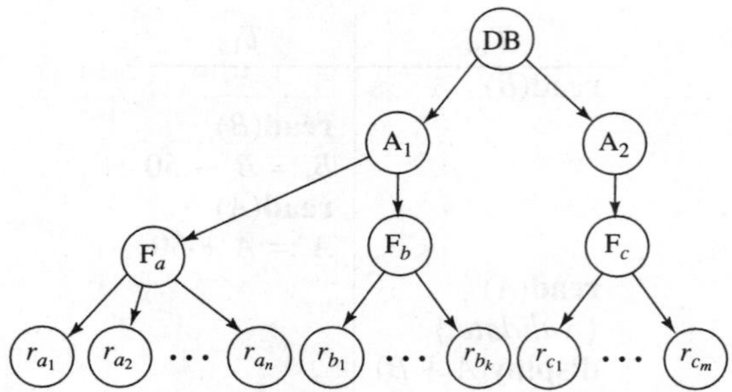

Figure 14.11 Granularity hierarchy.

records that are its child nodes, and no record can be present in more than one file.

Each node in the tree can be locked individually. As we did in the two-phase locking protocol, we shall use *shared* and *exclusive* lock modes. When a transaction locks a node, in either *shared* or *exclusive* mode, the transaction also has locked all the descendants of that node in the same lock mode. For example, if transaction T_i locks *explicitly* file F_c of Figure 14.11, in exclusive mode, then it has locked *implicitly* in exclusive mode all the records belonging to that file. It does not need to lock the individual records of F_c *explicitly*.

Suppose that transaction T_j wishes to lock record r_{b_6} of file F_b. Since T_i has locked F_b explicitly, it follows that r_{b_6} is also locked (implicitly). But, when T_j issues a lock request for r_{b_6}, r_{b_6} is not explicitly locked! How does the system determine whether T_j can lock r_{b_6}? T_j must traverse the tree from the root to record r_{b_6}. If any node in that path is locked in an incompatible mode, then T_j must be delayed.

Suppose now that transaction T_k wishes to lock the entire database. To do so, it simply must lock the root of the hierarchy. Note, however, that T_k should not succeed in locking the root node, since T_i is currently holding a lock on part of the tree (specifically, on file F_b). But how does the system determine if the root node can be locked? One possibility is for it to search the entire tree. This solution, however, defeats the whole purpose of the multiple-granularity locking scheme. A more efficient way to gain this knowledge is to introduce a new class of lock modes, called *intention* lock modes. If a node is locked in an intention mode, explicit locking is being done at a lower level of the tree (that is, at a finer granularity). Intention locks are put on all the ancestors of a node before that node is locked explicitly. Thus, a transaction does not need to search the entire tree to determine whether it can lock a node successfully. A transaction wishing to lock a node—say, Q—must traverse a path in the tree from the root to Q. While traversing the tree, the transaction locks the various nodes in an intention mode.

There is an intention mode associated with *shared* mode, and there is one with *exclusive* mode. If a node is locked in *intention-shared* (IS) mode, explicit locking is being done at a lower level of the tree, but with only shared-mode locks.

	IS	IX	S	SIX	X
IS	true	true	true	true	false
IX	true	true	false	false	false
S	true	false	true	false	false
SIX	true	false	false	false	false
X	false	false	false	false	false

Figure 14.12 Compatibility matrix.

Similarly, if a node is locked in *intention-exclusive* (IX) mode, then explicit locking is being done at a lower level, with exclusive-mode or shared-mode locks. Finally, if a node is locked in *shared and intention-exclusive* (SIX) mode, the subtree rooted by that node is locked explicitly in shared mode, and that explicit locking is being done at a lower level with exclusive-mode locks. The compatibility function for these lock modes is presented in Figure 14.12.

The multiple-granularity locking protocol that follows ensures serializability. Each transaction T_i can lock a node Q, using the following rules:

1. The lock-compatibility function of Figure 14.12 must be observed.
2. The root of the tree must be locked first, and can be locked in any mode.
3. A node Q can be locked by T_i in S or IS mode only if the parent of Q is currently locked by T_i in either IX or IS mode.
4. A node Q can be locked by T_i in X, SIX, or IX mode only if the parent of Q is currently locked by T_i in either IX or SIX mode.
5. T_i can lock a node only if it has not previously unlocked any node (that is, T_i is two-phase).
6. T_i can unlock a node Q only if none of the children of Q are currently locked by T_i.

Observe that the multiple-granularity protocol requires that locks be acquired in top-down (root-to-leaf) order, whereas locks must be released in bottom-up (leaf-to-root) order.

As an illustration of the protocol, consider the tree of Figure 14.11 and the following transactions:

- Suppose that transaction T_{18} reads record r_{a_2} in file F_a. Then, T_{18} needs to lock the database, area A_1, and F_a in IS mode (and in that order), and finally to lock r_{a_2} in S mode.
- Suppose that transaction T_{19} modifies record r_{a_9} in file F_a. Then, T_{19} needs to lock the database, area A_1, and file F_a in IX mode, and finally to lock r_{a_9} in X mode.
- Suppose that transaction T_{20} reads all the records in file F_a. Then, T_{20} needs to lock the database and area A_1 (in that order) in IS mode, and finally to lock F_a in S mode.

- Suppose that transaction T_{21} reads the entire database. It can do so after locking the database in S mode.

We note that transactions T_{18}, T_{20}, and T_{21} can access the database concurrently. Transaction T_{19} can execute concurrently with T_{18}, but not with either T_{20} or T_{21}.

This protocol enhances concurrency and reduces lock overhead. It is particularly useful in applications that include a mix of

- Short transactions that access only a few data items
- Long transactions that produce reports from an entire file or set of files

There is a similar locking protocol that is applicable to database systems in which data granularities are organized in the form of a directed acyclic graph. See the bibliographic notes for additional references. Deadlock is possible in the protocol that we have, as it is in the two-phase locking protocol. There are techniques to reduce deadlock frequency in the multiple-granularity protocol, and also to eliminate deadlock entirely. These techniques are referenced in the bibliographic notes.

14.5 Multiversion Schemes

The concurrency-control schemes discussed thus far ensure serializability by either delaying an operation or aborting the transaction that issued the operation. For example, a **read** operation may be delayed because the appropriate value has not been written yet; or it may be rejected (that is, the issuing transaction must be aborted) because the value that it was supposed to read has already been overwritten. These difficulties could be avoided if old copies of each data item were kept in a system.

In *multiversion* database systems, each **write**(Q) operation creates a new version of Q. When a **read**(Q) operation is issued, the system selects one of the versions of Q to be read. The concurrency-control scheme must ensure that the selection of the version to be read is done in a manner that ensures serializability. It is also crucial, for performance reasons, that a transaction be able to determine easily and quickly which version of the data item should be read.

14.5.1 Multiversion Timestamp Ordering

The most common technique used among multiversion schemes is timestamping. With each transaction T_i in the system, we associate a unique static timestamp, denoted by TS(T_i). This timestamp is assigned before the transaction starts execution, as described in Section 14.2.

With each data item Q, a sequence of versions $<Q_1, Q_2, ..., Q_m>$ is associated. Each version Q_k contains three data fields:

- **Content** is the value of version Q_k.

- **W-timestamp**(Q_k) is the timestamp of the transaction that created version Q_k.
- **R-timestamp**(Q_k) is the largest timestamp of any transaction that successfully read version Q_k.

A transaction—say, T_i—creates a new version Q_k of data item Q by issuing a **write**(Q) operation. The content field of the version holds the value written by T_i. The W-timestamp and R-timestamp are initialized to TS(T_i). The R-timestamp value is updated whenever a transaction T_j reads the content of Q_k, and R-timestamp(Q_k) < TS(T_j).

The multiversion timestamp scheme presented next ensures serializability. The scheme operates as follows. Suppose that transaction T_i issues a **read**(Q) or **write**(Q) operation. Let Q_k denote the version of Q whose write timestamp is the largest write timestamp less than or equal to TS(T_i).

1. If transaction T_i issues a **read**(Q), then the value returned is the content of version Q_k.
2. If transaction T_i issues a **write**(Q), and if TS(T_i) < R-timestamp(Q_k), then transaction T_i is rolled back. Otherwise, if TS(T_i) = W-timestamp(Q_k), the contents of Q_k are overwritten, otherwise a new version of Q is created.

The justification for rule 1 is clear. A transaction reads the most recent version that comes before it in time. The second rule forces a transaction to abort if it is "too late" in doing a write. More precisely, if T_i attempts to write a version that some other transaction would have read, then we cannot allow that write to succeed.

Versions that are no longer needed are removed based on the following rule. Suppose that there are two versions, Q_k and Q_j, of a data item, and that both versions have a W-timestamp less than the timestamp of the oldest transaction in the system. Then, the older of the two versions Q_k and Q_j will not be used again, and can be deleted.

The multiversion timestamp-ordering scheme has the desirable property that a read request never fails and is never made to wait. In typical database systems, where reading is a more frequent operation than is writing, this advantage may be of major practical significance.

The scheme, however, suffers from two undesirable properties. First, the reading of a data item also requires the updating of the R-timestamp field, resulting in two potential disk accesses, rather than one. Second, the conflicts between transactions are resolved through rollbacks, rather than through waits. This alternative may be expensive. An algorithm to alleviate this problem is described in Section 14.5.2.

14.5.2 Multiversion Two-Phase Locking

The multiversion two-phase locking protocol attempts to combine the advantages of multiversion concurrency control with the advantages of two-phase locking.

This protocol differentiates between read-only transactions and update transactions. *Update transactions* perform rigorous two-phase locking; that is, they hold all locks up to the end of the transaction. Thus, they can be serialized according to their commit order. Each data item has a single timestamp. The timestamp in this case is not a real clock-based timestamp, but rather is a counter, which we will call the **ts_counter**, that is incremented during commit processing.

We assign a timestamp to read-only transactions by reading the current value of **ts_counter** before they start execution; they follow the multiversion timestamp-ordering protocol for performing reads. Thus, when a read-only transaction T_i issues a **read**(Q), the value returned is the contents of the version whose timestamp is the largest timestamp less than TS(T_i).

When an update transaction reads an item, it gets a shared lock on the item, and reads the latest version of that item. When an update transaction wants to write an item, it first gets an exclusive lock on the item, and then creates a new version of the data item. The write is performed on the new version, and the timestamp of the new version is initially set to a value ∞, which value is greater than that of any possible timestamp.

When the update transaction T_i completes its actions, it carries out commit processing as follows: First, T_i sets the timestamp on every version it has created to 1 more than the value of **ts_counter**; then, T_i increments **ts_counter** by 1. Only one update transaction is allowed to perform commit processing at a time.

As a result, read-only transactions that start after T_i increments **ts_counter** will see the values updated by T_i, whereas those that start before T_i increments the **ts_counter** will see the value before the updates by T_i. In either case, read-only transaction never need to wait for locks.

Versions are deleted in a manner similar to that of multiversion timestamp ordering. Suppose there are two versions, Q_k and Q_j, of a data item, and that both versions have a timestamp less than the timestamp of the oldest read-only transaction in the system. Then, the older of the two versions Q_k and Q_j will not be used again and can be deleted.

Multiversion two-phase locking or variations of it are used in some commercial database systems.

14.6 Deadlock Handling

A system is in a deadlock state if there exists a set of transactions such that every transaction in the set is waiting for another transaction in the set. More precisely, there exists a set of waiting transactions $\{T_0, T_1, ..., T_n\}$ such that T_0 is waiting for a data item that is held by T_1, and T_1 is waiting for a data item that is held by T_2, and ..., and T_{n-1} is waiting for a data item that is held by T_n, and T_n is waiting for a data item that is held by T_0. None of the transactions can make progress in such a situation. The only remedy to this undesirable situation is for the system to invoke some drastic action, such as rolling back some of the transactions involved in the deadlock.

There are two principal methods for dealing with the deadlock problem. We can use a *deadlock-prevention* protocol to ensure that the system will *never* enter a deadlock state. Alternatively, we can allow the system to enter a deadlock state, and then try to recover using a *deadlock-detection and deadlock-recovery* scheme. As we shall see, both methods may result in transaction rollback. Prevention is commonly used if the probability that the system would enter a deadlock state is relatively high; otherwise, detection and recovery are more efficient.

Note that a detection and recovery scheme requires overhead that includes not only the run-time cost of maintaining the necessary information and of executing the detection algorithm, but also the potential losses inherent in recovery from a deadlock.

14.6.1 Deadlock Prevention

There are two approaches to deadlock prevention. One approach ensures that no cyclic waits can occur by ordering the requests for locks, or requiring all locks to be acquired together. The other approach is closer to deadlock recovery, and performs transaction rollback instead of waiting for a lock, whenever the wait could potentially result in a deadlock.

The simplest scheme under the first approach requires that each transaction locks all its data items before it begins execution. Moreover, either all are locked in one step or none are locked. There are two main disadvantages to this protocol. First, it is often hard to predict, before the transaction begins, what data items need to be locked. Second, *data-item utilization* may be very low, since many of the data items may be locked but unused for a long time.

Another scheme for preventing deadlocks is to impose a partial ordering of all data items, and to require that a transaction lock a data item only in the order specified by the partial order. We have seen one such scheme in the tree protocol.

The second approach for preventing deadlocks is to use preemption and transaction rollbacks. In preemption, when a transaction T_2 requests a lock that is held by a transaction T_1, the lock granted to T_1 may be *preempted* by rolling back of T_1, and granting of the lock to T_2. To control the preemption, we assign a unique timestamp to each transaction. The system uses these timestamps only to decide whether a transaction should wait or roll back. Locking is still used for concurrency control. If a transaction is rolled back, it retains its *old* timestamp when restarted. Two different deadlock-prevention schemes using timestamps have been proposed:

1. The **wait–die** scheme is based on a nonpreemptive technique. When transaction T_i requests a data item currently held by T_j, T_i is allowed to wait only if it has a timestamp smaller than that of T_j (that is, T_i is older than T_j). Otherwise, T_i is rolled back (dies). For example, suppose that transactions T_{22}, T_{23}, and T_{24} have timestamps 5, 10, and 15, respectively. If T_{22} requests a data item held by T_{23}, then T_{22} will wait. If T_{24} requests a data item held by T_{23}, then T_{24} will be rolled back.
2. The **wound–wait** scheme is based on a preemptive technique and is a counterpart to the *wait–die* scheme. When transaction T_i requests a data item currently held by T_j, T_i is allowed to wait only if it has a timestamp larger

than that of T_j (that is, T_i is younger than T_j). Otherwise, T_j is rolled back (T_j is *wounded* by T_i). Returning to our previous example, with transactions T_{22}, T_{23}, and T_{24}, if T_{22} requests a data item held by T_{23}, then the data item will be preempted from T_{23}, and T_{23} will be rolled back. If T_{24} requests a data item held by T_{23}, then T_{24} will wait.

Whenever transactions are rolled back, it is important to ensure that there is no *starvation*—that is, no transaction gets rolled back repeatedly and is never allowed to make progress.

Both the wound–wait and the wait–die schemes avoid starvation: At any time, there is a transaction with the smallest timestamp. This transaction *cannot* be required to roll back in either scheme. Since timestamps always increase, and since transactions are *not* assigned new timestamps when they are rolled back, a transaction that is rolled back will eventually have the smallest timestamp. Thus, it will not be rolled back again.

There are, however, significant differences in the way that the two schemes operate.

- In the *wait–die* scheme, an older transaction must wait for a younger one to release its data item. Thus, the older the transaction gets, the more it tends to wait. By contrast, in the *wound–wait* scheme, an older transaction never waits for a younger transaction.
- In the *wait–die* scheme, if a transaction T_i dies and is rolled back because it requested a data item held by transaction T_j, then T_i may reissue the same sequence of requests when it is restarted. If the data item is still held by T_j, then T_i will die again. Thus, T_i may die several times before acquiring the needed data item. Contrast this series of events with what happens in the *wound–wait* scheme. Transaction T_i is wounded and rolled back because T_j requested a data item that it holds. When T_i is restarted and requests the data item now being held by T_j, T_i waits. Thus, there may be fewer rollbacks in the *wound–wait* scheme.

The major problem with both of these schemes is that unnecessary rollbacks may occur.

14.6.2 Timeout-Based Schemes

Another simple approach to deadlock handling is based on *lock timeouts*. In this approach, a transaction that has requested a lock waits for at most a specified amount of time. If the lock has not been granted within that time, the transaction is said to time out, and it rolls itself back and restarts. If there was in fact a deadlock, one or more transactions involved in the deadlock will time out and roll back, allowing the others to proceed. This scheme falls somewhere between deadlock prevention, where a deadlock will never occur, and deadlock detection and recovery, which is discussed in Section 14.6.3.

The timeout scheme is particularly easy to implement, and works well if transactions are short, and if long waits are likely to be due to deadlocks. However, in general it is hard to decide how long a transaction must wait before timing out. Too long a wait results in unnecessary delays once a deadlock has occurred. Too short a wait results in transaction rollback even when there is no deadlock, leading to wasted resources. Starvation is also a possibility with this scheme. Hence, the timeout-based scheme has limited applicability.

14.6.3 Deadlock Detection and Recovery

If a system does not employ some protocol that ensures deadlock freedom, then a detection and recovery scheme must be used. An algorithm that examines the state of the system is invoked periodically to determine whether a deadlock has occurred. If one has, then the system must attempt to recover from the deadlock. To do so, the system must

- Maintain information about the current allocation of data items to transactions, as well as any outstanding data item requests.
- Provide an algorithm that uses this information to determine whether the system has entered a deadlock state.
- Recover from the deadlock when the detection algorithm determines that a deadlock exists.

In this section, we elaborate on these issues.

14.6.3.1 Deadlock Detection

Deadlocks can be described precisely in terms of a directed graph called a *wait-for graph*. This graph consists of a pair $G = (V,E)$, where V is a set of vertices and E is a set of edges. The set of vertices consists of all the transactions in the system. Each element in the set E of edges is an ordered pair $T_i \rightarrow T_j$. If $T_i \rightarrow T_j$ is in E, then there is a directed edge from transaction T_i to T_j, implying that transaction T_i is waiting for transaction T_j to release a data item that it needs.

When transaction T_i requests a data item currently being held by transaction T_j, then the edge $T_i \rightarrow T_j$ is inserted in the wait-for graph. This edge is removed only when transaction T_j is no longer holding a data item needed by transaction T_i.

A deadlock exists in the system if and only if the wait-for graph contains a cycle. Each transaction involved in the cycle is said to be deadlocked. To detect deadlocks, the system needs to maintain the wait-for graph, and periodically to invoke an algorithm that searches for a cycle in the graph.

To illustrate these concepts, consider the wait-for graph in Figure 14.13, which depicts the following situation:

- Transaction T_{25} is waiting for transactions T_{26} and T_{27}.
- Transaction T_{27} is waiting for transaction T_{26}.

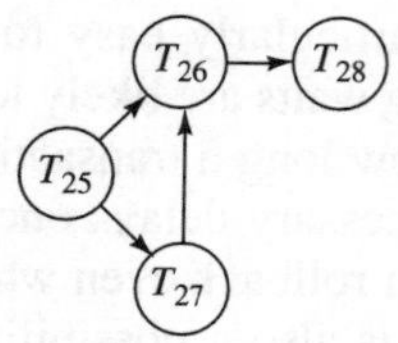

Figure 14.13 Wait-for graph with no cycle.

- Transaction T_{26} is waiting for transaction T_{28}.

Since the graph has no cycle, the system is not in a deadlock state.

Suppose now that transaction T_{28} is requesting an item held by T_{27}. The edge $T_{28} \rightarrow T_{27}$ is added to the wait-for graph, resulting in a new system state as depicted in Figure 14.14. This time, the graph contains the cycle

$$T_{26} \rightarrow T_{28} \rightarrow T_{27} \rightarrow T_{26}$$

implying that transactions T_{26}, T_{27}, and T_{28} are all deadlocked.

Consequently, the question arises: When should we invoke the detection algorithm? The answer depends on two factors:

1. How often does a deadlock occur?
2. How many transactions will be affected by the deadlock?

If deadlocks occur frequently, then the detection algorithm should be invoked more frequently than usual. Data items allocated to deadlocked transactions will be unavailable to other transactions until the deadlock can be broken. In addition, the number of cycles in the graph may also grow. In the worst case, we would invoke the detection algorithm every time a request for allocation could not be granted immediately.

14.6.3.2 Recovery from Deadlock

When a detection algorithm determines that a deadlock exists, the system must *recover* from the deadlock. The most common solution is to roll back one or more transactions to break the deadlock. Three actions need to be taken:

1. **Selection of a victim**. Given a set of deadlocked transactions, we must determine which transaction (or transactions) to roll back to break the deadlock.

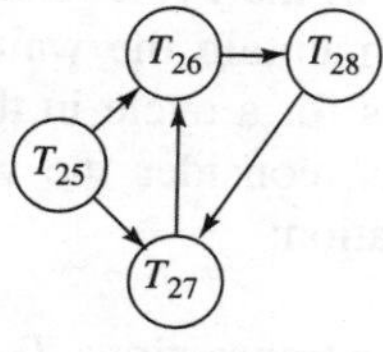

Figure 14.14 Wait-for graph with a cycle.

We should roll back those transactions that will incur the minimum cost. Unfortunately, the term *minimum cost* is not a precise one. Many factors may determine the cost of a rollback, including

a. How long the transaction has computed, and how much longer the transaction will compute before it completes its designated task.

b. How many data items the transaction has used.

c. How many more data items the transaction needs for it to complete.

d. How many transactions will be involved in the rollback.

2. **Rollback**. Once we have decided that a particular transaction must be rolled back, we must determine how far this transaction should be rolled back. The simplest solution is a total rollback: Abort the transaction and then restart it. However, it is more effective to roll back the transaction only as far as necessary to break the deadlock. But this method requires the system to maintain additional information about the state of all the running transactions. See the bibliographic notes section for relevant references.

3. **Starvation**. In a system where the selection of victims is based primarily on cost factors, it may happen that the same transaction is always picked as a victim. As a result, this transaction never completes its designated task. This situation is called *starvation*. We must ensure that transaction can be picked as a victim only a (small) finite number of times. The most common solution is to include the number of rollbacks in the cost factor.

14.7 Insert and Delete Operations

Until now, we have restricted our attention to **read** and **write** operations. This restriction limits transactions to data items already in the database. Some transactions require not only access to existing data items, but also the ability to create new data items. Others require the ability to delete data items. To examine how such transactions affect concurrency control, we introduce the following additional operations:

- **delete**(Q) deletes data item Q from the database.
- **insert**(Q) inserts a new data item Q into the database and assigns Q an initial value.

An attempt by a transaction T_i to perform a **read**(Q) operation after Q has been deleted results in a logical error in T_i. Likewise, an attempt by a transaction T_i to perform a **read**(Q) operation before Q has been inserted results in a logical error in T_i. It is also a logical error to attempt to delete a nonexistent data item.

14.7.1 Deletion

To understand how the presence of **delete** instructions affects concurrency control, we must decide when a **delete** instruction conflicts with another instruction. Let I_i and I_j be instructions of T_i and T_j, respectively, that appear in schedule S in consecutive order. Let I_i = **delete**(Q). We consider several instructions I_j

- I_j = **read**(Q). I_i and I_j conflict. If I_i comes before I_j, T_j will have a logical error. If I_j comes before I_i, T_j can execute the **read** operation successfully.
- I_j = **write**(Q). I_i and I_j conflict. If I_i comes before I_j, T_j will have a logical error. If I_j comes before I_i, T_j can execute the **write** operation successfully.
- I_j = **delete**(Q). I_i and I_j conflict. If I_i comes before I_j, T_i will have a logical error. If I_j comes before I_i, T_i will have a logical error.
- I_j = **insert**(Q). I_i and I_j conflict. Suppose that data item Q did not exist prior to the execution of I_i and I_j. Then, if I_i comes before I_j, a logical error results for T_i. If I_j comes before I_i, then no logical error results. Likewise, if Q existed prior to the execution of I_i and I_j, then a logical error results if I_j comes before I_i, but not otherwise.

We can conclude that, if two-phase locking is used, an exclusive lock is required on a data item before that item can be deleted. Under the timestamp-ordering protocol, a test similar to that for a **write** must be performed. Suppose that transaction T_i issues **delete**(Q).

- If TS(T_i) < R-timestamp(Q), then the value of Q that T_i was to delete has already been read by a transaction T_j with TS(T_j) > TS(T_i). Hence, the **delete** operation is rejected, and T_i is rolled back.
- If TS(T_i) < W-timestamp(Q), then a transaction T_j with TS(T_j) > TS(T_i) has written Q. Hence, this **delete** operation is rejected, and T_i is rolled back.
- Otherwise, the **delete** is executed.

14.7.2 Insertion

We have already seen that an **insert**(Q) operation conflicts with a **delete**(Q) operation. Similarly, **insert**(Q) conflicts with a **read**(Q) operation or a **write**(Q) operation. No **read** or **write** can be performed on a data item before the latter exists.

Since an **insert**(Q) assigns a value to data item Q, an **insert** is treated similarly to a **write** for concurrency-control purposes:

- Under the two-phase locking protocol, if T_i performs an **insert**(Q) operation, T_i is given an exclusive lock on the newly created data item Q.
- Under the timestamp-ordering protocol, if T_i performs an **insert**(Q) operation, the values R-timestamp(Q) and W-timestamp(Q) are set to TS(T_i).

14.7.3 The Phantom Phenomenon

Consider a transaction T_{29}, that executes the following SQL query on the bank database:

select sum(*balance*)
from *account*
where *branch-name* = "Perryridge"

Transaction T_{29} requires access to all tuples of the *account* relation pertaining to the Perryridge branch.

Let T_{30} be a transaction which executes the following SQL insertion:

insert into *account*
values ("Perryridge", A-201, 900)

Let S be a schedule involving T_{29} and T_{30}. We expect there to be potential for a conflict for the following reasons:

- If T_{29} uses the tuple newly inserted by T_{30} in computing **sum**(*balance*), then T_{29} read a value written by T_{30}. Thus, in a serial schedule equivalent to S, T_{30} must come before T_{29}.
- If T_{29} does not use the tuple newly inserted by T_{30} in computing **sum**(*balance*), then in a serial schedule equivalent to S, T_{29} must come before T_{30}.

The second of these two cases is curious. T_{29} and T_{30} do not access any tuple in common, yet they conflict with each other! In effect, T_{29} and T_{30} conflict on a phantom tuple. Thus, the phenomenon we have just described is called the *phantom phenomenon*. If concurrency control is performed at the tuple granularity, this conflict would go undetected.

To prevent the phantom phenomenon, we allow T_{29} to prevent other transactions from creating new tuples in the *account* relation with *branch-name* = "Perryridge."

To find all *account* tuples with *branch-name* = "Perryridge", T_{29} must search either the whole *account* relation, or at least an index on the relation. Up to now, we have assumed implicitly that the only data items accessed by a transaction are tuples. However, T_{29} is an example of a transaction that reads information about what tuples are in a relation, and T_{30} is an example of a transaction that updates that information. Clearly, it is not sufficient merely to lock the tuples that are accessed; locking also is required for the information about what tuples are in the relation.

The simplest solution to this problem is to associate a data item with the relation itself. Transactions, such as T_{29}, that read the information about what tuples are in a relation would then have to lock the data item corresponding to the *account* relation in shared mode. Transactions, such as T_{30}, which update the information about what tuples are in a relation would have to lock the data item in exclusive mode. Thus, T_{29} and T_{30} would conflict on a real data item, rather than on a phantom.

Do not confuse the locking of an entire relation, as in multiple granularity locking, with the locking of the data item corresponding to the relation. By locking the data item, a transaction only prevents other transactions from updating information about what tuples are in the relation. Locking is still required on tuples. A transactions that directly accesses a tuple can be granted a lock on the tuples even when another transaction has an exclusive lock on the data item corresponding to the relation itself.

The major disadvantage of locking a data item corresponding to the relation is the low degree of concurrency— two transactions that insert different tuples into a relation are prevented from executing concurrently.

A better solution is the *index-locking* technique. Any transaction that inserts a tuple into a relation must insert information into every index maintained on the relation. We eliminate the phantom phenomenon by imposing a locking protocol for indices.

As we saw in Chapter 11, every search-key value is associated with either an index record or a bucket. A query will usually use one or more indices to access a relation. An insert must insert the new tuple in all indices on the relation. In our example, we assume that there is an index on *account* for *branch-name*. Then, T_{30} must modify the Perryridge bucket. If T_{29} read the Perryridge bucket to locate all tuples pertaining to the Perryridge branch, then T_{29} and T_{30} conflict on that bucket.

The index-locking protocol takes advantage of the availability of indices on a relation by turning instances of the phantom phenomenon into conflicts on locks on index buckets. The protocol operates as follows:

- Every relation must have at least one index.
- A transaction T_i may lock a tuple t_i of a relation in S-mode only if it holds an S-mode lock on an index bucket that contains a pointer to t_i.
- A transaction T_i may lock a tuple t_i of a relation in X-mode only if it holds an X-mode lock on an index bucket that contains a pointer to t_i.
- A transaction T_i may not insert a tuple t_i into a relation r without updating all indices to r. T_i must obtain locks in X-mode on all index buckets that it modifies.
- The rules of the two-phase locking protocol must be observed.

Variants of the index-locking technique exist for eliminating the phantom phenomenon under the other concurrency-control protocols presented in this chapter.

14.8 Concurrency in Index Structures

It is possible to treat access to index structures like any other database structure, and to apply the concurrency-control techniques discussed earlier. However, since indices are accessed frequently, they will become point of great lock contention, leading to a low degree of concurrency. Luckily, indices do not have to be treated like other database structures, since they provide the high-level abstraction of mapping search keys to tuples in the database. It is perfectly acceptable for a transaction to look up an index twice, and to find that the structure of the index has changed in-between, as long as the index lookup returns the correct set of tuples. Thus, it is acceptable to have nonserializable concurrent access to an index, as long as the accuracy of the index is maintained.

We show a technique for managing concurrent access to B^+-trees. The bibliographic notes reference other techniques for B^+-trees, as well as techniques for other index structures.

The technique that we present for B^+-trees is based on locking, but neither two-phase locking nor the tree protocol is employed. The algorithms for lookup, insertion, and deletion are those used in Chapter 11, with only minor modifications. We require that every node (rather than just the leaves) maintain a pointer to its right sibling. Trees meeting this requirement are called *B-link trees*. This pointer is required because a lookup that occurs while a node is being split may have to search not only that node but also that node's right sibling (if one exists). We shall illustrate this technique with an example after we present the modified procedures.

- **Lookup**. Each node of the B^+-tree must be locked in shared mode before it is accessed. This lock is released before any lock on any other node in the B^+-tree is requested. If a split occurs concurrently with a lookup, the desired search-key value may no longer appear within the range of values represented by a node accessed during lookup. In such a case, the search-key value is represented by a sibling node, which the system locates by following the pointer to the right sibling.

- **Insertion and deletion**. The system follows the rules for lookup to locate the node into which the insertion or deletion is to be made. The shared-mode lock on this node is upgraded to exclusive mode, and the insertion or deletion is performed.

- **Split**. If a node is split, a new node is created according to the algorithm of Section 11.3. The right-sibling pointers of both the original node and the new node are set. Following this, the exclusive lock on the original node is released, and an exclusive lock is requested on the parent, so that a pointer to the new node can be inserted.

- **Coalescence**. If a node has too few search-key values after a deletion, the node with which it will be coalesced must be locked in exclusive mode. Once these two nodes have been coalesced, an exclusive lock is requested on the parent so that the deleted node can be removed. At this point, the lock on the coalesced node is released. Unless the parent node must be coalesced also, its lock is released.

It is important to observe that an insertion or deletion may lock a node, unlock it, and subsequently relock it. Furthermore, a lookup that runs concur-

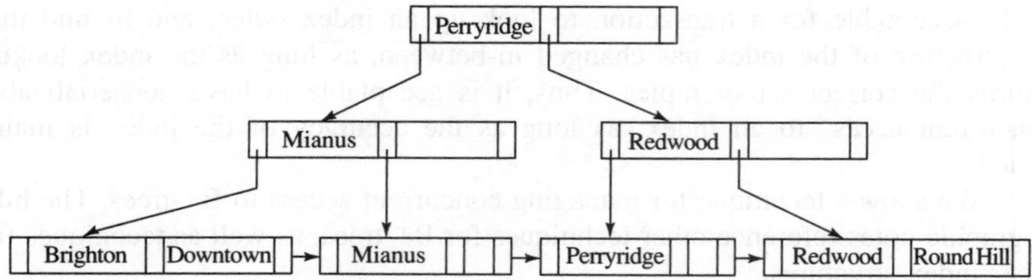

Figure 14.15 B^+-tree for *account* file with $n = 3$.

rently with a split or coalescence operation may find that the desired search key has been moved to the right-sibling node by the split or coalescence operation.

As an illustration, consider the B^+-tree in Figure 14.15. Assume that there are two concurrent operations on this B^+-tree:

1. Insert "Clearview"
2. Lookup "Downtown"

Let us assume that the insertion operation begins first. It does a lookup on "Clearview," and finds that the node into which "Clearview" should be inserted is full. It therefore converts its shared lock on the node to exclusive mode, and creates a new node. The original node now contains the search-key values "Brighton" and "Clearview." The new node contains the search-key value "Downtown."

Now assume that a context switch occurs that results in control passing to the lookup operation. This lookup operation accesses the root, and follows the pointer to the left child of the root. It then accesses that node, and obtains a pointer to the left child. This left-child node originally contained the search-key values "Brighton" and "Downtown." Since this node is currently locked by the insertion operation in exclusive mode, the lookup operation must wait. Note that, at this point, the lookup operation holds no locks at all!

The insertion operation now unlocks the leaf node and relocks its parent, this time in exclusive mode. It completes the insertion, leaving the B^+-tree as shown in Figure 14.16. The lookup operation proceeds. However, it is holding a pointer to an incorrect leaf node. It therefore follows the right-sibling pointer to locate the next node. If this node, too, turns out to be incorrect, that node's right-sibling pointer is followed. It can be shown that, if a lookup holds a pointer to an incorrect node, then, by following right sibling pointers, the lookup must eventually reach the correct node.

Lookup and insertion operations cannot lead to deadlock. Deletion can lead to deadlock if a lookup has locked the parent of nodes being coalesced. The simplest way to avoid such deadlocks is to leave nodes uncoalesced. This solution results in nodes that contain too few search-key values and that violate some properties of B^+-trees. In most databases, however, insertions are more frequent

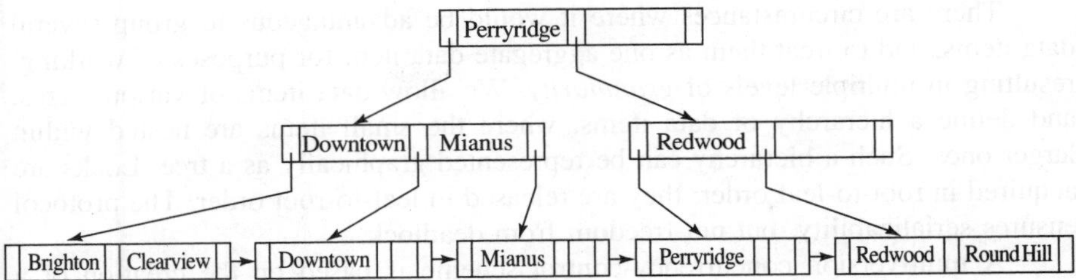

Figure 14.16 Insertion of "Clearview" into the B^+-tree of Figure 14.15.

than deletions, so it is likely that nodes that have too few search-key values will gain additional values relatively quickly.

14.9 Summary

When several transactions execute concurrently in the database, the consistency of data may no longer be preserved. It is necessary for the system to control the interaction among the concurrent transactions, and this control is achieved through one of a variety of mechanisms called *concurrency-control* schemes.

To ensure serializability, we can use various concurrency-control schemes. All these schemes either delay an operation or abort the transaction that issued the operation. The most common ones are locking protocols, timestamp-ordering schemes, validation techniques, and multiversion schemes.

A locking protocol is a set of rules, the members of which state when a transaction may lock and unlock each of the data items in the database. The *two-phase* locking protocol allows a transaction to lock a new data item only if that transaction has not yet unlocked any data item. The protocol ensures serializability, but not deadlock freedom. In the absence of information concerning the manner in which data items are accessed, the two-phase locking protocol is both necessary and sufficient for ensuring serializability.

A timestamp-ordering scheme ensures serializability by selecting an ordering in advance between every pair of transactions. A unique fixed timestamp is associated with each transaction in the system. The timestamps of the transactions determine the serializability order. Thus, if the timestamp of transaction T_i is smaller than the timestamp of transaction T_j, then the scheme ensures that the produced schedule is equivalent to a serial schedule in which transaction T_i appears before transaction T_j. It does so by rolling back a transaction whenever such an order is violated.

A validation scheme is an appropriate concurrency-control method in cases where the majority of transactions are read-only transactions, and thus the rate of conflicts among these transactions is low. A unique fixed timestamp is associated with each transaction in the system. The serializability order is determined by the timestamp of the transaction. A transaction in this scheme is never delayed. It must, however, pass a validation test, to complete. If it does not pass the validation test, it is rolled back to its initial state.

There are circumstances where it would be advantageous to group several data items, and to treat them as one aggregate data item for purposes of working, resulting in multiple levels of *granularity*. We allow data items of various sizes, and define a hierarchy of data items, where the small items are nested within larger ones. Such a hierarchy can be represented graphically as a tree. Locks are acquired in root-to-leaf order; they are released in leaf-to-root order. The protocol ensures serializability, but not freedom from deadlock.

A multiversion concurrency-control scheme is based on the creation of a new version of a data item for each transaction that writes that item. When a read operation is issued, the system selects one of the versions to be read. The concurrency-control scheme ensures that the version to be read is selected in a manner that ensures serializability, by using timestamps. A read operation always succeeds. In multiversion timestamp ordering, a write operation may result in the rollback of the transaction. In multiversion two-phase locking, write operations may result in a lock wait or, possibly, in deadlock.

Various locking protocols do not guard against deadlocks. One way to prevent deadlock is to use preemption and transaction rollbacks. To control the preemption, we assign a unique timestamp to each transaction. These timestamps are used to decide whether a transaction should wait or roll back. If a transaction is rolled back, it retains its *old* timestamp when restarted. The wait–die and wound–wait schemes are two preemptive schemes. Another method for dealing with deadlock is to use a deadlock detection and recovery scheme. To do so, a wait-for graph is constructed. A system is in a deadlock state if and only if the wait-for graph contains a cycle. When a detection algorithm determines that a deadlock exists, the system must recover from the deadlock. It does so by rolling back one or more transactions to break the deadlock.

A **delete** operation may be performed only if the transaction deleting the tuple has an exclusive lock on the tuple to be deleted. A transaction that inserts a new tuple into the database is given an X-mode lock on the tuple. Insertions can lead to the phantom phenomenon, in which an insertion conflicts with a query even though the two transactions may access no tuple in common. The index-locking technique solves this problem by requiring locks on certain index buckets. These locks ensure that all conflicting transactions conflict on a real data item, rather than on a phantom.

Special concurrency-control techniques can be developed for special data structures. Often, special techniques are applied in B^+-trees to allow greater concurrency. These techniques allow nonserializable access to the B^+-tree, but they ensure that the B^+-tree structure is correct, and ensure that accesses to the database itself are serializable.

Exercises

14.1. Show that the two-phase locking protocol ensures conflict serializability, and that transactions can be serialized according to their lock points.

14.2. Consider the following two transactions:

T_{31}: **read**(A);
read(B);
if $A = 0$ **then** $B := B + 1$;
write(B).

T_{32}: **read** (B);
read (A);
if $B = 0$ **then** $A := A + 1$;
write(A).

Add lock and unlock instructions to transactions T_{31} and T_{32}, so that they observe the two-phase locking protocol. Can the execution of these transactions result in a deadlock?

14.3. What benefit is provided by strict two-phase locking? What disadvantages result?

14.4. What benefit is provided by rigorous two-phase locking? How does it compare with other forms of two-phase locking?

14.5. The concurrency-control manager of a database system must decide whether to grant a lock request or to cause the requesting transaction to wait. Design a space-efficient data structure that allows the concurrency-control manager to make this decision quickly.

14.6. Most implementations of database systems use strict two-phase locking. Suggest three reasons for the popularity of this protocol.

14.7. Consider the following extension to the tree-locking protocol, which allows both shared and exclusive locks:

- A transaction can be either a read-only transaction, in which case it can request only shared locks, or an update transaction, in which case it can request only exclusive locks.
- Each transaction must follow the rules of the tree protocol. Read-only transactions may lock any data item first, whereas update transactions must lock the root first.

Show that the protocol ensures serializability and deadlock freedom.

14.8. Consider a database organized in the form of a rooted tree. Suppose that we insert a dummy vertex between each pair of vertices. Show that, if we follow the tree protocol on the new tree, we get better concurrency than if we follow the tree protocol on the original tree.

14.9. Consider the following graph-based locking protocol, which allows only exclusive lock modes, and which operates on data graphs that are in the form of a rooted directed acyclic graph.

- A transaction can lock any vertex first.
- To lock any other vertex, the transaction must be holding a lock on the majority of the parents of that vertex.

Show that the protocol ensures serializability and deadlock freedom.

14.10. Show by example that there are schedules possible under the tree protocol that are not possible under the two-phase locking protocol, and vice versa.

14.11. Consider the following graph-based locking protocol that allows only exclusive lock modes, and that operates on data graphs that are in the form of a rooted directed acyclic graph.

- A transaction can lock any vertex first.
- To lock any other vertex, the transaction must have visited all the parents of that vertex, and must be holding a lock on one of the parents of the vertex.

Show that the protocol ensures serializability and deadlock freedom.

14.12. Consider a variant of the tree protocol called the *forest* protocol. The database is organized as a forest of rooted trees. Each transaction T_i must follow the following rules:

- The first lock in each tree may be on any data item.
- The second, and all subsequent, locks in a tree may be requested only if the parent of the requested mode is currently locked.
- Data items may be unlocked at any time.
- A data item may not be relocked by T_i after it has been unlocked by T_i.

Show that the forest protocol does *not* ensure serializability.

14.13. Consider a database system that includes an atomic **increment** operation, in addition to the **read** and **write** operations. Let V be the value of data item X. The operation

increment(X) by C

sets the value of X to $V + C$ in an atomic step. The value of X is not available to the transaction unless the latter executes a **read**(X). Figure 14.17 shows a lock-compatibility matrix for three lock modes: share mode, exclusive mode, and incrementation mode.

(*a*) Show that, if all transactions lock the data that they access in the corresponding mode, then two-phase locking ensures serializability.

(*b*) Show that the inclusion of **increment** mode locks allows for increased concurrency. (Hint: Consider check-clearing transactions in our bank example.)

14.14. In timestamp ordering, **W-timestamp**(Q) denotes the largest timestamp of any transaction that executed **write**(Q) successfully. Suppose that, in-

	S	X	I
S	true	false	false
X	false	false	false
I	false	false	true

Figure 14.17 Lock-compatibility matrix.

stead, we defined it to be the timestamp of the most recent transaction to execute **write**(Q) successfully. Would this change in wording make any difference? Explain your answer.

14.15. When a transaction is rolled back under timestamp ordering, it is assigned a new timestamp. Why can it not simply keep its old timestamp?

14.16. In multiple-granularity locking, what is the difference between implicit and explicit locking?

14.17. Although SIX mode is useful in multiple-granularity locking, an exclusive and intend-shared (XIS) mode is of no use. Why is it useless?

14.18. Use of multiple-granularity locking may require more or fewer locks than an equivalent system with a single lock granularity. Provide examples of both situations, and compare the relative amount of concurrency allowed.

14.19. Consider the validation-based concurrency-control scheme of Section 14.3. Show that by choosing Validation(T_i), rather than Start(T_i), as the timestamp of transaction T_i, we can expect better response time provided that conflict rates among transactions are indeed low.

14.20. Show that there are schedules that are possible under the two-phase locking protocol, but are not possible under the timestamp protocol, and vice versa.

14.21. For each of the following protocols, describe aspects of practical applications that would lead you to suggest using the protocol, and aspects that would suggest not using the protocol:

- Two-phase locking
- Two-phase locking with multiple granularity locking
- The tree protocol
- Timestamp ordering
- Validation
- Multiversion timestamp ordering
- Multiversion two-phase locking

14.22. For each of the timestamp-based protocols, check whether it is cascadeless, and whether it is recoverable.

14.23. Under a modified version of the timestamp protocol, we require that a commit bit be tested to see whether a **read** request must wait. Explain how the commit bit can prevent cascading abort. Why is this test not necessary for **write** requests?

14.24. Under what conditions is it less expensive to avoid deadlock than to allow deadlocks to occur and then to detect them?

14.25. If deadlock is avoided, is starvation still possible? Explain your answer.

14.26. Explain the phantom phenomenon. Why may this phenomenon lead to an incorrect concurrent execution despite the use of the two-phase locking protocol?

14.27. Devise a timestamp-based protocol that avoids the phantom phenomenon.

14.28. Suppose that we use the tree protocol of Section 14.1.4 to manage concurrent access to a B^+-tree. Since a split may occur on an insert that affects the root, it appears that an insert operation cannot release any locks until it has completed the entire operation. Under what circumstances is it possible to release a lock earlier?

14.29. Locking is not done explicitly in persistent programming languages. Rather, objects (or the corresponding pages) must be locked when the objects are accessed. Most modern operating systems allow the user to set access protections (no-access, read, write) on pages, and memory access that violate the access protections result in a protection violation (see the Unix `mprotect` command, for example). Describe how the access-protection mechanism can be used for page-level locking in a persistent programming language. (Hint: The technique is somewhat similar to that used for hardware swizzling in Section 10.9.3.2).

Bibliographic Notes

The two-phase locking protocol was introduced by Eswaran et al. [1976]. The tree-locking protocol is from Silberschatz and Kedem [1980]. Other non–two-phase locking protocols that operate on more general graphs were developed by Yannakakis et al. [1979], Kedem and Silberschatz [1983], and Buckley and Silberschatz [1985]. General discussions concerning locking protocols are offered by Lien and Weinberger [1978], Yannakakis et al. [1979], Yannakakis [1981], and Papadimitriou [1982]. Korth [1983] explores various lock modes that can be obtained from the basic shared and exclusive lock modes. Various algorithms for concurrent access to dynamic search trees were developed by Bayer and Schkolnick [1977], Ellis [1980a, 1980b], Lehman and Yao [1981], and Manber and Ladner [1984]. Exercise 14.7 is from Kedem and Silberschatz [1983]. Exercise 14.8 is from Buckley and Silberschatz [1984]. Exercise 14.9 is from Kedem and Silberschatz [1979]. Exercise 14.11 is from Yannakakis et al. [1979]. Exercise 14.13 is from Korth [1983].

The timestamp-based concurrency-control scheme is from Reed [1983]. An exposition of various timestamp-based concurrency-control algorithms is presented by Bernstein and Goodman [1980a]. A timestamp algorithm that does not require any rollback to ensure serializability is presented by Buckley and Silberschatz [1983]. The validation concurrency-control scheme is from Kung and Robinson [1981]. A single-site and distributed validation concurrency-control scheme is presented by Bassiouni [1988].

The locking protocol for multiple-granularity data items is from Gray et al. [1975]. A detailed description is presented by Gray et al. [1976]. The effects of locking granularity are discussed by Ries and Stonebraker [1977]. Korth [1983] formalizes multiple-granularity locking for an arbitrary collection of lock modes (allowing for more semantics than simply read and write). This approach includes a class of lock modes called *update* modes to deal with lock conversion. Carey [1983] extends the multiple-granularity idea to timestamp-based concurrency control. An extension of the protocol to ensure deadlock freedom is presented by Korth [1982]. Multiple-granularity locking for object-oriented database systems is discussed in Lee and Liou [1996].

Discussions concerning multiversion concurrency control are offered by Bernstein et al. [1983]. A multiversion tree-locking algorithm appears in Silberschatz [1982]. Multiversion timestamp order was introduced in Reed [1978, 1983]. Lai and Wilkinson [1984] describes a multiversion two-phase locking certifier.

Dijkstra [1965] was one of the first and most influential contributors in the deadlock area. Holt [1971, 1972] was the first to formalize the notion of deadlocks in terms of a graph model similar to the one presented in this chapter. The timestamp deadlock-detection algorithm is from Rosenkrantz et al. [1978]. An analysis of the probability of waiting and deadlock is presented by Gray et al. [1981b]. Theoretical results concerning deadlocks and serializability are presented by Fussell et al. [1981], and by Yannakakis [1981].

Cycle-detection algorithms can be found in standard algorithm textbooks, such as Cormen et al. [1990], and Aho et al. [1983].

Concurrency in B^+-trees was studied by Bayer and Schkolnick [1977] and Johnson and Shasha [1993]. The technique presented in Section 14.8 is based on Kung and Lehman [1980], and on Lehman and Yao [1981]. Related work includes Kwong and Wood [1982], Manber and Ladner [1984], and Ford and Calhoun [1984]. Shasha and Goodman [1988] present a good characterization of concurrency protocols for index structures. Ellis [1987] presents a concurrency-control technique for linear hashing. B-link trees are discussed in Lomet and Salzberg [1992]. Concurrency-control algorithms for other index structures appear in Ellis [1980a, 1980b].

A comprehensive survey paper on concurrency control and recovery is presented by Gray [1978]. Textbook discussions are offered by Date [1983a], Bernstein et al. [1987], Papadimitriou [1986], and Gray and Reuter [1993]. Transaction-processing in object-oriented database systems is discussed in Garza and Kim [1988]. Transaction processing in design and software-engineering applications is discussed in Korth et al. [1988], Kaiser [1990], and Weikum [1991]. Theoretical aspects of multi-level transactions are presented in Lynch et al. [1988], and Weihl and Liskov [1990].

The ARIES transaction manager, developed at the IBM Almaden Research Center has had significant influence on transaction management. It is discussed in a series of papers including Mohan [1990a, 1990b], Mohan et al. [1991, 1992], and Mohan and Narang [1994, 1995].

CHAPTER 15

RECOVERY SYSTEM

A computer system, like any other mechanical or electrical device, is subject to failure. There is a variety of causes of such failure, including disk crash, power failure, software error, a fire in the machine room, or even sabotage. In each of these cases, information may be lost. Therefore, the database system must take actions in advance to ensure that the atomicity and durability properties of transactions, introduced in Chapter 13, are preserved, in spite of such failures. An integral part of a database system is a recovery scheme that is responsible for the restoration of the database to a consistent state that existed prior to the occurrence of the failure.

15.1 Failure Classification

There are various types of failure that may occur in a system, each of which needs to be dealt with in a different manner. The simplest type of failure to deal with is one that does not result in the loss of information in the system. The failures that are more difficult to deal with are those that result in loss of information. In this chapter, we shall consider only the following types of failure:

- **Transaction Failure.** There are two types of errors that may cause a transaction to fail:
  - **Logical error**. The transaction can no longer continue with its normal execution, owing to some internal condition, such as bad input, data not found, overflow, or resource limit exceeded.
  - **System error**. The system has entered an undesirable state (for example, deadlock), as a result of which a transaction cannot continue with its normal execution. The transaction, however, can be reexecuted at a later time.

- **System crash**. There is a hardware malfunction, or a bug in the database software or the operating system, that causes the loss of the content of volatile storage, and brings transaction processing to a halt. The content of nonvolatile storage remains intact, and is not corrupted.

  The assumption that hardware errors and bugs in the software bring the system to a halt, but do not corrupt the nonvolatile storage contents, is known as the *fail-stop* assumption. Well-designed systems have numerous internal checks, at the hardware and the software level, which bring the system to a halt when there is an error. Hence, the fail-stop assumption is a reasonable one.
- **Disk failure**. A disk block loses its content as a result of either a head crash or failure during a data transfer operation. Copies of the data on other disks, or archival backups on tertiary media, such as tapes, are used to recover from the failure.

To determine how the system should recover from failures, we need to identify the failure modes of those devices used for storing data. Next, we must consider how these failure modes affect the contents of the database. We can then propose algorithms to ensure database consistency and transaction atomicity despite failures. These algorithms are known as recovery algorithms, although they have two parts:

1. Actions taken during normal transaction processing to ensure that enough information exists to allow recovery from failures.
2. Actions taken following a failure to recover the database contents to a state that ensures database consistency, transaction atomicity, and durability.

15.2 Storage Structure

As we saw in Chapter 10, the various data items in the database may be stored and accessed in a number of different storage media. To understand how to ensure the atomicity and durability properties of a transaction, we must gain a better understanding of these storage media and their access methods.

15.2.1 Storage Types

There are various types of storage media; they are distinguished by their relative speed, capacity, and resilience to failure.

- **Volatile storage**. Information residing in volatile storage does not usually survive system crashes. Examples of such storage are main memory and cache memory. Access to volatile storage is extremely fast, both because of the speed of the memory access itself, and because it is possible to access any data item in volatile storage directly.
- **Nonvolatile storage**. Information residing in nonvolatile storage survives system crashes. Examples of such storage are disk and magnetic tapes. Disks are

used for online storage, whereas tapes are used for archival storage. Both, however, are subject to failure (for example, head crash), which may result in loss of information. At the current state of technology, nonvolatile storage is slower than volatile storage by several orders of magnitude. This distinction is the result of disk and tape devices being electromechanical, rather than based entirely on chips, as is volatile storage. In database systems, disks are used for most nonvolatile storage. Other nonvolatile media are normally used only for backup data.

- **Stable storage**. Information residing in stable storage is *never* lost (*never* should be taken with a grain of salt, since theoretically *never* cannot be guaranteed — for example, it is possible, although extremely unlikely, that a black hole may envelop the earth and permanently destroy all data!). Although stable storage is theoretically impossible to obtain, it can be closely approximated by techniques that make data loss extremely unlikely. Stable-storage implementation is discussed in Section 15.2.2.

The distinctions among the various storage types are often less clear in practice than in our presentation. Certain systems provide battery backup, so that some main memory can survive system crashes and power failures. Alternative forms of nonvolatile storage, such as optical media, provide an even higher degree of reliability than do disks.

15.2.2 Stable-Storage Implementation

To implement stable storage, we need to replicate the needed information in several nonvolatile storage media (usually disk) with independent failure modes, and to update the information in a controlled manner to ensure that failure during data transfer does not damage the needed information.

Recall (from Chapter 10) that RAID systems guarantee that the failure of a single disk (even during data transfer) will not result in loss of data. The simplest and fastest form of RAID is the mirrored disk, which keeps two copies of each block, on separate disks. Other forms of RAID offer lower costs, but at the expense of lower performance.

RAID systems, however, cannot guard against data loss due to disasters such as fires or flooding. Many systems store archival backups of tapes off-site to guard against such disasters. However, since tapes cannot be carried off-site continually, updates since the most recent time that tapes were carried off-site could be lost in such a disaster. More secure systems keep a copy of each block of stable storage at a remote site, writing it out over a computer network, in addition to storing the block on a local disk system. Since the blocks are output to a remote system as and when they are output to local storage, once an output operation is complete, the output is not lost, even in the event of a disaster such as a fire or flood.

In the remainder of this section, we discuss how storage media can be protected from failure during data transfer. Block transfer between memory and disk storage can result in

- **Successful completion**. The transferred information arrived safely at its destination.
- **Partial failure**. A failure occurred in the midst of transfer, and the destination block has incorrect information.
- **Total failure**. The failure occurred sufficiently early during the transfer that the destination block remains intact.

We require that, if a data-transfer failure occurs, the system detects it and invokes a recovery procedure to restore the block to a consistent state. To do so, the system must maintain two physical blocks for each logical database block; in the case of mirrored disks, both blocks are at the same location; in the case of remote backup, one of the blocks is local, whereas the other is at a remote site. An output operation is executed as follows:

1. Write the information onto the first physical block.
2. When the first write completes successfully, write the same information onto the second physical block.
3. The output is completed only after the second write completes successfully.

During recovery, each pair of physical blocks is examined. If both are the same and no detectable error exists, then no further actions are necessary. If one block contains a detectable error, then we replace its content with the content of the second block. If both blocks contain no detectable error, but they differ in content, then we replace the content of the first block with the value of the second. This recovery procedure ensures that a write to stable storage either succeeds completely (that is, updates all copies) or results in no change.

The requirement of comparing every corresponding pair of blocks during recovery is expensive to meet. We can reduce the cost greatly by keeping track of block writes that are in progress, using a small amount of nonvolatile RAM. On recovery, only blocks for which writes were in progress need to be compared.

The protocols for writing out a block to a remote site are similar to the protocols for writing blocks to a mirrored disk system, which we examined in Chapter 10, and particularly in Exercise 10.4.

We can extend this procedure easily to allow the use of an arbitrarily large number of copies of each block of stable storage. Although a large number of copies reduces the probability of a failure to even lower than with two copies, it is usually reasonable to simulate stable storage with only two copies.

15.2.3 Data Access

As we saw in Chapter 10, the database system resides permanently on nonvolatile storage (usually disks), and is partitioned into fixed-length storage units called

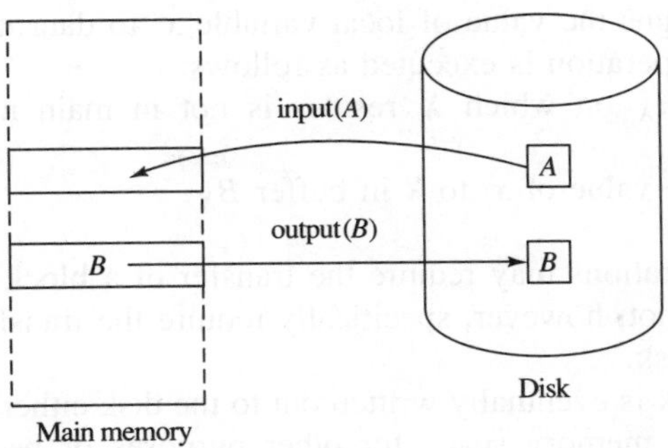

Figure 15.1 Block storage operations.

blocks. Blocks are the units of data transfer to and from disk, and may contain several data items. We shall assume that no data item spans two or more blocks. This assumption is realistic for most data-processing applications, such as our banking example.

Transactions input information from the disk to main memory, and then output the information back onto the disk. The input and output operations are done in block units. The blocks residing on the disk are referred to as *physical blocks*; the blocks residing temporarily in main memory are referred to as *buffer blocks*. The area of memory where blocks reside temporarily is called the *disk buffer*.

Block movements between disk and main memory are initiated through the following two operations:

1. **input**(B) transfers the physical block B to main memory.
2. **output**(B) transfers the buffer block B to the disk, and replaces the appropriate physical block there.

This scheme is illustrated in Figure 15.1.

Each transaction T_i has a private work area in which copies of all the data items accessed and updated by T_i are kept. This work area is created when the transaction is initiated; it is removed when the transaction either commits or aborts. Each data item x kept in the work area of transaction T_i is denoted by x_i. Transaction T_i interacts with the database system by transferring data to and from its work area to the system buffer. We transfer data using the following two operations:

1. **read**(X) assigns the value of data item X to the local variable x_i. This operation is executed as follows:
   a. If the block B_X on which X resides is not in main memory, then issue **input**(B_X).
   b. Assign to x_i the value of X from the buffer block.

2. **write**(X) assigns the value of local variable x_i to data item X in the buffer block. This operation is executed as follows:
   a. If block B_X on which X resides is not in main memory, then issue **input**(B_X).
   b. Assign the value of x_i to X in buffer B_X.

Note that both operations may require the transfer of a block from disk to main memory. They do not, however, specifically require the transfer of a block from main memory to disk.

A buffer block is eventually written out to the disk either because the buffer manager needs the memory space for other purposes or because the database system wishes to reflect the change to B on the disk. We shall say that the database system *force-outputs* buffer B if it issues an **output**(B).

When a transaction needs to access a data item X for the first time, it must execute **read**(X). All updates to X are then performed on x_i. After the transaction accesses X for the final time, it must execute **write**(X) to reflect the change to X in the database itself.

The **output**(B_X) operation for the buffer block B_X on which X resides does not need to take effect immediately after **write**(X) is executed, since the block B_X may contain other data items that are still being accessed. Thus, the actual output takes place later. Notice that, if the system crashes after the **write**(X) operation was executed but before **output**(B_x) was executed, the new value of X is never written to disk and, thus, is lost.

15.3 Recovery and Atomicity

Consider again our simplified banking system and transaction T_i that transfers \$50 from account A to account B, with initial values of A and B being \$1000 and \$2000, respectively. Suppose that a system crash has occurred during the execution of T_i, after **output**(B_A) has taken place, but before **output**(B_B) was executed, where B_A and B_B denote the buffer blocks on which A and B reside. Since the memory contents were lost, we do not know the fate of the transaction; thus, we could invoke one of two possible recovery procedures.

- **Reexecute** T_i. This procedure will result in the value of A becoming \$900, rather than \$950. Thus, the system enters an inconsistent state.
- **Do not reexecute** T_i. The current system state is values of \$950 and \$2000 for A and B, respectively. Thus, the system enters an inconsistent state.

In either case, the database is left in an inconsistent state, and thus this simple recovery scheme does not work. The reason for this difficulty is that we have modified the database without having assurance that the transaction will indeed commit. Our goal is to perform either all or no database modifications made by T_i. However, if T_i performed multiple database modifications, several output operations may be required, and a failure may occur after some of these modifications have been made, but before all of them are made.

To achieve our goal of atomicity, we must first output information describing the modifications to stable storage, without modifying the database itself. As we shall see, this procedure will allow us to output all the modifications made by a committed transaction, despite failures. There are two ways to perform such outputs; we study them in Sections 15.4 and 15.5. In these two sections, we shall assume that *transactions are executed serially*; that is, only a single transaction is active at a time. We shall describe how to handle concurrently executing transactions later, in Section 15.6.

15.4 Log-Based Recovery

The most widely used structure for recording database modifications is the *log*. The log is a sequence of *log records*, and maintains a record of all the update activities in the database. There are several types of log records. An *update log record* describes a single database write, and has the following fields:

- **Transaction identifier** is the unique identifier of the transaction that performed the **write** operation.
- **Data-item identifier** is the unique identifier of the data item written. Typically, it is the location on disk of the data item.
- **Old value** is the value of the data item prior to the write.
- **New value** is the value that the data item will have after the write.

Other special log records exist to record significant events during transaction processing, such as the start of a transaction and the commit or abort of a transaction. We denote the various types of log records as follows:

- <T_i **start**>. Transaction T_i has started.
- <T_i, X_j, V_1, V_2>. Transaction T_i has performed a write on data item X_j. X_j had value V_1 before the write, and will have value V_2 after the write.
- <T_i **commit**>. Transaction T_i has committed.
- <T_i **abort**>. Transaction T_i has aborted.

Whenever a transaction performs a write, it is essential that the log record for that write be created before the database is modified. Once a log record exists, we can output the modification to the database if that is desirable. Also, we have the ability to *undo* a modification that has already been output to the database. We undo it by using the old-value field in log records.

For log records to be useful for recovery from system and disk failures, the log must reside in stable storage. For now, we assume that every log record is written to the end of the log on stable storage as soon as it is created. In Section 15.7, we shall see when it is safe to relax this requirement so as to reduce the overhead imposed by logging. In Sections 15.4.1 and 15.4.2, we shall introduce two techniques for using the log to ensure transaction atomicity despite failures. Observe that the log contains a complete record of all database activity. As a result, the volume of data stored in the log may become unreasonably large. In Section 15.4.3, we shall show when it is safe to erase log information.

15.4.1 Deferred Database Modification

The deferred-modification technique ensures transaction atomicity by recording all database modifications in the log, but deferring the execution of all **write** operations of a transaction until the transaction partially commits. Recall that a transaction is said to be partially committed once the final action of the transaction has been executed. The version of the deferred-modification technique that we describe in this section assumes that transactions are executed serially.

When a transaction partially commits, the information on the log associated with the transaction is used in executing the deferred writes. If the system crashes before the transaction completes its execution, or if the transaction aborts, then the information on the log is simply ignored.

The execution of transaction T_i proceeds as follows. Before T_i starts its execution, a record <T_i **start**> is written to the log. A **write**(X) operation by T_i results in the writing of a new record to the log. Finally, when T_i partially commits, a record <T_i **commit**> is written to the log.

When transaction T_i partially commits, the records associated with it in the log are used in executing the deferred writes. Since a failure may occur while this updating is taking place, we must ensure that, prior to the start of these updates, all the log records are written out to stable storage. Once they have been written, the actual updating takes place, and the transaction enters the committed state.

Observe that only the new value of the data item is required by the deferred-modification technique. Thus, we can simplify the general update-log record structure that we saw in the previous section, by omitting the old-value field.

To illustrate, let us reconsider our simplified banking system. Let T_0 be a transaction that transfers $50 from account A to account B. This transaction is defined as follows:

T_0: **read**(A)
$A := A - 50$
write(A)
read(B)
$B := B + 50$
write(B)

Let T_1 be a transaction that withdraws $100 from account C. This transaction is defined as

T_1: **read**(C)
$C := C - 100$
write(C)

Suppose that these transactions are executed serially, in the order T_0 followed by T_1, and that the values of accounts A, B, and C before the execution took place were $1000, $2000, and $700, respectively. The portion of the log containing the relevant information on these two transactions is presented in Figure 15.2.

<T_0 **start**>
<T_0, A, 950>
<T_0, B, 2050>
<T_0 **commit**>
<T_1 **start**>
<T_1, C, 600>
<T_1 **commit**>

Figure 15.2 Portion of the database log corresponding to T_0 and T_1.

There are various orders in which the actual outputs can take place to both the database system and the log as a result of the execution of T_0 and T_1. One such order is presented in Figure 15.3. Note that the value of A is changed in the database only after the record <T_0, A, 950> has been placed in the log.

Using the log, the system can handle any failure that results in the loss of information on volatile storage. The recovery scheme uses the following recovery procedure:

- **redo**(T_i) sets the value of all data items updated by transaction T_i to the new values.

The set of data items updated by T_i and their respective new values can be found in the log.

The **redo** operation must be *idempotent*; that is, executing it several times must be equivalent to executing it once. This characteristic is required of we are to guarantee correct behavior even if a failure occurs during the recovery process.

After a failure has occurred, the recovery subsystem consults the log to determine which transactions need to be redone. Transaction T_i needs to be redone if and only if the log contains both the record <T_i **start**> and the record <T_i **commit**>. Thus, if the system crashes after the transaction completes its execution, the information in the log is used in restoring the system to a previous consistent state.

As an illustration, let us return to our banking example with transactions T_0 and T_1 executed one after the other in the order T_0 followed by T_1. Figure 15.2

Log	**Database**
<T_0 **start**>	
<T_0, A, 950>	
<T_0, B, 2050>	
<T_0 **commit**>	
	$A = 950$
	$B = 2050$
<T_1 **start**>	
<T_1, C, 600>	
<T_1 **commit**>	
	$C = 600$

Figure 15.3 State of the log and database corresponding to T_0 and T_1.

shows the log that results from the complete execution of T_0 and T_1. Let us suppose that the system crashes before the completion of the transactions, so that we can see how the recovery technique restores the database to a consistent state. Assume that the crash occurs just after the log record for the step

write(B)

of transaction T_0 has been written to stable storage. The log at the time of the crash is as shown in Figure 15.4a. When the system comes back up, no redo actions need to be taken, since no commit record appears in the log. The values of accounts A and B remain \$1000 and \$2000, respectively. The log records of the incomplete transaction T_0 can be deleted from the log.

Now, let us assume the crash comes just after the log record for the step

write(C)

of transaction T_1 has been written to stable storage. In this case, the log at the time of the crash is as shown in Figure 15.4b. When the system comes back up, the operation **redo**(T_0) is performed, since the record

<T_0 **commit**>

appears in the log on the disk. After this operation is executed, the values of accounts A and B are \$950 and \$2050, respectively. The value of account C remains \$700. As before, the log records of the incomplete transaction T_1 can be deleted from the log.

Lastly, assume that a crash occurs just after the log record

<T_1 **commit**>

is written to stable storage. The log at the time of this crash is as shown in Figure 15.4c. When the system comes back up, two commit records are in the log: one for T_0 and one for T_1. Therefore, the operations **redo**(T_0) and **redo**(T_1) must be performed. After these operations are executed, the values of accounts A, B, and C are \$950, \$2050, and \$600, respectively.

Finally, let us consider a case in which a second system crash occurs during recovery from the first crash. Some changes may have been made to the database as a result of the **redo** operations, but all changes may not have been made. When the system comes up after the second crash, recovery proceeds exactly as in the

(a)	(b)	(c)
<T_0 **start**>	<T_0 **start**>	<T_0 **start**>
<T_0, A, 950>	<T_0, A, 950>	<T_0, A, 950>
<T_0, B, 2050>	<T_0, B, 2050>	<T_0, B, 2050>
	<T_0 **commit**>	<T_0 **commit**>
	<T_1 **start**>	<T_1 **start**>
	<T_1, C, 600>	<T_1, C, 600>
		<T_1 **commit**>

Figure 15.4 The same log as that in Figure 15.3, shown at three different times.

preceding examples. For each commit record

<T_i **commit**>

found in the log, the operation **redo**(T_i) is performed. In other words, the recovery actions are restarted from the beginning. Since **redo** writes values to the database independent of the values currently in the database, the result of a successful second attempt at **redo** is the same as though **redo** had succeeded the first time.

15.4.2 Immediate Database Modification

The immediate-update technique allows database modifications to be output to the database while the transaction is still in the active state. Data modifications written by active transactions are called *uncommitted modifications*. In the event of a crash or a transaction failure, the system must use the old-value field of the log records described in Section 15.4 to restore the modified data items to the value they had prior to the start of the transaction. This restoration is accomplished through the **undo** operation described next.

Before a transaction T_i starts its execution, the record <T_i **start**> is written to the log. During its execution, any **write**(X) operation by T_i is *preceded* by the writing of the appropriate new update record to the log. When T_i partially commits, the record <T_i **commit**> is written to the log.

Since the information in the log is used in reconstructing the state of the database, we cannot allow the actual update to the database to take place before the corresponding log record is written out to stable storage. We therefore require that, prior to execution of an **output**(B) operation, the log records corresponding to B be written onto stable storage. We shall return to this issue in Section 15.7.

As an illustration, let us reconsider our simplified banking system, with transactions T_0 and T_1 executed one after the other in the order T_0 followed by T_1. The portion of the log containing the relevant information concerning these two transactions is presented in Figure 15.5.

One possible order in which the actual outputs took place to both the database system and the log as a result of the execution of T_0 and T_1 is described in Figure 15.6. Notice that this order could not be obtained in the deferred-modification technique of Section 15.4.1.

Using the log, the system can handle any failure that does not result in the loss of information on nonvolatile storage. The recovery scheme uses two

<T_0 **start**>
<T_0, A, 1000, 950>
<T_0, B, 2000, 2050>
<T_0 **commit**>
<T_1 **start**>
<T_1, C, 700, 600>
<T_1 **commit**>

Figure 15.5 Portion of the system log corresponding to T_0 and T_1.

Log	**Database**
<T_0 **start**>	
<T_0, A, 1000, 950>	
<T_0, B, 2000, 2050>	
	$A = 950$
	$B = 2050$
<T_0 **commit**>	
<T_1 **start**>	
<T_1, C, 700, 600>	
	$C = 600$
<T_1 **commit**>	

Figure 15.6 State of system log and database corresponding to T_0 and T_1.

recovery procedures:

- **undo**(T_i) restores the value of all data items updated by transaction T_i to the old values.
- **redo**(T_i) sets the value of all data items updated by transaction T_i to the new values.

The set of data items updated by T_i and their respective old and new values can be found in the log.

The **undo** and **redo** operations must be idempotent to guarantee correct behavior even if a failure occurs during the recovery process.

After a failure has occurred, the recovery scheme consults the log to determine which transactions need to be redone, and which need to be undone. This classification of transactions is accomplished as follows:

- Transaction T_i needs to be undone if the log contains the record <T_i **start**>, but does not contain the record <T_i **commit**>.
- Transaction T_i needs to be redone if the log contains both the record <T_i **start**> and the record <T_i **commit**>.

As an illustration, let us return to our banking example, with transaction T_0 and T_1 executed one after the other in the order T_0 followed by T_1. Let us suppose that the system crashes before the completion of the transactions. We shall consider three cases. The state of the logs for each of these cases is shown in Figure 15.7.

First, let us assume that the crash occurs just after the log record for the step

write(B)

of transaction T_0 has been written to stable storage (Figure 15.7a). When the system comes back up, it finds the record <T_0 **start**> in the log, but no corresponding <T_0 **commit**> record. Thus, transaction T_0 must be undone, so an **undo**(T_0) is

(a)	(b)	(c)
$<T_0$ **start**$>$	$<T_0$ **start**$>$	$<T_0$ **start**$>$
$<T_0, A, 1000, 950>$	$<T_0, A, 1000, 950>$	$<T_0, A, 1000, 950>$
$<T_0, B, 2000, 2050>$	$<T_0, B, 2000, 2050>$	$<T_0, B, 2000, 2050>$
	$<T_0$ **commit**$>$	$<T_0$ **commit**$>$
	$<T_1$ **start**$>$	$<T_1$ **start**$>$
	$<T_1, C, 700, 600>$	$<T_1, C, 700, 600>$
		$<T_1$ **commit**$>$

Figure 15.7 The same log, shown at three different times.

performed. As a result, the values in accounts A and B (on the disk) are restored to \$1000 and \$2000, respectively.

Next, let us assume that the crash comes just after the log record for the step

write(C)

of transaction T_1 has been written to stable storage (Figure 15.7b). When the system comes back up, two recovery actions need to be taken. The operation **undo**(T_1) must be performed, since the record $<T_1$ **start**$>$ appears in the log, but there is no record $<T_1$ **commit**$>$. The operation **redo**(T_0) must be performed, since the log contains both the record $<T_0$ **start**$>$ and the record $<T_0$ **commit**$>$. At the end of the entire recovery procedure, the values of accounts A, B, and C are \$950, \$2050, and \$700, respectively. Note that the **undo**(T_1) operation is performed before the **redo**(T_0). In this example, the same outcome would result if the order were reversed. However, the order of doing **undo** operations first, and then **redo** operations, is important for the recovery algorithm that we shall see in Section 15.6.

Finally, let us assume that the crash occurs just after the log record

$<T_1$ **commit**$>$

has been written to stable storage (Figure 15.7c). When the system comes back up, both T_0 and T_1 need to be redone, since the records $<T_0$ **start**$>$ and $<T_0$ **commit**$>$ appear in the log as do the records $<T_1$ **start**$>$ and $<T_1$ **commit**$>$. After the recovery procedures **redo**(T_0) and **redo**(T_1) are performed, the values in accounts A, B, and C are \$950, \$2050, and \$600, respectively.

15.4.3 Checkpoints

When a system failure occurs, we must consult the log to determine those transactions that need to be redone and those that need to be undone. In principle, we need to search the entire log to determine this information. There are two major difficulties with this approach:

1. The search process is time-consuming.
2. Most of the transactions that, according to our algorithm, need to be redone have already written their updates into the database. Although redoing them will cause no harm, it will nevertheless cause recovery to take longer.

To reduce these types of overhead, we introduce *checkpoints*. During execution, the system maintains the log, using one of the two techniques described in Sections 15.4.1 and 15.4.2. In addition, the system periodically performs checkpoints, which require the following sequence of actions to take place:

1. Output onto stable storage all log records currently residing in main memory.
2. Output to the disk all modified buffer blocks.
3. Output onto stable storage a log record <**checkpoint**>.

Transactions are not allowed to perform any update actions, such as writing to a buffer block or writing a log record, while a checkpoint is in progress.

The presence of a <**checkpoint**> record in the log allows the system to streamline its recovery procedure. Consider a transaction T_i that committed prior to the checkpoint. For such a transaction, the <T_i **commit**> record appears in the log before the <**checkpoint**> record. Any database modifications made by T_i must have been written to the database either prior to the checkpoint or as part of the checkpoint itself. Thus, at recovery time, there is no need to perform a **redo** operation on T_i.

This observation allows us to refine our previous recovery schemes. (We continue to assume that transactions are run serially.) After a failure has occurred, the recovery scheme examines the log to determine the most recent transaction T_i that started executing before the most recent checkpoint took place. It can find such a transaction by searching the log backward, from the end of the log, until it finds the first <**checkpoint**> record (since we are searching backward, the record found is the final <**checkpoint**> record in the log); then it continues the search backward until it finds the next <T_i **start**> record. This record identifies a transaction T_i.

Once transaction T_i has been identified, the **redo** and **undo** operations need to be applied to only transaction T_i and all transactions T_j that started executing after transaction T_i. Let us denote these transactions by the set T. The remainder (earlier part) of the log can be ignored, and can be erased whenever desired. The exact recovery operations to be performed depend on whether the immediate-modification technique or the deferred-modification technique is being used. The recovery operations that are required if the immediate-modification technique is employed are as follows:

- For all transactions T_k in T that have no <T_k **commit**> record in the log, execute **undo**(T_k).
- For all transactions T_k in T such that the record <T_k **commit**> appears in the log, execute **redo**(T_k).

Obviously, the **undo** operation does not need to be applied when the deferred-modification technique is being employed.

As an illustration, consider the set of transactions $\{T_0, T_1, ..., T_{100}\}$ executed in the order of the subscripts. Suppose that the most recent checkpoint took place during the execution of transaction T_{67}. Thus, only transactions $T_{67}, T_{68}, ..., T_{100}$

need to be considered during the recovery scheme. Each of them needs to be redone if it has committed; otherwise, it needs to be undone.

In Section 15.6.3, we consider an extension of the checkpoint technique for concurrent transaction processing.

15.5 Shadow Paging

An alternative to log-based crash-recovery techniques is *shadow paging*. The shadow-paging technique is essentially an improvement on the shadow-copy technique that we saw in Section 13.3. Under certain circumstances, shadow paging may require fewer disk accesses than do the log-based methods discussed previously. There are, however, disadvantages to the shadow-paging approach, as we shall see. For example, it is hard to extend shadow paging to allow multiple transactions to execute concurrently.

As before, the database is partitioned into some number of fixed-length blocks, which are referred to as *pages*. The term *page* is borrowed from operating systems, since we are using a paging scheme for memory management. Let us assume that there are n pages, numbered 1 through n. (In practice, n may be in the hundreds of thousands.) These pages do not need not to be stored in any particular order on disk (there are many reasons why they do not, as we saw in Chapter 10). However, there must be a way to find the ith page of the database for any given i. We use a *page table*, as shown in Figure 15.8, for this purpose. The page table has n entries — one for each database page. Each entry contains a pointer to a page on disk. The first entry contains a pointer to the first page of the database, the second entry points to the second page, and so on. The example in Figure 15.8 shows that the logical order of database pages does not need to correspond to the physical order in which the pages are placed on disk.

The key idea behind the shadow-paging technique is to maintain *two* page tables during the life of a transaction: the *current* page table and the *shadow* page table. When the transaction starts, both page tables are identical. The shadow page table is never changed over the duration of the transaction. The current page table may be changed when a transaction performs a **write** operation. All **input** and **output** operations use the current page table to locate database pages on disk.

Suppose that the transaction performs a **write**(X) operation, and that X resides on the ith page. The **write** operation is executed as follows:

1. If the ith page (that is, the page on which X resides) is not already in main memory, then issue **input**(X).
2. If this is the write first performed on the ith page by this transaction, then modify the current page table as follows:
   a. Find an unused page on disk. Typically, the database system has access to a list of unused (free) pages, as we saw in Chapter 10.
   b. Delete the page found in step 2a from the list of free page frames.
   c. Modify the current page table such that the ith entry points to the page found in step 2a.
3. Assign the value of x_j to X in the buffer page.

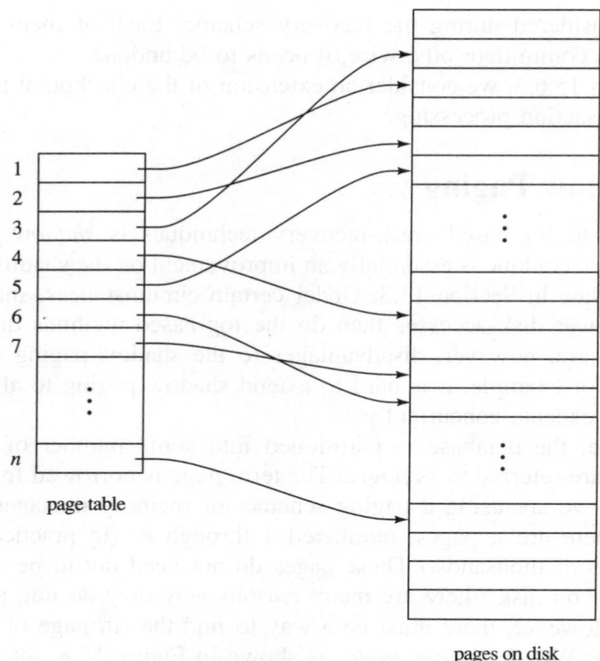

Figure 15.8 Sample page table.

Let us compare the preceding action for a **write** operation with that described in Section 15.2. The only difference is that we have added a new step. Steps 1 and 3 above correspond to steps 1 and 2 in Section 15.2. The added step, step 2, manipulates the current page table. Figure 15.9 shows the shadow and current page tables for a transaction performing a write to the fourth page of a database consisting of 10 pages.

Intuitively, the shadow-page approach to recovery is to store the shadow page table in nonvolatile storage, so that the state of the database prior to the execution of the transaction can be recovered in the event of a crash, or transaction abort. When the transaction commits, the current page table is written to nonvolatile storage. The current page table then becomes the new shadow page table, and the next transaction is allowed to begin execution. It is important that the shadow page table be stored in nonvolatile storage, since it provides the only means of locating database pages. The current page table may be kept in main memory (volatile storage). We do not care whether the current page table is lost in a crash, since the system recovers using the shadow page table.

Successful recovery requires that we find the shadow page table on disk after a crash. A simple way of finding it is to choose one fixed location in stable storage that contains the disk address of the shadow page table. When the system comes back up after a crash, we copy the shadow page table into main memory, and use it for subsequent transaction processing. Because of our definition of the

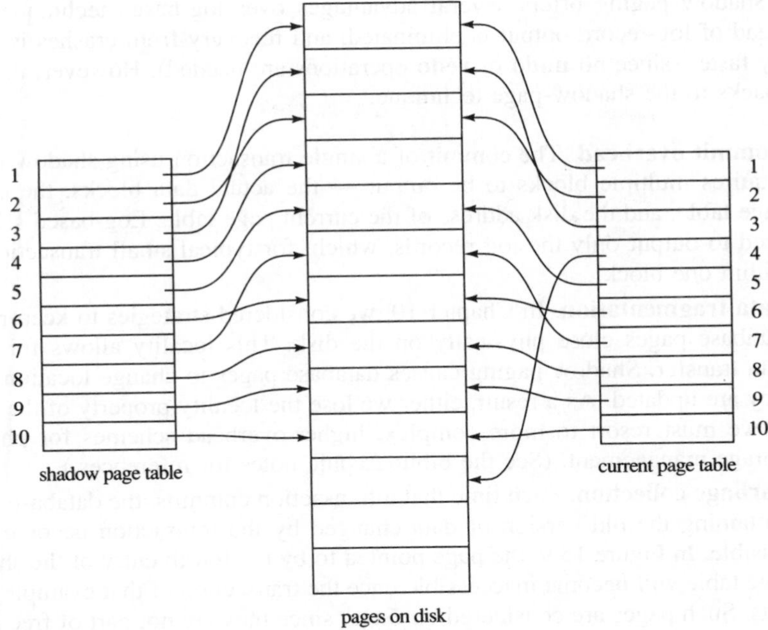

Figure 15.9 Shadow and current page tables.

write operation, we are guaranteed that the shadow page table will point to the database pages corresponding to the state of the database prior to any transaction that was active at the time of the crash. Thus, aborts are automatic. Unlike our log-based schemes, no **undo** operations need to be invoked.

To commit a transaction, we must do the following:

1. Ensure that all buffer pages in main memory that have been changed by the transaction are output to disk. (Note that these output operations will not change database pages pointed to by some entry in the shadow page table.)
2. Output the current page table to disk. Note that we must not overwrite the shadow page table, since we may need it for recovery from a crash.
3. Output the disk address of the current page table to the fixed location in stable storage containing the address of the shadow page table. This action overwrites the address of the old shadow page table. Therefore, the current page table has become the shadow page table, and the transaction is committed.

If a crash occurs prior to the completion of step 3, we revert to the state just prior to the execution of the transaction. If the crash occurs after the completion of step 3, the effects of the transaction will be preserved; no **redo** operations need to be invoked.

Shadow paging offers several advantages over log-based techniques. The overhead of log-record output is eliminated, and recovery from crashes is significantly faster (since no **undo** or **redo** operations are needed). However, there are drawbacks to the shadow-page technique:

- **Commit overhead**. The commit of a single transaction using shadow paging requires multiple blocks to be output — the actual data blocks, the current page table, and the disk address of the current page table. Log-based schemes need to output only the log records, which, for typical small transactions, fit within one block.
- **Data fragmentation**. In Chapter 10, we considered strategies to keep related database pages close physically on the disk. This locality allows for faster data transfer. Shadow paging causes database pages to change location when they are updated. As a result, either we lose the locality property of the pages or we must resort to more complex, higher-overhead schemes for physical storage management. (See the bibliographic notes for references.)
- **Garbage collection**. Each time that a transaction commits, the database pages containing the old version of data changed by the transaction become inaccessible. In Figure 15.9, the page pointed to by the fourth entry of the shadow page table will become inaccessible once the transaction of that example commits. Such pages are considered *garbage*, since they are not part of free space and do not contain usable information. Garbage may be created also as a side effect of crashes. Periodically, it is necessary to find all the garbage pages, and to add them to the list of free pages. This process, called *garbage collection*, imposes additional overhead and complexity on the system. There are several standard algorithms for garbage collection. (See the bibliographic notes for references.)

In addition to the drawbacks of shadow paging, that we have just mentioned, shadow paging is more difficult than logging to adapt to systems that allow several transactions to execute concurrently. In such systems, some logging is typically required, even if shadow paging is used. The System R prototype, for example, used a combination of shadow paging and a logging scheme similar to that presented in Section 15.4.2. It is relatively easy to extend the log-based recovery schemes to allow concurrent transactions, as we shall see in Section 15.6. For these reasons, shadow paging is not widely used.

15.6 Recovery with Concurrent Transactions

Until now, we considered recovery in an environment where only a single transaction at a time is executing. We now discuss how we can modify and extend the log-based recovery scheme to deal with multiple concurrent transactions. Regardless of the number of concurrent transactions, the system has a single disk buffer and a single log. The buffer blocks are shared by all transactions. We allow immediate updates, and permit a buffer block to have data items updated by one or more transactions.

15.6.1 Interaction with Concurrency Control

The recovery scheme depends greatly on the concurrency-control scheme that is used. To roll back a failed transaction, we must undo the updates performed by the transaction. Suppose that a transaction T_0 has to be rolled back, and a data item Q that was updated by T_0 has to be restored to its old value. Using the log-based schemes for recovery, we restore the value using the undo information in a log record. Suppose now that a second transaction T_1 has performed yet another update on Q *before* T_0 is rolled back. Then, the update performed by T_1 will be lost if T_0 is rolled back.

Therefore, we require that, if a transaction T has updated a data item Q, no other transaction may update the same data item until T has committed or been rolled back. We can ensure this requirement easily by using strict two-phase locking — that is, two-phase locking with exclusive locks held until the end of the transaction.

15.6.2 Transaction Rollback

We roll back a failed transaction, T_i, using the log. The log is scanned backward; for every log record of the form <T_i, X_j, V_1, V_2> found in the log, the data item X_j is restored to its old value V_1. The scanning of the log terminates when the log record <T_i, **start**> is found.

Scanning the log backward is important, since a transaction may have updated a data item more than once. As an illustration, consider the pair of log records

<T_i, A, 10, 20>
<T_i, A, 20, 30>

The log records represent a modification of data item A by T_i, followed by another modification of A by T_i. Scanning the log backward sets A correctly to 10. If the log were scanned in the forward direction, A would be set to 20, which value is incorrect.

If strict two-phase locking is used for concurrency control, locks held by a transaction T may be released only after the transaction has been rolled back as described. Once transaction T (that is being rolled back) has updated a data item, no other transaction could have updated the same data item, due to the concurrency-control requirements mentioned previously. Therefore, restoring the old value of the data item will not erase the effects of any other transaction.

15.6.3 Checkpoints

In Section 15.4.3, we used checkpoints to reduce the number of log records that must be scanned when the system recovers from a crash. Since we assumed no concurrency, it was necessary to consider only the following transactions during recovery:

- Those transactions that started after the most recent checkpoint
- The one transaction, if any, that was active at the time of the most recent checkpoint

The situation is more complex when transactions can execute concurrently, since several transactions may have been active at the time of the most recent checkpoint.

In a concurrent transaction-processing system, we require that the checkpoint log record be of the form <**checkpoint** L>, where L is a list of transactions active at the time of the checkpoint. Again, we assume that transactions do not perform updates either on the buffer blocks or on the log, while the checkpoint is in progress.

The requirement that transactions must not perform any updates to buffer blocks or to the log during checkpointing can be bothersome, since transaction processing will have to halt while a checkpoint is in progress. A *fuzzy checkpoint* is a checkpoint where transactions are allowed to perform updates even while buffer blocks are being written out. The bibliographic notes provide references to extensions of the recovery techniques to allow checkpoints to be fuzzy. Fuzzy checkpointing schemes are described in Section 15.9.5.

15.6.4 Restart Recovery

When the system recovers from a crash, it constructs two lists: The *undo-list* consists of transactions to be undone, and the *redo-list* consists of transactions to be redone.

These two lists are constructed on recovery as follows. Initially, they are both empty. We scan the log backward, examining each record, until the first <**checkpoint**> record is found:

- For each record found of the form <T_i **commit**>, we add T_i to *redo-list*.
- For each record found of the form <T_i **start**>, if T_i is not in *redo-list*, then we add T_i to *undo-list*.

When all the appropriate log records have been examined, we check the list L in the checkpoint record. For each transaction T_i in L, if T_i is not in *redo-list* then we add T_i to the *undo-list*.

Once the redo-list and undo-list have have been constructed, the recovery proceeds as follows:

1. Rescan the log from the most recent record backward, and perform an **undo** for each log record that belongs transaction T_i on the *undo-list*. Log records of transactions on the *redo-list* are ignored in this phase. The scan stops when the <T_i **start**> records have been found for every transaction T_i in the *undo-list*.

2. Locate the most recent <**checkpoint** L> record on the log. Notice that this step may involve scanning the log forward, if the checkpoint record was passed in step 1.
3. Scan the log forward from the most recent <**checkpoint** L> record, and perform **redo** for each log record that belongs to a transaction T_i that is on the *redo-list*. Ignore log records of transactions on the *undo-list* in this phase.

It is important in step 1 to process the log backward, to ensure that the resulting state of the database is correct.

After all transactions on the *undo-list* have been undone, those transactions on the *redo-list* are redone. It is important, in this case, to process the log forward. When the recovery process has completed, transaction processing resumes.

It is important to undo the transaction in the *undo-list* before redoing transactions in the *redo-list*, using the preceding algorithm. Otherwise, the following problem may occur. Suppose that data item A initially has the value 10. Suppose that a transaction T_i updated data item A to 20 and aborted; transaction rollback would restore A to the value 10. Suppose that another transaction T_j then updated data item A to 30 and committed, following which the system crashed. The state of the log at the time of the crash is

$<T_i, A, 10, 20>$
$<T_j, A, 10, 30>$
<T_j **commit**>

If the redo pass is performed first, A will be set to 30; then, in the undo pass, A will be set to 10, which is wrong. The final value of Q should be 30, which we can ensure by performing undo before performing redo.

15.7 Buffer Management

In this section, we consider several subtle details that are essential to the implementation of a crash-recovery scheme that ensures data consistency and imposes a minimal amount of overhead on interactions with the database.

15.7.1 Log-Record Buffering

Earlier, we assumed that every log record is output to stable storage at the time it is created. This assumption imposes a high overhead on system execution for the following reasons. Typically, output to stable storage is in units of blocks. In most cases, a log record is much smaller than a block. Thus, the output of each log record translates to a much larger output at the physical level. Furthermore, as we saw in Section 15.2.2, the output of a block to stable storage may involve several output operations at the physical level.

The cost of performing the output of a block to stable storage is sufficiently high that it is desirable to output multiple log records at once. To do so, we write log records to a log buffer in main memory, where they stay temporarily until they are output to stable storage. Multiple log records can be gathered in the log buffer, and output to stable storage in a single output operation. The order of log records in the stable storage must be exactly the same as the order in which they were written to the log buffer.

Due to the use of log buffering, a log record may reside in only main memory (volatile storage) for a considerable time before it is output to stable storage. Since such log records are lost if the system crashes, we must impose additional requirements on the recovery techniques to ensure transaction atomicity:

- Transaction T_i enters the commit state after the <T_i **commit**> log record has been output to stable storage.
- Before the <T_i **commit**> log record can be output to stable storage, all log records pertaining to transaction T_i must have been output to stable storage.
- Before a block of data in main memory can be output to the database (in nonvolatile storage), all log records pertaining to data in that block must have been output to stable storage.

  The latter rule is called the *write-ahead logging* (WAL) rule. (Strictly speaking, the WAL rule requires only that the undo information in the log have been output to stable storage, and permits the redo information to be written later. The difference is relevant in systems where undo and redo information is stored in separate log records.)

Writing the buffered log to disk is sometimes referred to as a *log force*. The preceding rules state situations in which certain log records *must* have been output to stable storage. There is no problem resulting from the output of log records *earlier* than necessary. Thus, when the system finds it necessary to output a log record to stable storage, it outputs an entire block of log records, if there are enough log records in main memory to fill a block. If there are insufficient log records to fill the block, all log records in main memory are combined into a partially full block, and are output to stable storage.

15.7.2 Database Buffering

In Section 15.2, we described the use of a two-level storage hierarchy. The database is stored in nonvolatile storage (disk), and blocks of data are brought into main memory as needed. Since main memory is typically much smaller than the entire database, it may be necessary to overwrite a block B_1 in main memory when another block B_2 needs to be brought into memory. If B_1 has been modified, B_1 must be output prior to the input of B_2. As discussed in Section 10.5.1 in Chapter 10, this storage hierarchy is the standard operating system concept of *virtual memory*.

The rules for the output of log records limit the freedom of the system to output blocks of data. If the input of block B_2 causes block B_1 to be chosen for output, all log records pertaining to data in B_1 must be output to stable storage before B_1 is output. Thus, the sequence of actions by the system would be as follows:

- Output log records to stable storage until all log records pertaining to block B_1 have been output.
- Output block B_1 to disk.
- Input block B_2 from disk to main memory.

It is important that no writes to the block B_1 be in progress while the preceding sequence of actions is carried out. We can ensure that they are not by using a special means of locking, as follows. Before a transaction performs a write on a data item, it must acquire an exclusive lock on the block in which the data item resides. The lock can be released immediately after the update has been performed. Before a block is output, the system obtains an exclusive lock on the block, to ensure that no transaction is updating the block. The lock is released once the block output has completed. Locks that are held for a short duration are often called *latches*. Latches are treated as distinct from locks used by the concurrency-control system. As a result, they may be released without regard to any locking protocol, such as two-phase locking, required by the concurrency-control system.

To illustrate the need for the preceding sequence of actions, we consider our banking example with transactions T_0 and T_1. Suppose that the state of the log is

<T_0 **start**>
<T_0, A, 1000, 950>

and that transaction T_0 issues a **read**(B). Assume that the block on which B resides is not in main memory, and that main memory is full. Suppose that the block on which A resides is chosen to be output to disk. If the system outputs this block to disk and then a crash occurs, the values in the database for accounts A, B, and C are \$950, \$2000, and \$700, respectively. This database state is inconsistent. However, due to the preceding requirements, the log record

<T_0, A, 1000, 950>

must be output to stable storage prior to output of the block on which A resides. The system can use the log record during recovery to bring the database back to a consistent state.

15.7.3 Operating System Role in Buffer Management

We can manage the database buffer using one of two approaches:

1. The database system reserves part of main memory to serve as a buffer that it, rather than the operating system, manages. The database system manages data-block transfer in accordance with the requirements that we discussed.

   This approach has the drawback of limiting flexibility in the use of main memory. The buffer must be kept small enough that other applications have sufficient main memory available for their needs. However, even when the other applications are not running, the database will not be able to make use of all the available memory. Likewise, nondatabase applications may not use that part of main memory reserved for the database buffer, even if some of the pages in the database buffer are not being used.

2. The database system implements its buffer within the virtual memory of the operating system. Since the operating system knows about the memory requirements of all processes in the system, ideally it should be in charge of deciding what buffer blocks must be force-output to disk, and when. But, to ensure the write-ahead logging requirements that we discussed, the operating system should not write out the database buffer pages itself, but instead should request the database system to force-output the buffer blocks. The database system in turn would force-output the buffer blocks to the database, after writing relevant log records to stable storage.

   Unfortunately, almost all current-generation operating systems retain complete control of virtual memory. The operating system reserves space on disk for storing virtual-memory pages that are not currently in main memory; this space is called *swap space*. If the operating system decides to output a block B_x, that block is output to the swap space on disk, and there is no way for the database system to get control of the output of buffer blocks.

   Therefore, if the database buffer is in virtual memory, transfers between database files and the buffer in virtual memory must be managed by the database system, which enforces the write-ahead logging requirements that we discussed.

   This approach may result in extra output of data to disk. If a block B_x is output by the operating system, that block is not output to the database. Instead, it is output to the swap space for the operating system's virtual memory. When the database system needs to output B_x, the operating system may need first to input B_x from its swap space. Thus, instead of a single output of B_x, we require two outputs of B_x (one by the operating system, and one by the database system) and one extra input of B_x.

Although both approaches suffer from some drawbacks, one or the other must be chosen unless the operating system is designed to support the requirements of database logging. Only a few current operating systems, such as the Mach operating system, support these requirements.

15.8 Failure with Loss of Nonvolatile Storage

Until now, we have considered only the case where a failure results in the loss of information residing in volatile storage while the content of the nonvolatile storage remains intact. Although failures in which the content of nonvolatile storage is lost are rare, we nevertheless need to be prepared to deal with this type of failure. In this section, we discuss only disk storage. Our discussions apply as well to other nonvolatile storage types.

The basic scheme is to *dump* the entire content of the database to stable storage periodically — say, once per day. For example, we may dump the database to one or more magnetic tapes. If a failure occurs that results in the loss of physical database blocks, the most recent dump is used in restoring the database to a previous consistent state. Once this restoration has been accomplished, the system uses the log to bring the database system to the most recent consistent state.

More precisely, no transaction may be active during the dump procedure, and a procedure similar to checkpointing must take place:

1. Output all log records currently residing in main memory onto stable storage.
2. Output all buffer blocks onto the disk.
3. Copy the contents of the database to stable storage.
4. Output a log record <**dump**> onto the stable storage.

Steps 1, 2, and 4 correspond to the three steps used for checkpoints in Section 15.4.3.

To recover from the loss of nonvolatile storage, we restore the database to disk using the most recent dump. Then, the log is consulted, and all the transactions that have committed since the most recent dump occurred are redone. Notice that no **undo** operations need to be executed.

A dump of the database contents is also referred to as an *archival dump*, since we can archive the dumps and use them later to examine old states of the database. Dumps of a database and checkpointing of buffers are similar.

The simple dump procedure described here is costly for the following two reasons. First, the entire database must be be copied to stable storage, resulting in considerable data transfer. Second, since transaction processing is halted during the dump procedure, CPU cycles are wasted. *Fuzzy dump* schemes have been developed, which allow transactions to be active while the dump is in progress. They are similar to fuzzy checkpointing schemes; see the bibliographic notes for more details.

15.9 Advanced Recovery Techniques

The recovery techniques described in Section 15.6 require that, once a transaction updates a data item, no other transaction may update the same data item until the first commits or is rolled back. We ensure that the condition by using strict two-phase locking. Although strict two-phase locking is acceptable for records in relations, as discussed in Section 14.8, it causes a significant decrease in concurrency when applied to certain specialized structures, such as B^+-tree index pages.

To increase concurrency, we can use the B^+-tree concurrency-control algorithm described in Section 14.8 to allow locks to be released early, in a non–two-phase manner. As a result, however, the recovery techniques from Section 15.6 will become inapplicable. Several alternative recovery techniques, applicable even with early lock release, have been proposed. We describe one such recovery technique in this section.

15.9.1 Logical Undo Logging

For actions where locks are released early, we cannot perform the undo actions by simply writing back the old value of the data items. Consider a transaction T that inserts an entry into a B^+-tree, and, following the B^+-tree concurrency-control protocol, releases some locks after the insertion operation completes, but before the transaction commits. After the locks are released, other transactions may perform further insertions or deletions, thereby causing further changes to the B^+-tree pages.

Even though the operation releases some locks early, it must retain enough locks to ensure that no other transaction is allowed to execute any conflicting operation (such as reading the inserted value, or deleting the inserted value). For this reason, the B^+-tree concurrency-control protocol that we studied earlier holds locks on the leaf level of the B^+-tree until the end of the transaction.

Now let us consider how to perform transaction rollback. If the old values of the internal B^+-tree nodes (before the insertion operation was executed) are written back during transaction rollback, some of the updates performed by later insertion or deletion operations executed by other transactions could be lost. Instead, the insertion operation has to be undone *logically* — that is, by execution of a delete operation.

Therefore, when the insertion action completes, before it releases any locks, it writes a log record $<O_i$, **operation-end**, $U>$, where the U denotes undo information, and O_i denotes an identifier for the operation. For example, if the operation inserted an entry in a B^+-tree, the undo information U would indicate what to delete from the B^+-tree. Such logging of information about operations is called *logical logging*. In contrast, logging of old-value and new-value information is called *physical logging*, and the corresponding log records are called *physical log records*.

The insertion and deletion operations are examples of a class of operations that requires logical undo operations since it releases locks early; we call such operations *logical operations*. Before a logical operation begins, it writes a log record $<O_i$, **operation-begin**$>$, where O_i is the identifier for the operation. While the operation is being executed, logging is done in the normal fashion for all updates performed by the operation. Thus, the usual old-value and new-value information is written out for each update. When the operation finishes, an **operation-end** log record is written as described earlier.

15.9.2 Transaction Rollback

Let us first consider transaction rollback during normal operation (that is, not during recovery from system failure). The log is scanned backward, and we use log records belonging to the transaction to restore the old values of data items. Unlike before, we write out special redo-only log records of the form $<T_i,\ X_j,\ V>$

containing the value V being resored to data item X_j during the rollback. These log records are sometimes called compensation log records. Whenever a log record $<O_i$, **operation-end**, $U>$ log record is found, special actions are taken:

1. We roll back the operation by using the undo information U in the log record. The updates performed during the rollback of the operation are logged just like updates performed when the operation was first executed. Further, **operation-begin** and an **operation-end** log records are generated just like during normal operation execution.
2. When the backward scan of the log continues, we skip all log records of the transaction until we find the log record $<O_i$, **operation-begin**$>$. After the **operation-begin** log record is found, log records of the transaction are processed in the normal manner again.

When the transaction T_i has been rolled back, a record <T_i **abort**> is added to the log.

If failures occur while a logical operation is in progress, the **operation-end** log record for the operation will not be found when the transaction is rolled back. However, for every update performed by the operation, undo information — in the form of the old value in the physical log records — is available in the log. The physical log records will be used to roll back the incomplete operation. Observe that skipping over physical log records when the **operation-end** log record is found during rollback ensures that the old values in the physical log record are not used for rollback, once the operation completes.

If locking is used for concurrency control, locks held by a transaction T may be released only after the transaction has been rolled back as described.

15.9.3 Checkpoints

Checkpointing is performed as described in Section 15.6. Updates to the database are temporarily suspended, and the following actions are carried out:

1. Output onto stable storage all log records currently residing in main memory.
2. Output onto stable storage a log record <**checkpoint** L>, where L is a list of all active transactions.
3. Output to the disk all modified buffer blocks.

15.9.4 Restart Recovery

Recovery actions, when the database system is restarted after a failure, are carried out in two phases:

1. In the *redo phase*, we replay updates of *all* transactions by scanning the log forward from the last checkpoint. The log records that are replayed include log records for transactions that were rolled back before system crash, and those that had not committed when the system crash occurred. The log

records replayed include the usual log records of the form <T_i, X_j, V_1, V_2> and the special log records of the form <T_i, X_j, V_2>; the value V_2 is written to data item X_j in either case. This phase also determines all transactions that are either in the transaction list in the checkpoint record, or started later, but did not have either a <T_i **abort**> or a <T_i **commit**> record in the log. All these transactions have to be rolled back, and their transaction identifiers are put in an *undo-list*.

2. In the *undo phase*, we roll back all transactions in the *undo-list*. We perform rollback by scanning the log backward from the end. Whenever a log record belonging to a transaction in the *undo-list* is found, undo actions are performed in exactly the same manner as though the log record were found during the rollback of a failed transaction. Thus, log records of a transaction preceding an **operation-end** record, but after the corresponding **operation-begin** record, are ignored.

   When a <T_i **start**> log record is found for a transaction T_i in *undo-list*, a <T_i **abort**> log record is written out to the log. Scanning of the log stops when <T_i **start**> log records have been found for all transactions in the *undo-list*.

The redo phase of restart recovery replays every physical log record since the most recent checkpoint record. In other words, this phase of restart recovery repeats all the update actions that were executed after the checkpoint, and whose log records reached the stable log. The actions include actions of incomplete transactions and the actions carried out to roll failed transactions back. The actions are repeated in the same order in which they were carried out; hence, this process is called *repeating history*. Repeating history simplifies recovery schemes greatly.

15.9.5 Fuzzy Checkpointing

The checkpointing technique described in Section 15.6.3 requires that all updates to the database be temporarily suspended while the checkpoint is in progress. It is possible to modify the technique to permit updates to start once the **checkpoint** record has been written, but before the modified buffer blocks are written to disk. The checkpoint thus generated is a *fuzzy checkpoint*.

The idea is as follows. Instead of scanning backward in the log to find a checkpoint record, we store the location in log of the last checkpoint record in a fixed position **last_checkpoint** on disk. However, this information is not updated when the **checkpoint** record is written. Instead, before the **checkpoint** record is written, a list of all modified buffer blocks is created. The **last_checkpoint** information is updated only after all buffer blocks in the list of modified buffer blocks have been written to disk. The write-ahead log protocol must be followed when buffer blocks are output.

Note that, in our scheme, logical logging is used only for undo purposes, whereas physical logging is used for redo and undo purposes. There are recovery schemes that use logical logging for redo purposes. However, such schemes cannot be used with fuzzy checkpointing, and are therefore not widely used.

15.10 Summary

A computer system, like any other mechanical or electrical device, is subject to failure. There is a variety of causes of such failure, including disk crash, power failure, and software errors. In each of these cases, information concerning the database system is lost. In addition to system failures, transactions may also fail for various reasons, such as violation of integrity constraints or deadlocks. An integral part of a database system is a recovery scheme that is responsible for the detection of failures and for the restoration of the database to a state that existed prior to the occurrence of the failure.

The various types of storage in a computer are volatile storage, nonvolatile storage, and stable storage. Data in volatile storage, such as in RAM, are lost when the computer crashes. Data in nonvolatile storage, such as disk, are not lost when the computer crashes, but may occasionally be lost due to failures such as disk crashes. Data in stable storage are never lost. Stable storage that must be accessible online is approximated with mirrored disks, or other forms of RAID, which provide redundant data storage. Offline, or archival, stable storage may consist of multiple tape copies of data stored in a physically secure location.

In case of failure, the state of the database system may no longer be consistent; that is, it may not reflect a state of the world that the database is supposed to capture. To preserve consistency, we require that each transaction be atomic. It is the responsibility of the recovery scheme to ensure the atomicity property. There are basically two different schemes for ensuring atomicity.

- **Log-based**. All updates are recorded on the log, which must be kept in stable storage. In the deferred-modifications scheme, during the execution of a transaction, all the **write** operations are deferred until the transaction partially commits, at which time the information on the log associated with the transaction is used in executing the deferred writes. In the immediate-modifications scheme, all updates are applied directly to the database. If a crash occurs, the information in the log is used in restoring the state of the system to a previous consistent state. To reduce the overhead of searching the log and redoing transactions, we can use the checkpointing technique.
- **Shadow paging**. Two page tables are maintained during the life of a transaction: the current page table and the shadow page table. When the transaction starts, both page tables are identical. The shadow page table is never changed during the duration of the transaction. The current page table may be changed when a transaction performs a **write** operation. All **input** and **output** operations use the current page table to locate database pages on disk. When the transaction partially commits, the shadow page table is discarded, and the current table becomes the new page table. If the transaction aborts, the current page table is simply discarded.

If multiple transactions are allowed to execute concurrently, the shadow-paging technique is not applicable, but the log-based technique can be used. No transaction can be allowed to update a data item that has already been updated by an incomplete transaction. We can use strict two-phase locking to ensure this condition.

Transaction processing is based on a storage model in which main memory holds a log buffer, a database buffer, and a system buffer. The system buffer holds pages of system object code and local work areas of transactions.

Efficient implementation of a recovery scheme requires that the number of writes to the database and to stable storage be minimized. Log records may be kept in volatile log buffer initially, but must be written to stable storage when one of the following conditions occurs:

- Before the <T_i **commit**> log record may be output to stable storage, all log records pertaining to transaction T_i must have been output to stable storage.
- Before a block of data in main memory is output to the database (in nonvolatile storage), all log records pertaining to data in that block must have been output to stable storage.

To recover from failures that result in the loss of nonvolatile storage, we must dump the entire contents of the database onto stable storage periodically — say, once per day. If a failure occurs that results in the loss of physical database blocks, we use the most recent dump in restoring the database to a previous consistent state. Once this restoration has been accomplished, we use the log to bring the database system to the most recent consistent state.

Advanced recovery techniques have been developed to support high-concurrency locking techniques, such as those used for B^+-tree concurrency control. These techniques are based on logical (operation) undo, and follow the principle of repeating history. When recovering from system failure, we perform a redo pass using the log, followed by an undo pass on the log to roll back incomplete transactions.

Exercises

15.1. Explain the difference between the three storage types — volatile, nonvolatile, and stable — in terms of cost.

15.2. Stable storage cannot be implemented.
(*a*) Explain why it cannot be.
(*b*) Explain how database systems deal with this problem

15.3. Compare the deferred- and immediate-modification versions of the log-based recovery schemes, in terms of ease of implementation and overhead cost.

15.4. Assume that immediate modification is used in a system. Show, by an example, how an inconsistent database state could result if log records for a transaction are not output to stable storage prior to committing of that transaction.

15.5. Explain the purpose of the checkpoint mechanism. How often should checkpoints be performed? How does the frequency of checkpoints affect

- System performance when no failure occurs
- The time it takes to recover from a system crash
- The time it takes to recover from a disk crash

15.6. When the system recovers from a crash (see Section 15.6.4), it constructs an undo-list and a redo-list. Explain why log records for transactions on the undo-list must be processed in reverse order, while those log records for transactions on the redo-list are processed in a forward direction.

15.7. Compare the shadow-paging recovery scheme with the log-based recovery schemes in terms of ease of implementation and overhead cost.

15.8. Consider a database consisting of 10 consecutive disk blocks (block 1, block 2, ..., block 10). Show the buffer state and a possible physical ordering of the blocks after the following updates, assuming that shadow paging is used, that the buffer in main memory can hold only three blocks, and that a least recently used (LRU) strategy is used for buffer management.

> **read** block 3
> **read** block 7
> **read** block 5
> **read** block 3
> **read** block 1
> **modify** block 1
> **read** block 10
> **modify** block 5

15.9. Explain how the buffer manager may cause the database to become inconsistent if some log records pertaining to a block are not output to stable storage before the block is output to disk.

15.10. Explain the recovery procedure that needs to take place after a disk crash.

15.11. Explain the benefits of logical logging. Give examples of one situation where logical logging is preferable to physical logging and one situation where physical logging is preferable to logical logging.

15.12. Explain the reasons why recovery of interactive transactions is more difficult to deal with than is recovery of batch transactions. Is there a simple way to deal with this difficulty? (Hint: Consider an automatic teller machine transaction in which cash is withdrawn.)

15.13. Logging of updates is not done explicitly in persistent programming languages. Describe how page access protections provided by modern operating systems can be used to create before- and after-images of pages that are updated. Hint: See Exercise 14.29.

Bibliographic Notes

Two early papers that present initial theoretical work in the area of recovery are Davies [1973] and Bjork [1973]. Chandy et al. [1975], which describes analytic models for rollback and recovery strategies in database systems, is another early work in this area.

Most of the recovery mechanisms introduced in this chapter are based on those used in System R. An overview of the recovery scheme of that system is presented by Gray et al. [1981a]. The shadow-paging mechanism of System R is described by Lorie [1977]. A fast transaction-oriented logging scheme is presented by Reuter [1980].

Tutorial and survey papers on various recovery techniques for database systems are presented by Gray [1978], Lindsay et al. [1980], and Verhofstad [1978]. The concepts of fuzzy checkpointing and fuzzy dumps are described in Lindsay et al. [1980]. A comprehensive presentation of the principles of recovery is offered by Haerder and Reuter [1983]. Basic textbook discussions are offered by Date [1983a], and Bernstein et al. [1987]. Gray and Reuter [1993] is an excellent textbook source of information about recovery, including interesting implementation and historical details.

The state of the art in recovery methods is best illustrated by the ARIES recovery method, described in Mohan et al. [1992], Mohan and Narang [1995], and by Mohan [1990b]. The recovery technique described in Section 15.9 is loosely based on the ARIES recovery method. Specialized recovery techniques for index structures are described in Mohan and Levine [1992], and in Mohan [1993]; Mohan and Narang [1994] describe recovery techniques for client–server architectures.

Remote backup for disaster recovery (loss of an entire computing facility by, for example, fire, flood, or earthquake) is considered in Polyzois and Garcia-Molina [1994] and King et al. [1991].

Operating-system issues for database management are discussed in Stonebraker [1981], Traiger [1982, 1983], and Haskin et al. [1988]. References pertaining to long-duration transactions and related recovery issues are listed in Chapter 20.

CHAPTER 16

DATABASE SYSTEM ARCHITECTURES

The architecture of a database system is greatly influenced by the underlying computer system on which the database system runs. Aspects of computer architecture—such as networking, parallelism, and distribution—are reflected in the architecture of the database system.

- Networking of computers allows some tasks to be executed on a server system, and some tasks to be executed on client systems. This division of work has led to the development of *client–server* database systems.
- Parallel processing within a computer system allows database-system activities to be speeded up, allowing faster response to transactions, as well as more transactions per second. Queries can be processed in a manner that exploits the parallelism offered by the underlying computer system. The need for parallel query processing has lead to the development of *parallel* database systems.
- Distributing data across sites or departments in an organization allows those data to reside where they are generated or most needed, but still to be accessible from other sites and from other departments. Keeping multiple copies of the database across different sites also allows large organizations to continue their database operations even when one site is affected by a natural disaster, such as flood, fire, or earthquake. *Distributed* database systems have been developed to handle geographically or administratively distributed data spread across multiple database systems.

We study the architecture of database systems in this chapter, starting with the traditional centralized systems, and covering client–server, parallel, and distributed database systems.

16.1 Centralized Systems

Centralized database systems are those that run on a single computer system and do not interact with other computer systems. Such systems span a range from single-user database systems running on personal computers to high-performance database systems running on mainframe systems.

A modern, general-purpose computer system consists of one to a few CPUs and a number of device controllers that are connected through a common bus that provides access to shared memory (Figure 16.1). The CPUs have local cache memories that store local copies of parts of the memory, to speed up access to data. Each device controller is in charge of a specific type of device (for example, a disk drive, an audio device, or a video display). The CPU and the device controllers can execute concurrently, competing for memory access. Cache memory reduces the contention for memory access, since it reduces the number of times that the CPU needs to access the shared memory.

We distinguish two ways in which computers are used: as single-user systems and as multiuser systems. Personal computers and workstations fall into the first category. A typical *single user system* is a desktop unit used by a single person, has only one CPU and one or two hard disks, and has an operat-

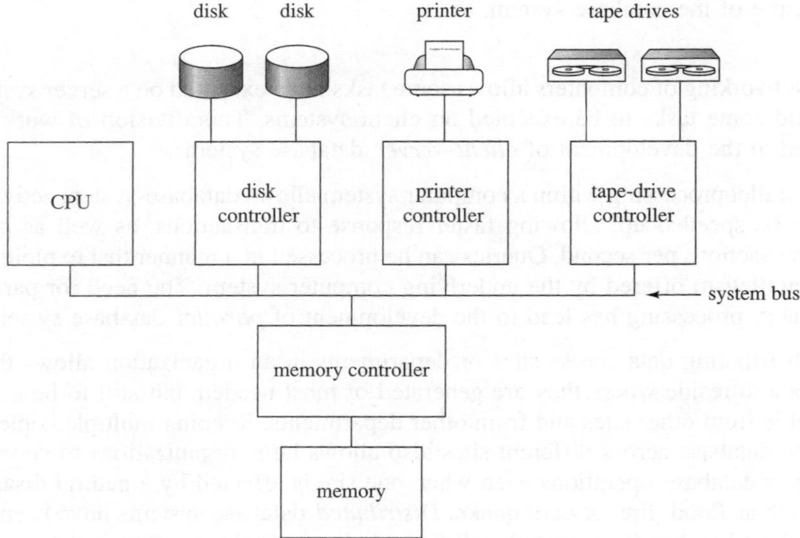

Figure 16.1 A centralized computer system.

ing system that may support only one user. A typical *multiuser system*, on the other hand, has more disks and more memory, may have multiple CPUs, and has a multiuser operating system. It serves a large number of users who are connected to the system via terminals. Such systems are often called *server* systems.

Database systems designed for single-user systems, such as personal computers, typically do not provide many of the facilities that a multiuser database provides. In particular, they do not support concurrency control, which is not required when only a single user can generate updates. The crash-recovery facilities in such systems are either absent or primitive—for example, simply making a backup of the database before any update. Many such systems do not support SQL, and provide a simpler query language, such as a variant of QBE.

Although general-purpose computer systems today have multiple processors, they have *coarse-granularity* parallelism, with only a few processors (about two to four, typically), all sharing main memory. Databases running on such machines typically do not attempt to partition a single query among the processors; instead, each query is run on a single processor, allowing multiple queries to run concurrently. Thus, such systems support a higher throughput; that is, they allow a greater number of transactions to run per second, although individual transactions do not run any faster.

Databases designed for single-processor machines already provide multitasking, allowing multiple processes to run on the same processor in a time-shared manner, giving a view to the user of multiple processes running in parallel. Thus, coarse-granularity parallel machines logically appear to be identical to single-processor machines, and database systems designed for time-shared machines can be easily adapted to run on them.

In contrast, *fine-granularity* parallel machines have a large number of processors, and database systems running on such machines attempt to parallelize single tasks (queries, for example) submitted by users. We study the architecture of parallel database systems in Section 16.3.

16.2 Client–Server Systems

As personal computers have become faster, more powerful, and cheaper, there has been a shift away from the centralized system architecture. Terminals connected to centralized systems are now being supplanted by personal computers. Correspondingly, user-interface functionality that used to be handled directly by the centralized systems is increasingly being handled by the personal computers. As a result, centralized systems today act as *server systems* that satisfy requests generated by *client systems*. The general structure of a client–server system is depicted in Figure 16.2.

Database functionality can be broadly divided into two parts—the front-end and the back-end—as shown in Figure 16.3. The back-end manages access structures, query evaluation and optimization, concurrency control, and recovery. The front-end of a database system consists of tools such as *forms*, *report writers*,

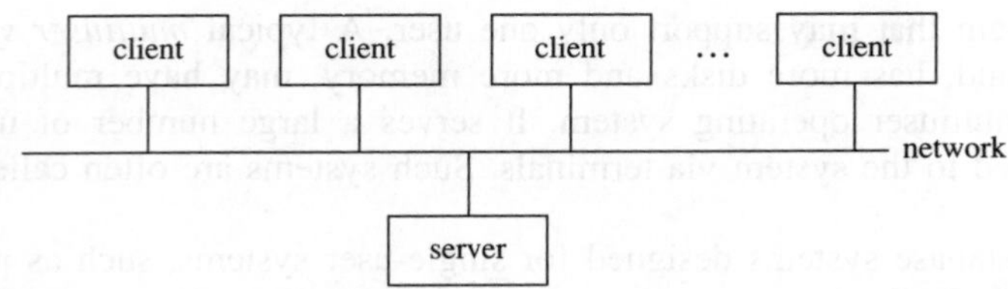

Figure 16.2 General structure of a client–server system.

and graphical user-interface facilities. The interface between the front-end and the back-end is through SQL, or through an application program.

Server systems can be broadly categorized as transaction servers and data servers.

- *Transaction-server* systems, also called *query-server* systems, provide an interface to which clients can send requests to perform an action, in response to which they execute the action and send back results to the client. Users may specify requests in SQL, or through an application program interface, using a *remote-procedure-call* mechanism.
- *Data-server systems* allow clients to interact with the servers by making requests to read or update data, in units such as files or pages. For example, file servers provide a file-system interface where clients can create, update, read, and delete files. Data servers for database systems offer much more functionality; they support units of data—such as pages, tuples, or objects—that are smaller than a file. They provide indexing facilities for data, and provide transaction facilities so that the data are never left in an inconsistent state if a client machine or process fails.

We shall elaborate on the transaction-server and data-server architectures in Sections 16.2.1 and 16.2.2.

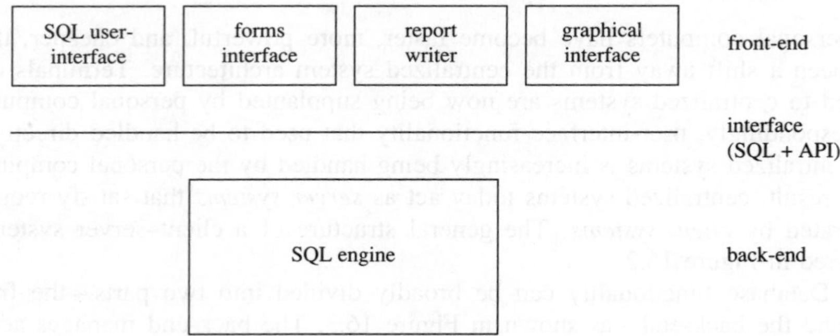

Figure 16.3 Front-end and back-end functionality.

16.2.1 Transaction Servers

In centralized systems, the front-end and the back-end are both executed within a single system. However, the transaction-server architecture follows the functional division between the front-end and the back-end. Due to the greater processing requirements of graphical user-interface code, and the increasing power of personal computers, front-end functionality is supported on personal computers. The personal computers act as *clients* of the server systems, which store large volumes of data and support the back-end functionality. Clients ship transactions to the server systems where those transactions are executed, and results are shipped back to clients that are in charge of displaying the data.

Standards such as *Open Database Connectivity* (ODBC), have been developed for interfacing of clients with servers. ODBC is an application program interface that allows clients to generate SQL statements that are sent to a server, where the statements are executed. Any client that uses the ODBC interface can connect to any server that provides the interface. In earlier-generation database systems, the lack of such standards necessitated that the front-end and the back-end be provided by the same software vendor.

With the growth of interface standards, the front-end tools and the back-end server are increasingly provided by different vendors. Gupta SQL and PowerBuilder are examples of front-end systems that are independent of the back-end servers. Further, certain application programs, such as spreadsheets and statistical-analysis packages, use the client–server interface directly to access data from a back-end server. In effect, they provide front-ends specialized for particular tasks.

Client–server interfaces other than ODBC are also used in some transaction-processing systems. They are defined by an application programming interface, using which clients make *transactional remote procedure calls* on the server. These calls appear like ordinary procedure calls to the programmer, but all the remote procedure calls from a client are enclosed in a single transaction at the server end. Thus, if the transaction aborts, the server can undo the effects of the individual remote procedure calls.

The fact that individual small machines are now cheaper to buy and maintain has resulted in an industry-wide trend toward *down-sizing*. Many companies are replacing their mainframes with networks of workstations or personal computers connected to back-end server machines. The advantages include better functionality for the cost, more flexibility in locating resources and expanding facilities, better user interfaces, and easier maintenance.

16.2.2 Data Servers

Data-server systems are used in local-area networks, where there is a high-speed connection between the clients and the server, the client machines are comparable in processing power to the server machine, and the tasks to be executed are compute intensive. In such an environment, it makes sense to ship data to client machines, to perform all processing at the client machine (which may take a while), and then to ship the data back to the server machine. Note that this architecture requires full back-end functionality (see Figure 16.3) at the clients. Data-server architectures have been particularly popular in object-oriented database systems.

Interesting issues arise in such an architecture, since the time cost of communication between the client and the server is high compared to that of a local memory reference (milliseconds, versus less than 100 nanoseconds).

- **Page shipping versus item shipping**. The unit of communication for data can be coarse granularity, such as a page, or fine-granularity, such as a tuple (or an object, in the context of object-oriented database systems). We use the term *item* to refer to both tuples and objects.

  If the unit of communication is a single item, the overhead of message passing is high compared to the number of data transmitted. Instead, when an item is requested, it makes sense also to send back other items that are likely to be used in the near future. Fetching items even before they are requested is called *prefetching*. Page shipping can be considered a form of prefetching if multiple items reside on a page, since all the items in the page are shipped when a process desires to access a single item in the page.

- **Locking**. Locks are usually granted by the server for the data items that it ships to the client machines. A disadvantage of page shipping is that client machines may be granted locks of too coarse a granularity— a lock on a page implicitly locks all items contained in the page. Even if the client is not accessing some items in the page, it has implicitly acquired locks on all prefetched items. Other client machines that require locks on those items may be blocked unnecessarily. Techniques for *lock deescalation* have been proposed, where the server can request its clients to transfer back locks on prefetched items. If the client machine does not need a prefetched item, it can transfer locks on the item back to the server, and the locks can then be allocated to other clients.

- **Data caching**. Data that are shipped to a client on behalf of a transaction can be *cached* at the client, even after the transaction completes, if sufficient storage space is available. Successive transactions at the same client may be able to make use of the cached data. However, cache coherency is an issue: Even if a transaction finds cached data, it must make sure that those data are up to date, since they may have been updated by a different client after they were cached. Thus, a message must still be exchanged with the server to check validity of the data, and to acquire a lock on the data.

- **Lock caching**. If the use of data is mostly partitioned among the clients, with clients rarely requesting data that are also requested by other clients, locks can also be cached at the client machine. Suppose that a data item is found in the cache, and that the lock required for an access to the data item is also found in the cache. Then, the access can proceed without any communication with the server. However, the server must keep track of cached locks; if a client requests a lock from the server, the server must *call back* all conflicting locks on the data item from any other client machines that have cached the locks. The task becomes more complicated when machine failures are taken into account. This technique differs from lock deescalation in that lock caching is done across transactions; otherwise, the two techniques are similar.

The bibliographic references provide more information about client–server database systems.

16.3 Parallel Systems

Parallel systems improve processing and I/O speeds by using multiple CPUs and disks in parallel. Parallel machines are becoming increasingly common, making the study of parallel database systems correspondingly more important. The driving force behind parallel database systems has been the demands of applications that have to query extremely large databases (of the order of terabytes—that is, 10^{12} bytes) or that have to process an extremely large number of transactions per second (of the order of thousands of transactions per second). Centralized and client–server database systems are not powerful enough to handle such applications.

In parallel processing, many operations are performed simultaneously, as opposed to in serial processing, in which the computational steps are performed sequentially. A *coarse-grain* parallel machine consists of a small number of powerful processors; a *massively parallel* or *fine-grain* machine uses thousands of smaller processors. Most high-end machines today offer some degree of coarse-grain parallelism: Two or four processor machines are common. Massively parallel computers can be distinguished from the coarse-grain parallel machines by the much larger degree of parallelism that they support. Parallel computers with hundreds of CPUs and disks are available commercially.

There are two main measures of performance of a database system. The first is *throughput*: the number of tasks that can be completed in a given time interval. The second is *response time*: the amount of time it takes to complete a single task from the time it is submitted. A system that processes a large number of small transactions can improve throughput by processing many transactions in parallel. A system that processes large transactions can improve response time as well as throughput by performing subtasks of each transaction in parallel.

16.3.1 Speedup and Scaleup

Two important issues in studying parallelism are speedup and scaleup. *Speedup* refers to running a given task in less time by increasing the degree of parallelism. *Scaleup* refers to handling larger tasks by increasing the degree of parallelism.

Consider a database application running on a parallel system with a certain number of processors and disks. Now suppose that we increase the size of the system by increasing the number or processors, disks, and other components of the system. The goal is to process the task in time inversely proportional to the number of processors and disks allocated. Suppose that the execution time of a task on the larger machine is T_L, and that the execution time of the same task on the smaller machine is T_S. The speedup due to parallelism is defined as T_S/T_L.

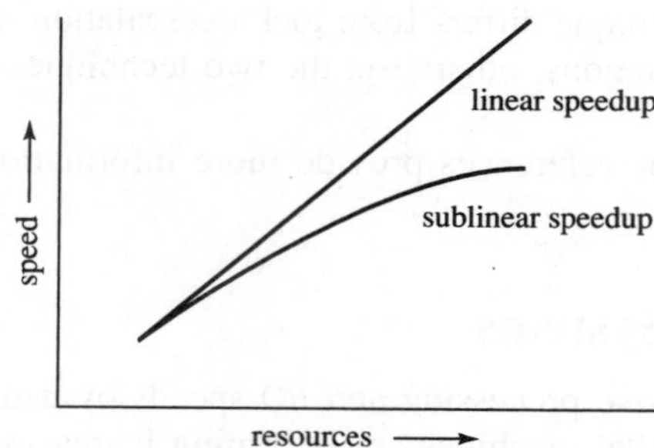

Figure 16.4 Speedup with increasing resources.

The parallel system is said to demonstrate *linear speedup* if the speedup is N when the larger system has N times the resources (CPU, disk, and so on) of the smaller system. If the speedup is less than N, the system is said to demonstrate *sublinear speedup*. Figure 16.4 illustrates linear and sublinear speedup.

Scaleup relates to the ability to process larger tasks in the same amount of time by providing more resources. Let Q be a task, and let Q_N be a task that is N times bigger than Q. Suppose that the execution time of task Q on a given machine M_S is T_S, and the execution time of task Q_N on a parallel machine M_L, which is N times larger than M_S, is T_L. The scaleup is then defined as T_S/T_L. The parallel system M_L is said to demonstrate *linear scaleup* on task Q if $T_L = T_S$. If $T_L > T_S$, the system is said to demonstrate *sublinear scaleup*. Figure 16.5 illustrates linear and sublinear scaleups. There are two kinds of scaleup that are relevant in parallel database systems, depending on how the size of the task is measured:

- In *batch scaleup*, the size of the database increases, and the tasks are large jobs whose runtime depends on the size of the database. An example of such a task is a scan of a relation whose size is proportional to the size of the database. Thus, the size of the database is the measure of the size

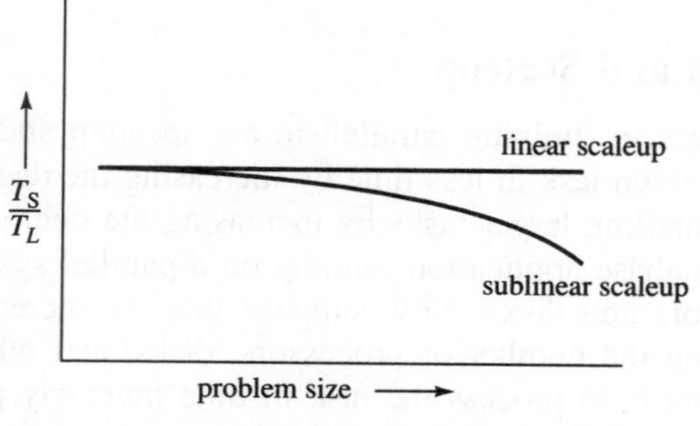

Figure 16.5 Scaleup with increasing problem size.

of the problem. Batch scaleup also applies in scientific applications, such as executing a query at an N-times finer resolution or performing an N-times longer simulation.

- In *transaction scaleup*, the rate at which transactions are submitted to the database increases and the size of the database increases proportional to the transaction rate. This kind of scaleup is what is relevant in transaction-processing systems where the transactions are small updates—for example, a deposit or withdrawal from an account—and transaction rates grow as more accounts are created. Such transaction processing is especially well adapted for parallel execution, since transactions can run concurrently and independently on separate processors, and each transaction takes roughly the same amount of time, even if the database grows.

Scaleup is usually the more important metric for measuring efficiency of parallel database systems. The goal of parallelism in database systems is usually to make sure that the database system can continue to perform at an acceptable speed, even as the size of the database and the number of transactions increases. Increasing the capacity of the system by increasing the parallelism provides a smoother path for growth for a company than does replacing a centralized system by a faster machine (even assuming that such a machine exists). However, we must also look at absolute performance numbers when using scaleup measures; a machine that scales up linearly may perform worse than a machine that scales less than linearly, simply because the latter machine is much faster to start off with.

A number of factors work against efficient parallel operation and can diminish both speedup and scaleup.

- **Startup costs.** There is a startup cost associated with initiating a single process. In a parallel operation consisting of thousands of processes, the *startup time* may overshadow the actual processing time, affecting speedup adversely.
- **Interference.** Since processes executing in a parallel system often access shared resources, a slowdown may result from the *interference* of each new process as it competes with existing processes for commonly held resources, such as a system bus, or shared disks, or even locks. Both speedup and scaleup are affected by this phenomenon.
- **Skew.** By breaking down a single task into a number of parallel steps, we reduce the size of the average step. Nonetheless, the service time for the single slowest step will determine the service time for the task as a whole. It is often difficult to divide a task into exactly equal-sized parts, and the way that the sizes are distributed is therefore *skewed*. For example, if a task of size 100 is divided into 10 parts, and the division is skewed, there may be some tasks of size less than 10 and some tasks of size more than 10; if even one task happens to be of size 20, the speedup obtained by running the tasks in parallel is only five, instead of ten, as we would have hoped.

16.3.2 Interconnection Networks

Parallel systems consist of a set of components (processors, memory and disks) that can communicate with each other via an *interconnection network*. Examples of interconnection networks include:

- **Bus**. All the system components can send data on and receive data from a single communication bus. The bus could be an ethernet, or a parallel interconnect. Bus architectures work well for small numbers of processors. However, they do not scale well with increasing parallelism since the bus can handle communication from only one component at a time.
- **Mesh**. The components are arranged as nodes in a grid, and each component is connected to all its adjacent components in the grid. In a two-dimensional mesh each node is connected to four adjacent nodes, while in a three-dimensional mesh each node is connected to six adjacent nodes. Nodes that are not directly connected can communicate with one another by routing messages via a sequence of intermediate nodes that are directly connected to one another. The number of communication links grows as the number of components grows, and the communication capacity of a mesh therefore scales better with increasing parallelism.
- **Hypercube**. The components are numbered in binary, and a component is connected to another if the binary representations of their numbers differ in exactly one bit. Thus, each of the n components is connected to $log(n)$ other components. It can be verified that in a hypercube interconnection a message from a component can reach any other component by going via at most $log(n)$ links. In contrast, in a mesh a component may be $\sqrt{n} - 1$ links away from some of the other components (or $\sqrt{n}/2$ links away, if the mesh interconnection wraps around at the edges of the grid). Thus communication delays in a hypercube are significantly lower than in a mesh.

16.3.3 Parallel Database Architectures

There are several architectural models for parallel machines. Among the most prominent ones are those shown in Figure 16.6 (in the figure, M denotes memory, P denotes a processor, and disks are shown as cylinders):

- **Shared memory**. All the processors share a common memory. This model is depicted in Figure 16.6a.
- **Shared disk**. All the processors share a common disk. This model is depicted in Figure 16.6b. Shared-disk systems are sometimes called as *clusters*.
- **Shared nothing**. The processors share neither a common memory nor common disk. This model is depicted in Figure 16.6c.
- **Hierarchical**. This model is depicted in Figure 16.6d; it is a hybrid of the preceding architectures.

In Sections 16.3.3.1 through 16.3.3.4, we elaborate on each of these models.

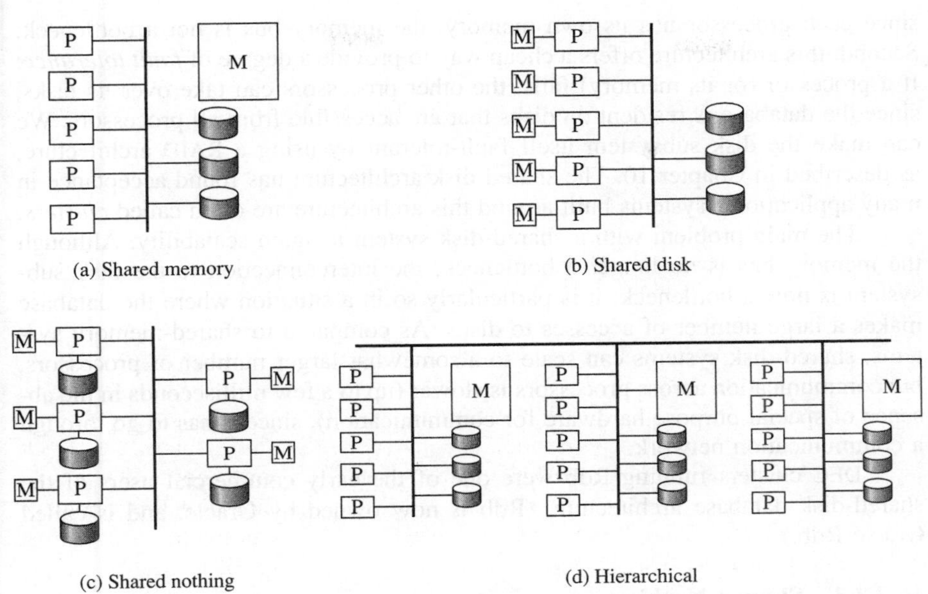

Figure 16.6 Parallel database architectures.

16.3.3.1 Shared Memory

In a shared-memory architecture, the processors and disks have access to a common memory, typically via a bus or through an interconnection network. The benefit of shared memory is extremely efficient communication between processors—data in shared memory can be accessed by any processor without being moved with software. A processor can send messages to other processors using memory writes, which messages are much faster (less than a microsecond usually) than are messages sent with a communication mechanism. The downside of shared-memory machines is that the architecture is not scalable beyond 32 or 64 processors, since the bus or the interconnection network becomes a bottleneck (since it is shared by all processors). Adding more processors does not help after a point, since the processors will spend most of their time waiting for their turn on the bus to access memory. Shared-memory architectures usually have large memory caches at each processor, so that referencing of the shared memory is avoided whenever possible. However, at least some of the data will not be in the cache, and accesses will have to go to the shared memory. Consequently, shared-memory machines are not capable of scaling up beyond a point; current shared-memory machines cannot support more than 64 processors.

16.3.3.2 Shared Disk

In the shared-disk model, all processors can access all disks directly via an interconnection network, but the processors have private memories. There are two benefits for a shared-disk architecture over a shared-memory architecture. First, since each processor has its own memory, the memory bus is not a bottleneck. Second, this architecture offers a cheap way to provide a degree of *fault tolerance*: If a processor (or its memory) fails, the other processors can take over its tasks, since the database is resident on disks that are accessible from all processors. We can make the disk subsystem itself fault-tolerant by using a RAID architecture, as described in Chapter 10. The shared-disk architecture has found acceptance in many applications; systems built around this architecture are often called *clusters*.

The main problem with a shared-disk system is again scalability. Although the memory bus is no longer a bottleneck, the interconnection to the disk subsystem is now a bottleneck; it is particularly so in a situation where the database makes a large number of accesses to disks. As compared to shared-memory systems, shared-disk systems can scale to a somewhat larger number of processors, but communication across processors is slower (up to a few milliseconds in the absence of special purpose hardware for communication), since it has to go through a communication network.

DEC clusters running Rdb were one of the early commercial users of the shared-disk database architecture. (Rdb is now owned by Oracle, and is called Oracle Rdb.)

16.3.3.3 Shared Nothing

In a shared-nothing system, each node of the machine consists of a processor, memory, and one or more disks. The processors at one node may communicate with another processor at another node using a high-speed interconnection network. A node functions as the server for the data on the disk or disks that the node owns. Since local disk references are serviced by local disks at each processor, the shared-nothing model overcomes the disadvantage of requiring all I/O to go through a single interconnection network; only queries, accesses to nonlocal disks, and result relations are passed through the network. Moreover, the interconnection networks for shared-nothing systems are usually designed to be scalable, so that their transmission capacity increases as more nodes are added. Consequently, shared-nothing architectures are more scalable and can easily support a large number of processors. The main drawback of shared-nothing systems are the costs of communication and of nonlocal disk access, which are higher than in a shared-memory or shared-disk architecture since sending data involves software interaction at both ends.

The Teradata database machine was among the earliest commercial systems to use the shared-nothing database architecture. The Grace and the Gamma research prototypes were also built on shared-nothing architectures.

16.3.3.4 Hierarchical

The hierarchical architecture combines the characteristics of shared-memory, shared-disk, and shared-nothing architectures. At the top level, the system consists of nodes that are connected by an interconnection network, and do not share disks or memory with one another. Thus, the top level is a shared-nothing architecture. Each node of the system could actually be a shared-memory system with a few processors. Alternatively, each node could be a shared-disk system, and each of the systems sharing a set of disks could be a shared-memory system. Thus, a system could be built as a hierarchy, with shared-memory architecture with a few processors at the base, and a shared-nothing architecture at the top, with possibly a shared-disk architecture in the middle. Figure 16.6d illustrates a hierarchical architecture with shared-memory nodes connected together in a shared-nothing architecture. Commercial parallel database systems today run on several of these architectures.

Attempts to reduce the complexity of programming such systems have resulted in *distributed virtual-memory* architectures, where logically there is a single shared memory, but physically there are multiple disjoint memory systems; the virtual-memory–mapping hardware coupled with extra software supports a single virtual-memory area view of these disjoint memories.

16.4 Distributed Systems

In a distributed database system, the database is stored on several computers. The computers in a distributed system communicate with one another through various communication media, such as high-speed networks or telephone lines. They do not share main memory or disks. The computers in a distributed system may vary in size and function, ranging from workstations up to mainframe systems.

The computers in a distributed system are referred to by a number of different names, such as *sites* or *nodes*, depending on the context in which they are mentioned. We mainly use the term *site*, to emphasize the physical distribution of these systems. The general structure of a distributed system is shown in Figure 16.7.

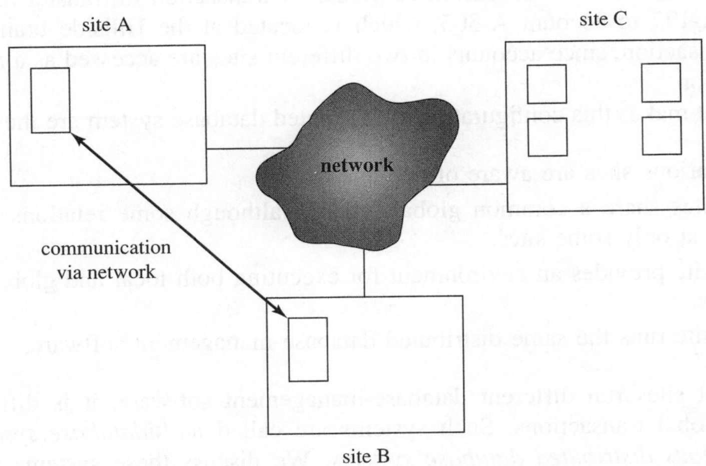

Figure 16.7 A distributed system.

The main differences between shared-nothing parallel databases and distributed databases are that distributed database are typically geographically separated, are separately administered, and have a slower interconnection. Another major difference is that, in a distributed system, we differentiate between *local* and *global* transactions. A local transaction is one that accesses data in the *single* site at that the transaction was initiated. A global transaction, on the other hand, is one which either accesses data in a site different from the one at which the transaction was initiated, or accesses data in several different sites.

16.4.1 Illustrative Example

Consider a banking system consisting of four branches located in four different cities. Each branch has its own computer, with a database consisting of all the accounts maintained at that branch. Each such installation is thus a site. There also exists one single site that maintains information about all the branches of the bank. Each branch maintains (among others) a relation *account*(*Account-schema*), where

Account-schema = (*branch-name*, *account-number*, *balance*)

The site containing information about the four branches maintains the relation *branch*(*Branch-schema*), where

Branch-schema = (*branch-name*, *branch-city*, *assets*)

There are other relations maintained at the various sites; we ignore them for the purpose of our example.

To illustrate the difference between the two types of transactions, we consider the transaction to add $50 to account number A-177 located at the Valleyview branch. If the transaction was initiated at the Valleyview branch, then it is considered local; otherwise, it is considered global. A transaction to transfer $50 from account A-177 to account A-305, which is located at the Hillside branch, is a global transaction, since accounts in two different sites are accessed as a result of its execution.

What makes this configuration a distributed database system are these facts:

- The various sites are aware of one another.
- The sites share a common global schema, although some relations may be stored at only some sites.
- Each site provides an environment for executing both local and global transactions.
- Each site runs the same distributed database-management software.

If different sites run different database-management software, it is difficult to manage global transactions. Such systems are called *multidatabase systems* or *heterogeneous distributed database systems*. We discuss these systems in Section 18.9, where we show how to achieve a degree of global control despite the heterogeneity of the component systems.

16.4.2 Tradeoffs

There are several reasons for building distributed database systems, including sharing of data, autonomy, and availability.

- **Sharing data.** The major advantage in building a distributed database system is the provision of an environment where users at one site may be able to access the data residing at other sites. For instance, in the distributed banking-system example from Section 16.4.1, it is possible for a user in one branch to access data in another branch. Without this capability, a user wishing to transfer funds from one branch to another would have to resort to some external mechanism that would couple existing systems.
- **Autonomy.** The primary advantage of sharing data by means of data distribution is that each site is able to retain a degree of control over data that are stored locally. In a centralized system, the database administrator of the central site controls the database. In a distributed system, there is a global database administrator responsible for the entire system. A part of these responsibilities is delegated to the local database administrator for each site. Depending up the design of the distributed database system, each administrator may have a different degree of *local autonomy*. The possibility of local autonomy is often a major advantage of distributed databases.
- **Availability.** If one site fails in a distributed system, the remaining sites may be able to continue operating. In particular, if data items are replicated in several sites, a transaction needing a particular data item may find that item in any of several sites. Thus, the failure of a site does not necessarily imply the shutdown of the system.

  The failure of one site must be detected by the system, and appropriate action may be needed to recover from the failure. The system must no longer use the services of the failed site. Finally, when the failed site recovers or is repaired, mechanisms must be available to integrate it smoothly back into the system.

  Although recovery from failure is more complex in distributed systems than in centralized systems, the ability of most of the system to continue to operate despite the failure of one site results in increased availability. Availability is crucial for database systems used for real-time applications. Loss of access to data by, for example, an airline may result in the loss of potential ticket buyers to competitors.

The primary disadvantage of distributed database systems is the added complexity required to ensure proper coordination among the sites. This increased complexity takes various forms:

- **Software-development cost**. It is more difficult to implement a distributed database system; thus, it is more costly.
- **Greater potential for bugs**. Since the sites that constitute the distributed system operate in parallel, it is harder to ensure the correctness of algorithms,

especially operation during failures of part of the system, and recovery from failures. The potential exists for extremely subtle bugs.

- **Increased processing overhead**. The exchange of messages and the additional computation required to achieve intersite coordination are a form of overhead that does not arise in centralized systems.

In choosing the design for a database system, the designer must balance the advantages against the disadvantages of distribution of data. There are several approaches to distributed database design, ranging from fully distributed designs to ones that include a large degree of centralization. We study them in Chapter 18.

16.5 Network Types

Distributed databases and client–server systems are built around communication networks. There are basically two types of networks: *local-area networks* and *wide-area networks*. The main difference between the two is the way in which they are distributed geographically. Local-area networks are composed of processors that are distributed over small geographical areas, such as a single building or a number of adjacent buildings. Wide-area networks, on the other hand, are composed of a number of autonomous processors that are distributed over a large geographical area (such as the United States, or the entire world). These differences imply major variations in the speed and reliability of the communication network, and are reflected in the distributed operating-system design.

16.5.1 Local-Area Networks

Local-area networks (LANs) emerged in the early 1970s, as a way for computers to communicate and to share data with one another. People recognized that, for many enterprises, numerous small computers, each with its own self-contained applications, are more economical than a single large system. Because each small computer is likely to need access to a full complement of peripheral devices (such as disks and printers), and because some form of data sharing is likely to occur in a single enterprise, it was a natural step to connect these small systems into a network.

LANs are usually designed to cover a small geographical area (such as a single building, or a few adjacent buildings) and are generally used in an office environment. All the sites in such systems are close to one another, so the communication links tend to have a higher speed and lower error rate than do their counterparts in wide-area networks. The most common links in a local-area network are twisted pair, baseband coaxial cable, broadband coaxial cable, and fiber optics. Communication speeds range from 1 megabyte per second, for networks such as Appletalk and IBM's slow token ring, to 1 gigabit per second for experimental optical networks. Ten megabits per second is most common, and is the speed of the standard Ethernet. The optical-fiber–based FDDI network and Fast Ethernet run at 100 megabits per second. Networks based on a protocol called

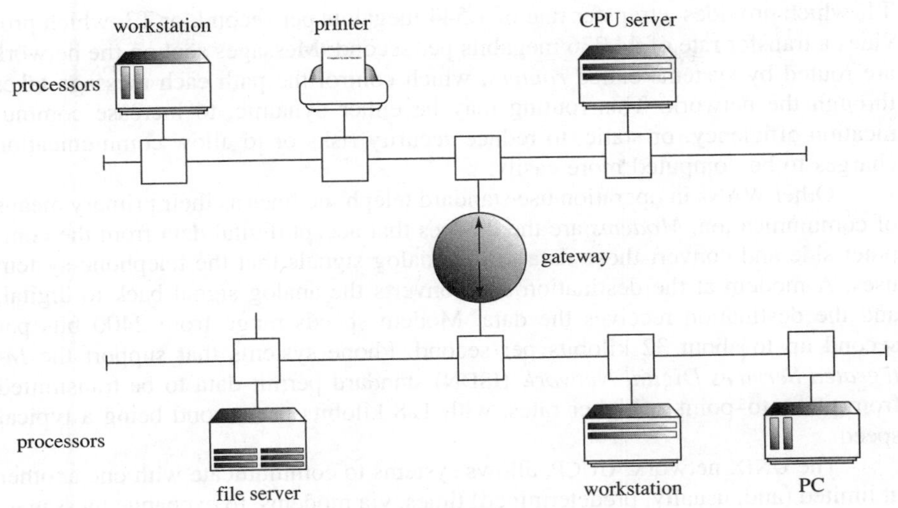

Figure 16.8 Local-area network.

asynchronous transfer mode (*ATM*) can run at even higher speeds, such as 144 megabits per second, and are growing in popularity.

A typical LAN may consist of a number of different workstations, one or more server systems, various shared peripheral devices (such as laser printers or magnetic-tape units), and one or more gateways (specialized processors) that provide access to other networks (Figure 16.8). An Ethernet scheme is commonly used to construct LANs.

16.5.2 Wide-Area Networks

Wide-area networks (WANs) emerged in the late 1960s, mainly as an academic research project to provide efficient communication among sites, allowing hardware and software to be shared conveniently and economically by a wide community of users. Systems that allowed remote terminals to be connected to a central computer via telephone lines were developed in the early 1960s, but they were not true WANs. The first WAN to be designed and developed was the *Arpanet*. Work on the Arpanet began in 1968. The Arpanet has grown from a four-site experimental network to a worldwide network of networks, the Internet, comprising millions of computer systems. Typical links in a WAN are telephone circuits, which are carried on fiber-optic lines and (sometimes) satellite channels.

As an example, let us consider the Internet network, which connects computers across the globe. The system provides an ability for hosts at geographically separated sites to communicate with one another. The host computers typically differ from one another in type, speed, word length, operating system, and so on. Hosts are generally on LANs, which are connected to regional networks. The regional networks are interlinked with routers to form the worldwide network. Connections between networks frequently use a telephone-system service called

T1, which provides a transfer rate of 1.544 megabits per second, or T3, which provides a transfer rate of 44.736 megabits per second. Messages sent on the network are routed by systems called *routers*, which control the path each message takes through the network. This routing may be either dynamic, to increase communication efficiency, or static, to reduce security risks or to allow communication charges to be computed more easily.

Other WANs in operation use standard telephone lines as their primary means of communication. *Modems* are the devices that accept digital data from the computer side and convert those data to the analog signals that the telephone system uses. A modem at the destination site converts the analog signal back to digital, and the destination receives the data. Modem speeds range from 2400 bits per second up to about 32 kilobits per second. Phone systems that support the *Integrated Services Digital Network* (ISDN) standard permit data to be transmitted from point–to–point at higher rates, with 128 kilobits per second being a typical speed.

The UNIX network, UUCP, allows systems to communicate with one another at limited (and, usually, predetermined) times, via modems, to exchange messages. The messages are then routed to other nearby systems and, in this way, either are propagated to all hosts on the network (public messages) or are transferred to their destination (private messages).

WANs can be classified into two types:

- In **discontinuous connection** WANs, such as those based on UUCP, hosts are connected to the network only part of the time.
- In **continuous connection** WANs, such as the Internet, hosts are connected to the network at all times.

The design of distributed database systems is influenced strongly by the type of underlying WAN. True distributed database systems can run on only those networks that are connected continuously—at least during the hours when the distributed database is operational.

Networks that are not continuously connected typically do not allow transactions across sites, but may keep local copies of remote data, and refresh the copies periodically (every night, for instance). For applications where consistency is not critical, such as sharing of documents, groupware systems such as Lotus Notes allow updates of remote data to be made locally, and the updates are then propagated back to the remote site periodically. There is a potential for conflicting updates at different sites, which have to be detected and resolved. A mechanism for detecting conflicting updates is described later, in Section 21.7.4; the resolution mechanism for conflicting updates is, however, application dependent.

16.6 Summary

Centralized database systems run entirely on a single computer. All database systems were initially centralized. With the growth of personal computers and local-area networking, the database front-end functionality has been moved increasingly to clients, and the back-end functionality is provided by server systems. Client–server interface protocols have helped the growth of client–server database systems. Servers can be either transaction servers or data servers.

Parallel database systems consist of multiple processors and multiple disks connected by a fast interconnection network. Speedup measures how much we can increase processing speed by increasing parallelism, for a single transaction. Scaleup measures how well we can handle an increased number of transactions by increasing parallelism. Parallel database architectures include the shared-memory, shared-disk, shared-nothing, and hierarchical architectures. These architectures have different tradeoffs on scalability versus communication speed.

A distributed database is a collection of partially independent databases that share a common schema, and coordinate processing of transactions that access nonlocal data. The processors communicate with one another through a communication network that handles routing and connection strategies.

Principally, there are two types of communication networks: local-area networks and wide-area networks. Local-area networks are composed of processors that are distributed over small geographical areas, such as a single building or a few adjacent buildings. Wide-area networks are composed of processors distributed over a large geographical area. Computers in a wide-area network may be connected to one another continuously or only periodically, such as once per day or a few times per day.

Exercises

16.1. Why is it relatively easy to port a database from a single processor machine to a multi-processor machine if individual queries need not be parallelized?

16.2. Transaction server architectures are popular for client-server relational databases, where transactions are short. On the other hand, data server architectures are popular for client-server object-oriented database systems, where transactions are expected to be relatively long. Give two reasons why data servers may be popular for object-oriented databases but not for relational databases.

16.3. In typical client-server systems the server machine is much more powerful than the clients, that is, its processor is faster, it may have multiple processors, and it has more memory and disk capacity. Consider instead a scenario where client and server machines have exactly the same power. Would it make sense to build a client-server system in such a scenario? Why? Which scenario would be better suited to a data-server architecture?

16.4. Consider an object-oriented database system based on a client-server architecture, with the server acting as a data server.

(*a*) What is effect of the speed of the interconnection between the client and the server on the choice between object and page shipping?

(*b*) If page shipping is used, the cache of data at the client can be organized either as an object cache or a page cache. The page cache stores data in units of a page, while the object cache stores data in units of objects.

Assume objects are smaller than a page. Describe one benefit of an object cache over a page cache.

16.5. What is lock de-escalation, and under what conditions is it required? Why is it not required if the unit of data shipping is an item?

16.6. Suppose you were in charge of the database operations of a company whose main job is to process transactions. Suppose the company is growing rapidly each year, and has outgrown its current computer system. When you are choosing a new parallel computer, what measure is most relevant—speedup, batch scale-up, or transaction scale-up? Why?

16.7. Suppose a transaction is written in C with embedded SQL, and about 80 percent of the time is spent in the SQL code, with the remaining 20 percent spent in C code. How much speedup can one hope to attain if parallelism is used only for the SQL code? Explain.

16.8. What are the factors that can work against linear scale-up in a transaction processing system? Which of the factors are likely to be the most important in each of the following architectures: shared memory, shared disk, and shared nothing?

16.9. Consider a bank which has a collection of sites, each running a database system. Suppose the only way the databases interact is by electronic transfer of money between one another. Would such a system qualify as a distributed database? Why?

16.10. Consider a network based on dial-up phone lines, where sites communicate periodically, such as every night. Such networks are often configured with a server site and multiple client sites. The client sites connect only to the server, and exchange data with other clients by storing data at the server and retrieving data stored at the server by other clients. What is the advantage of such an architecture over one where a site can exchange data with another site only by first dialing it up?

Bibliographic Notes

The textbooks of Patterson and Hennessy [1995] and Stone [1993] provide a good introduction to the area of computer architecture.

Gray and Reuter [1993] provides a textbook description of transaction processing, including the architecture of client-server and distributed systems. Geiger [1995] and Signore et al. [1995] describe the ODBC standard for client-server connectivity. North [1995] describes the use of a variety of tools for client-server database access.

Carey et al. [1991] and Franklin et al. [1993] describe data-caching techniques for client-server database systems. Biliris and Orenstein [1994] survey object storage management systems, including client-server related issues. Franklin et al. [1992] and Mohan and Narang [1994] describe recovery techniques for client-server systems.

A survey of parallel computer architectures is presented by Duncan [1990]. General discussions concerning multiprocessing are given by Jones and Schwarz

[1980]. Multiprocessor hardware is discussed by Satyanarayanan [1980]. Performance of multiprocessor systems is presented by Agrawal et al. [1986] and Bhuyan et al. [1989]. Dubois and Thakkar [1992] is a collection of papers on scalable shared-memory architectures.

DeWitt and Gray [1992] describe parallel database systems, including their architecture and performance measures. Ceri and Pelagatti [1984] and Bell and Grimson [1992] provide textbook coverage of distributed database systems. Further references pertaining to parallel and distributed database systems appear in the bibliographic notes of Chapters 17 and 18, respectively.

Comer [1995] and Thomas [1996] describe the computer networking and the Internet. Tanenbaum [1996] and Halsall [1992] provided general overviews of computer networks. Fortier [1989] presented a detailed discussion of networking hardware and software. Discussions concerning ATM Networks and switches are offered by Prycker [1993]. The general state of networks is described by Quarterman [1990].

CHAPTER 17

PARALLEL DATABASES

In this chapter, we discuss fundamental algorithms used in parallel database systems that are based on the relational data model. In particular, we focus on the placement of data on multiple disks and the parallel evaluation of relational operations, which have been instrumental in the success of parallel databases.

17.1 Introduction

In the past decade, parallel database systems have advanced from being nearly written off by even some of their staunchest advocates, to being successfully marketed by companies such as Teradata, Tandem, and Oracle. Fueling this transition are the following trends:

- The transaction requirements of organizations have grown with increasing use of computers.
- Organizations are using increasingly large volumes of transaction processing data—such as data about what items people buy, or when people make telephone calls—to plan their activities and pricing. Queries used for such purposes are called *decision-support* queries, and the data requirements for such queries may run into terabytes. Single-processor systems are not capable of handling such large volumes of data at the required rates.
- Commercial parallel database systems, such as the Teradata DBC series of computers, and research systems, such as Grace and Gamma, have clearly demonstrated the feasibility of parallel database queries. In fact, the set-oriented nature of database queries naturally lends itself to parallelization.

- With microprocessors having become cheap, parallel machines have become common and relatively inexpensive.

As we discussed in Chapter 16, parallelism is used to provide speedup, where queries are executed faster because more resources, such as processors and disks, are provided. Parallelism is also used to provide scaleup, where increasing workloads are handled without increased response time, via an increase in the degree of parallelism.

We outlined in Chapter 16 the different architectures for parallel database systems: shared-memory, shared-disk, shared-nothing, and hierarchical architectures. Briefly, in shared-memory architectures, all processors share a common memory and disks; in shared-disk architectures, processors have independent memories, but share disks; in shared-nothing architectures, processors share neither memory nor disks; and hierarchical architectures have nodes that share neither memory nor disks with each other, but internally each node has a shared-memory or a shared-disk architecture.

17.2 I/O Parallelism

In it simplest form, *I/O parallelism* refers to reducing the time required to retrieve relations from disk by partitioning the relations on multiple disks. The most common form of data partitioning in a parallel database environment is *horizontal partitioning*. In horizontal partitioning, the tuples of a relation are divided (or declustered) among many disks, such that each tuple resides on one disk. Several partitioning strategies have been proposed.

17.2.1 Partitioning Techniques

We present three basic data-partitioning strategies. We assume that there are n disks, $D_0, D_1, \ldots, D_{n-1}$, across which the data are to be partitioned.

- *Round-robin*. The relation is scanned in any order and the ith tuple is sent to disk numbered $D_{i \ mod \ n}$. The round-robin scheme ensures an even distribution of tuples across disks; that is, each disk has approximately the same number of tuples as do the others.
- *Hash partitioning*. In this declustering strategy, one or more attributes from the given relation's schema are designated as the partitioning attributes. A hash function is chosen whose range is $\{0, 1, \ldots, n-1\}$. Each tuple of the original relation is hashed on the partitioning attributes. If the hash function returns i, then the tuple is placed on disk D_i.
- *Range partitioning*. This strategy distributes contiguous attribute-value ranges to each disk. A partitioning attribute, A, is chosen, as is a *partitioning vector*. Let $[v_0, v_1, \ldots, v_{n-2}]$ denote the partitioning vector, such that, if $i < j$, then $v_i < v_j$. The relation is partitioned as follows. Consider a tuple t such that $t[A] = x$. If $x < v_0$, then t is placed on disk D_0. If $x \geq v_{n-2}$, then t is placed on disk D_{n-1}. If $v_i \leq x < v_{i+1}$, then t is placed on disk D_{i+1}.

17.2.2 Comparison of Partitioning Techniques

Once a relation has been partitioned among several disks, we can retrieve it in parallel using all the disks. Similarly, when a relation is being partitioned, it can be written to multiple disks in parallel. Thus, the transfer rates for reading or writing an entire relation are much faster with I/O parallelism than without it. However, reading an entire relation, or *scanning a relation*, is only one kind of access to data. Access to data can be classified as follows:

1. Scanning the entire relation
2. Locating a tuple associatively, (for example, *employee-name* = "Campbell"); these queries, called *point* queries, seek tuples that have a specified value for a specific attribute
3. Locating all tuples such that the value of a given attribute lies within a specified range (for example, $10000 < salary < 20000$); these queries are called *range* queries

The different partitioning techniques support these types of access at different levels of efficiency:

- *Round-robin*. The scheme is ideally suited for applications that wish to read the entire relation sequentially for each query. However, with this scheme, both point queries and range queries are complicated to process, since each of the n disks must be used for the search.
- *Hash partitioning*. This scheme is best suited for point queries based on the partitioning attribute. For example, if a relation is partitioned on the *telephone-number* attribute, then we can answer the query "Find the record of the employee with *telephone-number* = 555-3333" by applying the partitioning hash function to 555-3333 and then searching that disk. Directing a query to a single disk saves the startup cost of initiating a query on multiple disks, and leaves the other disks free to process other queries.

  Hash partitioning is also useful for sequential scans of the entire relation. If the hash function is a good randomizing function, and the partitioning attributes form a key of the relation, then the number of tuples in each of the disks is approximately the same, without much variance. Hence, the time taken to scan the relation is approximately $1/n$ of the time required to scan the relation in a single disk system.

  The scheme, however, is not well suited for point queries on nonpartitioning attributes. Hash-based partitioning is also not well suited for answering range queries, since, typically, hash functions do not preserve proximity within a range. Therefore, all the disks need to be scanned for range queries to be answered.
- *Range partitioning*. This scheme is well-suited for point and range queries on the partitioning attribute. For point queries, we can consult the partitioning vector to locate the disk where the tuple resides. For range queries, we consult the partitioning vector to find the range of disks on which the tuples may

reside. In both cases, the search is narrowed to exactly those disks that might have any tuples of interest.

This feature is both an advantage and a disadvantage. The advantage is that, if there are only a few tuples in the queried range, then the query is typically sent to one disk, as opposed to all the disks. Since other disks can be used to answer other queries, range partitioning results in higher throughput while maintaining good response time. On the other hand, if there are many tuples in the queried range (as there are when the queried range is a larger fraction of the domain of the relation), many tuples have to be retrieved from a few disks, resulting in an I/O bottleneck (hot spot) at those disks. In this example of *execution skew*, all processing occurs in one—or only a few—partitions. In contrast, hash partitioning and round-robin partitioning would engage all the disks for such queries, giving a faster response time for approximately the same throughput.

The type of partitioning also affects other relational operations, such as joins, as we shall see in Section 17.5. Thus, the choice of partitioning technique also depends on the operations that need to be executed. In general, hash partitioning or range partitioning are preferred to round-robin partitioning.

In a system with many disks, the number of disks across which to partition a relation can be chosen as follows. If a relation contains only a few tuples that will fit into a single disk block, then it is better to assign the relation to a single disk. Large relations are preferably partitioned across all the available disks. If a relation consists of m disk blocks and there are n disks available in the system, then the relation should be allocated $\mathbf{min}(m, n)$ disks.

17.2.3 Handling of Skew

The distribution of tuples when a relation is partitioned (except for round-robin) may be skewed, with a high percentage of tuples placed in some partitions and fewer tuples in other partitions. The ways that skew may appear are classified as follows:

- Attribute-value skew
- Partition skew

Attribute-value skew refers to the fact that some values appear in the partitioning attributes of many tuples. All the tuples with the same value for the partitioning attribute end up in the same partition, resulting in skew. *Partition skew* refers to the fact that there may be load imbalance in the partitioning, even when there is no attribute skew.

Attribute-value skew can result in skewed partitioning regardless of whether range partitioning or hash partitioning is used. If the partition vector is not chosen carefully, range partitioning may result in partition skew. Partition skew is less likely with hash partitioning, if a good hash function is chosen.

As we noted in Section 16.3.1, even a small skew can result in a significant decrease in performance. Skew becomes an increasing problem with a higher degree of parallelism. For example, if a relation of 1000 tuples is divided into 10 parts, and the division is skewed, then there may be some partitions of size less than 100 and some partitions of size more than 100; if even one partition happens to be of size 200, the speedup that we would obtain by accessing the partitions in parallel is only five, instead of the ten for which we would have hoped. If the same relation has to be partitioned into 100 parts, a partition will have 10 tuples on an average. If even one partition has 40 tuples (which is possible, given the large number of partitions) the speedup that we would obtain by accessing them in parallel would be 25, rather than 100. Thus, we see that the loss of speedup due to skew increases with parallelism.

If the partitioning attributes form a key for the relation, a good range-partitioning vector can be constructed by means of sorting, as follows. The relation is first sorted on the partitioning attributes. The relation is then scanned in sorted order. After every $1/n$ of the relation has been read, the value of the partitioning attribute of the next tuple is added to the partition vector. Here, n denotes the number of partitions to be constructed. The disadvantage of this method is the extra I/O overhead incurred in doing the initial sort.

17.3 Interquery Parallelism

In *interquery parallelism*, different queries or transactions execute in parallel with one another. Transaction throughput can be increased by this form of parallelism. However, the response times of individual transactions are no faster than they would be if the transactions were run run in isolation. Thus, the primary use of interquery parallelism is to scale up a transaction-processing system to support a larger number of transactions per second.

Interquery parallelism is the easiest form of parallelism to support in a database system—particularly in a shared-memory parallel system. Database systems designed for single-processor systems can be used with few or no changes on a shared-memory parallel architecture, since even sequential database systems support concurrent processing. Transactions that would have operated in a time-shared concurrent manner on a sequential machine operate in parallel in the shared-memory parallel architecture.

Supporting interquery parallelism is more complicated in a shared-disk or shared-nothing architecture. Processors have to perform some tasks, such as locking and logging, in a coordinated fashion, and that requires that they pass messages to each other. A parallel database system must also ensure that two processors do not update the same data independently at the same time. Further, when a processor accesses or updates data, the database system must ensure that the processor has the latest version of the data in its buffer pool. The latter problem is known as the *cache-coherency* problem.

Various protocols have been developed to guarantee cache coherency; often, cache-coherency protocols are integrated with concurrency-control protocols so that their overhead is reduced. One such protocol for a shared-disk system is as follows:

1. Before any read or write access to a page, a transaction locks the page in shared or exclusive mode, as appropriate. Immediately after the transaction obtains either a shared or exclusive lock on a page, it also reads the most recent copy of the page from the shared disk.
2. Before a transaction releases an exclusive lock on a page, it flushes the page to the shared disk; then, it releases the lock.

The preceding protocol ensures that, when a transaction sets a shared or exclusive lock on a page, it gets the correct copy of the page.

More complex protocols have been developed to avoid the repeated reading and writing to disk required by the preceding protocol. With such protocols, pages are not written to disk when exclusive locks are released. When a shared or exclusive lock is obtained, if the most recent version of a page is in the buffer pool of some processor, the page is obtained from there. The protocols have to be designed to handle concurrent requests. The shared-disk protocols can be extended to shared-nothing architectures as follows. Each page has a *home* processor P_i, and is stored on disk D_i. When other processors want to read or write the page, they send requests to the home processor P_i of the page, since they cannot directly communicate with the disk. The other actions are the same as in the shared-disk protocols.

The Oracle 7 and Oracle Rdb systems are examples of shared-disk parallel database systems that support interquery parallelism.

17.4 Intraquery Parallelism

Intraquery parallelism refers to the execution of a single query in parallel on multiple processors and disks. Using intraquery parallelism is important for speeding up long-running queries. Interquery parallelism does not help in this task, since each query is run sequentially.

To illustrate the parallel evaluation of a query, we consider a query that requires a relation to be sorted. Suppose that the relation has been partitioned across multiple disks by range partitioning on some attribute, and the sort is requested on the partitioning attribute. The sort operation can be implemented as follows: each partition is sorted in parallel, and the sorted partitions are concatenated to get the final sorted relation.

Thus, we can parallelize a query by parallelizing individual operations. There is another source of parallelism in evaluating a query: The *operator tree* for a query can contain multiple operations. We can parallelize the evaluation of the operator tree by evaluating in parallel some of the operations that do not depend on one another. Further, as mentioned in Chapter 12, we may be able to pipeline the output of one operation to another operation. The two operations can be executed in parallel on separate processors, one generating output that is consumed by the other, even as it is generated.

In summary, the execution of a single query can be parallelized in two ways:

- *Intraoperation parallelism.* We can speed up processing of a query by parallelizing the execution of each individual operation, such as sort, select, project, and join. We consider intra-operation parallelism in Section 17.5.
- *Interoperation parallelism.* We can speed up processing of a query by executing in parallel the different operations in a query expression. We consider this form of parallelism in Section 17.6.

The two forms of parallelism are complementary, and can be used simultaneously on a query. Since the number of operations in a typical query is small, compared to the number of tuples processed by each operation, the first form of parallelism can scale better with increasing parallelism. However, with the relatively small number of processors in typical parallel systems today, both forms of parallelism are important.

In the following discussion on parallelization of queries, we assume that the queries are *read only*. The choice of algorithms for parallelizing query evaluation depends on the machine architecture. Rather than presenting algorithms for each architecture separately, we use a shared-nothing architecture model in our description. Thus, we explicitly describe when data have to be transferred from one processor to another. We can simulate this model easily using the other architectures, since transfer of data can be done via shared-memory in a shared-memory architecture, and via shared disks in a shared-disk architecture. Hence, algorithms for shared-nothing architectures can be used on the other architectures too. We mention occasionally how the algorithms can be further optimized for shared-memory or shared-disk systems.

To simplify the presentation of the algorithms, we assume that there are n processors, $P_0, \ldots, P_{n-1}$, and n disks $D_0, \ldots, D_{n-1}$, where disk D_i is associated with processor P_i. A real system may have multiple disks per processor. It is not hard to extend the algorithms to allow multiple disks per processor: We simply allow D_i to be a set of disks. However, for simplicity of presentation, we assume here that D_i is a single disk.

17.5 Intraoperation Parallelism

Since relational operations work on relations containing large sets of tuples, we can parallelize the operations by executing them in parallel on different subsets of the relations. Since the number of tuples in a relation can be large, the degree of parallelism is potentially enormous. Thus, intraoperation parallelism is natural in a database system. We shall study parallel versions of some common relational operations in Sections 17.5.1 through 17.5.3.

17.5.1 Parallel Sort

Suppose that we wish to sort a relation that resides on n disks $D_0, D_1, \ldots, D_{n-1}$. If the relation has been range partitioned on the attributes on which it is to be sorted, then, as we noted in Section 17.2.2, we can sort each partition separately, and can concatenate the results to get the full sorted relation. Since the tuples are partitioned on n disks, the time required for reading the entire relation is reduced due to parallel access.

If the relation has been partitioned in any other way, we can sort it in one of two ways:

1. We can range partition it on the sort attributes, and then sort each partition separately
2. We can use a parallel version of the external sort–merge algorithm

17.5.1.1 Range-Partitioning Sort

When we sort by range partitioning the relation, it is not necessary to range partition the relation on the same processors or disks as those on which that relation is stored. Suppose that we choose processors $P_0, \ldots, P_m$, where $m < n$ to sort the relation. There are two steps involved in this operation:

1. We redistribute the relation using a range-partition strategy, such that all tuples that lie within the ith range are sent to processor P_i, which stores the relation temporarily on disk D_i. This step requires disk I/O and communication overhead.
2. Each of the processors sorts its partition of the relation locally, without interaction with the other processors. Each processor executes the same operation—namely, sorting—on a different data set. (Execution of the same operation in parallel on different sets of data is called *data parallelism.*)

   The final merge operation is trivial, because the range partitioning in the first phase ensures that, for $1 \leq i < j \leq m$, the key values in processor P_i are all less than the key values in P_j.

As we noted earlier in Section 17.2.3, we must do range partitioning using a load-balanced partition vector, so that each partition will have approximately the same number of tuples.

17.5.1.2 Parallel External Sort–Merge

Using *parallel external sort–merge* is an alternative to range partitioning. Suppose that the relation has already been partitioned among disks $D_0, \ldots, D_{n-1}$ (it does not matter how the relation has been partitioned). Parallel external sort–merge then works as follows:

1. Each processor P_i locally sorts the data on disk D_i.
2. The sorted runs on each processor are then merged to get the final sorted output.

The merging of the sorted runs in step 2 can be parallelized as follows:

1. The sorted partitions at each processor P_i are range partitioned (using the same partition vector) across the processors $P_0, \ldots, P_{m-1}$. The tuples are sent in sorted order, so that each processor receives the tuples in sorted streams.
2. Each processor P_i performs a merge on the streams as they are received, to get a single sorted run.
3. The sorted runs on processors $P_0, \ldots, P_{m-1}$ are concatenated to get the final result.

Some machines, such as the Teradata DBC series machines, use specialized hardware to perform merging. The Y-net interconnection network in the Teradata DBC machines can merge output from multiple processors to give a single sorted output.

17.5.2 Parallel Join

The join operation requires that we test pairs of tuples to see whether they satisfy the join condition; if they do, the pair is added to the join output. Parallel join algorithms attempt to split over several processors the pairs to be tested. Each processor then computes part of the join locally. Then, we collect the results from each processor to produce the final result.

17.5.2.1 Partitioned Join

For certain kinds of joins, such as equi-joins and natural joins, it is possible to *partition* the two input relations across the processors, and to compute the join locally at each processor. Suppose that we are using n processors, and that the relations to be joined are r and s. Then, the relations are each partitioned into n partitions, denoted $r_0, r_1, \ldots, r_{n-1}$ and $s_0, s_1, \ldots, s_{n-1}$. The partitions r_i and s_i are sent to processor P_i, where their join is computed locally.

The preceding technique works correctly only if the join is an equi-join (for example, $r \bowtie_{r.A=s.B} s$), and, if we partition r and s using the same partitioning function on their join attributes. The idea of partitioning is exactly the same as the idea behind the partitioning step of hash–join. However, there are two different ways of partitioning r and s:

- Range partitioning on the join attributes
- Hash partitioning on the join attributes

In either case, the same partitioning function must be used for both relations. For range partitioning, the same partition vector must be used for both relations. For hash-partitioning, this means that the same hash function must be used on both relations. Figure 17.1 depicts the partitioning used in a partitioned parallel join.

Once the relations are partitioned, we can use any join technique locally at each processor P_i to compute the join of r_i and s_i. For example, hash–join,

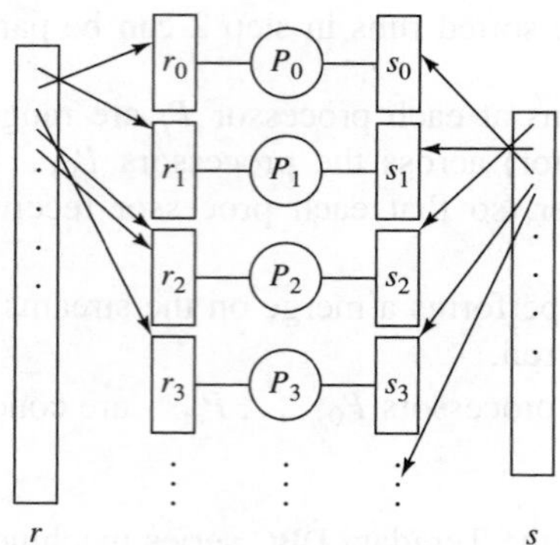

Figure 17.1 Partitioned parallel join.

merge–join, or nested-loop join could be used. Thus, we can use partitioning to parallelize any join technique.

If one or both of the relations r and s are already partitioned on the join attributes (via either hash partitioning or range partitioning), the work needed for partitioning is reduced greatly. If the relations are not partitioned, or are partitioned on attributes other than the join attributes, then the tuples need to be repartitioned. Each processor P_i reads in the tuples on disk D_i, computes for each tuple t the partition j to which t belongs, and sends tuple t to processor P_j. Processor P_j stores the tuples on disk D_j.

We can optimize the join algorithm used locally at each processor to reduce I/O by not writing some of the tuples to disk, but instead buffering them in memory. We describe such optimizations in Section 17.5.2.3.

Skew presents a special problem when range partitioning is used, since a partition vector that splits one relation of the join into equal-sized partitions may split the other relations into partitions of widely varying size. The partition vector should be such that $| r_i | + | s_i |$ (that is, the sum of the sizes of r_i and s_i) is roughly equal over all the $i = 0, 1, \ldots, n-1$. With a good hash function, hash partitioning is likely to have a smaller skew, except when there are many tuples with the same values for the join attributes.

17.5.2.2 Fragment-and-Replicate Join

Partitioning is not applicable to all types of joins. For instance, if the join condition is an inequality, such as $r \bowtie_{r.a<s.b} s$, it is possible that all tuples in r join with some tuple in s (and vice versa). Thus, there may be no nontrivial means of partitioning r and s such that tuples in partition r_i join with only tuples in partition s_i.

We can parallelize such joins using a technique called *fragment and replicate*. We first consider a special case of fragment and replicate—*asymmetric fragment-and-replicate*—which works as follows.

1. One of the relations—say, r—is partitioned. Any partitioning technique can be used on r, including round-robin partitioning.

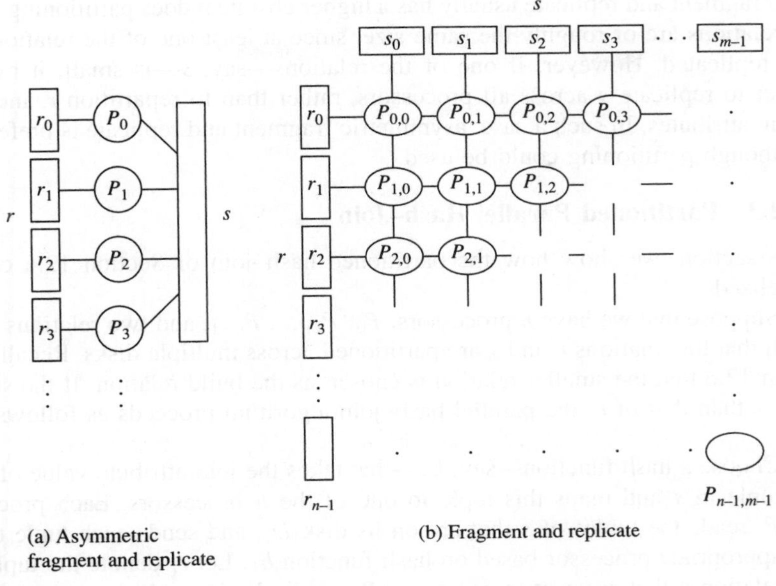

(a) Asymmetric fragment and replicate (b) Fragment and replicate

Figure 17.2 Fragment-and-replicate schemes.

2. The other relation, s, is replicated across all the processors.
3. Processor P_i then locally computes the join of r_i with all of s, using any join technique.

The asymmetric fragment-and-replicate scheme is shown in Figure 17.2a. If r is already stored by partitioning, there is no need to partition it further in step 1. All that is required is to replicate s across all processors.

The general case of fragment and replicate is shown in Figure 17.2b; it works as follows. Relation r is partitioned into n partitions, $r_0, r_1, \ldots, r_{n-1}$, and s is partitioned into m partitions, $s_0, s_1, \ldots, s_{m-1}$. As before, any partitioning technique may be used on r and on s. The values of m and n do not need to be equal, but they must be chosen such that there are at least $m * n$ processors. Asymmetric fragment and replicate is simply a special case of general fragment and replicate, where $m = 1$. Fragment and replicate reduces the sizes of the relations at each processor, as compared to asymmetric fragment and replicate.

Let us label the processors as $P_{0,0}, P_{0,1}, \ldots, P_{0,m-1}, P_{1,0}, \ldots, P_{n-1,m-1}$. Processor $P_{i,j}$ computes the join of r_i with s_j. To do so, r_i is replicated to processors $P_{i,0}, P_{i,1}, \ldots, P_{i,m-1}$ (which form a row in Figure 17.2b), and s_i is replicated to processors $P_{0,i}, P_{1,i}, \ldots, P_{n-1,i}$ (which form a column in Figure 17.2b). Any join technique can be used at each processor $P_{i,j}$.

Fragment and replicate works with any join condition, since every tuple in r can be tested with every tuple in s. Thus, it can be used where partitioning cannot be.

Fragment and replicate usually has a higher cost than does partitioning, when both relations are of roughly the same size, since at least one of the relations has to be replicated. However, if one of the relations—say, s—is small, it may be cheaper to replicate s across all processors, rather than to repartition r and s on the join attributes. In such a case, asymmetric fragment and replicate is preferable, even though partitioning could be used.

17.5.2.3 Partitioned Parallel Hash–Join

In this section, we show how the partitioned hash–join of Section 12.6 can be parallelized.

Suppose that we have n processors, $P_0, P_1, \ldots, P_{n-1}$, and two relations r and s, such that the relations r and s are partitioned across multiple disks. Recall from Section 12.6 that the smaller relation is chosen as the build relation. If the size of s is less than that of r, the parallel hash–join algorithm proceeds as follows.

1. Choose a hash function—say, h_1—that takes the join attribute value of each tuple in s and maps this tuple to one of the n processors. Each processor P_i reads the tuples of s that are on its disk D_i, and sends each tuple to the appropriate processor based on hash function h_1. Let r_i denote the tuples of relation r that are sent to processor P_i; similarly, let s_i denote the tuples of relation s that are sent to processor P_i.
2. As the tuples of s_i are received at the destination processor P_i, they are further partitioned using another hash function, h_2, which the processor uses to compute the hash–join locally. The partitioning at this stage is exactly the same as in the partitioning phase of the sequential hash–join algorithm. Each processor P_i executes this step independently from the other processors.
3. Once the tuples of s have been distributed, the system redistributes the larger relation r across the m processors using the hash function h_1, in the same way as before. As each tuple is received, the destination processor repartitions it using the function h_2, just as the probe relation is partitioned in the sequential hash–join algorithm.
4. Each processor P_i executes the build and probe phases of the hash–join algorithm on the local partitions r_i and s_i of r and s to produce a partition of the final result of the hash–join.

The hash–join performed at each processor is independent of that performed at other processors, and receiving the tuples of r_i and s_i is similar to reading them from disk. Therefore, any of the optimizations of the hash–join described in Chapter 12 can be applied as well to the parallel case. In particular, we can use the hybrid hash–join algorithm to cache some of the incoming tuples in memory, and thus to avoid the costs of writing them and of reading them back in.

17.5.2.4 Parallel Nested-Loop Join

To illustrate the use of fragment-and-replicate based parallelization, we consider the case where the relation s is much smaller than relation r. Suppose also that relation r is stored by partitioning; the attribute on which it is partitioned is irrelevant. Finally, suppose that there is an index on a join attribute of relation r at each of the partitions of relation r.

We use asymmetric fragment and replicate, with relation s being replicated, and with the existing partitioning of relation r. Each processor P_j where a partition of relation s is stored reads the tuples of relation s stored in D_j, and replicates the tuples to every other processor P_i. At the end of this phase, relation s is replicated at all sites that store tuples of relation r.

Now, each processor P_i performs an indexed nested-loop join of relation s with the ith partition of relation r. We can overlap the indexed nested-loop join with the distribution of tuples of relation s, to reduce the costs of writing the tuples of relation s to disk, and of reading them back. However, the replication of relation s must be synchronized with the join so that there is enough space in the in-memory buffers at each processor P_i to hold the tuples of relation s that have been received but that have not yet been used in the join.

17.5.3 Other Relational Operations

The evaluation of other relational operations also can be parallelized:

- *Selection*. Let the selection be $\sigma_\theta(r)$. Consider first the case where θ is of the form $a_i = v$, where a_i is an attribute, and v is a value. If the relation r is partitioned on a_i, the selection is performed at a single processor. If θ is of the form $l \leq a_i \leq u$—that is, θ is a range selection—and the relation has been range-partitioned on a_i, then the selection is performed at each processor whose partition overlaps with the specified range of values. In all other cases, the selection is performed in parallel at all the processors.
- *Duplicate elimination*. Duplicate elimination can be performed by sorting; either of the parallel sort techniques can be used, with the optimization of eliminating duplicates as soon as they are found during sorting. We can also parallelize duplicate elimination by partitioning the tuples (using either range or hash partitioning) and performing duplicate elimination locally at each processor.
- *Projection*. Projection without duplicate elimination can be performed as tuples are read in from disk in parallel. If duplicate elimination is to be performed, the techniques just described can be used.
- *Aggregation*. Consider an aggregation operation. We can parallelize the operation by partitioning the relation on the grouping attributes, and then computing the aggregate values locally at each processor. Either hash partitioning or range partitioning can be used. If the relation is already partitioned on the grouping attributes, the first step can be skipped.

  We can reduce the cost of transferring tuples during partitioning by partly computing aggregate values before partitioning, at least for the commonly used aggregate functions. Consider an aggregation operation on a relation r, using the **sum** aggregate function on attribute B, with grouping on attribute A. The operation can be performed at each processor P_i on those r tuples stored on disk D_i. This computation results in tuples with partial sums at each processor; there is one tuple at P_i for each value for attribute A present in r tuples stored on D_i. The result of the local aggregation is partitioned on the grouping attribute A, and the aggregation is performed again (on tuples with the partial sums) at each processor P_i to get the final result.

As a result of this optimization, fewer tuples need to be sent to other processors during partitioning. This idea can be extended easily to the **min** and **max** aggregate functions. Extensions to the **count** and **avg** aggregate functions are left for you to do in Exercise 17.8.

The parallelization of other operations is covered in several of the the exercises.

17.5.4 Cost of Parallel Evaluation of Operations

We achieve parallelism by partitioning the I/O among multiple disks, and partitioning the CPU work among multiple processors. If such a split is achieved without any overhead, and if there is no skew in the splitting of work, a parallel operation using n processors will take $1/n$ times as long as will the same operation on a single processor. We already know how to estimate the cost of an operation such as a join or a selection. The time cost of parallel processing would then be $1/n$ of the time cost of sequential processing of the operation.

We must also account for the following costs:

- Startup costs for initiating the operation at multiple processors
- Skew in the distribution of work among the processors, with some processors getting a larger number of tuples than others
- Contention for resources—such as memory, disk, and the communication network—resulting in delays
- Cost of assembling the final result by transmitting partial results from each processor

The time taken by a parallel operation can be estimated as

$$T_{\text{part}} + T_{\text{asm}} + \max(T_0, T_1, \ldots, T_{n-1})$$

where T_{part} is the time for partitioning the relations, T_{asm} is the time for assembling the results and T_i the time taken for the operation at processor P_i. Assuming that the tuples are distributed without any skew, the number of tuples sent to each processor can be estimated as $1/n$ of the total number of tuples. Ignoring contention, T_i, the cost of the operations at each processor P_i can then be estimated via the techniques described in Chapter 12.

The preceding estimate will be an optimistic estimate, since skew is common. Even though breaking down a single query into a number of parallel steps reduces

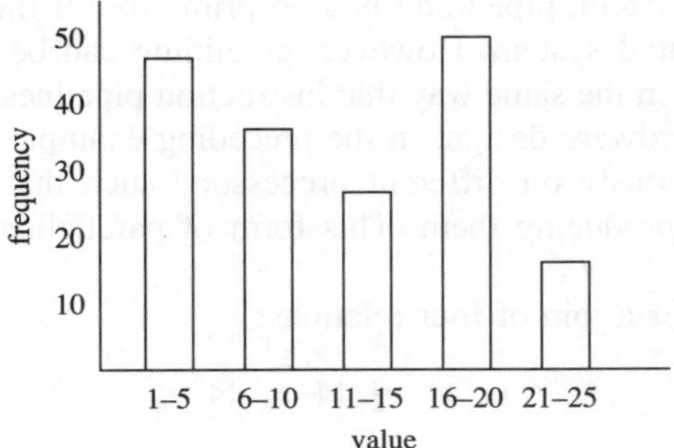

Figure 17.3 Example of histogram.

the size of the average step, it is the time for processing the single slowest step that determines the time taken for processing the query as a whole. A partitioned parallel evaluation, for instance, is only as fast as the slowest of the parallel executions. Thus, performance is greatly affected by any skew in the distribution of the work across processors.

The problem of skew in partitioning is closely related to the problem of partition overflow in sequential hash–joins (Chapter 12). We can use overflow resolution and avoidance techniques developed for hash–joins to handle skew when hash partitioning is used.

One technique to handle skew in joins with range partitioning is to construct and store a frequency table, or *histogram*, of the attribute values for each attribute of each relation. Figure 17.3 shows an example of a histogram for an integer-valued attribute that takes values in the range 1 to 25. We then construct a load-balanced range-partitioning function using histograms on the join attributes of the relations, to make the distribution of tuples more even. Approaches that construct the histogram based on sampling the relations, using only tuples from a randomly chosen subset of the disk blocks of the relation, have also been proposed to reduce the I/O overhead.

17.6 Interoperation Parallelism

There are two forms of *interoperation parallelism*: pipelined parallelism, and independent parallelism.

17.6.1 Pipelined Parallelism

As we discussed in Chapter 12, pipelining forms an important source of economy of computation for database query processing. Recall that, in pipelining, the output tuples of one operation, A, are consumed by a second operation, B, even before the first operation has produced the entire set of tuples in its output. The major advantage of pipelined execution in a sequential evaluation is that we can carry out a sequence of such operations without writing any of the intermediate results to disk.

In a parallel system, pipelining is used primarily for the same reason that it is used in a sequential system. However, pipelining can be used as a source of parallelism as well, in the same way that instruction pipelines are used as a source of parallelism in hardware design. In the preceding example, it is possible to run A and B simultaneously on different processors, such that B consumes tuples in parallel with A producing them. This form of parallelism is called *pipelined parallelism.*

Let us consider a join of four relations:

$$r_1 \bowtie r_2 \bowtie r_3 \bowtie r_4$$

We can set up a pipeline that allows the three joins to be computed in parallel. Let processor P_1 be assigned the computation of $temp_1 \leftarrow r_1 \bowtie r_2$, and let P_2 be assigned the computation of $r_3 \bowtie temp_1$. As P_1 computes tuples in $r_1 \bowtie r_2$, it makes these tuples available to processor P_2. Thus, P_2 has available to it some of the tuples in $r_1 \bowtie r_2$ before P_1 has finished its computation. P_2 can use those tuples that are available to begin computation of $temp_1 \bowtie r_3$, even before $r_1 \bowtie r_2$ is fully computed by P_1. Likewise, as P_2 computes tuples in $(r_1 \bowtie r_2) \bowtie r_3$, it makes these tuples available to P_3, which computes the join of these tuples with r_4.

Pipelined parallelism is useful with a small number of processors, but does not scale up well. First, pipeline chains generally do not attain sufficient length to provide a high degree of parallelism. Second, it is not possible to pipeline relational operators that do not produce output until all inputs have been accessed, such as the set-difference operation. Third, only marginal speedup is obtained for the frequent cases in which one operator's execution cost is much higher than are those of the others. Thus, when the degree of parallelism is high, the importance of pipelining as a source of parallelism is secondary to that of partitioned parallelism. The most important reason for using pipelining is that pipelined executions can avoid writing intermediate results to disk.

17.6.2 Independent Parallelism

Operations in a query expression that do not depend on one another can be executed in parallel. This form of parallelism is called *independent parallelism*.

Let us again consider the join $r_1 \bowtie r_2 \bowtie r_3 \bowtie r_4$. Clearly, we can compute $temp_1 \leftarrow r_1 \bowtie r_2$ in parallel with $temp_2 \leftarrow r_3 \bowtie r_4$. When these two computations complete, we compute

$$temp_1 \bowtie temp_2$$

To obtain further parallelism, we can pipeline the tuples in $temp_1$ and $temp_2$ into the computation of $temp_1 \bowtie temp_2$, which is itself carried out via a pipelined join (Section 12.8.2.2).

Like pipelined parallelism, independent parallelism does not provide a high degree of parallelism, and is less useful in a highly parallel system, although it is useful with a lower degree of parallelism.

17.6.3 Query Optimization

An important factor in the success of relational technology has been the successful design of query optimizers. Recall that a query optimizer takes a query, and finds the cheapest execution plan among the many possible execution plans that give the same answer.

Query optimizers for parallel query evaluation are more complicated than are query optimizers for sequential query evaluation. First, the cost models are more complicated, since partitioning costs have to be accounted for, and issues such as skew and resource contention must be taken into account. More important is the issue of how to parallelize a query. Suppose that we have somehow chosen an expression (from among those equivalent to the query) to be used for evaluating the query. The expression can be represented by an operator tree, as discussed in Section 12.8.

To evaluate an operator tree in a parallel system, we must make the following decisions:

- How to parallelize each operation, and how many processors to use for it
- What operations to pipeline across different processors, what operations to execute independently in parallel, and what operations to execute sequentially, one after the other

These decisions constitute the task of *scheduling* the execution tree.

Determining the resources of each kind—such as processors, disks, and memory—that should be allocated to each operation in the tree is another aspect of the optimization problem. For instance, it may appear wise to use the maximum amount of parallelism available, but it is a good idea not to execute certain operations in parallel. Operations whose computational requirements are significantly smaller than the communication overhead should be clustered with one of their neighbors. Otherwise, the advantage of parallelism is negated by the overhead of communication.

One concern when pipelining is used is that long pipelines do not lend themselves to good resource utilization. Unless the operations are coarse grained, the final operation of the pipeline may wait for a long time to get inputs, while holding precious resources, such as memory. Hence, long pipelines should be avoided.

The number of parallel evaluation plans from which to choose is much larger than is the number of sequential evaluation plans. Optimizing parallel queries by considering all alternatives is therefore much more expensive than is optimizing sequential queries. Hence, we usually adopt heuristic approaches to reduce the number of parallel execution plans that we consider. We describe two popular heuristics here.

The first heuristic is to consider only evaluation plans that parallelize every operation across all processors, and that do not use any pipelining. This approach is used in the Teradata DBC series machines. Finding the best such execution plan is similar to doing query optimization in a sequential system. The main differences lie in how the partitioning is performed, and in what cost-estimation formula are used.

The second heuristic is to choose the most efficient sequential evaluation plan, and then to parallelize the operations in that evaluation plan.

Yet another dimension of optimization is the design of physical-storage organization to speed up queries. The optimal physical organization differs for different queries. The database administrator must choose a physical organization that is believed to be good for the expected mix of database queries. Thus, the area of parallel query optimization is complex, and is still an area of active research.

17.7 Design of Parallel Systems

So far, in this chapter, we have concentrated on parallelization of data storage and of query processing. Since large-scale parallel database systems are used primarily for storing large volumes of data, and for processing decision-support queries on those data, these topics are the most important in a parallel database system. Parallel loading of data from external sources is an important requirement, if we are to handle large volumes of incoming data.

A large parallel database system must also address the following availability issues:

- Resilience to failure of some processors or disks
- On-line reorganization of data and schema changes

We consider these issues here.

With a large number of processors and disks, the probability that at least one processor or disk will malfunction is significantly greater than in a single-processor system with one disk. A poorly designed parallel system will stop functioning if any component (processor or disk) fails. Assuming that the probability of failure of a single processor or disk is small, the probability of failure of the system goes up linearly with the number of processors and disks. If a single processor or disk would fail once every 5 years, a system with 100 processors would have a failure every 18 days.

Therefore, large-scale parallel database systems, such as Tandem and Teradata machines, are designed to operate even if a processor or disk fails. Data are replicated across at least two processors. If a processor fails, the data that it stored can still be accessed from the other processors. The system keeps track of failed processors and distributes the work among functioning processors. Requests for data stored at the failed site are automatically routed to the backup sites that store a replica of the data. If all the data of a processor A are replicated at a single processor B, B will have to handle all the requests to A as well as those to itself, and that will result in B becoming a bottleneck. Therefore, the replicas of the data of a processor are partitioned across multiple other processors.

When we are dealing with large volumes of data (ranging in the terabytes), simple operations, such as creating indices, and changes to schema, such as adding a column to a relation, can take a long time — perhaps hours or even days.

Therefore, it is unacceptable for the database system to be unavailable while such operations are in progress. Parallel database systems, such as the Tandem systems, allow such operations to be performed *on-line*.

Consider, for instance, on-line index construction. A system that supports this feature allows insertions, deletions, and updates to be performed on a relation even as an index is being built on the relation. The index-building operation therefore cannot lock the entire relation in shared mode, as it would have done otherwise. Instead, the process keeps track of updates that occur while it is active, and incorporates the changes into the index being constructed.

17.8 Summary

Parallel databases have gained significant commercial acceptance in the past 15 years. In I/O parallelism, relations are partitioned among available disks so that retrieval can be made faster. Three commonly used partitioning techniques are round-robin partitioning, hash partitioning, and range partitioning. Skew is a major problem, especially with increasing degrees of parallelism.

In interquery parallelism, we run different queries concurrently to increase throughput. Intraquery parallelism attempts to reduce the cost of running a query. There are two types of intraquery parallelism: intraoperation parallelism and interoperation parallelism.

We use intraoperation parallelism to execute relational operations, such as sorts and joins, in parallel. Intraoperation parallelism is natural for relational operations, since they are set oriented. There are two basic approaches to parallelizing a binary operation such as a join. In partitioned parallelism, the relations are split into several parts, and tuples in r_i are joined with only tuples from s_i. In asymmetric fragment and replicate, one of the relations is replicated while the other is partitioned. Unlike partitioned parallelism, fragment and replicate can be used with any join condition. Both parallelization techniques can be used in conjunction with any join technique.

In independent parallelism, different operations that do not depend on one another are executed in parallel. In pipelined parallelism, processors send the results of one operation to another operation as those results are computed, without waiting for the entire operation to finish. Query optimization in parallel databases is significantly more complex than is query optimization in sequential databases.

Exercises

17.1. For each of the three partitioning techniques, namely round-robin, hash-partitioning, and range-partitioning, give an example of a query for which that partitioning technique would provide the fastest response.

17.2. When performing a range selection on a range-partitioned attribute, it is possible that only one disk may need to be accessed. Describe the benefits and drawbacks of this property.

17.3. What factors could result in skew when a relation is partitioned on one of its attributes using:
(*a*) Hash-partitioning
(*b*) Range-partitioning
In each case above, what can be done to reduce the skew?

17.4. What form of parallelism (inter-query, inter-operation, or intra-operation) is likely to be the most important for each of the following tasks.
(*a*) Increasing the throughput of a system with many small queries.
(*b*) Increasing the throughput of a system with a few large queries, when the number of disks and processors is large.

17.5. With pipelined parallelism, it is often a good idea to perform several operations in a pipeline on a single processor, even when many processors are available.
(*a*) Explain why.
(*b*) Would the above arguments hold if the machine used has a shared-memory architecture? Explain why or why not?
(*c*) Would the above arguments hold with independent parallelism? (That is, are there cases where even if the operations are not pipelined, and there are many processors available, it is still a good idea to perform several operations on the same processor?)

17.6. Give an example of a join that is not a simple equi-join, for which partitioned parallelism can be used. What attributes should be used for partitioning?

17.7. Consider join processing using symmetric fragment and replicate with range partitioning. How can you optimize the evaluation if the join condition is of the form $| r.A - s.B | \leq k$, where k is a small constant. Here, $| x |$ denotes the absolute value of x. A join with such a join condition is called a *band join*.

17.8. Describe a good way to parallelize each of the following.
(*a*) The difference operation.
(*b*) Aggregation using the **count** operation.
(*c*) Aggregation using the **count distinct** operation.
(*d*) Aggregation using the **avg** operation.
(*e*) Left outer join, if the join condition involves only equality.
(*f*) Left outer join, if the join condition involves comparisons other than equality.
(*g*) Full outer join, if the join condition involves comparisons other than equality.

17.9. Recall that histograms are used for constructing load balanced range partitions.
(*a*) Suppose you have a histogram where values are between 1 and 100, and are partitioned into 10 ranges, 1 – 10, 11 – 20, . . . , 91 – 100, with frequencies 15, 5, 20, 10, 10, 5, 5, 20, 5, and 5, respectively. Give a load balanced range partitioning function to divide the values into 5 partitions.

(*b*) Give an algorithm for computing a load-balanced range partition with p partitions, given a histogram of frequency distributions containing n ranges.

17.10. Describe the benefits and drawbacks of using pipelined parallelism.

17.11. Some parallel database systems store an extra copy of each data item on disks attached to a different processor, to avoid loss of data if one of the processors fails.

(*a*) Why is it a good idea to partition the copies of the data items of a processor across multiple processors?

(*b*) What are the benefits and drawbacks of using RAID storage instead of storing an extra copy of each data item?

Bibliographic Notes

Relational database systems began appearing in the marketplace in 1983; now, they dominate it. By the late 1970s and early 1980s, as the relational model gained reasonably sound footing, people recognized that relational operators are highly parallelizable and have good dataflow properties. A commercial system, Teradata, and several research projects, such as GRACE (Kitsuregawa et al. [1983], Fushimi et al. [1986]), GAMMA (DeWitt et al. [1986, 1990]), and Bubba (Boral et al. [1990]), were launched in quick succession. Researchers used these parallel database systems to investigate the practicality of parallel execution of relational operators. Subsequently, in the late 1980s and the 1990s, several more companies—such as Tandem, Oracle, Informix, and Red-Brick—have entered the market. Research projects in the academic world include XPRS (Stonebraker et al. [1989]) and Volcano (Graefe [1990]).

Locking in parallel databases is discussed in Joshi [1991], and in Mohan and Narang [1991, 1992b]. Cache-coherency protocols for parallel database systems are discussed by Dias et al. [1989], Mohan and Narang [1991, 1992], and Rahm [1993]. Carey et al. [1991] discuss caching issues in a client–server system. Parallelism and recovery in database systems are discussed by Bayer et al. [1980].

Graefe [1993] presents an excellent survey of query processing, including parallel processing of queries. Parallel sorting is discussed in DeWitt et al. [1992]. Parallel join algorithms are described by Nakayama et al. [1984], Kitsuregawa et al. [1983], and Richardson et al. [1987], Schneider and DeWitt [1989], Kitsuregawa and Ogawa [1990, Lin et al. [1994], and Wilschut et al. [1995], among other works. Parallel join algorithms for shared-memory architectures are described by Tsukuda et al. [1992], Deshpande and Larson [1992], and by Shatdal and Naughton [1993]. Skew handling in parallel joins is described by Walton et al. [1991], Wolf [1991], and DeWitt et al. [1992]. Sampling techniques for parallel databases are described by Seshadri and Naughton [1992] and Ganguly et al. [1996].

Graefe [1990, 1993] advocates a model of parallelization called the *exchange-operator* model, which uses existing implementations of operations, operating on local copies of data, coupled with an exchange operation that moves data around. Our description of parallelization of operations is based loosely on this model.

Parallel query-optimization techniques are described by Lu et al. [1991], Hong and Stonebraker [1991], Ganguly et al. [1992], Lanzelotte et al. [1993], and Hasan and Motwani [1995].

CHAPTER 18

DISTRIBUTED DATABASES

In Chapter 16, we discussed the basic structure of distributed systems. Unlike parallel systems, in which the processors are tightly coupled and constitute a single database system, a distributed database system consists of loosely coupled sites that share no physical components. Furthermore, the database systems that run on each site may have a substantial degree of mutual independence.

Each site may participate in the execution of transactions that access data at one site, or several sites. The main difference between centralized and distributed database systems is that, in the former, the data reside in one single location, whereas in the latter, the data reside in several locations. This distribution of data is the cause of many difficulties in transaction processing and query processing. In this chapter, we address these difficulties.

We start with the question of how to store data in a distributed database, in Section 18.1. In Section 18.2, we consider issues of network transparency and of naming of data items. Several techniques have been developed for processing queries in a distributed database; they are examined in Section 18.3.

The next few sections address transaction processing. The basic model and problems caused by different kinds of failures are examined in Section 18.4. Commit protocols designed to provide atomic transaction commit, in spite of these problems, are described in Section 18.5. Recovery issues related to selecting new coordinators when a site designated as a coordinator fails are considered in Section 18.6. Concurrency control in distributed systems is examined in Section 18.7; the issue of handling deadlocks is dealt with in Section 18.8.

In recent years, the need has arisen for accessing and updating data from a variety of preexisting databases, which differ in their hardware and software environments, and in the schemas under which data are stored. A *multidatabase system* is a software layer that enables such a heterogeneous collection of databases to be treated like a homogeneous distributed database. Section 18.9 deals with query-processing and transaction-processing issues related to multidatabase systems.

18.1 Distributed Data Storage

Consider a relation *r* that is to be stored in the database. There are several approaches to storing this relation in the distributed database:

- **Replication**. The system maintains several identical replicas (copies) of the relation. Each replica is stored at a different site, resulting in data replication. The alternative to replication is to store only one copy of relation *r*.
- **Fragmentation**. The relation is partitioned into several fragments. Each fragment is stored at a different site.
- **Replication and fragmentation**. The relation is partitioned into several fragments. The system maintains several replicas of each fragment.

In the following subsections, we elaborate on each of these techniques.

18.1.1 Data Replication

If relation *r* is replicated, a copy of relation *r* is stored in two or more sites. In the most extreme case, we have *full replication*, in which a copy is stored in every site in the system.

There are a number of advantages and disadvantages to replication.

- **Availability**. If one of the sites containing relation *r* fails, then the relation *r* can be found in another site. Thus, the system can continue to process queries involving *r*, despite the failure of one site.
- **Increased parallelism**. In the case where the majority of accesses to the relation *r* result in only the reading of the relation, then several sites can process queries involving *r* in parallel. The more replicas of *r* there are, the greater the chance that the needed data will be found in the site where the transaction is executing. Hence, data replication minimizes movement of data between sites.
- **Increased overhead on update**. The system must ensure that all replicas of a relation *r* are consistent; otherwise, erroneous computations may result. Thus, whenever *r* is updated, the update must be propagated to all sites containing replicas. The result is increased overhead. For example, in a banking system, where account information is replicated in various sites, it is necessary to ensure that the balance in a particular account agrees in all sites.

In general, replication enhances the performance of **read** operations and increases the availability of data to read-only transactions. However, update transactions incur greater overhead. Controlling concurrent updates by several transactions to replicated data is more complex than is using the centralized approach to concurrency control that we saw in Chapter 14. We can simplify the management of replicas of relation r by choosing one of them as the *primary copy of* r. For example, in a banking system, an account can be associated with the site in which the account has been opened. Similarly, in an airline-reservation system, a flight can be associated with the site at which the flight originates. We shall examine the options for distributed concurrency control in Section 18.7.

18.1.2 Data Fragmentation

If relation r is fragmented, r is divided into a number of *fragments* $r_1, r_2, ..., r_n$. These fragments contain sufficient information to allow reconstruction of the original relation r. As we shall see, this reconstruction can take place through the application of either the union operation or a special type of join operation on the various fragments. There are two different schemes for fragmenting a relation: *horizontal* fragmentation and *vertical* fragmentation. Horizontal fragmentation splits the relation by assigning each tuple of r to one or more fragments. Vertical fragmentation splits the relation by decomposing the scheme R of relation r in a special way that we shall discuss. These two schemes can be applied successively to the same relation, resulting in a number of different fragments. Note that some information may appear in several fragments.

We discuss the various ways for fragmenting a relation in Sections 18.1.2.1 to 18.1.2.3. We shall illustrate these approaches by fragmenting the relation *account*, with schema

Account-schema = (*branch-name*, *account-number*, *balance*)

The relation *account* (*Account-schema*) is shown in Figure 18.1.

18.1.2.1 Horizontal Fragmentation

The relation r is partitioned into a number of subsets, $r_1, r_2, ..., r_n$. Each tuple of relation r must belong to at least one of the fragments, so that the original relation can be reconstructed, if needed.

A fragment can be defined as a *selection* on the global relation r. That is, we use a predicate P_i to construct fragment r_i as follows:

$$r_i = \sigma_{P_i}(r)$$

branch-name	*account-number*	*balance*
Hillside	A-305	500
Hillside	A-226	336
Valleyview	A-177	205
Valleyview	A-402	10000
Hillside	A-155	62
Valleyview	A-408	1123
Valleyview	A-639	750

Figure 18.1 Sample *account* relation.

branch-name	*account-number*	*balance*
Hillside	A-305	500
Hillside	A-226	336
Hillside	A-155	62

$account_1$

branch-name	*account-number*	*balance*
Valleyview	A-177	205
Valleyview	A-402	10000
Valleyview	A-408	1123
Valleyview	A-639	750

$account_2$

Figure 18.2 Horizontal fragmentation of relation *account*.

We obtain the reconstruction of the relation r by taking the union of all fragments; that is,

$$r = r_1 \cup r_2 \cup ... \cup r_n$$

As an illustration, suppose that the relation r is the *account* relation of Figure 18.1. This relation can be divided into n different fragments, each of which consists of tuples of accounts belonging to a particular branch. If the banking system has only two branches—Hillside and Valleyview—then there are two different fragments:

$$account_1 = \sigma_{branch\text{-}name\ =\ \text{"Hillside"}}\ (account)$$
$$account_2 = \sigma_{branch\text{-}name\ =\ \text{"Valleyview"}}\ (account)$$

These two fragments are shown in Figure 18.2. Fragment $account_1$ is stored in the Hillside site. Fragment $account_2$ is stored in the Valleyview site.

In our example, the fragments are disjoint. By changing the selection predicates used to construct the fragments, we can have a particular tuple of r appear in more than one of the r_i. This form of data replication is discussed further at the end of this section.

18.1.2.2 Vertical Fragmentation

In its simplest form, vertical fragmentation is the same as decomposition (see Chapter 7). Vertical fragmentation of $r(R)$ involves the definition of several subsets of attributes $R_1, R_2, ..., R_n$ of the schema R such that

$$R = R_1 \cup R_2 \cup ... \cup R_n$$

Each fragment r_i of r is defined by

$$r_i = \Pi_{R_i}(r)$$

branch-name	*account-number*	*customer-name*	*balance*
Hillside	A-305	Lowman	500
Hillside	A-226	Camp	336
Valleyview	A-177	Camp	205
Valleyview	A-402	Kahn	10000
Hillside	A-155	Kahn	62
Valleyview	A-408	Kahn	1123
Valleyview	A-639	Green	750

Figure 18.3 Sample *deposit* relation.

The fragmentation should be done such that we can reconstruct relation r from the fragments by taking the natural join

$$r = r_1 \bowtie r_2 \bowtie r_3 \bowtie \ldots \bowtie r_n$$

One way of ensuring that the relation r can be reconstructed is to include the primary-key attributes of R in each of the R_i. More generally, any superkey can be used. It is often convenient to add a special attribute, called a *tuple-id*, to the schema R. The tuple-id value of a tuple is a unique value, used to distinguish the tuple from all other tuples. The tuple-id attribute thus serves as a candidate key for the augmented schema, and is included in each of the R_is. The physical or logical address for a tuple can be used as a tuple-id, since each tuple has a unique address.

To illustrate vertical fragmentation, we consider for our bank database an alternative database design that includes the schema†

Deposit-schema = (*branch-name*, *account-number*, *customer-name*, *balance*)

Figure 18.3 shows the *deposit* relation for our example. In Figure 18.4, we show the relation *deposit′*: the *deposit* relation of Figure 18.3 with tuple-ids

branch-name	*account-number*	*customer-name*	*balance*	*tuple-id*
Hillside	A-305	Lowman	500	1
Hillside	A-226	Camp	336	2
Valleyview	A-177	Camp	205	3
Valleyview	A-402	Kahn	10000	4
Hillside	A-155	Kahn	62	5
Valleyview	A-408	Kahn	1123	6
Valleyview	A-639	Green	750	7

Figure 18.4 The *deposit* relation of Figure 18.3 with tuple-ids.

† Although the highly normalized database design that we use elsewhere in this text can be vertically fragmented, such fragmentation is not particularly useful. Vertical fragmentation is more meaningful for a schema such as the one we use here.

branch-name	*customer-name*	*tuple-id*
Hillside	Lowman	1
Hillside	Camp	2
Valleyview	Camp	3
Valleyview	Kahn	4
Hillside	Kahn	5
Valleyview	Kahn	6
Valleyview	Green	7

$deposit_1$

account-number	*balance*	*tuple-id*
A-305	500	1
A-226	336	2
A-177	205	3
A-402	10000	4
A-155	62	5
A-408	1123	6
A-639	750	7

$deposit_2$

Figure 18.5 Vertical fragmentation of relation *deposit*.

added. Figure 18.5 shows a vertical decomposition of the schema *Deposit-schema* ∪ {*tuple-id*} into

Deposit-schema-1 = (*branch-name*, *customer-name*, *tuple-id*)
Deposit-schema-2 = (*account-number*, *balance*, *tuple-id*)

The two relations shown in Figure 18.5 result from computing

$$deposit_1 = \Pi_{Deposit\text{-}schema\text{-}1}\,(deposit')$$
$$deposit_2 = \Pi_{Deposit\text{-}schema\text{-}2}\,(deposit')$$

To reconstruct the original *deposit* relation from the fragments, we compute

$$\Pi_{Deposit\text{-}schema}\,(deposit_1 \bowtie deposit_2)$$

Note that the expression

$$deposit_1 \bowtie deposit_2$$

is a special form of natural join. The join attribute is *tuple-id*. Although the *tuple-id* attribute facilitates the implementation of vertical partitioning, it must not be visible to users, since it is an internal artifact of the implementation, and violates data independence — which is one of the main virtues of the relational model.

18.1.2.3 Mixed Fragmentation

The relation r is divided into a number of fragment relations $r_1, r_2, ..., r_n$. Each fragment is obtained as the result of application of either the horizontal-fragmentation or vertical-fragmentation scheme on relation r, or on a fragment of r that was obtained previously.

As an illustration, suppose that the relation r is the *deposit* relation of Figure 18.3. This relation is divided initially into the fragments $deposit_1$ and $deposit_2$, as defined previously. We can now further divide fragment $deposit_1$, using the horizontal-fragmentation scheme, into the following two fragments:

$$deposit_{1a} = \sigma_{branch\text{-}name\ =\ \text{"Hillside"}}\ (deposit_1)$$
$$deposit_{1b} = \sigma_{branch\text{-}name\ =\ \text{"Valleyview"}}\ (deposit_1)$$

Thus, relation r is divided into three fragments: $deposit_{1a}$, $deposit_{1b}$, and $deposit_2$. Each of these fragments may reside in a different site.

18.1.3 Data Replication and Fragmentation

The techniques described in Sections 18.1.1 and 18.1.2 for data replication and data fragmentation can be applied successively to the same relation. That is, a fragment can be replicated, replicas of fragments can be fragmented further, and so on. For example, consider a distributed system consisting of sites S_1, $S_2, ..., S_{10}$. We can fragment *deposit* into $deposit_{1a}$, $deposit_{1b}$, and $deposit_2$, and, for example, store a copy of $deposit_{1a}$ at sites S_1, S_3, and S_7; a copy of $deposit_{1b}$ at sites S_7 and S_{10}; and a copy of $deposit_2$ at sites S_2, S_8, and S_9.

18.2 Network Transparency

In Section 18.1, we saw that a relation r can be stored in a variety of ways in a distributed database system. It is essential that the system minimize the degree to which a user needs to be aware of how a relation is stored. As we shall see, a system can hide the details of the distribution of data in the network. We call this hiding *network transparency*, and define it as the degree to which system users can remain unaware of the details of how and where the data items are stored in a distributed system.

We shall consider the issues of transparency from the points of view of

- Naming of data items
- Replication of data items
- Fragmentation of data items
- Location of fragments and replicas

18.2.1 Naming of Data Items

Data items—such as relations, fragments, and replicas — must have unique names. This property is easy to ensure in a centralized database. In a distributed database, however, we must take care to ensure that two sites do not use the same name for distinct data items.

One solution to this problem is to require all names to be registered in a central *name server*. The name server helps to ensure that the same name does not get used for different data items. We can also use the name server to locate a data item, given the name of the item. This approach, however, suffers from two major disadvantages. First, the name server may become a performance bottleneck when data items are located via their names, resulting in poor performance. Second, if the name server crashes, it may not be possible for any site in the distributed system to continue to run.

An alternative approach is to require that each site prefix its own site identifier to any name that it generates. This approach ensures that no two sites generate the same name (since each site has a unique identifier). Furthermore, no central control is required. This solution, however, fails to achieve network transparency, since site identifiers are attached to names. Thus, the *account* relation might be referred to as *site*17.*account*, rather than as simply *account*.

To overcome this problem, the database system can create a set of alternative names or *aliases* for data items. A user may thus refer to data items by simple names that are translated by the system to complete names. The mapping of aliases to the real names can be stored at each site. With aliases, the user can be unaware of the physical location of a data item. Furthermore, the user will be unaffected if the database administrator decides to move a data item from one site to another.

Each replica of a data item and each fragment of a data item must also have a unique name. It is important that the system be able to determine those replicas that are replicas of the same data item and those fragments that are fragments of the same data item. We adopt the convention of postfixing ".*f*1", ".*f*2", . . . , ".*fn*" to fragments of a data item, and ".*r*1", ".*r*2", . . . , ".*rn*" to replicas. Thus

*site*17.*account*.*f*3.*r*2

refers to replica 2 of fragment 3 of *account*, and tells us that this item was generated by site 17.

It is undesirable to expect users to refer to a specific replica of a data item. Instead, the system should determine which replica to reference on a **read** request, and should update all replicas on a **write** request. We can ensure that it does so by maintaining a catalog table, which the system uses to determine all replicas for the data item.

Similarly, a user should not be required to know how a data item is fragmented. As we observed earlier, vertical fragments may contain *tuple-ids*. Horizontal fragments may involve complicated selection predicates. Therefore, a distributed database system should allow requests to be stated in terms of the unfragmented data items. This requirement presents no major difficulty, since it is always possible to reconstruct the original data item from its fragments. However, it may be inefficient to reconstruct data from fragments. Returning to our horizontal fragmentation of *account*, consider the query

$$\sigma_{branch\text{-}name = \text{"Hillside"}}\ (account)$$

```
if name appears in the alias table
    then expression := map (name)
    else expression := name;

function map (n)
    if n appears in the replica table
        then result := name of a replica of n;
    if n appears in the fragment table
        then begin
                result := expression to construct fragment;
                for each n' in result do begin
                    replace n' in result with map (n');
                end
             end
    return result;
```

Figure 18.6 Name-translation algorithm.

We could answer this query using only the $account_1$ fragment. However, fragmentation transparency requires that the user not be aware of the existence of fragments $account_1$ and $account_2$. If we reconstruct *account* prior to processing the query, we obtain the expression

$$\sigma_{branch\text{-}name = \text{"Hillside"}} \; (account_1 \; \cup \; account_2)$$

The optimization of this expression is left to the query optimizer (see Section 18.3).

Figure 18.6 shows the complete translation scheme for a given data-item name. To illustrate the operation of the scheme, we consider a user located in the Hillside branch (site S_1). This user uses the alias *local-account* for the local fragment *account.f1* of the *account* relation. When this user references *local-account*, the query-processing subsystem looks up *local-account* in the alias table, and replaces *local-account* with *S1.account.f1*. It is possible that *S1.account.f1* is replicated. If so, the system must consult the replica table in order to choose a replica. This replica could itself be fragmented, requiring examination of the fragmentation table. In most cases, only one or two tables must be consulted. However, the name-translation scheme of Figure 18.6 is sufficiently general to deal with any combination of successive replication and fragmentation of relations.

18.2.2 Transparency and Updates

Providing transparency for users that update the database is somewhat more difficult than is providing transparency for readers. The main problems are ensuring that all replicas of a data item are updated, and that all affected fragments are updated.

In its full generality, the update problem for replicated and fragmented data is related to the problem of view maintenance—that is, to the problem of keeping materialized views up-to-date when the database relations are updated (Section 3.7.1). Consider our example of the *account* relation, and the insertion of the tuple

("Valleyview", A-733, 600)

If *account* is fragmented horizontally, there is a predicate P_i associated with the ith fragment. We apply P_i to the tuple ("Valleyview", A-733, 600) to test whether that tuple must be inserted in the ith fragment. Using our example of *account* being fragmented into

$$account_1 = \sigma_{branch\text{-}name = \text{"Hillside"}} (account)$$
$$account_2 = \sigma_{branch\text{-}name = \text{"Valleyview"}} (account)$$

the tuple would be inserted into $account_2$.

Now consider a vertical fragmentation of deposit into $deposit_1$ and $deposit_2$. The tuple ("Valleyview", A-733, "Jones", 600) must be split into two fragments: one to be inserted into $deposit_1$, and one to be inserted into $deposit_2$.

If an update is made to a replicated relation, the update must be applied to all replicas. This requirement presents a problem if there is concurrent access to the relation, since it is possible that one replica will be updated earlier than another. We consider this problem in Section 18.7.

18.3 Distributed Query Processing

In Chapter 12, we saw that there is a variety of methods for computing the answer to a query. We examined several techniques for choosing a strategy for processing a query that minimize the amount of time that it takes to compute the answer. For centralized systems, the primary criterion for measuring the cost of a particular strategy is the number of disk accesses. In a distributed system, we must take into account several other matters, including

- The cost of data transmission over the network
- The potential gain in performance from having several sites process parts of the query in parallel

The relative cost of data transfer over the network and data transfer to and from disk varies widely depending on the type of network and on the speed of the disks. Thus, in general, we cannot focus solely on disk costs or on network costs. Rather, we must find a good tradeoff between the two.

18.3.1 Query Transformation

Let us consider an extremely simple query: "Find all the tuples in the *account* relation." Although the query is simple — indeed, trivial—processing of this query is not trivial, since the *account* relation may be fragmented, replicated, or both, as we saw in Section 18.1. If the *account* relation is replicated, we have a choice of replica to make. If no replicas are fragmented, we choose the replica for which the transmission cost is lowest. However, if a replica is fragmented, the choice is not so easy to make, since we need to compute several joins or unions to reconstruct the *account* relation. In this case, the number of strategies for our simple example may be large. Query optimization by exhaustive enumeration of all alternative strategies may not be practical in such situations.

Fragmentation transparency implies that a user may write a query such as

$$\sigma_{branch\text{-}name = \text{“Hillside”}}\ (account)$$

Since *account* is defined as

$$account_1 \cup account_2$$

the expression that results from the name translation scheme is

$$\sigma_{branch\text{-}name = \text{“Hillside”}}\ (account_1 \cup account_2)$$

Using the query-optimization techniques of Chapter 12, we can simplify the preceding expression automatically. The result is the expression

$$\sigma_{branch\text{-}name = \text{“Hillside”}}\ (account_1) \cup \sigma_{branch\text{-}name = \text{“Hillside”}}\ (account_2)$$

which includes two subexpressions. The first involves only $account_1$, and thus can be evaluated at the Hillside site. The second involves only $account_2$, and thus can be evaluated at the Valleyview site.

There is a further optimization that can be made in evaluating

$$\sigma_{branch\text{-}name = \text{“Hillside”}}\ (account_1)$$

Since $account_1$ has only tuples pertaining to the Hillside branch, we can eliminate the selection operation. In evaluating

$$\sigma_{branch\text{-}name = \text{“Hillside”}}\ (account_2)$$

we can apply the definition of the $account_2$ fragment to obtain

$$\sigma_{branch\text{-}name = \text{“Hillside”}}\ (\sigma_{branch\text{-}name = \text{“Valleyview”}}\ (account))$$

This expression is the empty set, regardless of the contents of the *account* relation.

Thus, our final strategy is for the Hillside site to return $account_1$ as the result of the query.

18.3.2 Simple Join Processing

As we saw in Chapter 12, a major aspect of the selection of a query-processing strategy is choosing a join strategy. Consider the following relational-algebra expression:

$$account \bowtie depositor \bowtie branch$$

Assume that the three relations are neither replicated nor fragmented, and that *account* is stored at site S_1, *depositor* at S_2, and *branch* at S_3. Let S_I denote the site at which the query was issued. The system needs to produce the result at site S_I. Among the possible strategies for processing this query are the following:

- Ship copies of all three relations to site S_I. Using the techniques of Chapter 12, choose a strategy for processing the entire query locally at site S_I.
- Ship a copy of the *account* relation to site S_2, and compute $temp_1$ = *account* ⋈ *depositor* at S_2. Ship $temp_1$ from S_2 to S_3, and compute $temp_2 = temp_1$ ⋈ *branch* at S_3. Ship the result $temp_2$ to S_I.
- Devise strategies similar to the previous one, with the roles of S_1, S_2, S_3 exchanged.

No one strategy is always the best one. Among the factors that must be considered are the volume of data being shipped, the cost of transmitting a block of data between a pair of sites, and the relative speed of processing at each site. Consider the first two strategies listed. If we ship all three relations to S_I, and indices exist on these relations, we may need to recreate these indices at S_I. This recreation of indices entails extra processing overhead and extra disk accesses. However, the second strategy has the disadvantage that a potentially large relation (*customer* ⋈ *account*) must be shipped from S_2 to S_3. This relation repeats the address data for a customer once for each account that the customer has. Thus, the second strategy may result in extra network transmission, as compared with the first strategy.

18.3.3 Semijoin Strategy

Suppose that we wish to evaluate the expression $r_1 \bowtie r_2$, where r_1 and r_2 are stored at sites S_1 and S_2, respectively. Let the schemas of r_1 and r_2 be R_1 and R_2. Suppose that we wish to obtain the result at S_1. If there are many tuples of r_2 that do not join with any tuple of r_1, then shipping r_2 to S_1 entails shipping tuples that fail to contribute to the result. It is desirable to remove such tuples before shipping data to S_1, particularly if network costs are high.

A strategy can be implemented as follows:

1. Compute $temp_1 \leftarrow \Pi_{R_1 \cap R_2}(r_1)$ at S_1.
2. Ship $temp_1$ from S_1 to S_2.
3. Compute $temp_2 \leftarrow r_2 \bowtie temp_1$ at S_2.
4. Ship $temp_2$ from S_2 to S_1.
5. Compute $r_1 \bowtie temp_2$ at S_1. The resulting relation is the same as $r_1 \bowtie r_2$.

Before considering the efficiency of this strategy, let us verify that the strategy computes the correct answer. In step 3, $temp_2$ has the result of $r_2 \bowtie \Pi_{R_1 \cap R_2}(r_1)$. In step 5, we compute

$$r_1 \bowtie r_2 \bowtie \Pi_{R_1 \cap R_2}(r_1)$$

Since join is associative and commutative, we can rewrite this expression as

$$(r_1 \bowtie \Pi_{R_1 \cap R_2}(r_1)) \bowtie r_2$$

Since $r_1 \bowtie \Pi_{(R_1 \cap R_2)}(r_1) = r_1$, the expression is, indeed, equal to $r_1 \bowtie r_2$.

This strategy is particularly advantageous when relatively few tuples of r_2 contribute to the join. This situation is likely to occur if r_1 is the result of a relational-algebra expression involving selection. In such a case, $temp_2$ may have significantly fewer tuples than r_2. The cost savings of the strategy result from having to ship only $temp_2$, rather than all of r_2, to S_1. Additional cost is incurred in shipping $temp_1$ to S_2. If a sufficiently small fraction of tuples in r_2 contribute to the join, the overhead of shipping $temp_1$ will be dominated by the savings of shipping only a fraction of the tuples in r_2.

This strategy is called a *semijoin strategy*, after the semijoin operator of the relational algebra, denoted $\ltimes$. The semijoin of r_1 with r_2, denoted $r_1 \ltimes r_2$, is

$$\Pi_{R_1}(r_1 \bowtie r_2)$$

Thus, $r_1 \ltimes r_2$ selects those tuples of r_1 that contributed to $r_1 \bowtie r_2$. In step 3, $temp_2 = r_2 \ltimes r_1$.

For joins of several relations, this strategy can be extended to a series of semijoin steps. A substantial body of theory has been developed regarding the use of semijoins for query optimization. Some of this theory is referenced in the bibliographic notes.

18.3.4 Join Strategies that Exploit Parallelism

Implementing intraoperation parallelism by redistributing tuples is generally not considered viable in a distributed system, due to the small degree of parallelism and the high cost of communication. However, interoperation parallelism, including pipelined parallelism and independent parallelism (Section 17.6), can be useful in a distributed system.

For example, consider a join of four relations:

$$r_1 \bowtie r_2 \bowtie r_3 \bowtie r_4$$

where relation r_i is stored at site S_i. Assume that the result must be presented at site S_1. There are many possible strategies for parallel evaluation; for example, any of the strategies described in Section 17.6 may be used. In one such strategy, r_1 is shipped to S_2, and $r_1 \bowtie r_2$ computed at S_2. At the same time, r_3 is shipped to S_4, and $r_3 \bowtie r_4$ computed at S_4. Site S_2 can ship tuples of $(r_1 \bowtie r_2)$ to S_1 as they are produced, rather than waiting for the entire join to be computed. Similarly, S_4 can ship tuples of $(r_3 \bowtie r_4)$ to S_1. Once tuples of $(r_1 \bowtie r_2)$ and $(r_3 \bowtie r_4)$ arrive at S_1, the computation of $(r_1 \bowtie r_2) \bowtie (r_3 \bowtie r_4)$ can begin, with the pipelined join technique of Section 12.8.2.2. Thus, computation of the final join result at S_1 can be done in parallel with the computation of $(r_1 \bowtie r_2)$ at S_2, and with the computation of $(r_3 \bowtie r_4)$ at S_4.

18.4 Distributed Transaction Model

Access to the various data items in a distributed system is usually accomplished through transactions, which must preserve the ACID properties (Section 13.1). There are two types of transaction that we need to consider. The *local* transactions are those that access and update data in only one local database; the *global* transactions are those that access and update data in several local databases. Ensuring the ACID properties of the local transactions can be done in a manner similar to that discussed in Chapters 13, 14, and 15. However, in the case of global transactions, this task is much more complicated, since several sites may be participating in execution. The failure of one of these sites, or the failure of a communication link connecting these sites, may result in erroneous computations.

18.4.1 System Structure

Each site has its own *local transaction manager*, whose function is to ensure the ACID properties of those transactions that execute at that site. The various transaction managers cooperate to execute global transactions. To understand how such a manager can be implemented, we define an abstract model of a transaction system. Each site of the system contains two subsystems:

- The **transaction manager** manages the execution of those transactions (or subtransactions) that access data stored in a local site. Note that each such transaction may be either a local transaction (that is, a transaction that executes at only that site) or part of a global transaction (that is, a transaction that executes at several sites).
- The **transaction coordinator** coordinates the execution of the various transactions (both local and global) initiated at that site.

The overall system architecture is depicted in Figure 18.7.

The structure of a transaction manager is similar in many respects to the structure used in the centralized-system case. Each transaction manager is responsible for

- Maintaining a log for recovery purposes
- Participating in an appropriate concurrency-control scheme to coordinate the concurrent execution of the transactions executing at that site

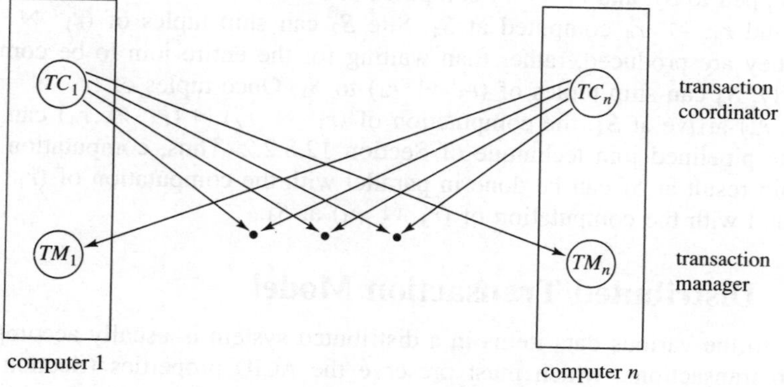

Figure 18.7 System architecture.

As we shall see, we need to modify both the recovery and concurrency schemes to accommodate the distribution of transactions.

The transaction coordinator subsystem is not needed in the centralized environment, since a transaction accesses data at only a single site. A transaction coordinator, as its name implies, is responsible for coordinating the execution of all the transactions initiated at that site. For each such transaction, the coordinator is responsible for

- Starting the execution of the transaction
- Breaking the transaction into a number of subtransactions, and distributing these subtransactions to the appropriate sites for execution
- Coordinating the termination of the transaction, which may result in the transaction being committed at all sites or aborted at all sites

18.4.2 System Failure Modes

A distributed system may suffer from the same types of failure that a centralized system does (for example, software errors, hardware errors, or disk crashes). There are, however, additional types of failure with which we need to deal in a distributed environment. The basic failure types are

- Failure of a site
- Loss of messages
- Failure of a communication link
- Network partition

The loss or corruption of messages is always a possibility in a distributed system. The system uses transmission-control protocols, such as TCP/IP, to handle such errors. Information about such protocols may be found in standard textbooks on networking (see the bibliographic notes).

To understand the effect of failures of communication links, and of network partition, we must first understand how sites in a distributed system are interconnected. The sites in the system can be connected physically in a variety of ways. Some of the most common configurations are depicted in Figure 18.8.

Each configuration has advantages and disadvantages. The configurations can be compared with one another, based on the following criteria:

- **Installation cost**. The cost of physically linking the sites in the system
- **Communication cost**. The cost in time and money to send a message from site *A* to site *B*
- **Availability**. The degree to which data can be accessed despite the failure of some links or sites

The various topologies are depicted in Figure 18.8 as graphs whose nodes correspond to sites. An edge from node *A* to node *B* corresponds to a direct

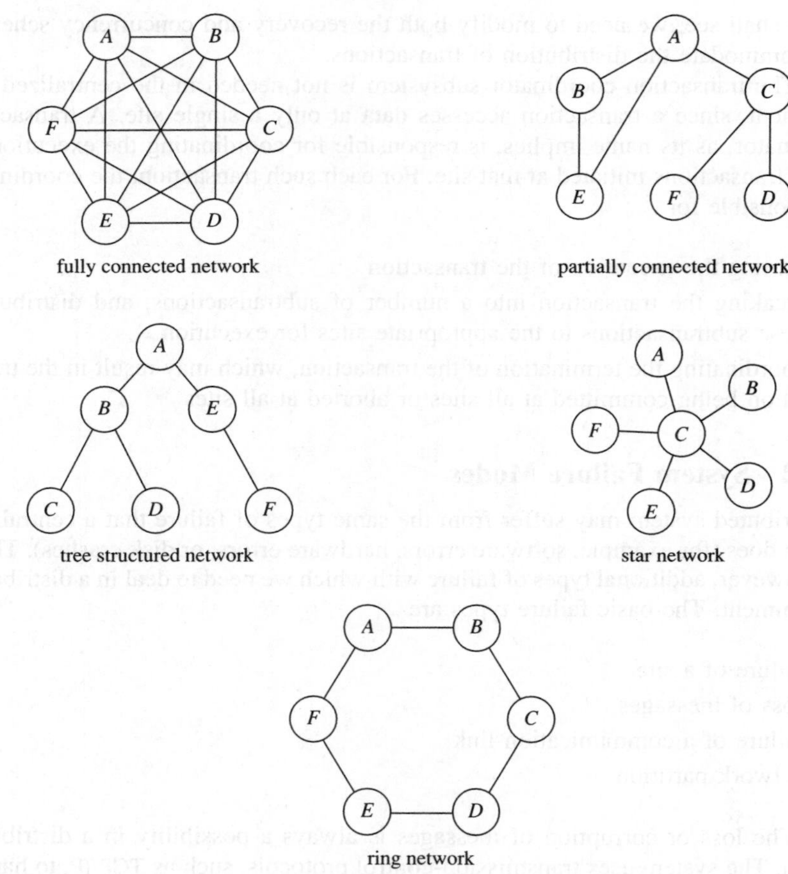

Figure 18.8 Network topology.

communication link between the two sites. In a fully connected network, each site is directly connected to every other site. However, the number of links grows as the square of the number of sites, resulting in a huge installation cost. Therefore, fully connected networks are impractical in any large system.

In a *partially connected network*, direct links exist between some—but not all—pairs of sites. Hence, the installation cost of such a configuration is lower than that of the fully connected network. However, if two sites *A* and *B* are not directly connected, messages from one to the other must be *routed* through a sequence of communication links. This requirement results in a higher communication cost.

If a communication link fails, messages that would have been transmitted across the link must be rerouted. In some cases, it is possible to find another route through the network, so that the messages are able to reach their destination. In other cases, a failure may result in there being no connection between some pairs of sites. A system is *partitioned* if it has been split into two (or more) subsystems, called *partitions*, that lack any connection between them. Note that, under this definition, a subsystem may consist of a single node.

The different partially connected network types shown in Figure 18.8 have different failure characteristics and installation and communication costs. Installation and communication costs are relatively low for a tree-structured network. However, the failure of a single link in a tree-structured network can result in the network becoming partitioned. In a ring network, at least two links must fail for partition to occur. Thus, the ring network has a higher degree of availability than does a tree structured network. However, the communication cost is high, since a message may have to cross a large number of links. In a star network, the failure of a single link results in a network partition, but one of the partitions has only a single site. Such a partition can be treated as a single-site failure. The star network also has a low communication cost, since each site is at most two links away from every other site. However, the failure of the central site results in every site in the system becoming disconnected.

18.4.3 Robustness

For a distributed system to be robust, it must *detect* failures, *reconfigure* the system so that computation may continue, and *recover* when a processor or a link is repaired.

The different types of failures are handled in different ways. Message loss is handled by retransmission. Repeated retransmission of a message across a link, without receipt of an acknowledgment, is usually a symptom of a link failure. The network usually attempts to find an alternative route for the message. Failure to find such a route is usually a symptom of network partition.

It is generally not possible, however, to differentiate clearly between site failure and network partition. The system can usually detect that a failure has occurred, but it may not be able to identify the type of failure. For example, suppose that site S_1 is not able to communicate with S_2. It could be that S_2 has failed. However, another possibility is that the link between S_1 and S_2 has failed, resulting in network partition.

Suppose that site S_1 has discovered that a failure has occurred. It must then initiate a procedure that will allow the system to reconfigure, and to continue with the normal mode of operation.

- If replicated data are stored at the failed site, the catalog should be updated so that queries do not reference the copy at the failed site.
- If transactions were active at the failed site at the time of the failure, these transactions should be aborted. It is desirable to abort such transactions promptly, since they may hold locks on data at sites that are still active.
- If the failed site is a central server for some subsystem, an *election* must be held to determine the new server (see Section 18.6.2). Examples of central servers include a name server, a concurrency coordinator, or a global deadlock detector.

Since it is, in general, not possible to distinguish between network link failures and site failures, any reconfiguration scheme must be designed to work correctly in case of a partitioning of the network. In particular, the following situations must be avoided:

- Two or more central servers are elected in distinct partitions.
- More than one partition updates a replicated data item.

Reintegration of a repaired site or link into the system also requires care. When a failed site recovers, it must initiate a procedure to update its system tables to reflect changes made while it was down. If the site had replicas of any data items, it must obtain the current values of these data items and ensure that it receives all future updates. Reintegration of a site is more complicated than it may seem to be at first glance, since there may be updates to the data items processed during the time that the site is recovering. An easy solution is temporarily to halt the entire system while the failed site rejoins it. In most applications, however, such a temporary halt is unacceptably disruptive. Techniques have been developed to allow failed sites to reintegrate while allowing concurrent updates to data items. If a failed link recovers, two or more partitions can be rejoined. Since a partitioning of the network limits the allowable operations by some or all sites, it is desirable to inform all sites promptly of the recovery of the link. See the bibliographic notes for more information on recovery in distributed systems.

18.5 Commit Protocols

If we are to ensure atomicity, all the sites in which a transaction T executed must agree on the final outcome of the execution. T must either commit at all sites, or it must abort at all sites. To ensure this property, the transaction coordinator of T must execute a *commit protocol*.

Among the simplest and most widely used commit protocols is the *two-phase commit* protocol (2PC), which is described in Section 18.5.1. An alternative is the *three-phase commit* protocol (3PC), which avoids certain disadvantages of the 2PC protocol but adds to complexity and overhead. The 3PC protocol is described in Section 18.5.2.

18.5.1 Two-Phase Commit

Let T be a transaction initiated at site S_i, and let the transaction coordinator at S_i be C_i.

18.5.1.1 The Commit Protocol

When T completes its execution—that is, when all the sites at which T has executed inform C_i that T has completed—C_i starts the 2PC protocol.

- **Phase 1**. C_i adds the record **<prepare** T> to the log, and forces the log onto stable storage. It then sends a **prepare** T message to all sites at which T

executed. On receiving such a message, the transaction manager at that site determines whether it is willing to commit its portion of T. If the answer is no, it adds a record <**no** T> to the log, and then responds by sending an **abort** T message to C_i. If the answer is yes, it adds a record <**ready** T> to the log, and forces the log (with all the log records corresponding to T) onto stable storage. The transaction manager then replies with a **ready** T message to C_i.

- **Phase 2.** When C_i receives responses to the **prepare** T message from all the sites, or when a prespecified interval of time has elapsed since the **prepare** T message was sent out, C_i can determine whether the transaction T can be committed or aborted. Transaction T can be committed if C_i received a **ready** T message from all the participating sites. Otherwise, transaction T must be aborted. Depending on the verdict, either a record <**commit** T> or a record <**abort** T> is added to the log and the log is forced onto stable storage. At this point, the fate of the transaction has been sealed. Following this point, the coordinator sends either a **commit** T or an **abort** T message to all participating sites. When a site receives that message, it records the message in the log.

A site at which T executed can unconditionally abort T at any time prior to its sending the message **ready** T to the coordinator. The **ready** T message is, in effect, a promise by a site to follow the coordinator's order to commit T or to abort T. The only means by which a site can make such a promise is if the needed information is stored in stable storage. Otherwise, if the site crashes after sending **ready** T, it may be unable to make good on its promise.

Since unanimity is required to commit a transaction, the fate of T is sealed as soon as at least one site responds **abort** T. Since the coordinator site S_i is one of the sites at which T executed, the coordinator can decide unilaterally to abort T. The final verdict regarding T is determined at the time that the coordinator writes that verdict (commit or abort) to the log and forces that verdict to stable storage. In some implementations of the 2PC protocol, a site sends an **acknowledge** T message to the coordinator at the end of the second phase of the protocol. When the coordinator receives the **acknowledge** T message from all the sites, it adds the record <**complete** T> to the log.

18.5.1.2 Handling of Failures

We now examine in detail how the 2PC protocol responds to various types of failures.

- **Failure of a participating site.** If the coordinator C_i detects that a site has failed, it takes the following actions. If the site fails before responding with a **ready** T message to C_i, it is assumed to have responded with an **abort** T message. If the site fails after the coordinator has received the **ready** T message from the site, the rest of the commit protocol is executed in the normal fashion, ignoring the failure of the site.

  When a participating site S_k recovers from a failure, it must examine its log to determine the fate of those transactions that were in the midst of execution when the failure occurred. Let T be one such transaction. We consider each of the possible cases:

- The log contains a <**commit** T> record. In this case, the site executes **redo**(T).
- The log contains an <**abort** T> record. In this case, the site executes **undo**(T).
- The log contains a <**ready** T> record. In this case, the site must consult C_i to determine the fate of T. If C_i is up, it notifies S_k regarding whether T committed or aborted. In the former case, it executes **redo**(T); in the latter case, it executes **undo**(T). If C_i is down, S_k must try to find the fate of T from other sites. It does so by sending a **query-status** T message to all the sites in the system. On receiving such a message, a site must consult its log to determine whether T has executed there, and if T has, whether T committed or aborted. It then notifies S_k about this outcome. If no site has the appropriate information (that is, whether T committed or aborted), then S_k can neither abort nor commit T. The decision concerning T is postponed until S_k can obtain the needed information. Thus, S_k must periodically resend the **query-status** message to the other sites. It continues to do so until a site recovers that contains the needed information. Note that the site at which C_i resides always has the needed information.
- The log contains no control records (**abort, commit, ready**) concerning T. Thus, we know that S_k failed before responding to the **prepare** T message from C_i. Since the failure of S_k precludes the sending of such a response, by our algorithm C_i must abort T. Hence, S_k must execute **undo**(T).

- **Failure of the coordinator**. If the coordinator fails in the midst of the execution of the commit protocol for transaction T, then the participating sites must decide the fate of T. We shall see that, in certain cases, the participating sites cannot decide whether to commit or abort T, and therefore these sites must wait for the recovery of the failed coordinator.
  - If an active site contains a <**commit** T> record in its log, then T must be committed.
  - If an active site contains an <**abort** T> record in its log, then T must be aborted.
  - If some active site does *not* contain a <**ready** T> record in its log, then the failed coordinator C_i cannot have decided to commit T, because a site that does not have a <**ready** T> record in its log cannot have sent a **ready** T message to C_i. However, the coordinator may have decided to abort T, but not to commit T. Rather than wait for C_i to recover, it is preferable to abort T.
  - If none of the preceding cases holds, then all active sites must have a <**ready** T> record in their logs, but no additional control records (such as <**abort** T> or <**commit** T>). Since the coordinator has failed, it is impossible to determine whether a decision has been made, and if one has, what that decision is, until the coordinator recovers. Thus, the active sites must wait for C_i to recover. Since the fate of T remains in doubt, T may continue to hold system resources. For example, if locking is used, T may

hold locks on data at active sites. Such a situation is undesirable, because it may be hours or days before C_i is again active. During this time, other transactions may be forced to wait for T. As a result, data items may be unavailable not only on the failed site (C_i), but on active sites as well. This situation is called the *blocking* problem, because T is blocked pending the recovery of site C_i.

- **Network partition**. When a network partitions, two possibilities exist:
  1. The coordinator and all its participants remain in one partition. In this case, the failure has no effect on the commit protocol.
  2. The coordinator and its participants belong to several partitions. From the viewpoint of the sites in one of the partitions, it appears that the sites in other partitions have failed. Sites that are not in the partition containing the coordinator simply execute the protocol to deal with failure of the coordinator. The coordinator and the sites that are in the same partition as the coordinator follow the usual commit protocol, assuming that the sites in the other partitions have failed.

Thus, the major disadvantage of the 2PC protocol is that coordinator failure may result in blocking, where a decision either to commit or to abort T may have to be postponed until C_i recovers.

18.5.1.3 Recovery and Concurrency Control

When a failed site restarts, we can perform recovery using, for example, the recovery algorithm described in Section 15.9. To deal with distributed commit protocols (such as 2PC and 3PC), the recovery procedure must treat *in-doubt* transactions specially; in-doubt transactions are transactions for which a <**ready** *T*> log record is found, but neither a <**commit** *T*> log record, nor an <**abort** *T*> log record, is found. The recovering site must determine the commit–abort status of such transactions by contacting other sites, as described in Section 18.5.1.2.

If recovery is done as just described, however, normal transaction processing at the site cannot begin until all in-doubt transactions have been committed or rolled back. Finding the status of in-doubt transactions can be slow, since multiple sites may have to be contacted. Further, if the coordinator has failed, and no other site has information about the commit–abort status of an incomplete transaction, recovery potentially could become blocked if 2PC is used. As a result, the site performing restart recovery may remain unusable for a long period.

To circumvent this problem, recovery algorithms typically provide support for noting lock information in the log. (We are assuming here that locking is used for concurrency control.) Instead of a <**ready** *T*> log record being written, a <**ready** *T*, *L*> log record is written out, where L is a list of all locks held by the transaction T when the log record is written. At recovery time, after performance of local recovery actions, for every in-doubt transaction T, all the locks noted in the <**ready** *T*, *L*> log record (read from the log) are reacquired.

After lock reacquisition is complete for all in-doubt transactions, transaction processing can start at the site, even before the commit–abort status of the in-doubt transactions is determined. The commit or rollback of in-doubt transactions is performed concurrently with the execution of new transactions. Thus, site recovery is faster, and never gets blocked. Note that new transactions that have a lock conflict with any in-doubt transactions will be unable to make progress until the conflicting in-doubt transactions have been committed or rolled back.

18.5.2 Three-Phase Commit

The 3PC protocol is designed to avoid the possibility of blocking in a restricted case of possible failures. The version of the 3PC protocol that we describe requires that

- No network partition can occur.
- At most K participating sites can fail while the 3PC protocol is being executed for a transaction. K is a parameter indicating the resiliency of the protocol to site failures.
- At any point, at least $K + 1$ sites must be up.

The protocol achieves the nonblocking property by adding an extra phase in which a preliminary decision is reached regarding the fate of T. The information made available to the participating sites as a result of this preliminary decision allows a decision to be made despite the failure of the coordinator.

18.5.2.1 The Commit Protocol

As before, let T be a transaction initiated at site S_i, and let the transaction coordinator at S_i be C_i.

- **Phase 1**. This phase is identical to phase 1 of the 2PC protocol.
- **Phase 2**. If C_i receives an **abort** T message from a participating site, or if C_i receives no response within a prespecified interval from a participating site, then C_i decides to abort T. The abort decision is implemented in the same way as is the 2PC protocol. If C_i receives a **ready** T message from every participating site, C_i makes the preliminary decision to *precommit* T. Precommit differs from commit in that T may still be aborted eventually. The precommit decision allows the coordinator to inform each participating site that all participating sites are ready. C_i adds a record <**precommit** T> to the log and forces the log onto stable storage. Then, C_i sends a **precommit** T message to all participating sites. When a site receives a message from the coordinator (either **abort** T or **precommit** T), it records that message in its log, forces this information to stable storage, and sends a message **acknowledge** T to the coordinator.
- **Phase 3**. This phase is executed only if the decision in phase 2 was to precommit. After the **precommit** T messages are sent to all participating sites, the coordinator must wait until it receives at least K **acknowledge** T messages. Then, the coordinator reaches a commit decision. It adds a <**commit** T>

record to its log, and forces the log to stable storage. Then, C_i sends a **commit** T message to all participating sites. When a site receives that message, it records the information in its log.

Just as in the 2PC protocol, a site at which T executed can unconditionally abort T at any time prior to sending the message **ready** T to the coordinator. The **ready** T message is, in effect, a promise by a site to follow the coordinator's order to commit T or to abort T. In contrast to the 2PC protocol, in which the coordinator can unconditionally abort T at any time prior to sending the message **commit** T, the **precommit** T message in the 3PC protocol is a promise by the coordinator to follow the participant's order to commit T.

Since phase 3 always leads to a commit decision, it may seem to be of little use. The role of the third phase becomes apparent when we look at how the 3PC protocol handles failures.

In some implementations of the 3PC protocol, a site sends a message **ack** T to the coordinator upon receipt of the **commit** T message. (Note the use of **ack** to distinguish this term from the **acknowledge** messages that were used in phase 2.) When the coordinator receives the **ack** T message from all sites, it adds the record <**complete** T> to the log.

18.5.2.2 Handling of Failures

We now examine in detail how the 3PC protocol responds to various types of failures.

- **Failure of a participating site**. If the coordinator C_i detects that a site has failed, the actions that it takes are similar to the actions taken in 2PC. If the site fails before responding with a **ready** T message to C_i, it is assumed to have responded with an **abort** T message. Otherwise, the rest of the commit protocol is executed in the normal fashion, ignoring the failure of the site.

  When a participating site S_j recovers from a failure, it must examine its log to determine the fate of those transactions that were in the midst of execution when the failure occurred. Let T be one such transaction. We consider each of the possible cases:

  - The log contains a <**commit** T> record. In this case, the site executes **redo**(T).
  - The log contains an <**abort** T> record. In this case, the site executes **undo**(T).
  - The log contains a <**ready** T> record, but no <**abort** T> or <**precommit** T> record. In this case, the site attempts to consult C_i to determine the fate of T. If C_i responds with a message that T aborted, the site executes **undo**(T). If C_i responds with a message **precommit** T, the site (as in phase 2) records this information in its log, and resumes the protocol by sending an **acknowledge** T message to the coordinator. If C_i responds with a message that T committed, the site executes **redo**(T). In the event that C_i fails to respond within a prespecified interval, the site executes a coordinator failure protocol (see next list entry).

◦ The log contains a <**precommit** T> record, but no <**abort** T> or <**commit** T> record. As before, the site consults C_i. If C_i responds that T aborted or committed, the site executes **undo**(T) or **redo**(T), respectively. If C_i responds that T is still in the precommit state, the site resumes the protocol at this point. If C_i fails to respond within a prescribed interval, the site executes the coordinator-failure protocol.

- **Failure of the coordinator**. When a participating site fails to receive a response from the coordinator, for whatever reason, it executes the *coordinator-failure protocol*. This protocol results in the selection of a new coordinator. When the failed coordinator recovers, it does so in the role of a participating site. It no longer acts as coordinator; rather, it must determine the decision that has been reached by the new coordinator.

18.5.2.3 Coordinator-Failure Protocol

The coordinator-failure protocol is triggered by a participating site that fails to receive a response from the coordinator within a prespecified interval. Since we assume no network partition, the only possible cause for this situation is the failure of the coordinator.

1. The active participating sites select a new coordinator using an election protocol (see Section 18.6).
2. The new coordinator, C_{new}, sends a message to each participating site requesting the local status of T.
3. Each participating site, including C_{new}, determines the local status of T:
   - **Committed**. The log contains a <**commit** T> record.
   - **Aborted**. The log contains an <**abort** T> record.
   - **Ready**. The log contains a <**ready** T> record, but contains no <**abort** T> or <**precommit** T> record.
   - **Precommitted**. The log contains a <**precommit** T> record, but contains no <**abort** T> or <**commit** T> record.
   - **Not ready**. The log contains neither a <**ready** T> nor an <**abort** T> record.

   Each participating site sends its local status to C_{new}.
4. Depending on the responses received, C_{new} decides either to commit or abort T, or to restart the 3PC protocol:
   - If at least one site has local status = **committed**, then C_{new} commits T.
   - If at least one site has local status = **aborted**, then C_{new} aborts T. (Note that it is not possible for some site to have local status = **committed** while another has local status = **aborted**.)
   - If no site has local status = **aborted**, and no site has local status = **committed**, but at least one site has local status = **precommitted**, then C_{new} resumes the 3PC protocol by sending new **precommit** messages.
   - Otherwise, C_{new} aborts T.

The coordinator-failure protocol allows the new coordinator to obtain knowledge about the state of the failed coordinator, C_i.

If any active site has a <**commit** T> in its log, then C_i must have decided to commit T. If an active site has <**precommit** T> in its log, then C_i must have reached a preliminary decision to precommit T, and that means that all sites, including any that may have failed, have reached **ready** states. It is therefore safe to commit T. However, C_{new} does not commit T unilaterally; doing so would create the same blocking problem, if C_{new} fails, as in 2PC. It is for this reason that phase 3 is resumed by C_{new}.

Consider the case where no active site has received a precommit message from C_i. We must consider three possibilities:

1. C_i had decided to commit T prior to C_i failing.
2. C_i had decided to abort T prior to C_i failing.
3. C_i had not yet decided the fate of T.

We shall show that the first of these alternatives is not possible, and that, therefore, it is safe to abort T.

Suppose that C_i had decided to commit T. Then, at least K sites must have decided to precommit T and have sent acknowledge messages to C_i. Since C_i has failed, and we assume that at most K sites fail while the 3PC protocol is executed for a transaction, at least one of the K sites must be active, and hence at least one active site would inform C_{new} that it has received a precommit message. Thus, if no active site had received a precommit message, a commit decision certainly could not have been reached by C_i. Therefore, it is indeed safe to abort T. It is possible that C_i had not decided to abort T, so it may still be possible to commit T. However, detecting that C_i had not decided to abort T would require waiting for C_i (or for some other failed site that had received a precommit message) to recover. Hence, the protocol aborts T if no active site has received a precommit message.

In the preceding discussion, if more than K sites could fail while the 3PC protocol is executed for a transaction, it may not be possible for the surviving participants to determine the action taken by C_i prior to failing; this situation would force blocking to occur until C_i recovers. Although a large value for K is best from this standpoint, it forces a coordinator to wait for more responses before deciding to commit—thus delaying routine (failure-free) processing. Further, if fewer than K participants (in addition to the coordinator) are active, it may not be possible for the coordinator to complete the commit protocol, resulting in blocking. Thus, the choice of a value for K is crucial, as it determines the degree to which the protocol avoids blocking.

Our assumption of no network partitions is crucial to our discussion. As mentioned earlier, it is, in general, impossible to differentiate between network failure and site failure. Thus, network partitioning could lead to the election of two new coordinators (each of which believes that all sites in partitions other than its own have failed). The decisions of the two coordinators may not agree, resulting in the transaction being committed in some sites while being aborted in others.

18.5.3 Comparison of Protocols

The 2PC protocol is widely used, despite its potential for blocking. The probability of blocking occurring in practice is usually sufficiently low that the extra cost of the 3PC protocol is not justified. The vulnerability of 3PC to link failures is another practical issue. This disadvantage can be overcome by network-level protocols, but that solution adds overhead.

We can streamline both protocols to reduce the number of messages sent, and to reduce the number of times that records must be forced to stable storage. The 3PC protocol can be extended to allow more than K failures, provided that not more than K sites fail before the new coordinator makes a commit decision. The bibliographic notes contain references to several such techniques.

18.6 Coordinator Selection

Several of the algorithms that we have presented require the use of a coordinator. If the coordinator fails because of a failure of the site at which it resides, the system can continue execution only by restarting a new coordinator on another site. It can do so by maintaining a backup to the coordinator that is ready to assume responsibility if the coordinator fails. Or, it can choose the new coordinator after the coordinator has failed. The algorithms that determine where a new copy of the coordinator should be restarted are called *election* algorithms.

18.6.1 Backup Coordinators

A *backup coordinator* is a site that, in addition to other tasks, maintains enough information locally to allow it to assume the role of coordinator with minimal disruption to the distributed system. All messages directed to the coordinator are received by both the coordinator and its backup. The backup coordinator executes the same algorithms and maintains the same internal state information (such as, for a concurrency coordinator, the lock table) as does the actual coordinator. The only difference in function between the coordinator and its backup is that the backup does not take any action that affects other sites. Such actions are left to the actual coordinator.

In the event that the backup coordinator detects the failure of the actual coordinator, it assumes the role of coordinator. Since the backup has all the information available to it that the failed coordinator had, processing can continue without interruption.

The prime advantage to the backup approach is the ability to continue processing immediately. If a backup were not ready to assume the coordinator's responsibility, a newly appointed coordinator would have to seek information from all sites in the system so that it could execute the coordination tasks. Frequently, the only source of some of the requisite information is the failed coordinator. In this case, it may be necessary to abort several (or all) active transactions, and to restart them under the control of the new coordinator.

Thus, the backup-coordinator approach avoids a substantial amount of delay while the distributed system recovers from a coordinator failure. The disadvantage is the overhead of duplicate execution of the coordinator's tasks. Furthermore, a coordinator and its backup need to communicate regularly to ensure that their activities are synchronized.

In short, the backup-coordinator approach incurs overhead during normal processing to allow fast recovery from a coordinator failure. In Section 18.6.2, we consider a lower-overhead recovery scheme that requires somewhat more effort to recover from a failure.

18.6.2 Election Algorithms

Election algorithms require that a unique identification number be associated with each active site in the system. For ease of notation, we shall assume that the identification number of site S_i is i. Also, to simplify our discussion, we assume that the coordinator always resides at the site with the largest identification number. The goal of an election algorithm is to choose a site for the new coordinator. Hence, when a coordinator fails, the algorithm must elect the active site that has the largest identification number. This number must be sent to each active site in the system. In addition, the algorithm must provide a mechanism by which a site recovering from a crash can identify the current coordinator.

The various election algorithms usually differ in terms of the network configuration. In this section, we present one of these algorithms: the *bully* algorithm.

Suppose that site S_i sends a request that is not answered by the coordinator within a prespecified time interval T. In this situation, it is assumed that the coordinator has failed, and S_i tries to elect itself as the site for the new coordinator.

Site S_i sends an election message to every site that has a higher identification number. Site S_i then waits, for a time interval T, for an answer from any one of these sites. If it receives no response within time T, it assumes that all sites with numbers greater than i have failed, and it elects itself as the site for the new coordinator and sends a message to inform all active sites with identification numbers lower than i that it is the site at which the new coordinator resides.

If S_i does receive an answer, it begins a time interval T', to receive a message informing it that a site with a higher identification number has been elected. (Some other site is electing itself coordinator, and should report the results within time T'.) If no message is received within T', then the site with a higher number is assumed to have failed, and site S_i restarts the algorithm.

After a failed site recovers, it immediately begins execution of the same algorithm. If there are no active sites with higher numbers, the recovered site forces all sites with lower numbers to let it become the coordinator site, even if there is a currently active coordinator with a lower number. It is for this reason that the algorithm is termed the *bully* algorithm.

18.7 Concurrency Control

In this section, we show how some of the concurrency-control schemes discussed earlier can be modified such that they can be used in a distributed environment.

We assume that each site participates in the execution of a commit protocol to ensure global transaction atomicity.

18.7.1 Locking Protocols

The various locking protocols described in Chapter 14 can be used in a distributed environment. The only change that needs to be incorporated is in the way the lock manager is implemented. We present several possible schemes that are applicable to an environment where data can be replicated in several sites. As in Chapter 14, we shall assume the existence of the *shared* and *exclusive* lock modes.

18.7.1.1 Single-Lock-Manager Approach

The system maintains a *single* lock manager that resides in a *single* chosen site—say, S_i. All lock and unlock requests are made at site S_i. When a transaction needs to lock a data item, it sends a lock request to S_i. The lock manager determines whether the lock can be granted immediately. If the lock can be granted, the lock manager sends a message to that effect to the site at which the lock request was initiated. Otherwise, the request is delayed until it can be granted, at which time a message is sent to the site at which the lock request was initiated. The transaction can read the data item from *any* one of the sites at which a replica of the data item resides. In the case of a write, all the sites where a replica of the data item resides must be involved in the writing.

The scheme has the following advantages:

- **Simple implementation**. This scheme requires two messages for handling lock requests, and one message for handling unlock requests.
- **Simple deadlock handling**. Since all lock and unlock requests are made at one site, the deadlock-handling algorithms discussed in Chapter 14 can be applied directly to this environment.

The disadvantages of the scheme include the following:

- **Bottleneck**. The site S_i becomes a bottleneck, since all requests must be processed there.
- **Vulnerability**. If the site S_i fails, the concurrency controller is lost. Either processing must stop, or a recovery scheme must be used so that a new site can take over lock management from S_i, as described in Section 18.6.

18.7.1.2 Multiple Coordinators

A compromise between the advantages and disadvantages just noted can be achieved through a *multiple-coordinator approach*, in which the lock-manager function is distributed over several sites.

Each lock manager administers the lock and unlock requests for a subset of the data items. Each lock manager resides in a different site. This approach reduces the degree to which the coordinator is a bottleneck, but it complicates deadlock handling, since the lock and unlock requests are not made at a single site.

18.7.1.3 Majority Protocol

In a majority protocol, each site maintains a local lock manager whose function is to administer the lock and unlock requests for those data items that are stored in that site. When a transaction wishes to lock data item Q, which is not replicated and resides at site S_i, a message is sent to the lock manager at site S_i requesting a lock (in a particular lock mode). If data item Q is locked in an incompatible mode, then the request is delayed until it can be granted. Once it has determined that the lock request can be granted, the lock manager sends a message back to the initiator indicating that it has granted the lock request. The scheme has the advantage of simple implementation. It requires two message transfers for handling lock requests, and one message transfer for handling unlock requests. However, deadlock handling is more complex. Since the lock and unlock requests are no longer made at a single site, the various deadlock-handling algorithms discussed in Chapter 14 must be modified, as we shall discuss in Section 18.8.

If data item Q is replicated in n different sites, then a lock-request message must be sent to more than one-half of the n sites in which Q is stored. Each lock manager determines whether the lock can be granted immediately (as far as it is concerned). As before, the response is delayed until the request can be granted. The transaction does not operate on Q until it has successfully obtained a lock on a majority of the replicas of Q.

This scheme deals with replicated data in a decentralized manner, thus avoiding the drawbacks of central control. However, when there is replication of data, it suffers from the following disadvantages:

- **Implementation**. The majority protocol is more complicated to implement than are the previous schemes. It requires $2(n/2 + 1)$ messages for handling lock requests, and $(n/2 + 1)$ messages for handling unlock requests.
- **Deadlock handling**. Since the lock and unlock requests are not made at one site, the deadlock-handling algorithms must be modified (see Section 18.8). In addition, it is possible for a deadlock to occur even if only one data item is being locked. As an illustration, consider a system with four sites and full replication. Suppose that transactions T_1 and T_2 wish to lock data item Q in exclusive mode. Transaction T_1 may succeed in locking Q at sites S_1 and S_3, while transaction T_2 may succeed in locking Q at sites S_2 and S_4. Each then must wait to acquire the third lock; hence, a deadlock has occurred. Luckily, we can avoid such deadlocks with relative ease, by requiring all sites to request locks on the replicas of a data item in the same predetermined order.

18.7.1.4 Biased Protocol

The *biased protocol* is based on a model similar to that of the majority protocol. The difference is that requests for shared locks are given more favorable treatment than requests for exclusive locks. The system maintains a lock manager at each site. Each manager manages the locks for all the data items stored at that site. *Shared* and *exclusive* locks are handled differently.

- **Shared locks**. When a transaction needs to lock data item Q, it simply requests a lock on Q from the lock manager at one site that contains a replica of Q.
- **Exclusive locks**. When a transaction needs to lock data item Q, it requests a lock on Q from the lock manager at all sites that contain a replica of Q.

As before, the response to the request is delayed until it can be granted.

The biased scheme has the advantage of imposing less overhead on **read** operations than does the majority protocol. This savings is especially significant in common cases in which the frequency of **read** is much greater than the frequency of **write**. However, the additional overhead on writes is a disadvantage. Furthermore, the biased protocol shares the majority protocol's disadvantage of complexity in handling deadlock.

18.7.1.5 Primary Copy

In the case of data replication, we can choose one of the replicas as the primary copy. Thus, for each data item Q, the primary copy of Q must reside in precisely one site, which we call the *primary site of Q*.

When a transaction needs to lock a data item Q, it requests a lock at the primary site of Q. As before, the response to the request is delayed until it can be granted.

Thus, the primary copy enables concurrency control for replicated data to be handled in a manner similar to that for unreplicated data. This similarity allows for a simple implementation. However, if the primary site of Q fails, Q is inaccessible, even though other sites containing a replica may be accessible.

18.7.2 Timestamping

The principal idea behind the timestamping scheme discussed in Section 14.2 is that each transaction is given a *unique* timestamp that the system uses in deciding the serialization order. Our first task, then, in generalizing the centralized scheme to a distributed scheme is to develop a scheme for generating unique timestamps. Then, our previous protocols can be applied directly to the nonreplicated environment.

There are two primary methods for generating unique timestamps, one centralized and one distributed. In the centralized scheme, a single site is chosen for distributing the timestamps. The site can use a logical counter or its own local clock for this purpose.

In the distributed scheme, each site generates a unique local timestamp using either a logical counter or the local clock. We obtain the unique global timestamp by concatenating the unique local timestamp with the site identifier, which also must be unique (Figure 18.9). The order of concatenation is important! We use the site identifier in the least significant position to ensure that the global timestamps

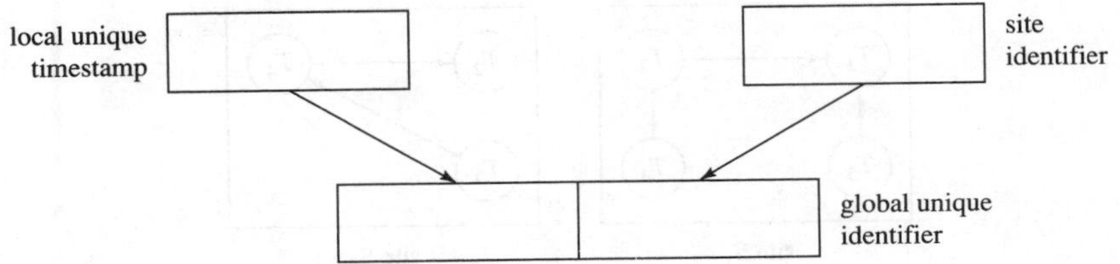

Figure 18.9 Generation of unique timestamps.

generated in one site are not always greater than those generated in another site. Compare this technique for generating unique timestamps with the one that we presented earlier for generating unique names.

We may still have a problem if one site generates local timestamps at a rate faster than that of the other sites. In such a case, the fast site's logical counter will be larger than that of other sites. Therefore, all timestamps generated by the fast site will be larger than those generated by other sites. What we need is a mechanism to ensure that local timestamps are generated fairly across the system. We define within each site S_i a *logical clock* (LC_i), which generates the unique local timestamp. The logical clock can be implemented as a counter that is incremented after a new local timestamp is generated. To ensure that the various logical clocks are synchronized, we require that a site S_i advance its logical clock whenever a transaction T_i with timestamp $<x,y>$ visits that site and x is greater than the current value of LC_i. In this case, site S_i advances its logical clock to the value $x + 1$.

If the system clock is used to generate timestamps, then timestamps are assigned fairly, provided that no site has a system clock that runs fast or slow. Since clocks may not be perfectly accurate, a technique similar to that used for logical clocks must be used to ensure that no clock gets far ahead of or behind another clock.

18.8 Deadlock Handling

The deadlock-prevention and deadlock-detection algorithms presented in Chapter 14 can be used in a distributed system, provided that modifications are made. For example, we can use the tree protocol by defining a *global* tree among the system data items. Similarly, the timestamp-ordering approach could be directly applied to a distributed environment, as we saw in Section 18.7.2.

Deadlock prevention may result in unnecessary waiting and rollback. Furthermore, certain deadlock-prevention techniques may require more sites to be involved in the execution of a transaction than would otherwise be the case.

If we allow deadlocks to occur and rely on deadlock detection, the main problem in a distributed system is deciding how to maintain the wait-for graph. Common techniques for dealing with this issue require that each site keep a *local* wait-for graph. The nodes of the graph correspond to all the transactions (local as well as nonlocal) that are currently either holding or requesting any of the items local to that site. For example, Figure 18.10 depicts a system consisting of two sites,

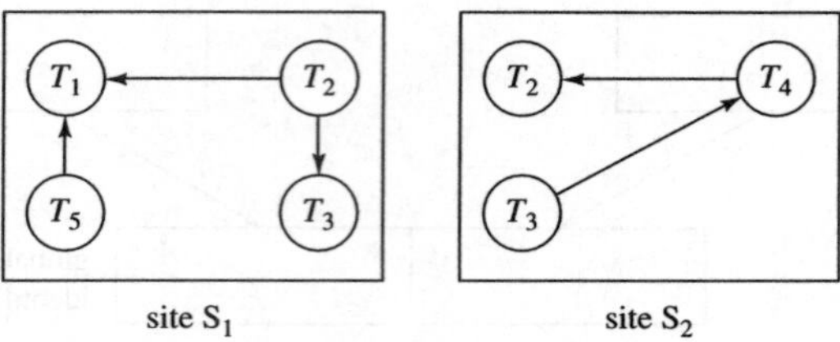

Figure 18.10 Local wait-for graphs.

each maintaining its local wait-for graph. Note that transactions T_2 and T_3 appear in both graphs, indicating that the transactions have requested items at both sites.

These local wait-for graphs are constructed in the usual manner for local transactions and data items. When a transaction T_i on site S_1 needs a resource in site S_2, a request message is sent by T_i to site S_2. If the resource is held by transaction T_j, an edge $T_i \rightarrow T_j$ is inserted in the local wait-for graph of site S_2.

Clearly, if any local wait-for graph has a cycle, deadlock has occurred. On the other hand, the fact that there are no cycles in any of the local wait-for graphs does not mean that there are no deadlocks. To illustrate this problem, we consider the local wait-for graphs of Figure 18.10. Each wait-for graph is acyclic; nevertheless, a deadlock exists in the system because the *union* of the local wait-for graphs contains a cycle. This graph is shown in Figure 18.11.

Several common schemes for organizing the wait-for graph in a distributed system are described in Sections 18.8.1 and 18.8.2.

18.8.1 Centralized Approach

In the *centralized approach*, a global wait-for graph (union of all the local graphs) is constructed and maintained in a *single* site: the deadlock-detection coordinator. Since there is communication delay in the system, we must distinguish between two types of wait-for graphs. The *real* graph describes the real but unknown state of the system at any instance in time, as would be seen by an omniscient observer. The *constructed* graph is an approximation generated by the controller during the execution of the controller's algorithm. Obviously, the constructed graph must be generated such that, whenever the detection algorithm is invoked, the reported results are correct in the sense that, if a deadlock exists, it is reported promptly, and if the system reports a deadlock, it is indeed in a deadlock state.

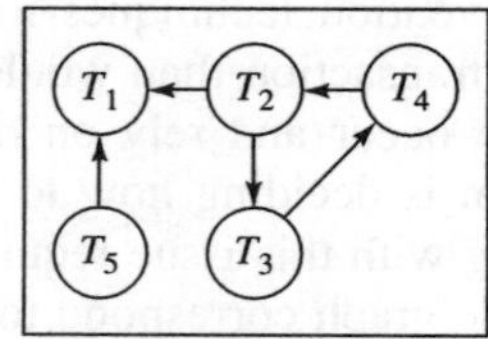

Figure 18.11 Global wait-for graph for Figure 18.10.

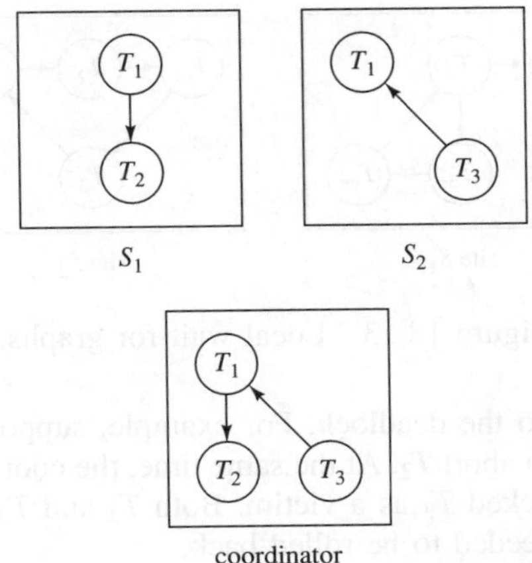

Figure 18.12 False cycles in the global wait-for graph.

The global wait-for graph can be constructed under these conditions:

- Whenever a new edge is inserted in or removed from one of the local wait-for graphs.
- Periodically, when a number of changes have occurred in a local wait-for graph.
- Whenever the coordinator needs to invoke the cycle-detection algorithm.

When the deadlock-detection algorithm is invoked, the coordinator searches its global graph. If a cycle is found, a victim is selected to be rolled back. The coordinator must notify all the sites that a particular transaction has been selected as victim. The sites, in turn, roll back the victim transaction.

We note that this scheme may produce unnecessary rollbacks, as a result of one of the following:

- *False cycles* may exist in the global wait-for graph. As an illustration, consider a snapshot of the system represented by the local wait-for graphs of Figure 18.12. Suppose that T_2 releases the resource that it is holding in site S_1, resulting in the deletion of the edge $T_1 \rightarrow T_2$ in S_1. Transaction T_2 then requests a resource held by T_3 at site S_2, resulting in the addition of the edge $T_2 \rightarrow T_3$ in S_2. If the **insert** $T_2 \rightarrow T_3$ message from S_2 arrives before the **remove** $T_1 \rightarrow T_2$ message from S_1, the coordinator may discover the false cycle $T_1 \rightarrow T_2 \rightarrow T_3$ after the **insert** (but before the **remove**). Deadlock recovery may be initiated, although no deadlock has occurred.

  Note that the preceding example could not occur under two-phase locking. Indeed, the likelihood of false cycles is usually sufficiently low that false cycles do not cause a serious performance problem.
- Unnecessary rollbacks may also result when a *deadlock* has indeed occurred and a victim has been picked, while one of the transactions was aborted for

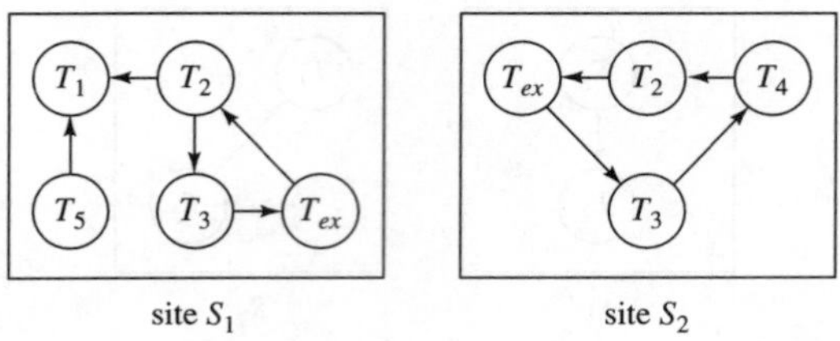

Figure 18.13 Local wait-for graphs.

reasons unrelated to the deadlock. For example, suppose that site S_1 in Figure 18.10 decides to abort T_2. At the same time, the coordinator has discovered a cycle, and has picked T_3 as a victim. Both T_2 and T_3 are now rolled back, although only T_2 needed to be rolled back.

18.8.2 Fully Distributed Approach

In the *fully distributed* deadlock-detection algorithm, all controllers share equally the responsibility for detecting deadlock. In this scheme, every site constructs a wait-for graph that represents a part of the total graph, depending on the dynamic behavior of the system. The idea is that, if a deadlock exists, a cycle will appear in (at least) one of the partial graphs. We present one such algorithm that involves construction of partial graphs in every site.

Each site maintains its own local wait-for graph. A local wait-for graph differs from the wait-for graph described previously in that we add one additional node T_{ex} to the graph. T_{ex} represents transactions that are external to the local site. An arc $T_i \rightarrow T_{\text{ex}}$ exists in the graph if T_i is waiting for a data item in another site that is being held by *any* transaction. Similarly, an arc $T_{\text{ex}} \rightarrow T_j$ exists in the graph if a transaction at another site is waiting to acquire a resource currently being held by T_j in this local site.

As an illustration, consider the two local wait-for graphs of Figure 18.10. The addition of the node T_{ex} in both graphs results in the local wait-for graphs shown in Figure 18.13.

If a local wait-for graph contains a cycle that does not involve node T_{ex}, then the system is in a deadlock state. However, the existence of a cycle involving T_{ex} implies that there is a *possibility* of a deadlock. To ascertain whether a deadlock really exists, we must invoke a distributed deadlock detection algorithm.

Suppose that site S_i contains in its local wait-for graph a cycle involving node T_{ex}. This cycle must be of the form

$$T_{\text{ex}} \rightarrow T_{k_1} \rightarrow T_{k_2} \rightarrow \ldots \rightarrow T_{k_n} \rightarrow T_{\text{ex}}$$

which indicates that transaction T_{k_n} in S_i is waiting to acquire a data item in some other site — say, S_j. On discovering this cycle, site S_i sends to site S_j a deadlock-detection message containing information about that cycle.

When site S_j receives this deadlock-detection message, it updates its local wait-for graph with the new information that it has obtained. Next, it searches

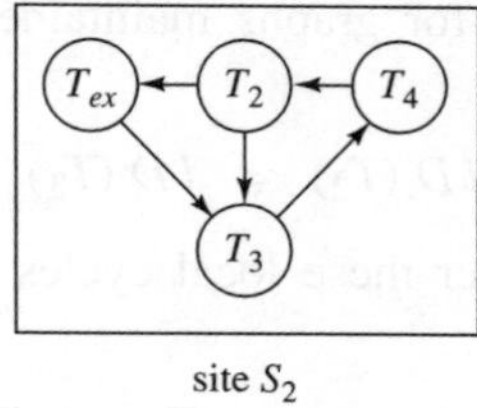

site S_2

Figure 18.14 Local wait-for graph.

the newly constructed wait-for graph for a cycle not involving T_{ex}. If one exists, a deadlock is found, and an appropriate recovery scheme is invoked. If a cycle involving T_{ex} is discovered, then S_j transmits a deadlock-detection message to the appropriate site — say, S_k. Site S_k, in return, repeats the previous procedure. Thus, after a finite number of rounds, if a deadlock exists, it is discovered; if no deadlock exists, the deadlock-detection computation halts.

As an illustration, consider the local wait-for graphs of Figure 18.13. Suppose that site S_1 discovers the cycle

$$T_{ex} \rightarrow T_2 \rightarrow T_3 \rightarrow T_{ex}$$

Since T_3 is waiting to acquire a data item in site S_2, a deadlock-detection message describing that cycle is transmitted from site S_1 to site S_2. When site S_2 receives this message, it updates its local wait-for graph, obtaining the wait-for graph of Figure 18.14. This graph contains the cycle

$$T_2 \rightarrow T_3 \rightarrow T_4 \rightarrow T_2$$

which does not include node T_{ex}. Therefore, the system is in a deadlock state, and an appropriate recovery scheme must be invoked.

Note that the outcome would be the same if site S_2 discovered the cycle first in its local wait-for graph, and sent the deadlock-detection message to site S_1. In the worst case, both sites discover the cycle at about the same time, and two deadlock-detection messages are sent: one by S_1 to S_2, and another by S_2 to S_1. This unnecessary message transfer adds to overhead in updating the two local wait-for graphs and searching for cycles in both graphs.

To reduce message traffic, we assign to each transaction T_i a unique identifier, which we denote by $ID(T_i)$. When site S_k discovers that its local wait-for graph contains a cycle involving node T_{ex} of the form

$$T_{ex} \rightarrow T_{K_1} \rightarrow T_{K_2} \rightarrow \ldots \rightarrow T_{K_n} \rightarrow T_{ex}$$

it will send a deadlock-detection message to another site only if

$$ID(T_{K_n}) < ID(T_{K_1})$$

Otherwise, site S_k continues its normal execution, leaving the burden of initiating the deadlock-detection algorithm to some other site.

Consider again the wait-for graphs maintained at sites S_1 and S_2 in Figure 18.13. Suppose that

$$ID(T_1) < ID(T_2) < ID(T_3) < ID(T_4)$$

Assume that both sites discover these local cycles at about the same time. The cycle in site S_1 is of the form

$$T_{ex} \rightarrow T_2 \rightarrow T_3 \rightarrow T_{ex}$$

Since $ID(T_3) > ID(T_2)$, site S_1 does not send a deadlock-detection message to site S_2.

The cycle in site S_2 is of the form

$$T_{ex} \rightarrow T_3 \rightarrow T_4 \rightarrow T_2 \rightarrow T_{ex}$$

Since $ID(T_2) < ID(T_3)$, site S_2 does send a deadlock-detection message to site S_1. On receiving the message, S_1 updates its local wait-for graph, searches for a cycle in the graph, and discovers that the system is in a deadlock state.

18.9 Multidatabase Systems

In recent years, new database applications have been developed that require data from a variety of preexisting databases located in a heterogeneous collection of hardware and software environments. Manipulation of information located in a heterogeneous database requires an additional software layer on top of existing database systems. This software layer is called a *multidatabase system*. The local database systems may employ different logical models and data-definition and data-manipulation languages, and may differ in their concurrency-control and transaction-management mechanisms. A multidatabase system creates the illusion of logical database integration without requiring physical database integration.

Full integration of existing systems into a *homogeneous* distributed database–the kind of distributed environment we have considered up to this point–is often difficult or impossible:

1. **Technical difficulties.** The investment in application programs based on existing database systems may be huge, and the cost of converting these applications may be prohibitive.
2. **Organizational difficulties.** Even if integration is *technically* possible, it may not be *politically* possible, due to the existing database systems belonging to different corporations or organizations.

In the second case, it is important for a multidatabase system to allow the local database systems to retain a high degree of *autonomy* over the local database and transactions running against that data.

For these reasons, multidatabase systems offer significant advantages that outweigh their overhead. In this section, we provide an overview of the challenges faced in constructing a multidatabase environment from the standpoints of data definition and transaction management.

18.9.1 Unified View of Data

Each local DBMS may use a different data model. That is, some may employ modern data models, such as the relational model, whereas others may employ older data models, such as the network model (see Appendix A) or the hierarchical model (see Appendix B).

Since the multidatabase system is supposed to provide the illusion of a single, integrated database system, a common data model must be used. The natural choice is the relational model, with SQL as the common query language. Indeed, there are several systems available today that allow SQL queries to a nonrelational DBMS.

Another difficulty is the provision of a common conceptual schema. Each local DBMS provides its own conceptual schema. The multidatabase system must integrate these separate schemas into one common schema. Schema integration is a complicated task, mainly due to the semantic heterogeneity.

Schema integration is not simply straightforward translation between data-definition languages. The same attribute names may appear in different local DBMSs but with different meanings. The data types used in one system may not be supported by other systems, and translation between types may not be simple. Even for identical data types, problems may arise due to the physical representation of data. One system may use ASCII, another EBCDIC. Floating-point representations may differ. Integers may be represented in *big-endian* or *little-endian* form. At the semantic level, an integer value for length may be inches in one system and millimeters in another, thus creating an awkward situation in which equality of integers is only an approximate notion (as is always the case for floating-point numbers). The same name may appear in different languages in different systems. For example, a system based in the United States may refer to the city "Cologne," whereas one in Germany refers to it as "Köln".

All these seemingly minor distinctions must be properly recorded in the common global conceptual schema. Translation functions must be provided. Indices must be annotated for system-dependent behavior (for example, the sort order of nonalphanumeric characters is not the same in ASCII as in EBCDIC). As we noted earlier, the alternative of converting each database to a common format may not be feasible without obsoleting existing application programs.

Under these circumstances, query processing is complex. Query optimization at the global level is difficult. The usual solution is to rely on only local-level optimization.

18.9.2 Transaction Management

A multidatabase system supports two types of transactions:

1. **Local transactions**. These transactions are executed by each local DBMS, outside of the multidatabase system's control.
2. **Global transactions**. These transactions are executed under the multidatabase system's control.

The multidatabase system is aware of the fact that local transactions may run at the local sites, but it is not aware of what specific transactions are being executed, or of what data they may access.

Ensuring the local autonomy of each DBMS requires making no changes to the local DBMS software. A DBMS at one site thus is not able to communicate directly with a DBMS at any other sites to synchronize the execution of a global transaction active at several sites.

Since the multidatabase system has no control over the execution of local transactions, each local DBMS must use a concurrency-control scheme (for example, two-phase locking or timestamping) to ensure that its schedule is serializable. In addition, in case of locking, the local DBMS must be able to guard against the possibility of local deadlocks.

The guarantee of local serializability is not sufficient to ensure global serializability. As an illustration, consider two global transactions T_1 and T_2, each of which accesses and updates two data items, A and B, located at sites S_1 and S_2, respectively. Suppose that the local schedules are serializable. It is still possible to have a situation where, at site S_1, T_2 follows T_1, whereas, at S_2, T_1 follows T_2, resulting in a nonserializable global schedule. Indeed, even if there is no concurrency among global transactions (that is, a global transaction is submitted only after the previous one commits or aborts), local serializability is not sufficient to ensure global serializability (see Exercise 18.20).

There are many protocols for ensuring consistency despite concurrent execution of global and local transactions in multidatabase systems. Some are based on imposing sufficient conditions to ensure global serializability. Others ensure only a form of consistency weaker than serializability, but achieve this consistency by less restrictive means. We consider one of the latter schemes: *two-level serializability*. Section 20.4 describes further approaches to consistency without serializability; other approaches are cited in the bibliographic notes.

18.9.2.1 Two-Level Serializability

Two-level serializability (2LSR) ensures serializability at two levels of the system:

- Each local DBMS ensures local serializability among its local transactions, including those that are part of a global transaction.
- The multidatabase system ensures serializability among the global transactions alone — *ignoring the orderings induced by local transactions.*

Each of these serializability levels is simple to enforce. Local systems already offer guarantees of serializability; thus, the first requirement is easy to achieve. The second requirement applies to only a projection of the global schedule in which local transactions do not appear. Thus, the MBDS can ensure the second requirement using standard concurrency-control techniques (the precise choice of technique does not matter).

The two requirements of 2LSR are not sufficient to ensure global serializability. However, under the 2LSR-based approach, we adopt a requirement weaker than serializability, called *strong correctness*:

1. Preservation of consistency as specified by a set of consistency constraints
2. Guarantee that the set of data items read by each transaction is consistent

It can be shown that certain restrictions on transaction behavior, combined with 2LSR, are sufficient to ensure strong correctness (although not necessarily to ensure serializability). We list several of these restrictions.

In each of the protocols, we distinguish between *local* and *global* data. Local data items belong to a particular site and are under the sole control of that site. Note that there cannot be any consistency constraints between local data items at distinct sites. Global data items belong to the multidatabase system, and, though they may be stored at a local site, are under the control of the multidatabase system.

The *global-read protocol* allows global transactions to read, but not to update, local data items, while disallowing all access to global data by local transactions. The global-read protocol ensures strong correctness if all the following hold:

1. Local transactions access only local data items.
2. Global transactions may access global data items, and may read local data items (although they must not write local data items).
3. There are no consistency constraints between local and global data items.

The *local-read protocol* grants local transactions read access to global data, but disallows all access to local data by global transactions. In this protocol, we need to introduce the notion of a *value dependency*. A transaction has a value dependency if the value that it writes to a data item at one site depends on a value that it read for a data item on another site.

The local-read protocol ensures strong correctness if all the following hold:

1. Local transactions may access local data items, and may read global data items stored at the site (although they must not write global data items).
2. Global transactions access only global data items.
3. No transaction may have a value dependency.

The *global-read–write/local-read protocol* is the most generous in terms of data access of the protocols that we have considered. It allows global transactions to read and write local data, and allows local transactions to read global data. However, it imposes both the value-dependency condition of the local-read protocol, and the condition from the global-read protocol that there be no consistency constraints between local and global data.

The global-read–write/local-read protocol ensures strong correctness if all of the following hold:

1. Local transactions may access local data items, and may read global data items stored at the site (although they must not write global data items).

2. Global transactions may access global data items as well as local data items (that is, they may read and write all data).
3. There are no consistency constraints between local and global data items.
4. No transaction may have a value dependency.

18.9.2.2 Ensuring Global Serializability

Early multidatabase systems restricted global transactions to be read only. They thus avoided the possibility of global transactions introducing inconsistency to the data, but were not sufficiently restrictive to ensure global serializability. We leave it to the reader to demonstrate that it is indeed possible to get such global schedules, and to develop a scheme to ensure global serializability (Exercise 18.21).

There are a number of general schemes to ensure global serializability in an environment where update as well read-only transactions can execute. Several of these schemes are based on the idea of a *ticket*. A special data item called a ticket is created in each local DBMS. Every global transaction that accesses data at a site must write the ticket at that site. This requirement ensures that global transactions conflict directly at every site they visit. Furthermore, the global transaction manager can control the order in which global transactions are serialized, by controlling the order in which the tickets are accessed. References to such schemes appear in the bibliographic notes.

If we want to ensure global serializability in an environment where no direct local conflicts are generated in each site, some assumptions must be made about the schedules allowed by the local DBMSs. For example, if the local schedules are such that the commit order and serialization order are always identical, we can ensure serializability by controlling only the order in which transactions commit.

The problem with schemes that ensure global serializability is that they may restrict concurrency unduly. They are particularly likely to do so because most transactions submit SQL statements to the underlying DBMS, rather than submitting individual **read**, **write**, **commit**, and **abort** steps. Although it is still possible to ensure global serializability under this assumption, the level of concurrency may be such that other schemes, such as the two-level serializability technique discussed previously, are attractive alternatives.

18.10 Summary

A distributed database system consists of a collection of sites, each of which maintains a local database system. Each site is able to process local transactions: those transactions that access data in only that single site. In addition, a site may participate in the execution of global transactions; those transactions that access data in several sites. The execution of global transactions requires communication among the sites.

There are several reasons for building distributed database systems, including sharing of data, reliability and availability, and speedup of query processing. However, along with these advantages come several disadvantages, including higher software-development cost, greater potential for bugs, and increased processing overhead. The primary disadvantage of distributed database systems is the added complexity required to ensure proper coordination among the sites.

There are several issues involved in storing a relation in the distributed database, including replication and fragmentation. It is essential that the system minimize the degree to which a user needs to be aware of how a relation is stored.

A distributed system may suffer from the same types of failure that can afflict a centralized system. There are, however, additional failures with which we need to deal in a distributed environment, including the failure of a site, the failure of a link, loss of a message, and network partition. Each of these problems needs to be considered in the design of a distributed recovery scheme. If the system is to be robust, therefore, it must detect any of these failures, reconfigure itself such that computation may continue, and recover when a processor or a link is repaired.

If we are to ensure atomicity, all the sites in which a transaction T executed must agree on the final outcome of the execution. T either commits at all sites or aborts at all sites. To ensure this property, the transaction coordinator of T must execute a commit protocol. The most widely used commit protocol is the two-phase commit protocol.

The two-phase commit protocol may lead to blocking: a situation in which the fate of a transaction cannot be determined until a failed site (the coordinator) recovers. To avoid blocking, we can use the three-phase commit protocol.

The various concurrency-control schemes that can be used in a centralized system can be modified for use in a distributed environment. In the case of locking protocols, the only change that needs to be incorporated is in the way that the lock manager is implemented. There is a variety of different approaches here. One or more central coordinators may be used. If, instead, a distributed approach is taken, replicated data must be treated specially. Protocols for handling replicated data include the majority, biased, and primary-copy protocols. In the case of timestamping and validation schemes, the only needed change is to develop a mechanism for generating unique global timestamps. We can develop one by either concatenating a local timestamp with the site identification or advancing local clocks whenever a message arrives with a larger timestamp.

The primary method for dealing with deadlocks in a distributed environment is deadlock detection. The main problem is deciding how to maintain the wait-for graph. Different methods for organizing the wait-for graph include a centralized approach, a hierarchical approach, and a fully distributed approach.

Some of the distributed algorithms require the use of a coordinator. If the coordinator fails owing to the failure of the site at which it resides, the system can continue execution only by restarting a new copy of the coordinator on some other site. It can do so by maintaining a backup to the coordinator that is ready to assume responsibility if the coordinator fails. Another approach is to choose the new coordinator after the coordinator has failed. The algorithms that determine where a new copy of the coordinator should be restarted are called election algorithms.

A multidatabase system provides an environment in which new database applications can access data from a variety of preexisting databases located in various heterogeneous hardware and software environments. The local database systems may employ different logical models and data-definition and data-manipulation languages, and may differ in their concurrency-control and transaction-management mechanisms. A multidatabase system creates the illusion of logical database integration, without requiring physical database integration.

Exercises

18.1. Discuss the relative advantages of centralized and distributed databases.

18.2. Explain how the following differ: fragmentation transparency, replication transparency, and location transparency.

18.3. How might a distributed database designed for a local-area network differ from one designed for a wide-area network?

18.4. When is it useful to have replication or fragmentation of data? Explain your answer.

18.5. Explain the notions of transparency and autonomy. Why are these notions desirable from a human-factors standpoint?

18.6. Consider a relation that is fragmented horizontally by *plant-number*:

employee (*name, address, salary, plant-number*)

Assume that each fragment has two replicas: one stored at the New York site, and one stored locally at the plant site. Describe a good processing strategy for the following queries entered at the San Jose site.

(*a*) Find all employees at the Boca plant.
(*b*) Find the average salary of all employees.
(*c*) Find the highest-paid employee at each of the following sites: Toronto, Edmonton, Vancouver, Montreal.
(*d*) Find the lowest-paid employee in the company.

18.7. Consider the relations

employee (*name, address, salary, plant-number*)
machine (*machine-number, type, plant-number*)

Assume that the *employee* relation is fragmented horizontally by *plant-number*, and that each fragment is stored locally at its corresponding plant site. Assume that the *machine* relation is stored in its entirety at the Armonk site. Describe a good strategy for processing each of the following queries.

(*a*) Find all employees at the plant that contains machine number 1130.
(*b*) Find all employees at plants that contain machines whose type is "milling machine."
(*c*) Find all machines at the Almaden plant.
(*d*) Find employee $\bowtie$ machine.

18.8. For each of the strategies of Exercise 18.7, state how your choice of a strategy depends on:

(*a*) The site at which the query was entered
(*b*) The site at which the result is desired

18.9. Compute $r \ltimes s$ for the following relations:

A	B	C
1	2	3
4	5	6
1	2	4
5	3	2
8	9	7

C	D	E
3	4	5
3	6	8
2	3	2
1	4	1
1	2	3

18.10. Is $r_i \ltimes r_j$ necessarily equal to $r_j \ltimes r_i$? Under what conditions does $r_i \ltimes r_j = r_j \ltimes r_i$ hold?

18.11. To build a robust distributed system, you must know what kinds of failures can occur.
(*a*) List possible types of failure in a distributed system.
(*b*) Which items in your list from part a are also applicable to a centralized system?

18.12. Consider a failure that occurs during 2PC for a transaction. For each possible failure that you listed in Exercise 18.11a, explain how 2PC ensures transaction atomicity despite the failure.

18.13. Repeat Exercise 18.12 for 3PC.

18.14. List those types of failure that 3PC cannot handle. Describe how failures of these types could be handled by lower-level protocols.

18.15. Consider a distributed deadlock-detection algorithm in which the sites are organized in a hierarchy. Each site checks for deadlocks local to the site, and for global deadlocks that involve descendant sites in the hierarchy. Give a detailed description of this algorithm. Argue that the algorithm detects all deadlocks. Compare the relative merits of this hierarchical scheme with those of the centralized scheme and of the fully distributed scheme.

18.16. Consider a distributed system with two sites, *A* and *B*. Can site *A* distinguish among the following?

- *B* goes down.
- The link between *A* and *B* goes down.
- *B* is extremely overloaded and response time is 100 times longer than normal.

What implications does your answer have for recovery in distributed systems?

18.17. If we apply a distributed version of the multiple-granularity protocol of Chapter 14 to a distributed database, the site responsible for the root of the DAG may become a bottleneck. Suppose we modify that protocol as follows:

- Only intention-mode locks are allowed on the root.
- All transactions are given all possible intention-mode locks on the root automatically.

Show that these modifications alleviate this problem without allowing any nonserializable schedules.

18.18. Discuss the advantages and disadvantages of the two methods that we presented in Section 18.7.2 for generating globally unique timestamps.

18.19. Consider the following deadlock-detection algorithm. When transaction T_i, at site S_1, requests a resource from T_j, at site S_3, a request message with timestamp n is sent. The edge (T_i, T_j, n) is inserted in the local wait-for of S_1. The edge (T_i, T_j, n) is inserted in the local wait-for graph of S_3 only if T_j has received the request message and cannot immediately grant the requested resource. A request from T_i to T_j in the same site is handled in the usual manner; no timestamps are associated with the edge (T_i, T_j). A central coordinator invokes the detection algorithm by sending an initiating message to each site in the system.

On receiving this message, a site sends its local wait-for graph to the coordinator. Note that such a graph contains all the local information that the site has about the state of the real graph. The wait-for graph reflects an instantaneous state of the site, but it is not synchronized with respect to any other site.

When the controller has received a reply from each site, it constructs a graph as follows:

- The graph contains a vertex for every transaction in the system.
- The graph has an edge (T_i, T_j) if and only if
  - There is an edge (T_i, T_j) in one of the wait-for graphs.
  - An edge (T_i, T_j, n) (for some n) appears in more than one wait-for graph.

Show that, if there is a cycle in the constructed graph, then the system is in a deadlock state, and that, if there is no cycle in the constructed graph, then the system was not in a deadlock state when the execution of the algorithm began.

18.20. Consider a multidatabase system in which it is guaranteed that at most one global transaction is active at any time, and every local site ensures local serializability.

(*a*) Suggest ways in which the multidatabase system can ensure that there is at most one active global transaction at any time.

(*b*) Show by example that it is possible for a nonserializable global schedule to result despite the assumptions.

18.21. Consider a multidatabase system in which every local site ensures local serializability, and all global transactions are read-only.

(*a*) Show by example that nonserializable executions may result in such a system.

(*b*) Show how you could use ticket scheme to ensure global serializability.

Bibliographic Notes

Computer networks are discussed in Tanenbaum [1996] and Halsall [1992]. A survey paper discussing major issues concerning distributed database systems has been written by Rothnie and Goodman [1977]. Textbook discussions are offered by Bray [1982], Date [1983], Ceri and Pelagatti [1984], and Ozsu and Valduriez [1991].

Distributed query processing is discussed in Wong [1977], Epstein et al. [1978], Hevner and Yao [1979], Epstein and Stonebraker [1980], Apers et al. [1983], Ceri and Pelagatti [1983], and Wong [1983]. Selinger and Adiba [1980], and Daniels et al. [1982], discuss the approach to distributed query processing taken by R* (a distributed version of System R). Mackert and Lohman [1986] provide a performance evaluation of query-processing algorithms in R*. The performance results also serve to validate the cost model used in the R* query optimizer. Theoretical results concerning semijoins are presented by Bernstein and Chiu [1981], Chiu and Ho [1980], Bernstein and Goodman [1981b], and Kambayashi et al. [1982].

The implementation of the transaction concept in a distributed database are presented by Gray [1981], Traiger et al. [1982], Spector and Schwarz [1983], and Eppinger et al. [1991]. The 2PC protocol was developed by Lampson and Sturgis [1976], and by Gray [1978]. The three-phase commit protocol is from Skeen [1981]. Mohan and Lindsay [1983] discuss two modified versions of 2PC, called *presume commit* and *presume abort*, that reduce the overhead of 2PC by defining default assumptions regarding the fate of transactions.

The bully algorithm presented in Section 18.6.2 is from Garcia-Molina [1982]. Distributed clock synchronization is discussed in Lamport [1978].

Papers covering distributed concurrency control are offered by Rosenkrantz et al. [1978], Bernstein et al. [1978, 1980a], Menasce et al. [1980], Bernstein and Goodman [1980a, 1981a, 1982], and Garcia-Molina and Wiederhold [1982]. The transaction manager of R* is described in Mohan et al. [1986].

Concurrency control for replicated data that is based on the concept of voting is presented by Gifford [1979] and Thomas [1979]. Validation techniques for distributed concurrency-control schemes are described by Schlageter [1981], Ceri and Owicki [1983], and Bassiouni [1988]. Discussions concerning semantic-based transaction-management techniques are offered by Garcia-Molina [1983], and by Kumar and Stonebraker [1988]. Recently, the problem of concurrent update to replicated data has re-emerged as an important research issue in the context of data warehouses. Problems in this environment are discussed in Gray et al. [1996].

Attar et al. [1984] discuss the use of transactions in distributed recovery in database systems with replicated data. A survey of techniques for recovery in distributed database systems is presented by Kohler [1981].

Distributed deadlock-detection algorithms are presented by Gray [1978], Rosenkrantz et al. [1978], Menasce and Muntz [1979], Gligor and Shattuck [1980], Chandy and Misra [1982], and Chandy et al. [1983]. Knapp [1987] surveys the distributed deadlock-detection literature. The algorithm presented in Section 18.8.2 comes from Obermark [1982]. Exercise 18.19 is from Stuart et al. [1984].

Transaction processing in multidatabase systems is discussed in Breitbart [1990], Breitbart et al. [1991, 1992], Soparkar et al. [1991], and Mehrotra et al. [1992a, 1992b]. The ticket scheme is presented in Georgakopoulos et al. [1994]. 2LSR is introduced in Mehrotra et al. [1991]. An earlier approach, called *quasi-serializability*, is presented in Du and Elmagarmid [1989].

CHAPTER 19

SPECIAL TOPICS

In earlier chapters, we covered the basic principles of database design and implementation. In this and subsequent chapters, we briefly cover a number of special topics in the area of database systems. In Chapter 20, we discuss advanced transaction processing schemes. In Chapter 21, we consider new applications of database systems, and the challenges that they pose to database system design. The bibliographic notes at the end of these chapters provide references for each topic; they can serve as a starting point for detailed study.

19.1 Security and Integrity

The data stored in the database need to be protected from unauthorized access, malicious destruction or alteration, and accidental introduction of inconsistency. In Chapter 6, we saw how integrity constraints can be specified. In Chapter 7, we saw how databases can be designed to facilitate checking of integrity constraints. In Chapters 13, 14, and 15, we saw how to preserve integrity despite failures, crashes, and potential anomalies from concurrent processing. In Chapters 17 and 18, we saw how to preserve integrity in parallel and distributed systems. Until now, we have considered only how to prevent the accidental loss of data integrity. In this section, we examine the ways in which data may be misused or intentionally made inconsistent. We then present mechanisms to guard against such occurrences.

19.1.1 Security and Integrity Violations

Misuse of the database can be categorized as being either intentional (malicious) or accidental. Accidental loss of data consistency may result from

- Crashes during transaction processing

- Anomalies caused by concurrent access to the database
- Anomalies caused by the distribution of data over several computers
- Logical errors that violate the assumption that transactions preserve the database consistency constraints

It is easier to protect against accidental loss of data consistency than to protect against malicious access to the database. Among the forms of malicious access are the following:

- Unauthorized reading of data (theft of information)
- Unauthorized modification of data
- Unauthorized destruction of data

Absolute protection of the database from malicious abuse is not possible, but the cost to the perpetrator can be made sufficiently high to deter most if not all attempts to access the database without proper authority. Database *security* usually refers to protection from malicious access, whereas *integrity* refers to the avoidance of accidental loss of consistency. In practice, the dividing line between security and integrity is not always clear. We shall use the term *security* to refer to both *security* and *integrity* in cases where the distinction between these concepts is not essential.

To protect the database, we must take security measures at several levels:

- **Physical**. The site or sites containing the computer systems must be physically secured against armed or surreptitious entry by intruders.
- **Human**. Users must be authorized carefully to reduce the chance of any such user giving access to an intruder in exchange for a bribe or other favors.
- **Operating system**. No matter how secure the database system is, weakness in operating-system security may serve as a means of unauthorized access to the database.
- **Network**. Since almost all database systems allow remote access through terminals or networks, software-level security within the network software is as important as physical security, both on the Internet and in networks private to an enterprise.
- **Database system**. Some database-system users may be authorized to access only a limited portion of the database. Other users may be allowed to issue queries, but may be forbidden to modify the data. It is the responsibility of the database system to ensure that these authorization restrictions are not violated.

Security at all these levels must be maintained if database security is to be ensured. A weakness at a low level of security (physical or human) allows circumvention of strict high-level (database) security measures.

It is worthwhile in many applications to devote considerable effort to preserving the integrity and security of the database. Large databases containing payroll or other financial data are inviting targets to thieves. Databases that contain data pertaining to corporate operations may be of interest to unscrupulous competitors. Furthermore, loss of such data, whether via accident or fraud, can seriously impair the ability of the corporation to function.

In the remainder of this section, we shall address security at the database-system level. Security at the physical and human levels, although important, is far beyond the scope of this text. Security within the operating system is implemented at several levels, ranging from passwords for access to the system to the isolation of concurrent processes running within the system. The file system also provides some degree of protection. The bibliographic notes reference coverage of these topics in operating-system texts. Finally, network-level security has gained widespread recognition as the Internet has evolved from an academic research platform to the basis of international electronic commerce. The bibliographic notes list textbook coverage of the basic principles of network security. We shall present our discussion of security in terms of the relational data model, although the concepts of this chapter are equally applicable to all data models.

19.1.2 Authorization

A user may have several forms of authorization on parts of the database. Among them are the following:

- **Read authorization** allows reading, but not modification, of data.
- **Insert authorization** allows insertion of new data, but not modification of existing data.
- **Update authorization** allows modification, but not deletion, of data.
- **Delete authorization** allows deletion of data.

A user may be assigned all, none, or a combination of these types of authorization.

In addition to these forms of authorization for access to data, a user may be granted authorization to modify the database schema:

- **Index authorization** allows the creation and deletion of indices.
- **Resource authorization** allows the creation of new relations.
- **Alteration authorization** allows the addition or deletion of attributes in a relation.
- **Drop authorization** allows the deletion of relations.

The **drop** and **delete** authorization differ in that **delete** authorization allows deletion of tuples only. If a user deletes all tuples of a relation, the relation still exists, but it is empty. If a relation is dropped, it no longer exists.

The ability to create new relations is regulated through **resource** authorization. A user with **resource** authorization who creates a new relation is given all privileges on that relation automatically.

Index authorization may appear unnecessary, since the creation or deletion of an index does not alter data in relations. Rather, indices are a structure for performance enhancements. However, indices also consume space, and all database modifications are required to update indices. If **index** authorization were granted to all users, those who performed updates would be tempted to delete indices, whereas those who issued queries would be tempted to create numerous indices. To allow the *database administrator* to regulate the use of system resources, it is necessary to treat index creation as a privilege.

The ultimate form of authority is that given to the database administrator. The database administrator may authorize new users, restructure the database, and so on. This form of authorization is analogous to that provided to a *superuser* or operator for an operating system.

19.1.3 Authorization and Views

In Chapter 3, we introduced the concept of *views* as a means of providing a user with a personalized model of the database. A view can hide data that a user does not need to see. The ability of views to hide data serves both to simplify usage of the system and to enhance security. System usage is simplified because the user is allowed to restrict attention to the data of interest. Although a user may be denied direct access to a relation, the user may be allowed to access part of that relation through a view. Thus, a combination of relational-level security and view-level security can be used to limit a user's access to precisely the data that user needs.

In our banking example, consider a clerk who needs to know the names of all customers who have a loan at each branch. This clerk is not authorized to see information regarding specific loans that the customer may have. Thus, the clerk must be denied direct access to the *loan* relation. But, if she is to have access to the information needed, the clerk must be granted access to the view *cust-loan*, which consists of only the names of customers and the branches at which they have a loan at. This view can be defined in SQL as follows:

> **create view** *cust-loan* **as**
> (**select** *branch-name, customer-name*
> **from** *borrower, loan*
> **where** *borrower.loan-number* = *loan.loan-number*)

Suppose that the clerk issues the following SQL query:

> **select** *
> **from** *cust-loan*

Clearly, the clerk is authorized to see the result of this query. However, when the query is translated by the query processor into a query on the actual relations in the database, we obtain a query on *borrower* and *loan*. Thus, authorization must be checked on the clerk's query before query processing begins.

Creation of a view does not require **resource** authorization. A user who creates a view does not necessarily receive all privileges on that view. Such a user receives only those privileges that provide no additional authorization beyond those that he already had. For example, a user cannot be given **update** authorization on a view without having **update** authorization on the relations used to define the view. If a user creates a view on which no authorization can be granted, the view creation request is denied. In our example using *cust-loan* view, the creator of the view must have **read** authorization on both the *borrower* and *loan* relations.

19.1.4 Granting of Privileges

A user who has been granted some form of authorization may be allowed to pass on this authorization to other users. However, we must be careful how authorization may be passed among users, to ensure that such authorization can be revoked at some future time.

Consider, as an example, the granting of update authorization on the *loan* relation of the bank database. Assume that, initially, the database administrator grants update authorization on *loan* to users U_1, U_2, and U_3, who may in turn pass on this authorization to other users. The passing of authorization from one user to another can be represented by an *authorization graph*. The nodes of this graph are the users. An edge $U_i \rightarrow U_j$ is included in the graph if user U_i grants update authorization on *loan* to U_j. The root of the graph is the database administrator. A sample graph appears in Figure 19.1. Observe that user U_5 is granted authorization by both U_1 and U_2; U_4 is granted authorization by only U_1.

A user has an authorization *if and only if* there is a path from the root of the authorization graph (namely, the node representing the database administrator) down to the node representing the user.

Suppose that the database administrator decides to revoke the authorization of user U_1. Since U_4 has been granted authorization from U_1, that authorization should be revoked as well. However, U_5 was granted authorization by both U_1 and U_2. Since the database administrator did not revoke **update** authorization on *loan* from U_2, U_5 retains **update** authorization on *loan*. If U_2 eventually revokes authorization from U_5, then U_5 loses the authorization.

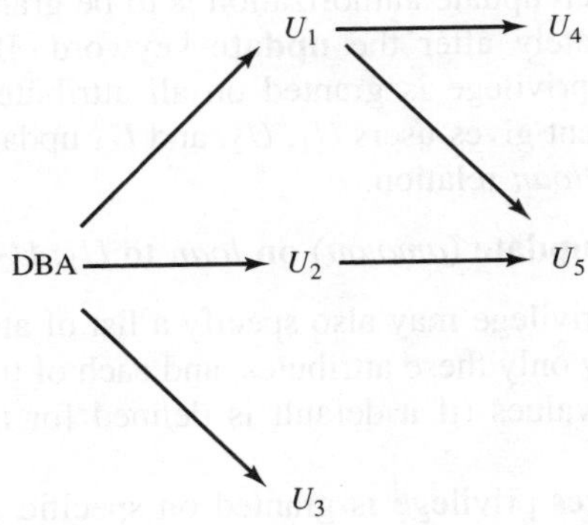

Figure 19.1 Authorization-grant graph.

A pair of devious users might attempt to defeat the rules for revocation of authorization by granting authorization to each other, as shown in Figure 19.2a. If the database administrator revokes authorization from U_2, U_2 retains authorization through U_3, as shown in Figure 19.2b. If authorization is revoked subsequently from U_3, U_3 appears to retain authorization through U_2, as shown in Figure 19.2c. However, when the database administrator revokes authorization from U_3, the edges from U_3 to U_2 and from U_2 to U_3 are no longer part of a path starting with the database administrator. We require that all edges in an authorization graph be part of some path originating with the database administrator. These edges are deleted; the resulting authorization graph is as shown in Figure 19.3.

19.1.5 Security Specification in SQL

The SQL data-definition language includes commands to grant and revoke privileges. The SQL standard includes **delete**, **insert**, **select**, and **update** privileges. The **select** privilege corresponds to the **read** privilege. SQL also includes a **references** privilege that restricts a user's ability to declare foreign keys when creating relations. If the relation to be created includes a foreign key that references attributes of another relation, the user must have been granted **references** privilege on those attributes. The reason that the **references** privilege is a useful feature is somewhat subtle, and is explained later in this section.

The **grant** statement is used to confer authorization. The basic form of this statement is as follows:

grant <privilege list> **on** <relation name or view name> **to** <user list>

The *privilege list* allows the granting of several privileges in one command. The following **grant** statement grants users U_1, U_2, and U_3 **select** authorization on the *branch* relation:

grant select on *branch* **to** U_1, U_2, U_3

The **update** authorization may be given either on all attributes of the relation or on only some. If **update** authorization is included in a **grant** statement, the list of attributes on which update authorization is to be granted optionally appears in parentheses immediately after the **update** keyword. If the list of attributes is omitted, the update privilege is granted on all attributes of the relation. The following **grant** statement gives users U_1, U_2, and U_3 update authorization on the *amount* attribute of the *loan* relation:

grant update (*amount*) **on** *loan* **to** U_1, U_2, U_3

In SQL-92, the **insert** privilege may also specify a list of attributes; any inserts to the relation must specify only these attributes, and each of the remaining attributes is either given default values (if a default is defined for the attribute) or set to null.

The SQL **references** privilege is granted on specific attributes in a manner similar to that shown for the **update** privilege. The following **grant** statement allows user U_1 to create relations that reference the key *branch-name* of the

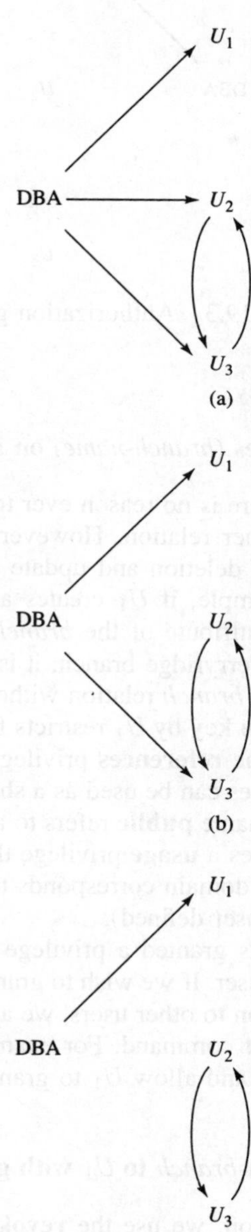

Figure 19.2 Attempt to defeat authorization revocation.

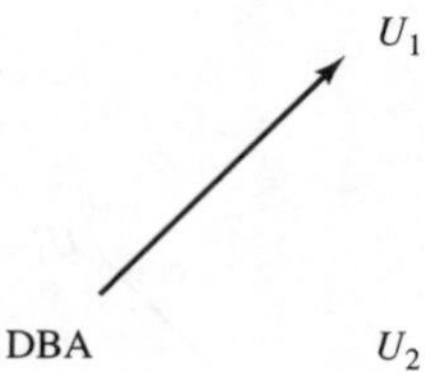

Figure 19.3 Authorization graph.

branch relation as a foreign key:

grant references (*branch-name*) **on** *branch* **to** U_1

Initially, it may appear that there is no reason ever to prevent users from creating foreign keys referencing another relation. However, recall from Chapter 6 that foreign-key constraints restrict deletion and update operations on the referenced relation. In the preceding example, if U_1 creates a foreign key in a relation r referencing the *branch-name* attribute of the *branch* relation, and then inserts a tuple into r pertaining to the Perryridge branch, it is no longer possible to delete the Perryridge branch from the *branch* relation without also modifying relation r. Thus, the definition of a foreign key by U_1 restricts future activity by other users; therefore, there is a need for the **references** privilege.

The privilege **all privileges** can be used as a short form for all the allowable privileges. Similarly, the user name **public** refers to all current and future users of the system. SQL-92 also includes a **usage** privilege that authorizes a user to use a specified domain (recall that a domain corresponds to the programming-language notion of a type, and may be user defined).

By default, a user who is granted a privilege in SQL is not authorized to grant that privilege to another user. If we wish to grant a privilege and to allow the recipient to pass the privilege on to other users, we append the **with grant option** clause to the appropriate **grant** command. For example, if we wish to allow U_1 the **select** privilege on *branch* and allow U_1 to grant this privilege to others, we write

grant select on *branch* **to** U_1 **with grant option**

To revoke an authorization, we use the **revoke** statement. It takes a form almost identical to that of **grant**:

revoke <privilege list> **on** <relation name or view name>
from <user list> [**restrict** | **cascade**]

Thus, to revoke the privileges that we granted previously, we write

> **revoke select on** *branch* **from** U_1, U_2, U_3 **cascade**
> **revoke update** (*amount*) **on** *loan* **from** U_1, U_2, U_3
> **revoke references** (*branch-name*) **on** *branch* **from** U_1

As we saw in Section 19.1.4, the revocation of a privilege from a user may cause other users also to lose that privilege. This behavior is called *cascading of the revoke*. The **revoke** statement may also specify **restrict**:

> **revoke select on** *branch* **from** U_1, U_2, U_3 **restrict**

In this case, an error is returned if there are any cascading revokes, and the revoke action is not carried out. The following **revoke** statement revokes only the grant option, rather than the actual **select** privilege.

> **revoke grant option for select on** *branch* **from** U_1

The SQL-92 standard specifies a primitive authorization mechanism for the database schema: Only the owner of the schema can carry out any modification to the schema. Thus, schema modifications—such as creating or deleting relations, adding or dropping attributes of relations, and adding or dropping indices—may be executed by only the owner of the schema. Several database implementations have more powerful authorization mechanisms for database schemas, similar to those discussed earlier, but these mechanisms are nonstandard.

19.1.6 Encryption

The various provisions that a database system may make for authorization may not provide sufficient protection for highly sensitive data. In such cases, data may be *encrypted*. It is not possible for encrypted data to be read unless the reader knows how to decipher (*decrypt*) them.

There is a vast number of techniques for the encryption of data. Simple encryption techniques may not provide adequate security, since it may be easy for an unauthorized user to break the code. As an example of a weak encryption technique, consider the substitution of each character with the next character in the alphabet. Thus,

Perryridge

becomes

Qfsszsjehf

If an unauthorized user sees only "Qfsszsjehf," she probably has insufficient information to break the code. However, if the intruder sees a large number of encrypted branch names, she could use statistical data regarding the relative frequency of characters (for example, *e* is more common than *f*) to guess what substitution is being made.

A good encryption technique has the following properties:

- It is relatively simple for authorized users to encrypt and decrypt data.
- The encryption scheme depends not on the secrecy of the algorithm, but rather on a parameter of the algorithm called the *encryption key*.
- It is extremely difficult for an intruder to determine the encryption key.

One approach, the *Data Encryption Standard* (DES), does both a substitution of characters and a rearrangement of their order on the basis of an encryption key. For this scheme to work, the authorized users must be provided with the encryption key via a secure mechanism. This requirement is a major weakness, since the scheme is no more secure than the security of the mechanism by which the encryption key is transmitted.

Public-key encryption is an alternative scheme that avoids some of the problems that we face with the DES. It is based on two keys; a *public key* and a *private key*. Each user U_i has a public key E_i and a private key D_i. All public keys are published: They can be seen by anyone. Each private key is known to only the one user to whom the key belongs. If user U_1 wants to store encrypted data, U_1 encrypts them using public key E_1. Decryption requires the private key D_1.

Because the encryption key for each user is public, it is possible to exchange information securely using this scheme. If user U_1 wants to share data with U_2, U_1 encrypts the data using E_2, the public key of U_2. Since only user U_2 knows how to decrypt the data, information is transferred securely.

For public-key encryption to work, there must be a scheme for encryption that can be made public without making it easy for people to figure out the scheme for decryption. In other words, it must be hard to deduce the private key, given the public key. Such a scheme does exist and is based on the following:

- There is an efficient algorithm for testing whether or not a number is prime.
- No efficient algorithm is known for finding the prime factors of a number.

For purposes of this scheme, data are treated as a collection of integers. We create a public key by computing the product of two large prime numbers: P_1 and P_2. The private key consists of the pair (P_1, P_2), and the decryption algorithm cannot be used successfully if only the product P_1P_2 is known. Since all that is published is the product P_1P_2, an unauthorized user would need to be able to factor P_1P_2 to steal data. By choosing P_1 and P_2 to be sufficiently large (over 100 digits), we can make the cost of factoring P_1P_2 prohibitively high (on the order of years of computation time, on even the fastest computers).

The details of public-key encryption and the mathematical justification of this technique's properties are referenced in the bibliographic notes.

Although public-key encryption using the scheme described is secure, it is also computationally expensive. A hybrid scheme used for secure communication is as follows: DES keys are exchanged via a public-key–encryption scheme, and DES encryption is used on the data transmitted subsequently.

Another interesting application of cryptography is in *digital signatures*, which play the electronic role of physical signatures used to verify authenticity of data. One scheme for digital signatures uses public-key encryption in reverse: The private key is used to encode data, and the encoded data can be made public. Anyone can decode them using the public key, but no one could have generated the encoded data without having the private key. Thus, we can verify that the data were indeed created by the person who claims to have created them.

19.1.7 Statistical Databases

Suppose that, in our banking example, the bank wants to grant an outsider access to its database under the condition that only statistical studies (averages, medians, and so on) are made on the data, and that information about individual customers is not divulged. In this section, we examine the difficulty of ensuring the privacy of individuals while allowing use of data for statistical purposes.

One possible approach is to give the outsider access to only those views that provide relevant aggregate data, such as sum and count. One weakness in such a statistical database is unusual cases. For example, suppose that a user asks for the total bank-account balances for all customers living in Smalltown. If only one customer happens to live in Smalltown, the system has divulged information about an individual. Of course, a security breach has occurred only if the user knows that only one customer lives in Smalltown. However, that information is easily determined by the statistical query "Find the number of customers living in Smalltown."

A simple way to deal with potential security breaches like that just described is for the system to reject any query that involves fewer than some predetermined number of individuals. Suppose that this predetermined number is n. A malicious user who has an account with the bank can find an individual's balance in two queries. Suppose that the user wants to find the account balance of Rollo. The user chooses $n - 1$ customers and issues two queries to compute:

- x, the total balances for the malicious user and the $n - 1$ customers
- y, the total balances for Rollo and the $n - 1$ customers

Rollo's total balance is

$$y - x + \text{the malicious user's balance}$$

The critical flaw that was exploited in this example is that the two queries referred to many of the same data items. The number of data items that the two queries have in common is called their *intersection*.

Thus, in addition to requiring that a query reference data pertaining to at least n individuals, we may require that no two queries have an intersection larger than m. By adjusting n and m, we can increase the difficulty a user will face in determining data about an individual, but we cannot upgrade it to an impossibility.

These two restrictions do not preclude the possibility of some extremely clever query that divulges individual data. However, if, in addition, all queries are restricted to computing sums, counts, or averages, and if a malicious user knows only the data value for himself, then we can show that it will take at least $1 + (n - 2)/m$ queries for the malicious user to determine data about another individual. The proof of this assertion is beyond the scope of this text; it is referenced in the bibliographic notes. This fact is, nonetheless, only partially reassuring. We can limit a user to fewer than $1 + (n - 2)/m$ queries, but a conspiracy of two malicious users can result in data being divulged.

Another approach to security is *data pollution*, or the random falsification of data provided in response to a query. This falsification must be done such that the statistical significance of the response is not destroyed. A similar technique involves random modification of the query itself. For both of these techniques, the goals involve a tradeoff between accuracy and security.

Regardless of the approach taken to security of statistical data, it is possible for a malicious user to determine individual data values. However, good techniques can make the expense, in terms of cost and time, sufficiently high that it serves as a deterrent.

19.2 Standardization

Standards define the interface of a software system; for example, standards define the syntax and semantics of a programming language, or the functions in an application-program interface, or even a data model (such as the object-oriented–database standards). Today, database systems are complex, and are often made up of multiple independently created parts that need to interact. For example, client programs may be created independently of back-end systems, but the two must be able to interact with each other. A company that has multiple heterogeneous database systems may need to exchange data between the databases. Given such a scenario, standards play an important role.

Formal standards are developed by a standards organization, or by industry groups, through a public process. Dominant products sometimes become *de facto standards*, in that they become generally accepted as standards without any formal process of recognition. Some formal standards, like many aspects of the SQL-92 standard, are *anticipatory standards* that lead the marketplace; they define features that vendors then implement in products. In other cases, the standards, or parts of the standards, are *reactionary standards*, in that they attempt to standardize features that some vendors have already implemented, and that may even have become de facto standards. SQL-89 was in many ways reactionary, since it standardized features, such as integrity checking, that were already present in the IBM SAA SQL standard, and in other databases.

Formal standards committees are typically composed of representatives of the vendors, and members from user groups and standards organizations such as the International Standards Organization (ISO) or the American National Standards Institute (ANSI), or professional bodies, such as the Institute for Electrical and Electronic Engineers (IEEE). Formal standards committees meet periodically, and members present proposals for features to be added to or modified in the standard. After a (usually extended) period of discussion, modifications to the proposal, and public review, members vote on whether to accept or reject a feature. Some time after a standard has been defined and implemented, its shortcomings become clear, and new requirements become apparent. The process of updating the standard then begins, and a new version of the standard is typically released after a few years. This cycle typically repeats every few years, until eventually (perhaps many years later) the standard becomes technologically irrelevant, or loses its user base.

The DBTG CODASYL standard for network databases, formulated by the Database Task Group, was one of the early formal standards in the area of databases. IBM database products used to establish de facto standards, since IBM commanded much of the database market. With the growth of relational databases came a number of new entrants in the database business; hence, the need for formal standards arose.

Since SQL is the most widely used query language, much work has been done on standardizing it. ANSI and ISO, with the various database vendors, have played a leading role in this work. The SQL-86 standard was the initial version. The IBM Systems Application Architecture (SAA) standard for SQL was released in 1987. As people identified the need for more features, updated versions of the formal SQL standard were developed, called SQL-89 and SQL-92. The next version of the SQL standard, currently called SQL-3, is under development, and will add a variety of object-oriented features to SQL.

Today, database systems are often organized as a front-end client that provides a graphical user interface, and a back-end database server. So that users will have maximum flexibility in choosing front-ends and back-ends, standards for client-server interconnectivity have evolved. In the personal-computer end of the market, the most commonly used standard for client–server interconnection is the *Open DataBase Connectivity* (*ODBC*) standard for client–server application-program interfaces (APIs) defined by Microsoft.

ODBC is based on the SQL *Call-Level Interface* (CLI) standards developed by the *X/Open* industry consortium and the SQL Access Group, but has several extensions. Figure 19.4 schematically illustrates the role of the ODBC standard. ODBC basically defines an API that client programs can use to connect to database systems and to issue SQL commands. Clients, such as graphical user interfaces, statistics packages, or spreadsheets, can make use of the same ODBC API to

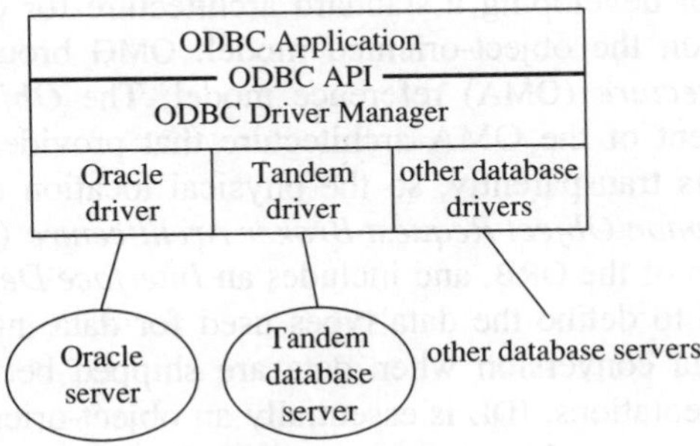

Figure 19.4 ODBC architecture

connect to any database server that supports ODBC. Each database system provides a driver that is controlled by the ODBC driver manager at the client end, and is responsible for connecting to and communicating with the server, as well as for doing any data and query format translations that may be required.

The ODBC API defines a CLI, an SQL syntax definition, and rules about permissible sequences of CLI calls. The standard also defines conformance levels for the CLI and the SQL syntax. For example, the core level of the CLI has commands to connect to a database, to prepare and execute SQL statements, to get back results or status values, and to manage transactions. The next level of conformance (level 1) requires support for catalog information retrieval and some other features over and above the core-level CLI; level 2 requires further features, such as ability to send and retrieve arrays of parameter values, and to retrieve more detailed catalog information.

ODBC allows a client to connect simultaneously to multiple data sources and to switch among them, but transactions on each are independent; ODBC does not support two-phase commit.

A distributed system provides a more general (and more complex) environment than that provided by a client–server system. The X/Open consortium has also developed the *X/Open XA* standards for interoperation of databases. These standards define transaction-management primitives (such as transaction begin, commit, abort, and prepare-to-commit) that compliant databases should provide; a transaction manager can invoke these primitives, to implement distributed transactions using two-phase commit. The XA standards are independent of the data model and of the specific interfaces between clients and databases to exchange data. Thus, we can use the XA protocols to implement a distributed transaction system where a single transaction can access relational as well as object-oriented databases, yet the transaction manager ensures global consistency via two-phase commit.

Standards in the area of object-oriented databases have so far been driven primarily by OODB vendors. The Object Database Management Group (ODMG), is a group formed by OODB vendors to standardize the data model and language interfaces to OODBs. The C++ language interface specified by ODMG was discussed in Chapter 8. The ODMG has also specified a Smalltalk interface.

The *Object Management Group* (*OMG*) is a consortium of companies, formed with the objective of developing a standard architecture for distributed software applications based on the object-oriented model. OMG brought out the *Object Management Architecture* (OMA) reference model. The *Object Request Broker* (*ORB*) is a component of the OMA architecture that provides message dispatch to distributed objects transparently, so the physical location of the object is not important. The *Common Object Request Broker Architecture* (*CORBA*) provides a detailed specification of the ORB, and includes an *Interface Description Language* (*IDL*) which is used to define the data types used for data interchange. The IDL helps to support data conversion when data are shipped between systems with different data representations. IDL is essentially an object-oriented data-definition language, and people are working to create a unified version of IDL and the ODMG object-definition language (ODL).

The bibliographic notes at the end of the chapter provide references to detailed descriptions of the standards mentioned in this section.

19.3 Performance Benchmarks

As database servers become more standardized, the differentiating factor among the products of different vendors is those products' performance. Performance benchmarks are suites of tasks that are used to quantify the performance of software systems.

19.3.1 Suites of Tasks

Since most software systems, such as databases, are complex, there is a good deal of variation in their implementation by different vendors. As a result, there is a significant amount of variation in their performance on different tasks. One system may be the most efficient on a particular task; another may be the most efficient on a different task. Hence, a single task is usually insufficient to quantify the performance of the system. Instead, the performance of a system is measured by a suite of tasks, called a *performance benchmark*.

Combining the performance numbers from multiple tasks must be done with care. Suppose that we have two tasks, T_1 and T_2, and that we measure the throughput of a system as the number of transactions of each type that run in a given amount of time—say, 1 second. Suppose that system A runs T_1 at 99 transactions per second, and that T_2 runs at 1 transaction per second. Similarly, let system B run both T_1 and T_2 at 50 transactions per second. Suppose also that a workload has an equal mixture of the two types of transactions.

If we took the average of the two pairs of numbers (that is, 99 and 1, versus 50 and 50), it might appear that the two systems have equal performance. However, it is *wrong* to take the averages in this fashion—if we ran 50 transactions of each type, system A would take about 50.5 seconds to finish, whereas system B would finish in just 2 seconds!

The preceding example shows that a simple measure of performance is misleading if there is more than one type of transaction. The right way to average out the numbers is to take the *time to completion* for the workload, rather than the average *throughput* for each transaction type. We can then compute system performance accurately in transactions per second for a specified workload. Thus, system A takes 50.5/100, which is 0.505 seconds per transaction, whereas system B takes 0.02 seconds per transaction, on an average. In terms of throughput, system A runs at an average of 1.98 transactions per second, whereas system B runs at 50 transactions per second. Assuming that transactions of all the types are equally likely, the correct way to average out the throughputs on different transaction types is to take the *harmonic mean* of the throughputs. The harmonic mean of n throughputs $t_1, \ldots, t_n$ is defined as

$$\frac{n}{(\frac{1}{t_1} + \frac{1}{t_2} + \ldots + \frac{1}{t_n})}.$$

For our example, the harmonic mean for the throughputs in system A is 1.98. For system B, it is 50. Thus, system B is approximately 25 times faster than system A on a workload consisting of an equal mixture of the two example types of transactions.

19.3.2 Database-Application Classes

Online transaction processing (OLTP) and decision support (including online analytical processing (OLAP)) are two broad classes of applications handled by database systems. These two classes of tasks have different requirements. High concurrency and clever techniques to speed up commit processing are required for supporting a high rate of update transactions. On the other hand, good query-evaluation algorithms and query optimization are required for decision support. The architecture of some database systems has been tuned to transaction processing; that of others, such as the Teradata DBC series of parallel database systems, has been tuned to decision support. Other vendors try to strike a balance between the two tasks.

Applications typically have a mixture of transaction-processing and decision-support requirements. Hence, which database system is best for an application depends on what mix of the two requirements the application has.

Suppose that we have throughput numbers for the two classes of applications separately, and the application at hand has a mix of transactions in the two classes. We must be careful even about taking the harmonic mean of the throughput numbers, due to *interference* between the transactions. For example, a long-running decision-support transaction may acquire a number of locks, which may prevent all progress of update transactions. The harmonic mean of throughputs should be used only if the transactions do not interfere with one another.

19.3.3 The TPC Benchmarks

The *Transaction Processing Performance Council* (TPC), is an organization that has defined a series of benchmark standards for database systems.

The first in the series was the TPC-A benchmark, which was defined in 1989. The TPC-A benchmark measures performance in update-intensive database environments typical in *on-line transaction processing* (*OLTP*) applications. Such environments have multiple on-line terminal sessions, have significant disk I/O, and require transaction integrity. This benchmark simulates a typical bank application, using a single type of transaction that models cash withdrawal and deposit at a bank teller. The transaction updates several relations—such as the bank balance, the teller's balance, and the customers balance—and adds a record to an audit trail relation. Moreover, the benchmark also incorporates communication with terminals, to model the end-to-end performance of the system realistically.

The TPC benchmarks are defined in great detail. They define the set of relations, and the sizes of the tuples. The benchmarks define the number of tuples in the relations not as a fixed number, but rather as a multiple of the number of claimed transactions per second, to reflect that a larger rate of transaction execution is likely to be correlated with a larger number of accounts. The performance metric used is throughput, expressed as *transactions per second* (*TPS*). When its performance is measured, the system must provide a response time within certain bounds, so that a high throughput cannot be obtained at the cost of very long response times. Further, for business applications, cost is of great importance. Hence, the TPC benchmark also measures performance in terms of *price per TPS*. A large system may have a high number of transactions per second, but may be expensive (that is, have a high price per TPS). Moreover, a company cannot claim TPC benchmark numbers for its systems *without* an external audit that ensures that the system faithfully follows the definition of the benchmark, including full support for the ACID properties of transactions.

The TPC-B benchmark was designed to test the core performance of the database system, along with the operating system on which the system runs. It removes the parts of the TPC-A benchmark that deal with users, communication, or terminals, to focus on the back-end database server. The TPC-B benchmark is relatively less widely used.

The TPC-C benchmark was designed to model a more complex system than that modeled by the TPC-A benchmark. The TPC-C benchmark concentrates on the main activities in an order-entry environment, such as entering and delivering orders, recording payments, checking status of orders, and monitoring levels of stock.

The TPC-D benchmark was designed to test the performance of database systems on decision-support queries. Decision-support systems are becoming increasingly important today. The TPC-A, TPC-B, and TPC-C benchmarks measure performance on transaction-processing workloads, and should not be used as a measure of performance on decision-support queries. The "D" in TPC-D can be understood as standing for decision support. The benchmark consists of a set of 17 queries modeling decision-support systems; the queries must be implemented in SQL. Some of the queries make use of complex SQL features, such as aggregation.

19.3.4 The OODB Benchmarks

The nature of applications in an OODB is different from that of typical transaction-processing applications. Therefore, a different set of benchmarks has been proposed for OODBs. The Object Operations benchmark, version 1, popularly known as the OO1 benchmark, was an early proposal. The OO7 benchmark is widely used today. This benchmark follows a philosophy different from that of the TPC benchmarks. The TPC benchmarks provide one or two numbers (in terms of average transactions per second, and transactions per second per dollar); the OO7 benchmark provides a set of numbers, containing a separate benchmark number for each of several different kinds of operations. The reason for this approach is that it is not yet clear what is the *typical* OODB transaction. It is clear that such a transaction will carry out certain operations, such as traversing a set of connected objects, or retrieving all objects in a class, but it is not clear exactly what mix of these operations will be used. Hence, the benchmark provides separate numbers for each class of operations; the numbers can be combined in an appropriate way, depending on the specific application.

19.4 Performance Tuning

Tuning the performance of a system involves adjusting various parameters and design choices to improve its performance for a specific application. Various aspects of a database-system design—ranging from high-level aspects such as the schema and transaction design, to database parameters such as buffer sizes, down to hardware issues such as number of disks—affect the performance of an application. Each of these aspects can be adjusted such that performance is improved.

19.4.1 Location of Bottlenecks

The performance of most systems (at least before they are tuned) is limited primarily by the performance of one or a few components, which are called *bottlenecks*. For instance, a program may spend 80 percent of its time in a small loop deep in the code, and the remaining 20 percent of the time distributed across the rest of the code; the small loop then is a bottleneck. Improving the performance of a component that is not a bottleneck does little to improve the overall speed of the system; in the preceding example, improving the speed of the rest of the code cannot lead to more than a 20 percent improvement overall, whereas improving the speed of the bottleneck loop could result in an improvement of nearly 80 percent overall, in the best case.

Hence, when tuning a system, we must first try to discover what are the bottlenecks, and then to eliminate the bottlenecks by improving the performance of the components causing the bottlenecks. When one bottleneck is removed, it may turn out that another component becomes the bottleneck. In a well-balanced system, no single component is the bottleneck. If the system contains bottlenecks, components that are not part of the bottleneck are underutilized, and could perhaps have been replaced by cheaper components with lower performance.

For simple programs, the time spent in each region of the code determines the overall execution time. However, database systems are much more complex, and can be modeled as *queueing systems*. A transaction requests various services from the database system, starting from entry to a server process, disk reads during execution, CPU cycles, and locks for concurrency control. Each of these services has a queue associated with it, and small transactions may spend most of their time waiting in queues—especially in disk I/O queues—rather than executing code. Figure 19.5 illustrates some of the queues in a database system.

As a result of the numerous queues in the database, bottlenecks in a database system typically show up in the form of long queues for a particular service, or, equivalently, in high utilizations for a particular service. If requests are spaced exactly uniformly, and the time to service a request is less than or equal to the time when the next request arrives, then each request will find the resource idle and can therefore start execution immediately without waiting. Unfortunately,

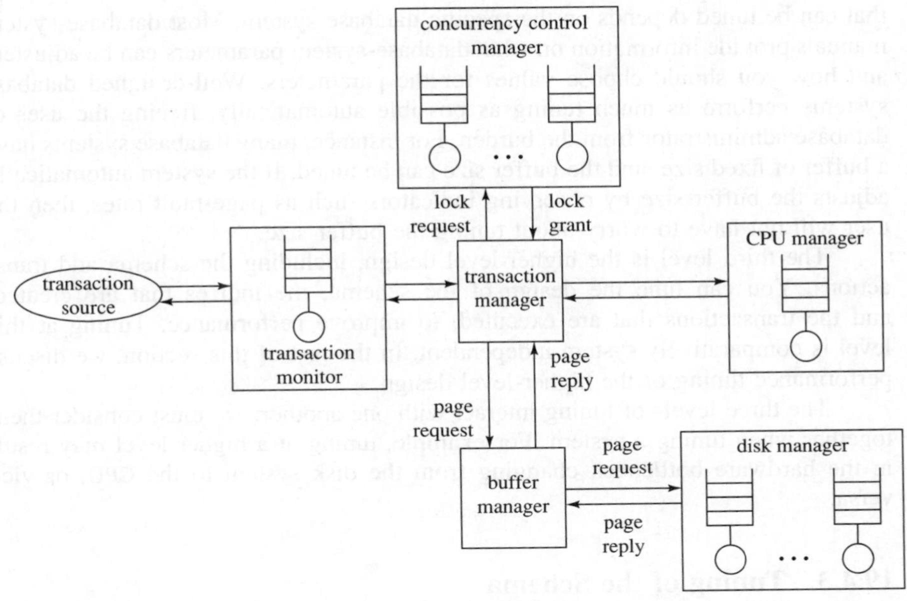

Figure 19.5 Queues in a database system

the arrival of requests in a database system is never so uniform, and is instead random.

If a resource, such as a disk, has a low utilization, then, when a request is made, the resource is likely to be idle, in which case the waiting time for the request will be 0. Assuming uniformly randomly distributed arrivals, the length of the queue (and correspondingly the waiting time) go up exponentially with utilization; as utilization approaches 100 percent, the queue length increases sharply, resulting in excessively long waiting times. The utilization of a resource should be kept low enough that queue length is short. As a rule of the thumb, utilizations of around 70 percent are considered to be good, and utilizations above 90 percent are considered excessive, since they will result in significant delays. To learn more about the theory of queueing systems, generally referred to as *queueing theory*, you can consult the references cited in the bibliographic notes.

19.4.2 Tunable Parameters

Database administrators can tune a database system at three levels. The lowest level is at the hardware level. Options for tuning systems at this level include adding disks or using a RAID system if disk I/O is a bottleneck, adding more memory if the disk buffer size is a bottleneck, or moving to a faster processor if CPU use is a bottleneck.

The second level consists of the database-system parameters, such as buffer size and checkpointing intervals. The exact set of database-system parameters that can be tuned depends on the specific database system. Most database-system manuals provide information on what database-system parameters can be adjusted, and how you should choose values for the parameters. Well-designed database systems perform as much tuning as possible automatically, freeing the user or database administrator from the burden. For instance, many database systems have a buffer of fixed size, and the buffer size can be tuned. If the system automatically adjusts the buffer size by observing indicators such as page-fault rates, then the user will not have to worry about tuning the buffer size.

The third level is the higher-level design, including the schema and transactions. You can tune the design of the schema, the indices that are created, and the transactions that are executed, to improve performance. Tuning at this level is comparatively system independent. In the rest of this section, we discuss performance tuning of the higher-level design.

The three levels of tuning interact with one another; we must consider them together when tuning a system. For example, tuning at a higher level may result in the hardware bottleneck changing from the disk system to the CPU, or vice versa.

19.4.3 Tuning of the Schema

Within the constraints of the normal form adopted, it is possible to partition relations vertically. For example, consider the *account* relation, with the schema

account (*branch-name, account-number, balance*)

for which *account-number* is a key. Within the constraints of the normal forms (BCNF and third normal forms), we can partition the *account* relation into two relations as follows:

account-branch (*account-number, branch-name*)
account-balance (*account-number, balance*)

The two representations are logically equivalent, since *account-number* is a key, but they have different performance characteristics.

If most accesses to account information look at only the *account-number* and *balance*, then they can be run against the *account-balance* relation, and access is likely to be somewhat faster, since the *branch-name* attribute is not fetched. For the same reason, more tuples of *account-balance* will fit in the buffer than corresponding tuples of *account*, again leading to faster performance. This effect would be particularly marked if the *branch-name* attribute were large. Hence, a schema consisting of *account-branch* and *account-balance* would be preferable to a schema consisting of the *account* relation in this case.

On the other hand, if most accesses to account information require both *balance* and *branch-name*, using the *account* relation would be preferable, since the cost of the join of *account-balance* and *account-branch* would be avoided. Also, the storage overhead would be lower, since there would be only one relation, and the attribute *account-number* would not be replicated.

Another trick used to improve performance is to store a denormalized relation, such as a join of *account* and *depositor*, where the information about branch-names and balances is repeated for every account holder. More effort has to be expended to make sure the relation is consistent whenever an update is carried out. However, a query that fetches the names of the customers and the associated balances will be speeded up, since the join of *account* and *depositor* will have been precomputed. If such a query is executed frequently, and has to be performed as efficiently as possible, use of the denormalized relation could be beneficial. Another approach supported by some databases is to cluster records that would match in the join, on the same disk page, so that the join can be computed efficiently.

19.4.4 Tuning of Indices

We can tune the indices in a system to improve performance. If queries are the bottleneck, we can often speed them up by creating appropriate indices on relations. If updates are the bottleneck, there may be too many indices, which have to be updated when the relations are updated. Removing indices may speed up updates.

The choice of the type of index also is important. Some database systems support different kinds of indices, such as hash indices and B-tree indices. If range queries are common, B-tree indices are preferable to hash indices. Whether or not to make an index a clustered index is another tunable parameter. Only one index on a relation can be made clustered; generally, the one that benefits the most number of queries and updates should be made clustered.

19.4.5 Tuning of Transactions

Both read-only and update transactions can be tuned. In the past, optimizers on many database systems were not particularly good, so how a query was written would have a big influence on how it was executed, and therefore on the performance. Today, optimizers are advanced, and can transform even badly written queries and execute them efficiently. However, optimizers have limits on what they can do. Most systems provide a mechanism to find out the exact execution plan for a query, and to use it to tune the query.

In embedded SQL, if a query is executed frequently with different values for a parameter, it may help to combine the calls into a more set-oriented query that is executed only once. The costs of communication of SQL queries can be high in client–server systems, so combining the embedded SQL calls is particularly helpful in such systems. For example, consider a program that steps through each department specified in a list, invoking an embedded SQL query to find the total expenses of the department using the **group by** construct on a relation *expenses*(*date*, *employee*, *department*, *amount*). If the *expenses* relation does not have a clustered index on *department*, each such query will result in a scan of the relation. Instead, we can use a single embedded SQL query to find total expenses of every department, and to store the total in a temporary relation; the query can be evaluated with a single scan. The relevant departments can then be looked up in this (presumably much smaller) temporary relation.

Another technique used widely in client–server systems to reduce the cost of communication and SQL compilation is to use stored procedures, where queries are stored at the server in the form of procedures, which may be precompiled. Clients can invoke these stored procedures, rather than communicate entire queries.

Concurrent execution of different types of transactions can sometimes lead to poor performance due to contention on locks. Consider, for example, a banking database. During the day, numerous small update transactions are executed almost continuously. Suppose that a large query that computes statistics on branches is run at the same time. If the query performs a scan on a relation, it may block out all updates on the relation while it runs, and that can have a disastrous effect on the performance of the system. Such large queries are best executed when updates are few or nonexistent, such as late at night.

Long update transactions can cause performance problems with system logs, and with the time taken to recover from system crashes. If the transactions performs many updates, the system log may get full even before the transaction completes, in which case the transaction will have to be rolled back. If an update transaction runs for a long time (even with few updates), it may block deletion of old parts of the log, if the logging system is not well designed. Again, this blocking could lead to the log getting filled up.

To avoid such problems, many database systems impose strict limits on the number of updates that a single transaction can carry out. Even if the system does not impose such limits, it is often helpful to break up a large update transaction into a set of smaller update transactions where possible. For example, a transaction that gives a raise to every employee in a large corporation could be split up into a series of small transactions, each of which updates a small range of employee-ids. Such transactions are called *mini-batch* transactions. However, mini-batch transactions must be used with care. First, if there are concurrent updates on the set of employees, the result of the set of smaller transactions may not be equivalent to that of the single large transaction. Second, if there is a failure, the salaries of some of the employees would have been increased by committed transactions, but salaries of other employees would not. To avoid this problem, as soon as the system recovers from failure, we must execute the transactions remaining in the batch.

19.4.6 Performance Simulation

To test the performance of a database system even before it is installed, we can create a performance-simulation model of the database system. Each service shown in Figure 19.5, such as the CPU, each disk, the buffer, and the concurrency control is modeled in the simulation. Instead of modeling details of a service, the simulation model may capture only some aspects of each service, such as the *service time*—that is, the time taken to finish processing a request once processing has begun. Thus, the simulation can model a disk access based on just the average disk access time.

Since requests for a service generally have to wait their turn, each service has an associated queue in the simulation model. A transaction consists of a series of requests. The requests are queued up as they arrive, and are serviced according to the policy for that service, such as first come first served. The models for services such as CPU and the disks conceptually operate in parallel, to account for the fact that these subsystems operate in parallel in a real system.

Once the simulation model for transaction processing is built, a number of experiments can be run on it. Experiments with simulated transactions arriving at different rates are used to find how the system would behave under various load conditions. Other experiments could vary the service times for each service to find out how sensitive the performance is to each of them. System parameters can be varied, so that performance tuning can be don on the simulation model.

19.5 Time in Databases

A database models the state of some aspect of the real world outside itself. Typically, databases model only one state—the current state—of the real world, and do not store information about past states, except perhaps as audit trails. When the state of the real world changes, the database gets updated, and information about the old state gets lost. However, in many applications, it is important to store and retrieve information about past states. For example, a patient database must store information about the medical history of a patient. A factory monitoring system may store information about current and past readings of sensors in the factory, for analysis. Databases that store information about states of the real world across time are called *temporal databases*.

When considering the issue of time in database systems, we must distinguish between time as measured by the system and time as observed in the real world. The *valid time* for a fact is the set of time intervals during which the fact is true in the real world. The *transaction time* for a fact is the time interval during which the fact is current within the database system. This latter time is based on the transaction serialization order and is generated automatically by the system. Note that valid-time intervals, being a real-world concept, cannot be generated automatically and must be provided to the system.

A *temporal relation* is one where each tuple has an associated time when it is true; the time may be either valid time or transaction time. Of course, both valid time and transaction time can be stored, in which case the relation is said to be a *bitemporal relation*. Figure 19.6 shows an example of a temporal relation. To simplify the representation, each tuple has only one time interval associated with it; thus, a tuple is represented once for every disjoint time interval in which it is true. Intervals are shown here as a pair of attributes *from* and *to*; an actual implementation would have a structured type, perhaps called *Interval*, that contains both fields. Note that some of the tuples have a "*" in the *to* time column; these asterisks indicate that the tuple is true until the value in the *to* time column is changed; thus, the tuple is true at the current time. Although times are shown in textual form, they can be stored in a more compact form, such as in the number

branch-name	*account-number*	*balance*	*from*	*to*
Downtown	A-101	500	94/1/1 9:00	94/1/24 11:30
Downtown	A-101	100	94/1/24 11:30	*
Mianus	A-215	700	95/6/2 15:30	95/8/8 10:00
Mianus	A-215	900	95/8/8 10:00	95/9/5 8:00
Mianus	A-215	700	95/9/5 8:00	*
Brighton	A-217	750	94/7/5 11:00	95/5/1 16:00

Figure 19.6 A temporal *account* relation.

of seconds since some fixed time on a fixed date, which can be translated back to the normal textual form.

19.5.1 Time Specification in SQL-92

The SQL-92 standard defines the types **date**, **time**, and **timestamp**. The type **date** contains four digits for the year (1–9999), two digits for the month (1–12), and two digits for the date (1–31). The type **time** contains two digits for the hour, two digits for the minute, and two digits for the second, plus optional fractional digits. The seconds field can go beyond 60, to allow for leap seconds that are added during some years to correct for small variations in the speed of rotation of the earth. The type **timestamp** contains the fields of **date** and **time**, with six fractional digits for the seconds field. The SQL-92 times are specified in the *Universal Coordinated Time* (*UTC*), which is a standard for specifying time. (The standard abbreviation is UTC, rather than UCT, since it is an abbreviation of "Universal Coordinated Time" written in French as *universel temps coordonné*. SQL-92 also supports two types, **time with time zone**, and **timestamp with time zone** which specify the time as a local time plus the offset of the local time from UTC. For instance, the time could be expressed in terms of U.S. Eastern Standard time, with an offset of −6:00, since U.S. Eastern Standard time is 6 hours behind UTC.

SQL-92 supports a type called **interval** (which more properly ought to have been called *span*), which allows us to refer to a period of time such as "1 day" or "2 days and 5 hours," without specifying a particular time when this period starts. This notion differs from the notion of interval used previously, which is to an interval of time with specific starting and ending times.

19.5.2 Temporal Query Languages

A database relation, as we have defined it in this text, is sometimes called a *snapshot relation*, since it reflects the state in a snapshot of the real world. Thus, a snapshot of a temporal relation at a point in time t is the set of tuples in the relation that are true at time t, with the time-interval attributes projected out. The snapshot operation on a temporal relation gives the snapshot of the relation at a specified time (or the current time, if the time is not specified).

A *temporal selection* is a selection that involves the time attributes; a *temporal projection* is a projection where the tuples in the projection inherit their times from the tuples in the original relation. A *temporal join* is one where the time of a tuple in the result is the intersection of the times of the tuples from which it is derived. If the times do not intersect, the tuple is removed from the result.

The predicates *precedes*, *overlaps*, and *contains*, can be applied on intervals; their meanings should be clear. The *intersect* operation can be applied on two intervals, to give a single (possibly empty) interval. However, the union of two intervals may or may not be a single interval.

Functional dependencies must be used with care in a temporal relation. Although the account number may functionally determine the balance at any given point in time, obviously the balance can change over time. A temporal functional dependency $X \xrightarrow{\tau} Y$ holds on a relation schema R if, for all legal instances r of R, all snapshots of r satisfy the functional dependency $X \rightarrow Y$.

Several proposals have been made for extending query languages such as QUEL and SQL to improve their support of temporal data. The proposal that currently has the widest support is TSQL2, which extends SQL-92. The bibliographic notes provide references on TSQL2.

19.6 User Interfaces

User interfaces for databases have progressed a long way from the early days when the only interface to the database was through procedure calls. Today, database systems provide a variety of tools that allow specialized interfaces, for tasks such as order entry and report generation, to be constructed quickly.

User interfaces to a database can be broadly classified in the following categories:

- Line-oriented interfaces
- Forms interfaces
- Report writers
- Graphical user interfaces

Unfortunately, there are no standards for user interfaces, and each database system typically has its own user interface. In this section, we describe the basic concepts, without going into the details of any particular user interface.

Line-oriented interfaces are the most basic user interfaces. For example, interactive SQL systems allow users to type in queries, and display answers to the queries in tabular form. Although line-oriented interfaces are good for ad hoc querying, they are not convenient for repetitive tasks, such as those performed by bank tellers and salespersons.

Forms interfaces are widely used for entering data into databases. Online forms have a visual appearance much like a paper form. A common example of the use of forms is the entry of orders; Figure 19.7 shows an example of such a form. Forms are also useful for retrieving certain kinds of information from a

Acme Supply Company Inc. **Component Order Form**

Customer Name: __________ Date: __________

Customer Number: __________ Order No.: __________

Address: __________

Phone Number: __________

Part Number	Part Description	Unit Price	Quantity	Subtotal
			Total	

Figure 19.7 An order-entry form.

database. For example, the order-entry form can also be used for retrieving old orders, when the order number or customer name is provided.

Creating a forms interface using a programming language such as Pascal or C is a tedious task. Most database systems provide forms packages that allow users to create forms in an easy declarative fashion, using form-editor programs. Users can define the type, size, and format of each field in a form using the form editor. System actions can be associated with user actions, such as hitting a function key on the keyboard, or typing the enter key in a specified field. For instance, the execution of a transaction to register a filled-in order may be associated with typing the enter key in a field labeled *Submit*. As another example, the action associated with entering a value for the customer-id field may retrieve customer information from a database, and may automatically fill in values for other fields, such as customer name and address.

We can perform simple error checks by defining constraints on the fields in the form. For example, a constraint on the item-number field may check that the item number typed in by the user corresponds to an actual item in the database. Although such constraints can be checked when the transaction is executed, detecting errors early allows the forms system to indicate which field in the form has the error. Forms packages also provide features such as menus that indicate the valid values that can be entered in a field. The ability to control such features

Acme Supply Company Inc.
Quarterly Sales Report

Period: Jan. 1 to March 31, 1996

Region	Category	Sales	Subtotal
North	Computer Hardware	1,000,000	
	Computer Software	500,000	
	All categories		1,500,000
South	Computer Hardware	200,000	
	Computer Software	400,000	
	All categories		600,000
		Total Sales	2,100,000

Figure 19.8 A formatted report.

declaratively reduces the effort greatly, as compared to creating a form directly using a programming language.

Report writers are another form of user interface supported by many database systems. People often query databases to detect trends—examples of such queries include include finding the total sales in the past month, and comparing the total sales in the past month with the sales in the corresponding month in the previous year. The output of such queries needs to be properly formatted in the form of a report that can be given to managers. Moreover, such reports need to be generated regularly—for example, at the end of each month. Report-writer packages provide a clean way to combine text formatting for creating reports, with database querying to generate the data that goes into the report.

We specify report formats using the text-formatting facilities provided by the report writer. Variables can be used to store parameters such as the month and the year, and fields in the report can be defined with these variables. Tables, graphs, bar charts, or other graphics can be defined via queries on the database. The query definitions can make use of the parameter values stored in the variables. Once we have defined a report structure using a report-writer facility, we can store it, and can execute it at any time to generate a report. Report-writer systems provide a variety of facilities for structuring tabular output, such as defining table and column headers, displaying subtotals for each group in a table, automatically splitting long tables into multiple pages, and displaying subtotals at the end of each page.

Figure 19.8 shows an example of a formatted report. The data in the report can be generated by aggregation on information about orders.

The collections of application-development tools provided by database systems, such as forms packages and report writers, are often referred to as *fourth-generation languages* (4GLs). The name emphasizes that these tools offer a programming paradigm different from the imperative programming paradigm offered by third-generation programming languages, such as Pascal and C.

In recent years, personal computers that support graphical user interfaces have replaced terminals in many data-entry applications. Graphical user interfaces support interaction based on the point-and-click paradigm, using features such as menus and icons. Forms systems can be thought of a primitive type of graphical user interfaces. Graphical interfaces also provide an excellent means of displaying data, by using bar charts, pie charts, graphs, and other such devices. Numerous tools have been developed to simplify the creation of graphical interfaces to databases. Power Builder, Gupta SQL, and the user interface of the Microsoft Access database system are examples of such tools.

The most recent addition to the family of graphical user interfaces to databases has been the World Wide Web, often called simple the Web. (See Chapter 21 for more information about the World Wide Web.) Within a short period of the development of the Web standards, numerous vendors have announced Web interfaces to their databases. Web interfaces to databases are based primarily on the graphical-forms facilities provided by the *Hypertext Markup Language* (*HTML*). The Web is an area of intense development, and new graphical user interface facilities are likely to emerge on the Web.

19.7 Active Databases

Early-generation database systems stored data passively, and performed only actions explicitly requested by a user transaction. In contrast, an active database system not only stores data, but also carries out actions in response to events, such as changes in the data. *Active rules* specify when to carry out actions, and what actions to carry out.

The *event–condition–action* model for active rules is widely used. The general form of rules in this model is as follows:

on *event*
if *condition*
then *action*

Changes to the database—such as insertions, deletions, and updates to tuples—are modeled as *events*. In an object-oriented database, an event could be an action, such as creating or deleting an object, or the execution of a method on the object. Other examples of events are temporal events, such as "at 11:59 P.M. on 31 December, 1999", or "at 12:00 A.M. every weekday."

When an event occurs, one or more rules may be *triggered*. The event is called the *triggering event* of the rules. Once a rule is triggered, the *conditions* of the rule are checked. Examples of conditions to check include whether inventory levels have fallen below a minimum, or whether the update has left the database in an inconsistent state.

If the conditions are satisfied, the *actions* of the rule are executed. Examples of actions are the ordering of fresh stock if the inventory level has fallen below a minimum, or rollback of the transaction (if the update would make the database inconsistent).

Active rules can be used for diverse purposes. An example application is *alerting*, where the rules monitor the system and notify the administrator or user if an unusual event has occurred. Active rules also can be used for checking integrity constraints. Another example of the use of active rules is in maintenance of derived data, such as indices and materialized views. If a view has been materialized (that is, computed and stored), it needs to be updated in response to changes to the database relations on which it is defined. The actions needed for keeping the view up to date can be encoded as active rules.

Suppose that we want to enforce a constraint that, when an employee record is inserted into the *employee* relation, the salary of the employee must be less than the salary of the employee's manager. The following rule can be used to enforce the constraint:

```
define trigger employee-sal
on insert employee
if employee.salary >
        (select E.salary from employee as E
         where E.name = employee.manager)
then abort
```

The **define trigger** clause serves to give a name to the trigger. As an alternative to aborting the transaction, the rule designer could have specified some other action, such as reducing the employee's salary to that of the manager.

The syntax for active rules is not yet standardized, and may differ across systems. The trigger facility described in Chapter 6 is an example of an active-rule facility.

Rules are typically stored in the database, just like regular data, so that they are persistent and are accessible to all database operations. Once a rule is entered into the database, the database system takes on the responsibility of executing the action whenever the specified event occurs and the corresponding condition is satisfied.

If the database system does not support triggers, some applications can manage with *polling*. That is, a process periodically queries (polls) the database to see whether any event of interest has occurred, and then carries out necessary condition checks and actions. However, detecting that an event—such as insertion or deletion—has occurred can be expensive if proper support is not available from the database, since a large relation may have to be scanned each time. Further, since the transaction that performed the update could have committed before polling occurs, actions such as aborting the transaction cannot be implemented. Hence, polling is not practical for many applications. The use of active rules avoids the problems of polling.

When you are designing a collection of active rules, there are several points that you should keep in mind:

- **Termination**. The execution of the actions of a rule may cause the occurrence of some new events. These events may, in turn, trigger other rules. These in turn could potentially trigger others, leading to possible chains of triggering.

If a rule occurs twice in a chain, there is a potential for the execution of the rule to (indirectly) trigger itself. In such a case, there is a possibility that an infinite chain of triggering could occur, and the triggering of rules might never terminate. Note that the presence of a rule twice in a chain does not necessarily imply that an infinite loop will occur, since the rule may have been triggered on updates of different tuples. The designer of a rule system must ensure that no update on an consistent state of the database can result in an infinite chain of rule triggering.

- **Priority**. If several rules are triggered by the same event, they have to be executed in some order. Rule systems usually provide a means of specifying a priority value for each rule. If multiple rules are triggered, they are executed in the order of their priority value. Some systems allow multiple rules to have the same priority value. If several rules with the same priority are triggered, the system makes a nondeterministic (that is, arbitrary) choice of the order of execution of those rules.

- **Event-execution binding**. The event-execution binding specifies when a rule gets executed. For instance, if the binding is specified as *immediate*, the rule gets executed as soon as the triggering event (such as insertion or deletion of a tuple) occurs. The rule execution is treated as part of the transaction that performed the update. If the binding is specified as *deferred*, the rule gets executed at the end of the transaction that performed the update, as part of the same transaction. If the binding is specified as *decoupled*, the rule gets executed in a separate transaction, after the transaction that performed the update has committed. Decoupled binding requires support from the recovery system to ensure that the actions will get executed eventually, even if there are intervening system failures after the triggering transaction commits. Some rule systems provide more powerful means for specifying when rules are to be executed, allowing, for example, a choice between *before* or *after* the triggering event.

- **Error handling.** If the execution of a rule results in a run-time error, error recovery must be initiated. As long as the event-execution binding is either immediate or deferred, the rule execution is part of the transaction that performed the update. In a well-designed rule system, such an error probably reflects an error in the transaction, rather than in the rule itself. Error recovery could then just roll back the transaction.

  Error recovery is much harder if the event-execution binding is decoupled. In this case, when the error is detected, it is too late to roll back the transaction. Not executing the rule could result in some forms of inconsistency in the database. Thus, it is not clear, in general, exactly how to deal with an error in a decoupled rule execution. Manual intervention may be needed to deal with the error. It is therefore important to design the rule system such that run-time errors do not occur during the execution of decoupled rules.

19.8 Summary

The data stored in the database need to be protected from unauthorized access, malicious destruction or alteration, and accidental introduction of inconsistency. It is easier to protect against accidental loss of data consistency than to protect against malicious access to the database. Absolute protection of the database from malicious abuse is not possible, but the cost to the perpetrator can be made sufficiently high to deter most, if not all, attempts to access the database without proper authority.

A user may have several forms of authorization on parts of the database. Authorization is a means by which the database system can be protected against malicious or unauthorized access. A user who has been granted some form of authority may be allowed to pass on this authority to other users. However, we must be careful about how authorization can be passed among users if we are to ensure that such authorization can be revoked at some future time.

The various authorization provisions in a database system may not provide sufficient protection for highly sensitive data. In such cases, data can be *encrypted*. Only a reader who knows how to decipher (*decrypt*) the encrypted data can read them.

It is difficult to ensure the privacy of individuals while allowing use of data for statistical purposes. A simple way to deal with potential security breaches is for the system to reject any query that involves fewer than some predetermined number of individuals. Another approach to security is data pollution, or the random falsification of data provided in response to a query. A similar technique involves random modification of the query itself. For both of these techniques, the goals involve a tradeoff between accuracy and security. Regardless of the approach taken to security of statistical data, it is possible for a malicious user to determine individual data values. However, good techniques can make the expense in terms of cost and time sufficiently high that it becomes a deterrent.

Standards are important in database systems, due to the latter's complexity and the need for interoperation. Formal standards exist for SQL. De-facto standards, such as ODBC, and standards adopted by industry groups, such as CORBA, have played an important role in the growth of client–server database systems. Standards for object-oriented databases, such as ODMG, are being developed by industry groups.

Performance benchmarks play an important role in comparisons of database systems, especially as systems become more standards compliant. The TPC benchmark suites are widely used, and the different TPC benchmarks are useful for comparing the performance of databases under different workloads. Tuning of the database-system parameters, as well as the higher-level database design—such as the schema, indices and transactions—is important for achieving good performance. Tuning is best done by identifying bottlenecks, and eliminating them.

Time plays an important role in database systems. Databases are models of the real world. Whereas most databases model the state of the real world at a point in time (at the current time), temporal databases model the states of the real world across time. Facts in temporal relations have associated times when they are valid, which can be represented as a union of intervals. Temporal query languages have been proposed to simplify modeling of time, as well as time-related queries.

There are several types of user interfaces to databases, ranging from command-line interfaces to graphical user interfaces. Form interfaces are widely used for data entry and for some types of packaged queries. Forms packages help programmers to construct forms in a simple declarative manner. Report writers are used for generating reports based on data in the database. They combine text formatting with data retrieval from the database. Languages for defining forms and report-writer languages constitute what are known as fourth-generation languages (4GLs).

Active databases support the specification and execution of rules in the database. In the event–condition–action model, rules are triggered by events; the database system checks the conditions of rules that have been triggered; and, if the conditions are satisfied, the database system executes the actions specified by the rules. Rules are used for a variety of purposes such as for alerting users to unusual activity, for reordering stock, or for enforcing integrity constraints. We must be careful to ensure that the rule set will terminate, if the action of a rule can cause an event that (directly or indirectly) triggers the same rule.

Exercises

19.1. Make a list of security concerns for a bank. For each item on your list, state whether this concern relates to physical security, human security, operating-system security, or database security.

19.2. Using the relations of our sample bank database, write an SQL expression to define the following views:
(*a*) A view containing the account numbers and customer names (but not the balances) for all accounts at the Deer Park branch.
(*b*) A view containing the names and addresses of all customers who have an account with the bank, but do not have a loan.
(*c*) A view containing the name and average account balance of every customer of the Rock Ridge branch.

19.3. For each of the views that you defined in Exercise 19.2, explain how updates would be performed (if they should be allowed at all). *Hint*: See the discussion of views in Chapter 3.

19.4. In Chapter 3, we described the use of views to simplify access to the database by users who need to see only part of the database. In this chapter, we described the use of views as a security mechanism. Do these two purposes for views ever conflict? Explain your answer.

19.5. What is the purpose of having separate categories for index authorization and resource authorization?

19.6. Database systems that store each relation in a separate operating-system file may use the operating system's security and authorization scheme, rather than defining a special scheme themselves. Discuss an advantage and a disadvantage of such an approach.

19.7. What are two advantages of encrypting data stored in the database?

19.8. How does data encryption affect the index schemes of Chapter 11? In particular, how might it affect schemes that attempt to store data in sorted order?

19.9. Suppose that the bank of our running example maintains a statistical database containing the average balances of all customers. The schema for this relation is (*customer-name*, *customer-city*, *avg-balance*). Assume that, for security reasons, the following restrictions are imposed on queries against this data:

- Every query must involve at least 10 customers.
- The intersection of any pair of queries, that is, the number of customers involved in both queries in the pair, may be at most 5.

Construct a series of queries to find the average balance of a customer. *Hint*: This can be done in fewer than seven queries.

19.10. Perhaps the most important data items in any database system are the passwords that control access to the database. Suggest a scheme for the secure storage of passwords. Be sure that your scheme allows the system to test passwords supplied by users who are attempting to log into the system.

19.11. List some benefits and drawbacks of an anticipatory standard as compared to a reactionary standard.

19.12. Suppose a system runs three types of transactions. Transactions of type A run at the rate of 50 per second, transactions of type B run at 100 per second, and transactions of type C run at 200 per second. Suppose the mix of transactions has 25 percent of type A, 25 percent of type B, and 50 percent of type C.

(*a*) What is the average transaction throughput of the system, assuming there is no interference between the transactions.

(*b*) What factors may result in interference between the transactions of different types, leading to the calculated throughput being incorrect?

19.13. List some of the features of the TPC benchmarks that help make them realistic and dependable measures.

19.14. (*a*) What are the three broad levels at which a database system can be tuned to improve performance?

(*b*) Give two examples of how tuning can be done, for each of the levels.

19.15. What is the motivation for splitting a long transaction into a series of small one? What problems could arise as a result, and how can these problems be averted?

19.16. What are the two types of time, and how are they different. Why does it make sense to have both types of time associated with a tuple?

19.17. Will functional dependencies be preserved if a relation is converted to a temporal relation by adding a time attribute? How is the problem handled in a temporal database?

19.18. Consider a view *branch-cust* defined as follows:

> **create view** *branch-cust* **as**
> **select** *branch-name, customer-name*
> **from** *depositor, account*
> **where** *depositor.account-number* = *account.account-number*

Suppose that the view is *materialized*, that is, the view is computed and stored. Write active rules to *maintain* the view, that is, to keep it up to date on insertions to and deletions from *depositor* or *account*. Do not bother about updates.

Bibliographic Notes

Security aspects of computer systems in general are discussed in Bell and LaPadula [1976], and by the U.S. Department of Defense [1985]. Security aspects of SQL are discussed in detail in ANSI [1992], and are summarized in Date and Darwen [1993] and in Melton and Simon [1993]. Stonebraker and Wong [1974] discuss the Ingres approach to security, which involves modification of users' queries so as to ensure that users do not access data for which authorization has not been granted. Denning and Denning [1979] survey database security. Database systems that can produce incorrect answers when necessary for security maintenance are discussed in Winslett et al. [1994] and Tendick and Matloff [1994].

Work on security in relational databases includes that of Lunt et al. [1990], Stachour and Thuraisingham [1990], Jajodia and Sandhu [1990], Kogan and Jajodia [1990], and Qian and Lunt [1996]. Rabitti et al. [1988,1991] and Thomas and Sandhu [1996] discuss security in object-oriented databases. Lunt [1995] provides an overview of issues in authorization.

Operating-system security issues are discussed in most operating-system texts, including Silberschatz and Galvin [1994].

Chin and Ozsoyoglu [1981] discuss the design of statistical databases. Several papers provide mathematical analysis of the number of queries required to break privacy in a database under a variety of assumptions. Among these are Kam and Ullman [1977], Chin [1978], DeMillo et al. [1978], Dobkin et al. [1979], Yao [1979a], Denning [1980], and Leiss [1982b].

Another aspect of security that has been studied from a mathematical standpoint is data encryption. The Data Encryption Standard is presented by the U.S. Dept. of Commerce [1977]. Public-key encryption is discussed by Rivest et al. [1978]. Other discussions on cryptography include Diffie and Hellman [1979], Lempel [1979], Simmons [1979], Davies [1980], Fernandez et al. [1981], Denning [1982], Leiss [1982a], and Akl [1983].

The American National Standard SQL-86 is described in ANSI [1986]. The IBM Systems Application Architecture definition of SQL is defined by IBM [1987]. The standards for SQL-89 and SQL-92 are available as ANSI [1989] and ANSI [1992] respectively. The X/Open SQL call-level interface is defined in X/Open [1993]; the ODBC API is described in Microsoft [1992]. The X/Open XA interface is defined in X/Open [1991]. The ODMG-93 standard is defined in Catell [1994].

An early proposal for a database-system benchmark (the Wisconsin benchmark) was made by Bitton et al. [1983]. The TPC A, B and C benchmarks are described in Gray [1993]. An online version of all the TPC benchmarks descriptions, as well as benchmark results, is available on the World Wide Web at the URL http://www.tpc.org; the site also contains up-to-date information about new benchmarks such as TPC-E, a proposed extension of TPC-C. The OO1 benchmark for OODBs is described in Catell and Skeen [1992]; the OO7 benchmark is described in Carey et al. [1993]. In contrast to the TPC benchmarks, the OODB benchmarks were designed by individuals, rather than by a council.

Kleinrock's two volumes [1975, 1976] are popular textbooks on queueing theory. Shasha [1992] provides a good overview of database tuning. O'Neil's textbook [1994] describes performance measurement and tuning. Brown et al. [1994] describe an approach to automated tuning.

The incorporation of time into the relational data model is discussed in Snodgrass and Ahn [1985], Clifford and Tansel [1985], Gadia [1986, 1988], Snodgrass [1987], Tansel et al. [1993], Snodgrass et al. [1994], and Tuzhilin and Clifford [1990]. Stam and Snodgrass [1988] and Soo [1991] provide surveys on temporal data management. Jensen et al. [1994] presents a glossary of temporal-database concepts, aimed at unifying the terminology. Snodgrass et al. [1994] present the TSQL2 proposal. Tansel et al. [1993] is a collection of articles on different aspects of temporal databases. Chomicki [1995] presents techniques for managing temporal integrity constraints. A concept of completeness for temporal query languages analogous to relational completeness (equivalence to the relational algebra) is given in Clifford et al. [1994].

The user interfaces of commercial database systems—in particular, their forms and report-writer interfaces—are described in the respective user manuals. Nguyen and Srinivasan [1996] describe the World Wide Web interface to the IBM DB2 database system.

The trigger subsystem of System R is described by Eswaran and Chamberlin [1975]. McCarthy and Dayal [1989] discuss the architecture of an active database system based on the event–condition–action formalism. Widom and Finkelstein [1990] describe the architecture of a rule system based on set-oriented rules; the implementation of the rule system on the Starburst extensible database system is presented in Widom et al. [1991]. Consider an execution mechanism that allows a nondeterministic choice of which rule to execute next. A rule system is said to be *confluent* if, regardless of the rule chosen, the final state is the same. Issues of termination, nondeterminism, and confluence of rule systems are discussed in Aiken et al. [1995]. Modularity as a means to manage large rule bases in considered in Baralis et al. [1996].

CHAPTER 20

ADVANCED TRANSACTION PROCESSING

In Chapters 13, 14, and 15, we introduced the concept of a transaction, which is a program unit that accesses—and possibly updates—various data items, and whose execution ensures the preservation of the ACID properties. We discussed in those chapters a variety of schemes for ensuring the ACID properties in an environment where failure can occur, and where the transactions may run concurrently. In this chapter, we go beyond the basic schemes discussed previously, and cover more advanced transaction-processing concepts, including remote backup systems, transaction-processing monitors, high-performance transaction systems, long-duration transactions, nested transactions, real-time transaction systems, and transaction systems that ensure a level of consistency weaker than serializability.

20.1 Remote Backup Systems

Traditional transaction-processing systems are centralized or client–server systems. Such systems are vulnerable to environmental disasters such as fire, flooding, or earthquakes. Increasingly, there is a need for transaction-processing systems that offer high availability, and that can function in spite of environmental disasters.

We can achieve *high availability* by using a distributed database where the data are replicated, and transactions update all copies of the data. Two-phase commit can be used for synchronization of the sites. If a site fails, transaction processing can still continue, using other sites. However, actions such as concurrency control, which were earlier performed at a single site, now require synchronization

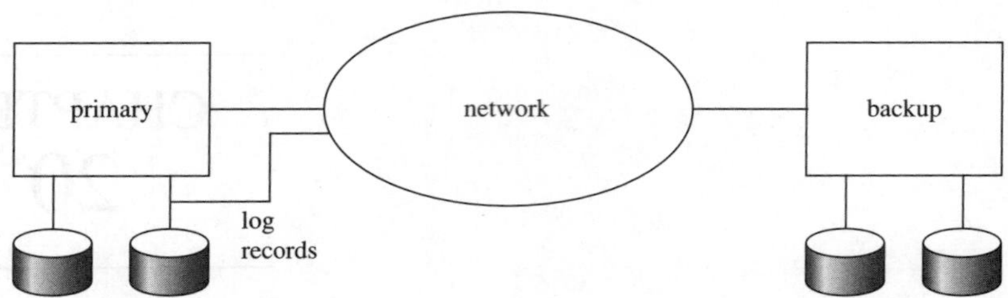

Figure 20.1 Architecture of remote-backup system.

across multiple sites, with the resultant delays. Further, two-phase commit itself is expensive. Hence, transaction throughput suffers under such a scheme.

An alternative is to perform transaction processing at a single site, called the *primary* site, but to have a *remote backup* site, where all the data from the primary site are replicated. The remote backup site is sometimes also called the *secondary* site. The remote site must be kept synchronized with the primary site, as updates are performed at the primary. We achieve synchronization by sending all log records from primary site to the remote backup site. The remote backup site must be physically separated from the primary—for example, we can locate it in a different state—so that a disaster at the primary does not damage the remote backup site. Figure 20.1 shows the architecture of a remote backup system.

When the primary site fails, the remote backup site takes over processing. First, however, it performs recovery, using its (perhaps outdated) copy of the data from the primary, and the log records received from the primary. In effect, the remote backup site is performing recovery actions that would have been performed at the primary site when the latter recovered. Standard recovery algorithms, with minor modifications, can be used for recovery at the remote backup site. Once recovery has been performed, the remote backup site starts processing transactions.

Availability is greatly increased over a single-site system, since the system can recover even if all data at the primary site are lost. The performance of a remote backup system is better than the performance of a distributed system with two-phase commit.

Several issues for you to address when you are designing a remote backup system follow:

- **Detection of failure.** As it is in failure-handling protocols for distributed system, it is important for the remote backup system to detect when the primary has failed. Failure of communication lines can fool the remote backup into believing that the primary has failed. To avoid this problem, we maintain several communication links with independent modes of failure between the primary and the remote backup. For example, in addition to the network connection, there may be a separate modem connection over a telephone line, with services provided by different telecommunication companies. These connections may be backed up via manual intervention by operators, who can communicate over the telephone system.

- **Transfer of control.** When the primary fails, the backup site takes over processing and becomes the new primary. When the original primary site recovers, it can either play the role of remote backup, or take over the role of primary site again. In either case, the old primary must receive a log of updates carried out by the backup site while the old primary was down.

  The simplest way of transferring control is for the old primary to receive redo logs from the old backup site, and to catch up with the updates by applying them locally. The old primary can then act as a remote backup site. If control must be transferred back, the old backup site can pretend to have failed, resulting in the old primary taking over.

- **Time to recover.** If the log at the remote backup grows large, recovery will take a long time. The remote backup site can periodically process the redo log records that it has received, and can perform a checkpoint, so that earlier parts of the log can be deleted. The delay before the remote backup takes over can be significantly reduced as a result.

  A *hot-spare* configuration can make takeover by the backup site almost instantaneous. In this configuration, the remote backup site continually processes redo log records as they arrive, applying the updates locally. As soon as the failure of the primary is detected, the backup site completes recovery by rolling back incomplete transactions; it is then ready to process new transactions.

- **Time to commit.** So that we ensure that the updates of a committed transaction are durable, a transaction must not be declared committed until its log records have reached the backup site. This delay can result in a longer wait to commit a transaction, and some systems therefore permit lower degrees of durability. The degrees of durability can be classified as follows.

  - **One-safe.** A transaction commits as soon as its commit log record is written to stable storage at the local site.

    The problem with this scheme is that the updates of a committed transaction may not have made it to the backup site, when the backup site takes over processing. Thus, the updates may appear to be lost. When the primary site recovers, the lost updates cannot be merged in directly, since the updates may conflict with later updates performed at the backup site. Thus, human intervention may be required to bring the database to a consistent state.

  - **Two-very-safe.** A transaction commits as soon as its commit log record is written to stable storage at the primary and the backup site.

    The problem with this scheme is that transaction processing cannot proceed if either the primary or the backup site is down. Thus, availability is actually less than in the single-site case, although the probability of data loss is much less.

  - **Two-safe.** This scheme is the same as two-very-safe if both primary and backup sites are active. If only the primary is active, the transaction is allowed to commit as soon as is commit log record is written to stable storage at the local site.

This scheme provides better availability than does two-very-safe, while avoiding the problem of lost transactions faced by the one-safe scheme. It results in a slower commit than the one-safe scheme, but the benefits generally outweigh the cost.

Several commercial shared-disk systems provide a level of fault tolerance that is intermediate between centralized and remote backup systems. In these systems, the failure of a CPU does not result in system failure, Instead, other CPUs take over, and they carry out recovery. Recovery actions include rollback of transactions running on the failed CPU, and recovery of locks held by those transactions. Since data are on a shared disk, there is no need for transfer of log records. However, we should safeguarded the data from disk failure by using, for example, a RAID disk organization.

20.2 Transaction-Processing Monitors

Database systems have traditionally been viewed as monolithic systems. In the real world, however, data are often partitioned across multiple database systems, file systems, and applications, all of which may run on different machines. Users may need to run updates on several of these systems, as part of a single transaction. Thus, the transactional properties for consistency and recovery from failures are essential. The two-phase commit protocol forms a building block for supporting transactions that span multiple databases. However, layers of software, and corresponding software architectures, are needed to coordinate the execution of such tasks. *Transaction-processing* (*TP*) *monitors* are systems that provide such support.

TP monitors were developed in the 1970s and 1980s, initially in response to a need to support a large number of remote terminals (such as airline-reservation terminals) from a single computer. The term *TP monitor* initially stood for *teleprocessing monitor*. These systems have since evolved to provide the core support for distributed transaction processing, and the term *TP monitor* has acquired its current meaning. Commercial TP monitors (in rough order of introduction) include the IMS system and CICS (introduced in the 1970s) from IBM, Pathway from Tandem (1979), ACMS and RTR from Digital Equipment (1981 and 1987), Tuxedo and Top End from NCR (1985 and 1991), and Encina from Transarc (1993).

20.2.1 TP-Monitor Architectures

In a typical operating system today, users log in and execute one or more processes. Consider an airline-reservation system with thousands of reservation terminals active at a time, all connected to a central computer. The operating system has considerable memory overhead for each login session, and the memory overhead would be excessive if each user of a terminal had to log in to the computer system. Further, for reasons of security, it is not a good idea to let many remote users have full access to the operating system via login sessions.

Instead of having one login session per terminal, an alternative is to have a server process that communicates with the terminal, and handles authentication

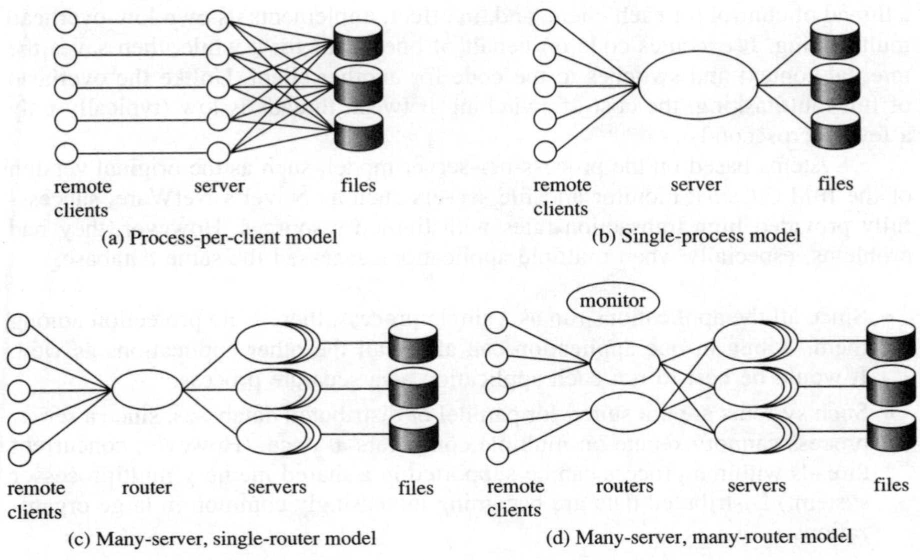

Figure 20.2 TP-monitor architectures.

and executes actions requested by the terminal. This *process-per-client* model is illustrated in Figure 20.2a. This model presents several problems with respect to memory utilization and processing speed:

- Per-process memory requirements are high. Even if memory for program code is shared by all processes, each process consumes memory for local data and open file descriptors, as well as for operating-system overhead, such as page tables to support virtual memory.
- The operating system divides up available CPU time among processes by switching among them; this technique is called *multitasking*. Each *context switch* between one process and the next has considerable CPU overhead; even on today's fast systems, a context switch can take hundreds of microseconds.

With this model, given the limited memory and processor power available in the 1970s and 1980s, it would have been impossible to serve more than tens to hundreds of users at a time without running out of memory and CPU resources.

To avoid these problems, systems such as IBM CICS introduced the concept of a *teleprocessing monitor*. These systems had a single server process to which all remote terminals connect; this model is called the *single-server* model, and is illustrated in Figure 20.2b. Remote terminals send requests to the server process, which then executes those requests. This model is also used in client–server environments, where clients send requests to a single server process. The server process handles tasks, such as user authentication, that would normally be handled by the operating system. To avoid blocking other clients when processing a long request for one client, the server process is *multithreaded*: The server process has a thread of control for each client, and, in effect, implements its own low-overhead multitasking. It executes code on behalf of one client for a while, then saves the internal context and switches to the code for another client. Unlike the overhead of full multitasking, the cost of switching between threads is low (typically only a few microseconds).

Systems based on the process-per-server model, such as the original version of the IBM CICS TP monitor and file servers such as Novel's NetWare, successfully provided high transaction rates with limited resources. However, they had problems, especially when multiple applications accessed the same database:

- Since all the applications run as a single process, there is no protection among them. A bug in one application can affect all the other applications as well. It would be best to run each application as a separate process.
- Such systems are not suited for parallel or distributed databases, since a server process cannot execute on multiple computers at once. (However, concurrent threads within a process can be supported in a shared-memory multiprocessor system.) Distributed data are becoming increasingly common in large organizations.

One way to solve these problems is to run multiple application-server processes that access a common database, and to let the clients communicate with the application through a single communication process that routes requests. This model is called the *many-server, single-router* model, and is illustrated in Figure 20.2c. This model supports independent server processes for multiple applications; further, each application can have a pool of server processes, any one of which can handle a client session. The request can, for example, be routed to the most lightly loaded server in a pool. As before, each server process can itself be multithreaded, so that it can handle multiple clients concurrently. As a further generalization, the application servers can run on different sites of a parallel or distributed database, and the communication process can handle the coordination among the processes.

A more general architecture has multiple processes, rather than just one, to communicate with clients. The client communication processes interact with one or more router processes, which route their requests to the appropriate server. Later-generation TP monitors therefore have a different architecture, called the *many-server, many-router* model, illustrated in Figure 20.2d. A controller process starts up the other processes, and supervises their functioning. Tandem Pathway is an example of the later-generation TP monitors that use this architecture.

The detailed structure of a TP monitor is shown in Figure 20.3. A TP monitor does more than simply pass messages to application servers. When messages arrive, they have to be queued; thus, there is a *queue manager* for incoming messages. The messages may even be logged on stable storage, so that, once received, they will be processed eventually, regardless of system failures. Authorization and application-server management (e.g., server startup, and routing of messages to servers) are further functions of a TP monitor. TP monitors often provide log-

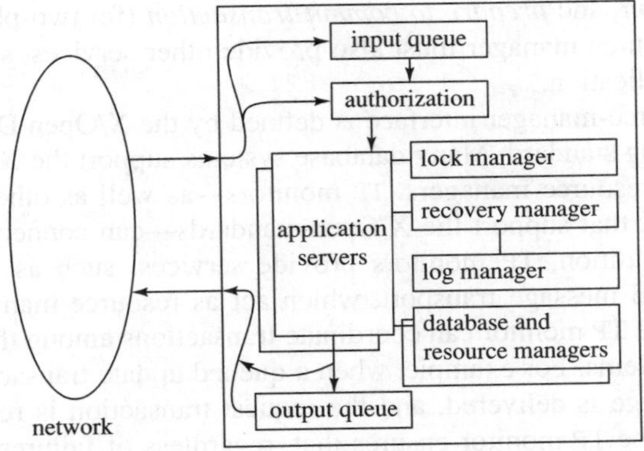

Figure 20.3 TP-monitor components.

ging, recovery, and concurrency-control facilities, allowing application servers to implement the ACID transaction properties directly if required.

Finally, TP monitors also provide durable queueing for outgoing messages. Thus, a server can send a message as part of a transaction; the TP monitor guarantees that the message will be delivered if (and only if) the transaction commits, thereby providing ACID properties not just for the actions within a database, but also for messages sent outside the database.

In addition to these facilities, many TP monitors also provide *presentation facilities* for dumb clients such as terminals; the presentation facilities help to create menu and form interfaces.

20.2.2 Application Coordination Using TP monitors

Applications today often have to interact with multiple databases. They may also have to interact with legacy systems,† such as special-purpose data-storage systems built directly on file systems. Finally, they may have to communicate with users or other applications at remote sites. Hence, they also have to interact with communication subsystems. It is important to be able to coordinate data accesses, and to implement ACID properties for transactions across such systems.

Modern TP monitors provide support for the construction and administration of such large applications, built up from multiple subsystems such as databases, legacy systems, and communication systems. A TP monitor treats each subsystem as a *resource manager* that provides transactional access to some set of resources. The interface between the TP monitor and the resource manager is defined by a set of transaction primitives, such as *begin_transaction*, *commit_transaction*,

† Legacy systems are older-generation systems that are incompatible with current-generation standards and systems. Such systems may still contain valuable data, and may support critical applications. Porting these applications to a more modern environment is often costly in terms of both time and money. Thus, it is important to support these older-generation, or legacy, systems, and to facilitate their interoperation with newer systems.

abort_transaction, and *prepare_to_commit_transaction* (for two-phase commit). Of course, the resource manager must also provide other services, such as supplying data, to the application.

The resource-manager interface is defined by the X/Open Distributed Transaction Processing standard. Many database systems support the X/Open standards, and can act as resource managers. TP monitors—as well as other products, such as SQL systems, that support the X/Open standards—can connect to the resource managers. In addition, TP monitors provide services, such as persistent queue management and message transport, which act as resource managers supporting transactions. The TP monitor can coordinate transactions among these services and the database systems. For example, when a queued update transaction is executed, an output message is delivered, and the request transaction is removed from the request queue; the TP monitor ensures that, regardless of failures, either all these actions occur, or none occurs.

In client–server systems, clients often interact with servers via a *remote-procedure-call* (*RPC*) mechanism, where a client invokes a procedure call, which is actually executed at the server, with the results sent back to the client. As far as the client code that invokes the RPC is concerned, the call looks like a local procedure-call invocation. TP monitor systems, such as Encina, provide a *transactional RPC* interface to their services. In such an interface, the RPC mechanism provides calls that can be used to enclose a series of RPC calls within a transaction. Thus, updates performed by an RPC are carried out within the scope of the transaction, and can be rolled back if there is any failure.

We can also use TP monitors to administer complex client–server systems consisting of multiple servers and a large number of clients. Each server behaves like a resource manager, and registers with the TP monitor. The TP monitor coordinates activities, such as system checkpoints and shutdowns. It provides security and authentication of clients. It administers server pools by adding servers or removing servers without interruption of the system. Finally, it controls the scope of failures. If a server fails, the TP monitor can detect this failure, abort the transactions in progress, and restart the transactions. If a node fails, the TP monitor can migrate transactions to servers at other nodes, again backing out incomplete transactions. When failed nodes restart, the TP monitor can govern the recovery of the node's resource managers.

Modern database systems support replication of databases; updates performed at a primary site are carried out automatically on the replicas of the site as well. If the primary site fails, one of the secondary sites takes over processing (see Section 20.1). TP monitors can be used to hide database failures in such replicated systems; transaction requests are sent to the TP monitor, which relays the messages to one of the database replicas. If one site fails, the TP monitor can transparently route messages to a backup site, masking the failure of the first site.

20.3 High-Performance Transaction Systems

To allow a high rate of transaction processing (hundreds or thousands of transactions per second), we must use high-performance hardware, and must exploit parallelism. These techniques alone, however, are insufficient to obtain high performance in transaction processing, for the following reasons:

- Disk I/O remains a bottleneck—about 10 milliseconds are required for each I/O, and this number has not decreased at a rate comparable to the increase in processor speeds. Disk I/O is often the bottleneck for reads, as well as for transaction commits.
- Transactions running in parallel may attempt to read or write the same data item, resulting in data conflicts that reduce effective parallelism. This problem is exacerbated by long-running transactions.

In Sections 20.3.1 and 20.3.2, we discuss techniques to reduce the influence of these problems.

20.3.1 Main-Memory Databases

Usually, the performance of database systems is limited by the speed at which data are read from and written to disk. We can reduce the degree to which a database system is disk bound by increasing the size of the database buffer. Advances in main-memory technology have made it possible for us to construct large main memories at relatively low cost. Today, there are commercial 64-bit systems that can support main memories as large as 14 gigabytes.

The long disk latency (about 10 milliseconds average) increases not only the time to access a data item, but also limits the number of accesses per second. Therefore, for some applications, such as in real-time control, it is necessary to store data in main memory to meet performance requirements. The memory size required for most such systems is not exceptionally large, although there are at least a few applications that require multiple gigabytes of data to be memory resident. As memory sizes grow, more applications can be expected to have data that fit into main memory.

Large main memories allow faster processing of transactions, since data are memory resident. However, there are still disk-related limitations:

- Log records must be written to stable storage before a transaction is committed. The improved performance made possible by a large main memory may result in the logging process becoming a bottleneck. We can reduce commit time by creating a stable log buffer in main memory, using battery backed-up memory (also called *nonvolatile RAM*). The overhead imposed by logging can also be reduced by the *group-commit* technique discussed next. Throughput (number of transactions per second) is still limited by the data-transfer rate of the log disk.
- Buffer blocks marked as modified by committed transactions still have to be written so that the amount of log that has to be replayed at recovery time is reduced. If the update rate is extremely high, the disk data-transfer rate may become a bottleneck.

- If the system crashes, all of main memory is lost. On recovery, the system has an empty database buffer, and data items must be input from disk when they are accessed. Therefore, even after recovery is complete, it takes some time before the database is fully loaded in main memory and high-speed processing of transactions can resume.

On the other hand, main-memory database provide opportunities for optimizations:

- Since memory is costlier than disk space, internal data structures in main-memory databases have to be designed to reduce space requirements. However, data structures can have pointers crossing multiple pages unlike in disk databases, where the cost of the I/Os to traverse multiple pages would be excessively high. For example, tree structures in main-memory databases can be relatively deep, unlike B^+-trees, but should minimize space requirements.
- There is no need to pin buffer pages in memory before data are accessed, since buffer pages will never be replaced.
- Query-processing techniques should be designed to minimize space overhead, so that main memory limits are not exceeded while a query is being evaluated; that situation would result in paging to swap area, and would slow down query processing.
- Once the disk I/O bottleneck is removed, operations such as locking and latching may become bottlenecks. Such bottlenecks must be eliminated by improvements in the implementation of these operations.
- Recovery algorithms can be optimized, since pages rarely need to be written out to make space for other pages.

Additional information on main-memory databases is given in the references provided in the bibliographic notes.

20.3.2 Group Commit

The process of committing a transaction *T* requires the following to be written to stable storage:

- All log records associated with *T* that have not been output to stable storage
- The <T **commit**> log record

These output operations frequently require the output of blocks that are only partially filled. To ensure that nearly full blocks are output, we use the *group-commit* technique. Instead of attempting to commit *T* when *T* completes, the system waits until several transactions have completed. It then commits this group of transactions together. Blocks written to stable storage may contain records of several transactions. By careful choice of group size, the system can ensure that blocks are full when they are written to stable storage. This technique results, on average, in fewer output operations per committed transaction.

Although group commit reduces the overhead imposed by logging, it results in transactions being delayed in committing until a sufficiently large group of transactions is ready to commit. The delay is acceptable in high-performance transaction systems, since it does not take much time for a group of transactions to be ready to commit.

20.4 Long-Duration Transactions

The transaction concept was developed initially in the context of data-processing applications, in which most transactions are noninteractive and of short duration. Although the techniques presented here and earlier in Chapters 13, 14, and 15 work well in those applications, serious problems arise when this concept is applied to database systems that involve human interaction. Such transactions have the following key properties:

- **Long duration**. Once there is any human interaction with an active transaction, that transaction becomes a long-duration transaction from the perspective of the computer, since human response time is slow relative to computer speed. Furthermore, in design applications, the human activity being modeled may involve hours, days, or an even longer period. Thus, transactions may be of long duration in human terms, as well as in machine terms.
- **Exposure of uncommitted data**. Data generated and displayed to a user by a long-duration transaction are uncommitted, since the transaction may abort. Thus, users—and, as a result, other transactions—may be forced to read uncommitted data. If several users are cooperating on a design, user transactions may need to exchange data prior to transaction commit.
- **Subtasks**. An interactive transaction may consist of a set of subtasks initiated by the user. The user may wish to abort a subtask without necessarily causing the entire transaction to abort.
- **Recoverability**. It is unacceptable to abort a long-duration interactive transaction because of a system crash. The active transaction must be recovered to a state that existed shortly before the crash so that relatively little human work is lost.
- **Performance**. Good performance in an interactive transaction system is defined as fast response time. This definition is in contrast to that in a noninteractive system, in which high throughput (number of transactions per second) is the goal. Systems with high throughput make efficient use of system resources. However, in the case of interactive transactions, the most costly resource is the user. If the efficiency and satisfaction of the user is to be optimized, response time should be fast (from a human perspective). In those cases where a task takes a long time, response time should be predictable (that is, the variance in response times should be low), so that users can manage their time well.

In Sections 20.4.1 through 20.4.5, we shall see why these five properties are incompatible with the techniques presented thus far, and shall discuss how those techniques can be modified to accommodate long-duration interactive transactions.

20.4.1 Nonserializable Executions

The properties that we discussed make it impractical to enforce the requirement used in earlier chapters that only serializable schedules be permitted. Each of the concurrency-control protocols of Chapter 14 has adverse effects on long-duration transactions:

- **Two-phase locking**. When a lock cannot be granted, the transaction requesting the lock is forced to wait for the data item in question to be unlocked. The duration of this wait is proportional to the duration of the transaction holding the lock. If the data item is locked by a short-duration transaction, we expect that the waiting time will be short (except in case of deadlock or extraordinary system load). However, if the data item is locked by a long-duration transaction, the wait will be of long duration. Long waiting times lead to both longer response time and an increased chance of deadlock.
- **Graph-based protocols**. Graph-based protocols allow for locks to be released earlier than under the two-phase locking protocols, and they prevent deadlock. However, they impose an ordering on the data items. Transactions must lock data items in a manner consistent with this ordering. As a result, a transaction may have to lock more data than it needs. Furthermore, a transaction must hold a lock until there is no chance that the lock will be needed again. Thus, long-duration lock waits are likely to occur.
- **Timestamp-based protocols**. Timestamp protocols never require a transaction to wait. However, they do require transactions to abort under certain circumstances. If a long-duration transaction is aborted, a substantial amount of work is lost. For noninteractive transactions, this lost work is a performance issue. For interactive transactions, the issue is also one of user satisfaction. It is highly undesirable for a user to find that several hours' worth of work have been undone.
- **Validation**. Like timestamp-based protocols, validation protocols enforce serializability by means of transaction abort.

Thus, it appears that the enforcement of serializability results in long-duration waits, in abort of long-duration transactions, or in both. There are theoretical results, cited in the bibliographic notes, that substantiate this conclusion.

Further difficulties with the enforcement of serializability arise when we consider recovery issues. We previously discussed the problem of cascading rollback, in which the abort of a transaction may lead to the abort of other transactions. This phenomenon is undesirable, particularly for long-duration transactions. If locking is used, exclusive locks must be held until the end of the transaction, if cascading rollback is to be avoided. This holding of exclusive locks, however, increases the length of transaction waiting time.

Thus, it appears that the enforcement of transaction atomicity must either lead to an increased probability of long-duration waits or create a possibility of cascading rollback.

These considerations are the basis for the alternative concepts of correctness of concurrent executions and transaction recovery that we consider in the remainder of this section.

20.4.2 Concurrency Control

The fundamental goal of database concurrency control is to ensure that concurrent execution of transactions does not result in a loss of database consistency. The concept of serializability can be used to achieve this goal, since all serializable schedules preserve consistency of the database. However, not all schedules that preserve consistency of the database are serializable. Let us illustrate this assertion by considering again a bank database consisting of two accounts A and B, with the consistency requirement that the sum $A + B$ be preserved. For example, although the schedule of Figure 20.4 is not conflict serializable, it nevertheless preserves the sum of $A + B$. It also illustrates two important points about the concept of correctness without serializability.

- Correctness depends on the specific consistency constraints for the database.
- Correctness depends on the properties of operations performed by each transaction.

It is of prohibitive computational cost to perform an automatic analysis of low-level operations by transactions, and of their potential effect on a fully specified database consistency constraint. However, there are simpler, less costly techniques. One is to use the database consistency constraints as the basis for a split of the database into subdatabases on which concurrency can be managed separately. Another is to treat some operations besides **read** and **write** as fundamental low-level operations, and to extend concurrency control to deal with them.

T_1	T_2
read(A) $A := A - 50$ **write**(A)	
	read(B) $B := B - 10$ **write**(B)
read(B) $B := B + 50$ **write**(B)	
	read(A) $A := A + 10$ **write**(A)

Figure 20.4 A non–conflict-serializable schedule.

The bibliographic notes reference other techniques for ensuring consistency without requiring serializability. Many of these techniques exploit variants of multiversion concurrency control (see Section 15.6). For older data-processing applications that need only one version, multiversion protocols impose a high space overhead to store the extra versions. Since many of the new database applications require the maintenance of versions of data, concurrency-control techniques that exploit multiple versions are practical.

20.4.3 Nested and Multilevel Transactions

A long-duration transaction can be viewed as a collection of related subtasks or subtransactions. By structuring a transaction as a set of subtransactions, we are able to enhance parallelism, since it may be possible to run several subtransactions in parallel. Furthermore, it is possible to deal with failure of a subtransaction (due to abort, system crash, and so on) without having to roll back the entire long-duration transaction.

A nested or multilevel transaction T consists of a set $T = \{t_1, t_2, \ldots, t_n\}$ of subtransactions and a partial order P on T. A subtransaction t_i in T may abort without forcing T to abort. Instead, T may either restart t_i or simply choose not to run t_i. If t_i commits, this action does not make t_i permanent (unlike the situation in Chapter 15). Instead, t_i *commits to* T, and may still abort (or require compensation—see Section 20.4.4) if T aborts. An execution of T must not violate the partial order P. That is, if an edge $t_i \rightarrow t_j$ appears in the precedence graph, then $t_j \rightarrow t_i$ must not be in the transitive closure of P.

Nesting may be several levels deep, representing a subdivision of a transaction into subtasks, subsubtasks, and so on. At the lowest level of nesting, we have the standard database operations **read** and **write** that we have used previously.

If a subtransaction of T is permitted to release locks on completion, T is called a *multilevel* transaction. When a multilevel transaction represents a long-duration activity, the transaction is sometimes referred to as a *saga*. Alternatively, if locks held by a subtransaction t_i of T are automatically assigned to T on completion of t_i, T is called a *nested transaction*.

Although the main practical value of multi-level transactions arises in complex, long-duration transactions, we shall use the simple example of Figure 20.4 to show how nesting can create higher-level operations that may enhance concurrency. We rewrite transaction T_1 using subtransactions $T_{1,1}$ and $T_{1,2}$ that perform increment or decrement operations:

- T_1 consists of
  - $T_{1,1}$, which subtracts 50 from A
  - $T_{1,2}$, which adds 50 to B

Similarly, we rewrite transaction T_2 using subtransactions $T_{2,1}$ and $T_{2,2}$ that perform increment or decrement operations:

- T_2 consists of
  - $T_{2,1}$, which subtracts 10 from B
  - $T_{2,2}$, which adds 10 to A

No ordering is specified on $T_{1,1}$, $T_{1,2}$, $T_{2,1}$, and $T_{2,2}$. Any execution of these subtransactions will generate a correct result. The schedule of Figure 20.4 corresponds to the schedule $< T_{1,1}, T_{2,1}, T_{1,2}, T_{2,2} >$.

20.4.4 Compensating Transactions

To reduce the frequency of long-duration waiting, we arrange for uncommitted updates to be exposed to other concurrently executing transactions. Indeed, multilevel transactions may allow this exposure. However, the exposure of uncommitted data creates the potential for cascading rollbacks. The concept of *compensating transactions* helps us to deal with this problem.

Let transaction T be divided into several subtransactions $t_1, t_2, \ldots, t_n$. After a subtransaction t_i commits, it releases its locks. Now, if the outer-level transaction T has to be aborted, the effect of its subtransactions must be undone. Suppose that subtransactions $t_1, \ldots, t_k$ have committed, and that t_{k+1} was executing when the decision to abort is made. We can undo the effects of t_{k+1} by aborting that subtransaction. However, it is not possible to abort subtransactions $t_1, \ldots, t_k$, since they have committed already.

Instead, we execute a new subtransaction ct_i, called a *compensating transaction* to undo the effect of a subtransaction t_i. Each subtransaction t_i is required to have a compensating transaction ct_i. The compensating transactions must be executed in the inverse order $ct_k, \ldots, ct_1$. We give several examples of compensation here:

- Consider the schedule of Figure 20.4, which we have shown to be correct, although not conflict serializable. Each subtransaction releases its locks once it completes. Suppose that T_2 fails just prior to termination, after $T_{2,2}$ has released its locks. We then run a compensating transaction for $T_{2,2}$ that subtracts 10 from A and a compensating transaction for $T_{2,1}$ that adds 10 to B.
- Consider a database insert by transaction T_i that, as a side effect, causes a B$^+$-tree index to be updated. The insert operation may have modified several nodes of the B$^+$-tree index. Other transactions may have read these nodes in accessing data other than the record inserted by T_i. As discussed in Section 15.9, we can run undo the insertion by deleting the record inserted by T_i. The result is a correct, consistent B$^+$-tree, but is not necessarily one with exactly the same structure as the one we had before T_i started. Thus, deletion is a compensating action for insertion.
- Consider a long-duration transaction T_i representing a travel reservation. Transaction T has three subtransactions: $T_{i,1}$, which makes airline reservations; $T_{i,2}$,

which reserves rental cars; and $T_{i,3}$, which reserves a hotel room. Suppose that the hotel cancels the reservation. Instead of undoing all of T_i, we compensate for the failure of $T_{i,3}$ by deleting the old hotel reservation and making a new one.

If the system crashes in the middle of executing an outer-level transaction, its subtransactions must be rolled back when it recovers. The techniques described in Section15.9 can be used for this purpose.

Compensation for the failure of a transaction requires use of semantics of the failed transaction. For certain operations, such as incrementation or insertion into a B^+-tree, the corresponding compensation is easily defined. For more complex transactions, the application programmers may have to define the correct form of compensation at the time that the transaction is coded. For complex interactive transactions, it may be necessary for the system to interact with the user to determine the proper form of compensation.

20.4.5 Implementation Issues

The transaction concepts discussed in this section create serious difficulties for implementation. We present a few of them here, and discuss how we can address these problems.

Long-duration transactions must survive system crashes. We can ensure that they will by performing a **redo** on committed subtransactions, and by performing either an **undo** or compensation for any short-duration subtransactions that were active at the time of the crash. However, these actions solve only part of the problem. In typical database systems, such internal system data as lock tables and transactions timestamps are kept in volatile storage. For a long-duration transaction to be resumed after a crash, these data must be restored. Therefore, it is necessary to log not only changes to the database, but also changes to internal system data pertaining to long-duration transactions.

Logging of updates is made more complex by the types of data items that may exist in the database. A data item may be a CAD design, text of a document, or another form of composite design. Such data items are physically large. Thus, storing both the old and new values of the data item in a log record is undesirable.

There are two approaches to reducing the overhead of ensuring the recoverability of large data items:

- **Operation logging**. Only the operation performed on the data item and the data-item name are stored in the log. Operation logging is also called *logical logging*. For each operation, an inverse operation must exist. We perform **undo** using the inverse operation, and **redo** using the operation itself. Recovery through operation logging is more difficult, since **redo** and **undo** are not idempotent. Further, using logical logging for an operation that updates multiple pages is greatly complicated by the fact that some, but not all, of the updated pages may have been written to the disk, so it is hard to apply either the **redo** or the **undo** of the operation on the disk image during recovery.

- **Logging and shadow paging**. Logging is used for modifications to small data items, but large data items are made recoverable via a shadow-page technique (see Section 15.5). When we use shadowing, only those pages that are actually modified need to be stored in duplicate.

Regardless of the technique used, the complexities introduced by long-duration transactions and large data items complicate the recovery process. Thus, it is desirable to allow certain noncritical data to be exempt from logging, and to rely instead on offline backups and human intervention.

20.5 Real-Time Transaction Systems

The constraints that we have considered thus far pertain to the values stored in the database. In certain applications, the constraints include *deadlines* by which a task must be completed. Examples of such applications include plant management, traffic control, and scheduling. When deadlines are included, correctness of an execution is no longer solely an issue of database consistency. Rather, we are concerned with how many deadlines are missed, and by how much time they are missed. Deadlines are characterized as follows:

- **Hard**. The task has zero value if it is completed after the deadline.
- **Soft**. The task has diminishing value if it is completed after the deadline, with the value approaching zero as the degree of lateness increases.

Systems with deadlines are called *real-time* systems.

Transaction management in real-time systems must take deadlines into account. If the concurrency-control protocol determines that a transaction T_i must wait, it may cause T_i to miss the deadline. In such cases, it may be preferable to preempt the transaction holding the lock, and to allow T_i to proceed. Preemption must be used with care, however, because the time lost by the preempted transaction (due to rollback and restart) may cause the transaction to miss its deadline. Unfortunately, it is difficult to determine whether rollback or waiting is preferable in a given situation.

A major difficulty in supporting real-time constraints arises from the variance in transaction execution time. In the best case, all data accesses reference data in the database buffer. In the worst case, each access causes a buffer page to be written to disk (preceded by the requisite log records), followed by the reading from disk of the page containing the data to be accessed. Because the two or more disk accesses required in the worst case take several orders of magnitude more time than the main-memory references required in the best case, transaction execution time can be estimated only very poorly if data are resident on disk. Hence, main-memory databases are often used if real-time constraints have to be met. However, even if data are resident in main memory, variances in execution time arise from lock waits, transaction aborts, and so on.

In high-performance transaction systems (see Section 20.3), speed is the critical issue. In real-time systems, deadlines, rather than absolute speed, are the most important issue. Designing a real-time system involves ensuring that there is enough processing power exists to meet deadlines without requiring excessive hardware resources. Achieving this objective, despite the variance in execution time resulting from transaction management, remains a challenging problem. The bibliographic notes provide references to research in the area of real-time databases.

20.6 Weak Levels of Consistency

In Chapter 14, the concept of serializability was presented, and protocols were defined to ensure that only serializable schedules are possible. Serializability is a useful concept because it allows programmers to ignore issues related to concurrency when they code transactions. If every transaction has the property that it maintains database consistency if executed alone, then serializability ensures that concurrent executions maintain consistency. However, the protocols required to ensure serializability may allow too little concurrency for certain applications. In these cases, weaker levels of consistency are used. The use of weaker levels of consistency places additional burdens on programmers for ensuring database correctness.

20.6.1 Degree-Two Consistency

The purpose of *degree-two consistency* is to avoid cascading aborts without necessarily ensuring serializability. The locking protocol for degree-two consistency uses the same two lock modes as we used for the two-phase locking protocol: shared (S) and exclusive (X). A transaction must hold the appropriate lock mode when it accesses a data item.

In contrast to the situation in two-phase locking, S-locks may be released at any time, and locks may be acquired at any time. Exclusive locks cannot be released until the transaction either commits or aborts. Serializability is not ensured by this protocol. Indeed, a transaction may read the same data item twice and obtain different results. In Figure 20.5, T_3 reads the value of Q before and after that value is written by T_4.

The potential for inconsistency under degree-two consistency makes this approach undesirable for many applications.

20.6.2 Cursor Stability

Cursor stability is a form of degree-two consistency designed for programs written in general-purpose, record-oriented languages such as Pascal, C, Cobol, PL/I, or Fortran. Such programs often iterate over the tuples of a relation. Rather than locking the entire relation, cursor stability ensures that

- The tuple that is currently being processed by the iteration is locked in shared mode.
- Any modified tuples are locked in exclusive mode until the transaction commits.

T_3	T_4
lock-S(Q)	
read(Q)	
unlock(Q)	
	lock-X(Q)
	read(Q)
	write(Q)
	unlock(Q)
lock-S(Q)	
read(Q)	
unlock(Q)	

Figure 20.5 Nonserializable schedule with degree-two consistency.

These rules ensure that degree-two consistency is obtained. Two-phase locking is not required. Serializability is not guaranteed. Cursor stability is used in practice on heavily accessed relations as a means of increasing concurrency and improving system performance. Applications that use cursor stability must be coded in a way that ensures database consistency despite the possibility of nonserializable schedules. Thus, the use of cursor stability is limited to specialized situations with simple consistency constraints.

20.7 Transactional Workflows

A *workflow* is an activity involving the coordinated execution of multiple tasks performed by different processing entities. A *task* defines some work to be done and can be specified in a number of ways, including a textual description in a file or an electronic-mail message, a form, a message, or a computer program. A *processing entity* that performs the tasks may be a person or a software system (for example, a mailer, an application program, or a database-management system).

Figure 20.6 shows examples of such workflows. A simple example of a workflow is in an electronic-mail system. The delivery of a single mail message

Workflow application	Typical tasks	Typical processing entities
electronic-mail routing	electronic-mail message	mailers
loan processing	form processing	humans, application software
purchase-order processing	form processing	humans, application software, DBMSs

Figure 20.6 Examples of workflows.

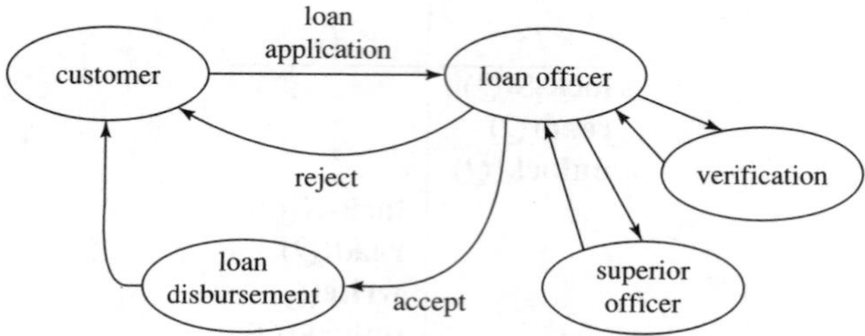

Figure 20.7 Workflow in loan processing.

may involve several mailer systems that receive and forward the mail message, until the message reaches its destination, where it is stored. Each mailer performs a task—namely, forwarding the mail to the next mailer—and the tasks of multiple mailers may be required to route mail from source to destination. Other terms used in the database and related literature to refer to workflows include *task flow* and *multisystem applications*. Tasks are also sometimes called *steps*.

In general, workflows may involve one or more humans. For instance, consider the processing of a loan. The relevant workflow is shown in Figure 20.7. The person who wants a loan fills out a form, which is then checked by a loan officer. An employee who processes loan applications verifies the data in the form using sources such as credit-reference bureaus. When all the required information has been collected, the loan officer may decide to approve the loan; that decision may then have to be approved by one or more superior officers, after which the loan can be made. Each human here performs a task; in a bank that has not automated the task of loan processing, the coordination of the tasks is typically carried out via passing of the loan application, with attached notes and other information, from one employee to the next. Other examples of workflows include processing of expense vouchers, of purchase orders, and of credit-card transactions.

Today, all the information related to a workflow is more than likely to be stored in a digital form on one or more computers, and, with the growth of networking, information can be easily transferred from one computer to another. Hence, it is feasible for organizations to automate their workflows. For example, to automate the tasks involved in loan processing, we can store the loan application and associated information in a database. The workflow itself then involves handing of charge from one human to the next, and possibly even to programs that can automatically fetch the required information. Humans can coordinate their activities using means such as electronic mail.

We have to address two problems, in general, to automate a workflow. The first is the *specification* of a workflow: detailing the tasks that must be carried out, and defining the execution requirements. The second problem is the *execution* of workflows, which we must do while providing the safeguards of traditional database systems related to computation correctness, data integrity and durability.

For example, it is not acceptable for a loan application or a voucher to be lost, or to be processed multiple times, because of a system crash. The idea behind transactional workflows is to use and extend the concepts of transactions to the context of workflows.

Both problems are complicated by the fact that many organizations use multiple independently managed information-processing systems that, in most cases, were developed separately to automate different functions. Workflow activities may require interactions among several such systems, each performing a task, as well as interactions with humans.

A number of workflow systems have been developed in recent years. Here, we study properties of workflow systems at a relatively abstract level, without going into the details of any particular system.

20.7.1 Workflow Specification

The idea of a workflow can be traced to the job-control language (JCL) of batch operating systems, which allowed the user to specify a job as a collection of steps. Each step was an invocation of a program, and the steps were executed in sequence. Some steps could be executed conditionally—for example, only if the previous step was successful, or if that step failed. Thus, a JCL specification can be thought of as an example of a workflow specification.

Internal aspects of a task do not need to be modeled for the purpose of workflow management. In an abstract view of a task, a task may use parameters stored in its input variables, may retrieve and update data in the local system, may store its results in its output variables, and may be queried about its execution state. At any time during the execution, the *state of a workflow* consists of the collection of states of the workflow's constituent tasks, and the states (values) of all variables in the workflow specification.

The coordination of tasks can be specified either statically or dynamically. In a static specification, the tasks and dependencies among them are defined before the execution of the workflow begins. For instance, the tasks in an expense-voucher workflow may consist of the approvals of the voucher by a secretary, a manager, and an accountant, in that order, and finally by the delivery of a check. The dependencies among the tasks may be simple—each task has to be completed before the next begins.

A generalization of this strategy is to have a precondition for execution of each task in the workflow, so that all possible tasks in a workflow and their dependencies are known in advance, but only those tasks whose preconditions are satisfied are executed. The preconditions can be defined through dependencies such as the following:

- *Execution states* of other tasks—for example, "task t_i cannot start until task t_j has ended," or "task t_i must abort if task t_j has committed"
- *Output values* of other tasks—for example, "task t_i can start if task t_j returns a value greater than 25," or "the manager-approval task can start if the secretary-approval task returns a value of OK"

- *External variables* modified by external events—for example, "task t_i cannot be started before 9 AM GMT," or "task t_i must be started within 24 hours of the completion of task t_j."

We can combine the dependencies using the regular logical connectors (**or**, **and**, **not**) to form complex scheduling preconditions.

An example of dynamic scheduling of tasks is an electronic-mail routing system. The next task to be scheduled for a given mail message depends on what the destination address of the message is, and on which intermediate routers are functioning.

20.7.2 Failure-Atomicity Requirements of a Workflow

Based on the semantics of a workflow, the workflow designer may specify the *failure-atomicity* requirements of the workflow. The traditional notion of failure atomicity would require that a failure of any task results in the failure of the workflow. However, a workflow can, in many cases, survive the failure of one of its tasks—for example, by executing a functionally equivalent task at another site. Therefore, we should allow the designer to define failure-atomicity requirements of a workflow. The system must guarantee that every execution of a workflow will terminate in a state that satisfies the failure-atomicity requirements defined by the designer. We call those states *acceptable termination states* of a workflow. All other execution states of a workflow constitute a set of *nonacceptable termination states*, in which the failure-atomicity requirements may be violated.

An acceptable termination state can be designated as committed or aborted. A *committed acceptable termination state* is an execution state in which the objectives of a workflow have been achieved. In contrast, an *aborted acceptable termination state* is a valid termination state in which a workflow has failed to achieve its objectives. If an aborted acceptable termination state has been reached, all undesirable effects of the partial execution of the workflow must be undone in accordance with that workflow's failure-atomicity requirements.

A workflow must reach an acceptable termination state *even in the presence of system failures*. Thus, if a workflow was in a nonacceptable termination state at the time of failure, during system recovery it must be brought to an acceptable termination state (whether aborted or committed).

For example, in the loan-processing workflow, in the final state, either the loan applicant is told that a loan cannot be made, or the loan is disbursed. In case of failures such as a long failure of the verification system, the loan application could be returned to the loan applicant with a suitable explanation; this outcome would constitute an aborted acceptable termination. A committed acceptable termination would be either the acceptance or the rejection of the loan.

In general, a task can commit and release its resources before the workflow reaches a termination state. However, if the multitask transaction later aborts, its failure atomicity may require that we undo the effects of already completed tasks (for example, committed subtransactions) by executing compensating tasks (as subtransactions). The semantics of compensation requires that a compensating transaction eventually completes its execution successfully, possibly after a number of resubmissions.

In an expense-voucher–processing workflow, for example, a department-budget balance may be reduced based on an initial approval of a voucher by the manager. If the voucher is later rejected, whether due to failure or for other reasons, the budget may have to be restored by a compensating transaction.

20.7.3 Execution of Workflows

The execution of the tasks may be controlled by a human coordinator or by a software system called a *workflow-management system*. A workflow-management system consists of a scheduler, task agents, and a mechanism to query the state of the workflow system. A task agent controls the execution of a task by a processing entity. A scheduler is a program that processes workflows by submitting various tasks for execution, monitoring various events, and evaluating conditions related to intertask dependencies. A scheduler may submit a task for execution (to a task agent), or may request that a previously submitted task be aborted. In the case of multidatabase transactions, the tasks are subtransactions, and the processing entities are local DBMSs. In accordance with the workflow specifications, the scheduler enforces the scheduling dependencies and is responsible for ensuring that tasks reach acceptable termination states.

There are three architectural approaches to the development of a workflow-management system. A centralized approach has a single scheduler that schedules the tasks for all concurrently executing workflows. The partially distributed approach is to have one (instance of) a scheduler for each workflow. When the issues of concurrent execution can be separated from the scheduling function, the latter option is a natural choice. A fully distributed approach has no scheduler, but the task agents coordinate their execution by communicating with one another to satisfy task dependencies and other workflow execution requirements.

The simplest workflow-execution systems follow the fully distributed approach just described, and are based on electronic mail. Each site has a task agent that executes tasks received over electronic mail. Execution may also involve presenting electronic mail to humans, who have then to carry out some action. When a task is completed at a site, and needs to be processed at another site, the task agent dispatches an electronic-mail message to the next site. The message contains all relevant information about the task to be performed. Such electronic-mail–based workflow systems are particularly useful in networks that may be disconnected for part of the time, such as dial-up networks.

The centralized approach is used in workflow systems where the data are stored in a central database. The scheduler notifies various agents, such as humans or computer programs, that a task has to be carried out, and keeps track of task completion. It is easier to keep track of the state of a workflow with a centralized approach than it is with a fully distributed approach.

The scheduler must guarantee that a workflow will terminate in one of the specified acceptable termination states. Ideally, before attempting to execute a workflow, the scheduler should examine that workflow to check whether the workflow may terminate in a nonacceptable state. If the scheduler cannot guarantee that a workflow will terminate in an acceptable state, it should reject such specifications without attempting to execute the workflow. As an example, let us consider a workflow consisting of two tasks represented by subtransactions S_1 and S_2, with the failure-atomicity requirements indicating that either both or neither of the subtransactions should be committed. If S_1 and S_2 do not provide prepared-to-commit states (for a two-phase commit), and further do not have compensating transactions, then it is possible to reach a state where one subtransaction is committed and the other aborted, and there is no way to bring both to the same state. Therefore, such a workflow specification is *unsafe*, and should be rejected.

Safety checks such as the one just described may be impossible or impractical to implement in the scheduler; it then becomes the responsibility of the person designing the workflow specification to ensure that the workflows are safe.

20.7.4 Recovery of a Workflow

The objective of failure recovery in workflow management is to enforce the failure atomicity of workflows. The recovery procedures must make sure that, if a failure occurs in any of the workflow-processing components (including the scheduler), the workflow will eventually reach an acceptable termination state (whether aborted or committed). For example, the scheduler could continue processing after failure and recovery, as though nothing happened, thus providing forward recoverability. Otherwise, the scheduler could abort the whole workflow (that is, reach one of the global abort states). In either case, some subtransactions may need to be committed or even submitted for execution (for example, compensating subtransactions).

We assume that the processing entities involved in the workflow have their own local recovery systems and handle their local failures. To recover the execution-environment context, the failure-recovery routines need to restore the state information of the scheduler at the time of failure, including the information about the execution states of each task. Therefore, the appropriate status information must be logged on stable storage.

We also need to consider the contents of the message queues. When one agent hands off a task to another, the handoff should be carried out exactly once: if the handoff happens twice a task may get executed twice; if the handoff does not occur, the task may get lost.

If a persistent message mechanism is used, the messages are stored in stable storage and are not lost in case of failure. The persistent message system is then responsible for making sure that messages get delivered eventually, even in the presence of system failures. Persistent message support may be provided by a transaction-processing monitor, or may be provided directly by the operating system, as it is in the mailboxes provided by the DEC VMS operating system. Before an agent commits, it writes to the persistent message queue whatever messages need to be sent out. The message system at the receiving end must also log requests in stable storage so that it can detect multiple receipts of a request.

20.8 Summary

Remote backup systems provide a high degree of availability, allowing transaction processing to continue even if the primary site is destroyed by a fire, flood, or earthquake. Transaction processing is faster than in a replicated distributed system.

Transaction-processing monitors were initially developed as multithreaded servers that could service large numbers of terminals from a single process. They have since evolved, and today they provide the infrastructure for building and administering complex transaction-processing systems that have a large number of clients and multiple servers. They provide services such as presentation facilities to simplify the writing of user-interface applications, persistent queueing of client requests and server responses, routing of client messages to servers, and coordination of two-phase commit when transactions access multiple servers.

Large main memories are exploited in certain systems to achieve high system throughput. In such systems, logging is a bottleneck. Under the group-commit concept, the number of outputs to stable storage can be reduced, thus releasing this bottleneck.

The efficient management of long-duration interactive transactions is more complex, because of the long-duration waits, and because of the possibility of aborts. Since the concurrency-control techniques used in Chapter 14 use waits, aborts, or both, alternative techniques must be considered. These techniques must ensure correctness without requiring serializability. A long-duration transaction is represented as a nested transaction with atomic database operations at the lowest level. If a transaction fails, only active short-duration transactions abort. Active long-duration transactions resume once any short-duration transactions have recovered. We can do recovery using the **undo** mechanism discussed in Chapter 15. However, it is often possible to use a compensating transaction, instead of an **undo**. A compensating transaction corrects, or compensates for, the failure of a transaction, without causing cascading rollback.

In systems with real-time constraints, correctness of execution involves not only database consistency but also deadline satisfaction. The wide variance of execution times for read and write operations complicates the transaction-management problem for time-constrained systems.

We can sometimes use alternative notions of consistency that do not ensure serializability, to improve performance. Cursor stability and degree-two consistency ensure that no transaction can read data written by an uncommitted transaction. However, nonserializable executions are possible.

Workflows are activities that involve the coordinated execution of multiple tasks performed by different processing entities. They exist not just in computer applications, but also in almost all organizational activities. With the growth of networks, and the existence of multiple autonomous database systems, workflows provide a convenient way of carrying out tasks that involve multiple systems. Although the usual ACID transactional requirements are too strong or are unimplementable for such workflow applications, workflows must satisfy a limited set of transactional properties that guarantee that a process is not left in an inconsistent state.

Exercises

20.1. Explain the difference between a system crash and a "disaster."

20.2. Explain the difference between data replication in a distributed system and the maintenance of a remote backup site.

20.3. For each of the following requirements, identify the best choice of degree of durability:

(*a*) Data loss must be avoided but some loss of availability may be tolerated.

(*b*) Transaction commit must be accomplished quickly, even at the cost of loss of some committed transactions in a disaster.

(*c*) A high degree of availability and durability is required, but a longer running time for the transaction commit protocol is acceptable.

20.4. Explain how a TP monitor manages memory and processor resources more effectively than a typical operating system.

20.5. If the entire database fits in main memory, do we still need a database system to manage the data? Explain your answer.

20.6. Consider a main-memory database system recovering from a system crash. Explain the relative merits of

- Loading the entire database back into main memory before resuming transaction processing.
- Loading data as it is requested by transactions.

20.7. In the group-commit technique, how many transactions should be part of a group? Explain your answer.

20.8. Let T_1 and T_2 be transactions that each modify two data items. Assume that 100 log records fit on one block. How many block writes are required if T_1 and T_2 are committed separately? How many are required if T_1 and T_2 are committed as a group?

20.9. Explain why it may be impractical to require serializability for long-duration transactions.

20.10. Discuss the modifications that need to be made in each of the recovery schemes covered in Chapter 15 if we allow nested transactions. Also, explain any differences that result if we allow multilevel transactions.

20.11. What is the purpose of compensating transactions? Present two examples of their use.

20.12. Is a high-performance transaction system necessarily a real-time system? Why or why not?

20.13. In a database system using write-ahead logging, what is the worst-case number of disk accesses required to read a data item? Explain why this presents a problem to designers of real-time database systems.

20.14. Explain the reason for the use of degree-two consistency. What disadvantages does this approach have?

20.15. Workflow systems require concurrency and recovery management as do database systems. List 3 reasons why we cannot simply apply a relational DBMS using 2PL, WAL, and 2PC

Bibliographic Notes

Gray and Edwards [1995] provide an overview of TP monitor architectures; Gray and Reuter [1993] provide a detailed (and excellent) textbook description of transaction-processing systems, including chapters on TP monitors. Our description of TP monitors is modeled on these two sources. X/Open [1991] defines the X/Open XA interface. Transaction processing in Tuxedo is described in Huffman [1993]. Wipfler [1987] is one of several texts on application development using CICS.

There has been much work on high-performance transaction systems. Garcia-Molina and Salem [1992] provide an overview of main-memory databases. Jagadish et al. [1993] describe a recovery algorithm designed for main-memory databases. A storage manager for main-memory databases is described in Jagadish et al. [1994]. Degree-two consistency was introduced in Gray et al. [1975].

Nested and multilevel transactions are presented by Lynch [1983], Moss [1982, 1985], Lynch and Merritt [1986], Fekete et al. [1990a, 1990b], Korth and Speegle [1994], and Pu et al. [1988]. Several extended-transaction models have been defined including sagas (Garcia-Molina and Salem [1987]), ACTA (Chrysanthis and Ramamritham [1994]), the ConTract model (Wächter and Reuter [1992]), ARIES (Mohan et al. [1992]), and the NT/PV model (Korth and Speegle [1994]). Splitting transaction to achieve higher performance is addressed in Shasha et al. [1995]. A model for concurrency in nested transactions systems is presented in Beeri et al. [1989]. Relaxation of serializability is discussed in Garcia-Molina [1983], and in Sha et al. [1988]. Recovery in nested transaction systems is discussed by Moss [1987], Haerder and Rothermel [1987], and Rothermel and Mohan [1989]. Multilevel transaction management is discussed in Weikum [1991]. Gray [1981], Skarra and Zdonik [1989], and Korth and Speegle [1988, 1990] discuss long-duration transactions. Transaction processing for long-duration transactions is considered by Weikum and Schek [1984], Haerder and Rothermel [1987], Weikum et al. [1990], and Korth et al. [1990a]. Salem et al. [1994] present an extension of 2PL for long-duration transactions by allowing the early release of locks under certain circumstances.

Transaction processing in real-time databases is discussed by Abbot and Garcia-Molina [1992], and by Dayal et al. [1990]. Barclay et al. [1982] describe a real-time database system used in a telecommunications switching system. Complexity and correctness issues in real-time databases are addressed by Korth et al. [1990b], and Soparkar et al. [1995]. Concurrency control and scheduling in real-time databases are discussed by Haritsa et al. [1990], Hong et al. [1993], and Pang et al. [1995]. Ozsoyoglu and Snodgrass [1995] is a survey of research in real-time and temporal databases.

Security considerations in transaction processing are addressed by Smith et al. [1996].

The levels of consistency – or isolation – offered in SQL-92 are explained and critiqued in Berenson et al. [1995].

Our description of workflows follows the model of Rusinkiewicz and Sheth [1995], who discuss the specification and execution of transactional workflows. Reuter [1989] presents ConTracts, a method for grouping transactions into multitransaction activities. Some issues related to workflows were addressed in the work on long-running activities by Dayal et al. [1990, 1991]. They propose event–condition–action rules as a technique for specifying workflows. Jin et al. [1993] describe workflow issues in telecommunication applications. A reference model for workflows, proposed by the Workflow Management Coalition, is presented in Hollinsworth [1994].

CHAPTER 21

NEW APPLICATIONS

Relational databases have been in use for over two decades. A large portion of the applications of relational databases have been in the commercial world, supporting such tasks as transaction processing for banks and stock exchanges, sales and reservations for a variety of businesses, and inventory and payroll for almost all companies. We study several new applications, which have become increasingly important in recent years.

- **Decision-support systems**. As the online availability of data has grown, businesses have begun to exploit the available data to make better decisions about their activities, such as what items to stock and how best to target customers to increase sales. We can extract much information for decision suppert by using simple SQL queries. Recently, however, people have felt the need for better decision support based on data analysis and data mining, or knowledge discovery, using data from a variety of sources. Section 21.1 presents an overview of decision-support systems. Data analysis is described in Section 21.2; data mining in described in Section 21.3; data warehousing is described in Section 21.4.
- **Spatial databases**. Spatial databases include geographic databases, which store maps and associated information, and computer-aided–design databases, which store information such as integrated-circuit or building designs. Applications of spatial data initially stored data as files in a file system, as did early-generation business applications. But as the complexity and volume of the data, and the number of users, have grown, ad hoc approaches to storing and retrieving data in a file system have proved insufficient for the needs of applications that use spatial data. Spatial-data applications require facilities

offered by a database system—in particular, the ability to store and query large amounts of data efficiently. Some applications may also require other database features, such as atomic updates to parts of the stored data, durability, and concurrency control. In Section 21.5, we study the extensions needed to traditional database systems to support spatial data.

- **Multimedia databases**. In Section 21.6, we study the features required in database systems that store data such as image, video, and audio data. The main distinguishing feature of video and audio data is that the display of the data requires retrieval at a steady, predetermined rate; hence, such data are called *continuous-media* data.
- **Mobile databases**. In Section 21.7, we study the database requirements of the new generation of mobile computing systems, such as notebook computers and palmtop computing devices, which are connected to base stations via wireless digital communications networks. Such computers need to be able to operate while disconnected from the network, unlike the distributed database systems discussed in Chapter 18. They also have limited storage capacity, and thus require special techniques for memory management.
- **Information retrieval**. In parallel with the field of database systems, the field of information systems has seen large growth in the last few decades. Information systems have much in common with database systems—in particular, the storage and retrieval of data on secondary storage. However, the emphasis in the field of information systems has been different from that in database systems, concentrating on issues such as querying based on keywords; the relevance of documents to the query; and the analysis, classification and indexing of documents. In Section 21.8, we study issues that arise in information-retrieval systems.
- **Distributed information retrieval**. In recent years computer networking has grown enormously, and today tens of millions of computers are connected on the global *internet*. Many of the users (people as well as organizations) have information stored on these computers that they would like to share with the rest of the world. Distributed information systems deal with the problem of how to present a uniform interface to the information, and how to allow a user to locate information in which she is interested from amidst the vast amount of information that is available on the internet. We discuss issues and challenges in distributed information systems in Section 21.9.

21.1 Decision-Support Systems

Database applications can be broadly classified into transaction processing and decision support (Section 19.3.2). Transaction-processing systems are widely used today, and companies have accumulated a vast amount of information generated by these systems.

For example, company databases often contain enormous quantities of information about customers and transactions. The size of the information storage required may range into gigabytes, or even terabytes for large retail chains. Transaction information for a retailer may include the name or identifier (such as credit-card number) of the customer, the items purchased, the price paid, and the dates on which the purchases were made. Information about the items purchased may include the type of item, the manufacturer, the model number, the color, and the size. Customer information may include credit history, annual income, residence, age, and even educational background.

Such large databases can be treasure troves of information for making business decisions, such as what items to stock, or what discounts to offer. For instance, a retail company may notice a sudden spurt in purchases of flannel shirts in the Pacific Northwest, may realize that there is a trend, and may start stocking a larger number of such shirts in shops in that area. As another example, a car company may find, on querying its database, that most of its small sports cars are bought by young women whose annual incomes are above \$50,000. The company may then target its marketing to attract more such women to buy its small sports cars, and may avoid wasting money trying to attract other categories of people to buy those cars. In both cases, the company has identified patterns in customer behavior, and has used the patterns to make business decisions.

The storage and retrieval of data for decision support raises several issues:

- Although many decision support queries can be written in SQL, others either cannot be expressed in SQL or cannot be expressed easily in SQL. Several SQL extensions have therefore been proposed. In Section 21.2, we study a few such extensions that simplify the task of generating summary data.
- Database query languages are not suited to the performance of detailed *statistical analyses* of data. There are several packages, such as S++, that help in statistical analysis. Such packages have been interfaced with databases, to allow large volumes of data to be stored in the database and retrieved efficiently for analysis. The field of statistical analysis is a large discipline on its own, and we shall not discuss it here; see the references in the bibliographic notes for more information.
- Knowledge-discovery techniques, developed by the artificial-intelligence community, attempt to discover automatically statistical rules and patterns from data. The field of *data mining* combines ideas about knowledge discovery with efficient implementation techniques that enable them to be used on extremely large databases. Data mining is discussed in Section 21.3.
- Large companies have diverse sources of data that they need to use for making business decisions. The sources may store the data under different schemas. For performance reasons (as well as for reasons of organization control), the data sources usually will not permit other parts of the company to retrieve data on demand.

  To execute queries efficiently on such diverse data, companies have started building *data warehouses*. Data warehouses gather data from multiple sources under a unified schema, at a single site. Thus, they provide the user a single uniform interface to data. We study issues in building and maintaining a data warehouse in Section 21.4.

21.2 Data Analysis

Although complex statistical analysis is best left to statistics packages, databases should support simple, commonly used, forms of data analysis. Since the data stored in databases are usually large in volume, they need to be summarized in some fashion if we are to derive information that humans can use. Aggregate functions are commonly used for this task.

The SQL aggregation functionality is limited, so several extensions have been implemented by different databases. For instance, although SQL defines only a few aggregate functions, many database systems provide a richer set of functions, including variance, median, and so on. Some systems also allow users to add new aggregate functions.

Histograms are frequently used in data analysis. A histogram partitions the values taken by an attribute into ranges, and computes an aggregate, such as sum, over the values in each range. For example, a histogram on salaries values might count the number of people whose salaries fall in each of the ranges 0 to 20000, 20001 to 40000, 40001 to 60000, and above 60000. Using SQL to construct such a histogram efficiently would be cumbersome. We leave it as an exercise for you to verify our claim. Extensions to the SQL syntax that allow functions to be used in the **groupby** clause have been proposed to simplify the task. For instance, the *N_tile* function supported on the Red Brick database system divides values into percentiles. Consider the following query:

> **select** *percentile*, **avg**(*balance*)
> **from** *account*
> **groupby** *N_tile*(*balance, 10*) **as** *percentile*

Here, *N_tile*(*balance*, 10) divides the values for *balance* into 10 consecutive ranges, with an equal number of values in each range; duplicates are not eliminated. Thus, the first range would have the bottom 10 percent of the values, and the tenth range would have the top 10 percent of the values. The rest of the query performs a groupby based on these ranges, and returns the average balance for each range.

Statistical analysis often requires aggregation on multiple attributes. Consider an application where a shop wants to find out what kinds of clothes are popular. Let us suppose that clothes are classified based on color and size, and that we have a relation *sales* with the schema *Sales*(*color*, *size*, *number*). To analyze the sales by color (light versus dark) and size (small, medium, large), a manager may want to see data laid out as shown in the table in Figure 21.1.

The table in Figure 21.1 is an example of a *cross-tabulation (cross-tab)*. Many report writers provide support for such tables. In this case, the data are two-dimensional, since they are based on two attributes: *size* and *color*. In general, the data can be represented as a multidimensional array, with a value for each element of the array. Such data are called *multidimensional* data.

	Small	Medium	Large	Total
Light	8	35	10	53
Dark	20	10	5	35
Total	28	45	15	88

Figure 21.1 Cross tabulation of *sales* by *size* and *color*.

The data in a cross-tabulation cannot be generated by a single SQL query, since totals are taken at several different levels. Moreover, we can see easily that a cross-tabulation is not the same as a relational table. We can represent the data in relational form by introducing a special value **all** to represent subtotals, as shown in Figure 21.2.

Consider the tuples (Light, **all**, 53) and (Dark, **all**, 35). We have obtained these tuples by eliminating individual tuples with different values for *size*, and by replacing the value of *number* by an aggregate—namely, sum. The value **all** can be thought of as representing the set of values for *size*. Moving from finer-granularity data to a coarser granularity by means of aggregation is called doing a *rollup*. In our example, we have rolled up the attribute *size*. The opposite operation—that of moving from coarser-granularity data to finer-granularity data—is called *drill down*. Clearly, finer-granularity data cannot be generated from coarse-granularity data; they must be generated either from the original data, or from yet-more-fine–granularity summary data.

The number of different ways in which the tuples can be grouped for aggregation can be large, as you can verify easily from the table in Figure 21.2. In fact, for a table with n dimensions, rollup can be performed on each of the 2^n subsets of the n dimensions. Consider a three-dimensional version of the *sales* relation, with attributes *size*, *color*, and *price* as the three dimensions. Figure 21.3 shows the subsets of attributes of the relation as corners of a three-dimensional cube;

Color	Size	Number
Light	Small	8
Light	Medium	35
Light	Large	10
Light	**all**	53
Dark	Small	20
Dark	Medium	10
Dark	Large	5
Dark	**all**	35
all	Small	28
all	Medium	45
all	Large	15
all	**all**	88

Figure 21.2 Relational representation of the data in Figure 21.1.

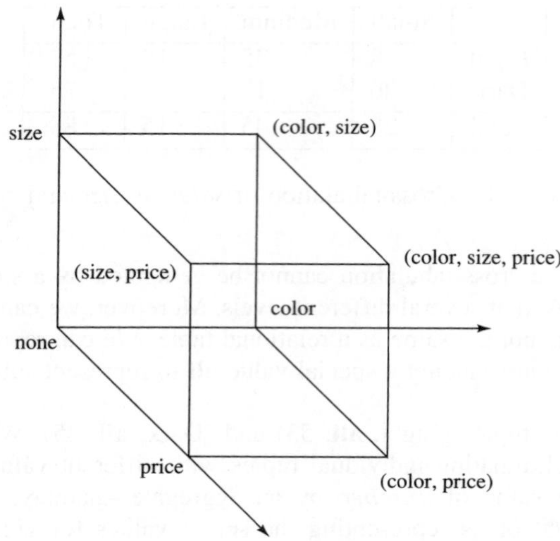

Figure 21.3 Three-dimensional data cube.

rollup can be performed on each of these subsets of attributes. In general, the subsets of attributes of an n-dimensional relation can be visualized as the corners of a corresponding n-dimensional cube.

Although we can generate tables such as the one in Figure 21.2 using SQL, doing so is cumbersome. The query involves the use of the **union** operation, and can be long; we leave it to you as an exercise to generate the rows containing **all** from a table containing the other rows.

There have been proposals to extend the SQL syntax with a **cube** operator. For instance, the following extended SQL query would generate the table shown in Figure 21.2:

select *color, size,* **sum**(*number*)
from *sales*
groupby *color, size* **with cube**

21.3 Data Mining

The term *data mining* refers loosely to finding relevant information, or "discovering knowledge," from a large volume of data. Like knowledge discovery in artificial intelligence, data mining attempts to discover statistical rules and patterns automatically from data. However, data mining differs from machine learning in that it deals with large volumes of data, stored primarily on disk.

Knowledge discovered from a database can be represented by a set of *rules*. The following is an example of a rule, stated informally: "Young women with annual incomes greater than $50,000 are the most likely people to buy small sports cars."

We first describe the structure of rules used to represent knowledge, in Section 21.3.1. We then consider several classes of data-mining applications, to explain the need for data mining, in Section 21.3.2. We can discover rules from database using one of two models:

- In the first model, the user is involved directly in the process of knowledge discovery. This model is discussed in Section 21.3.3.
- In the second model, the system is responsible for automatically discovering knowledge from the database, by detecting patterns and correlations in the data. This model is covered in more detail in Section 21.3.4.

Knowledge-discovery systems may have elements of both models, with the system discovering some rules automatically, and the user guiding the process of rule discovery.

21.3.1 Knowledge Representation Using Rules

Rules provide a common framework in which to express various types of knowledge. Rules are of the general form

$$\forall \overline{X} antecedent \Rightarrow consequent$$

where $\overline{X}$ is a list of one or more variables with associated ranges. Let the database contain a relation *buys* that specifies what was bought in each transaction. The following is an example of a rule:

$$\forall\ transactions\ \ T,\ buys(T, bread) \Rightarrow buys(T, milk)$$

Here, T is a variables whose range is the set of all transactions. The rule says that, if there is a tuple $(t_i, bread)$ in the relation *buys*, there must also be a tuple $(t_i, milk)$ in the relation *buys*.

The range of a variable defines a set of values that the variable can take. The cross-product of the ranges of the variables in the rule forms the *population*. Many data-mining systems restrict a rule to have a single variable.

Rules have an associated *support*, as well as an associated *confidence*.

- *Support* is a measure of what fraction of the population satisfies the both the antecedent and the consequent of the rule.

  For instance, if 0.001 percent of all transactions include the purchase of milk and bread, the support for the rule

  $$\forall\ transactions\ \ T,\ buys(T, bread) \Rightarrow buys(T, milk)$$

  is low. The rule may not even be statistically significant—perhaps there was only a single transaction that purchased both bread and milk. Businesses are often not interested in rules that have low support, since the latter involve few customers, and are not worth bothering about. On the other hand, if 50 percent of all transactions involve the purchase of milk and bread, then support is relatively high, and the rule is worth attention. Exactly what minimum degree of support is considered desirable depends on the application.

- *Confidence* is a measure of how often the consequent is true when the antecedent is true. For instance, the rule

$$\forall\ transactions\ \ T,\ buys(T, bread) \Rightarrow buys(T, milk)$$

has a confidence of 80 percent if 80 percent of the transactions that include the purchase of bread also include the purchase of milk. A rule with a low confidence is not meaningful. In business applications, rules usually have confidences significantly less than 100 percent, whereas in other domains, such as in physics, rules may have high confidences.

21.3.2 Classes of Data-Mining Problems

Two important classes of problems in data mining are *classification* and *association rules*.

Classification involves finding rules that partition the given data into disjoint groups. For instance, suppose that a credit-card company wants to decide whether or not to give a credit card to an applicant. The company has a variety of information about the person—such as her age, educational background, annual income, current debts, and housing location—which it can use for making a decision.

Some of this information could be relevant to the credit worthiness of the applicant, whereas some may not be. To make the decision, the company assigns a credit-worthiness level of excellent, good, average, or bad to each of a sample set of *current* customers. The assignment of credit worthiness is based on the customer's payment history. Then, the company attempts to find rules that classify its current customers into excellent, good, average, or bad, based on the information about the person, other than the actual payment history (which is unavailable for new customers). Let us consider just two attributes: education level (highest degree earned) and income. The rules may be of the following form:

$$\forall person\ \ P,\ P.degree = Masters\ \textbf{and}\ P.income \geq 75000 \Rightarrow P.credit = excellent$$

$$\forall\ person\ \ P,\ P.degree = Bachelors\ \textbf{or}\ (P.income \geq 25000\ \textbf{and}\ P.income < 75000) \Rightarrow P.credit = good$$

Similar rules would also be present for the other credit worthiness levels (average and bad).

Other important uses of classification include making loan approvals, setting insurance premiums, deciding whether or not to stock a particular item in a shop based on statistical information about customers, and so on.

Retail shops are often interested in *associations* between different items that people buy. For instance, someone who buys bread is quite likely also to buy milk — an association represented by the rule that we saw earlier:

$$\forall\ transactions\ \ T,\ buys(T, bread) \Rightarrow buys(T, milk)$$

with an associated confidence level and support.

Association information can be used in several ways. A shop may decide to place bread close to milk, to help shoppers finish their task faster. Or the shop may place them at opposite ends of a row, and place other associated items inbetween to tempt people to buy those items as well, as the shoppers walk from one end of the row to the other. A shop that offers discounts on one associated item may not offer a discount on the other, since the customer will probably buy the other anyway.

Another important class of data-mining applications is sequence correlations. Time-series data, such as stock prices on a sequence of days, form an example of sequence data. Stock-market analysts want to find correlations among stock-market price sequences. An example of such a correlation is the following rule: "Whenever bond rates go up, the stock prices go down within 2 days." Discovering such correlations between sequences can help us to make intelligent investment decisions.

21.3.3 User-Guided Data Mining

In the user-guided model for data mining, the user has primary responsibility for discovering rules, and the database system plays a supporting rule. Typically, the user makes up a hypothesis, and runs tests on the database to verify or refute that hypothesis. For instance, a user may have a hypothesis that people who hold master's degrees are the most likely to have an excellent credit rating, and may use the database to verify his hypothesis. The data may indicate that people who hold master's degrees are more likely than others to have an excellent credit rating.

The user may then come up with a new hypothesis, or may refine the existing hypothesis, and may verify it against the database. Thus, there may be several iterations, involving successive refinement of the hypothesis, as the user tests more refined versions.

For instance, since people who hold master's degrees have been detected to be slightly more likely to have an excellent credit rating than others, perhaps a subclass of such people are even more likely to have an excellent credit rating. The user may come up with a hypothesis that customers who hold master's degrees *and* who earn \$75,000 or more per year are likely to have an excellent credit rating. The confidence and support for the rule can be derived from the database. Now, the confidence may be high (close to 1), and the user may stop at this point, having derived a rule of the form

$$\begin{aligned}\forall\ people\ P,\ P.degree = Masters\ \textbf{and}\ C.income \geq 75,000 \\ \Rightarrow\ C.credit = excellent\end{aligned}$$

with the appropriate confidence and support levels.

Data-visualization systems help users to examine large volumes of data, and to detect patterns visually. Visual displays of data—such as maps, charts, and other graphical representations—allow data to be presented compactly to users. A single graphical screen can encode as much information as can a far larger number of text screens.

For example, if the user wants to find out whether production problems at plants are correlated to the location of the plants, the problem locations can be encoded in a special color—say, red—on a map. The user can then quickly discover locations in which problems are occurring. The user may then form hypotheses about why problems are occurring in those locations, and may verify the hypotheses quantitatively against the database.

As another example, information about values can be encoded as a color, and can be displayed with as little as one pixel of screen area. To detect associations between pairs of items, we can use a two-dimensional pixel matrix, with each row and each column representing an item. The percentage of transactions that buy both items can be encoded by the color intensity of the pixel. Items with high association will show up as bright pixels in the screen — easy to detect against the darker background.

21.3.4 Automatic Discovery of Rules

Work on automatic discovery of rules has been influenced strongly by work in the artificial-intelligence community on machine learning. The main differences lie in the volume of data handled in databases, and in the need to access disk. Specialized data-mining algorithms have been developed to handle large volumes of disk-resident data efficiently.

The manner in which rules are discovered depends on the class of data-mining application. We illustrate rule discovery using two application classes: classification and associations.

21.3.4.1 Discovery of Classification Rules

The process of discovery of classification rules starts from a sample of data, called a *training set*. For each tuple in the training set, the grouping is already known. For instance, the training set for a credit-card application may be the existing customers, with their credit worthiness determined from their payment history. The actual data, or population, may consist of all people, including those who are not existing customers.

The example from Section 21.3.3 of finding which class of people have an excellent credit rating illustrates not only how a human would discover rules, but also hints at how a data-mining system can discover rules.

The data-mining system starts first with antecedents consisting of only a simple condition on a single attribute. The possible conditions on the degree attribute are $P.degree = None$, $P.degree = Bachelors$, $P.degree = Masters$, and $P.degree = Doctorate$, if these are the only possible degrees. For attributes whose value is numeric, the data-mining system divides up the possible values into intervals; the salary-attribute value could be divided into intervals 0 to 25,000,

25,000 to 50,000, 50,000 to 75,000, and over 75,000. Thus, if we consider any attribute, the conditions based on that attribute partition the set of tuples into disjoint groups.

If, for any attribute, all or most of the tuples in each group have the same classification value (the credit worthiness, in our example), a set of rules based on that attribute can be output, and data mining stops. More likely, this situation will not hold. Rules based on the *degree* attribute or the *income* attribute alone will not be sufficient to classify the data properly.

In this case, one of the attributes is chosen—usually, the one that best partitions the data. The data are divided into groups based on the conditions on this attribute, and then classification is done separately, based on the other attributes, for each group. Suppose that *degree* is chosen as the attribute on which to partition. Consider the partition corresponding to *Masters*. The partitioning at the next level would be made on one of the other attributes; in our example, we use the attribute *income*. The rules in the group for *Masters* would have a condition of the form *degree* = *Masters*, in addition to the condition on *income*, in their antecedent. The other partitions, with *degree* = *None* and so on, would be separately classified in the same manner.

This method generates a *classification tree* from the top down. Part of the classification tree for our problem is shown in Figure 21.4. Each node of the tree partitions the data into groups based on one attribute. The construction of a path in the tree stops when either the attribute has properly classified the data, or all attributes have been considered. In our example, within each partition based on degree, the partitions defined by *income* adequately classify the tuples. Tree construction stops at this level for each partition based on degree. In general, different branches of the tree could grow to different levels.

Numerous improvements on the basic technique have been developed. The number of rules generated can be reduced by means of merging rules together—

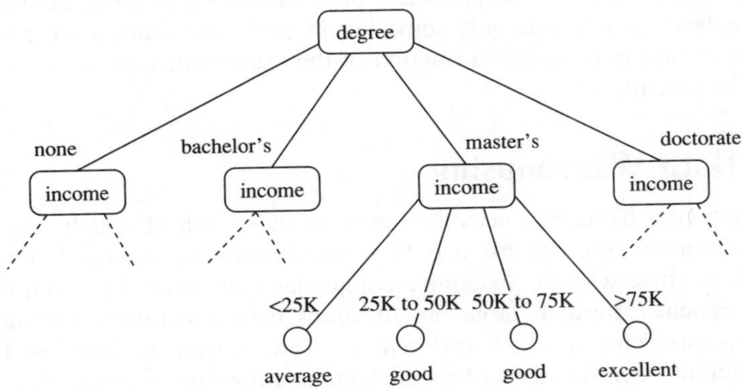

Figure 21.4 Classification tree.

for instance, if adjacent intervals belong to the same classification group. The I/O cost can be reduced by techniques that grow multiple branches of a tree with a single scan of the tuples. See the bibliographic notes for more information.

21.3.4.2 Discovery of Association Rules

Consider our earlier example of an association rule:

$$\forall\ transactions\ \ T,\ buys(T, bread) \Rightarrow buys(T, milk)$$

We can derive rules such as this one efficiently by associating a bitmap with each transaction, with one bit per item of interest in the shop. This approach is reasonable if the number of items of interest is not large. Even if the initial set of items is large, users will typically want only those rules that have strong support, which will involve only items purchased in a significant percentage of the transactions. Thus, the set of relevant items can be deduced quickly, and is likely to be small.

Now, to discover association rules of the form

$$\forall\ transactions\ \ T,\ buys(T, i_1)\ \textbf{and}\ \ldots\ \textbf{and}\ buys(T, i_n) \Rightarrow buys(T, i_0)$$

we must consider all subsets of the set of relevant items, and, for each set, must check whether there is a sufficient number of transactions in which all the items in the set are purchased.

If the number of such sets is small, a single pass over the transactions suffices to detect the level of support for all the sets. A count is maintained for each set, initially set to 0. When a transaction is fetched, the count is incremented for each set of items, all of whose bits are set in the transaction's bitmap. Those sets with a sufficiently high count at the end of the pass correspond to items that have a high degree of association.

If the number of sets is high, the cost of processing each transaction becomes correspondingly large. Techniques have been developed that use multiple passes on the database, considering only some sets in each pass. Once a set is eliminated because it occurs in too small a fraction of the transactions, none of its supersets needs to be considered.

21.4 Data Warehousing

Large companies have presences at numerous sites, each of which may generate a large volume of data. For instance, large retail chains have shops at hundreds or thousands of sites, whereas insurance companies may have data from thousands of local branches. Further, large organizations have a complex internal organization structure, due to which different data are present in different locations, or on different operational systems, and under different schemas. For instance, manufacturing-problem data and customer-complaints data may be stored on different database systems. Corporate decision makers require access to information

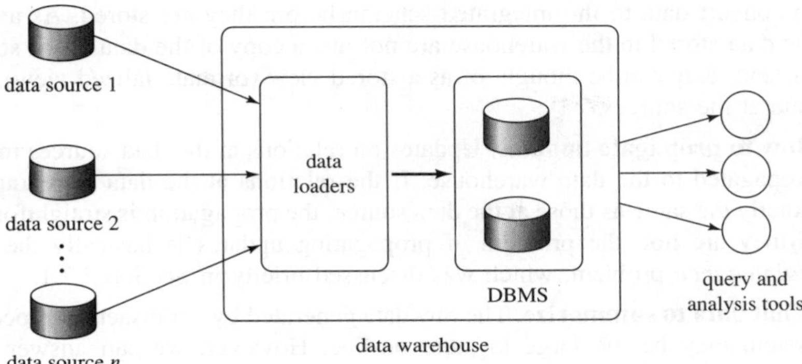

Figure 21.5 Data-warehouse architecture.

from all such sources. Setting up queries on individual sources is both cumbersome and inefficient. Moreover, the sources of data may store only current data, whereas decision makers may need access to past data as well; for instance, information about how purchase patterns have changed in the past year could be of great importance. Data warehouses provide a solution to these problems.

A *data warehouse* is a repository (or archive) of information gathered from multiple sources, stored under a unified schema, at a single site. Once gathered, the data are stored for a long time, permitting access to historical data. Thus, data warehouses provide the user a single consolidated interface to data, making decision-support queries easier to write. Moreover, by accessing information for decision support from a data warehouse, the decision maker ensures that on-line transaction-processing systems are not affected by the decision-support workload.

Figure 21.5 shows the architecture of a typical data warehouse, and illustrates the gathering of data, the storage of data, and the querying and data-analysis support. Among the issues to be addressed in building a warehouse are the following:

- **When and how to gather data.** In a source-driven architecture for gathering data, the data sources transmit new information, either continually, as transaction processing takes place, or periodically, such as each night. In a destination-driven architecture, the data warehouse periodically sends requests for new data to the sources.

  Unless updates at the sources are replicated at the warehouse via two-phase commit, the warehouse will never be quite up to date with the sources. Two-phase commit is usually far too expensive to be an option, so data warehouses typically have slightly out-of-date data. That, however, is usually not a problem for decision-support systems.

- **What schema to use.** Data sources that have been constructed independently are likely to have different schemas. In fact, they may even use different data models. Part of the task of a warehouse is to perform schema integration, and to convert data to the integrated schema before they are stored. As a result, the data stored in the warehouse are not just a copy of the data at the sources. Instead, they can be thought of as a stored view (or materialized view) of the data at the sources.

- **How to propagate updates.** Updates on relations at the data sources must be propagated to the data warehouse. If the relations at the data warehouse are exactly the same as those at the data source, the propagation is straightforward. If they are not, the problem of propagating updates is basically the *view-maintenance* problem, which was discussed briefly in Section 3.7.1.
- **What data to summarize.** The raw data generated by a transaction-processing system may be too large to store on-line. However, we can answer many queries by maintaining just summary data obtained by aggregation on a relation, rather than maintaining the entire relation. For example, instead of storing data about every sale of clothing, we can store total sales of clothing by category.

  Suppose that a relation r has been replaced by a summary relation s. Users may still be permitted to pose queries as though the relation r were available on-line. If the query requires only summary data, it may be possible to transform it into an equivalent one using s instead. This transformation can be done as follows. The stored summary relation s is defined as a view on the original relation. However, s is a materialized view, rather than a view computed on demand. The query optimizer must then decide whether it can replace uses of r in the given query by s, with some other associated changes, based on analysis of the given query and the view definition of s. See the bibliographic notes for more information.

21.5 Spatial and Geographic Databases

Spatial databases store information related to spatial locations, and provide support for efficient querying and indexing based on spatial locations. For example, suppose that we want to store a set of polygons in a database, and to query the database to find all polygons that intersect a given polygon. We cannot use standard index structures, such as B-trees or hash indices, to answer such a query efficiently. A spatial database would use special-purpose index structures, such as R-trees (which we study later) for the task.

Two types of spatial databases are particularly important:

- *Design databases*, or computer-aided-design (CAD) databases, are spatial databases used to store design information about how objects—such as buildings, cars, or aircraft—are constructed. Other important examples of computer-aided–design databases are integrated-circuit and electronic-device layouts.
- *Geographic databases* are spatial databases used to store geographic information, such as maps. Geographic databases are often called *geographic information systems.*

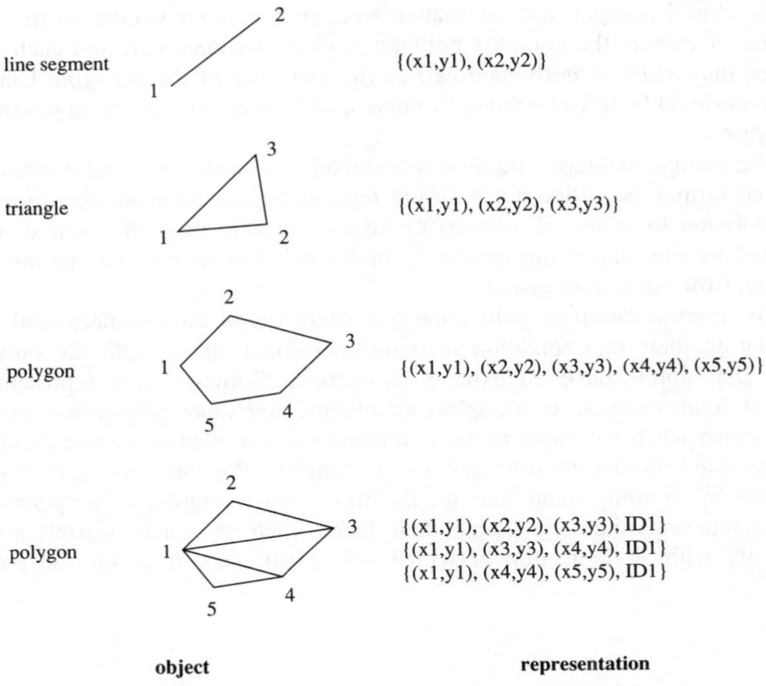

Figure 21.6 Representation of geometric constructs.

21.5.1 Representation of Geometric Information

Figure 21.6 illustrates how various geometric constructs can be represented in a database, in a normalized fashion. We stress here that geometric information can be represented in several different ways, only some of which we describe.

A line segment can be represented by the coordinates of its endpoints. We can approximately represent an arbitrary curve by partitioning it into a sequence of segments. To allow the use of fixed-size tuples, we can give the curve an identifier, and can represent each segment as a separate tuple that also carries with it the identifier of the curve. This representation is useful for two-dimensional features such as roads; here, the width of the road is small enough relative to the size of the full map that it can be considered two dimensional. For a map database, the two coordinates of a point would be its latitude and longitude.

We can represent a polygon by listing its vertices in order, as shown in Figure 21.6. The list of vertices actually specifies the boundary of a polygonal region. For simplicity, we consider only *closed polygons*—that is, polygons where the starting vertex in the list is the same as the ending vertex in the list. The interior of the boundary forms the polygonal region.

In an alternative representation, a closed polygon can be divided into a set of triangles, as shown in Figure 21.6. This process is called *triangulation*, and any closed polygon can be triangulated. In a manner similar to the representation of curves, the complex polygon is given an identifier, and each of the triangles into which it is divided carries the identifier of the polygon. Complex two-dimensional features bounded by curves, such as circles, can be approximated by polygons.

The triangulated representation is designed to be stored in a first-normal-form relational format. Non–first-normal-form representations, such as ones representing a polygon by a list of vertices or edges, are also used in practice, where supported by the underlying database. Such list-based representations are often convenient for query processing.

The representation of points and line segments in three-dimensional space is similar to their representation in two-dimensional space, with the only difference that points have an extra z component. Similarly, the representation of planar figures—such as triangles, rectangles, and other polygons—does not change much when we move to three dimensions. Tetrahedrons and cuboids can be represented similar to triangles and rectangles. We can represent arbitrary polyhedra by dividing them into tetrahedrons, like triangulating polygons. We can also represent them by listing their faces, each of which is itself a polygon, along with an indication of which side of the face is inside the polyhedron.

21.5.2 Design Databases

Computer-aided design (CAD) has been in use for many years now. CAD systems traditionally stored data in memory during editing or other processing, and wrote the data back to a file at the end of a session of editing. The drawbacks of such a scheme include the cost (programming complexity, as well as time cost) of transforming data from one form to another, and the need to read in an entire file even if only parts of it are required. For large designs, such as the design of a large-scale integrated circuit, or the design of an entire airplane, it may be impossible to hold the complete design in memory. Designers of object-oriented databases were motivated in large part by the database requirements of CAD systems. Components of the design are represented as objects, and the connections between the objects indicate how the design is structured.

The objects stored in a design database are generally geometric objects. Simple two-dimensional geometric objects include points, lines, triangles, rectangles, and, in general, polygons. Complex two-dimensional objects can be formed from simple objects by means of union, intersection, and difference operations. Similarly, complex three-dimensional objects may be formed from simpler objects such as spheres, cylinders, and cuboids, by union, intersection, and difference operations, as illustrated in Figure 21.7. Three-dimensional surfaces may also be represented by *wireframe* models, which essentially model the surface as a set of simpler objects, such as line segments, triangles, and rectangles.

Design databases also store nonspatial information about objects, such as the material from which the objects are constructed. We can usually model such

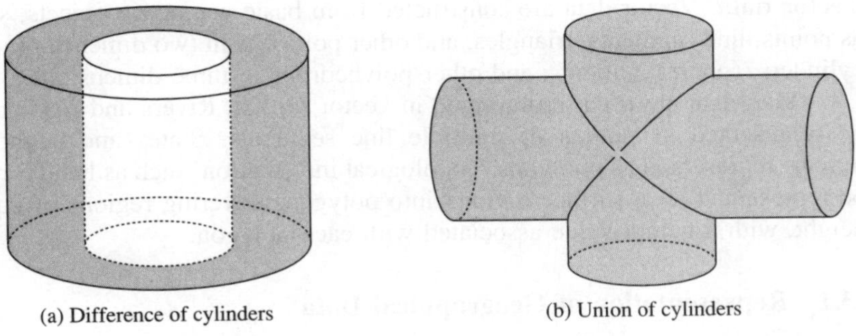

(a) Difference of cylinders (b) Union of cylinders

Figure 21.7 Complex three-dimensional objects.

information using standard data-modeling techniques. We concern ourselves here with only the spatial aspects.

Various spatial operations must be performed on the design. For instance, the task may be to retrieve that part of the design that corresponds to a particular region of interest. Spatial-index structures, discussed in Section 21.5.5, are useful for such tasks. Such spatial-index structures are multidimensional, dealing with two- and three-dimensional data, rather than dealing with just the simple one-dimensional ordering provided by the B^+-trees.

Spatial-integrity constraints, such as "two pipes should not be in the same location," are important in design databases. Such errors often occur if the design is performed manually, and are detected only when a prototype is being constructed. As a result, these errors can be expensive to fix. Database support for spatial-integrity constraints helps people to avoid design errors, thereby keeping the design consistent. Implementing such integrity checks again depends on the availability of efficient multidimensional index structures.

21.5.3 Geographic Data

Geographic data are spatial in nature, but differ from design data in certain ways. Maps and satellite images are typical examples of geographic data. Maps may provide not only location information—such as boundaries, rivers and roads—but also much more detailed information associated with locations, such as elevation, soil type, land usage, and annual rainfall.

Geographic data can be categorized into two types:

- **Raster data**. Such data consist of bit maps or pixel maps, in two or more dimensions. A typical example of a two-dimensional raster image is a satellite image of cloud cover, where each pixel stores the cloud visibility in a particular area. Such data can be three-dimensional—for example, the temperature at different altitudes at different regions, again measured with the help of a satellite. Time could form another dimension—for example, the surface temperature measurements at different points in time. Design databases generally do not store raster data.

- **Vector data**. Vector data are constructed from basic geometric objects, such as points, line segments, triangles, and other polygons in two dimensions, and cylinders, spheres, cuboids, and other polyhedrons in three dimensions.

  Map data are often represented in vector format. Rivers and roads may be represented as unions of multiple line segments. States and countries may be represented as polygons. Topological information, such as height, may be represented by a surface divided into polygons covering regions of equal height, with a height value associated with each polygon.

21.5.3.1 Representation of Geographical Data

Geographical features, such as states and large lakes, are represented as complex polygons. Some features, such as rivers, may be represented either as complex curves or as complex polygons, depending on whether their width is relevant.

Geographic information related to regions, such as annual rainfall, can be represented as an array—that is, in raster form. For space efficiency, the array can be stored in a compressed form. In Section 21.5.5, we study an alternative representation of such arrays using a data structure called a *quadtree*.

As described earlier, we can represent region information in vector form, using polygons, where each polygon is a region within which the array value is the same. The vector representation is more compact than the raster representation in some applications. It is also more accurate for some tasks, such as depicting roads, where dividing the region into pixels (which may be fairly large) leads to a loss of precision in location information. However, the vector representation is unsuitable for applications where the data are intrinsically raster based, such as satellite images.

21.5.3.2 Applications of Geographic Data

Geographic databases have a variety of uses, including vehicle-navigation systems; distribution-network information for public-service utilities such as telephone, electric-power and water-supply systems; and land-usage information for ecologists and planners.

Vehicle-navigation systems store information about roads and services for the use of drivers. Such information includes the layout of roads, speed limits on roads, road conditions, connections between roads, and one-way restrictions. At the simplest level, these systems can be used to generate on-line maps for humans. An important benefit of on-line maps is that it is easy to scale the map to the desired size—that is, to zoom in and out to locate relevant features. With this additional information about roads, the maps can be used for automatic trip planning. Users can query on-line information about services to locate, for example, hotels, gas stations, or restaurants with desired offerings and price ranges.

Vehicle-navigation systems are typically mobile, and are mounted on the dashboard of a vehicle. A useful addition to a mobile geographic information system is a *Global Positioning System (GPS)* unit, which uses information broadcast from GPS satellites to find the current location with an accuracy of tens of meters.

With such a system, a driver can never† get lost—the GPS unit finds the location in terms of {latitude, longitude, elevation} and the geographic database can be queried to find where and on which road the vehicle is currently located.

Geographic databases used for public-utility information are becoming increasingly important as the network of buried cables and pipes grows. Due to a lack of detailed maps, work carried out by one utility may damage the cables of another utility, resulting in large-scale disruption of service. Geographic databases, coupled with location-finding systems, promise the hope of avoiding such disasters in the future.

So far, we have explained why people use spatial databases. In the rest of the section, we shall study technical details, such as representation and indexing of spatial information.

21.5.4 Spatial Queries

There are a number of types of queries that involve spatial locations.

- *Nearness queries* request objects that lie near a specified location. A query to find all restaurants that lie within a given distance of a given point is an example of a nearness query. The *nearest-neighbor query* requests the object that is nearest to a specified point. For example, we may want to find the nearest gasoline station. Note that this query does not have to specify a limit on the distance, and hence we can ask it even if we have no idea how far the nearest gasoline station lies.
- *Region queries* deal with spatial regions. Such a query can ask for objects that lie partially or fully inside a specified region. A query to find all retail shops within the geographic boundaries of a given town is an example.
- Queries may also request **intersections** and **unions** of regions. For example, given region information, such as annual rainfall and population density, a query may request all regions with a low annual rainfall as well as a high population density.

Queries that compute intersections of regions can be thought of as computing the *spatial join* of two spatial relations—one representing rainfall and the other representing population density—with the location playing the role of join attribute. In general, given two relations, each containing spatial objects, the spatial join of the two relations generates either pairs of objects that intersect, or the intersection regions of such pairs.

Several join algorithms have been developed that compute efficiently spatial joins on vector data. Although nested-loop join and indexed nested-loop join (with spatial indices) can be used, hash joins and sort–merge joins cannot be used on spatial data. Join techniques based on coordinated traversal of spatial index

† Well, hardly ever!

structures on the two relations have also been proposed. See the bibliographic notes for more information.

In general, queries on spatial data may have a combination of spatial and nonspatial requirements. For instance, we may want to find the nearest restaurant that has vegetarian selections, and that charges less than $10 for a meal.

Since spatial data are inherently graphical, we typically query them using a graphical query language. Results of such queries are also displayed graphically, rather than in tables. The user can invoke various operations on the interface, such as choosing an area to be viewed (for example, by pointing and clicking on suburbs west of Manhattan), zooming in and out, choosing what to display based on selection conditions (for example, houses with more than three bedrooms), overlay of multiple maps (for example, houses with more than three bedrooms overlayed on a map showing areas with low crime rates), and so on. The graphical interface constitutes the front-end. Extensions of SQL have been proposed as a back-end, allowing relational databases to store and retrieve spatial information, and also allowing queries to mix spatial and nonspatial conditions. Extensions include allowing abstract data types, such as lines, polygons, and bit maps, and allowing spatial conditions, such as *contains* or *overlaps*.

21.5.5 Indexing of Spatial Data

Indices are required for efficient access to spatial data. Traditional index structures, such as hash indices and B-trees, are not suitable, since they only deal with one-dimensional data, whereas spatial data are typically of two or more dimensions.

21.5.5.1 k-d Trees

To understand how to index spatial data consisting of two or more dimensions, we consider first the indexing of points in one-dimensional data. Tree structures, such as binary trees and B-trees, operate by successively dividing space into smaller parts. For instance, each internal node of a binary tree partitions a one-dimensional interval in two. Points that lie in the left partition go into the left subtree; points that lie in the right partition go into the right subtree. In a balanced binary tree, the partition is chosen such that approximately one-half of the points stored in the subtree fall in each partition. Similarly, each level of a B-tree splits a one-dimensional interval into multiple parts.

We can use that intuition to create tree structures for two-dimensional space, as well as in higher-dimensional spaces. A tree structure called a *k-d tree* was one of the early structures used for indexing in multiple dimensions. Each level of a k-d tree partitions the space into two. The partitioning is done along one dimension at the node at the top level of the tree, along another dimension in nodes at the next level, and so on, cycling through the dimensions. The partitioning is done such that, at each node, approximately one-half of the points stored in the subtree fall on one side, and one-half fall on the other. Partitioning stops when a node has less than a given maximum number of points. Figure 21.8 shows a set of points in two-dimensional space, and a k-d tree representation of the set of points. Each line corresponds to a node in the tree, and the maximum number of points in a

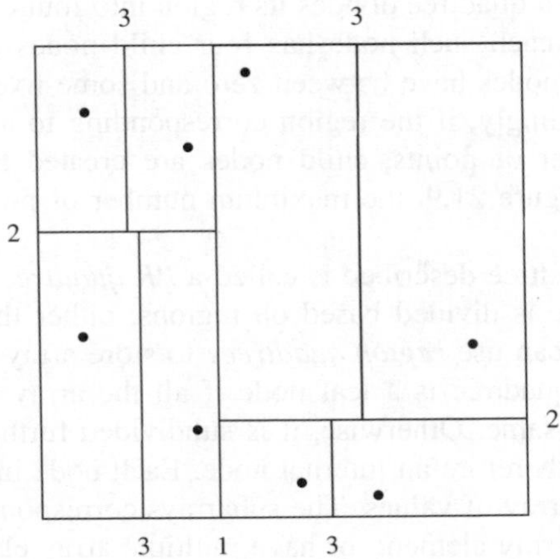

Figure 21.8 Division of space by a k-d tree.

leaf node has been set at 1. Each line in the figure (other than the outside box) corresponds to a node in the k-d tree. The numbering of the lines in the figure indicates the level of the tree at which the corresponding node appears.

The *k-d-B tree* extends the k-d tree to allow multiple child nodes for each internal node, just as a B-tree extends a binary tree, to reduce the height of the tree. k-d-B trees are better suited for secondary storage than are k-d trees.

21.5.5.2 Quadtrees

An alternative representation for two-dimensional data is a *quadtree*. An example of the division of space by a quadtree is shown in Figure 21.9. The set of points is the same as that used in Figure 21.8. Each node of a quadtree is associated with a rectangular region of space. The top node is associated with the entire target space.

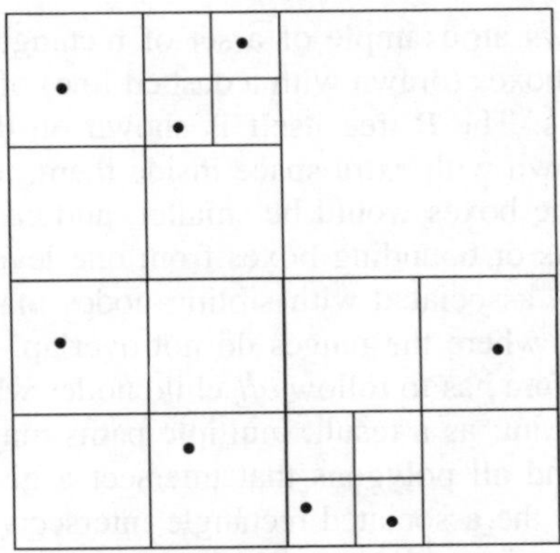

Figure 21.9 Division of space by a quadtree.

Each nonleaf node in a quadtree divides its region into four equal-sized quadrants, and correspondingly each such node has four child nodes corresponding to the four quadrants. Leaf nodes have between zero and some fixed maximum number of points. Correspondingly, if the region corresponding to a node has more than the maximum number of points, child nodes are created for that node. In the example shown in Figure 21.9, the maximum number of points in a leaf node is set to 1.

The type of quadtree described is called a *PR quadtree*, to indicate it stores points, and that space is divided based on regions, rather than on the actual set of points stored. We can use *region quadtrees* to store array (raster) information. A node in a region quadtree is a leaf node if all the array values in the region that it covers are the same. Otherwise, it is subdivided further into four children of equal area, and is therefore an internal node. Each node in the region quadtree corresponds to a subarray of values. The subarrays corresponding to leaves either contain just a single array element, or have multiple array elements, all of which have the same value.

Indexing of line segments and polygons presents new problems. There are extensions of k-d trees and quadtrees for this task. However, a line segment or polygon may cross a partitioning line. If it does, it has to be split and represented in each of the subtrees in which its pieces occur. Multiple occurrences of a line segment or polygon can result in inefficiencies in storage, as well as inefficiencies in querying.

21.5.5.3 R-Trees

A storage structure called an *R-tree* is useful for indexing of rectangles and other polygons. An R-tree is a balanced tree structure, much like a B-tree; however, instead of a range of values, a rectangular *bounding box* is associated with each tree node. Polygons are stored in only leaf nodes. The bounding box of a leaf node is the smallest rectangle (parallel to the axes) that contains all objects stored in the leaf node. The bounding box of internal nodes is similarly the smallest rectangle (parallel to the axes) that contains the bounding boxes of its child nodes.

Figure 21.10 shows an example of a set of rectangles (drawn with a solid line) and the bounding boxes (drawn with a dashed line) of the nodes of an R-tree for the set of rectangles. The R-tree itself is shown on the right. Note that the bounding boxes are shown with extra space inside them, to make them stand out pictorially. In reality, the boxes would be smaller, and each side would touch at least some of the objects or bounding boxes from one level down.

The bounding box associated with sibling nodes may overlap, unlike with k-d trees and quadtrees, where the ranges do not overlap. A search for polygons containing a point therefore has to follow *all* child nodes whose associated bounding boxes contain the point; as a result, multiple paths may have to be searched. Similarly, a query to find all polygons that intersect a given polygon has to go down every node where the associated rectangle intersects the polygon.

When we insert a polygon into an R-tree, we select a leaf node to hold the polygon. If the node is already full, node splitting is performed (and propagated

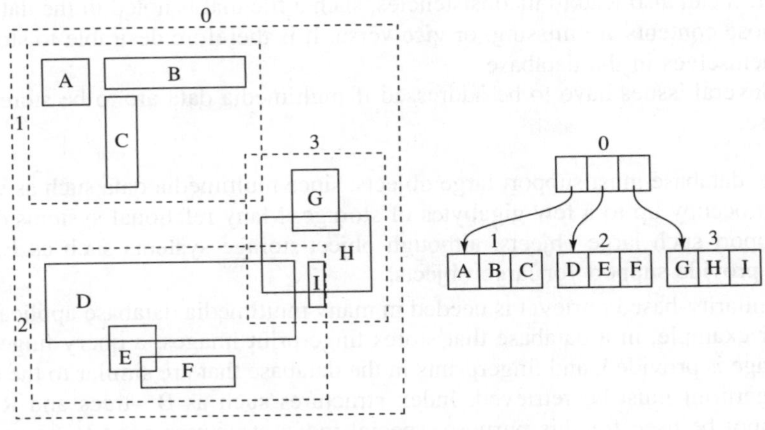

Figure 21.10 An R-tree.

upward if required) in a manner similar to B^+-tree insertion. The insertion algorithm ensures that the tree remains balanced, and the bounding boxes of leaf as well as internal nodes, remain consistent. There are multiple ways in which to split a node that is overfull; see the bibliographic references for more details on R-trees, as well as on variants of R-trees, called R^*-trees or R^+-trees.

The storage efficiency of R-trees is better than that of k-d trees or quadtrees, since a polygon is stored only once, and we can ensure easily that each node is at least half full. However, querying may be slower, since multiple paths have to be searched. Spatial joins are simpler using quadtrees than using R-trees, since all quadtrees on a region are partitioned in the same manner. However, because of their better storage efficiency, and their similarity to B-trees, R-trees and their variants have proved popular in database systems that support spatial data.

21.6 Multimedia Databases

Recently, there has been much interest in databases that store multimedia data, such as images, audio, and video. Today, multimedia data typically are stored outside the database, in file systems. When the number of multimedia objects is relatively small, features provided by databases are usually not important.

Database functionality becomes important when the number of multimedia objects stored is large. Issues such as transactional updates, querying facilities, and indexing then become important. Multimedia objects often have descriptive attributes, such as those indicating when they were created, who created them, and to what category they belong. One approach to building a database for such multimedia objects is to use databases for storing the descriptive attributes, and for keeping track of the files in which the multimedia objects are stored.

However, storing multimedia outside the database makes it harder to provide database functionality, such as indexing on the basis of actual multimedia data content. It can also lead to inconsistencies, such a file that is noted in the database, but whose contents are missing, or vice versa. It is therefore desirable to store the data themselves in the database.

Several issues have to be addressed if multimedia data are to be stored in a database.

- The database must support large objects, since multimedia data such as videos can occupy up to a few gigabytes of storage. Many relational systems do not support such large objects, although object-storage systems such as Exodus do provide support for large objects.
- Similarity-based retrieval is needed in many multimedia database applications. For example, in a database that stores fingerprint images, a query fingerprint image is provided, and fingerprints in the database that are similar to the query fingerprint must be retrieved. Index structures such as B^+-trees and R-trees cannot be used for this purpose; special index structures need to be created. We discuss similarity-based retrieval in Section 21.6.1
- The retrieval of some types of data, such as audio and video, has the requirement that data delivery must proceed at a guaranteed steady rate. Such data are sometimes called *isochronous data*, or *continuous-media data*. For example, if audio data are not supplied in time, there will be gaps in the sound. If the data are supplied too fast, system buffers may overflow, resulting in loss of data. We discuss continuous-media data in Section 21.6.2.

21.6.1 Similarity-Based Retrieval

In many multimedia applications, data are described only approximately in the database. We noted previously the example of fingerprint data. Other examples follow:

- **Pictorial data.** Two pictures or images that are slightly different as represented in the database may be considered the same by a user. For instance, a database may store trademark designs. When a new trademark is to be registered, the system may need first to identify all similar trademarks that were registered previously.
- **Audio data.** Speech-based user interfaces are being developed that allow the user to give a command or identify a data item by speaking. The input from the user must then be tested for similarity to those commands or data items stored in the system.
- **Handwritten data.** Handwritten input can be used to identify a handwritten data item or command stored in the database. Here again, similarity testing is required.

The notion of similarity is often subjective and user specific. However, similarity testing is often more successful than speech or handwriting recognition, because the input can be compared to data already in the system and, thus, the set of choices available to the system is limited.

Several algorithms for finding the best matches to a given input using similarity testing exist. Some systems, including a dial-by-name, voice-activated telephone system, have been deployed commercially. Details of these algorithms are beyond the scope of this text; see the bibliographic notes for references.

21.6.2 Continuous-Media Data

The most important types of continuous-media data are video and audio data (for example, a database of movies). Continuous-media systems are characterized by their high data volumes and real-time information-delivery requirements:

- Data must be delivered sufficiently fast that no gaps in the audio or video result.
- Data must be delivered at a rate that does not cause overflow of system buffers.
- Synchronization among distinct data streams must be maintained. This need arises, for example, when the video of a person speaking must show lips moving synchronously with the audio of the person speaking.

21.6.2.1 Multimedia Data Formats

Because of the large number of bytes required to represent multimedia data, it is essential that the latter be stored and transmitted in compressed form. For image data, the most widely used format is JPEG, named after the standards body that created it, the Joint Picture Experts Group. We can store video data by encoding each frame of video using JPEG format, but such an encoding is wasteful, since successive frames of a video are often nearly the same. The Motion Picture Experts Group (MPEG) has developed standards for encoding video and audio data that use commonalities among a sequence of frames to achieve a greater degree of compression. The MPEG-1 standard stores a minute of 30-frame-per-second video and audio in approximately 12.5 megabytes (as compared with approximately 75 megabytes for video using only JPEG). However, MPEG-1 encoding introduces some loss of video quality, to a level roughly comparable to that of VHS video tape. The MPEG-2 standard is designed for digital broadcast systems and digital video disks (DVD); it introduces only a negligible loss of video quality. MPEG-2 compresses 1 minute of video and audio to approximately 17 megabytes.

21.6.2.2 Video Servers

Video-on-demand servers are being developed by many vendors. Current systems are based on file systems, because existing database systems do not meet the need that these applications have for real-time response. The basic architecture of a video-on-demand system consists of the following:

- **Video server.** Multimedia data are stored on several disks (usually in a RAID configuration). Systems containing a large volume of data may use tertiary storage for less frequently accessed data.

- **Terminals.** People view multimedia data through various devices collectively referred to as *terminals*. Examples of such devices include personal computers or televisions attached to a small, inexpensive computer called a *set-top box*.
- **Network.** Transmission of multimedia data from a server to multiple terminals requires a high-capacity network. Asynchronous-transfer-mode (ATM) networks are used frequently for this purpose.

We envision that video-on-demand service eventually will become ubiquitous, in the way that cable and broadcast television are currently. At present, the main applications of video-server technology are in offices (for training, viewing recorded talks and presentations, and the like), in hotels, and in video-production facilities.

21.7 Mobility and Personal Databases

Large-scale, commercial databases have traditionally been stored in central computing facilities. In the case of distributed database applications, there has usually been strong central database and network administration. Two technology trends have combined to create applications in which this assumption of central control and administration is not entirely correct:

1. The increasingly widespread use of personal computers, and, more important, of laptop or "notebook" computers
2. The development of a relatively low-cost wireless digital communication infrastructure, based on wireless local-area networks, cellular digital packet networks, and other technologies

Mobile computing has proved useful in many applications. Many business travelers use laptop computers to enable them to work and to access data en route. Delivery services use mobile computers to assist in package tracking. Emergency-response services use mobile computers at the scene of disasters, medical emergencies, and the like to access information and to enter data pertaining to the situation. New applications of mobile computers continue to emerge.

Wireless computing creates a situation where machines no longer have fixed locations and network addresses. This complicates query processing, since it becomes difficult to determine the optimal location at which to materialize the result of a query. In some cases, the location of the user is a parameter of the query. An example is a traveler's information system that provides data on hotels, roadside services, and the like to motorists. Queries about services that are ahead on the current route must be processed based on knowledge of the user's location, direction of motion, and speed.

Energy (battery power) is a scarce resource for mobile computers. This limitation influences many aspects of system design. Among the more interesting consequences of the need for energy efficiency is the use of scheduled data broadcasts to reduce the need for mobile systems to transmit queries.

Increasing amounts of data may reside on machines administered by users, rather than by database administrators. Furthermore, these machines may, at times, be disconnected from the network. In many cases, there is a conflict between the user's need to continue to work while disconnected and the need for global data consistency.

In Sections 21.7.1 through 21.7.4, we discuss techniques in use and under development to deal with the problems of mobility and personal computing.

21.7.1 A Model of Mobile Computing

The mobile-computing environment consists of mobile computers, referred to as *mobile hosts*, and a wired network of computers. Mobile hosts communicate with the wired network via computers referred to as *mobile support stations*. Each mobile support station manages those mobile hosts within its *cell*—that is, the geographical area that it covers. Mobile hosts may move between cells, thus necessitating a *handoff* of control from one mobile support station to another. Since mobile hosts may, at times, be powered down, a host may leave one cell and rematerialize later at some distant cell. Therefore, moves between cells are not necessarily between adjacent cells. Within a small area, such as a building, mobile hosts may be connected by a wireless local-area network that provides lower-cost connectivity than would a wide-area cellular network, and that reduces the overhead of handoffs.

It is possible for mobile hosts to communicate directly without the intervention of a mobile support station. However, such communication can occur between only nearby hosts.

The size and power limitations of many mobile computers have led to alternative memory hierarchies. Instead of, or in addition to, disk storage, flash memory, which we discussed in Section 10, may be included. If the mobile host includes a hard disk, the disk may be allowed to spin down when it is not in use, to save energy.

21.7.2 Routing and Query Processing

A consequence of the mobile-computing model is that the route between a pair of hosts may change over time if one of the two hosts is mobile. This simple fact has a dramatic effect at the network level, since location-based network addresses are no longer constants within the system. These networking issues are beyond the scope of this text.

Another consequence of the mobile-computing model directly affects database query processing. As we saw in Chapter 18, we must consider communication costs when we choose a distributed query-processing strategy. Mobility results in dynamically changing communication costs, thus complicating the optimization process. Furthermore, there are competing notions of cost to consider:

- **User time** is a highly valuable commodity in many business applications

- **Connection time** is the unit by which monetary charges are assigned in some cellular systems
- **Number of bytes, or packets, transferred** is the unit by which charges are computed in digital cellular systems
- **Time-of-day based charges** vary based on whether communication occurs during peak or off-peak periods
- **Energy** is limited. Often, battery power is a scarce resource whose use must be optimized. A basic principle of radio communication is that it requires less energy to receive than to transmit radio signals. Thus, transmission and reception of data impose different power demands on the mobile host.

21.7.3 Broadcast Data

It is often desirable for frequently requested data to be broadcast in a continuous cycle by mobile support stations, rather than transmitted to mobile hosts on demand. A typical application of broadcast data is stock-market price information. There are two reasons for using broadcast data. First, the mobile host avoids the energy cost for transmitting data requests. Second, the broadcast data can be received by a large number of mobile hosts at once, at no extra cost. Thus, the available transmission bandwidth is utilized more effectively.

Mobile hosts can then receive data when those data are transmitted, rather than consuming energy by transmitting a request. The mobile host may have local nonvolatile storage available to cache the broadcast data when those data are received, for possible later use. Given a query, the mobile host may optimize energy costs by determining whether it can process that query using only cached data. If the cached data are insufficient, there are two options: Wait for the data to be broadcast, or transmit a request for data. To make this decision, the mobile host must know when the relevant data will be broadcast.

Broadcast data may be transmitted according to a fixed schedule or a changeable schedule. In the former case, the mobile host uses the known fixed schedule to determine when the relevant data will be transmitted. In the latter case, the broadcast schedule must itself be broadcast at a well-known radio frequency and at well-known time intervals.

In effect, the broadcast medium can be modeled as a disk with a high latency. Requests for data can be thought of as being serviced when the requested data are broadcast. The transmission schedules behave like indices on the disk. The use of broadcast data as part of a mobile-information-system environment is under study. The bibliographic notes list recent research papers in this area.

21.7.4 Disconnectivity and Consistency

Since wireless communication may be paid for on the basis of connection time, there is an incentive for certain mobile hosts to be disconnected for substantial periods. During these periods of disconnection, the mobile host may remain in operation. The user of the mobile host may issue queries and updates on data that reside or are cached locally. This situation creates several problems, among which the most noteworthy are the following:

- **Recoverability:** Updates entered on a disconnected machine may be lost if the mobile host experiences a catastrophic failure. Since the mobile host represents a single point of failure, stable storage cannot be simulated well.
- **Consistency:** Locally cached data may become out of date, but the mobile host cannot discover this situation until it is reconnected. Likewise, updates occurring in the mobile host cannot be propagated until reconnection occurs. We explored this problem in Chapter 18, where we discussed network partitioning, and we elaborate on it here.

In wired distributed systems, partitioning is considered to be a failure mode; in mobile computing, partitioning via disconnection is part of the normal mode of operation. It is therefore necessary to allow data access to proceed despite partitioning, even at the risk of some loss of consistency.

For data updated by only the mobile host, it is a simple matter to propagate those updates when the mobile host reconnects. However, if the mobile host caches read-only copies of data that may be updated by other computers, the cached data may become inconsistent. When the mobile host is connected, it can be sent *invalidation reports* that inform it of out-of-date cache entries. However, when the mobile host is disconnected, it may miss an invalidation report. A simple solution to this problem is to invalidate the entire cache on reconnection, but such an extreme solution is highly costly. Several caching schemes are cited in the bibliographic notes.

If updates can occur at both the mobile host and elsewhere, detecting conflicting updates is more difficult. Version-numbering–based schemes have been developed to allow updates of shared files from disconnected hosts. These schemes do not guarantee that the updates will be consistent. Rather, they guarantee that, if two hosts independently update the same version of a document, the clash will be detected eventually, when the hosts exchange information either directly or through a common host. The basic idea is for each host i to store, with its copy of each document d, a *version vector*—that is, a set of version numbers $\{V_{d,i,j}\}$, with one entry for each other host j on which the document could potentially be updated. When a host i updates a document d, it increments the version number $V_{d,i,i}$.

Whenever two hosts i and j connect with each other, they exchange updated documents, so that both obtain new versions of the documents. However, before exchanging documents, the hosts have to discover whether the copies are consistent:

1. If the version vectors are the same on both hosts—that is, for each k, $V_{d,i,k} = V_{d,j,k}$—then the copies of document d are identical.
2. If, for each k, $V_{d,i,k} \leq V_{d,j,k}$, and the version vectors are not identical, then the copy of document d at host i is older than the one at host j. That is, the copy of document d at host j was obtained by one or more modifications

of the copy of the document at host i. Host i replaces its copy of d, as well as its copy of the version vector for d, with the copies from host j.

3. If there is a pair of hosts k and l such that $V_{d,i,k} < V_{d,j,k}$ and $V_{d,i,l} > V_{d,j,l}$, then the copies are *inconsistent*; that is, the copy of d at i contains updates performed by host k that have not been propagated to host j, and, similarly, the copy of d at j contains updates performed by host l that have not been propagated to host i. Then, the copies of d are inconsistent, since two or more updates have been performed on d independently. Manual intervention may be required to merge the updates.

The preceding version-vector scheme was initially designed to deal with failures in distributed file systems. The scheme gained importance because mobile computers often store copies of files that are also present on server systems, in effect resulting in a distributed file system that is often disconnected. Another application of the scheme has been in groupware systems, where hosts are connected periodically, rather than continuously, and must exchange updated documents. The version-vector scheme also has applications in replicated databases.

The version-vector scheme, however, fails to address the most difficult and most important issue arising from updates to shared data—the reconciliation of inconsistent copies of data. Many applications can perform reconciliation automatically by executing in each computer those operations that had performed updates on remote computers during the period of disconnection. This solutions works if update operations commute—that is, they generate the same result, regardless of the order in which they are executed. Alternative techniques may be available in certain applications; in the worst case, however, it must be left to the users to resolve the inconsistencies. Dealing with such inconsistency automatically, and assisting users in resolving inconsistencies that cannot be handled automatically, remains an area of research.

Another weakness is that the version-vector scheme requires substantial communication between a reconnecting mobile host and that host's mobile support station. Consistency checks can be delayed until the data are needed, although this delay may increase the overall inconsistency of the database.

The potential for disconnection and the cost of wireless communication limit the practicality of transaction-processing techniques discussed in Chapter 18 for distributed systems. Often, it is preferable to let users prepare transactions on mobile hosts, but to require that, instead of executing the transactions locally, they submit transactions to a server for execution. Transactions than span more than one computer and that include a mobile host face long-term blocking during transaction commit, unless disconnectivity is rare or predictable.

21.8 Information-Retrieval Systems

The field of *information retrieval* has developed in parallel with the field of databases. The traditional model used in this field is as follows. Information is organized into documents, and it is assumed that there is a large number of documents. The process of information retrieval consists of locating relevant documents, based on user input, such as keywords or example documents.

Typical examples of information-retrieval systems are online library catalogs, and online document-management systems such as those that store newspaper articles. The data in such systems are organized as a collection of *documents*; a newspaper article or a catalog entry (in a library catalog) are examples of documents. A user of such a system may want to retrieve a particular document or a particular class of documents. The intended documents are typically described by a set of *keywords*—for example, the keywords "database system" may be used to locate books on database systems, and the keywords "stock" and "scandal" may be used to locate articles about stock-market scandals. Documents have associated with them a set of keywords, and documents whose keywords contain those supplied by the user are retrieved.

There are several differences between this model and the models used in traditional database systems.

- Database systems deal with several operations that are not addressed in information-retrieval systems. For instance, database systems deal with updates, with the associated transactional requirements of concurrency control and durability. These matters are viewed as less important in information systems. Similarly, database systems deal with structured information organized with relatively complex data models (such as the relational model or object-oriented data models), whereas information-retrieval systems traditionally have used a much simpler model, where the information in the database is organized simply as a collection of unstructured documents.
- Information-retrieval systems deal with several issues that have not been addressed adequately in database systems. For instance, the field of information retrieval has dealt with the problems of managing unstructured documents, such as approximate searching using keywords, and of retrieving documents based on the degree of relevance of the documents to the query.

21.8.1 Queries

Keyword-based information retrieval is common not only in information systems that store text data, but also in systems that store other kinds of data, such as multimedia data (audio or video clips, or still-picture images). Descriptive keywords can be created for multimedia data. A movie may have associated with it keywords such as its title, director, actors, type, and so on.

Information-retrieval systems based on keywords often allow queries to use expressions formed out of the keywords. A user could ask for all documents that contain the keywords "motorcycle *and* maintenance," or documents that contain the keywords "computer *or* micro-processor," or even documents that contain the keyword "computer *but not* database."

Consider the problem of locating catalog entries for books about motorcycle maintenance using the keywords "motorcycle" and "maintenance." Suppose that the keywords for each catalog entry are the words in the title and the names of the authors. The catalog entry of a book called *Motorcycle Repair* would not be retrieved, since the word "maintenance" does not occur in its title.

We can solve that problem by making use of *synonyms*. Each word can have a set of synonyms defined, and the occurrence of a word can be replaced by the *or* of all its synonyms (including the word itself). Thus, the query "motorcycle *and* repair" can be replaced by "motorcycle *and* (repair *or* maintenance)." This query would find the desired catalog entry.

Another important issue in information retrieval is the degree of *relevance* of a document. Suppose that in addition to the title and authors, a list of topics covered in the book is created, and is used as a portion of the keywords in the catalog. There may be a number of books on car racing that include sections on cars and motorcycles, as well as a section on maintenance. The keywords "motorcycle" and "maintenance" would be associated with the catalog entry, and all these books would be retrieved in response to the query on motorcycle maintenance, in addition to the books on motorcycle maintenance. However, these other books are only of marginal relevance to the query. A book where the keywords "motorcycle" and "maintenance" occur close to each other is more likely to be relevant than one where they occur far apart. Some information-retrieval systems permit queries to specify that the two words should occur one after another in the text, or within the same sentence. In general, documents where the specified keywords occur close to one another is more likely to be relevant than one where they appear far apart. Documents that contain all the specified keywords can then be given a score of likely relevance based on the nearness of the keywords, and can be sorted in order of relevance when presented to the user. If the list is long, the system is free to present only the most relevant few documents.

Certain information-retrieval systems permit *similarity-based retrieval*. Here, the user can give the system a document A, and ask the system to retrieve documents that are "similar" to A. The similarity of two documents may be defined, for example, based on common keywords. If the set of documents similar to A is large, the system may present the user a few of the documents, allow him to choose the most relevant few, and start a new search based on similarity to A *and* to the chosen documents.

21.8.2 Indexing of Documents

An effective index structure is important for efficient processing of queries in an information-retrieval system. This system can locate documents that contain a specified keyword using an *inverted index*, which maps each keyword K_i to the set S_i of (identifiers of) the documents that contain K_i. To support relevance ranking based on proximity of keywords, such an index may provide not just identifiers of documents, but also a list of locations in the document where the keyword appears. Since such indices must be stored on disk, the index organization also attempts to minimize the number of I/O operations to retrieve the set of documents that contain a keyword. Thus, the system may attempt to keep the set of documents for a keyword in consecutive disk pages.

Each keyword may be contained in a large number of documents; hence, a compact representation is critical to keep space usage of the index low. Thus, the sets of documents for a keyword are maintained in a compressed form. So that storage space is saved, the index is sometimes stored such that the retrieval is approximate; a few relevant documents may not be retrieved (called a *false drop*), or a few irrelevant documents may be retrieved (called a *false positive*). A good index structure will not have *any* false drops, but may permit a few false positives; the system can filter them away later by looking at the keywords that they actually contain.

Two metrics are used to measure how well an information-retrieval system is able to answer queries. The first, *precision*, measures what percentage of the retrieved documents are actually relevant to the query. The second, *recall*, measures what percentage of the documents relevant to the query were retrieved.

The *and* operation finds documents that contain all of a specified set of keywords $K_1, K_2, \ldots, K_n$. We implement the *and* operation by first retrieving the sets of document identifiers $S_1, S_2, \ldots, S_n$ of all documents that contain the respective keywords. The intersection, $S_1 \cap S_2 \cap \ldots \cap S_n$, of the sets gives the document identifiers of the desired set of documents. The *or* operation gives the set of all documents that contain at least one of the keywords $K_1, K_2, \ldots, K_n$; We implement the *or* operation by computing the union, $S_1 \cup S_2 \cup \ldots \cup S_n$, of the sets. The *but not* operation finds documents that do not contain a specified keyword K_i. Given a set of document identifiers S, we can eliminate documents that contain the specified keyword K_i by taking the difference $S - S_i$, where S_i is the set of identifiers of documents that contain the keyword K_i.

A *full-text index* on a document uses every word in the document as a keyword; such an index can be used on short documents. However, almost all text documents contain words such as "and," "or," "a," and so on, and hence these words are useless for indexing purposes. Information-retrieval systems define a set of words called *stop words*, containing one-hundred or so of the most common words, and remove this set from the document when indexing; such words are not allowed as keywords in queries either.

21.8.3 Browsing and Hypertext

Information systems were initially conceived primarily as catalog systems, such as library catalogs. The actual documents were stored outside the system. However, as disk capacities have increased greatly and more documents are created and stored online, information-retrieval systems are now being used to store the actual documents as well. Therefore, current-generation information systems allow the user to view documents that are stored online.

A typical library user may use a catalog to locate a book for which she is looking. When she retrieves the book from the shelf, however, she is likely to *browse* through other books that are located nearby. Libraries organize books such that related books are kept close together. Hence, a book that is physically near the desired book may be of interest as well, making it worthwhile for users to browse through such books.

To keep related books close together, libraries use a *classification hierarchy*. Books on science are classified together. Within this set of books, there is a finer classification, with computer-science books organized together, mathematics

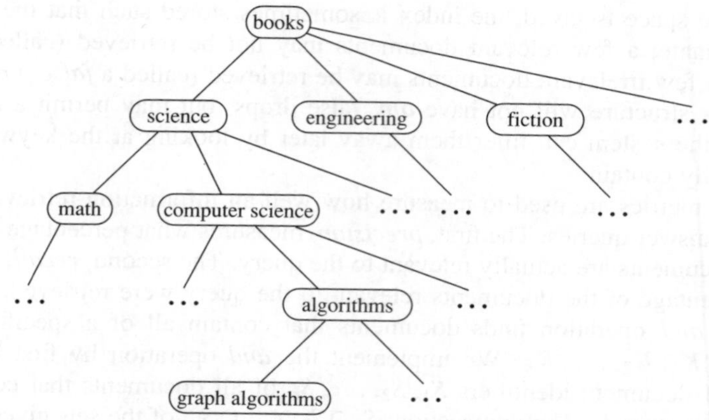

Figure 21.11 A classification hierarchy for a library system.

books organized together, and so on. Since there is a relation between mathematics and computer science, relevant sets of books are stored close to each other physically. At yet another level in the classification hierarchy, computer-science books are broken down into subareas, such as operating systems, languages, or algorithms. Figure 21.11 illustrates a classification hierarchy that may be used by a library. Because books can be kept at only one place, each book in a library is classified into exactly one spot in the classification hierarchy.

In an information-retrieval system, there is no great need to store related documents close together—the speed of disk access is high enough that disk-arm movement is typically not a major performance issue in such systems. However, such systems need to *organize documents logically* so as to permit browsing. Thus, such a system could use a classification hierarchy similar to one that libraries use, and, when a particular document is displayed, it can display a brief description of books that are close in the hierarchy.

In an information-retrieval system, there is no need to keep a document in a single spot in the hierarchy. A book that talks of mathematics for computer scientists could be classified under mathematics as well as under computer science. All that is stored at each spot is an identifier of the document (that is, a pointer to the document), and it is easy to fetch the contents of the document by using the identifier.

As a result of this flexibility, not only can a book be classified under two locations, but also a subarea in the classification hierarchy can itself occur under two areas. The class of "graph algorithm" books can appear both under mathematics and under computer science. Thus, the classification hierarchy is now a directed acyclic graph (DAG), as shown in Figure 21.12. A graph-algorithm book may appear in a single location in the DAG, but can be reached via multiple paths.

In response to a query, the information-retrieval system can not only display related documents, but also even display related classes in the classification hierarchy. The user can then look at all books (or subclasses) within that class.

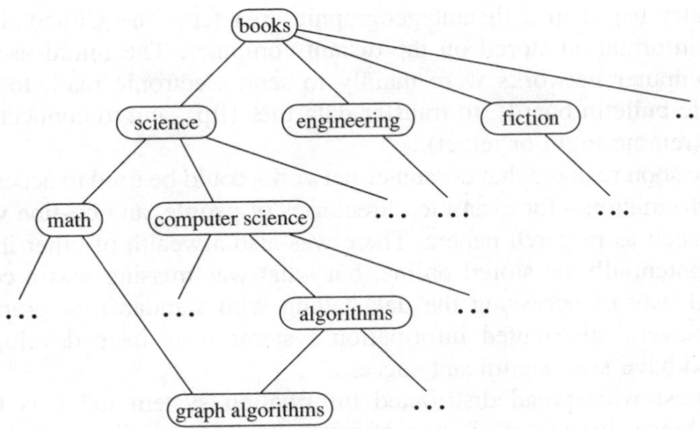

Figure 21.12 A classification DAG for a library information-retrieval system.

A typical document, such as a textbook or a research paper, has a list of references to other documents that provide related information. The references provide the name of the document, the authors, the publisher; the system uses these keywords to locate the document. However, if the document is already in the system, the user can provide an identifier of the document with the reference, avoiding the need for a query using keywords.

Hypertext systems are based on this idea of storing identifiers of other documents; they provide a powerful facility where the user can easily switch from the first document to the others. Typically, she does so using a point-and-click interface, where a simple mouse click on the display screen on top of the referred document retrieves and displays the document. *Hypertext* systems also permit references to specific locations within the or other documents. A click on such a link takes the user to the desired position within the document. Hypertext systems provide an extremely convenient way of browsing documents.

An early hypertext system was HyperCard, introduced on the Apple Macintosh computer systems. *Hypermedia* systems provide not only text, but also other media, such as images, videos, audio clips, and so on. The popular *online encyclopedias* today provide such facilities, as well as keyword-based retrieval. Unlike traditional encyclopedias, which provide only text and images, these systems include audio and video segments. We shall use the word *hypertext* to refer to hypermedia systems as well.

Today, *distributed hypertext* systems even permit references to documents stored at other sites in a distributed system. We study the most popular such system, the World Wide Web, in Section 21.10.

21.9 Distributed Information Systems

One of the most important developments in the field of computer science in recent years has been the rise of long-distance computer networks, in particular the global Internet. It is now easy for a person located in one area (say, India) to connect to a computer based in a distant geographic area (say, the United States), and to retrieve information stored on the distant computer. The initial uses of long-distance computer networks were mainly to send electronic mail, to post news on electronic bulletin boards, to transfer data files (ftp), and to connect to remote computers (remote login or telnet).

People soon realized that computer networks could be used to access a wealth of useful information—for example, directories of people, and on-line versions of documents such as research papers. There was also a wealth of other information that could potentially be stored online, but what was missing was a convenient, standardized way of accessing the data, along with standardized graphical user interfaces. Several distributed information systems have been developed to fill this gap, and have seen significant success.

The most widespread distributed information system today is the *World Wide Web*. Since this system is one of much interest, we discuss it in detail in Section 21.10.

The Internet *Gopher* from the University of Minnesota, and the *Wide Area Information System*, were two of the early distributed information systems, that predated the World Wide Web. They represent two distinct approaches to organizing and retrieving information in a distributed system.

A Gopher system consists of servers and clients. A Gopher server organizes data into directories, much like a classification hierarchy. The Gopher client initially communicates with a server, and displays the top-level directory of the server hierarchy as a menu, as illustrated in Figure 21.13. The user can then choose an item in the menu, which can be another directory in the hierarchy, or a document, or a link to a directory on another server. If the chosen item is a directory in the hierarchy, the data in the directory are displayed as a menu. If the chosen item is a document, the document is displayed. If the chosen item is a link

```
              Internet Gopher Information Client 2.0 pl8

      University of XYZ Computer Science Department Gopher

 -->  1.  WELCOME
      2.  Information About Gopher/
      3.  About the University of XYZ CS Department
      4.  University of XYZ Campus Information/
      5.  Search Gopher Titles at the Univ. of Minnesota <?>
      6.  University of Minnesota Gopher (Gopher Central)/
      7.  Libraries/
      8.  Phone Books/
      9.  Other Gopher and Information Servers/
      10. Internet file server (ftp) sites/


Press ? for Help, q to Quit, u to go up a menu      Page: 1/1
```

Figure 21.13 A sample Gopher client display.

to a directory on another Gopher server, the client connects to the new Gopher server and displays the directory as a menu. Thus, the Gopher system allows a seamless connection to remote servers. Logically, there is no difference between a local and a remote server.

The model of information retrieval in a Gopher system is based on browsing and navigating a directory hierarchy. However, an item in a Gopher directory may be a link to other kinds of servers, such as index servers, which can provide keyword-based indexing capabilities. Figure 21.13 illustrates typical topics stored on a Gopher server. The figure also illustrates menu items corresponding to documents, corresponding to index servers (with a "<?>" suffix), and corresponding to directories (with a "/" suffix)

The Wide Area Information System (WAIS) follows a different approach to information retrieval. The basic model in WAIS is the indexing of information by server systems. Each server stores information on one or more subjects, and supports a powerful keyword-based indexing mechanism on its local data. In addition, each server maintains a directory, or description, of other servers. The directory is a summary of what kind of information is stored at the server, and how to access that information. If a query is presented at a WAIS server, the server uses its directory information to tell the user what other servers may have relevant information. It is infeasible to run a query at every WAIS server in the Internet, since there is an enormous number of such servers. The directory provides a means of narrowing down the search, as well as a means of freeing the user from remembering which servers may contain relevant information for a query.

21.10 The World Wide Web

The *World Wide Web* (*WWW*, or *Web*) is a distributed information system based on hypertext. Documents stored under the Web can be of one of several types. The most common type are hypertext documents formatted according to the HyperText Markup Language (HTML), which itself is based on the Standard Generalized Markup Language (SGML). HTML documents contain text, font specifications, and other formatting instructions. Links to other documents (whether local or remote) can be associated with regions of the text. Images can also be referenced with appropriate formatting instructions (such as a link to an image file).

The user of a Web system sees formatted text along with images, rather than the raw text with formatting instructions. Formatted text with images is visually much more appealing than is plain text. Further, the displayed document is a hypertext document; with an appropriate browser, the user can click on a region that has a link associated with it, and the document pointed to by the link will be displayed. Thus, the hypertext interface to the Web forms a powerful and visually attractive browsing interface. More recently, Web browsers have begun to support a programming language called *Java*, which allows documents to contain programs that are executed at the user's site. Thus, documents can now be *active*, rather than just passive.

In Sections 21.10.1 through 21.10.5, we study the basic technology underlying the Web, and examine how the Web is likely to influence database systems.

21.10.1 Universal Resource Locators

Recall that a hypertext system must be able to store pointers to documents. In the Web, the functionality of pointers is provided by *Universal Resource Locator*s (URLs). The following is an example of an URL:

http://www.bell-labs.com/topic/book/db-book

The first part of the URL indicates how the document is to be accessed: "http" indicates that the document is to be accessed using the HyperText Transfer Protocol, which is a protocol for transferring HTML documents. The second part gives the unique name of a machine on the Internet. The rest of the URL is the path name of the file on the machine.

Thus, URLs provide a globally unique name for each document that can be accessed from a Web system. Since URLs are human readable, a human can use them directly to access a desired document, instead of navigating down a path from a predefined location. Since they allow the use of an Internet machine name, they are global in scope, and people can use them to create links across machines.

Unlike in the Gopher system, where what is displayed is either a document or a directory, a HTML document display is simultaneously a document and a directory. Another important difference is that, since URLs are human readable, and can specify a file in the system, it is easy for anyone on a machine connected to the Internet to create a document that other users can then access using the Web. Gopher systems tend to be set up and controlled by system administrators. The Web is much more open: Any user can create documents on the Web, and can give the URL to anyone else. In fact, as a result, the Web is almost anarchic—there is no central authority governing anything on the Web. Many Internet users today have *home pages* on the Web; such pages often contain information about users' personal and work lives.

The fact that a URL can specify how to access a document is also of importance. In addition to supporting http, Web clients support other protocols for transferring documents, such as the widely used file transfer protocol (ftp). The Web client even provides a hypertext-based front-end to the ftp services.

21.10.2 Web Servers

HTTP provides powerful features, beyond the simple transfer of documents, such as encryption for security. The document name in a URL may identify an executable program that, when run, generates a HTML document. When a HTTP server receives a request for such a document, it executes the program, and sends back the HTML document that is generated. Further, the Web client can pass extra arguments with the name of the document; they are then passed as arguments when the program is executed. Thus, the generated document can depend on the arguments that were passed in.

As a result of these features, a Web server can easily serve as a front-end to a variety of information services. To install a new service on the Web, a person needs only to create and install an executable program that provides the service. The language supported by the Web, HTML, provides a graphical user interface to the information service.

21.10.3 Display Languages

Today's computer systems not only provide a simple character-based interface, but also support graphics, multiple fonts, color, and so on, which options can greatly enhance the quality of displayed information. However, there is a variety of standards for graphical displays, and different kinds of computers have different interfaces. It is hard to write a program that can support multiple display interfaces directly. Page-description languages, such as PostScript, and standard text-formatting languages, such as nroff or TEX/LATEX, provide standardized interfaces, but have a large set of features, making them slow and thus unsuitable for interactive use.

Text-markup languages, such as the Standard Generalized Markup Language (SGML), were developed to fill a void between plain text and page-description or text-formatting languages. The markup languages provide simple formatting commands, such as paragraph separators and numbered or itemized lists, as well as a degree of control over displayed fonts. Thus, they provide a standard output interface for programs.

Text-markup languages are particularly important for general-purpose distributed information systems, since the information to be displayed ought to be formatted in a pleasing manner, rather than being merely plain text. An alternative way to implement such formatting would be for each information service to run a special-purpose program at the client site—which solution is obviously inconvenient for a user who wants to access many information services.

21.10.3.1 HyperText Markup Language

SGML provides a grammar for specifying document formats based on standard markup annotations. HTML is a general-purpose hypertext display language, based on SGML. It specifies a document format that allows text-formatting commands, as well as hypertext-link commands and image-display commands. Figure 21.14 shows an example of the source of a HTML document. Figure 21.15 shows the displayed image corresponding to the same document.

HTML also provides limited input features. For example, an HTML document can specify that a form should be displayed. The HTML display program (that is, the Web client) allows the user to fill in entries in the form. Menus and other graphical input facilities are also provided, and let the user select a menu item, move a slider bar to select a value in a range, point to and click on a location in an image (such as a map), and so on. When the user has finished entering values, she can press a "submit" button.

At this point, values entered by the user are collected, and the Web client sends a request for the document, with the values entered by the user as arguments.

```
<title>WWW Home Page</title>
<img src="lucent_logo.gif"> <img src="iitb-logo.gif">
<hr>
<h3> <a href=
     "http://www.bell-labs.com/topic/books/db-book">
     Database System Concepts:  Home Page </a>
</h3>
<h3> Information Services </h3>
<dl>
     <dd> <a href="http://www.altavista.digital.com">
           The Altavista Information
           Gathering Service</a>
     <dd> <a href=
           "http://www.informatik.uni-trier.de/~ley/db">
           Database and Logic Programming
           Bibliography</a>
     <dd> <a href="http://cs.indiana.edu/cstr/search">
           Indiana University's Unified
           CS Tech. Report Service</a>
     <dd> <a href="http://www.ncstrl.org">
           Networked Computer Science
           Tech. Report Library</a>
</dl>
```

Figure 21.14 A portion of an HTML source text.

This document is an executable program, and the Web server invokes the program with the specified arguments. As described earlier, the program generates an HTML document, which is then sent back to be displayed

The actual layout of the screen, and the specific forms to be filled and menu items to be chosen, are all under the control of the HTML document. Thus, HTML provides a graphical user interface that can run on almost any computer. However, there is no continuous connection between the client and the server; the server keeps no history of its interaction with the client, and all state information has to be stored at the client and sent to the server with each communication. In spite of these limitations (which may well be removed in the future), HTML it is likely to prove of increasing importance to distributed information systems in the future.

21.10.3.2 Java

A more recent development has been the release of the Java language, which allows documents to be *active*, carrying out activities such as animation by executing programs at the local site, rather than just presenting passive text and graphics. The Java language, developed by Sun, is an interpreted language that resembles C++. The Java language also provides standardized libraries of graphical user-interface functions. When a Java program is compiled, instead of generating machine code, the compiler generates byte code, which can be executed

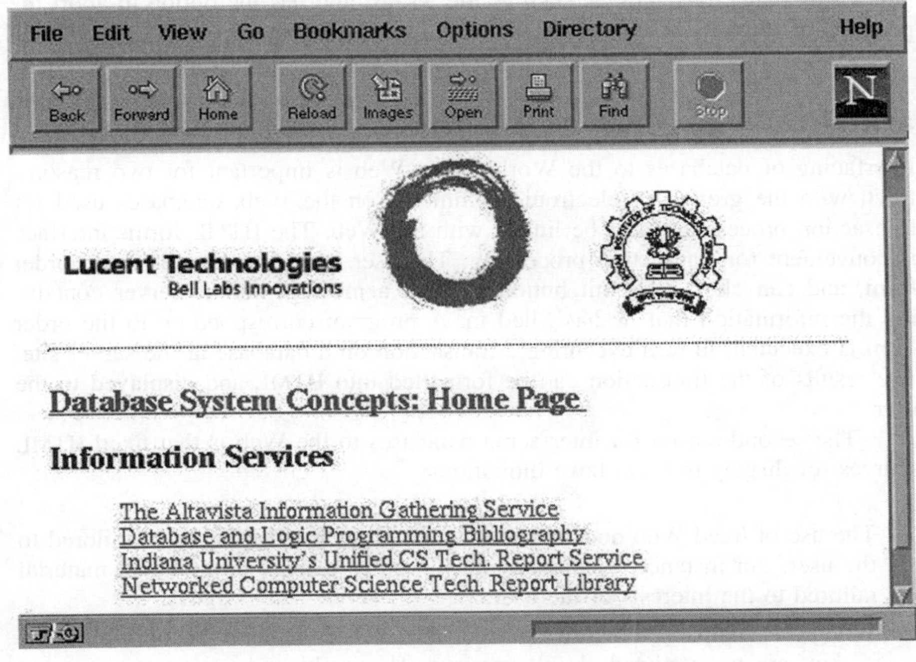

Figure 21.15 Display of HTML source from Figure 21.14.

on an interpreter. Java interpreters have been written for practically every platform (combination of hardware and operating system), and hence the same Java program can run on practically any platform.

As a result of the uniformity of the Java environment, Java programs can be stored at server sites just like HTML documents, and can be downloaded and executed by any client site, regardless of the client platform. Thus, Java provides a convenient way of distributing (small) programs. The primary use of such programs is flexible interaction with the user, beyond the limited interaction power provided by HTML and HTML forms. Further, executing programs at the client site speeds up interaction greatly, compared to every interaction being sent to a server site for processing.

With the power of downloading and executing programs at the click of a button comes the danger of downloaded programs causing damage, such as deleting files, at the client site. Unlike system programs, downloaded programs have no authority, such as a vendor, which has checked them for absence of malicious behavior. Therefore, it is important that Java programs be allowed only those facilities that can cause no permanent damage, such as displaying data on the screen, and that they not be allowed to make system calls directly. Hence, Java interpreters have a security system built in. The security system ensures that the Java code does not make any system calls directly. The user is notified about potentially dangerous actions, such as file writes, and has the option to abort the program or to continue execution.

21.10.4 Web Interfaces to Databases

Interfacing of databases to the World Wide Web is important for two reasons. First, with the growth of electronic commerce on the Web, databases used for transaction processing must be linked with the Web. The HTML forms interface is convenient for transaction processing. The user can fill in details in an order form, and can click a submit button to send a message to the server containing the information that he has filled in. A program corresponding to the order form is executed, in turn executing a transaction on a database at the server site. The results of the transaction can be formatted into HTML and displayed to the user.

The second reason for interfacing databases to the Web is that fixed HTML sources for display to users have limitations:

- The use of fixed Web documents does not allow the display to be tailored to the user. For instance, a company may want to display promotional material tailored to the interests of the user.
- When the company data are updated, the Web documents become outdated if they are not updated simultaneously. The problem becomes more acute if multiple Web documents replicate important data, and all must be updated.

We can fix these problems by generating Web documents dynamically. When a document is requested, a program can be executed at the server site, which runs queries on the database, and generates a document based on the query results. The Web document displayed can be tailored to the user, based on user information stored in the database. Data in Web documents can also be defined by queries on a database, so that, whenever relevant data in the database are updated, the Web documents will be up-dated too.

Translating variables defined in HTML forms to SQL can involve making format conversions. Translating tables and other data generated by a database query into HTML can be even more tedious, since the programmer has to know about details such as field formats and sizes, and the number of tuples generated. Web interfaces to databases simplify these tasks. These interfaces are similar to report writers (see Section 19.6); in fact, the main difference is that, instead of generating formatted text, they generate HTML documents. The programmer can define a HTML document in a macro language with embedded SQL queries. Variables defined in HTML forms can be used directly in the embedded SQL queries. When the document is requested, a macro processor executes the SQL queries, and generates the actual HTML document that is sent to the user. The HTML document written in the macro language may have two parts — a forms-input interface, and a result-display interface. Interaction then occurs in two phases. In the first, the forms part of the HTML document is generated and is sent back to the client. When the client submits the form, the result part of the document is generated and is sent back.

21.10.5 Locating of Information on the Web

The Web provides a convenient way to get to, and to interact with, information sources across the Internet. However, a persistent problem facing the Web is the explosion of stored information, with little guidance to help the user to locate what is interesting.

One simple way in which users can find out about interesting information is simply to ask friends! In fact, that is how most information about interesting Web sites gets propagated even today. A second way, which is slightly more sophisticated, but is perhaps less useful, is for a user to note in her home page a list of the most interesting Web sites that she has seen. Other people can follow these links to locate interesting sites. Neither of these techniques is a particularly efficient means for locating information.

Let us step back and look at the world of tourism—visiting a place physically has similarities to visiting a place on the Web, to retrieve a document or to use an information service. Whereas time and money are constraints for tourism, time is usually the only constraint for visiting places on the Web. How do you decide what geographic places to visit? One source of information is friends who have traveled. Guide books tell you about places to visit. Libraries, with their classification of books, help you to browse related guide books easily. Finally, a library catalog lets you locate specific books.

There are rough counterparts to each of these sources on the Web. There are Web sites that provide information about other Web sites in a fashion similar to a guide book. Some of these sites even act as online shopping malls, collecting at one site services that let you shop for various goods via the Web. Some sites maintain a classification hierarchy of information about sites on the Web. You can follow the hierarchy to find desired Web sites.

The equivalent of the library catalog is the hardest information source to implement on the Web. In a library, every book that is purchased goes through the librarian, who adds an entry to the catalog. No such librarian exists on the Web. Who is to find what Web sites exist, and what they contain? A similar problem also exists for other information systems, such as the Gopher.

Distributed information-gathering systems perform the task of finding out what information exists on the Web. Whereas WAIS systems send queries to remote systems when users ask for information, distributed information-gathering systems periodically fetch information from remote systems, and create an index locally. The systems thus combines at one site information from multiple sources. Client programs can access the distributed information-gathering system and can pose queries, which the system answers using its locally stored index. Due to disk-space limitations, the documents typically are not stored within the information-gathering system; instead, pointers to the remotely located documents are returned as answers to a query.

An early example of such a system was the Computer Science Technical Report Index, which collects information about computer-science technical reports stored on-line at various ftp sites. A more ambitious system of this kind is the Archie system, which automatically follows Gopher links to locate information, and creates a centralized index of information found from various sites.

Various information-gathering systems, generically called *Web crawlers*, have been developed for locating and gathering information on the Web. They recursively follow hypertext links present in known documents to find other documents. The documents are retrieved, and information found in the document is added to a combined index; again, the document is not stored. These services run a daemon process in the background to find new sites by following links, obtain updated information from known sites, and discard sites that no longer exist, so that the information in the index is kept reasonably up to date.

With the explosive growth of the Web today, the workload of Web crawlers becomes progressively heavier, as more sites need to be indexed. Further, with a huge number of sites, a query may generate a correspondingly huge number of answers, and good techniques for distinguishing relevant sites from irrelevant sites will be required. However, Web crawlers have the significant advantage that no central authority is required for registering documents, so it is easy for users to create new documents and to have people locate the documents via an index. Indexing of data on the Web is an area of ongoing research.

Finding documents based on keywords is a simplistic form of query processing, compared to the query functionality provided by database systems. The problem with supporting more complex queries is that data on the Web typically are in the form of unstructured text, unlike the highly structured data stored in relational databases. *Semistructured data* are data that are mostly unstructured and have only some degree of structure. For instance, documents that are tagged with values for some or all of the attributes *author:*, *title:*, *subject:* and *keywords:* could be considered semistructured data. Query processing using semistructured data is another topic of ongoing research.

21.11 Summary

Decision-support systems are gaining in importance, as companies realize the value of the on-line data collected by their on-line transaction-processing systems. Proposed extensions to SQL, such as the **cube** operation, help to support generation of summary data. Data mining seeks to discover knowledge automatically, in the form of statistical rules and patterns from large databases. Data-visualization systems help humans to discover such knowledge visually. A data warehouse is a repository (or archive) of information gathered from multiple sources, stored under a unified schema, at a single site. Once gathered, the data are stored for a long period, permitting access to historical data for decision-support purposes.

Spatial databases are finding increasing use today to store computer-aided–design data as well as geographic data. Design data are stored primarily as vector data; geographic data consist of a combination of vector and raster data. Spatial-integrity constraints are important for design data. Vector data can be encoded as first-normal-form data, or can be stored using non–first-normal-form structures, such as lists. Special-purpose index structures are particularly important for accessing spatial data, and for processing spatial queries. R-trees are a two-dimensional extension of B-trees; with variants such as R+-trees and R*-trees, they have proved popular in spatial databases. Index structures that partition space in a regular fashion, such as quadtrees, help in processing spatial join queries.

Multimedia databases are growing in importance. Issues such as similarity-based retrieval and delivery of data at guaranteed rates are topics of current research.

Mobile computing systems have become common, leading to interest in database systems that can run on such systems. Query processing in such systems may involve lookups on server databases. The query cost model must include the cost of communication, including monetary cost and battery-power cost, which is relatively high for mobile systems. Broadcast is much cheaper per recipient than is point-to-point communication, and broadcast of data such as stock-market data helps mobile systems to pick up data inexpensively. Disconnected operation, use of broadcast data, and caching of data are three important issues being addressed in mobile computing.

Information-retrieval systems use a simpler data model than do database systems, but provide more powerful querying capabilities within the restricted model. Queries attempt to locate documents that are of interest by specifying, for example, sets of keywords. The query that a user has in mind usually cannot be stated precisely; hence, information-retrieval systems order answers based on potential relevance.

Distributed information systems that run on the Internet have seen explosive growth in recent years. The World Wide Web system supports browsing such information using the hypertext paradigm. Tools that integrate HTML with SQL ease the task of creating HTML front-ends to databases. Distributed information-gathering systems help people to find information on the Web.

Exercises

21.1. Consider the *balance* attribute of the *account* relation. Write an SQL query to compute a histogram of *balance* values, dividing the range 0 to the maximum account balance present, into three equal ranges.

21.2. Consider the *sales* relation from Section 21.2. Write an SQL query to compute cube operation on the relation, giving the relation shown in Figure 21.2. Do not use the **with cube** construct.

21.3. Suppose there are two classification rules, one which says that people with salaries between 10, 000 and 20, 000 have a credit rating of *good*, and another which says that people with salaries between 20, 000 and 30, 000 have a credit rating of *good*. Under what conditions can the rules be replaced, without any loss of information, by a single rule that says people with salaries between 10, 000 and 30, 000 have a credit rating of *good*.

21.4. Suppose half of all the transactions in a clothes shop purchase jeans, and one third of all transactions in the shop purchase t-shirts. Suppose also that half of the transactions that purchase jeans also purchase t-shirts. Write down all the (non-trivial) association rules you can deduce from the above information, giving support and confidence of each rule.

21.5. Consider the problem of finding *frequent item-sets*, that is, sets of items that are frequently purchased together. The *support* of an item-set is the number of transactions that purchase that every item in the item-set. An item-set is a frequent item-set if its support is greater than k, for some pre-defined k.

(*a*) Describe how to find the support for a given collection of item-sets using a single scan of the data. Assume that the item-sets and associated information, such as counts, will fit in memory.

(*b*) Suppose an item-set has support less than j. Show that no superset of this item-set can have support greater than or equal to j.

(*c*) Due to memory limitations, it is possible to find the support for only a small number of item-sets (as many as will fit in memory) in one scan of the data. Devise an algorithm for reducing the number of scans of the data (and thereby, the I/O required) for finding frequent item-sets, by finding support for as few item-sets as possible.

21.6. Describe benefits and drawbacks of a source-driven architecture for gathering of data at a data-warehouse, as compared to a destination-driven architecture.

21.7. Suppose you have a relation containing the x,y coordinates and names of restaurants. Suppose also that the only queries that will be asked are of the following form: the query specifies a point, and asks if there is a restaurant exactly at that point. Which type of index would be preferable: R-tree or B-tree? Why?

21.8. Consider two-dimensional vector data where the data items do not overlap. Is it possible to convert such vector data to raster data? If so, what are the drawbacks of storing raster data obtained by such conversion, instead of the original vector data?

21.9. Suppose you have a spatial database that supports region queries (with circular regions) but not nearest-neighbor queries. Describe an algorithm to find the nearest neighbor by making use of multiple region queries?

21.10. Suppose you want to store line segments in an R-tree. If a line segment is not parallel to the axes, the bounding box for it can be large, containing a large empty area.

- Describe the performance effect of having large bounding boxes, on queries that ask for line segments intersecting a given region.
- Briefly describe a technique to improve performance for such queries and give an example of its benefit.

  Hint: you can divide segments into smaller pieces.

21.11. What problems can occur in a continuous-media system if data is delivered either too slowly or too fast?

21.12. Describe how the ideas behind the RAID organization (Section 10.3) can be used in a broadcast-data environment, where there may occasionally be noise that prevents reception of part of the data being transmitted.

21.13. List 3 main features of mobile computing over wireless networks that are distinct from traditional distributed systems.

21.14. List 3 factors that need to be considered in query optimization for mobile computing that are not considered in traditional query optimizers.

21.15. Define a model of broadcast data in which the broadcast medium is a virtual disk. Describe how seek time, latency, and data-transfer rate for this virtual disk differ from the corresponding values for a typical hard disk.

21.16. Consider a database of documents in which all documents are kept in a central database. Copies of some documents are kept on mobile computers. Suppose that mobile computer A updates a copy of document 1 while it is disconnected, and, at the same time, mobile computer B updates a copy of document 2 while it is disconnected. Show how the version-vector scheme can ensure proper updating of the central database and mobile computers when a mobile computer re-connects.

21.17. Give an example to show that the version-vector scheme does not ensure serializability. (Hint: Use the example from Exercise 21.16, with the assumption that documents A and B are available on both mobile computers A and B, and take into account the possibility that a document may be read with it being updated.)

21.18. What is the difference between a false positive and a false drop? If it is essential that no relevant information be missed by an information retrieval query, is it acceptable to have either false positives or false drops? Why?

21.19. Suppose you want to find documents that contain at least k of a given set of n keywords. Suppose also you have a keyword index that gives you a (sorted) list of identifiers of documents that contain a specified keyword. Give an efficient algorithm to find the desired set of documents.

21.20. Give three main features of HTML that have lead to its enormous success.

21.21. Describe the main feature provided by Java that HTML lacks, and some of the benefits of this feature.

21.22. Describe some benefits of dynamic generation of Web pages from data stored in a database.

21.23. Describe three distinct ways a user can find information on the Web.

Bibliographic Notes

Gray et al. [1995] describe the data-cube operator. Harinarayan et al. [1996] describe techniques for efficient lazy implementation of the data-cube operator, to generate required aggregates on demand.

Fayyad et al. [1995] present an extensive collection of articles on knowledge discovery and data mining. Agrawal et al. [1993] provide an early overview of data mining in databases. Agrawal et al. [1992] describe data-mining techniques for classification; Ng and Han [1994] describe data-mining techniques based on spatial clustering. Srikant and Agrawal [1996] present techniques for deducing quantitative association rules.

Poe [1995] and Mattison [1996] provide textbook coverage of data warehousing. Zhuge et al. [1995] describe view maintenance in a data-warehousing environment. Larson and Yang [1985] and Dar et al. [1996] describe how to use materialized relations to answer queries.

There has been a great deal of work on spatial index structures, and Samet [1995b] provides a recent overview of the field. Samet [1990] provides a textbook coverage of spatial data structures. An early description of the quad tree is provided by Finkel and Bentley [1974]; Samet [1990, 1995b] describes numerous variants of quad trees. Bentley [1975] describes the k-d tree, and Robinson [1981] describes the k-d-B tree. The R-tree was originally presented in Guttman [1984]. Extensions of the R-tree are presented by Sellis et al. [1987], who describe the R^+ tree; Beckmann et al. [1990], who describe the R^* tree; and Kamel and Faloutsos [1992], who describe a parallel version of the R-tree.

Brinkhoff et al. [1993] discuss an implementation of spatial joins using R-trees. Lo and Ravishankar [1996], and Patel and DeWitt [1996] present partitioning-based methods for computation of spatial joins. Samet and Aref [1995] provide an overview of spatial data models, spatial operations, and the integration of spatial and nonspatial data. Indexing of handwritten documents is discussed in Aref et al. [1995a, 1995b], and Lopresti and Tomkins [1993]. Joins of approximate data are discussed in Barbará et al. [1992]. Evangelidis et al. [1995] present a technique for concurrent access to indices on spatial data.

Samet [1995a] describes research issues in multimedia database. Indexing of multimedia data is discussed in Faloutsos and Lin [1995]. Video servers are discussed in Anderson et al. [1992], Rangan et al. [1992], Özden et al. [1994], Freedman and DeWitt [1995], and Özden et al. [1996a]. Fault tolerance is discussed in Berson et al. [1995] and Özden et al. [1996b]. Reason et al. [1996] suggest alternative compression schemes for video transmission over wireless networks. Disk storage management techniques for video data are described in Chen et al. [1995], Chervenak et al. [1995], Özden et al. [1995a], and Özden et al. [1995b].

Information management in systems that include mobile computers is studied in Alonso and Korth [1993] and Imielinski and Badrinath [1994]. Imielinski and Korth [1996] present an introduction to mobile computing and a collection of research papers on the subject. Indexing of data broadcast over wireless media is considered in Imielinski et al. [1995]. Caching of data in mobile environments is discussed in Barbará and Imielinski [1994] and Acharya et al. [1995]. Disk management in mobile computers is addressed in Douglis et al. [1994].

The version-vector scheme for detecting inconsistency in distributed file systems is described by Popek et al. [1981], and by Parker et al. [1983].

Salton's book [1989] is a good textbook source for material on information-retrieval systems. Other work on text databases includes Gravano et al. [1994] and Tomasic et al. [1994]. There are numerous books about the Internet, which include material on the distributed information systems described in this chapter. Krol [1994] presents a description of the information systems, along with a directory of sources of information on the Internet. Most of the popular distributed information systems are available free of charge on the Internet; the most effective way to learn more about these systems is to use them. Nguyen and Srinivasan [1996] describe an interface between HTML and SQL, based on embedding SQL queries in HTML documents. There are several distributed information-gathering and indexing systems on the Web, one of the more popular of which is the Digital Altavista system at the URL http://www.altavista.digital.com. The Yahoo system, at the URL http://www.yahoo.com, provides an extensive classification hierarchy for Web sites.

APPENDIX A

NETWORK MODEL

In the relational model, the data and the relationships among data are represented by a collection of tables. The network model differs from the relational model in that data are represented by collections of *records*, and relationships among data are represented by *links*.

A.1 Basic Concepts

A network database consists of a collection of records connected to one another through links. A record is in many respects similar to an entity in the entity–relationship (E-R) model. Each record is a collection of fields (attributes), each of which contains only one data value. A link is an association between precisely two records. Thus, a link can be viewed as a restricted (binary) form of relationship in the sense of the E-R model.

As an illustration, consider a database representing a *customer-account* relationship in a banking system. There are two record types, *customer* and *account*. As we saw earlier, we can define the *customer* record type, using Pascal-like notation, as follows:

type *customer* = **record**
customer-name: string;
customer-street: string;
customer-city: string;
end

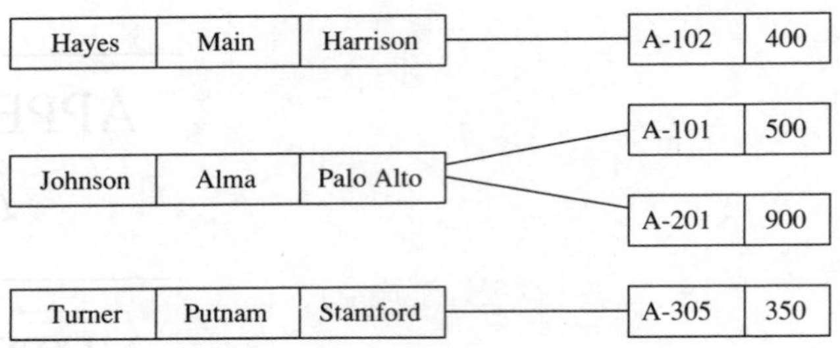

Figure A.1 Sample database.

The *account* record type can be defined as follows:

> **type** *account* = **record**
> *account-number*: string;
> *balance*: integer;
> **end**

The sample database in Figure A.1 shows that Hayes has account A-102, Johnson has accounts A-101 and A-201, and Turner has account A-305.

A.2 Data-Structure Diagrams

A *data-structure diagram* is a schema representing the design of a network database. Such a diagram consists of two basic components: boxes, which correspond to record types, and lines, which correspond to links. A data-structure diagram serves the same purpose as an E-R diagram; namely, it specifies the overall logical structure of the database. E-R diagrams can be translated into corresponding data-structure diagrams.

To illustrate, consider the E-R diagram of Figure A.2a, consisting of two entity sets, *customer* and *account*, related through a binary, many-to-many relationship *depositor*, with no descriptive attributes. This diagram specifies that a customer may have several accounts, and that an account may belong to several different customers. The corresponding data-structure diagram is illustrated in Figure A.2b. The record type *customer* corresponds to the entity set *customer*. It includes three fields—*customer-name*, *customer-street*, and *customer-city*—as defined above. Similarly, *account* is the record type corresponding to the entity set *account*. It includes the two fields *account-number* and *balance*. Finally, the relationship *depositor* has been replaced with the link *depositor*. If the relationship *depositor* were one to many from *customer* to *account*, then the link *depositor* would have an arrow pointing to *customer* record type. Similarly, if the relationship *depositor* were one to one, then the link *depositor* would have two arrows: one pointing to *account* record type, and one pointing to *customer* record type.

Consider the E-R diagram of Figure A.3a, which consists of three entity sets—*account*, *customer*, and *branch*—related through the general relationship *CAB* with no descriptive attribute. This diagram specifies that a customer may

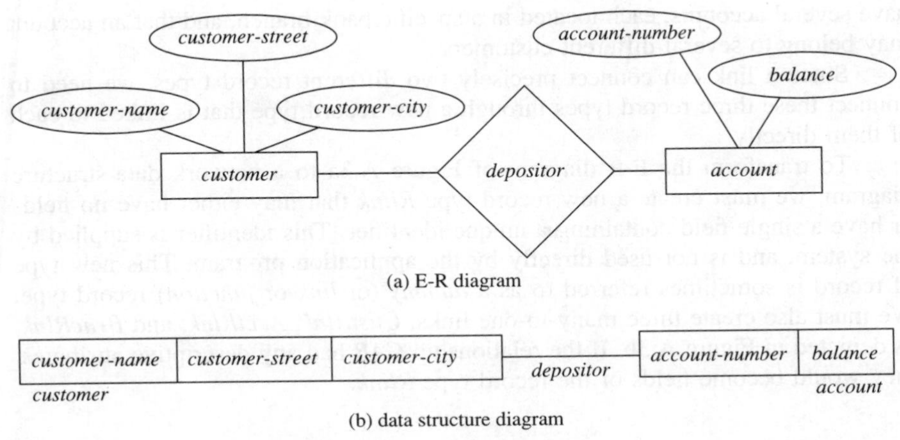

Figure A.2 E-R diagram and its corresponding data-structure diagram.

branch-city
branch-name
assets
branch
customer-street
account-number
balance
customer-name
customer-city
customer
CAB
account

(a) E-R diagram

customer-name
customer-street
customer-city
customer
branch-name
branch-city
assets
branch
account-number
balance
account
CustRlnk
AcctRlnk
BrnchRlnk
Rlink

(b) data structure diagram

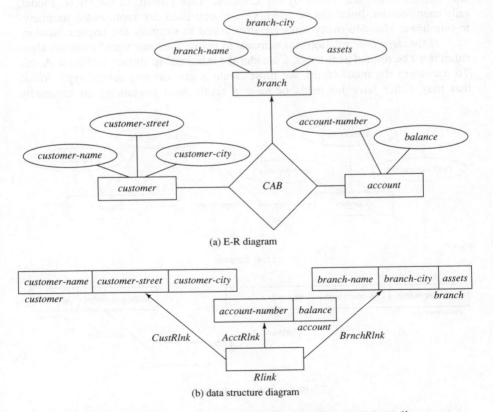

Figure A.3 E-R diagram and its corresponding data-structure diagram.

have several accounts, each located in a specific bank branch, and that an account may belong to several different customers.

Since a link can connect precisely two different record types, we need to connect these three record types through a new record type that is linked to each of them directly.

To transform the E-R diagram of Figure A.3a to a network data-structure diagram, we must create a new record type *Rlink* that may either have no fields or have a single field containing a unique identifier. This identifier is supplied by the system, and is not used directly by the application program. This new type of record is sometimes referred to as a *dummy* (or *link* or *junction*) record type. We must also create three many-to-one links, *CustRlnk*, *AcctRlnk*, and *BrncRlnk*, as depicted in Figure A.3b. If the relationship *CAB* had any descriptive attributes, they would become fields of the record type *Rlink*.

A.3 The DBTG CODASYL Model

The first database-standard specification, called the CODASYL DBTG 1971 report, was written in the late 1960s by the Database Task Group. In the DBTG model, only many-to-one links can be used. One-to-one links are represented as many-to-one links. Many-to-many links are disallowed to simplify the implementation.

If the *depositor* relationship is many to many, then our transformation algorithm must be refined as follows. Consider the relationship shown in (Figure A.4a). To transform the relationship, we must create a new dummy record type, *Rlink*, that may either have no fields or have a single field containing an externally

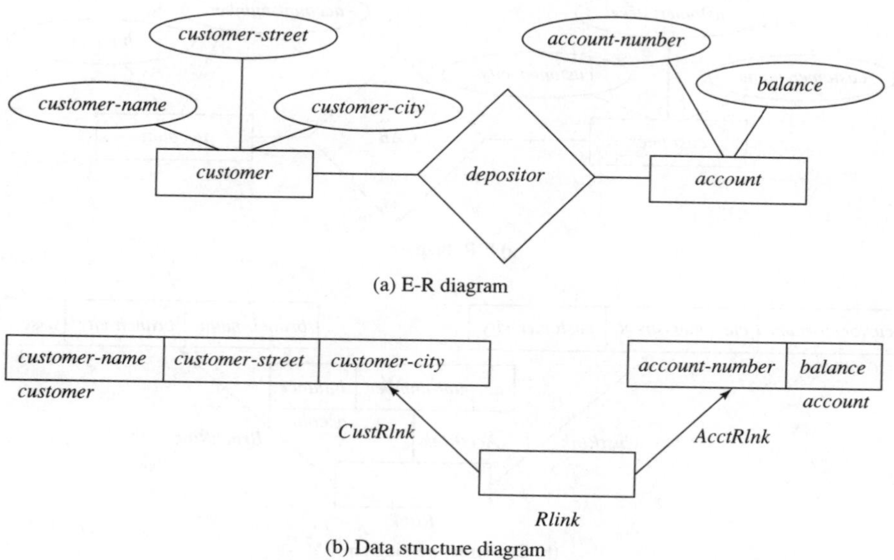

Figure A.4 E-R diagram and its corresponding data-structure diagram.

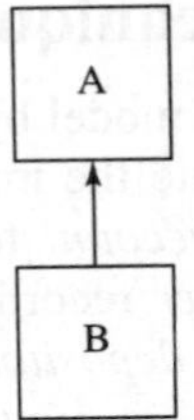

Figure A.5 DBTG-set.

defined unique identifier, and two many-to-one links *CustRlnk* and *AcctRlnk* as depicted in Figure A.4b.

Given that only many-to-one links can be used in the DBTG model, a data-structure diagram consisting of two record types that are linked together has the general form of Figure A.5. This structure is referred to in the DBTG model as a *DBTG set*. The name of the set is usually chosen to be the same as the name of the link connecting the two record types.

In each such DBTG set, the record type *A* is designated as the *owner* (or *parent*) of the set, and the record type *B* is designated as the *member* (or *child*) of the set. Each DBTG set can have any number of *set occurrences*—that is, actual instances of linked records. For example, in Figure A.6, we have three set occurrences corresponding to the DBTG set of Figure A.5.

Since many-to-many links are disallowed, each set occurrence has precisely one owner, and has zero or more member records. In addition, no member record of a set can participate in more than one occurrence of the set at any point. A member record, however, can participate simultaneously in several set occurrences of *different* DBTG sets.

The data-manipulation language of the DBTG proposal consists of commands that are embedded in a host language. The commands enable the programmer to select records from the database based on the value of a specified field, and to iterate over the selected records by repeated commands to get the next record. The programmer is also provided with commands find the owner of a set in which a record participates, and to iterate over the members of the set. And of course, there are commands to update the database.

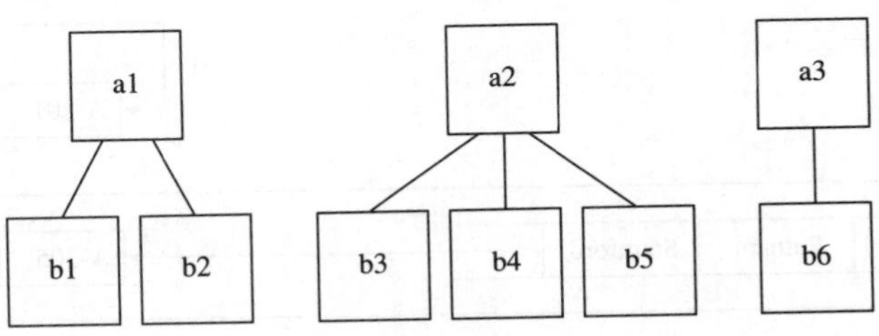

Figure A.6 Three set occurrences.

A.4 Implementation Techniques

Links are implemented in the DBTG model by adding *pointer fields* to records that are associated via a link. To illustrate the implementation, suppose the *depositor* relationship is many-to-one from *account* to *customer*. An *account* record can be associated with only one *customer* record. Thus, we need only one pointer in the *account* record to represent the *depositor* relationship. However, a *customer* record can be associated with many *account* records. Rather than using multiple pointers in the *customer* record, we can use a *ring structure* to represent the entire occurrence of the DBTG set *depositor*. In a ring structure, the records of both the owner and member types for a set occurrence are organized into a circular list. There is one circular list for each set occurrence (that is, for each record of the owner type).

Figure A.7 shows the ring structure for the example of Figure A.1. Let us examine the DBTG-set occurrence owned by the "Johnson" record. There are two member-type (*account*) records. Rather than containing one pointer to each member record, the owner (Johnson) record contains a pointer to only the first member record (account A-101). This member record contains a pointer to the next member record (account A-201). Since the record for account A-201 is the final member record, it contains a pointer to the owner record.

It is significantly harder to implement many-to-many links using pointers. Hence the DBTG model restricted links to be many-to-one. The implementation strategy for the DBTG model also provided the basis for the DBTG data retrieval facility.

A.5 Discussion

It is clear from the preceding discussion that the network model is closely tied to the implementation. As we saw earlier, the database designer has to create artificial record types even to implement simple many-to-many relationships. Unlike in the

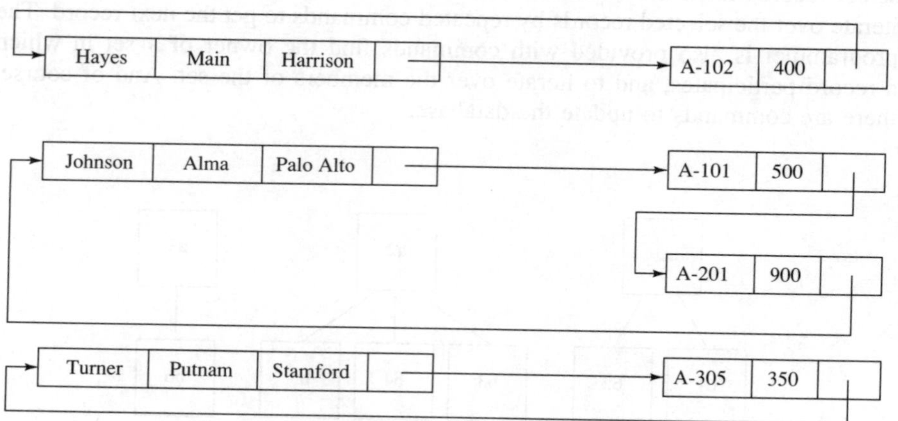

Figure A.7 Ring structure for instance of Figure A.1.

relational model, where querying can be done in a simple, declarative, manner, querying is significantly more complicated. The programmer is forced to think in terms of links, and how to traverse them to get at needed information; data-manipulation in the network model is hence said to be *navigational*.

Thus, the network model significantly increases the burden on the programmer, for database design as well as for data manipulation, as compared to the relational model. It held up against the relational model for many years since the implementations of the relational model were initially rather inefficient. Today, there are excellent implementations of the relational model, and the network model has therefore been losing importance. Hence it is no longer covered in detail in this book.

However, a detailed description of the network model is available on the Web for the benefit of those who wish to study it, at the URL:

`http://www.bell-labs.com/topic/books/db-book`

or via anonymous FTP from `ftp.research.bell-labs.com` in the subdirectory `dist/db-book`

APPENDIX B

HIERARCHICAL MODEL

In the network model, the data are represented by collections of *records*, and relationships between data are represented by *links*. This structure holds for the hierarchical model as well. The only difference is that, in the hierarchical model, records are organized as collections of trees, rather than as arbitrary graphs.

B.1 Basic Concepts

A hierarchical database consists of a collection of *records* that are connected to each other through *links*. A record is similar to a record in the network model. Each record is a collection of fields (attributes), each of which contains only one data value. A link is an association between precisely two records. Thus, a link here is similar to a link in the network model.

Consider a database that represents a *customer-account* relationship in a banking system. There are two record types: *customer* and *account*. The *customer* record type can be defined in the same manner as in Appendix A. It consists of three fields: *customer-name*, *customer-street*, and *customer-city*. Similarly, the *account* record consists of two fields: *account-number* and *balance*.

A sample database appears in Figure B.1. It shows that customer Hayes has account A-305, customer Johnson has accounts A-101 and A-201, and customer Turner has account A-305.

Note that the set of all customer and account records is organized in the form of a rooted tree, where the root of the tree is a dummy node. As we shall see, a hierarchical database is a collection of such rooted trees, and hence forms a forest. We shall refer to each such rooted tree as a *database tree*.

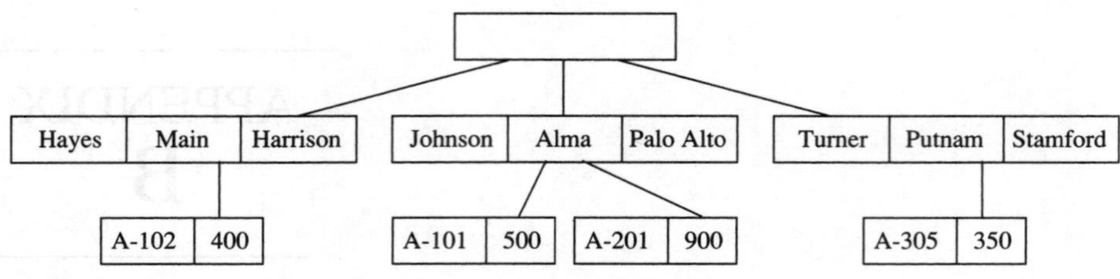

Figure B.1 Sample database.

B.2 Tree-Structure Diagrams

A *tree-structure diagram* is the schema for a hierarchical database. Such a diagram consists of two basic components: *boxes*, which correspond to record types, and *lines*, which correspond to links. A tree-structure diagram serves the same purpose as does an (E-R) diagram; namely, it specifies the overall logical structure of the database. A tree-structure diagram is similar to a data-structure diagram in the network model. The main difference is that, in the former, record types are organized in the form of a *rooted tree*, whereas in the latter, record types are organized in the form of an arbitrary graph. There can be no cycles in the underlying graph of a tree-structure diagram. However, we can still transform E-R diagrams into corresponding tree-structure diagrams.

To illustrate, consider the E-R diagram of Figure B.2a; it consists of the two entity sets *customer* and *account* related through a binary, one-to-many relationship *depositor*, with no descriptive attributes. This diagram specifies that a customer can have several accounts, but an account can belong to only one

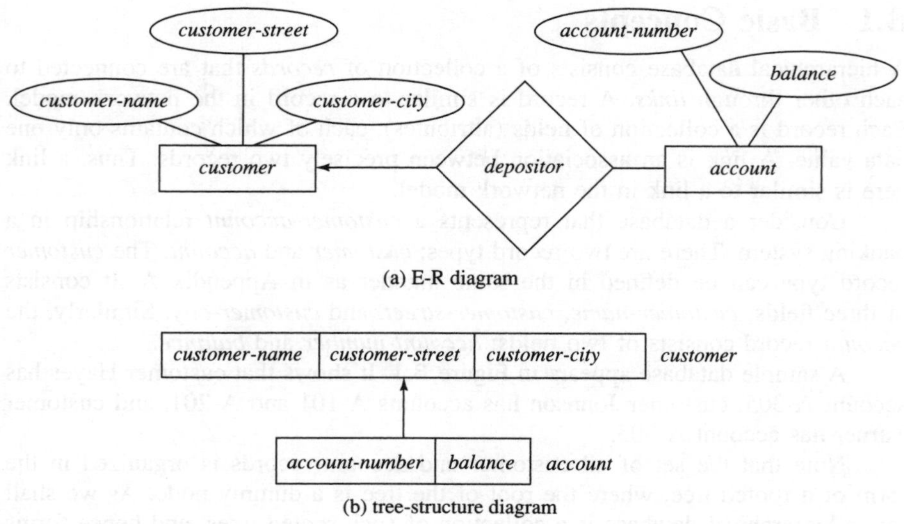

Figure B.2 E-R diagram and its corresponding tree-structure diagram.

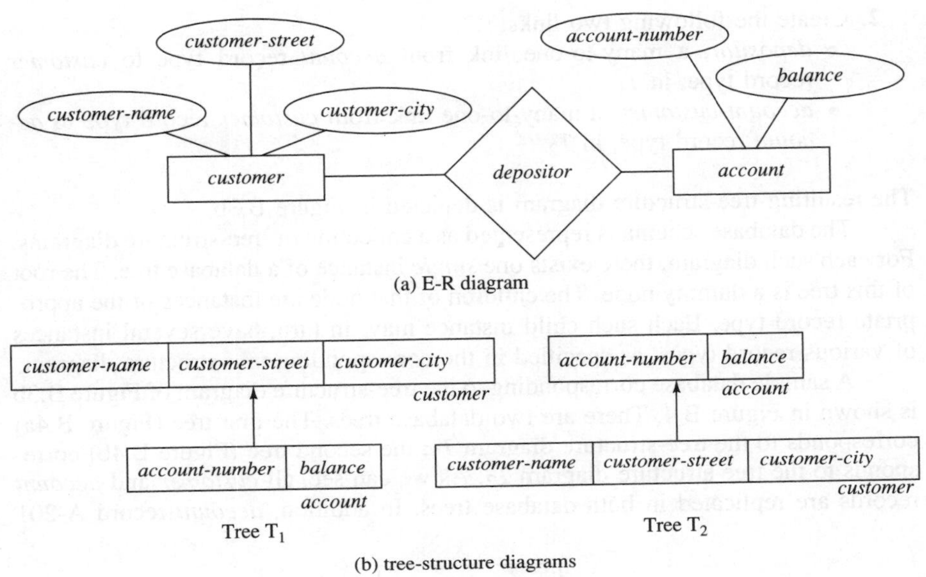

Figure B.3 E-R diagram and its corresponding tree-structure diagrams.

customer. The corresponding tree-structure diagram is depicted in Figure B.2b. The record type *customer* corresponds to the entity set *customer*. It includes three fields: *customer-name*, *customer-street*, and *customer-city*. Similarly, *account* is the record type corresponding to the entity set *account*. It includes two fields: *account-number* and *balance*. Finally, the relationship *depositor* has been replaced with the link *depositor*, with an arrow pointing to *customer* record type.

An instance of a database corresponding to the described schema may thus contain a number of *customer* records linked to a number of *account* records, as shown in Figure B.1. Since the relationship is one to many from *customer* to *account*, a customer can have more than one account, as does Johnson, who has both accounts A-101 and A-201. An account, however, cannot belong to more than one customer; none do in the sample database.

If the relationship *depositor* is many to many (see Figure B.3a), then the transformation from an E-R diagram to a tree-structure diagram is more complicated. Only one-to-many and one-to-one relationships can be directly represented in the hierarchical model.

To transform the E-R diagram of Figure B.3a to a tree-structure diagram, we do the following:

1. Create two separate tree-structure diagrams, T_1 and T_2, each of which has the *customer* and *account* record types. In tree T_1, *customer* is the root; in tree T_2, *account* is the root.

2. Create the following two links:
   - *depositor*, a many-to-one link from *account* record type to *customer* record type, in T_1
   - *account-customer*, a many-to-one link from *customer* record type to *account* record type, in T_2

The resulting tree-structure diagram is depicted in Figure B.3b.

The database schema is represented as a collection of tree-structure diagrams. For each such diagram, there exists one *single* instance of a database tree. The root of this tree is a dummy node. The children of that node are instances of the appropriate record type. Each such child instance may, in turn, have several instances of various record types, as specified in the corresponding tree-structure diagram.

A sample database corresponding to the tree-structure diagram of Figure B.3b is shown in Figure B.4. There are two database trees. The first tree (Figure B.4a) corresponds to the tree-structure diagram T_1; the second tree (Figure B.4b) corresponds to the tree-structure diagram T_2. As we can see, all *customer* and *account* records are replicated in both database trees. In addition, *account* record A-201

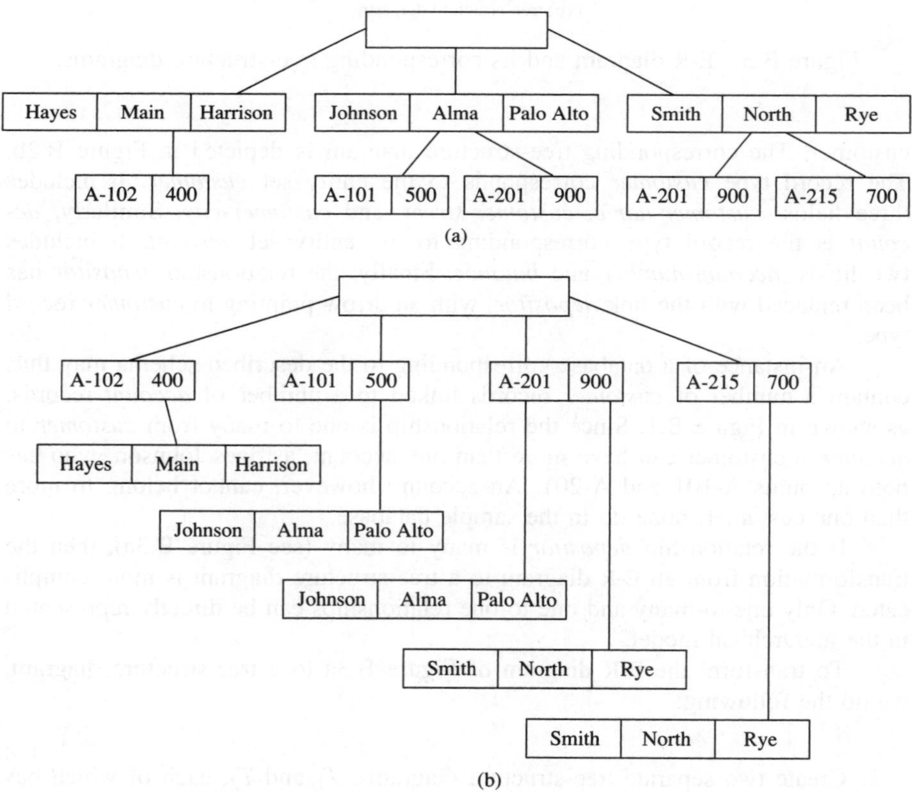

Figure B.4 Sample database corresponding to diagram of Figure B.3b.

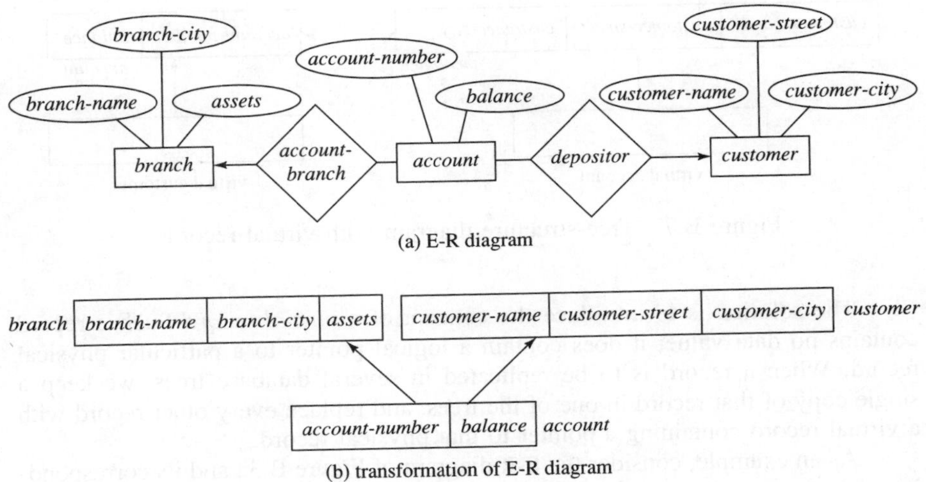

(a) E-R diagram

(b) transformation of E-R diagram

Figure B.5 E-R diagram and its transformation.

appears twice in the first tree, whereas *customer* records Johnson and Smith appear twice in the second tree.

Consider the E-R diagram of Figure B.5a. By applying the transformation algorithm described earlier the relationships *account-branch* and *depositor*, we obtain the diagram of Figure B.5b. This diagram is not a rooted tree, since the only possible root can be the record type *account*, but this record type has many-to-one relationships with both its children, and that violates our definition of a rooted tree. To transform this diagram into one that is in the form of a rooted tree, we replicate the *account* record type, and create two separate trees, as shown in Figure B.6. Note that each such tree is indeed a rooted tree. Thus, in general, we can split such a diagram into several diagrams, each of which is a rooted tree.

B.3 Implementation Techniques

Record replication has two major drawbacks:

1. Data inconsistency may result when updating takes place.
2. Waste of space is unavoidable.

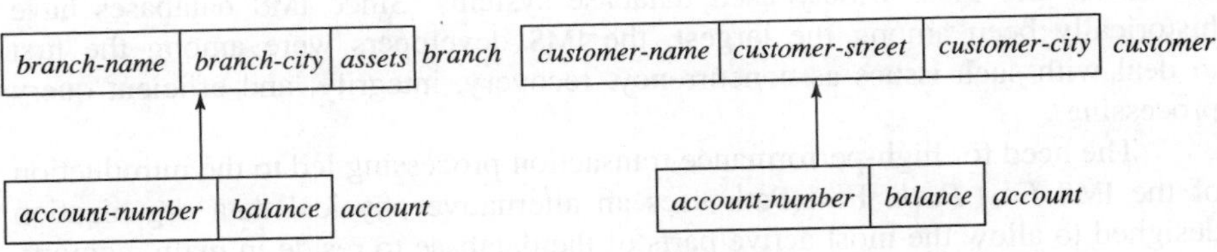

Figure B.6 Tree-structure diagram corresponding to Figure B.5a.

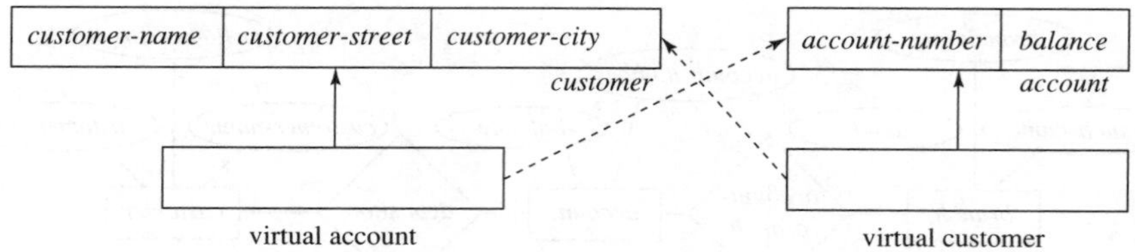

Figure B.7 Tree-structure diagram with virtual records.

The solution is to introduce the concept of a *virtual record* Such a record contains no data value; it does contain a logical pointer to a particular physical record. When a record is to be replicated in several database trees, we keep a single copy of that record in one of the trees, and replace every other record with a virtual record containing a pointer to that physical record.

As an example, consider the E-R diagram of Figure B.3a and its corresponding tree-structure diagram, which comprises two separate trees, each consisting of both *customer* and *account* record types (Figure B.3b).

To eliminate data replication, we create two virtual record types: *virtual-customer* and *virtual-account*. We then replace record type *account* with record type *virtual-account* in the first tree, and replace record type *customer* with record type *virtual-customer* in the second tree. We also add a dashed line from *virtual-customer* record to *customer* record, and a dashed line from *virtual-account* record to *account* record, to specify the association between a virtual record and its corresponding physical record. The resulting tree-structure diagram is depicted in Figure B.7.

An instance of a tree-structure diagram can be implemented using *leftmost-child* and *next-sibling* pointers. A record has only two pointers. The leftmost-child pointer points to one child. The next-sibling pointer points to another child of the same parent. Figure B.8 shows this structure for the database tree of Figure B.1. Under this structure, every record has exactly two pointers. Thus, fixed-length records retain their fixed length when we add the necessary pointers.

B.4 The IMS Database System

The hierarchical model is significant primarily because of the importance of IBM's IMS database system. The IBM Information Management System (IMS) is one of the oldest and most widely used database systems. Since IMS databases have historically been among the largest, the IMS developers were among the first to deal with such issues as concurrency, recovery, integrity, and efficient query processing.

The need for high-performance transaction processing led to the introduction of the IMS *Fast Path*. Fast Path uses an alternative physical data organization designed to allow the most active parts of the database to reside in main memory, and is a forerunner of work in main-memory database systems.

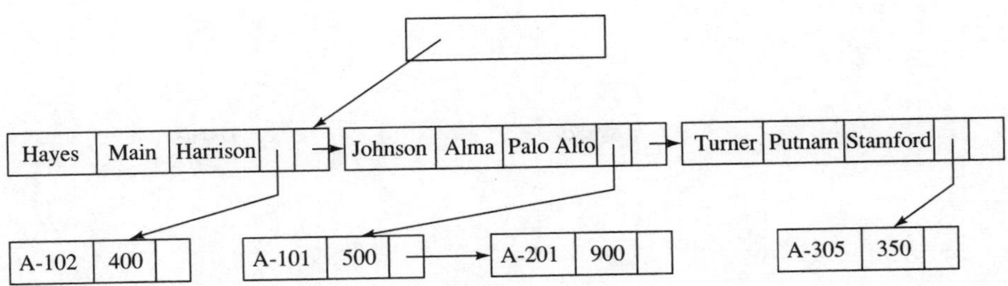

Figure B.8 Implementation with leftmost child and next-sibling pointers.

The data-manipulation language for hierarchical databases consists of commands that are embedded in a host language. It is similar in flavor to the data-manipulation language for network databases, although there are differences in the facilities provided. The data-manipulation language of the IMS database system is called DL/I.

B.5 Discussion

The hierarchical model suffers from the same shortfalls as the network model. The complexity of the tree-structure diagrams, and the restrictions to many-to-one links makes the design of databases a rather complex task. Further, the lack of declarative querying facilities, and the need for navigation of pointers to access needed information make querying rather complex.

Like the network model, the hierarchical model held up against the relational model for many years since the implementations of the hierarchical model, such as IMS were superior to implementations of the relational model. Today, there are excellent implementations of the relational model, and the hierarchical model has therefore lost its importance. Hence it is no longer covered in detail in this book.

However, a detailed description of the hierarchical model is available on the Web for the benefit of those who wish to study it, at the URL:

`http://www.bell-labs.com/topic/books/db-book`

or via anonymous FTP from `ftp.research.bell-labs.com` in the subdirectory `dist/db-book`.

BIBLIOGRAPHY

[Abbott and Garcia-Molina 1992] R. Abbott and H. Garcia-Molina, "Scheduling Real-Time Transactions: A Performance Evaluation," *ACM Transactions on Database Systems*, Volume 17, Number 3 (September 1992), pages 513–560.

[Abiteboul and Kanellakis 1989] S. Abiteboul and P. Kanellakis, "Object Identity as a Query Language Primitive," *Proceedings of the ACM SIGMOD International Conference on the Management of Data* (1989), pages 159–173.

[Abiteboul et al. 1989] S. Abiteboul, P. C. Fischer, and H. J. Schek (Editors), *Nested Relations and Complex Objects in Databases*, Lecture Notes in Computer Science 361, Springer-Verlag (1989).

[Abiteboul et al. 1995] S. Abiteboul, R. Hull, and V. Vianu, *Foundations of Databases*, Addison-Wesley, Reading, MA (1995).

[Acharya et al. 1995] S. Acharya, R. Alonso, M. Franklin, and S. Zdonik, "Broadcast Disks: Data Management for Asymmetric Communication Environments," *Proceedings of the ACM SIGMOD International Conference on Management of Data* (1995), pages 19–210. Also appears in **[Imielinski and Korth 1996]**, Chapter 12.

[Agrawal and Gehani 1989] R. Agrawal and N. Gehani, "Ode (Object Database and Environment): The Language and the Data Model," *Proceedings of the ACM SIGMOD International Conference on Management of Data* (May 1989), pages 36–45.

[Agrawal et al. 1986] D. P. Agrawal, V. K. Janakiram, and G. C. Pathak, "Evaluating the Performance of Multicomputer Configurations," *Communications of the ACM*, Volume 29, Number 5 (May 1986), pages 23–37.

[Agrawal et al. 1992] R. Agrawal, S. P. Ghosh, T. Imielinski, B. R. Iyer, and A. N. Swami, "An Interval Classifier for Database Mining Applications," *Proceedings of the International Conference on Very Large Data Bases* (1992), pages 560–573.

[Agrawal et al. 1993] R. Agrawal, T. Imielinski and A. N. Swami, "Database Mining: A Performance Perspective," *IEEE Transactions on Knowledge and Data Engineering*, Volume 5, Number 6 (1993), pages 914–925.

[Aho and Ullman 1979] A. V. Aho and J. D. Ullman, "Optimal Partial Match Retrieval When Fields Are Independently Specified," *ACM Transactions on Database Systems*, Volume 4, Number 2 (June 1979), pages 168–179.

[Aho et al. 1974] A. V. Aho, J. E. Hopcroft, and J. D. Ullman, *The Design and Analysis of Computer Algorithms*, Addison-Wesley, Reading, MA (1974).

[Aho et al. 1979a] A. V. Aho, Y. Sagiv, and J. D. Ullman, "Equivalences among Relational Expressions," *SIAM Journal of Computing*, Volume 8, Number 2 (June 1979), pages 218–246.

[Aho et al. 1979b] A. V. Aho, C. Beeri, and J. D. Ullman, "The Theory of Joins in Relational Databases," *ACM Transactions on Database Systems*, Volume 4, Number 3 (September 1979), pages 297–314.

[Aho et al. 1979c] A. V. Aho, Y. Sagiv, and J. D. Ullman, "Efficient Optimization of a Class of Relational Expressions," *ACM Transactions on Database Systems*, Volume 4, Number 4 (December 1979), pages 435–454.

[Aho et al. 1983] A. V. Aho, J. E. Hopcroft, and J. D. Ullman, *Data Structures and Algorithms*, Addison-Wesley, Reading, MA (1983).

[Aho et al. 1986] A. V. Aho, R. Sethi, and J. D. Ullman, *Compilers: Principles, Techniques, and Tools*, Addison-Wesley, Reading, MA (1986).

[Aiken et al. 1995] A. Aiken, J. Hellerstein, and J. Widom, "Static Analysis Techniques for Predicting the Behavior of Active Database Rules," *ACM Transactions on Database Systems*, Volume 20, Number 1 (March 1995), pages 3–41.

[Akl 1983] S. Akl, "Digital Signatures, A Tutorial Survey," *IEEE Computer*, Volume 16, Number 2 (February 1983), pages 15–24.

[Alonso and Korth 1993] R. Alonso and H. F. Korth, "Database System Issues in Nomadic Computing," *Proceedings of the ACM SIGMOD International Conference on Management of Data* (1993), pages 388–392.

[Ammon et al. 1985] G. J. Ammon, J. A. Calabria, and D. T. Thomas, "A High-Speed, Large-Capacity, 'Jukebox' Optical Disk System," *IEEE Computer*, Volume 18, Number 7 (July 1985), pages 36–48.

[Anderson et al. 1992] D. P. Anderson, Y. Osawa, and R. Govidan, "A File System for Continuous Media," *ACM Transactions on Computer Systems*, Volume 10, Number 4 (November 1992), pages 311–337.

[ANSI 1975] "Study Group on Data Base Management Systems: Interim Report," *FDT*, Volume 7, Number 2, ACM, New York, NY (1975).

[ANSI 1986] "American National Standard for Information Systems: Database Language SQL," *FDT*, ANSI X3,135–1986, American National Standards Institute, New York (1986).

[ANSI 1989] "Database Language SQL With Integrity Enhancement," ANSI X3,135–1989, American National Standards Institute, New York (1989). Also available as ISO/IEC Document 9075:1989.

[ANSI 1992] "Database Language SQL," ANSI X3,135–1992, American National Standards Institute, New York (1992). Also available as ISO/IEC Document 9075:1992.

[Apers et al. 1983] P. M. G. Apers, A. R. Hevner, and S. B. Yao, "Optimization Algorithms for Distributed Queries," *IEEE Transactions on Software Engineering*, Volume SE-9, Number 1 (January 1983), pages 57–68.

[Apt and Pugin 1987] K. R. Apt and J.-M. Pugin, "Maintenance of Stratified Database Viewed as a Belief Revision System," *Proceedings of the ACM SIGACT-SIGMOD Symposium on the Principles of Database Systems* (1987), pages 136–145.

[Aref et al. 1995a] W. Aref, D. Barbará, and P. Vallabhaneni, "The Handwritten Trie: Indexing Electronic Ink," *Proceedings of the ACM SIGMOD International Conference on Management of Data* (1995), pages 151–162.

[Aref et al. 1995b] W. Aref, D. Barbará, D. Lopresti, and A. Tomkins, "Ink as a First-Class Multimedia Object," in **[Jajodia and Subramanian 1995]**.

[Armstrong 1974] W. W. Armstrong, "Dependency Structures of Data Base Relationships," *Proceedings of the 1974 IFIP Congress* (1974), pages 580–583.

[Astrahan et al. 1976] M. M. Astrahan, M. W. Blasgen, D. D. Chamberlin, K. P. Eswaran, J. N. Gray, P. P. Griffiths, W. F. King, R. A. Lorie, P. R. McJones, J. W. Mehl, G. R. Putzolu, I. L. Traiger, B. W. Wade, and V. Watson, "System R, A Relational Approach to Data Base Management," *ACM Transactions on Database Systems*, Volume 1, Number 2 (June 1976), pages 97–137.

[Astrahan et al. 1979] M. M. Astrahan, M. W. Blasgen, D. D. Chamberlin, J. N. Gray, W. F. King, B. G. Lindsay, R. A. Lorie, J. W. Mehl, T. G. Price, G. R. Putzolu, M. Schkolnick, P. G. Selinger, D. R. Slutz, H. R. Strong, P. Tiberio, I. L. Traiger, B. W. Wade, and R. A. Yost, "System R: A Relational Database Management System," *IEEE Computer*, Volume 12, Number 5 (May 1979), pages 43–48.

[Attar et al. 1984] R. Attar, P. A. Bernstein, and N. Goodman, "Site Initialization, Recovery, and Backup in a Distributed Database System," *IEEE Transactions on Software Engineering*, Volume SE-10, Number 6 (November 1984), pages 645–650.

[Atzeni and De Antonellis 1993] P. Atzeni and V. De Antonellis, *Relational Database Theory*, Benjamin Cummings, Menlo Park, CA (1993).

[Bachman 1969] C. W. Bachman, "Data Structure Diagrams," *Journal of ACM SIGBDP* Volume 1, Number 2 (March 1969), pages 4–10

[Bachman and Williams 1964] C. W. Bachman and S. S. Williams, "A General Purpose Programming System for Random Access Memories," *Proceedings of the Fall Joint Computer Conference*, Volume 26, AFIPS Press (1964), pages 411–422.

[Badal and Popek 1979] D. S. Badal and G. Popek, "Cost and Performance Analysis of Semantic Integrity Validation Methods," *Proceedings of the ACM SIGMOD International Conference on Management of Data* (1979), pages 109–115.

[Bancilhon and Buneman 1990] F. Bancilhon and P. Buneman, *Advances in Database Programming Languages,* ACM Press, New York, NY (1990).

[Bancilhon and Ramakrishnan 1986] F. Bancilhon and R. Ramakrishnan, "An Amateur's Introduction to Recursive Query-Processing Strategies," *Proceedings of the ACM SIGMOD International Conference on Management of Data* (1986), pages 16–52.

[Bancilhon and Spyratos 1981] F. Bancilhon and N. Spyratos "Update Semantics and Relational Views," *ACM Transactions on Database Systems,* Volume 6, Number 4 (December 1981), pages 557–575.

[Bancilhon et al. 1985a] F. Bancilhon, W. Kim, and H. F. Korth, "A Model of CAD Transactions," *Proceedings of the International Conference on Very Large Data Bases* (1985), pages 25–31.

[Bancilhon et al. 1985b] F. Bancilhon, W. Kim, and H. F. Korth, "Transactions and Concurrency Control in CAD Databases," *Proceedings of the IEEE International Conference on Computer Design: VLSI in Computers* (1985).

[Bancilhon et al. 1989] F. Bancilhon, S. Cluet, and C. Delobel, "A Query Language for the O_2 Object-Oriented Database," *Proceedings of the Second Workshop on Database Programming Languages* (1989).

[Banerjee et al. 1987a] J. Banerjee, H. T. Chou, J. F. Garza, W. Kim, D. Woelk, N. Ballou, and H. J. Kim, "Data Model Issues for Object-Oriented Applications," *ACM Transactions on Office Information Systems* (January 1987).

[Banerjee et al. 1987b] J. Banerjee, W. Kim, H. J. Kim, and H. F. Korth, "Semantics and Implementation of Schema Evolution in Object-Oriented Databases," *Proceedings of the ACM SIGMOD International Conference on Management of Data* (1987), pages 311–322.

[Baralis et al. 1996] E. Baralis, S. Ceri, and S. Paroboschi, "Modularization Techniques for Active Rules Design," *ACM Transactions on Database Systems*, Volume 21, Number 1 (March 1996), pages 1–29.

[Barbará and Imielinski 1994] D. Barbará and T. Imielinski, "Sleepers and Workaholics: Caching Strategies in Mobile Environments," *Proceedings of the ACM SIGMOD International Conference on Management of Data* (1994), pages 1–12.

[Barbará et al. 1992] D. Barbará, H. Garcia-Molina, and D. Porter, "The Management of Probabilistic Data," *IEEE Transactions on Knowledge and Data Engineering*, Volume 4, Number 5 (October 1992), pages 487–502.

[Barclay et al. 1982] D. K. Barclay, E. R. Byrne, and F. K. Ng, "A Real-Time Database Management System for No.5 ESS," Bell System Technical Journal, Volume 61, Number 9 (November 1982), pages 2423–2437.

[Barsalou et al. 1991] T. Barsalou, N. Siambela, A. Keller, and G. Wiederhold, "Updating Relational Databases Through Object-Based Views," *Proceedings of the ACM SIGMOD International Conference on the Management of Data* (1991).

[Bassiouni 1988] M. Bassiouni, "Single-site and Distributed Optimistic Protocols for Concurrency Control," *IEEE Transactions on Software Engineering*, Volume SE-14, Number 8 (August 1988), pages 1071–1080.

[Batini et al. 1992] C. Batini, S. Ceri, and S. Navathe, *Database Design: An Entity-Relationship Approach*, Benjamin Cummings, Redwood City, CA (1992).

[Batini et al. 1986] C. Batini, M. Lenzerini, and S. Navathe, "A Comparative Analysis of Methodologies for Database Schema Integration," *ACM Computing Surveys*, Volume 18, Number 4 (1986), pages 323–364.

[Batory and Gotlieb 1982] D. S. Batory and C. C. Gotlieb, "A Unifying Model of Physical Databases," *ACM Transactions on Database Systems*, Volume 7, Number 4 (December 1982), pages 509–539.

[Bayer 1972] R. Bayer, "Symmetric Binary B-trees: Data Structure and Maintenance Algorithms," *Acta Informatica*, Volume 1, Number 4 (1972), pages 290–306.

[Bayer and McCreight 1972] R. Bayer and E. M. McCreight, "Organization and Maintenance of Large Ordered Indices," *Acta Informatica*, Volume 1, Number 3 (1972), pages 173–189.

[Bayer and Schkolnick 1977] R. Bayer and M. Schkolnick, "Concurrency of Operating on B-trees," *Acta Informatica*, Volume 9, Number 1 (1977), pages 1–21.

[Bayer and Unterauer 1977] R. Bayer and K. Unterauer, "Prefix B-trees," *ACM Transactions on Database Systems*, Volume 2, Number 1 (March 1977), pages 11–26.

[Bayer et al. 1978] R. Bayer, R. M. Graham, and G. Seegmuller (Editors), *Operating Systems: An Advanced Course*, Springer-Verlag, Berlin, Germany (1978).

[Bayer et al. 1980] R. Bayer, H. Heller, and A. Reiser, "Parallelism and Recovery in Database Systems," *ACM Transactions on Database Systems*, Volume 5, Number 2 (June 1980), pages 139–156.

[Beckmann et al. 1990], N. Beckmann, H. P. Kriegel, R. Schneider, and B. Seeger, "The R*-tree: An Efficient and Robust Access Method for Points and Rectangles," *Proceedings of the ACM SIGMOD International Conference on Management of Data* (May 1990), pages 322–331.

[Beech 1988] D. Beech, "OSQL: A Language for Migrating from SQL to Object Databases," *Proceedings of the International Conference on Extending Database Technology* (March 1988).

[Beeri and Ramakrishnan 1991] C. Beeri and R. Ramakrishnan, "On the Power of Magic," *Journal of Logic Programming*, Volume 10, Numbers 3 and 4 (1991), pages 255–300.

[Beeri et al. 1977] C. Beeri, R. Fagin, and J. H. Howard, "A Complete Axiomatization for Functional and Multivalued Dependencies," *Proceedings of the ACM SIGMOD International Conference on Management of Data* (1977), pages 47–61.

[Beeri et al. 1983] C. Beeri, R. Fagin, D. Maier, and M. Yannakakis, "On the Desirability of Acyclic Database Schemes," *Journal of the ACM*, Volume 30, Number 3 (July 1983), pages 479–513.

[Beeri et al. 1989] C. Beeri, P. A. Bernstein, and N. Goodman, "A Model for Concurrency in Nested Transactions Systems," *Journal of the ACM*, Volume 36, Number 2 (April 1989).

[Bell and Grimson 1992] D. Bell and J. Grimson, *Distributed Database Systems*, Addison-Wesley, Reading, MA (1992).

[Bell and LaPadula 1976] D. E. Bell and L. J. LaPadula, "Secure Computer Systems: Unified Exposition and Multics Interpretation," Mitre Corporation, Bedford, MA (1976).

[Benneworth et al. 1981] R. L. Benneworth, C. D. Bishop, C. J. M. Turnbull, W. D. Holman, and F. M. Monette, "The Implementation of GERM, an Entity-Relationship Data Base Management System," *Proceedings of the International Conference on Very Large Data Bases* (1981), pages 478–484.

[Bentley 1975] J. L. Bentley, "Multidimensional Binary Search Trees Used for Associative Searching," *Communications of the ACM*, Volume 18, Number 9 (September 1975), pages 509–517.

[Berenson et al. 1995] H. Berenson, P. Bernstein, J. Gray, J. Melton, E. O'Neil, and P. O'Neil, "A Critique of ANSI SQL Isolation Levels," *Proceedings of the ACM SIGMOD International Conference on Management of Data* (1995), pages 1–10.

[Bernstein 1976] P. A. Bernstein, "Synthesizing Third Normal Form Relations from Functional Dependencies," *ACM Transactions on Database Systems*, Volume 1, Number 4 (December 1976), pages 277–298.

[Bernstein and Chiu 1981] P. A. Bernstein and D. W. Chiu, "Using Semijoins to Solve Relational Queries," *Journal of the ACM*, Volume 28, Number 1 (January 1981), pages 25–40.

[Bernstein and Goodman 1980a] P. A. Bernstein and N. Goodman, "Timestamp-based Algorithms for Concurrency Control in Distributed Database Systems," *Proceedings of the International Conference on Very Large Data Bases* (1980), pages 285–300.

[Bernstein and Goodman 1980b] P. A. Bernstein and N. Goodman, "What Does Boyce-Codd Normal Form Do?," *Proceedings of the International Conference of Very Large Data Bases* (1980), pages 245–259.

[Bernstein and Goodman 1981a] P. A. Bernstein and N. Goodman, "Concurrency Control in Distributed Database Systems," *ACM Computing Surveys*, Volume 13, Number 2 (June 1981), pages 185–221.

[Bernstein and Goodman 1981b] P. A. Bernstein and N. Goodman, "The Power of Natural Semijoins," *SIAM Journal of Computing*, Volume 10, Number 4 (December 1981), pages 751–771.

[Bernstein and Goodman 1982] P. A. Bernstein and N. Goodman, "A Sophisticate's Introduction to Distributed Database Concurrency Control," *Proceedings of the International Conference on Very Large Data Bases* (1982), pages 62–76.

[Bernstein et al. 1978] P. A. Bernstein, N. Goodman, J. B. Rothnie, Jr., and C. H. Papadimitriou, "Analysis of Serializability of SDD-1: A System of Distributed Databases (the Fully Redundant Case)," *IEEE Transactions on Software Engineering*, Volume SE-4, Number 3 (May 1978), pages 154–168.

[Bernstein et al. 1980a] P. A. Bernstein, D. W. Shipman, and J. B. Rothnie, Jr., "Concurrency Control in a System for Distributed Databases (SDD-1)," *ACM Transactions on Database Systems*, Volume 5, Number 1 (March 1980), pages 18–51.

[Bernstein et al. 1980b] P. A. Bernstein, B. Blaustein, and E. Clarke, "Fast Maintenance of Semantic Integrity Assertions Using Redundant Aggregate Data," *Proceedings of the International Conference on Very Large Data Bases* (1980).

[Bernstein et al. 1983] P. A. Bernstein, N. Goodman, and M. Y. Lai, " Analyzing Concurrency Control when User and System Operations Differ," *IEEE Transactions on Software Engineering*, Volume SE-9 Number 3 (May 1983), pages 233–239.

[Bernstein et al. 1987] A. Bernstein, V. Hadzilacos, and N. Goodman, *Concurrency Control and Recovery in Database Systems*, Addison-Wesley, Reading, MA (1987).

[Berson et al. 1995] S. Berson, L. Golubchik, and R. R. Muntz, "Fault Tolerant Design of Multimedia Servers," *Proceedings of the ACM SIGMOD International Conference on Management of Data* (1995), pages 364–375.

[Bertino and Kim 1989] E. Bertino and W. Kim, "Indexing Techniques for Queries on Nested Objects," *IEEE Transactions on Knowledge and Data Engineering* (October 1989).

[Bhuyan et al. 1989] L. N. Bhuyan, Q. Yang, and D. P. Agrawal, "Performance of Multiprocessor Interconnection Networks," *IEEE Computer*, Volume 22, Number 2 (February 1989), pages 25–37.

[Biliris and Orenstein 1994] A. Biliris and J. Orenstein, "Object Storage Management Architectures," in **[Dogac et al. 1994]**, pages 185–200.

[Biskup et al. 1979] J. Biskup, U. Dayal, and P. A. Bernstein, "Synthesizing Independent Database Schemas," *Proceedings of the ACM SIGMOD International Conference on Management of Data* (1979), pages 143–152.

[Bitton and Gray 1988] D. Bitton and J. N. Gray, "Disk Shadowing," *Proceedings of the International Conference on Very Large Data Bases* (1988), pages 331–338.

[Bitton et al. 1983] D. Bitton, D. J. DeWitt, and C. Turbyfill, "Benchmarking Database Systems: A Systematic Approach," *Proceedings of the International Conference on Very Large Data Bases* (1983).

[Bjork 1973] L. A. Bjork, "Recovery Scenario for a DB/DC System," *Proceedings of the ACM Annual Conference* (1973), pages 142–146.

[Bjorner and Lovengren 1982] D. Bjorner and H. Lovengren, "Formalization of Database Systems and a Formal Definition of IMS," *Proceedings of the International Conference on Very Large Data Bases* (1982), pages 334–347.

[Blakeley et al. 1986] J. A. Blakeley, P. Larson, and F. W. Tompa, "Efficiently Updating Materialized Views," *Proceedings of the ACM SIGMOD International Conference on Management of Data* (1986), pages 61–71.

[Blakeley et al. 1989] J. Blakeley, N. Coburn, and P. Larson, "Updating Derived Relations: Detecting Irrelevant and Autonomously Computable Updates," *ACM Transactions on Database Systems*, Volume 14, Number 3 (1989), pages 369–400.

[Blasgen and Eswaran 1976] M. W. Blasgen and K. P. Eswaran, "On the Evaluation of Queries in a Relational Database System," *IBM Systems Journal*, Volume 16 (1976), pages 363–377.

[Bohl 1981] M. Bohl, *Introduction to IBM Direct Access Storage Devices*, Science Research Associates, Chicago, IL (1981).

[Bolour 1979] A. Bolour, "Optimal Retrieval Algorithms for Small Region Queries," *Journal of the ACM*, Volume 26, Number 2 (April 1979), pages 721–741.

[Boral et al. 1990] H. Boral, W. Alexander, L. Clay, G. Copeland, S. Danforth, M. Franklin, B. Hart, M. Smith, and P. Valduriez, "Prototyping Bubba, a Highly Parallel Database System," *IEEE Transactions on Knowledge and Data Engineering* Volume 2, Number 1 (March 1990).

[Boyce et al. 1975] R. Boyce, D. D. Chamberlin, W. F. King, and M. Hammer, "Specifying Queries as Relational Expressions," *Communications of the ACM*, Volume 18, Number 11 (November 1975), pages 621–628.

[Bracchi and Nijssen 1979] G. Bracchi and G. M. Nijssen (Editors), *Data Base Architecture*, North Holland, Amsterdam, The Netherlands (1979).

[Bradley 1978] J. Bradley, "An Extended Owner-Coupled Set Data Model and Predicate Calculus for Database Management," *ACM Transactions on Database Systems*, Volume 3, Number 4 (December 1978), pages 385–416.

[Bray 1982] O. H. Bray, *Distributed Database Management Systems*, Lexington Books (1982).

[Brinkhoff et al. 1993] T. Brinkhoff, H-P. Kriegel, and B. Seeger, "Efficient Processing of Spatial Joins Using R-trees," *Proceedings of the ACM SIGMOD International Conference on Management of Data* (May 1993), pages 237–246.

[Brown et al. 1994] K. P. Brown, M. Mehta, M. Carey, and M. Livny, "Towards Automated Performance Tuning for Complex Overloads," *Proceedings of the International Conference on Very Large Data Bases* (September 1994).

[Buckley and Silberschatz 1983] G. Buckley and A. Silberschatz, "Obtaining Progressive Protocols for a Simple Multiversion Database Model," *Proceedings of the International Conference on Very Large Data Bases* (1983), pages 74–81.

[Buckley and Silberschatz 1984] G. Buckley and A. Silberschatz, "Concurrency Control in Graph Protocols by Using Edge Locks," *Proceedings of the ACM SIGACT-SIGMOD Symposium on the Principles of Database Systems* (1984), pages 45–50.

[Buckley and Silberschatz 1985] G. Buckley and A. Silberschatz, "Beyond Two-Phase Locking," *Journal of the ACM*, Volume 32, Number 2 (April 1985), pages 314–326.

[Buneman and Frankel 1979] P. Buneman and R. Frankel, "FQL: A Functional Query Language," *Proceedings of the ACM SIGMOD International Conference on the Management of Data* (1979), pages 52–58.

[Burkhard 1976] W. A. Burkhard, "Hashing and Trie Algorithms for Partial Match Retrieval," *ACM Transactions on Database Systems*, Volume 1, Number 2 (June 1976), pages 175–187.

[Burkhard 1979] W. A. Burkhard, "Partial-match Hash Coding: Benefits of Redundancy," *ACM Transactions on Database Systems*, Volume 4, Number 2 (June 1979), pages 228–239.

[Campbell et al. 1985] D. Campbell, D. Embley, and B. Czejdo, "A Relationally Complete Query Language for the Entity-Relationship Model," *Proceedings of the International Conference on Entity-Relationship Approach* (1985).

[Cannan and Otten 1993] S. Cannan and G. Otten, *SQL—The Standard Handbook*, McGraw-Hill International, Maidenhead, UK (1993).

[Carey 1983] M. J. Carey, "Granularity Hierarchies in Concurrency Control," *Proceedings of the ACM SIGACT-SIGMOD Symposium on the Principles of Database Systems* (1983), pages 156–165.

[Carey et al. 1986] M. J. Carey, D. DeWitt, J. Richardson, and E. Shekita, "Object and File Management in the EXODUS Extensible Database System," *Proceedings of the International Conference on Very Large Data Bases* (1986), pages 91–100.

[Carey et al. 1990] M. J. Carey, D. DeWitt, G. Graefe, D. Haight, J. Richardson, D. Schuh, E. Shekita, and S. Vandenberg, "The EXODUS Extensible DBMS Project: An Overview," in **[Zdonik and Maier 1990]**, pages 474–499.

[Carey et al. 1991] M. Carey, M. Franklin, M. Livny, and E. Shekita, "Data Caching Tradeoffs in Client-Server DBMS Architectures," *Proceedings of the ACM SIGMOD International Conference on the Management of Data* (May 1991).

[Carey et al. 1993] M. J. Carey, D. DeWitt, and J. Naughton, "The OO7 Benchmark," *Proceedings of the ACM SIGMOD International Conference on Management of Data* (May 1993).

[Casanova et al. 1984] M. A. Casanova, R. Fagin, and C. Papadimitriou, "Inclusion Dependencies and Their Interaction with Functional Dependencies," *Journal of Computer and System Sciences*, Volume 28, Number 1 (January 1984), pages 29–59.

[Cattell 1994] R. Cattell (Editor), *The Object Database Standard: ODMG – 93*, Release 1.1, Morgan Kaufmann, San Francisco, CA (1994).

[Cattell and Skeen 1992] R. Cattell and J. Skeen, "Object Operations Benchmark," *ACM Transactions on Database Systems,* Volume 17, Number 1 (March 1992).

[Ceri and Owicki 1983] S. Ceri and S. Owicki, "On the Use of Optimistic Methods for Concurrency Control in Distributed Databases," *Proceedings of the Sixth Berkeley Workshop on Distributed Data Management and Computer Networks* (1983).

[Ceri and Pelagatti 1983] S. Ceri and G. Pelagatti, "Correctness of Query Execution Strategies in Distributed Databases," *ACM Transactions on Database Systems*, Volume 8, Number 4 (December 1983), pages 577–607.

[Ceri and Pelagatti 1984] S. Ceri and G. Pelagatti, *Distributed Databases: Principles and Systems*, McGraw-Hill, NY (1984).

[Chakravarthy et al. 1990] U. S. Chakravarthy, J. Grant, and J. Minker, "Logic-Based Approach to Semantic Query Optimization," *ACM Transactions on Database Systems,* Volume 15, Number 2 (June 1990), pages 162–207.

[Chamberlin and Boyce 1974] D. D. Chamberlin and R. F. Boyce, "SEQUEL: A Structured English Query Language," *Proceedings of the ACM SIGMOD Workshop on Data Description, Access, and Control* (1974), pages 249–264.

[Chamberlin et al. 1976] D. D. Chamberlin, M. M. Astrahan, K. P. Eswaran, P. P. Griffiths, R. A. Lorie, J. W. Mehl, P. Reisner, and B. W. Wade, "SEQUEL 2: A Unified Approach to Data Definition, Manipulation, and Control," *IBM Journal of Research and Development*, Volume 20, Number 6 (November 1976), pages 560–575.

[Chamberlin et al. 1981] D. D. Chamberlin, M. M. Astrahan, M. W. Blasgen, J. N. Gray, W. F. King, B. G. Lindsay, R. A. Lorie, J. W. Mehl, T. G. Price, P. G. Selinger, M. Schkolnick, D. R. Slutz, I. L. Traiger, B. W. Wade, and R. A. Yost, "A History and Evaluation of System R," *Communications of the ACM*, Volume 24, Number 10 (October 1981), pages 632–646.

[Chandra and Harel 1982] A. K. Chandra and D. Harel, "Structure and Complexity of Relational Queries," *Journal of Computer and System Sciences*, Volume 15, Number (January 1982), pages 99–128.

[Chandy and Misra 1982] K. M. Chandy and J. Misra, "A Distributed Algorithm for Detecting Resource Deadlocks in Distributed Systems," *Proceedings of the ACM SIGACT-SIGOPS Symposium on the Principles of Distributed Computing* (1982), pages 157–164.

[Chandy et al. 1975] K. M. Chandy, J. C. Browne, C. W. Dissley, and W. R. Uhrig, "Analytic Models for Rollback and Recovery Strategies in Database Systems," *IEEE Transactions on Software Engineering*, Volume SE-1, Number 1 (March 1975), pages 100–110.

[Chandy et al. 1983] K. M. Chandy, L. M. Haas, and J. Misra, " Distributed Deadlock Detection," *ACM Transactions on Computer Systems*, Volume 1, Number 2 (May 1983), pages 144–156.

[Chaudhuri and Shim 1994] S. Chaudhuri and K. Shim, "Including Group-By in Query Optimization," *Proceedings of the International Conference on Very Large Data Bases* (1994).

[Chen 1976] P. P. Chen, "The Entity-Relationship Model: Toward a Unified View of Data," *ACM Transactions on Database Systems*, Volume 1, Number 1 (January 1976), pages 9–36.

[Chen and Patterson 1990] P. Chen and D. Patterson, "Maximizing Performance in a Striped Disk Array," *Proceedings of the Seventeenth Annual International Symposium on Computer Architecture* (May 1990).

[Chen et al. 1994] P. M. Chen, E. K. Lee, G. A. Gibson, R. H. Katz, and D. A. Patterson, "RAID: High-Performance, Reliable Secondary Storage," *ACM Computing Surveys*, Volume 26, Number 2 (June 1994).

[Chen et al. 1995] M.-S. Chen, H.-I. Hsiao, C.-S. Li, and P. S. Yu, "Using Rotational Mirrored Declustering for Replica Placement in a Disk Array Based Video Server," *Proceedings of the Third ACM International Multimedia Conference and Exhibition* (1995), pages 121–130.

[Chervenak et al. 1995] A. L. Chervenak, D. A. Patterson, and R. H. Katz, "Choosing the Best Storage System for Video Service," *Proceedings of the Third ACM International Multimedia Conference and Exhibition* (1995), pages 109–120.

[Chi 1982] C. S. Chi, "Advances in Computer Mass Storage Technology," *IEEE Computer*, Volume 15, Number 5 (May 1982), pages 60–74.

[Chin 1978] F. Y. Chin, "Security in Statistical Databases for Queries with Small Counts," *ACM Transactions on Database Systems*, Volume 3, Number 1 (January 1978), pages 92–104.

[Chin and Ozsoyoglu 1981] F. Y. Chin and G. Ozsoyoglu, "Statistical Database Design," *ACM Transactions on Database Design*, Volume 6, Number 1 (January 1981), pages 113–139.

[Chiu and Ho 1980] D. M. Chiu and Y. C. Ho, "A Methodology for Interpreting Tree Queries into Optimal Semi-join Expressions," *Proceedings of the ACM SIGMOD International Conference on the Management of Data* (1980), pages 169–178.

[Chomicki 1992a] J. Chomicki, "History-less checking of Dynamic Integrity Constraints," *Proceedings of the International Conference on Data Engineering* (1992).

[Chomicki 1992b] J. Chomicki, "Real-Time Integrity Constraints," *Proceedings of the ACM SIGACT-SIGMOD-SIGART Symposium on the Principles of Database Systems* (1992).

[Chomicki 1995] J. Chomicki, "Efficient Checking of Temporal Integrity Constraints Using Bounded History Encoding," *ACM Transactions on Database Systems*, Volume 20, Number 2 (June 1995), pages 149–186.

[Chou et al. 1985] H-T. Chou, D. J. Dewitt, R. H. Katz, A. C. Klug, "The Wisconsin Storage System Software," *Software—Practice and Experience*, Volume 15, Number 10 (October 1985), pages 943–962.

[Chou and DeWitt 1985] H. T. Chou and D. J. Dewitt, "An Evaluation of Buffer Management Strategies for Relational Database Systems," *Proceedings of the International Conference on Very Large Data Bases* (1985), pages 127–141.

[Christodoulakis and Faloutsos 1986] S. Christodoulakis and C. Faloutsos, "Design and Performance Considerations for an Optical Disk-Based Multimedia Object Server," *IEEE Computer*, Volume 19, Number 12 (December 1986), pages 45–56.

[Chrysanthis and Ramamritham 1994] P. Chrysanthis and K.Ramamritham, "Synthesis of Extended Transaction Models Using ACTA," *ACM Transactions on Database Systems*, Volume 19, Number 3 (September 1994) pages 450–491.

[Clemons 1978] E. K. Clemons, "An External Schema Facility to Support Data Base Update," in **[Schneiderman 1978]**, pages 371–398.

[Clemons 1979] E. K. Clemons, "An External Schema Facility for CODASYL 1978," *Proceedings of the International Conference on Very Large Data Bases* (1979), pages 119–128.

[Clifford and Tansel 1985] J. Clifford and A. Tansel, "On an Algebra for Historical Relational Databases: Two Views," *Proceedings of the ACM SIGMOD International Conference on Management of Data* (1985), pages 247–267.

[Clifford et al. 1994] J. Clifford, A. Croker, and A. Tuzhilin, "On Completeness of Historical Relational Query Languages," *ACM Transactions on Database Systems*, Volume 19, Number 1 (March 1994), pages 64–116.

[Cluet et al. 1989] S. Cluet, C. Delobel, C. Lecluse, and P. Richard, "Reloop: An Algebra-Based Query Language for an Object-Oriented Database System," *Proceedings of the International Conference on Deductive and Object-Oriented Databases* (December 1989).

[CODASYL 1971] "CODASYL Data Base Task Group April 71 Report," ACM, New York, NY (1971).

[CODASYL 1978] CODASYL *Data Description Language Journal of Development*, Material Data Management Branch, Department of Supply and Services, Ottawa, Ontario (1978).

[Codd 1970] E. F. Codd, "A Relational Model for Large Shared Data Banks," *Communications of the ACM*, Volume 13, Number 6 (June 1970), pages 377–387.

[Codd 1972a] E. F. Codd, "Further Normalization of the Data Base Relational Model," in **[Rustin 1972]**, pages 33–64.

[Codd 1972b] E. F. Codd, "Relational Completeness of Data Base Sublanguages," in **[Rustin 1972]**, pages 65–98.

[Codd 1979] E. F. Codd, "Extending the Database Relational Model to Capture More Meaning," *ACM Transactions on Database Systems*, Volume 4, Number 4 (December 1979), pages 397–434.

[Codd 1982] E. F. Codd, "The 1981 ACM Turing Award Lecture: Relational Database: A Practical Foundation for Productivity," *Communications of the ACM*, Volume 25, Number 2 (February 1982), pages 109–117.

[Codd 1990] E. F. Codd, *The Relational Model for Database Management: Version 2*, Addison-Wesley, Reading, MA (1990).

[Comer 1979] D. Comer, "The Ubiquitous B-tree," *ACM Computing Surveys*, Volume 11, Number 2 (June 1979), pages 121–137.

[Comer 1995] D. Comer, *The Internet Book: Everything You Need to Know about Computer Networking*, Prentice-Hall, Englewood Cliffs, NJ (1995).

[Cormen et al. 1990] T. Cormen, C. Leiserson, and R. Rivest, *An Introduction to Algorithms*, McGraw-Hill, New York, NY (1990).

[Corrigan and Gurry 1993] P. Corrigan and M. Gurry, *ORACLE Performance Tuning*, O'Reilly and Associates, Inc. (1993).

[Cosmadakis and Papadimitriou 1984] S. S. Cosmadakis and C. H. Papadimitriou, "Updates of Relational Views," *Journal of the ACM*, Volume 31, Number 4 (October 1984), pages 742–760.

[Cosmadakis et al. 1990] S. Cosmadakis, P. Kanellakis, and M. Vardi, "Polynomial-Time Implication Problems for Unary Inclusion Dependencies," *Journal of the ACM,* Volume 37, Number 1 (January 1990), pages 15–46.

[Cox 1986] B. J. Cox, *Object-Oriented Programming: An Evolutionary Approach*, Addison-Wesley, Reading, MA (1986).

[Dahl and Bubenko 1982] R. Dahl and J. Bubenko, "IDBD: An Interactive Design Tool for CODASYL DBTG Type Databases," *Proceedings of the International Conference on Very Large Data Bases* (1982), pages 108–121.

[Daniels et al. 1982] D. Daniels, P. G. Selinger, L. M. Haas, B. G. Lindsay, C. Mohan, A. Walker, and P. F. Wilms, "An Introduction to Distributed Query Compilation in R*," in **[Schneider 1982]**.

[Dar et al. 1996] S. Dar, H. V. Jagadish, A. Levy, and D. Srivastava, "Answering Queries with Aggregation Using Views," *Proceedings of the International Conference on Very Large Data Bases* (1996).

[Date 1983a] C. J. Date, *An Introduction to Database Systems*, Volume II, Addison-Wesley, Reading, MA (1983).

[Date 1983b] C. J. Date, "The Outer Join," *IOCOD-2*, John Wiley and Sons, New York, NY (1993), pages 76–106.

[Date 1986] C. J. Date, *Relational Databases: Selected Writings,* Addison-Wesley, Reading, MA (1986).

[Date 1987] C. J. Date, *A Guide to Ingres*, Addison-Wesley, Reading, MA (1987).

[Date 1990] C. J. Date, *Relational Database Writings, 1985-1989*, Addison-Wesley, Reading, MA (1990).

[Date 1993] C. J. Date, "How SQL Missed the Boat," *Database Programming and Design* Volume 6, Number 9 (September 1993).

[Date 1995] C. J. Date, *An Introduction to Database Systems*, Sixth Edition, Addison-Wesley, Reading, MA (1995).

[Date and Darwen 1993] C. J. Date and G. Darwen, *A Guide to the SQL Standard*, Third Edition, Addison-Wesley, Reading, MA (1993).

[Date and White 1989] C. J. Date and C. J. White, *A Guide to SQL/DS*, Addison-Wesley, Reading, MA (1989).

[Date and White 1993] C. J. Date and C. J. White, *A Guide to DB2*, Fourth Edition, Addison-Wesley, Reading, MA (1993).

[Davies 1980] D. W. Davies, "Protection," in *Distributed Systems: An Advanced Course*, Springer-Verlag, Berlin, Germany (1980), pages 211–245.

[Davies 1973] C. T. Davies, Jr., "Recovery Semantics for a DB/DC System," *Proceedings of the ACM Annual Conference* (1973), pages 136–141.

[Davis et al. 1983] C. Davis, S. Jajodia, P. A. Ng, and R. Yeh (Editors), *Entity-Relationship Approach to Software Engineering*, North Holland, Amsterdam, The Netherlands (1983).

[Davison and Graefe 1994] D. L. Davison and G. Graefe, "Memory-Contention Responsive Hash Joins," *Proceedings of the International Conference on Very Large Data Bases* (September 1994).

[Dayal 1987] U. Dayal, "Of Nests and Trees: A Unified Approach to Processing Queries that Contain Nested Subqueries, Aggregates and Quantifiers," *Proceedings of the International Conference on Very Large Data Bases* (1987), pages 197–208.

[Dayal and Bernstein 1978] U. Dayal and P. A. Bernstein, "The Updatability of Relational Views," *Proceedings of the International Conference on Very Large Data Bases* (1978), pages 368–377.

[Dayal and Bernstein 1982] U. Dayal and P. A. Bernstein, "On the Correct Translation of Update Operations on Relational Views," *ACM Transactions on Database Systems*, Volume 3, Number 3 (September 1982), pages 381–416.

[Dayal et al. 1982] U. Dayal, N. Goodman, and R. H. Katz, "An Extended Relational Algebra with Control over Duplicate Elimination," *Proceedings of the ACM SIGACT-SIGMOD Symposium on Principles of Database Systems* (1982).

[Dayal et al. 1990] U. Dayal, M. Hsu, and R. Ladin, "Organizing Long-Running Activities with Triggers and Transactions," *Proceedings of the ACM SIGMOD International Conference on the Management of Data* (1990), pages 204–215.

[Dayal et al. 1991] U. Dayal, M. Hsu, and R. Ladin, "A Transactional Model for Long-Running Activities," *Proceedings of the International Conference on Very Large Data Bases* (September 1991), pages 113–122.

[DeMillo et al. 1978] R. A. DeMillo, D. P. Dobkin, A. K. Jones, and R. J. Lipton, *Foundations of Secure Computation*, Academic Press, New York, NY (1978).

[Denning 1980] D. E. Denning, "Secure Statistical Databases with Random Sample Queries," *ACM Transactions on Database Systems*, Volume 5, Number 3 (September 1980), pages 291–315.

[Denning 1982] P. J. Denning, *Cryptography and Data Security*, Addison-Wesley, Reading, MA (1982).

[Denning and Denning 1979] D. E. Denning and P. J. Denning, "Data Security," *ACM Computing Surveys*, Volume 11, Number 3 (September 1979), pages 227–250.

[Deshpande and Larson 1992] V. Deshpande and P. A. Larson, "The Design and Implementation of a Parallel Join Algorithm for Nested Relations on Shared-Memory Multiprocessors," *Proceedings of the International Conference on Data Engineering* (1992), page 68.

[Derr et al. 1993] M. A. Derr, S. Morishita, and G. Phipps, "Design and Implementation of the Glue-Nail Database System," *Proceedings of the ACM SIGMOD International Conference on Management of Data* (1993), pages 147–156.

[Deux et al. 1991] O. Deux et al., "The O_2 System," *Communications of the ACM*, Volume 34, Number 10 (October 1991), pages 34–49.

[DeWitt and Gray 1992] D. DeWitt and J. Gray, "Parallel Database Systems: The Future of High Performance Database Systems," *Communications of the ACM*, Volume 35, Number 6 (June 1992), pages 85–98.

[DeWitt et al. 1984] D. DeWitt, R. Katz, F. Olken, L. Shapiro, M. Stonebraker, and D. Wood, "Implementation Techniques for Main Memory Databases," *Proceedings of the ACM SIGMOD International Conference on Management of Data* (1984), pages 1–8.

[DeWitt et al. 1986] D. DeWitt, R. Gerber, G. Graefe, M. Heytens, K. Kumar, and M. Muralikrishna, "GAMMA — A High Performance Dataflow Database Machine," *Proceedings of the International Conference on Very Large Data Bases* (1986).

[DeWitt et al. 1990] D. DeWitt et al., "The Gamma Database Machine Project," *IEEE Transactions on Knowledge and Data Engineering* Volume 2, Number 1 (March 1990).

[DeWitt et al. 1992] D. DeWitt, J. Naughton, D. Schneider, and S. Seshadri, "Practical Skew Handling in Parallel Joins," *Proceedings of the International Conference on Very Large Data Bases* (1992).

[Dias et al. 1989] D. Dias, B. Iyer, J. Robinson, and P. Yu, "Integrated Concurrency-Coherency Controls for Multisystem Data Sharing," *IEEE Transactions on Software Engineering*, Volume 15, Number 4 (April 1989), pages 437–448.

[Di Battista and Lenzerini 1989] G. Di Battista and M. Lenzerini "A Deductive Method for Entity-Relationship Modeling," *Proceedings of the International Conference on Very Large Data Bases* (1989), pages 13–22.

[Diffie and Hellman 1979] W. Diffie and M. E. Hellman, "Privacy and Authentication," *Proceedings of the IEEE*, Volume 67, Number 3 (March 1979), pages 397–427.

[Dijkstra 1965] E. W. Dijkstra, "Cooperating Sequential Processes," Technical Report EWD-123, Technological University, Eindhoven, The Netherlands (1965); reprinted in **[Genuys 1968]**, pages 43–112.

[Dippert and Levy 1993] B. Dippert and M. Levy, *Designing with FLASH Memory,* Annabooks 1993.

[Dittrich 1988] K. Dittrich (Editor), *Advances in Object-Oriented Database Systems*, Lecture Notes in Computer Science 334, Springer-Verlag (1988).

[Dobkin et al. 1979] D. Dobkin, A. K. Jones, and R. J. Lipton, "Secure Databases: Protection Against User Inference," *ACM Transactions on Database Systems*, Volume 4, Number 1 (March 1979), pages 97–106.

[Dodd 1969] G. G. Dodd, "APL-A Language for Associative Data Handling in PL/I," *Proceedings of the Fall Joint Computer Conference* (1969), pages 667–684.

[Dogac et al. 1994] A. Dogac, M. T. Ozsu, A. Biliris, and T. Selis (Editors), *Advances in Object-Oriented Database Systems*, Computer and Systems Sciences, NATO ASI Series F, Volume 130, Springer-Verlag (1994).

[Douglis et al. 1994] F. Douglis, R. Cáceres, B. Marsh, F. Kaashoek, K. Li, and J. Tauber, "Storage Alternatives for Mobile Computers," *Proceedings of the Symposium on Operating Systems Design and Implementation* (1994), pages 25–37. An updated version appears as **[Douglis et al. 1996]**.

[Douglis et al. 1996] F. Douglis, R. Cáceres, M. F. Kaashoek, P. Krishnan, K. Li, B. Marsh, and J. Tauber, "Storage Alternatives for Mobile Computers," in **[Imielinski and Korth 1996]**, Chapter 18.

[Du and Elmagarmid 1989] W. Du and A. Elmagarmid, "Quasi Serializability: A Correctness Criterion for Global Database Consistency in InterBase," *Proceedings of the International Conference on Very Large Data Bases* (1989), pages 347–356.

[Dubois and Thakkar 1992] M. Dubois and S. Thakkar (Editors), *Scalable Shared Memory Multiprocessors*, Kluwer Academic Publishers, Boston, MA (1992).

[Duncan 1990] R. Duncan, "A Survey of Parallel Computer Architectures," *IEEE Computer*, Volume 23, Number 2 (February 1990), pages 5–16.

[Ellis 1980a] C. S. Ellis, "Concurrent Search and Insertion in 2–3 Trees," *Acta Informatica*, Volume 14 (1980), pages 63–86.

[Ellis 1980b] C. S. Ellis, "Concurrent Search and Insertion in AVL Trees," *IEEE Transactions on Computers*, Volume C-29, Number 3 (September 1980), pages 811–817.

[Ellis 1987] C. S. Ellis, "Concurrency in Linear Hashing" *ACM Transactions on Database Systems*, Volume 12, Number 2 (June 1987), pages 195–217.

[Elmasri and Larson 1985] R. Elmasri and J. Larson, "A Graphical Query Facility for E-R Databases," *Proceedings of the International Conference on Entity-Relationship Approach* (1985).

[Elmasri and Navathe 1994] R. Elmasri and S. B. Navathe, *Fundamentals of Database Systems*, Second Edition, Benjamin Cummings, Redwood City, CA (1994).

[Elmasri and Wiederhold 1981] R. Elmasri and G. Wiederhold, "GORDAS: A Formal High-Level Query Language for the Entity-Relationship Model," *Proceedings of the International Conference on Entity-Relationship Approach* (1981).

[English and Stepanov 1992] R. M. English and A. A. Stepanov, "Loge: A Self-Organizing Disk Controller," *Proceedings of the Winter 1992 USENIX Conference*, San Francisco, CA (January 1992), pages 238–252.

[Eppinger et al. 1991] J. L Eppinger, L. B. Mummert and A. Z. Spector, *Camelot and Avalon: A Distributed Transaction Facility*, Morgan Kaufmann Publishers, Inc. (1991).

[Epstein and Stonebraker 1980] R. Epstein and M. R. Stonebraker, "Analysis of Distributed Database Processing Strategies," *Proceedings of the International Conference on Very Large Data Bases* (1980), pages 92–110.

[Epstein et al. 1978] R. Epstein, M. R. Stonebraker, and E. Wong, "Distributed Query Processing in a Relational Database System," *Proceedings of the ACM SIGMOD International Conference on Management of Data* (1978), pages 169–180.

[Escobar-Molano et al. 1993] M. Escobar-Molano, R. Hull, and D. Jacobs, "Safety and Translation of Calculus Queries with Scalar Functions," *Proceedings of the ACM SIGACT-SIGMOD-SIGART Symposium on the Principles of Database Systems* (1993), pages 253–264.

[Eswaran and Chamberlin 1975] K. P. Eswaran and D. D. Chamberlin, "Functional Specifications of a Subsystem for Database Integrity," *Proceedings of the International Conference on Very Large Data Bases* (1975), pages 48–68.

[Eswaran et al. 1976] K. P. Eswaran, J. N. Gray, R. A. Lorie, and I. L. Traiger, "The Notions of Consistency and Predicate Locks in a Database System," *Communications of the ACM*, Volume 19, Number 11 (November 1976), pages 624–633.

[Evangelidis et al. 1995] G. Evangelidis, D. Lomet and B. Salzberg, "The hB-Pi Tree: A Modified hB-tree Supporting Concurrency, Recovery and Node Consolidation." *Proceedings of the International Conference on Very Large Data Bases* (1995), pages 551–561.

[Fagin 1977] R. Fagin, "Multivalued Dependencies and a New Normal Form for Relational Databases," *ACM Transactions on Database Systems*, Volume 2, Number 3 (September 1977), pages 262–278.

[Fagin 1979] R. Fagin, "Normal Forms and Relational Database Operators," *Proceedings of the ACM SIGMOD International Conference on Management of Data* (1979), pages 153–160.

[Fagin 1981] R. Fagin, "A Normal Form for Relational Databases That Is Based on Domains and Keys," *ACM Transactions on Database Systems*, Volume 6, Number 3 (September 1981), pages 387–415.

[Fagin 1983] R. Fagin, "Types of Acyclicity of Hypergraphs and Relational Database Schemes," *Journal of the ACM*, Volume 30, Number 3 (July 1983), pages 514–550.

[Fagin et al. 1979] R. Fagin, J. Nievergelt, N. Pippenger, and H. R. Strong, "Extendible Hashing — A Fast Access Method for Dynamic Files," *ACM Transactions on Database Systems*, Volume 4, Number 3 (September 1979), pages 315–344.

[Fagin et al. 1982] R. Fagin, A. O. Mendelzon, and J. D. Ullman, "A Simplified Universal Relation Assumption and Its Properties," *ACM Transactions on Database Systems*, Volume 7, Number 3 (September 1982), pages 343–360.

[Faloutsos and Lin 1995] C. Faloutsos and K.-I. Lin, "Fast Map: A Fast Algorithm for Indexing, Data-Mining and Visualization of Traditional and Multimedia Datasets," *Proceedings of the ACM SIGMOD International Conference on Management of Data* (1995), pages 163–174.

[Fayyad et al. 1995] U. Fayyad, G. Piatetsky-Shapiro, P. Smyth, and R. Uthurusamy, *Advances in Knowledge Discovery and Data Mining*, MIT Press, Cambridge, MA (1995).

[Fekete et al. 1990a] A. Fekete, N. Lynch, and W. Weihl, "A Serialization Graph Construction for Nested Transactions," *Proceedings of the ACM SIGACT-SIGMOD-SIGART Symposium on the Principles of Database Systems* (1990), pages 94–108.

[Fekete et al. 1990b] A. Fekete, N. Lynch, M. Merritt, and W. Weihl, "Commutativity-Based Locking for Nested Transactions," *Journal of Computer and System Sciences* (August 1990), pages 65–156.

[Fernandez et al. 1981] E. Fernandez, R. Summers, and C. Wood, *Database Security and Integrity*, Addison-Wesley, Reading, MA (1981).

[Finkel and Bentley 1974] R. A. Finkel and J. L. Bentley, "Quad Trees: A Data Structure for Retrieval on Composite Keys," *Acta Informatica*, Volume 4 (1974), pages 1–9.

[Finkelstein 1982] S. Finkelstein, "Common Expression Analysis in Database Applications," *Proceedings of the ACM SIGMOD International Conference on Management of Data* (1982), pages 235–245.

[Finkelstein et al. 1988] S. Finkelstein, M. Schkolnick, and P. Tiberio, "Physical Database Design for Relational Databases," *ACM Transactions on Database Systems*, Volume 13, Number 1 (March 1988), pages 53–90.

[Fischer and Thomas 1983] P. C. Fischer and S. Thomas, "Operators for Non-First-Normal-Form Relations," *Proceedings of the International Computer Software Applications Conference* (1983), pages 464–475.

[Fishman et al. 1990] D. Fishman, D. Beech, H. Cate, E. Chow, T. Connors, J. Davis, N. Derrett, C. Hoch, W. Kent, P. Lyngbaek, B. Mahbod, M. Neimat, T. Ryan, and M. Shan, "IRIS: An Object-Oriented Database Management System," in **[Zdonik and Maier 1990]**, pages 216–226.

[Ford and Calhoun 1984] R. Ford and J. Calhoun, "Concurrency Control Mechanism and the Serializability of Concurrent Tree Algorithms," *Proceedings of the ACM SIGACT-SIGMOD Symposium on the Principles of Database Systems* (1984), pages 51–60.

[Fortier 1989] P. J. Fortier, *Handbook of LAN Technology,* McGraw Hill, New York, NY (1989).

[Franklin et al. 1992] M. J. Franklin, M. J. Zwilling, C. K. Tan, M. J. Carey, and D. J. DeWitt, "Crash Recovery in Client-Server EXODUS," *Proceedings of the ACM SIGMOD International Conference on Management of Data* (June 1992), pages 165–174.

[Franklin et al. 1993] M. J. Franklin, M. Carey, and M. Livny, "Local Disk Caching for Client-Server Database Systems," *Proceedings of the International Conference on Very Large Data Bases* (August 1993).

[Fredkin 1960] E. Fredkin, "Trie Memory," *Communications of the ACM*, Volume 4, Number 2 (September 1960), pages 490–499.

[Freedman 1983] D. H. Freedman, "Searching for Denser Disks," *Infosystems* (September 1983).

[Freedman and DeWitt 1995] C. S. Freedman and D. J. DeWitt, "The SPIFFI Scalable Video-on-Demand Server," *Proceedings of the ACM SIGMOD International Conference on Management of Data* (1995), pages 352–363.

[Fry and Sibley 1976] J. Fry and E. Sibley, "Evolution of Data-Base Management Systems," *ACM Computing Surveys*, Volume 8, Number 1 (March 1976), pages 7–42.

[Fujitani 1984] L. Fujitani, "Laser Optical Disk: The Coming Revolution in On-Line Storage," *Communications of the ACM,* Volume 27, Number 6 (June 1984), pages 546–554.

[Furtado 1978] A. L. Furtado, "Formal Aspects of the Relational Model," *Information Systems,* Volume 3, Number 2 (1978), pages 131–140.

[Fushimi et al. 1986] S. Fushimi, M. Kitsuregawa, and H. Tanaka, "An Overview of the Systems Software of a Parallel Relational Database Machine: GRACE," *Proceedings of the International Conference on Very Large Databases* (August 1986).

[Fussell et al. 1981] D. S. Fussell, Z. Kedem, and A. Silberschatz, "Deadlock Removal Using Partial Rollback in Database Systems," *Proceedings of the ACM SIGMOD International Conference on the Management of Data* (1981), pages 65–73.

[Gadia 1986] S. K. Gadia, "Weak Temporal Relations," *Proceedings of the ACM SIGACT-SIGMOD Symposium on the Principles of Database Systems* (1986), pages 70–77.

[Gadia 1988] S. K. Gadia, "A Homogeneous Relational Model and Query Language for Temporal Databases," *ACM Transactions on Database Systems*, Volume 13, Number 4 (December 1988), pages 418–448.

[Gait 1988] J. Gait, "The Optical File Cabinet: A Random-Access File System for Write-Once Optical Disks," *IEEE Computer*, Volume 21, Number 6 (June 1988).

[Galindo-Legaria 1994] C. Galindo-Legaria, "Outerjoins as Disjunctions," *Proceedings of the ACM SIGMOD International Conference on Management of Data* (1994).

[Galindo-Legaria and Rosenthal 1992] C. Galindo-Legaria and A. Rosenthal, "How to Extend a Conventional Optimizer to Handle One- and Two-Sided Outerjoin," *Proceedings of the International Conference on Data Engineering* (1992), pages 402–409.

[Gallaire and Minker 1978] H. Gallaire and J. Minker (Editors), *Logic and Databases*, Plenum Press, New York, NY (1978).

[Gallaire et al. 1984] H. Gallaire, J. Minker, and J. M. Nicolas, "Logic and Databases: A Deductive Approach," *ACM Computing Surveys*, Volume 16, Number 2 (June 1984), pages 154–185.

[Ganguly et al. 1992] S. Ganguly, W. Hasan and R. Krishnamurthy, "Query Optimization for Parallel Execution," *Proceedings of the ACM SIGMOD International Conference on Management of Data* (1992).

[Ganguly et al. 1996] S. Ganguly, P. Gibbons, Y. Matias, and A. Silberschatz, "A Sampling Algorithm for Estimating Join Size," *Proceedings of the ACM SIGMOD International Conference on Management of Data* (May 1996).

[Ganski and Wong 1987] R. A. Ganski and H. K. T. Wong, "Optimization of Nested SQL Queries Revisited," *Proceedings of the ACM SIGMOD International Conference on Management of Data* (May 1987).

[Garcia-Molina 1982] H. Garcia-Molina, "Elections in Distributed Computing Systems," *IEEE Transactions on Computers*, Volume C-31, Number 1 (January 1982), pages 48–59.

[Garcia-Molina 1983] H. Garcia-Molina, "Using Semantic Knowledge for Transaction Processing in a Distributed Database," *ACM Transactions on Database Systems*, Volume 8, Number 2 (June 1983), pages 186–213.

[Garcia-Molina and Salem 1992] H. Garcia-Molina and K. Salem, "Main Memory Database Systems: An Overview," *IEEE Transactions on Knowledge and Data Engineering,* Volume 4, Number 6 (December 1992), pages 509–516.

[Garcia-Molina and Wiederhold 1982] H. Garcia-Molina and G. Wiederhold, "Read-only Transactions in a Distributed Database," *ACM Transactions on Database Systems*, Volume 7, Number 2 (June 1982), pages 209–234.

[Gardarin and Valduriez 1989] G. Gardarin and P. Valduriez, *Relational Databases and Knowledge Bases,* Addison-Wesley, Reading, MA (1989).

[Garey and Johnson 1979] M. R. Garey and D. S. Johnson, *Computers and Intractability: A Guide to the Theory of NP-Completeness*, Freeman, New York, NY (1979).

[Garza and Kim 1988] J. Garza and W. Kim, "Transaction Management in an Object-Oriented Database System," *Proceedings of the ACM SIGMOD International Conference on the Management of Data* (1988), pages 37–45.

[Gehani and Jagadish 1991] N. Gehani and H. Jagadish, "Ode as an Active Database: Constraints and Triggers," *Proceedings of the International Conference on Very Large Data Bases* (1991).

[Gehani et al. 1992] N. Gehani, H. Jagadish, and O. Shmueli, "Composite Event Specification in Active Databases: Model and Implementation," *Proceedings of the International Conference on Very Large Data Bases* (1992).

[Geiger 1995] K. Geiger, *Inside ODBC*, Microsoft Press, Redmond, WA (1995).

[Genuys 1968] F. Genuys (Editor), *Programming Languages*, Academic Press, London, England (1968).

[Georgakopoulos et al. 1994] D. Georgakopoulos, M. Rusinkiewicz, and A. Seth, "Using Tickets to Enforce the Serializability of Multidatabase Transactions," *IEEE Transactions on Knowledge and Data Engineering,* Volume 6, Number 1 (February 1994), pages 166–180.

[Gerritsen 1975] R. Gerritsen, "A Preliminary System for the Design of DBTG Data Structures," *Communications of the ACM*, Volume 18, Number 10 (October 1975) pages 551–557.

[Gifford 1979] D. K. Gifford, "Weighted Voting for Replicated Data," *Proceedings of the ACM SIGOPS Symposium on Operating Systems Principles* (1979), pages 150–162.

[Gligor and Shattuck 1980] V. D. Gligor and S. H. Shattuck, "On Deadlock Detection in Distributed Systems," *IEEE Transactions on Software Engineering*, Volume SE-6, Number 5 (September 1980), pages 435–439.

[Gogolla and Hohenstein 1991] M. Gogolla and U. Hohenstein, "Towards a Semantic view of an Extended Entity-Relationship Model," *ACM Transactions on Database Systems*, Volume 16, Number 3 (September 1991), pages 369–416.

[Goldberg and Robson 1983] A. Goldberg and D. Robson, *Smalltalk-80: The Language and Its Implementation*, Addison-Wesley, Reading, MA (1983).

[Goodman 1995] N. Goodman, "An Object-Oriented DBMS War Story: Developing a Genome Mapping Database in C++," in **[Kim 1995]**, pages 216–237.

[Gotlieb 1975] L. R. Gotlieb, "Computing Joins of Relations," *Proceedings of the ACM SIGMOD International Conference on the Management of Data* (1975), pages 55–63.

[Graefe 1990] G. Graefe, "Encapsulation of Parallelism in the Volcano Query Processing System," *Proceedings of the ACM SIGMOD International Conference on Management of Data* (1990), pages 102–111.

[Graefe 1993] G. Graefe, "Query Evaluation Techniques for Large Databases," *ACM Computing Surveys*, Volume 25, Number 2 (June 1993), pages 73–170.

[Graefe and McKenna 1993] G. Graefe and W. McKenna, "The Volcano Optimizer Generator," *Proceedings of the International Conference on Data Engineering* (1993), pages 209–218.

[Graham et al. 1986] M. H. Graham, A. O. Mendelzon, and M. Y. Vardi, "Notions of Dependency Satisfaction," *Journal of the ACM*, Volume 33, Number 1 (January 1986), pages 105–129.

[Gravano et al. 1994] L. Gravano, H. Garcia-Molina, and A. Tomasic, "The Effectiveness of GIOSS for the Test Database Discovery Problem," *Proceedings of the ACM SIGMOD International Conference on Management of Data* (1994), pages 126–137.

[Gray 1978] J. Gray, "Notes on Data Base Operating System," in **[Bayer et al. 1978]**, pages 393–481.

[Gray 1981] J. Gray, "The Transaction Concept: Virtues and Limitations," *Proceedings of the International Conference on Very Large Data Bases* (1981), pages 144–154.

[Gray 1991] J. Gray, *The Benchmark Handbook for Database and Transaction Processing Systems,* Second Edition, Morgan-Kaufmann, San Mateo, CA (1991).

[Gray and Edwards 1995] J. Gray and J. Edwards, "Scale Up with TP Monitors," *Byte*, Volume 20, Number 4 (April 1995), pages 123–130.

[Gray and Reuter 1993] J. Gray and A. Reuter, *Transaction Processing: Concepts and Techniques*, Morgan Kaufmann, San Mateo, CA (1993).

[Gray et al. 1975] J. Gray, R. A. Lorie, and G. R. Putzolu, "Granularity of Locks and Degrees of Consistency in a Shared Data Base," *Proceedings of the International Conference on Very Large Data Bases* (1975), pages 428–451.

[Gray et al. 1976] J. Gray, R. A. Lorie, G. R. Putzolu, and I. L. Traiger, "Granularity of Locks and Degrees of Consistency in a Shared Data Base," in **[Nijssen 1976]**, pages 365–395.

[Gray et al. 1981a] J. Gray, P. R. McJones, and M. Blasgen, "The Recovery Manager of the System R Database Manager," *ACM Computing Surveys*, Volume 13, Number 2 (June 1981), pages 223–242.

[Gray et al. 1981b] J. Gray, P. Homan, H. F. Korth, and R. Obermarck, "A Straw Man Analysis of the Probability of Waiting and Deadlock," Research Report RJ3066, IBM Research Laboratory, San Jose, CA (1981).

[Gray et al. 1990] J. Gray, B. Horst, and M. Walker, "Parity Striping of Disc Arrays: Low-Cost Reliable Storage with Acceptable Throughput," *Proceedings of the International Conference on Very Large Data Bases* (1990), pages 148–161.

[Gray et al. 1995] J. Gray, A. Bosworth, A. Layman, and H. Pirahesh, "Data Cube: A Relational Aggregation Operator Generalizing Group-By, Cross-Tab and Sub-Totals," Technical Report MSR-TR-95-22, Microsoft Research (November 1995).

[Gray et al. 1996] J. Gray, P. Helland, and P. O'Neil, "The Dangers of Replication and a Solution," *Proceedings of the ACM SIGMOD International Conference on Management of Data* (1996), pages 173–182.

[Griffin and Libkin 1995] T. Griffin and L. Libkin, "Incremental Maintenance of Views with Duplicates," *Proceedings of the ACM SIGMOD International Conference on Management of Data* (1995).

[Gupta and Mumick 1995] A. Gupta and I. S. Mumick, "Maintenance of Materialized Views: Problems, Techniques and Applications," *IEEE Data Engineering Bulletin*, Volume 18, Number 2 (June 1995).

[Guttman 1984] A. Guttman, "R-Trees: A Dynamic Index Structure for Spatial Searching," *Proceedings of the ACM SIGMOD International Conference on Management of Data* (1984), pages 47–57.

[Haas et al. 1989] L. M. Haas, J. C. Freytag, G. M. Lohman, and H. Pirahesh, "Extensible Query Processing in Starburst," *Proceedings of the ACM SIGMOD International Conference on Management of Data* (1989), pages 377–388.

[Haerder and Reuter 1983] T. Haerder and A. Reuter, "Principles of Transaction-Oriented Database Recovery," *ACM Computing Surveys*, Volume 15, Number 4 (December 1983), pages 287–318.

[Haerder and Rothermel 1987] T. Haerder and K. Rothermel, "Concepts for Transaction Recovery in Nested Transactions," *Proceedings of the ACM SIGMOD International Conference on Management of Data* (1987), pages 239–248.

[Hall 1976] P. A. V. Hall, "Optimization of a Single Relational Expression in a Relational Database System," *IBM Journal of Research and Development*, Volume 20, Number 3 (1976), pages 244–257.

[Halsall 1992] F. Halsall, *Data Communications, Computer Networks, and Open Systems*, Addison-Wesley, Reading, MA (1992).

[Hammer and McLeod 1975] M. Hammer and D. McLeod, "Semantic Integrity in a Relational Data Base System," *Proceedings of the International Conference on Very Large Data Bases* (1975), pages 25–47.

[Hammer and McLeod 1981] M. Hammer and D. McLeod, "Database Description with SDM: A Semantic Data Model," *ACM Transactions on Database Systems*, Volume 6, Number 3 (September 1980), pages 351–386.

[Hammer and Sarin 1978] M. Hammer and S. Sarin, "Efficient Monitoring of Database Assertions," *Proceedings of the ACM SIGMOD International Conference on Management of Data* (1978).

[Harinarayan et al. 1996] V. Harinarayan, J. D. Ullman, and A. Rajaraman, "Implementing Data Cubes Efficiently," *Proceedings of the ACM SIGMOD International Conference on the Management of Data* (1996).

[Haritsa et al. 1990] J. Haritsa, M. Carey, and M. Livny, "On Being Optimistic about Real-Time Constraints," *Proceedings of the ACM SIGACT-SIGMOD Symposium on Principles of Database Systems* (April 1990).

[Harker et al. 1981] J. M. Harker, D. W. Brede, R. E. Pattison, G. R. Santana, and L. G. Taft, "A Quarter Century of Disk File Innovation," *IBM Journal of Research and Development,* Volume 25, Number 5 (September 1981), pages 677–689.

[Hasan and Motwani 1995] W. Hasan and R. Motwani, "Coloring Away Communication in Parallel Query Optimization," *Proceedings of the International Conference on Very Large Data Bases* (1995).

[Haskin and Lorie 1982] R. Haskin and R. A. Lorie, "On Extending the Functions of a Relational Database System," *Proceedings of the ACM SIGMOD International Conference on the Management of Data* (1982), pages 207–212.

[Haskin et al. 1988] R. Haskin, Y. Malachi, W. Sawdon, and G. Chan, "Recovery Management in Quicksilver," *ACM Transactions on Computer Systems*, Volume 6, Number 1 (January 1988), pages 82–108.

[Hevner and Yao 1979] A. R. Hevner and S. B. Yao, "Query Processing in Distributed Database Systems," *IEEE Transactions on Software Engineering*, Volume SE-5, Number 3 (May 1979), pages 177–187.

[Hinrichs 1985] K. H. Hinrichs, "The Grid File System: Implementation and Case Studies of Applications," Ph.D. thesis, Swiss Federal Institute of Technology, Zurich, Switzerland (1985).

[Hoagland 1985] A. S. Hoagland, "Information Storage Technology — A Look at the Future," *IEEE Computer*, Volume 18, Number 7 (July 1985), pages 60–68.

[Hollinsworth 1994] D. Hollinsworth, "The Workflow Reference Model," *Workflow Management Coalition,* Number TC00-1003 (December 1994).

[Holt 1971] R. C. Holt, "Comments on Prevention of System Deadlocks," *Communications of the ACM*, Volume 14, Number 1 (January 1971), pages 36–38.

[Holt 1972] R. C. Holt, "Some Deadlock Properties of Computer Systems," *ACM Computing Surveys*, Volume 4, Number 3 (September 1972), pages 179–196.

[Hong and Stonebraker 1991] W. Hong and M. Stonebraker, "Optimization of Parallel Query Execution Plans in XPRS," *Proceedings of the International Symposium on Parallel and Distributed Information Systems* (1991), pages 218–225.

[Hong et al. 1993] D. Hong, T. Johnson, S. Chakravarthy, "Real-Time Transaction Scheduling: A Cost Conscious Approach," *Proceedings of the ACM SIGMOD International Conference on Management of Data* (April 1993).

[Horowitz and Sahni 1976] E. Horowitz and S. Sahni, *Fundamentals of Data Structures*, Computer Science Press, Rockville, MD (1976).

[Hsu and Imielinski 1985] A. Hsu and T. Imielinski, "Integrity Checking for Multiple Updates," *Proceedings of the ACM SIGMOD International Conference on Management of Data* (1985), pages 152–168.

[Hudson and King 1989] S. E. Hudson and R. King, "Cactis: A Self-Adaptive, Concurrent Implementation of an Object-Oriented Database Management System," *ACM Transactions on Database Systems,* Volume 14, Number 3 (September 1989), pages 291–321.

[Huffman 1993] A. Huffman, "Transaction Processing with TUXEDO," *Proceedings of the International Symposium on Parallel and Distributed Information Systems* (1993).

[Hull and King 1987] R. Hull and R. King, "Semantic Database Modeling: Survey, Applications and Research Issues," *ACM Computing Surveys*, Volume 19, Number 3 (September 1987), pages 201–260.

[IBM 1978a] IBM Corporation, *Information Management System/Virtual Storage General Information,* IBM Form Number GH20–1260, SH20–9025, SH20–9026, SH20–9027.

[IBM 1978b] IBM Corporation, *Query-by Example Terminal Users Guide,* IBM Form Number SH20–20780 (1978).

[IBM 1987] IBM Corporation, *Systems Application Architecture: Common Programming Interface, Database Reference*, IBM Form Number SC26–4348–0 (1987).

[Imielinski and Badrinath 1994] T. Imielinski and B. R. Badrinath, "Mobile Computing — Solutions and Challenges," *Communications of the ACM*, Volume 37, Number 10 (October 1994).

[Imielinski and Korth 1996] T. Imielinski and H. F. Korth (Editors), *Mobile Computing,* Kluwer Academic Publishers (1996).

[Imielinski et al. 1995] T. Imielinski, S. Viswanathan, and B. R. Badrinath, "Energy Efficient Indexing on the Air," *Proceedings of the ACM SIGMOD International Conference on Management of Data* (1995), pages 25–36.

[Ioannidis and Christodoulakis 1993] Y. Ioannidis and S. Christodoulakis, "Optimal Histograms for Limiting Worst-Case Error Propagation in the Size of Join Results," *ACM Transactions on Database Systems*, Volume 18, Number 4 (December 1993), pages 709–748.

[Ioannidis and Kang 1990] Y. Ioannidis and Y. Kang, "Randomized Algorithms for Optimizing Large Join Queries," *Proceedings of the ACM SIGMOD International Conference on Management of Data* (1990), pages 312–321.

[Ioannidis and Poosala 1995] Y. E. Ioannidis and V. Poosala, "Balancing Histogram Optimality and Practicality for Query Result Size Estimation," *Proceedings of the ACM SIGMOD International Conference on Management of Data* (1995), pages 233–244.

[Ioannidis and Wong 1987] Y. E. Ioannidis and E. Wong, "Query Optimization by Simulated Annealing," *Proceedings of the ACM SIGMOD International Conference on Management of Data* (1987), pages 9–22.

[Ioannidis et al. 1992] Y. E. Ioannidis, R. T. Ng, K. Shim, and T. K. Sellis, "Parametric Query Optimization," *Proceedings of the International Conference on Very Large Data Bases* (1992), pages 103–114.

[Ishikawa et al. 1993] H. Ishikawa, F. Suzuki, F. Kozakura, A. Makinouchi, M. Miyagishima, Y. Izumida, M. Aoshima, and Y. Yamana, "The Model, Language, and Implementation of an Object-Oriented Multimedia Knowledge Base Management System," *ACM Transactions on Database Systems*, Volume 18, Number 1 (March 1993), pages 1–50.

[Jaeschke and Schek 1982] G. Jaeschke and H. J. Schek, "Remarks on the Algebra of Non First Normal Form Relations," *Proceedings of the ACM SIGACT-SIGMOD Symposium on Principles of Database Systems* (1982), pages 124–138.

[Jagadish and Qian 1992] H. V. Jagadish and X. Qian, "Integrity Maintenance in an Object-Oriented Database," *Proceedings of the International Conference on Very Large Data Bases* (1992).

[Jagadish et al. 1993] H. V. Jagadish, A. Silberschatz, and S. Sudarshan, "Recovering from Main-Memory Lapses," *Proceedings of the International Conference on Very Large Data Bases* (August 1993).

[Jagadish et al. 1994] H. Jagadish, D. Lieuwen, R. Rastogi, A. Silberschatz, and S. Sudarshan, "Dali: A High Performance Main Memory Storage Manager," *International Conference on Very Large Databases* (September 1994).

[Jajodia and Sandhu 1990] S. Jajodia and R. Sandhu, "Polyinstantiation Integrity in Multilevel Relations," *Proceedings of the IEEE Symposium on Research in Security and Privacy* (1990), pages 104–115.

[Jajodia and Subramanian 1995] S. Jajodia and V. S. Subramanian (Editors), *Multimedia Database Systems: Issues and Research Directions*, Springer-Verlag (1995).

[Jarke and Koch 1984] M. Jarke and J. Koch, "Query Optimization in Database Systems," *ACM Computing Surveys*, Volume 16, Number 2 (June 1984), pages 111–152.

[Jensen et al. 1994] C. S. Jensen and others, "A Consensus Glossary of Temporal Database Concepts," *ACM SIGMOD Record*, Volume 23, Number 1 (March 1994), pages 52–64.

[Jin et al. 1993] W. Jin, L. Ness, M. Rusinkiewicz, and A. Sheth, "Concurrency Control and Recovery of Multidatabase Work Flows in Telecommunication Applications," *Proceedings of the ACM SIGMOD International Conference on Management of Data* (May 1993).

[Johnson and Shasha 1993] T. Johnson and D. Shasha, "The Performance of Concurrent B-Tree Algorithms," *ACM Transactions on Database Systems*, Volume 18, Number 1 (March 1993).

[Jones and Schwarz 1980] A. K. Jones and P. Schwarz, "Experience Using Multiprocessor Systems — A Status Report," *Computing Surveys*, Volume 12, Number 2 (June 1980), pages 121–165.

[Joshi 1991] A. Joshi, "Adaptive Locking Strategies in a Multi-Node Shared Data Model Environment," *Proceedings of the International Conference on Very Large Data Bases* (1991).

[Kaiser 1990] G. Kaiser, "A Flexible Transaction Model for Software Engineering," *Proceedings of the International Conference on Data Engineering* (1990).

[Kam and Ullman 1977] J. B. Kam and J. D. Ullman, "A Model of Statistical Databases and Their Security," *ACM Transactions on Database Systems*, Volume 2, Number 1 (January 1977), pages 1–10.

[Kambayashi et al. 1982] Y. Kambayashi, M. Yoshikawa, and S. Yajima, "Query Processing for Distributed Databases Using Generalized Semi-joins," *Proceedings of the ACM SIGMOD International Conference on the Management of Data* (1982), pages 151–160.

[Kamel and Faloutsos 1992] I. Kamel, and C. Faloutsos, "Parallel R-Trees," *Proceedings of the ACM SIGMOD International Conference on Management of Data* (June 1992).

[Katz and Wong 1982] R. H. Katz and E. Wong, "Decompiling CODASYL DML into Relational Queries," *ACM Transactions on Database Systems*, Volume 7, Number 1 (March 1982), pages 1–23.

[Katz et al. 1989] R. H. Katz, G. A. Gibson, and D. A. Patterson, "Disk System Architectures for High Performance Computing," *Proceedings of the IEEE*, Volume 77, Number 12 (December 1989).

[Kedem and Silberschatz 1979] Z. M. Kedem and A. Silberschatz, "Controlling Concurrency Using Locking Protocols," *Proceedings of the Annual IEEE Symposium on Foundations of Computer Science* (1979), pages 275–285.

[Kedem and Silberschatz 1983] Z. M. Kedem and A. Silberschatz, "Locking Protocols: From Exclusive to Shared Locks," *Journal of the ACM*, Volume 30, Number 4 (October 1983), pages 787–804.

[Keller 1985] A. M. Keller, "Updating Relational Databases Through Views," Ph.D. thesis, Department of Computer Science, Stanford University, Stanford, CA (1985).

[Kenville 1982] R. F. Kenville, "Optical Disk Data Storage," *IEEE Computer*, Volume 15, Number 7 (July 1982), pages 21–26.

[Khoshafian and Copeland 1990] S. Khoshafian and G. P. Copeland, "Object Identity," in **[Zdonik and Maier 1990]**, pages 37–46.

[Kifer et al. 1992] M. Kifer, W. Kim, and Y. Sagiv, "Querying Object Oriented Databases," *Proceedings of the ACM SIGMOD International Conference on the Management of Data* (1992), pages 393–402.

[Kim 1982] W. Kim, "On Optimizing an SQL-like Nested Query" *ACM Transactions on Database Systems*, Volume 3, Number 3 (September 1982), pages 443–469.

[Kim 1984] W. Kim, "Query Optimization for Relational Database Systems," in **[Unger et al. 1984]**.

[Kim 1989] W. Kim, "A Model of Queries for Object-Oriented Databases," *Proceedings of the International Conference on Very Large Data Bases* (1989).

[Kim 1990a] W. Kim, "Architectural Issues in Object-Oriented Databases," *Journal of Object-Oriented Programming* (March/April 1990).

[Kim 1990b] W. Kim, *Introduction to Object-Oriented Databases*, MIT Press, Cambridge, MA (1990).

[Kim 1995] W. Kim (Editor), *Modern Database Systems,* ACM Press/Addison Wesley (1995).

[Kim and Lochovsky 1989] W. Kim and F. Lochovsky (Editors), *Object-Oriented Concepts, Databases, and Applications*, Addison-Wesley, Reading, MA (1989).

[Kim et al. 1984] W. Kim, R. Lorie, D. McNabb, and W. Plouffe, "Transaction Mechanism for Engineering Design Databases," *Proceedings of the International Conference on Very Large Data Bases*, (August 1984), pages 355-362.

[Kim et al. 1985] W. Kim, D. S. Reiner, and D. S. Batory (Editors), *Query Processing in Database Systems*, Springer-Verlag, Berlin, Germany (1985).

[Kim et al. 1988] W. Kim, N. Ballou, J. Banerjee, H. T. Chou, J. F. Garza, and D. Woelk, "Integrating an Object-Oriented Programming System with a Database System," *Proceedings of the International Conference on Object-Oriented Programming Systems, Languages, and Applications* (1988).

[Kim et al. 1989] W. Kim, K. C. Kim, and A. Dale, "Indexing Techniques for Object-Oriented Databases," in **[Kim and Lochovsky 1989]**, pages 371–394.

[King 1981] J. J. King, "QUIST: A System for Semantic Query Optimization in Relational Data Bases," *Proceedings of the International Conference on Very Large Data Bases* (1981), pages 510–517.

[King et al. 1983] R. P. King, H. F. Korth, and B. E. Willner, " Design of a Document Filing and Retrieval Service," *Proceedings of the ACM SIGMOD-SIGBDB Database Week* (1983).

[King et al. 1991] R. P. King, N. Halim, H. Garcia-Molina, and C. Polyzois, "Management of a Remote Backup Copy for Disaster Recovery," *ACM Transactions on Database Systems*, Volume 16, Number 2 (June 1991), pages 338–368.

[Kitsuregawa and Ogawa 1990] M. Kitsuregawa and Y Ogawa, "Bucket Spreading Parallel Hash: A New, Robust, Parallel Hash Join Method for Skew in the Super Database Computer," *Proceedings of the International Conference on Very Large Data Bases* (1990), pages 210–221.

[Kitsuregawa et al. 1983] M. Kitsuregawa, H. Tanaka, and T. MotoOka, "Application of Hash to a Database Machine and its Architecture," *New Generation Computing*, Number 1 (1983), pages 62–74.

[Kleinrock 1975] L. Kleinrock, *Queuing Systems, Volume 1: Theory,* John Wiley and Sons Publishers, New York, NY (1975).

[Kleinrock 1976] L. Kleinrock, *Queuing Systems, Volume 2: Computer Applications,* John Wiley and Sons Publishers, New York, NY (1976).

[Klug 1982] A. Klug, "Equivalence of Relational Algebra and Relational Calculus Query Languages Having Aggregate Functions," *Journal of the ACM*, Volume 29, Number 3 (July 1982), pages 699–717.

[Knapp 1987] E. Knapp, "Deadlock Detection in Distributed Databases," *ACM Computing Surveys,* Volume 19, Number 4 (December 1987).

[Knuth 1973] D. E. Knuth, *The Art of Computer Programming, Volume 3: Sorting and Searching*, Addison-Wesley, Reading, MA (1973).

[Koch and Loney 1995] G. Koch and K. Loney, *Oracle: The Complete Reference*, Third Edition, Osborne, McGraw-Hill, Oracle (1995).

[Kogan and Jajodia 1990] B. Kogan and S. Jajodia, "Concurrency Control in Multilevel-secure Databases Using Replicated Architecture," *Proceedings of the ACM SIGMOD International Conference on the Management of Data* (1990), pages 153–162.

[Kohler 1981] W. H. Kohler, "A Survey of Techniques for Synchronization and Recovery in Decentralized Computer Systems," *ACM Computing Surveys*, Volume 13, Number 2 (June 1981), pages 149–183.

[Korth 1982] H. F. Korth, " Deadlock Freedom Using Edge Locks," *ACM Transactions on Database Systems*, Volume 7, Number 4 (December 1982), pages 632–652.

[Korth 1983] H. F. Korth, "Locking Primitives in a Database System," *Journal of the ACM*, Volume 30, Number 1 (January 1983), pages 55–79.

[Korth and Speegle 1988] H. F. Korth and G. Speegle, "Formal Model of Correctness Without Serializability," *Proceedings of the ACM SIGMOD International Conference on Management of Data* (1988), pages 379–386.

[Korth and Speegle 1990] H. F. Korth and G. Speegle, "Long Duration Transactions in Software Design Projects," *Proceedings of the International Conference on Data Engineering* (1990), pages 568–575.

[Korth and Speegle 1994] H. F. Korth and G. Speegle, "Formal Aspects of Concurrency Control in Long Duration Transaction Systems Using the NT/PV Model," *ACM Transactions on Database Systems*, Volume 19, Number 3 (September 1994), pages 492–535.

[Korth et al. 1988] H. F. Korth, W. Kim, and F. Bancilhon, "On Long Duration CAD Transactions," *Information Science*, Volume 46 (October 1988), pages 73–107.

[Korth et al. 1990a] H. F. Korth, E. Levy, and A. Silberschatz, "A Formal Approach to Recovery by Compensating Transactions," *Proceedings of the International Conference on Very Large Data Bases* (1990), pages 95–106.

[Korth et al. 1990b] H. F. Korth, N. Soparkar, and A. Silberschatz, "Triggered Real-Time Databases with Consistency Constraints," *Proceedings of the International Conference on Very Large Data Bases* (1990), pages 71–82.

[Krol 1994] E. Krol, *The Whole Internet: Users Guide and Catalog,* Second Edition, O'Reilly & Associates, Sebastopol, CA (1994).

[Kumar and Stonebraker 1988] A. Kumar and M. Stonebraker, "Semantics Based Transaction Management Techniques for Replicated Data," *Proceedings of the ACM SIGMOD International Conference on Management of Data* (1988), pages 117–125.

[Kung and Lehman 1980] H. T. Kung and P. L. Lehman, "Concurrent Manipulation of Binary Search Trees," *ACM Transactions on Database Systems*, Volume 5, Number 3 (September 1980), pages 339–353.

[Kung and Robinson 1981] H. T. Kung and J. T. Robinson, " Optimistic Concurrency Control," *ACM Transactions on Database Systems*, Volume 6, Number 2 (June 1981), pages 312–326.

[Kwong and Wood 1982] Y. S. Kwong and D. Wood, "Method for Concurrency in B+-trees," *IEEE Transactions on Software Engineering*, Volume SE-8, Number 3 (March 1982), pages 211–223.

[Lai and Wilkinson 1984] M. Y. Lai and W. K. Wilkinson "Distributed Transaction Management in JASMIN," *Proceedings of the International Conference on Very Large Data Bases* (1984), pages 466–472.

[Lamb et al. 1991] C. Lamb, G. Landis, J. Orenstein, and D. Weinreb, "The ObjectStore Database System," *Communications of the ACM*, Volume 34, Number 10 (October 1991), pages 51–63.

[Lamport 1978] L. Lamport, "Time, Clocks, and the Ordering of Events in a Distributed System," *Communications of the ACM*, Volume 21, Number 7 (July 1978), pages 558–565.

[Lampson and Sturgis 1976] B. Lampson and H. Sturgis "Crash Recovery in a Distributed Data Storage System," Technical Report, Computer Science Laboratory, Xerox, Palo Alto Research Center, Palo Alto, CA (1976).

[Langerak 1990] R. Langerak, "View Updates in Relational Databases with an Independent Scheme," *ACM Transactions on Database Systems,* Volume 15, Number 1 (March 1990), pages 40–66.

[Lanzelotte et al. 1993] R. Lanzelotte, P. Valduriez, and M. Zat, "On the Effectiveness of Optimization Search Strategies for Parallel Execution Spaces," *Proceedings of the International Conference on Very Large Data Bases* (1993).

[Larson 1978] P. Larson, "Dynamic Hashing," *BIT*, 18 (1978).

[Larson 1982] P. Larson, "Performance Analysis of Linear Hashing with Partial Expansions," *ACM Transactions on Database Systems*, Volume 7, Number 4 (December 1982), pages 566–587.

[Larson 1988] P. Larson, "Linear Hashing with Separators — A Dynamic Hashing Scheme Achieving One-Access Retrieval," *ACM Transactions on Database Systems*, Volume 19, Number 3 (September 1988), pages 366–388.

[Larson and Yang 1985] P. Larson and H. Z. Yang, "Computing Queries from Derived Relations," *Proceedings of the International Conference on Very Large Data Bases* (1985), pages 259–269.

[Lecluse et al. 1988] C. Lecluse, P. Richard, and F. Velez, "O2: An Object-Oriented Data Model," *Proceedings of the ACM International Conference on the Management of Data* (1988), pages 424–433.

[Lee and Liou 1996] S. Y. Lee and R. L. Liou, "A Multi-Granularity Locking Model for Concurrency Control in Object-Oriented Database Systems," *IEEE Transactions on Knowledge and Data Engineering,* Volume 8, Number 1 (February 1996), pages 144–156.

[Leiss 1982a] E. Leiss, *Principles of Data Security*, Plenum Press, New York, NY (1982).

[Leiss 1982b] E. Leiss, "Randomizing: A Practical Method for Protecting Statistical Databases Against Compromise," *Proceedings of the International Conference on Very Large Data Bases* (1982), pages 189–196.

[Lehman and Yao 1981] P. L. Lehman and S. B. Yao, "Efficient Locking for Concurrent Operations on B-trees," *ACM Transactions on Database Systems*, Volume 6, Number 4 (December 1981), pages 650–670.

[Lempel 1979] A. Lempel, "Cryptography in Transition," *ACM Computing Surveys*, Volume 11, Number 4 (December 1979), pages 286–303.

[Lenzerini and Santucci 1983] M. Lenzerini and C. Santucci, "Cardinality Constraints in the Entity Relationship Model," in **[Davis et al. 1983]**.

[Lien and Weinberger 1978] Y. E. Lien and P. J. Weinberger, "Consistency, Concurrency and Crash Recovery," *Proceedings of the ACM SIGMOD International Conference on Management of Data* (1978), pages 9–14.

[Lin et al. 1994] E. T. Lin, E. R. Omiecinski, and S. Yalamanchili, "Large Join Optimization on a Hypercube Multiprocessor," *IEEE Transactions on Knowledge and Data Engineering,* Volume 6, Number 2 (April 1994), pages 304-315.

[Lindsay et al. 1980] B. G. Lindsay, P. G. Selinger, C. Galtieri, J. N. Gray, R. A. Lorie, T. G. Price, G. R. Putzolu, I. L. Traiger, and B. W. Wade, "Notes on Distributed

Databases," in [*Distributed Data Bases*, Draffen and Poole [Ed.] Cambridge University Press, Cambridge, England (1980)], pages 247–284.

[Litwin 1978] W. Litwin, "Virtual Hashing: A Dynamically Changing Hashing," *Proceedings of the International Conference on Very Large Data Bases* (1978), pages 517–523.

[Litwin 1980] W. Litwin, "Linear Hashing: A New Tool for File and Table Addressing," *Proceedings of the International Conference on Very Large Data Bases* (1980), pages 212–223.

[Litwin 1981] W. Litwin, "Trie Hashing," *Proceedings of the ACM SIGMOD International Conference on Management of Data* (1981), pages 19–29.

[Lo and Ravishankar 1996] M.-L. Lo and C. V. Ravishankar, "Spatial Hash-Joins," *Proceedings of the ACM SIGMOD International Conference on the Management of Data* (1996).

[Lomet 1981] D. G. Lomet, "Digital B-trees," *Proceedings of the International Conference on Very Large Data Bases* (1981), pages 333–344.

[Lomet and Salzberg 1992] D. Lomet and B. Salzberg, "Access Method Concurrency with Recovery," *Proceedings of the ACM SIGMOD International Conference on Management of Data* (1992), pages 351–360. A new version will appear in *The VLDB Journal* (1997).

[Lopresti and Tomkins 1993] D. P. Lopresti and A. Tomkins, "Approximate Matching of Hand Drawn Pictograms," *Proceedings of the INTERCHI 93 Conference* (1993).

[Lorie 1977] R. A. Lorie, "Physical Integrity in a Large Segmented Database," *ACM Transactions on Database Systems*, Volume 2, Number 1 (March 1977), pages 91–104.

[Lorie et al. 1985] R. Lorie, W. Kim, D. McNabb, W. Plouffe, and A. Meier, "Supporting Complex Objects in a Relational System for Engineering Databases," in **[Kim et al. 1985]**, pages 145–155.

[Lu et al. 1991] H. Lu, M. Shan, and K. Tan, "Optimization of Multi-Way Join Queries for Parallel Execution," *Proceedings of the International Conference on Very Large Data Bases* (1991), pages 549–560.

[Lunt 1995] T. F. Lunt, "Authorization in Object-Oriented Databases," in **[Kim 1995]**, pages 130–145.

[Lunt et al. 1990] T. F. Lunt, D. E. Denning, R. R. Schell, M. Heckman, and W. R. Shockley, "The SeaView Security Model," *IEEE Transactions on Software Engineering,* Volume SE-16, Number 6 (June 1990), pages 593–607.

[Lynch 1983] N. A. Lynch, "Multilevel Atomicity–A New Correctness Criterion for Database Concurrency Control," *ACM Transactions on Database Systems*, Volume 8, Number 4 (December 1983), pages 484–502.

[Lynch and Merritt 1986] N. A. Lynch and M. Merritt, "Introduction to the Theory of Nested Transactions," *Proceedings of the International Conference on Database Theory* (1986).

[Lynch et al. 1988] N. A. Lynch, M. Merritt, W. Weihl, and A. Fekete, "A Theory of Atomic Transactions," *Proceedings of the International Conference on Database Theory* (1988), pages 41–71.

[Lynch et al. 1994] N. A. Lynch, M. Merritt, W. Weihl, and A. Fekete, *Atomic Transactions*, Morgan Kaufmann Publishers, Inc., San Mateo, CA (1994).

[Lyngbaek and Vianu 1987] P. Lyngbaek and V. Vianu, "Mapping a Semantic Database Model to the Relational Model," *Proceedings of the ACM SIGMOD International Conference on the Management of Data* (1987), pages 132–142.

[Mackert and Lohman 1986] L. F. Mackert, G. M. Lohman, "R* Optimizer Validation and Performance Evaluation for Distributed Queries," *Proceedings of the International Conference on Very Large Data Bases* (August 1986).

[Maier 1983] D. Maier, *The Theory of Relational Databases*, Computer Science Press, Rockville, MD (1983).

[Maier and Stein 1986] D. Maier and J. Stein, "Indexing in an Object-Oriented DBMS," *Proceedings of the International Workshop on Object-Oriented Database Systems* (1986).

[Maier et al. 1986] D. Maier, J. Stein, A. Otis, and A. Purdy, "Development of an Object-Oriented DBMS," *Proceedings of the International Conference on Object-Oriented Programming Systems, Languages, and Applications* (1986), pages 472–482.

[Makinouchi 1977] A. Makinouchi, "A Consideration of Normal Form on Not-necessarily Normalized Relations in the Relational Data Model," *Proceedings of the International Conference on Very Large Data Bases* (1977), pages 447–453.

[Malamud 1989] C. Malamud, *Ingres: Tools for Building an Information Architecture*, Van Nostrand Reinhold (1989).

[Malley and Zdonick 1986] C. Malley and S. Zdonick, "A Knowledge-Based Approach to Query Optimization," *Proceedings of the International Conference on Expert Database Systems* (1986), pages 329–344.

[Manber and Ladner 1984] U. Manber and R. E. Ladner, "Concurrency Control in a Dynamic Search Structure," *ACM Transactions on Database Systems*, Volume 9, Number 3 (September 1984), pages 439–455.

[March et al. 1981] S. T. March, D. G. Severance, and M. Wilens, "Frame Memory: A Storage Architecture to Support Rapid Design and Implementation of Efficient Databases," *ACM Transactions on Database Systems*, Volume 6, Number 3 (September 1981), pages 441–463.

[Markowitz and Raz 1983] V. Markowitz and Y. Raz, "ERROL: An Entity-Relationship, Role Oriented, Query Language," in **[Davis et al. 1983]**.

[Markowitz and Shoshani 1992] V. M. Markowitz and A. Shoshani, "Represented Extended Entity-Relationship Structures in Relational Databases," *ACM Transactions on Database Systems*, Volume 17 (1992), pages 385–422.

[Martin et al. 1989] J. Martin, K. K. Chapman, and J. Leben, *DB2: Concepts, Design, and Programming*, Prentice-Hall, Englewood Cliffs, NJ (1989).

[Mattison 1996] R. Mattison, *Data Warehousing: Strategies, Technologies, and Techniques*, McGraw-Hill, New York, NY (1996).

[McCarthy and Dayal 1989] D. McCarthy and U. Dayal, "The Architecture of an Active Database Management System," *Proceedings of the ACM SIGMOD International Conference on Management of Data* (1989), pages 215–224.

[McCune and Henschen 1989] W. W. McCune and L. J. Henschen, "Maintaining State Constraints in Relational Databases: A Proof Theoretic Basis," *Journal of the ACM*, Volume 36, Number 1 (January 1989), pages 46–68.

[McGee 1977] W. C. McGee, "The Information Management System IMS/VS Part I: General Structure and Operation," *IBM Systems Journal*, Volume 16, Number 2 (June 1977), pages 84–168.

[Mehrotra et al. 1991] S. Mehrotra, R. Rastogi, H. F. Korth, and A. Silberschatz, "Non-Serializable Executions in Heterogeneous Distributed Database Systems," *Proceedings of the First International Conference on Parallel and Distributed Information Systems* (December 1991).

[Mehrotra et al. 1992a] S. Mehrotra, R. Rastogi, H. F. Korth, A. Silberschatz, and Y. Breitbart, "The Concurrency Control Problem in Multidatabases: Characteristics and Solutions," *Proceedings of the ACM SIGMOD International Conference on Management of Data* (1992).

[Mehrotra et al. 1992b] S. Mehrotra, R. Rastogi, Y. Breitbart, H. F. Korth, and A. Silberschatz, "Ensuring Transaction Atomicity in Multidatabase Systems," *ACM SIGACT-SIGMOD Symposium on the Principles of Database Systems* (1992).

[Melton 1993] J. Melton (Editor), *ISO/ANSI Working Draft: Database Language SQL (SQL3)*, X3H2-93-091/ISO DBL YOK-003.

[Melton 1996] J. Melton, "An SQL-3 Snapshot," *Proceedings of the International Conference on Data Engineering* (1996), pages 666–672.

[Melton and Simon 1993] J. Melton and A. R. Simon, *Understanding The New* SQL*: A Complete Guide*, Morgan Kaufmann, San Francisco, CA (1993).

[Menasce and Muntz 1979] D. A. Menasce and R. R. Muntz, "Locking and Deadlock Detection in Distributed Databases," *IEEE Transactions on Software Engineering*, Volume SE-5, Number 3 (May 1979), pages 195–202.

[Menasce et al. 1980] D. A. Menasce, G. Popek, and R. Muntz, "A Locking Protocol for Resource Coordination in Distributed Databases," *ACM Transactions on Database Systems*, Volume 5, Number 2 (June 1980), pages 103–138.

[Mendelzon and Maier 1979] A. O. Mendelzon and D. Maier, "Generalized Mutual Dependencies and the Decomposition of Database Relations," *Proceedings of the International Conference on Very Large Data Bases* (1979), pages 75–82.

[Meng et al. 1995] W. Meng, C. Yu, and W. Kim, "A Theory of Translation from Relational to Hierarchical Queues," *IEEE Transactions on Knowledge and Data Engineering*, Volume 7, Number 2 (April 1995), pages 228–245.

[Microsoft 1992] *ODBC Programmer's Reference*, Microsoft Press (1992).

[Minker 1988] J. Minker, *Foundations of Deductive Databases and Logic Programming*, Morgan-Kaufmann, San Mateo, CA (1988).

[Mohan 1990a] C. Mohan, "ARIES/KVL: A Key-Value Locking Method for Concurrency Control of Multiaction Transactions Operations on B-Tree indexes," *Proceedings of the International Conference on Very Large Data Bases* (1990), pages 392–405.

[Mohan 1990b] C. Mohan, "Commit-LSN: A Novel and Simple Method for Reducing Locking and Latching in Transaction Processing Systems," *Proceedings of the International Conference on Very Large Data Bases* (1990), pages 406–418.

[Mohan 1993] C. Mohan, "IBM's Relational Database Products: Features and Technologies," *Proceedings of the ACM SIGMOD International Conference on Management of Data* (1993).

[Mohan and Levine 1992] C. Mohan and F. Levine, "ARIES/IM: An Efficient and High-Concurrency Index Management Method Using Write-Ahead Logging," *Proceedings of the ACM SIGMOD International Conference on Management of Data* (1992).

[Mohan and Lindsay 1983] C. Mohan and B. Lindsay, "Efficient Commit Protocols for the Tree of Processes Model of Distributed Transactions," *Proceedings of the Second ACM SIGACT-SIGOPS Symposium on the Principles of Distributed Computing* (1983).

[Mohan and Narang 1991] C. Mohan and I. Narang, "Recovery and Coherency-Control Protocols for Fast Intersystem Page Transfer and Fine-Granularity Locking in a Shared Disks Transaction Environment," *Proceedings of the International Conference on Very Large Data Bases* (September 1991).

[Mohan and Narang 1992] C. Mohan and I. Narang, "Efficient Locking and Caching of Data in the Multisystem Shared Disks Transaction Environment," *Proceedings of the International Conference on Extending Database Technology* (1992).

[Mohan and Narang 1994] C. Mohan and I. Narang, "ARIES/CSA: A Method for Database Recovery in Client-Server Architectures," *Proceedings of the ACM SIGMOD International Conference on Management of Data* (May 1994), pages 55–66.

[Mohan et al. 1986] C. Mohan, B. Lindsay, and R. Obermarck, "Transaction Management in the R* Distributed Database Management System," *ACM Transactions on Database Systems,* Volume 11, Number 4 (December 1986), pages 378–396.

[Mohan et al. 1991] C. Mohan, D. Haderle, B. Lindsay, H. Pirahesh, and P. Schwarz, "ARIES: A Transaction Recovery Method Supporting Fine-Granularity Locking and Partial Rollback Using Write-Ahead Logging," *ACM Transactions on Database Systems* (1991).

[Mohan et al. 1992] C. Mohan, "ARIES: A Transaction Recovery Method Supporting Fine-Granularity Locking and Partial Rollbacks Using Write-Ahead Logging," *ACM Transactions on Database Systems*, Volume 17, Number 1 (March 1992).

[Mok et al. 1996] W. Y. Mok, Y.-K. Ng, and D. W. Embley, "A Normal Form for Precisely Characterizing Redundancy in Nested Relations," *ACM Transactions on Database Systems*, Volume 21, Number 1 (March 1996), pages 77–106.

[Moss 1982] J. E. B. Moss, "Nested Transactions and Reliable Distributed Computing," *Proceedings of the Symposium on Reliability in Distributed Software and Database Systems* (1982).

[Moss 1985] J. E. B. Moss, *Nested Transactions: An Approach to Reliable Distributed Computing,* MIT Press, Cambridge, MA (1985).

[Moss 1987] J. E. B. Moss, "Log-Based Recovery for Nested Transactions," *Proceedings of the International Conference on Very Large Data Bases* (1987), pages 427–432.

[Moss 1990] J. E. B. Moss, "Working with Objects: To Swizzle or Not to Swizzle," Technical Report COINS TR 90-38, Computer and Information Science, University of Massachusetts, Amherst (1990).

[MRI 1974] MRI Systems Corporation, "System 2000 Reference Manual," Document UMN-1 (1974).

[MRI 1979] MRI Systems Corporation, "Language Specification Manual: The DEFINE Language," Document LSM-DEF-10 (1979).

[Mumick et al. 1996] I. S. Mumick, S. Finkelstein, H. Pirahesh, and R. Ramakrishnan, "Magic Conditions," *ACM Transactions on Database Systems*, Volume 21, Number 1 (March 1996), pages 107–155.

[Nakayama et al. 1984] T. Nakayama, M. Hirakawa, and T. Ichikawa, "Architecture and Algorithm for Parallel Execution of a Join Operation," *Proceedings of the International Conference on Data Engineering* (1984).

[Naqvi and Tsur 1988] S. Naqvi and S. Tsur, *A Logic Language for Data and Knowledge Bases*, Computer Science Press, Rockville, MD (1988).

[Nelson and Cheng 1992] B. Nelson and Y. Cheng, "How and Why SCSI is better than IPI for NFS," *Proceedings of the Winter 1992 USENIX Conference,* San Francisco, CA, (January 1992), pages 253–270.

[Ng and Han 1994] R. T. Ng and J. Han, "Efficient and Effective Clustering Methods for Spatial Data Mining," *Proceedings of the International Conference on Very Large Data Bases* (1994).

[Nguyen and Srinivasan 1996] T. Nguyen and V. Srinivasan, "Accessing Relational Databases from the World Wide Web," *Proceedings of the ACM SIGMOD International Conference on the Management of Data* (1996).

[Nievergelt et al. 1984] J. Nievergelt, H. Hinterberger, and K. C. Sevcik, "The Grid File: An Adaptable Symmetric Multikey File Structure," *ACM Transactions on Database Systems*, Volume 9, Number 1 (March 1984), pages 38–71.

[Nijssen 1976] G. M. Nijssen (Editor), *Modeling in Data Base Management Systems*, North Holland, Amsterdam, The Netherlands (1976).

[North 1995] K. North, *Windows Multi-DBMS Programming: Using C++, Visual Basic, ODBC, OLE2, and Tools for DBMS Projects*, John Wiley and Sons, New York, NY (1995).

[Obermarck 1980] R. Obermarck "IMS/VS Program Isolation Feature," Research Report RJ2879, IBM Research Laboratory, San Jose, CA (1980).

[Obermarck 1982] R. Obermarck, "Distributed Deadlock Detection Algorithm," *ACM Transactions on Database Systems*, Volume 7, Number 2 (June 1982), pages 187–208.

[O'Leary and Kitts 1985] B. T. O'Leary and D. L. Kitts, "Optical Device for a Mass Storage System," *IEEE Computer*, Volume 18, Number 7 (July 1985).

[Olsen and Kenley 1989] R. P. Olsen and G. Kenley, "Virtual Optical Disks Solve the On-Line Storage Crunch," *Computer Design,* Volume 28, Number 1 (January 1989), pages 93–96.

[O'Neil 1994] P. O'Neil, *Database: Principles, Programming, Performance*, Morgan Kaufmann Publishers, Inc. (1994).

[Oracle 1992] Oracle Corporation, *Oracle 7 Concepts Manual,* Redwood Shores, Ca (1992).

[Orestein 1982] J.A. Orestein, "Multidimensional Tries Used for Associative Searching," *Information Processing Letters*, Volume 14, Number 4 (June 1982), pages 150–157.

[Ozden et al. 1994] B. Özden, A. Biliris, R. Rastogi, and A. Silberschatz, "A Low-cost Storage Server for a Movie on Demand Database," *International Conference on Very Large Databases* (September 1994).

[Ozden et al. 1995a] B. Özden, R. Rastogi, and A. Silberschatz, "A Framework for the Storage and Retrieval of Continuous Media Data," *IEEE International Conference on Multimedia Computing and Systems* (May 1995).

[Ozden et al. 1995b] B. Özden, R. Rastogi, and A. Silberschatz, "Research Issues in Multimedia Storage Servers," *ACM Computing Surveys*, Volume 27, Number 4 (December 1995), pages 617–620.

[Ozden et al. 1996a] B. Özden, R. Rastogi, and A. Silberschatz, "On the Design of a Low-Cost Video-on-Demand Storage System," *Multimedia Systems Journal*, Volume 4, Number 1 (February 1996), pages 40–54.

[Ozden et al. 1996b] B. Özden, R. Rastogi, P. Shenoy, and A. Silberschatz, "Fault-Tolerant Architectures for Continuous Media Servers," *ACM-SIGMOD International Conference on Management of Data* (May 1996).

[Ozsoyoglu and Snodgrass 1995] G. Ozsoyoglu and R. Snodgrass, "Temporal and Real-Time Databases: A Survey," *IEEE Transactions on Knowledge and Data Engineering*, Volume 7, Number 4 (August 1995), pages 513–532.

[Ozsoyoglu and Yuan 1987] G. Ozsoyoglu and L. Yuan, "Reduced MVDs and Minimal Covers," *ACM Transactions on Database Systems*, Volume 12, Number 3 (September 1987), pages 377–394.

[Ozsoyoglu et al. 1987] G. Ozsoyoglu, Z. M. Ozsoyoglu, and V. Matos, "Extending Relational Algebra and Relational Calculus with Set-Valued Attributes and Aggregate Functions," *ACM Transactions on Database Systems*, Volume 12, Number 4 (December 1987), pages 566–592.

[Ozsu and Valduriez 1991] T. Ozsu and P. Valduriez, *Principles of Distributed Database Systems*, Prentice-Hall, Englewood Cliffs, NJ (1991).

[Pang et al. 1995] H.-H. Pang, M. J. Carey, and M. Livny, "Multiclass Scheduling in Real-Time Database Systems," *IEEE Transactions on Knowledge and Data Engineering*, Volume 7, Number 4 (August 1995), pages 533-551.

[Papadimitriou 1979] C. H. Papadimitriou, "The Serializability of Concurrent Database Updates," *Journal of the ACM*, Volume 26, Number 4 (October 1979), pages 631–653.

[Papadimitriou 1982] C. H. Papadimitriou, "A Theorem in Database Concurrency Control," *Journal of the ACM*, Volume 29, Number 5 (October 1982), pages 998–1006.

[Papadimitriou 1986] C. H. Papadimitriou, *The Theory of Database Concurrency Control*, Computer Science Press, Rockville, MD (1986).

[Papadimitriou et al. 1977] C. H. Papadimitriou, P. A. Bernstein, and J. B. Rothnie, "Some Computational Problems Related to Database Concurrency Control," *Proceedings of the Conference on Theoretical Computer Science* (1977), pages 275–282.

[Parent and Spaccapietra 1985] C. Parent and S. Spaccapietra, "An Algebra for a General Entity-Relationship Model," *IEEE Transactions on Software Engineering*, Volume SE-11, Number 7 (July 1985), pages 634–643.

[Parker et al. 1983] D. S. Parker, G. J. Popek, G. Rudisin, A. Stoughton, B. J. Walker, E. Walton, J.M. Chow, D. Edwards, S. Kiser, and C. Kline, "Detection of Mutual

Inconsistency in Distributed Systems," *IEEE Transactions on Software Engineering*, Volume 9, Number 3 (May 1983), pages 240–246.

[Patel and DeWitt 1996] J. Patel and D. J. DeWitt, "Partition Based Spatial-Merge Join," *Proceedings of the ACM SIGMOD International Conference on the Management of Data* (1996).

[Patterson and Hennessy 1995] D. A. Patterson and J. L. Hennessy, *Computer Architecture: A Quantitative Approach*, Second Edition, Morgan Kaufmann Publishers, Inc., San Mateo, CA (1995).

[Patterson et al. 1988] D. A. Patterson, G. Gibson, and R. H. Katz, "A Case for Redundant Arrays of Inexpensive Disks (RAID)," *Proceedings of the ACM SIGMOD International Conference on the Management of Data* (1988), pages 109–116.

[Pecherer 1975] R. M. Pecherer, "Efficient Evaluation of Expressions in a Relational Algebra," *Proceedings of the ACM Pacific Conference* (1975), pages 17–18.

[Pechura and Schoeffler 1983] M. A. Pechura and J. D. Schoeffler, "Estimating File Access Time of Floppy Disks," *Communications of the ACM,* Volume 26, Number 10 (October 1983), pages 754–763.

[Peckham and Maryanski 1988] J. Peckham and F. Maryanski, "Semantic Data Models," *Computing Surveys,* Volume 20, Number 3 (September 1988), pages 153–189.

[Penney and Stein 1987] J. Penney and J. Stein, "Class Modification in the GemStone Object-Oriented DBMS," *Proceedings of the International Conference on Object-Oriented Programming Systems, Languages, and Applications* (1987).

[Pless 1989] V. Pless, *Introduction to the Theory of Error-Correcting Codes*, Second Edition, John Wiley and Sons, New York, NY (1989).

[Poe 1995] V. Poe, *Building a Data Warehouse for Decision Support*, Prentice-Hall, Englewood Cliffs, NJ (1995).

[Polyzois and Garcia-Molina 1994] C. Polyzois and H. Garcia-Molina, "Evaluation of Remote Backup Algorithms for Transaction-Processing Systems," *ACM Transactions on Database Systems*, Volume 19, Number 3 (September 1994), pages 423–449.

[Poosala et al. 1996] V. Poosala, Y. E. Ioannidis, P. J. Haas, and E. J. Shekita, "Improved Histograms for Selectivity Estimation of Range Predicates," *Proceedings of the ACM SIGMOD International Conference on Management of Data* (1996), pages 294–305.

[Popek at al. 1981] G. J. Popek, B. J. Walker, J. M. Chow, D. Edwards, C. Kline, G. Rudisin, and G. Thiel, "LOCUS: A Network Transparent, High Reliability Distributed System," *Proceedings of the Eighth Symposium on Operating System Principles*, (1981), pages 169–177.

[Prycker 1993] M. de Prycker, *Asynchronous Transfer Mode: Solution for Broadband ISDN*, Second Edition, Ellis Horwood (1993).

[Pu et al. 1988] C. Pu, G. Kaiser, and N. Hutchinson, "Split-transactions for Open-Ended Activities," *Proceedings of the International Conference on Very Large Data Bases* (1988), pages 26–37.

[Qian and Lunt 1996] X. Qian and T. F. Lunt, "A MAC Policy Framework for Multilevel Relational Databases," *IEEE Transactions on Knowledge and Data Engineering,* Volume 8, Number 1 (February 1996), pages 3–15.

[Quarterman 1990] J. S. Quarterman, *The Matrix: Computer Networks and Conferencing Systems Worldwide,* Digital Press, Bedford, MA (1990).

[Rabitti et al. 1988] F. Rabitti, D. Woelk, and W. Kim, "A Model of Authorization for Object-Oriented and Semantic Databases," *Proceedings of the International Conference on Extending Database Technology* (1988), pages 231–250.

[Rabitti et al. 1991] F. Rabitti, E. Bertino, W. Kim, and D. Woelk, "A Model of Authorization for Next-Generation Database Systems," *ACM Transactions on Database Systems,* Volume 16, Number 1 (March 1991), pages 88–131.

[Rahm 1993] E. Rahm, "Empirical Performance Evaluation of Concurrency and Coherency Control Protocols for Database Sharing Systems," *ACM Transactions on Database Systems*, Volume 18, Number 2 (June 1993).

[Ramakrishna and Larson 1989] M. V. Ramakrishna and P. Larson, "File Organization Using Composite Perfect Hashing," *ACM Transactions on Database Systems,* Volume 14, Number 2 (June 1989), pages 231–263.

[Ramakrishnan and Ullman 1995] R. Ramakrishnan and J. D. Ullman, "A Survey of Deductive Database Systems," *Journal of Logic Programming,* Volume 23, Number 2 (1995), pages 125–149.

[Ramakrishnan et al. 1992a] R. Ramakrishnan, D. Srivastava, and S. Sudarshan, "CORAL: Control, Relations, and Logic," *Proceedings of the International Conference on Very Large Data Bases* (1992), pages 238–250.

[Ramakrishnan et al. 1992b] R. Ramakrishnan, D. Srivastava, and S. Sudarshan, "Efficient Bottom-up Evaluation of Logic Programs," in **[Vandewalle 1992]**.

[Ramakrishnan et al. 1992c] R. Ramakrishnan, D. Srivastava, and S. Sudarshan, "Controlling the Search in Bottom-up Evaluation," *Joint International Conference and Symposium on Logic Programming* (1992), pages 273–287.

[Ramakrishnan et al. 1993] R. Ramakrishnan, D. Srivastava, S. Sudarshan, and P. Seshadri, "Implementation of the CORAL Deductive Database System," *Proceedings of the ACM SIGMOD International Conference on Management of Data* (1993), pages 167–176.

[Ramesh et al. 1989] R. Ramesh, A. J. G. Babu, and J. P. Kincaid, "Index Optimization: Theory and Experimental Results," *ACM Transactions on Database Systems,* Volume 14, Number 1 (March 1989), pages 41–74.

[Ranft et al. 1990] M. Ranft, S. Rehm, and K. Dittrich, "How to Share Work on Shared Objects in Design Databases," *Proceedings of the International Conference on Data Engineering* (1990).

[Rangan et al. 1992] P. V. Rangan, H. M. Vin, and S. Ramanathan, "Designing an On-Demand Multimedia Service," *IEEE Communications Magazine*, Volume 1, Number 1 (July 1992), pages 56–64.

[Reason et al. 1996] J. M. Reason, L. C. Yun, A. Y. Lao, and D. G. Messerschmitt, "Asynchronous Video: Coordinated Video Coding and Transport for Heterogeneous Networks with Wireless Access," in **[Imielinski and Korth 1996]**, Chapter 10.

[Reed 1978] D. Reed, "Naming and Synchronization in a Decentralized Computer System," Ph.D. thesis, Department of Electrical Engineering, MIT, Cambridge, MA (1978).

[Reed 1983] D. Reed, "Implementing Atomic Actions on Decentralized Data," *ACM Transactions on Computer Systems*, Volume 1, Number 1 (February 1983), pages 3–23.

[Reuter 1980] A. Reuter, "A Fast Transaction-Oriented Logging Scheme for UNDO Recovery," *IEEE Transactions on Software Engineering*, Volume SE-6, Number 4 (July 1980), pages 348–356.

[Reuter 1989] A. Reuter, "ConTracts: A Means for Extending Control Beyond Transaction Boundaries," *Proceedings of the 3rd International Workshop on High Performance Transaction Systems* (September 1989).

[Richardson et al. 1987] J. Richardson, H. Lu, and K. Mikkilineni, "Design and Evaluation of Parallel Pipelined Join Algorithms," *Proceedings of the ACM SIGMOD International Conference on Management of Data* (1987).

[Ries and Stonebraker 1977] D. R. Ries and M. Stonebraker, "Effects of Locking Granularity in a Database Management System," *ACM Transactions on Database Systems*, Volume 2, Number 3 (September 1977), pages 233–246.

[Rissanen 1979] J. Rissanen, "Theory of Joins for Relational Databases - A Tutorial Survey," *Proceedings of the Symposium on Mathematical Foundations of Computer Science*, Springer-Verlag, Berlin, Germany (1979), pages 537–551.

[Rivest 1976] R. L Rivest, "Partial Match Retrieval Via the Method of Superimposed Codes," *SIAM Journal of Computing*, Volume 5, Number 1 (1976), pages 19–50.

[Rivest et al. 1978] R. L. Rivest, A. Shamir, and L. Adelman, "On Digital Signatures and Public Key Cryptosystems," *Communications of the ACM*, Volume 21, Number 2 (February 1978), pages 120–126.

[Robinson 1981] J. Robinson. "The k-d-B Tree: A Search Structure for Large Multidimensional Indexes," *Proceedings of the ACM SIGMOD International Conference on Management of Data* (1981), pages 10–18.

[Rosenblum and Ousterhout 1991] M. Rosenblum and J. K. Ousterhout, "The Design and Implementation of a Log-Structured File System," *Proceedings of the 13th ACM Symposium on Operating Systems Principles* (October 1991), pages 1–15.

[Rosenkrantz et al. 1978] D. J. Rosenkrantz, R. E. Stearns, and P. M. Lewis II, "System Level Concurrency Control For Distributed Data Base Systems," *ACM Transactions on Database Systems*, Volume 3, Number 2 (March 1978), pages 178–198.

[Rosenthal and Reiner 1984] A. Rosenthal and D. Reiner, "Extending the Algebraic Framework of Query Processing to Handle Outerjoins," *Proceedings of the International Conference on Very Large Databases* (August 1984), pages 334–343.

[Ross 1990] K. A. Ross, "Modular Stratification and Magic Sets for DATALOG Programs with Negation," *ACM SIGACT-SIGMOD Symposium on the Principles of Database Systems* (April 1990).

[Roth and Korth 1987] M. A. Roth and H. F. Korth, "The Design of ¬1NF Relational Databases into Nested Normal Form," *Proceedings of the ACM SIGMOD International Conference on Management of Data* (1987), pages 143–159.

[Roth et al. 1988] M. A. Roth, H. F. Korth, and A. Silberschatz, "Extended Algebra and Calculus for Nested Relational Databases," *ACM Transactions on Database Systems*, Volume 13, Number 4 (December 1988), pages 389–417.

[Roth et al. 1989] M. A. Roth, H. F. Korth, and A. Silberschatz, "Null Values in Nested Relational Databases," *Acta Informatica*, Volume 26 (1989), pages 615–642.

[Rothermel and Mohan 1989] K. Rothermel and C. Mohan, "ARIES/NT: A Recovery Method Based on Write-Ahead Logging for Nested Transactions," *Proceedings of the International Conference on Very Large Data Bases* (August 1989), pages 337–346.

[Rothnie and Goodman 1977] J. B. Rothnie, Jr. and N. Goodman, "A Survey of Research and Development in Distributed Database Management," *Proceedings of the International Conference on Very Large Data Bases* (1977), pages 48–62.

[Roussopoulos and Mylopoulos 1975] N. Roussopoulos and J. Mylopoulos, "Using Semantic Networks for Data Base Management," *Proceedings of the International Conference on Very Large Data Bases* (1975), pages 144–172.

[Ruemmler and Wilkes 1994] C. Ruemmler and J. Wilkes, "An Introduction to Disk Drive Modeling," *IEEE Computer*, Volume 27, Number 3 (March 1994), pages 17–27.

[Rusinkiewicz and Sheth 1995] M. Rusinkiewicz and A. Sheth, "Specification and Execution of Transactional Workflows," in **[Kim 1995]**, pages 592–620.

[Rustin 1972] R. Rustin (Editor), *Data Base Systems*, Prentice-Hall, Englewood Cliffs, NJ (1972).

[Sacks-Davis et al. 1995] R. Sacks-Davis, A. Kent, K. Ramamohanarao, J. Thom, and J. Zobel, "Atlas: A Nested Relational Database System for Text Applications," *IEEE Transactions on Knowledge and Data Engineering*, Volume 7, Number 3 (June 1995), pages 454–470.

[Sadri and Ullman 1982] F. Sadri and J. Ullman, "Template Dependencies: A Large Class of Dependencies in Relational Databases and Its Complete Axiomatization," *Journal of the ACM*, Volume 29, Number 2 (April 1982), pages 363–372.

[Sagiv and Yannakakis 1981] Y.Sagiv and M. Yannakakis, "Equivalence among Relational Expressions with the Union and Difference Operators," *Journal of the ACM*, Volume 27, Number 4 (November 1981).

[Salem and Garcia-Molina 1986] K. Salem and H. Garcia-Molina, "Disk Striping," *Proceedings of the International Conference on Data Engineering* (1986), pages 336–342.

[Salem et al. 1994] K. Salem, H. Garcia-Molina, and J. Sands, "Altruistic Locking," *ACM Transactions on Database Systems*, Volume 19, Number 1 (March 1994), pages 117–165.

[Salton 1989] G. Salton, *Automatic Text Processing*, Addison Wesley, Reading, MA (1989).

[Samet 1990] H. Samet, *The Design and Analysis of Spatial Data Structures*, Addison Wesley, Reading, MA (1990).

[Samet 1995a] H. Samet, "General Research Issues in Multimedia Database Systems," *ACM Computing Surveys*, Volume 27, Number 4 (1995), pages 630–632.

[Samet 1995b] H. Samet, "Spatial Data Structures," in **[Kim 1995]**, pages 361–385.

[Samet and Aref 1995] H. Samet and W. Aref, "Spatial Data Models and Query Processing," in **[Kim 1995]**, pages 338–360.

[Sarisky 1983] L. Sarisky, "Will Removable Hard Disks Replace the Floppy?" *Byte* (March 1983), pages 110–117.

[Satyanarayanan 1980] M. Satyanarayanan, *Multiprocessors: A Comparative Study*, Prentice-Hall, Englewood Cliffs, NJ (1980).

[Schenk 1974] K. L. Schenk, "Implementational Aspects of the CODASYL DBTG Proposal," *Proceedings of the IFIP Working Conference on Data Base Management Systems* (1974).

[Schlageter 1981] G. Schlageter, "Optimistic Methods for Concurrency Control in Distributed Database Systems," *Proceedings of the International Conference on Very Large Data Bases* (1981), pages 125–130.

[Schmid and Swenson 1975] H. A. Schmid and J. R. Swenson, "On the Semantics of the Relational Model," *Proceedings of the ACM SIGMOD International Conference on the Management of Data* (1975), pages 211-223.

[Schneider 1982] H. J. Schneider, "Distributed Data Bases," *Proceedings of the International Symposium on Distributed Databases* (1982).

[Schneider and DeWitt 1989] D. Schneider and D. DeWitt, "A Performance Evaluation of Four Parallel Join Algorithms in a Shared-Nothing Multiprocessor Environment," *Proceedings of the ACM SIGMOD International Conference on the Management of Data* (1989).

[Schneiderman 1978] B. Schneiderman (Editor), *Database: Improving Usability and Responsiveness*, Academic Press, New York, NY (1978).

[Sciore 1982] E. Sciore, "A Complete Axiomatization for Full Join Dependencies," *Journal of the ACM*, Volume 29, Number 2 (April 1982), pages 373–393.

[Selinger and Adiba 1980] P. G. Selinger and M. E. Adiba, "Access Path Selection in Distributed Database Management Systems," Research Report RJ2338, IBM Research Laboratory, San Jose, CA (1980).

[Selinger et al. 1979] P. G. Selinger, M. M. Astrahan, D. D. Chamberlin, R. A. Lorie, and T. G. Price, "Access Path Selection in a Relational Database System," *Proceedings of the ACM SIGMOD International Conference on the Management of Data* (1979), pages 23–34.

[Sellis 1988] T. K. Sellis, "Multiple Query Optimization," *ACM Transactions on Database Systems*, Volume 13, Number 1 (March 1988), pages 23–52.

[Sellis et al. 1987] T. K. Sellis, N. Roussopoulos, and C. Faloutsos, "The R^+-Tree: A Dynamic Index for Multi-Dimensional Objects," *Proceedings of the International Conference on Very Large Data Bases* (1987), pages 507–518.

[Seshadri and Naughton 1992] S. Seshadri and J. Naughton, "Sampling Issues in Parallel Database Systems," *Proceedings of the International Conference on Extending Database Technology* (1992).

[Sha et al. 1988] L. Sha, J. Lehoczky, and D. Jensen, "Modular Concurrency Control and Failure Recovery," *IEEE Transactions on Computing*, Volume 37, Number 2 (February 1988), pages 146–159.

[Shapiro 1986] L. D. Shapiro, "Join Processing in Database Systems with Large Main Memories," *ACM Transactions on Database Systems*, Volume 11, Number 3 (September 1986), pages 239–264.

[Shasha 1992] D. Shasha, *Database Tuning: A Principled Approach,* Prentice-Hall, Englewood Cliffs, NJ (1992).

[Shasha and Goodman 1988] D. Shasha and N. Goodman, "Concurrent Search Structure Algorithms," *ACM Transactions on Database Systems*, Volume 13, Number 1 (March 1988), pages 53–90.

[Shasha et al. 1995] D. Shasha, F. Llirabat, E. Simon, and P. Valduriez, "Transaction Chopping: Algorithms and Performance Studies," *ACM Transactions on Database Systems*, Volume 20, Number 3 (September 1995), pages 325–363.

[Shatdal and Naughton 1993] A. Shatdal and J. Naughton, "Using Shared Virtual Memory for Parallel Join Processing," *Proceedings of the ACM SIGMOD International Conference on the Management of Data* (1993).

[Sheard and Stemple 1989] T. Sheard and D. Stemple, "Automatic Verification of Database Transaction Safety," *ACM Transactions on Database Systems*, Volume 14, Number 3 (September 1989), pages 322–368.

[Shipman 1981] D. Shipman, "The Functional Data Model and the Data Language DAPLEX," *ACM Transactions on Database Systems*, Volume 6, Number 1 (March 1981), pages 140–173.

[Sibley 1976] E. Sibley, "The Development of Database Technology," *ACM Computing Surveys*, Volume 8, Number 1 (March 1976), pages 1–5.

[Sibley and Kerschberg 1977] E. Sibley and L. Kerschberg, "Data Architecture and Data Model Considerations," *Proceedings of the AFIPS National Computer Conference* (1977).

[Signore et al. 1995] R. Signore, J. Creamer, M. O. Stegman, *The ODBC Solution: Open Database Connectivity in Distributed Environments*, McGraw-Hill, New York, NY (1995).

[Silberschatz 1982] A. Silberschatz, "A Multi-Version Concurrency Control Scheme With No Rollbacks," *ACM SIGACT-SIGOPS Symposium on Principles of Distributed Computing* (1982), pages 216–223.

[Silberschatz and Galvin 1994] A. Silberschatz and P. Galvin, *Operating System Concepts,* Fourth Edition, Addison Wesley, Reading, MA (1994).

[Silberschatz and Kedem 1980] A. Silberschatz and Z. Kedem, "Consistency in Hierarchical Database Systems," *Journal of the ACM*, Volume 27, Number 1 (January 1980), pages 72–80.

[Silberschatz et al. 1990] A. Silberschatz, M. R. Stonebraker, and J. D. Ullman (Editors), "Database Systems: Achievements and Opportunities," *ACM SIGMOD Record,* Volume 19, Number 4 (1990).

[Silberschatz et al. 1996] A. Silberschatz, M. Stonebraker, and J. Ullman, "Database Research: Achievements and Opportunities into the 21st Century," Technical Report CS-TR-96-1563, Department of Computer Science, Stanford University, Stanford, CA (1996).

[Simmons 1979] G. J. Simmons, "Symmetric and Asymmetric Encryption," *ACM Computing Surveys*, Volume 11, Number 4 (December 1979), pages 304–330.

[Skarra and Zdonik 1986] A. Skarra and S. Zdonik, "The Management of Changing Types in an Object-Oriented Database," *Proceedings of the International Conference on Object-Oriented Programming Systems, Languages, and Applications* (1986).

[Skarra and Zdonik 1989] A. Skarra and S. Zdonik, "Concurrency Control in Object-Oriented Databases," in **[Kim and Lochovsky 1989]**, pages 395–421.

[Skeen 1981] D. Skeen, "Non-blocking Commit Protocols." *Proceedings of the ACM SIGMOD International Conference on the Management of Data* (1981), pages 133–142.

[Smith 1982] A. J. Smith, "Cache Memories," *ACM Computing Surveys,* Volume 14, Number 3 (September 1982), pages 473–530

[Smith and Barnes 1987] P. Smith and G. Barnes, *Files and Databases: An Introduction,* Addison Wesley, Reading, MA (1987).

[Smith and Smith 1977] J. M. Smith and D. C. P. Smith, "Database Abstractions: Aggregation and Generalization," *ACM Transactions on Database Systems,* Volume 2, Number 2 (March 1977), pages 105–133.

[Smith et al. 1996] K. P. Smith, B. T. Blaustein, S. Jajodia, L. Notargiacomo, "Correctness Criteria for Multilevel Secure Transactions," *IEEE Transactions on Knowledge and Data Engineering,* Volume 8, Number 1 (February 1996), pages 32–45.

[Snodgrass 1987] R. Snodgrass, "The Temporal Query Language TQuel," *ACM Transactions on Database Systems,* Volume 12, Number 2 (March 1987), pages 247–298.

[Snodgrass and Ahn 1985] R. Snodgrass and I. Ahn, "A Taxonomy of Time in Databases" *Proceedings of the ACM SIGMOD International Conference on the Management of Data* (1985), pages 236–246.

[Snodgrass et al. 1994] R. Snodgrass and others, "TSQL2 Language Specification," *ACM SIGMOD Record,* Volume 23, Number 1 (March 1994), pages 65–86.

[Soo 1991] M. Soo, "Bibliography on Temporal Databases," *ACM SIGMOD Record,* Volume 20, Number 1 (1991) pages 14–23.

[Soparkar et al. 1991] N. Soparkar, H. F. Korth, and A. Silberschatz, "Failure-Resilient Transaction Management in Multidatabases," *IEEE Computer,* Volume 24, Number 12 (December 1991), pages 28–36.

[Soparkar et al. 1995] N. Soparkar, H. F. Korth, and A. Silberschatz, "Databases with Deadline and Contingency Constraints," *IEEE Transactions on Knowledge and Data Engineering,* Volume 7, Number 4 (August 1995), pages 552–565.

[Spector and Schwarz 1983] A. Z. Spector and P. M. Schwarz, "Transactions: A Construct for Reliable Distributed Computing," *ACM SIGOPS Operating Systems Review,* Volume 17, Number 2 (1983), pages 18–35.

[Srikant and Agrawal 1996] R. Srikant and R. Agrawal, "Mining Quantitative Association Rules in Large Relational Tables," *Proceedings of the ACM SIGMOD International Conference on the Management of Data* (1996).

[Srivastava et al. 1995] D. Srivastava, S. Sudarshan, R. Ramakrishnan, and J. Naughton, "Space Optimization in Deductive Databases," *ACM Transactions on Database Systems,* Volume 20, Number 4 (December 1995), pages 472–516.

[Stachour and Thuraisingham 1990] P. D. Stachour and B. Thuraisingham, "Design of LDV: A Multilevel Secure Relational Database Management System," *IEEE Transactions on Knowledge and Data Engineering,* Volume 2, Number 2 (June 1990), pages 190–209

[Stam and Snodgrass 1988] R. Stam and R. Snodgrass, "A Bibliography on Temporal Databases," *Database Engineering,* Volume 7, Number 4 (December 1988), pages 231–239.

[Stefik and Bobrow 1986] M. Stefik and D. G. Bobrow, "Object-Oriented Programming: Themes and Variations," *The AI Magazine* (January 1986), pages 40–62.

[Stone 1993] H. S. Stone, *High-Performance Computer Architecture,* Third Edition, Addison Wesley, Reading, MA (1993).

[Stonebraker 1975] M. Stonebraker, "Implementation of Integrity Constraints and Views by Query Modification," *Proceedings of the ACM SIGMOD International Conference on the Management of Data* (1975), pages 65–78.

[Stonebraker 1980] M. Stonebraker, "Retrospection on a Database System," *ACM Transactions on Database Systems*, Volume 5, Number 2 (March 1980), pages 225–240. Also in **[Stonebraker 1986b]**, pages 46–62.

[Stonebraker 1981] M. Stonebraker, "Operating System Support for Database Management," *Communications of the ACM*, Volume 24, Number 7 (July 1981), pages 412–418. Also in **[Stonebraker 1986b]**, pages 172–182.

[Stonebraker 1986a] M. Stonebraker, "Inclusion of New Types in Relational Database Systems," *Proceedings of the International Conference on Data Engineering* (1986), pages 262–269.

[Stonebraker 1986b] M. Stonebraker (Editor), *The Ingres Papers*, Addison Wesley, Reading, MA (1986).

[Stonebraker 1987] M. Stonebraker, "The Design of the POSTGRES Storage System," *Proceedings of the International Conference on Very Large Data Bases* (1987).

[Stonebraker 1994] M. Stonebraker (Editor), *Readings in Database Systems*, Second Edition, Morgan Kaufmann Publishers, Inc., San Mateo, CA (1994).

[Stonebraker and Rowe 1986] M. Stonebraker and L. Rowe, "The Design of POSTGRES," *Proceedings of the ACM SIGMOD International Conference on the Management of Data* (1986).

[Stonebraker and Wong 1974] M. Stonebraker and E. Wong, "Access Control in a Relational Database Management System by Query Modification," *Proceedings of the ACM National Conference* (1974), pages 180–187.

[Stonebraker et al. 1976] M. Stonebraker, E. Wong, P. Kreps, and G. D. Held, "The Design and Implementation of INGRES," *ACM Transactions on Database Systems*, Volume 1, Number 3 (September 1976), pages 189–222. Also in **[Stonebraker 1986b]**, pages 1–45.

[Stonebraker et al. 1987a] M. Stonebraker, J. Anton, and E. Hanson, "Extending a Database System with Procedures," *ACM Transactions on Database Systems*, Volume 12, Number 3 (September 1987), pages 350–376.

[Stonebraker et al. 1987b] M. Stonebraker, E. Hanson, and C. H. Hong, "The Design of the POSTGRES Rule System," *Proceedings of the International Conference on Data Engineering* (1987), pages 356–374.

[Stonebraker et al. 1989] M. Stonebraker, P. Aoki, and M. Seltzer, "Parallelism in XPRS," *Proceedings of the ACM SIGMOD International Conference on the Management of Data* (1989).

[Stroustrup 1988] B. Stroustrup, "What Is Object-Oriented Programming?," *IEEE Software* (May 1988), pages 10–20.

[Stroustrup 1992] B. Stroustrup, *The C++ Programming Language*, Second Edition, Addison-Wesley, Reading, MA (1992).

[Stuart et al. 1984] D. G. Stuart, G. Buckley, and A. Silberschatz, "A Centralized Deadlock Detection Algorithm," Technical Report, Department of Computer Sciences, University of Texas, Austin, TX (1984).

[Swami and Gupta 1988] A. Swami and A. Gupta, "Optimization of Large Join Queries," *Proceedings of the ACM SIGMOD International Conference on Management of Data* (1988), pages 8–17.

[Tanenbaum 1996] A. S. Tanenbaum, *Computer Networks*, Third Edition, Prentice-Hall, Englewood Cliffs, NJ (1996).

[Tansel et al. 1993] A. Tansel, J. Clifford, S. Gadia, S. Jajodia, A. Segev, and R. Snodgrass, *Temporal Databases: Theory, Design and Implementation,* Benjamin Cummings, Redwood City, CA (1993).

[Taylor and Frank 1976] R. W. Taylor and R. L. Frank, "CODASYL Data Base Management Systems," *ACM Computing Surveys*, Volume 8, Number 1 (March 1976), pages 67–103

[Tendick and Matloff 1994] P. Tendick and N. Matloff, "A Modified Random Perturbation Method for Database Security," *ACM Transactions on Database Systems*, Volume 19, Number 1 (March 1994), pages 47–63.

[Teorey and Fry 1982] T. J. Teorey and J. P. Fry, *Design of Database Structures*, Prentice-Hall, Englewood Cliffs, NJ (1982).

[Teorey et al. 1986] T. J. Teorey, D. Yang, and J. P. Fry, "A Logical Design Methodology for Relational Databases Using the Extended Entity-Relationship Model," *ACM Computing Surveys*, Volume 18, Number 2 (June 1986), pages 197–222.

[Thomas 1979] R. H. Thomas, "A Majority Consensus Approach to Concurrency Control," *ACM Transactions on Database Systems*, Volume 4, Number 2 (June 1979), pages 180–219.

[Thomas 1996] S. A. Thomas, *IPng and the TCP/IP Protocols: Implementing the Next Generation Internet*, John Wiley and Sons, New York, NY (1996).

[Thomas and Sandhu 1996] R. K. Thomas and R. S. Sandhu, "A Trusted Subject Architecture for Multilevel Secure Object-Oriented Databases," *IEEE Transactions on Knowledge and Data Engineering,* Volume 8, Number 1 (February 1996), pages 16–31.

[Todd 1976] S. J. P. Todd, "The Peterlee Relational Test Vehicle - A System Overview," *IBM Systems Journal*, Volume 15, Number 4 (1976), pages 285–308.

[Tomasic et al. 1994] A. Tomasic, H. Garcia-Molina, and K. Shoens, "Incremental Updates of Inverted Lists for Text Document Retrieval," *Proceedings of the ACM SIGMOD International Conference on Management of Data* (1994), pages 289–300.

[Traiger 1982] I. L. Traiger, "Virtual Memory for Database Systems," *ACM SIGOPS Operating Systems Review*, Volume 16, Number 4 (1982), pages 26–48.

[Traiger 1983] I. L. Traiger, "Trends in Systems Aspects of Database Management," Research Report RJ3845, IBM Research Laboratory, San Jose, CA (1983).

[Traiger et al. 1982] I. L. Traiger, J. N. Gray, C. A. Galtieri, and B. G. Lindsay, "Transactions and Consistency in Distributed Database Management Systems," *ACM Transactions on Database Systems*, Volume 7, Number 3 (September 1982), pages 323–342.

[Tremblay and Sorenson 1985] J.-P. Tremblay and P. G. Sorenson, *The Theory and Practice of Compiler Writing*, McGraw-Hill, New York, NY (1985).

[Trivedi et al. 1980] K. S. Trivedi, R. A. Wagner, and T. M. Sigmon, "Optimal Selection of CPU Speed, Device Capacities and File Assignment," *Journal of the ACM*, Volume 7, Number 3 (July 1980), pages 457–473.

[Tsichritzis and Lochovsky 1976] D. C. Tsichritzis and F. H. Lochovsky, "Hierarchical Data-base Management: A Survey," *ACM Computing Surveys*, Volume 8, Number 1 (March 1976), pages 67–103.

[Tsou and Fischer 1982] D.-M. Tsou and P. Fischer, "Decomposition of a Relation Scheme into Boyce-Codd Normal Form," *ACM SIGACT News*, Volume 14, Number 3 (1982), pages 23–29.

[Tsukuda et al. 1992] S. Tsukuda, M. Nakano, M. Kitsuregawa, and M. Takagi, "Parallel Hash Join on Shared-Everything Multiprocessor," *Proceedings of the Eighth International Conference on Data Engineering* (1992).

[Tsur and Zaniolo 1986] S. Tsur and C. Zaniolo, "LDL: A Logic-Based Data-Language," *Proceedings of the International Conference on Very Large Data Bases* (1986), pages 33–41.

[Tuzhilin and Clifford 1990] A. Tuzhilin and J. Clifford, "A Temporal Relational Algebra as a Basis for Temporal Relational Completeness," *Proceedings of the International Conference on Very Large Data Bases* (1990), pages 13–23.

[UniSQL 1991] UniSQL Inc., *UniSQL/X Database Management System User's Manual: Release 1.2*, (1991).

[U.S. Dept. of Commerce 1977] United States Department of Commerce, *Data Encryption Standard*, National Bureau of Standards Federal Information Processing Standards Publication 46 (1977).

[U.S. Dept. of Commerce 1992] United States Department of Commerce, *Database Language SQL*, National Bureau of Standards Federal Information Processing Standards Publication 127-2 (1992).

[U.S. Dept. of Defense 1985] United States Department of Defense, "Department of Defense Trusted Computer System Evaluation Criteria," National Computer Security Center (1985).

[Ullman 1988] J. D. Ullman, *Principles of Database and Knowledge-base Systems*, Volume I, Computer Science Press, Rockville, MD (1988).

[Ullman 1989] J. D. Ullman, *Principles of Database and Knowledge-base Systems*, Volume II, Computer Science Press, Rockville, MD (1989).

[Unger et al. 1984] E. A. Unger, P. S. Fisher, and J. Slonim (Editors), *Advances in Data Base Management*, Volume 2, John Wiley and Sons, New York, NY (1984).

[Valduriez and Gardarin 1989] P. Valduriez and G. Gardarin, *Analysis and Comparison of Relational Database Systems*, Addison Wesley, Reading, MA (1989).

[Vandewalle 1992] J. Vandewalle (Editor), *The State of the Art in Computer Systems and Software Engineering*, Kluwer Academic Publishers (1992).

[Van Gucht 1987] D. Van Gucht, "On the Expressive Power of the Extended Relational Algebra for the Unnormalized Relational Model," *Proceedings of the ACM SIGACT-SIGMOD-SIGART Symposium on Principles of Database Systems* (1987), pages 302–312.

[Verhofstad 1978] J. S. M. Verhofstad, "Recovery Techniques for Database Systems," *ACM Computing Surveys*, Volume 10, Number 2 (June 1978), pages 167–195.

[Wächter and Reuter 1992] H. Wächter and A. Reuter, "The ConTract Model," in *Database Transaction Models for Advanced Applications*, Morgan Kaufmann Publishers, Inc. (1992).

[Walton et al. 1991] C. Walton, A. Dale, and R. Jenevein, "A Taxonomy and Performance Model of Data Skew Effects in Parallel Joins," *Proceedings of the International Conference on Very Large Data Bases* (1991).

[Weddell 1992] G. Weddell, "Reasoning About Functional Dependencies Generalized for Semantic Data Models," *ACM Transactions on Database Systems*, Volume 17, Number 1 (March 1992).

[Weihl and Liskov 1990] W. Weihl and B. Liskov, "Implementation of Resilient, Atomic Data Types," in **[Zdonik and Maier 1990]**, pages 332–344.

[Weikum 1991] G. Weikum, "Principles and Realization Strategies of Multilevel Transaction Management," *ACM Transactions on Database Systems,* Volume 16, Number 1 (March 1991).

[Weikum and Schek 1984] G. Weikum and H. J. Schek, "Architectural Issues of Transaction Management in Multi-Level Systems," *Proceedings of the International Conference on Very Large Data Bases* (1984), pages 454–465.

[Weikum et al. 1990] G. Weikum, C. Hasse, P. Broessler, and P. Muth, "Multi-Level Recovery," *Proceedings of the ACM SIGACT-SIGMOD-SIGART Symposium on Principles of Database Systems* (1990), pages 109–123.

[Weldon 1981] J. Weldon, *Data Base Administration*, Plenum Press, New York, NY (1981).

[Whang and Krishnamurthy 1990] K. Whang and R. Krishnamurthy, "Query Optimization in a Memory-Resident Domain Relational Calculus Database System," *ACM Transactions on Database Systems,* Volume 15, Number 1 (March 1990), pages 67–95.

[Whang et al. 1982] K. Whang, G. Wiederhold, and D. Sagalowicz, "Physical Design of Network Model Databases Using the Property of Separability," *Proceedings of the International Conference on Very Large Data Bases* (1982), pages 98–107.

[White and DeWitt 1992] S. J. White and D. J. DeWitt, "A Performance Study of Alternative Object Faulting and Pointer Swizzling Strategies," *Proceedings of the International Conference on Very Large Data Bases* (1992).

[White and DeWitt 1994] S. J. White and D. J. DeWitt, "QuickStore: A High Performance Mapped Object Store," *Proceedings of the ACM SIGMOD International Conference on the Management of Data* (1994).

[Widom and Finkelstein 1990] J. Widom and S. Finkelstein, "Set-Oriented Production Rules in Relational Database Systems," *Proceedings of the ACM SIGMOD International Conference on Management of Data* (1990).

[Widom et al. 1991] J. Widom, R. Cochrane, and B. Lindsay, "Implementing Set-Oriented Production Rules as an Extension to Starburst," *Proceedings of the International Conference on Very Large Data Bases* (1991).

[Wiederhold 1983] G. Wiederhold, *Database Design*, Second Edition, McGraw-Hill, New York, NY (1983).

[Wilkinson et al. 1990] K. Wilkinson, P. Lyngbaek, and W. Hasan, "The Iris Architecture and Implementation," *IEEE Transactions on Knowledge and Data Engineering* (March 1990), pages 63–75.

[Wilson 1990] P. R. Wilson, "Pointer Swizzling at Page Fault Time: Efficiently Supporting Huge Address Spaces on Standard Hardware," Technical Report UIC-EECS-90-6, University of Illinois at Chicago (December 1990).

[Wilschut et al. 1995] A. N. Wilschut, J. Flokstra, and P. M. Apers, "Parallel Evaluation of Multi-Join Queues," *Proceedings of the ACM SIGMOD International Conference on Management of Data* (1995), pages 115–126.

[Winslett et al. 1994] M. Winslett, K. Smith, and X. Qian, "Formal Query Languages for Secure Relational Databases," *ACM Transactions on Database Systems*, Volume 19, Number 4 (December 1994), pages 626–662.

[Wipfler 1987] A. J. Wipfler, *CICS: Application Development and Programming*, Macmillan Publishing, New York, NY (1987).

[Wolf 1991] J. Wolf, "An Effective Algorithm for Parallelizing Hash Joins in the Presence of Data Skew," *Proceedings of the Seventh International Conference on Data Engineering* (1991).

[Wong 1977] E. Wong, "Retrieving Dispersed Data from SDD-1: A System for Distributed Databases," *Proceedings of the Berkeley Workshop on Distributed Data Management and Computer Networks* (1977), pages 217–235.

[Wong 1983] E. Wong, "Dynamic Rematerialization-Processing Distributed Queries Using Redundant Data," *IEEE Transactions on Software Engineering*, Volume SE-9, Number 3 (May 1983), pages 228–232.

[Wong and Mylopoulos 1977] H. K. T. Wong and J. Mylopoulos, "Two Views of Data Semantics: A Survey of Data Models in Artificial Intelligence and Database Management," *INFOR*, Volume 15 (1977), pages 344–383.

[Wong and Youssefi 1976] E. Wong and K. Youssefi, "Decomposition-A Strategy for Query Processing," *ACM Transactions on Database Systems*, Volume 1, Number 3 (September 1976), pages 223–241.

[X/Open 1991] *X/Open Snapshot: X/Open DTP: XA Interface,* X/Open Company, Ltd. (1991).

[X/Open 1992] *Structured Query Language (SQL): CAE specification C201* (September 1992).

[X/Open 1993] *X/Open Data Management: SQL Call Level Interface (CLI),* X/Open Company, Ltd. (1993).

[Yannakakis 1981] M. Yannakakis, "Issues of Correctness in Database Concurrency Control by Locking," *Proceedings of the ACM Symposium on the Theory of Computing* (1981), pages 363–367.

[Yannakakis et al. 1979] M. Yannakakis, C. H. Papadimitriou, and H. T. Kung, "Locking Protocols: Safety and Freedom from Deadlock," *Proceedings of the IEEE Symposium on the Foundations of Computer Science* (1979), pages 286–297.

[Yao 1979a] A. C. Yao, "A Note on a Conjecture of Kam and Ullman Concerning Statistical Databases," *Information Processing Letters* (1979).

[Yao 1979b] S. Yao, "Optimization of Query Evaluation Algorithms," *ACM Transactions on Database Systems*, Volume 4, Number 2 (June 1979), pages 133–155

[Zaniolo 1976] C. Zaniolo, "Analysis and Design of Relational Schemata for Database Systems," Ph.D. thesis, Department of Computer Science, University of California, Los Angeles, CA (1976).

[Zaniolo 1979a] C. Zaniolo, "Design of Relational Views over Network Schemas," *Proceedings of the ACM SIGMOD International Conference on the Management of Data* (1979), pages 179–190.

[Zaniolo 1979b] C. Zaniolo, "Multimodel External Schemas for CODASYL Data Base Management Systems," in **[Bracchi and Nijssen 1979]**, pages 157–176.

[Zaniolo 1983] C. Zaniolo, "The Database Language GEM," *Proceedings of the ACM SIGMOD International Conference on the Management of Data* (1983), pages 207–218.

[Zdonik and Maier 1990] S. Zdonik and D. Maier, *Readings in Object-Oriented Database Systems*, Morgan Kaufmann Publishers, Inc., San Mateo, CA (1990).

[Zeller and Gray 1990] H. Zeller and J. Gray, "An Adaptive Hash Join Algorithm for Multiuser Environments," *Proceedings of the International Conference on Very Large Data Bases* (1990), pages 186–197.

[Zhang and Mendelzon 1983] Z. Q. Zhang and A. O. Mendelzon, "A Graphical Query Language for Entity-Relationship Databases," in **[Davis et al. 1983]**, pages 441–448.

[Zhuge et al. 1995] Y. Zhuge, H. Garcia-Molina, J. Hammer, and J. Widom, "View Maintenance in a Warehousing Environment," *Proceedings of the ACM SIGMOD International Conference on the Management of Data* (1995), pages 316–327.

[Zloof 1977] M. M. Zloof, "Query-by-Example: A Data Base Language," *IBM Systems Journal*, Volume 16, Number 4 (1977), pages 324–343.

INDEX

2PC protocol. *See* Two-phase commit protocol
3PC protocol. *See* Three-phase commit protocol

Aborted, 443
Access time, 298
ACID properties, 440, 466, 669, 675
Active rules, 660
Aggregation, 46, 57, 59
  functions, 96, 122, 125, 168, 284
  operations, 94
  operators, 161
Algorithms
  B^+-tree concurrency-control, 535
  election, 613
  deadlock-detection, 495, 620, 627
  deadlock-handling, 615
  parallel join, 573
  query-evaluation, 648
  recovery, 607, 678
Aliases, 594
American National Standards Institute (ANSI), 112
Application programs, 15
  interfaces (APIs), 645
Archival dump, 535
Armstrong's axioms, 207, 234
Arpanet, 559
Assertion, 200
Assignment operation, 85
Association rules, 704
  discovery, 708
Asymmetric fragment-and-replicate, 574
Asynchronous transfer mode (ATM), 559, 722
ATM. *See* Asynchronous transfer mode
Atomic domains, 275
Atomicity, 440, 445, 466, 511, 516
Attributes, 8, 24, 28, 51
  composite, 25, 284
  derived, 26
  descriptive, 28
  list, 371
  value skew, 568
Augmentation rule, 207, 234
Authorization, 112, 635, 663
  graph, 637
  restrictions, 634

Backup coordinator, 612
Batch scaleup, 550
Binary large objects (blobs), 331
Bit-interleaved parity organization, 305
Bit-level striping, 303
Blind writes, 455
Blocking, 612
Block-interleaved parity organization, 305, 306
Block-level striping, 303
Block-replacement strategy, 311
Bottlenecks, 650
Boxes, 756
  bounding, 718
  condition, 158
Boyce–Codd normal form (BCNF), 224
Browsing, 729
B^+-tree, 501, 504
  B^+-tree concurrency-control algorithm, 535
Bucket, 358
  skew, 360
Buffer management, 309, 311, 327, 333
Bus, 552
Byte-string representation, 315

Cache, 294
  coherency, 548, 569
CAD. *See* Computer-aided design
Call-level interface (CLI), 645
Candidate key, 69, 340
Canonical cover, 209, 228
Cartesian-product operation, 75
Cascading rollback, 457, 477
CASE. *See* Computer-aided software engineering
Checkpoints, 524, 529, 537
  fuzzy, 530, 538
CICS monitor, 672
Client systems, 545
Client–server, 543
  interface protocols, 561
Closure, 206
Clustering file organization, 319, 321, 322, 554
  indices, 340
Coalescence, 501
Coalescence rule, 234
Collection type, 266
Commit protocol, 604, 608
  2PC, 604, 609, 627, 646
  3PC, 604, 608, 609
Common object request broker architecture (CORBA), 646
Compact-disk read-only memory (CD-ROM), 294
Compatibility function, 472
Complementation rule, 234
Complete rules, 234
Complex types, 275, 287
Computer-aided design (CAD), 252, 271, 289, 712
Computer-aided software engineering (CASE), 252
Concurrency control, 607, 622, 681
  components, 14, 312, 442, 447, 451, 457, 466, 471, 485, 503, 529, 569, 613, 627
Conflict serializability, 451, 453, 466
  schedules, 458, 482
Consistency, 13, 440, 466, 725
  weak, 686
Constraints
  completeness, 45
  conditions-defined, 146
  consistency, 3
  disjointedness, 45
  referential-integrity, 195, 196, 210
Containment hierarchy, 262
Continuous connection, 560
Count aggregate function, 170
Crash-recovery subsystem, 312
Cursor stability, 686

Dangling pointers, 314, 325
Data
  abstract, 7
  abstraction from, 4
  archival, 295

audio and video data, 332
broadcast, 724
caching, 548
consistency, 193, 447, 531
continuous-media, 720, 721
dictionary, 12, 15, 322
directory, 12
distributed. storage, 588
encapsulating, 253
fragmentation, 528, 589
geographic, 713, 714
graphical, 332
inconsistency, 2
independence, 6, 19
integrity, 633
isochronous, 720
mining, 699, 702, 705
model, 7
multimedia formats, 721
naming, 593
object-oriented, 253
parallelism, 572
partitioning, 566
physical models, 11, 19
pollution, 644
redundancy, 2
relational models, 106, 565
replication, 588
semistructured, 740
storage, 293
striping, 303
structure definition, 331
diagram, 748
text, 332
transfer failure, 514
transmission cost, 596
uncommitted, 679
visualization, 706
warehouse, 699, 709, 740
Data encryption standard (DES), 642
Databases 1, 106
active system, 660, 664
administrator (DBA), 15, 636
applications, 271
buffer, 532–533
CAD, 28
centralized, 560
CODASYL DTBG 1991, 645, 750, 751
computer-aided–design, 697
design, 710, 712
distributed systems, 543, 555, 560, 587, 593
geographic, 697, 710
heterogeneous distributed, 556
hierarchical, 755
homogeneous distributed, 622
hypertext, 252
Illustra system, 278
Ingres system, 165
main-memory systems, 677, 760
management system (DBMS), 1, 19
Microsoft Access, 660
mobile, 698
modification of, 100, 163, 170
multimedia, 252, 698, 719, 741
multisystem, 556, 622, 623, 628
multiversion systems, 490
network, 747
object-oriented, 260, 288, 324
open connectivity (ODBC), 547, 645
parallel architectures, 552
parallel systems, 543, 551, 561, 565
relational, 63, 215, 697
schema, 65
security, 634
spatial, 697, 710, 740
specifications, standard, 750
statistical, 643
temporal, 655
Datalog, 106, 111, 153, 174, 188
rules, 176
fixpoint, 183
Data-server systems, 546, 547
DDL. *See* Languages, data-definition
Deadlines, 685
Deadlock, 490, 492
detection, 495, 620, 624, 627
handling, 493, 615
prevention, 492, 617

Deadlock (*continued*)
recovery, 496
Decision-support queries, 565
Decision-support systems, 697, 740
Decomposition, 217, 222
dependency-preserving, 237
lossless-join, 219, 222, 225, 239
lossy, 219
lossy-join, 219
rule, 207
Deferred modification, 518, 539
Degree-two consistency, 686
Deletion, 100, 131, 163, 170, 497, 501
Dense index, 341
Dependency preservation, 223
Dereferencing, 326
Derived relations, 129
Design constraints, 44
attribute-defined, 45
condition-defined, 44
user-defined, 45
Difference rule, 235
Digital signatures, 643
Digital video disk (DVD), 308
Directed acyclic graph (DAG), 259, 480
Disconnectivity, 724
Disjoint subtrees, 481
Disk mirroring, 305
Distributed environment, 613
Distributed hypertext systems, 731
Distributed information systems, 698
Distributed query processing, 596
Distributed transaction model, 599
Distributed virtual-memory architectures, 555
Division operation, 84
DKNF database. *See* Domain-key normal form
DML. *See* Languages, data-manipulation
Domain, 90
constraints, 193, 210
relational calculus, 90
types, 141
variable, 162
Domain-key normal form (DKNF) database, 242–243
Drill down, 701
Dump, 535
Duplicate elimination, 155
Durability, 13, 440, 445, 466, 511

Election algorithms, 613
Encina monitor, 672, 676
Encryption, 641
Enterprise schema, 23, 58
Entity, 23, 58
dominant, 34
set, 24, 28, 42, 44, 48, 51, 58
higher-level, 44
strong, 38, 53, 55, 58, 70
weak, 37, 40, 54, 55, 58, 70
subordinate, 34
Entity–relationship model, 7
attribute inheritance, 44
data model, 7, 23, 747
database schema, 47
diagram, 36, 37, 51
generalizaton 57, 58
E-R model. *See* Entity–relationship model
Ethernet, 559
Existence dependency, 33, 58

Fail-stop assumption, 512
Failures
detection, 692
disk, 512
link, 612
recovery, 692
log-based, 517
system, 446
Failure atomicity, 690
False cycles, 619
False drop, 729
False positive, 729
Fault tolerance, 554
File, 333
grid, 373
header, 314
organization, 300

sequential, 318, 319
structure, 318
system, 2, 312
log-based, 301
organization techniques, 318, 319, 324, 358
Fixed-length records, 312
Fixed-length representation, 317
Flash memory, 294
Foreign key, 144, 198, 640
Forms interfaces, 657
Fortran, 145
Fragment and replicate, 574, 576
asymmetric, 574
join, 574
Fragmentation
horizontal, 589
mixed, 593
vertical, 589, 591
Frame-memory model, 11
Free list, 314
Full replication, 588
Full-text index, 729
Functional dependencies, 202, 204, 206, 211, 232, 234
Fuzzy checkpoint, 530, 538
Fuzzy dump schemes, 535

Gamma system, 554, 565
Garbage collection, 528
Generalized-projection operation, 94
Geometric information, 711
Global Positioning System (GPS), 714
Global transaction, 556, 600
Grace system, 554, 565
Granularity, 504
coarse, 545, 549
fine, 545, 549
multiple, 487
Graphical user interface, 736
Graphs
authorization, 637
and data, 332
directed acyclic (DAG), 259, 480
histogram, 579
labeled precedence, 462, 467
local wait-for, 617
precedence, 467
wait-for, 495, 617
Group-commit technique, 677
Growing phase, 476

Hardware swizzling, 327, 330
Hashing, 358
closed, 361
dynamic, 363, 377
extendable, 364, 368, 377
file organization, 319, 358
function, 339, 358, 376
index, 339, 363, 378
linear, 369
open, 361
partitioning, 566, 574
static, 377
Heap file organization, 318
Hidden pointers, 331
Hierarchical architecture, 554
Hierarchical model, 10, 63, 755
High availability, 669
High-performance transaction systems, 676, 685
Histograms, 579
Home pages, 734
Hot-spare configuration, 671
HTML. *See* Languages, hypertext markup
HyperCard, 731
Hypercube interconnection, 552
Hypermedia systems, 731
Hypertext, 729, 731
databases, 252
distributed systems, 731
markup language (HTML), 660, 733
transfer protocol, 734

IBM Information Management System (IMS), 760
Identifying relationship, 40
IDL. *See* Languages, interface description
Immediate-modifications scheme, 539
Immediate-update technique, 521
IMS monitor, 672, 760

Inconsistent state, 441
Independent parallelism, 580, 599
Index, 339
  authorization, 636
  B-tree, 356
  B^+-tree, 346, 356, 377
  entry, 341
  locking, 500
  record, 341
  sequential file organization, 341, 346, 354, 369, 377
Indexing
  documents, 728
  spatial data, 716
Information retrieval, 698, 726, 727, 741
Information systems, distributed, 732
  Gopher, 732
  Internet, 635, 698
  World Wide Web (WWW), 732, 733, 738, 741
Inheritance, 257, 280
Insertion, 100, 133, 164, 171, 498, 501
Instance, 6, 254
Integrated services digital network (ISDN), 560
Integrity, 112, 634
  constraints, 193, 210, 633
Interconnection network, 552
Interface, 644
Internet, 635, 698
Interoperation parallelism, 571, 579, 583, 599
Interquery parallelism, 569, 583
Intersection rule, 235
Intraoperation parallelism, 571, 583, 599
Intraquery parallelism, 570, 583
Inverted index, 728
I/O parallelism, 566
Isolation, 440, 466

Java, 733, 736
Joins
  cross, 140
  dependent, 239
  fragment-and-replicate, 574
  full outer, 139
  left outer, 139
  lossless, 219, 222, 225, 239
  lossy, 219
  natural, 82, 138
  outer, 94, 95
  parallel, 573, 576
  project, 239, 242
  right outer, 139
  semi, 599
  union, 140
Joint Picture Experts Group (JPEG), 721
Jukebox, 294, 308

Key, 34, 202
Keyword-based information retrieval, 727
Knowledge-discovery systems, 703

Languages
  COBOL, 145, 440
  data-definition (DDL), 12, 19, 112, 260
  Datalog, 106, 111, 153, 174, 188
    rules, 176
    fixpoint, 183
    recursion, 183
  data-manipulation (DML), 12, 19, 112
    embedded, 112
  DL/I, 761
  Fortran, 145
  fourth-generation (4GLs), 148, 659
  hypertext markup (HTML), 660, 733, 735
  Illustra, 278, 287
  interface description (IDL), 646
  nonprocedural, 71, 86
  persistent programming, 263, 271, 275, 288, 289
  PL/I, 145
  procedural, 71
  QBE, 106, 111, 153, 188

Quel, 106, 111, 153, 165, 188
  and the tuple relational calculus, 174
query, 13, 71
  embedded, 264
SQL, 106, 111, 153, 246, 263, 275, 288, 440, 638
  embedded, 145, 287
  Gupta, 574, 660
  reference privilege, 638
  referential integrity, 197
  standard, 371, 644
SQL-89, 112
SQL-92, 112, 118, 120, 194
  privileges, 640
  time specification, 656
standard generalized markup (SGML), 733, 735
temporal query, 656, 664
text-markup, 735
TeX/LaTeX, 735
XSQL, 278
Latches, 533
Latency time, average, 299
Lattice, 44
Legacy systems, 675
Lexicographic ordering, 373
Linear scaleup, 550
Linear speedup, 550
Linked list, 314
Links, 750, 755
  failures, 612
Load-balanced partition vector, 572
Local autonomy, 557
Local-area networks (LANs), 558, 561
Locks, 471, 548
  deescalation, 548
  exclusive mode, 472, 476, 614, 616
  granting of, 476
  granularity, *See* Granularity
  intention mode, 488, 489
  protocol, 471, 475, 476, 488, 503, 614
  shared mode, 614, 616, 472, 476
  two-phase locking, 476, 478, 481, 488, 503, 680,
Log, 517
Log disk, 301
Logical clock, 617
Logical connectives, 167
Logical error, 511
Logical level, 4
Logical logging, 536, 684
Log-record buffering, 531
Long-distance computer networks, 731
Lotus Notes, 560

Magnetic tapes, 307
Magnetic-disk storage, 294, 296
Main memory, 294
Many-server, single-router model, 674
Mapping
  cardinalities, 8, 31, 51, 52, 58
  many to many, 31
  many to one, 31, 38, 55, 70
  objects to files, 324
  one to many, 31, 38
  one to one, 31, 38
Massively parallel, 549
Mesh, 552
Mirrored disk, 513
Mirroring, 302
Mobile-computing, 722, 723
Modems, 560
Monotonic systems, 187
Most recently used (MRU) strategy, 311
Motion Picture Experts Group (MPEG)
  MPEG-1 standard, 721
  MPEG-2 standard, 721
MPEG. *See* Motion Pictures Expert Group
Multilevel indices, 343
Multimedia data formats, 721
Multiple application-server processes, 674
Multiple inheritance, 259
Multiple-coordinator approach, 614
Multiple-key access, 372
Multiprogramming, 447
Multiset versions, 119
Multisystem applications, 688

Multitasking, 673
Multiuser system, 545
Multivalued attributes, 25, 56, 70
Multivalued augmentation rule, 234
Multivalued dependency, 232, 234
Multivalued transitivity rule, 234
Multivalued union rule, 235
Multiversion concurrency-control scheme, 504, 682
Multiversion timestamp-ordering scheme, 491

Name server, 594
Nested relational model, 276
  relations, 275, 278, 283, 285, 289
  subqueries, 125, 166
  transactions, 682
Networking of computers, 543
  database, 747
  model, 10, 63, 747
  partitions, 607
  security, 635
  transparency, 593
Nonatomic types, 289
Nonclustering indices, 340
Nonserializable executions, 680
Nonvolatile random-access memory (nonvolatile RAM), 300
Nonvolatile storage, 512, 534
Normal form, 215, 221, 224, 232
  Boyce-Codd normal form (BCNF), 224
  domain-key normal form (DKNF), 242–243
  first normal form (1NF), 247, 275
  fourth normal form (4NF), 232, 236
  project-join normal form, (PJNF)m 239, 242
  second normal form (2NF), 247
  third normal form (3NF), 228
Normalization, 239
NP-complete problems, 465
Null attributes, 26
Null values, 217, 245

Objects, 253, 275
  classes, 254
  complex, 276
  composite, 262
  database management group (ODMG), 267, 646
  definition language (ODL), 331
  identifiers (OID), 261, 325
    logical, 325
    physical, 325
  logical models, 7, 19
  management architecture (OMA), 646
  management group (OMG), 646
  and models, 7, 8, 251, 253
  persistence of, 264
  relational models, 275
  relational databases, 288
  relational systems, 263
Observable external writes, 444
Office information systems (OIS), 252
Off-line storage, 296
On-line analytical processing (OLAP), 648
On-line storage, 296
On-line transaction processing (OLTP), 648
Operations
  append, 171
  by, 119, 169
  delete, 497
  except, 120,121
  from, 115
  grant, 683
  group by, 161, 168
  intersect, 120, 121, 167
  join, 138
  lookup, 501
  range of, 167
  redo, 519
  rename, 76, 116
  replace, 172
  select, 113, 114
  undo, 521
  union, 120
  where, 115, 168
Optical disks, 307
Optical storage, 294

Oracle 7, 565, 570
Ordered indexing, 339, 369, 373

Page fault, 328
Parallel architecture, 552
Parallel database architectures, 552
Parallel database systems, 543, 551, 561, 565
Parallel evaluation of operations, cost of, 578
Parallel external sort–merge, 572
Parallel join algorithms, 573
Parallel sort, 571
Parallel systems, 549
Partially connected network, 602
Partitioning
  hashing, 373, 375, 376, 576
  horizontal, 566
  join, 573
  load-balanced, 572
  networks, 607
  range, 566, 574
  round-robin, 566
  skew, 568
  vector, 566
Pascal, 145, 264, 440
Passwords, 635
Pathway, 672
Performance benchmarks, 647
Performance tuning, 650
Performance-simulation model, 654
Persistent extensions, 288
Persistent pointer, 266, 324, 326, 330
Phantom phenomenon, 499
Physical logging, 536
Pipelined parallelism, 580, 599
Point queries, 567
Pointer fields, 752
Pointer swizzling, 326
Pointers, in-memory pointers, 326, 330
Postgres, 278
PostScript, 735
PowerBuilder, 547, 660
P+Q redundancy scheme, 306
Precedence graph, 467
  labeled, 462, 467
  test, 460
Precision, 729
Prefetching, 548
Primary copy, 589, 616
Primary index, 340, 377
Primary key, 35, 69, 142, 197, 340
Primary storage, 296
Private key, 642
Privileges, granting of, 637
Project operation, 72
Project-join normal form (PJNF), 239, 242
Prolog, 153, 174, 188
Protocols
  biased, 615
  client–server interface, 561
  commit, 604, 608
  concurrency-control, 569
  coordinator-failure, 610
  deadlock-prevention, 492
  global-read–write, 625
  graph-based, 479, 680
  local-read, 625
  lock, 471, 475, 489, 491, 503, 614
  multiple-granularity locking, 489
  multiversion two-phase locking, 491
  three-phase commit, 604, 608, 609
  timestamp-based, 680
  timestamp-ordering, 483, 484
  tree, 480
  tree-locking, 481
  two-phase commit, 604, 609, 627, 646
  two-phase locking, 476, 481, 488, 491, 503
    rigorous, 478
    strict, 477
  validation, 680
Pseudotransitivity rule, 207
Public-key encryption, 642

Queries, 13, 348
  complex types, 283
  evaluation algorithms, 648
  management facility (QMF), 154
  optimization, 16, 581, 623, 648

Queries (*continued*)
processing,16, 678, 723, 740
range, 567
relations, 287
server systems, 546
spatial, 715
subqueries, 128
Queues
manager, 674
systems, 650
theory, 651

RAID. *See* Redundant arrays of inexpensive disks
Read authorization, 635, 637
Read phase, 485
Real-time systems, 685
Rebuild performance, 307
Recall, 729
Records, 747
logical models, 9, 19
Recoverability, 456
large data items, 684
schedule, 457
Recovery, 516, 528, 607
restart, 530, 537
Recovery algorithms, 607, 678
Recovery scheme, 511, 531
Recovery-management component, 442
Recursion, 28, 183, 186
Redo-list, 530
Redundancy, 302
Redundant arrays of inexpensive disks (RAIDs), 302
levels, 304
systems, 513
Reed–Solomon codes, 306
Reference types, 282
References privilege, 638
Reflexivity rule, 207, 234
Relation schema, 65
Relational algebra, 71, 73, 80, 186, 597
Relational model, 9, 63, 747
Relational operations, 119, 182
composition of, 73
Relational systems, 289
Relationship set, 27, 29, 35, 51, 54, 58, 70
Reliability, 302
Remote backup site, 670
Remote backup systems, 669, 693
Remote-procedure-call (RPC), 546, 676
Replication rule, 234
Resource authorization, 635
Resource manager, 675, 676
Revoke statement, 640
Rigorous two-phase locking protocol, 478
Robustness, 603, 627
Rollback, 497
Rollup, 701
Rotational latency time, 299
Round-robin partitioning, 566
Routing, many-servers, single, 674
RTR monitors, 672
Rule, ground instantiation of, 178

Scaleup, 549
Scanning a relation, 567
Scheduling, 299, 449
Schema, 6, 142, 148
Search key, 340
Secondary indices, 340, 345, 377
Secondary site, 670
Secondary storage, 296
Sector, 297
Security specification, 638
Seek time, average, 298
Segmentation violation, 328
Select operation, 71
Semantics
of a program, 180
of a rule, 178
Serializability, 451, 466, 471, 686
order, 460
testing for, 459
two-level, 624
Server systems, 545
Set
comparison, 126
difference operation, 74

intersection, 81
membership, 125
operations, 120
valued fields, 324
Shadow copy, 445
Shadow paging, 525, 528, 539, 685
Shared Memory, 553
Shared-disk architecture, 553
Shared-disk model, 553
Shared-disk systems, 672
Shared-memory architecture, 553, 555
Shared-memory multiprocessor system, 674
Shared-nothing architectures, 554
Shrinking phase, 477
SGML. *See* Languages, standard generalized markup
Similarity-based retrieval, 720, 728
Simula 67, 251
Single relation schema, 160
Single user system, 544
Sites, 555
Skew, 574, 578, 583
Slotted-page structure, 317
Small computer-system interconnect (SCSI), 298
Smalltalk, 251, 264
Snapshot relation, 656
Software swizzling, 326
Sound rules, 234
Sparse index, 341
Specialization, 41, 58, 256
Specification, 688
Speedup, 549
Split, 501
Stable storage, 513
Standards, 644
Starvation, 476, 494, 497
Statistical analyses, 699
Storage manager, 19
Strict two-phase locking protocol, 477
String operations, 118
Strong correctness, 625
Subclasses, 256
Sublinear scaleup, 550
Sublinear speedup, 550
Subset dependencies, 195
Superkey, 34, 69, 340
Superuser, 636
System
application architecture database interface (SAA-SQL), 112
catalog, 322
clock, 482
crash, 512
error, 511
failure, 446
System R, 111, 337, 468, 430–431, 437, 438, 528, 542

Tables
combined, 70
page, 525
representations, 53
skeleton, 154, 160
Tandem, 565, 582
Tape storage, 295
Task flow, 688
Teleprocessing monitor, 673
Teradata database machine, 554, 565, 573, 581, 582
Termination states, 443
aborted, 690
acceptable, 690
committed, 690
nonacceptable, 690
Tertiary storage, 296, 307
Theft of information, 634
Thomas' write rule, 485
Three-phase commit protocol (3PC), 604, 608, 609
Timeout scheme, 495
Timestamp-based protocols, 680
Timestamp-ordering protocol, 483, 484
Timestamp-ordering scheme, 482, 503
Topological sorting, 460
Toss-immediate strategy, 311
Training set, 706
Transaction Processing Performance Council (TPC), 648
Transactions, 13, 439, 465, 669
committed, 443

Transactions (*continued*)
compensating, 443, 683, 693
complex interactive, 684
concurrency control, 447
control, 112
coordinator, 600
failure, 511
global, 556, 600
high-performance, 676, 685
local, 556, 599
long-duration, 679, 693
management, 19, 600, 622
multilevel, 689
multiple, 447, 528
nested, 682
processing, 672, 693, 698
remote procedure calls (RPC), 547, 676
rollback, 529, 536
scaleup, 551
server systems, 546
short-duration, 680
workflows, 687
Transient, 264
Transitive closure, 186
Transitive dependencies, 229
Transitivity rule, 207, 234
Trees
binary trees, 349
B^+-trees, 501, 504
concurrency-control algorithm, 535
file organization, 354, 369
index, 346, 356, 377
classification, 707
database, 755
disjoint subtrees, 481
in-memory structures, 349
k-d, 716
leftmost-child, 760
operator, 570
protocols, 480, 481
quadtree, 714, 717, 718
rooted, 756
R-trees, 373, 718
structure, 258, 756
Trigger, 201, 211, 660
Trivial multivalued dependency, 232
Tunable parameters, 651
Tuning, 663
Tuple relational calculus, 86
Tuple variables, 117
Tuple-id, 591
Two-phase commit protocol (2PC), 604, 609, 627, 646

Uncommitted modifications, 521
Undo-list, 530
Unifying model, 11
Union rule, 207
Unique identifier, 325
Unique-role assumption, 246
Universal resource locators (URLs), 734
Unnesting, 285
Unstructured documents, managing, 727
Updates, 101, 134, 165, 172
authorization, 635, 637
User interfaces, 657
User-coded functions, 287
User-guided data mining, 705

Validation phase, 486
Validation scheme, 503
Value dependency, 625
Variable-length records, 315
Version vector, 725
Video server, 721
Views, 102, 106, 112, 130, 636
equivalent, 455
level, 4
relation, 180
serializability, 451, 464, 466
maintenance problem, 710
Virtual memory, 532
Virtual record, 760
Volatile storage, 512

Wait–die scheme, 493
Wait-for graph, 495
local, 617
Web. *See* World Wide Web

Wide-area networks (WANs), 558, 559, 561
  transfer rates, 560
Workflow, 689, 690
  management, 691, 692
  specification, 689
    unsafe, 692
World Wide Web (WWW), 732, 733, 738, 741
  home pages, 734
  web crawlers, 740
  web server, 735
Wound–wait scheme, 493
Write phase, 486
Write-ahead logging, 532
Write-once, read-many (WORM), 308

X/open distributed transaction processing standard, 676

Pollution

Causes, Effects and Control

5th Edition